The **TIMEWEB CHRONICLES**

The TIMEWEB CHRONICLES

Books 1–3 of the Timeweb Chronicles

Brian Herbert

WordFire Press
Colorado Springs, Colorado

Contents

TIMEWEB

Book 1 of the Timeweb Chronicles

Brian Herbert

Dedication

Of all the books I have written, I owe the most to Jan for this one. You are the love of my life and my daily inspiration. Thank you for being so understanding while I spend much of my life in my study, taking fantastic journeys through space and time. You are a blessing beyond words.

Chapter One

We are but one of many galaxies, wheels moving the cart of the universe.
—Ancient Tulyan Legend

He stood profiled against the blood-red sunset as bulbous ships took off, a swarm of mechanical insects transporting contaminated materials to dump zones. It had been another long day. Normally the muscular, freckled man liked the buzz of activity in the air, the sense that he was restoring a planet that had been severely damaged by the industrial operations of the merchant princes. At the moment, however, he had something else on his mind, a surprising turn of events.

Noah Watanabe glanced again at a brief telebeam message, a black-on-white holo letter that floated in the air beside him. He had been estranged from his father, Prince Saito Watanabe, for so long that he had never expected to hear from the old tycoon again. Touching a signet ring on his right hand, Noah closed the message. In a wisp of smoke, it disappeared into the ring.

Brushing a hand through his reddish, curly hair, Noah considered the unexpected offer of a meeting between them. His initial thought had been to send a scathing response, or to simply ignore his father altogether. But other possibilities occurred to him.

In the din of aircraft, soil-processing machines, and the shouts of workers, he became aware of an oval-shaped hoverjet landing nearby, raising a cloud of dust. Moments later, the craft settled to the ground, and an underbelly hatch swung open, followed by a ramp that slid to the ground. Men wearing the green-and-brown uniforms of the Guardians—his ecological recovery force—hurried down the ramp, dragging with them a disheveled young woman, a prisoner. A trickle of blood ran down the side of her face. Her eyes were feral, and she kicked at her captors, without much success.

"Caught her trying to rig explosives to our biggest skyminer," one of the Guardians said, a rotund man with a purple birthmark on one cheek and chestnut hair combed straight back. In his early forties, Subi Danvar was Noah's trusted but sometimes outspoken adjutant. "She and two men—we killed both of them—stole one of our fast recon ships and locked onto the miner. They were about to set the whole rig off when we caught them and defused the charges."

"Who sent you?" Noah demanded, stepping close and looking down at her.

Sneering, the woman said, "I don't do anything for free. What will you give me if I answer your questions?"

"You're a mercenary, aren't you?"

"You haven't paid for my answer yet."

"Talk and we'll let you live," Subi snarled. "That's our offer." With a round belly and a puffy face he looked soft, but in reality he had the strength of three men.

Having never mistreated prisoners, Noah scowled at his adjutant, who should know better. The man was bluffing, but was doing so without Noah's authorization.

"Maybe the princes sent her," another Guardian suggested, a large man who held the woman's arms and danced away whenever she tried to kick him.

"Do you think it was your own father, Master Noah?" Danvar asked.

"I'm not sure," Noah said, recalling the telebeam message. Remarkably, old Prince Saito had offered an apology for their failed relationship, and had expressed the hope that they might be close again. But warning signals went off in Noah's mind; this could be a trick, even from his own father.

Noah and his Guardians had to be on constant alert against sabotage. In the past year, attacks had come from his business competitors and from enemies of the powerful Watanabe family, people who didn't believe the stories about the estrangement between the business mogul and his son, and thought they must be working together in some clandestine way.

"Take her away for interrogation," Noah said, with a dismissive gesture toward the young woman. "And treat her well, with respect."

The woman looked at him in astonishment. "No torture?"

"Of course not. We don't do things that way."

"I am very pleased to hear that." With a sudden movement, the woman writhed free of her captors and lunged toward Noah, brandishing a long dagger that she seemed to have produced from thin air. She moved with surprising speed.

Displaying athletic grace, Noah sidestepped the thrust and grabbed her weapon hand. But in his grip, her hand seemed to melt away, and the dagger, too.

"Mutati!" Danvar shouted.

It was a shapeshifter. For centuries Mutatis like this one had warred against the Merchant Prince Alliance. In a matter of seconds, her entire body metamorphosed into a long, serpentine form. She coiled, and struck out at Noah with deadly fangs.

But he whirled to one side and rolled away. His men fired a volley of ion-pistol shots at the creature, bursts of energy that flashed and sparkled in the air. Purple blood oozed from the Mutati, and the wounded creature began to change form again, this time to a startlingly large and ferocious beast with sharp barbs all over its body and face. But it only half metamorphosed, with its rear—more injured than the rest of the body—still a writhing snake. Using its front legs to propel itself forward, the monstrosity lunged at the Guardians, but they kept firing, and the Mutati finally fell, spurting gouts of blood.

On his feet, Noah drew his own sidearm and pointed it. Holding his fire, he took a step backward, watching the Mutati in fascination. His men stopped shooting.

Once more, the creature shapeshifted on its front, and the barbs on the face dissolved into torn and jagged flesh. A tiger-like beast began to take form, with desperate, wild eyes. But when it was only half formed, it abruptly shuddered and twitched, and then stopped moving entirely.

"Are you all right?" Subi Danvar asked, running to Noah's side.

"I'm not hurt. Doesn't look like any of you are, either."

"My fault, sir. I thought sure our prisoner was Human, but the red blood on the side of her face was obviously faked, something she wiped on her skin."

"They used a new trick on us," Noah said, "but that's no excuse. From now on, stick all the prisoners in the finger to see if they bleed purple. It's the one thing about their bodies they can't change."

"I'll check them myself," Danvar said, referring to half a dozen men and women saboteurs that they had captured here on the planet Jaggem in recent weeks.

"Guess this lets my father off the hook," Noah said, staring at the motionless blotch of purple flesh on the ground.

One of the men a knife to dig a small white object out of the body. "Implanted allergy protector," he said, holding it up. Mutatis were strongly allergic to Humans, so the shapeshifters often wore medical devices that encased the cells of their bodies in a prophylactic film.

After a worried, guilt-ridden nod toward his superior, Danvar departed with his men.

Shaking his head as he watched them go, Noah realized that he should have taken precautions earlier to prevent Mutati incursions. Especially here, on a planet that could have future significance to the Merchant Prince Alliance as a military outpost, by virtue of its strategic location. With all the planets that he had restored so far, Noah had never experienced even a hint of trouble from the shapeshifters, and for years he had relied on local police security operations to detect them if they ever tried to get through. The possibility of Mutati incursions had been in the back of his mind all that time, but from now on he needed to move such concerns to the forefront. He would have Subi Danvar work up new security measures in coordination with the MPA.

Noah's thoughts returned to the communication he had just received from his crusty, septuagenarian father. How odd to hear from him after all this time, after all the bad feelings and bitterness between the two of them. Their last encounter—more than fifteen years ago—had been a shouting match that had become physical when the prince struck his son in the face with a closed fist. The blow from the big man had been considerable, and Noah had reeled backward in surprise and shock. Out of a sense of honor, the younger man had not even considered striking back, not even for a moment. As a result of the altercation, he had not expected to ever see his father again, except on newsreels that documented the businessman's comings and goings.

Now he watched Danvar's hoverjet take off and thread its way through the crowded airspace, flying toward the Guardians' base of operations on a nearby plateau. The sky was deep purple, almost a foreboding Mutati shade, and Jaggem's small, silvery moon was just rising above a distant escarpment. He wished his father was here to see how successful he had become in his own right.

Noah had not needed any inheritance from Prince Saito. The younger Watanabe had become wealthy beyond anything he could ever hope to spend, from the ecological recovery operations he conducted on numerous planets around the Merchant Prince Alliance. Before embarking on that career, Noah had considered becoming the industrialist that his father wanted him to be.

But, after long consideration, Noah had come up with a better line of work, one that did not conflict with his own strongly held environmental beliefs. His ambitious, conniving sister Francella was more suited to following in their father's footsteps anyway, so by default Noah gave her what she wanted, his own spot as the heir apparent of the family's huge commercial operations, spanning countless star systems.

After making his momentous, life-changing decision, Noah had proceeded to carve out a business niche of his own, bringing efficiency to what had previously been a fledgling, loosely run industry. His timing had been exquisite, and now he ran the largest ecological recovery operation in the galaxy, with skilled teams working on blighted worlds, restoring them to habitability after their resources had been stripped by merchant prince industrialists.

It was a career path in which Noah restored many of the planets that his own father's operations had nearly destroyed. But he had not selected this particular business just to irritate the old man—at least not consciously. Noah had only done what he thought was right, and as a Watanabe he felt he had an obligation to make up for the environmental wrongs committed by his family.

In memory, he reread his father's short telebeam message. Then he activated his ring and transmitted a polite but reserved response, agreeing to the meeting.

Bordereau date de retour/Due date slip

Bibliothèque de Beaconsfield Library
514-428-4460
17 Jul 2019 07:45PM

Usager / Patron : 23872000149349

Date de retour/Date due: 07 Aug 2019
The marriage pact : a novel /

Date de retour/Date due: 07 Aug 2019
The Timeweb Chronicles /

Date de retour/Date due: 07 Aug 2019
The dead lands : a novel /

Date de retour/Date due: 07 Aug 2019
Secondhand souls /

Total : 4

HORAIRE D'ÉTÉ / SUMMER HOURS
Du 3 juin au 2 septembre
From June 3 to September 2
Lundi/Monday 13:00 - 21:00
Mardi au Vendredi 10:00 à 21:00
Tuesday to Friday 10:00 to 21:00
Samedi/Saturday FERMÉ / CLOSED
Dimanche/Sunday 13:00 - 17:00

La bibliothèque sera FERMÉE:
Les 1 et 2 septembre.

The library will be CLOSED:
On September 1 and 2.

Inscrivez-vous au Club de lecture d'été TD!
Pour les 0 - 17 ans

Sign up for the TD Summer Reading Club!
For 0 - 17 year olds

beaconsfieldbiblio.ca

Chapter Two

Lorenzo the Magnificent ... Should he be described as Machiavellian, or as a Renaissance man? Perhaps he is both: a leader who will do anything necessary to advance the business and scientific ideas that he holds dear.

—Succession: a Concise History of the Doges,
one of the underground press books

O f all the worlds in the Merchant Prince Alliance, none came close to rivaling the elegant capital world of Timian One, a domain of fabulous palazzos, villas, and country estates, with ambassadors and nobles coming and going on important business. The planet was guarded from space attack by orbital military platforms and by extensive installations on the surface.

And yet, in all of this opulence and grandeur, there existed on the homeworld of humankind a high and sprawling prison known as the Gaol of Brimrock, filled with bloodstained walls and floors, musty rooms, and filthy corridors ... a structure that reeked of bodily decay and the most excruciating, horrendous deaths. At any hour of the day and night, victims could be heard screaming as they were tortured and killed.

In the largest chamber of the gaol, a vaulted room with barbed straps hanging from the ceiling and hideous machines arrayed along the walls, the aged but still-spry Doge Lorenzo del Velli sat at the Judgment Table between a pair of princes. At one time the Doge had been a classically handsome man with a prominent chin, strong nose, and dark, penetrating eyes, but now the skin sagged on his cheeks and under his chin, and his gaze had lost its luster. The leathery face was etched with the concerns of high command and the depravities of endless nocturnal liaisons. He rarely ever smiled, and when he did, it had a steely edge to it. Lorenzo and his companions wore cloaks, brocaded surcoats, silkine shirts with dagged collars, and golden medallions. Their liripipe hats, in the varying colors of their noble houses, rested on the table in front of them.

The trio of noblemen watched dispassionately as their top military officer used a nerve induction rack to torture a flesh-fat Mutati. The air around the rack sparked and flashed with green light, from the strong threads of a jade laser held by the inflictor, a delicate little man in a baggy red uniform with gold braids and an oversized officer's cap. Supreme General Mah Sajak, despite his high rank, enjoyed coming here on occasion to perform tasks that were normally reserved for men in black hoods.

The high-intensity device, a golden staff that shot threads of green fire from the tip, had been manufactured by the Hibbil race, specialists in computers and high-performance machines. The electronic wand inhibited the movements of the Mutati, and was used in lieu of physical cords or other restraints.

An expert in the application of the laser, Sajak intentionally left small segments of the victim's flesh only lightly secured, thus providing apparent escape opportunities. Every few seconds, the Mutati would shapeshift and try to squirm through one of the "openings," but each time the General would quickly close it up, while leaving another space free.

It was all a game, and the Doge noted a cruel smile twitching at the edges of Sajak's scarred mouth. After each escape attempt, the officer adjusted controls on the nerve induction rack as punishment, to intensify the pain.

Looking puffy and red-faced, the victim coughed and sneezed, and emitted the foul odor of Mutati fear. In order to intensify the suffering, General Sajak had removed the creature's implanted allergy protector.

The agonized, high-pitched shrieks of the Mutati gave the Doge a warm, toasty feeling because he hated the shapeshifters so much and always had. From a young age he, like billions of people, had learned to loathe the arch enemies of humanity. He looked forward to these sessions as much as Sajak did, the way children looked forward to sugary treats.

On the wall behind Lorenzo hung a stylized painting of the Madonna holding technological devices. A composite artwork, it depicted a synthesis of the leading religious and scientific disciplines of humankind ... tenets that dated back to the origins of Human life on Earth eons ago, and to the subsequent migrations to Timian One, Siriki, Canopa, and other planets.

The ruler of all Humans, the stocky, wrinkled Doge Lorenzo was the ninety-fourth person to occupy the Palazzo Magnifico and sit upon the legendary Aquastar Throne. He held strong theoscientific beliefs himself, and employed them to keep his citizens in line. The officially sanctioned text of the Merchant Prince Alliance was the Scienscroll, whose origins lay in the murky, legendary past. An electronic copy lay open in front of the Doge, and he read a passage from it aloud while the Mutati screamed in agony. A wager box also sat on the table, a black mechanism that the three noblemen used to keep track of their bets concerning how long the victim would survive. Lorenzo loved games of chance.

This notorious prison was linked to the Palazzo Magnifico by a covered walking bridge over a narrow waterway, a man-made tributary of the Royal Canal that ran through the heart of Elysoo, the capital city. Named after a mythical economist of millennia past who led the first corporate migrations from Earth, Elysoo became the most beautiful of all cities created by the affluent princes, one of the Wonders of the Galaxy. Even Mutatis (those foolish but brave ones who ventured here in disguise) said so; everyone admired the magnificent municipal designs, and especially the intricate dancing lights on the canals and the illuminated, lambent waterfalls that made the metropolis such a magical wonderland at night.

To prevent the features of his beloved city from being duplicated elsewhere, the doges always blinded the architects and engineers after they had completed their work. But the biggest threat to the Merchant Prince Alliance was not the theft of urban designs, or even of industrial secrets. It came from the Mutati Kingdom. Lorenzo wanted to annihilate the entire race of shapeshifters and make them suffer as much physical pain and humiliation as possible in the process. In his view they were the lowest form of life imaginable, the biological dregs of creation. He could not understand why the Supreme Being had contrived such organisms, unless it was to test Humans, to see how they would respond to such a dreadful enemy. The Mutatis were not just a military threat; they were a supreme challenge to all that any decent person held sacred....

This hapless torture victim (captured in a space skirmish between Humans and Mutatis) was still trying to metamorphose his flesh in order to escape, but Sajak handled him deftly with the strong green threads of high-intensity light. As the Mutati assumed different physiques, the laser threads still held onto him, tightening their grip on his cellular structure and causing him to howl in agony and frustration. Exhausted, he reverted to his original fat, fleshy form.

With a sardonic laugh, the General turned up the pain amplification mechanism to its maximum setting, causing the Mutati to squirm even more frantically. The creature reached the highest note of a blood-curdling scream, and then babbled everything he knew about the military operations of his people. In a cracking voice, he said he was a mid-level officer, a sevencap who had been the adjutant for one of their top admirals.

"He has told all he knows," General Sajak announced triumphantly, as the victim slumped on the rack, bleeding purple fluid from his ears and giving off fitful gasps. The small officer stood over him, smiling....

One of the noblemen sitting in judgment with Lorenzo was the chisel-featured Jacopo Nehr, inventor of the "nehrcom," the instantaneous, cross-galactic communication system. Fabulously wealthy, he also manufactured efficient, low-cost robots in leased facilities on the Hibbil Cluster Worlds, and engaged in precious gem mining and distribution.

The other noble at the Judgment Table was Saito Watanabe of CorpOne, a tall, obese man with jowls that hung loosely on each side of his face. He and Nehr, both born commoners, had been promoted by the Doge to "Princes of the Realm," in honor of their business successes. Now their companies were affiliated with the all-pervasive Doge Corporation, which received a share of all merchant prince profits.

Prince Saito did not like these sessions, but attended them out of necessity, in order to maintain the favorable economic position of his own business empire. When the interrogation of a prisoner became most intense, he tried to tune it out discreetly and think of other matters. At the moment, he was remembering back a decade, to a time when his estranged son Noah had been in his late twenties and had worked for him. Once they had been close, though it had developed into a strained relationship, filled with disagreements over environmental issues.

He wondered if the young man had been right after all.

Sadness filled the Prince as he recalled their emotion-charged final argument. As the details came back, he felt tears forming in his eyes. With sudden resolve, he fought the emotion and pushed it deep inside, where it would not be noticed by his companions.

Only hours ago, Prince Saito had sent his son a letter suggesting a meeting. A telebeam response had arrived moments before this interrogation session, as indicated by a change in the color of Saito's signet ring, from ruby to emerald. He had not been able to look at it yet.

At long last the victim issued a horrendous, shuddering scream and died. As he did so, the wager box metamorphosed from black to gold, and cast a bright beam of light on the face of the victorious contestant. It was Lorenzo the Magnificent, as usual. He loved to win, and set the machines to make certain that he always did.

Presently, the Doge and Nehr went out the door, bantering back and forth over the results of the bet, while Saito remained at the table. Men in black hoods swung a hoist mechanism over the corpse of the prisoner. They grunted with exertion as they moved the heavy body onto a sling.

Prince Watanabe took a deep breath, anticipating a negative response from his proud, willful son. To activate the telebeam projector, he touched the stone of the signet ring. The mechanism identified him from DNA in the oil of his skin and flashed a black-on-white message in front of his eyes, floating in the air.

He read it, and allowed a tear of joy to fall down his cheek. Given a fresh opportunity, he would listen to his son this time, would do everything humanly possible to bring them back together again.

Chapter Three

There is a legend that the Creator of the Galaxy can alter his appearance, like a Mutati.

—From a Mutati children's story

P aradij, the fabled Mutati homeworld....
High atop his glittering Citadel overlooking the capital city, the Zultan Abal Meshdi stood on a clearglax floor inside a slowly spinning gyrodome. An immense terramutati who could take on many appearances, he now looked like a golden-maned lionoid in flowing robes and jewels, clinging with the suction of his bare feet to the moist, revolving surface.

Around the majestic leader spun two other compartments, visible to him through thick, clear plates. One contained waterborne Mutati variations that swam gracefully ... while the other enclosure was filled with genetic variations that flew about at hummingbird speed.

These were the three types of Mutatis—terramutatis, hydromutatis, and aeromutatis—functioning on the ground, in the water, and in the air. Within their own environments, the variations could shapeshift, becoming a panoply of exotic creatures.

From the gyrodome, Meshdi saw Royal Chancellor Aton Turba in the room outside, pacing back and forth as he awaited the instructions of his superior. A mass of flesh with a small head and centipede legs, Turba had been in this shape for less than a day.

If a Mutati remained in one form too long, his sensitive cellular structure locked into place, so that he could no longer metamorphose. Normally it was safe to maintain one appearance for weeks, but Turba changed himself on a much more frequent basis, fearful that if he didn't he might slip into cellular rigidity. And, despite the chancellor's fluid appearance he remained instantly recognizable to the Zultan, who possessed a rare gift. Meshdi was one of the few Mutatis who could look at another, no matter his appearance, and see beyond the surface to an intricate combination of aural hues and electrical charges that were unique to the individual.

The Zultan's gyrodome made a faint squealing noise specially tuned to give pleasure to him, and he smelled the sweetness of santhems, tiny airflowers that glowed faintly mauve in the moist, humid air ... a barely visible field of color.

Abal Meshdi inhaled deeply, absorbing millions of the scented flowerets. A sensation of deep relaxation permeated his entire body, and he sighed with pleasure.

A wonderful gift from his Adurian allies far across the galaxy, the gyrodome spun faster and faster, raising the pitch of its whine, heightening his pleasure to one of the highest levels he had ever experienced. Everything became a blur around him. The mechanism sent the Zultan into a trance in which all of the problems, decisions, and challenges of his position were aligned, and he could consider them in detail.

Foremost in his mind: the continued Human threat. Each day he considered what to do with the ones that were captured, assigning the trickle that came in from various sectors of the galaxy to hard labor or execution through horrific, screaming deaths. He enjoyed watching them die, since they suffered so much. Like his counterparts on Timian One, he knew how to heighten the pain of his enemies.

He also worried what to do with his own son, Hari'Adab, who seemed overly independent, almost rebellious at times. It especially troubled him that Hari had expressed opposition to him privately about the "Demolio" program, a top secret, highly ambitious military weapon that the Mutatis had under development. The Zultan, with no patience for naysayers, had thus far been unable to change the young Mutati's mind, but had obtained his sacred promise to keep his feelings to himself. And, in an effort to provide Hari with administrative experience for the maturation of his thinking processes, he had assigned him as Emir of another planet, Dij. For some time, however, Hari had not been submitting the required reports to his father. As a result, the Zultan would need to apply stern discipline.

Gradually the dome slowed, and Abal Meshdi stood upright. The water and air creatures around him had grown quiet, and the Zultan's head was clear and calm. By the time he emerged from the dome, he had made a decision about his arch enemies. The matter of his errant son would have to wait.

Aton Turba bowed, then stood submissively with his three hands clasped in front of his round belly.

Above all, the Zultan hated Humans. It was an enmity that went back for millennia, to disputes among the distant ancestors of both races. He didn't remember what started it all, but had an exacting memory of the events that had occurred during his own lifetime. There had been a number of military skirmishes, and in most of them Humans had prevailed. Because of limitations on space travel, however—with faster-than-light speed only achieved by mysterious, sentient podships that operated on their own schedules—neither side had been able to mount a large-scale attack on the other.

According to Mutati mythology, the galaxy was once pristine, before Humans defiled it tens of thousands of years ago. The Mutatis knew this from an oral tradition that went back to a time before Humans existed, when there were only a handful of galactic races.

The Zultan scowled at his chancellor and announced, "The gyrodome has just shown me exactly how to use the new weapon my researchers are developing."

Turba looked perplexed, for he had not been told anything about this. But he knew better than to ask questions of his superior. As always, the information would flow in due course, and the chancellor would be required to remember every detail.

"When the device is perfected I will institute a new policy," the Zultan announced in a pompous voice, "and trillions of Humans will be exterminated, like hordes of insects."

Abal Meshdi went on to explain the terrible new doomsday weapon to Turba, and told the astounded chancellor that he would need to tend more carefully to the affairs of the Citadel in the near future, since the Zultan would be occupied with other, more far-reaching, matters....

* * * * *

Within days, an elite corps of "outriders" was selected and trained ... Mutatis who were looking for opportunities to attack their enemies with the most frightful weapon of annihilation in the history of galactic warfare.

Overseeing the operation from his busy War Room in the capital city of Jadeen, the Zultan gazed out on banks of data processors that projected space-simulation images of the merchant prince worlds ... and of planets farther out, at the fringe of the enemy realm. A tiny spaceship, represented by a larger-than-scale point of orange light, flew toward one of the outer worlds.

Abal Meshdi chuckled, and thought, *The Humans believe they are such masters of technology, but we have a surprise for them.*

Chapter Four

Timeweb ensnares the past, the present, and the future. As each moment becomes the past, it folds into the web and seems to disappear without actually doing so. Simultaneously, in a great cosmic balance, the future opens up for us ... little by little.

—Tulyan Imprint

Seated in the back of a maglev limousine, the man gazed out a tinted window as the car hummed along a mountain track, snaking downhill. Through morning vistas that opened between sun-dappled trees, Noah Watanabe saw immense factories and office complexes below in the Valley of the Princes, facilities that were operated by the titans of industry who controlled the multi-planet Human Empire. For a few seconds, he barely made out the high-walled perimeter of his father's CorpOne compound, with its radically-shaped structures, an imaginative variety of geometric and artistic combinations.

On the opposite side of the valley, Rainbow City—the largest industrial metropolis on Canopa—clung to a shimmering, iridescent cliff. Workers occupied homes on the lower levels of the community, while the villas of wealthy noblemen studded the top like a crown of jewels. For decades Prince Saito had owned one of those palatial residences, and Noah recalled some happy times growing up there ... but only a few. There had been too many family problems.

It was early summer now, with the canopa pines and exotic grasses of the valley still bright green, having gorged themselves with moisture in anticipation of the coming dry months. Noah viewed it as a survival mechanism, and thought that plants were just as intelligent as other life forms, but in different ways. This and other controversial beliefs frequently put him at odds with the wealthy industrialists of the Merchant Prince Alliance, including his own father.

Noah wore a velvis surcoat and a high-collar shirt with a gold chain around the neck. His muscles bulged under the fabric. He was accompanied by six men dressed in the green-and-brown uniforms of the Guardians, his force of environmental activists who were known as "eco-warriors." The men were armed with high-caliber puissant rifles, as well as sidearms and an arsenal of stun-weapons, poisons, and plax-explosives. They sat silently, staring outside in all directions, ever on the alert for danger. Ahead of the black car and behind it on the maglev track—as arranged by Prince Saito—were nine other identical vehicles, thus preventing potential aggressors from targeting Noah too easily. An air escort of CorpOne attack hellees flew overhead, and the entire area around him had been scanned by infrared and other devices.

Enemies could still defeat any of these systems. Technology was that way; you could never be certain what your adversary knew, or what he had developed to use against you in the eternal dance of offensive and defensive advancements. People wishing to do Noah harm might still be lurking in the woods or in the air, but he believed in fate; if something was meant to get him, it would.

This was how he felt about the upcoming meeting with his father, which he had not expected to occur. Upon receiving the message from the old man, Noah had experienced a visceral sensation that a greater power was at work, drawing them together. Perhaps the two of them, who had disagreed so vehemently about industrial and environmental issues in the past, might find some common ground after all. Noah had always held onto a thread of hope that this might happen, but had taken no steps in that direction, until he replied to his father's recent message.

Noah's strong belief in fate did not mean that he just sat around and waited for things to occur. Far from it. The penultimate activist among activists, he was an assertive leader who constantly pushed events, implementing large-scale transformations on the worlds of the Human-controlled Merchant Prince Alliance.

In the process, Noah had become fabulously wealthy in his own right, so he cared nothing of rumors reaching him that he had been disowned by his father; he really only cared about the loss of a relationship with Prince Saito … the riches of emotion, knowledge, and experience that they were not sharing with each other. Maybe that was about to change.

The procession of maglev vehicles reached the valley floor, where the single track widened into ten, with a variety of conveyances whirring along on them … luxury cars, truck-trailer rigs, and buses filled with workers. Presently Noah and his entourage passed through a security beam at an ornate gate, and entered the CorpOne compound. A pair of diamonix elephants with red-jeweled eyes stood on either side of a grassy planting area just inside the entry. Ahead, Noah could see the main building. He knew it well, from having worked there with his father at one time, before their blowup.

A marvel of engineering and aesthetic design, Prince Saito Watanabe's office headquarters was an inverted pyramid, with the point down. As if by magic, the large structure balanced perfectly in that precarious position, while the foundation—a broad platform that included gardens, flagstones, and ornamental fountains—spun slowly beneath it. But Noah Watanabe (with his scientific knowledge and curiosity) knew how it worked; the structure was held in place by a slender core-pillar of pharium, the strongest metal in the galaxy. Elaborate geomagnetics were involved as well, and as a last recourse, a backup system would shoot stabilizing outriggers into receptacles if the tilt meters indicated trouble.

Noah's car hummed up to the edge of the slowly revolving platform and locked into position at the edge of an exotic rose garden. He gazed up at the improbable building above him as it rotated with the platform, and considered the practical benefits of such a design. As the headquarters spun, it gave off electronic pulses that absorbed and processed important data. The system could identify known agitators from all galactic races, profile criminal types, and make highly sophisticated statistical predictions.

Noah wondered what his father wanted; their emotion-charged enmity had lasted for a decade and a half. In memory, he went over the conciliatory message he had received from the old patriarch, reviewing every detail that had been in the telebeam. His father was a precise man, who said exactly what he intended every time he communicated in any form, but Noah suspected hidden meanings:

In the past we have not understood one another as a father and son should. I blame myself almost entirely, and you not at all. It is my duty to bridge our differences.

Brian Herbert

The electronic transmittal had gone on to suggest a time and a place for a meeting. Now, as Noah watched a white-uniformed escort secretary march primly toward the hover-limousine, he recollected his own written response:

Father: I appreciate your sentiments, and look forward to meeting with you as you have specified

* * * * *

From her office inside the inverted pyramid, Francella Watanabe stared in rage and disbelief at a closed-circuit screen that showed the escort secretary leading Noah and his entourage through a wide corridor. At various points along the route, Francella—as Corporate Security Chief—could activate detonations by remote control and kill the entire party. The thought was tempting, but she had something even more devastating in mind.

With a heavy sigh, she activated a copy of the telebeam messages her father and Noah had exchanged, and continued to seethe over them, as she had done since seeing them for the first time three days before. To the very depths of her soul she loathed her twin brother, resenting the preferential treatment he had always received at her expense. Before the big disagreement between Noah and his father over environmental issues, the young man had been the heir apparent, the favored one. In those days Noah had even dressed like his father, in a cloak, brocaded surcoat and liripipe hat, while she was expected to remain in the shadows and say very little. She was, after all, only a female in an interplanetary society run by men, for the benefit of men.

Now her bête noire had entered the building only a few floors down. She wished their father had consulted her about such an important matter, for she might have used her considerable wiles to steer him away from making the invitation. Recently, though, the old man had seemed distant and had been making excuses to avoid or delay the appointments she had requested with him.

He would regret that soon, because Francella had set in motion a new and climactic plan ... one that would take both her father and brother out of the picture, while allowing her to obtain everything she so richly deserved.

A two-pronged attack.

She wished it didn't have to be this way, and her conscience had been giving her some trouble over it. But she had been driven to do this, with no other choice. Events ... and people ... were conspiring against her, and she needed to strike fast, in order to protect her position.

Hearing familiar noises behind her, she felt her pulse quicken. Francella flipped off the telebeam and turned to see her aged father opening the door and lurching into the room in his stiff-jointed way, tapping the hardwood floor with one of his ornate walking sticks. He had arrived only the day before from Timian One, where he had been attending to his duties on the Council of Forty, a powerful clique of noblemen who ruled with the Doge.

Prince Saito Watanabe had a large collection of fancy canes, many of them carved in the images of animals. This one, of canopa white teak, had a bull elephant head carved on top of the handle and the end of an elephant snout at the bottom.

All around the CorpOne complex, as well as in his lavish homes and vehicles, the obese old man had representations of the grand, extinct beasts. Images of the pachyderms were on wall hangings, pillow cases, and statuary; even articles of furniture were carved in their likeness. In addition, Prince Watanabe had commissioned paleontology expeditions to Earth and other far planets where the creatures used to roam ... scientific ventures that brought back remains of elephants for genetic testing.

"You requested an urgent conference with me," the industrialist said to her, in a coarse tone. "I grant you five minutes, before my appointment with Noah."

"*Five minutes?*" She felt her face flush, and noticed her father looking at her closely with his intense, dark eyes.

"My schedule is very tight," he said.

"Too tight for your own daughter?"

"I'm sorry if it appears that way, but I have been planning for this important rendezvous with Noah, going over what I will say to him."

"Are you certain it is wise to do this now?" she asked, already knowing his answer.

Saito Watanabe studied his statuesque, redheaded daughter, who wore a white lace dress with gold brocade, and a high, star-shaped headdress. For an additional fashion statement, she had shaved off her eyebrows and hair at the front of her head, creating a high forehead.

He heard the displeasure in her voice, saw it etched on her face ... and wondered what had gone wrong with the relationship between her and Noah. For years Saito had not failed to notice the raw hatred between them, the destructive sparks and flames that flared whenever they were together.

"I will see your brother alone," he said to her. "It is best for the two of you to remain apart."

"Daddy, Noah hates us. Don't you realize that?"

With deep sadness, the heavyset man looked away. He felt his eyes misting over, and didn't say what had been in his heart for a long time, a primogenitary hope that Noah would take over for him.

A son should follow in his father's footsteps, the Prince thought. *It is the natural order of things.*

But Noah had been defiant and headstrong. So much so that the Prince had not expected him to accept the invitation. But he had.

What is Noah thinking? What are his wishes, his dreams?

"It is time," the Prince announced to his daughter. And he ordered her out of his office, hardly noticing the fiery glare she shot back at him.

* * * * *

The reception room where Noah had been told to wait was on the fourth level of the upside-down pyramid, with a wide picture window that looked out on the gardens and fountains below. Since each floor was larger than the one below it, he saw an overhang outside the window, and knew that each floor all the way to the top was like this as well, in a dizzying arrangement of inverted tiers.

He was pondering the upcoming session with his enigmatic father, and only half noticed a number of CorpOne security police in silver uniforms gathering on a flagstone area outside. Over their heads, blue-and-silver CorpOne banners fluttered, each bearing the stylized designs of elephants.

Suddenly he heard the violent pop-pop of gunfire. The private police took cover behind plants, benches, and fountains, and drew their weapons. But many of them were not quick enough, and they fell under the onslaught.

Stunned, Noah saw a squadron of green-and-brown uniformed soldiers running onto the flagstones, carrying shiny blue puissant rifles, setting up a ferocious volley of high-intensity fire that drove the defenders for cover. Many died in the onslaught.

The uniforms looked like those of Noah's own Guardians! But they couldn't possibly be his people. He had not ordered this! Oblivious to any danger, he pressed his face against the window glax. He didn't recognize any of the individuals. Who were they and why were they doing this?

Noah's thoughts went wild. He couldn't imagine what was occurring. Now the attackers were hurling explosives that detonated and shook the building.

Furious and confused, Noah hurried into the corridor, where he met his entourage of six Guardians, all with their weapons drawn. "Follow me!" he shouted. And he led them back the way they had come in.

* * * * *

Only moments before, Saito Watanabe had been standing at a window of his large office, considering what he would say to his son. It had been a long time since the two of them had spoken at all, so it would be an extremely awkward situation. Lifting a tall glass to his lips the old man took a long drink of sakeli, a syrupy liqueur, and admitted to himself that he was afraid the meeting would not go well. A tiny remark could set off yet another argument, so he would be careful about what he said … and try not to take offense too easily.

We need to get to know one another again.

His dark gaze flickered around the room and settled on a scroll attached to the wall. It was his Document of Patronage from Doge Lorenzo, the legal instrument attesting to the fact that Saito had been elevated to the status of a nobleman, even though he had not been born to such a station. Saito's entire corporate empire rested upon that piece of inscribed tigerhorse skin, and upon the ancient political system that supported it.

My son should receive this some day.

Like other merchant princes, Saito believed that a strong son could carry on the family traditions in ways that a daughter could never do. Francella had been trying to fill that role, but something had been missing. The Prince knew it, and she must as well.

Canopa, one of the wealthiest Human-ruled worlds, was dominated by CorpOne, the mega-company owned by Prince Saito Watanabe. Under grant from Doge del Velli, the Prince owned industrial facilities on more than a hundred moons and planets, including distant Polée, a mineral-rich but sparsely populated world that generated immense profits. With a wide range of operations, Watanabe was especially proud of his medical laboratories, which had developed remarkable products to extend and improve the quality of life through "cellteck"—advanced cellular technology.

In recent years, Noah had become wealthy in his own right as Master of the Guardians, demonstrating considerable business acumen. The young man's operations were on nowhere near the scale of the Prince's, but nonetheless they showed great ability. In sharp contrast, Francella had never done anything on her own. She just whiled away her time as an officer of the firm, without showing any creative spark of her own.

An eruption of gunfire brought the old man out of his thoughts. As if in a bad dream, he stared in shock at the outbreak of violence and pandemonium outside. Guardian forces were attacking CorpOne! He could not believe that his own son would commit such an atrocity against him, no matter the differences they'd had in the past. They were the same blood, the same heredity, and the Prince had sought a reconciliation with him. Was there no honor in Noah, no familial loyalty?

Dark fury infused Saito Watanabe, the raw, unforgiving rage brought on by deception and betrayal. Somehow his son's Guardians had disabled the building's electronic-pulse security system to gain entry!

Why would Noah do this?

All hope for rapprochement between the two of them exploded. A gloomy darkness settled around the Prince. Prior to this, he had been reconsidering his entire business philosophy, wondering if his son's environmental activist position might have some merit after all. Saito had wanted to suggest to Noah that perhaps CorpOne's polluting factories might be dismantled or redesigned after all, no matter the cost.

Now they would never have that conversation.

The door of Watanabe's office burst open, and his silver-uniformed security police rushed in. Their faces were red, their eyes wild. "This way, My Prince!" one of them shouted, a corporal.

The police formed a protective cocoon around the big man, and rushed him out into the corridor.

Chapter Five

The noble-born princes have too much time on their hands.

—Doge Lorenzo del Velli

General Mah Sajak stood impatiently while an Adurian slave put a clean red-and-gold uniform on him, replacing one that was covered with fresh purple blood stains. The General had been torturing a Mutati with an evisceration machine, and the prisoner of war had not died well.

The next time, Sajak would stand in a different position while supervising the interrogation and punishment process, to avoid being splattered with the filthy alien fluid. Sometimes when he got excited and stepped too close to a captive this sort of thing happened. It was all part of the job, he supposed, but he didn't like it. A stickler for decorum, he wanted everything clean and tidy, both in both his profession and his personal life.

"Hurry up, hurry up," Sajak admonished the slave, for the General was anxious to get back to Regimental HQ and take care of other business.

The captive Adurian was a male hairless homopod, a mixture of mammalian and insectoid features with a small head, bulbous eyes, and no bodily hair. His skin, a blotchy patchwork of faded colors, poked out around the wrinkled but clean rags he wore. He perspired profusely as he worked, and made the mistake of leaving spots of moisture on the General's new uniform. Because of this, Sajak marked him for death, but would keep it a secret until a suitable replacement had been trained, and administered the necessary psychological testing.

This one should have received a perspiration test.

"Sorry, sir," the Adurian said, as he noticed the sweat dripping from his own wide forehead onto the clothing. "Shall I get another jacket?"

"No time for that now," Mah Sajak growled. "Do you really think I have time to wait for such things?"

"No, sir. It's just that … " The slave's oversized eyes became even larger from fear, and he perspired even more, a torrent that ran from his brow down his face.

15

Grumbling to himself, Sajak left the nervous alien and stepped into the hot, silvery light of a security scanner that identified him and allowed him to pass through to a corridor. His body and uniform glowed faintly silver, and would until he reached the next security checkpoint.

A slideway transported him through a long series of corridors in the Gaol of Brimrock, past dismal cells, torture chambers, and body handling rooms. Unpleasant odors seeped into the hallways, mixed with sweet disinfectant sprays that never quite masked them. Other officers, guards, and civilians passed by, all glowing with metallic illumination that indicated which checkpoints they had been through. Here and there, through tiny windows, he caught glimpses of another world outside, the blue waters of the Grand Canal and the glittering buildings of the opulent city.

The officer barely noticed any of it, however, so engrossed was he in his own concerns, which were extremely important. Mah Sajak—in his oversized uniform and cap—took seriously his duties as Supreme General of the Merchant Prince Armed Forces. Eleven and a half years ago, he had dispatched a military fleet to attack the Mutati homeworld of Paradij, where the Zultan lived in his ostentatious citadel. That fleet should be arriving soon.

I'd like to hoist Meshdi's fat carcass onto one of my interrogation machines, the General thought, and he considered the wide array of torture devices at his disposal— automatic, semi-mechanized, and manual. Each had a specific, deadly purpose, and worked to great effect on the Mutati race.

Beneath the small, bony-featured officer, the slideway squeaked as it flowed forward jerkily. He gripped a shimmering electronic handrail that moved alongside.

So much responsibility on his shoulders, and sometimes it weighed heavily on him. Especially now, with the climactic moment approaching. The "Grand Fleet" of MPA fighter-bombers was aboard a bundle of vacuum rockets that had been traveling through space at sub-light speed for all those years, moving inexorably toward the Mutati homeworld of Paradij. He expected complete military success, but there were always little nagging worries that kept him awake at night.

The General had assured the Doge that all would go well. The renowned Mutati-killer, Admiral Nils Obidos, headed the task force, a man who had won two important military victories against the shapeshifters. He had selected more than twenty-four thousand of the finest men and women in the armed forces, including the top fighter-bomber pilots in the Merchant Prince Alliance. In addition, all ships had redundant mechanical systems and even a backup crew of the finest sentient robots from the Hibbil Cluster Worlds ... intelligent machines that could operate the whole fleet without Human involvement, if necessary. In some respects the General considered them better than Humans; if he told them what to do, they did it, without delays, complaints, or questions.

Doge Lorenzo del Velli was so convinced of a huge victory that he had begun preparations for a gala celebration on Timian One, with the exact date to be announced. It was widely known that there would be a festival, but the Doge had not told anyone what the occasion was. Rumors spread like fire on oil. The best entertainers—Human and alien—would be brought in from all over the galaxy. Even Mutati captives would participate. Under the high security of a huge containment field, terramutatis, hydromutatis, and aeromutatis would perform shapeshifting acts in a golden amphitheater.

At Sajak's thought command, he felt the tiny computer strapped to his wrist imprint his skin with a nubraille pattern, telling him what time it was at that moment. The device, containing a vast encyclopedia of information that he could access, required only that he think what he wanted to know, and the message would be received almost immediately. Now it was early evening, and in the zealousness of his interrogation he had neglected dinner.

During the first six years in which merchant prince fleet had been advancing toward the enemy, General Sajak had received coded nehrcom transmissions from the task force admiral informing him that the operation was progressing well. Nehrcoms (invented by Prince Jacopo Nehr) were audio-video signals transmitted across the galaxy at many times the speed of light ... an instantaneous communication system in which messages were fired from solar system to solar system at precise angles of deflection, using amplified solar energy. Nehrcom Industries, with a monopoly on the system, had installed transceivers in key sectors of the galaxy—sealed units that would detonate if anyone tried to scan or open them, thus protecting the priceless technological secrets. But the inventor still worried about military and industrial espionage by military enemies and business competitors, and refused to install transceivers in locations he did not consider secure.

And, although the remarkable transceivers could transmit instantaneously across space, they only operated to and from land-based facilities ... for reasons known only to the secretive Nehr. The General and his staff had discussed sending status reports via messengers on board podships ... but it had been known from the beginning that this would be an unreliable, dangerous method. Podships operated on their own schedules, often following circuitous routes with numerous pod station stops—thus risking detection by Mutati operatives. The mission planners agreed that it would be better to transmit no messages at all than to take such chances.

So, during the more than five years that the fleet had been beyond nehrcom range, the General had heard nothing at all. His huge task force was taking the long way to the Mutati homeworld, approaching it from an unexpected, poorly patrolled direction. If the Grand Fleet encountered Mutati forces, they would only be small ones, easily crushed.

The arrogant Jacopo Nehr irritated Sajak, for more reasons than one. The self-serving inventor should be forced to share his technology with the Merchant Prince Armed Forces, so that military strategists could employ it more effectively. It might even be possible to improve the system, so that it was no longer dependent upon land-based installations.

The Supreme General sucked in a deep breath. That would be a tremendous advance. But Nehr would not give up the information easily. Attempts had been made—through friendly persuasion and otherwise—and all had failed.

Jacopo Nehr and Prince Saito Watanabe were often seated beside the Doge during torture sessions that the General conducted. For Sajak, this created an awkward situation. Born to a noble station, he secretly resented princely appointments such as the ones received by the two business tycoons, and would prefer a return to the old ways. While Sajak had done well personally through his own efforts, many of his relatives and noble friends had suffered setbacks—having been supplanted by the new breed of entrepreneurs and inventors that the Doge favored. Even worse than his father, Doge Paolantonio IV, who started all of this foolishness, the merchant prince sovereign was surrounding himself with scientists and industrialists, upsetting the old, proven ways of doing things.

Someday the General would do something about that. It was one of his vows, and he always did what he set out to do. From an early age he had been that way. The trick was to conceal his desires from persons more powerful than he, so that they could not prevent him from achieving his goals. Fortunately for him, that list was quite small now, and one day it might not exist at all. He didn't mind taking orders from a commander in chief; but he had to respect the commands, and their source.

General Sajak stepped off the slideway and strolled through a short corridor, then paused at another security check point. This one scanned him with golden light and left him glowing that color when he left. He made his way down a short set of steps through a hallway where the lights were not functioning, and his own glow cast an eerie illumination on the walls. He took another slideway in a different direction.

At a casual wave of his hand, a red-cushioned seat popped up beside him on the conveyor, and he sat upon it. The transporter went through a long tunnel that sloped gently downward toward the Military HQ complex, a heavily fortified bunker deep underground.

In a few moments, he saw a cavern of bright white light ahead, and presently he was immersed in a scanner, this one with a rainbow of metallic colors that left him without a glow. Despite the security checkpoints, one could never be too careful when your mortal enemy was a race of expert shapeshifters.

Robotic guards greeted the General with stiff salutes as he stepped off the slideway and strode through a wide entrance into the War Chamber. Each of the mechanical sentinels was a weapon in itself, featuring a destructive array of guns and explosives that the General could set off at a thought command.

The machinery and personnel of tactics and strategy filled the immense War Chamber. Officers in red-and-gold uniforms rose stiffly and saluted as he entered. Those in his way stepped aside, enabling him to reach the red velvis command chair on a dais at the center.

"Give me a full report," General Sajak said, as he sat down and gazed about impatiently.

His adjutant, Major Edingow, was an angular, square-jawed man who favored single malt whiskey and the camaraderie of officers' clubs. He had halitosis, and to counteract it often chewed mints. This time he seemed to have forgotten his manners.

Irritated, Sajak stepped back to escape the stale odor.

Oblivious to the offense he was committing against his fastidious superior, the Major activated a telebeam bubble—a bright light that floated in the air—and moved it to a comfortable distance in front of the General. In a wordless broadcast, data flowed from the bubble into a receiver implanted in Sajak's brain, and from there traversed the circuitous neural pathways of his mind. He felt a soft hum inside his skull. The facts unfolded in an orderly fashion, and he considered them.

Concerned about the obsolescence of military technology in the eleven-year old attack force that he had dispatched, General Sajak had sent advance men to the Mutati homeworld, covert agents who were assigned to sneak in and commit acts of sabotage against Mutati infrastructures and military installations, softening them up for the bigger attack. Now he learned the results of the most recent forays, that many agents never got through, and that some were missing and possibly apprehended.

At the edge of the glistening data bubble, Sajak saw his staff officers watching him alertly, ready to comply with his commands the moment he issued them. At a snap of his fingers, the bubble popped and faded away.

Ignoring the faces that were turned toward him expectantly, General Mah Sajak considered the new information. For a century and a half—since galaxy-spanning podships first appeared mysteriously and began to increase contact between the races—Humans and Mutatis had been in an arms race, with huge research teams on both sides striving to make quantum leaps in military technology. He did not know what the Mutatis were working on now, but hoped it was not significant.

A career soldier, it had been frustrating for him to deal with the limited cargo capacities of podships, which had prevented him—and the enemy—from mounting large-scale offensives. He needed the element of surprise to work in favor of his forces ... but gnats of worry reminded him that the Mutatis might have their own surprise in store for him.

Chapter Six

These machines are designed to mimic only the best aspects of their creators. To permit the opposite, either through something intrinsic or of their own volition, would be to invite disaster.

—Hibbil product statement, sent out with each AI robot

The jewel-like volcanic planet of Ignem was a favorite for those who liked to travel the back ways of space. Shaped by a series of volcanic cataclysms that belched up rainbows of porous silica, the glittering world looked like an exotic treat for giant gods, one they could just scoop up and swallow as they flew past on one of their journeys across the cosmos.

Each day Ignem looked a little different, depending upon solar conditions and the amount of glassy dust that was kicked up by powerful winds blowing across the surface. No known life forms existed on the planet, since conditions were too severe for carbon-based, chemical, electrical, or other living creatures. Humans, Hibbils, Mutatis, Adurians, and other galactic races could only go on the surface in expensive, specially-crafted spacesuits that contained layered filter systems. Deep-space adventure companies took wealthy tourists to Ignem several times a year, and the visitors always returned home in amazement, gushing about the natural beauty they had seen.

All expeditions stopped first at the Inn of the White Sun, a comfortable machine-operated way station that had been constructed in a dense orbital ring more than eighty kilometers above the surface of the planet. At the inn, bubble-windowed rental spaces had been fitted with an atmosphere that was breathable to most of the galactic races. Adventurers checked their equipment and purchased anything they needed from a wide array of vending machines. At premium prices, of course.

Sales conventions were also held at the inn, usually for members of the Human-run Merchant Prince Alliance. At the moment, however, many of the rooms were filled with Heccians and Diffros, races of artisans and craftsmen from the far-off Golden Nebula of the Seventieth Sector. They were making quite a commotion as they drank foul-tasting venom extracted from snakes ... a traditional kickoff ceremony for their conventions.

Now it was the month of Dultaz in the White Sun solar system. A flat-bodied, gray robot named Thinker paced back and forth on the main observation deck of the Inn. The deck ran along the top of the thickest ring section, and was not atmospherically-controlled. Beneath him and stretching along the rings were the beehive-like rooms of the Inn, positioned so that they offered spectacular views of the shimmering jewel-like world below. For travelers on a budget, less expensive rooms were available without views, or with vistas of the twinkling darkness of deep space.

Far below the robot, Ignem glowed with a million colors as the last rays of the setting sun pierced the faceted, layered surfaces of the planet, lighting up the globe and the thin atmosphere surrounding it. He watched the hypnotically subtle chromatic changes, and the translucent effects on Ignem's surface, as the planet held onto the last rays of light before they were sucked away into the stygian night of space.

Thinker often came to this spot late in the day and stood by himself. These were reflective times for him, when he could consider significant issues, utilizing the immense amount of information in his data banks. As the leader of the sentient machines in this galactic subsector he had many responsibilities, and took them all seriously.

In a continual quest to improve himself, Thinker periodically went around the galaxy to collect material for his data banks, which he then brought back to the Inn of the White Sun to catalog. Whenever he traveled, he sought out other sentient machines, conversing with them and making interface connections, to download whatever data they had. Sometimes their security programs would not permit them to interface with him, and if that happened he had the ability to force a connection and override their internal firewalls. But he only rarely did that, not wishing to create controversy or call unnecessary attention to himself. Usually it was easier to just move on. There were always machines that would help him.

The sentient machines under his command had done quite well for themselves, rebuilding mechanical life forms that had been discarded by Humans and putting them back into operation. They even manufactured popular computer chips and sold them around the galaxy. Sometimes, though, they seemed overly dependent upon Thinker. At the moment, two of his assistants, Ipsy and Hakko, were standing at a thick glax door staring out at him, as if they could not do anything further without his advice. He waved them off dismissively, and they stepped back, out of his view. He knew, however, that they were still close by, waiting to talk with him the moment he went back inside.

I should reprogram them, he reminded himself. But this had occurred to him before, and he had never done anything about it. He knew why. Despite the minor irritations he actually enjoyed the relationships, because his subordinates made him feel needed.

Far off, in the perpetual night of the galaxy, he saw something flash and disappear. He would never know for certain what it was, and could only speculate. Perhaps it was a shooting star, a small sun going nova, or the glinting face of a comet before it turned and veered away from the reflective rays of sunlight that seemed to give it life.

It is so beautiful out there.

Since Thinker was a mechanical creature with few internal moving parts, he did not breathe, and was able to function outside the boundaries imposed upon biological life forms. The machines that operated this facility were the sentient remnants of merchant prince industrial efforts. Thrown away and left to rust and decay all over the galaxy, the intelligent robots had sought each other out and formed their own embryonic civilization.

Among Humans and other biological life forms that visited the inn, these mechanical men were something of a joke, and non-threatening. After all, the machines had an affection for Humans, referring to them in almost godlike terms as their "creators." The metal people were an eclectic assortment as well, and amusing in appearance to many people. Some of the robots were Rube Goldberg devices that performed tasks in laughable, inefficient ways, taking pratfalls and accomplishing very little. This explained why many of them were abandoned. Others had been cobbled together with spare parts. In all they looked quite different from the standardized robots manufactured by the Hibbils on their Cluster Worlds, under contract to the Doge and to the leaders of various galactic races.

Thinker didn't really care how he and his loyal compatriots were viewed. His emotional programs were limited in scope, and while he became mildly irritated at times he did not take offense easily. His thoughts tended toward the intellectual, toward questions of deep purpose and matters involving the origins of the universe. Most of all he found it exhilarating to stand out here in the vacuum of space, gazing into eternity … into all that was, and all that ever would be. Some marvelous power had created this galaxy, and in his most private thoughts he liked to imagine the Supreme Being as a machine, and not some cellular entity. It seemed plausible … perhaps even likely. The galaxy was a machine after all, one that operated on a vast scale, ticking along moment by moment in its journey through time.

Lights blinked on inside the rooms and public chambers of the Inn of the White Sun. Far below, Ignem gave up its ephemeral translucence and faded to darkness, casting an ebony shadow against the cloth of stars beyond.

The cerebral robot was about to go back inside when he felt a rumbling in the metal plates of his body, and his metal-lidded eyes detected a distortion in the fabric of the cosmos, with star systems twisted slightly out of their normal alignment. A section of space in front of him became opaque and amorphous, with a wobbly effect around the edges. He noted a slight change of pressure around him, too, as if a door into another dimension had opened for an instant, and something altogether different was entering.

Podship.

The opacity glowed bright green for a moment, then flickered. A blimp-shaped object took form and made its way toward a faint, barely visible pod station, floating nearby in the airless vacuum of space. The mottled, gray-and-black podship had a row of portholes on the side facing Thinker, with pale green light visible inside the passenger compartment. From his data banks the robot drew a comparison. The sentient creature was reminiscent of a whale of Earth, but without a tail or facial features, and cast off into space.

The pod station, after fading from view during the entry of the podship, solidified its appearance. A globular, rough-hewn docking facility, it was nearly as mysterious as the podships themselves. For tens of thousands of years the sentient podships—hunks of living cosmic material—had been traveling at faster-than-light speeds through the galaxy, on regular routes. The ships were of unknown origin, and so too were the orbiting pod stations at which they docked—utilitarian facilities positioned all over the galaxy, usually orbiting the major planets. Some of the galactic races said that the podships and their infrastructure were linked with the creation of the galaxy, and there were numerous legends concerning this. One, attributed to the Humans of ancient

21

Brian Herbert

Earth, held that the podships would come one day and transport religious and political leaders to the Supreme Being, where all of the great secrets would be revealed.

Thinker signaled for a sliding door to open, and then strode into the lobby of the inn on his stiff metal legs. There he encountered Ipsy and Hakko, who had been waiting for him, as he'd suspected. "Later," he told them. "For once, handle something on your own."

"We need to plan next month's sales convention," Hakko said, "so that the necessities can be ordered."

"Yes," Ipsy agreed. "There is a great deal of printing to be done— announcement cards, menus. You know the trouble we had at the last convention when we tried to serve Blippiq food to Adurians."

"Well, take care of it then," Thinker said, with mock impatience, since it was like playing a game with them.

He continued on his way, and entered a lift that took him down to the lowest level of the inn. There, through a thick glax floor, he could see the dark gray pod station floating perhaps a thousand meters away, and the sentient ship that had just entered one of its docking bays.

Presently he saw a shuttle emerge from the pod station, burning a blue exhaust flame as it closed the gap between the station and the orbital ring. The little craft locked onto a berthing slot, and Thinker saw men step out. He counted twenty-two.

His first impression was that they were Humans, a group of tourists. Unlike other galactic races, Humans did that sort of thing. They just went places to be there, to experience them. To most galactic races it seemed a waste of time, but Thinker understood. Like the Human technicians who created him, he had a sense of curiosity and wonder about the cosmos.

But the new arrivals were *not* Human. As they walked across a deck toward the main entrance to the Inn of the White Sun, he noted subtle differences that only a highly trained observer such as himself could detect. The bodily motions were slightly different. Oh, they were very close to authentic, but not quite right. They moved like what they really were.

What are Mutatis doing here?

In order to contemplate without distraction, Thinker folded his dull-gray body closed in a clatter of metal, tucking his head neatly inside. To an observer he might look like a metal box now, just sitting silently on the deck. Inside, though, he was deep in concentration, organizing the vast amount of information in his data banks, trying to solve the conundrum that had presented itself to him suddenly.

Unlike Humans, Mutatis never traveled for leisure. They always had some important purpose in mind ... usually military, political, or economic. In memory, Thinker recalled the bodily movements of the Human impostors. Remnants of their true identities could be seen in every step they took.

They were Mutati soldiers, led by an officer.

This worried Thinker, and he wondered if word had gotten out about the machine operations here. Down on the surface of the volcanic planet, in a region not visible from the orbital ring, the machines were secretly building a military force of their own, a collection of patched-together fighting robots. One day he would use them to prove that his sentient machines had value, that they should not have been discarded.

Were the Mutatis here to spy on that operation? Or had they come for another reason?

22

Chapter Seven

Our entire galaxy is in motion. The Scienscroll tells us this. But where is it going?

—Master Noah of the Guardians

At CorpOne headquarters on Canopa, Noah Watanabe had been shocked to see soldiers in green-and-brown Guardian uniforms, firing puissant rifles and setting off booming explosions. He came to realize that they were impersonating his own environmental activists, but there was no time to determine the reason. Instead, he'd led his small entourage to the rooftop of the main building, where they ran toward a dark blue, box-shaped aircraft.

From the days when he had worked there, Noah knew the layout of the complex, and the main building had not changed much in fifteen years. Here and there, doorways were marked differently, but the corridors and lifts remained the same, and it was unchanged on the roof. The aircraft, one of the grid-planes kept on the premises for Prince Watanabe and his top officers, was familiar to Noah, for this was a technology so successful that it had not been significantly altered in nearly a century. The onboard semi-automatic systems were relatively simple to operate, and many people knew how to handle them from an early age.

Noah and his men leaped aboard, and his adjutant Subi Danvar squeezed into the cockpit. Using voice commands and pressure pads, the rotund Danvar activated the takeoff sequence. Red and blue lights flashed across the instrument panel.

The vessel extended four short wings and lifted off. Within moments it engaged the multi-altitude electronic grid system that was part of a planet-wide transportation network. Through the open doorway of the cockpit just forward of Noah's seat, he saw automatic systems begin to kick in, as parallel yellow and blue lines on an instrument panel screen merged into each other, and became green.

Danvar activated touch pads beneath the screen, then reached down for something in the flight bag beside his chair. A scar on the back of his right hand marked where doctors had attached cloned knuckles and fingers, after he lost them in a grid plane crash. Noah had his own moral objections to cloned Human body parts, but he'd never tried to force his views on other people.

He felt a characteristic gentle bump as they locked into the grid, but this was followed moments later by a disturbingly sharp jolt. The screen flashed angry orange letters: TAIL SECTION DAMAGED BY PROJECTILE.

Before Noah could react, the screen flashed again, this time in yellow: BACKUP SYSTEMS ENGAGED.

The craft kept going with hardly a variation in its flight characteristics, and presently Noah felt a reassuring smooth sensation as the grid-plane accelerated to the standard speed of three hundred kilometers per hour.

"Permission to seal the cockpit," Danvar said. "I need to concentrate on the instruments."

"Do it," Noah responded. Almost before permission was granted, the pilot slid the cockpit door shut, placing a white alloy barrier between them.

Through a porthole Noah could see that they were leaving the Valley of the Princes behind, a landscape of trees and fields, spotted with industrial complexes. Had his father betrayed him, faking a Guardian attack to bring him and his organization into disfavor?

Unable to suppress his anger, Noah slammed his fist on the armrest of the chair, so hard that pain shot through the hand. He scanned the sky and the land below, looking for threats.

Obviously, Subi was concerned about this himself. He was Noah's most trusted Guardian, but somewhat eccentric at times, and very outspoken. Noah had learned to give him free rein, but new thoughts began to occur to him now.

Could this man betray me?

After all that he and Subi had been through together, it seemed a preposterous, paranoid thought, and Noah discarded it out of hand. While the two of them were careful to maintain their distance, keeping their relationship professional, Noah had always felt an affinity for the adjutant, a strong bond of friendship. The feeling seemed mutual.

Master Noah heaved a deep sigh. He sat back in his bucket seat and listened to the smooth purr of the grid-plane.

If I am meant to die today, so be it. If I am meant to live, that will happen instead. He flicked a speck of black off the long sleeve of his ruffled shirt, where the garment poked out from his surcoat.

Ever since boyhood, Noah Watanabe had sensed a presence guiding him, a force that was always there, constantly directing his actions. He often felt it viscerally, and was convinced that it told him whether or not he was doing the right thing. His stomach was calm now, but the sensation didn't always provide him with consistent indicators. It seemed to have lapses ... unpredictable and disconcerting gaps.

The grid-plane left the valley far behind and flew over a rugged mountain range, irregular peaks that looked like the heads of demons. On the far side of the mountains the aircraft streaked over an industrial city perched on the edge of a high cliff whose stony facets glittered and flashed in mid-morning sunlight.

Known as the "canyon planet," Canopa was unlike any other world in the charted galaxy, with deep rainbow-crystal gorges, powerful whitewater rivers and spectacular scenery. Cities such as the one they were flying over now were engineering marvels, clinging to cliff-faces of iridescent rock. Long ago, superstitious aborigines had lived in these areas, but had been driven out by Human traders who were the economic precursors of the modern-day merchant princes. Primitive people still lived on Canopa, but kept themselves out of view, with the exception of a few men and women who were captured on occasion and brought in for observation. Curiously, aboriginal children were never seen by outsiders, not even in pre-merchant times.

Canopa was steeped in mystery and legend, and was said to have been the domain in ancient times of a race of alien creatures ... people who had gone extinct, with their bodies now on display in museums. At a number of archaeological sites around the planet, their eerie exoskeletons and personal effects had been dug up. After studying the bodies, galactic anthropologists determined that they were a race of arthropods of high intelligence. Through rune stones that had been recovered, their language had been only partially deciphered. It was known that they had referred to themselves as Nops and that they had engaged in off-world trading, but very little else was learned about them.

Following an hour's flight, Noah's compound came into view atop a verdant plateau, bounded by river gorges on two sides. On land that had once been the site of industrial operations, he had restored and converted it to an impressive wildlife preserve and farm that he called his Ecological Demonstration Project, or "EDP." The facility was far more than just structures and compounds and set-aside areas. It was a high-concept dream shaped into reality, one that included projects designed to show how man could live in harmony with the environment.

One of Master Noah's oft-repeated admonitions to his loyal followers was, *Excess is waste.* This was linked to his concept of balance, which he saw as a necessary force in the cosmos, as true for microorganisms as it was for higher life forms.

This way of thinking had been a source of friction between Noah and his father, building up to their terrible argument. On that day, only moments after Prince Saito struck him, Noah had quit his job at CorpOne and stormed out, never expecting to return or even to speak with his father again. Noah's environmental militancy had proven too much for the Prince, who had refused to accept any of the concepts. Like Earthian bulls the two men had butted heads, with each of them holding fast to their political and economic beliefs.

After Noah's resignation, his father had publicly and vehemently disowned him. Noah wondered how much of a part his twin sister Francella had played in encouraging the old man's willful behavior. She had always hated Noah. Certainly there had been jealousy on her part; he had seen too many examples of it. But her feelings of enmity seemed to run even deeper, perhaps to her own biological need to survive and her feeling that Noah was a threat to the niche she wanted to occupy.

At the troubling thought, Noah cautioned himself. One of his father's criticisms of him might have been valid, the way Noah constantly saw situations in environmental terms. Sometimes when Noah caught himself doing this, he tried to pull back and look at things in a different way. But that did not always work. He was most comfortable thinking within a framework that he knew well, which he considered a blueprint for all life forms, from the simplest to the most complex.

The grid-plane locked into a landing beam. Subi Danvar opened the cockpit door, and Noah saw the parallel green lines on the instrument panel diverge, forming flashing yellow and blue lines.

"All systems automatic," Subi reported. He swung out of the pilot's chair and made his way aft, turning his husky body sideways to get past banks of instruments on each side.

Noah felt the grid-plane descend, going straight down like an elevator, protected by the electronic net over his EDP compound.

With a scowl on his birthmark-scarred face, Subi plopped his body into a chair beside Noah and announced, "I'm not getting any sleep until I get to the bottom of this. Somebody copied our uniforms exactly ... or stole them from us."

"I didn't see any of our people out there," Noah said.

"That doesn't mean they weren't involved, Master. I'll start with the most recent volunteers and work back from there. Maybe one of them is disgruntled."

"Could be."

In an organization as large as Noah's, with thousands of uniformed Guardians, it was impossible to keep every one of them happy all the time. It was company policy to recruit people with high ideals, capable of thinking in terms of large-scale issues ... rather than petty private matters. Still, there were always personality conflicts among workers, and unfulfilled ambitions.

The aircraft settled onto a paved landing circle and taxied toward a large structure that had gray shingle walls and elegant Corinthian columns, shining bright white in the midday sunlight. This was Noah's galactic base of operations, the main building in a complex of offices and scientific laboratories.

In his primary business, he performed ecological recovery operations around the galaxy, under contract to various governmental agencies, corporations, and individuals wanting to repopulate areas devastated by industrial operations. On some of the smaller worlds he also operated electric power companies, having patented his own environmentally-friendly energy chambers. The merchant princes, and not just his father, had shown absolutely no concern for ecology; they routinely raped each planet's resources and then moved on to other worlds. Canopa, despite the wild areas that still existed along the route Noah was flying now, was nowhere near what it used to be. Huge areas of the planet had been stripped of their resources and denuded of beauty, leaving deep geological scars that might never heal.

As far as Noah Watanabe was concerned, the galactic races tended to be interlopers in the natural order of things, and Humans were the worst of all. His ideas were much wider than humanity, though, or any of the races. While performing his business operations on a variety of worlds, he had begun to see relationships within relationships, and the vast, galaxy-wide systems in which they operated.

The grid-plane came to a stop and a double door whooshed open. As he stepped down onto a flagstone entry plaza, Noah inhaled a deep breath of warm, humid air, and watched aides as they hurried to greet him. This moment was a gift. For a while, he had not been certain if he would ever make it back here.

Chapter Eight

The art of business is not a pretty one; it requires blood-red pigment.
—Francella Watanabe, private reflections

In her white-and-gold dress and star-shaped headdress, Noah's sister gave the appearance of a lady of leisure. It was just one of the subterfuges the tall, redheaded woman employed to conceal the fact that she was responsible for the assault on CorpOne headquarters, and that she herself had received training in the most advanced styles of combat and tactical warfare.

"Faster!" Francella shouted to four company policemen who carried her injured, comatose father on a hover-bier. With her leading the way, they ran through a dimly-illuminated corridor, just one of the tunnels that formed a maze beneath the office-industrial complex of more than twenty buildings. Originally these subterranean passageways had been the streets of an ancient Nopan city, but the community had been abandoned long ago when the inhabitants fell victim to a mysterious malady.

Old Prince Saito, with his head bandaged, came to life suddenly on the bier. His eyes opened wide and he groaned loudly, then flopped one of his beefy arms over the side. "Noah?" he said, while lifting his head and looking toward Francella.

She wanted to scream her rage and pound on him, but instead pressed a small skin-colored pad against her own neck, right over a throbbing vein. Almost immediately she felt a custom drug take effect, deadening her emotions and dampening twinges of personal guilt she had been feeling, concerning the things she had to do.

Abruptly the nobleman's eyes closed again, but he kept murmuring Noah's abominable name. Finally he fell silent and his face went slack, though his chest heaved up and down as he clung stubbornly to life. She stared at a sapphire signet ring on his right hand and vowed that Noah would never possess it. She considered slipping it off the old man's finger at the first opportunity, but hesitated. Soon she would have everything she wanted anyway.

In order to maintain appearances, Francella fell back beside her father and re-secured his arm inside the electronic strap that had been holding it. His eyelids fluttered, but didn't open.

She spoke his name, but he did not respond. His breathing remained steady.

Prince Saito had been injured by a hail of alloy-jacketed projectiles fired into his office building by the phony Guardians, who were *conducci*, mercenaries she had hired secretly. Murdering her father had been the primary objective of the professional fighters, but they may not have succeeded. She hated sloppy workmanship.

"You'll be fine," she assured Prince Saito, though he seemed unable to hear her. "We're taking care of you."

"Noah?" he murmured, with his eyelids still closed.

"I'm *Francella*," she said, arching her hairless brows in displeasure. "Noah tried to kill you."

"He wouldn't do that … wouldn't do that … " Prince Saito's face became a twisted mask as he struggled to think, struggled for consciousness, and finally gave up the effort … but kept breathing.

She studied the heaving of his chest, and thought, *Die, damn you!*

They ascended a corrugated alloy ramp to a platform and ran across to the opposite side, where they boarded a small maglev rail car. Francella took a seat at the rear of the vehicle, while the others placed the bier on the floor in the center of the aisle, and then took seats themselves. Armored doors closed and the car accelerated quickly, throwing Francella against her seat back.

Only half an hour earlier, fifty-eight heavily armed *conducci* had attacked the CorpOne complex. She had hired them through a series of middlemen in such a circuitous chain that no one knew who had originally paid for their services. As the Security Chief for the company, Francella Watanabe had ways of getting things done discreetly. She had, however, put out the word that any mistakes would be handled brutally … and the killers had not done their job cleanly, as she had demanded.

The CorpOne policemen in the rail car with her had known nothing of the plot and had interfered, going to the aid of the Prince and whisking him off to safety, with Francella in tow … trying to figure out what to do.

Her thoughts racing, she touched an electronic transmitter at her waist, setting off explosives in the tunnel behind them. The company security men chattered excitedly and stared out the rear window of the railway car at the flaming tunnel.

But Francella had other matters on her mind. Privately, she was considering how best to finish the job on her father, but she needed to do it carefully, so that no one suspected a thing. For years she had been monitoring the old man's declining health, and had hastened it along by seeing to it that the "cellteck" life extension drugs and other medicines he took were of less effect than they should have been. With those products at full strength—many manufactured in

Brian Herbert

CorpOne laboratories—he might have lived to a hundred and ten, another twenty-seven years.

Too long for her to wait. She wanted control of all family corporate operations as soon as possible, before anything could erode her position.

The alterations in her father's pharmacopoeia had been slight but cumulative, so that over a period of years they undoubtedly subtracted time from his life. An actuary secretly in her employ (his services obtained through another circuitous series of middlemen) had prepared projections showing how much she had probably shortened the unnamed subject's life. Based upon raw medical data that she had provided for the actuary, he had originally estimated a reduced life span of seventeen months, twenty-four days, and a few hours.

Unfortunately that had been modified by the interference of the Prince himself, who had unwittingly compensated for her tricks by improving his diet and instituting a moderate exercise program. In the process, the big man, unaware of her actions, had been bragging that he'd lost two kilos over the past few weeks. Undoubtedly the net effect on his health had been minimal, since he had always been sedentary and had such an enormous girth. She had been waiting for him to slip back into his old ways, but the crisis had interfered ... the meeting between Noah and her father that she could not allow.

At Francella's instigation another explosion sounded behind the maglev car in which she rode. The vehicle shuddered, but kept going. It entered a brightly-illuminated tunnel, and moments later a heavy alloy door slammed shut behind them, keeping them safe from pursuers or the fire and detonations that she had set off.

A rapprochement between Francella's brother and father would have unraveled much of her carefully-crafted efforts over the past decade, allowing her hated brother to gain a toe-hold on CorpOne operations.

She and Noah, her fraternal twin, had never gotten along very well, and the problems started early. After the babies were born, they thrashed around on a table and gave each other bloody lips. Over the years there had been respites between them, cease-fires, but they were few and far between ... and tense. The siblings had always loathed one another, and had exchanged few words in the last fifteen years.

Their mother Eunicia, the only woman Prince Saito ever married, had almost died in childbirth. She had lived for years afterward, but never fully recovered, and was always a frail woman, finally dying in a grid-plane crash at the age of fifty-one. Prince Saito had never been the same afterward.

In recent weeks the old man had been wavering about Noah, and had mentioned the possibility of revamping his business operations in order to satisfy his son. This could involve bringing her hated twin back into the corporation, with all of his costly, meddlesome ideas about environmental issues. Francella could not tolerate that.

Upon learning of the scheduled meeting between the men, she had gone into a crisis mode. Setting aside her attempts to erode the Prince's health, she had moved forward quickly. Her military-style attack with phony Guardians was a risky course of action, but offered the potential of distinct benefits. It could eliminate the Prince much more quickly, while placing the blame for his "tragic death" on Noah.

It might still work, if the old man died of his head injury.

On the bier beside her, Prince Saito groaned again. Francella felt like stuffing something in his mouth to shut him up, but resisted the temptation. She would take the rational course, not letting her emotions get the better of her.

Chapter Nine

We Parviis are the most powerful of all galactic races.
And, with good reason, the most secretive.

—Woldn, *Eye of the Swarm*

A towering black cloud hung over Canopa's central plain like an anvil, threatening to strike the land with a hammer-blow of rain. Summer was late getting underway this year, as the weather had been unseasonably stormy and cold, almost a month into the season. There had been some warm days, but not many.

As Tesh Kori stood on cobblestones near the center of a large courtyard, she wished her boyfriend did not have such a quick temper. Dr. Hurk Bichette stood with his hands on his hips, shouting at the maintenance man for his country estate. The prominent physician had a strong jaw and closely-set green eyes. A vein bulged and throbbed at his temple, a sign that he was losing control.

"You're not paying enough attention to your duties," Bichette thundered in his basso voice. "It seems that other things interest you more." He shot a glance in Tesh's direction and glared at her for an instant before looking away. This courtyard was between the doctor's palatial home and the stables for his expensive tigerhorses. The buildings were constructed in the classical Canopan style, of smoky-white marble with inlaid ruby and emerald gemstones. A colorful kaleidoscope of imported tulips bloomed in flower beds around the perimeter of the courtyard, and in planter boxes on the balconies of the three-story main house.

The target of Dr. Bichette's rage, Anton Glavine, wore a short blue-and-white tunic buttoned down the front, with high, tight leggings, and black boots. Remaining calm all through the verbal onslaught, the blond, mustachioed maintenance man stood taller than the doctor, and stared down at him dispassionately, saying nothing in response.

Tesh tried to be understanding, but in recent weeks she had been growing increasingly irritated with her boyfriend's possessive, even paranoid, attitude. Bichette seemed to fear that he might be losing her affections to this rough-and-tumble young upstart, who enjoyed tramping around in the woods and living off the land. Glavine—only twenty years old—had been working on the opulent estate, performing handyman tasks and yard work.

Concerned that the situation would escalate, Tesh stepped forward and said, "Hurk, he's hardly spoken to me at all. I assure you, there's nothing for you to worry ... "

"You stay out of this," he snapped. With one arm, he shoved her away, and she stumbled backward before regaining her footing.

The muscles in Glavine's face tightened. He studied Tesh, as if to make certain she was all right.

Standing off to one side with her arms folded across her chest, Tesh had to admit to herself that she was physically attracted to Glavine. With a tan, ruddy complexion and hazel eyes, he carried himself with an air of maturity. Despite his youth, he was well-spoken and knowledgeable on a wide range of subjects. He had a tendency to exude an air of arrogance, though, and this seemed to grate on Dr. Bichette at times.

Human males have interesting means of combat, Tesh thought.

She hoped this pair didn't come to blows, but she had seen other Human men fight for her attentions, and even an unfortunate instance where one man had killed another. Among her own Parvii race this sort of verbal ... and potentially physical ... battling never occurred. But her true identity remained a complete secret here on the merchant prince planet of Canopa. With long black hair, emerald green eyes, and a full figure, Tesh looked like an attractive Human woman of around twenty-seven years.

But all of her people *looked* Human, with one significant exception. Parviis were exceedingly tiny, no taller than the little finger of a typical *humanus ordinaire*. In order to conceal their true identities when traveling to foreign planets such as this one, the diminutive humanoids used a personal magnification system that made each one of them look as large as the Humans of the merchant prince worlds. The ingenious apparatus, undetectable to scanners or the most sophisticated scientific instruments, even caused anyone touching Tesh's "skin" to think it was real, and permitted her to experience sensory feelings. Her projected skin and hair, and the atomic structure of the clothing she wore, were in reality crackling molecular energy fields, technologically-created illusions that involved no magic whatsoever.

Emerging from her thoughts, she noticed she that the doctor was taking a deep breath and gazing off into the distance. After several moments he resumed talking, in a lower, more controlled tone. He seemed to be holding back a little, perhaps because he knew that he could not easily find another person who would maintain the structures on the large estate as well as Glavine. In the few months that the young man had worked on the property, he had already completed important repairs to the larger of two stable buildings.

Among other operations here, Dr. Bichette provided a tigerhorse stud service for nobles on the merchant prince planets. This had been his family business for centuries, begun by a great-great grandfather and continued to the present day as a highly successful enterprise. Bichette himself had extensive veterinary knowledge, in addition to the medical services he offered to important noblemen and their ladies. A renowned medical expert with a handful of powerful clients, he was Saito Watanabe's personal physician. He also directed CorpOne's Medical Research Division.

Presuming that the dispute between the men would dissipate, Tesh went inward again. She did this sometimes in order to revisit the fondest places of her memory and heart, and for deeper ruminations, to better understand her position in a cosmos of staggering dimensions. The voices of the men droned on, a fuzzy background noise in her mind.

Linked inextricably to the fate of her own people, Tesh could extricate herself somewhat from them during occasional inward journeys in search of her own personal identity, but these were no more than ephemeral trips of the mind, vagrant sparks of thought that were soon washed away in the streams of time. She was linked to every other Parvii, part of a collective organism that stretched into the most distant sectors of the galaxy, into light and into darkness.

The personal magnification system of each Parvii provided only superficial benefits, a defense mechanism for each segment of the much larger organism that allowed it to avoid detection in certain situations ... and thus to survive.

The Parviis were a powerful race. Secretly, they held dominion over another galactic race, the Aopoddae, that fleet of podship spacecraft that carried travelers and goods across the entire galaxy. One tiny Parvii could, in fact, pilot a much larger sentient pod through deep space. It had been this way for countless millennia, since the early moments following the Moment of Creation. And

Tesh was herself a pilot. She had learned her skill from an early age, in the time-honored method by which all children of her race were trained.

However, since there were many more Parviis than podships, she had a great deal of time off-duty … as much as a decade without interruption. During the current interlude she had been getting to know Human men better, while on previous breaks she had dated the men of other star systems. By galactic standards she was quite old, much more than she appeared to be. It was like this with all of her kinsmen, but each Parvii was not eternal. On average they lived for twenty or twenty-five standard centuries, and sometimes for as long as thirty.

Parviis were a traveling breed, galactic gypsies without a homeworld. They lived all over the cosmos, and communicated with one another across vast distances through a mysterious, arcane medium that was known by many appellations, the most common of which was Timeweb.

Timeweb.

Even after the seven-plus centuries of her life, the thought of the gossamer connective tissue between star systems never failed to amaze and confound her. The web meant so many things beyond its physical reality.

A shout startled Tesh to awareness. It was the deep voice of Dr. Bichette, and she saw him shove Glavine in the chest. The younger man, much stronger than his feisty, smaller aggressor, hardly moved backward at all. Enraged, Bichette took a wild punch, which Glavine eluded with athletic ease, and then grabbed both arms of his boss to restrain him.

"Let go of me!" Bichette demanded, as he struggled unsuccessfully against the stronger man. "If you value your job, take your filthy hands off me!"

Instead, Glavine spun him around and forced him toward a wrought-alloy bench on one side of the patio. "Our relationship is no longer employer and employee," Glavine said in a flat tone. He glanced at Tesh, and then looked away as he shoved the doctor onto the bench. "Sit there until you're ready to talk reasonably."

"Nothing happened between you two?" Bichette looked first at her, then back at him.

In response, both of them shook their heads. But Tesh knew it was a lie; there *had* been sparks between her and the young maintenance man, a mutual attraction that they had not acted upon. Not yet. Parvii women, like their Human counterparts, knew such things intuitively.

With a sudden, startling clang, a heavy metal door slammed open on the perimeter of the courtyard, and a heavyset man in a purple uniform burst through. Wearing a frilly white shirt with lace at the collar and sleeves, he was a *messagèro*, one of the bonded couriers who worked for the Merchant Prince Alliance. Breathing heavily and perspiring, although his run had not been far from the circular parking area outside, he bowed as he reached Bichette.

"Doctor Sir," he gasped, "Most urgent news. A car awaits you."

Narrowing his eyes, Bichette accepted a pyruz from him, a rolled sheet of white ishay bark on which matters of life and death were written. The doctor touched an identity plate on the seal, causing the pyruz to unfurl and become rigid. He read it, then rose to his feet.

"We must continue this later," Bichette said to Glavine. "I am certain we can resolve it." Without another word, he handed the pyruz to Tesh and strode out of the courtyard, behind the sweating *messagèro*.

Tesh read the communication.

"Prince Saito has been gravely injured," she said to Anton Glavine. But as their gazes met, she knew they were thinking of something else, with each of them wondering where their relationship would go from there.

They stood near each other, and drew closer, with almost imperceptible movements. Out at the front entrance, the maglev car hummed. Then, with a high-pitched whine, the vehicle left.

Anton took Tesh in his arms and drew her to him. She had been waiting for this moment, expecting it. However, she had learned that one of the interesting things about physical relationships was that neither the timing nor the exact circumstances were ever known in advance. Of course, Tesh reminded herself, it was that way with the rest of life as well. But she had never anticipated anything quite as much as this particular first kiss, had never wondered about anything so much.

As Anton held her tightly, the Parvii woman had the pleasurable sensation of floating away, on a journey to a far-off place.

Chapter Ten

It is said of merchant prince schooners that they are as numerous as raindrops from a cloudburst. The small red-and-gold vessels, filled with the most wondrous products imaginable, are transported by podship to all sectors of the galaxy.
—*Jannero's Starships*, Tenth edition

On Timian One, the stocky, gray-haired Doge Lorenzo del Velli sat upon his great throne, perusing a folio that his Cipher Secretary had just delivered to him, the translation of an intercepted Mutati communiqué. The gangly secretary, Triphon Soro, stood at the foot of the dais, awaiting instructions.

Such messages (which the Mutati Kingdom sent by courier since they did not have nehrcom transceivers) were of interest to Lorenzo, but he always eyed them suspiciously. The shapeshifters were tricky, and had been known to plant false information.

The missive was brief, and he reread it several times, then spoke it aloud with a query in his voice, "'*Demolio is almost ready.*'" Leaning forward a little, he handed it back to Soro. "What in the inferno does this mean?"

Shrugging, the lanky man responded, "No one knows. It is the first time I have ever heard the word, but it might be a code name for something. Perhaps the letters: *d-e-m-o-l-i-o*, represent a deeper cipher, or an acronym. We are working on it."

"Well get on with it," the Doge snapped. He waved a hand dismissively, causing the royal functionary to scurry away.

With a sigh, the aged leader retrieved a rolled parchment from a golden receiving tray at his elbow. He opened the document and let it roll out so that it stretched all the way to the plush crimson carpet at his feet.

The immense chair on which he sat, the legendary Aquastar Throne, had been cut in the shape of a merchant schooner. Presented to Lorenzo the Magnificent by a wealthy nobleman in exchange for the granting of a lucrative trade route, it was the largest piece of blue aquastar ever found, and one of the Wonders of the Galaxy.

At the side of the royal dais and only peripherally noticed by the Doge, his Royal Attaché fidgeted, having signaled that he needed to speak with his superior ... an entreaty that had been ignored. Dressed in an oversized gold and platinum robe, Pimyt was a Hibbil, a soft-fleshed creature with black-and-white fur that made him look somewhat like an Earthian panda bear. Despite the cuddly appearance of his galactic race, they were vicious fighters, and extremely fast; no one could outrun them. Over the course of centuries, they had formed political and business alliances with Humans, and were most renowned for their innovative machines, which they manufactured on their Cluster Worlds and provided to Human allies at reasonable costs.

Pimyt was an extraordinary individual. Even though he was not Human, he was so trusted that he had been made the Regent of the Merchant Prince Alliance decades ago, when the princes on the Council of Forty could not agree on the election of a new leader. The aging Hibbil had flecks of gray fur and a thick, salt-and-pepper beard. His red eyes still remained bright and youthful, and at the moment they flashed impatiently as he moved around restlessly. He did not like to be kept waiting, but Doge Lorenzo sometimes made him do so anyway, just to remind him who was in charge.

"Your Magnificence," Pimyt said, "if you could just … " He paused, as Lorenzo raised a hand to quiet him, and read the long parchment.

The document was a long list of "requests" from the Princess Meghina of Siriki, whom he had married after divorcing three of his previous five wives and executing two others. He had married all of them for political reasons, to cement alliances between the noble houses and to gain assets. Everything was a business proposition for him, and the current spouse was the most expensive of all. Still, Meghina had undeniable physical talents to go with her excellent pedigree, and he intended to keep her around. This did not mean that he was faithful to her, or that he expected her to be, either. She was, after all, a celebrated courtesan … and they had reached an understanding in the beginning of their relationship that neither of them would ever be tethered. For his own part, Lorenzo had always liked to "dabble" with the females of the various galactic races.

In her mid-thirties, the Royal Consort was much younger than her husband, and he had given her virtually everything. On their wedding day Meghina had asked for her own golden palace, and he had commissioned one for her on the Human-ruled planet of Siriki, complete with two hundred servants and a private zoo of exotic, laboratory-bred animals.

Now she was pressing him for a larger ballroom and a royal hall to entertain important guests. The new construction would require adding another wing onto her palace. She also wanted a more modern stable for her thoroughbred tigerhorses, and sculpted carriages to be pulled by those powerful animals. This would require new access gates for the coaches to enter and leave the grounds, and a spiral ramp to traverse a steep incline down to the cobblestone streets of the village below.

Lorenzo fiddled with the gold medallion that hung from his neck. He was not feeling well this morning, from an attack of the gout. Within the hour his physician had administered a kaser injection, which had dulled, but not eliminated, the pain and swelling in his feet. He took a deep, exasperated breath and continued reading.

Meghina's document included a construction cost estimate, which he presumed she had inflated grossly—one of her many tricks to extract extra money from him. Adding to the expense, she wanted a fast-paced construction schedule, requiring some of the highest paid artisans in the galaxy. Fortunately, Doge Lorenzo had no shortage of funds. In his position at the top of the merchant prince food chain, he had an efficient tax collection network that brought in a massive flow of money. All of it was managed by his Finance

Minister, but the Doge—ever cautious and suspicious—had an elaborate system of checks and balances to prevent embezzlement.

In her transmittal, the Princess explained why it all had to be done quickly. She had given birth to the first of seven daughters for the Doge when she was only fifteen, and now Annyette—the eldest—was making her society debut. The party for her would be a grand affair, with guests invited from most of the galactic races ... with the exception of the Mutatis and their allies, of course.

With a sigh of acceptance, Lorenzo signed the parchment and instructed Pimyt to attend to the necessary details. As the Doge gave his orders, it amused him slightly to see the Hibbil twitching and clearing his throat, wishing to say whatever was on his mind but having to wait.

"Yes, yes," Pimyt said when he had heard the commands. "I will attend to all of them."

"*Immediately.*"

Confusion reigned in his expression. "Yes, of course, but don't you wish to hear ... "

"One matter at a time. I don't want anything to be forgotten. You would not wish to displease me or the Princess Meghina, would you?"

Stammering, he replied in a voice that squeaked with agitation: "N-no."

"Go then, and come back."

The furry man bowed and scurried away.

When he finally returned, it was nearly lunch time and the Doge could have put him off again. But he did not, and instructed him to speak.

"My Lord, I am sorry to report that Prince Saito Watanabe has been seriously injured and clings to life. He is the victim of an attack on CorpOne by a force of Guardians."

"Guardians?"

"They call themselves environmental warriors, Sire. They also use the term eco-warriors."

"Oh yes, now I remember. We only permit them to operate because they are led by Prince Saito's son. But why would they attack him?"

"No one knows. They have never done anything this rash before. Most of their efforts have been confined to political maneuvering and to ecological restoration projects on distant worlds. On a couple of occasions they have attempted to block certain industrial efforts, demanding changes in corporate practices ... but it was our understanding that the Prince was keeping them under rein."

"Obviously that understanding is wrong." Lorenzo scowled, and listened as Pimyt provided details on Prince Saito's medical condition. The corpulent industrialist was an important business and political associate of the Doge, one of the most trusted men in the Merchant Prince Alliance. This was a crisis situation that would require action at the highest level. He knew only too well how fragile allegiances could be.

Shifting on his throne, Lorenzo gazed out a stained glass window high on one wall, through which he could see dark gray clouds hovering. "I need accurate intelligence reports," he said in a sharp, urgent tone. "Important decisions must be made."

Chapter Eleven

In the final days of the galaxy, there will be many clever schemes and designs for power.

—Tulyan Prophecy

The Citadel of Paradij was not one of the Wonders of the Galaxy, but only for political reasons that the Zultan resented deeply. The quintessential example of neoclassical Mutati workmanship, the breathtaking structure seemed to float above the rugged surrounding plateau, with slender, glittering spires rising to impossible heights ... more ornamentation, it seemed, than practicality. Ordinary Mutati citizens never knew what really went on inside the palatial fortress, where Abal Meshdi kept some of the most remarkable technological devices ever developed. The people could only whisper among themselves, and imagine.

He stood inside a spire on one of the highest levels of the Citadel now, and peered through a window slit at the distant horizon. Silvery gray clouds and the pastel oranges of sunset were darkening, becoming the homogeneous indigo of night. Abal Meshdi liked to watch this transitional process of light into darkness, and the reverse as well, at dawn. It was a cosmic, eternal march of illumination and color. Sometimes he equated his interest with the fact that he was a changeling himself, a Mutati who could metamorphose into a panoply of shapes and functions.

He held the fleshy palm of his third hand against the window, and for several moments felt subtle temperature variations in the clearglax as it grew cooler, despite the warmth of his touch. Intrigued by change in its variety of forms, he had included this as a design feature of the fortress, with tiny sensors in the glax that transmitted data to him.

It was rumored among the common citizens that the spires of the Citadel contained electronic signaling or receiving units, for communicating across the entire galaxy. After all, Humans had the nehrcom instantaneous communication system ... and weren't Mutatis every bit as good as Humans when it came to the latest technological advancements? Hadn't the Mutati High Command halted the earlier flow of Human military victories, leading to the present stalemate?

He sighed at the questions, knowing there were still doubters among his people, despite his impassioned speeches. At least he had a refuge here from the problems of leadership.

The totality of secrets within the Citadel were known only to the Zultan himself. His closest advisers, as well as the scientists, architects, and builders they employed, knew some of the mysteries, but nowhere near all of them. Ever-wary, the Zultan liked to compartmentalize important information, letting it out piecemeal to those few aides that he trusted the most. In addition, his special police, the Dubak, had surveillance methods that provided him with reports on even the tiniest nooks and crannies of his empire.

Reports, reports, and more reports.

They arrived in a variety of forms, and for decades he had been thriving on the details contained within them. His grandfather once told him, "A ruler is only as good as the information he receives, and only as strong as the organization that supports his power." It had been excellent advice, and Abal Meshdi had never forgotten it.

This morning, however, he didn't feel like reading innocuous reports, or even receiving holosummaries of them. Normally he studied information from all over his realm during breakfast, and by midday he decided what to do about most of the matters. He was a leader who made many decisions, but at the moment he didn't feel like dealing with ordinary activities of state. He almost felt like canceling all of his appointments for the entire day with the exception of the Adurian ambassador who was calling on him … hopefully with progress information on the new doomsday weapon, their joint project.

With a little time available before the arrival of the foreign dignitary, Meshdi strolled around the Citadel and rode the lifts inside the spires to high vantage points, each of which provided him with a slightly different view of the fortress and the surrounding ornamental gardens. Sometimes he needed a break from the flow of information, curtailing its steady inward current. Especially now, after all the time he had spent in coordinating development of the ferocious weapon that would destroy humankind. He did not consider such breaks wasted time; far from it. They restored his mental capacities.

Dressed in a white-and-purple royal cloak, tunic, and matching beret, the Zultan had eight chins of fat beneath a puckish little mouth, a snout, and two oval, bright black eyes. His body, among the largest in the realm, was a lumpy mass of salmon-colored flesh with a broad hump across the shoulders. It had the traditional complement of three slender Mutati arms, along with six stout legs.

Often when he scuttled around the Citadel, he liked to make subtle alterations in his appearance, since it was so pleasurable for a Mutati to shapeshift. Large changes were extremely gratifying while small ones were lesser, but still sensual, joys. A complete transformation in the way he looked, however, could send a Mutati into waves of hedonistic ecstasy, from which he might not emerge for hours or even days on end. The Zultan, ever conscious of this and of the priorities required of his position, could not afford such a diversion now, not with the important visitor about to arrive.

As Meshdi exited the lift at the base of a spire, he scurried through a wide corridor. Set up on a grand scale, the main passageways of the Citadel of Paradij were as wide as boulevards. Commensurately, the ceilings in the great rooms were as high as government buildings, and were adorned with frescoes, lacy platinum filigrees, and even necropaintings, a macabre Mutati art style in which the artists prepared their pigments from the bone powders of Human corpses.

As the royal personage rounded a corner, he used his Mutati mental powers to shift his facial appearance slightly, adding one more fatty chin … so that he now had nine of them instead of eight. Just ahead, a black-uniformed guard noticed the alteration, and stared more closely than usual when the immense leader passed by, so that the guard saw beyond the outer shell of the Mutati leader and analyzed the spectral aura beneath.

Satisfied at the identity of his superior, the guard nodded stiffly and looked away.

On a whim, Abal Meshdi whirled and returned. He stood in front of the guard and studied him closely, peering all the way to the glowing yellow aura beyond the skin. "Is that really you in there, Beaustan?"

"I am here, Sire," the guard said, with the faintest hint of a smile. He tapped the butt of his jolong rifle once on the floor, a gesture of respect. For a Mutati, Beaustan was small, weighing only around one hundred and fifty kilograms. He had obtained his position by family connections, and was descended from a long line of loyal guards.

"I have a better idea," the Zultan said. "I don't feel much like attending to my duties today, so let's trade places." As he said this, he began unsnapping the golden clasps of his royal cloak.

"You want me to meet with the ambassador, too, Sire?" The guard looked shocked and frightened.

"Yes, he's scheduled to arrive at any moment. I think you'll do a fine job."

"But Sire, I am a much smaller terramutati than you are. Even if I shapeshifted to look like you to an outsider, I would not have the requisite mass."

"You aren't proficient at puffing up, expanding your cells? No? Well then, just tell him you've been on a diet. He can't see your aura, won't know the difference. It will be a good test to determine how smart he is, to see if he really believes it."

"Sire, I am not trained in diplomatic matters. I do not have your consummate interpersonal skills, and I do not wish to cause a galactic incident by making a major faux pas."

"You are much too intelligent to be a guard," Abal Meshdi said, nodding. "I have known that for some time. Perhaps I can find some more suitable job for you in my administration."

"I am happy wherever you assign me, Sire." He smiled nervously. "With certain exceptions, of course."

At that moment a white-uniformed aide ran through the corridor. Stopping in front of the Zultan he saluted and said, "The Adurian ambassador has arrived, Sire."

"Tell him I'll be right there," Meshdi said.

When the aide was out of earshot, the Zultan re-secured his tunic and said, "Perhaps you are right, Beaustan. We wouldn't want to create an embarrassing incident."

With a noticeable sigh of relief, the guard nodded, and stood even more rigidly at attention than before.

Actually, the Zultan had not intended to trade places with an underling. He had simply made the ludicrous suggestion on impulse, using absurdity to relieve (albeit only slightly) the matters that weighed so heavily on his mind. The Mutati leader was not known to have a sense of humor, which undoubtedly contributed to the confusion of the guard.

Meshdi shrugged his entire body in the way he had been trained to do by his dancée master, a spiritual counselor who taught him time-honored ways of controlling the mind and body. But even the most skilled dancée instructor could only do so much.

In his position, the Zultan needed more, and his magnificent gyrodome usually provided what he needed. He would reenter it later this evening.

* * * * *

In Abal Meshdi's opulent Salutation Chamber he greeted Ambassador VV Uncel of the Adurian Nebula, a region of spiral arm star systems. This large room in the west wing of the Citadel featured a mosaic dome, with rabesk designs on eight interior columns that supported the dome's weight. Statues of great Mutati statesmen filled alcoves around the perimeter of the room, next to high-backed merchant prince chairs that had been taken from the Humans in one of the Mutati military victories. Even the most petite Mutatis were too big to sit on these exquisitely-carved articles of furniture, but Meshdi liked to keep them around for display anyway, as reminders of past successes.

Larger, more practical chairs stood on an orange-carpeted section at the center of the chamber, furniture that had deep cushions bearing the likenesses of legendary Mutati rulers. The Zultan pointed in that direction, and led the way.

The Adurian diplomat had arrived with two attendants, who waited off to one side with a heavy gold and crystal chest, which they held by the handles with considerable difficulty. Like his assistants, Uncel was a hairless homopod, a mixture of mammalian and insectoid features with a small head, bulbous eyes, and no bodily hair. Dressed in a tight black suit and long white cape, the Ambassador's skin was, in contrast, a bright patchwork of pink, blue, green and red caste markings. The intense colors and arrangements symbolized his high social status, but the large chair made him look very small.

VV Uncel waited while a servant brought two trays filled with tiny ceramic cups of irdol, an imported wine that was reputed to enhance virility. One tray was placed in front of each of the dignitaries. Quickly, the Zultan quaffed a cup of the bright orange liquid, then hurled it to the floor with a small crash, grabbed another and drank it too, before his visitor had even reached for one.

The Adurian dignitary rubbed his wiry fingers together, making a grating sound, as if a microphone had been placed next to an insect. "I shall partake of your fine wine," he said in his whiny alien accent, "but first allow me to present you with a gift." He nodded toward his two attendants.

At his signal the homopods stepped forward, carrying the heavy chest. They set it down on the thick carpeting in front of Abal Meshdi and swung open the lid.

After discarding his irdol cup, the Zultan leaned forward expectantly and looked inside. Seeing a pale blue polyplax bubble sitting on black velvmink, he wondered if this was a prototype of the terrible weapon. He had been told that the device was easily transportable, but had no idea what it actually looked like. The Adurians, with their inventive and manufacturing skills, were building it on one of their industrial planets, using funds provided by the Mutatis.

"Is this a Demolio?" Abal Meshdi whispered. His ring-bedecked fingers danced over the top of the box. He wanted to touch the object, but was not entirely certain if it was a prototype.

Uncel laughed with an abruptness that startled the Zultan, causing him to recoil, and then to scowl.

"Certainly not," the diplomat said, in a squeaky voice. "This is a portable version of the full-size gyrodome that we gave you earlier. We call it a minigyro, and soon it will be the most prized thought-enhancement device in the entire galaxy. Everyone will want one, but few will be able to afford them. The gold and crystal chest is yours as well, with my personal compliments."

"But I thought you were bringing me news of my Demolio program."

"My apologies, Zultan. Did someone say I was?"

"No, but I assumed … the last reports I received said that it was very close to completion, requiring only a few more tests and some fine tuning. I thought you were bringing me the good news that it is ready."

"I am not a scientist, but I can report that I too have heard the same thing. I would be happy to check immediately upon my return and get right back to you. Will that be satisfactory?"

"Yes, yes, of course." Meshdi felt flush in the face, from embarrassment. He reached into the box and brought forth the polyplax bubble, which was lightweight.

"Here, permit me to show you how it works," Uncel said. "It is a minigyro, a small version of the gyro we gave you earlier."

"I can do it myself," the Zultan responded, for he was quite proud of his ability to figure things out. Soon, however, he gave up the effort. With an awkward grin, he shrugged and waved all three of his arms.

The Adurians were always creating new, wondrous objects from their marvelous collective imagination, often involving biological and biotech products. Like a small child, Meshdi was intrigued by the polyplax bubble. He felt a rush of excitement, and his pulse quickened.

"You wear it like this," the Adurian explained, as he placed the minigyro high on the Zultan's forehead, where it stuck to the skin with suction. When the device made contact it flashed on, bathing the Zultan's flesh-fat face in spinning circles of multicolored light.

"Intriguing," Abal Meshdi exclaimed, as images floated and gyrated in the air before his eyes like organisms under a scientist's high-powered magnifying glax.

The Adurian looked on, and finally said, "You are seeing Mutati cells. A precise mixture of them, including all three variations of your people—those that walk upon the ground, fly, and swim."

"*Cells?*" The pitch of the Zultan's voice rose in alarm. "But how did you acquire them? I thought they were too complex to extract."

"One of your own companies has developed a method." He smiled. "Quite expensive, I must say. It's one of the matters I would like to discuss with you. Perhaps you can help us obtain better prices."

The Zultan nodded as he continued to watch the dance of the organisms before his eyes, projections that came from inside the housing of the minigyro. He felt his thoughts merging with the mechanism, sorting themselves into categories that he could analyze in the same manner as the much larger gyrodome.

It was quite ingenious, really, which he came to realize when he used the thought-enhancement quality of the minigyro to determine some features of its design. As the Zultan removed the mechanism from his forehead and felt the effects diminish, he asked how many units had been manufactured.

With an enigmatic wink, the Adurian said, "The production lines will start soon, but I wanted to meet with you first to go over … details."

"Yes, that is wise." After a moment, Meshdi added, "I wish to be your only customer for the product." He turned the unit over in his hands, studying it from every angle. Through a clear plate on the underside he saw multicolored swirls, which Uncel explained were the Mutati cells, going about their tasks without complaint.

"You want our entire production?" Uncel said, after a moment of silence. "But we had hoped to export them all over the galaxy. The demand for something like this could be enormous."

"But you need my cooperation in order to obtain the most essential ingredients. At a word from me, I could put you out of business."

"That may or may not be true. We are talking about cells, after all, and the ones we have could be divided."

"Without a loss of quality? Remember, Mutati cells are unique in the galaxy, and very sensitive."

"Perhaps you are right. To be honest, I am not certain. In any event, I wish to be cooperative." The Ambassador narrowed his eyes. "But must you have *all* of our production?"

With a firm nod, the Zultan said, "I can arrange for excellent wholesale prices and I will pay you fairly. You deserve to be rewarded, but all minigyro manufacturing must be performed on Paradij, or on another planet in the Mutati Kingdom."

The Adurian's insectoid eyebrows arched. "Why, if I might ask?"

"We are concerned about security."

"With all appropriate respect, sir, I do not understand. You permit us to develop and manufacture Demolios on one of our own planets, but not minigyros?"

Meshdi nodded energetically, causing his many chins to quiver like the layers of a trifle. "The idea of extracted Mutati cells troubles me a great deal. It is no reflection upon your people, for I trust them completely. It is just that our cells are ... sacred ... and I do not wish to have them or your interesting product fall into the wrong hands." He spoke with all the solemnity of his high position. "There is tremendous potential for harm here as well as for benefit."

Abal Meshdi did not really trust the Adurians that much. With their permission he had stationed his own military forces on the industrial world where Demolios were being developed. Since it was well-known that Mutati forces were far superior to those of the Adurians, the conspirators agreed that it would be best to have the Mutatis provide security for this highly important, ultra-secret project. Still, the Adurian military had made significant advances recently and would need to be monitored, even if they were an ally....

VV Uncel hesitated, and considered the situation. He thought it would be better to do the work on Adurian property, but didn't envision problems doing it the Zultan's way. The Adurians were so adept at their biomanufacturing processes that they could keep certain information secret from the Mutatis, even if the shapeshifters were watching them all the time.

With authority from the Adurian Council to make his own decisions in this matter, the Ambassador proceeded to reach an agreement with the Mutati Zultan. The diplomat-salesman accepted a large order for the new minigyros, which he knew Meshdi would distribute to his own people, despite his professed security concerns. The gyrodome and minigyros would suggest this course of action to him subconsciously, and he would not be able to resist.

This Adurian was much more than a diplomat, or a salesman. As VV Uncel departed, he was exceedingly pleased. Soon a large segment of the Mutati population would be influenced in their decision-making processes by the minigyros.

The Zultan was not going to get what he expected.

Chapter Twelve

The love between father and son should be simple, but the reality is far different.
—Prince Saito Watanabe

On the grounds of his Ecological Demonstration Project, Master Noah Watanabe knelt in a meadow and dug his hands into soft, loamy soil around the roots of plants. The sun-warmed Canopan dirt had a calming effect on him, especially now, shortly after a warm summer rain. The muscular man wore a khaki, sleeveless tunic and short, matching breeches. His knees were damp, but he hardly noticed.

This planet is alive, he thought. *Just like the back country people say.*

He was thinking of a superstitious legend, one found all over the galaxy, among various sentient races. On Canopa the primitive people called their planet "Zehbu," while on other planets the living entity was referred to as "Gaea" or other names, but always in conjunction with a similar story. So-called intellectuals dismissed it as a commonly held myth, but Noah believed it was much more than that. Millennia ago there had also been a legend of a great flood that swept across the planet Earth, and another story about a race of sentient spaceships that traveled the galaxy at tremendous speeds. Both "myths" proved to be accurate, so he was confident that one day everyone would also come to accept the fact of living planetary organisms. He could only hope this would be the case. His entire environmental movement was closely allied with the concept.

Zehbu. The people living on your surface are only as healthy as you are.

A tiny yellow field sparrow swooped low, and landed on the grass a couple of meters away. As Noah watched from his kneeling position, the bird looked up at him, tilting its head comically.

Noah smiled softly, then gazed at the distant blue-green hills. Philosophically, he believed that all galactic races, as well as every genus of flora and species of fauna, functioned best if they worked in harmony, filling ecological niches. He loathed the rapacious industries of his father and the other merchant princes, valuing profits above all else. They were ruining every planet where they were involved, stripping minerals and polluting the air, water and ground, caring nothing of the future generations who might live in those places. Most Human businessmen took the short view of events, doing whatever it took to fill their purses with money. Noah, also an entrepreneur but with environmentally friendly operations, took what he considered to be a much longer view.

He had attempted to contact a number of third world alien races to enlist them into his activist organization, but the vast majority of them were suspicious of him, and preferred to keep to themselves. With the exception of the Tulyans, they scoffed openly or paid no heed when his representatives told them that his beliefs were similar to theirs, that all planets needed to be treated with respect and preserved for future generations. As far as most of them were concerned, no matter the promises or assurances of Noah Watanabe, he was not worthy of trust.

He was, after all, the son of a greedy merchant prince.

Something touched the back of Noah's shoulder, and he straightened. The little yellow bird came into view again, perched close to his face. After a few seconds, it chirped and flew away.

Noah heaved a sigh, and prepared to catch a shuttle. In less than an hour he would be inside EcoStation, his laboratory complex in geostationary orbit over Canopa, always directly above his unique wildlife preserve and farm. Up there he conducted genetic studies on exotic plants and animals under strict, uncontaminated conditions....

Just before boarding the shuttle, he received word about his father's grave injuries, and that he had fallen into a coma. Hearing the news, Noah went cold inside. Prince Saito Watanabe had betrayed his own son, and had somehow been caught in his own trap. It seemed fitting.

Nonetheless, a small part of Noah grieved.

* * * * *

Tesh no longer had feelings for him.

For almost a week, her former boyfriend had not returned to the country estate that was his principal residence. Instead, Dr. Bichette stayed in a CorpOne apartment near the Prince's cliffside villa, where his important patient lay, gravely wounded. According to a telebeam message that the doctor sent to Tesh at the estate, he wanted her to join him at the apartment.

But she wasn't interested.

His first message had arrived three days ago, and she had not responded to it yet. Additional demands arrived each day, and this morning he had sent her two more … each more importunate than the one before.

Since Bichette's departure, Tesh Kori and Anton Glavine had spent a lot of time together, but had remained in separate quarters. There had been no sexual intercourse, but not due to any reticence on her part. She had tempted the young man in every way she knew (short of disrobing), and he *had* shown considerable interest. He did not appear to be a homosexual in any sense, either, but for some reason he was resisting his own natural urges, holding back and not saying why. Perhaps he wanted to get to know her better before committing himself; he certainly asked her a lot of questions about her background.

But Tesh felt she was making progress anyway. They had taken walks together through the forests on Dr. Bichette's property, and Anton had kissed her once on the mouth for a few seconds before pulling away, revealing in his demeanor that he was struggling with his own willpower. Soon he would come to her; she sensed it.

In response to Anton's queries, Tesh had provided him with creative answers, fragments of truth painted on wide canvases of lies. She couldn't possibly reveal her real identity to him, for that was beyond the comprehension of a *humanus ordinaire.*

The Parvii race, like its distant Human cousins, required regenerative sleep, but not nearly as much. That night as Tesh slept alone, she remembered … and remembered. Her unconscious thoughts seemed to drift off into deep space, to a far-away galactic fold where her people swarmed by the millions whenever there was trouble….

She awoke with a start and opened her eyes. The images had seemed so real, as if she were again with all of her companions in their hidden sanctuary, responding to the commands of Woldn, their revered leader.

From her bed she heard a noise, and saw a crack of light at the doorway that soon widened, as illumination streamed in like yellow sunlight. A shape filled the doorway, profiled against the brightness.

Anton Glavine.

He closed the door, and she heard him moving around inside the room, without seeing him. Moments later he crawled into bed with her, and she felt the warmth of his body against hers. She had been hoping for this, and had kept her physical magnification system in operation, making her appear to be a normal-sized woman. Otherwise, she thought with a smile, he might not have been able to find her tiny body under the bed coverings.

Soon Tesh forgot about her dream, and about everything else. Except for her mounting passion.

Chapter Thirteen

Tulyans and Parviis pilot podships in different ways. In both methods, it involves telepathic control over the Aopoddae, but Tulyans—unlike Parviis—actually merge into the flesh of the pods, changing the appearance of the spacefaring vessels so that they develop scaly skin, protruding snouts and a pair of narrowly slitted eyes. Why, in view of that remarkable symbiosis, are we Parviis more dominant over podships than Tulyans? This is a great enigma, and a blessing from the Universal Creator.

—The Parvii View of Divinity

A creature with bronze, reptilian skin piloted a grid-plane low over the surface of Canopa, a small aircraft that bore the green-and-brown markings of the Guardians. From the air Eshaz surveyed conditions below, blinking his pale gray eyes as he searched for subtle signs on the ground, for even the smallest indications of trouble. Like all of the people of his race he was extremely old, dating back to a time when Tulyans were stewards of the entire galaxy.

Those times were long gone. Now the Tulyans filled in where they could, performing their specialized, unselfish tasks ... even if they had to work for others. Eshaz's Guardian superior, Noah Watanabe, had complete faith in him and in scores of other Tulyans in his employ, permitting them to operate unsupervised on a number of planets, monitoring ecological conditions. In the process, the reptilian men and women submitted regular reports to Noah ... but they also performed other tasks on their own that they could never reveal to any Human.

Wherever possible, Tulyans tried to meld into society, be it Human or otherwise. In the process, they visited planets, asteroids, moons, and mass clusters, and in some of those places they found environmental protection measures already in place. None, however, were as extensive or as well thought out as those instituted by Noah Watanabe and his Guardians. That one man had, to his credit, found a way to enhance and restore natural systems while making a great deal of money.

How odd Humans are, Eshaz thought. *The worst polluters imaginable, and the most careless, but they are the most creative, too.*

For a moment the Tulyan had an unexpected thought, that Humans, despite their glaring flaws, could possibly be the greatest hope for the salvation of the cosmos, for the restoration of Timeweb. How ironic that would be, if it proved to be true. But every Tulyan knew differently. Only Eshaz's own people could save the web, through the caretakers they sent out on clandestine missions.

As Eshaz flew over a dry river bed at the base of a cliff, a cloud of glassy dust rose from below and blocked the large front porthole of the grid-plane. The normally quiet engines whined and sputtered, and the craft spiraled toward the ground. He fought desperately for control, jabbing his fingers against the touch pads on the instrument panel.

Tulyans could live for hundreds of thousands, even millions of years, but were subject to accidental death. Eshaz bore the scars of countless injuries, yet he had been fortunate, exceedingly fortunate. He and his kinsmen were immune to disease or any form of bodily degeneration, and had remarkable powers of recovery from injury. But they were not immortal.

At the last possible moment, just before it touched the ground, the grid-plane pulled up and then swooped back into the sky, rising above a looming, rainbow-crystal cliff face. Eshaz went higher this time, to avoid whatever was occurring down there. Moments later he brought the plane around, circled the glittering cliff, and descended toward the riverbed. He saw the swirling dust again, but this time he remained at a safer altitude.

A small golden circle adorned the lapel of his Guardian uniform, which had been custom-fitted by a Human tailor to conform with the unusual contours of his alien body. The golden circle was the sigil of the Tulyan race, representing eternity. It was a design found everywhere in their arcane society: on their clothing, on the hulls of their ships, and on the sides of their buildings.

Today the mission of this highly intelligent race was much more limited than it had been in ancient times. Now a comparatively few Tulyans traveled the galactic sectors, performing fine ecological adjustments wherever necessary, trying to restore delicate environmental balances that had been disturbed by the careless practices of the galactic races. Humans were not alone in the damage they caused.

He brought the grid-plane as low as he could over the trouble spot, for a better look. Below him was a wide, dry riverbed with a rough, disturbed surface of crystalline soil and black volcanic rock. The disturbed area was pulsing, surging with ground and air action and then diminishing … as if breathing. He had seen this before, and needed to wait for just the right moment.

Most of Eshaz's people remained back at the Tulyan Starcloud, their home at the edge of the galaxy. In that sacred place they thought of the old days … or tried to forget them. His brethren harbored secrets that could never be discussed with any other race, things known only to the Tulyans since time immemorial, and perhaps even before that. Much of the highly restricted information had to do with Timeweb, the way everything in the galaxy was connected by gossamer threads that were only visible to certain sentients, and then only during heightened states of consciousness.

There had been signs of increasing problems on Canopa and in other sectors of the galaxy, causing the Tulyans great concern. Handling the touch-pad controls of the grid-plane expertly, Eshaz watched the swirls of glassy dust diminish. He would have to move quickly.

Without hesitation he set the aircraft down, off to one side of the broad riverbed, a couple of hundred meters from the debris. He didn't like to think about what would happen if Timeweb continued to decay.

It would mean the end of everything.

He stepped from the craft and made his way across the rough, rocky terrain. Every few steps Eshaz knelt to examine the ground, touching its disturbed surface, studying stones, small broken plants, and dirt. He moved closer, and confirmed his suspicions. This was no ordinary debris field, nothing that had been caused by the natural geological or weather forces of Canopa itself. He studied a blast-pattern of dirt and fragments that had been broken away from the planetary crust, and shook his head sadly. It was exactly as he had feared, a very serious situation indeed.

He watched as a patch of crystalline soil and debris began to swirl only a few meters from him, then faded from view. Unmistakably, he was looking at the early stage of a timehole, a defect in the cosmos through which matter could slip between the layers of the web and, for all practical purposes, disappear from the space-time continuum.

Bringing forth a sorcerer's bag that he always carried in a body pouch, Eshaz stepped forward carefully, until he reached the edge of the flickering area. He sprinkled a handful of green dust on it, raised his hands high and uttered the ancient incantation that had always been used to ward off Galara, the evil spirit of the undergalaxy.

"Galara, ibillunor et typliv unat Ubuqqo!"

Now the Tulyan bowed his scaly bronze head in reverence to Ubuqqo, the Sublime Creator of all that was known and all that was good, and uttered a private prayer for the salvation of the galaxy.

"Ubuqqo, anret pir huyyil."

This was the strongest form of invocation that he knew, for it did not request anything for himself, and not merely for this small section of Canopan crust, either, only a pinprick in the cosmos. Rather, Eshaz's prayer stretched and stretched along the cosmic web … the miraculous filament that connected everyone, ultimately, to the Sublime Creator.

But agitated by the Tulyan's magic, the timehole grew larger, and Eshaz felt the ground crumbling beneath him. Bravely, he held steady and refused to retreat. Each timehole was a little different, and all shared something in common: unpredictability. But this one seemed to be in its beginning stages.

Debris swirled all around him, and he felt a powerful force tugging at him, drawing him toward a realm of existence where he would no longer have thoughts and would no longer experience independent movements. It was not entropy, for that natural force of cosmic decay did not waste matter by discarding it into another realm. Entropy did not waste anything, and instead reused every little bit of matter in some other useful form.

No, this was something else … the eternal, unyielding and opportunistic force of the undergalaxy, working on every weakness, trying to exploit it for its own voracious purposes. He had no doubt that the undergalaxy—like the galaxy that he wanted so desperately to save—was a living entity, with a powerful force that drove it. And this timehole, like so many others, threatened to cast the galaxy into oblivion.

The ground cracked and shook, and the heavy Tulyan fell to one knee. He felt aches and pains in his joints and muscles, something he had never experienced before in his long life.

Timeweb's pain is my pain, he thought, since his own condition seemed to run parallel with the recent precipitous decline of the web.

He repeated the invocation.

"Galara, ibillunor et typliv unat Ubuqqo! … Ubuqqo, anret pir huyyil!"

A rift opened beneath him, as deep as a grave, and he tumbled into it. As he struggled to climb out, the ground rolled and knocked him back in. Swirling dirt piled on top of him, and though Tulyans did not breathe, he knew what might happen next. The hole could open up completely, and send him hurtling through into the stygian oblivion of the undergalaxy. Still, like an insect struggling to make its way through a storm, he fought to stand up and free himself.

Fumbling in his pocket, he located the sorcerer's pouch, and scattered its entire contents around him. A thunderous noise sounded, followed by a cacophonous grating sound, like huge continents rubbing together. He felt warm air.

Suddenly, with a flash of green light, he was tossed out of the hole and onto the rocky ground. The air was still, and there were no sounds. The rift had disappeared and the land looked almost normal, with hardly any sign of disturbance. Even his grid-plane, which he had parked away from the center of the disruption, appeared unharmed.

Eshaz rubbed a sore shoulder, and felt the pain diminishing already. With his recuperative powers it would not last long. He tested the surface of the ground carefully by putting a scaly foot on it, and then taking a step. It felt solid. Presently he walked on it, toward the waiting aircraft.

As he entered his plane to leave, worries assailed him like a swarm of insects. There had been too many timeholes appearing ... and too many missing Tulyans, who presumably were being sucked into the openings. Symptomatic of the heightening crisis, fifteen of his people had disappeared in the past year ... and hardly any before that.

The grid-plane lifted off, and he looked out through the window. Amazingly, the ground hardly looked disturbed at all, and even had wildflowers and small succulent plants growing on it. He clutched the empty sorcerer's pouch in one hand, and wondered if he had actually repaired that timehole, or if it had just shifted position in relation to the strands of Timeweb. He had ways of finding out, and would do so.

Eshaz tapped the touch pads of the instrument panel, causing the aircraft to accelerate along the planetary flight control system. With a little stretch of his imagination he could see similarities between this airgrid, with its unseen web of interlocked electronics, and Timeweb, which encompassed so much more. In each case, ships traveled along strands that guided them safely. Where Timeweb was the work of the Sublime Creator, however, the airgrid networks on various Human planets had been invented and installed by much lesser beings ... and the equipment operated on infinitely smaller scales. It could not be overlooked, either, that Timeweb was a *natural* system, while airgrids were not; they were intrusions. Airgrids were, however, ecologically benign, and not known to cause damage to plants, animals, or other aspects of nature.

The Tulyan wished he could do more for the empyrean web, that his people were again in control of podships as they had been in the long-ago days when he had been a pilot himself—before Parvii swarms came and took the pods away. At one time, Tulyans could travel freely around the galaxy, performing their essential work on a much larger scale.

An entire sorcerer's bag expended for one timehole. It would take him nearly a day to restore the ingredients in the repair kit. For a moment he despaired, as the efforts of the Tulyans seemed so inefficient. But in a few moments the feeling passed, and he vowed to continue his work for as long as possible.

He was fighting more than timeholes, or the inefficiencies of dealing with them. On top of everything else, Eshaz and other Tulyans had been experiencing bodily aches and pains ... for the first time in the history of their race. This suggested to them that their bodies might be undergoing a process of disintegration into homogeneous chemical soups and dust piles ... along with every other organism in the dying galaxy.

Chapter Fourteen

The Theoscientific Doctrine tells us that our religious and scientific principles are indistinguishable from one another.

—*Scienscroll*, 1 Neb 14-15

After gambling all night in the palazzo casino with members of the royal court, Doge Lorenzo took a ground-jet to the dagg races on the other side of the broad river that bisected the capital city of Elysoo. This was one of his favorite haunts for placing bets.

It was Monday morning, and he should be attending theoscientific services at the Cathedral of the Stars. Right about now, the Moral Instructors—elderly women in silver robes—would be reading passages from the *Scienscroll*, perhaps even admonishing the parishioners about the sins of gambling. He didn't care. The meddlesome old maids of the Cathedral would not dare to speak directly against him, the powerful leader of the Merchant Prince Alliance. Still, he would not want a confrontation with them; he was a devout believer in the holiest of all writings, the *Scienscroll*. He even knew the most famous verses by heart, such as the one from the Book of Visions:

Know ye the Way of the Princes,
for it is the path to gold and glory.

He liked another passage even more, and frequently quoted it:

May mine enemies tumble into space,
and crumble to dust!

There! he thought, after murmuring the verses to himself. *I've fulfilled my theoscientific obligations for the day.*

As usual, he went to the dagg track with no fanfare whatsoever, accompanied by only a handful of plainclothed security guards. His Hibbil attaché, Pimyt, went along as well. Dressed in red-and-brown capes and matching fez hats, the two of them entered the Doge's private box, which was decorated in wallpaper that featured sports calligraphy and holos of race champions in action.

Lorenzo stood at one of the windows of the enclosure and watched spectators stream into the stands. Out on the track—over slopes and around hairpin turns—daggs made practice runs, dusty brown-and-tan animals that resembled the canines of Earth but had tiny heads ... proportionately less than half as large as those of greyhounds. Each dagg had a large, bulbous eye in the center of its face—dominating the front like a headlight—and a snout-mouth beneath the boxlike jaw.

"While we await the first race, I thought you might like to use the time productively," Pimyt suggested. After removing his cap the furry Hibbil knelt and tried to open the clasps on a shiny black valise that he had brought with him. He pressed on the release buttons, but only two of the four fasteners popped open.

"Must we discuss business here?" Lorenzo protested, watching him with irritation. He heard the crowd roar and looked to see the daggs and their trainers—many of them alien—parade in front of the main viewing stands and private boxes.

"You've said yourself that every bit of time is useful, Sire, and you are extremely busy ... so there is hardly a moment available to show you the latest in Hibbil technology." He waved casually at the valise. "Of course, if you would prefer not to see this...."

The Doge sighed. "You know me too well, my friend. Aside from my weakness for betting, I do have a fondness for gadgets ... and for women, lest I forget, and not necessarily in that order."

With a curt smile, Pimyt struggled to open the lid of his valise. "I think you will like this, Sire." He slammed a furry fist on the bag, but the last clasp resisted him.

As Doge Lorenzo gazed dispassionately at his attaché, he had a hard time believing that Pimyt had once been the Regent of the Merchant Prince Alliance. A *Hibbil.* Though he hadn't realized it at the time (and still didn't), Pimyt had not been given any real power or responsibility during his term in office. It had only been ceremonial, and something of a well-concealed joke, a way of treading water between doge regimes while seeming to show respect for the Hibbil Republic, an important economic ally who provided the best machines available, at reasonable prices. His tenure in office had only lasted for a few months, until the Council of Forty elected a new leader, but it had helped cement relations between the Human and Hibbil societies.

Finally, Pimyt won his argument with the stubborn clasp and swung the lid of the valise open.

Intrigued, Lorenzo leaned closer to look.

"We call this a 'hibbamatic,'" Pimyt announced proudly, as he brought out several flat, geometric pieces and snapped them together on the floor, forming a box with octagonal sides. He slid open a little door on the structure, permitting Lorenzo to see that it glowed pale orange inside, as if with an internal fire.

"Strange device." The Doge reached out and placed a finger against one side of the box, which was around a meter in height. It felt cool to the touch.

"This is one of our smaller models, a machine that can be programmed to build a variety of small consumer and military devices out of programmable raw materials" Pimyt had noticeable pride in his voice. "Here, let me show you."

The Doge squinted as he watched the Hibbil remove a hand-sized cartridge from inside the lid of the valise. The selected cartridge had a keypad on one side, and Pimyt tapped a code into it. He then tossed the cartridge into the geometric structure and slid the door shut. Moments later, a tray opened on the opposite side and a small, red-handled weapon slid out and clattered onto the tray.

"An ion gun," Pimyt said. "Fully loaded. The hibbamatic can create anything except a copy of itself." He grinned. "Or so our promotional literature says. Assuming we provide enough raw materials."

"How about a beamvideo of *Capponi's Revenge?*" Lorenzo asked.

"Ah yes, that patriotic war story."

Seconds later, like a wish fulfilled by a genie, a silver-colored video cylinder clattered into the tray. After examining it, Lorenzo smiled craftily and said, "Now make me a nehrcom transceiver."

Since this was one of the most secret devices in the galaxy, with its workings known only to Prince Jacopo Nehr, the Hibbil responded, "Don't believe everything in our promotional literature, Sire."

With a guffaw, the merchant prince leader said, "Nonetheless, I rather like your hibbamatic, as a novelty item for the amusement of my court."

"Shall I transmit your order to my homeworld?"

"Later." Lorenzo glanced out the window. "The race is about to begin."

Twenty daggs in racing colors took off and dashed around the track, going up and down the slopes and around the sharp turns. But the top daggs were not as fast as usual. Doge Lorenzo smiled, for he had taken steps to influence the result, having arranged for the sedation of the favorites ... just enough to slow them down slightly.

As expected, Abeeya's Dowry, the underdagg he had bet on, won easily.

"Now I have enough to buy your products," Doge Lorenzo said. "Big payday ... minus operating expenses, of course."

Beside him, Pimyt smiled, but a bit too broadly for the occasion, as he envisioned the Hibbil-Adurian master plan unfurling, moment by moment. Timing was everything....

Chapter Fifteen

Life is about changes, and adapting to them.

—Tulyan Wisdom

O nly moments before the arrival of the *conducci*, Tesh Kori and Anton Glavine ran through the front gate of the estate and hid in the thick woods outside. Flushed with anger and outrage, Tesh parted the leaves of an aixberry bush and peered through the red-leafed foliage. A groundjet stopped at the gate and waited for it to slide open slowly. These mercenaries had their own transmitter key.

It was a warm afternoon, with hardly any clouds in the azure blue sky. Beside her, Anton breathed hard from the exertion of running across the large compound. His brow glistened with perspiration. In contrast, Tesh showed no signs of physical effort. Parviis, who could survive in outer space without the necessity of any breathing apparatus, did not have cardiovascular systems. Rather, they were complex electrochemical creatures, with tiny, highly sophisticated neurological systems.

Six large men wearing black coats and tinted eyeglasses sat inside the oval-shaped vehicle, which discharged orange flames from the rear as it idled. To Tesh they looked like barroom brawlers, or street thugs. The tip telebeamed to her by a girlfriend had been correct. Dr. Bichette had hired muscle to bring her back to him ... and had sent enough men to handle not only her, but Anton as well. Judging by the puissant rifles that Tesh saw in the rear of the passenger compartment, she judged that the men had been given strict orders to do whatever it took to accomplish the task.

She had long suspected that Bichette had a mean streak, and this confirmed it. Despite his attempts to show her a gentle, compassionate side she had seen behavioral lapses in him, moments when a darker aspect showed through and then scurried for cover, like a creature not wishing to be discovered. It had taken months for this nature to reveal itself, but it had not escaped her attention, as she noticed the way he treated servants and even his valuable tigerhorses when he didn't know anyone was watching. Two of the animals in his stable had died of poisoning, and while he had insisted that it must have been committed by an intruder, he had also collected large insurance payments. Humans could be so unethical.

"I have a bad feeling about this," Anton said. He held a four-barrel handgun that he had grabbed on the way out of the palatial home.

"So do I," she said. "Let's go deeper into the woods. Maybe there's a way out on the other side."

Not a person to run from a fight, no matter the odds, Anton hesitated.

She tugged at his arm. "Come on!"

The groundjet roared fire and entered the compound. The gate closed behind it with a hard click of metal. Tesh and Anton scrambled deeper into the woods, tromping their way over thorny underbrush and through stands of gray and yellow-barked trees.

Ten minutes later they heard a commotion behind them, barking daggs and shouting men. A second vehicle must have arrived, carrying the animals. To Tesh they sounded like keanu tuskies, known to be fast and deadly. A hundred years ago she had seen one run down a fugitive and chew off his legs before handlers arrived to collect what was left. Ever since, the memory had been etched indelibly in her mind.

"Faster!" she said, without explaining what she knew.

Anton didn't need any encouragement, but he had trouble keeping up with her. His hands were bloody from thorn bushes, but hers were not, since Parviis did not bleed.

Abruptly, Anton stopped and turned the other way. Kneeling, he flipped a toggle and pressed a button on the handgun. Flames belched out of all four barrels and ignited the tinder-dry underbrush. He scurried to one side and the other, setting up a wall of fire to block the pursuers.

Then he turned and rejoined her, where she awaited him. "That'll slow 'em down," he said. "My dad and uncle were hunters and had a lot of guns, including a couple like this one … handy for flushing wild treegeese out in the open."

"That doesn't sound very sporting," Tesh observed.

"Maybe not, but it works."

The pair sprinted ahead, while fire raged behind them, turning the brush and trees into a popping, exploding conflagration. Birds screeched and flew off.

"We have a favorable wind direction," Anton said. "It could switch on us, though. We need to hurry."

She glanced longingly at her companion as he ran alongside her. He seemed to be in complete control and unafraid … capable of handling virtually any situation.

In the seven centuries of her life, Tesh had enjoyed countless sexual experiences with the males of almost every galactic race. Two of the most memorable had been a tryst with a Vakeen swordsman in the Dardar Sector and months of lovemaking with a handsome Ilakai merchant, who entertained her at his various chateaux around the galaxy.

She sighed, remembering her first physical relationship, with a powerful Adurian lord who looked like a humanoid ant, with bulbous eyes and puffy black cheeks. She had been little more than a child at the time, and he had been so ruggedly handsome, enhanced by the keloid scars on his face and arms. The touch of his antennae had been almost electric on her skin, so stimulating that she had been hard-pressed to find anyone afterward who was anywhere near his sexual equal.

Her current love interest, Anton Glavine, was perhaps the most perplexing of all. In her many relationships, she had learned a great deal about the various races and cultures, including Humans. But this was an entirely new experience for her. She found him intelligent, sensitive, and extremely irritating. With males, she was used to getting her own way.

Their first night of lovemaking had been passionate, but nowhere near the most stimulating of her life. Still, the sexual experience had been adequate, and she'd wanted to continue the episodes, hoping they would improve with time. After that, though, Anton had refused to make love to her again, saying he'd made a regrettable mistake with her. He said he wanted to get to know her better before repeating what they had done.

"But it was so wonderful," she'd told him in exaggeration, blinking her emerald green eyes. She and Anton had been in the living room of the main house, sitting in front of a warm, cheery fireplace. Tesh had set it all up, even providing wine to lower his resistance.

With surprising determination, Anton had said, "I like to be in control of myself, and with you around that presents a challenge."

Then he put down his wineglass and gave her a hard stare, as if he could see through her superficiality. He seemed to look deep into her soul with his penetrating hazel eyes … through her personal magnification system to the tiny Parvii inside. Of course that was impossible, but she had been unnerved, and bewildered. He was not like any Human male she had ever encountered; instead he behaved more in the manner of a Human *female,* who typically wanted to develop an emotional relationship before becoming intimate.

Things were topsy-turvy. Tesh was even playing more the part of a Human male, as she pursued him aggressively. But she was not a *humanus ordinaire,* and could not be judged in the terms of that race. As a Parvii, she had her own ways, her own traditions and genetic makeup that drove her actions. She was not sure how to control this man; the more time she spent with him the more she wanted him, and the more he befuddled her.

Privately, she had to admit that she rather liked his gallantry, the way he treated her with courtesy and respect. He showed great bravery in the face of danger as well, and a strong desire to protect her from harm. She could outrun him, but usually held herself back and checked to see how he was doing.

Behind them, the keanu tuskies yelped in confusion. "The smoke of the fire is interfering with their ability to smell," he explained. "My uncle used them for hunting daggs, and said that was their weakness."

Tesh smelled the acrid odor of the fire.

"The wind is changing!" Anton shouted. He pointed down a steep, brushy hill, toward a small lake. "I think we've lost the daggs, but we need to get into the water."

Suddenly Tesh heard a loud noise overhead, and peered up through an opening in the trees. A green-and-brown grid-plane hovered above them for several moments, profiled against the sky, and then flew back toward the fire. She heard the popping of the flames, and loud hissing noises.

"That's a Guardian aircraft," he said "They're a bunch of radical environmentalists, and wouldn't be happy if they found out I started the fire. They're always patrolling Canopa, like self-proclaimed eco-police."

"You make them sound kooky."

"Actually, I admire them. I wouldn't have set fire to the woods if we weren't in a life or death situation. For days I've seen their spotter craft operating in the area, and hoped they would show up here … but not too soon. I just wanted to use the fire as a temporary shield, without causing too much damage. They'll put it out now."

"I see."

He helped her down a steep embankment, over granite boulders and through thorny bushes. The lake was only a short distance away, deep blue in a rock bowl.

The aircraft noise returned, and Tesh saw the same Guardian grid-plane fly low over the lake. Pontoons emerged from the undercarriage, and the aircraft set down on the water with a splash, near the closest shore. A hatch opened in the fuselage, and a reptilian creature stepped out onto the short wing. Larger than a Human, he had bronze, scaly skin and a protruding snout. He wore a green-and-brown uniform.

"One of the Tulyans who work for Noah Watanabe," Tesh said, identifying a race that was at least as ancient as, and perhaps even older, than her own … going all the way back to the earliest known days of galactic habitation.

"I'm familiar with them," Anton said in a low tone, "but I've never seen one this close. I hear they are non-violent?"

"That is correct."

"Hurry," the Tulyan said in a throaty voice. He motioned with one arm, which seemed too small for his substantial body.

Anton and Tesh looked at each other for a moment, then waded through cold water to the grid-plane and boarded it.

"What a coincidence," Anton said to the Tulyan as the two passengers found seats in the rear of the craft. "We were just on our way to see Noah Watanabe and volunteer as Guardians."

"We were?" Tesh said, surprised.

"I wanted to surprise you," Anton said. "Noah and I go way back."

The Tulyan looked at him skeptically through slitted, pale gray eyes, and said, "Your friends were asphyxiated by the fire. One of our crews picked up their bodies."

Tesh wanted to say they weren't friends, but caught Anton's hard stare and read the message there. It was best not to say anything about being chased, or about starting the fire.

The reptilian man identified himself as Ifnattil, and said he was a caretaker, responsible for protecting the natural resources in this region. With no further comment, he plopped his large body into a specially-designed pilot's seat and began tapping the instrument panel with stubby fingers. The grid-plane lifted off with a smooth whir into the smoky sky.

"Noah was a friend of my parents," Anton told Tesh. "Just working-class people, but he always took a special interest in me when I was growing up. Noah is seventeen years older than I am, like a big brother to me. I told him I wanted to join the Guardians someday, and engage in his style of environmental warfare."

Tesh grinned, and curled an arm around Anton's waist. "It looks like that someday is now," she said.

Chapter Sixteen

The path of honor is a narrow ridge, with deep crevasses on either side.
—Princess Meghina of Siriki

D r. Hurk Bichette wanted his patient to get better. Certainly he was administering every technique known to medical science, some of them the result of advice he had received from experts he'd brought in for consultation. Money was no object; Prince Saito Watanabe had unlimited funds.

But in Bichette's thoughts, grating on his conscience like sand between his skull and brain, he wished the Prince would just die, if that was going to occur anyway. It was irritating the way the old man kept straddling the fence between life and death, not heading in either direction.

From the foot of the bed, Bichette watched the regular breathing of the comatose man. Following brain surgery, the rotund patient had been fitted with a mediwrap around his head to enhance the healing of damaged functions, along with a clearplax life-support dome. The injury was severe, but with modern technology this patient could live indefinitely, well beyond his normal life span.

But this is not living, the doctor thought.

Two women stood on one side of the bed.... the Prince's redheaded daughter Francella and the blonde Princess Meghina, who had a distinctive heart-shaped face. Occasionally they glared at one another, without saying anything.

Located within the Prince's cliffside villa, this had been an elegant reception chamber, until its conversion to a high-tech hospital facility. The large room had gold Romanesque filigree on the walls, a vaulted ceiling with dark wood beams, and brightly-colored simoil murals. The paintings, by the renowned artist Tintovinci, depicted the life of Prince Saito Watanabe, from the time when he had been an itinerant street vendor to his years as a factory worker and his rise to the very highest echelons of merchant prince society.

Life-support equipment hummed and clicked softly as it kept the body's vital functions going. The big man's chest heaved up and down within the clearplax dome, and occasionally he coughed, but did not awaken.

Meghina wiped tears from her eyes, and appeared about to say something. Her generous lips parted, then clamped shut, as she seemed to change her mind. Though married to the Doge, she was also a well-known courtesan, and had relationships with a number of noblemen. She and her powerful husband lived separately—she in her Golden Palace on Siriki and he in his Palazzo Magnifico on Timian One. Though Bichette did not approve of such relationships himself, they were commonplace among MPA noblemen, and the source of much braggadocio.

Beside her, Francella Watanabe shifted uneasily on her feet. She had a reddish makeup splotch on her high forehead, but neither Meghina nor the doctor were about to tell her.

Dr. Bichette looked away from them, back at this great Prince who seemed so helpless now and so peaceful, with his eyes closed and a calm, almost pleased expression on his round face. Even if the doctor wanted to disconnect him for humanitarian reasons—or for other reasons—he could not do so. Watanabe had left specific, signed instructions that he was not to be taken off life support, not even if he became brain dead. He had not reached that stage yet, but his mental functions had been damaged by oxygen deprivation, and he seemed unlikely to recover. Since his injury he had lapsed in and out of consciousness several times, and had spoken a few garbled, unintelligible words.

Frustrated by the amount of time he had been required to spend here, Bichette would rather deal with Tesh instead, to see if they could resurrect their relationship ... a relationship that might be in worse shape than this patient. Bichette didn't like Anton Glavine, and didn't trust him around his attractive girlfriend.

A method of tipping the medical balance occurred to him. *If I make just a slight adjustment in the nutrient lines, or administer a quick injection of protofyt enzyme, Saito will slip away, with no evidence remaining of what I did.*

Anxiously, the doctor weighed the possibilities. Certainly this client paid him high fees, but there were other nobles who wanted his medical services, and if he lost this one he would have more time for the others. Prince Saito was something of a hypochondriac anyway, constantly summoning him for perceived, but not real, ailments. If he died, Dr. Bichette could take on three or four additional important clients who would pay him more in total, and cause less trouble.

Of course, there must be no suspicions cast upon me ... and no suggestions of incompetence, either.

He would decide what to do after speaking with Tesh. The *conducci* he had sent to retrieve her should be bringing her back at any moment, with or without Anton. If the maintenance man happened to get in the way and sustained an injury, so be it. Bichette would not even provide him with a healing pad.

* * * * *

Princess Meghina did not like the hard expressions on the faces of Francella and the doctor, the way they stared coldly at the man she loved, as if impatient for him to slip away. A highly sensitive woman, Meghina prided herself on her ability to detect the hidden emotions of others, picking up on little mannerisms, tones of voice, and ephemeral expressions that suggested hidden thoughts and motivations. It did not seem to her that either of these people were overly concerned about Saito's welfare. Rather, they appeared to be thinking of other matters, of other priorities. Meghina didn't see how that could be possible. Still, she was detecting this.

To protect Prince Saito, Meghina would spend more time at his side, to monitor what was being done for him. If he died, it would be a terrible tragedy, not only for him but for Meghina. Even though they were not married, they were deeply in love and by all rights should have at least another twenty-five years together. Yet, if this wonderful man was going to pass away, it seemed fitting for him to do it here, surrounded by murals depicting the stellar accomplishments of his life.

Fighting back tears, she envisioned one last painting of Saito Watanabe lying on his death bed, and her administering to him.

Hold on, my darling, she thought.

Princess Meghina loved the fine things that were provided for her by the Doge and other noblemen—fancy clothing and jewels, the best food and wine, luxurious living and travel arrangements. But above all, she had a special fondness for Saito, and had provided him with honest business and financial advice for CorpOne operations, in addition to her physical and mental comforts.

Meghina shot a sidelong glance at Francella, who gazed dispassionately at her father, a man she should care about. On a number of occasions, Saito had confided to Meghina that he suspected his daughter only wanted money and power from him, and nothing else. The woman seemed to bear no love for anyone but herself, but her father kept hoping he was wrong.

Princess Meghina shook her head sadly. Francella was probably everything he feared she was, and maybe even worse. It seemed obvious that she thought Meghina was interfering, preventing the old man from lavishing money on her. Francella treated the courtesan like an enemy, a competitor for her father's affections and wealth.

We live in a universe of secrets, Meghina thought. *Everyone has them.*

She considered her own secrets, especially one that would send shock waves across the entire Merchant Prince Alliance if it was ever revealed. Only two people knew it, herself and Prince Saito.

In reality, Princess Meghina was a Mutati who could not change back because she had remained in one shape—Human—for too long, allowing her cells to form irreversible patterns. This did not make her internal chemistry, or the arrangement of her organs, Human at all. Her DNA was radically different, and her blood was of a purplish hue. Thus it was quite easy for her to be revealed through a medical examination or a security scan—none of which had ever been required of her, because of her purported noble status and lofty connections. Even a pin prick could reveal her true identity, so she had to take extra care to avoid injury.

Meghina had in her possession falsified documents attesting that she was of noble merchant prince blood, the last surviving member of the House of Nochi. In fact she was a princess, but a *Mutati* one … a distant cousin of Zultan Abal Meshdi. Ever since her childhood on Paradij she had wanted to be Human, and now she was living her dream under an elaborate subterfuge. And, making her task somewhat easier, she was one of the few people of her race who did not display any of the typical allergies that Mutatis felt toward Humans. She had discovered that benefit inadvertently, after her implanted allergy protector stopped functioning.

The Princess had spent a great deal of time and money setting up her clandestine life, and each day she paid close attention to how well the artifice was going, and what she might do to strengthen it. For her own sake, and for that of Prince Saito, it was necessary to remain on constant guard. If anyone ever discovered her, it would ruin her and the Prince, since he knew her true identity and sheltered her. Without any doubt, it would rock the foundations of the Merchant Prince Alliance if the dirty little secret ever got out—despite the fact that she was, at heart, more Human than Mutati.

Her husband Lorenzo was at risk as well, though she did not love him. He was a cruel, selfish man who cared nothing for anyone but himself. Still, he was enamored of her, and provided her with the luxuries of a queen. She used her feminine wiles to manipulate him, like a flesh-and-bone puppet.

Purportedly, Meghina had given birth to seven daughters for the Doge. But each of her pregnancies had been false, since Humans and Mutatis could not interbreed. The "births" were among the most elaborate of her subterfuges, since she paid for children that had been carried in the wombs of other women, and she always went away to a remote planet, without her husband or any of his cronies, to "give birth."

Without realizing it, Princess Meghina had been holding one of the large, limp hands of Prince Saito, and had been massaging it. Suddenly he jerked free of her. His eyes opened wide, and his gaze darted around in all directions. Finally he looked in Meghina's direction, but not directly at her. Instead, he fixed his attention on a point somewhere beyond.

"Noah?" he murmured in a ghostly voice. "Is that you, Noah?"

Without waiting for an answer, he closed his eyes suddenly and slumped back on the bed.

* * * * *

Watching this, Francella grimaced. Nothing, it seemed, could dissuade the foolish old man from loving Noah. She had not planned on her father surviving the attack, so now she had to work on a contingency plan. As in a game of nebula chess, she needed to visualize several moves ahead.

Moments passed while she let the game play out in her mind. When a particularly delicious possibility occurred to her she smiled, just a little. Then, remembering suddenly where she was, she stiffened, and looked directly into Meghina's penetrating sea-green eyes.

Chapter Seventeen

The technology of war is a perilous, but fascinating game. As each side makes an advance, the other attempts to learn its secrets and counter it. Thus, the information provided by spies becomes the most precious commodity in the galaxy.
—Defense Commander Jopa Ilhamad of the Mutati Kingdom

The Citadel of Paradij glittered in morning sunlight like a huge, multifaceted bauble, casting emerald, ruby, and sapphire hues across the rooftops of the capital city. Despite the early hour, the air was already warm and the air conditioning system had broken down, causing the Zultan to perspire heavily and exude foul smells. Someone would die for this incompetence.

In Abal Meshdi's satin-gold dressing chamber, a small Vikkuyo slave stood on a step stool and placed a cone-shaped wax hat on the head of the Mutati leader. In the warmth, the hat would melt a little at a time, releasing perfumes that would mask his body odors. He would be calling upon his concubines today, and did not wish to offend them.

* * * * *

Eight hundred star systems away, General Mah Sajak paced the outdoor patio of his penthouse, fretting and muttering to himself. Around him towered the geometric buildings of Elysoo, the capital of Timian One. Between the structures he saw glimpses of the Halaru River and the snowy Forbidden Mountains in the distance. A cool breeze blew from that direction, and he shivered as it hit him.

The Grand Fleet should be arriving on far-away Paradij at any moment, and then victory would be his. Doge Lorenzo asked him about the progress of the assault force each day, since he wanted to stage one of his gala celebrations here on Timian One. Most of the preparations for the festivities had been completed, and the moment he received word of the victory everything would be brought out, including an immense selection of gourmet foods and exotic beverages for the people.

The surprise attack against the Mutati Kingdom had been thirteen years in the making, including the building and manning of the powerful space fleet, and the time to transport it across the galaxy. But General Sajak was a realist, and in any military venture there were risks … and unknowns.

He told himself to stop worrying, that everything would go perfectly. Just then, a blast of wind hit him squarely in the face, stinging his skin. He turned to go back inside the apartment.

At his approach, a glax door dilated open. The officer stepped through into a warm parlor that featured shifting electronic paintings on the walls and display cases filled with military memorabilia.

As a result of the anticipated triumph—the biggest in the history of Human-Mutati warfare—General Sajak would gain tremendous prestige. Basking in adulation, he would use his new influence to convince the Doge to stop converting commoners into noblemen, in violation of thousands of years of tradition. Since the days of yore, noblemen had been born into their positions, but under the most recent Doges this had changed drastically. Men were being appointed to high positions based upon a ridiculous premise—their scientific or business acumen—with no consideration given to the purity of their bloodline.

The General watched an electronic painting shift. The stylized image of a podship faded, giving way to a violent depiction of a supernova.

He'd better listen to me.

Having been trained in war college to think in terms of high-stakes games, General Sajak was considering the potential responses he might receive. If Doge Lorenzo chose to disregard the urgent entreaty, a new and drastic course of action would be undertaken.

* * * * *

As the Zultan Abal Meshdi rode a sedan chair across Alliq Plaza, the center of his fabulous city, he was surprised by the sudden coolness of the weather. In the last half hour the temperature had dropped precipitously. Most unusual for this time of year.

On impulse, he ordered the runners to set his chair down near a fountain, and then disembarked onto the flagstones of the plaza. Gazing up at the darkening sky, he didn't think he had ever seen clouds quite like those before, with striations of deep purple against gray that were like arteries about to burst open and rain blood on the planet.

* * * * *

The Mutati homeworld was guarded by a fleet of warships that conducted regular patrols over that galactic sector. On a cosmic scale, this did not comprise much area, but it was substantial in planetary terms. The mounting of such a comprehensive guard force required the allocation of a tremendous amount of personnel and hardware.

The patrol ships, while light, fast, and armed with heliomagnetic missiles, were not capable of traveling between star systems. To cross deep space, no practical alternative to podships existed. The distances were too great, making the costs involved with traveling by vacuum rocket or other conventional means prohibitive, because of the incredible fuel requirements that would be involved.

Prohibitive for most galactic races, that is. The Merchant Prince Alliance had more money and other resources than anyone else. It was from this seemingly bottomless treasury that General Mah Sajak drew funds to build the Grand Fleet and send it across light years of distance. It was all done with the permission of the Doge and the Council of Forty.

Sajak and his military brain trust knew about the Mutati patrols, and had taken steps to counteract them. For this assault force, timing was everything. At precisely the right moment, the admiral in charge of the fleet would implement the massive destruction plan. It would be horrible, and beautiful at the same moment.

In his mind's eye, the General envisioned the assault force waiting under the cover of an asteroid belt. This part of his imagination was fairly accurate, but beyond that the differences were significant.

* * * * *

When the Mutati patrol moved along to the other side of Paradij, the merchant prince warships made their long-anticipated move. Piercing the upper atmosphere of the Mutati homeworld, the Grand Fleet generated swirls of ionized hydrols around it which looked like large gray-and-white storm clouds, concealing the attackers from the inhabitants of the planet below. Even the sophisticated electronics of the Mutatis could not detect them.

Theoretically.

* * * * *

In the sedan chair far below the fleet, a communication transceiver crackled, and the Zultan heard Mutati battle language, chattering frantically. Paradij was under attack! The Humans had generated artificial storm clouds to conceal their forces.

Abal Meshdi stared upward, unmoving, and thought of all the defensive preparations that had been made by the Mutati High Command. They had not known exactly when the attack would occur, but had received a number of clues that it was coming, and—with the approval of the Zultan himself—had made certain clever arrangements.

The Mutati war program, after so many losses to Human forces, was two-pronged. The Zultan's doomsday weapon was undergoing final testing, and barring any unforeseen problems it would soon be launched against enemy planets, annihilating them to the last one.

He also had a shock in store for anyone daring to attack his worlds, as the commander of the enemy fleet was about to discover.

He smiled nervously, and prayed to God-On-High for the defense of sacred Paradij. He hoped that his people had taken adequate steps, because in war, anything could happen.

High in the atmosphere, the clouds roiled.

When Meshdi was a young emir in training for future responsibilities, his grandfather had said to him, "Preparation is the child of necessity." At the time, the boy had not understood the significance of the adage, but later it had become abundantly clear to him.

Thousands of years of hatred and armed conflict against Humans had led to this moment, a stepping stone in what he hoped would ultimately be Mutati dominion. Meshdi felt his pulse accelerate. Since the earliest moments of his recollection he had loathed Humans. Under his leadership, no expense had been spared and important programs had been initiated. Galactic espionage, for one.

Mutatis, by virtue of their ability to shapeshift, could work as spies on Human worlds more easily than the enemy could on Mutati planets ... provided that Mutatis controlled their strongly allergic reactions in the presence of their arch enemies. Implanted allergy protectors usually worked, but when they failed—as they did occasionally—the consequences could be disastrous. The best solution lay in a small percentage of Mutatis who for unknown reasons did not show any Human aversion—so it was from this group that spies were recruited. There had been a handful of incidents in which even they sometimes developed reactions, but the Zultan played the odds, and thus far his espionage operations had not been compromised.

Humans knew that these enemy incursions were occurring, and had their own safeguards, including regular physical examinations for persons in sensitive positions. Under even a cursory medical examination, a Mutati could be revealed. It just took a needle prick to reveal the color of the blood. But Humans were susceptible to bribes and other deceptions, and Mutati spies continued to ply their artful trade. Secrets were learned, bits and pieces of information that made their way back to Paradij and the Zultan.

In this manner the Mutatis learned—more than a decade ago—that a massive Human fleet was going to be sent against them, but at an unknown time. For years, the Mutatis waited. And waited. They knew ... or strongly suspected, based upon their knowledge of conventional cross-space transportation technology ... that a Human fleet could not possibly travel as fast as the mysterious podships. The sentient pods had never cooperated with any military venture, and in fact had undermined a number of attempts by various races to exploit them for warlike pur-poses. As a consequence, the Mutatis knew that Humans would need to transport their fleet on their own, without the assistance of podships.

As the clues arrived via their spy network, the Mutati High Command held emergency meetings. They floated an idea that the Humans might move their military hardware and personnel in disguise, a little at a time, using podships. In this manner, they could set up a staging area closer to the core of the Mutati Kingdom, at a place where they could launch their attack more quickly. In an attempt to discover such a location, the Mutatis sent out continual scouting parties in comprehensive, fanning search patterns.

Nothing surfaced. This suggested the probability that the Humans were sending their force en masse from one of their own military bases, which meant time would be needed to make the journey ... perhaps ten to fifteen years. It also suggested the possibility of obsolescence, since the hardware would be old by the time it arrived at its destination. Maybe the enemy was counting on the element of surprise.

At least we're taking that away from them, the Zultan thought. *But will it be enough?*

* * * * *

From the bridge of his flagship, Admiral Pan Obidos surveyed the protective cloud layer beneath his fleet of ten mother ships that had traveled across space in a bundle of vacuum rockets and were now spread out in attack formation. Minutes ago, each mother ship had disgorged thousands of small fighter-bombers that looked like silver fish flying in the upper atmosphere.

As he watched, the mother ships fired electronic probes into the artificial clouds every few seconds like lightning bolts, checking their thickness and integrity as a shield.

Going well so far, the Admiral thought. This renowned "Mutati-Killer," hero of two big military victories against his arch enemies, stood behind his command chair, with his hands gripping the back. A small man with a jutting jaw, he had a large mole over his left eyebrow.

Moment by moment, inexorably, the masking clouds dropped lower and lower, concealing the advancing fleet like an immense shield....

In order to make the clouds appear authentic, the attackers had initially generated them over a sparsely populated region of the Mutati homeworld, and had then moved them (as if blown by high atmospheric winds) in the direction the Admiral wanted to go, toward the capital city of Jadeen and the surrounding military installations.

A successful strike would be devastating to the Mutatis, cutting the rotten heart out of their entire kingdom.

Looking around the command bridge at the flagship officers who had endured the perils of this long voyage with him, he felt pride in their loyalty and dedication. None of the officers in the fleet had complained about their hardships, nor had the twenty-four thousand fighters under their command.

Jimu, a black, patched-together robot who was Captain of the sentient machines in the fleet, hurried up to Admiral Obidos, and saluted with a short metal arm. In his mechanical voice, the robot gave a concise report. Then, at a nod from his superior, he hurried off, to tend to his duties.

Despite prohibitions against it, a number of women under the Admiral's command had conceived and given birth to children in space—twenty-eight in all—and they were subsequently raised in a community facility. The unauthorized pregnancies had irritated Obidos, but such problems had been minor in comparison with other problems faced by the task force.

The huge vessel jostled, and the Admiral held onto side bars.

"Just turbulence," one of the officers reported.

Five years into the mission, most of the officers and crew came down with a serious space sickness, including Admiral Obidos. More than three hundred died before the fleet medics came up with a treatment, combining marrow and calcium injections.

After so many years of injections, however, there were side effects. Obidos and the other victims no longer had their own bones, as their entire skeletal structures—even the essential marrow—had dissipated and been replaced by artificial substances. The Admiral had been among those who had suffered the most physical pain—but each day he tried not to think about it.

As the assault force dropped lower and lower in the atmosphere, proceeding slowly and methodically behind the cloud cover, the Admiral felt cold, and shivered. Sliding a forefinger across a touch pad at his belt, he activated a warming mechanism. Within seconds, heat coursed through the artificial marrow cores and calcium deposits of his bones.

Nonetheless, he shivered again.

Obidos could not get warm, no matter how high he turned up the mechanism. There was no remedy for cold fear.

* * * * *

High over the Zultan's head, the storm clouds began to break up, revealing what looked like thousands of silver needles glistening in the sun. Ships ... and several much larger vessels behind them.

A merchant prince task force!

Abruptly, the flight pattern changed in the sky, and Abal Meshdi thought he detected disarray. He heard confirmation of this over the nearby communication transceiver, as it crackled in Mutati battle language. "We broke the electronic integrity of their shield, and they are attempting to regroup."

Over the open line he heard percussive blasts, and saw distant flashes in the atmosphere. The storm cover had been anticipated, based upon intelligence information that the Mutatis had received.

In short order, the attack turned into an epic debacle, as the Mutatis shot down everything in the merchant prince fleet except for the flagship, which they captured along with the officers and crew. They even took the Admiral prisoner, saved from his intended suicide by a fast-acting Mutati medic.

* * * * *

As he prepared to visit the captured officers in their electronic cells, Abal Meshdi wondered why the merchant princes had undertaken such a risky mission. He was about to board a lift platform, on his way to interrogate and torture the military leaders, when an aide rushed up to him, breathing hard and perspiring.

"Sire, their Admiral is dead!" he reported. He went on to explain that Obidos had taken his own life in a second suicide attempt—after obtaining poison in an unknown way.

Moments later, Meshdi burst into the cell and examined the body himself. There was no sign of life. Off to one side, a dented black mechanical man watched.

"He's the Captain of their machines," the aide said, pointing. "Calls himself Jimu."

An idea occurred to the Zultan, and he acted on it without delay. Within hours he sent the robot back to Timian One, carrying holos of the humiliating military defeat and of the Admiral's body. Jimu traveled by podship.

But that was only for entertainment, to make Abal Meshdi's prey suffer the most possible agony. Soon he would send them something even bigger, a storm of doomsday weapons.

Demolios.

Chapter Eighteen

There is a beginning point to everything, and an ending point, but it is not always possible to identify either one.
— Noah Watanabe, *Reflections on my Life*, Guardian Publications

At sunset a brown-and-black catus, one of the thick-furred persinnians that ran wild on the grounds of the Ecological Demonstration Project, stalked a bird. The feline remained low on the dry, yellowing grass, its front paws outstretched, and pulled itself toward a fat pazabird, moving forward only centimeters at a time without making a sound. The white-breasted bird dug around the roots of grass for worms, oblivious to danger.

Thinking he felt movement beneath his feet, Noah got down on all fours and placed an ear to the ground. He heard something, a distant rumbling noise, but could not determine the source. He wondered if it could be a nuisance that had been occurring on Canopa in recent years, groundtruck-sized digging machines that were left behind by mining companies. The "Diggers," with artificial intelligence and the ability to sustain themselves, had been burrowing deep underground and occasionally surfacing like claymoles, tearing up large chunks of real estate and damaging buildings. So far, Noah had been fortunate, but it was an increasingly widespread problem. The Doge himself had ordered their extermination on a variety of merchant prince planets, which amounted to commando raids against the machines in their burrows—going after them like pests.

The rumbling noise subsided, and he felt nothing in the ground. Looking up, he saw the catus pounce, filling the air with feathers. It was an efficient act of predation, with the kill completed in a matter of seconds. Now the catus played with the dead bird, lying on the ground and batting it around like a kittus with a ball.

With the last rays of sunlight kissing his face, he was reminded of an incident from his childhood. No more than seven years old at the time, he had been out in a forest, walking along a path that led from the village to his home. Upon hearing a repetitive thumping sound, he'd noticed a red-crested woodbird pecking away at a rotten log beside the trail. Instinctively, Noah had not moved and was careful not to make a sound. The bird seemed unaware of his presence, and the curious boy stood silently, watching it extract worms from the holes it was making in the soft wood. Presently the bird flew off, into the high branches of a pine tree. Perching there, it fed worms from its beak to hungry chicks that poked their heads out of a hole in the tree trunk.

Afterward, Noah had gone to the rotten log and pulled some of the wood away, enabling him to see many worms writhing around in their moist habitat, trying to burrow deeper into the log to escape him. He had gathered some of the wriggling creatures, taking them home to put in a jar with air holes in the lid. That afternoon, however, his sister Francella stole the worms and chopped them into pieces, just to watch the little segments keep moving. When he found out about this, Noah screamed, but it was too late.

The twins' governess, Ilyana Tinnel, had separated them as they fought. A kindly woman, she showed Noah other worms in the rich soil of her own garden and explained how they enriched the dirt, adding nutrients to it. She told him something that intrigued him, that soil, worms, and birds were all connected and that they worked together, as other life forms did, to enhance the ecology of Canopa. In her world-view, soil was a living organism, part of the vital, breathing planet.

Though his father discounted the concept of complex environmental relationships, it was an astounding revelation to the boy, and proved to be the starting point for his life's work. In his adulthood he extended his study to a number of planets ... and the roles that Humans and other galactic races played on each of them. Noah learned about incredibly long food chains, all the predators and prey, and marvelous plants that sentient creatures could use for medicines, herbs, and food. For each planet, all of the parts fit together like the pieces of a complicated jigsaw puzzle....

Now the catus, having grown tired of playing with the bird, devoured its prey, bones and all. It was an unpleasant sight for Noah to watch, but entirely necessary in the larger scheme of existence. He would not think of interfering.

His thoughts spun back again, to a time when he began to wonder how life forms survived in hostile environments, such as snow fleas on mountains, lichen on cliff faces, and desert succulents that stored water in their cellular structures. He had also been intrigued by chemical life forms thriving in the deepest ocean trenches where immense pressures would crush other creatures, and by alien races such as Tulyans, that did not need to breathe.

Noah had tried to put things together in new ways. He considered how seeds fell from trees and were carried by winds, so that saplings grew a few meters away, and even farther. It was a continual process of establishing new root systems, growing young plants, and then having seeds carried off again, to someplace new. When he put this information together with what he knew about comets and asteroids—heavenly bodies that carried living seeds around the galaxy in their cellular structures—he found his mind expanding, taking in more and more data. He envisioned fireballs entering atmospheres and spreading seeds ... not unlike the seeds transported around a planet by its own winds.

Such theoretical linkages had caused him to wonder if planetary ecosystems might possibly extend farther than previously imagined, into the cold vacuum of space. Could each planet, with its seemingly independent environment, actually be linked to others? The seeds carried by comets and asteroids suggested that that this might be possible, as did the gravitational pulls exerted by astronomical bodies on one another, and the fact that the same elements existed in widely-separated locations. It seemed connected, perhaps, to a huge explosion long ago, the legendary "Big Bang" that split an immense mass into the planets, suns, and other components of the galaxy.

It all boggled Noah's mind, but still another analogy had occurred to him. The galaxy was a sea of stars and planets and other cosmic bodies. A *sea*, with a myriad of mysterious interactions and interdependencies.

Now, thinking back on the events that had turned him into a galactic ecologist, Noah refocused on the grassy spot where the catus had devoured the bird. The feline was gone, and only feathers remained behind. Shadows stretched across the brown-brick and glax buildings of his compound, as if the encroaching night was a predator, sucking away the light. Guardians were leaving the offices, greenhouses, and laboratories on their way home, having completed their work for the day.

Deep in thought, Master Noah left the landscaped area and strode along a path, toward grass- and shrub-covered hills that were beginning to yellow as the summer season established itself. In waning daylight, trail lamps flickered on. He passed half a dozen workers going the other way, and barely noticed them. At the base of the nearest hill he reached a metal gate that covered a vaulted opening cut into the base of the slope. A pool of floodlights illuminated the area. A stocky little guard, armed with a puissant rifle over his shoulder, saluted him.

Passing into a plaxene-lined room beyond the gate, Noah took an *ascensore*—a high-speed lift mechanism—up to a private tram station on top of the hill. He crossed to the other side of a platform, where he boarded a green-and-brown tram car and sat on one of the seats inside the brightly-illuminated passenger compartment. The door slid shut and the vehicle went into motion, leaving the station and accelerating along an unseen electronic wire that transported him out over forested hills and small, shadowy lakes on top of the plateau.

As the car sped into increasing darkness on its invisible wire, Noah felt the buffeting effects of wind gusts. It was unusual for winds to be so strong at this time of year. Only a small event to the untrained eye, but a troubling one to him. Lately things seemed out of balance on Canopa, as if the forces of nature were refusing to continue business as usual. A steady stream of unusual occurrences were being reported by Guardian patrols ... sudden storms and geological upheavals in remote regions of the planet. One of the Tulyans in his employ, Eshaz, had provided him with some of the information, but he seemed to be holding things back. The Tulyans were a strange breed anyway, but in the years that Eshaz and his companions had worked as Guardians, Noah had never seen them this way.

Just ahead, bathed in floodlights on a landing pad, he saw the orange shuttle craft that would transport him up to EcoStation, his orbital laboratory and School of Galactic Ecology. He watched a team of Guardians run scanners with lavender lights over the craft to make certain it was safe to ride. In part of Noah's mind the need for such caution seemed preposterous. After all, the merchant princes had permitted him to operate freely for years, having done this out of deference to his powerful father. Now, though, following the attack on CorpOne headquarters, anything was possible. The feisty old Prince had tried to ruin his own son ... or worse.

Noah could not believe it had all happened. Things were more complicated than ever. Sometimes he wished he was a small boy again, examining flora and fauna with fresh eyes. But the more he learned, the more he realized that he had lost the innocence of youth. His lifelong quest for information, almost desperate because of the finite term of his life, had taken him far away from those early days. Sadness enveloped him now, for it seemed to him that innocence, once lost, could never be regained.

Master Noah boarded the shuttle, and it lifted off. As he looked up at the night sky through the bubble roof of the craft he remembered lying in a meadow one evening long ago, staring in awe and amazement at the stars above him. His life had been a tabula rasa at the time, a white slate extending into the future, waiting for him to make marks upon it.

In the years since that night he had not really learned that much after all, not in the vast scale of the cosmos. Still, as he lifted heavenward, his mind seemed suddenly refreshed and ready to absorb a great deal more, and he felt a new sense of wonder and excitement.

Chapter Nineteen

Sometimes I wish podships had never shown up at all. Our access to them on a limited basis has only whetted our appetites, making us think of astonishing, seemingly unattainable, possibilities. The concept of a starliner, for example, a trainlike arrangement of linked podships … or a startruck in which a podship pulls a long line of container trailers. Alas, such ideas seem destined to remain on the drawing boards.

—Wooton Ichiro, 107th Czar of Commerce
for the Merchant Prince Alliance

A dozen workmen slid the immense Aquastar Throne down a roller-ramp from the top of the dais, toward the floor of the elegant chamber. Having been awakened from his bed by the voices and other commotion in there, Doge Lorenzo stood off to one side, watching. He wore a bathrobe with the golden tigerhorse crest of his royal house on the lapel. His thinning gray hair stuck out at the sides.

Noticing him, a small man with a narrow face hurried to his side. "Is there anything you wish, Sire?" the work supervisor asked.

"No, no," Lorenzo said, for he was anxious to get the alterations taken care of, even if these men had made the mistake of beginning work too early in the morning. He didn't feel much like punishing anyone today.

The man bowed and was about to leave when the Doge said, "Wait. There is something. Have my breakfast tea brought to me here."

"Right away, Sire."

"And send for the Royal Attaché."

"Yes, Your Magnificence."

As his orders were carried out, the Doge's mind spun onto other matters. In his position, he had so much to think about. No other noblemen, not even the princes on the Council of Forty, could fully understand the extent of being a leader in wartime. Foremost in his thoughts, he looked forward to the gala celebration that would occur after the Grand Fleet won its glorious victory against the Mutatis. The announcement was due at any moment, and like a child forced to wait for a present, he was running out of patience.

Although nehrcom transceivers could transmit instantaneously across space, they only operated to and from secure, land-based facilities. With the aid of relay mechanisms, messages could be sent from a planet to nearby ships or space stations, but the reception quality was substantially diminished in the process.

No one except the nehrcom inventor, Prince Jacopo Nehr, knew why such a problem existed, and he was not divulging any secrets. As a consequence, the Grand Fleet had remained out of contact for years as it traveled through enemy star systems and other regions where there were no transceiver units. Some people thought this apparent "Achilles heel" in the communication network had to do with the gravitational or magnetic fields of planets and suns. Others were not so certain, but all agreed on one thing: nehrcoms were almost as mysterious as podships.

Despite the lack of contact, Doge Lorenzo del Velli remained confident of a huge victory over the Mutati Kingdom, and had been receiving nothing but the most glowing assurances to this effect from General Sajak. At the Doge's insistence, concise calculations had been completed by the most advanced Hibbil computers, showing exactly when the Grand Fleet should be filling the skies of Paradij ... and when the rain of destruction would be complete.

A day ago he had received updated calculations, and had been thinking about them ever since. Unfortunately they included variables and a lot of double-talk from the mathematicians and military advisers who supervised the work. The attack might occur anytime during a thirty day period, beginning with the upcoming weekend.

As he stood there watching the workmen settle his throne onto the floor with a soft thump, he thought back to a decision he had announced the night before, when he notified General Sajak that he was not going to wait for word from the task force before staging the festivities. Instead he wanted them scheduled on the earliest possible day of victory—this Saturday—without revealing in advance the nature of the occasion. Lorenzo was ebullient at the decision, but General Sajak had been oddly silent.

Was the officer worried about something going wrong? Of course not, Lorenzo assured himself. The plan of attack had been worked out in exquisite detail by the best military minds in the realm, and no expense had been spared.

This Saturday the Doge would open his present; the party would be one the most extravagant celebrations in the history of the Merchant Prince Alliance, overshadowed only by royal coronations and weddings. Covering more than three hundred square blocks of the city of Elysoo, it would be more impressive than the jubilee at the turn of the last century. In fact, as far as anyone could recall, this was slated to be the biggest open-invitation party ever held anywhere. It would be an opportunity for the common people to experience the finest foods, beverages, and entertainment available. As the most successful traders in the galaxy, the merchant princes had everything that the mind could imagine or the heart could want.

The Doge's breakfast tea arrived, and he sat upon his throne to sip it, while the activity continued around him. The workers were cutting open the top of the dais now, to install the lift mechanism that he had specified. Upon learning that an ancient Byzantine Emperor had been in possession of such an apparatus, the Doge vowed to have one, too. He had no idea how the original one operated—probably with slave labor—but he would have a mechanical system for his, and would use it during royal audiences. Up toward the heavens he would go, or down, depending upon his whim and upon the extent of awe and fear he wished to generate.

Pimyt entered the chamber just as the remaining tea was growing cold. Over the noise of ongoing work the two of them discussed the status of preparations for the celebration.

The aging, black-and-white Hibbil seemed more agitated than usual, undoubtedly because of all the arrangements he had been coordinating. His red eyes flashed with intensity. "Despite a high standard of living on Timian One," he said in a squeaky voice, "the event is likely to attract impoverished persons from the back country and a fair share of rowdies who will drink and party to excess."

"Well, take care of it," Lorenzo said, with a dismissive gesture. "Assign my entire special force to work the celebration."

"*All* of your Red Berets? I don't have the authority to do that."

"Stop whining. Prepare the necessary document and I will sign it."

"Yes. Mmmm, a large number of them should be plainclothesmen."

"Attend to it."

"I will, My Lord." The Hibbil concealed a scowl on his furry, graying face. Unknown to the Doge, he would have preferred no festivities at all, since he considered the whole affair a lot of wasted effort when he had more important matters to handle … things the Doge didn't know about. Though he concealed it well behind his innocent-looking, bearlike face, Pimyt did not like Humans at all, and he had taken certain steps to make them suffer.

When the Doge had no more orders to issue, the Royal Attaché took his leave.

That afternoon, crews began setting up temporary structures and hanging colorful banners from buildings. Curious crowds gathered in the streets of Elysoo to watch, and heard the scheduling announcement. By tomorrow the people would be jockeying for the best positions to camp, and street musicians, mimes, and jugglers would accelerate their practice sessions, putting the finishing touches on their routines.

And in only a few days, brightly-colored dirigibles would fill the sky, with their telebeam messages proclaiming the epic Human victory.

Chapter Twenty

Do you know what is exciting about the galaxy? The mystery of it, for this vast network of star systems, despite its great antiquity, continually shows us new and unpredictable faces.

—*Scienscroll*, Commentaries 1:29-30

In the bustling main kitchen of the Palazzo Magnifico, seven chefs in white smocks and gold caps hurried from counter to counter, inspecting the decorations on the mini-cakes, fruit biscuits, and other elegant desserts.

The five men and two women moved from section to section like wine tasters, sampling the imaginatively-shaped confections and expectorating into buckets on the floor. It was mid-afternoon, a warm day in the city of Elysoo and even warmer in the kitchen, because of the ovens.

A teenage culinary worker, Dux Hannah. wiped perspiration from his brow with a long white sleeve. He noticed a roachrat poking its long black antennae out of a bucket at the exact moment that a female chef was about to spit food into it.

Startled, the chef sprayed her mouthful all over a tray of decorated cookies. "Double damn!" she exclaimed, and swept a thick arm across the contaminated tray, sending it crashing to the floor. Then she gave chase to the fat, beetle-bodied rodent as it ran across the kitchen.

Looking on, the stocky head chef, Verlan Ladoux, flew into a rage. "Get this kitchen clean!" he shouted. "We feed people, not roachrats!"

Moments later, a team of exterminators appeared with their equipment. Solemnly, they inspected sonic traps under the counters, cleaned dead roachrats out of sealed compartments, and reset the devices.

Dux Hannah and Acey Zelk were members of a Human slave crew. Sixteen-year-old boys, they were first cousins, with no formal education. Acquired on the auction market by Doge del Velli's chief of staff, they had been enslaved because their people—the Barani tribe of Siriki's wild back country—had been negligent in paying taxes to the Merchant Prince Alliance. The boys did not look alike at all. Acey had bristly black hair and a wide face, while Dux was taller and thinner, with long blond hair that tended to fall across his eyes.

Owing to his considerable artistic talents, Dux had been ordered to decorate royal cakes and other delicacies, using frosting and sprinkle guns to create swirls, animals, hieroglyphics, and geometric designs. In contrast, Acey had mechanical skills, so he worked with the maintenance staff to keep food-service robots operable.

As the exterminators worked under the counters, slowing the pace of kitchen operations, Chef Ladoux paced about nervously. He was especially agitated today, since food was being prepared for the Doge's elaborate celebration, which had begun that morning. It was early afternoon now, and the kitchen—one of many servicing the festivities—had been operating at peak efficiency for more than a day. Until this interruption.

Acey and Dux exchanged glances, and nodded at each other. This was the moment the boys had long awaited, for they intended to use the confusion to activate their bold plan.

Acey slipped away first and entered a supply room. After shutting and locking the door he reprogrammed one of the robots. The brassex, semi-sentient machine was large and blocky, with a spacious interior where it carried food that it picked up and delivered—enough space for the two young men to hide, if the shelves were removed.

Still in the kitchen, Dux wrote a frosting message on a large ivory-chocolate cake: "I WOULDN'T EAT THIS IF I WERE YOU." He then covered the cake with a silver lid and knocked on the door of the supply room, three taps followed by a pause and then two more taps.

Moments later, the robot marched outside and clanked toward the central market of the city. When out of sight of the palazzo, the machine changed course and took the boys instead to a crowded depot. There they caught a shuttle that took them up to an orbital pod station, high above the atmosphere of the planet. They brought money with them—merchant prince liras—stolen from the chefs' locker room over a period of months.

Presently the boys stood at a broad glax window in a noisy, crowded waiting room, waiting for the next podship to arrive. The pod station was stark and utilitarian, made of unknown, impermeable materials and placed there by unknown methods ... as others like it had been established in orbital positions around the galaxy.

Below the pod station, through patchy white clouds, Acey and Dux watched early evening shadows creeping across the surface of Timian One as the sun dropped beneath the horizon.

"When do you think the next podship will arrive?" Acey asked.

Looking up at an electronic sign hanging from the ceiling, Dux answered, "Anytime in the next twelve hours."

"I'm not talking about what the podcasters say. Those guys are wrong all the time."

As both teenagers knew, podcasters were expert prognosticators employed by the various galactic races, performing jobs that computers purportedly could not do nearly as well. Working at each pod station, the professionals spent long hours making calculations, figuring podship arrival probabilities based upon past results. The calculations were elaborate, owing to a number of variables and the sometimes unexpected behavior of the podships. The jobs were demanding and required a great deal of education to obtain, including rigid testing procedures. In merchant prince society the positions were considered prestigious for commoners to hold, causing people to compete for entrance into the finest schools.

"Wrong?" Dux said, brushing his long golden hair out of his eyes. "I don't know about that."

"Maybe I've had bad luck, but I've spent days waiting for podships that were supposed to show up and didn't." Acey's chin jutted out stubbornly, as it often did when he debated a point.

"You mean on that cross-space trip you and Grandmamá took?"

"Uh huh, the contest she won."

"I hear there was a big shakeup in the podcaster ranks a couple of years afterward, so hopefully it's better now."

For a long moment, Dux stared at another electronic sign hanging from the ceiling, a display panel that reported information transmitted by "glyphreader" robots from the zero-G docking bays. This one was blank, since there were no podships present at the moment. Had one been docked, the glyphreader would have translated the hieroglyphic destination board on the fuselage and transmitted the results to the various electronic signs around the station. (The alien hieroglyphs were one of the few things that anyone had figured out about the spaceships—a revelation that enabled travelers to know where they were going before boarding one of the vessels.)

When the right opportunity presented itself, Acey and Dux sneaked aboard a podship ... without paying any attention to the destination....

Back on Timian One, in the broad *plaza mayore* of the capital city, the citizens went into shock as rumors began to circulate about a catastrophic military loss suffered by the merchant princes at far-away Paradij. It seemed impossible for the Mutatis—who had lost most of the battles fought against the Humans—to have scored such a huge victory. People couldn't believe it. Stunned and fearful, the crowds fell into murmurs. Were Mutati forces on the way here now?

In the throne room of the Palazzo Magnifico, Doge Lorenzo railed at General Sajak, who stood humbly before him in a wrinkled red-and-gold uniform, cap in hand. The furious ruler shouted so loudly that he could be heard all the way out in the corridors and public rooms. It was an embarrassment of epic proportions, the worst military defeat in the history of humanity.

Chapter Twenty-One

Nothing is entirely secure. No matter how many precautions are taken, no matter how much money and manpower are expended, a narrow crack of exposure always remains. Our mortal safety, then, depends upon the inability of an enemy to identify, or capitalize upon, each of his opportunities.
    —Admiral Monmouth del Velli, ancestor of Lorenzo the Magnificent

A slideway took Master Noah from the docked shuttle into EcoStation, an orbital structure that looked like something a child had fitted together with toy parts, but on a very large scale. A round doorway dilated open and Noah stepped through into a vaulted entrance chamber that featured exotic climbing plants visible through glax-plate walls.

He waited while a security officer in a hooded black suit checked him with a scanner beam. The wash of white light felt cool on his skin. Even though Noah suffered this inconvenience every time he came here, it was the result of his own orders, to prevent anyone from pretending to be him. If a saboteur ever got aboard, the entire facility could be destroyed.

Guardian headquarters and this orbiter had state-of-the-art security systems and a private military force, which Noah had ordered on full alert. He'd had nothing to do with the assault on CorpOne, but feared that someone had impersonated his activists in order to make him look bad—thus paving the way for attacks against his operations.

For a while, he thought his father had laid a trap for him, but he was coming to believe that such a malicious deception was something altogether different from their earlier quarrels, and almost beyond comprehension. The more Noah thought about it, the more he suspected that Francella had masterminded the plan to ruin his reputation at the very least, and quite possibly to kill him. He wondered if his father had participated in such a scheme, perhaps after having been duped and manipulated by his wily daughter. And—plots within plots—had Francella planned to kill both her brother and father in the same incident?

A chill ran down Noah's spine as possibilities curled around him like the tails of demons.

On the other side of a thick glax window, he saw the Adjutant of the Guardians, Subi Danvar, watching the security procedure. Loyal and efficient, he ran the entire Guardian organization whenever Noah was away on business.

Presently the hooded officer nodded stiffly, and on Noah's right the door to a glax-walled booth opened, sliding upward. Stepping inside, Noah waited while an ion mist bathed him and his clothing in a waterless decontamination shower. It only lasted a few seconds, during which he felt a slight warmth, and a tingling sensation. Then an interior door opened.

As the Guardian leader marched into the adjacent room, Subi bowed slightly and said, "I trust you are doing well, Master Noah?"

"Passably, thank you."

After the sound of a musical tone the adjutant said, "Excuse me for a moment, please." From a pocket of his surcoat he removed a headset, and put it on. Telebeam images danced in front of his face, a live connection. He tuned the device so that the color projections grew larger, and filled the air between him and Noah. Two people were shown.

"An urgent transmission from a friend of yours," Subi said. "He is at the entrance gate of the compound." The adjutant was referring to the Ecological Demonstration Project, down on Canopa.

Noah recognized one of the pair, a blond, mustachioed young man standing just outside the guard station. It was Anton Glavine, accompanied by an attractive woman. She had long black hair and a good figure. "You're looking fit, Anton," Noah said, looking away from her.

"I must speak with you."

"This is a busy time, but I can grant you three minutes. Proceed."

"In person. Please."

"I'll return the day after tomorrow. You may await me in one of the guest houses. Make yourself comfortable."

"I must see you now. *Please,* Noah. Allow me to come up there with you. I'd like to bring my girlfriend along, too. This is Tesh Kori."

The woman bowed and smiled. She had emerald green eyes that Noah found striking. But he tried not to look at her, and focused instead on Anton. There were many reasons why Noah would do anything for this young man, reasons that had never been revealed to Anton.

"Very well," Noah said after a long pause, "but I'm about to conduct a class. I will see you afterward."

"All right. Thank you."

Assuming that Anton wanted to express his sympathy over the life-threatening injury to Saito Watanabe, Noah told Subi to telebeam approval to the security people down at the compound, so that the young man and his companion could board a tram car and shuttle.

After Subi took care of this, he put away the headset and said, "Your class awaits you, Master."

The two men walked through a dimly-illuminated corridor. This was a section that had been added to the complex recently. EcoStation, always in geostationary orbit directly above Noah's wildlife preserve and farm, had originally been designed with modular elements. Hence it was easily enlarged with the addition of more units, an ongoing process as the need for more laboratory and classroom space constantly increased. Aside from the benefit of an uncontaminated, off-planet facility for genetic studies on exotic plants and animals, he liked the isolation that the orbiter provided for students, so that they could maximize the learning process. The students lived in dormitories on board.

Soon Noah heard the chattering and giggling of young voices, just ahead. Moments later he and his companion entered the classroom. The students, all new to the school, grew silent.

While the adjutant introduced Noah to thirty men and women dressed in unisex green smocks and trousers, Noah found himself impressed by their erect posture and bright, attentive expressions. They seemed eager to learn and become full-fledged Guardians, and he was just as eager to teach them.

The classroom was surrounded by dwarf oak and blue-bark canopa pines, simulating a forest environment. Birds and small woodland creatures flitted from branch to branch, kept separate from the classroom by an invisible electronic barrier. It was an entirely self-sufficient, small scale environment. Noah had designed it himself, and others that were similar. They doubled as air cleaning facilities for surrounding rooms.

"All of you are volunteers," Noah began, from the lectern, "and you are to be commended for not going to work in a polluting industry, and for instead committing yourselves to the preservation of the galactic environment. The term I have just used—'galactic environment'—is not easily defined, so I will take several moments to explain certain basic concepts to you.... "

He gestured with his hands as he spoke, and for almost an hour he went on uninterrupted, while the students listened in fascination, hardly stirring from their seats.

Then he rolled forth a large clearplax box on a cart, and explained that it contained a living organism he had saved from the planet Jaggem while performing ecological recovery operations there. The box held what looked like an amorphous hunk of dark brown flesh, writhing slowly, throbbing and pulsing. But Noah knew it was a lot more than that.

"Meet my friend Lumey," he said. "I named him that because he glows luminescent white when digesting his food."

Noah invited the students to gather around.

"As far as we can tell," he said, "Lumey belongs to a nearly extinct galactic race, and may be the last of his kind. We keep him in a sealed environment, and he might live there for a long time. Or, sadly, he might die before your very eyes. One thing is certain: We could not leave the little fellow on Jaggem, since industrial polluters there destroyed his entire food chain."

"How does he see?" one of the female students asked. "Where are his eyes?"

"According to my biologists, he doesn't have eyes, ears, or a sense of smell. Nonetheless, he uses other senses to get around, and has an innate ability to sense danger, and to survive."

"Is that a face?" one of the young men asked. "He keeps turning a portion of his body toward us." He pointed at a light brown area of flesh. "See. Just a small section that is different in color, and more smoothly textured than the rest of his body."

"Good observation," Noah said. "That seems to be a sensor pad, although we're still not sure what he detects with it. When we found the poor creature in a pile of industrial slag, he was living off his own residual body cells, withering away. We have created a mini environment here where he lives quite well on his own recycled air, and reprocessed waste as well, which exits his body in a mineral-rich condensation and is then scooped up by one of our inventions from eco-recovery. In this case it's a small-scale skyminer, which salvages important elements from the mini-atmosphere and converts them to food for Lumey."

As Noah spoke, he pointed to a miniature skyminer hovering inside the container, and a food processor on one wall. He was about to explain more, when suddenly he stopped in mid-sentence. Startling him, a nehrcom screen on the back wall—which previously had been as black as space—came to life, showing the fuzzy image of a large terramutati. Turning their heads to look back, several students cried out or screamed in horror.

The Mutati was, in its natural state, an almost incomprehensible amalgam of fatty tissue, with bony extrusions for its numerous arms and legs. A tiny head with oversized eyes was barely visible atop folds of fat, like the head of a turtle poking out of its shell. The creature had no mouth, but words came forth in synchronization, as its body quivered and pulsed like gelatin.

"Your security is rather feeble and easy to penetrate," the Mutati said in a crackling, eerie voice. The image on the screen and accompanying sounds, while weak, were the normal quality of a nehrcom transmission that had been relayed from the Canopa ground station. He saw what looked like nehrcom equipment in the background.

"Find out where this is coming from!" Noah barked to Subi. "And evacuate the classroom!" The adjutant ran out into the corridor and shouted for guards. A number of students followed him, but others tarried, staring with transfixed expressions at the screen.

"Get out of here!" Noah shouted at them. "All of you!" He gripped the lectern, and it rocked.

"Out there orbiting Canopa," the electronic intruder said in an irritating, calm tone, "you are not exactly at the center of the galaxy, are you? So I will tell you what has occurred today. A merchant prince assault fleet, sent to Paradij by devious design, has been demolished."

As if to emphasize what the Mutati had just said, a loud static pop sounded, and the last word echoed in the room: " ... demolished ... demolished ... demolished.... "

Stunned by the assertion, Noah was not certain if he should believe it. He had heard nothing of a military venture against Paradij. But could this possibly be true?

* * * * *

On the wall screen the Mutati sneezed, coughed, and twitched. The shapeshifter had sneaked onto Timian One, having assumed the identity of a Human and gained access to a nehrcom station while its electronic surveillance system was under repair.

As one of the Mutatis who did not normally show allergic reactions in the proximity of Humans, he had, for a time, experienced no adverse reactions. But eventually the allergies had surfaced and now they were now hitting him full force. Even the implanted allergy protector he had as a backup did not work.

* * * * *

As Noah watched the screen, he heard a static hiss, and then saw a gray fog surround the Mutati. Previously Noah had seen captive shapeshifters do this when under stress.

Out of the fog came words. "Abal Meshdi, his Eminence the Zultan of the Mutati Kingdom, has instructed me to present a generous offer to you. We would like to join forces with your Guardians against the evil industrial polluters of the Merchant Prince Alliance. We can provide you with technical advice, even highly portable military hardware to use against the corporations. We have a common enemy."

Unnoticed by Noah, he had been joined in the classroom by two people who entered from a side door, and stood beside him.

"Interesting proposition," one of them said.

Startled, Noah glanced to his left. "Anton!"

"You gave me some kind of high priority clearance to come aboard. Hey, I must be pretty important to you, huh?" He nodded toward his companion. "Meet Tesh Kori."

Noah nodded toward her, but only briefly.

"You're not going to accept that creep's proposal, are you?" Anton asked.

"Of course not. I'd never sell out to the Mutatis."

"I didn't think so." The blond young man looked up at the screen and shouted at it. "He says no! Do you understand?"

"Too bad," the Mutati said. He produced a shiny, metallic device, which he held in front of his face. "I was prepared to offer this to you and your Guardians." Tiny wings popped out of the side of the apparatus. "Stealth bomb. It's undetectable, can fly past any security system and blow up an entire factory. Just think of how much that would help the environment."

"You heard what my friend said," Noah responded.

"Is that your final decision?"

"It is!"

"In that case," the Mutati said, "we wouldn't want this to go to waste." The flying bomb glowed red, and exploded. The transmission flashed bright red and orange, then went dark abruptly, leaving the wall screen black again.

"Did you hear him talking about a Mutati military victory against merchant prince forces?" Noah asked.

"No," Anton said.

Noah went on to relate what he had been told, then said, "Let's hope it isn't true." He paused. "What do you want to see me about?"

"We came to help," Anton replied. "And it looks like you can use it." He put his arm around Tesh. "We want to become Guardians."

"This is not a good time. I thought you were here because of my father's injury."

Anton's face darkened. "I'm sorry that happened, and I hope he gets better. Look, I always told you I wanted to join the Guardians someday, but you gave me a bunch of excuses. You're not going to do that again, are you?"

Noah hesitated. He did not want Anton to do anything dangerous, and was considering how to respond. For years, Noah had concealed from Anton the true identity of the young man's parents ... that his mother was Noah's sister Francella, making Noah his uncle. The identity of the father was even more shocking.

At that moment, two security men burst into the classroom, apologizing profusely. Seeing the screen dark, one of them said, "We don't know how he got through, sir, but it won't happen again. We'll make sure of it."

Noah didn't see how they would accomplish that if they didn't know what had happened in the first place. He told the men to have their commander submit a full report to Subi Danver within the hour. Nervously, the pair saluted and hurried away.

Refocusing, Noah saw his nephew standing with Tesh Kori, waiting for a response. He met their hopeful gazes, then looked away for a moment.

Francella had become pregnant after one of her trysts with the Doge Lorenzo himself and had kept the information from him—for reasons that she never revealed. After she gave birth, Noah learned about her indiscretion and insisted upon making certain that the child was cared for properly. Reluctantly, she had given Noah the responsibility of maintaining contact with her son, while she paid the bills for the child's support. It was one of the few things on which she and Noah had ever agreed.

Knowing what he did about his sister's nature, however—her cruelties and selfishness—Noah always wondered why she had not just aborted the fetus. It had given him some hope that she might have a modicum of humanity after all. But Francella always had a way of dashing such sentiments.

Out of concern for the safety of his nephew, Noah had discouraged him from joining the Guardians, and now it was more dangerous than ever. Still, the organization was in desperate need of good people, and Anton certainly qualified. He was a hard worker, honest, and resourceful.

During several moments when Tesh Kori was looking in another direction, Noah studied her exquisite profile, the way she stood tall and proud and beautiful. She glanced at him before he could look away, and he felt drawn into her hypnotic, emerald green eyes.

Finally he looked at Anton, and met the young man's anxious gaze. With a smile, Noah shook his hand briskly and said, "Welcome to the Guardians." He then shook Tesh's hand. "Both of you. It won't be easy. You'll have to undergo a rigorous training process. Some make it, and some don't."

"We will," Anton said, in a determined voice.

Chapter Twenty-Two

How many aspects of love are there? How many people have ever lived? These are the questions, and the answers.

—Princess Meghina of Siriki, *Critiques of a Courtesan*

Princess Meghina hardly thought of her magnificent Golden Palace on far-away Siriki. Instead, she spent sixteen hours a day at Prince Saito's bedside in his villa, and took surreptitious steps to obtain the best medical care for him. Inside the elegant, mural-walled reception room that had been converted to a hospital room, two doctors stood behind her, looking at the patient through a clearplax life-support dome and whispering between themselves. In order to avoid a confrontation with Dr. Bichette and Francella, she had identified them as friends, and they were dressed in common daysuits. Now they were alone in the room with Meghina and the ailing Prince.

On the staff of the renowned Nottàmbulo Hospital of Meghina's homeworld, these men were specialists in comas induced by head injuries. The Sirikans had studied the Prince's medical charts that Meghina obtained secretly, and had told her that Bichette, despite bringing in high-priced specialists, had not selected the best people.

One of the Sirikans, Dr. Woods Masin, was a tall black man with a square jaw and gray hair. His companion, Dr. Kydav Uleed, had primitive, rough-boned features like those of a back country Human, with a high, sloping forehead and large, protruding cheekbones.

Unable to hear everything they were whispering behind her, the blonde noblewoman stared sadly at the simoil murals on the walls, depicting the fascinating life of the man she loved. A breeze rustled the curtains by an open window, and out beyond the high cliff she saw one of the Prince's flying yachts anchored in the air.

Meghina shifted uneasily on her feet. She wished she had met this great man earlier, and that they might have married. Instead she had been required—for political reasons—to become the wife of Doge Lorenzo del Velli. Her dual life, as royal spouse and courtesan to many of the leading nobles of the realm, was not easy for her. It also made her husband a cuckold, but he didn't seem to mind. He had his own stable of women to satisfy his physical needs, and sometimes he even dangled Meghina's favors in front of influential princes in order to obtain what he wanted from them. It was one of the most unusual marriages anyone had ever heard of, and was conducted without any pretenses.

She gazed at the comatose form of Prince Saito on the bed, which was oversized to accommodate his bulk. It seemed unfair to her that this vital, very *alive* man had been stricken down and reduced to such a sad state, dependent for every breath upon the medical technology that was connected to him. Much, but not all, of the equipment had been provided by the medical division of his own corporation.

At least I've had time with you, my love. For that I shall always be grateful.

"May we open the dome?" It was Dr. Masin, leaning close to her and speaking in a low tone.

"No one is around," Dr. Uleed added.

Nervously, Princess Meghina looked behind her. The main door and a side door were closed. "Be quick about it!" she husked.

The tall, gray-haired Masin swung the life-support dome open and checked the Prince's eyes with a small silvery medical tube, while Uleed held another device on the patient's temple. "He needs to be moved to a hospital," Uleed announced.

"Preferably Nottàmbulo," his companion added.

Suddenly the side door crashed open and Dr. Hurk Bichette burst in. "What is going on here?" he demanded.

"These are specialists from Siriki," Princess Meghina answered, almost shouting at him in return. In a near-breaking voice she introduced them by name, and added that the Prince's condition had worsened. Whereas earlier he had been semi-comatose, with brief periods of enigmatic conversation, now he was trapped in a full coma and had not spoken for more than a week.

"Get away from my patient!" Dr. Bichette roared. He closed the lid of the life-support dome and physically pushed the other doctors away. Bichette's face was flushed, and a large vein throbbed at his temple.

"I want all of you to leave," he insisted. "You are interfering with my medical procedures, and I want this room cleared immediately." He waved his hands at the other doctors and at the Princess.

"How dare you speak to me in that manner?" Meghina exclaimed. "I am of noble blood, the wife of the Doge, and the … " Her voice trailed off, since the rest of her résumé could not be put into words that sounded dignified. "I am the … favorite … of Prince Saito," she added, softly.

For a moment Bichette glared defiantly at her. Then, belatedly, he looked down at the floor and bowed slightly. "I apologize, My Lady. Perhaps the stress of the occasion and the long hours I have devoted to Prince Saito have dulled my manners."

"Step aside, please," Meghina said in a firm tone, "so that my doctors may continue their examination."

With a scowl, Bichette moved away from the bed.

As the Sirikan doctors resumed their work, one on each side of the Prince, Bichette said, "You will find that I have done everything possible."

"You are a general practitioner," Dr. Uleed said, with a quick glance at the target of his words. "This case appears to be beyond the scope of your knowledge."

"A specialist performed the surgery, and I have experts advising me."

"We are familiar with their names … and *credentials*," Uleed snapped. "Let's just say that their reputations are rather limited."

Bichette chewed at his lower lip, and muttered something unintelligible in return.

Hearing a noise behind her, Princess Meghina turned and saw Francella Watanabe standing just inside the main doorway. She appeared to have been observing for a while. Francella's shaved brows had been tinted cherry red, matching her lipstick and her sleeveless damask dress, a garment that featured a plunging neckline, exposing her naval. She wore white gloves that extended to her elbows.

"You should have obtained my permission before bringing these men here," Francella said, locking gazes with Meghina. "In my father's diminished state, I have complete power of attorney to make decisions about his medical care."

"I also have a special relationship with your father," the blonde Princess retorted, "and I have certain rights."

"You are his wife in name only, with limited rights. Nonetheless, out of courtesy for you, I will not banish you from his presence. You are never again, however, to bring anyone in here to examine my father without my permission. Is that understood?"

In low tones, Meghina conferred with the Sirikan doctors. Wrinkles of concern etched her heart-shaped face. Finally she said to Francella, "Your father needs specialized care at a facility such as the Nottàmbulo Hospital."

"He will not be moved off-world!"

"Don't you want the best for him?"

"I resent your tone."

"This is not a time for petty feelings. We must consider the welfare of Prince Saito."

"It is probable that he will never awaken," Francella said. "Sadly, I must say this."

"You base that statement upon the opinion of a general practitioner."

"And his specialists."

"Who happen to belong to his own drinking club."

"See here," Dr. Bichette interjected. "I will not have my integrity impugned in this manner."

"Be quiet," Francella snapped. "I will take care of this." She pointed at Masin and Uleed. "Leave this room immediately and don't ever come back."

Meghina nodded to them, affirming the command. She would make an attempt to discuss the matter with Francella at a later date, after tempers had calmed.

The Sirikan doctors departed, while Meghina remained behind. She went to the bedside and held Prince Saito's hand. Across the room, beyond her hearing, Francella and Dr. Bichette conferred.

The Prince's hand was cold to the touch, but he clung to life, his chest rising and falling regularly. With a wistful smile Meghina remembered some of their favorite times together, and how startled he'd been upon discovering she was a Mutati. They'd already had sexual relations dozens of times, so he could hardly believe it when she admitted her true physical form to him. She had never, however, shown her Mutati body to him, fearing his revulsion. "I would rather be Human anyway," she had whispered to him.

After that, she had not changed back, and in a matter of weeks, remaining in that state for too long, she no longer had the cellular flexibility to metamorphose at all. She had never felt comfortable as a Mutati anyway, and ever since her childhood had preferred the beauty and functional utility of the Human physical form.

Her decision had not been without its sacrifices. Despite her rank as a Mutati princess, it had rendered her an outcast among her people, preventing her from ever assimilating with them again. In losing her ability to shapeshift, she gave up an act that was extremely pleasurable, even to her. It provided a Mutati with the highest form of bliss—higher even than sex, and left the Mutati in a state of satiated euphoria for an extended period. (A potentially dangerous time, since it made the shapeshifter vulnerable to attack).

Now Meghina looked Human, and would for the rest of her life. She had not contemplated all of the problems that this would entail, such as the signs of aging that had a way of creeping up on this race. Mutatis, in contrast, went at full-vitality through old age, until the moment of their death. In her present form she had to think about face creams and laser treatments in order to remain youthful in appearance, something she would never have bothered to consider in her original bodily structure.

Come back to me, my love, she thought. A tear ran down her cheek as she gazed at the nearly lifeless form of her lover.

Chapter Twenty-Three

Dying is easy. Life is infinitely more difficult.

—Prince Saito Watanabe

As Francella left the room where her father lay and strolled along a loggia, she concealed a smile. The confrontation between Dr. Bichette and the two Sirikan doctors had not disturbed her in the least. Oh, Bichette was upset about his competency was being called into question, but that fool didn't matter to her. No criticism could possibly be directed at her for leaving him in charge. After all, he had been Prince Saito's hand-picked personal physician, and an important director of CorpOne's Medical Research Division. On the surface, Francella could not have selected a more appropriate person.

Her father's cliffside villa, with its red tile roof and white stucco walls, overlooked the Valley of the Princes, with the office and industrial complexes of some of the wealthiest corporations in the Alliance. His regal dwelling had been styled in the manner of an ancient Earthian home found in the ruined town of Herculaneum. Roman emperors had enjoyed walkways like this one, with its open-air gallery of imperial statues. The eagle fountain in the terrace courtyard, visible to Francella now through ornate columns lining the loggia, had actually been brought back from Herculaneum, and so had the mosaic tile floor in the opulent private bath building.

As for Meghina, she would bear watching. Hidden camviewers recorded her every move at the villa, and Francella had been monitoring the medical confrontation from another room, until deciding it was time to intervene.

Noah's fraternal twin waved a hand across a pale yellow identity beam that protected a doorway. After a momentary pause, a heavy alloy door slid open with a smooth click, revealing her father's study—a place he called "the inner sanctum." This room had always been off-limits to Francella and her brother when they were growing up, so it gave her special pleasure to be here now. It was from this study that she had been watching the confrontation in the other room.

No Roman emperor had ever been in possession of the technology that was arrayed on exquisite teakoak and marbelite tables and desks. Tiny computer monitors—each looking like a small electronic eye on the end of a long flexible neck—stood on one side. At a voice command the units were capable of filling the air with holo and telebeam images. This was a data and communications nerve center, not only of this house but also of her father's mega-company,

CorpOne. Because of her position as Corporate Security Chief, he had provided her with access codes.

What he'd failed to notice, though, was her dissatisfaction over the way she had been treated in comparison with Noah, and how her resentment had built up over the years into a deep-seated anger. Francella now had an intense and all-consuming need for money, power, and prestige, and wanted to enjoy it all before she grew too old to appreciate such things. In her late thirties, with her vitality enhanced by CorpOne medical products, she was in perfect physical and mental condition to assume control of everything right now—including this study and villa. Her father was too elderly to enjoy such things anyway, so she was doing him a favor by rushing things along. What could be wrong with speeding up the timetable a little?

Glancing at a bank of camviewer screens on the wall, she satisfied herself that Princess Meghina was no longer causing any trouble. Unaware of the surveillance equipment himself, Dr. Bichette sat in a large chair, scowling as he concentrated on the blonde courtesan at the bedside.

Francella sighed. Unfortunately, her father still clung to life like an injured spider on a web, and Dr. Bichette had no idea how long he might continue in that condition. It could go on for years, the nervous doctor had said ... or the old mogul might just give up and die at any moment. One of Meghina's specialists said that the patient's mind, even in its damaged condition, was making decisions about whether to live or die.

Somewhere in Prince Saito's subconscious he fought on, perhaps out of a powerful desire to be with his courtesan harlot again, or to make decisions about his vast riches. He even had an ultra-high-security treasure room in the villa, where he kept priceless jewels, manuscripts, and artworks. Undoubtedly part of his mind wanted to go in there again, and wallow in his wealth. The way he had it piled up in there, he probably swam in it.

One day the treasure room, like everything else, would belong to her, so she ignored it for the moment. There were easier riches to take. Her father had done exceedingly well as a merchant prince; few had ever done better. Francella only had one regret: she wished she could bottle him up and let him continue making business decisions for her—perhaps as a sentient robot that was completely under her control and had her father's mind. Or a disembodied brain that did what she told it to do and just kept making more and more money for her. Yes, that would be perfect.

Men should do that for women anyway, whether they were fathers, husbands, or lovers: providing money for ladies to spend. Even her brother should get in on the act and send her a steady stream of funds. He was prosperous enough. In fact, it surprised her how he did so well himself; like a junkyard king he made money from dirt, minerals, and plants, performing ecological recovery operations on various worlds and selling environmentally friendly products. In effect, Noah had squeezed money out of nothing.

She had to admire both her father and her brother for their business acumen. They were more alike than either of them realized. And she hated them, with every breath she took.

Keeping them apart for years had been a major victory for her. After the attack on CorpOne headquarters she had leaked phony evidence that it had been committed by Noah and his Guardians, without ever letting anyone know—not even her closest associates—that she was the source of the information, and of the attack itself.

Francella crossed the large study and stood at one of the computers, a segregated unit that kept track of CorpOne's off-planet holdings. Earlier that morning, data in another segregated terminal had referred her to this one, stipulating that it contained information that would enable her to shift assets around. Even with her father's injury, Francella wasn't sure how long he would live, and she wanted to get her hands on as much as she could, as fast as possible. Things could still go wrong, and Noah—against all odds—might still worm his way back into the old man's affections, drastically reducing her share or even cutting her off entirely.

Now she would begin with the saphonium mines of the Veldic Asteroid Belt, where Prince Saito had a subterranean storehouse of uncut gemstones that were among the rarest and most precious in the Merchant Prince Alliance. Delivery of the hoard had been held up by unexplained changes in podship schedules; only recently had the strange vessels resumed calling on that region.

Francella had only to shift the destination codes to her own warehouses on Timian Four, and the treasure-trove would be hers. In anticipation of this (and a lot more), she'd hired private construction crews to work on her property for some time now, putting up more buildings and beefing up the security systems. According to an encrypted nehrcom message she had just received, the job was almost complete.

She kept her plans completely secret, because as far as she was concerned, no one could be trusted. Relationships always had a nasty habit of changing, and if that happened here, if the wrong people learned too much about her operations, she would have to take drastic action. So, by keeping her activities secret and working anonymously through intermediaries, she was actually committing a kindness, making it unnecessary for her to commit violence.

It all made perfect sense to her.

Not that it was unkind to kill. In fact, she would soon do her father a favor by putting him to rest. At his age, it was too difficult for him to control such a huge empire anyway. One or more of his employees—or a corporate competitor—would take advantage of him sooner or later, and that would only upset him. She was avoiding the inevitable unhappiness for him, doing a very nice thing for her aged father.

Without question, it all made perfect sense.

Casually, she nudged the long neck of the computer terminal, and heard the internal whir of the machine. In a moment the eyelike monitor would flash on and project a telebeam, allowing her to review the data as it danced in front of her vision.

At this terminal, however, the tiny screen was illuminated red instead of the normal amber, and did not project at all. Francella caught her breath. None of the other data processors had done this. She took a step back just as the eye changed to bright green and began to project something.

A serpent with glistening fangs lunged at her, coming out of the screen.

Since this had to be an electronic image, Francella felt intuitively that it could not possibly harm her. But she tumbled backward anyway, and scrambled for safety.

The green snake grew longer and chased her, hissing through the air.

She rolled under a table with the mechanical creature right behind her. On the other side she leaped to her feet, changed direction, and tumbled over the top of a desk, scattering a dictocam machine and shiny silver tubes of cartridges that had been stacked there.

The fangs were only centimeters from her. The jaws snapped, but missed.

Desperately, she grabbed one of the tubes, which was heavy from all of the cartridges it contained. Whirling, she slammed it down as hard as she could on the snake-head, expecting her blow to pass through the air without hitting anything. But to her surprise the tube struck something and the creature recoiled, as if in pain.

The serpent turned sickly yellow and crashed noisily onto the tile floor. Tiny metal parts sprayed through the air, and one glanced off Francella's browless forehead, drawing blood. Finally the reptile went silent on the floor. Its shattered carcass did not move.

Confused, Francella went to one of the other computer terminals, and took the tube, now dented, along with her for protection. Carefully, she nudged the neck to turn on the machine. The computer spun through its cycles normally. This time she went through a deep search mechanism, using her passwords to look for all security systems in the room. She should have done so before, but had assumed that her identity would allow her to do anything.

Finally, she set the makeshift weapon aside.

In a few minutes, she found what she was looking for in the database. The snake had been one of several deadly traps in the room, activated under certain circumstances. She shuddered as she looked down at her feet. One of the large tiles to her right was a trap door that would cast her into a drowning pool beneath the villa if she stepped on it. She had narrowly missed it several times.

The tricky old man was even dangerous on his death bed.

Death bed.

She had not used this term previously because of the way her father kept hanging on, but now she did, and liked the sound of it. One way or another, even if it involved additional risk to her, she would finish him off.

With her adrenaline surging from the close escape, Francella spent the rest of the day and night in the study, without eating or drinking anything. After disabling the traps, she used her access codes to divert the Veldic saphonium and rifled his corporate bank accounts, even pilfering tax account funds that had been earmarked for the Doge. She proceeded to steal more assets than the value of an industrialized planet, and covered her trail expertly, so that it looked as if the holdings were still there.

When it was finished, she sat at her father's desk and grinned. He had always encouraged her to excel at data processing.

Her gaze lifted to one of the camviewer screens on the wall. Prince Saito lay alone in the room, sleeping with an almost serene expression on his face. Obviously the old tycoon thought he had taken care of every necessary detail, but he was wrong.

Chapter Twenty-Four

Indecision has killed more people than all the battles of history.
—Supreme General Mah Sajak, Merchant Prince of Armed Forces

The noble-born princes had been seething for years over their loss of prestige, a trend that began when Lorenzo's father, the Doge Paolantonio IV, began appointing successful businessmen and inventors to princely positions. This policy was amplified under the regime of Lorenzo, causing widespread resentment among the royals.

In the past decade, the disaffected noblemen Prince Giancarlo Paggatini began organizing regular social events for the noble-born princes. These were held at a prestigious resort on Parma, one of the moons of Timian One. In actuality, the gatherings were fronts for meetings, which were attended by a group of malcontents, including General Mah Sajak.

On Parma the most popular attraction was Vius, an immense active volcano with a three hundred kilometer-wide crater. Through a unique network of lava tubes and subterranean currents, Vius circulated the lava so that the caldera was always molten, like a thick, red-hot lake on top of the mountain.

Though nervous about it, General Sajak had been looking forward to this meeting for weeks. He had an agenda in mind, one that he had kept under close wraps. As he passed through airlocks to enter a small terminal building at the edge of the fiery lava cone, he considered what he would say to his comrades, and how he might convince them to take a dangerous step, one that could put all of their lives at risk. He wore his usual baggy red-and-gold uniform and oversized cap, with metallic dress trim on the trousers and on the arms of the jacket.

Behind him, the black, patched-together robot Jimu clanked along … the same one that had been in charge of sentient machines in the Grand Fleet, and which was dispatched with evidence of the terrible defeat to the merchant princes. The General, while irritated about the noise Jimu made, had not bothered to have him repaired, since he didn't plan to keep him around for much longer.

Supposedly the terminal building was hermetically sealed in order to keep out toxic gases exuded by the lava, and likewise the gangway that led to a ceramic-hulled luxury yacht that floated in the lake. Still, Sajak smelled fumes as he boarded the craft … evidence that there must be a leak somewhere. His nose twitched. Gradually, after walking down a short flight of steps to the spacious dining salon, he no longer noticed the odors, perhaps because they were overridden by mouth-watering cooking aromas from the adjacent galley … meat sauces, garlic, exotic spices from all over the galaxy. Through thick-plated windows around the dimly-lit room he saw the red, menacing glow of lava outside, against the starry blackness of night.

The owner of the volcano resort, Prince Giancarlo, rose from the head of a long table as the General strolled in, followed by the clattering robot. Almost all of the seats were filled with noblemen dressed in their silkine and lace finery. They sipped aperitifs from tall, thin goblets, but none of their ladies were present, since the subjects discussed at these meetings were considered private. To the men's way of thinking, women—even those of noble birth—could never occupy the lofty social positions of men.

"Welcome, welcome," Giancarlo Paggatini said, motioning toward a reserved high-back chair on his right. A chubby, rosy-cheeked man, he wore an exquisite platinum-tint shirt with wide, flared sleeves. The consummate host, he always served the finest foods and wines. He grasped the General's hand and shook it energetically.

Trying to conceal his own shaking knees and hands, Sajak instructed the robot to remain off to one side. The officer removed his hat and placed it on a rack under the proffered chair, then sat down quickly. Three little glasses of aperitif were arrayed on the table in front of him, one pink, one green, and one blue.

"You have some catching up to do," the rotund host said.

"With respect, I must decline," the small, bony-featured man said, trying to make his voice sound firm even though his insides churned. "I have important matters to discuss this evening, and do not wish to be impaired."

"You're not going to get serious on us, are you?" protested a prince on the other side of the table. A tall, loose-jowled man with a monocle dangling from his neck, Santino Aggi was already showing the signs of alcohol. He motioned for a waiter to bring him another drink.

"I'm afraid so, my friends," Sajak said. He took a long breath, and waited.

The rest of the noblemen arrived, and finally the boat pulled slowly away from the terminal, out into the cauldron of liquid fire. Within moments the ceramic craft was planing over hot lava and the captain activated its skimmers—temperature-resistant extrusions on the underside of the hull—that caused a kaleidoscope of colors to flash around the boat.

Some of the men on the other end of the table gasped at the spectacular beauty, but those seated nearest to the General remained quiet, as they wondered what he was about to say to them. It disgusted him that some of them didn't want to consider serious political matters, and preferred to just collect earnings that they had inherited. To his credit, Prince Giancarlo was not like that. With a gesture of dismissal and a barked command, the host stopped the waiters from bringing any more drinks and ordered them out of the salon. As they left, they closed all doors.

Conversation ceased around the table as the air of anticipation intensified.

"I'm sorry to dampen the tone of our meeting so early," Sajak said, rising to his feet. "As you know, we normally do little more than commiserate when we get together, sharing tales of woe and our desire for political change."

Two of the princes on the General's side of the table took offense at this remark, and muttered between themselves.

Nervously, the officer fingered a cluster of war medals on his chest, and began. "I presume that all of you have heard of our military defeat at the hands of the Mutati. Our plan of attack should have succeeded, so the failure had to be due to sabotage, a traitorous act. We are investigating the matter and will take all necessary action."

"One moment, please," Prince Giancarlo said, rising from his chair, his beefy arms extended to reveal shiny rings on his hands.

As he spoke, slots along the center of the long table opened, and dishes of hot, steaming food rotated to the top. Little mechanical robots, dressed like waiters, stood beside each serving dish.

Wielding large utensils, the metal men loaded food onto the diner's plates. However—pursuant to instructions they had received from the host—they did not pour any additional drinks, and only filled water glasses. Some of the princes muttered their displeasure. When their serving tasks were complete, the diminutive robots dropped into the open slots, and the compartments closed behind them.

To the clinking of forksticks—combination eating and cutting implements used by the diners—Sajak continued. "I won't deny it was a personal setback for me ... I had hoped to gain prestige with a great victory. Nonetheless, I will probably remain Supreme General of the Armed Forces. The Doge has stated openly that he wants me to step down, but I won't do it. I have enough political clout to resist. For awhile, anyway."

"Bravo," Giancarlo Paggatini said, as he stuffed a dripping chunk of Huluvian pheasant into his mouth.

"Times have been changing," the General agreed, ignoring his own food. "Noble birth means much less than ever before. We lost good men and women at Paradij, and a lot of expensive military hardware."

The princes murmured in concurrence.

With a nervous motion, Sajak signaled for the dented, scratched robot to step forward, which it did.

"This is Jimu," the General announced. "I told you about him, but I want you to hear firsthand what he has to say, and what he has to show you."

Dutifully, the robot reported in a hesitating, mechanical voice what he had already told the General, how the Mutatis seemed to be waiting for them and had defeated the attacking fleet at every turn. As he spoke, his artificial eyes glowed yellow, alternately dimming and brightening. Then, opening a compartment in his chest, Jimu projected blue light into the air, the holo evidence that the Mutatis had sent back with him. The images were similar to telebeams, but of an inferior, grainy quality.

When the robot finished and put away the projection mechanism, General Sajak rose and went to him. Jimu, around the height of the small officer, blinked his eyes as he awaited further instructions. Without saying anything, Sajak drew a pearl-handled puissant pistol from a holster at his waist and fired it into the control panel in the center of Jimu's chest.

The robot sputtered a garbled sentence, sparked, and fell with a thud on the deck. He went silent and motionless.

"As you have just seen and heard," Sajak said, holstering his weapon, "the Mutatis have provided information that they could only know if they had actually won the battle. It's obvious how far our Doge has gone to undermine my authority … and yours, by association. The Mutatis couldn't have defeated such a force without inside help. I'm sorry to say this, but Lorenzo sacrificed thousands of my people and caused our defeat … just to keep me from gaining political influence that might threaten his soft, pampered position."

"What evidence do you have of Lorenzo's involvement?" one of the princes wanted to know.

"The very scale of the debacle proves it, you dolt! We had a perfect mission plan. It couldn't fail. This had to come from the very top."

Taking a deep breath to calm himself, Sajak resumed his seat. He grabbed the blue glass of aperitif in front of him and quaffed the syrupy sweet drink. Thoughtfully, he placed the glass back on the table, while considering how to phrase his comments. "What I am about to propose is risky," he said. "I won't deny that. But I must remind you of the vows we took as members of the Society of Princes, this most secret of organizations."

"Honor to the death!" the men shouted, in unison.

"Every one of us could die for the cause," Sajak said. "I'd hoped it wouldn't come to this, but I'm afraid it's time for us to move against the Doge and his political appointees. Such drastic action has not been necessary for more than a thousand years, so I do not propose it lightly. Lorenzo's attitude, however, leaves us no choice. Each day that we delay, our position erodes."

As he spoke, images appeared on a wall screen behind him. For several moments the nobles watched the Doge at some of his public and private appearances. In each instance he was accompanied by Princess Meghina, or, when she wasn't around, by other women.

"Lorenzo has an open marriage," the officer said. "They both sleep with other people."

"That's nothing new," Santino Aggi said, putting on his monocle. He reached across the table, snared one of the remaining glasses of aperitif in front of the General and sipped it. "I've enjoyed the pleasures of the courtesan myself."

"Don't you see?" Sajak said. "This sort of behavior is a sign of moral decay. It is unseemly for our Doge and his wife to behave as they do, or for us to condone it."

Many of the princes nodded their heads in agreement, and whispered among themselves. Others sat motionless.

The images on the screen shifted, to a scrolling list of names and dates.

"This is the family pedigree claimed by Princess Meghina," the General said, "purportedly all the way back to Ilrac the Conqueror. A close examination of her documentation, however, reveals significant irregularities. We'll have to research it more, including the source of her dowry, but take a look at what I have learned so far...."

For the rest of the evening, as the dinner boat plied the flowing, molten lake, the intense General Sajak presented his information to the assembled lords, and outlined his plan to discredit, and assassinate, the Doge Lorenzo del Velli.

But unknown to any of the noblemen, the robot lying on the floor had not been completely deactivated. Despite his rather rough appearance, Jimu was a sophisticated machine, with a number of customized internal features installed by his Hibbil builders. Silently, his backup brain core heard everything that was said in the dining salon, and recorded it.

Chapter Twenty-Five

Oh, the challenges of leadership! Can I achieve what God-On-High expects of me? This I vow: I shall never stop trying.

—Citadel Journals

His Exalted Magnificence the Zultan Abal Meshdi received many messages and reports—from around his realm and from his allies—but never anything like this. With all he had put into the Demolio project—the funds, the manpower, the time, and the angst—this was the most anticipated communication he had ever received.

Everything rode upon the precious research project that he had commissioned.

The shapeshifter stared at a purple-and-gold pyramid in the hands of the young royal messenger who fluttered in front of him in the audience hall, his tiny feet not touching the mosaic floor. The slender youth, an aeromutati who had ridden a podship from the Adurian Republic to Paradij, could fly with his short white wings, but not through space. After arriving at the orbital pod station above Paradij, he had taken a shuttle to the ground depot, and from there had flown to the Citadel overlooking the city.

The messenger shivered slightly, perhaps from the chilly air outside, but more likely from fear.

Hesitating, the Zultan did not reach out to accept the communication pyramid. He wondered if there had been unforeseen problems with the Demolio program, or—as he hoped and prayed—had the final testing gone smoothly?

Suddenly, Meshdi grabbed for the pyramid with his middle arm, startling the bearer and causing him to drop it on the hard tile floor with a loud clatter.

Apologizing profusely, the functionary retrieved it. As he fumbled with the device, however, the seal mechanism released and the sides of the pyramid lit up, casting bright light around it.

Disgusted with the ineptitude, the Zultan hand-signaled to a black-uniformed guard in the doorway. The rotund Mutati guard opened fire with his jolong rifle, shooting high-speed projectiles that smashed the aeromutati back against a wall, leaving him a blood-purple mass of torn flesh and broken wings. He slumped to the floor, dead.

As the guard rushed toward the body, the Zultan shouted, "I meant for you to remove him from my sight. It was not necessary to kill him."

"Sorry, Sire. I thought you ... uh, I ... misinterpreted your signal."

Abal Meshdi realized that he had himself sent the wrong hand signal. No matter. He would have the guard put to death anyway. The Zultan did not tolerate mistakes. Except his own, of course.

Glaring in feigned disapproval, Meshdi retrieved the communication pyramid and activated it. Through a magnification mechanism on one of the faces of the device, he peered into a deep space sector that he did not recognize ... a small blue sun, a pink planet, high meteor activity. Something streaked toward the planet from space, and moments later the world detonated, hurtling chunks of debris into the cosmos.

The pyramid glowed brightly for a moment, then went dark.

The audience hall was full of armed guards now, chattering nervously and searching for threats. Calmly, the Zultan again pressed the activation button of the pyramid. The same scene repeated itself, an unknown planet destroyed. No written communication accompanied the display, but under the circumstances he did not need one.

Gazing calmly at the guard who had fired his weapon, Meshdi said sternly, "Beaustan, with your long family history of service to this throne, you should know that it is never good form to kill the bearer of *good* news."

"I'm terribly sorry," the black-uniformed Mutati said. He looked confused, and terrified.

Noting a pool of perspiration forming on the floor beneath his guard, the Zultan smiled. "Well, we can always get new messengers." *And new guards*, he thought. The Zultan pointed a long, bony finger. "Remove the body and bring contractors to repair the damage."

"Immediately, Sire."

As the men worked, Meshdi stood and watched. This was excellent news indeed, and he had worried unnecessarily.

But isn't that the job of a Zultan, he mused, *to worry?* He found himself in a rare, giddy mood.

His secret research program, which had lasted for decades, was about to pay dividends. Finally, Adurian scientists, funded and supervised by Mutatis, had perfected the doomsday weapon. The planet he had just seen explode on the screen had been an uninhabited backwater world, a test case ... blasted into space trash.

He absolutely *loved* the extrapolation: the entire Merchant Prince Alliance blown to bits and drifting through space like garbage.

Humans are garbage.

Just to play it safe, the detonation of the planet—and its aftermath—were camouflaged behind a veiling spectral field that made it look as if nothing had occurred at all. It had been an insignificant world in an immense galaxy, but the Zultan did not like to take chances.

Two guards carried the broken body of the royal messenger past him, while others cleaned up blood and feathers from the spot where he fell. A team of contractors—four Mutati females wearing tight coveralls over their lumpy bodies—hurried into the hall carrying tools and equipment.

Now the Zultan of the Mutati Kingdom had only to fund the training of an elite corps of "Mutati outriders" and manufacture enough Demolios to keep them busy—the high-powered torpedo-bombs that were capable of causing so much destruction. Any one of the projectiles could split through the crust and mantle of a planet and penetrate to the molten core within seconds. There it would go nuclear, with catastrophic results.

In this manner, the gleeful Mutati leader would destroy every merchant prince world. Then, to completely eradicate Humans, he would proceed to wipe out even planets that were capable of sustaining their form of life—those having water, the proper atmospheric conditions, and circular orbits that provided them with the most stable environments. By contrast, Mutatis could live on worlds their enemy would find intolerable, where conditions were too hot or too cold, or with atmospheres that were too thin or too thick, and even with gravities that were too heavy or too light. Mutatis—life forms based upon carbon-crystal combinations—were one of the most highly adaptable races in the galaxy. Hence, they could live in many places.

Meshdi, however, had decided to draw a line in space. After having been driven from planet to planet by the aggressive Humans, he would not be pushed back any further. The successful defense of Paradij had been a warning shot fired across their bow.

The Zultan intended to commence his extermination program with Human fringe worlds, where habitation was low and military defenses were weak, or even nonexistent. Ultimately he planned to strike the key merchant prince planets where hundreds of billions lived, but that would be far more difficult, and would require meticulous planning. Those worlds were on the main podways, and Human agents constantly boarded vessels along the way, searching for dangers with highly effective Mutati detection equipment.

If he focused on less guarded worlds it would provide the advantage of cutting off escape routes from the more populated planets, leaving the Humans no place to run.

Chapter Twenty-Six

Sometimes a storm of the heart is more uncomfortable than any other kind.
—Mutati Saying

On a rocky promontory, Noah and Eshaz peered through thin plates of binocular glax that floated in front of their eyes. Automatically, the respective focal points shifted to accommodate their vision, and presently Noah made out the details of an encampment in the canopa pine woods below them. It was early morning on a cloudy day, and thirty Humans were arising in the camp, crawling out of their lean-tos and lighting a community fire to cook breakfast. It had rained heavily the night before, and those who had not constructed adequate shelters looked wet and miserable.

"Anton and the girl are on the right side of the clearing," Noah said, pointing. He had a reddish stubble of beard.

"I see them."

Noah watched as Tesh stood in front of the foliage-roofed, blue-bark structure that she shared with Anton. He was sitting inside on his sleeping mat of soft jalapo leaves, stretching and yawning. He looked dry. Outside, Tesh pulled on a coat and blew on her hands to warm them. Up on the promontory, Noah was cold himself. If he hadn't known it was midsummer, he might have thought snow was coming.

The rock outcropping on which he stood was five kilometers from his administration building but still on the grounds of the Ecological Demonstration Project. He and Eshaz had flown a grid-plane there, an aircraft that was parked on a flat area just above them.

Anton and Tesh lived in the primitive encampment with other Guardian trainees, and every day they had to trek back to the administration-education complex for classes. In the evenings they studied under dim lantern lights in their simple structures—a battery of classes that included Outdoor Survival, Cellular Mathematics, and Planetary Ecology. It was a challenging life, a test of the students' endurance and ability to live in harmony with nature. They were provided with only a limited quantity of packaged foods (such as capuchee jerky and puya coffee), and had to forage and hunt for the rest ... according to instructions they received in class.

So as not to interfere with important ecological relationships, they could only kill certain animals (such as claymoles and abundant birds), and only for food. With respect to the flora, they were also restricted. Monitors in the woods graded their performance.

Through his floating binocular glax Noah saw Tesh carrying a covered bowl over to contribute to the community breakfast. Based upon a report Noah had seen, she planned to prepare a protein paste from wild ingredients: kanoberries, ground grub worms and red ants, and honey. Anton was nursing several bee stings from going after the honey the day before. Tesh had been with him, but according to the report the bees had not bothered her at all.

Now she was urging Anton to get up; he appeared groggy, and kept trying to lie back down. She wouldn't let him, and finally dragged him out of the shelter, half-dressed. Other campers gathered around to watch, and were obviously enjoying the show. Even at this distance Noah could hear them laughing and clapping. But around the perimeter of the group, some people were looking up at the sky instead, which Noah did as well. The clouds were an ominous shade of dark gray, as if they were about to disgorge their heavy, wet contents on the land.

In a few minutes Anton was up and moving around, carrying a big coffee cup. He seemed to have as much energy as most people in the class ... but nowhere near as much as Tesh. A Human dynamo, she seemed able to call upon some inner reservoir of vitality.

Tesh had a bucket now, and carried it down a steep path to a nearby creek, for water. Noah followed her movements, watching her closely.

"She *is* strikingly beautiful, isn't she?" Eshaz said.

"What?" Noah felt his face flush hot.

"I'm referring to Queen Zilaranda of the Vippandry Protectorate."

"Huh?"

"Just kidding. I mean Tesh Kori."

"Anton's girlfriend? I hadn't noticed."

"Is that so? Then I must have mistaken that gleam in your eyes, my friend."

Noah began to gesture with his hands as he spoke. "Well, she is attractive, but I would never think of showing her any interest—other than professional, of course. She's my ... friend's ... girlfriend."

An exceedingly observant sentient, Eshaz had noted with interest Noah's hesitation over the word "friend" ... but he said nothing of it. Eshaz wondered, though. If young Anton was not a friend, what was he? Certainly not an enemy, or Noah would not have permitted him to train for a position with the Guardians. A rival, perhaps? Had they competed for women in the past? But Noah was at least fifteen years older, and maybe a bit more than that.

A light flashed on in Eshaz's head. At a voice command he increased the power of his binocular glax, which enabled him to study the face of Anton Glavine. To his surprise, the Tulyan noted similarities with the way Noah looked: strong chin, aquiline nose, and wide-spaced hazel eyes.

Could Anton be Noah's son?

As for the young woman, Eshaz found her extraordinary himself, in more than just her beauty, her high energy level, and her resistance to bee stings. The Tulyan had noted in brief conversations with her how quick she was, how obviously intelligent. He could see it in the glint and flash of her emerald green eyes, could hear it in her well-chosen words. In his own intellectual way, Eshaz found her eminently fascinating, but solely for the quality of her mind. Yes, Tesh Kori would make an excellent Guardian one day, and should receive rapid promotions.

Inevitably she might work closely with Noah, perhaps even on his staff. Eshaz envisioned problems between the "friends" if that occurred. In the realm of Human relationships, some things were quite obvious and predictable to the Tulyan.

In the camp below, Tesh brought the bucket of water back ... while Noah continued to watch her.

Just as the campers finished their breakfast, snow began to fall, only a little at first, and then a blizzard. They ran for cover, while Noah and Eshaz took shelter in their grid-plane and put on warm coats and insulated boots. Hours passed, with no slackening. By mid-afternoon, a meter of white lay on the ground.

During the unexpected snowfall, Noah stayed in touch with his headquarters via the onboard telebeam transmitter. Finally, when the storm let up, he confirmed that a rescue team was about to set out in snow trucks. Concerned that this would take too long, he transmitted back that he and Eshaz were going to inspect the camp, and would meet them there.

Noah and his trusted aide slid open the door of their small aircraft and cleared snow away so that they could get out. With Noah wearing a backpack full of survival gear, the two of them slogged through deep, pristine snow to the edge of the hill. From there, Noah fired a wire at a tree down in the woods and then connected a sling and descent clip to the wire. Glancing back at Eshaz, who held another sling and clip, he said, "Follow me." And he jumped over the edge.

One after the other, the two of them went down the steeply-angled wire. The descent clips had braking mechanisms that squeaked, but they worked properly, enabling the pair to proceed at a controlled rate of speed.

When they descended as far as they could on the wire, they switched on motors to lower their slings to the ground. Reaching the camp a short while later, Noah feared the worst. Heavy snow had caved in many of the roofs, and the air was still. He detected no signs of life.

Then he heard something, and looked to the right. On the creek side of the camp, snow shifted, breaking away with soft thumps, and he heard voices from that direction. "It's about time you got here!" a woman shouted, cheerily. Noah recognized Tesh. As she stepped out from what looked like a snow cave, he counted four others behind her, including Anton.

Eshaz got to them first, and looked inside the opening. Moments later, he reported, "They're all here ... and all are smiling."

"We're OK, except one of the boys has a broken wrist," Tesh said to Noah. She wore a sweater and jeans, and with a bare hand brushed snow from her shoulders and arms. Then, while Eshaz tended to the injured student, Tesh told Noah that the entire class had been caught unawares, but had pooled their resources, especially when some of the lean-to structures failed. As snow pummeled them, they had built a larger shelter, and huddled together inside.

"Do we all get A's?" Anton asked, with a wide grin.

"You can count on it," Noah promised. "But this is crazy. It never snows around here in the summer."

As if to show him how wrong he was, a howling arctic wind blasted through the trees, and the temperature dropped precipitously. Noah and Eshaz joined the others inside the makeshift shelter. This further delayed the rescuers in their snow machines, but they finally rolled noisily into to the camp....

* * * * *

At well past midnight, Noah and Eshaz stood in the large lobby of the Guardian administration building, wearing dry clothes and drinking hot chocolate. Around them their companions chattered excitedly about the unexpected adventure. Curiously, the temperature had been rising quickly in the last few hours, and snow was melting outside, with water running off the rooftop and overflowing the gutters.

Standing nearby, Tesh and Anton had been bundled up in warm coats, but heat coming in from outside forced them to remove them. Others were doing the same, and no one understood what was occurring. With one exception.

"Canopa is not healthy," Eshaz murmured, as he gazed into the distance.

* * * * *

By the following morning, even with the sun shining, the temperature began to drop once more, and snow accompanied the plunge, although considerably less than before. By evening the temperature rose and melted away the blanket of white, but it did not get as warm as the first night. Another day and night of this ensued—three in all—with the odd reversal of expected patterns repeating themselves, but in diminishing form.

On the third night, Noah and Eshaz stood outside the main building, gazing up at a starry sky. To a certain extent Noah understood the Tulyan's remark about Canopa. Both of them believed that planets were vital organisms, and that the galaxy was populated by living, Gaea-type worlds. They had discussed this subject in the past, but only in general terms that never quite satisfied Noah's desire for information.

It always seemed to him that Eshaz knew more than he was revealing about the subject. Even though Noah had coined the phrase "galactic ecology," he did not really feel like an expert on the subject. He was only a student himself, with a great deal to learn.

"Perhaps one day you will decide to tell me more," Noah said.

"Perhaps," came the response.

Chapter Twenty-Seven

The wise merchant prince emulates the predator.
—"Discourses on Power," confidential memo from Doge Lorenzo

For weeks Prince Saito had clung to life, sustained by the life-support dome over him and the auxiliary medical equipment connected to his failing body. Since the injury he had lost more than forty kilograms, and looked pale. Princess Meghina felt as if she was caught in a nightmare, unable to save the man she loved. Each day was like the one before it and the one that followed, and she fell into a dismal routine.

She had been staying in an elegant hotel, only a short distance away by groundjet. In view of her high social status and special relationship with the Prince she might have stayed in his villa, but Francella had proffered no invitation and Meghina had too much pride to push the issue. Hence, the Princess had decided to go somewhere else, where she could have a little breathing room.

Each morning at eight o'clock, her groundjet left the hotel and took her to the Prince's villa high on the cliff, a short ride. She then remained at his side until late evening, talking to him, holding his hand, massaging his shoulders ... and never giving up hope that he might regain consciousness. Sometimes she sustained herself by dipping into her memory vault and reliving wonderful moments the two of them had shared.

"Remember that time we went on a sand-skiing holiday to Lost Lake Desert, and I tumbled down a huge dune and disappeared? You rushed down to rescue me, my gallant knight. I'll never forget how you cleared away the sand so that I could breathe, and then you kissed me. I carry that kiss with me every day, and so many others, my darling...."

While recounting the anecdote for him she held his hand, and thought she felt his pulse quicken for a moment.

A quick learner, Meghina had developed an understanding of the cell meters, immuno monitors, and other machines connected to his body. She began to memorize the results and compare them with prior outcomes, while asking a lot of questions of any doctor or nurse who happened to be in her proximity.

Late one night, after staying with the Prince all day, she kissed him gently and felt the coldness of his lips, so cruelly different from the passion they had shared not so long ago. During the groundjet ride back afterward, she'd cried, afraid that he would never recover. But it had been only a short trip and only a short cry. By the time she arrived at her hotel suite she reminded herself that she needed to be strong for him, and she prepared for the next day.

Upon returning to the villa the following morning, however, she walked into the sick room and found the life-support dome sitting on the floor by the bed, with a blanket over the Prince, including his face.

No one else was in the room; just the two of them.

"My love. No! Please, no, not you...."

Gasping in shock and disbelief, she removed the blanket from his head and kissed him one last time, dropping Mutati tears on his lifeless face. He looked so small and fragile, where once he had been such a powerhouse of a man. She glanced around, but saw no one. Prince Saito was gone, leaving the courtesan with only her memories.

A short while later, Dr. Bichette marched into the room, followed by two large men in black tunics, capes, and fez hats. *Undertakers*, Meghina thought, unable to stop the flow of tears. A motorized gurney rolled behind them, controlled by a transmitter held by one of the men. Bichette looked stern and impatient, as if other matters were more important to him than this one, and he had been delayed by the inconvenience of Prince Saito's injury.

Despite her abiding sadness and the tears that continued to flow, Princess Meghina thought of Saito's daughter, and how she must be hurting. Presumably Francella was in the house, and had been with her father earlier in the morning, perhaps before he died. Meghina hoped that he had felt the warmth of his daughter's touch during his final moments.

Resolving to offer her condolences to Francella, despite the past animosity between them, Meghina walked out to the loggia and peered into room after room. She took several deep breaths. This was not an easy thing for her to do. But she lifted her head high and continued looking. Her noble prince would have wanted her to rise above personal conflict, and she would make every effort to do exactly that.

At the far end of the loggia she passed a hand through the pale yellow identity beam that protected the Prince's study. Presently the heavy alloy door slid open with a smooth click, and she stepped through.

"What are you doing here?" It was Francella, looking up from a long-necked computer terminal just inside the doorway. Her face was filled with rage and hatred.

"I ... I just wanted to offer my condolences for your loss."

Unaffected by the deep sadness on the face of the blonde woman, Francella shouted at her, "You were his whore, but I am his heir. Now get out!"

Maintaining her composure, Meghina gazed down the bridge of her nose and retorted, "I am a *courtesan*. There is a difference." Not wishing to get into an emotional argument so soon after a death, she whirled smoothly and left....

A short while later, Francella went to the local nehrcom transmitting station and sent a message to Doge del Velli, requesting an audience with him, so that they might discuss their new working relationship. Actually, she had forged important documents that she wanted him to sign, and she knew exactly how to gain his cooperation. It was the sort of behavior that the merchant princes liked and expected anyway, and no one enjoyed this sort of interaction more than Lorenzo, even if he had to give something up in the process.

Chapter Twenty-Eight

Sometimes when you want to think big, it is necessary to begin with the very small.

—*Scienscroll*, Commentaries 8:55

After completing their outdoor survival training and a battery of preliminary classes, Tesh Kori and Anton Glavine were promoted to the School of Galactic Ecology on the orbital EcoStation. There they began more advanced studies, including Correlated Astronomy, Planetary Reclamation, and Eco-Activism. Tesh excelled in her studies, while

Anton did acceptable, but not outstanding, work. Both of them were still only probationary Guardians, and could not become full-fledged members until they graduated.

During a lunch break inside EcoStation's crowded automatic cafeteria, they sat at a small table by a window that afforded a distant view of Canopa, beyond wind-sculpted clouds below them. One of the cloud formations made Tesh giggle, since it resembled a corpulent Mutati, with a small head and a lumpy body.

Upon hearing her, Anton looked up from an electronic book that he had been reading. His eyes were bloodshot from staying up late the night before, studying for his first examination in Eco-Activism. He had been pushing himself, trying to prove to Tesh that he could keep up with her. She smiled gently at the thought of this mere *humanus ordinaire* trying to match her own performance levels, an utter and complete impossibility. Perhaps she should diminish her accomplishments, as a kindness to him. Human males, so competitive with everyone in their spheres, didn't like to be shown up by females, and especially not by females with whom they were having relationships.

Several tables away, the scaly-skinned, reptilian Eshaz was deep in conversation with Noah Watanabe. On a cart beside them, Noah had brought along the nearly extinct alien he had rescued from Jaggem, the amorphous creature he called Lumey. Surprising everyone, and Noah more than anyone, Lumey no longer needed to be kept inside the sealed container. Perhaps in response to Noah's loving attention, the creature had healed, and was now living off a variety of foods. At the moment, Noah had the case open, and was tossing occasional scraps of food inside. As each morsel arrived, Lumey slithered his body over it and absorbed it into his skin, glowing luminescent white for a few moments at a time during the digestive process. But Tesh was more interested in another, much larger creature. Eshaz.

The Tulyan, while an ancient rival of her own Parvii race, had not appeared to recognize her true self … the tiny person hiding inside. She had never heard of a Tulyan seeing through a Parvii magnification system, but it was said that they knew such devices existed. Although Tesh did not go out of her way to talk with Eshaz, she did not attempt to avoid him, either. She was not overly worried, since the energy field around her worked to conceal her identity from all galactic races, even defeating the most sophisticated scanners.

As she gazed at him now, he glanced suddenly in her direction, but only for a moment before continuing his discussion. He placed a hand gently on Noah's shoulder, leading her to believe that he might be expressing his condolences to the Guardian leader over the death of his father.

This Tulyan was unlike others that Tesh had observed in her seven hundred years of life, in that he socialized easily with Humans and even ate their food in large portions. Normally Tulyans were insular, sticking to their own kind and the ways of their own people. Considering the cuisine of alien races far inferior to their own, they were fussy about what they ate and drank, too. Curiously, though, Eshaz seemed to actually *prefer* Human food—even the barely adequate fare of this school cafeteria. As for Tesh, she didn't concern herself with taste in the least; she was capable of experiencing it, but enjoyed other senses more. She simply ate what was nutritious.

Based upon her miniature racial physique, one might think that she could only consume half a thimbleful of lunch. But this was not the case at all: she ate (or seemed to eat) as much as any other woman. In reality, however, almost all of her food was being diverted by the magnification system into a concealed food chamber that she could dump later, at her convenience. The chamber was much larger than she was in her natural Parvii state, and it occupied a space below the location of her true form.

Unknown to anyone gazing upon her, Tesh (like any magnified Parvii) floated inside the brain section of the image, with the shimmering light of the enlargement mechanism all around her. Her secret, comparatively immense food chamber became only a sac with the thinnest of membranes after she emptied it—so that whenever she wished to return to her normal size, the sac compressed to an object as small as a Parvii marble, which she could carry about in a pocket. Thus she could easily exist in two realms, and was able to shift quickly between them.

In recent days she and Anton had begun to make love again. After their passionate first encounter, he had refused to do it again for a time, telling her that they should develop their relationship more first. Assuming it was some misguided Human sense of guilt combined with gallantry, she had not argued. Gradually her seductive methods worked anyway, and his resistance melted away like an ice sculpture in the tropics. Human men, even if they tried, could not resist a beautiful woman forever. He had been a challenge—she had to admit that—but only for awhile.

Thinking of this, and of the sexuality of Human men in general, her gaze wandered over to the table where Noah Watanabe sat with the Tulyan. Engrossed in conversation, the Guardian leader didn't appear to notice her at all. In fact, whenever they encountered one another in the corridors or classrooms of the space station he seemed to make a point of avoiding her. It was not simply disinterest on his part, either. To her it looked like considerably more than that, as if he had a strong emotional feeling about her—either attraction or loathing—which he tried to manifest as detachment. Whatever he felt toward her, he was not concealing it entirely, though, and she intended to pursue the matter further.

Another challenge....

Chapter Twenty-Nine

Danger: Never tamper with the inner workings of a sentient machine. For service, contact one of our factory-trained technicians.

—Hibbil product statement, sent sent out with each AI robot

After General Sajak shot Jimu, the robot had been left for the mechanical equivalent of dead. Servants on the dinner boat had been told to toss him into the molten lava lake of the volcano, but in private they had attempted to reactivate him instead, thinking he might perform some of their more menial chores. It was a risky enterprise, but with the noblemen gone they thought they could get away with it—while taking care to keep the robot hidden whenever the wrong people were around.

Operating on one of his backup systems, Jimu had heard every word spoken at the clandestine meeting of the noble-born princes, and had recorded all of it into his core processing unit. He was conscious now, as the servants worked on his mechanisms in an attempt to resuscitate him. He could not see anything, but based upon the position of his body and the sounds around him

Jimu guessed that he was on a table or a counter, in a small room. Detecting the odors of grime and decaying food, he thought it might be a lunchroom.

One of the men had experience with robots, but not enough to understand the sophisticated internal workings of this one. Jimu could tell what they were doing at every moment, as they attempted to rebuild and reconnect fiber optics, trillian capacitors, and data transmission zips, but these guys were not that smart and were doing it all wrong, causing more damage than good.

In fact, the way these servants were going they wouldn't get anything working, and might give up. Most of all, Jimu didn't want them to throw him in the hot lava. If they did that, he might not ever recover.

He checked data in his systems. The central core with which he was thinking at this very moment—in essence the soul of the machine—was protected by a ten centimeter thick shell, designed to withstand the impact of falling from great heights or being hit by a groundtruck. Constructed of ascarb fiber materials, the box was resistant to fire as well, up to twelve hundred and fifty degrees Celsius for a ten hour period. He paused and asked himself a question: What was the temperature of molten lava? His data banks provided the answer: a little less than twelve hundred degrees.

As Jimu thought more about it, he realized that this was not a margin of comfort for him. Within a few minutes of immersion in the lava, every part in his body with the exception of the core shell would melt away. He would be left with ten final hours to think, followed by the disintegration of the central shell itself. That might take another thirty minutes at most before molten material started leaking in.

His survival depended upon staying out of the lava lake.

But he was helpless to act. While he had a self-functioning repair system, it only worked with raw materials provided by the Hibbils under factory conditions.

He could only wait, and hope....

Agonizing hours went by, during which time Jimu began to despair. The Humans kept doing the wrong things, making incorrect connections. It would never work. Then, he sensed something strange.

"Look!" one of the Humans exclaimed. "His arm just moved!"

"I didn't see it."

Jimu hesitated. Then, ever so slightly, he moved the arm again ... no more than a twitch.

How can this possibly be happening? he wondered.

Jimu analyzed the repairs, and confirmed that they were not done properly. Then he examined them more carefully, and was astounded. The Humans had found an alternative way of making his arm operate, but without its full range of movement.

Excited Human: "There! Did you see it?"

"Yeah."

"I saw it, too," another voice said.

Feverishly, they continued working on the control panel, and soon both of the mechanical arms were moving, and the fists were flexing open and closed. The Humans brought his legs to life next, and the components of his metal face. All functioned in only a very limited fashion, without the capabilities he'd had before.

Finally, peering through narrowly open eyes, Jimu took a playful swing at one of the servants, and narrowly missed his jaw.

"Whoa!" the man exclaimed, as he easily dodged the blow.

"Do you think he's dangerous?" another asked.

You bet I am, Jimu thought. He opened his glowing yellow eyes all the way and sat up, causing quite a start from the servants. There were four Humans in the room, staring wide-eyed at him as if he were the ancient Frankenstein monster of Earthlore, come back to life.

Chapter Thirty

The concept of a soul is one of the pillars of fear-based religions, suggesting that there is no escape from the wrath of the Supreme Being, even after death. This is a clever deceit, designed to control followers. We can do as we please.

—Halama Erstad, Chairman of Merchant Priests

Noah stood with a crowd inside the gated hillside necropolis, squinting in afternoon sunlight that flashed through puffy clouds. He could see the Valley of the Princes below, and the inverted pyramid of the CorpOne headquarters building, with bolts of lightning flashing across the sky beyond. It was warm and he felt no breeze, a respite from the freak weather of recent days that had postponed the funeral of Prince Saito Watanabe. Now nine days after his death, it was finally taking place.

But the funeral procession seemed like too much of a festive parade, and Noah detested every moment of it. On one level, he fully understood the concept of celebrating the life of a prominent man. Certainly Prince Saito Watanabe had been one of the most admired noblemen in the entire Merchant Prince Alliance. No one had more business acumen than he; no one possessed more ability to generate immense profits. But at what cost? As Master of the Guardians, Noah understood only too well the wholesale destruction of galactic environments by CorpOne and its competitors, and could never forgive his father for his part in that. Not even now.

On no account did he feel like honoring the life of such a man. The old mogul had not been a good person by any definition. Noah was simply paying his respects. He stood on a grassy elevation beside a narrow one-way road, with his adjutant Subi Danvar and a squad of armed Guardian security men keeping vigilance nearby. Eshaz had come along as well, but he remained a little downhill from Noah, saying he did not wish to intrude.

In a display of great pageantry and fanfare—with trumpets, court jugglers, drummers, and scantily-clad female dancers—a noisy procession made its way past the onlookers and began to ascend the steepest portion of the road. A jeweled monolith crowned the top of the hill, a magnificent mausoleum that Prince Saito had commissioned for his final resting place. But it was like no other funerary structure that had ever been built.

Across the road from Noah and his small entourage the Doge Lorenzo del Velli wore a golden surcoat and matching liripipe hat. A large group surrounded him, including his blonde wife, the Princess Meghina, in a spectacular gown of golden leaves and a rubyesque tiara. The most famous courtesan in the galaxy and the lover of many a nobleman, she stood proudly with her chin uplifted, and seemed out of place in the company around her, as if they were rabble and she their queen.

This enigmatic woman had been the paramour of Prince Saito, and everyone knew it, even her own powerful husband. Noah had never met her himself, since she had begun her relationship with his father after the blowup that sent Noah off on his own. She looked so elegant over there, so proud and haughty.

Near the Doge, Francella Watanabe wore a tight, shimmering red dress with a low neckline and a tall red hat. She had no eyebrows at all, not even her customary painted ones, and above the long slope of her forehead the red hat had twin antennae, so that she looked like an insect in Human skin. She smoked a long fumestik while chattering incessantly and smiling, as if she were attending a gay soiree.

Francella and Noah gave each other periodic dirty looks across the roadway, but had not spoken to one another today. Noah had separated himself from her intentionally in order to avoid a scene, even though he knew she was working her manipulative, seductive wiles with Lorenzo and his sycophants. She had publicly accused Noah of murder, and he had denied it. A full-scale investigation—ordered by the Doge—was underway, but thus far Noah had not followed the advice of his aides, and had not hired his own legal team to defend himself. He thought that would only make him look guilty and worried, when he was neither.

Someone had hired phony Guardian soldiers to attack CorpOne headquarters, and Noah's loathsome sister undoubtedly played a key role in the planning and financing. Conceivably, Francella may have even suggested the staged event to the old man, twisting facts to get him involved in it. Noah conjectured as well what part, if any, Princess Meghina may have had in the conspiracy. He had a lot of questions, and no answers.

Behind the procession of entertainers, twenty hover-floats moved slowly uphill, providing garish displays of CorpOne products. Right after them came a black, robot-operated hearse, with the blue-and-silver elephant-design banners of CorpOne fluttering on the fenders. The great man lay inside, on his way to his final destination. Noah felt a wave of bereavement over the loss, but tried to suppress it with righteous anger.

As the hearse passed a high jadeglax structure by the roadway, a white-robed Merchant Priest on a high platform scattered holy water, and read passages from the *Scienscroll* over a blaring loudspeaker system. Noah could not make out the words, but didn't care.

A small number of noblemen and ladies stood on Noah's side of the roadway, but maintained their distance from him. One was Jacopo Nehr, accompanied by his brother Giovanni and by Jacopo's unmarried, fortyish daughter Nirella. A reserve colonel in the Doge's paramilitary Red Berets, Jacopo Nehr wore a red-and-gold uniform decked with medals and ribbons, while his brother had on a blue tunic, leggings, and a surcoat.

Gazing at the chisel-featured brothers, Noah envied their close relationship and wished that he and his twin sister might have gotten along, and even been close. But it was too late for such sentiments. Far too late.

Despite his efforts to feel otherwise, Noah could not help grieving for his father, and thought back to better times they shared, especially when Noah's mother was alive. Noah, working for CorpOne at the time, had been trying unsuccessfully to get his father to change his business practices. After Noah's mother died in that grid-plane crash, the two men no longer had a buffer between them, and the inevitable explosion occurred. Francella had reveled in the breakup, not concealing her glee in the least, and not even showing much emotion over the death of their mother.

Noah hated to think about his own family relationships, as they made him sick to his stomach. But here, under the solemn circumstances, he couldn't help himself.

With the sun warming his face and shoulders, it almost seemed like a normal summer day to him. He felt anything but normal, though. Things seemed horribly out of balance.

The entertainers and corporate floats at the head of the procession split off onto side roads, while the robot-operated hearse continued uphill, to the jeweled mausoleum on top. Wide, diamonix-faceted doors slid open on the structure, and the hearse entered. Not long afterward Noah heard a small explosion, and the building turned fiery red as Prince Saito Watanabe—one of the greatest industrialists in history—was cremated inside the very building that would become his tomb. The unusual funerary arrangement had been specified in his will, and reportedly had been carried out with considerable difficulty.

Just then the ground rumbled and shook beneath Noah's feet, nearly causing him to fall over. A huge bolt of lightning accompanied by a thunderous explosion struck near the monolith. The ground rumbled and broke away, and the ornate structure tilted, then tumbled with a tremendous crash onto its side, still glowing red.

The mourners panicked and ran in all directions, but Noah remained in place, watching the others scatter. A short distance downhill, Eshaz stayed where he was, too.

The shaking of the ground ceased, and the sky began to clear....

* * * * *

"This planet is dying," Eshaz murmured to himself. "And the web as well."

He sensed forces at work that could not be controlled by any galactic race, and which he might not even be able to identify.

A shudder passed through his body.

In a very real sense it seemed to Eshaz that the Great Unknown was a black box filled with nasty surprises, and something was opening the box a little at a time, permitting the contents to escape. It was an enormous cosmic mystery, and he feared it. But he also felt like a detective, with an immense and intriguing enigma to solve.

He saw Noah studying him, perhaps guessing at his thoughts. This remarkable man, so advanced in his thinking, had asked for more information. And Eshaz, while he had lived for almost a million years and knew much more than he had revealed to his friend, did not possess nearly all of the answers himself.

The Elders would not want Eshaz to discuss such matters with a mere Human, but for such an extraordinary example of the race he thought an exception might be in order.

* * * * *

Over the better part of a week, Jimu worked in secrecy for the servants of the Parma dining salon, performing menial chores when management was not around. At night the conspirators locked their prized robot in a storage room and went home to small cabins that were provided for them a short distance away.

One evening when all was quiet, Jimu broke out and fled into the surreal, red-glowing darkness of the volcanic moon. By the following day he reached a depot, where he mingled with the robots of a work crew and boarded a shuttle with them.

He soon discovered that they were headed for Canopa, where laborers were needed to work on a damaged mausoleum....

Chapter Thirty-One

A secret within a secret. This is the most difficult to unravel.

—Anonymous

A t the conclusion of the funeral, the Nehr brothers took a shuttle to the nearest pod station, and from there caught a podship to Timian One, the breathtaking capital world of the Merchant Prince Alliance.

Now, as the pair rode a ground-jet back to the headquarters of Nehrcom Industries, Giovanni Nehr considered how to say something important. He was slumped into one of the soft, deep seats in the passenger cabin, while Jacopo sat across from him, studying an electronic copy of the quasi-religious *Scienscroll.*

The Great Inventor, Gio thought bitterly. It was a title commonly applied to his graying older brother, for developing the nehrcom cross-galaxy transceiver.

His big secret.

Gio touched a combination of toggles on a small vending machine between the seats, causing the Hibbil device to manufacture a pill according to his specifications. A bright red capsule tumbled into a receptacle. With a shaking hand he grabbed the narcotic and gulped it, and seconds later felt it take effect on his mind. He inhaled several deep breaths, and tried to maintain control over his emotions. The drug only helped a little, but he didn't want to consume more right away, since he had such a sensitive constitution.

For the past two generations, secrets had been the economic life blood of the Nehr family. His parents had made a fortune by sending hunters out into the galaxy to capture Mutatis, which were subsequently used—under extreme secrecy—as biological factories, processing foreign substances in their bodies and metamorphosing them into hallucinogenic drugs.

On Forzin, a remote moon of the Canopa Star System, the family had kept Mutatis penned up like farm animals for the production of the drugs. The prisoners were force fed carefully-selected substances such as ravenflower hips, bacchanal barley, and toxilia, powerful agents that overwhelmed Mutati immune systems and tapped into their shapeshifting cores. In this manner the transformative powers of the Mutatis were rerouted, causing the creatures to change the extrinsic substances into exotic hallucinogens instead of metamorphosing their own flesh.

Each captive Mutati created a different narcotic, which was extracted from his blood. The Nehrs called their products "powerdrugs," since the procedure always resulted in something highly potent. The wide variation and unpredictability made the substances extremely exciting ... and expensive.

The drugs, as individual as each Mutati, all bore letter and numerical code names, from P-1 through P-1725 ... meaning that a total of one thousand, seven hundred twenty-five of the creatures had been captured and forced to produce. Some of the narcotics were more popular than others, such as P-918, which simulated Human flight when the user took it. But when the Mutati producing that variation finally died, the drug was gone forever ... with the exception of any that might have been stockpiled. Like rare vintages of wine, preferred varieties went up in value, and people could make money by trading them on galactic commodities markets.

The business all came to a sudden, violent end when the last Mutati broke free, killed Gio's parents, and destroyed the manufactory. Jacopo had been fifteen at the time, and Gio barely three.

As Gio grew up he followed a different course from his famous sibling, and became something of a ne'er-do-well', failing in a number of risky business ventures. Two years ago, Jacopo rescued him from a bad drug overdose and gave him a job in administration with Nehrcom Industries.

Gio, however, was less than appreciative, as he did not like Jacopo's condescending attitude toward him. The younger Nehr also felt extreme jealousy toward his brother ... and while he fought to suppress it, he rarely succeeded. Like a toxic leak that could not be sealed, the feelings continued to seep into his mind, poisoning it.

Although the pair resembled one another in their chiseled facial features, the similarity ended there. Gio was taller and heavier, with a muscular physique that he had developed with sterisone drugs and regular visits to Hibbil body-enhancement facilities. If he wanted to, he could break his brother's body in half with his bare hands, and sometimes thought about doing exactly that. Jacopo often wore a reserve military officer's uniform, but that was just for show; he was not tough at all.

Across the passenger cabin, Jacopo continued to read his electronic copy of the *Scienscroll*.

Gio glared at him and thought, smugly, *I have secrets too, Big Brother. And you're not going to like them.* He bit his lower lip. *OK, let's start with this one.*

In the most pleasant of tones, Gio announced, "I will be resigning soon."

The great man looked up from his reading and lifted an eyebrow in surprise, but only a little. "To do what?"

"I don't know. I need to try something new."

Jacopo showed little reaction. It was exactly as Gio expected, and made him doubly glad that he was about to steal something important—the secret of his brother's nehrcom transceiver. For some unknown reason, Jacopo fully trusted only one person, his own daughter Nirella, and had given her responsibility for protecting information about the invention.

But Nirella had made a mistake, and her opportunistic uncle was about to capitalize upon it.

Chapter Thirty-Two

What is the origin of the pods? If we could answer that, it might reveal much about the nature and purpose of our galaxy.
— "Great Questions" (Mutati Royal Astronomical Society)

The podship emerged from space in a burst of green luminescence, having traveled the arcane, faster-than-light pathways known only to these sentient spacecraft. With glowing green particles clinging to the mottled, blimp-shaped hull and dissipating around it, the vessel approached a pod station that flickered in and out of view. The arrival seemed like tens of thousands that had preceded it, and even more that were expected to follow.

The intelligent ship carried a small red-and-gold vessel in its hold, ostensibly one of the Doge's merchant schooners on a trading mission. Purportedly it was filled with wondrous products from exotic ports near and far, such as Churian teas, Kazupan silkine gowns, Hibbil machines, Adurian organics, glax lenses, and pearlian spices.

But inside the faux schooner sat a Mutati outrider disguised as a Human. In a trance, he quoted aloud from *The Holy Writ* of his people, the purity-extolling religious text that was the doctrinal basis for the annihilation of unclean Humans throughout the galaxy.

The podship docked at a zero-G berth inside the orbital station. Momentarily, without a creak or a squeak, doors opened in the vessel's gray-and-black, living tissue underbelly.

The disguised Mutati craft inside the cargo hold dropped like a child from a cosmic womb. The engines of the fake schooner surged on, and the pilot guided it past loading docks and walkways. All pod stations were built essentially the same, and so were the interrelated podships, so the pilot—even though he had never been to this particular station before—knew his way around.

As the outrider taxied, he passed a "glyphreader" robot patrolling the sealed walkways, one of the sentient machines that scanned and translated the pinkish-red geometric designs on arriving podships, which indicated their routes. It was one of the few mysteries about podships that the galactic races had been able to figure out—the way the markings changed constantly, like destination screens on jet-buses. The robot had an electronic sign atop its head, a small version of larger display panels that hung from ceilings. All were written in Galeng, the common language of the galactic races.

Smoothly, engines purring, the Mutati guided his little ship out of the station and dropped down into weightless space, with a blue-green planet visible far below. Twin jets of white-hot exhaust shot out of the double tail of the clandestine schooner, and the craft accelerated downward. Within seconds, instruments told the pilot he was inside the atmospheric envelope of the planet, and he saw ionized orange sparks from the friction of the hull as it skimmed the air.

The Mutati, his senses deadened by focal drugs, had no ancillary thoughts in his mind. He recalled nothing of his life or family or career, none of which existed for him anymore. His entire *raison d'être*, everything he had done in his life up to this point, culminated in this one task. The assignment had come directly from the Zultan Abal Meshdi himself.

I cannot fail.

He studied his console of instruments and electronic charts. The globe below had a crust of thirty-three kilometers in thickness, with sedimentary materials and an upper shell of granite. Basalt, gabbro, and other rock types were beneath that ... then the mantle, and the molten core.

Switching on a prismatic timer, the outrider set the torpedo, which in reality was his entire schooner. The doomsday device ... a Demolio ... screamed down toward the ice-covered southern continent of the planet.

Thousands of years ago this had been an important world to the Humans, where billions of people lived. Stripped bare by endless wars and the insatiable appetites of Human industry, it now contained a mere thirty million inhabitants.

"Earth," the Mutati muttered as his suicide torpedo penetrated the crust. Seconds later, it reached the fiery core and went nuclear. The planet was obliterated in an explosion, so sudden and immense that it consumed the pod station and the podship as well, before it could set course for a new star system.

Chapter Thirty-Three

Reputedly, Doge Lorenzo del Velli is the greatest patron of business and science in history ... but this is his own propaganda, cleverly disguised as fact.
—Succession: a Concise History of the Doges (one of the banned books)

O n distant Canopa, Francella Watanabe rode a slideway from a shuttle depot to a white, bubble-shaped nehrcom transmitting station. In a hurry, she wore a simple black dress and no makeup, so that her bald eyebrows and forehead glistened in bright morning sunlight.

The cross-space transmission facility sat in a hollow at the perimeter of the Valley of Princes, and was protected from attack by an implosive energy shield that encircled it, both above and below ground. It was a new structure, replacing one that had been blown up by a Mutati suicide bomber. The landscaping and other finishing touches were still under construction.

As she stepped off the sliding walkway and climbed wide marble steps Francella felt the invisible electronic field all around her, and experienced a shortness of breath from the anxiety this always gave her. The system read her identity at every imaginable level, and she wondered if it would make a mistake and not recognize her. These highly sensitive security units required a great deal of maintenance; they were always breaking down and under repair. During one of the down-times at the former station, a disguised Mutati sneaked in and sent messages, before destroying the facility.

Because of the high degree of concern over security, there were stories of mistaken arrest, and even one instance where a noble-born prince was misidentified and died from the stress of it. Francella felt strong enough to endure any rigid, probing procedures that the mechanism might put her through, but she hated the thought of wasted time. She had so many important things to do, secret things, and hardly enough time to complete them.

The electronic system emitted a friendly beep, allowing her to pass. The rooms inside the building were a brilliant, almost blinding white, with complex geometric ceilings but few furnishings, as if the contents had not arrived yet, or as if the designer expected to receive additional objects at some later date. But she knew the interior was complete. All of the stations were like this.

In an immense room beneath a glax dome stood one of the ultra-secret, platinum-cased nehrcom transceivers, with chromatic surveillance beams darting in all directions around it. For a few seconds, a rainbow of color washed across her, then moved on. Reportedly Jacopo Nehr, ever paranoid about keeping his priceless business secrets, continually rotated his security systems, to keep potential thieves off balance. This particular apparatus looked the same as the last time she had been here, but she suspected subtle differences.

The platform on which the nehrcom sat resembled a religious shrine, and not by accident, some people asserted, considering the reverence with which the instantaneous communication device was held. Arguably the greatest feat of technology ever conceived by the galactic races, it was second in its impact only to a concoction that was generally attributed to the Supreme Being himself ... an entire race of sentient podships.

In a new security upgrade, users of the transceiver were not permitted to touch it or even to go near it, and instead had to remain behind a glowing blue railing that encircled the center of the room. Francella stepped up to the elec-

Brian Herbert

tronic barrier and touched one of the buttons on a panel, indicating that she
wanted to pick up a message.

Presently a hatch opened in the floor on the other side of the railing and a
platform rose, bearing a nehrcom operator dressed in a black robe with a nebula
swirl on the chest. When the mechanism came to a rest he stepped off and
approached Francella.

"Here is your message, Lady Watanabe," he said.

As she accepted a folded sheet of brown parchment it irritated her that she
had been required to come here personally to pick it up, but the Doge
sometimes made this a requirement when he sent transmittals, even the most
innocuous of them. As a rule, nehrcoms were entrusted for delivery to *messagèros*,
the bonded couriers who worked for the Merchant Prince Alliance.

While the operator waited, Francella read the Doge's brief communication.
He had consented to the audience that she had requested, and told her what
time to appear for it.

"Please inform the Doge I will be there," she said.

The operator nodded.

As she left and descended the steps outside, one of the CorpOne vice-
presidents stopped her, a toothy man with a bald head. "Did you hear about the
catastrophe?" he asked.

When she gazed at him blankly, he told her that Earth had been destroyed.
"It's gone," he said, "with only space debris left."

"What happened?"

"No one knows. A huge comet, maybe."

"No matter," Francella said. "It was only a backwater planet, of little
concern to the Alliance."

With that she hurried away, to complete her scheming tasks.

Chapter Thirty-Four

I care nothing if my people love me. The primary emotion I wish to elicit is fear.
—Doge Lorenzo del Velli, as told by the Hibbil Pimyt

Princess Meghina strolled along a narrow path that overlooked the
grounds of the Palazzo Magnifico and its fabulous orange-and-yellow
Daedalian Labyrinth. A mini-forest formed in an intricate web of natural
mazes around a Minotaur statue, it was a great delight to members of the
royal court and to scientists as well, who frequently came to study the plants and
take samples of them. The only such forest in existence, it was of unknown
origin, and resisted all efforts to transplant it.

Meghina had been on Timian One for two weeks following the disastrous
funeral on Canopa. Even though she and the Doge had the most famous open
marriage in the Merchant Prince Alliance, there had been tension between them
over her long-standing relationship with Prince Saito, and even jealousy on the
day of the tycoon's ceremony. Afterward, the Doge had insisted that she come
to the capital for an indeterminate period, and he had been displaying her at
state functions, making her remain at his side like a living, ornamental doll. It
was childish on his part, but no one could defy him when he really wanted
something.

Doge Lorenzo had respected Prince Saito, even revered him for his
business acumen. As long as the Prince was alive, the Doge looked the other

way and said little about the relationship with Meghina. There were important professional connections between the men, and noble princes never let women come between them. Now that Saito was gone, however, the situation was different.

At dinner each evening, with only Lorenzo and his pretty blonde wife seated at an immense table in the Grand Banquet Hall, he continually harped at her, demanding to know personal details about her affair with the dead man. She tried to answer his questions, but no response seemed sufficient, and he kept snapping at her and digging deeper, asking additional questions.

The Doge had been watching her every move, mostly through his agents but often on his own. At the moment he was attempting to conceal himself on the pathway behind her, thinking she would not notice him if he dressed in the garb of an ordinary court noble ... royal blue surcoat, leggings, and liripipe hat. She smiled to herself, but it was more a grimace than anything else.

He could behave so immaturely at times. She didn't understand the double standard involved here. Well, actually, she did *understand* it as the chauvinistic manner of the merchant princes, but it was not fair. Her husband performed sexual acts with more than a hundred women a year, while her tally was a scant tenth of that, and only with noblemen of the highest stations. The sin she had committed in Lorenzo's eyes, however, had been to care deeply about one of them without making any attempt to camouflage her feelings.

She missed Saito so much that it hurt, and her husband knew it.

Pausing to catch her breath, she pretended to examine a poppy garden, while actually looking peripherally at her husband, at least fifty meters down trail. He had stopped, and was acting as if he was cleaning something off his shoes with a stick.

Part of her wanted to go back there and confront him, shouting her feelings at the top of her voice. But a proper lady would never conduct herself in that manner. The noblewomen of the Merchant Prince Alliance were all trained in civilized behavior ... known as *urbanitas* ... from an early age. She needed to comport herself at all times as if she was actually one of those ladies. An uncultured, or *rusticitas* person, was not welcome in court society.

All of her life, going back to the early years in which she had grown up as a Mutati princess on Paradij, the Princess had longed to be a beautiful, elegantly-dressed Human lady, socializing with handsome Human men. She had always considered Mutatis ugly in their natural state, with their rolling mounds of fat, tiny heads, and oversized eyes. She had run away from the Mutati Kingdom in order to live out her fantasy, and for years it had gone well. Meghina achieved all of the wealth and social position that a woman could want, and had enjoyed the affections of a man she loved. But after the death of Prince Saito her fantasy seemed to burst. Everything looked dark and dismal to her now, and she wondered if she had made a terrible mistake when she abandoned her roots.

With a deep and abiding sadness, she picked a bright yellow pollenflower to remind her of her lost love, and continued along the path, away from her observer.

* * * * *

At dinner that evening, as expected, Lorenzo lay in waiting for her. A valet reported to the Princess that the aged Doge had been sitting at the table for more than an hour, drinking wine and getting meaner by the minute. He had thrown crystal glasses and candlesticks at servants, shouted epithets at them, and even threatened to kill one on the spot and use his body as a centerpiece for the table.

His behavior hardly qualified as civilized, but in his position he could do anything he pleased.

As Meghina swept into the Grand Banquet Hall she wore a shimmering gown of metallic blue Sirikan cloth, with golden lace at the bodice that revealed her ample breasts. Above her heart-shaped face, her blonde hair rose in an elaborate structure, with wings at the sides and a ruby tiara gracing the front.

Her husband did not rise for her, and hardly looked in her direction when a servant helped her onto a high-backed chair. She sat on the Doge's right, not a safe distance away.

"Good evening, Your Magnificence," she said in a melodic tone. Meghina wore a subtle floral perfume that she knew he liked.

Lorenzo gulped a glass of red wine and glared at her with dark, watery eyes that suggested things he did to Mutati prisoners in one of the gaol's torture chambers. If he ever discovered her true identity, she had no doubt of her fate.

"Are you my wife or aren't you?" he demanded. His gaze focused on the scant lace over her bosom.

"I am your wife, Sire ... and more. I serve nobility." It was a rather open-ended response, but one that presented her position to him clearly—she had informed him in the very beginning that she wished to be a courtesan and not merely a wife.

A servant came to pour more wine, but had to duck and run for cover when the old man pummeled him with tableware that crashed and broke on the floor.

"Get out!" Lorenzo thundered to the hapless fellow. "Can't you see I want peace and quiet?"

When they were alone in the great hall, Lorenzo gripped Meghina's wrist on top of the table and rasped, "After your lover's funeral, you ordered the restoration of his mausoleum, didn't you?"

"Yes," she admitted, "but I thought you would want that. He was your friend and an important prince."

"It is unseemly for you to arrange for the work personally." He squeezed her wrist tightly. "You see that, don't you?"

"I had hoped to remove the worry from you, Sire, since you are so busy." *Busy following me around,* she thought.

A cruel smile cut the features of his leathery face, with a bit of drool sliding from one side of his mouth. "How thoughtful of you," he said in a low, menacing tone, "toward me and my late friend."

"I had hoped to be," she said. Tugging slightly at her wrist, she protested, "You're hurting me."

"What?" He looked down, saw his own knuckles white from squeezing, and let go.

She rubbed her reddened wrist to get circulation going again. If she had known how violent Human noblemen could be, she might have taken steps to safeguard herself more after shapeshifting into Human form. Certain protective features could have been concealed in the flesh. As it was now, she could never change back again and was as vulnerable to injury or death as any Human female.

"Is work on the mausoleum finished?" he asked in an annoyed tone. He glanced around, as if looking for an inattentive servant to injure.

"They should be lifting it back onto its foundation about now."

"And the contractor's invoices?" He raised his voice. "You aren't *paying* them personally, are you?"

"I advanced some funds in order to get things going. I was only trying to remove the burden from you."

"All costs must be born by the state, and not by the wife of the Doge. Have the bills sent to me!"

"As you wish, My Lord. Shall we dine now?" Noting his continued interest in her bosom, she smiled sweetly and asked, "Or would you prefer your dessert first?"

His face provided the answer. Human men were so transparent when they wished to have intercourse. But she would tease this one first, with a sexually-charged dance of bewitchment.

* * * * *

On Canopa, Jimu had been one of hundreds of robots assigned to lift and repair the damaged mausoleum of Prince Saito Watanabe. The mechanical man melted into the background and did as he was told by the Human work bosses.

The structure rested in its proper position now, but the jeweled walls had been fractured, and were undergoing repair by a team of specialists who worked on low scaffolds. The work bosses had described the powerful lightning strike and ground tremor that caused all this damage as a freak act of nature. Jimu didn't know anything about that. He focused on his assignment, retrieving and listing the priceless gems that were scattered around the site.

At the top of the hill, he added a bucketful of jewels to a growing pile. Security was everywhere, with armed soldiers watching every move that he and his companions made, like the guards for a prison work crew. After a while Jimu peered through a broken wall in the mausoleum. Inside stood a glassy statue of the dead prince, with both arms broken off. Workers were repairing them.

Despite high security, Jimu had the intelligence to circumvent it, and he sneaked away, this time making his way onto a podship bound for the Inn of the White Sun. He had heard about a group of sentient robots that operated a way station there, and wanted to see what it was like for machines to control their own destinies....

Chapter Thirty-Five

Is there anything larger than the galaxy? And even if there is, what difference does it make?

—Anonymous note, found inside a piece of
malfunctioning Hibbil machinery

When Jimu arrived at the Inn of the White Sun, he was astounded by the ingenious architecture of this hivelike way station that had been constructed in an orbital ring. The views of the planet Ignem, far below, were spectacular through bubble windows, and unlike anything he had ever seen before. The world looked like the largest gemstone in the galaxy, and it changed moment by moment, displaying different color combinations in shifting light.

"So you've heard of us, eh?" a flat-bodied robot said, as they stood on an observation deck. Within an hour of his arrival, Jimu had been introduced to

Thinker, the leader of the mechanical colony. Narrowing his metal-lidded eyes, Thinker added, "What is it you've heard?"

"That you control your own destinies." With one hand, Jimu rubbed a small dent on his own torso. He rather liked the feeling, for it made him think of the adversities he had overcome.

"I mean, what is it you've been told we do here?"

"That you run this inn, and make a great deal of money at it. Robots all over the galaxy speak of this place with affection and admiration."

"Anything else?"

"No, nothing."

"That is good, very good."

Not wishing to conceal anything from this important robot, Jimu said, "I was Captain of the sentient machines on the Human Grand Fleet. You may have heard of it ... the force that attacked the Mutati Kingdom and lost."

"Yes," Thinker said, staring at Jimu's dented, scratched body. "And a military disaster does not look good on your résumé."

"I wasn't to blame for it, but listen to this." In his concise, mechanical voice Jimu described General Sajak's suspicion that Doge Lorenzo had sabotaged the fleet.

"Preposterous," Thinker said. "The Doge would never do that."

"Nonetheless, General Sajak is convinced of it, and is conspiring to assassinate Lorenzo."

Without warning, Thinker inserted a flexible probe into Jimu's control panel. Jimu went numb, like a patient under anesthetic.

"You are telling me the truth," Thinker announced presently, in a flat voice. He withdrew the probe, then asked, "Who set up your control box? I've never seen connections like this."

"A Human food-service worker. He had only a little experience with machines, I'm afraid."

"You don't have full range of movement do you? I noticed considerable stiffness as you walked."

"You're right." Jimu lifted an arm, but not very high, then showed how the elbow didn't bend as far as it should. He demonstrated similar problems with other joints.

"We'll have to get you into the shop. But first, I want to show you our operation here. As a military robot, you will appreciate it." The cerebral leader paused. "In fact, with your credentials, you deserve to be an officer again. Let's make it Captain, all right?"

"In what force?" Jimu's glowing yellow eyes opened wide.

He pointed a steely finger at Ignem. "We are building an army down there."

"And you've already decided to make me a part of it?"

"I make quick decisions," Thinker said. "That's why I'm in charge here. Besides, nothing eludes my interface probe. In only a few seconds, I learned all about you."

Later that day, Thinker escorted Jimu down to the surface of Ignem, to a camouflaged headquarters building that had been made to look like no more than a high spot on the surrounding black obsidian plain. There the newcomer was introduced to five other officers, all matching his own rank. One, a tall machine named Gearjok, had served as a technical robot on a Merchant Prince warship, responsible for maintaining mechanical systems. The other captains— Whee, Nouter, Fivvul, and Qarmax—had all worked in various machine supervisory roles for the armed forces of the Humans. In each case the robots had been discarded at the end of their useful lives, and had been salvaged by Thinker.

After a while, Gearjok slapped Jimu on his metal backside and said, "Enough of this. Now let's introduce you to the others."

As the mechanical men strolled outside, it pleased Jimu that none of his new comrades seemed to envy him for his quick promotion to their own level. He had seen such feelings of animosity in machine groups before, metastasizing like cancers and destroying the ability of the robots to work together. It was one of the undesirable traits of Humans that some mechanicals had acquired, but here it seemed to have been programmed out.

Jimu followed the others into a vacuum tube, which transported them with whooshes and thumps up to the roof of the headquarters, which they called the Command Center. From the top, he saw volcanoes in the distance, suddenly active and spewing fire and smoke into the atmosphere. Overhead, through the increasingly murky sky, he barely made out the orbital ring of the Inn of the White Sun.

Hearing a rumbling noise, he lowered his gaze and saw black plates slide open on the floor of the obsidian plain. Thousands of machines poured out, like fat, oddly-shaped insects from a burrow. He gaped in disbelief.

The robots began to form into ranks, but a number of them had problems and bumped into each other or stopped functioning. One, a round-backed mechanism who resembled a silver beetle, fell onto his back at the front of the ranks and could not right himself. Very few of them were shiny; most had unsightly dents and patch marks.

"As you can see, we still have some kinks to work out," Thinker said. "But believe me, we've made a lot of progress."

The worst robots were taken away for more repairs, and soon the remaining machines—around three thousand of them—were arrayed in neat infantry formations, identifiable to Jimu as the boxy ranks of ancient Earthian legions. He had mixed feelings about what he was seeing. In one respect, this was not a very impressive display. But in another, at least it existed.

A machine army!

He noted that only a small number of the troops carried weapons, and those were mostly outdated pelleteers and slingknives, with a few modern puissant rifles. Some of the robots seemed to know how to handle their implements of war, while others did not. This certainly was a motley gathering of individuals and equipment.

"We'll have to send them back to barracks shortly," Thinker said. "We keep maneuvers out here to a minimum, to avoid detection by enemies."

"And who are our enemies?" Jimu inquired.

"There are always enemies. The trick is identify them in time and take appropriate action."

"I see." Jimu nodded, but made a creaking sound as he did so. One more thing to fix.

With a sudden clatter of metal, Thinker folded closed, so that he looked like a dull-gray metal box.

"He does that sometimes," Gearjok said, "when he needs to consider something really important. It gives him absolute darkness and silence. The trouble is, when he thinks about deep philosophical matters he tends to fall asleep in the quiet darkness, with all of his senses blocked or shut off. Whenever that happens, we reactivate him by shaking him gently."

Moments later, Thinker opened back up, and said, "I've been meaning to offer our services to mankind one day, in repayment for inventing sentient machines in the first place."

"But Humans discarded these machines," Jimu said.

"We still owe them some loyalty for creating us. Never forget that, Jimu. You and I would not be having this conversation at all if not for Humans. I think they threw us away in error, and I've been looking for an opportunity to prove it. I assure you, that despite the fumbling appearance of my troops, it is a skillful deception." He touched a long scratch on his own torso. "Conventional wisdom holds that a well-run military force should be spotless and polished, thus instilling a sense of pride and personal self-worth into the organization. But there are distinct advantages to a less-than-perfect appearance. It can cause an opponent to underestimate your abilities."

"That makes sense," Jimu admitted. "Do you mean to tell me that even the machines that stopped functioning out on the parade ground did so by design?"

Thinker cut a jagged grin across his metal face. "Not exactly, but things *are* getting better."

"The robots here are independently self-replicating," Gearjok said to Jimu, "and you can be, too, with a little updating."

Thinker explained that he had developed a sentient machine manufacturing process that did not exist anywhere else in the galaxy. His metal men were able to make copies of themselves by finding their own raw materials and making their own parts, even recycling old items as necessary. He mentioned what Jimu already knew, that there were other machines that could self-replicate (such as those of the Hibbils), but only in regimented factories, with raw materials provided for them under assembly line conditions.

"Is that why the robots are not uniform?" Jimu asked.

"Precisely. They use whatever materials are available to them."

"With my own scrapes and dents, I should fit in nicely around here."

"You'll get a lot more before you're through," Thinker said. He paused, and added, "I am troubled about the assassination plot against Doge Lorenzo. It seems to me that this is the opportunity we've been looking for."

Solemnly, Thinker placed a metal hand on Jimu's shoulder and said, "I want you to lead a small force of our best fighting robots to Timian One and inform the Doge that he is in danger."

"Me?"

"I like what I see in you, Jimu. You have experience, but even more importantly you have special qualities of leadership ... your own way of solving problems. And you heard the conspirators yourself."

"I'm honored, but ..."

"You will inform him of the danger, and come right back. I need you here, to assist with the army we are forming."

"I don't feel ready for such an important assignment."

"Nonsense. We just need to update your operating systems and data banks, clean you up a bit, and you'll be ready to go. Another advantage that we have over Humans. With us, the learning curve is almost immediate."

"You're going to intervene in Human politics?"

"Doge Lorenzo is in danger, and we must do something!"

"Then I'm your robot. But first I must confess, anxiety is heating up my circuits. Could you ask the programmers to take care of that too, please?"

"Don't worry. We'll get you in shape for the assignment." Exuberantly, Thinker slapped his new comrade on the back, leaving one more dent, a little one.

Chapter Thirty-Six

The soil beneath your feet is never as solid as it looks. You must continually probe and turn over rocks, never letting your guard down.

—From The Tulyan Compendium

Noah led Tesh along a path that skirted his own home, with its gray shingle walls and white columns, matching the main administration building and complex of buildings that were partially visible downhill, through a stand of canopa oaks. Focused on the ecological training he was giving to her, he hardly noticed where they were. For the past three days, he had been spending private time with this intellectually gifted young woman, the top student in his school, sharing his personal insights with her, grooming her for the important position he hoped she would hold one day with the Guardians.

He had another matter on his mind as well. Word had reached him that Earth had been destroyed in a sudden, mysterious explosion that left the original home of humanity a debris field, floating in space. The most widely accepted theory was that a comet had hit the sparsely-populated planet, or a meteor, but astronomers had not seen anything unusual in that sector prior to the detonation. Another theory held that it might have been a huge volcanic chain reaction, and still another suggested that the Mutatis had done it. Every one of these ideas seemed far-fetched to the experts, and Noah wasn't sure himself.

As an ecologist, he would be analyzing all available data as it came in. Under the circumstances, though, with the death of his father and the suspicions that had been cast in his direction about that incident, he didn't want to go anywhere near the remains of Earth, or engage any of his own investigators. His own advisers suggested that he maintain a low profile, or his enemies would find a way to blame Earth on him, too. He and Subi were convinced that Noah's enemies—undoubtedly including Francella—wanted to discredit him and his planetary recovery operations. Many of the corporate princes were opposed to his environmental policies and recommendations, and considered him a thorn in their collective side. Now, with the influential Saito Watanabe out of the way, the son had become an even easier target.

Bending down, Noah selected a large oak leaf and held it up, so that midday sunlight revealed the gold-and-brown details of its pattern. "Look at the perfect symmetry of these lines," he said, passing a finger over the leaf. "Amazing, isn't it? I've seen such perfection all over the galaxy, in leaves, seashells, spider webs, and in so many other amazing objects of nature. It shows an interconnectedness, that planets are linked to one another."

"Your concept of galactic ecology," she said, "the interconnectedness of life in remote star systems."

He nodded. "A controversial concept, but I've never shied away from controversy. I think life sprouted in similar forms all over the galaxy, and probably all over the universe."

"Like the theory of parallel evolution," she observed, "but bigger than the similar life forms found on the continents or islands of one planet. You're talking about each planet as an island in a cosmic sea, with parallel life forms sprouting all over the place."

"That's correct," he said, beaming at her.

"I've been wondering about something," she said, looking at him intently with her bright green eyes. "Your writings are silent on this point, but do you think a cosmic wind carries seeds and cells from planet to planet?"

He tried not to think about the physical attraction he felt for her, and as before he set it aside. "Perhaps, and perhaps not. I've never been able to prove it one way or another."

"Doesn't all this prove the existence of a higher power, holding sway over everything, creating perfect beauty? Doesn't it prove that there really is a God?"

"It doesn't prove anything of the kind, only that there is an interconnectedness."

"I see. You're a scientist, not a religious scholar."

He smiled. "The universe is an incredible mystery. We see what we want to see in it, and delight in its boundless wonders." Noah let the leaf go, and a gust of wind picked it up, lifting it gracefully into the sky and carrying it through an opening in the trees, toward his headquarters on the land below. He watched the leaf until it eventually drifted down, out of view.

Placing a hand on his arm, Tesh said, "Perhaps I shouldn't say this, but I feel something between us." Slowly, hesitantly, he looked at her, and she moved around in front him, so that he could not avoid her easily.

"I don't know what you mean," he said, lying. The wind whipped his curly, reddish hair.

Abruptly, she stretched up and kissed him on the mouth, so passionately that he had difficulty pulling away, but finally did so.

Folding her arms across her chest, she said, "I suppose you have this problem with many of your female students, and I'm sorry if I make you uncomfortable, but I've always been direct."

"I'm your professor, that's all." Noah was not entirely surprised by her forwardness, having noticed the way she looked at him seductively with her emerald eyes , and the gentle, alluring tones of her voice whenever she spoke to him. He had been trying to maintain his distance from her, but she must have noticed something in his demeanor, a weakness that she could exploit. He didn't entirely trust her, or any women who used their looks and wiles to lure men. Too many were like Sirens, he thought, enticing men onto dangerous shoals.

His eyes flashed as he looked at her. Despite his misgivings, Noah longed for a closer relationship with her, but fought his emotions, trying to retain his professional demeanor. Other female students had made overtures toward him, and he had always taken the high road, never succumbing to the desires he had felt for them. By avoiding embarrassing and compromising entanglements, he had remained proud of himself. But now, more than ever before, he felt vulnerable.

"You're Anton's girlfriend," Noah said, flatly. He looked away, at the sun dappled trees on the slope below them. "He's like a … younger brother … to me, and I could never consider betraying him."

"I've made no promises to him," she said.

"But I've made promises to myself."

"And I respect that. She moved away a little. Look, I've always been a flirt. I've dated men of many galactic races, have always been a traveler. Maybe you're better off avoiding me."

As Noah led the way on a trail back downhill, he had no inkling of the extent of her travels, that she could actually guide podships on fantastic journeys across the galaxy, that she had already lived for more than seven centuries, and that she was not at all what she appeared to be.

"Are you going to kick me out of school for this?" she asked.

"Of course not. You're an exceptional student. You just need to understand that I have boundaries."

"At least you know I wasn't doing anything to influence my grades," she said with a laugh. "I already have the highest test scores."

He laughed with her, but didn't like what he was feeling. Aside from the professional distance he wanted from his students, he felt what could only be described as a prurient desire for her, and it wasn't right. He was not that sort of a person … at least, he didn't think he was.

As they reached the glax-walled main entrance of the administration building, his adjutant Subi Danvar rushed up, wearing the green-and-brown uniform of the Guardians. "We have a problem," the rotund man said, wiping perspiration from his brow. "Diggers."

"They're on our property?" he asked.

"Southwest corner of the compound," Danvar said. "They came up underneath a maintenance building and tore up the floor pretty bad before diving back into the ground. We lost a lot of equipment. Some of it damaged, and some just disappeared into the hole with them."

"More than one Digger?"

"Three of the mechanical pests. Two big ones and a little one. Like a small family of them."

Nodding, Noah said, "Form an extermination squad to go after them in their burrows."

"It will be done, sir. We have a man who served on one of the Doge's extermination squads before joining us. I'll get his advice."

"Good."

"Can I join the squad?" Tesh asked.

"What?" Noah said. "But you have no experience."

"I'm a fast learner, and it sounds like important work to me."

"What about your studies?" Noah asked.

"To tell you the truth, it's become too easy for me. I need a change of pace, if it's all right with you, sir. Call it penance."

Not understanding what she meant, the adjutant crinkled his brow.

"Just a private joke," Noah said to him. Glancing at the young woman, he told her, "All right. We'll give you extracurricular credit for the work. The machines are tearing up the environment, after all, so it is related to your studies."

* * * * *

The following morning, Anton Glavine was waiting at Noah's office when he arrived for work. With an infusercup of strong coffee in his hand, Noah greeted him, and let him in.

"I want to join the extermination squad, too," Anton announced, as Noah went around and sat at his desk.

"Out of the question. You need to complete your studies."

"So does Tesh. She says you're giving her extracurricular credit for Digger duty."

"That's true, but she's way ahead of you in her lessons, and can afford to take time away from the classroom. You don't have that luxury."

The young man chewed at the blond mustache on his upper lip. "I need to watch out for her, make sure she's safe."

"Tesh can take care of herself."

"I don't agree. This is a new operation." His hazel eyes narrowed. "It's really important to me, Noah. I won't be any good in class at all if you don't let me go."

Noah still had not told Anton who his parents were—Doge Lorenzo and Noah's own sister Francella—but he knew he could not keep the secret forever. Anton was no longer a child, and had a right to know. He was behaving like a man right now, taking responsibility for the woman he cared about, the woman Noah couldn't help caring about himself.

A long period of silence ensued between the men. Finally, Noah said to his nephew, "All right."

Shortly after Anton left his office, Noah received encouraging news from Subi Danvar. The extermination squads used by Doge Lorenzo had developed relatively safe, efficient means of combating the mechanical pests, and had designed their own remote-controlled probes and tunneling machines … equipment that Subi Danvar was purchasing. The adjutant had also been able to hire more experienced men and women to join the squad, and was referring to them as commandos.

"It'll be safer than riding up to EcoStation," Subi assured him.

"I hope you're right," Noah said.

Chapter Thirty-Seven

It is said that God made the Tulyan Starcloud in the image of heaven.
                                        —From The Book of Tulyan Lore

On an orbital pod station, Eshaz stood at the end of a line of passengers, waiting to board a mottled gray-and-black spacecraft. He was returning to the starcloud for a regularly scheduled session of the Council of Elders, to report to them on his travels and activities … a requirement for all of his people who spent time away from home. The passengers included scores of other Tulyans—web caretakers like himself—along with a colorful assortment of galactic races.

Eshaz touched the side of the large, bulging vessel, felt the slight warmth and barely discernible pulse of living tissue. "Hello, old friend," he whispered, thinking back to a halcyon time long ago when Tulyans held dominion over this podship and its brethren.

Now, in direct contact with the creature, Eshaz felt his own thoughts trying to penetrate and read the ancient mind of the podship, in a way that Tulyans could do with members of their own race, and with other galactic races. But this podship was not amenable to having its thoughts read. It was under the control of another entity, another galactic race.

The throb on the thick skin quickened just a little, and then slowed as the podship's tiny but powerful Parvii pilot detected the alien intrusion and warded it off.

Feeling a deep sadness for millions of years past and what could never be recaptured, Eshaz withdrew his hand and moved closer to the stout Huluvian man ahead of him in line. Others joined the queue behind Eshaz. His joints and muscles were aching again, the condition that seemed to run parallel with the decline of Timeweb.

The old Tulyan set his personal discomfort aside. His thoughts drifted off.

Contrary to popular belief, the Mutatis were not the most important shapeshifters in the galaxy. Certainly, they were the most numerous and caused the most trouble, especially for the Humans who were their mortal enemies. But they had a rival in the magical art of appearance modification, a race that was the glue of the galaxy, the podships that provided faster-than-light space travel to everyone at no charge.

Widely considered the greatest mystery in the cosmos, the pods were of uncertain origin and purpose. Even Tulyans, who knew the migration patterns of the whale-like creatures and had the ability to pilot them in ancient times, never discovered the spacefarers' deepest, most profound secrets. Eshaz's people were well aware of their shape-shifting abilities, however, the way the living, sentient Aopoddae were all of a similar blimp shape, but morphed the cellular structures of their interior spaces to provide compartments for passengers, complete with portholes, and even destination boards on the outsides of the hulls. The Tulyans knew, as well, how to reach the sectoid chamber at the core of each podship, where Eshaz's kinsmen used to navigate the spacecraft, but which was now blocked to them by the superior powers of the Parviis.

A hatch opened in the hull of the podship, like a mouth on the side. The line began to move forward, and moments later Eshaz stepped aboard and took a seat on one of the utilitarian dark-gray benches. Looking around, he noted the features of the passenger compartment, the similarities and subtle differences in comparison with other pods … the patterns of gray-and-black streaks and pale yellow veins.

Passengers did not need any form of breathing apparatus, since the interior of the podship had an oxygen and nutrient-rich life support system generated by the mysterious biological workings of the creature—enabling different types of life forms to survive in their confines.

Most of the benches accommodated three passengers, but Eshaz was so large that there was only enough space for one tall, slender Vandurian to sit beside him. The two of them exchanged stiff glances, without words. Strangers usually didn't talk at all during these voyages, and not just because of the shortness of the trips—only a few minutes to traverse vast distances of space. Instead, they were silent to a great extent because of the sense of awe and infinite, cosmic serenity that the podships inspired in their passengers. Some races revered the podships as godlike creatures, or as messengers of the Supreme Being, or even as incarnations of the Supreme Being.

From his seat Eshaz noticed a slight pulsing of the interior wall beside him, and he touched it gently with a bronze, scaly hand, feeling the warm skin of the sentient creature. Again, the vibration quickened when he touched it, but only for a moment. Eshaz liked to think that the podship was trying to reach out to him, longing for the ancient times as much as he was himself.

"So long, old friend," the Tulyan said, withdrawing his hand.

Beside him, the Vandurian scowled and blinked his oversized eyes, but said nothing.

According to Tulyan legend, one day the podships would transport their passengers to an ethereal realm, a place so enchanted that it was beyond words. Eshaz had always tried to visualize what that magical province might look like, and how it would engage his seven senses, but always he returned to the same conundrum. How could that ultimate realm be any more impressive that his own solar system, the Tulyan Starcloud? The possibility seemed unimaginable.

He felt the sentient spacecraft engage with one podway and then another in rapid succession, making course changes in seconds and fractions of seconds. In what seemed like the blink of an eye, Eshaz had traversed a million star systems, and he stepped off onto the pod station orbiting Tulé, the largest planet in his beloved Tulyan Starcloud.

Far below the pod station he saw the immense Council Chamber, an inverted dome that floated above the planet in a hazy, milky sky, illuminated by a pair of weak suns. From the soft golden glow of the chamber, he knew that the Elders were inside, awaiting him. But the news he brought for them was not good this time.

Timeweb—the connective tissue of the entire galaxy—was showing further, ominous signs of disintegration.

Chapter Thirty-Eight

Your enemy is not really defeated as long as he still exists. He can always regroup, gain strength and strike a lethal blow.

—Mutati Saying

In a foul mood, the Zultan Abal Meshdi strolled along an arcade, a circle of arches and columns around the Citadel's grandest, most famous fountain. Morning sunlight played off the cascading water, but even the beauty and serenity of this special place did not calm him. He had affairs of state on his mind, matters to consider away from the clatter and clutter of advisers and attendants.

Inside the deep, aquamarine water of the fountain's pond, twenty hydromutatis swam energetically, whirling and swooping in a traditional water dance while metamorphosing from exotic sea creatures to asexual humanoids with fins and tails. As they concluded the performance, the hydromutatis merged into one large gargantufish—an ancient, exotic life form—and leaped over the fountain with elegant power, landing in water on the other side with hardly a splash.

The Zultan was a terramutati himself, the most common form of his species. This gave him some advantages, but also presented him with a number of challenges. He was not telepathic like hydromutatis, and could not fly like aeromutatis. The three groups were essentially political factions, cooperating as they needed to while constantly competing for business advantages and political offices.

Feeling sudden heat from a medallion that hung around his neck, the Zultan knew that an important message had arrived for him. Since he was not in his throne room, and had prohibited anyone from calling upon him out here where he liked to relax, he knew it had to be something critical. During this time of war, the news could be really bad. It probably was, he decided gloomily, as he watched the gargantufish swim around the pond.

Transmitting a thought signal, he felt the information materialize in his brain, just five concise words:

Earth destroyed by our Demolio

Summoning additional details, a holovideo appeared in the air before the Zultan's eyes, with three-dimensional color and percussive sound. Taken by the heroic Mutati outrider who piloted the doomsday weapon into the planet, cracking it open, the holovideo survived because he transmitted a signal to a Mutati deep-space observation post.

Elation filled Abal Meshdi. Here at last was proof positive that his gallant outriders could get past Human security and destroy one of their most beloved planets, the ancient cradle of their despicable civilization. Prior to its destruction Earth had not sustained much population, having declined over the centuries as people emigrated to other worlds. It had retained symbolic value to the Merchant Prince Alliance, however, and its loss was sure to inflict serious emotional distress on them.

Tears of joy formed in his eyes. He was so proud of the brave Mutati outrider who had completed this suicide mission, submitting to the will of God On-High and permitting himself to be consumed in the detonation of the planet.

We will build a monument to him in this Citadel, the Zultan thought, a fine statue showing him riding the Demolio into the heart of Earth, and the planet shattering.

The image pleased him immensely.

Heroes had stepped forth from the very beginning of the doomsday program, even in the years of the testing process. The outriders—all volunteers from the three factions of Mutati society—understood their collective fate clearly, and it served to energize them, the opportunity to take the ultimate trip to eternal glory. From the outset, the Zultan had received more volunteers than he needed, enabling his officers to select only the best candidates, improving the odds of success.

Many of the volunteers wore Adurian minigyros, which the Zultan distributed in large numbers to the populace, so that they would better understand the decisions he made. The devices made them closer to God On-High, a benefit that the Zultan had thus far concealed from the Adurians, to keep them from raising the price.

The telepathic hydromutatis, who were prohibited from intruding on the Zultan's inner thoughts, seemed to have done so anyway, because they divided again and began to perform a celebratory dance, skimming along the surface of the pond like race boats, then diving and soaring up out of the water into the air and diving back down, in perfect synchronization. Abal Meshdi was actually pleased that they had violated a rule this time, since they were making him feel even better. Perhaps he would not punish them much for their infraction.

Presently, the twenty hydromutatis assumed their natural appearance structures, masses of swimming, fatty tissue with tiny heads. They formed a circle in the water and spun faster and faster until they were a blur and the water churned like a large blender. They were the fastest, most impressive swimmers he had ever seen. But they seemed agitated, undoubtedly because they knew what the Zultan had in mind. They were telepaths after all, and continued their unlawful acts, using their powers to violate the serenity and privacy of his royal thoughts.

From a fatty fold of his body, Abal Meshdi brought forth a black jolong rifle and fired it into the pond, causing the water to run purple. He peppered the fountain with projectiles, then paused. One hydromutati continued to move. It twitched and writhed, and tried to make its way to an edge of the pond.

Meshdi pressed the firing button, but his weapon jammed. With a curse, he attempted to hurl the rifle like a spear, but it flipped over and over in the air. His aim was fortunate, though, because the butt of the rifle hit the hydromutati squarely on the head, knocking brain matter loose and causing the creature to stop moving entirely.

Twenty bodies floated on top of the purple pond now, with fountain spray misting over them. Meshdi thought it was a surprisingly pretty sight, despite the unfortunate circumstances.

The Zultan shook his head in dismay. He didn't like to kill such beautiful, perfect organisms, but they had violated his rules and he could not tolerate that, no matter their intention to help him.

He accepted no excuses from anyone, even if this resulted in political repercussions, the inevitable complaints from hydromutati leaders. Rules were rules, after all.

With that matter resolved for the moment, Meshdi thought about beautiful Mutati planets that had been overrun by aggressive Humans over the centuries, worlds that had ample water, breathable atmospheres, and stable, circular orbits. Aside from their constant business pursuits, the merchant princes invariably targeted the most scenic planets for takeover. In this regard, Humans and Mutatis were similar—they enjoyed picturesque landscapes, seascapes, and mountainscapes.

While Mutatis could adapt to virtually any environment or climate, Abal Meshdi resented having to retreat. Centuries ago, the two races had tried to live side by side, but problems soon ensued. Humans were exceedingly combative, belligerent, and offensive. Even with the aid of anti-allergenic implants, Mutati revulsion against disgusting Humans could not be overcome. There had been numerous battles and wars for control of particular planets and star systems. With inferior technology, the Mutatis were usually beaten back and driven out, and finally sought refuge on planets that were of little interest to Humans.

It had been a long, humiliating journey, harmful to the pride of the Mutati people, but that was about to change. Earth was a first step, and there would be many more.

The Demolio—his doomsday weapon—made that possible. Payback time.

While the Zultan had been thinking of annihilating the Humans, he had wavered a bit recently, since his own son Hari'Adab disagreed with his aggressive approach. Perhaps Meshdi would simply teach the Humans a lesson by killing only a few hundred billion of them and wiping out half their planets.

God On-High will guide me.

Chapter Thirty-Nine

All documents are rooted in falsehood anyway. I only filed my papers that way to protect myself.

—Francella Watanabe, journal notes

On the morning of her scheduled audience with the glorious Doge Lorenzo del Velli, Francella entered the Audience Hall of the Palazzo Magnifico. The tall, redheaded woman carried a sheath of documents under one arm, and found a place to stand in the designated waiting area of the immense marble floor.

It was an intimidating chamber, as large as a prince's villa, with a platinum filigree ceiling towering seven stories overhead. On the walls and ceiling were frescoes depicting Human technology, trade, religion, and science, along with heroic portrayals of the most famous doges in history. At the center of the great room, Lorenzo sat upon a throne carved in the shape of a merchant schooner, typical of the commercial vessels that carried his goods to the farthest reaches of the galaxy, inside the bellies of podships.

For a moment, she caught his gaze, but he didn't smile, as he normally did upon seeing her. He seemed preoccupied, agitated, and looked away....

The peculiar and as yet unexplained destruction of Earth two weeks ago had unsettled Lorenzo's mind, and he really didn't know if he could ever recover from the shock. As a boy, he and his family had gone there on pilgrimages and vacations, and he had always felt roots on that world, strong connections that were unseen but nevertheless existed. Everywhere he went in those days, he learned the ancient histories of the armies and passions that had flowed across the landscapes, the hopes and dreams of mankind that had eventually spread into the rest of the galaxy as they reached for the stars and built spaceships to take them there. In the centuries before the appearance of podships, Humans had settled a dozen solar systems—and had expanded from there with the sudden and mysterious gift of faster-than-light travel.

The podships had been such an unexplained boon to mankind's desires to spread throughout the galaxy. But were they really a boon, after all? Hadn't they brought severe problems as well as benefits? The terrible, never-ending war against the Mutati Kingdom, for one thing, a conflict that had undoubtedly caused the demise of Earth. Humans and Mutatis hadn't even known one another existed until the strange, sentient spaceships brought them together. Was that done by design, to cause a war that would result in the destruction of two civilizations?

Or only one? he thought nervously. *If our enemies were responsible for what happened to Earth, there may be no safe refuge from them in the entire galaxy. How could the Mutatis possibly have accomplished such a terrible thing?*

It galled the greatest prince in the realm that he had to be dependent upon the mute podships, which showed up regularly and performed their tasks day after day, year after year, at no charge. Aside from his suspicions about their intent, it was a failure of Human technology, and a big one, that the mysterious system of space travel could not be figured out and duplicated—or exceeded.

Unaware of the fact that Tulyans controlled podships in ancient times, and Parviis did in modern times, Lorenzo thought that all attempts to capture podships were doomed to failure. He knew of examples in which Humans—and other races that used these creatures for transport—got too aggressive, causing the large pods to react forcefully, shutting their transport systems down and disappearing into space. A decade ago, a squad of Vandurian troops had tried to commandeer one of the podships by force of arms, while riding inside as passengers. None of them survived the attempt, or at least they were never seen again. For a year afterward, the podships refused to provide any transport service to or from Vandurian planets, and then, as if lifting the suspension, the services resumed. All without any explanation or communication of any sort. Just ships showing up or not showing up.

It was all very unsettling, and he wished that the princes and their allies had not grown so dependent on such strange, uncommunicative creatures.

Podships were, without question, *living* organisms. Anyone traveling aboard one sensed a strong presence around him, and felt a faint pulse within the walls. Some passengers even claimed to have seen the vessels change their appearances in small degrees, slight adjustments in the cabins or basic amenities. The process by which the creatures fashioned themselves into spacecraft was not at all understood, nor was it known from where they came. One theory, among many, held that they were cosmic chunks of space debris, each bearing a speck of the soul of God....

With such far-reaching issues on his mind, the gray-haired Doge raised a jeweled tigerhorse scepter to begin the audience session. His attaché, the furry Hibbil Pimyt, guided an old woman to the base of the dais, and then whispered, seemingly to himself. In reality, he was speaking into a comm-unit, transmitting to a receiver implanted in Lorenzo's ear.

"She was your mother's most trusted housekeeper, Takla Shoshobi."

"Nice to see you again, Takla," Lorenzo said, although he didn't recognize her at all, or recall the name.

"I don't wish to waste your valuable time," the crone said in a croaking voice, "I just wanted to thank you for everything you've done for my family."

"Yes, yes, of course. I am pleased that you are here." With a broad smile, he looked around the audience chamber, as if she was just one of many examples of his magnanimity.

"I am the last of my family," she said. "All of the others died in the war, in your prisons, or of starvation in one of your roachrat-infested ghettos."

"My ghettos? I have no *ghettos*!"

"Then why are they called 'lorenzos?'"

The Doge caught Pimyt's gaze. Looking suddenly alarmed, the Hibbil grabbed her by the arm and dragged her away.

"Thanks for nothing!" she shouted. "All of our allegiance to you, all of our sacrifices, and what do you give us in return? Nothing!"

Guards took charge of the struggling, ranting old woman and escorted her out of the chamber.

"That was all staged for your entertainment," Lorenzo exclaimed to the men and women in the chamber, with a twisted smile. "Just a little change of pace to get things going."

Uneasy laughter carried through the great room.

"I'm very sorry," Pimyt whispered over the private communications link. "So terribly sorry. She said she wanted to give you a blessing, and since her credentials were above suspicion, I thought it would be all right. Of course, I should have known that no one is above suspicion. It won't happen again, Sire."

Lorenzo the Magnificent rolled his eyes, but actually felt pleased with himself for the way he had handled the situation. Leadership was like that. He had to respond to unexpected problems, always maintaining his composure and never allowing the bubble to burst, never permitting his subjects to see through the barriers he had set up.

For the rest of the morning, he conducted a typical audience session, responding to commoners and dignitaries as they come to him with requests. He granted and denied favors with a wave of his tigerhorse scepter, and finally gazed down upon the last person—Francella Watanabe. According to her appointment summary, she had estate documents for his review and approval. She handed them to Pimyt, and he scurried up the stairs of the dais with them.

Looking over the estate papers, Lorenzo said, "I'm very sorry about the death of your father, the eminent Prince Saito. He was a great man, one of the beacons of the Alliance."

Murmurings of concurrence passed through the chamber.

"Thank you, My Lord," Francella said, with a pretty smile.

The Doge pretended to read the papers in detail, although he had already reviewed them beforehand. A commoner by birth, she was applying to be made a Princess of the Realm, which the Doge could grant to important families. With her father gone, as she stated in the papers, she was the logical person to be elevated in status. To support her case, she included a certified copy of Prince Saito's will, which had already been filed and probated. He had bequeathed everything to her and nothing to her twin brother. Additional documents showed that he had formally disinherited Noah.

Asking her a few official-sounding questions, Lorenzo nodded solemnly at her answers. The two of them had known each other for years, on the most intimate basis. She was an attractive, statuesque woman, and as she addressed him, the womanizing Doge found himself increasingly captivated by the comeliness of her figure and her dark brown eyes.

For several minutes, they engaged in a formal discussion for the sake of the onlookers, but her submission was a fait accompli. Finally, waving aside the whispered concerns of his attaché, Pimyt, he openly invited her to his private chamber to discuss the matter further. There, they pulled one another's clothes off and made love, as they had done so many times before.

Then, while the scheming woman was dressing, Lorenzo summoned Pimyt, and formally approved her documents, making her a Princess of the Realm.

In reality, even though Saito Watanabe told many people that he had disowned his son, he had never actually completed the necessary documents, hoping that he and Noah would reconcile one day. Without the Doge's knowledge, Francella had brought forged estate papers with her.

In the actual documents, which she had destroyed, Prince Saito had left half of his estate to his son.

Chapter Forty

A secret is never meant to be kept. It is always trying to break out of the box confining it.

—Graffiti, Gaol of Brimrock

The shuttle trip down to the surface of the Mutati homeworld would take longer than his entire cross-space journey to the Paradij pod station, covering millions of parsecs. This seemed incongruous to Giovanni Nehr, but it was the reality nonetheless. Hyper-fast podships were one of the greatest mysteries in the universe, but he had another one with him, in the heavy parcel he carried under his arm.

Boarding the shuttle, he was confronted by two Mutati guards, their large, pulpy bodies draped in black uniforms. They ran the yellow beam of a scanner over his body and the package, to make certain he wasn't carrying anything dangerous.

During the procedure, Gio smiled confidently. In reality, he *was* carrying something explosive—but not in the usual sense of the word. Speaking to them in common Galeng, he provided his name and demanded to see the Zultan Abal Meshdi himself.

Surprised, the guards laughed, a peculiar squeaky sound. "Our Zultan?" one of them said. "Don't you know he hunts down your kind and tortures them?"

"Tell him I am Giovanni Nehr, brother of Jacopo Nehr, inventor of the nehrcom. You are familiar with that device?"

The guards looked at him stupidly.

"Just tell him I'm a very important person," Gio added.

"Our scanner shows you are carrying rocks," the shorter of the guards said. "Are they pretty stones?"

"Oh yes, pretty stones for your Zultan. He will like them."

The taller guard reached out and was about to touch the parcel, when he started to sneeze and sniffle. His companion's eyes began to water, and he coughed.

In proximity to the Human, both guards were becoming uncomfortable, not having bothered to wear implanted allergy protectors near their own homeworld. Their small fleshy faces reddened and they stepped back, taking seats on the shuttle as far away from Gio as possible. There were no other passengers.

"What sort of a fool are you?" the taller of the guards asked, eyeing him with contempt. His large eyes had become purple-veined and watery.

"A *Human* fool," his companion answered. He sniffled and laughed, then sneezed.

After the shuttle landed, four guards replaced the initial pair. Staying as far away from Giovanni as possible, they took him by groundjet to the imposing Citadel.

After a careful security screening and a check of his identity documents, the visitor was escorted through a long portico and then into a maze of interior corridors and lifts that took them to one of the upper levels of the Citadel. The parcel was carried by a guard, who put gloves on before touching it. As Gio's escort of Mutati men sniffled, sneezed, and wiped tears from their eyes, they spoke to him in Galeng.

"Are you brave or just crazy?" one asked.

"Perhaps both," came the reply.

"You are fortunate that the Zultan has consented to see you. As the brother of the nehrcom inventor, you are an important person in the Merchant Prince Alliance."

"Ah, so you know what a nehrcom is?" Gio asked.

"I've heard of it," the guard said, although he did not elaborate.

Ahead of them, two immense doors carved with space battle scenes swung open, revealing a glittering audience hall beyond. An immense Mutati in a jeweled golden robe sat in the center, on a high throne. Curiously, he had some sort of a blue bubble attached to his forehead, a device with internal workings that bathed his face in spinning circles of multicolored light.

Gio took a deep breath, for this had to be the Zultan Abal Meshdi himself. As Gio approached, the Mutati removed the bubble device and handed it to an attendant. With a scowl on his face, the Zultan stared down silently at his visitor as if observing every detail, absorbing information without words.

The hall was nearly empty, except for a few attendants around the perimeter. Gio noticed a hairless alien standing off to one side as well, and judged him to be an Adurian, a race that was said to be allied with the Mutatis. This one wore a black suit and a white cape, and he had a number of colorful caste markings on his face and forearms.

"Greetings, bold Human," the Zultan said. "You have a gift for me? I like gifts."

The guards halted Gio at the base of the throne. He felt very small in this immense chamber, like a tiny child in the midst of the oversized Mutatis and furnishings.

Looking up, he bowed and said, "Your Eminence, I bring a gift for all of your people, not just for you personally."

"What?" He looked displeased. "Not for me personally, you say?"

"Of course, you don't have to share it if you don't want to," Gio added hastily. He glanced sidelong at the parcel held by one of the guards.

"What sort of strange offering do you bring?" Meshdi demanded.

"Unlike anything you have ever seen. It will enable your great kingdom to compete with the Merchant Prince Alliance."

From his quivering, pulsating mound of fat, the Zultan sneezed and then responded huffily. "What makes you think we wish to *compete* with our inferiors?" Surveying the fearless Human, he added, "Nonetheless, what is your gift? If it is a good one, I will be pleased."

At a signal from the Zultan, the guard stepped up to the throne, and handed him the parcel.

Meshdi examined the package, turning it over and over without opening it. "The scanner report says that there are rocks inside," he said, with a sly expression. "I think you have rocks in your head, too."

The Adurian, having moved closer for a better view, snickered.

"I have not brought you common rocks, Your Eminence." Gio motioned. "Please, open your gift."

Beaming like a fat child, the Zultan tore off the plaxene wrapping, then lifted the lid of a box inside. A wash of green light startled him, and he almost dropped everything.

The guards clicked their weapons, but Meshdi waved them off.

"Jewels?" he exclaimed, looking at them with his eyes wide. "These glitter in ways I have never seen before." He selected one of the small green gems and held it up to the light. A peculiar fascination filled his face.

"You hold in your hand a great military secret," Gio said, "the secret of the nehrcom transceiver, sometimes referred to as the Nehr Cannon."

With a perplexed expression, the Mutati asked, "Instantaneous communication across space? This is the secret?"

"It is."

He looked confused, but his dark eyes glinted with pleasure. "But how does it work?" He put the gem back in the box, picked up another.

Having penetrated his brother's computer system to learn the secret of the cross-space transmission device, Gio began to spew forth information, telling how to cut the rare stones and align them for perfect transmission, holding nothing back. He knew it was foolhardy to do this, and perhaps even suicidal, but he didn't care. After working closely with his brother, and seeing the decadence and debauchery of the merchant princes, Gio had decided it was only a matter of time before the determined Mutatis defeated them, and he wanted to be on the winning side. Even if he never saw that day and these shapeshifters put him to death, he would go to his grave knowing he had knocked the arrogant Jacopo Nehr off his pedestal.

The transmitter wasn't really a cannon at all, Gio announced. The term "Nehr Cannon" was merely selected to confuse and misdirect the curious. He even told the Zultan how to mine for the deep-shaft piezoelectric emeralds, and that they could be found on a number of planets around the galaxy, including some that had no military defenses. He provided a list.

Finally, Giovanni Nehr fell silent.

"Is that all you know?" the Zultan inquired.

"It is, Majesty."

"Then of what use are you to me anymore?"

"I assumed you would be grateful." Feeling a surge of unexpected panic, he added a lie: "Besides, my expertise will still be needed to perfect your own galactic communication system, to work out any problems that you are bound to encounter."

"But if you betrayed your own people—including your own brother—we cannot trust you, either. Your disloyalty marks you as dangerous and unreliable. If what you have said is true—and we recorded all of it—we have scientists capable of replicating the nehrcom transceiver and dealing with problems. We don't need you."

"But I brought you a gift! You should be grateful!"

"You said yourself that it was not for me personally, that it was for my people. Thus, you committed a social gaffe, an unforgivable faux pas in our culture." His large eyes narrowed. "You should have researched more carefully."

With a cruel smile, Abal Meshdi motioned for the guards to take the sputtering, suddenly terrified man away. "Foolish Human, you will not live long enough to learn how to bargain."

* * * * *

Under tight security, Gio was taken to a prison moon orbiting the planet Dij. He recognized the name the moment he heard it. This was one of the worlds stripped of all resources and abandoned by the Merchant Prince Alliance.

He did not know, however, that on the surface of Dij, under the direction of Hari'Adab Meshdi—the Emir and eldest son of the Zultan—planet-busting Demolio torpedoes were being constructed.

Chapter Forty-One

Disaster—and salvation—usually come from unexpected sources.
—Data Banks, sentient machine repository

A polyglax bubble stood in the middle of a circle of standing noblemen, all dressed in jerkins, capes, and liripipe hats. Inside the clear enclosure—a combat rink—a pair of crimson eagles fluttered and ripped at each other with beaks and talons, powerful birds shrieking and tearing each other to shreds, spattering blood on the bubble's interior. Their wings had been cropped, so that they could not fly.

"Kill him!" one of the men shouted, his voice hardly rising above the noise of the birds.

"Rip his heart out!" another shouted.

As the birds gouged each other, making feathers fly, spectators threw merchant prince liras and platinum coins in a wide dish on top of the bubble, making bets and raising them or dropping out of the game, depending on the progress of their feathered champions.

Lorenzo del Velli had placed a wager on the larger bird, but it was losing to its smaller, faster, competitor. The Doge was not pleased, but still was not yet ready to give up. With a scowl, he threw more money on the pile. It was late evening, and he was in the illuminated courtyard of his Palazzo Magnifico, with young members of his royal court. Around them, most of the lights in the palace were out.

He liked to associate with people much younger than he was. They gave him energy, almost making him forget what an old man he was becoming. Even with all of his wealth—no prince had more money—he could not slow the advances of age. Time was like a thief, and a sneaky one at that, taking what rightfully belonged to him when he was unaware, moment by moment.

And unknown to him, another time thief lurked in the shadows behind shrubbery, looking on....

* * * * *

In all of the realm of the merchant princes, there was perhaps no more loyal robot than Jimu. This had something to do with his original programming, since all MPA robots were programmed to be loyal to their Human creators. But it had even more to do with his sentient character, which he had developed on his own, through devotion and hard work.

As a robot, Jimu had been maltreated by Humans for decades. They had always overworked him and kept him going with whatever parts they could lay their hands on, no matter how that decreased his operating abilities. His Human masters could have installed new program modules in him, or the latest grappling arms, but had not bothered to do so. They just kept cobbling him together while awaiting new automaton models, always intending to replace him. But Jimu fooled them.

By the force of his personality, his dogged determination and will to survive, he had basically maintained himself, locating or rebuilding his own parts, all the while remaining cheerful and making himself useful. In his machine unit he had risen to the rank of a noncommissioned officer—a duty sergeant—but still people spoke constantly of getting rid of him in favor of a newer, more efficient model.

Several times Jimu had felt the end was near, especially during the Battle of Irriga years ago, when his undercarriage was shot out from under him. Thinking he was useless, soldiers dumped his mangled metal body in a pile of scraps and forgot about him. But he still had his upper body and backup battery pack, and managed to pull himself around until he found another machine with the parts he needed. Within hours, he put himself back together and reported for duty.

That created quite a stir in the ranks of Humans, and the soldiers took him on as a mascot, symbolizing the fighting spirit of their unit. They promoted him to Captain of Machines—a rank that put him in charge of six thousand other robots. For a while, Jimu felt basically invulnerable, as the soldiers maintained him passably well, even knocking out some of his dents and polishing him up. But personalities changed around him as his military friends moved on to other assignments, and one day Jimu again felt forgotten, and had to fend for himself with new troops, who didn't know his personal story or care about him.

But he hadn't blamed them for that. Humans were Humans and machines were only machines, even with the enhancement of sentient programming. Machines would not exist at all if not for the inventive, godlike spark of the Human minds that designed and built them in the first place.

Of all living Humans, Jimu felt that the Doge Lorenzo most deserved his loyalty and dedication, since that nobleman was the titular head of the revered Humans, the prince who was so admired by his peers that they elevated him to the highest station in the galaxy.

So it was that Jimu and his force of twenty fighting robots, having come all the way from the Inn of the White Sun to serve the Doge, found themselves watching the eagles fight, or more precisely, watching over Lorenzo to make certain he was safe.

Brian Herbert

Several days ago, Jimu had marched up to one of the palazzo guard stations and stated his business to the Red Beret soldier on duty there. "I'm here to warn the Doge that people intend to harm him," Jimu had said.

The soldier had taken one look at him, with his dented, scraped body and glowing yellow eyes, and he cut loose with a belly laugh. Then, looking closely at the rest of the patched-up robots who had accompanied Jimu, he laughed even more.

Jimu had not taken offense, for he'd seen Humans like this before, the shallow types who made judgments based upon appearances. It was one of the biggest weaknesses of human nature, their inability to avoid superficiality, but he forgave them for it.

"The Doge is in great danger," Jimu said.

"And I suppose you're here to protect him?"

"If necessary, yes."

More guards came over, weapons at the ready. They stood around, smirking, laughing, and hurling insults at the visitor. "You and your pals look like zombie robots," one said. "Who dug you up?"

"Zombiebots," another said. And they laughed uproariously.

Jimu didn't respond to any of those insults, for they had nothing to do with his mission. He and his companions concealed their own weaponry within compartments on their metal bodies, and he knew he could easily overwhelm these fools and enter the palazzo. But that would only cause more Red Berets to come, and a wild battle would ensue. No, that would never do.

"I can see you do not understand," Jimu finally said. "There is nothing more for me to do here." With that, he turned and departed, and took his odd little squadron with him.

But the following morning, Jimu and his robots got into the palazzo anyway. Having put the royal home under observation, he knew that household robots ran errands, getting food and other supplies. In an alley behind one of the markets, Jimu had cornered one of the robots and then interfaced with it, programming it to open a servant's door later that night.

Normally this would not have been possible, since all of the Doge's robots had built-in security measures that prevented tampering. After General Sajak shot Jimu, however, the servants who reactivated him accidentally tapped into a deep data transmission zip that had been installed by the Hibbils. This opened up programs to Jimu that he had not previously realized he had. Later, after Thinker had him overhauled, Jimu found that he functioned with new mental acuity, beyond any of the programs installed in ordinary robots. That superior knowledge had enabled him to easily bypass the security barriers of the Doge's household robot.

Thus the entire squadron got in, and they set up clandestine positions around the palazzo....

For days and nights afterward, without any break, Jimu and his squad concealed themselves carefully around the royal palazzo, their powerful puissant rifles at the ready, weapons that had been hidden inside their motley assortment of mechanical bodies....

Now they stood on balconies and rooftops, looking down on the courtyard, at the boisterous activities of the Doge and his royal companions. The Humans were getting louder as they gambled and drank.

Suddenly, in the shadows below, Jimu saw a hunched-over man run between bushes, moving from the concealment of one to another. Then he saw three more hunched-over shapes, doing the same.

He sent an electronic signal to his companions, cocked his own rifle. Around him, he heard the faint buzzing of their activated weapons.

The robots fired in synchronization, lighting the shrubbery on fire with powerful blasts, making flares out of all of the bushes around the perimeter of the courtyard. Simultaneously, half of the robot force surged into the courtyard from the lower level.

Men shouted and scattered on the flagstones. The fighting eagles got loose, but with their cropped wings they could only fly a few feet off the ground before crashing into someone and flopping onto the courtyard. Blood and feathers filled the air.

In the melee, four hooded, black figures emerged from their hiding places and tried to flee, firing handguns at robots that pursued them. But the robots were not deterred, and knocked them onto the flagstones, then snapped restraint cables on them.

Jimu hurried down to the courtyard, which was illuminated by the crackling, burning bushes. The palace staff rushed forward to douse water on the flames, keeping them from catching the buildings on fire. Under Jimu's watchful gaze, the robots removed hoods from the captives. He recognized one of them, and so did the noblemen gathering around.

"You!" Doge Lorenzo shouted. "General Sajak, why are you dressed like that?"

"Some things are best not delegated," Sajak said, with a sneer. "I wanted to do this job myself."

Dragging the small, slender man to his feet, Jimu said, "He intended to assassinate you."

"Is that true?" Lorenzo asked.

The General smiled. His eyes burned with hatred.

Searching his data banks, Jimu said, "He doesn't like your politics, Doge Lorenzo, and feels that only noble-born princes should hold high office—not entrepreneurs and inventors."

Moments later, Lorenzo was surrounded by his special police, the Red Berets. They were heavily armed men in red uniforms and floppy caps.

"And where were you when I needed you?" the Doge asked, of the squad leader.

The uniformed man looked embarrassed.

"These robots saved my hide," Lorenzo said, patting Jimu on his metal backside. "Maybe you should give them your uniforms."

"I'm sorry, sir," the squad leader said. "We didn't expect any problems from your royal court, and General Sajak must have used his security clearance to get through. This was totally unexpected."

"Then why were these robots on alert? Are they smarter than you?"

"I'm sorry, Doge Lorenzo. It won't happen again."

"With all due respect, Sire," Jimu said, "Your household security could use considerable improvement." He told how he had waylaid a household robot and reprogrammed it to allow him to gain access to the palazzo, and how he had originally learned of the assassination plot at the lava lake on one of the moons of Timian One. He provided as many names as he knew, including that of Prince Giancarlo Paggatini, the nobleman who organized the secret meetings of General Sajak and his conspirators.

"The way you got in here is very interesting," Lorenzo said. "And quite disturbing. Fortunately for me, you're not one of their agents."

With a gesture at the Red Beret squad leader, the Doge barked, "Go! Get out of my sight, all of you! Take Sajak and his goons with you. The arrogant fool! He wanted to kill me himself. You are to interrogate them, and I mean *interrogate*. Find out everything. See who's involved in the conspiracy. I want every name."

"It will be done, sir."

Like whipped daggs, the Red Berets left, handling the men in black roughly. Despite their shortcomings, Jimu knew that the special police were a fierce bunch, highly motivated and dedicated in their own way. An ancient law enforcement group, they had their own secret rituals, language, and symbols. If anyone could get the answers Lorenzo wanted, they could.

"Come with me, robots," Lorenzo said. "I'm going to show you how to bet on an eagle fight." With that, he put his arm around Jimu's rounded shoulders, and led him back to the bubble enclosure. Fresh eagles were brought in, and the entertainment resumed.

Chapter Forty-Two

Infinity beckons.

—Parvii Inspiration

Perched inside the core of the most unusual biological organism in the galaxy, the tiny man noticed a hesitation in the sentient spacecraft. He had just established a course, but the podship had not yet responded.

Seconds passed. This had never happened to him before. By now, they should be speeding along the podways, racing past star systems, bound for the farthest regions of the galaxy.

The diminutive Parvii pilot required no food or water for sustenance, and none of the other nutrients commonly needed by the galactic races. And, while the various chambers of the large podship contained an ample supply of oxygen, the pilot didn't require any. He could fly free in the vacuum of space, and in a swarm with other members of his race could reach tremendous speeds.

Until moments ago, Woldn had been in total control of the podship, having captured and tamed it with millions of his miniature followers, who subsequently departed for other duties. They were like wranglers of wild tigerhorses, and Woldn was the most skilled of them all. He was the Eye of the Swarm, commanding decillions of Parviis, an entire galactic race. Now he was performing a task he normally delegated, in order to keep his piloting and navigation skills sharp.

Finally, Woldn felt the great ship shudder into motion and accelerate.

In its wordless way, the podship was communicating with him, sending a stream of messages that filled Woldn's brain. Through the sentient creature's far-reaching eyes—indiscernible cells all over the outside of its body—Woldn peered deep with the podship, into the curving green webs of time and space.

Way off in the distance and directly ahead, an orange light flashed.

The blimp-shaped podship—carrying a variety of galactic races in its passenger compartment and cargo hold—accelerated onto the web on a new course, wrenching command away from the Parvii leader, though he struggled mightily, invoking the most severe guidance-and-control words in his repertoire. Mysteriously, his efforts were to no avail.

Within minutes, the spacecraft slowed near a debris field and circled it at a safe distance. Through the mind he shared with the pod, Woldn felt a tremendous sense of loss because a podship had just died here, along with its Parvii pilot.

Most unusual, a Parvii death here, and he'd received no signal of distress along the telepathic connections he maintained with all of his people, stretching across the entire galaxy. This suggested to him that there had either been a psychic breakdown, which occurred occasionally, or that the violent event had been so sudden and unexpected that the pilot had not had time to send a signal.

Woldn got his bearings and figured out where he was … and what was missing. A planet had exploded, a world the Humans called Mars. Within moments, he saw other podships approach and circle nearby, with Parviis inside their sectoid control chambers, helpless to control the spacecraft, trying to comprehend. This was the same solar system where an earlier explosion had occurred, the one that took Earth with it.

Both planets and their inhabitants had been dispatched to oblivion, their remnants scattered in space.

Was something wrong in this sector, causing a natural disaster—or could there be another explanation? Woldn would return to his people, and order a full investigation.…

Chapter Forty-Three

Our young must always learn the most important lessons of life firsthand. It has been this way since time immemorial, and always will be.

—Mutati Observation

Two of the passengers on board Woldn's podship were Acey Zelk and Dux Hannah, the teenage Humans who had escaped from Timian One. Crowded with others at the membranous portholes, they saw a large debris field outside.

"Where are we?" Acey asked, as he and Dux tried to maintain their spot by a porthole, while an assortment of creatures pushed for better views.

"I have no idea," Dux said.

With difficulty the boys held their position. Only a small percentage of the passengers were Human, or even humanoid. In close proximity to so many different races, Dux picked up odors he'd never experienced before. Not all of the smells were unpleasant, though some certainly were. He also picked up a musk odor from the skin of the podship.

A pale-skinned Kichi woman beside them gasped as body parts floated by, most of them Human … arms, legs, and heads with crusts of blood frozen on them. One completely intact body drifted into view, a young woman fully clothed in layers of unsoiled skirts, her face frozen in a broad smile, as if someone had pulled her picture out of a photo album and put a three-dimensional form to it. She showed no signs of trauma, which seemed remarkable to Dux in view of the obvious violence that had occurred here. He wondered what could possibly have caused such a catastrophe.

"Might have been a merchant prince planet," a man said.

"It was," another said. Dux saw a Jimlat man standing taller than the throng, his blockish head shaved. Blinking his tiny gray eyes, the Jimlat studied a brassplax instrument. "They called it Mars."

"Mars?" Dux said. "Then it's completely gone, destroyed?"

"That'd be my bet. Course, some of it remains." With a facetious smile, he nodded toward the nearest porthole. "Out there."

"Maybe you'd like me to climb up there are rearrange your ugly face," Acey said, making a move toward him.

Dux grabbed his cousin's arm to restrain him. "What are his fighting capabilities?" Dux asked in a low tone.

"If you let go of me, I'll find out."

"Don't chance it. We don't need to look for trouble." He looked around, at the hostile gazes of some of the aliens, and their gleaming eyes. Obviously, they wanted to see a fight, and probably didn't care if Acey got hurt … or worse. A number of races around the galaxy resented Humans for the financial and military successes of the merchant princes, so the young men had to be on constant alert for potential trouble. Acey lost his temper too much, didn't always think through the consequences of his actions.

Hearing a thump beside him, Dux looked at the porthole, and recoiled in horror. A little Huluvian girl screamed, and was consoled by her mother. The bloody face of a man bobbed against the outside of the window, seeming to stare into the passenger compartment. The face, and its torn body, drifted away.

The podship, still moving slowly, proceeded through the shocking milieu, passing floating fragments of what had once been a vibrant world on one of the main merchant prince trading routes. Machine parts, building fragments, and many shredded body parts, some of them so small that they must have belonged to children. Dux could hardly bear to look any more but did nonetheless, in horrified fascination. Around him, hardly anyone spoke anymore. Most of the noises were sobbing sounds, and whimpering cries of disbelief, even from non-Humans. An alien in a business suit said the planet must have been hit by a meteor, and several onlookers agreed.

After only a few minutes that seemed like an eternity, the podship changed course. It headed away from the debris field and picked up speed. Soon they flashed by star systems, spiral nebulas, and glowing asteroid belts. For a fraction of a second, a comet seemed to try to keep up with them, then fell back.

The podship resumed a normal route, making its regular stops, as shown on route boards at both ends of the passenger compartment. Some of the passengers moved away from the windows, but many remained standing, numb with shock. Along the way, the various races disembarked, and others got aboard. Odors changed. Dialects drifted through the cabin. New passengers heard the terrible news about Mars, and no one understood what could have happened.

Finally the boys disembarked at Nui-Lin in a remote sector of the galaxy, an exotic world they had heard about in their travels, where they hoped to secure jobs. They had with them the address of a residential construction project where the pay was said to be excellent, and the name of a man who had put out a call for workers.

The shuttle was unlike any they had seen before, resembling a broad green leaf with a tiny bubble of a cabin on the underside. The craft descended, and when it reached the atmosphere the engines shut off and it drifted down, landing gently on the black pavement of a spaceport.

The terminal building abutted a thick jungle, draped with vines. They caught a jitney driven by a long-eared Cogg, one of the natives of this world. They told him where they wanted to go, as did many the other passengers as they boarded, and he promised to let the new riders know when he reached their various destinations.

He was not a very good driver, though, or didn't seem able to talk and drive at the same time, as he insisted on delivering a monologue about the various types of flora and fauna as he sped past them. Some of them he scraped with the vehicle, and once he very nearly drove off a precipice into a tree-choked crevasse. Those passengers who were Coggs didn't show any fear, but other races were on the edges of their seats, and some demanded to get off. Ignoring their pleas, the driver refused to stop. In some places a thick canopy of trees overhung the road, creating a tunnel effect that required him to turn on a bright headlamp.

They passed through a town that looked like a village in a fairy tale, with narrow cobblestone streets and quaint homes that were not constructed entirely straight, or which had fallen into a pattern of leaning to one side or the other for what might have been centuries. The majority of the Coggs and the most fearful foreigners got out in the town, and then the jitney continued on its way, along a narrow highway that skirted a silvery sea. Immense birds soared out over the water, with sunlight glinting off their golden wings, making the birds look as if they were really built out of gold, and should be too heavy to fly.

The driver kept chattering, babbling like a tour guide. Then he began talking about galactic politics, and his comments about the Merchant Prince Alliance were less than complimentary. This surprised Dux, since Coggs were supposedly neutral. He shrugged. This must be an oddball, an eccentric fellow who was out of step with his people.

"This is it," the driver announced, as he pulled levers on the dashboard to squeak the bus to a stop. Carrying their bags, Acey and Dux stepped off at a narrow path, which the driver told them to take. "The construction site is just a short distance," he said, pointing toward a cluster of one-story buildings in a clearing.

The boys found signs written in the common galactic language of Galeng, telling them where to report to apply for work. Inside a large, open-walled hut, they located the very Cogg whose name they had been given far across the galaxy, Bibby Greer. As the long-eared work supervisor introduced himself to them and shook their hands, he smiled in such a friendly fashion that Dux thought he would be the best boss they ever had. He could not have been more wrong. The experience would, in fact, be exactly the opposite.

Suddenly the tentacles of a plant darted in through the open walls and wrapped themselves around the boys, so that they could not escape. Before their eyes, the Cogg metamorphosed into a tremulous mound of fat, with a tiny head and oversized eyes. A Mutati!

Dux felt a sinking sensation.

"Welcome to our fly trap," Bibby Greer announced with a nasty grin.

Chapter Forty-Four

It as if the entire galaxy is being sucked downward, into the black void of the undergalaxy. Is there life in that Stygian realm? I shudder to imagine it.

—Eshaz, Remarks to the Council

T he green-and-brown groundjet sped across a broad meadow of flowers, passing over the plants like a windless whisper, not disturbing them at all. This was a specially modified craft that Noah had ordered, with hover capabilities that could be activated when going over sensitive environmental areas.

"It is good to see you back," Noah said to Eshaz, who sat beside him in the passenger seat, his large body overflowing the chair and draping off the sides. Noah piloted the machine. "I trust you had a pleasant visit with your Elders?"

"Oh, the Tulyan Starcloud is the most wondrous place in all of creation," he replied, "and my people are the most pleasant to be around. No offense to present company, of course."

"I understand. There's no place like home, the old saying goes."

"How true it is."

"Your people are pacifists, aren't they?"

"We pride ourselves on non-violence, but I would not go so far as to say that we are complete pacifists. We do not claim to be perfect, only that we strive to be so. We are not political in any way. Tulyans try to go about their daily lives peacefully while contributing to their environs, instead of detracting from them."

"The peaceful nature of Tulyans explains why it must be so nice to be with them on the Starcloud. I can't visualize a single argument there. It must be total bliss, almost a fantasy land."

"Well, we do have rather heated discussions, but for the most part you're not far off." Eshaz smiled, but to Noah it seemed forced.

Noah steered toward a maintenance building at the southwest corner of his compound. Diggers had torn through the floor of the building, creating a lot of damage. Subi Danvar and the commando team he had organized were using this as a staging area to launch extermination efforts, and over the weeks they had experienced some success against the renegade machines.

"I would like to see the Tulyan Starcloud someday," Noah said, as he had on occasion before. "I know, you said how rare it is for outsiders to be permitted there, but perhaps you could mention my name to the Elders as a possibility."

"I already have," Eshaz said with a decidedly pained expression. "Perhaps someday we can do it, my friend."

It seemed to Noah that his trusted companion was sadder than he should be, that his demeanor did not match his words. Perhaps he was just tired. This Tulyan was quite an old fellow, after all. Noah wasn't certain exactly how old, and Eshaz always shunted such questions aside, but he thought it might be around a hundred or more standard years of age. With no idea how much of a colossal underestimation this was, Noah worried about the health of the old fellow.

Eshaz was a valued contributor to the Ecological Demonstration Project on Canopa and had helped with a number of planetary recovery operations around the galaxy. He always seemed to know more about local environments than anyone, and gave advice about exactly what would work best—from flora to fauna to geology. But he was also a man of secrets, as were the other Tulyans who worked for Noah. They liked to spend a lot of time by themselves, wandering around planets and communing with nature in their arcane ways.

As Noah drew near the maintenance building, he noticed new holes in the ground beyond the structure, gaping excavations that he was certain his own people had not made. "Looks like more trouble here," he said, as he brought the groundjet to a stop near a team of his uniformed Guardians. He recognized Subi Danvar, Tesh Kori, and Anton Glavine.

"There is trouble everywhere," Eshaz said.

With a nod, but not totally understanding what he meant, Noah stepped out. The two of them went their separate ways.

* * * * *

Taking a walk through the nearby woods, Eshaz contemplated the troubles he had seen, and the troubles that he saw coming.

The meeting with the Council of Elders had gone much more poorly than he had anticipated, even considering the bad news that he brought to them. As it turned out, he was not the only caretaker of Timeweb to report an acceleration of problems they had noticed earlier, an increasingly serious deterioration of the vital strands holding the galaxy together. The situation had, in fact, reached crisis proportions.

Upon entering the inverted dome of the Council Chamber for the regularly scheduled meeting, Eshaz had found himself in a raucous throng of his peers, all clamoring to tell their stories. While he had observed serious damage himself, the most grave report of all came from Ildawk, who described a complete web collapse in the Huluvian Sector, and the disappearance of two entire solar systems with it, decimating the Huluvian race.

Listening solemnly, the Elders had absorbed the information and conferred among themselves. First Elder Kre'n, a broad-necked female who was the head of the Council, then made a solemn pronouncement:

"All of you must redouble your efforts, or soon the galaxy will reach a state of critical mass, where the deterioration cannot be reversed."

Turning to Eshaz, who stood at the front of the throng of caretakers, Kre'n then said, "Tell us what you see."

Most Tulyans were prescient, with an ability to peer into paranormal realms, even into other time periods—and Eshaz was among the best with this ability. It gave him special value, but he didn't like to use the talent. Often, it upset him too much.

Feeling exasperated, he closed his heavy-lidded eyes and peered into the time continuum of the cosmos, but saw nothing this time, not even a flicker of activity. Was that a foretelling in itself, an indication of what was to come? Utter, motionless blackness?

With a shudder, Eshaz opened his eyes. Standing before his superiors, he shook his bronze-scaled head and said, "I see nothing, First Elder. There is too much disturbance in the galaxy. It is blocking me."

In a sense, this excuse was true, but not completely. He strongly suspected something else was interfering, a personal failure.

Kre'n nodded. "So it is. So it must be."

The other Elders nodded, and whispered among themselves. Normally stoic, they were showing signs of emotion this time. He heard a sad edge to Kre'n's voice, as if in realization that the end of the galaxy might be approaching. He saw worried glints in the eyes of these ancients, slight frowns on their faces.

In the past Eshaz had predicted the emergence of black holes, of suns going nova, and of gas giant planets erupting. Now, however, he felt useless, and angry with himself. He was beginning to wonder if it was not a cosmic disturbance at all, but was instead his own increasing stress, causing him to lose his timeseeing ability at a moment when he—and his people—most needed it. He felt as if he was letting them down, as if he was letting all of the galactic races down. Life ... so fragile, and his own abilities were disintegrating. Almost everywhere, Timeweb was crumbling.

A possibility occurred to him. There had been no signs of web deterioration anywhere near his beloved Tulyan Starcloud, so he wondered if that sector of the galaxy could possibly be spared.

What will become of my people? he wondered, *if our sector is spared and we have nothing left to caretake?*

The twenty old women and men of the Council were the foremost web masters in the galaxy, Tulyans who were ancient and sagacious when Eshaz was born almost a million standard years ago. The Elders knew so much more than he did about the galaxy—it was like his own knowledge in comparison with that of the most enlightened Human ... Noah Watanabe, for example. The differences were so great that there was no fair comparison, and in his own limited state Eshaz could only defer to these ancient Tulyans, and hope he would himself become as wise and revered one day.

For that to happen, though, the galaxy needed to survive. And at the moment, the prospects for that did not look good at all....

Having made his report to the wise old Tulyans, Eshaz was back on Canopa now, working with Noah and his Guardians. The Council of Elders had ordered Eshaz and all other web caretakers to amplify their ecological preservation efforts, and now they were to report more frequently than before. Because of the ominous signs noted by Eshaz and his peers in the field, the Council had also decided to dispatch more caretaker observers around the galaxy. They would serve under various guises, because Tulyans were not permitted to tell other races what they were doing, not even ecologically conscious individuals such as Noah Watanabe. No one but a Tulyan could possibly understand the enormity of the responsibilities they had.

"We are a race of givers," Kre'n said once, "while the other races are takers, users, destroyers."

It was true, so tragically true. And now all of the abuses of civilization were taking their terrible toll.

To aid in their caretaking efforts, the Tulyans did have a few podships that had been captured in the wild reaches of space, from intercepting the ancient migration routes of the creatures. But the pods had to be hidden carefully in order to avoid having them taken by Parvii swarms ... or by the ravenous demons of the undergalaxy. With only limited resources, the dedicated Tulyans could not do much ... nowhere near what they achieved in ancient, bygone times.

Emerging from his walk in the woods, Eshaz stared for a long while at the Humans bustling around the new Digger holes. The exterminators were dropping probes into the openings, to search for the malfunctioning machines.

Eshaz rather liked these Humans, especially Noah, who had more upstanding qualities than any other alien he'd ever encountered. In his long life, Eshaz had known many persons of various races, and some of them were extraordinary historical figures, males and females who were much honored by their people. Always, though, the Tulyan had tried to maintain his distance from aliens he admired. In large part this was to preserve his own emotional balance, since it was too difficult to get attached to sentients who had such short life spans in comparison with his own.

But now, for the first time, Eshaz was breaking that hard-and-fast rule. No matter how much he had tried to avoid it, he could not help feeling tremendous esteem for Noah Watanabe ... and a strong bond of affection. While some of the reasons for this were obvious to Eshaz, he also felt something ineffable toward the Human, an almost instinctual sensation that was as inexplicable to him as his inability to peer through the veils of time.

Chapter Forty-Five

I only collect on promises. I don't fulfill them.

—Doge Lorenzo del Velli

The Doge Lorenzo del Velli prided himself on his nefarious plots and schemes. He liked to do things behind the scenes to effect important changes, so that the persons targeted were blind-sided, and never figured out what happened to them. It was a game he liked to play. In his position, of course, he didn't have to do that, because he was the most powerful man in the galaxy. But he preferred subtle methods rather than using hammers. He liked to compare his "little tricks," as he called them, to a whispering wind that slipped up behind the victim unawares and suddenly transformed itself into a hurricane.

Several years ago, a warlord prince had been openly critical of Lorenzo's administration, making the ridiculous assertion that the Doge was doing such a terrible job that he should relinquish his throne to the first person who asked for it—since anyone could do better. It was such an absurd idea that it didn't deserve a response, at least not a direct one.

So, after considering the matter at length, Lorenzo and his Royal Attaché came up with a way to silence the outspoken critic. Pimyt spread a convincing rumor, complete with falsified evidence, that the grumbling Prince was having an affair with General Mah Sajak's attractive, flirtatious wife. The General, who was often away from home in battles against the Mutatis, became so convinced of the story that he hired assassins to go after the Prince.

It all went perfectly, and when Lorenzo received confirmation of the killing, Pimyt could hardly control his elation, for he claimed that he had come up with the plan. The furry little Hibbil did four back flips and half a dozen spinning rolls, landing on his feet at the base of the Doge's throne.

"Whatever do you think you're doing?" Lorenzo had asked. "It was my idea, not yours." This was not true, and the Doge knew it. But he also knew he could win any argument with the Hibbil.

"Oh, my mistake," Pimyt said, in a tone that bordered on the sarcastic. Then, as if to sublimate any anger he could not express, he did the reverse of the gymnastics he had just accomplished, with six reverse spinning rolls followed by four front flips.

"There," Pimyt said. "That neutralizes my little celebration, as if it never happened."

Now the Doge had another serious problem, one that his lover Francella Watanabe wanted taken care of. She had told him about it in bed, asserting what a terrible, deceptive man her own brother was. Of course, Lorenzo was not foolish enough to believe all of those distortions, for he knew Noah personally and also knew how to spin his own tales. But he let on that he believed her, and she was most grateful for the sympathy he expressed, just one of his many skills.

That night—in return for his promise to have Noah killed at the first opportunity—Francella bestowed her generous personal favors on him. In the morning Lorenzo set in motion his own plan to accomplish the assassination. After all, he had plenty of excellent ideas himself, and didn't need to always rely upon that fur-ball Pimyt to solve every problem.

Having solved that for the moment, Lorenzo turned to other matters, and conferred with his royal astronomers over the Earth-Mars disasters. They cited examples of other odd events occurring around the galaxy ... ground giving way underneath people, exposing immense, seemingly bottomless sinkholes, and large chunks of planets (or entire small planets) disappearing into voids. Survivors told harrowing tales, and investigators were working on the problem, but thus far had not come up with any solutions.

"How could entire planets disappear?" Lorenzo asked them.

"If it were only Earth and Mars, we might think it was a problem with the yellow sun in that solar system," the lead astronomer said, a grizzled old man who dressed impeccably. "We've seen at least one example of a sun giving off destructive solar energy that destroyed all of the planets orbiting it, one by one. But that can't be the case here. The problem is too widespread, and the results differ. Sometimes we find space debris, and other times there's nothing left ... a complete vanishing act."

"My grandfather used to tell me about Earth and Mars," Lorenzo said. "He said that Human migrations departed from them thousands of years ago, spreading the seeds of our race across hundreds of star systems."

"It's a big loss," the old astronomer said, shaking his head sadly.

Afterward, when he had time to think by himself, the Doge was left with an unsettled feeling. What if something terrible were to happen to Canopa or Siriki ... or even worse, to Timian One? He could hardly imagine such events, and yet, something told him they were entirely possible.

Chapter Forty-Six

Thanks to medical technology, the average lifespan of a human being has risen steadily in modern times. It now stands at 106.4 years for women, and 94.1 years for men ... with men lagging in large part because of war deaths.

—MPA Actuarial Office

On the grounds of his Ecological Demonstration Project, Noah Watanabe stood inside an energy production chamber, surrounded by crystalglax tanks and tubes. Checking gauges and meters, he monitored the progress of one of the experiments. This particular test system was the brainchild of a team of his brightest students. Designed to harness and amplify energy generated by thousands of green plants, it had sounded far-fetched to him at first, but just might work after all. Using collection units that floated over the plants, from field to field, they collected energy from various botanical species, for the purpose of observing differences between them and optimizing future Human exploitation of the technology.

Speaking into a computer, Noah instructed it to provide day by day comparisons for the past six months. Long charts scrolled down the monitor, providing field by field and species by species analyses. Curiously, imported Sirikan sporeweeds were beginning to outperform the other plants, whereas initially they had not done well at all. In recent days the technicians had found a way of tweaking the sensitive organisms, irritating them to create more oxygen and other cellular exhalants, for transfer to the EDP's energy production chamber.

Subi Danvar opened the chamber door and entered, but it closed so hard behind him that the images on the screen jiggled. "Master Noah, you don't need to perform these tasks," the heavyset man said as he lumbered across the floor. We have people to do them for you."

"This is turning into an important test program," Noah said. "I want to check it firsthand."

"You have thousands of employees, so that you can free yourself from such responsibilities." His tone became acidic. "It's called delegation."

"Are you saying I don't know how to manage people?" Noah asked, with a twinkle in his eye.

"Well," Subi said, with his own blue-eyed sparkle, "you've never figured out how to keep *me* in line, have you?"

"I'll grant you that, old friend." He paused. "Of course, I could fire you."

"Then who would protect your well-exposed backside?" Subi rubbed the purple birthmark on his own cheek, and it seemed to brighten.

"Is that all you are, Subi, padding for my derriere?"

"I could say something to devastate you now," he countered, "but I'll give you a break this time."

"Sure, sure."

They exchanged mock scowls.

The two men were not angry with each other, not in the least. It was just a typical bantering session between them, with each trying to gain a verbal leg up on the other. A mental wrestling match. It didn't keep either of them from focusing on their work, and had actually proved to be a way of reducing the natural stresses of their jobs. They always took great care not to exchange sharp repartees in front of other employees, however, not wishing to give anyone the impression that the men did not respect one another.

Noah ordered a printout, then had to grab hold of a thick vertical tube when the chamber started to shake, accompanied by a loud rumbling noise.

"Uh oh," Subi said. "I hope it's not what I think it is."

They hurried to leave, but stumbled and fell together when the konker floor buckled and cracked beneath them. Struggling back to their feet, they made it to the door, but it was stuck and would not open. Behind them, the floor was breaking apart, and the noise had become deafening. Cracking, roaring sounds, and loud engine noises.

"Diggers!" Noah shouted, as he and Subi pulled with all of their strength at the door. It budged, just a little.

The floor of the chamber erupted, with a deafening roar.

Noah and Subi got the door open and ran outside. Moments later, the walls and ceiling of the chamber collapsed and fell into a newly made hole. Noah barely got a glimpse of the tail end of a Digger as it dove back into the ground with the debris. The elongated, silvery machine was covered in dirt; it had huge treads, and large, spinning drill bits on its body. Anyone coming close to one would be torn apart, but Noah's extermination squads had modern, remote controlled boring machines of their own to chase down the pesky, mole-like Diggers and wipe them out.

The most danger occurred if people were inside a building, because it often took so long to get outside and damage to the structure—as had almost happened to Noah and Subi—could prevent escape. If people were outside, however, they could usually get away from the errant machines without harm, since the contraptions made so much noise when they were coming that people had time to get out of the way.

But the renegade machines seemed to get irritated whenever they were attacked, and might even be self-replicating. For each one that was destroyed, two more seemed to pop out of the ground. The very act of chasing the Diggers down seemed to trigger a survival instinct in them. Still, reports reaching Noah showed that the population of the machines on Canopa was actually dwindling. Their behavior was decidedly curious.

Under Subi Danvar's command, Anton Glavine and Tesh Kori, along with other anti-Digger commandos, dropped explosive depth-probes into the hole. Moments later, detonations sounded, and the ground shook.

"We've got 'em on the run now," Subi said. He started to grin, but Noah saw it fade suddenly, and heard more machinery noises, and gunfire.

On a handheld surveillance monitor, Noah saw silver vehicles approaching along the main road into the compound, and uniformed men running beside them. He recognized blue-and-silver CorpOne banners fluttering over the military squadron. His own sister Francella was in control of the family corporation now, and Noah was certain that this was no welcoming party. Not content to acquire all of the wealth of their father, she had apparently decided to go on the offensive against her twin.

As Noah and his adjutant ran for shelter and shouted commands into transmitters, his mind whirled. Did she hope to capture or kill him? There had been rumors that she wanted to make Noah the scapegoat for the death of Prince Saito Watanabe, and perhaps they were true after all.

Blue tracer fire hissed over their heads. Noah and Subi ducked into a bolt hole that they had opened with an electronic signal, and the hatch closed behind them. They joined hundreds of green-and-brown uniformed Guardians running for emergency stations. Everyone had done this drill before, and knew the priorities.

Noah continued to wonder. He had expected Francella's attempt to blame him for the death of their father, but had not anticipated a military onslaught from her. That was far too brash, so she must have the backing of Doge Lorenzo for something like this. Yes, that was undoubtedly it. They were lovers, after all.

Guardians cleared the way for Noah and Subi, and the two of them boarded a grid-plane. Just as they jumped aboard, Noah noticed Tesh and Anton with a group of other Digger exterminators, all of them covered in dirt from the recent attack.

"Bring those two with us," Noah ordered, and as many others as we can. Tell everyone possible to take off for EcoStation. Priority One. From there we might have time to figure out what to do."

He knew that his Guardian Security Force was defending against the attack. He'd seen them beginning to fight back just before he and Subi made it into the bolt hole. But he also knew what CorpOne could throw against them, and worried about whether they had the firepower to defend the compound. He would stay there and man the guns himself, but Subi had developed contingency plans to keep enemies from getting to Noah, and Noah knew that his followers needed him for inspiration.

"You're the soul of this organization," the loyal adjutant had said to him on more than one occasion.

Now Noah nodded to Anton and Tesh as they boarded with him. Moments later, the grid-plane rocketed out of its underground bunker, followed by other green-and-brown escape aircraft, at irregular intervals.

* * * * *

On board EcoStation, high in orbit over the planet, Noah reviewed security procedures with Subi and three Guardian officers. After they left his office, he stood at a wide window, gazing down at Canopa below, at the continents and oceans that looked so calm from this distance. Touching a transmitter on his wrist, he activated the magnaview feature of the glax, and it zoomed in on his Ecological Demonstration Project compound. The resolution was so clear that he could see uniformed soldiers hurrying in and out of the vehicles and structures.

His blood boiled, as he thought of all the ecological work that those idiots would trample on, desecrating years of effort. It looked like a military base down there now, with vehicles and aircraft pouring in. And not just those of CorpOne, either, he noticed with a sinking feeling. Doge Lorenzo's forces were there as well, in their cardinal red uniforms.

Atop the administration building, his green-and-brown flag still fluttered defiantly in a slight breeze. Then he saw it being lowered.

"You asked to see me?" a man said.

Turning, Noah saw the mustachioed Anton Glavine enter the office and stand by the desk, looking nervous and upset. His black trousers were torn, and one of his knees was bloodied.

Noah switched off the viewer. "I have something to say to you," he began. At a wave of his hand, the office door closed, and he blocked all intercom systems.

"Tesh and I appreciate what you've done for us," Anton said. "OK if I sit down? I injured my leg in a fall."

"Sure. Go ahead."

Anton slid into one of three chairs that fronted the desk.

Too agitated to sit, Noah paced back and forth by the window. "I should have told you this earlier," he said, "but for your sake I thought it was best to hold back the information. I hope you're not angry with me, because I always had your welfare in mind."

"I would never question that." The younger man looked perplexed. His hazel eyes looked straight at Noah.

"I've always acted like a big brother to you," Noah said. "You thought I started out as a friend of your parents, but that isn't the whole story." He took a deep breath. "They weren't really your parents, not birth parents anyway."

"Sitting straight up, Anton said, "What?"

"You and I are related by blood."

"You're not my ... father? We are only seventeen years apart."

He shook his head. "I'm your uncle."

Stopping the pacing, Noah could see Anton's mind churning through the possibilities, behind the gaze of his eyes.

"My uncle?" His face contorted. "My mother isn't Francella? God, I hope not!"

"She is, unfortunately." Noah folded his arms across his chest. "After you were born, she paid for your care, but never bothered to see you again or even ask about you. I doubt if she even remembers the name of the family that took you in, or your own given name that they provided for you. I'm really sorry, Anton."

Anger filled the young man's face. "You should have told me. I'm twenty years old, not a baby."

"It never seemed like a good time. I wanted to spare you. Now isn't the greatest time, either, but I don't feel I can wait any longer. We're all in danger, and in case something more happens...." Noah's eyes misted over, and he choked up.

"OK," Anton said. He went to his newly discovered uncle, half-smiled. "I know you mean the best."

"Don't be too quick to forgive me. I have something more to tell you."

"Worse than what you already told me?"

"It depends on how you look at it."

"Well?" Anton stood up, went over to the window by Noah.

"Doge Lorenzo is your father."

"Now I know you're kidding."

"Look at me, boy. Do I look like I'm kidding?" Noah stared hard at him, unblinking.

"Is that all you have to tell me? Or does it get even worse?"

"Lorenzo doesn't know about you. My sister didn't want him to know she was pregnant, so she stayed away from him until after you were born, and then said she had been tending to family business matters."

He looked numb. "I need time to absorb this."

Noah went on to tell Anton about the military insignias he had seen through the magnaviewer, that Francella and Lorenzo appeared to have combined their forces to attack the compound. They might even be down there together right now.

"I wish they were," Anton replied, "and that we could drop a bomb on them." He sulked toward the door, opened it.

Just before he left, Noah said, "Be cautious with the information. Revealing it to anyone could put you at more risk."

"Everything's dangerous nowadays," Anton said, and he closed the door behind him.

Chapter Forty-Seven

No one is ever totally free. Everyone is confined by his own mortality.
—Jacopo Nehr

On the Mutati prison moon of Omo, Giovanni Nehr lamented his situation. He had hoped to get rich by turning the nehrcom secret over to the shapeshifters, but it had not worked out that way at all. In the process, he had also hoped to avenge himself on his smug, overbearing brother Jacopo, but he might never learn if that happened. Gio should not have proceeded without knowing the outcome in advance. In retrospect, he realized that he should have envisioned the possibilities better before committing himself.

Now he toiled in white-hot sunlight, carrying stones from one side of a field to another. Obviously, the work had no purpose whatsoever except to occupy and annoy the prisoners, because there were other men like him moving the stones again, to another place. Back and forth and around and around hundreds of Human men in checkered prison garb went, only occasionally getting water breaks, and then only to drink a brackish, green liquid that looked positively lethal. He swallowed as little of the slimy fluid as possible.

During one of the breaks, he sat cross-legged on a flat rock and struck up a conversation with two young men standing nearby, who identified themselves as Acey Zelk and Dux Hannah. The pair had been discussing the destruction of the planet Mars, wondering how it could have happened. Upon hearing the boys say they'd seen the debris field, Gio asked for more information. They described the horrors of the aftermath, and said some of the onlookers theorized a meteor may have hit the planet.

"Must have been quite a blast," Gio said.

To Dux, the man didn't seem very sympathetic. The teenager had heard that Mars was only lightly populated and not on any important commercial routes, but that still meant the loss of hundreds of thousands of people.

For several moments, the three of them gazed off into the distance at shimmering bubbles of air that floated between the moon and the planet Dij, a large ball that looked like it was below the moon.

"Those bubbles are strangely beautiful," Dux said.

The others agreed, and then Gio expressed his opinion about the uselessness of their labor, just carrying rocks around.

Grinning in a disarming way, Acey said, "Try to see the positive side, friend. We're getting a good workout, keeping our bodies in shape."

"Unless this green water gets us," Dux added, spitting it out and making a face.

"Where are you from?" Gio asked.

"Siriki," Acey said.

"Ah yes, the world of Princess Meghina. Do you know her?"

"Do we look like her social set?" Acey asked.

"I guess not. I'm from Canopa myself, the most beautiful planet in the galaxy."

"We've seen a lot of worlds," Dux said to the older man. "Canopa is nice, but not exotic enough for me."

"Yeah," Acey agreed. "Too civilized." He paused, and asked the Canopan, "How did the Mutatis get you?"

Gio grimaced, shook his head. "I'd rather not say. Something dumb I did, dumb and embarrassing."

"Could say the same for us," Dux admitted. "We were snared on a Mutati-controlled vacation planet, like insects in a fly trap, they said to us."

Into the throng of prisoners strutted six guards, fleshy creatures who moved with remarkable speed despite their great girths. The shapeshifters stood in the center, each of them looking in a different direction at the relaxing men.

Without warning, lances of orange fire shot from weapons attached to their wrists, hitting many of the prisoners. "Back to work, you slackers!" they shouted with cruel glee, as the captives cried out in pain and surprise, and jumped in attempts to get out of the way.

On a second burst of fire, Dux was struck in the shoulder, burning through his thin shirt to the skin. Acey was hit on one arm—but both boys refused to cry out. They just moved back into the work detail and did as they were told.

These guards were bored, Dux realized. They had rousted the prisoners from breaks before, but never like this. Previously it had been with shouts, threats, and strange curses, and once they had hurled small, stinging stones at the men. On rare occasions, the Mutati overseers were even pleasant, but Dux came to realize that this was just a sadistic game with them, as they easily shifted back to cruel behavior.

* * * * *

The next time they had a chance to talk, following an evening meal, the two young prisoners and their new friend discussed an escape plan. The moon on which they were incarcerated, in low orbit over Dij, was connected to the Mutati-controlled world by airvators, shimmering capsules of air that rose and descended with passengers inside. From air pressure, they had firm interior walls, floors, and ceilings, but they had no real substance. To observers looking upward, it seemed like the passengers were floating on air bubbles … which, in fact, they were doing. Each airvator was controlled by an operator inside who wore a pressure-regulator, strapped around his torso.

Pursuant to a plan that Dux developed, Acey—who was mechanically inclined—stole one of the regulators and put it on, then generated a pale yellow bubble around them.

"It's easy to operate," Acey said. The mechanism made a soft hiss. "Hang on," he said. "Here we go!"

Looking around, Dux grabbed a railing as they lifted into the air. His companions did the same, and barely in the nick of time, because the capsule flipped over, tossing them around.

"Sorry," Acey said. He righted the airvator, increased the power, and they went higher into the air.

Dux felt lightness in his feet, the gravity field weakening as they moved farther from the moon.

"I'm turning on artificial gravity now," Acey said.

Dux felt it kick on, as his feet settled firmly to the deck of the airvator.

"Beyond the moon's atmosphere now," Acey reported. "We're in a narrow band of space between Omo and Dij. In a few moments, we'll enter the stratosphere of the planet."

But as they descended toward Dij, Mutati guards in another airvator spotted them and opened fire.

Acey changed course, and inside the enclosure the three of them tried to duck. Projectiles hit their airvator, puncturing the seal and damaging the pressure mechanism.

Acey tried to re-inflate, but they began to lose pressure. and tumbled rapidly. Dux saw a gaping hole on one side of the bubble, an opening that shifted when Gio moved around.

"Stay away from the hole!" Acey yelled. "Watch out!"

Gio lunged at Dux and said, "Careful! You could fall a long way!" He gave Dux a hard push toward the cavity.

Dux was nearly as tall as his attacker, but thinner and less muscular. The older man was stronger, and had the added element of surprise. Still, the youth had wiry strength, and fought desperately to avoid falling to his certain death.

He lost his grip on the railing, but tumbled to the other side of the capsule and grabbed hold again.

"Just a mistake," Gio said. "It wasn't what it must have looked like. I was just trying to keep my balance, didn't mean to push you."

"Like hell," Dux said.

Acey struggled with the regulator and managed to increase the air pressure, but only a little.

The airvator hurtled downward, spinning.

Suddenly an emergency system went on, and the hole sealed over. The airvator began to descend at a normal speed until it settled onto the ground. As it landed, the mechanism shut down, and the shimmering bubble disappeared entirely, leaving only a wisp of color behind that soon dissipated in the air. The three of them ran from the guards, whose airvator landed moments later. Gio ran in a separate direction from the boys.

Acey and Dux scampered across a storage compound enclosed by energy-field fences. They hurried by a faceless servobot and boarded a small gray ship, slipping into the cargo hold amidst large crates, bags, and barrels. The pair were barely inside when the hatch slid shut behind them, and the craft lifted off.

Peering through a porthole, Dux saw the vessel speeding toward the setting sun on the horizon, skimming over grassy hills and treetops. Acey showed interest in something else, an arched doorway in the forward bulkhead of the hold. He strode through, and disappeared for several moments.

When Dux followed, he found his cousin standing at a control panel on the bridge of the ship, examining the instruments. Glancing back, Acey said, "This thing's on automatic, a programmed route."

"To where?"

"Can't tell." He tapped a light green screen, said, "This is the destination board, full of numbers and letters. We're on course for Destination 1-A, wherever that is. My guess is this is a supply ship, and after we deliver cargo there, it keeps going on its route, to other destinations."

"Too bad we're so low to the ground," Dux said. "I'd give *your* right arm for a pod station right now."

"And I'd give your right eye," said the other, with a wink and a grin. He glanced out the front window. "Whoa, what's that?"

Ahead, Dux saw a building that at first appeared to be one-story. As they neared the structure—which was constructed of patterned geometric blocks—he realized it was at least ten stories in height, with huge open doorways and ships inside that look like merchant schooners, even painted the red-and-gold of the Merchant Prince Alliance. Lights began to flicker on as the sun dipped below the horizon.

"Something doesn't look right here," Dux said. "Our princes would never buy ships from the Mutatis, or sell anything to them."

Inside the facility, he identified the lumpy shapes of Mutati workmen, fitting some sort of hardware into one of the vessels. A complex of smaller buildings was adjacent, surrounded by a high fence. He saw hundreds of blue-uniformed shapeshifters on the grounds, and more of the schooner-like vessels.

"What is this place?" Dux asked.

"Looks like a manufacturing facility," Acey said. "Military, from the look of it, and the level of security."

"Something to do with fake merchant prince schooners," Dux said.

"That'd be my bet."

Their ship set down a short distance away on a shadowy landing field, where only servobots awaited them, simpleton machines that were programmed to perform a limited number of tasks, repetitively. Moments later, a hatch opened in the floor of the cargo hold, and a ramp extended down to the pavement. On-board systems began sliding items down the ramp, where the bots loaded them onto a groundtruck.

In the cargo hold, Acey used a strip of metal to pry open a crate. "Just food," he said, peering inside. While the unloading operation continued, he avoided the flexing servo-arms of the bots and broke into another crate, followed by another.

"I know what this is," he said, pulling out a black field gun. Rummaging around in the crate, he found ammunition, which he began loading into the weapon.

"What are you doing?" Dux asked.

"You want to join the fun, or are you just going to watch?"

"Uh, I don't ..."

Acey grabbed another gun and more ammunition from of the crate just before a servomechanism grabbed the open container and slid it down the ramp, followed by the others he had opened. Finally the hatch closed, and the ship began to lift off. Acey handed the first weapon to Dux, then loaded the second one and fired it at a porthole, blasting it open. Hefting the heavy gun and touching the firing pad, Dux blew open another porthole.

The boys exchanged quick glances, and grinned at each other. Mutatis were the mortal enemies of all Humans, and these two had been indoctrinated in this belief system from an early age.

Without another word, they fired into the building with the powerful field guns, hitting the schooners and barrels of chemicals, which exploded into flames. In a matter of seconds the entire facility was ablaze and alarm klaxons were sounding. Like ants in a frenzy, uniformed Mutatis scurried around, trying to figure out what had happened. The boys emptied their guns into the soldiers, dropping many of them and sending others scrambling for cover.

The cargo ship flew on its programmed course past the flames, while the teenagers shouted in glee at the unexpected bonus, and reloaded their weapons. At last they were getting even for what the Mutatis had done to them, and in the process had undoubtedly saved the lives of Humans who might have been the victims of whatever weapons systems they were constructing inside that building.

Acey ran back onto the bridge, and smashed something. "They're coming after us!" he shouted. "I see two blips on the scanscreen."

Dux hurried to the back of the hold and blasted open another porthole. He saw a pair of fighter ships speeding after them, with the factory burning behind them. Dux opened fire on them, and they fired back.

Just then, the cargo vessel banked left and surged upward, in a burst of acceleration. Dux held on and kept firing the field gun. He hit the short wing of one of the pursuit ships, and the craft spun out of control.

"I overrode the program!" Acey shouted. "This baby really has power!"

"I got one of them!" Dux yelled. His field gun was more powerful than the armaments of the fighter ships, and had a longer range. One ship hit the ground and exploded in a fireball, and then he hit the other one, which blew up in midair.

The cargo vessel, lifting higher and higher into the sky, had proven to be more versatile than Acey or Dux could have possibly imagined. They flew to a pod station, jumped onto a deck and used the field guns to shoot their way past any Mutatis they encountered.

Boarding a podship that arrived a few minutes later, they left chaos in their wake. The sentient spacecraft departed for deep space....

When they were safely off-planet, Acey and Dux talked about what they would like to do to that slimy Canopan—Giovanni Nehr—if they ever saw him again.

Chapter Forty-Eight

Opportunities are all around you, waiting to be plucked like gemstones from a jeweler's tray.

—Malbert Nehr, to his sons

Giovanni Nehr was not as skilled as the boys in getting away from the Mutati world. He hid in the marshland for two days, drinking rainwater and not eating anything. Seeing shuttles lift off regularly in the distance, he made his way through swamp and jungle to the edge of the transport station. For most of a day he watched the shuttles taking off and landing. Early that evening, in geostationary orbit high overhead, he saw a bright light, which he judged must be a pod station.

Darkness dropped like a thick black blanket over the land. It was a moonless, starless night, illuminated only by the pod station and the landing lights of the shuttles. Gradually, he built up his courage, and crept across the landing field.

Concealing himself behind a stack of shipping crates, he watched Mutati soldiers supervise robots that were loading a shuttle, using heavy equipment. On occasion the Mutatis came close to Gio, only a couple of meters away, without seeing him in the shadows.

As he watched, he discovered something very interesting. Even when he was relatively near the shapeshifters, they showed no signs of anti-Human, allergic reactions ... apparently as long as they could not see him, as long as they were unaware of his presence.

Gio learned something else as well, of even greater significance. From his place of concealment, waiting for an opportunity to sneak aboard a shuttle, he overheard two Mutati officers supervising the loading operation, giving the robots voice commands in Galeng. The pair also talked between themselves about impending military missions against the Humans ... stepped-up attacks.

"It's nothing like the merchant princes have ever seen before," one of the Mutatis said. "They can't defend against it."

"The Demolio program is brilliant, isn't it?" said the other. "This will be the deciding factor in the war."

The voices drifted off as the Mutatis moved farther away. When they returned, they were discussing the same subject, but there were no specifics. They kept referring to something called "Demolio."

Demolio?

Whatever it was, it sounded big to Gio, and he wondered if he could get a reward for tipping off the merchant princes about it. But for his next venture he vowed do more research in advance, so that he didn't get into trouble again, the way he did with the Mutatis. Always the opportunist, Gio knew there was a great potential for profit during wartime. If he could only escape and take advantage of the situation....

The loading took the better part of an hour, after which the Mutatis and robots boarded a motocart and sped away across the landing field.

With the shuttle unattended, Gio made his way to a loading hatch and sneaked aboard the craft. Hours passed while he waited inside in the darkness of a cargo hold.

He drifted off to sleep on the hard deck, then awoke hours later at the sound of voices, and the rumble of an engine as it surged on and vibrated the vessel. He hoped the interior air would be breathable when they reached orbital space. Dim light filtered into the hold, making him think it might be dawn.

Gio yawned and stretched. His muscles were sore, and hunger gnawed at his stomach, like a creature consuming his body from the inside out. He felt air circulating in the hold, and heard the whir of fans. The ship lifted off.

In only a few minutes, he felt weightless, then the craft's gravitational system kicked on. Presently, he heard what he judged to be the sound of a docking mechanism engaging, perhaps at a pod station or space station.

Soon he heard voices again, an angry confrontation outside. Peeking around the edge of an open hatchway, he saw the Mutatis on the loading platform of a pod station, arguing with a pair of pale-skinned Kichi men. The Kichis claimed that the Mutatis had taken their docking berth, and they were quite upset.

"Take another berth," one of the Mutati officers said. He pointed the forefingers of his three hands to another docking spot, a short distance away.

"No," the tallest Kichi said. "We reserved this one for a freighter arriving in the next half hour."

"What difference does it make which berth you get?" the Mutati asked. "They're all the same, just holding spots until a pod takes us aboard."

"It makes a lot of difference, you fat pile of ugly. You have five minutes to get out of here, or we're going to cut your piece of junk loose." He spit on the Mutati vessel.

Enraged Mutatis surrounded them. But the Kichis activated a long, high-pitched signal, and moments later a throng of them came running toward the platform.

During the wild melee, Gio saw a podship arrive in one of the zero-g docking berths at the center of the station, where passengers were already lined up to board. On impulse, he ran for the ship, but had to pass the fighting aliens to get there.

A Mutati guard spotted him as he crept out of the shuttle, and opened fire with a jolong rifle. Sparkling blue projectiles whizzed by his head, and thumped into the thick gray-and-black skin of the podship. The vessel shuddered.

Gio ran to the front of the line and pushed his way on, out of turn.

"Who do you think you are?" a Jimlat dwarf shouted, after Gio shoved him aside and he fell to the dock.

Ignoring him, Gio found a seat on a bench at the rear of the passenger compartment. A handful of additional passengers boarded, but not the dwarf. Without warning, before the normal amount of time allowed for boarding, the podship hatch closed, and the large sentient vessel got underway.

The cabin wasn't even half full, but apparently the podship had been agitated by the projectiles hitting its side, even though it would take more firepower than that to harm one of the creatures. Some of the passengers glared back at Gio, but he ignored them.

Noticing a stinging on his left arm, he examined it. Just a flesh wound visible through the torn sleeve of his shirt, with a little trickle of blood. Nothing to dampen the ebullience he was feeling. He had gotten away from the Mutatis, and was free now.

Chapter Forty-Nine

My mind cuts in many directions. The gyrodome makes the blades sharper.
—Zultan Abal Meshdi

It was difficult to imagine that anyone could be unhappy living in the magnificent Citadel of Paradij. As the Zultan of the Mutati Kingdom, Abal Meshdi possessed everything a shapeshifter could desire, including a harem of the most stunning and sensual Mutati women in all of creation, each of them rounded heaps of rolling fat. On a terraced hillside, his private baths offered a broad selection of mineral and spirit waters from all over the galaxy, for soothing his tired bones and renewing his energy, which had been sapped by endless affairs of state. Tens of thousands of Mutatis, robots, and the slaves of various races (other than allergy-producing Humans) worked for him in the Citadel, a virtual city within the capital city, attending to his every need, his every whim.

Originally, Paradij had not been a world that appealed to any galactic race for habitation, since it was covered with arid deserts and vast salt flats. But the planet featured deep aquifers, essentially subterranean seas. The Mutatis—driven there by Human attacks against their other planets—had set up a massive hydraulic engineering project to bring the water to the surface, which they then used to create rivers, lakes, and irrigation canals for crops and forests. The costs in money and the expenditure of time had been enormous, but the marvelous result had been a source of inspiration to all Mutatis. It showed what they could do in even the most difficult environments, and that the greedy, aggressive Humans could not take everything away from them.

He lived in such exquisite luxury that he didn't really need to go to war against the merchant princes. But they had insulted him and his people, driving them from one world to the next, never letting up.

And Mutatis did not take insults lightly.

With many important matters weighing heavily on his mind, the big shapeshifter shuffled toward the clearglax bubble of his gyrodome, which he'd had moved to one of the highest rooms in the Citadel, where he could be closer to God-on-High. The platform inside the dome spun slowly now as it awaited him, making a faint, inviting hum. Pursuant to his instructions, the mind-enhancing unit was in its simplest, most basic configuration, without the customized compartments that could be fitted on the outside to contain aeromutatis and hydromutatis. Sometimes he did not want such distractions.

Just then an aide interrupted him and said, "Pardon me, Your Eminence, but there is a messenger to see you. He says it is important."

Shaking his tiny head in dismay, since he really needed what he had come to call his "morning gyro treatment," the Zultan said, "Very well, send him in."

Moments later a uniformed aeromutati flew into the chamber, and hovered in the air. It was one of the small, speedy flyers who were best suited for such tasks. "There are two messages, Sire. I carry one"—he held a small communication pyramid in one hand—"and the other is outside."

"Outside?" Abal Meshdi said.

"Look over there, My Zultan," the messenger said. He pointed to a small window on the narrow north end of the chamber.

Hurrying to the window, Meshdi beheld a sight that surprised him, and filled him with patriotic pride. He counted ten outrider schooners flying in formation over the capital city, swooping this way and that.

"They are performing for you, Sire, in honor of the glory they will achieve when you send them into battle."

"But I thought there was a delay in production," the Zultan said. "I was told that the vessels would not be ready for another month."

"Apparently they solved the problem," the messenger said, with a shrug of his narrow shoulders. "Look, Sire, the outriders have come to receive your blessing before departing on their holy missions and giving up their lives."

Filled with pride, the Zultan watched the bomb-laden schooners, each a beautiful doomsday machine capable of annihilating an entire enemy planet. Such a magnificent, perfect design. Truly, his researchers were inspired by God-on-High when they developed this most perfect and deadly of all weapons!

The Zultan felt tremendously humbled by all of this. As the leader of trillions of Mutatis, he was still only a tool of the Almighty, put here on Paradij to further the hallowed Mutati mission. Today, his sacred duty was to dispatch these outriders.

Already two fringe planets under enemy control—Earth and Mars—had fallen victim to his deadly design. And one additional outrider had been sent as well, with orders to strike against a third planet in the future at a predetermined time, on a Mutati holy day. Now—glory of glories!—ten more magnificent weapons were ready to go, and only needed his blessing before surging off into space.

The opening salvos of the Demolio program were all according to a precise, sacred pattern of numerology, following mathematical formulas laid out in *The Holy Writ* of his people. Two, one, and ten were sacred numbers, referring to a sequence of events that occurred long ago in Mutati history, leading to the most celebrated of military victories.

Until now.

It was not necessary to wait for confirmation of the third kill—the outrider who was still out there—before sending more of his brethren into the fray. The excited Zultan knew nothing could go wrong with any of the attacks, and that the third one would go off without a hitch, scattering another merchant prince planet to the cosmic winds. Then there would be ten more.

And many more after that.

'Everything is predetermined,' he thought, quoting from the ancient sacred text of *The Holy Writ*.

The Zultan felt euphoria sweeping over him, and then noticed the aeromutati fluttering its short wings, still waiting to deliver the second message. "Oh yes," Meshdi said, extending a hand, palm up.

The messenger placed the gleaming communication pyramid on his palm. Afterward, the aeromutati tried to leave, but Abal Meshdi shouted after him, "Wait! I might send a response."

* * * * *

The Zultan didn't want to believe the message.

Angrily, he hurled the communication pyramid at the aeromutati and hit him square in the head, dropping him out of the air, where he had been hovering. The flying Mutati thudded heavily to the floor, didn't even twitch. He was dead, but this didn't make the Zultan feel any better.

"It's not possible!" he bellowed.

According to the missive, his son Hari'Adab had barely escaped with his life when enemy commandos destroyed the Demolio manufacturing plant, along with the adjacent outrider training facility. The ten planet-busting schooners now at Paradij had been dispatched shortly before the disaster, and—for reasons of military security—had flown across the solar system by conventional hydion propulsion.

Two attendants ran into the chamber. "Your Eminence?" one of them said. "is everything all right?"

Reaching into the pockets of his robe with his two outer hands, Meshdi brought out a pair of long knives. Thunk. Thunk. The motions were smooth as he hurled the blades expertly at the terramutatis, hitting each of them in their torsos. The attendants dropped into piles of pulpy, bleeding flesh, beside the messenger.

For months, the Zultan had been practicing with his knives, throwing them at target boards. Fortunately for his aim, the attendants had been wide, easy targets. But he still didn't feel any better.

I need to kill Humans, not my own people.

Extremely agitated, he entered the gyrodome and stood on the whirling floor. Closing his eyes, he felt the mechanism probing his overburdened mind, trying to purge it of the weight of vital duties and decisions. But it only made him feel worse.

When he finally stepped out of the gyrodome, the Zultan felt confused and uncertain. Now he would need to wait for instructions from God-on-High before proceeding. Clearly, it was not enough to only destroy ten merchant prince planets, since the enemy had hundreds, with military industrial facilities on many of them. With only a limited number of doomsday weapons and no manufacturing facility to replace them, Abal Meshdi needed to rework his war plan.

As he watched the gyrodome stop spinning and shut down, he made a new vow. The destruction of his Demolio facility would slow the Zultan down, but he would resume operations as quickly as possible at another location, diverting all possible resources to the project.

And next time there would be no security breach.

Chapter Fifty

There are so many ways to kill a prisoner, and so many ways to make it entertaining.

—Supreme General Mah Sajak

Princess Meghina sat beside her husband in the royal box, with immense red-and-gold banners fluttering overhead, each emblazoned with the golden tigerhorse crest of the House of del Velli. They gazed down on the broad central square of the capital city, thronged with people who came to see the public executions. It was a cloudy afternoon, and she shivered as a breeze picked up from the west.

At the near end of the square, a platform had been constructed with a simple-looking chair mounted atop it ... a device that her husband had said was actually a newly-designed execution machine. Perhaps a meter away, and around the same height as the empty chair, stood an alloy framework with a black tube on top of it. Wishing to spare herself some of the horror of whatever they had in mind for the prisoner, she had not asked him for details, and had silenced him when he tried to tell her. But in her high station, she still had to attend the event.

Now she gasped as a blue flame surged straight in the air from the top of the alloy stand, coming from the tube. The crowd roared its mindless approval, and then grew even louder when four guards escorted the condemned man toward the platform. Sajak wore a red hood over his head, and a simple red smock; without his uniform he looked very small and thin. Onlookers moved aside as the guards pressed their way through.

Meghina, the most famous noblewoman in the Merchant Prince Alliance, loathed these macabre spectacles that Lorenzo staged too frequently, and disliked the way he made her observe them whenever they were together. She and the Doge could not be any different, but eighteen years ago she had consented to marry him for the sake of her own House of Siriki, to give her people enhanced military protection and commercial benefits.

Over the time that they had been married—living much of the time on different worlds—she had tried to see good things in him, and on occasion his small kindnesses surfaced. But she felt no passion for the nobleman, no spark, not the way she had cherished Prince Saito. Such a distinguished old gentleman the industrialist had been, and what a terrible loss when he didn't come out of his coma. She wondered if the rumors were true, that his own son had attacked CorpOne, leading to his death. If so, she hoped he got what he deserved.

In front of the Doge and his lady, entertainers wandered through the crowd, playing music, singing songs, and juggling, throwing glimmerballs high in the air. Hawkers worked the perimeter, selling gourmet foods to the excited people who had come to see fifteen traitors die.

How ironic this whole scenario was, Meghina thought, as she watched two black-robed men take custody of the hooded prisoner and lead him up the steps of the platform. General Mah Sajak had been a renowned torturer of Mutatis, and now Lorenzo promised he was going to die as horribly as he always gave it out himself. Fittingly, according to her husband, today's means of execution was a device of Sajak's own invention, a machine that he had been developing, and which no one had ever put to use. Until now.

Atop the platform, one of the robed men removed Sajak's hood with a flourish, which seemed odd to Meghina. Normally it was the other way around; they put a hood on a victim just before executing him, a gesture of compassion at the end. But there was nothing normal about today's event. General Sajak had been the most trusted military officer in the entire Merchant Prince Alliance, and had committed the ultimate betrayal.

Seeing the chair and the blue flame beside it, Sajak began to scream in terror, and tried unsuccessfully to free himself. The crowd grew quiet, except for the call of a food hawker, an odd sound drowned out by the General's panicked shrieks.

"No, no!" he pleaded. "Not this! Please, not this! I'll give you more names, people who conspire against the Doge!" Even from her distance of perhaps thirty meters away, Meghina saw the terror on the disgraced officer's gaunt face, the way his eyes seemed twice their normal size.

Doge Lorenzo waved one hand, and a holo-image appeared in the air over the execution machine, a three-dimensional schematic drawing of the device.

"General Mah Sajak invented this machine himself!" a mechanical voice proclaimed over the loudspeaker system. "These are his own drawings!"

The image spun slowly, so that all could see it.

The elegant Princess didn't want to watch this terrible event, but knew she had no choice. Her husband and the crowd would expect it, and she could not lose face by disappointing them.

"No!" Sajak screamed. He tried to kick one of the robed men in the groin, but a thick garment prevented this. In response, the man backhanded the prisoner, sending him sprawling. Forcefully, the ominously-attired pair then dragged Sajak to the chair and strapped him to it, while he continued to scream and shout his promises to reveal new information.

It did him no good, for his fate had been sealed. A black, rather dented robot climbed the platform, and removed the tube that was shooting the blue flame, so that it was now a mobile torch.

Pointing it toward the sky, the robot turned the flame up, to double its previous size. The crowd thundered its approval.

Even over that noise, Meghina heard Sajak's screams.

"Louder," Doge Lorenzo said, to an aide.

Moments later, someone turned up the volume on a fireproof microphone that Sajak wore on his person. His shuddering screams reverberated across the square, sending the crowd into a frenzy of pleasure.

* * * * *

Holding the torch, the sentient robot activated a laser eye on it, and directed a bright red light at the prisoner's booted left foot. Jimu moved closer, and a metallic strap shot out of the device in his hand, wrapping itself around Sajak's lower left leg, just above his ankle.

"No!" he screamed. "Don't do this to me!"

The blue flame darted forward hungrily, and consumed the boot and the General's foot. His screams intensified, but the robot paid no attention. This evil man had tried to assassinate the Doge, the greatest Human in the galaxy.

Where there had been a foot only moments before, nothing but a charred, cauterized stump remained now.

Moments later, Jimu burned the right foot off. The robot expected Sajak to pass out from the pain, but he didn't, and kept wailing and crying for mercy. An expert at torture himself, the General was suffering indignity on top of indignity at the hands of the robot. The lower legs followed, then the thighs. Piece by piece, Jimu melted the body from the feet up. When he got to the lower torso, Sajak finally grew quiet and motionless.

The crowd cheered and clapped. Children giggled and played. Musicians struck up joyous tunes, and acrobats performed.

In a cruel spectacle, other robots under Jimu's command then executed General Sajak's co-conspirators the same way, one by one and piece by piece. Princess Meghina nearly gagged at the odor of charred flesh. Admittedly, these were all bad people, but she couldn't avoid her feelings of intense sadness. Faking a little sneeze, she leaned forward and wiped tears from her eyes, not wanting anyone to see.

Through it all, she sat silently beside Lorenzo, showing the Doge and the public one face, while concealing another one.

* * * * *

Following the executions, Doge Lorenzo appointed the famed inventor Jacopo Nehr to a new position, surprising many people. Nehr—previously only a reserve colonel—became Supreme General of the Merchant Prince Armed Forces, taking control away from the noble-born princes, whose champion had been Sajak. The new military commander owned several machine manufacturing plants on Hibbil worlds, and preferred the uniformity of those new machines to Jimu and his motley bunch. Still, Nehr could not deny their loyalty or accomplishments, so he rewarded them by commissioning all of them Red Beret officers.

In the process, Jimu was initiated into the rituals and secrets of the elite paramilitary organization, whose primary mission was to protect the Doge. This pleased the robot immensely, but he found himself troubled by the memory of the terrible defeat suffered by the Grand Fleet at Paradij ... the biggest military loss in merchant prince history. Sadness and guilt permeated his mechanical brain, but his logical circuitry told him that he had not been at fault, and that he had done his best possible job as Captain of the sentient machines.

Even so, he felt an inexplicable need to make up for the loss, in some manner. The loyal robot vowed to work even harder on behalf of Doge Lorenzo.

Chapter Fifty-One

We have been taught from birth to never trust any member of another race, not even those who profess to be our greatest, most virtuous friends.

—Hibbil Instruction

He knew he must be a comical sight this morning, a furry little Hibbil in the saddle of an immense tigerhorse, but Pimyt didn't care.

Far ahead, at the edge of a clearing, the Royal Attaché heard barking hounds and the shouts of other riders, who were barely visible to him as they hunted an elusive ivix. Pimyt sat sidesaddle on a magnificent bay steed at the rear of the pack, thinking about how much he hated having to get up so early, without time for a civilized breakfast. Hunger pangs gnawed at his stomach.

He tried to put such thoughts aside, knowing that his opportunity to get even for such discomforts would come. Very soon.

An ivix? Who cared about running one of those tiny horned creatures to ground and taking it home to stuff as a trophy? Pimyt had much more important prey in mind.

Purportedly, his own people were to Humans what Adurians were to Mutatis—allies, advisers, and legitimate business associates. But none of that was really true. It was all a deadly ruse. The extent of the treachery was immense and so cleverly fabricated that it spanned an entire galaxy.

The web of deceit permeated both Human and Mutati society at the highest levels.

As the Doge Lorenzo del Velli's most trusted associate, Pimyt exerted a great deal of influence over affairs of the realm. In the past, the furry, innocent-looking little fellow had even been appointed temporary Regent of the entire Merchant Prince Alliance, until the princes decided upon a new leader.

But Hibbils had never been loyal to Humans, nor had Adurians ever been allegiant to Mutatis. The Hibbils and Adurians were, in fact, secretly allied with one another in what they called the HibAdu Coalition, and for centuries had developed a diabolical scheme to overthrow both the Merchant Prince Alliance and the Mutati Kingdom.

Lorenzo was somewhere up ahead with most of the other riders, on the heels of the barking hounds and the little ivix that they all sought. It hardly seemed worth the effort to Pimyt. But he participated anyway, as he was expected to do. Not being of noble blood himself, some of the riders resented his presence, but he didn't care about any of that, the petty politics of Human society.

To his credit, Doge Lorenzo didn't care much about the pedigree of noble blood, even though it coursed through his own veins. Rather, he preferred to promote people on the basis of merit, regardless of the circumstances of birth. But that was not enough to redeem himself in the eyes of Pimyt or his Hibbil brethren. No Human could ever do that, and especially not the leader of their damnable kind.

In his years as a trusted confidant of Doge Lorenzo, Pimyt had accomplished a great deal, and in the process he had learned not to trust anyone. The downside of a lapse or oversight was too great. Better not to rely on anyone except his own people. Promises made between races were notoriously unreliable. Even the alliance between the Hibbils and the Adurians had its dangers, which his people were monitoring carefully.

Abruptly, Pimyt noticed that the hounds were running toward him, barking loudly, and the rest of the hunters were following them. Then he noticed something running low to the ground just ahead of the daggs, a little horned creature with fur that glinted gold when morning sunlight hit it.

Concealing himself and his mount in a thicket of leyland maples, he waited until the ivix ran by, then fired a shot from his vest-pocket gun at it, hitting the animal square in the side of its body. This was not a proper thing to do, so he quickly rode away through the trees, to avoid detection. Coming around behind the hunters again, he sat atop his tigerhorse, looking down at the fallen ivex.

"Looks like it's been shot," said a fop from the royal court.

"Who would do such an unsportsmanlike thing?" Lorenzo asked, looking from face to face. Since he trusted Pimyt explicitly, however, his gaze hardly touched the Hibbil.

No one seemed to know the answer.

As they rode back to the stables together, Pimyt felt very pleased. Now that this consummate waste of time was over, he could sit down for a decent meal. Despite his small stature, he had a voracious appetite. All of his people were this way, so it was a wonder that they didn't grow any larger.

* * * * *

That evening at his private apartment in the capital city, Pimyt received a coded message chip, containing very interesting information from his Adurian co-conspirators. With information from an unlikely source—Jacopo Nehr's own brother Giovanni—the Mutatis now had the secret of the nehrcom cross-space communication system. This was highly useful information to Pimyt. Not for the technology, but for the *lack of it* ... and the leverage this gave him. Jacopo Nehr had always been so secretive about the workings of the device, and now it turned out that it was not so complicated after all. With the message, Pimyt received a holo replica of the entire nehrcom transceiver, showing its simple inner workings.

* * * * *

The following afternoon, Pimyt plodded into Jacopo Nehr's private offices for an appointment he had requested, ostensibly to discuss details of their new working relationship. Behind his gleaming sirikan teak desk, Nehr looked more rested than usual, perhaps reflecting his contentment at having been selected as the top military officer in the Alliance.

"Congratulations on your appointment, General Nehr."

"Thank you."

"I would have thought you'd be out drilling your officers on your new programs," Pimyt said, as he climbed onto a chair that was too large for him and plopped himself down.

Nehr beamed. "As a businessman, I've learned how to delegate."

"I see. And how to manage crises, I presume?"

The man's eyes narrowed, just a little. "Of course. That comes with the territory."

"We'll see how good you are at it, then."

Leaning forward nervously, Nehr asked, "What do you mean?"

At a snap of his fingers, Pimyt produced a holo-image of the nehrcom transceiver, showing all of its inner workings. Like a bubble, it floated in front of the startled inventor, whose eyes looked more like an owl's now than those of a Human. The Hibbil suppressed a smile.

"W-where did you g-get this?" he stammered.

Ignoring the question, Pimyt said, "So, your famous transceiver is only a box of piezoelectric emeralds cut precisely and then arranged and linked in a specific way to open up the cross-galactic transmission lines. Interesting, isn't it, how the most important ideas are often so simple?"

"But h-how?.... w-where did you ... ?" Undoubtedly envisioning his galactic corporation crumbling around him, Nehr could hardly complete a sentence.

"I have my sources, shall we say? Let me caution you, before we go any farther, that I have given copies of this holo to certain key ... associates for safekeeping. And if anything were to happen to me ... " He smiled. "I need not go into detail, do I?"

Astounded, Nehr stared at the holo of precisely-arranged gems inside its box.

The Royal Attaché smiled, and said, "*Great* inventor! What a joke that is. As a Hibbil, with a long tradition of innovative manufacturing and development techniques, I know the difference."

"I've had my suspicions about you for a long time," Nehr muttered.

"And you consider yourself a fine judge of character, I presume?"

"What are you driving at?"

Rubbing his furry chin, Pimyt decided not to reveal what was on the verge of passing over his lips, that Nehr's own brother had betrayed him. No need to reveal that yet. There might be an opportunity to gain an advantage over the brother, too.

"Well?"

Delaying his response, Pimyt studied his new captive, considering how best to leash him and prevent him from biting. Nehr was red-faced. Perspiration trickled down his brow, into his eyes.

"If you don't cooperate with me," Pimyt said, "I'm in a position to ruin you. If I reveal your nehrcom secrets, you will no longer have a monopoly on instantaneous communication across the galaxy. There's also the little matter of your machine-manufacturing plants on Hibbil worlds. They could easily be nationalized, taken away from you."

"Get to the point. What is it you want?"

"Not so much. Just a little arrangement." Again, he hesitated, this time for dramatic effect. Nehr was getting more red-faced, sweating more.

"Here is what you will do," Pimyt finally said. "Periodically, I will give you communiqués, which you are to transmit to all planets in the Merchant Prince Alliance."

"Concerning what?"

"You are in no position to ask questions. And do not discuss this with anyone but me, in private. Not even Doge Lorenzo. Understood?"

The inventor nodded, reluctantly. He looked displeased and trapped.

Pimyt smiled. Unrevealed to Jacopo or any other Human, the Hibbils and Adurians had a military agenda of their own, and were now in a position to influence the placement and strength of Human forces. Some of the messages, in the midst of innocuous ones, would involve military matters....

Chapter Fifty-Two

People change, and so do worlds. The universe remains constant.
                                                              —Saying of the Sirikan Hill People

Inside an oval chamber on the lowest level of EcoStation, Noah stood at the most powerful magnaviewer window aboard, providing him with a high-resolution picture of the planet below the geostationary orbiter. Once, Canopa had been his world. He had known it well, and especially his beloved Ecological Demonstration Project there.

Subi Danvar wanted him to leave the orbital platform and seek refuge on some distant planet. But that was against Noah's nature. He didn't like to run away from anything, no matter how much sense it made to do so. Earlier, when he'd been caught in the surprise attack on CorpOne headquarters, he'd only been accompanied by a small entourage, and it had seemed prudent to escape quickly and analyze the situation. Now he hesitated, searching for alternatives.

Having received telebeam reports from the ground, and having watched through his magnaviewer, he knew that his security force had fought valiantly, and still held tenuous control over the southwest corner of the compound. But they had been unable to defend the main buildings, which had fallen to superior Red Beret and CorpOne forces. Such a disturbing alliance between his own sister Francella and Doge Lorenzo, and Subi had intercepted reports that more of their forces were on the way. It was only a matter of time until the brave Guardian defenders lost what little ground they still held.

And EcoStation would be next. The orbital platform had armoring and other defensive features, but could never hold out against a full-scale onslaught.

Several days ago, Noah had relayed an urgent nehrcom message directly to the Palazzo Magnifico, demanding an explanation for the attack and an emergency meeting with the Doge. So far there had been no response, but he continued to hold out hope.

He had not anticipated his sister's military aggression, nor her devious strategy of aligning herself with the man whom Noah had thought was no longer her lover. Those assumptions seemed to have been entirely wrong, and were costly mistakes. She might have stepped up the Lorenzo relationship with her lies and tricks, falsely accusing Noah of killing their father. Or perhaps she and the Doge had collaborated from the very beginning in the murder of Prince Saito, to take control of his business empire and blame the death on Noah.

He wanted to believe the best about Lorenzo del Velli, that the powerful leader had only been duped after the CorpOne attack, and that he and Francella had not collaborated in the murder. Lorenzo had been a patron to both Saito Watanabe and Jacopo Nehr, neither of whom had been noble born but whose careers had been advanced because of the support of the Doge.

Gazing down through the magnification window at his besieged compound, Noah felt rage and confusion, seeing the Doge's elite Red Beret soldiers setting up their own military installations. Some of the Doge's long-range artillery pieces were pointed up, aimed ominously at the orbiter. Nonetheless, Noah did not order an emergency change in the orbital path.

No matter the lies Francella told him, he couldn't believe that Lorenzo would try to blow him out of space. Not after what the Watanabe family had done for the Merchant Prince Alliance, far beyond the munitions plants that were part of Prince Saito's diverse corporate empire. Noah himself had contributed substantially to the war effort, restoring the ecology of the formerly worthless planet of Jaggem, so that it could be used as a key military outpost by the Alliance. The Doge had even visited Jaggem during the final stages of the reconstruction, to commend Noah and his Guardians for their excellent work. Noah always wanted to believe the best about people.

Suddenly, he saw a flash on the ground. One of the artillery pieces!

Then a flash from another gun, and an explosion in midair.

* * * * *

Having gotten into bed with Francella Watanabe in more ways than one, Doge Lorenzo del Velli had ordered the stationing of his elite Red Beret troops at her brother's ecological demonstration compound. Military personnel worked all around him now, setting up a command center in Noah Watanabe's former office. Lorenzo had stopped by to inspect the facility.

He had been frustrated by the holdouts in the southwest corner of the compound. Noah's security forces still held onto the maintenance and warehouse building there, but they wouldn't last long. He had more troops and weapons on the way.

As for EcoStation orbiting high overhead, the Doge had initially ordered its destruction, as Francella had demanded. She wanted him to "blast it out of orbit" with one of the big artillery pieces, and the final countdown had been initiated.

At the last possible moment, he had received an intelligence report that contained startling information. Lorenzo had shouted to stop the firing of the weapon, but he had been too late, and it had gone off. Thinking quickly, he had ordered an immediate intercepting shot, which followed in seconds, at an even higher velocity. The two projectiles had exploded in midair.

Now, breathing a heavy sigh of relief, the Doge reread the report. So perplexing. Supposedly his illegitimate son, Anton Glavine, was on board EcoStation … a son he didn't even know he had, and Francella Watanabe was the mother. The report contained purported evidence of the parentage, which would still require confirmation. If accurate, though, Francella would have a lot of explaining to do.

Could it possibly be true? Lorenzo had been told by a doctor that he could not father any more children, and had given up hope. But somehow, miraculously....

He caught himself, didn't dare hope, not without confirmation. But if the young man really was the only male child sired by Lorenzo the Magnificent, that was not something to be destroyed easily.

The Doge would have to take other measures to kill Noah Watanabe, no matter what Francella wanted.

Chapter Fifty-Three

It is said of Francella Watanabe that she should have been born a man, and that she has spent her life trying to make up for this affront.
                    —From *Red Rage*, the unauthorized biography

I t had not been their typical bedroom encounter. Usually the passion of the two lovers was physical, but now it filled the air. They had been about to make love and had taken off their clothes in a frenzy, throwing them in all directions, hardly able to wait. Then he told her.

"You spared EcoStation?" Francella screamed, rolling away from Lorenzo and sitting up on the bed. "Even though you knew my brother was up there, a sitting duck? How could you, after what he did to my father?" Furious, she pulled a long chartreuse blouse over her nakedness and clasped one of the buttons.

"You haven't been entirely truthful with me, have you?" he shouted back at her, only inches from her face. He grabbed the blouse and ripped it open.

She slapped him across the face. "I told you everything, the way Noah had my father killed, and all the other terrible things he did."

With a curse, Lorenzo held her wrists, preventing her from striking him again. "I'm not talking about Noah, although perhaps I should. As for your father, there are other more likely suspects."

"Which means?"

He smiled savagely. "For another time, my sweet. We want to save things to argue about later." Then, holding both of her hands with one, he used his other to smooth her long red hair. "I so enjoy it when we make up."

Glaring, Francella tried to pull away, but he held her tightly.

"You are a woman of secrets, aren't you?"

"Every woman has her secrets, you fool."

"But not nearly as interesting as yours. Would you like to tell me about our love child?"

He saw her face tighten, the knotting of muscles on her cheeks. "What do you mean?" she asked.

"The boy you concealed from me. My own *son*, damn you!"

She reddened. He saw the guilt all over her, didn't need any other confirmation.

"After he was born, I sent him away," she admitted, unable to hold gazes with him.

"And had your evil brother take care of him."

"No, I put the boy with a foster family."

Letting her go, Lorenzo pushed her away, against the headboard of the bed. "From what I hear, Noah has been monitoring his care for years, and recently made the boy one of his Guardians."

"One of his Guardians?"

"Our son is on EcoStation with Noah."

"So what? Kill them both, for all I care."

"But I have no other sons, don't you see? Princess Meghina has born only daughters for me. Our love child, it seems, is the rightful heir to my legacy. Assuming the Council of Forty proclaims him Doge, that is. Just think of it, Francella, history will call him The Bastard Doge."

"That wouldn't be any different from now," she snapped. "We already have a bastard in that position."

After a look of shock and anger, he let loose a deep, resounding guffaw, and said, "You're only saying that because you mean it." Laughing, he chased her around the bedroom, not letting her get to the door. Finally, exhausted and furious, she tumbled to the floor.

He took her in his arms, and finished ripping off her blouse.

Chapter Fifty-Four

The Human mind contains a universe of secrets.

—Noah Watanabe

An electronic field veiled the assault ship, making it invisible to the security force on the space station. This was accomplished with a stealth skin that projected images from one side of the large vessel's skin to the other, shifting seamlessly as the craft moved. The noise and heat signatures had been masked as well, and like a ghost the craft docked, undetected, on the underside of the immense orbiter.

A hatch door slid open on the vessel, followed by a large circular hatch on the space station, activated by a signal that kept the alarm system from going off. Hundreds of men in red uniforms slipped into a shadowy corridor, each of them made invisible by computerized images projected from one side of each body to the other, as if the person was not there at all.

All were Red Berets, the Doge's elite, fiercely loyal fighting force.

Through visors on their helmets, the men saw their companions, all dressed in red uniforms with caps. Heavily armed, they rushed through one corridor and another, using silencers on their handguns to kill any green-and-brown Guardians they encountered. With holo-schematics of the orbiter, images that danced on the visors in front of their eyes, they thought they knew the proper route. The route program had not been updated for all of the changes that had been made to the modular station, however, and the squad ran right past an entrance hatch to the classroom section. They then took a high-speed elevator to a lower level, the wrong one.

The Red Berets also had not taken precautions to bring weapons whose projectiles would not penetrate the skin of the space station. Errant shots went through exterior walls, activating the orbiter's emergency systems, which closed bulkhead doors and sealed holes to prevent catastrophic depressurization.

Alarm systems went off, and something in the jangle of electronics shut down their computerized image projectors. Suddenly the intruders were visible to guards, who fired stunner pellets at them, hitting one of the men and dropping him to the metal deck. The others ran on, leaving him behind.

* * * * *

Earlier, Noah had seen the artillery flashes, and his security advisers had confirmed to him that the second flash had been an intercepting shot. This had given him some measure of reassurance that Doge Lorenzo was not going to do anything rash. The first shot appeared to have been an equipment malfunction, which they had corrected immediately.

Now, as the alarms went off Noah stood in the school module, having just conducted a meeting with a number of his Guardians, trying to answer their questions and allay their fears. He had spoken truthfully to his loyal followers, not wishing to conceal anything from them.

None of his people had expressed any desire to abandon EcoStation, but he thought that might change when they were alone and not under the attentive eyes of their peers, not trying to prove anything to anyone or show courage they didn't really feel. They were all brave enough, Noah realized, but few of them were trained fighters. Only the security personnel. The rest were students, and support staff for the orbital platform.

The meeting had just ended, and he had been conferring with Tesh and Anton, considering what to do next. In a few minutes, Noah was scheduled for a one-on-one conference with Subi Danvar to consider alternatives.

Just then, the three of them heard the screaming wail of alarm klaxons. On a wall-mounted security screen, they saw Red Beret soldiers running through the corridors, firing weapons. Activating sound, Noah heard the squadron leader shouting to his companions.

"We're on the wrong level!" he shouted. "Glavine has classes on Level Four!"

"They're looking for me!" Anton said. "Why?"

"Your father's special forces," Tesh said. "And they don't look friendly."

"Somehow they know your schedule," Noah said, wondering how they had gotten the information, and what they hoped to do with it.

"My father either wants to kill me or kidnap me," Anton said.

Noah took a deep, agitated breath. He remembered what his adjutant Subi Danvar always told him, that he was the soul of the Guardians and needed to survive for the sake of the organization and all they stood for. In his desire to fight back against his sister and the Doge, Noah had not wanted to follow the advice for his own welfare, and had only gone along with it reluctantly. Now he needed to survive and fight another day, for his vital cause and for the people who believed in him.

Some time ago he had asked the Doge for an emergency meeting to explain the attack against the ecology compound, and at last he had his answer. Noah saw no advantage in being taken to any meeting by force, or in dying here.

Speaking sharply into a lapel microphone, he told Subi to broadcast a general evacuation order to everyone on the station, readying ships that would disperse his people to predetermined locations on Canopa. Then he commanded the adjutant to prepare a grid-plane for him, and provided a short list of passengers he wanted to accompany him. Over the communication link, Danvar confirmed receiving the message, and said he would take care of it all right away.

"Hurry!" Noah urged, leading the way through a door at the rear of the classroom. The trio ran through a narrow corridor to a spiral stairway and bounded up four levels, taking two steps at a time.

They reached the top and ran through a wide doorway onto a metalloy platform. Grid-planes were tethered on the other side of a bubble window, their green-and-brown hulls floating in zero gravity. Guardians ran toward the three people on the platform, their boots making echoing sounds. Subi Danvar, moving quickly despite his broad girth, led them.

"I issued your evacuation order, Master Noah," Subi reported, "and all ships are ready."

Seeing Eshaz reach the platform, which was on his short list of priority passengers, Noah motioned for him to join them.

The group hurried through an airlock and boarded one of the grid-planes. Subi Danvar took the controls, and powered up the engines. The sleek craft surged out of the docking bay into orbital space.

Through a porthole, Noah saw two red gunships, more of the Doge's force. One of them opened fire with automatic weapons, ripping holes through the cabin. Noah heard the hiss of escaping air, and the whistle of repair systems going on, sealing the holes in the hull.

"Get this crate going!" he shouted to Subi. "We're faster than they are!"

"I'm trying!" Subi shouted. "Hold on. Here we go!"

The supercharged grid-plane picked up speed, and the passengers found things to hold onto: seat backs, bulkheads, railings. Through a porthole, Noah saw other escape ships scattering away from the station, using their superior speed and on-board scanning equipment to elude the Doge's electronic grids. Noah knew that some of his followers would still be captured or killed, but all of them had the same opportunity to get away that he did.

"We need to get to a podship," Noah said. "There's a planet we can go where our environmental activists have a clandestine support network. I've told some of you about it ... Plevin Four."

"I'll do the best I can," Subi said, "but the Doge may already have gunships around the pod station."

Anton asked a question about Plevin Four, said he was unfamiliar with it. Tesh told him it was an abandoned world, that it had a history alternating between Mutati and MPA control.

Just as Noah started to tell his nephew more about Plevin Four, projectiles ripped through the passenger compartment. He felt something sting his arm, and the side of his head. Then something tore into his left foot. Terrible pain, and dizziness. He lost consciousness and fell in a bloody heap on the carpeted deck....

Sitting by Noah, Tesh held his bleeding head on her lap, as the grid-plane accelerated and automatic repair systems repaired the hull damage. A wall and ceiling of the cabin were torn up. Anton popped open a first-aid kit, began applying gauze bandages on the wounds. Eshaz came over and stood silently, looking down at the fallen Master of the Guardians.

Tesh had never understood Tulyans, the way they kept their emotions bottled up, never revealing their inner thoughts. She knew that Noah thought highly of this one, so she tried to show him respect. But it was not easy. Her own Parvii people and the Tulyans were natural enemies, ancient competitors for dominion over the galactic herds of podships. So far Eshaz had shown no indication of recognizing her—the Parvii magnification system was a closely guarded secret—but she didn't trust him.

"We're beginning to outdistance them!" Subi shouted. "Almost out of range now."

Looking up, Tesh saw blue tracers zip by a porthole, but nothing more hit them. She heard Subi say the vessel's on-board repair systems were continuing to seal the holes.

"Noah needs medical attention," Tesh said. "His head is bleeding, and his foot is torn up bad." She checked the bandages, and it occurred to her how Human bodies, like this ship, had automatic repair systems—but how much better it would be if people were capable of healing themselves from even the most serious wounds. She worried about Noah, having grown to admire him, and hoped for more between them.

"I'll see what I can find," Subi said, "but we need to leave Canopa as soon as possible. It's too hot for us here." He steered down into the atmosphere of Canopa, causing sparks to fly off the underside of the hull during reentry. When they were a couple of thousand meters above the planet, he leveled out and slowed.

Going over to a porthole, Tesh surveyed the trees and farms of the countryside below, then pointed and said, "Head that way: northeast, I think. I know a doctor." She glanced at her wristchron, which had adjusted itself to their locale, and saw that it was late afternoon. "He should be home now, too."

A few minutes later, they set down on a wide parking area between the sprawling main house and the tigerhorse stables. Half a dozen men emerged from the front of the house, dressed in cloaks and brocaded surcoats. Ladies in shimmering evening gowns stood on the broad porch behind them, some holding drinks.

One of the men, square-jawed, went down the steps and strode toward the grid-plane. Tesh recognized Dr. Hurk Bichette, her former lover. The two of them exchanged glares.

She led Subi and Anton, and introduced them. "Sorry to interrupt your dinner party," Tesh said, "but we have an emergency. Noah Watanabe is on board, and he's seriously injured."

"Head wound," Subi said. "But that looks like a glancing blow. His left foot might be the worst of it. He passed out after he got hit there."

"I'll get my bag," Bichette said, in his deep voice. He ran inside the house, and emerged moments later, carrying a black bag and a large packet with a clear covering, showing a variety of healing pads inside, of varying sizes.

"Let me help you with that," Tesh said, taking the packet from him and then following him aboard the grid-plane.

While Bichette knelt over Noah and tended to him on the deck, Tesh helped. Looking up, she saw Subi step forward with a handgun. "I'm afraid we'll have to borrow you for a while," he told the doctor. "We'll send apology cards to your dinner guests."

"What do you mean?" Bichette asked.

"It's no longer safe for us on Canopa," Anton said, accepting the gun as Subi handed it to him. "We have another planet in mind, and you're going with us."

She looked over at Eshaz. The large, bronze-scaled Tulyan stood silently, watching, taking it all in as if he was looking into another realm, as if he were not actually here.

"But I can't!" Bichette protested. "This isn't an ordinary dinner party. It's an important business meeting. My guests are wealthy investors, considering a business proposition I made to them."

"Business can wait," Subi said, as he slipped into the command chair. Safety restraints snapped automatically into place around him, but he shoved them away. "Lives can't."

"Listen to me. Noah needs a hospital. We can't have him bouncing around in a grid-plane." The vein on Bichette's temple throbbed.

"I'll take off smoothly," Subi said. "We don't have any way of securing him, of strapping him down."

"Stop thinking about yourself," Tesh said to Bichette, "and tend to your patient."

The doctor glowered at her, but did as she demanded.

Tesh felt the grid-plane's rocket system kick on, but as promised they made a smooth ascent. In a matter of minutes, they reached the upper atmosphere, then surged into orbital space, with the vessel's gravitational system on.

"Where are we going?" Tesh asked.

"Plevin Four," Subi said. "That's where Noah told me to go."

"But he's been injured, needs a hospital."

"They have a medical facility on Plevin Four," Subi said.

Through the wide front window, Tesh saw the globular pod station ahead, floating. Subi drew near, then circled the station twice, without entering any of the docking bays. "Keep your eyes open for bad guys," he said, looking at the ships that were lined up inside. Tesh only saw two, and neither of them was emblazoned with the Doge's or CorpOne's colors.

Warily, Subi guided the vessel into one of the docking bays and found a berth. "We got here fast," he said, "but our pursuers aren't far behind us."

Just then, Tesh felt a pressure change inside the cabin, and heard a faint, familiar pop. Looking out a side windowport, she saw green luminescence around a podship as it floated toward the main docking bay of the station. As seconds passed, the luminescence dissipated, leaving the mottled gray-and-black exterior of the vessel. All of the sentient spacecraft looked essentially the same to the untrained eye, but Tesh recognized the characteristic streaks and other markings on this one. She had been in the Parvii swarm that originally captured it in deep space, more than five centuries ago. While the Parviis had taken control of the vast majority of podships long before that, there were always wild pods wandering through the cosmos, strays to be rounded up.

Presently, a wide door opened on the side of the podship. All three of the waiting vessels floated aboard into the cavernous cargo hold, and their crews secured them to tethers.

They got underway quickly, engaging with the podways of deep space, connective fibers so fine that they could not be seen by anyone except the podships, and a handful of other races. Parviis were among the select few, but in their case it was only while at the helms of podships. Tesh was not certain who the pilot of this craft was, since assignments changed regularly. She could go into the sectoid chamber and find out—perhaps it was an old friend—but it was risky to do so, since she might be observed while changing her personal magnification system, getting smaller and later getting larger again. Usually, she did not take the chance, and certainly not this time, when she wanted to be near Noah and do whatever she could to keep him alive.

At least he was breathing regularly, and from the expression on his face he did not appear to be in any pain. Such an attractive man, she thought, with his freckles and curly red hair. He was the strong, take-charge type, so certain of his purpose in life and able to inspire others around him.

You certainly inspired me, she thought. Gently, she touched his temple on the uninjured side of his head, and felt the reassuring pulse of his heartbeat.

She caught a hard gaze from Anton, who sat by a porthole, intermittently looking out into the cargo hold or at her. Since picking up Dr. Bichette, Tesh had noticed Anton acting irritably, as if jealous of her former lover. She felt nothing for Bichette anymore, not for months now. That relationship was over.

Or was Anton jealous of Noah instead? While expressing concern for his injured uncle, Anton might actually resent the attention she was giving him herself. And she really did care about him. Maybe Anton had noticed something. She didn't care. In her long lifetime, Tesh had known many men, and always knew that she would have to end each relationship one day. Her lifespan was much longer than theirs, after all, and she didn't want to stay with a person who was going to die. She didn't think it was cruel on her part. In reality, she was overly sensitive and always tried to keep from getting too close to anyone, since that only made it more difficult. Her feelings for Noah were developing, but different from anything she had experienced before. She felt excitement at this, and fear.

The podship made only two brief stops along the way, at pod stations in remote sectors where there was not much activity. On board the grid-plane, Tesh and Dr. Bichette rounded up pillows, blankets, and anything else they could find to make the patient more comfortable. Once, Noah had moved his hands, as if gesturing with them while he talked, and his lips moved, without making any sounds. Then he became motionless again, except for his regular breathing and pulse.

Through it all, Eshaz said nothing, did nothing. To Tesh, it was very strange. She thought he should be doing something to help.

Only a few minutes after leaving Canopa and journeying far across the galaxy, the sentient spacecraft arrived at a pod station orbiting the planet of Plevin Four, in a belt of dead galactic stars. Subi provided details as he guided the grid-plane out of the cargo hold, then through a docking bay of the pod station, and out into orbital space. He shifted the propulsion system to conventional hydion, since they were away from the grid-system of Canopa.

"This world was stripped of its natural resources long ago by CorpOne mining operations," he said. "PF—its common name—is technically still owned by the corporation but is valued on their balance sheets at virtually nothing. We Guardians have been 'squatting' here for years without detection, using it as a training station and bolt-hole."

"Doesn't look like much," Anton said, studying a report on the ship's computer. "Hardly any natural beauty, bad weather, irritable natives. I see why you weren't noticed here."

"It's a good training ground," Subi said.

The craft headed down through a hazy atmosphere, toward the surface of the planet, with its gray-and-yellow hills, rivers, and lakes. "We do terraforming experiments here, practicing our ecological engineering methods for use elsewhere."

Through the front window of the grid-plane, Tesh saw a deep scar running for perhaps a thousand kilometers on the surface of PF. She asked about it, and when the adjutant did not reply Anton checked the on-board computer terminal.

"CorpOne leased it out to a strip mining operation," he said. "Doesn't say here what they took out, but whatever it was, they must have gotten all that was worth getting. Looks dead down there now."

The grid-plane flew low over the terrain. In six hours they reached the dark side of the planet, and Tesh made out a dark, serpentine river below. They flew over it for a distance, then slowed and hovered in front of a high embankment, illuminated by spotlights from the aircraft. Two big doors yawned open in the river bank, revealing a large, dark chamber beyond. With the aircraft's spotlights probing ahead, making fingers of illumination, they flew into the chamber. Looking back, Tesh saw the cliff doors close.

As Subi landed and shut down the engines, he said, "Centuries ago, PF was under Mutati control. How the MPA took it away from them, I don't know. This is a military bunker. originally built by Mutati civil engineers. A short ways downriver, it empties into a swirling, pale yellow sea."

"Sounds picturesque," Anton said, his voice caustic. "Can't wait to see it tomorrow." He caught a sharp glance of displeasure from Tesh, who then went to check on Noah. She watched Dr. Bichette replace the healing pads on his patient's injured foot.

"Head's OK but his foot doesn't look any better," Bichette said. "It's badly mangled and in need of more than these pads."

Tesh felt tears welling in her eyes. She looked away. Through the portholes and front window, she saw that they had landed below the level of the river. Murky water could be seen through thick glax viewing plates and airlocks.

"Wonder where everyone is," Subi said. He stood at the open hatch of the grid-plane, gazing out into the cavern. Behind him, a heavy plate slid over the control panel of the aircraft, apparently preventing anyone from stealing it. Tesh noticed him slip something into his pocket.

Deep in thought, the big adjutant bounded down the steps to the rock floor of the chamber, then ducked around the tail of the aircraft to the other side. She saw him open a heavy metal door and stride through, into what looked like a room, or perhaps a corridor. A while later, he returned. By then, Tesh and Anton were outside the grid-plane, looking around themselves. Dr. Bichette and Eshaz were still inside with Noah.

Subi said, "Hundreds of Guardians are supposed to be here, but it doesn't look like anyone's been here for months."

"What do we do now?" Tesh asked. "This doesn't look like any place to stay, especially with Noah's condition. You said it had a medical facility."

"That wasn't entirely true," Subi admitted, rubbing the purple birthmark on his cheek. "They used to have a small clinic here, but I was hoping that Master Noah would come back to consciousness, especially after we got the doctor. Noah wanted to come here, so I thought I should do what he wanted."

She frowned. "But you've been to other planets with him, all the ecological reconstruction projects around the galaxy. Surely one of them is better than this place?"

He shook his head. "They're all well known, so the Doge probably sent forces to them, taking control of the projects. In fact, any of the main merchant princes worlds are a problem now, because of the dragnet that's out for us."

"I see." Tesh felt frustrated, and angry that Noah wasn't getting the care he needed.

She heard what sounded like an anguished cry, coming from the grid-plane. Worried, she ran up the steps into the passenger cabin.

Dr. Bichette held a bloody white cloth, wrapped around something.

"One of Noah's feet was so badly shot up that I had to amputate it," he said, in an emotionless voice.

Horrified, Tesh looked down at the unfortunate Noah, who lay on the deck, face up. His head rested on a pillow, and he had a thin blanket over him. Another bloody white cloth was wrapped around the stump where his foot used to be. He slept, as before, except now his face was a mask of anguish.

"You fool!" Tesh screamed. "Why did you do that?"

"I did what I had to do. It was either that, or infection would have set in and he would have lost his entire leg. Or his life."

"But the healing pads ..."

He shook his head. "They don't solve everything. I had no choice."

"Why didn't you consult with the rest of us? Maybe we could have figured out another place to go, where they have medical facilities. Damn you, Hurk!"

"And you, Eshaz!" she howled, glaring at the motionless Tulyan. "Why didn't you stop him?"

"I'm not a doctor, madam."

Turning back to Bichette, she started beating on his chest. The doctor backed up, looking surprised and shocked.

Anton pulled her off him, and forced her to sit on the deck, where he knelt beside her. "You need to calm down," he said. "The doctor only did what he thought was best. He couldn't consult with us. As Eshaz said, we aren't doctors. The decision was Dr. Bichette's alone."

"Let go of me," she demanded, trying to pull free of his strong grip.

But he held on. "Not until you promise to calm down."

Stubbornly, she shook her head, and Anton held tight....

The surgical procedure had been a traumatic event for his uncle, but Anton couldn't suppress feeling envy, having noticed that Tesh was overly interested in Noah.

It was driving the young man crazy.

Chapter Fifty-Five

A thought has no dimensions, no weight, no color, no texture, no way to look at it, touch it, or hold it in your hands. And yet, it has substance. It is the spark of every galactic race, the flame of their hopes and dreams. It is the spark of the robot race.

—Thinker, Contemplations

It looked like no more than a dull gray metal box, sitting on an observation deck at the Inn of the White Sun. Inside, a sentient robot was in deep contemplation, having folded himself inward to avoid distractions and interruptions.

In the decades since Hibbils had manufactured him on their Cluster Worlds, Thinker had interacted with countless Humans. Some he liked and some he did not, but always he treated them with deference and respect, since Humans had designed him and paid for his manufacture and he was honorbound to serve their needs. Even now, after they discarded him in a trash heap, and he and others like him had to regenerate themselves, he bore no feelings of malice toward the people who threw him away.

That may, in fact, have been a blessing to him.

By virtue of his own ingenuity and perseverance, Thinker had developed a considerable degree of independence from Humans. Certainly, he did not serve them on a daily basis anymore, and saw far fewer of them than he used to. In addition, he had discovered new abilities that he didn't know he had, and which he didn't think had ever been programmed into him.

He had thought up the idea of creating a machine army out of discarded robots, and for more than a year they had been training down on the surface of Ignem. Not so long ago, Jimu led a squad of his soldiers on a mission to save Doge Lorenzo from an assassination attempt, and they were so gloriously successful that the Doge had invited them to join his special force, the prestigious Red Berets.

Sensing something, Thinker unfolded himself into the familiar form of a flat-bodied robot, the way he had looked when Humans first designed him, before he later added the folding feature himself.

Out in space not far from the inn, he saw a burst of green luminescence as a podship arrived, seeming to pop out of another dimension into this one. The gray-and-black vessel, making one of the stops on its route, proceeded to the pod station.

Thinker hurried to the lobby of the inn, to see if there were any guest arrivals. He was not the innkeeper; other robots did that for him. But as one of the machines who founded the inn, he liked to break his intense contemplation routines on occasion to see the colorful galactic races and robots that stopped off here on their various personal, business, and government missions.

Ten minutes later, only one passenger stepped into the lobby of the machine-run lodge in the orbital ring, having taken a shuttle from the pod station. Carrying no luggage, he strode to the registration desk, and spoke to the robot clerk. Curious, Thinker eavesdropped from a short distance away.

"My name is Giovanni Nehr," the man said. "I'm on my way to Timian One, but first I need a little R and R."

Searching his data banks, Thinker found entries about this tall, sharp-featured man, and visuals to confirm the identity. This was the younger brother of the famous nehrcom inventor, Jacopo Nehr. He had a healing pad on his left arm, over the bicep.

"Seven nights, please," the visitor said. Reaching into his pocket, he dumped a handful of lira chips into a hopper. The alloy pieces rattled around, and the machine dropped his change into a tray. Nehr stuffed the smaller denominations into his pocket.

"I see you are hurt," Thinker said, stepping closer with a clatter.

After looking him over, Nehr said, "It's nothing. Just a nick."

"Would you like us to look at it?"

"No, thank you." The smile was stiff, making Thinker suspicious, as if he might be hiding something.

"That looks like a Mutati healing pad," the robot observed. "It has a distinctive fold and color."

"Oh? I wasn't aware of that. A passenger on the podship handed it to me."

"A *Mutati* passenger?"

The man reddened. "If so, I wasn't aware of it. He looked Human to me. He seemed kind enough, and wouldn't have cared about me if he really was a Mutati. Would he?"

"You wouldn't think so. Unless he was trying to get information out of you. Did he ask a lot of questions?"

"Like you, you mean?" Nehr smiled stiffly.

"Yes."

"Well, come to think of it, he was rather curious."

"And what did you tell him?"

"Mmmm, not much. The cross-space journey was brief, only a few minutes."

"Forgive my questions, but we are very security conscious here, and our data banks require information."

"I am quite tired," Nehr said, "so if you will forgive me, I'd like to go to my room now."

But Thinker took a step closer, and his voice intensified, since he always worried about what Mutatis were up to, and the harm they constantly inflicted on Humans. "Did you see any Mutatis that were recognizable?"

"By name, you mean? I'm not personally acquainted with their kind."

"By *race*, Mr. Nehr. Did you see any shapeshifters in their natural, fleshy form, perhaps in the neutral confines of the podship?"

"Yes. They travel, as all of the races do."

"I'm sensing something more. Forgive me, Mr. Nehr, but I am very perceptive. I have developed my mind and senses to very high levels. Sometimes I wonder if I have what you Humans refer to as a sixth sense. Am I mistaken about you?"

Chewing at the inside of his mouth, Nehr said, "Not exactly." He paused, and leaned back against the registration desk. "I went to a planet called Nui-Lin for a vacation, and found out it was a Mutati front. They took me prisoner and put me on a prison moon. I barely escaped with my life." He touched his injured arm.

Thinker detected a mélange of truth and fiction, but didn't press any more, and bade the man good day. As Nehr followed a bellhop robot to his room, Thinker sorted through what he had just heard, and combined it with what he had been learning from other travelers. The Mutatis were more active along the space corridors than they had been in many years. Historically, this meant they were up to something big, perhaps a surprise military attack. They were a race of devious tricksters, able to assume many guises and sneak behind enemy lines to learn information.

Quickly, Thinker dictated a letter into his internal word processor and transferred it to a disk cylinder, for delivery to the Doge Lorenzo del Velli. With no nehrcom transmitter available at the Inn of the White Sun, the missive would go out on the next podship, carried to the merchant prince capital by Agar, a repaired messenger robot.

Unfortunately, due to a programming glitch, Agar would become lost in deep space and never make it to his destination. No one ever would ever hear from him again.

Chapter Fifty-Six

Dreams are the products of imagination, and the fuel of civilization.
                                                            —Chia, a merchant prince poet

Back when they were small boys, Dux Hannah and his cousin Acey Zelk used to dream of running away to space together and sharing grand adventures, of meeting beautiful girls and getting richer than the grandest princes in the realm.

Living in the wild back country of Siriki, their plans had been vague in those days, more the fantasies of fanciful children than reality. Then they were enslaved, first by merchant princes and later by Mutatis, before using their wiles to escape from both. Thus, before their seventeenth birthdays, they had been abused by both sides of the ongoing galactic war. This might have left them feeling put upon and filled with hatred toward their captors, but it had done nothing of the kind. On the contrary, they remained upbeat, and harkened back to the "old days" when they planned to share fabulous journeys together.

Through all that they had shared, the boys had forged a bond between them, a friendship that extended far beyond the familial blood they shared. Their camaraderie had been forged in a crucible of perilous escapades, when any moment might have been their last. But they persevered through what they called "misadventures," and lived to look back on the experiences, and even to laugh about them.

After escaping from the Mutati prison moon, Dux and Acey stowed away on conventional spacecraft and podships, vagabonding from one star system to another, from one pod station to another. If a place interested them, perhaps after talking with strangers along the way, they went down to the planet and investigated it.

Now they were on the third such world they had visited in the past few weeks, each time having to panhandle for shuttle fares, since they had no money. While podship trips were free of charge—traveling routes developed by the mysterious, sentient pods—shuttle trips usually were not. This could have left them stranded in space if they had not been able to figure out ways to get down to the planets.

It was risky leaving the pod stations and venturing down, so before venturing to the surface, they developed the habit of asking as many questions as they could. If they didn't like the answers, or if they could not get enough information to make them feel comfortable, they remained in space and caught the next podship, bound for unknown sectors. This caused them to avoid both MPA and Mutati worlds, and to shun planets controlled by the allies of both sides as well, principally those of the Hibbils and the Adurians.

Such caution did not restrict their movements that much. The galaxy was a vast place, filled with colorful races and exotic worlds. In spite of their youth, Dux and Acey became good judges of character. That didn't mean someone couldn't slip something by them, but they did work hard at it, and they were both quite intelligent, despite having no formal education....

On Vippandry, their shuttle descended past the Floating Airgardens, one of the Wonders of the Galaxy. The gardens, circular tiers of flowers and lawns that floated in the lower atmosphere, rose more than seven kilometers into the air and covered many cubic meters. They looked to the naked eye like holo projections, but were real, kept aloft by exotic, lighter-than-air plants from all over the galaxy, selected by master gardeners.

The shuttle pilot, a Vippandry with billowing white hair, acted like a tour guide for the trip down from the pod station. "You're lucky," he said. "The gardeners are at work now." He laughed. "I should have charged you more."

The passengers—an assortment of shapes and races—thronged to the windows, pushing for better views. They oohed and awed in their native languages, while gardeners wearing jet packs pruned the plants and added aerosol nutrients to the lighter-than-air soils. Dux thought they looked like bees or hummingbirds tending flowers, nurturing them.

At the Airgarden Gift Shop, Dux and Acey read a computerized bulletin board, looking for jobs. They paused to peruse enlistment ads for Noah Watanabe's Guardians, and learned of the ecological engineering work they performed on several planets. The work sounded interesting to the boys, and they liked a good cause, but they had something more adventurous in mind.

They spent more than a day panhandling around the shuttleport, and on the narrow, cobblestone streets of the nearby old city. The following day they made it back to the orbital pod station.

While waiting for the next podship into space, they wandered along the sealed walkways of the station. Looking through plax viewing windows at the ships out in the zero-g docking bays, they watched the crews as they performed various tasks or just stood around chatting. One mixed group of aliens and Humans had a mechanical problem with their spaceclipper. Wearing breather suits, they had one of the engine compartments open, with parts scattered on the adhesive surface of a work platform. An old vessel, it had maroon-and-vermillion swirls on the sides, and the graceful structural lines of a bygone era. Somehow its crew had managed to keep it going this long, but to Dux it looked like the end of the line. The name of the vessel was emblazoned on its side in golden letters, "*Avelo.*"

As the two teenagers looked on, a Hibbil crewman stepped through an airlock and approached them, a rugged-looking little fellow dressed in black. He wore an eye patch, and a sword in a scabbard.

"Where you boys headed?" he asked in a squeaky voice.

"Deep space," Acey said.

"That covers a lot of territory, doesn't it?" He rubbed his furry chin. "No place in particular?"

They shook their heads.

"We're a treasure ship," the Hibbil said, gripping the handle of his sword. "I'm Mac Golden, official purser on the ship. I keep track of everything important for the captain." The little fellow beamed proudly. "He considers me the most trustworthy person on the crew."

"Your ship is full of treasure?"

"Sometimes it is, sometimes it isn't. On this run, we've had a streak of bad luck, more trouble than you could...." He paused, and stared at a podship as it entered the docking bay. Simultaneously, the crew of the treasure ship stopped working, to look.

The podship swung wildly and bumped into the Hibbil's vessel, almost jerking it free of its moorings. Then the podship continued on its way, to the main docking bay at the center of the pod station. When it was safe, the crew returned to their work on the engine.

"That's the third time one of those pods has nudged us," Mac Golden said. "They seem impatient with us, but we can't leave yet."

"C'mon," Dux said to Acey. "Let's go catch our ride."

But Acey hesitated. He watched the crew at work, then went over and spoke to them through a wall speaker. "These hydion drives can be temperamental, eh?" Acey said.

"You know anything about them?" one of the crew asked from out in the docking bay, a tall, black-bearded Ordian.

"Yeah, a little."

A short while later the podship left, again bumping into the *Avelo*, and then continuing on its way.

Saying he might be able to help, Acey talked them into loaning him a breather suit. He went out and immersed himself in the engine work, examining the pieces carefully, discussing them with the crew, asking questions like a doctor diagnosing the symptoms of a patient. One of the men took an interest in Acey, a gray-beard who wore a dirty white shirt and a red sash around his waist.

"That's Wimm Yuell," Mac said. "Our captain."

Dux nodded. A while later, a dark-skinned alien—small and swarthy, with a pointed snout—emerged from the ship and passed food bars around to the crew as they worked. He didn't wear a breather, making Dux wonder where he was from. Dux got one of the bars from Mac. He found it delicious, but with fruity flavors that he couldn't identify.

Acey kept working with the captain and the others, and they seemed to be following his advice. The crew was putting the engine back together, while Acey used diagnostic devices to test the components.

Bored and wanting to leave, Dux strolled down the walkway. He learned from a glyphreader panel hanging from the ceiling that the next podship wasn't due for a couple of days.

Dux took his time, exploring the walkways and the waiting room, looking at reading material that had been left behind. He spent some time chatting with an old man who called himself the manager of the pod station, though Dux didn't think any such position existed. He seemed a little touched in the head, but harmless enough.

By the time Dux returned, the crew was excited and smiling. They had the engine running, and were patting Acey on the back.

Coming over to Dux, Mac Golden said, "Your cousin asked just the right questions to get the mechanics thinking along the proper lines."

"I was afraid he'd ruin something," Dux said, glancing at the tough-looking little Hibbil.

"Welcome to the *Avelo*," Mac said, reaching up and shaking Dux's hand energetically.

When they were underway in space, Dux and Acey met the whole crew, an eclectic group of androids, Humans, and aliens who followed treasure maps, tips, and hunches all over the galaxy. They looked like a rough-and-tumble bunch, but took a liking to the young men.

Captain Yuell said to them, "You each get half shares to start, with the opportunity of working your way up."

"That's great, sir," Acey said. "You can count on us. We can do men's work, you'll see."

"We specialize in searching for merchant shipwrecks," the captain said. "But it takes more than maps."

"Well if you're looking for luck," Acey said, "I can provide that."

"Luck has a way of changing around here," Mac Golden said. "Don't get too full of yourself. Not yet."

Acey's face reddened, and he said, "Yes, sir. Sorry...."

The young men found themselves on a voyage unlike anything they had ever imagined, bound for unknown parts, with undiscovered adventures and treasures awaiting them.

Chapter Fifty-Seven

If not for the magic of perception,
Nothing would exist.
It is the spark of the universe.

——Parvii Inspiration

Like a visitor to a municipal aquarium, the woman stood in front of a large clearglax plate, gazing out at the marine shapes swimming in the water, but it was murky out there and she was having some difficulty discerning what she was seeing.

Nothing was as it seemed here. This was not an aquarium, and she was not a full-sized human. Tesh Kori felt dampness in the air, and pulled her coat tighter around her shivering body. Back at the grid-plane, Noah still had not returned to consciousness after almost two days. She'd been worrying about him when she went to the window wall, and had tried to calm herself by looking out into the flowing river. But it was having the opposite, disturbing effect on her. She tried to peer deeper into the water.

On her right, she heard her companions working to open a stone door that none of them had noticed before, in what had appeared to be a solid rock wall. That morning, Anton had discovered the almost unnoticeable door, and now they were using cutting tools on it.

Standing at what looked like a wall of water, she'd been thinking about perception, and the old Parvii saying about it being the spark of the universe. She wondered, as she had before, what the architect of that aphorism had in mind when he or she came up with it. Didn't perception extend to all of the senses, and not just to what you could see? Yes, of course, and at the moment she considered her various known senses and one that was not so easy to identify, lying just beneath the surface of her consciousness. Humans and their tiny Parvii cousins called it the sixth sense, but other races had a different number for it, since they had more or less senses. But the various sentient races were in universal agreement: this level of awareness existed.

Through the clear plates, Tesh saw frothing out in the river, and large, blurry shapes swimming toward her and then veering off to one side or the other, getting enticingly close to the glax without allowing her to see what they were. She touched the thick window wall, the coolness of it, and frowned.

There is danger here, she thought. And she was about to call for her companions when she heard Anton shout.

"Tesh! Get over here!" He stood in an open doorway, where there had been none before. The others were behind him, moving around inside another chamber. Their voices were murmurous, agitated.

Hurrying over there, she saw an additional chamber fronting the river. While smaller than the main chamber, it had a window wall as high as the other one. She went inside, and her nostrils wrinkled as she picked up a revolting stench.

Death.

In one corner, she saw the blackened, charred bodies of Humans jammed up against the rock wall—men and women who seemed to have been trying to escape but had no way out. She noted burned, bloody Guardian uniforms on some of them, while the clothing of others, and most of their skin, had been burned off. The victims had pitted eye sockets, seared-off hair, and scorch marks on their melted, horribly burned faces.

"This explains where thirty of the missing Guardians are," Dr. Bichette said.

Anton shone a flashbeam on the walls, went around and rubbed his hands over the surfaces, checking them. "But what could have killed these people?" he asked. "We came through the only door, and it was sealed from the inside."

"A locked-door mystery," Eshaz said. His bronze-scaled face, usually taciturn, showed concern now, in the downturn of the reptilian snout and the nervous gaze of the slitted eyes. "I don't like it in here."

"This was supposed to be a safe room," Anton said, "where they could get away from attackers. I suspect the other Guardians are around here somewhere, too, in additional safe rooms, or maybe up on the surface. They were trying to get away from something."

"And it got them anyway," Bichette said. "I think Eshaz is right. This place gives me the creeps. Let's go."

"I was just about to call for all of you," Tesh said, as the group moved toward the door. She pointed at the window wall and the blurry, swimming shapes out in the current. They had moved over to this chamber now and were continuing their strange water dance, getting closer and closer without revealing details of their features. They were large, the size of canopan sharks or dolphins.

Something flashed in the water, but for only a second, a glint of color. Red.

"Hurry," Eshaz said, pushing his Human companions toward the door. "Those are hydromutatis, swimming shapeshifters. They're still here from the time when this planet was controlled by the Mutati Kingdom."

As they reached the grid plane and boarded, Eshaz added, "I have heard of worlds with large bodies of water, where all of the hydromutatis could not be killed off by the Humans who took over."

"I've heard the same," Tesh said. "Hydromutatis are much more elusive than terramutatis or aeromutatis, and are very difficult to hunt down."

Eshaz nodded his scaly bronze head. The grid-plane shook as he boarded, from his great weight.

"But the hydromutatis are sealed off from the chambers," Anton said. "They couldn't have killed the Guardians."

"The creatures are rumored to have telepathic powers," Eshaz said. "They are also called Seatels."

As Tesh took a seat and watched Subi Danvar work the controls, she felt a tingle in her mind, and heard what sounded like pounding against the walls of the bunker, like a heavy surf slamming into a bulkhead. Or like Diggers burrowing their way through rock and dirt.

She heard a mechanical whine as Subi tried to start the engines. But they didn't catch. At the window wall, she saw scores of Seatels, their features clearly visible now, with smoldering red eyes and undersized heads.

Suddenly, a lance of light from one of the Seatels hit the grid-plane and fried the engines, so that they would not start....

Chapter Fifty-Eight

From birth to death, life is a game of chance.

—Old Sirikan Saying

E ven Doge Lorenzo del Velli, the richest and most powerful Human in the galaxy, liked to keep a little extra spending money around. He was not certain exactly why he felt the need to carry liras around with him in the pockets of his royal robe, but he did anyway. Perhaps just to reassure himself that the assets were available if he ever needed them, an eventuality that would require catastrophic changes in his life. He would have to lose his magnificent palazzo, all of his corporate holdings, and find himself tossed out in the street. All utterly impossible, but he felt helpless to avoid the feelings, the chronic fear.

This theory carried through the rest of his life. In secret places all over the galaxy, he had stashed his treasures, culled from the legitimate and illegitimate profits of his business and governmental enterprises. This went far beyond liras, although he had plenty of those in various places. Of critical importance, he didn't want to depend on the solvency of the merchant prince economy. To protect against that, he owned, among other things, some of the largest and most valuable gemstones in all of creation. This included the famous Veldic Saphostone, which disappeared from the Intergalactic Museum one day and found its way—through a circuitous path—to him.

The men who had taken it for him had been put to death. Now no one knew his little secret.

Each morning, as he was doing now, Lorenzo strolled through his ornamental Galeng gardens, passed a guard station, and entered a scaled-down version of his Palazzo Magnifico that had the same number of rooms and the same configuration, but with much smaller dimensions. He rather liked his "Palazzito" for its coziness, but it was not a suitable place for contemplation, or a place to be alone. It was, instead, where he practiced what he most enjoyed doing.

Gambling at the most sophisticated gaming tables in the galaxy.

The first to arrive in his private casino, the Doge went from machine to machine in the Blue Chamber, activating the programs, seeing how well he could do at the mechanical games of chance. His favorite, where he stood the longest this morning, was a simulated suicide machine, called Spheres. He didn't have to put money or chips in it, because he owned the establishment. After a scanner identified him, he could play it to his heart's content.

By voice command, he selected the means of "death" that he preferred, and instantly the ominous hologram of a Mutati with a huge handgun appeared on one side of him, with the weapon pointed at his head.

Next, he specified the amount of his wager, which in reality wasn't anything at all. But he provided a number anyway, and the screen in front of him filled with hundreds of tiny spheres, each with a different color and number on them. He had only two minutes. With a foot pedal, he directed the motion of the balls, trying to balance them on a narrow bar.

In only a minute, he had seven spheres lined up, and his score appeared on the screen: 17,252. It had to be higher than the last time he played the game, or the holo shapeshifter would fire, and a holo of blood would be all over his head and clothing.

The last time he played, his score was 17,251, and he liked to play it close, only increasing by one point at a time. This was the most risky way to play, dancing on the edge of the proverbial sword, but it energized him.

Game after game, he increased by one point, without fail. He became aware of a crowd of men and women streaming into the chamber around him, the royal court. They cheered him on and chanted his name. He liked that, playing the hero. One day, he might even use the threat of a real Mutati with a weapon, instead of a hologram.

Presently, Francella came in and sat by him. She wore a low-cut black lace dress, with a long red fall of hair cascading over her shoulders.

Only she and Lorenzo knew that he could not lose here, not in his own casino. If he didn't measure up at any game that involved skill or if a game of chance did not go his way, the machine compensated, and he won anyway. It did not work that way for the other players, and they lost a lot of money on a regular basis. But as members of the Doge's royal court, they had no choice. If they wanted to remain in his favor, they needed to participate in what Lorenzo called "friendly exchanges."

Actually, this meant transferring their funds to the casino, and ultimately into one of the Doge's secret stashes. It was an additional source of income for him, one of many.

And he needed all he could get, he thought, as he looked into Francella's dark brown eyes. She was an expensive mistress.

Chapter Fifty-Nine

For as long as there has been warfare, there has been subterfuge. It can be the key to victory.

—Mutati military handbook

Just above the hazy atmospheric envelope of Plevin Four, a podship emerged from space in a burst of translucent green light, having traveled the faster-than-light podways known to the sentient space travelers. It settled into a docking station at the little-used pod station.

A cargo hold opened like a mouth in the side of the podship, and a long black transport ship slipped out into the docking bay, followed by what looked like a red-and-gold merchant schooner.

But this vessel was not that at all.

The Mutati outrider at the controls taxied out into space, and went through the detailed checklist he had learned at the training camp on Dij, just prior to its destruction. He had prepared carefully for this moment, and would only get one opportunity to make good.

Today my life and death meet, he thought, feeling supreme joy at the prospect of his final journey to heaven.

This Demolio suicide mission had been dispatched prior to the attack against the factory by a pair of Human escapees from a Mutati prison moon. The vessel had no long-range communication device aboard, so the pilot didn't know what had happened. He also could not be called back by the Zultan and diverted to a more significant planet. The timing of the attack had been predetermined, and he had waited in deep space for the moment to arrive.

The pilot looked forward to his own glorious death, and to his ascension into heaven. It would be wonderful, but in a way he wished he might have gone on the Demolio mission later. In recent weeks he'd been hearing intriguing rumors of an instantaneous cross-galactic communication system under development by the Mutati Kingdom. Everyone was curious about how it worked, and how it would enhance the war effort.

But it all seemed like another universe to him, another life. The fate of the galactic communication system was just one of many loose ends he had left behind, along with family, friends, and his career as a construction superintendent.

He would never know that the Mutatis were investigating the Human's own cross-space nehrcom system, based upon information secretly provided by Jacopo Nehr's brother. Through their own experiments the Mutatis had confirmed what they were told by the turncoat Human, that nehrcoms only operated between land-based, planetary installations. The only exceptions to this were the lower quality relay transmissions that could be made to and from space stations or spaceships that were near nehrcom planets. At that very moment, the Mutatis were building nehrcom stations on distant star systems, to conduct their initial tests.

Nor would the pilot ever learn the strategy behind his own demise. The Mutati High Command was willing to sacrifice not only terramutati outriders such as himself, but any Mutatis, such as Seatels, who might still reside on Human-controlled planets. He only had a narrow view of his mission, the scant but focused information that had been drilled into his mind by his trainers.

All thoughts faded now. The shapeshifter had completed his final checklist, making all of the necessary settings. The kamikaze torpedo was heading for its target, accelerating....

* * * * *

From somewhere, Tesh Kori heard a piercing, high-pitched whine that hurt her ears, followed by a rumbling sound, and a huge explosion.

Chapter Sixty

I cannot bear the thought of my own death. If only there were a way to prevent it, I would give anything. Well, almost anything. I'd have to keep something to sustain me in my long life, after all.

—Doge Lorenzo del Velli, private notes

The elegant nobleman hated "up-shuttles." Even when he ordered the pilots to ascend as slowly as possible through the atmosphere, the Doge Lorenzo del Velli always got nosebleeds. They were more of an irritation and an embarrassment than anything else, since trillions of his followers in the Alliance gave him superhuman, almost godlike attributes. But inside shuttles, doing something commonplace, just going from planet to pod station, Lorenzo had to sit with a white handkerchief over his nose, glaring around to make sure that no one was staring at him.

At mid-morning, he rode with a handful of military officers, bureaucrats, and his usual entourage of personal attendants. None of them seemed to pay any attention to his condition, and certainly none dared mention it to him. From experience, they knew he snapped back whenever that particular subject came up.

For this up-shuttle ride, he was not, however, going to a pod station. Instead, he was making his first inspection trip to EcoStation, having received confirmation from his officers that they had taken control of it away from the remnants of Noah Watanabe's defenders. He wanted to see the famous orbital facility firsthand and make decisions about the future of the asset. His first inclination had been to destroy it, now that his son was not there, but his bankers had told him he could make money with the operation, just as Noah did. This intrigued the Doge.

The southwest corner of the Ecological Demonstration Project compound had not been so easy to take over, but that morning the Guardians had finally fallen there, too. His troops had captured some of them, but most had disappeared into the surrounding forests and hills, melting away with high efficiency. His Red Berets had searched for them and had found a few. They were living off the land, surviving like animals in the wild. Noah Watanabe, the master ecologist, must have taught them how to do that.

The Doge smiled bitterly as he dabbed at his nose. Those forest rats were more trouble than they were worth. He had called off the search operations, since they were too costly and not worth the effort. Noah's Guardians were useless as a fighting force now. Lorenzo didn't worry about them anymore.

Still, he had a certain amount of grudging respect for them.

Of course, he could throw mininukes or pulse bombs in the woods, but he didn't want the political fallout that would certainly result from the use of such controversial weapons. No, it wasn't worth it at all.

Doge Lorenzo had not taken a complete inventory, but it seemed to him that every bone in his body ached from the night of ardor he'd spent with Francella. They had made love in virtually every room of her brother's house, which was on the grounds of the Ecological Demonstration Project that the Guardians had abandoned. For days, the woman had been in a frenzy that alternated between rage and passion. One moment she would tear apart Noah's offices or the parlor of his home, and the next she would want Lorenzo to make love to her, right in the middle of the rubble.

The Doge had not participated in the destruction himself, except as an observer, but he had found the violence tremendously exciting, and stimulating. Francella's emotions and sexuality were raw and almost primal, although she was also highly intelligent, with a wide knowledge of business and cultural matters. She could speak at length about virtually any subject. Then, in the privacy of a bedroom (or any other room for that matter), she might become someone entirely different, as if a switch had been activated.

He sighed. Lorenzo had never met anyone like her, and didn't expect that he ever would.

Only the day before, he had received a paternity report that he had requested. His investigators had confirmed to him that Anton Glavine really was his son, and Francella was the mother.

Initially, Lorenzo had been angry at her for concealing such an important matter from him for all of these years. In the face of his rage she finally apologized in tears, and insisted that she'd only done it for his own good, since she hadn't thought that he wanted a bastard child to interfere with any sons he might have sired through marriage. With years passing, and the Doge having only daughters, Francella had claimed she'd wanted to tell him the truth, but had never found the right opportunity to do so. She also admitted not feeling comfortable as a parent herself, and hoping against hope that Lorenzo would one day father a son by legitimate means, thus creating an untainted noble heir.

Eventually Lorenzo had told her he forgave her, and this was true for the most part, since he had never been able to stay angry with Francella for any reason during the more than two decades of their relationship. On a certain level, just below his full consciousness, he had always known that he was a slave to his passion for her. He always tried not to dwell on any negative thoughts about her, or the way he felt for her. He only knew for certain that he could not live without her, despite her selfish ways....

The shuttle floated into a docking berth on the space station, and airlocks clicked into place. Lorenzo sniffled blood up his nostrils, trying not to be too loud. Gradually, as he stepped into the corridors of the space station with his officers, his nose stopped bleeding and he began to feel better.

Robots wearing red caps stood guard at doorways along the way. Some of the sentient machines were black, and others silver. Many had dents and metal patches. Lorenzo liked this group despite their appearance, and had rewarded them for saving his life by making them full-fledged Red Berets. They looked particularly proud this morning. As he rounded a corner, he saw their leader Jimu using a probe to interface with another machine.

Jimu had been expanding the number of machines under Doge Lorenzo's command, cleverly replicating them without the need for Human intervention. They recycled old parts, found their own raw materials, and fabricated replacement parts. The machines were loyal, efficient, and cost him very little, since they took care of themselves. It was an ideal situation.

But as he looked around at the green-and-brown walls and peered into empty classrooms and offices, knowing his son Anton had been there before him, his mood darkened. He worried over the young man's welfare. Both anxious and furious at the situation, he swung an arm at a hanging plant in one of the lunchrooms, and became entangled in it. The whole thing ripped loose from its ceiling hooks, and he fell with it over a table, cursing.

"Are you all right, Sire?" one of his aides said, running over to free him from the snarl of vines and leaves. "Oh Sire, you're injured."

"It's only a little nosebleed, you fool! I'm fine, fine. Now, get away from me."

Pushing the man out of the way and nearly tripping as he stepped away from the plant, the Doge issued a stream of expletives.

"Sorry, Sire, sorry," the hapless man said as he tripped and fell himself.

"How am I supposed to run the Alliance when I'm surrounded by idiots?" Lorenzo, asked, as he returned to the corridor and rejoined the officers who were showing him around.

The Doge was extremely worried about his newly-discovered son, and suspected that Noah was trying to maintain control over him as a means of leverage, for his own selfish ends. Francella had said that Noah knew all along about the real parentage of Anton, and that he had assumed the role of an attentive family friend when he knew all along that he was really the young man's genetic uncle.

It enraged Lorenzo how Noah was putting Anton in danger to further his own schemes. The Doge was even beginning to believe Francella's claim that Noah had been responsible for the death of his own father and for other crimes, while putting up the public persona of the great galactic ecologist.

As far as Lorenzo was concerned, the meeting that Noah had demanded with him must have only been a stalling technique, to give him more time to escape, undoubtedly with treasures he had stolen from Canopa. Noah Watanabe had proven himself to be anything but a man of high morals.

The inspection tour took until early afternoon, after which Lorenzo caught a shuttle back to Canopa. He was especially looking forward to another tryst with Francella, which should put him in a better mood than he was in now.

His attaché Pimyt met him at the shuttle station. The furry little Hibbil strutted up and asked, "Any sign of Noah or your son?"

"Nothing."

The Hibbil spoke nervously as he walked beside his much taller superior. "I have a groundjet waiting to take you back to Elysoo, Sire."

"I'm going back to the compound first," Lorenzo said.

"But you've conquered it, and the space station, too. What more do you need to do?"

"Since when do you question me, or direct my actions? I will notify you when I am ready to return."

"But much important business needs your attention, Sire. Diplomats and other dignitaries are at the palazzo, anxious to speak with you."

Stopping, Lorenzo confronted the little alien. "I don't answer to you," he said, "or to any of the *dignitaries*, as you call them."

"It's that CorpOne woman, isn't it, Sire? Pardon me for saying so, but she's dangerous. I hear she holds aspirations of becoming Doge herself."

"Preposterous! There has never been a female Doge, and there never will be!"

"I'm sure you're right, Sire. I'm just providing you with the information, for you to handle as you see fit."

"As for 'that CorpOne woman,' I'll spend as much time with her as I please, whenever I please."

"Of course. My apologies, Doge Lorenzo. I only have your welfare in mind."

"When you get back to the palazzo, send for my wife. Have her waiting for me when I return."

"When will that be?"

"Just get her there. And say nothing to her of my whereabouts, or the military operation we conducted against Noah Watanabe."

The furry little attaché bowed very low to the ground, and hurried off to do as he was told.

Priding himself on his ability to manage relationships with several women at once, Lorenzo intended to make love to both Meghina and Francella in the next few days, but would keep them far apart because of the loathing the women felt toward each other.

Chapter Sixty-One

In sentient machines, as in biological creatures, allegiance is always emotion-based. And that makes it notoriously unreliable.

—Thinker, internal observation

On the planet Ignem, far beneath the orbital ring containing the Inn of the White Sun, the flat-bodied robot moved with uncharacteristic vigor, examining each mechanical soldier in the parade formation, using his interface probe to check their operating programs.

Thinker had to move quickly. There wasn't much time to get the army ready. Beyond the formation, he saw smoke drifting over a volcano. But that was normal for Ignem, and certainly not the problem that had him so very, very concerned.

Thinker's sensor probe darted out of one hand and snapped into a port on the side of the robot in front of him, making its interface connection.

Data poured into Thinker's analytical brain. After only a few seconds, he shook his head. Another defective machine. Too many of them. Simultaneously, his officer robots moved along the ranks, checking the battle fitness of other soldiers.

"Remove this robot from the ranks," Thinker said to an aide behind him, "and take him in for servicing." Thinker downloaded a list of needed repairs into the robot, disconnected his probe, and moved on to the next one.

The next in line was not really a robot at all. Giovanni Nehr stood ramrod straight, wearing machinelike armor that he had received after volunteering to serve the mechanical army. Gio's request had been unusual, and totally unanticipated by the robot leader. At first, Thinker had resisted.

"I'll be the best fighter in the army, sir," he had promised. "Just give me the chance to prove myself, please." He went on to admit that he'd had a falling out with his famous brother, and would prefer to follow an entirely new career.

"Well, this would certainly qualify as that," Thinker had said.

The two of them had laughed and clasped hands, metal against flesh.

Now, Thinker thought the new recruit looked quite good despite the dents in his armor. It occurred to the robot leader, though, that he could not interface with this Human to download the contents of his mind, the way he could with the mechanical soldiers. How useful it would be, Thinker realized, if he had that ability, since he still had questions about Giovanni Nehr.

For several seconds, Thinker paused and allowed his internal programming to search through the various data banks, determining if a complete machine to Human interface was possible. The data revealed a number of obstacles, but he thought it just might be possible. At the first opportunity he would perform a deeper analysis, and see if the technology could be developed.

Saying nothing to Nehr, Thinker moved on down the line.

The recycled fighting robots looked at their commander with sensor-blinking surprise as he hurried among them, inspecting components and issuing terse commands. In the past he had moved slowly and deliberately, a robot of thought, not of action. But he always knew he could get around quicker if he had to; it had only been necessary to activate one of the backup programs he had for emergencies.

The situation he faced at this time was exactly that....

In the afternoon, Thinker inspected his manufacturing and assembly plants, a hive of buildings constructed at the jewel-like base of a volcano. Like the robots under his command, and like himself for that matter, the structures and machinery inside were all cobbled together from whatever parts the enterprising robots could locate, scavenged from dump heaps all over the galaxy and brought here.

He could order replacement parts from the Hibbils, but that would be prohibitively expensive. Besides, he didn't trust those deceptive little fur balls, having discovered some of the insidious programs they had installed in sentient machines. Thinker preferred to make his own new parts, or rebuild old ones. Here on Ignem, his blast furnaces heated up metals, plax, and other materials for re-use. He had assembly lines in which mobile and fixed robots worked on old bodies and interior components.

Deep in thought, Thinker strutted down the main aisle of his largest assembly plant. For a moment he paused to watch the blue light of a laser soldering machine as it fused the sealing strip on a synaptic board, one of the brain components of a Series 1405 automaton. He hated using such old machines, since they didn't have nearly as many features as the newer ones, but at least this series had always been reliable.

Yet, his thoughts were elsewhere.

Jimu and his squad were supposed to have returned by now. Instead, Thinker had learned they were staying with the Doge, as members of his elite Red Beret corps. From the reports reaching Thinker, he knew that the initial mission had been successful, as Jimu had saved the Doge's life. But in doing so, the infernal robot had ingratiated himself so much to Lorenzo that the nobleman had praised Jimu and offered him a career in the Red Berets ... an offer that was accepted.

Jimu is no longer under my command, Thinker thought. He had sent numerous messages to Jimu by courier, but had received no responses. Still, Thinker had obtained a great deal of information about his activities.

At this very moment, the wayward robot was doing something very, very troubling. On the resource-rich planet of Canopa, under the auspices of the powerful Doge, he was increasing the number of fighting robots under his own command. The original squadron of twenty had multiplied, and at last report comprised more than four hundred. Jimu was highly intelligent, with fine internal programming. On more than one occasion, he had proven his survival abilities, and Thinker, recognizing talent, had promoted him.

But perhaps the promotion had been premature. In retrospect, it seemed to him that Jimu had been exceedingly emotional by robotic standards, overzealous and too dedicated to Humans. It was a fine line, but clearly Jimu had gone too far. He should have completed his mission, saving the Doge's life, and returned. Now he was something of a loose cannon.

This concerned Thinker greatly, but not for selfish reasons, not because Jimu was in a position of high influence and becoming well-known in his own right. To the contrary, Thinker's motivations were pure, and he honestly believed that Jimu needed guidance. A sentient robot couldn't just go off half-cocked and start building an army. He needed extensive education and preparation before taking that step. He needed a great deal of wisdom and moral instruction, and a huge amount of specific knowledge in his data banks. Otherwise, the army would not receive the proper programming, and could become a liability instead of an asset.

In particular, without the fail-safe mechanisms that Thinker always installed in the programming of sentient machines who followed him, they could go out of control and cause a lot of damage. Thinker had seen it happen before. It was called a robotic chain reaction. After one machine went bad it infected others, and they all went bad. Like a mob or a wolf pack, they took on new and menacing personalities, wreaking havoc against any biological organism unfortunate enough to cross their path.

Jimu had the fail-safe in his own programming. Thinker had installed it himself when he interfaced with him. But Jimu still didn't know how to build an army; he didn't know how to reprogram other robots to keep them from breaking down, and perhaps going berserk.

Thinker had no personal concerns, no petty jealousies. If Jimu had expressed a desire to build an army himself, and if it made sense to do so, Thinker would have set him on a training course to make it possible. But that had never occurred. The proper procedures had not been followed.

I should have handled him more carefully, he thought glumly, *given him a tight internal program that compelled him to complete the one mission only. I'm no perfect army builder myself.*

Hearing a machine voice, Thinker swiveled his head and looked around. The plant superintendent, Saccary, stood behind him. A small robot with an unusual porcelain-like face containing synthetic Human features, Saccary asked, "I have a hundred more of these automatons backed up for repairs, with worn out synaptic board sealing strips , but I'm running out of parts."

"I'll see what I can do."

"Thank you, sir. May I give you a list of other parts we need?"

Thinker nodded stiffly and then moved on, accompanied by the superintendent.

With the Jimu matter dominating his concerns, Thinker slipped into a deep mental state in which he split his exterior self away from the inner core of his consciousness. The exterior self continued to interact with Saccary, accessing data banks for information and conversing with him, but at the core of his conscience Thinker didn't hear or sense any of that. A volcano could erupt, sending everything flying and tumbling, and if his brain survived he might go on with his line of deep, uninterrupted thought.

In all of the galaxy, no robot was more altruistic or loyal to Humans than Thinker, more totally selfless. He knew this to be so with an almost absolute certainty, since he had downloaded the programs of thousands of robots into his own circuitry, and had analyzed them. Thinker did not consider himself morally superior out of any sense of pride; rather, he knew it to be the simple, unadorned truth.

Now he needed to deal with the crisis quickly, before Jimu built a force that was too large. At the pace the rogue robot had been increasing his numbers, he would one day exceed Thinker's own army, which had slowed its growth rate due to a limited availability of key raw materials. Jimu, with his central location and the blessing of Doge Lorenzo del Velli, had no such limitations.

And Thinker had another reason in mind, a very deep and specific worry, beyond any general concern about robotic breakdowns and chain reactions. Thinker had heard about the Doge's attacks on Noah Watanabe, and was horrified by them. As far as Thinker was concerned, Noah was the machine leader's own Human equivalent, the most altruistic and untainted of his kind. From the reports of travelers stopping at the Inn of the White Sun, Thinker had been inspired by stories of Noah Watanabe and the idealistic mission of the Guardians. He had always hoped to meet the man one day, and perhaps that day was coming.

Noah was the most indispensable member of his race, just as Thinker himself was to his own. Even robots, in Thinker's alternate but highly informed way of looking at things, constituted a racial type. The mechanicals were sentient, after all, and had emotions and desires, just like biologicals. Intelligent machines were born in a sense, could reproduce themselves, and could die. Just because they had no flesh or cellular structures meant nothing. Thinker had his own definitions.

Of supreme importance, Thinker did not want Jimu's force to contribute to the annihilation of Noah Watanabe … and he intended to counter that. He would still make efforts to contact Jimu and talk sense into him, but didn't hold out much hope for that.

Like a sleepwalker, Thinker strutted across a landing field toward a gleaming white shuttle. With only a surface awareness of his surroundings. he boarded the craft for the ride up to the Inn of the White Sun.

In the few minutes required for the trip, Thinker searched his data banks for important information. With all of the facts that he collected around the galaxy, constantly interfacing with thousands of robots, he had the equivalent of an intelligence operation—a spy network—within his own internal circuitry. Following sightings of Noah Watanabe and his grid-plane on podships and in pod stations, Thinker traced the Guardian leader's travels around the galaxy in recent weeks.

In actuality, the robot was going through a probability program. There were gaps in the information, but he had enough to determine that Noah was no longer on Canopa, and no longer on board his orbital station high over the planet, either.

The fugitive and a small entourage had—with near statistical certainty—escaped to a remote planet in the Plevin Star System.

Chapter Sixty-Two

We Parviis are greatly advantaged by our size, or lack of it, depending upon your perspective. With the enhancement of our magnification systems we can appear to be what we are not, while still retaining what Humans are not.

—The Parvii View of Evolution

I n the thunder and blur of the mysterious explosion, Tesh, Anton and their companions felt an emptiness in the pits of their stomachs, and a sensation of extreme speed. Subi shouted that stabilizers had automatically extruded from the undercarriage of the grid-plane, attaching the craft to the floor of the bunker. Inside the cabin of the plane, objects were flying around and things were slamming into the outside of the fuselage.

Everyone held on, and they made heroic efforts to protect the still-unconscious Noah. After attempts by the others, Eshaz was able to reach Noah and wedge himself in a corner by the command console, while keeping a powerful, protective grip on the Human.

The movement settled down, and as Tesh looked at Eshaz, who was shifting his hold on Noah, she thought the Tulyan looked almost maternal, the way he cradled the unconscious man's head and kept a blanket over him. It seemed incongruous for her to be feeling positive thoughts about one of her mortal enemies, but she couldn't avoid the feelings.

As if he were a doctor himself, Eshaz checked the healing pad on one side of Noah's head, satisfying himself that it was still secure and pumping nutrients into the wound. The reptilian Tulyan looked up. For a moment he exchanged glances with Tesh, and she saw kindness in his slitted, pale gray eyes. Then Eshaz again focused his attention on Noah, and whispered something to him.

Through the thick windowglax of the bunker, Tesh saw that the river was no longer visible. Instead it looked like they were in outer space, with blackness and flickering dots of light marking distant suns.

She heard Anton and Subi wondering if the cosmic view might be caused by some sort of a projection mechanism, but suddenly she had an entirely different, much more startling idea. Could it possibly be?

Abruptly, she ran to the exit hatch and touched a button to open it. Without waiting for the automatic stairway to descend and lock into place, she jumped out of the grid-plane and landed on the floor of the bunker.

"I'll be right back!" she shouted. "Everyone wait here."

Before Anton or any of the others could react, she ran for a passageway.

She heard shouts of confusion and concern behind her, with Anton running after her with the others, calling her name. "Tesh! Tesh! Where are you going? Come back!"

But none of them could keep up with her, or begin to imagine where she had gone....

Tesh did something only a Parvii could do. To anyone observing her, she seemed to disappear. She was miniature now, having switched off the magnification system that made her look as large as the giant Humans. She ran with a blur of speed, much faster than she could have moved in her magnified state, which interfered with her natural abilities. Like most Parviis, Tesh preferred her normal size. It provided her with so many more intriguing options, involving speed, access, and personal safety.

She stood in what looked like a rocky passageway now. She touched the walls around her, felt the cold hardness. And knew something with absolute certainty.

This is not rock.

Finding the subtle but telltale burrowing marks she was looking for, she entered a minuscule opening in the stony surface, like a bee entering a hive hole. Once inside, she followed the traditional maze of passageways and now-dormant signal scramblers, designed to keep intruders and probing electronics out. She knew the way well. It was essentially the same in every podship.

Within moments, she located the large sectoid chamber, the nerve center of the pod, still glowing with a faint green luminescence and humming in a barely audible tone. This surprised her, and gave her hope. But the walls were hard, as if fossilized. Could the creature regenerate itself, coming back from its long dormancy? She had heard of cases where this had actually occurred, and of others in which the sectoid chamber was the last portion of the creature to die, like a heart that continued to beat but no longer had the strength to sustain the rest of the body.

Tesh's own metabolism had been going at full speed, driving her forward. Suddenly it slowed, and she moved ahead cautiously. In shock, she stared at the unmistakable remains of a skeleton lying on the floor ahead of her, humanoid like herself and around the same diminutive size, with streaks of dark green and black on the bones.

A long-dead Parvii, one of her own people.

She murmured an ancient, silent prayer over the body, felt an immense welling of emotion. Even though her kinsmen were numerous, she had always been taught that even one death was significant, since it was a loss suffered by the swarm.

If uninterrupted by calamity, Parviis lived comparatively long lives, substantially more than her own seven hundred twelve years, but they were still mortal. They could be killed in accidents, or could fall victim to specific, odious diseases.

While this one lay on its side now, it appeared to have died and rigidified in a crouching position, as if it had wanted to spring out into space and rejoin a swarm, but perhaps had been too injured to do so. Crouching for a time after death, the Parvii's flesh and internal organs had fallen away, and sometime afterward the bones fell over.

It was as Tesh had suspected. Their grid-plane had not landed in an abandoned Mutati military bunker at all. Rather, they had entered the cargo hold of what had originally been a podship that crashed into the riverbank centuries ago—and which was subsequently found by Mutatis and converted to their purposes. Hence the thick glax windows, ceramic airlocks, and added rooms. The Mutatis must have had some means of communicating with their hydromutati cousins from there, the Seatels, perhaps through some sort of technology that interacted with the telepathy of the Seatels.

Later, perhaps from an adverse military operation, or a disease, the Mutatis no longer occupied the bunker. For some reason, the Seatels were left behind. Then, when Noah's Guardians arrived, the hydromutati telepaths killed them ... and were about to kill Noah, Tesh, and the rest of their group when the planet exploded.

But why had the podship crashed on Plevin Four in the first place? Something must have gone wrong with the Parvii pilot ... an illness, a misjudgment? Or some failure by the podship itself. Such events were rare, but over the course of millenniums did occur.

Another realization hit her.

We are no longer on Plevin Four. It doesn't exist anymore.

The cosmic blackness and flickering, distant suns were stark confirmation, seen around drifting chunks of the dead world. The podship, even with improvised Mutati window walls, had survived the explosion. In its present state, with the body as cold and hard as stone, the podship had effectively armored itself against the explosion, and this had not been compromised by the Mutati alterations.

The planet is gone, and we are drifting in space. What happened?

She could not imagine. An entire planet! She had been in the midst of a huge explosion.

Above all, Tesh could not shake the intense sadness over her lost comrade, even though she had never known him personally. But she had no time for emotion.

Podships were hardy creatures, and it might just be possible to revive this one. She had to hurry. The bunker was tightly sealed, but soon her companions could run out of air. She did not have that problem. It was one of the principle advantages of Parvii evolution.

Chapter Sixty-Three

The Eye of the Swarm is in telepathic contact with his Parvii swarms, all over the galaxy. It is a vast morphic field, but has been subject to increasing problems, running parallel with the disintegration of the cosmic web.

—Thinker's data bank: *Galactic Leaders*

They were as thick as locusts, but did not fly over hills and crops, looking for plants to ravage. Instead, they journeyed from one star system to another on a mission that was nearly as old as the galaxy itself. A distant observer might have wondered what was moving so rapidly through the heavens, and would have undoubtedly guessed wrong.

At Woldn's command, the swarm appeared to take the shape of a comet, then an asteroid belt, and then a string of planets flung out of orbit by God. These were shapeshifters on an immense scale, a malleable multitude that covered much of a galactic sector at a time … and even more, if they switched on their personal magnification systems simultaneously. But individually, they were exceedingly small, like tiny pixies or fairies.

For more than a thousand years, Woldn had been the Eye of the Swarm, the leader of the entire Parvii race. At the center of the formation, he flew with them now, speeding past brilliant suns and multicolored nebulas, swooping, diving, circling, going faster than podships or as slow as a Human walking through space. At times, Woldn felt like an artist of movement, the conductor of a great galactic symphony.

Some of his followers rose through the ranks because they displayed special talents, the most gifted of whom were wranglers who specialized in the capture of wild, migrating podships, and pilots who could guide the mysterious sentient spacecraft on long journeys.

Periodically, the wranglers and pilots were given rest between assignments, time on their own that could last for years in succession. In the typical lifetime of a Parvii, that was not very long at all. Woldn himself had lived for nearly two millennia.

I am the Eye of the Swarm.

At will, Woldn's thoughts expanded and contracted as he guided his beloved throng, directing their movements telepathically, knowing their collective and individual thoughts as if they were part of his own body. He made them curve upward and then down, like a rollercoaster in space, and then formed them into a twisting Mobius strip that looked like a contorted conveyor belt.

He was in fact the eye of many, many Parvii swarms in all sectors of the galaxy, controlling them with his powerful beaming thoughts, keeping track of them at all times, no matter how far away they were. His minions had telepathic powers as well, but on nowhere near the scale of his. Woldn's abilities—while still subject to the limitations of psychic breakdowns that affected all members of his race, and inhibited by an increasing number of telepathic dead zones in the galaxy—were historically unparalleled. He was the chosen one, the most gifted of the gifted, capable of wrangling and piloting podships, capable of stretching his thoughts, and his swarms, across vast distances.

It was his raison d'être to capture and control every podship possible. His swarms were relentless, and he would send millions of the tiny breed on a mission to capture just a few podships, or only one. That's how valuable the sentient Aopoddae were to them, for they were the best means by which the various galactic races could travel across vast distances of space at hyper speeds.

Had they been savvy businessmen, with avaricious hearts like those of the merchant princes, the Parviis could have turned this monopoly into huge profits and used the funds to build an empire. But they had no use for money; it was not the currency of their existence. They did not live on planets or have any desire for worldly things. Beautiful objects meant nothing to them. They did not even need the oxygen of a planet, and traveled through space without any sort of breathing apparatus.

Parviis measured their accomplishments in terms of the success of their race. In the overall perspective, the individual was of little consequence to them, for he could do almost nothing without the collective strength of his companions.

Even so, one Parvii inside the sectoid chamber of a podship—when trained and entrusted with that position—could control that marvelous creature, guiding it though the treacherous pathways of space. But as many podships as they controlled, there were always wild pods out in the far reaches. Though some of their migration patterns were known, no one knew where Aopoddae came from originally, whether they were generated through some sexual liaison or just appeared out of the ether.

Woldn led his swarm to the dark side of the Tulyan Starcloud, a region where the sun never shone. He had received intelligence reports from Parvii operatives that this was where the bronze, scaly Tulyans were hiding podships, reports that he had picked up telepathically. They told him exactly where to look.

But the ships were not there anymore. Were they all out on the podways, transporting Tulyans to unknown regions?

Stretching his swarm out and using all of the eyes of its members, Woldn picked up their thoughts, and beheld a region of space as large as four ordinary solar systems. Though he usually paid little attention to beauty, here he felt truly stirred to the depths of his soul. This was one of the most spectacular regions he had ever seen, very nearly as lovely as the Parvii Fold, that sacred galactic region where his people bred, and where they went to die when their long lifetimes wound down.

Cosmic mists floated through the starcloud, a rainbow of swirling gas that at times seemed to take on magical shapes. He'd heard a legend that the mists conformed to the vivid, collective imaginations of the Tulyans themselves, and that the entire region, with its islands of land, were products of their minds.

Woldn doubted if that could be true. The Tulyans had not been powerful enough to defeat his people, so he did not see how such an extrasensory feat could be possible. After all, if they were that powerful they could just visualize weapons to defeat the Parviis, something customized to block the telepathic signals that controlled the swarms. He and his minions had been here before, and occasionally made captures of hidden podships in this region. But the Tulyans were clever, with a variety of tricks in their repertoire.

He steered the swarm through a thick mist that grew intensely red as he got into it, and then became darker and completely encompassed the multitude of Parviis. Soon Woldn could see nothing at all. He sensed the fear and mounting panic of his people around him, but ordered them to change the configuration of the formation and continue on, which they did, in the shape of a wide, spinning fan blade.

Faster and faster they spun as they flew, in an effort to dissipate the mist by sweeping it out of position, but Woldn felt something resisting his efforts, as if the legend was true and the Tulyans really were holding the mist in place through the collective power of their minds.

Then he felt something give way. The mist separated, and Woldn saw dozens of podships floating in the vacuum of space, tethered together. For a moment, he hesitated, as this was more than they usually had at one time. In the clearing, shuttles approached the podships, and Woldn saw Tulyans inside the shuttles, peering out of the portholes with their slitted gray eyes. They were so peculiar in appearance, looking in his direction, seeing their Parvii enemies.

He felt his swarm wanting to surge forward, but he held them back, and watched as the shuttles moved between the gray-and-black pods, depositing Tulyans into each spaceship. Woldn was amused by their pathetic effort to escape.

As the Tulyan pilots took control of the podships, the vessel hulls metamorphosed, taking on scaly, reptilian skin and Tulyan facial features. The podships got underway, and accelerated. But as fast as they were, they could not escape, not even on the podways. The pursuing swarm split into as many segments as there were pods and ran each of them down. Woldn remained behind, but experienced the simultaneous captures telepathically.

In short order, the Parviis took control of the small fleet, and as their pilots went to work the podships changed back to their original blimp-like appearances. The Eye of the Swarm had all of the sentient spacecraft brought to him, and ordered his people to imprison the Tulyans inside the shuttles. He didn't kill his enemies, but refused to listen when they protested that they needed the podships to perform important ecological work on a galactic scale.

"I sentence all of you to retirement!" Woldn shouted. As he spoke, his people uttered the words simultaneously to the Tulyans inside the shuttles, producing an eerie synchronized voice.

Muttering with displeasure, the bronze-scaled aliens did not fight back. As big as they were, Tulyans had traditionally been a non-violent race. They also knew they were powerless against such a formidable enemy.

In short order Woldn led his swarm, the captured podships, and the imprisoned Tulyans to a point in deep space, where he assigned a pilot to each craft and turned them loose on the podways, increasing the galactic transport fleet under his command.

This had all happened before, an eternal cycle of dispute between the two races. The Tulyans, no matter their losses and inadequacies, continually tried to regain control of podships and hide them from their unrelenting Parvii competitors, using different methods of concealment.

And these newly captured Tulyans, like others before them, would be used as bargaining chips for timeseeing services the Parviis wanted from those few Tulyans who had such abilities, so that the Parviis could obtain reports on events a short distance in the future. While the most gifted timeseers had only imperfect abilities, it was, nonetheless, a highly-desired service to the tiny, swarming creatures.

Chapter Sixty-Four

In a special corner of my imagination there is no distinction between thought and reality, as one melds gently into the other, along a vast continuum. There, perception takes on substance, and thoughts are as tangible as anything perceived with the known senses.

—Noah Watanabe, *Drifting in the Ether* (unpublished notes)

A short while ago, the dreaming man had been immersed in a cacophony of chaos.

In the din and violence of his physical awareness, he had tried to prepare himself for a realm where he would have no more need for thoughts, no worries or desires to clutter his mind. He had been wondering what sort of reality that might be, and if, on some level, he would still be conscious of it. The answer to these questions meant a great deal to him.

But clarity was elusive.

For some time now, Noah Watanabe had been seeking doorways out of the darkness that encompassed him. He had been sending mental probes in various directions, searching for escape from the barless prison of his comatose mind.

His mind was the key to his body, for his physical form could not function without mental impulses. But he sensed that his intellect was also the key to something far greater than one mortal body and all of the trivial details that made up its daily routines. He felt a tremendous frustration as he realized this with absolute certainty, while his brain was completely locked up and unable to attain its potential.

Once more he tried to escape, and again he failed. Unable to come out of the coma, Noah's thoughts focused on a prison within a prison. He re-experienced the onslaught on EcoStation by Red Beret forces, saw them running through the corridors, shouting commands. In painstaking detail he relived the attack, and his escape in the grid-plane.

Through the porthole, he saw the Doge's red gunships again, firing at the escaping vessel, tearing through the hull just as Subi was increasing the acceleration. Only moments away from freedom.

In the void between the spacecraft, Noah saw the path of enemy projectiles as they sped toward him. As yet, nothing had hit Noah or any of his companions.

For a long, lingering moment, Noah awaited the inevitable, knowing there was no escape from that fate, or the one that held him tightly now. Silence encased him, the eerie stillness of impending death.

The grid-plane was not going fast enough!

The projectiles drew closer. They were right outside the porthole now, only a fraction of a second from impact. He flinched, then felt searing pain. He tried to scream, but in the vault of darkness he had no voice.

Chapter Sixty-Five

Visual observation is not the same as confirmation.
—Sulu Granby, Philosopher of Old Mars

Resembling a small, bronze-scaled dragon, Eshaz knelt beside the comatose form of Noah, who lay on the carpeted deck of the grid-plane, with a blanket over him and a pillow beneath his head. His Human friend had not been doing well; the vital signs had declined precipitously to a dangerous level. In addition, the Tulyan's own bodily aches and pains had been worsening of late—the apparent link with the decline in Timeweb—but he tried not to think about all those things.

Instead, he gazed off into the distance, seeing through the walls of the grid-plane and the damaged, stranded podship that encompassed it and floated in space. Debris from the planetary explosion bobbed near them like flotsam on the sea, great chunks of rock and turf. But none of that inhibited his vision in the least. He saw through it all, to the other side.

With slitted gray eyes, Eshaz peered far into the galaxy, as if through a child's looking glass. But this was no juvenile activity. Nothing ever had been for him, since he had always taken his responsibilities seriously. His ancient ability permitted him to gaze far across the galaxy, to stars and planets and his own starcloud, floating like an oasis in a vast wasteland, most of which was entirely devoid of life.

Home.

Whenever he peered into the galaxy, he always liked to start out this way, making certain the sacred Tulyan homeland was still intact, that the Council Chamber was lit, and everything was all right. Considering the tenuous state of the galaxy, this was not always a certainty. There were no distance or time factors diminishing the sighting. He was peering into the present, not the past. Like using a super zoom lens that spanned the curvatures, folds, and distances of time and space.

A tear of relief ran down the bronze, scaly skin of his face. The legendary Tulyan Starcloud floated serenely in space, looking no different from this distant vantage than it had long ago. He knew, because he had lived for nearly a million standard years.

The visual confirmation gave him great comfort, but on this occasion he took only a moment to look in that direction, because of a pressing matter that required his attention. Sadly, there were so many of them nowadays, an acceleration of bad events.

Refocusing, he saw a tiny Parvii woman exploring the hidden passageways and chambers of the stranded podship that contained his grid-plane. As was the case with all Tulyans, Eshaz's ability to see Parviis in this paranormal manner was limited: for unknown reasons, he and his comrades could not see their tiny enemies in swarms, but occasionally they could see individuals, especially when the individual was far from the center of a swarm.

With a start, Eshaz recognized the Parvii woman.

Tesh!

He'd thought something was strange about her, but had been unable to determine what. Though he knew Parviis could alter their size, he hadn't suspected her of being one of them. But he had no time for personal reproach. Something was far more important than that, or than the control of a single sentient pod.

Eshaz, like all Tulyans, could see Timeweb, the exceedingly strong, hidden strands that connected an entire galaxy. He saw that this podship was hung up on one of the strands, and that it had been propelled into that position by the explosion on Plevin Four. What caused such a catastrophe? He had no idea.

He spotted a tiny rip in the web adjacent to the podship—a defect just starting to form in the fabric of space. It was an early stage timehole, barely discernible by his trained eye, and not visible to other galactic races at all. If left unchecked, it would grow in severity, eventually reaching a dangerous advanced stage, when it was visible to Humans and other races. The most severe timeholes, if they occurred in proximity to planets, could rip portions of earth and rock away, sucking them into bottomless holes in the cosmos.

It was frustrating to him. Wherever he went in the galaxy he fixed these web defects, or thought he did, but frequently another one appeared only a short distance away. He had hoped that these ominous signs of galactic disintegration would reverse and either heal themselves or stop appearing, but that had not been the case at all.

This one, while small, was in a bad location, out in the middle of space by a vital, structural fold in the galaxy, where it could easily enlarge and cause serious havoc in an entire sector.

But he wasn't thinking so much about that. He had another thought in mind. Still kneeling by Noah, but not looking at him, he placed a scaly hand over the man's forehead, and felt the life ebbing away.

I must move quickly.

On impulse, Eshaz was about to attempt something he should not do without approval from the Council of Elders. But Noah Watanabe was a rare person, one who behaved more like a Tulyan than a Human. He truly cared about the environment, and for more than just one planet. Noah saw—or *sensed*—an interconnectedness spanning the galaxy, and galaxies linked with other galaxies.

But is he the one spoken of in our legends?

So many important questions, and so little time. Eshaz only knew one thing for certain, a visceral sense that saving Noah was far more important than trying to gain control of this podship, or even repairing the rip in Timeweb.

Using his free hand, the Tulyan reached overhead, and onlookers were startled to see him and Noah flicker in and out of view. Unknown to them, Eshaz had his scaly hand pressed against a torn spot on the web just above him.

With a shudder, he felt energy flowing from the rift, coursing through his body into Noah Watanabe....

Chapter Sixty-Six

How do we measure the accomplishments of our lives? By this do we measure our happiness, or our despair.

—Anton Glavine, *Reflections*

The crew of the *Avelo*, following one of Captain Yuell's rare and prized treasure maps, made several passes around Wuxx Reef, in a blue binary star system. The yellowing parchment, which he had spread open on the bridge of the ship, described fully laden merchant prince schooners that were missing in that sector, but without precise information on the exact location of the wrecks.

In only a few hours, the adventurers struck pay dirt, locating a spice schooner that had crashed into a cave within the floating rock formation, so that it was not visible from the outside. They only found it by sending a scouting party into the cave in a speedplane, with the red-sashed captain at the controls.

The wreck contained a cargo of exotic Old Earth spices, in sealed, largely undamaged containers. Captain Yuell, with a wide-ranging knowledge of commodities and values, said that he would investigate before selling the salvaged goods, since some of the spices might be irreplaceable, now that Earth was destroyed.

"This cargo might even be needed by scientists to regenerate seeds," he theorized as Acey, Dux, and other crewmen loaded bags, chests, and barrels into the *Avelo*. "In fact, even without knowing what we can get for the haul, I'm going to award all of you a bonus. We're overdue for a celebration."

When the loading was completed, he patted Acey on the back, and added, "You and your cousin have done fine work for our little enterprise, and now you'll learn how we let our hair down." Ever since helping with the repair of the hydion engine, Acey had become one of his favorites, almost like a son....

The following day, Captain Yuell took his treasure ship crew to the dusty planet of Adurian for a celebration. As the men strutted into a dimly-lit saloon they wore their finest clothes, with eye patches, bandanas, baggy trousers, and gleaming knives at their waists. Captain Yuell and the little Hibbil Mac Golden wore ceremonial swords.

"Stick with me, lads," the captain said to Acey and Dux, "and I'll teach you how to have a good time."

Most of the patrons in the crowded tavern were Adurians, looking like humanoids with small, antlike heads and bulbous, oversized eyes. But there were a handful of other races as well, chubby Kichis, tall Vandurians, and bearded Ordians. As the treasure crew entered, conversation halted, but resumed soon afterward when the visitors glared around.

"They don't want trouble with us," Mac Golden said, keeping his hand near his sword.

A curvaceous Jimlat woman, with a pretty but blockish face, smiled at Dux, causing the young man to blush.

"You like that one?" Yuell asked.

"Uh, I have a girlfriend waiting for me at home," Dux said, lying.

"Well, this is where we keep ourselves tuned up in the love department," Yuell said, with a wide grin. "Don't want to get rusty on these long voyages." He and the men laughed.

Like ancient Earth cowboys after a cattle drive, the crew drank heavily and gambled in the smoky main room. More Jimlat women emerged from back rooms, and mingled with the men. Even Acey had one on his lap, but Dux, being more shy, kept his distance. For a while, Dux even tried to avoid gambling, since he and Acey had already lost so much. But after a couple of "high-du" drink injections, he joined his friends in a card game.

By the time Dux slipped into one of the high-backed chairs, the game was getting boisterous, with the participants shouting at each other, and not always good-naturedly. As Mac Golden explained in his squeaky little voice, this was Endo, the favorite pastime of the hairless, homopod Adurians—a fast moving competition in which electronic cards changed their faces and numbers in the blink of an eye, reducing or increasing their values.

Each player had an electronic screen on the table in front of him, with cards flashing across the surface. If certain card combinations showed up, the player had to press a button quickly to select it, or lose the hand. Acey had the best luck with the cards that came up, and the quickest reactions of anyone at the table. No one, not even Dux , could even come close.

"Time to quit!" Captain Yuell exclaimed finally, as he rose to his feet. "We better get Acey out of here before he ruins the whole Adurian economy."

But just as he said this, Dux got his own winning hand on the screen, and he pressed the button. The screen locked in place, showing the faces of six Adurian women, side by side, each of them wearing matching sunbonnets. The word "WINNER" appeared on his screen in Galeng.

"Hey, look at this!" one of the treasure hunters exclaimed. "We've got another big winner here!"

But before Dux could celebrate, the faces on his screen changed, to pictures of Acey Zelk and Dux Hannah at the center, along with four blank faces, two on each side.

"What the...." Unable to comprehend what he was seeing, Dux leaned close to the screen, and blinked his eyes in disbelief. The blank cards changed, to four uniformed men wearing hats marked "POLICE."

Dux's companions all said they had the same screens.

"Let's get outta here," Captain Yuell said, leading the way to the exit.

Just then, the front door of the saloon burst open, and white-uniformed Adurian police officers swarmed in. Yuell and Golden charged into their midst with swords drawn, scattering the officers with the aggressive attack. The rest of the treasure ship crew waded in behind them, swinging chairs, clubs, bottles, and anything else they could get their hands on. Acey got on top of the bar and leaped down on two officers, smashing both of them to the floor hard. This knocked one unconscious, and Acey head-butted the other one into a similar state, then jumped over the motionless Adurians and attacked others.

Dux did what he could himself, but he wasn't the fighter the others were. An Adurian officer hit him in the side of the face with a stun club, sending him reeling and tumbling back under a table. Dux tried to sit up, but felt a little dizzy. Nonetheless, he climbed out and hurtled himself against the police, swinging his fists and screaming obscenities at them.

The police officers had apparently expected their numerical superiority to be enough to take the motley treasure ship crew into custody, but soon discovered how wrong they were. The Adurians tried to draw their pistols from holsters, but only one of them pulled a gun free, and he didn't get an opportunity to use it, because Mac Golden severed his arm at the elbow with a swish of his sword. The injured Adurian ran from the saloon into the street, screaming and spurting gouts of blood. Other officers ran after him in terror, and most of those remaining in the saloon were on the floor, either unconscious or dead.

Just as Dux was fighting another, having punched him in the face, he heard someone shout, "Duck, Dux!"

Without delaying to consider why, Dux did as he was told. A fraction of a second later Captain Yuell fired one of the officers' own guns, a thunderous blast that blew the alien's head off only inches away from a startled Dux.

The captain then led a retreat. They made it to a shuttle and lifted off just before the shuttleport filled with police vehicles. As they rocketed upward, Dux saw police aircraft arrive and circle the landing field below.

"I didn't see any other shuttles down there," Mac Golden said, as he wiped his bloody sword on a cloth. "It'll take 'em awhile to mount a pursuit, and by then we should be long gone."

"But they can still catch us at the pod station," Acey said, "while we're waiting for a podship."

"Not so," the Hibbil said. "I checked the glyphreader before we went down to the surface. We'll have a wait of maybe fifteen minutes after arriving at the station, and then we're off on our next adventure."

The furry little Hibbil, who prided himself on keeping track of important matters for the captain, proved to be correct.

* * * * *

When the entire crew was safely in outer space aboard their treasure ship, everyone surrounded Dux and Acey. "What did you do to the Adurians?" Captain Yuell asked. "You guys are on their most wanted list."

"We didn't do much," Acey said.

"Aw, come on," Yuell said. "They had pictures of both of you."

"Well," Dux said, looking at Acey and then the captain, "maybe we should have told you this before, but we didn't think you would care."

"This sounds serious," Mac Golden said, moving close and staring up at Dux.

The teenagers went on to describe how they had destroyed the Mutati manufacturing facility on Dij, and how they had barely escaped with their lives.

"You should have told us that earlier," Captain Yuell said, scowling. "You put my entire crew at peril."

"We didn't think it would hurt going to an Adurian world," Acey said.

"Oh you didn't, did you?" Mac Golden said. The little Hibbil stomped his foot angrily. "Don't you boys know anything about politics?"

"Uh, we grew up in the backwoods of Siriki," Dux said. "We don't know much about stuff like that."

"Don't you know that the Mutatis and Adurians are allies?" Golden shouted.

Dux felt a flush of hotness in his face, and caught the nervous gaze of Acey. The two of them shrugged....

Captain Yuell did not kick the boys off the ship. He said that they had learned their lesson, but obtained their promises not to keep any more important secrets from their crewmates. "We're your family now," he said. "I'm your Dad and Golden here is your Mom."

"Hey!" the Hibbil said. "I don't like the sound of that." He and the captain sparred playfully with swords, while the boys and the rest of the crew laughed and shouted insults....

But none of them, with the exception of Mac Golden, knew that the Hibbils and Adurians were secretly allied with each other, and intended to destroy both the Humans and the Mutatis. The HibAdu Coalition had placed sleeper agents all over the galaxy, with standing orders to await further instructions. Golden was one of those agents himself, but he had recently decided not to follow activation orders, if he ever got them.

Like Acey and Dux, the furry little Hibbil had found a new family. He liked these Humans, and would never consider betraying them. But he fell short of revealing what he knew about the HibAdu Coalition's scheme, and the danger it presented to the entire Human race.

Golden didn't want to think about all of that, and hoped the whole situation would just go away, without harming any of the people who had grown close to him.

Chapter Sixty-Seven

No one can ever see all of the interesting places in this galaxy. At least, I used to think that way.

—Noah Watanabe

H is friends who attended to him would have confirmed that Noah did not leave the deck of the grid-plane, where he lay in deep sleep, not having awakened or even moved for days. Untended, his reddish beard had been growing. But his mind was more active than ever, and—unknown to the Guardians around him—he was about to take a fantastic mental journey.

Sitting on the carpeted deck beside Noah's supine form, Eshaz talked soothingly to him, massaging the man's forehead as gently as he could with one scaly hand.

On the surface of his consciousness, Noah was aware of his alien friend, and of a mysterious healing treatment he had administered. But Noah made no effort to respond to the Tulyan, or to communicate with him in any manner. His attentions were focused elsewhere.

He heard Tesh say, excitedly, "Look, his eyelids are fluttering!"

And he heard a murmuring of conversation around him, as the others came over to see if Noah was coming back to consciousness. It almost seemed to him that he could if he really wanted to, but something much more important drew him away from them ... and he felt his mind expanding, questing outward.

Noah felt drawn by something momentous he needed to discover. Instinct told him it would most certainly be dangerous, and that if he went too deeply into his subconscious, he might never be able to wake up. The experience might kill him, but he to take it anyway.

He felt a beckoning, something tugging at his mind, teasing it, promising unknown delights. In his mind's eye, he saw a dark cloud in space, with a faint illumination beyond, delineating the shape of the mass. Every few seconds, something flashed behind the cloud, making its outline sharper. It was like a lightning storm, but that did not seem possible, since he was in deep space, far beyond any atmospheric envelope.

Earlier, Noah had heard Tesh and Eshaz discussing the explosion of Plevin Four, and it occurred to him now that a chunk of atmosphere might have lifted into space, sealed inexplicably, and that it was beyond a cloud of space dust now, flashing. The wild beauty could be like a last hurrah before the pocket of air disappeared forever, along with the planet.

Of course, none of that seemed possible. But still, he wondered. The visual effect was compelling.

As if released from his body, Noah's mind felt like it was floating in space, similar to the atmosphere that appeared to have broken away from the dead planet. His consciousness drifted on an empyrean current, taking him past blindingly spectacular sights. A massive yellow sun went nova in an awe-inspiring burst of destructive beauty, and in the next star system an even larger sun, a red giant, dropped into a black hole and then faded abruptly, like a dramatic sunset with all of its light suddenly sucked away.

He felt a mental click, and the scene before his inner eye shifted. Noah was no longer floating, no longer just observing. He found himself spread-eagled, connected to an immense gossamer web, but he was not a prisoner of it. It was the most marvelous sensation!

To his astonishment he was able to flip from one section of the pale green web to another—left, right, up, down, forward, and backward. Awkwardly, he went in several directions, one after the other, and then found he could gain better control over his movements. On impulse, he accelerated into deep space and spun into the cosmos, passing by asteroids, worlds, star systems, and even passing completely *through* other ghostly, acrobatic figures like him, of various recognizable races.

But there were other phantom creatures out there as well, some spinning, some darting, and others seeming to run in space, their appendages dancing along the webbing. Some were humanoid, while others looked like mythological animals, such as he had never seen before.

One with a lion head and serpentine body approached and kept pace beside him, staring at him as if trying to decide whether to devour him or not. Concerned, Noah tried to go faster than before, but the ghostly creature stayed with him.

Unable to get away, Noah wanted to cry out in terror, but knew his voice would make no sound in the airless void of space. Like a man in the wilderness facing a ferocious beast, he attempted to show no fear, and made a defiant, aggressive face at the would-be predator, along with wildly dramatic hand gestures.

Finally, apparently bored, the beast drifted off into the tail of a passing comet, and disappeared entirely.

Noah went on to cartwheel across the galaxy, a cosmic voyager in a realm he had never known existed. He was a mote in the heavens. With surprising ease, he gained new skills flying in this realm, and was able to increase his speed and maneuverability. He kept up with other creatures, following them for a while and then breaking off to go his own way. There seemed no limit to the places he could go, but none of them seemed tangible. It was all dreamlike, as if he was peering into a dimension that did not really exist.

And a disturbing thought intruded: *The Doge tried to kill me, and my sister put him up to it. Has she succeeded? Am I dead, or dying? Is that true of the others out here, too?*

He thought back on the near-death stories he had heard—of a person's life flashing in front of his eyes in seconds or fractions of seconds, and of a light at the end of a tunnel, beckoning him to go through and discover the light, beckoning him to....

For the first time, Noah wasn't certain if passing through meant dying or living. In the past he'd always thought if he went to the other side of the tunnel he would die, and that the light was heaven, drawing him like a magnet. But now he wasn't so certain. Couldn't the light represent life instead, pulling him out of the darkness of death?

He saw no tunnel at all now, though it seemed appropriate to him that he should. After all, wasn't he on the brink of death? Hadn't he chosen not to swim to the top of his consciousness where his friends were? Instead, he'd gone in a different, very dangerous direction. But a fascinating direction, where he had so much to learn, so much to experience.

Somehow, through everything, his personal fate seemed of little importance.

He was out in the middle of the vast galaxy where the lifetime of a human being was so infinitesimal in the scale of time that it hardly mattered at all. But could a life form only alive briefly still accomplish something meaningful? The common fruit fly lived but a few hours, and some organisms even less than that. Could the death of that fly affect events on the other side of the universe?

Noah thought it was possible, an extrapolation of a "butterfly flapping its wings" theory his mother had once told him, how that seemingly inconsequential occurrence could affect events on the other side of a planet.

He thought of the theories of relativity, of quantum mechanics, and of macro systems—of worlds orbiting stars, of entire galaxies hurtling through the cosmos, and of the all-encompassing universe expanding, fleeing from the singularity where the Big Bang was supposed to have occurred.

But his lingering physical reality interfered rudely with the serenity of such ruminations.

My sister tried to kill me!

The galactic images faded, and his eyes fluttered open. For an instant, he saw the scaly, reptilian face of Eshaz and his gray-slitted alien eyes, peering hard at him. A universe of caring in those eyes. The Tulyan had always been a giver, quick to do whatever he could for his friends, and for the environment.

But those eyes harbored a universe of secrets.

Abruptly, of his own volition, Noah found himself back in the strange cosmic realm again, spread-eagled on the gossamer web, spinning, cartwheeling across the galaxy. He peered into places where Humans could not look, and not knowing what he saw, he failed to comprehend.

Noah's mind filled to bursting. He wanted to come back again some other time and re-experience this ... if the opportunity ever presented itself to him. Logically, it seemed to him that he must be going stark, raving mad, but he felt the opposite, that he was more focused than ever before in his life. In the spaceship of his mind he journeyed far from anyplace he had ever been before, on an expedition that his physical body, subject to its corporeal limitations, could not possibly undertake.

With his new awareness, he didn't see how the concept of a physical form fit into a realm that seemed to be constructed of something else entirely, and where the spiritual meant more than anything he could touch. His eyes were transmitting extraordinary images to him.

The faint green webbing curved and stretched off into infinity, surrounding and penetrating him, connecting him with all that had ever been and all that ever would be. He could not comprehend how he knew this, only that he did, and that he had always known it, and always would, since he would never die as long as he remained connected to this marvelous galactic structure. He felt it giving him life, renewed energy, and that this was one of the secrets in Eshaz's eyes.

But there were more, many more.

As Noah spun away into this alternate dimension, he saw his friend's eyes superimposed over the cosmic tableau, and felt the Tulyan's presence with him, sharing the connection the two of them had with the webbing. Eshaz was making this experience available for him; Eshaz was saving his life by showing him ... what? Heaven?

Most astonishing. The slenderest threads connected Noah to a hidden network that spanned everything in existence, a godlike web that gave life and took it away. Despite the guidance of his friend, Noah feared that he would lose contact and never find his way back to this realm again. What a tragedy that would be, what a fathomless loss. He realized with a start that he hadn't been moving at all, that he had been connected to one strand, and that the web had been folding and refolding and unfolding around him, in a magical display of empyrean origami.

Such beauty he had never before beheld or even imagined possible, as he saw sunlight glistening off the green webbing in star system after star system. Exquisitely perfect in its design, this galactic mesh appeared to be an extrapolation of elegant patterns seen on planets ... of the designs in spider webs, leaves, and seashells. It all seemed linked to him, and all of it had to be the achievement of a remarkable higher power.

There could be no other possible explanation.

For a moment his vision shifted, and he saw green-and-brown skymining ships floating over the surface of a planet, scooping air and processing important elements out of it. On a plateau below the ships he saw his company's base of operations for that world, which he recognized as Jaggem. It gave him reassurance to see the important work continuing, despite his own absence. He had left good people in charge.

Then he saw a contingent of red-uniformed men supervising the operations, and his spirits dropped. The Doge's Red Berets.

Presently the images faded, replaced by the twinkling void of deep space and the pale green filigree. Ahead, he saw chunks of matter hurtling through the cosmos, some pieces without apparent direction, while others ... *podships!* ... were racing along the gossamer web strands. Appearing Lilliputian in comparison with the immensity of his own form, they sped right through him without apparent harm. Such a peculiar sensation. He felt as if he was stretched across a vast distance. A mental stretch, he believed, and not a physical one, but the mind had brought along an enlarged ghost of its body.

The folding images seemed to fade now, although Noah beheld a curvature of webbing stretched to infinity, faintly fluttering on a cosmic wind. Again he had the illusion of whirling and spinning along the strands himself, and he saw once more that the web was really doing tricks around him, creating the most wondrous of all illusions.

On impulse, Noah thought of grabbing the podships as they sped around him and through him. How incredible that would be, if he could only stop one and examine it closely, without harming anything. But as he considered this more it didn't seem wise, even if he could accomplish it. Noah did not want to interfere in natural processes, didn't want to disturb the exquisite perfection of the heavens. He didn't think it was possible anyway; it would be like trying to reach from one dimension into another one.

Again, his brain clicked, and the focus of his inner eye shifted.

* * * * *

Eshaz felt Noah pulling away from him, and he tried to prevent it. But this Human had grown too strong for even a large Tulyan to keep under control. He pushed Eshaz away with surprising strength, and the bronze-scaled creature tumbled backward, onto the deck of the grid-plane.

Timeweb's healing powers had worked. But spiders of worry scuttled through the Tulyan's thoughts.

What have I done?

* * * * *

As the podships continued to speed by, Noah discovered that he could make mental linkages with them one at a time, only for a few moments in each case, but enough for him to obtain information. He saw inside the living, spacefaring vessels and understood how they operated. Everyone knew that the podships were living organisms, but their inner workings had always been mysterious. He learned for the first time that they were piloted by tiny humanoid creatures, who guided the ships across the far reaches of space. Two very different organisms were working together ... perhaps the strangest of all symbiotic relationships, it seemed to Noah.

The images were clear at times but kept slipping in and out of focus and blurring.

Some podships carried a number of merchant ships in their cargo holds—typically fifteen or twenty—while others had a wild assortment of passengers on board: Humans, Mutatis, machines, various aliens. One pod was transporting the Doge Lorenzo del Velli and Noah's twin sister toward Canopa. He heard them in the grand salon of their private yacht, talking about most of Noah's Guardians having scattered into the woods and hills, where they were living off the land.

"They're not worth going after," Francella said to the Doge in an eerie, distant voice. "We need to focus our forces on finding Noah and killing him. Only then will I be satisfied."

Lorenzo nodded, and said something unintelligible. He seemed to be in acquiescence.

From afar, Noah felt a chill as he stared at his fraternal twin's hardened face, with her treacherous dark eyes and bald eyebrows. She had become his bête noire, or perhaps she always had been, and he hadn't paid enough attention to the danger. Her image grew fuzzy and then sharpened again.

First she kills our father and cleverly blames me. Now she seeks to assassinate me, and the manipulated Doge thinks she is justified.

Noah tried not to hate her, didn't want to carry such a burden in his heart. But it was not easy to fight the strong feelings.

Abruptly and without his impetus, the images of Francella and Lorenzo, and of the podship carrying their yacht, vanished.

Inside the cargo hold of another sentient pod, a motley assortment of sentient machines from the White Sun star system were aboard at least a dozen battered transport ships, also bound for Canopa. While most of the robots were silent and packed in close quarters, Noah determined their origin and destination from a conversation their leader, a flat-bodied machine, was having with a subordinate. But the cosmic eavesdropper could not determine why they were en route.

In the hold of yet another podship, he saw a peculiar pilot at the controls of a spacecraft that looked exactly like a merchant prince schooner, including the red-and-gold colors on the hull. Visible through the thick plax of the front window, the pilot had shapeshifted to make himself look Human. But Noah—he wasn't sure how—could tell that he wasn't Human at all.

What is a Mutati doing with one of our ships?

Our ships? The thought stuck in his throat, because he and Doge Lorenzo were mortal enemies now. Noah wasn't certain where his own home was any more, but his allegiance to humankind had never faltered.

Gazing past the Mutati, he scanned the schooner's interior and saw a strange array of gleaming tubes built into the hull, an arrangement he could not identify. He tried to see more, but the image faded and disappeared. Moments later it flickered back, and he saw the podship arrive at the orbital station over Ilbao, one of the Mutati worlds. The pilot offloaded his schooner and took it out into orbital space, perhaps fifty kilometers away. There, he held a geostationary position.

With new eyes, Noah scanned the podways. Images blurred and clarified, shifted out of focus and grew sharper. Floating near various pod stations around the galaxy, he saw a total of ten matching schooners, each with a solitary Mutati aboard, and each with the odd, unidentifiable tubes inside the vessels. It was extremely peculiar, but undoubtedly the Merchant Prince Alliance had already sighted the vessels, and would take action against them.

Or had they? Looking back, he realized that all of the strange schooners were stationed over Mutati worlds, inside enemy territory. Perhaps they were listening posts, part of a defensive network. But why were they all merchant prince schooners, or made to look like them? Most perplexing.

His focus shifted, and Noah saw something he hadn't noticed before. A podship lay motionless in space, and he sensed difficulty there, that the spacecraft was marooned and in need of assistance. If he could help, it would not be interfering; he would be going to the aid of a stranded traveler.

But can I do anything?

Zooming in, he absorbed a vision of the vessel into his mind, and saw a green-and-brown grid-plane in the cargo hold, and—to his amazement—his own Human form lying comatose inside the plane, with Eshaz tending to him.

We're on board a podship? But how? The answer eluded him.

Letting his mind permeate the rest of the podship, Noah focused on a green, glowing chamber at the core, and he seeped inside. Touching the core with his probing thoughts, he suddenly felt the craft lurch into motion, which at first surprised him. Then, as he thought about it, the experience seemed oddly familiar, though he could not determine why. He only knew one thing for certain, that the sentient podship was responding to his mental commands, leaping onto a different cosmic strand than the one it had been on before, a different podway headed in a different direction.

Gaining control was a fantastic sensation, and Noah Watanabe had a destination in mind.

Canopa.

He had decided to return home, and saw clearly how to get there. He gave instructions to the podship, through the mental linkage they shared.

Then Noah sensed another entity in the navigation chamber with him, and saw a tiny, barely discernible creature clinging to one of the walls. Incredibly, it was struggling to take command of the pod away from him....

Chapter Sixty-Eight

We are taught from birth to never let our guard down, and how to protect ourselves against mortal enemies. But this aggression, I never anticipated.

—Tesh Kori

T esh had been stunned to find another entity—one she saw as a looming, shadowy form—take control of the podship away from her and send it in wild, spinning dives through space, finally locking onto a course for Canopa. It had been a surprise takeover.

Now Tesh went through the ritualistic steps involved with occupying this sacred chamber, this womb within a womb, and she uttered a litany of ancient *benedictios*, the guidance-and-control phrases her people had employed for millions of years.

The podship quivered, and started to respond to her commands, but only for a few seconds before it stopped, as the intruder fought for control.

This was unlike any battle Tesh had ever experienced, as she faced a specter that kept coming at her and neutralizing her strength. She never felt her foe touch her, only the numbing effects of its ghostly power.

Normally, when a Parvii entered a sectoid chamber, that was enough to control the creature. If they used ancient words and a gentle touch anyplace on a sectoid wall, the commands were understood. Now, however, the podship was confused, as it was receiving conflicting orders from different entities, different galactic races. Her opponent was not a Parvii. She knew that for certain, but little else. She didn't think it was a Tulyan, either, for she had never known them to behave this way.

The powerful phantom stood inside the sectoid chamber, but details of its body were not discernible. Only a distorted shadow of whatever it was. It almost looked Human in shape, but with gross distortions on the head and appendages, as if something had pulled it, stretching it out.

Scurrying along the wall in front of the shadow, Tesh gained access to the core of the creature's body by pressing her hands hard on a small, bright green wall section of the sectoid chamber, which was the nerve center of the creature. This technique, known as the "Parvii Hold," was used by the wranglers of wild pods out in the galaxy, to tame particularly rebellious pods. She'd learned it from an old veteran. On the downside, the trick would only work for a few minutes before the pod shifted the location of its nerve center, moving the bright patch of color to another place.

But that might just be enough time.

As she pressed against the tough flesh with both hands, pushing this way and that to steer and send acceleration signals, the pod finally began to follow her commands.

Tesh needed to focus all of her considerable powers, not letting up for even a fraction of a second. By means of her connection, she saw through the visual sensors of the pod creature. Ahead, the faint green strands of the web seemed limitless, although an ancient legend said they did stop somewhere, at the end of the galaxy.

She saw the intruder's shadow move. Focusing, she tried again to see bodily and facial features, but none were apparent. Her adversary—she couldn't determine the gender—seemed much larger than she was, but she could not even tell if it had a face, in the common sense. From the humanoid shadow, she wondered if it might be a rogue Parvii using some sort of modified magnification mechanism. Looking around carefully, she saw no evidence of this. But her opponent continued to cause her trouble.

Receiving mental impulses from Tesh's mysterious opponent, the pod began to slow. She pressed even harder on the green nerve center, which had not shifted position yet. The podship shuddered, and resumed the speed she wanted.

Tesh felt no more opposition, and she saw no sign of the shadowy form. She hoped it was gone, but kept her guard up. It took only a few minutes for her to cross space, but seemed like much longer.

Feeling uneasy, she guided the craft to a remote pod station, not on the busiest podways. As she pulled into the main docking bay of the station, she saw no other spacecraft at all, exactly as she had anticipated. Tesh needed to keep control of this pod, and did not want any distractions.

The podship seemed edgy. It didn't shift its nerve center, but if it did she vowed to locate it again, doing whatever was necessary to maintain the upper hand.

The pod station orbited over a world that had not been inhabited for more than three hundred years. It no longer had shuttle service, so anyone wishing to go down to the surface needed to bring their own landing craft, which she didn't have. She just wanted to focus on the podship, keeping it from breaking free of her, or from falling under the control of her unseen competitor.

Where was that shadowy form now? She saw no sign of it. Perhaps on the journey across space it had fallen away, and would no longer be any trouble to her. Either that, or it had died in the struggle to oppose her superior powers.

Looking through the visual sensors of the agitated podship, Tesh saw that the station was as she recalled it from earlier in her life, an unadorned structure orbiting over the tundra of a small, icy planet.

Chapter Sixty-Nine

Each life is a journey, from birth to death, from wake to slumber.

—Parvii Inspiration

After searching the sectoid chamber carefully and finding nothing out of the ordinary, Tesh became convinced that her mysterious adversary had departed. It had been the strangest experience of her life.

Playing it safe, upon leaving the core chamber she sealed it with her own private command signal to the podship, making it impossible for anyone to gain access without her permission. No one, not even Woldn himself, the Eye of the Swarm, could override a Parvii command signal to a podship. The bond between pilot and beast was too strong.

In a shadowy corridor of the spacecraft, Tesh then enlarged herself by switching on her personal magnification system. She felt the energy field crackle on the surface of her skin.

After waiting a few seconds for the familiar but uncomfortable sensation to pass, she hurried back through the maze of passageways. Rounding a turn, she encountered a worried Anton Glavine.

"Where have you been?" he demanded.

"You wouldn't believe me if I told you," she said with an enigmatic smile.

"Try me."

"Perhaps another time."

Though he tried to block her way while demanding answers, she pushed past him and climbed the short stairway into the passenger cabin of the grid-plane, which was still inside the podship's cargo hold.

There she saw Noah lying comatose on the deck, as before, with a blanket over him and the healing pad bulging on one side of his head. His body jerked and he flailed his arms for several seconds, before going motionless again.

Dr. Bichette sat on a pillow beside him, tending to him, while Eshaz loomed over both of them, looking on....

* * * * *

Moments before, Noah had felt the podship settle into a docking berth. He had almost, but not quite, been able to pilot the sentient vessel. Most remarkable. But something ... or someone ... had overridden him. During the cross-space journey, the spacecraft had stopped complying with his commands. It all seemed like a dream.

Previously, Noah had been content to remain physically unconscious, so that he could journey in his mind. But now he struggled to awaken. He heard Dr. Bichette's excited voice, then felt the rough, scaly touch of Eshaz on his hand. And he heard other voices.

Like a diver short on air, swimming frantically toward a luminous surface, he struggled with all of his strength, pulling upward, using his arms. The voices became a little louder. In addition to the doctor, he recognized Tesh, Anton, and Subi.

Must reach them. Must see them.

Heavy. Too heavy. He felt himself sinking, and the voices fading.

Swim harder.

Just when he thought he would never make it, and would fade away to oblivion, he finally reached the surface and gasped for air. He felt an odd sensation in his left foot, but tried to put it out of his mind.

"We cannot remain here!" Noah shouted, flailing his arms and struggling to fill his lungs with air. "I tried to go to Canopa, but the podship wouldn't cooperate."

He opened his eyes, blinked, and saw Tesh staring at him. She looked stunned.

"He's babbling something about the podship," Bichette said.

"I'm not babbling, you fool!" Noah snapped. "I was in the navigation chamber, don't you understand? For a few moments, I had the podship under control! It was an incredible feeling!"

"He's delusional," the doctor said. "Must be the anesthesia I had to give him. Poor fellow. I wish I could have saved the foot."

Foot? With the blanket gone, Noah looked down. A thick white healing pad was on the bottom of his left leg, where his foot should be.

I'm not awake yet.

But he felt Tesh's hand on his, the gentle caress of her touch. He tried to stand up, but could not support himself on one foot. Eshaz kept him from falling, and eased him back down. Bewildered, Noah looked around.

His gaze met Dr. Bichette's. Sadness there, and guilt. "I'm sorry," he said. "I had to amputate."

Again, Noah felt Tesh's touch, this time on his forearm. "We're so sorry," she whispered.

He looked at her, and saw that she still appeared to be stunned, presumably over his tragic operation. Bichette was spouting medical details, but Noah tuned him out. His foot was gone, and nothing could be done about that now, since he had moral objections to the cloning of Human body parts. Somehow, as sad as he was, and as angry as he was at the doctor, Noah felt great comfort from Tesh. He could not take his eyes off her.

But something seemed different about her. He couldn't quite tell what, but he was sure of it.

Chapter Seventy

The proper course of honor is not always clear. Is it more honorable to follow a family tradition, or to follow what is in your heart?

—Emir Hari'Adab

A tall metalloy platform stood at the center of the construction site, with a bubble cab atop the platform and eight crane booms extending from the core, like the legs of an immense spider. Eight robots inside the high cab operated the system, and with them stood a young Mutati in a purple-and-gold robe, watching the progress.

Hari'Adab Meshdi—son of the Zultan—could just as easily have supervised from the ground, but this high perch gave him a better vantage point. Besides, he felt dismal about the project, and wouldn't mind too much if the whole rig toppled over and took him with it.

A gust of wind buffeted the cab, but the Emir didn't bother to hold on. Dejectedly, he bumped against a window and leaned there for a moment before straightening himself.

The explosives belt under his robe felt uncomfortable against the soft flesh of his Mutati belly, and reaching under his clothing he loosened it a little.

One of the robots, a ball of rivets with red eyes, turned toward him without comprehension, then looked away and resumed its work. The cranes moved in synchronization, sliding mezzanine floor pieces into slots in vertical posts, and then snapping on the interior walls.

In only a few violent seconds, Hari could halt the rapid, efficient progress by blowing everything up himself. But disaster engineers combing through the wreckage afterward would figure out what he did, and it would smear his name. Already the name was tenuous, because of the successful enemy strike on the Demolio facility, a defensive failure that had been his personal responsibility.

One of his three hands rested on the detonation trigger. It wouldn't take much, just a moment of courage. At least that would slow reconstruction of the immoral facility.

Just beyond a grassy rise, the debris of the former manufacturing site still remained, exactly as it had been left a few weeks ago, with destroyed torpedoes inside and the bodies of four hundred Mutatis who died in the sneak attack. Hari could have died with them. Earlier that day he had been inspecting the facility, and had left Dij by shuttle only moments before the unexpected offensive.

To a large extent the Mutatis had assumed that the previous facility would be protected by secrecy and its remote location—and they were still investigating how the young Human commandos got through. The episode had caused the Mutatis to close down their "fly trap" system of capturing and imprisoning small numbers of Humans, in order to get intelligence information out of them. Now an entire division of Mutati soldiers guarded the new Demolio manufacturing and training facility, armed with the latest detection technology. This facility could not be destroyed by outside attack again, not even if the enemy sent a huge force against it.

Following the surprise attack, his father had proclaimed the site sacred ground, and decreed that it was not to be disturbed. Just beyond the ruins of the largest building, facing the holy direction of sunrise, a monument had been erected to honor the fallen workers, brave martyrs who died in that brief but effective attack.

"Our enemy is without honor," the Zultan had announced at the dedication ceremony the week before. "They will regret this dirty business."

A crowd of well-dressed Mutatis, all in their natural flesh-fat forms, had cheered and called for the blood of every Human in the galaxy, annihilating them to the last man, woman, and child. Sitting on the stage as his father spoke, Hari'Adab had been deeply troubled by the aggressive statements, but had tried to conceal his feelings. Certainly all human beings could not possibly be evil. He'd heard of their magnificent historical religious leaders, such as Jesus, Muhammad, Buddha, Mohandas Gandhi, and Mother Theresa, any one of whom matched the stature of the greatest Mutati prophets.

And by all accounts, one of the most altruistic of modern Humans was Noah Watanabe. Not openly religious, he nonetheless professed a deep reverence for the sacred, interconnected nature of planets, and for the need to restore them after the damage caused by industrial operations. Such Humans did not deserve to die. The galaxy would not be a better place without them, or without future leaders like that.

Hari'Adab could not condone genocide.

Sadly, his own father and other Mutati leaders were so filled with blind hatred toward their enemies that they had lost touch with decency, with altruism. Instead, they continually looked for passages from *The Holy Writ* to support their positions, citing scripture that called for the complete destruction of all enemies of the Mutati people. But *The Holy Writ* had plenty of other passages that called for compassion and justice as well, and for reasoned diplomacy instead of warfare. The Mutati leadership, however, was only citing passages to support their militaristic positions, while ignoring other, even more significant scriptures.

In their fanatic zeal, they had become tunnel minded.

The Mutati Kingdom's Demolio program was the exact antithesis of everything that Noah Watanabe stood for. If Watanabe learned about this deadly technology, the whole idea of cracking planets open would chill him to his soul, and Hari felt the same way. Such a program had no basis in morality. And yet, Hari found himself managing the industrial facility that built the torpedoes, and the training program for Mutati outriders.

As the Zultan's eldest son, the Emir would assume the throne from his father someday, but that would be too late. Already, psychotic Mutati military commanders had destroyed three enemy planets, and many more were planned. It was terrible, just terrible. He didn't care if the technology could be the turning point in the centuries-long long war, swinging the tide decisively in favor of his people.

Winning that way was not victory.

One of the Emir's closest friends had even suggested that they arrange to have the Zultan killed, for the sake of the Mutati Kingdom, and to prevent continued bloodshed. No one could even remember why Mutatis and Humans were mortal enemies. A regime change seemed like the only way to break the continuing cycles of retribution and violence.

At first Hari had refused to consider patricide, one of the very worst sins that a Mutati could commit. In a huff, he had sent his friend away, and had not spoken to him since.

But maybe the idea had merit. It might just might end this folly once and for all. What if he brought the Zultan up here, along with some of the top generals, and blew them up with the Demolio facility? Hari would need to set up a political coup team to take over during the power vacuum, and he would not be around to run the government himself.

He'd always disliked his father anyway, couldn't ever recall feeling close to him. The explosion would solve a lot of problems at once.

Hari loathed the Demolio program his father was sponsoring, could not comprehend the suffering and death one of the planet-buster torpedoes inflicted on human beings when it hit a planet. That was a fate he wouldn't wish on even his most-despised enemies. He hadn't even been aware of the diabolical extent of the program when his father commanded him to supervise it. The Zultan had only told him that it was an important military operation, and a secret that he didn't want to entrust to anyone but his own son and heir apparent. The trust had been surprising considering their lack of closeness, but somewhat flattering, of only for a short while until he discovered what horrors the Demolio program entailed.

Still, the Emir had accepted the wishes of his father. In Mutati society, the young—even if they held an opposing opinion—were expected to show respect for their elders. Now Hari was in too deep to slide gracefully out of this Demolio assignment. His father would brand him a coward, and a traitor to the cause. The repercussions were severe if he didn't do what he was told, if he didn't carry on the militaristic family tradition of following orders and never questioning them.

But the repercussions were even more severe if he looked away, if he didn't follow his conscience.

Thus far he had, at least, refused to wear the Adurian minigyro that his father gave to him. A proud young man, Hari did not need a mechanical device to help him make decisions. He'd never trusted the bubble-eyed aliens anyway, and certainly didn't want their technology interfering with his thought processes.

If only it was possible to reach a peace accord with the Humans. The fighting didn't make sense to Hari, just killing an enemy because it had been that way for a long time. There had to be a better way.

Chapter Seventy-One

There are many ways of getting from one place to another. When it comes to space travel, however, the options are strictly limited to podships—if you want to get there efficiently, not wasting time or money.

—From a merchant prince transportation analysis

Despite the tragic loss of his foot, Noah insisted on leaving the grid-plane. He had just shaved and cleaned up. "It's cramped in here," he said, hobbling around with a pair of crutches that Subi made by fusing together pieces of scrap alloy. "I need fresh air."

"There's something I'd like to discuss with you," Tesh said, looking at him earnestly. "It's very important."

Noah nodded, though something about her still bothered him. For an unknown reason, he wasn't sure if he could trust her. He would rather be alone to sort through his thoughts, and the shocking medical procedure that had been performed on him. But he had trouble saying no to her. Even trying to look past her beauty, he found her an intriguing, persuasive woman.

Leaning on the crutches, Noah led the way into the cargo hold of the former podship, then hobbled through an airlock to one of the sealed walkways of the pod station, where the air was breathable.

For several moments, he paused to stare through a filmy window at the podship in its berth, trying to comprehend some of the mysteries of the sentient creatures.

Intruding on his thoughts, Tesh said, "Your bunker on Plevin Four was actually a podship that crashed centuries ago, and then was modified. After the podship regenerated and shifted its skin back into position, the window walls fell away, and so did interior rooms that your Guardians added. The vessel now has a typical passenger compartment and a cargo hold, containing your grid-plane."

"This podship lay dormant for centuries?"

"Yes."

"And how do you know that?" Noah looked intensely at her, deep into her emerald green eyes.

Without answering, she began to walk beside the podship.

Keeping up with her, Noah almost fell, and she reached out to help him. Pushing her hand away, he supported himself on his own. The stump of his lower leg throbbed with pain.

"You said you were in a navigation chamber," Tesh said, as they made their way along the walkway, past empty berths in the docking bay. "What did you mean by that?"

"Are you in the habit of responding to a question with a question?"

"I need you to bear with me, Noah. I know it's difficult, but please trust me."

"I trust you."

"I don't think you do, not entirely."

He hesitated, then said, "The navigation chamber may have only been in my dream, but it seemed fantastically real. I felt as if I was at the controls of the podship, speeding through deep space. Without touching anything, I was using my brain signals to direct the vessel. It responded for awhile, then wouldn't anymore. It was like ..."

"Like what?"

The two of them were standing outside the waiting room of the pod station. Noah considered how to answer her, but his thoughts drifted away, like balloons floating up on a sudden breeze, just beyond a child's grasp. He stared at the wall next to them, then looked along the walkway.

Like podships themselves, pod stations were mottled gray and black, with not-quite clear, filmy sections for windows. He'd heard that pod stations were also living creatures, just as the podships were, but they didn't travel the podways of deep space like the ships. That left open the question as to how the pod stations—which were much larger than the sentient spacecraft—ever got sprinkled around the galaxy in the first place.

Perhaps the stations had once been spacefaring vessels themselves, and went into retirement. Or maybe they were amalgams of retired podships, having fused themselves together into different shapes. In any event, all of the ships and stations had an obvious symbiotic relationship, like different parts of one immense galactic organism. Noah had more questions than answers.

With a start, he realized that Tesh had been saying something to him.

"I'm sorry," he said. "Guess I'm not totally out of my coma. As I said, when I was asleep all that time, I had strange, vivid dreams."

"You thought you were in some kind of a navigation chamber?"

"That's right."

"You said the podship responded for awhile, and then wouldn't do so any longer. You were about to say something more."

"Well, it seemed like someone else was in the chamber too, fighting me for control of the podship."

"You *did* have a strange dream," Tesh said.

"Now tell me how that thing changed from a bunker to a podship," Noah said, nodding his head toward the vessel.

"Perhaps that's best answered inside," she said, leading the way back to the ship.

Intrigued, Noah hobbled along beside her, thumping the crutches on the walkway.

Just as they stepped from the airlock into the cargo hold, Anton greeted them. He looked nervous and upset.

"We need to talk," the young man said to Tesh.

"This is a not a good time," she said. "Maybe later?" Tesh looked at him inquisitively, as if concerned about his welfare. This was one of the things that Noah thought he liked about her, the way she seemed so caring, so nurturing. Assuming it was not all an act. He didn't think it was, but couldn't quite overcome his feelings of doubt.

"We used to be close," Anton said, trying to move in front of her. "What went wrong?"

"I'll talk to you later," she promised. "I told you, this isn't a good time."

As she attempted to walk on, Anton grabbed her arm. She shook him loose, raised her voice. "Well, what is it?" she demanded. "What's so important?"

"It's about us, about our relationship."

"And you've chosen to interrupt me when I'm busy? Why is it so urgent?"

"It's urgent to *me*," he said, "but I can see it isn't to you."

"That's not true at all!"

"Then why are you and my uncle acting so cozy?"

"The green of jealousy is not a good color on you, Anton...."

Noah leaned against a bulkhead of the cargo hold. With his arm he felt the leathery flesh of the podship, and he pressed his face against the creature. In the background of his consciousness, the animated voices of Tesh and Anton continued, but faded and blurred. They were occupied with their mounting argument, and weren't looking at the man with the cane.

They did not notice that Noah's eyes were closed, and that his eyelids were fluttering, as if in a REM dream state. But he was not sleeping. Far from it ...

Chapter Seventy-Two

It is said that success in life is about focus, and lacking that, nothing meaningful can be accomplished. But is that old adage really true? Can't the wandering heart, the questing soul, achieve even more? Aren't the highest achievements in God's universe the simplest, the most pure?

—*The Holy Writ* of the Mutatis

From the open hatch of the grid-plane, Eshaz had been watching Tesh and Anton as they engaged in an animated conversation, and saw Noah Watanabe with them. Despite his injury, Noah was showing grit and tenacity, a desire to continue his life and not complain about his personal misfortune. He had lost his foot, but thanks to the healing nutrients of the timehole, he was out of his coma.

The man had come back from the dead.

But if the Council of Elders ever discovered what Eshaz had done, he would be in a lot of trouble. His mission was to repair timeholes and no more, using proven methods of patching up damage to the sacred web, anywhere in the galaxy. He was not authorized to go beyond that, not sanctioned to use any ancillary skills he had developed over the nine hundred and eighty thousand years of his lifetime. The reason was clear, and he understood it well. Primarily, it was all about concentration, about adhering to priorities. If he did other things, by definition that meant he was neglecting his essential Timeweb maintenance duties.

But Eshaz was, among other things, a timeseer, one of the few Tulyans with the ability to see—though imperfectly—into the future, and into the past. If ordered to do so by the high council, he used that skill for the benefit of the Tulyan race and Timeweb. On occasion, he even did it for other galactic races, for the sometimes-arcane political purposes of the Tulyan Elders. One thing in exchange for another.

Eshaz also knew how to draw beneficial nutrients from a rip in the web, as he had done for Noah's sake, but this was one of the greatest infractions a Tulyan could commit. Only the most ancient of the ancients were authorized to do that, Tulyan sorcerers who were much older than he was, and who knew much more. He had learned the skill from one of them, with all of the dire warnings that went along with it. A mistake, holding the web open improperly, could result in a huge cataclysm, the collapse of an entire galactic sector.

Thankfully, that calamity had not occurred in this case, and he had repaired the web defect after the healing procedure, along with others he found in the vicinity of the planetary explosion. Still, he could not conceal his transgression from the Elders. The next time he visited the Tulyan Starcloud, he would have to tell his superiors what he had done, and face the consequences.

After healing Noah with the Timeweb connection, Eshaz had noticed a change in his own body, as the aches and pains in his muscles and joints diminished. Physically, he began to feel more like his old self again.

Following the radical procedure, Eshaz had tried to take control of the podship himself, by gaining entrance to the sectoid chamber and merging into the flesh of the creature in the way of his people, but he was prevented from doing so. A Parvii already had it....

Now, as he stood watching the argument between Tesh and Anton, he noticed that Noah was leaning against a bulkhead, and not looking at all well. His eyes were closed, and he seemed about to fall over.

Eshaz ran to help his friend.

Chapter Seventy-Three

By deeds does a man measure his own personality, and his own worth.
—Anton Glavine, *Reflections*

Following the harrowing escape of the treasure crew from the Adurian planet, Acey and Dux gambled their remaining bonus money, and lost all of it to their more experienced mates. Even so, the young men didn't feel they had lost anything at all. They had begun the space adventure with no assets, only their lives and the clothes on their backs, and now they were distinctly ahead of that. They possessed a newfound wealth of experience, something that could not be purchased at any price or found in any treasure chest.

On the bridge the *Avelo*, the crew huddled around Captain Yuell as he examined one of many parchments in his possession. In his early years the gray-bearded old man had been the heir to a great merchant prince fortune, and had used much of his money to purchase old documents, especially galactic treasure maps. Eventually, his family had fallen into political disfavor and had lost their property and fortune. So, in his middle years, he had run off to space, taking his precious charts with him. He had spent the decades afterward exploring the galaxy, following the documents and discovering that most of them were either erroneous or fraudulent.

But a few were accurate. He had already proven that at Wuxx Reef, and at other spots around the galaxy, according to stories the teenagers had heard about him.

"There," the old adventurer said, pointing at a star system at the top right corner of the parchment. "We go there!"

* * * * *

On the way, a two day journey to a region where podships supposedly did not venture, Captain Yuell regaled the crew with tales from his own treasure trove of lore. He told of the most unusual aliens in the "wide, wide galaxy," of Wolfen midgets and lighter-than-air creatures, of humanoids five meters tall, and of the renowned mind-readers of Eleo.

Then, just as the battered but venerable *Avelo* entered a small solar system whose red dwarf sun glistened off the craft, the captain said, "But none are more unusual than the Gamboliers of Ovinegg. That's their primary planet," he said, pointing to a world that glistened a dreary shade of brown in the diminished light. Moment by moment, the oval shape of Ovinegg drew closer.

An air of anticipation filled the passenger cabin of the ship. Thus far, however, as the world loomed larger and larger, Dux was less than impressed. Through the hazy atmosphere he didn't see any bodies of water down there at all, and wondered if they were brown and polluted, like the seemingly treeless landscape. From the edge of the atmospheric envelope, he didn't see mountains or any other topographical features, either.

"It looks like a misshapen rubber ball," Dux said.

"Is that why the people are called Gamboliers?" one of the men asked, "because they bounce and jump around on the surface?"

"Nice guess," Captain Yuell said, "but that's not even close. The Treasure of Ovinegg awaits us, lads, but the question is, which of you are brave enough to go get it?"

"I am, sir!" Acey said. "And so's my cousin Dux." The two of them stepped forward, but Dux did not feel as enthusiastic as his cousin. He hoped Acey's bravado didn't get them into trouble.

"I'm ready too, sir," the Hibbil Mac Golden said, pushing the youngest crewmen aside. "Just tell us where to find the goods, and we'll bring 'em back."

"Well," the captain responded with a broad smile, "the goods are just lying down there for the picking. Piles of priceless gems, and they don't even need to be mined."

"If it's that easy," one of the crewmen said, "why haven't we heard of this place before?"

"Because you're stupid," one of the men shouted.

Laughter ensued. But all around, Dux heard his mates talking about how none of them had heard of the Treasure of Ovinegg, or the Gamboliers, or this solar system.

"Here's how it works," Captain Yuell said. "The Gamboliers don't allow foreign spacecraft to land on their homeworld. All visitors must leap from a shuttle no closer than two thousand meters above the planet."

He paused, and looked from face to face. "Without parachutes," he added.

"We just jump like rocks?" Mac Golden asked in his squeaky voice. Nervously, he adjusted his eye patch, and inched a couple of steps back.

"They're supposed to catch you. The Gamboliers are quite expert at catching people as they fly out of the sky, with fire rescue nets and other techniques. After you land, they bestow great wealth on you for your bravery."

"Why don't we just sneak down there and gather treasure?" Acey asked.

"Because they'll catch us and kill us. They promise a horrendous death for anyone who doesn't follow the rules. Oh, one more thing. I didn't mention it before, but I never got any money from being in a wealthy merchant prince family. I made my whole life story up. Actually, I got my money here, on Ovinegg when I was a young man, not much older than you two. I earned it and spent it, and now I need to replenish my stockpile."

"And the rules are still the same down there?" one of the crewmen asked.

"Those rules have been around for millennia, and when I was there I saw no sign of anything changing. That was forty-four years ago, not long to a civilization like theirs."

A palpable, worried silence filled the cabin.

"I'd like to see us all go home rich," Captain Yuell said, "but if I'm the only one going, that's fine, too. In case something goes wrong, you'll find my will on the ship's computer, with my virtual signature. I leave the *Avelo* to all of you equally."

Again, he looked from face to face. "Are any of you still with me?"

At first, no one answered.

Then Acey said. "I'm with you, Captain. And so is my cousin Dux." He looked at Dux, and smiled. "Right, buddy?"

Reluctantly, Dux nodded.

There were no other volunteers.

At Captain Yuell's command, the pilot steered the vessel into position, cutting down into the atmosphere, a couple of thousand meters above the surface. Then Yuell and his two young devotees jumped into the hazy sky and plunged downward.

Chapter Seventy-Four

No matter the excellence of your skills, no matter how superior you think you are, there is always someone who surpasses you, and there is always be someone to outdo him as well. It is this way across the entire galaxy, and throughout every eon of time. Most of us think there is only one zenith of attainment, in God Almighty. But is he the supreme being of only one galaxy? Or are there other galaxies, and superior gods?

—*Scienscroll* Apocrypha

Probing with his mind, Noah determined that someone had sealed the entrance to the navigation chamber, undoubtedly the mysterious, barely discernible adversary who had taken control of the podship away from him. He remembered being inside the core room, and now his memory scanned over every feature he had seen in there earlier, the glowing, pale green walls, with veins of gray and black, and a small, bright green patch high on one wall.

During the struggle for control of the vessel, his tiny opponent had moved with blurring speed, climbing a wall to the bright green section, and had done something there to take control away from him. But what had been done there?

As he continued to probe now, he could not see that section, or anything at all inside the navigation chamber. His thoughts moved around the outside of the sealed enclosure, and he noted how it was connected by a thick membrane to the rest of the sentient spaceship. Finally, he noticed that a small portion of the mottled gray exterior of the chamber was a slightly different color, a shade of bright green.

Could this be the other side of the green patch on the other side? He wasn't certain. Previously, the spot had been high on a wall, and this was lower. But could it have shifted position?

Focusing all of his energy on the bright green section, he tried to use it as an entrance to the chamber. He visualized penetrating it and going through, as if his thoughts were a laser cutting device.

Moments passed, with no apparent effect.

Then, abruptly, the thick flesh began to pulse and throb, and Noah heard a squeal, as if from a yelping animal. The flesh quivered, and parted to reveal an opening. Noah shot through, into the interior of the navigation chamber.

I'm in! he thought.

But looking back at the patch, which was also bright green on this side, Noah saw to his dismay that he had injured the creature. The flesh was torn and oozed clear liquid, giving the surface a sickly sheen. Cautiously, Noah's shadowy, remote-controlled form floated back to the spot and placed a hand over the wound. He felt moisture, a bit of warmth, and the agitation of the podship.

I'm sorry, Noah thought.

The creature shuddered. Then, as if able to read the intruder's thoughts, the podship grew calmer. In a few seconds, the wound began to heal, and the injured tissue faded, closing the opening.

Cautiously, Noah withdrew his ghostlike touch, and drifted back to the center of the chamber. There could be no more exotic control center in the entire galaxy than the one he occupied now. All his life he had wondered how these sentient space vessels operated, and now he felt the mystery revealing itself to him, opening up like the petals of a magnificent flower.

Physically, he knew he wasn't really inside the navigation chamber at all, and that he still stood beside Anton and Tesh in the cargo hold of the podship. He had extended himself to the chamber by what he could only call mental projection, an expansion of his mind that permitted him to travel telepathically, just as he had previously journeyed across vast stretches of the galaxy. All of it had all been very real, not a dream at all.

The days when Noah had performed ecological recovery operations with his Guardians seemed like long ago to him, but they weren't, really. Only a matter of weeks, or perhaps months. He had lost track of time, at least the way he had measured it previously. That all seemed like a prior incarnation to him, operating under different, less meaningful, parameters.

He sensed something around him now, the powerful psychic presence of very alien creatures who had been inside this chamber before him … commanding the mysterious podship, piloting it across the galaxy. Then a powerful thought projected itself into his awareness, overwhelming all others.

I am the first of my race to accomplish this.

He found the realization exhilarating, and something else even more so. He didn't understand how he knew it, but he had an eerie, undeniable sensation that his power to command podships was greater than that of any other pilot in history. For awhile—as he developed his extrasensory ability—an unknown adversary had been able to keep him at bay and maintain control of the vessel. But that time was gone. No one could ever do it to him again.

The sensation gave him pause. He needed to use his new power well, and carefully.

His vision clouded over, then cleared. In his mind he held the image of the podship's interior, from bow to stern, as if he could see through the creature's tough skin. He felt his power and dominance permeating the entire vessel, entering every cell of the sentient creature.

He saw Tesh running across the cargo hold, then into a passageway.

What is she doing? he wondered.

Abruptly, she seemed to disappear.

Refocusing, he saw her in a much smaller form, climbing walls like an insect, frantically looking for something she could no longer find. The entrance to the navigation chamber. Now he knew the identity of his adversary.

And he smiled to himself....

* * * * *

Noah's mind controlled his body.

In itself, this was not a revolutionary concept, since the minds of all creatures controlled their bodily movements. But in Noah's case, his cognitive center could roam great distances beyond his corporal form, and still move the body by remote control. After Tesh ran off, he sent a telepathic command, causing his physical self to walk calmly to the grid-plane and climb the short staircase into the craft. It was a peculiar sensation, like a puppet master operating strings.

Then, filling the navigation chamber with his mental energy, he set the podship into motion. Following his thought commands, the vessel hyper-accelerated onto the podways.

* * * * *

Another extraordinary event was about to occur.

Thinking back on it afterward, Noah would not recall being aware of the crisis beforehand. Perhaps the temporary fusion of his mind with the consciousness of the podship had caused a state of hyper awareness, an ability to see something far away and react to it in a fraction of a second. Maybe time stood still and permitted it all to happen, something to do with the vast galactic web and the space-time continuum. In his mind, the possibilities were as limitless as the stars in the sky.

Anyone looking at a chart of the galaxy would see that the remote region where Tesh had taken the podship was a long way from the scene of the crisis. But podships could cross great distances in little more than the blink of an eye, so the customary ways of thinking were not always useful. Alternate thought processes were required, different ways of looking at things.

Certainly, all was not as it appeared to be, and Noah was not the only one to notice it, and wonder at the possibilities.

According to Eshaz, Noah Watanabe was the most remarkable human being ever born, and his life had been well worth the risk the web caretaker had taken in saving it. Only a short time after receiving the mysterious healing treatment administered by the Tulyan, Noah had been able to take a fantastic mental journey across the galaxy ... and perhaps that continuing ability, combined with his innate sense of goodness, led to the remarkable events that took place in the hazy atmosphere over a remote planet....

Ovinegg.

A world where the inhabitants used to wait for treasure hunters to fall out of the sky and save them with nets, had become a ghost planet, its population devastated by plagues. But many of those facts would not surface until later. Still, on some level Noah, and perhaps the podship to which he was linked, might have had this information, at some level of consciousness.

Or, in a universe of chance, that's exactly what it was. Mere happenstance.

But no matter the reasons, which were always debatable, the reality could not be denied. Only seconds after three people tumbled out of a spacefaring vessel that had entered the lower atmosphere of Ovinegg, a flash of green split the sky beneath them, and the daredevils never reached the ground.

The podship absorbed them into its skin and dropped them gently into its passenger compartment. Then it continued on its way, leaping back onto the podways and accelerating.

* * * * *

Noah could not explain what had happened, but in the moments after the rescue he felt that he again had control of the vessel. With uncertainties and questions swimming through his mind, he directed the podship across space to the pod station orbiting Canopa—a cross-space journey of only a few more minutes.

Inside the grid-plane, Noah sat in one of the passenger seats, with his eyes closed. He felt an odd sensation as his thoughts occupied two places at once, and he sensed that even more was possible. The idea amazed and frightened him. In the passenger compartment of the podship, he saw two young men leaning over a gray-bearded man who lay on the deck, tending to him. Something seemed to be wrong. The image faded.

Opening his eyes, Noah saw Tesh seated beside him. She was saying something to him but he only saw her lips moving, and didn't hear her voice. She seemed upset. Something clicked in his ears, like a pressure change, and he heard her.

"Why aren't you answering me?" she demanded.

"What?"

"What do you know about this?"

"About the trip to Canopa, you mean?"

"That's where we are?"

"We'll discuss it later," he said. Then, looking at Dr. Bichette, he said, "Go to the passenger compartment of the podship and see what you can do. A man needs your attention."

Bichette frowned. "But all of us are aboard this grid-plane, in the cargo hold."

"It's someone else. Go! Now!"

Looking perplexed, the doctor hurried away.

Turning to his rotund adjutant, Noah said, "When Bichette returns, Subi, I want you to off-load this grid-plane from the podship."

"Are we going down to Canopa, sir?" The big man slipped into the command chair, began checking the controls.

"That is my intent," Noah said.

"But it's too dangerous down there," Tesh sputtered.

"I need to check on the Guardians," Noah said. "They're at risk because of me, and I need to go to them. The Doge and my sister have captured some, and others have taken refuge in the forests near our compound."

"How do you know all that?"

Without answering her, not telling her what he had overheard Francella and the Doge say during Noah's own fantastic mental journey through the galaxy, he said instead, "Maybe I can find enough of our people to organize a resistance movement. This may be too dangerous for the rest of you, so you can leave anytime you wish."

Noah's companions fell silent, as his comments sank in.

Presently, Noah took Tesh and Anton aside, and said to them, "Remember, you told me the Diggers had made a tunnel system that honeycombed much of my compound? Could you draw me a map, using the ship's computer system?"

"Maybe," Anton said. "We've been in those tunnels chasing the Diggers and shutting them down, but they were just burrowing in all directions, without any organized plan."

"If you could recall the main passageways, including any beneath my old administration buildings, that would be a big help." It occurred to Noah that he might journey there mentally, but he did not feel entirely comfortable—or safe—in that realm yet. The rapid growth of his paranormal powers opened up an exciting new realm to him, but it was also terrifying, like walking a tightrope between extreme mental clarity and complete lunacy. For now, he preferred to obtain the information this way.

"I think we could do that," Tesh said. "Between the two of us."

"All right," Noah said. "Get to work on it."

Presently, Dr. Bichette returned to the grid-plane, accompanied by two teenage boys. "We've got a dead man in the passenger compartment," the doctor said. "These young people were with him, and are telling a fantastic story, that they were plucked out of thin air and taken aboard. It sounds like a lot of gibberish to me, but I want you to hear it for yourself."

Gazing beyond the doctor, Noah met the gazes of the two youths he had previously remote-viewed in the passenger compartment. They appeared to be confused, and were obviously quite upset at the death of their companion. They exchanged introductions with Noah and the others, then repeated their story for Noah, adding details.

After listening intently, Noah had little to say in response. He decided privately that the matter would require more thought and analysis, in a manner that he could best do on his own.

"You're free to go," Noah said to the boys, "or we can take you into our organization." He identified himself and provided them with basic information about the Guardians and their ecological mission, but didn't mention what he had in mind yet, an attempt to reestablish his operations on Canopa.

Acey Zelk described again how he and his cousin had jumped out of the treasure ship with the captain, and asked what had happened to them, how they had been pulled out of the air.

"We're not sure," Noah said, and this was mostly true. He saw no benefit in speculation, or in saying anything more about the matter.

"We're treasure hunters," Dux Hannah said, "but I'd say we're out of a job now. Speaking for Acey here—and he's gotten me into trouble by speaking for me—I'd say you have two new recruits, Mr. Watanabe."

"First I need to tell you more about what you're getting into," Noah said. "I'm heading into real danger, going after the people who stole my property and killed the Guardians who worked for me. Our enemies are powerful, the Doge Lorenzo himself, and my own turncoat sister."

Acey whistled. "Sounds worse than jumping out of a ship with no parachute."

"Could be," Noah said. He looked around the compartment, at the others. "I think I know what Subi's answer is, but I'm giving all of you, including him, the opportunity to leave right now. If necessary, I'll proceed without any of you. I can fly this grid-plane myself, maybe not as well as Subi, but I can get it down to the surface, and the on-board scanning system should enable me elude the Doge's surveillance grid. The risk is obvious, but it's critical for me to get down there and rally the Guardians against the schemes of Lorenzo and my sister."

"I'm with you, Master Noah," Subi said, without any hesitation.

"So am I," Anton said, from a chair at the computer terminal.

"We are, too," Dux said. Beside him, Acey nodded.

Looking at Eshaz and seeing him nod his large, scaly head, Noah didn't need to hear him speak to know he would risk his own life with theirs. The two of them had an affinity that transcended galactic races and star systems, and even time itself. Noah felt like they had been friends forever, though he knew that could not possibly be the case. The Guardian leader sensed extreme dangers ahead of him—it could be a suicide mission—but he had to face these particular enemies himself and not flee or send in surrogates to do his bidding.

"I'm not getting off this ride yet," Tesh said. She made an adjustment to the tunnel map that Anton was drawing on the computer.

Staring at Dr. Bichette, whose silence had been palpable, Noah said, "We have no real need for your services any more, so I wish I could allow you to return to your home on Canopa. Unfortunately, I can't do that, though, because you're a security risk. Even if you tried to keep your mouth shut, the Doge would take you in for questioning in his notorious Gaol of Brimrock."

The doctor shot a lingering look at his old girlfriend, then scowled and asked, "How old are you, anyway? You've never told me."

"And I never will," she answered, with a sly smile.

Noah thought about her broken relationships with Dr. Hurk Bichette and the shaky subsequent relationship with Anton Glavine. He didn't want to be the next victim on her trail of broken hearts, but couldn't help the feelings of attraction that he felt for her.

Standing in front of Noah with her hands on her hips, Tesh said, "The only reason I'm sticking around is because you have some explaining to do."

"I see it the other way around," he snapped.

She bit her lip and muttered to herself. A mixture of emotions played across her face: shock, anger, and confusion.

As Noah saw the situation, the two of them were growing farther and farther apart. In one respect, he thought this was a shame, since he was attracted to her, though he would never admit his feelings to anyone, or act on them. Honoring Anton's obvious love for her, Noah wanted to keep his distance from any entanglement. In the past she had been flirtatious toward him, but he couldn't imagine having any relationship with her.

"So, you're with me, Tesh?" Noah asked.

"I just said I was." Angrily, she looked away.

With an exasperated sigh, Noah gave instructions for Anton and the boys to bring the dead captain on board the grid-plane, so that they could make proper arrangements for his body.

* * * * *

Half an hour later, Subi guided the grid-plane out of the cargo hold and into a docking berth of the pod station, where they connected and awaited their turn to depart. There were other grid-planes in the berths of this busy facility, and larger merchant vessels. Four large podships loomed in the central docking bay, including their own craft.

"Uh oh," Subi said. He pointed through the front window, and Noah saw around a dozen Red Beret officers on a nearby platform, looking at Noah's grid-plane and talking among themselves.

"Our ship is still painted Guardian colors," Anton said.

The Red Beret commander did not take long to make his decision. He and his men hurried to board their own ship, several berths away.

Subi activated his weapons system, causing panels to slide open on the side of the grid-plane, revealing high caliber puissant guns. The barrels glowed blue. At a nod from Noah, Subi backed out into the airless vacuum of the docking bay. Just as the Red Beret vessel attempted to do the same, Subi opened fire on it, riddling the hull with holes.

A weapons panel opened on the Red Beret craft, but too late. Subi's shots struck their mark, and the vessel exploded in a ball of blue and orange. Debris and the bodies of the Doge's soldiers floated in the docking bay.

One of the nearby merchant vessels was hit by the explosion, and within seconds small robots scurried onto the hull, making repairs. The damage appeared to be superficial, and not near the engines. Then an odd assortment of sentient machines streamed out of that craft and others moored by it, scurrying through airlocks onto the walkway. The machines were dented, scuffed, and dull. They looked like refugees from a scrap pile, but were moving efficiently, and took positions on the walkway.

Just then, more Red Beret soldiers appeared on the walkway, running toward empty airlocks, including the one where Noah's grid-plane had been berthed. The men wore breather shields over their faces, which would permit them to open the airlocks and fire through them.

But the sentient machines lifted their robotic arms in synchronization, and their hands became an assortment of glistening weapons: guns, mini-crossbows, and dart shooters. They opened fire on the Red-Berets, cutting them down on the walkway and in the airlocks.

"We have unexpected allies," Noah said. He and Subi scanned the ships and walkways, looking for more opponents. None appeared. The machines mopped up the rest of the soldiers, killing them to the last, while only losing a couple from their own ranks.

"Who are those guys?" Anton said.

"I don't know," Noah responded. The engines of several machine vessels were firing, glowing orange in their exhaust tubes.

Then he recalled the fantastic mental excursion he had taken, when he saw podships crossing the galaxy, and one of them was filled with robot ships journeying from the Inn of the White Sun to Canopa. These must be the same sentient machines, a small army of them. And they had come to his aid. But he kept the information to himself for the moment.

Now most of the armed robots reboarded their ships, but some stayed on the body-strewn walkway. One of the machines became apparent now, the flat-bodied robot that Noah remembered seeing in his earlier vision. The others gathered around him and waved their mechanical hands—no longer showing weapons—in the direction of Noah's grid-plane.

"Pull back into the dock," Noah ordered. "Let's see why they helped us."

Chapter Seventy-Five

One of the great delights of life is the discovery of new friends.

—Noah Watanabe

T he leader of the robot force was one of the most peculiar sentient machines that Noah had ever encountered. His flat-bodied appearance was somewhat seedy—dull gray with a small dent on the front of his face plate, and numerous scuff marks. Most robots that looked that bad were no longer operating. His companions didn't look any better.

The robot featured a hinge arrangement at the center of its body, by which Noah had earlier seen him fold open and closed. "I am called Thinker," this one announced. "We saw you blow up the Red Beret vessel, and noticed the green-and-brown colors of your grid-plane. Obviously, you are Guardians."

Noah did not reply, nor did those who stood with him, his companions on the trip here.

"And you are Master Noah Watanabe," Thinker said.

Stepping up beside Noah, Subi feigned a laugh and said, "He just resembles Watanabe."

"We might point you in the right direction, though," Noah added, "but first tell us why you want to see him."

"I must contemplate this," the leader of the robots said. Abruptly, he folded shut again, tucking himself away like a metal version of a turtle.

Scowling, Subi rested his hand on a holstered pistol that he had put on, just before going to talk with the machines.

Moving close, Tesh walked around the flat-bodied machine, which was now motionless. The other machines stood nearby rigidly, but in non-threatening postures. "What's he doing?" she asked.

They didn't answer.

Moments later, the machine leader folded open. His metal-lidded eyes blinked yellow and then green. He faced Noah, and said, "I have considered the facts, and I was not mistaken. You are Noah Watanabe."

Noah did not respond, nor did his companions.

"Your identity is obvious to me," the machine said. "Even without the vast amount of data available to me, you are a well-known fugitive."

"Why did you help us?" Noah asked, ignoring the assertion.

"Consider it our employment application," Thinker said. "We wish to join the Guardians, and thought this battle would look good on our résumés."

"We want to be Guardians!" the machines shouted in unison.

A chill of delight ran down Noah's spine, but still he hesitated. Calmly, he walked from machine to machine, examining them closely, looking into their metal eyes and checking their blinking, multicolored sensors. Halting at one of the heavily armored sentient machines, he did a double take.

"This is not a machine," he announced. Through the visor of the face plate, he saw the unmistakable glint of Human eyes, and the skin of a Caucasian.

Moving to Noah's side, Thinker said, "Quite right, my new friend. This is the brother of your famous inventor Jacopo Nehr."

"Giovanni Nehr?" Noah said. Surprised, he looked more closely.

The armored man nodded.

While Noah had never met the younger Nehr, he had seen him in public, and knew his reputation as a proud man who never got along well with his famous brother. Because of the strained relationship Noah had with his own father, a renowned man like Jacopo Nehr, he thought he might have something in common with this strange soldier.

Suddenly, the armored man appeared to get very nervous, and looked in the direction of Acey and Dux, who were whispering between themselves and pointing angrily at Nehr.

Then, before anyone could stop them, the boys rushed at Nehr. They knocked him down and began pummeling him through openings in his armor. Robots pulled them apart.

"It seems that we have a minor problem," Thinker said.

Giovanni Nehr, despite his superior size and armor, appeared terrified of the boys. Blood trickled from his nose.

"What's the problem here?" Noah asked. He glared at the teenagers.

"Nothing we can't work out ourselves," Acey said.

Dux didn't add anything to that.

"What do you have to say?" Noah said, looking at the man. All three of the combatants had been released by the robots now, and looked very angry.

"Same," Nehr said. "Just a little misunderstanding, that's all. We'll work it out. I promise you, sir, this won't happen again."

"They don't seem to like you," Noah said. "I want to know why."

"Uh," Nehr said, "we were in an airvator together, escaping from a Mutati prison moon, and the guards shot us up pretty good. I was just trying to keep my balance and almost pushed Dux out through a hole, entirely by accident. I didn't mean to stumble against him. Fortunately he held on, but he was understandably angry."

Dux muttered something.

Turning to Dux, Noah asked, "Could you have been mistaken? Is he telling the truth?"

"Sir," the young man said, "Speaking for myself, I'm prepared to let the matter drop. I promise you that. Whatever I thought about him before is nowhere near as important as the mission you want us to accomplish. We'll set our differences aside."

"Right," Acey said, nodding. But his expression, and Dux's, looked less than convincing.

"One of the disadvantages of your race," Thinker said, stepping closer to Noah. "Personalities inevitably get in the way." The lights on his face plate glowed a cheery orange. "Now my machines, on the other hand, have no such problems. I tell them what to do, and they do it."

"Your point is well taken," Noah said.

"We have come all the way from the Inn of the White Sun to join your force of environmental activists," Thinker said. "We even have our own flying ships," he boasted, "faster than your grid-plane." He pointed at the battered vessels berthed in the docking bay, "We have many ships at this pod station, filled with more than thirty-five hundred fighting machines. The Red Berets only discovered us today, and began asking questions. We cannot remain here now."

Noah could not believe his own ears. Pensively, he rubbed his chin. "So you think I'm Noah Watanabe, eh?" he said, resting a hand on Thinker's shoulder.

"I know you are … sir. In my data banks, I have images of you, and voice prints, to mention only a couple of the identity markers."

"Welcome to the Guardians," Noah said, with a broad smile. He clasped the metal hand of the robot and shook it briskly. "I hereby formally commission all of you."

"And we formally accept." The machine leader raised both hands over his head, and the pod station filled with the roar of thousands of machines.

"Well, here's something that's not in your data banks," Noah said, with an intense stare. He took Thinker aside, and told him where he would like to land on Canopa, and that he needed to scout the area first by making a low fly-over with the grid-plane, while the other ships waited a safe distance away.

"We're going around to the dark side of the planet," Noah said. "We'll be looking through infrared, with the ship blacked out and our scanning system activated. Do you have those capabilities?"

"Are you kidding? We've got the latest gadgets, and even the latest gadgets for our gadgets. Well, maybe I shouldn't boast too much. Everything's a few years old, but we do have night vision capability and the ability to evade surveillance grids. When you activate your systems, we'll do the same."

"Good." Noah provided coordinates to the leader of the sentient robots, and the two of them agreed upon arrangements for the scouting and subsequent reconnoitering.

Moments later, the motley-looking force of spaceships taxied toward the exit tunnels.

Chapter Seventy-Six

Noah Watanabe was unable to conceal the locations of many of his ecological recovery projects and other enterprises. We found documents and computer files concerning his galactic operations, and employees who responded to our questions, though only under torture. Still, we suspect there are more operations, as yet unrevealed. He's out there somewhere, with the ragtag remnants of his company, but we don't know where. He's like a ghost in the galaxy.

—File NW27, Report to the Doge Lorenzo del Velli

Noah's grid-plane led a procession of ships down toward the surface of Canopa. Seated by a porthole in the passenger compartment, he was struck by the raw natural beauty of his homeworld as he entered its atmosphere, with its deep green forests, pale blue seas, and snow-capped mountains. To the west, the late afternoon sky glowed a soft golden hue, rimmed by an orange line along the horizon. Such a glorious view. He was glad to be back.

He was just thinking that the planet must be putting on a show for his benefit, in honor of his return, when he looked to the north. In that direction the weather was quite different, with roiling clouds and jagged flashes of lightning. At the controls of the small ship, Subi reported that the storm was heading toward them. It was an unusually deep disturbance, he said, with powerful winds in the upper and lower atmospheres.

"Can we outrun it?" Noah asked.

"I don't know if we want to. This weather could actually be a blessing in disguise, covering our approach."

Noah glanced at the navigation desk, on one end of the instrument console. Anton and Tesh sat at the nav-computer, putting finishing touches on the tunnel map that Noah had ordered. A half hour ago, they had shown him an earlier version on the screen. Based on that, Noah had decided to scout the southwest corner of his former ecological demonstration compound, looking for a possible landing site there. With luck, he would be able to enter the tunnels and set up a base there for his resistance operation, in a place where the Red Beret and CorpOne forces would never to think to look.

"We can fly through this storm, then?" Noah rose and went over behind Subi, where he held onto the chair-back and looked over the adjutant's shoulder at the instrument console, with its dials, meters, and gauges.

"We can, but I don't know about those space jalopies behind us."

"I suspect the machines may be tougher than they look," Eshaz said, clumping heavily across the deck and standing by Noah. "And their vessels, too."

"We're about to find out," Subi said. "Take your seats, and get into your safety harnesses."

As Noah got into his own harness, he saw the big Tulyan showing Acey and Dux how to engage theirs. He had developed a liking for the boys, had told Noah privately that they were brave young adventurers, and he thought they were fine additions to the Guardians.

Eshaz barely had time to get into his own large harness when the grid-plane rattled as it entered the storm and bumped through the air currents.

It grew darker outside Noah's window. He squinted as a flash of lightning lit up the sky, like a high-powered ethereal spotlight.

When the flash dissipated, he could see a portion of Canopa clearly, but the view was framed by dark, rain-saturated clouds.

My beautiful Canopa, he thought.

Of all the worlds he had known in his travels around the galaxy, this one was by far the most pleasing to the eye. Even more important than that, it held a special place in his heart.

Without a moment's hesitation, Subi plunged the grid-plane through the slot in the clouds. Looking out the wide aft porthole, Noah saw the machine ships following. He counted them, and none were missing.

He had never expected to find so many recruits awaiting him upon his arrival at the pod station, and now he took a few seconds to consider his good fortune. Thinker, while unusual in his appearance and mannerisms, just might prove to be exactly what Noah needed, perhaps breaking the string of bad luck he'd been going through.

Inside the aerial tunnel, lightning flashed on all sides, brilliant orange zigzags in the clouds. Behind him, he heard Dr. Bichette cry out in surprise and fear.

Noah thought back to the images of Mutatis in merchant schooners that he saw in the cosmic web. They had been floating in space near pod stations in Mutati territory, and he had not been able to determine why. It had seemed like an odd dream, but one that overlapped into reality.

What did I see, and why was it accessible to me?

Aside from his desire to rescue any Guardians who had been captured or who had fled into the countryside, Noah had another reason for returning to Canopa. He felt mentally and physically stronger on his homeworld, as if invigorated by the living energy of the planet. Even before landing (and despite the bumpiness of the ride), he felt more animated, more able to carry on his important work. He knew the large planet well, and looking down saw the rugged canyons where he often went on retreat in earlier years. One day he would like to take new Guardian recruits there to teach them about ecology, the interdependence of life forms in harsh environments. He had made detailed notes on how such classes might be conducted, but had not yet put them into effect.

The grid-plane leveled out, and headed toward the night side of the planet, crossing over a remote, unpopulated region that was only intermittently visible through turbulent, swirling clouds.

On the way, Noah noted how Subi was able to adjust the guidance and power to make the ride more smooth, like a person in a groundcar avoiding ruts and potholes. Noah also knew that the smoothness was not entirely dependent on the pilot's skill. Some of it was attributable to a computer program that reacted to the gusts of wind with equal and opposite forces. Elementary physics. But there were always surprises, both in intensity and direction, and some time ago Subi had explained to him that Humans were frequently better at reacting to unexpected situations than machines were.

In less than an hour, they began to pass into darkness.

"Switching to night vision," Subi finally said. Thirty seconds later, the passenger cabin changed to an eerie infrared darkness, including all computer screens. Looking through the aft porthole, Noah confirmed that Thinker and his robot force had done the same. The ships were shadows against the starlit night sky.

Down on the surface of the planet, Noah made out only occasional lights, marking widely spaced Human settlements.

"The descendants of ancient Canopans live in wild, hostile regions down there," Noah said. In the darkness of the cabin, he saw his companions as ghostlike shapes, from the infrared mechanism that provided interior and exterior visibility for the pilot and passengers. "With our scanner on it probably wouldn't matter if we switched on our lights," Noah said, "but I don't want to take any chances."

Presently, Subi reported that they were approaching the plateau where the robot ships were to wait, by pre-arrangement. He circled the area, then looped upward and sped off. Thinker's ships went into holding patterns.

Noah went to the nav-computer and studied the tunnel map. A small screen on one side showed the terrain of this region of Canopa, with them flying toward the Ecological Demonstration Project compound. Subi, ever conscious of security, had fitted this grid-plane with its long-range scanning system, one that could not only detect hostile forces at a great distance, but would also neutralize the surveillance features of the planet's electronic grid system.

"All clear in the southwest corner of the compound," Subi reported. "I'm picking up activity over at the main administration building in the center of the compound, but that's what we expected."

Noah's ecology complex was immense, covering many hectares of land. As the grid-plane swooped over one corner of the land, he saw the maintenance building that Diggers had damaged, and gaping holes from the activity of the rampant machines and the counter operations of his own commandos.

From those missions and the new computer map that he now had, Noah knew that there were hundreds of deep tunnels beneath his compound and the adjacent land, and that all Diggers down there had either been destroyed or disabled. Anton and Tesh, commandos themselves, had shown him how to gain access to a network of burrows in the remote hills east of the maintenance building, far enough away that they might go undetected. With that as his base of operations, Noah intended to organize a resistance force, hoping to eventually regain control of his land and space station.

"Let's go get our new army," Noah said.

Subi nodded, and accelerated out toward the plateau where the machine ships were waiting. As Noah's aircraft rose up to the top of the plateau and burst into the sky, he was pleased to see the twelve machine ships still in a holding pattern. They blinked their infrared lights, and followed Subi's lead.

Undetected by Canopa's electronic grid system, Noah's force skimmed the ground and reached the eastern hills. After landing, they tucked their wings and hover-floated into the largest burrow, which led to an immense cavern. The burned-out hulks of three Digger machines were near the entrance.

As Noah stepped from the grid-plane to the floor of the cavern, he saw Thinker and summoned him. The scholarly robot clanked over, and bowed slightly. "Sir?" he said.

"Send robots back to seal the entrance behind us," Noah commanded. Looking back at Tesh and Anton, he ordered them to go with the robots, and to help Thinker supervise the operation.

The three of them marched off, and at a signal from Thinker they were joined by many sentient machines. While the physical camouflage work was being accomplished, Subi set up a multi-function scrambling device to prevent scanner detection from above. He was quick to say as he activated the system, however, that it still needed to be calibrated to the surrounding terrain and tunnel system, which could take several days.

Studying the scrambler machinery, Thinker said, "Perhaps I can speed up the calibration, and even improve the system. I will work on it."

"All right," Noah said.

Thinker and Noah accompanied Subi as the beefy adjutant made final settings to the scrambler system, which was supposed to erase heat and sound signatures, making them undetectable to their enemies aboveground and in adjacent tunnels. Finally the robot folded his body flat, saying he wanted to contemplate how to improve the system.

"What do you say we call this place Diggerville?" Subi asked, looking at Noah. "Our new headquarters ... or should I say, our new digs?" He looked tired, and seemed a little giddy.

"Fine, fine." Noah smiled stiffly.

Leaving Thinker where he was, Noah and the crew of his grid-plane settled in for their first night underground, sleeping in the cabin of the aircraft while the machines stood guard.

Just before Noah drifted off to sleep he thought of Tesh, who slept not far from him on the carpeted deck. He heard the regular breathing and snoring of his companions, but in the shadows could only identify the regular, deep snorts of Eshaz, and saw his hulking form profiled against the low light of the instrument panel.

At the first opportunity, he wanted to have a conversation with Tesh. The two of them needed to clear the air.

Chapter Seventy-Seven

All living forms are dying. It is a vast and glorious empyrean curve, gaining strength and vitality, reaching a zenith, and then fading.

—Noah Watanabe

In the darkness of the grid-plane cabin, Noah cried out in his sleep, but no one seemed to hear him. He sat up, or thought he did, and wondered why he could no longer hear the snoring of his companions, and why he could no longer see the slumbering form of Eshaz profiled against the light of the instrument panel.

He barely made out a flickering light that seemed to be way off in the distance. Presently it came into focus, a tiny pinpoint of illumination. Then another appeared beside it, and another, and another. With a start, he realized that they were stars, and that he was gazing into deep space. He felt the intense cold of the void, but could endure it nonetheless.

His mind told him that he was underground in a Digger burrow, and that this should not be happening, but he recalled his previous experience in which he cartwheeled across the galaxy on a fantastic cosmic journey. At the time, he had wondered if it had really occurred, or if it had only been a vivid dream. Subsequently, however, he'd had another paranormal experience, in which he took control of the podship and flew it to Canopa.

Now, he realized that he only had his left eye open.

Lifting the other eyelid, his body shuddered at what he saw, a strange split vision in which the tableau of space and the interior of the grid-plane cabin were superimposed over one another, as in old double photographic images. He heard rumbling breathing, and saw the broken image of Eshaz in the shadows, and this time he saw Tesh as well, and Anton. All were asleep, breathing and snoring regularly.

Noah closed the eye with which he had been peering into space, and abruptly the cosmic panorama disappeared, leaving only the interior of the cabin, with its warmth and Human noises. He felt queasy, then uncertain and fearful. A shuddering shock shook his body, and it took him several moments to stop shaking.

Testing, he looked through one eye or the other, and sometimes both, to confirm the bizarre reality that had overtaken him. Why this was happening he could not determine, but through each eye he beheld a different reality— confusing double images. Each eye saw something entirely different, and with it opened up the sounds, smells, and other senses. All of his senses were now oddly linked to his vision.

First I journeyed across the cosmos in my mind, he thought, and then *did that physically when I piloted the podship.*

So odd, two realities—one ethereal and the other physical—overlapping at times and separate at times. His brain had capabilities that he had never imagined possible, and now each eye seemed to be linked to different aspects of that brain. He felt freakish, as if he was splitting into parts, with no control over the changes.

Opening only one eye at a time, he found that he could completely change his reality. With his left eye he saw—and telepathically *entered*—the cold cosmic-web realm, while with his right eye he saw the low light of the grid-plane cabin, and felt the warmth and nearness of his friends. This at least was an aspect of control, albeit minimal, as he could open and shut the two realities. But he couldn't make his brain and eyes stop generating the peculiar, disturbing phenomenon.

Abruptly, he felt something odd where his left foot used to be, a tingling sensation where nothing remained any longer. Noah had heard of that happening to injury victims, in which they seemed to feel missing limbs and appendages. Looking down along his body, he saw a faint illumination around the bottom of his left leg, where he knew the stump was.

He moved his left leg, and to his amazement saw what looked like his missing foot in the soft ambient glow.

Not possible. I'm only imagining this.

The illumination faded, and with it his foot seemed to disappear, and he felt nothing there at all. Darkness enveloped him and he saw nothing, heard nothing and felt nothing, not even the warmth of the cabin or the hard carpet under him. He found himself unable to reach out and check, or move his body at all. With one exception,

His eyes.

Trying to sort it all out, he closed both eyes and sat in the silence of his thoughts. But something interfered, refusing to leave him in serenity. He felt drawn outward, as if by a magnet. Cautiously, he opened his left eye just a little, and peered through the slit between his eyelids.

Noah could not resist the temptation to see more of the bizarre cosmic domain, to *experience* more of it. Once again, his thoughts surged out into the mysterious void of space, along a mystical cosmic webway. Every element of the web surrounded him, enfolded him, welcomed and embraced him. He was part of it, and looking back found that he could observe himself. There was no ground beneath him and no sky overhead, only the gossamer strands connecting him with every other point in the galaxy.

He was a Human inside a navigation chamber; he was a podship itself; he was every member of every galactic race.

By following the curving web, spinning through it, Noah found that he could reach virtually any point in the imagination of the Supreme Being who had created this wondrous kingdom of stars—and that he could move from point to point almost instantaneously. Everything floated around him, as if he was underwater. He did not seem to breathe or to have a heartbeat.

As before, he became aware of other cosmic voyagers spinning along the web—people, podships, and passengers going this way and that, passing over, under and through him, just as he did with them, in a realm that seemed to be non-physical. Who were these web travelers? Were they like him?

During his first paranormal voyage like this, he had wondered if he was dead or dying, and if the others out there were as well. He had been deathly ill then, in a comatose state. His health was much improved now. Or was it? In his sleep, had he again slipped into a coma?

And out in the cosmos, in the non-physical realm, he felt his missing foot again, and knew his body had grown a new one. In an epiphany, he realized that his corporal form had undergone a remarkable transformation. He was not dying at all. It was exactly the opposite. His injury had been healed by the web when Eshaz connected him to it. More than healed. His genetic structure had been altered in the procedure, with the gene that activated the aging process switched off.

I am immortal.

But how could that have happened? The answer did not come to him, but another did. In its original form it was a wordless answer, but the Human portion of his mind translated it for him, so that he could begin to understand.

The magical realm that saved him was an eternal continuum in which vast distances were covered in infinitesimal fragments of time. Time began billions of years ago, but the complete life of the galaxy might encompass only a few moments. Before him, the webbing expanded, folded, compressed, and took shapes he could barely imagine—while unimagined secrets remained concealed from him.

From somewhere far away Noah heard voices, and almost recognized them. They were calling for him by name, asking if he was all right. He struggled and opened both eyes, lifting the lids with great difficulty as if they were very heavy.

The split images returned, one tableau superimposed over another.

He heard himself cry out again, and saw Dr. Bichette and the robot leader Thinker standing over him, engaged in a worried conversation about his welfare. They seemed to be floating out in space, no longer on the deck of the grid-plane. Like a Human-sized god or an angel, the doctor hovered over Noah, and began checking his vital signs.

As moments passed, the split images ceased, and with both eyes he saw that the doctor and Thinker were standing in the grid-plane cabin again, this time with Tesh, Anton, and Subi.

"Are you all right?" Tesh asked. Noah felt the warmth of her hand in his, and knew he had returned to the living. He was lying on the deck, with his legs under a blanket.

Slowly, deliberately, he moved the blanket and looked at his own left leg, where there had been a stump.

The foot was there, and when he saw the expressions of horrified fascination on the faces of the others, he knew it was no apparition. Even Eshaz, who rarely showed any emotion at all, looked utterly astounded.

Chapter Seventy-Eight

Life is a sea of darkness, with islands of light.

—From a Sirikan folk tale

The following day, Noah experienced no recurrence of the split visions, the odd straddling of two dimensions, the one physical and the other ethereal. It had all been like a dream, but a tangible souvenir of it remained.

His re-grown foot.

He felt emotionally lifted, and excited. Something truly remarkable had happened to him. He knew this for certain when he confirmed over and over that the body part had in fact regenerated, like the appendage of a reptile. Squeezing the flesh of the new foot and toes with his fingers, he felt the remarkable bone and tissue growth beneath his left ankle. It was almost as if the doctor had never amputated, but the new growth was tender, and he limped when he tried to walk on it. He still had to use the crutches that Subi had improvised for him.

Noah wondered if this miracle was an aspect of his immortality.

Encountering him in the cavern outside the grid-plane, a bewildered Dr. Bichette said, "I want to bring a bone specialist in to look at you." Eshaz, Tesh, Anton, and Subi were with him. Earlier, he had examined the foot.

"And what would he tell us?" Noah asked, waving one of his alloy crutches around. "That it's impossible, that it couldn't possibly have happened? I'd be put under a microscope, asked to go on a medical sideshow tour as a freak."

Bichette stared at the regenerated foot, which Noah had covered with a sock and a shoe.

"I don't have time for all that nonsense," Noah said. "I have more important things to do now; I need to maintain security and lead the resistance movement." He looked from face to face, and settled on the scaly bronze countenance of Eshaz, whom he had always considered as much a friend as an employee. "You know what happened to me, don't you?"

"Some will say I should not have done what I did," Eshaz said, "that it was too dangerous."

"And what did you do to Noah, exactly?" Tesh asked.

The big Tulyan hung his head. "I've said all I can say here. I must report to the Council of Elders, and accept their punishment. You will probably never see me again afterward."

"Whatever Eshaz did to me," Noah said to the others, "I'm grateful to him. But I don't want the rest of you to discuss my medical condition with anyone, not even the robots. Is that understood?"

He waited until he got a nod from each of them, but didn't notice when Subi shook his head afterward.

"Tell everyone I have a prosthetic foot now," Noah said. He walked away stiffly, but was beginning to feel a little better with each step.

* * * * *

After the group separated, Tesh switched off her personal magnification system and in her tiny form began to spy on Noah in the cavern and connecting tunnels, scrambling around behind him unseen.

Rounding a corner, she came face to face with a roachrat. The creature, around her height, stared at her with dark, beady eyes. Its antennae twitched, and it bared its sharp teeth. A moment later, the animal squealed and ran away.

* * * * *

Noah slipped into a small side cavern. Then, looking around to make certain no one was watching, he drew a knife from its sheath and slashed his own left wrist. Pointing the wrist away from his clothes, he watched in fascination as the blood flow stopped and the wound healed itself, in a matter of minutes. No sign of the injury remained. He even felt his internal chemistry converting reserves and restoring the lost blood.

Taking a deep breath to summon his courage, Noah then attempted something even more drastic.

Holding the handle of the knife with both hands, he plunged it into his own heart, feeling it crack through bone and cartilage and pierce the organ. He gasped and cried out, then toppled over onto the ground, with gouts of blood spurting from his chest. All bodily functions ceased.

Seconds passed.

Then, like Lazarus, he rose from the dead and stood in his own blood, as his cells regenerated themselves.

* * * * *

In horror and fascination, Tesh watched Noah's drastic self experimentation and a walking frenzy he went into, hurrying this way and that around the cavern. She saw him throw the crutches away and actually begin to run around the cavern, slowly at first and then faster. Noah looked elated, and this frightened her.

What sort of creature is this? she wondered. *What has Eshaz done to him?*

Unexpected thoughts assailed her. Tesh began to consider ways to destroy Noah, incinerating his body in such a conflagration that he could not possibly regenerate himself. In her lifetime, and from what she had been told by Woldn, there were no immortal creatures in the entire universe. Even those that seemed to be were not. They all had an Achilles heel.

Somehow, Noah had embarked on a dangerous, intrusive course of evolution, a fantastic mutation of the genetic process. If his dangerous bloodline was permitted to continue, there could be others like him, a race of powerful Humans who could commit terrible acts, including taking podships away from the Parviis who had held dominion over them for hundreds of thousands of years. Just as Tesh's Parviis had once replaced the Tulyans, so too could another race prove itself superior and gain dominion. Woldn, the Eye of the Swarm, had long warned of this. It was the subject of legends.

She just hoped it was not too late to stop the mutant....

Later that day, she crept away from the tunnel compound, a minuscule form that none of them noticed leaving. Like an insect, Tesh emitted a faint, wingless buzzing noise and flew all the way to the orbital pod station. (In swarms Parviis could fly much farther, even across the galaxy, but not by themselves). The tiny airborne humanoid reached the podship, but found herself unable to gain entrance to the sectoid chamber, unable to make the vessel move at all. The stubborn vessel proved unresponsive to her commands.

In the ancient podship's passenger compartment and on the walkway of the pod station outside, she scuttled about like a bug, eavesdropping on Red Beret officers, scientists, and others who wondered why the sentient vessel did not depart like a normal podship and resume its route around the galaxy. The investigators were poring over it, trying to discover its secrets. So far they had not found the hidden passageways or the sectoid chamber, and Tesh didn't think that they could.

But she'd never thought that a full-sized Human could have piloted the spacecraft, either. The Parviis had long known that there was more than one way to control podships. Long ago, Tulyans had their method, and Parviis had their own. Now the likelihood of yet another terrified her.

She envisioned a universe of untapped secrets.

* * * * *

Thinker thought the four Humans and the Tulyan were behaving strangely. That evening he watched as they slipped into a shadowy side tunnel. Moments later he heard them arguing, their voices escaping from the darkness into the dimly lit main cavern. Listening, he picked out their voices—Tesh, Subi, Anton, Dr. Bichette, and Eshaz.

Abruptly, a rotund man emerged from the tunnel and hurried across the cavern with surprising speed, heading for the main entrance. Moving as quietly as he could while maintaining his distance, Thinker followed.

He watched as Subi Danvar used his own code to bypass the security system, then slipped around large rocks and shrubs that the robots had placed over the entrance, and disappeared into the night.

Chapter Seventy-Nine

All of us see life through the lens of personal experience, and how limited those experiences are! The sum total of all Human knowledge is but a pinprick in the universe. So it is with each star system as well, in relation to all other star systems. A universe of pinpricks.

—Master Noah Watanabe

As required under the most ancient procedures of his people, Eshaz prepared to send a message to the Council of Elders, informing them of his unforgivable transgressions, violating the most consecrated of rules. In the transmittal, to be sent by touching the web and sending a telepathic transmission through it, he would not attempt to mitigate what he had done, because that would only make matters worse. It was hard to imagine how he could be in more trouble, considering the risks he had taken to save just one life, and that of a mere Human. The web was the most sacred object in the entire galaxy, and tampering with it was a most grievous offense. Since time immemorial there had been carefully prescribed regulations for its use and maintenance, and he had always followed them.

Until the episode with Noah.

Just before one of the prescribed times for telepathic transmissions, Eshaz prepared to place a scaly bronze finger against a strand of web. He was about to reach out of the commonly perceived physical dimension and touch another that was on a higher, more ethereal level.

Timeweb.

His fingers moved close, but he did not yet make contact.

* * * * *

Subi Danvar knew the back ways well, for he had walked and driven them for years as one of Noah Watanabe's faithful Guardians. But this evening was like none other. He was alone out here, in a moonlit wilderness of unknown perils, running along a paved road, breathing hard, pushing his physical limits.

Reaching the shuttle landing field at the perimeter of the compound, he saw half a dozen stock groundjets parked behind a storage building, and no visible security. With one of those vehicles he could reach Rainbow City, and obtain a good doctor for Noah. Ever conscious of safety measures, Subi thought it would have been too risky to take Noah's grid-plane or one of the robot ships on this mission. They were better left where they were, since he had just received an intelligence report that Doge Lorenzo was making improvements to the planet's surveillance grid system, and he wanted to find out what had been done before going airborne again.

He ran for one of the groundjets, staying low, hugging the shadows.

* * * * *

For moments, Eshaz had been reconsidering, forming all sorts of rationalizations in his mind for delaying his transmission or not making it all, defenses he might use if ever summoned before the Council of Elders on this matter. Of utmost importance, he wanted to protect Noah Watanabe, the remarkable Human who had shown more concern for the interrelationships between planets and star systems than anyone in the history of his people. As only three races knew—the Tulyans, the Parviis, and the Aopoddae—the entire galaxy was connected by a gossamer but strong and essential web that spanned time and space. This made Noah's own concept of galactic ecology all the more remarkable, though he could not possibly know how right he was. Eshaz wasn't sure how to tell him, either; Humans were not one of the privy races, so Noah was not supposed to be informed about such secrets.

Still, Eshaz felt Noah had already expanded the knowledge of his race with what he had done, and that he had the potential to do much more. In Eshaz's mind, this was linked directly to his own primary assignment from the Council of Elders, which was to protect and maintain the web. He felt he had done exactly that by saving Noah's life, but his bold (the council might say brash) decision would still require considerable explanation on his part.

The prescribed time arrived, and Eshaz placed a quivering fingertip against a slender strand of web, touching it ever so gently. He did not transmit, but felt the coursing energy of the web, the distant podships traveling on their various routes, along with the mental communications of Tulyans who reported to the Elders and received orders from them. He also heard the subtle but disturbing noises of breakage in the web, the disintegration that was continuing, no matter the efforts of the Tulyans to prevent it.

At the very last possible second, a message arrived from the Council of Elders, sent to him personally like a whisper across the cosmos: *Return to the Starcloud immediately.*

His heart sank. They must know, or suspect what he had done, and intended to interrogate him.

In fear, Eshaz removed his finger from the web and hunched over, his entire body trembling. The next transmission time would not take place for seven galactic days, and the Elders wanted him to report sooner than that. He could reach the Tulyan Starcloud today if he made the next podship, and tomorrow at the latest. The pod station here at Canopa was one of the busiest in the galaxy, with ships arriving and departing regularly, connecting the world with all points of the astronomical compass.

Now he would have to confess under less-than-ideal circumstances, enduring the suspicious glares of his superiors. It would have been better if he had volunteered the information.

Eshaz expected the worst, although they probably didn't have the evidence against him that they needed yet. If they'd had it, they might have dispatched someone to execute him on the spot—a punishment that had been used in the past, on rare occasions. If they did have the proof already, the Elders might still want to conduct a public tribunal and use him as an example, to keep anyone else from tapping into the web improperly. He felt certain that he would be declared one of the worst criminals in the history of his people, and that his name would go down in infamy.

At his trial, he could at least explain why he drained critical nutrients from the web without first asking for permission from the Council, and how he needed to move quickly to save Noah Watanabe's life, since the Human's vital signs had declined rapidly and he was on the verge of death. Eshaz doubted if it would do any good to present a defense, but if given the opportunity he would lay it all out, including the full and remarkable story of Noah Watanabe ... a man whose life mattered much more than his own.

* * * * *

Schemes flowed through Giovanni Nehr's mind like the currents of an ocean, deep beneath the surface.

The day before, he had overheard Acey Zelk and Dux Hannah telling Noah how they hid inside the storage compartment of a food delivery robot to escape from a slave crew in the Doge's Palazzo Magnifico. The story had given Gio an idea.

During the time that he had worked with Thinker's army of robots, Gio had learned a great deal about machines and their internal operating systems. Moving quickly, under the guise of fine tuning two large robots, he had programmed changes into them. These were unmarked mechanical units, of a type that the Guardians planned to send into nearby towns on reconnaissance missions, in conjunction with Human operatives.

Then, in the shadows of a tunnel, Gio had knocked the teenagers out with drugdarts, using one of the weapons that Thinker had given to him. He then stuffed Accy into a large compartment inside one of the robots, and Dux inside the other robot.

Giovanni Nehr did not dislike the boys, and did not wish them any real harm. But he needed to deal with them for his own survival and advancement, which were his highest priorities. Other stories that he'd heard the boys telling the Guardians would provide him with an excellent cover, in particular their boastful tales of stowing away on ships and vagabonding around the galaxy. People would think they ran off for more adventures.

Gio didn't have the stomach to kill the teenagers, and hoped they didn't die because of his actions. But he knew he was putting them in danger, casting them into the perilous ocean of space. Now he watched on a remote camera screen as the robots did their work, and projected images back to him....

The sentient machines, carrying their unusual cargoes, entered the nearest shuttleport, and studied the electronic labels on space-cargo boxes in a storage yard, showing that they were being shipped to a variety of star systems and planets. As programmed, the robots selected the farthest, most remote destination.

When no one was looking, the sentient machines loaded the motionless bodies into a cargo container filled with crates of computer parts, after removing some of the contents and then making sure there were air holes in the box.

Observing it all on the small screen, Gio thought, *If they're meant to live, they'll live. If they're meant to die, they'll die.* He had done everything necessary to keep his own conscience clear, taking steps to save their lives by assuring them of air.

As programmed, the robots waited in shadows while a mechanized crew loaded the containers on board a shuttle. Satisfied, Gio watched while the shuttle lifted off. Now he didn't have to sleep with one eye open. If the boys survived, they had no assets and would have a hard time finding their way back here. He didn't expect to ever see them again.

* * * * *

Subi slipped into the command chair of the groundjet. Taking a deep breath, he activated the controls and saw the instrument panel light up with shimmering, lambent colors. His fingers moved expertly, and he waited to hear the engines turn over.

But they didn't start, even though the hydion charges were full.

He cursed, hit the backup button. Nothing happened.

Spotlights lit up the parking area outside. Men shouted, and he heard the sounds of boots running on pavement.

Red Beret soldiers surrounded the vehicle, and took him into custody.

Chapter Eighty

Each of us must face a judgment day.

—Ancient Saying

T he following afternoon ...
After crossing space and arriving at the pod station over the Tulyan Starcloud, Eshaz passed through an airlock. Pausing, he watched four robots loading space-cargo boxes onto a walkway. In other places around the galaxy, especially at merchant prince worlds, this would not have been extraordinary, since products were always being picked up and delivered. But in this remote star system it was highly unusual. Largely self-sufficient, Tulyans did not import very many articles.

Working hurriedly, the robots accidentally dropped one of the large boxes as they were trying to hoist it on top of the others, and it split open. To Eshaz's shock, two Human bodies tumbled out, along with crates of computer parts, which spilled their contents all over the walkway.

Eshaz saw one of the bodies move, and then the other. He recognized Acey Zelk and Dux Hannah. As they struggled to their feet, the teenagers looked dazed and confused, and had bumps and cuts on their faces.

The robots chattered among themselves, and sent beeping electronic signals back and forth. Then, leaving the mess behind them, they hurried back through the airlock and reboarded the podship. Moments later, the vessel departed.

"You boys all right?" Eshaz asked.

"I think so," Dux said, as he looked at his shorter cousin, who was testing a bruise on his forehead.

"I have a terrible headache," Acey said.

"Me too," Dux said. "I think we were drugged."

"I don't know about that," Eshaz said, narrowing his already slitted eyes, "but there may have been low oxygen in the cargo hold of the podship. Whatever the cause, this should make you feel better." Bringing a small bag out of a body pouch in his side, he opened it and scattered green dust on the boys. Within moments their injuries healed, and the teenagers said their headaches were gone, too.

"How did we get in that cargo box?" Dux asked, as he and Acey accompanied the Tulyan along the walkway.

"You didn't crawl in yourselves?"

"No disrespect intended," Dux said, "but I wouldn't have asked the question if we had."

"Maybe someone doped you and put you in the box," Eshaz said. "There is a likely candidate, but you should not jump to conclusions."

"Giovanni Nehr," Acey said. "I can't wait to get my hands on him!"

Showing that he was the more introspective of the two, Dux said, "We need to cool off before we deal with him. I don't think we should go back to Canopa right now, or we might do something we'll regret."

With a nod, Eshaz said, "That would be wise. The personal feud between you and the inventor's brother could be destructive. Keep in mind, too, that Master Noah does not need that sort of conflict around him, not with all the important matters he must attend to."

Acey sulked as he walked along.

"There is no proof that Gio did it," Eshaz said, "but perhaps the truth will surface."

"Where are we?" Dux asked.

Eshaz answered the question, then offered to put the boys under his protection for a while. "I feel responsible for you now," he said, "and I won't hear of letting you go off on your own."

"So we have no choice in the matter?" Acey said.

"Sure you do." Eshaz stopped on the walkway, and briefly touched the faces of Acey and Dux, one after the other. In this manner, he read their thoughts, and confirmed the story they had told him, that they had not run away from the Guardians. It was one of the abilities that Tulyans had in interacting openly with their own kind, and secretly with other galactic races.

As Eshaz removed his hand from Dux, he noted intelligence and sincerity in the boy's dark brown eyes.

"I'm going to catch a shuttle now," Eshaz said, "and you can either go with me or wait for the next podship ride. But you'll be missing out on a great place if you go. I think I can get you into a fantastic facility that's usually reserved for visiting dignitaries. At no charge, of course."

"We qualify as dignitaries," Dux said with a broad grin.

"I think we should hit the podways," Acey said.

"Aw, come on," Dux said, nudging his cousin in the side. "If we don't like it around here, we'll go somewhere else."

Hesitation. Then, "All right."

"I'll send a message to Noah," Eshaz said, "and let him know you're both safe."

"It might be better not to," Dux said. "We don't want the perpetrator to find out where we are. But if it is Gio, do you think he's a threat to Noah? Or do we just have a problem with the guy?"

"I will need to give that some thought," Eshaz said.

* * * * *

Eshaz was not allowed to bring visitors to any of the worlds in the Tulyan Starcloud, so he left the teenagers at the orbital Visitor's Center, floating in space over the mist-enshrouded starcloud below. The guests were each given an opulent suite, the kind usually reserved for ambassadors and other high government officials. The Tulyan desk clerk and a security officer appeared to be surprised upon seeing the young Humans, but acceded to Eshaz's wishes, in deference to his position. Eshaz told them he was personally responsible for the boys' safety, after having rescued them, and that they worked for Noah Watanabe, as he did himself. Then he hurried away by himself, to meet with the Council of Elders.

The Visitor's Center was globular, like a pod station and around the same size, but the resemblance stopped there. This was a glittering spacetel, not a mottled, gray-and-black docking station. As they followed the bellhop into a room, he explained that the rooms were interconnected in what he called suites; the boys had never heard of anything like this.

The bellhop, a tall Churian with thick, white eyebrows and a guttural voice, said, "This is Mr. Zelk's suite. Yours is next door, Mr. Hannah."

The boys exchanged surprised, pleased glances.

The Churian showed them through room after room, in just the first suite. Impressively, each room had a view of the misty Tulyan Starcloud below, which the bellhop explained was a trick of electronics. Dux scratched his head. It looked incredibly realistic, and he couldn't see how it worked. Soft music played in the background, blending into different tunes in each room.

"This place is bigger than the entire crew quarters on our ship," Acey said. Leaning over, he touched the plush black carpet in the sitting area, then laid on it and said it was softer than any bed on which he'd ever slept. "I'll just sleep on the floor tonight. I don't want to get too comfortable, or I might not be able to go back to my real life."

Dux laughed, but the Churian, a very proper alien, frowned intensely, causing his bushy eyebrows to cover his eyes. To Dux, this looked very comical, but he tried not to smile, or laugh anymore. It looked like the fellow had hairy eyes. For several moments, the bellhop paced around without crashing into anything, so he must have had some way of seeing where he was going, or perhaps a backup sonrad system.

* * * * *

A lone reptilian figure stood before a bench with twenty robed judges seated at it, gazing down at him sternly. Eshaz had a solid floor beneath him, but could not see it under his feet; he seemed to float on air, with the curvature of the inverted dome visible far below him, and the stars of space twinkling through the ethereal mists beyond.

He knew that the Visitor's Center staff had probably reported him, so he expected the aged leaders to ask him about the boys. Eshaz had an explanation ready—that he couldn't just cast them adrift after their narrow escape from death—but he hoped he didn't have to defend himself on that issue. He was already in enough trouble.

Nervously, the web caretaker gazed from face to face, searching for something in their expressions to tell him what to do. He wanted to spill all of the information he knew but resisted the urge, and instead awaited the comments and commands of his superiors. The council members looked hostile, with downturned mouths and glaring expressions.

"Reports have reached us that give us grave concern about the condition of the web," First Elder Kre'n said, rubbing her scaly chin. One of the oldest Tulyans, she was reputed to have been the first of her race ever to pilot a podship across the vast reaches of space.

Eshaz steeled himself, waiting for the hammer of authority to smash down on him.

"Truly, this is a dire crisis," she said. Then she paused and conferred in whispers with the Elders on either side of her.

Eshaz's mind raced with visions of horrible fates, as he imagined the worst things that could happen to him.

"For hundreds of thousands of years, you have been one of our Web Technicians, responsible for the care of the connective strands, and we can ill afford to lose your services when they are needed so much now."

She's regretting what they're about to do to me, Eshaz thought. He wished he could be anywhere but here. Even dead.

Kre'n nodded to a towering Tulyan on her left, whom Eshaz recognized as Dabiggio, one of the more severe Elders who had been responsible for strict sentences in the past. Eshaz steeled himself, then jerked in surprise when the robed dignitary said, "You will remain at the Starcloud until further notice."

Scrunching up his face in confusion, Eshaz said, "But there is no punishment facility here. It's on Colony L."

"Who said you were going to a punishment facility?" Dabiggio asked.

"I thought you were going to pronounce sentence on me for something I did wrong. I, uh...."

"Personally, I do not approve of your behavior," Dabiggio said. "As a web caretaker, you took a risky, unprecedented action with respect to Noah Watanabe, but you have your supporters on this council."

"You know what I did, then?"

"I have my sources," the imposing Elder said.

"But now is not the time for punishment," Kre'n interjected. She locked gazes with Dabiggio, and Eshaz detected some disagreement between them.

"I was about to transmit my confession to you," Eshaz said, "when your orders arrived for me to report to the Starcloud. I am prepared to tell all now." Convinced of the correctness of his actions, Eshaz lifted his chin confidently. "I offer no excuses, only an explanation."

At a nod from Kre'n, Eshaz went on to describe Noah on the verge of death, and the crisis Eshaz faced, with only one way to save a remarkable man who had come up with his own theory of the interconnectedness of the galaxy. Then he said, "To me, Noah Watanabe has always seemed more Tulyan than Human, he might be the one spoken of in our legends, the ... " He paused, afraid to utter the word.

"A *Human* Savior?" Dabiggio exclaimed. "How utterly revolting and preposterous!"

"With respect sir, our legends say the Savior will appear from an unexpected source. Given the selfish and destructive record of humanity, could there be a more unexpected source?" Eshaz noticed several other Elders, including Kre'n, nodding their heads, just a little. At least they seemed open to the possibility.

"We have already decided to defer the matter of your punishment," Kre'n announced, with a stiff smile. "Your long and illustrious record has not gone unnoticed by this council, and we are willing to reserve judgment during this time of crisis."

"I appreciate that very much," Eshaz said, dipping his head in a slight bow. "One thing more. As you know, I used a web defect to heal Watanabe—an early stage timehole in the vicinity of the destroyed planet. I also found other defects around the site of the explosion, and repaired them."

"We are aware of that," Kre'n said. "Your peers found similar web damage around the Earth and Mars debris fields, and they, too, implemented repairs. The question is, did web defects cause the planets to blow up, or was it the reverse?"

"The chicken or the egg," one of the Elders said.

"And why are merchant prince planets the ones affected?" another asked.

"These are disturbing questions," Kre'n said, staring at Eshaz. "But now we have another important assignment for you, as a timeseer."

Eshaz lifted his eyebrows. The last time he had been asked to timesee, he had been blocked—either by chaos in the universe or by his own failing. It disturbed him to look into the future, because he didn't know what he would see there. Especially now, with the rapid decline of the web, which portended ultimate, if not imminent, disaster on an immense scale.

He heard a drone, and looking toward a side door saw what appeared to be insects flying into the large chamber, a swarm of them in various shades of color. As they drew closer he identified them as Parviis, each dressed in ornate outfits. They looked like tiny flying dolls, and set down on top of the judicial bench. The buzzing sound in his ears was not from wings, because Parviis had none, but from their hyper-accelerated metabolisms, which enabled them to fly in some mysterious fashion.

"I'd hoped I wouldn't have to do this again," Eshaz protested.

"Then you should not have demonstrated your talents so well," one of the Parviis said in a tiny, high-pitched voice.

Eshaz recognized him as Woldn, their leader. He wore a carmine red suit, with billowing sleeves and trousers. The Tulyan felt anger welling up inside, but knew better than to say anything more. This was a political matter, perhaps involving an exchange of his services for Tulyan captives taken by the Parviis in their constant raids around the galaxy. He hated providing such a valuable service to the enemies of his people, but had to do as he was told. The last time he had demonstrated his limited prescience for the Parviis, they had treated it like a carnival side show act, an amusing diversion.

"You will accompany the delegation to an antechamber," Kre'n said. "And there you will tell them what you see."

While wishing another Tulyan timeseer had been summoned in his place, Eshaz nonetheless said nothing. Deep in thought, he traipsed toward one of the many smaller chambers ringing the central council room, enclosures that had clear walls, floors, and ceilings, and were only discernible by faint construction outlines around the edges. As before, everything he said would be recorded, so that the Elders would have the information, too. Theoretically, Eshaz's timeseeing report would not benefit either side. In many ways, however, this seemed worse to him than the most serious punishments he had imagined for his Timeweb infraction. It seemed like treason, even though technically it wasn't, since he was being ordered by the Elders to do it.

Still, a citizen could disobey an order if he found it unconscionable.

Chapter Eighty-One

Sentience [one of 56 definitions]: A thinking creature with the ability to deceive another of its kind.

—Thinker, Reserve Data Bank

s days passed and Subi failed to return, Noah asked constant questions, so many that the others could not maintain the lie. "We were concerned about you and sent him for a bone specialist," Tesh finally admitted.

The two of them sat in a small lunchroom that the robots had built in the main cavern, using scrap parts from the damaged hulks of Digger machines. Adjacent to that structure, the robots had also constructed sleeping quarters for the Humans and for Eshaz, who still had not returned from his visit to the Tulyan Starcloud.

"Another doctor?" Noah exclaimed. "I ordered you to keep my condition a secret!"

"You've been behaving so strangely," Tesh said. "We're worried about you."

"And where is Subi now?" Noah demanded.

"We don't know," Tesh said. She stirred a bowl of soup with her spoon, didn't taste it.

"And those young men—Dux and Acey—any sign of them yet?"

She shook her head. "People think they ran off to space again. They probably stowed away on a ship, looking for a new adventure."

"Maybe not. I wonder if they're with Subi instead, wherever he is," Noah said.

"Doubtful."

"I wish you'd gone instead of Subi," Noah said. He glared at her. "I hold you personally responsible for anything that happens to him."

"You've never liked me, have you?"

Noah continued glaring, didn't respond. Then he lunged to his feet and stomped away.

* * * * *

Weeks passed, still with no sign of Subi Danvar.

During that period, several of Thinker's robots were able to blend in with other sentient machines in the cities, and used their new contacts to obtain food, construction materials, and various supplies needed by the Guardians. The robots paid for the articles with earnings from the lucrative Inn of the White Sun, and from the popular computer chips that Thinker manufactured for resale. The robots also obtained intelligence reports on the movement of Red Beret and CorpOne troops.

While Noah felt deep sadness at the loss of his loyal adjutant, he was heartened when Human Guardians in dirty, ragged uniforms began to filter back into his ranks. Some had escaped from the space station, while others had been in hiding in the woods and hills surrounding his commandeered ecology compound.

He sent out Human agents in plain clothes, along with robots, to look for Subi, but nothing turned up. Not a clue or any sign of him. Noah tried to hold onto slender strands of hope, but felt his grip slipping. There was no sign of the missing teenagers, either, and no word on their whereabouts. Maybe they ran away to space, as people were suggesting. Worrying that the location of his underground headquarters might be compromised because of the missing Guardians, Noah ordered the implementation of even more security measures, developed by Thinker. Primarily this involved additional covert patrols and hardening of the entrances to the tunnels and chambers. He also reviewed a report that Subi had given him before leaving, concerning unknown improvements that the Doge was making to the planet's surveillance grid system, and how this made air travel riskier than normal for Noah's and his forces.

Each day Noah went for walks around the perimeter of the cavern, past piles of scrap metal that the robots had scavenged and organized. He was walking normally or running now, without any pain. The regeneration of his foot was a minor miracle, and so was his recovery from the self-inflicted knife wound to the heart. He had even given himself a poisonous bioshot, and had survived. He had confirmed his own immortality.

Despite his astounding new physical powers, Noah found the expansion of his mental resources even more remarkable. At will, he could go in and out of the alternate, extrasensory realm and journey across the galaxy in his mind— without having to undergo the oddly disconcerting double visions he'd experienced earlier, which seemed to have only been a transitional phase. Now he just had to close his eyes and focus, and his thoughts vaulted into the cosmos … a dimension and reality that allowed him to see his own physical form as a tiny mote in a vast galactic sea.

The physical is part of the ethereal, he thought in an epiphany. *My body is an aspect of something far greater.*

All sorts of possibilities occurred to him. While he could journey in his mind, the excursions didn't always provide him with answers, at least not those that were of huge importance to him, and which should matter to all sentient creatures. He felt like a tourist in the galaxy, seeing and experiencing things on a limited basis, while not learning much about what lay deeper. There were gaps in his abilities: places he could not go and places he could not see.

So many twists and turns, he thought, *trying to unravel the mysteries of existence. The meaning of life.*

Abruptly, he reeled his far-reaching thoughts back, like a fisherman about to head home for the day. 'The meaning of life.' Such a cliché, but that did not make it an insignificant line of inquiry.

In the caverns, the Master of the Guardians stood watching robots construct more of their kind from scrap parts. Near him, Thinker was in his folded-shut mode, as if he, too, had been contemplating matters of great import.

Noah was making no further attempts to pilot the podship that had become so familiar to him. For the moment, Canopa was where he wanted to be physically, and he didn't want to get lost out in the ethereal realm or realms, and find himself unable to return. He came to the realization that he had been holding something back in his cosmic journeys; Noah feared getting lost out there and finding himself unable to return to consciousness, to his familiar corporal form and all of its traditional links.

As just one example, he could have made attempts to commandeer podships as he saw them flying by on the web, but had not, and had no intention of doing so. He did not want to interfere or inflict himself on anything, did not want to cause harm to the galactic environment.

Even so, this did not prevent Noah Watanabe's mind from taking fantastic, dreamlike journeys each night as he slept.

* * * * *

Upon awaking one morning and looking out into the cavern, Noah saw the robots moving around, as they did constantly to complete their myriad tasks. For several minutes, he stood at the window of the improvised structure, watching them. He wore shorts and a tee-shirt.

To his amazement, he suddenly saw Subi Danvar limp into the cavern, carrying a large black bag. Thinker and another robot hurried to the man's assistance, while Noah ran out of the small sleeping structure, still dressed in his night clothes.

"Subi!" he shouted. "I thought I'd never see you again!"

The adjutant hung his head. "Look," he said, "I'm sorry, but I tried to get you … " His right leg was bandaged, with the trousers cut away. He had shadows under his eyes, matted hair, and a stubble of beard.

"I already know about that, and I forgive you."

"Your loving sister and the Doge have turned the top level of our administration building into a prison and torture chamber," Subi said. "They put me in there, but I escaped. No one knew who I was; they thought I was just another Guardian."

Noah nodded, knowing that Subi had always maintained a low profile, so that the background information on him was limited. "I assume you checked for tracking devices before coming back here?"

In a perturbed tone Subi said, "You don't even need to ask."

"Don't take offense, old friend."

"All right. Guess I'm just tired and irritable."

"So the rumors are true about our old headquarters." Noah shook his head sadly. "Did they torture you?"

"I decided to cancel the appointment they had scheduled for me." Subi grinned. "This leg is nothing, just a minor injury I got when they captured me. It took six of them to take me down."

"You've lost a little weight," Noah observed.

"Yeah. I didn't like the chef." The big man scowled. "Some of our guys are still in there."

"Are those teenage boys there, Dux and Acey?"

"No. They're not here?"

"They disappeared shortly after you left."

"I hope they're OK," Subi said.

"We'll get even for this," Noah vowed. "Already we've found thousands of our Guardians who were living off the land, and we have Thinker's loyal robots. I promise you, my friend, we'll get justice."

"Maybe this will help," Subi said. He zipped open the large bag and brought out a black-and-tan machine that was perhaps a meter and a half tall, which he placed on the dirt floor of the cavern. "This makes my whole trip worthwhile. I borrowed it from our friend the Doge."

Crouching, Noah looked the machine over. It had what looked like a hopper on top, and a chute on one side that could be pulled out to make it longer. On the side opposite the chute were control toggles, buttons, and what looked like a voice-activation speaker.

Tesh and Anton joined them, and greeted their comrade. "What have you got there?" she asked.

"It's a hibbamatic," Subi said, "a popular diversion in royal courts around the MPA, this one can create any number of small devices. Larger models are also available."

Nearby, Thinker made a hissing sound. He stared with the metal-lidded eyes on his face plate.

Retrieving several small pieces of metal and plax from a nearby pile, Subi stuffed them in the hopper, then made settings and spoke into the voice-activator. "Salducian dagger," he said.

The machine whirred on, and the raw materials were sucked noisily down into the hopper. Moments later, an object clanked through the chute and landed in Subi's waiting hand, a dagger in a red plax sheath. He slid the shiny silver weapon out and showed it off. The handle was made of the same material as the sheath.

Subi continued to demonstrate his new treasure, making progressively more complex objects: a pair of night-vision goggles, a projectile gun, and a heat-and-motion sensor that he said could fly around, watching for intruders.

"Most impressive," Noah said.

"I beg to differ," Thinker interjected. "It is just a novelty item." The hissing noise increased, and he spoke over it. "Hibbil products have become increasingly inferior. Their new robots are always breaking down, whereas old models like myself—with minor tune-ups, of course—are much more reliable."

"Very well," Noah said. "As commander of my machines, you are in charge of this one, too."

"Is that wise?" Subi asked. "We could get a lot of use out of this thing."

"The hibbamatic is not even sentient," Thinker scoffed. The hiss stopped, and he added, "All right, I will agree that it is an interesting product, and of potential use. But the units require constant maintenance by Hibbil technicians. This one appears to be out of adjustment."

Thinker retrieved the dagger from the ground where Subi had left it, and smacked the blade against a piece of scrap metal. "Look at that," the intelligent robot said, holding the blade up afterward. "It chipped."

"Can you get the machine working properly?" Subi asked.

"Perhaps, but we might not be able to manufacture more of them. Hibbamatics contain materials that are not easily obtainable, especially rare Ilkian fiber optics." Orange lights around his face plate glowed. "Of course, the hibbamatics can't make anything that we can't make ourselves, assuming we can locate the necessary raw materials."

Noah watched as Subi nodded reluctantly. Obviously, he had gone to a lot of trouble to obtain this device, adding to the peril of his escape.

Emitting a little click, Thinker sent an electronic signal to a robot that stood nearby, and the subordinate took the hibbamatic away.

* * * * *

In ensuing weeks, Subi and Thinker supervised the training of the Human and robot Guardians, turning them into a cohesive fighting force. On one training exercise, they located two non-functioning Digger machines inside a deep tunnel, units that had gotten into trouble on their own or been decommissioned by Noah's commandos.

Hearing of this, Noah went to investigate. The silvery machines appeared to be intact, although some of the drill bits studding their hulking bodies were broken or chipped.

"I think we should reactivate them," Thinker suggested, standing at Noah's side. "They could be programmed to do beneficial work."

"What about their tendency to go off on rampages of destruction?" Noah asked.

Abruptly, Thinker closed in a clatter of metal so that he could consider the matter in absolute darkness and silence. In less than a minute he opened back up and announced, confidently, "It's nothing a good programmer can't straighten out."

"Do it, then," Noah ordered.

"Very well. Oops." Thinker's internal programming whirred and made a little popping sound. On the robot's chest, a screen flashed on with an image of Noah and the tunnel surroundings. Their entire conversation was played back, sounding somewhat tinny. At the end, as before, the recorded Noah said, "Do it, then."

"You've been recording all of my words?" Noah asked.

"Not just yours. I absorb data from all directions. That's why I'm so smart. I used to travel around the galaxy collecting data and storing it away. Now I'm too busy for that."

Opening a panel below the screen, the robot tinkered with the controls, then slammed the cover shut and said, "Sorry about the little glitch. If you ever want me to play anything back, just let me know."

"I don't know how I feel about being recorded," Noah said, scratching his freckled forehead.

"Would you like me to disconnect it whenever you and I talk?" Thinker inquired.

"No. I hereby designate you our official historian, along with your other duties."

* * * * *

Soon the restored Diggers began to excavate large underground living chambers out of rocky areas, upgrading the previous barrack arrangements. They also made improvements to the labyrinthine tunnel system beneath the woods and hills outside his former compound, and even explored existing tunnels that were directly under the old administration buildings. At Thinker's command, Giovanni Nehr supervised much of the work, improving upon the original subterranean map that Anton and Tesh drew up.

Noah came to rely on the new armored Guardian, although Gio seemed somewhat vain and self absorbed, constantly admiring his shiny armor in any mirror he passed. But little did Noah know that Gio was also a shameless opportunist, intent on watching for the perfect time to take advantage of his surroundings ... like waiting for fruit to ripen on someone else's tree.

It must be noted however, that Giovanni Nehr's feelings were not simplistic by any means. While he looked out for his own interests above all others, he was still a long-time admirer of Noah Watanabe. The discontented son of an industrialist, Noah had tweaked the noses of the merchant princes on more than one occasion—including Gio's own famous, insufferable brother Jacopo. So, Gio was loyal to the man the Guardians called "Master," but only as much as an egocentric man like him could be....

Noah had a mission in mind, and not necessarily the obvious one of retaking control of his Ecological Demonstration Project and orbital EcoStation, at least not right away. First he intended to lead his Guardians in guerrilla raids against industrial polluters, with the hope of making Francella, Doge Lorenzo, and their allies suffer.

Chapter Eighty-Two

Even after seeing all of the evidence, it remains difficult for me to believe, and brings tears to my eyes. But the truth is that my brother attacked CorpOne headquarters and mortally wounded our father. One of the great merchant princes and industrial geniuses, Saito Watanabe, is gone forever because of Noah's treachery. I promise you this: his crime will not go unpunished.
— Francella Watanabe, speech to CorpOne employees

Despite his paranormal abilities, Noah Watanabe still had significant blind spots.

One morning he explored the subterranean tunnels and caverns, probing ahead with a flashbeam visor, and did not notice Tesh—tiny and silent—following him everywhere, watching everything he did, listening to everything he said. Noah had dual realities, an ability to venture into two dimensions, realms that at times overlapped and folded over one another in ways that he had not yet fully sorted out. He was in the physical reality now, running at a good clip over dirt and rock, rebuilding his strength.

Earlier, after taking control of the podship away from Tesh, he had secretly watched her in her tiny form as she tried to regain control of the vessel, but found herself unable to reenter the navigation chamber that he had sealed. Now, though he remained alert and looked around, he did not see her at all. She wasn't invisible, but she could move so quickly that she approached invisibility in this dimension.

Deep underground, Noah slowed and walked through one of the older burrows that the rampant Diggers had excavated. He was taking the time to wander, but not aimlessly; he had a purpose in mind. Through an internal survival mechanism that had surfaced recently, he found that he could not get lost, at least not physically. No matter how far off the subterranean map he ventured, he always seemed able to find his way back to the main cavern and his companions.

This gave him increasing comfort, and he was thinking about reentering a podship and taking control of it to surge out into the vast reaches of the galaxy, where the power of his mind controlled his reality. In that mystical realm, he could stretch into the cosmos mentally, or he could take his body along, and not just as an afterthought. There actually was a physical aspect where podships traveled and carried their passengers to fantastic places.

But the domain of podships, while astounding and intriguing, gave him considerable pause. It was so infinitely beautiful out there, so alluring and yet so dangerous.

As he wandered the tunnels now, he recognized that the scene before him was not entirely corporeal. He only saw it, felt it, smelled it, and heard it because his mind permitted him to do so … and his mind could change focus. He wondered how many other realities remained unexplored. The possibilities enticed him.

Previously when he piloted a podship, he had done so by extrasensory means, while inside the cargo hold. From there, he had mentally projected himself into the navigation chamber and caused the vessel to lurch into motion, taking him physically and cerebrally across space.

Now it was different. He was not inside any portion of the podship, but he wondered if he could still reach out with his thoughts, if he could still seep like a mist into the operational core of the spacecraft and take control of it, if he could still guide it across space.

But even if he could do that, Noah remained cautious. If he piloted a podship again, and tried to get lost, would his internal compass continue to function, always permitting him to return?

Moments passed, as temptation and curiosity buffeted him. He could not avoid thoughts that drifted in and out of his conscious mind. Now that he'd had the paranormal experiences, he needed to experience them again.

Summoning his courage, he dipped into the ethereal web, and on the internal screen of his mind he saw the faint green cosmic filigree stretching into infinity, wavering ever so slightly, as if from a gentle breeze. Focusing closer, he again saw flickering images of the podship he had left at the Canopa pod station, with Red Beret officers and scientists continuing to crawl over it, still not finding the secret passageways or the navigation chamber.

But as Noah seeped into the podship now, the interior was a little out of focus. Like a phantom, he floated silently through a wide corridor, then darted into a narrow one that the Red Berets had not been able to enter, or even see. Just ahead, Noah made out the entrance to the navigation chamber that he had previously sealed, to keep Tesh and any other intruders out.

Mentally, he gave the instruction to unseal it, so that he could pass through the flesh of the podship, into its most sacred and sheltered chamber, the heart and mind of the creature. Cautiously, Noah's ghost-self moved forward, and pressed itself against the entryway.

He entered the navigation chamber.

But something was happening back in the tunnel, where his physical form remained....

Shifting his focus, Noah felt something cold and hard against his jugular.

"I should cut your throat," a woman's voice whispered. "But would you die?"

With a quick movement, Noah grabbed the knife by its razor-sharp blade, cutting deeply into his hand. Despite the blood and pain, he tried to pull the weapon from her grip, but could not. She was extremely strong. Blood spurted from the hand as he pulled it away, but within seconds it coagulated. In the low light, he watched with her as the skin healed. The searing pain stopped.

She withdrew the knife from his neck. "Talk," Tesh demanded, glaring at him.

"I am indestructible. You cannot kill me. I cannot even commit suicide. I've been doing little tests lately, self-inflicted stab wounds, even injected poison into my arm. I always heal perfectly. Do you know why this is happening to me?"

"I don't know *what* you are," she responded.

I don't know what you are, either, Noah thought, as he remembered seeing Tesh in her tiny, secret form, trying to gain entrance to the navigation chamber. "Let's go for a walk," he said. "We need to talk."

She sheathed the knife at her waist, and followed his lead.

* * * * *

The two of them trekked upward along a circuitous route of tunnels to the main cavern, crossed it and went out through the camouflaged main entrance, after using Noah's security alarm code. It was much warmer outside, with the foliage and ground baked by a late afternoon sun. They climbed to a knoll and sat on it, gazing out across the countryside toward the southern edge of his former ecological demonstration compound.

From this vantage, Noah could not see any of the buildings, only the familiar sloping hills and dark green trees of his beloved land. He longed to have it back, to free himself from the yoke of the misfortunes that had befallen him. If only he and his father had not become estranged, perhaps this whole unfortunate chain of events would never have occurred.

"I have something to tell you," Tesh said. Sunlight sparkled on her long black hair, and her emerald eyes were filled with concern.

"And I have a lot of questions," he said.

They talked well past sunset, when a cool night breeze began to pick up, rustling the nearby shrubs and canopa trees. Noah offered her his coat in case she was cold. She accepted, and he sat there shivering without it, while trying to keep his mind on other things. High overhead, the moon peeked around from behind a cloud, casting low illumination on the landscape, creating strange shadows around them.

She revealed to him that she was a Parvii, a major—but clandestine— galactic race that had held dominion over another race, the Aopoddae, since ancient times. Tesh spoke of her magnification system, and demonstrated it as they spoke, but Noah did not admit having previously seen her in her natural state.

"We Parviis do not confide in other races," she said as she switched the magnification system back on. "But in view of my unparalleled experiences with you, and the unfortunate condition of the galaxy ... I must trust you. Please understand, it is not easy for me."

Pausing, Tesh looked at him. He saw her eyes glint in the low light. The wind blew her hair forward, and with one hand she brushed it out of her eyes, and continued.

"In part from time dilation during space travel, my people live for centuries. Before dying, our oldest person attained the age of three thousand and eighty-eight standard years, while I am more than seven hundred myself. Even so, we can still die of diseases and injuries."

"My story is not so clear," he said. "You and I seem to have shared a paranormal experience in which we fought for control of a podship. I suspect that each of us has information ... and abilities ... that the other does not."

"I agree," she said. "It's all part of a vast galactic puzzle, and we must solve it together." She paused. Then: "You are ... or *were* ... a primitive Human on the evolutionary scale, but Eshaz altered that with one brash act."

Even when he'd seen Tesh in her tiny size, she'd looked Human to Noah. Was that the future of humanity—to get smaller and live longer?

"Eshaz should never have granted you access to Timeweb," she said, "which he did when he healed you. He committed a terrible, dangerous act, and will surely pay the price for it. His action is unprecedented, and so, to my knowledge, are you. I do not believe that you are immortal, however. Our leader, Woldn, has always told us that there are no deathless creatures in the universe. Some are just harder to kill than others, that's all."

Noah actually did feel immortal, but said only, "Well, I'm definitely hard to kill. Anyway, I didn't try to do anything wrong, so don't be angry with me. I still don't understand what happened to me, or ... you called it Timeweb?"

She nodded. "It's a vast web that holds the entire cosmos together, but it's extremely fragile. Think of an immense ecosystem, with planetary and other organisms intricately woven together and utterly dependent upon each other ... a large-scale version of what it is like on each world. Your concept of galactic ecology is very close to the truth."

He struggled to comprehend. "But it sounds more complicated than anything I imagined."

"The old ways of the galaxy are in chaos, and this may have permitted you to gain unprecedented access to the web. I cannot say, but I do know this. You and I must journey into Timeweb in a podship ... together."

"With you?" He wasn't sure how he felt about that idea.

"I sense great danger, and we must move quickly. Do you know that our podship has been sitting at the pod station, exactly where we ... where you ... left it?"

He nodded. "I, too, sense peril, but have not known how to deal with it, or if I am the right one to deal with it."

"We might be able figure it out as a team. Something is afoot in the galaxy, and we must discover what it is."

Noah considered her proposal, wondering if it might be a trick, so that she could take control of the sentient spacecraft away from him. In the moonlight, he stared at the knife that she had sheathed.

As if to answer his unspoken concerns, she smiled gently and said, "You are, as we have learned from our podship experience, stronger than I am in Timeweb."

"But you know your way around better than I do."

"Perhaps I only know different aspects of it than you do."

He told her about the fantastic vision in which he journeyed in his mind across space, and saw Francella and the Doge Lorenzo del Velli in a podship,

241

and overheard her saying she wanted Noah killed. Noah also told of seeing Thinker and his small army of robots in another podship, and of seeing Mutatis at the controls of ten schooners that were painted with merchant prince colors, all with unidentifiable tube mechanisms built into their hulls.

"The Mutatis were in orbit over their own planets," Noah said. "Some sort of defensive operation, I guess, maybe listening posts. But why are they using merchant ships?"

"They probably stole them," Tesh suggested. "But with that devious race, nothing is as it seems. Woldn has long warned of Mutati treachery, saying they are a danger to the entire galaxy, and not just to Humans."

"Sometimes I wonder if the galaxy would be better off without Mutatis or Humans," Noah said.

"Don't say that. You know the goodness of humankind."

"And the evils."

"We'd better get out there and see what the Mutatis are up to," she said, pressing.

He didn't respond, and didn't tell her he had been conducting a remote experiment when she interrupted him, to see if he could get into the core while not physically on board the podship. He'd proven to himself he could, and had no doubt that he could also pilot the ship remotely. But the less she knew about his powers the better—this Parvii female probably had more tricks than he could imagine.

"Will you go with me to the podship?" she asked.

"You could shrink yourself and sneak past the guards at the ship," he said.

"That wouldn't do me any good. You sealed the navigation chamber, and I can't get in without you."

"So it seems." Looking into her seductive, moonlit eyes, Noah wondered if he could ever trust her. "I need time to process all of this," he said.

"When will you have an answer?" Her voice sounded anxious.

"I'll let you know. You can't get into the navigation chamber without my help."

"So it seems." She touched his hand. He felt warmth from her, which was remarkable considering her magnification system.

Gently, Noah pushed her hand away. He gazed into the night sky, scanning the twinkling, distant stars. Doubts about her assailed him. She was using her physical beauty and charm to get what she wanted, obviously a method she was accustomed to using.

She pulled his face to hers, and their lips met—or seemed to—but for only a fraction of a second. Quickly, Noah pulled away. The more attraction he felt for her, the more it worried him.

Tesh tried again, and this time Noah was more forceful in response. "I will make my decision logically," he snapped, "not emotionally."

And he stalked off.

* * * * *

Alone in the darkness of his room, Noah probed the vast cosmic domain, his thoughts skipping along the faint green filigree of Timeweb. He needed to conduct an experiment to discover if he really could pilot a podship by remote control, but he decided it would be best to try other sentient vessels, not the one at the Canopa pod station. He didn't want to disturb that one now, not until he determined how best to put it to use. Aside from his concern about keeping information from Tesh, he was afraid that something might go wrong in a remote takeover attempt, preventing him from ever controlling that ship.

At random, he selected a podship speeding along the web, and zeroed in on it. His mind seeped inside, first into the passenger compartment and cargo hold, and then into the green, glowing navigation chamber at the core of the vessel. He saw a Parvii clinging to a wall there, guiding the ship along one galactic strand and another.

Focusing all of his mental energy, Noah tried to commandeer the ship, and for a moment he felt a mental linkage with the mysterious creature, though not as strong as he had experienced previously, with the other vessel. This time he caused the podship to slow, just a little. Then he felt increasing resistance, and noticed that the tiny humanoid had moved to another section of wall, a bright green patch.

The podship followed the Parvii's commands now and disregarded Noah's, no matter how much he tried. Finally giving up the effort to overcome the other pilot, Noah wondered how much his difficulty had to do with the remote connection, and if he had more power when he was actually on board a craft before attempting to pilot it.

Moments later, the podship pulled into a pod station and docked.

While passengers and small vessels unloaded from the ship, Noah again touched the core with his probing thoughts, and once more he experienced a men-tal linkage with the sentient creature. The Parvii resisted him as expected, but only briefly this time, before losing the battle.

I did it! Noah thought.

He waited for the unloading to finish, but before any passengers or cargo could be loaded, he ordered the podship to close the entrance hatches and leave the dock. To his elation, these commands were followed. He then took the vessel out on the podways and guided it along one strand and another, as he pleased.

Eventually he let the connection go, and allowed the disturbed Parvii pilot to resume control.

During the next hour, Noah conducted additional experiments on other podships around the galaxy. In each case he found that he could not maintain control of a pod that was already in motion, but he could if the vessel was docked when he made the attempt.

Noah was gaining skills in Timeweb, like a child learning how to walk.

Chapter Eighty-Three

There are countless ways to destroy a foe … and to destroy yourself. You must take care that one does not lead to the other.

—Mutati Wisdom

Two Mutatis stood high inside one of the spires of the Citadel of Paradij, gazing out on the jeweled buildings of the capital city, the glittering colors in afternoon sunlight. One of the shapeshifters—the Zultan Abal Meshdi—was the more massive, though his son could not be considered petite.

In the time that had passed since the enemy attack on his Demolio manufacturing facility, the Zultan had restored the program. Now there were hundreds of doomsday machines, and they had been dispatched to strategic locations in the Mutati Kingdom and in other star systems, where their outriders had been told to await further instructions.

Those final commands would be sent via his new instantaneous cross-space communication system. Pursuant to the information received from the turncoat Giovanni Nehr, the Mutatis had established deep-shaft emerald mines on a number of planets, and had been harvesting the piezoelectric gems that were required for nehrcom transceivers.

The new communication program was ancillary to the overall doomsday plan, and would facilitate the obliteration of merchant prince planets. Meshdi could have distributed the deadly torpedoes without the instantaneous communication system, by sending outriders with predetermined attack schedules (as he had done in the past), but he had been waiting for instructions from God-on-High.

Finally, while inside his gyrodome the day before, the Zultan had been told what to do. The blessed Creator of the Galaxy had appeared to him, as if from a cosmic mist, and had commanded him to make Humans suffer by destroying them progressively—rather than all at once. But unknown to Meshdi, it had not really been a divine directive at all. Rather, it had been the result of psychic influences exerted by the Adurian gyrodome and minigyros—mechanisms that swayed his decisionmaking processes and caused him to preserve the most valuable merchant prince worlds, which the clandestine HibAdu Coalition wanted as prizes of war.

Abal Meshdi had been feeling disappointment all day, and had summoned his eldest son Hari'Adab to this private meeting, to discuss what to do next. Now the Zultan snapped his fingers, causing a clearplax door in front of them to slide open. He led the way out onto a balcony, and felt the floor flex under their combined weight.

"I wish you hadn't asked for my advice this time," the younger Mutati said. He placed three hands on the balcony railing, and gazed blankly out on the city. "You know how I feel about your Demolio program."

"As my heir apparent, you must accept it anyway, just as I must accept the will of God-on-High. Each of us has our superior, you see, and we cannot alter what is meant to be, the natural order of affairs. If I had my way it would all be over quickly. I would attack every enemy world simultaneously, blasting them all to oblivion." He paused. "Beyond oblivion, I hate Humans so much."

Hari'Adab did not respond.

"We will annihilate them," the Zultan said. He tasted the destructive word and smiled to himself, forming a tiny curvature of the mouth atop his impressive mountain of fat. Such a delicious, salivating sound to it.

"We will *annihilate* them!" he repeated.

"If I had my way, Father, I would negotiate with the merchant princes and form a lasting peace. Our militarism only generates more of the same by our opponents. I say this to you with all respect, My Zultan, for the ultimate decision is yours and I would not think to question it. I only offer my humble opinion."

"I've heard that all before from you, Hari, and you would be wise not to press me further on that issue, considering how far you have to fall if I decide to tip you over the railing." He grinned at his son, and caught an angry glance in return. Then Hari'Adab looked away and stared into the distance, as if wishing he could be anywhere else.

Shifting on his feet and feeling the balcony floor move again, Meshdi said, "Maybe I shouldn't be so disappointed at the order from God-on-High. Perhaps it is for the best, after all. By inflicting anguish on our enemy in stages, we will strike more terror into their black little hearts. Think of it, Hari! They will know the end is coming without being able to stop it!"

Almost imperceptibly—but not quite—the young Emir shook his undersized head, but said nothing, obviously trying to show the proper respect for his elder, as required in Mutati society. Hari had, however, refused to wear the Adurian gyro that his father shipped to him. A proud young terramutati, he'd said that he did not need a mechanical device to help him make decisions. It had been another disappointment for Abal Meshdi, and he had been struggling to overcome it.

But at the thought of making his enemies suffer, the Zultan cheered up and trembled with excitement. "Let them scramble like ants from a fire, trying to save themselves," he said. "It will do them no good."

Chapter Eighty-Four

The symbiosis of man and machine. That may be the best way to describe my relationship with the robot leader.

—Noah Watanabe

In the weeks they had known one another, Noah and Thinker were developing a surprisingly close friendship, something neither of them had anticipated, since they seemed so different. This is not to say that they failed to notice one another's faults. Early one morning as they ventured outside the tunnel complex, the robot commented that Noah had a tendency to be overly trustful of people he met, always trying to see the good in them, even if he had to struggle to do so.

"Perhaps you're right," Noah admitted, feeling the comfortable warmth of the sun on his face. "Essentially I'm an optimist, I suppose, looking for light instead of darkness."

They walked a path that led into the canopa woods. The deciduous trees were in full leaf, deep green from the seasonal rains. As the forest embraced them, Noah felt secure, sheltered by its living force.

"Perhaps that's how you got your environmental recovery company going," Thinker said as he clanked along, "Pessimists aren't usually successful."

"I'm not much of a success any more," Noah replied. "Hopefully some of my company is still operational, but I'm sure Francella and Lorenzo are scouring the galaxy, searching for anything associated with me."

"But you have new friends," Thinker said.

They paused at a clearing where gray-and-brown mushrooms grew, and Noah made his own observation in return. "I appreciate your loyalty, but I must say, you're overly boastful and egotistical at times."

"I don't boast and I have no ego whatsoever," Thinker said, "for those are Human frailties, and have nothing to do with machines."

"We could argue that point for a long time, because I have seen signs of emotions in machines. Call them internal operating programs or whatever you want, but the result is the same."

"It is possible to refute everything you say," Thinker said.

"I'm sure you're right."

"As for your accusation about an ego, I simply tell the truth, and here is an example: I am the smartest sentient machine in the entire galaxy, with a virtually unlimited capacity for data absorption."

"Speaking of that, do you recall our discussion a few days ago, when I found out that you were recording everything we said, and that you could play the data back?"

"Of course. I never forget anything."

They scaled a steep, wooded hillside together. Noah knew the area well, and kept off the main trail to avoid detection. For a long while, he said nothing as they tramped along, and Thinker did not press him. The Guardian leader thought of Tesh's proposal that they explore Timeweb together, and of the possibilities—and perils—this presented. Preliminary evidence suggested to Noah that he had become immortal, but as he considered this at length he had reservations. His own tests had been limited, and perhaps there was a way to kill him after all.

He cared little for his own personal safety, but his legacy was a different matter altogether. It had importance beyond the breaths he took and the beating of his heart. It meant something to the entire galaxy.

He smiled bitterly to himself as they approached the crest of the hill, where the trees thinned out and it was brighter. A short while ago, Noah had accused Thinker of being egotistical, but he had that fault himself. In a sense, though, and Noah hoped he had the right edge on it himself, an ego could be a good thing, for without it his word would mean a lot less to his followers and his message might not always be respected.

"Hold it," Noah said, raising a hand.

Thinker went motionless beside him.

"Wait here," Noah said. Keeping low, he crept ahead as silently as possible, avoiding sticks, making the minimum amount of noise possible. At the edge of the trees he peered beyond, toward a grassy expanse dotted with low trees and the doberock remains of a long-dead settlement. For several minutes he stood silently, scanning in all directions, listening intently to the calls of the birds and the sounds of the wind, until satisfied that it was safe to proceed. He wondered if weapons fire would erupt anyway, and if he could still heal himself, no matter the severity of the wounds.

Safety was only a matter of degree, he realized. Nothing was completely secure. If his entire cellular structure was destroyed, he might be rendered incapable of regenerating himself, thus leaving no mechanism for him to come back.

That is, if the renewal process actually worked that way, if it was a physical, cellular phenomenon. Or was it a form of miraculous recovery, a resurrection? He shivered at the thought. In any event, he could not conceal himself forever in the tunnels of Canopa, or here at the edge of the trees. He had to take risks.

That's what life is all about, he thought.

With a wave of his hand, Noah strode boldly out of the trees, onto the sunlit grass, which sloped gently upward. Thinker followed.

At the rock pile of a fallen-down building, "Noah said, "This is an ancient archaeological site, where the original inhabitants of Canopa once lived. It's very spiritual here, a place where I like to think about important matters."

"I simply fold into myself whenever I want to do that," Thinker said. "Much more efficient."

"Perhaps," Noah agreed, "but efficiency is not always the best thing."

"I must contemplate that," the robot said. With a small clatter of metal he closed himself, folding neatly into a box. He did not move.

While waiting for him to return, Noah sat on an adjacent rock and recalled coming to this site not so long ago in terms of time, only a few months. So much had occurred since then that it seemed like much longer. The people he used to know were like specters from the past, like the phantoms of this long-dormant settlement.

Presently, Thinker folded open and said, "Efficiency is always best. You have made an inaccurate statement."

"We'll debate it another time, my friend. First, I want to ask you something about your data collection and playback system."

"Do you want to see and hear something you said to me, perhaps information you are having trouble remembering?" Thinker asked. "I can put you on the screen right away."

"No, it's not that. Well, it is, but in a larger sense." He hesitated. Then: "Can you dig into my memories, sort of like an archaeologist, and resurrect all of the events I've experienced? Things that occurred before I met you, and which you could not have recorded?"

"You have already made me the official historian of the Guardians. Now you wish me to be your own personal archivist as well?"

"Can you do it?"

"Possibly. I've been working on a method of interfacing with Humans, similar to the way I do it with my own kind, to download data. When Giovanni Nehr joined my army, it occurred to me that I had no way of analyzing the thoughts in his brain. Since then, I have come up with a method, and I even constructed the biotechnology to accomplish data transfer."

He hesitated. "But I have encountered certain … internal programming obstacles. You might refer to them as moral issues. As a robot, I find that I do not feel comfortable forcing the probe on a human being, not even one who is ostensibly under my command. Humans created robots in the first place, before Hibbils ever got involved, and we honor that fact."

"That's a nice sentiment," Noah said.

As if ashamed, the robot looked down with his metal-lidded eyes and added, "I fear that my researches have gone too far."

"Could you transfer my thoughts without harming me?" Noah asked.

"Of course. All of my internal operating tests confirm this."

"Then, what if I give you permission to download my memories?"

"You would permit yourself to be a guinea pig? Don't you consider that dangerous?"

"Not at all," Noah said. "I have supreme confidence in your abilities. And in your friendship."

A tentacle snaked out of Thinker's alloy head and hovered over Noah. "This is an organic interface," the robot explained. "Are you sure you want to go through with this?"

Noah took a step back, and said, "I've been wondering if a mental replica of me could be made. As Guardian leader, I've been thinking about my own mortality, and I want to make sure my philosophy is imparted clearly to my followers, in case something happens to me. I have written a number of handbooks, but it would be nice to leave something more personal behind."

"But you are still comparatively young, with much of your life to live."

"I am a hunted, wanted man. And even if I weren't, I've been doing dangerous things, guiding podships across the galaxy and the like."

"Even so, I see great strength in you, an ability to survive and overcome great obstacles. You are no ordinary man, Noah Watanabe."

"Perhaps not." He looked up at the organic interface, with its array of needles, and shuddered. But he stepped forward, so that he was again directly beneath the tentacle head. "I'm ready," he said. And he closed his eyes.

A moment later, Noah felt the tentacle connect to the top of his head, and needles of pain all over his skull. In a surge of panic, he wanted to pull away, but could not move. The sharp points of pain reminded him of stars in distant space, and how his own mind could expand into the cosmos and take incredible journeys....

Thinker sent the probes deeper into Noah's brain, and data began to flow into the machine's computer brain, downloading every bit of information comprising Noah's life, including not only his memories but the chemical makeup of his body. After several moments the robot withdrew, and Noah's excruciating pain ceased.

"Now I know what you had for breakfast on your fifth birthday," Thinker said.

Noah opened his eyes, squinted in the sunlight. "And that was?"

"A poached gooselet egg. You only ate half of it, and said you were full. Then you sneaked into another room and gorged yourself on a stash of candy."

"I'd almost forgotten all that," Noah said.

"What would you like me to do with the information? I can erase it, analyze it, or store it."

"Store it," Noah ordered. "I want you to keep a backup copy of me, and update it regularly."

* * * * *

In his Canopa office, Pimyt considered the coded nehrcom message he had received within the hour, on a sheet of folded parchment. Enraged at the terrible news, he had been stomping around the room, muttering and cursing to himself.

On every merchant prince planet, the influential Hibbil had sent fake communiqués, ostensibly from the Doge. They had been passed through Jacopo Nehr and resulted in the dismantling of many Human military forces, and the positioning of others in out-of-the way locations without adequate armaments, thus rendering them useless. In addition, Hibbil officers were in key positions throughout the armed forces of the Merchant Prince Alliance, ready to take the necessary actions when ordered to do so.

My part of the plan is in perfect order, he thought.

Disgusted, the covert agent kicked the parchment under his desk, trying to get it out of his sight. The problem had to do with the Adurian side of the conspiracy, the control they were supposed to be exerting over the Zultan Abal Meshdi and all military operations of the Mutati Kingdom.

Despite being under the influence of Adurian gyros, the Zultan had still dispatched an outrider to attack and destroy Timian One, the wealthiest of all merchant prince worlds. This was a big potential setback for the HibAdu Coalition, a planet-busting torpedo that could not be called back. Meshdi was supposed to send it against another fringe planet, not the MPA capital world!

Across much of the Mutati Kingdom, the Adurians had used gyro-manipulation to twist the thoughts of the Zultan and his minions, causing them to overlook certain military anomalies, such as the preponderance of Adurian officers in leadership positions. Gyro-manipulation had also been used to establish and carry out the essentially futile Demolio torpedo program, which had diverted Mutati military assets into dead ends and permitted the shapeshifters to destroy three Human fringe worlds that were of little value— Earth, Mars, and Plevin Four.

Now came this unexpected problem involving Timian One, which should never have happened, since the HibAdu Coalition wanted to preserve that valuable planet and others for their own uses after their great victory. Many of those worlds had important assets that the wealthy merchant princes had set up, and some had untapped natural resources, minerals that were only valuable to the Hibbils and the Adurians. They were supposed to be spoils of war.

To prevent further undesirable losses, the Adurians were making emergency adjustments to the signals being transmitted to Mutatis who used gyrodomes and portable gyros for decision-making. Pimyt hoped it worked.

* * * * *

Upon returning to the underground encampment, Noah found Tesh waiting for him, just inside the entrance. She rose from a rock where she had been sitting and said to him, "Well? Do you have an answer for me yet?"

"As a matter of fact I do," Noah replied. "My friend and I had some business to take care of first."

"I'm not asking where you were," she said in an impertinent tone.

He looked at her calmly, while Thinker stood beside him.

"Your answer is no, isn't it?" Tesh said.

"My answer may not be what you expect." Noah smiled stiffly, then brushed by her and went toward the cafeteria.

"That's all you have to say?" she yelled after him.

"Be ready to leave first thing in the morning," Noah shouted.

"Did he say what I think he said?" Tesh asked, looking wide-eyed at Thinker.

"He answered yes," the robot said. "I see no other alternative, even though I do not know the question. Perhaps you asked him to marry you, which is something Humans are known to do."

"We're not quite ready for that," Tesh said.

Chapter Eighty-Five

The future is a tapestry woven with disappearing threads. Sometimes it seems to come into view, but only ephemerally, providing titillating but confusing glimpses of what is to come.

—From a Parvii Legend

Disguised as ordinary travelers, Tesh and Noah took a crowded city shuttle up to the orbital pod station, ostensibly to await the next podship from deep space.

In reality, they were looking for the one that still sat in its docking berth, where they had left it. Uniformed Red Berets and technicians were poring over the craft, searching for answers. Never before had a sentient spacecraft remained in place for so long.

As they approached the vessel, Tesh reduced her pace and touched Noah's arm, causing him to slow as well. The two of them were dressed in black robes, like the garb of a religious sect.

"What is it?" he asked in a low tone.

"Nothing, nothing," she said, lying. They proceeded together, more slowly. The walkway was crowded with passengers and Red Beret soldiers.

She couldn't tell him what she was feeling. Despite the fact that she had invited Noah to accompany her into space, it troubled her that this sacred spacefaring vessel was being violated by so many nosy, meddling Humans. She hoped they had not been able to gain access to the innermost secrets of the creature, its sectoid chamber and other workings that she knew so well as a Parvii.

In the past, whenever podships were abused by Humans, Vandurians, and certain other races, the sentient vessels reacted, sealing themselves up and closing off all sections to intruders, suffocating anyone aboard and then speeding off into space. Now, however, this creature was behaving differently, and Tesh didn't know why.

Throughout history there had been examples of Parvii pilots taking heroic actions to save their vessels. In his younger years the Eye of the Swarm, Woldn, had done so himself, saving an entire herd of rampaging, panicked podships.

Tesh wondered if the battle she and Noah had fought for control of this vessel had confused or traumatized it. Perhaps it would take the two of them to restore balance to the creature, or the harm might be irreversible. She hoped not, prayed that it was not too late.

* * * * *

Unknown to either her or Noah, Anton Glavine had followed them in a separate shuttle, and now he was mingling into the crowd at the pod station. In a dark blue cape and liripipe hat, the typical garb of a nobleman, Anton watched with considerable interest as Noah and Tesh found a place off to one side of the walkway and conversed in low tones.

The young man was no longer jealous, and had all but given up any hope of having a close relationship with Tesh again. But he was seriously concerned about her, and wanted to make absolutely certain she was safe. It was more than concern, he admitted to himself now. He loved her. And he only wanted the best for her, even if that meant giving her up entirely.

* * * * *

Perhaps twenty meters from the podship, Tesh and Noah were keeping an eye on activity around the vessel, watching for the first opportunity to slip on board.

Tesh had her own complex feelings, but they were for the man beside her. She cared deeply for Noah with an unrequited passion, but he was an interloper in Timeweb and had control of a podship that should be hers. It made for an internal tug of war between her personal and professional needs.

The two of them had not spoken much that morning, with tension still lingering. Now they exchanged only terse comments about the movements of the investigators and soldiers who were going in and out of the passenger compartment and cargo hold of the podship.

They fell silent for several long moments. Then she said, "We Parviis express ourselves differently than our larger Human cousins, a race we call 'humanus ordinaire.' When we find a person we like, we are quite aggressive. If I have offended you I am sorry, but that is our way."

He glared down at her with hardness in his hazel eyes.

Seemingly unperturbed, she explained with surprising frankness how Parviis and Humans—she kept calling them "humanus ordinaire"—could have sex together, and that it was potentially quite pleasurable. They could not, however, conceive children ... even though the Human race was a genetic Mutation of the Parviis, a split that occurred millions of years ago. Now they were two of the major galactic races, none of which could interbreed.

"I'm trying to figure out where a galactic playgirl fits into all of this," he said, "scattering hearts across the cosmos."

"That might have been a fair comment about me once," she admitted, "but not anymore. Not since I met you."

He looked at her skeptically.

As she continued to speak to him, he said little in response. In his sparse words and demeanor he appeared to be trying to maintain his emotional distance from her, but in his eyes she detected his difficulty doing that. Periodically, he locked gazes with her, and seemed to soften. Then he would stiffen and pull away.

From a personal standpoint, these were good signs to her. It was only a matter of time.

* * * * *

When the technicians and soldiers wrapped up their work for the day, two black-robed figures took advantage of a lapse in security. Slipping through the airlock, they sneaked aboard the disabled podship. In a shadowy corner of the passenger compartment, Noah pressed a hand against the interior wall, touching the rough, leathery skin of the sentient spacecraft. It felt unusually cool, but he sensed life.

The faint pulse quickened, and he withdrew his hand. But as he did so, he still felt the pulse.

"Follow me to the navigation chamber," he said. But he did not move physically.

Closing his eyes, Noah watched while Tesh became small and ran behind his own ghostlike form as it entered a passageway that led to the core of the podship. He was making her think he had to be in physical contact with the ship before being able to get into the navigation chamber, still not revealing his earlier remote entry.

At the end of the passage, he hesitated, then seeped through the wall of the central chamber, leaving her behind. Seconds passed, and he sensed her impatience growing.

Then he released the seal on the entrance and let her in....

* * * * *

Outside, Anton Glavine approached the podship, but was noticed by a Red Beret guard who had just gone on duty. "Stay back," the soldier commanded tersely. "This vessel is out of service."

Obediently, Anton backed up. "Sorry," he said. "I thought this was my ship."

"Read the destination boards and pay attention to berth numbers, you idiot."

"Yes sir." Anton blended back into the walking, milling traffic.

* * * * *

In the soft green glow of the navigation chamber, at the nerve center of the podship, Noah concentrated the power of his mind, and felt the ship pulse into motion.

Just inside the enclosure, Tesh stood motionless, not challenging him.

Under Noah's direction, the vessel proceeded slowly through the docking bay. From the walkway, Red Beret soldiers fired puissant rifles at the craft, but to no effect. Some of the uniformed men scrambled into a pursuit ship and fired up the engine, making a flash of orange in the exhaust tubes.

But the podship surged away from the orbital station and leapt onto the podways with surprising vigor, then accelerated out into the frigid void, leaving the Red Berets far behind.

From the passenger compartment, Noah shared the joy of the creature.

And he felt the podship still under his control, turning this way and that along the cosmic filigree. Presently, he brought the vessel to a complete halt in outer space, and as he did so he sensed the creature come to a new awareness, watching warily with its visual sensors, looking for the approach of other podships.

Noah commanded the sentient vessel to disengage, and it floated free of the cosmic web, into the vacuum of space. He felt the creature grow calmer.

Keeping his eyes closed, Noah gazed telepathically into the boundless galaxy. He was startled to behold a sea of shimmering suns in much better focus than before.

"It's so clear this time. I can't believe it."

His mind soared, and he began to see other podships speeding along the pale green webbing. As before, he could only probe one of the sentient vessels at a time, so he telescoped in on several in succession. Again he saw their passengers and heard them speaking, but in much sharper visual and auditory clarity than previously. Now he could hold the links more strongly, as if his mind had suddenly grown talons and he was digging them in deeply. But the conversations were innocuous, and of no interest to him.

Instead, he let the podship connections go, and zoomed in on one of the red-and-gold merchant schooners he had seen earlier, the one that had gone into geostationary orbit over the Mutati world of Ilbao. Inside the vessel, he again saw the Mutati pilot, and once more Noah scanned the interior of the hull, where the peculiar array of gleaming alloy tubes remained.

This time, the tubes looked far more sinister. Able to probe deeper into the tubes themselves, he saw even more tubes inside. These were smaller, filled with dry chemical powders that were interspersed with unknown, solid elements and liquid-filled capsules, all connected to multiple warheads and trigger devices.

The schooners were not listening posts at all. They were warships, mobile bombs.

Agitated, Noah stretched his mental power and searched the other Mutati worlds where he had seen the strange vessels. Previously, there had been ten. Now he saw hundreds of them around the Mutati Kingdom, each orbiting a different planet. Expanding his search radius, he found more of the schooners in other star systems. In all cases, the vessels were near pod stations.

Another even more disturbing pattern became apparent to him: Mutati warships were surrounding the Merchant Prince Alliance.

In a frenzy, Noah zoomed one by one to the Earth, Mars, and Plevin Four debris fields, where worlds had exploded under mysterious circumstances. It was all becoming clear to him. The Mutatis intended to stage a huge attack against every Human-ruled planet, striking from all directions!

A woman's voice came to him from afar. Tesh. "Terrible weapons!" she exclaimed.

"You can see this?" Noah asked.

"I've been with you all the way, by touching the nerve center of the podship."

With his voice drifting across the cosmos, Noah told her how he had seen only a few of the schooners earlier, and how there were many more now. "They're getting ready to do something big," he said. "Each ship seems to have enough explosive power to destroy a planet, taking everything in the vicinity with it … podships and pod stations have been wiped out, too."

"That's why you examined the three debris fields," she said.

"Exactly. Those planets may have been destroyed in a weapons testing program. But why are you seeing this with me? Previously, I was able to take a mental journey through the galaxy on my own. And why is my vision so much clearer now?"

"I'm not sure, but maybe I'm boosting your power. During my career piloting podships, I have occasionally had paranormal experiences caused by my mental linkages to the creatures. From what we call sectoid chambers—and which you have been referring to as navigation chambers—we Parvii pilots gaze out at the galaxy through the eyes of the creatures. Usually, we see visions of deep space, the galactic webbing on which we travel and the like. But occasionally the podships seem to peer into alternate dimensions for brief moments, and we are taken along with them."

"What do they see?"

"Woldn teaches it could be the future, the present, or even the past, since Timeweb is linked to time and space." She paused. "Eons ago, Tulyans such as Eshaz held dominion over podships, before we took control of the sentient vessels away from them. Some Tulyans of today are known to have timeseeing abilities, but not all of them, only a few. Woldn theorizes that this power is linked to the abilities of the podships themselves, and that the capacity of the Tulyans to peer into time is weakening … from the lack of connection to their ancient allies."

"Regarding the Mutati war schooners, are we seeing them in the future or in the present?" Noah asked. "I assume it's not the past."

"They are in the present," she said flatly.

"How do you know that?"

"I am trained to know," she said. "There are certain indicators, which I am not at liberty to discuss with you."

"I'm supposed to trust you, but you keep secrets from me?"

"If I could reveal them, I would."

"They are Parvii secrets, then, not personal ones?"

"That is correct. But I do not have all the answers, not even close. It is most unusual—unheard of—how we are sharing the Timeweb experience. Perhaps it is because we are working together now, while previously we were at counter purposes. Perhaps I am boosting your power, and you are doing the same for me. We are in turn mutually enhanced by our connection to the podship itself, since we are looking through the eyes of the spacefaring creature."

She went on to explain that the multiple eyes of the big, whale-like creatures were concealed in its mottled exterior skin, and didn't look like eyes. But they were, nonetheless.

The two of them grew silent for awhile. As Noah and Tesh focused, the faintly green strands of the web appeared to them, only slightly visible and dancing ever so faintly in cosmic winds.

"We are seeing what is not visible to the naked eye," Tesh said. "An alternate dimension. Legend holds that it is one of many layers of Timeweb, that it goes deeper and deeper, beyond anything a Parvii has ever seen or experienced."

"Legends," Noah said. At his impetus, the image shifted, and he gazed at a miniature Tesh where she still stood inside what she called the sectoid chamber. He zoomed in on her tiny features, saw the classic loveliness of her face, the seductive green eyes.

"There are many ancient legends," she said. "Perhaps one of them involves what is happening to the galaxy now. If we survive this, I will ask Woldn. He knows all of the old stories."

"We must return to Canopa and tell the Doge what we have seen," Noah said. "Sadly, there are bigger enemies than Lorenzo or my sister. I fear a plot against all of humanity."

The eyes of the miniature woman widened. "Are you crazy? Lorenzo will kill us."

"I intend to go along. Remember, I am somewhat difficult to kill."

"Alone? You'd leave me in control of this podship?"

"Yes. Contemplating the worst, I've also left Subi Danvar in charge of the Guardians ... he understands the possibility that I might never return."

"Don't say that!"

"At a time like this, I need to be realistic. My Guardians are important, even critical, but I must give the Mutati threat an even higher priority." He paused, and added, "You may take the helm now. Just drop me off at the pod station."

"I hope you know what you're doing," she said.

Without responding, Noah relinquished his mental hold on the craft. He watched Tesh move into position in the sectoid chamber, and heard her utter the ancient *benedictios* of her people, like magic words.

The sentient spacecraft lifted onto the webbing, then came around like a galactic sailboat and pointed back the way they had come, toward Canopa.

With his mind separated from Tesh, Noah wondered if she had penetrated his thoughts moments ago, the inner workings of his mind, especially his intentions. He had been unable to read her thoughts at all, even though they had shared images of the cosmic web, and information from it. He hoped she could not read his mind, because if she could, she would not be pleased with what he intended to do. Noah had omitted certain key details from the plan he had related to her.

With the Merchant Prince Alliance surrounded by Mutati warships, Noah's ability to remote control podships was not enough. He could only pilot one of the sentient vessels at a time in that manner, while the shapeshifters were poised to load their superweapons into different podships and strike from hundreds of directions at once. To counter that, Noah had to take drastic action.

His podship sped toward Canopa. He just watched, anticipating that he could take control of the vessel away from the Parvii woman again if necessary, even if he was not physically on board it. But it occurred to him now, as it had before, that she might have new ways to block him, more than she had shown him before.

Noah had never felt entirely comfortable with Tesh, and didn't think he ever would. She and her people harbored secrets that went far beyond the brief time that he had been formulating his own.

Chapter Eighty-Six

Our universe is in chaos.

—From Eshaz's timeseer report to the Parviis

To avoid attention, Tesh brought the podship into one of the secondary docking bays of the Canopa pod station, where fewer vessels went and the walkways were not so crowded. As they connected to a berth, Noah saw no sign of the Doge's Red Berets.

Wearing a khaki tunic and dark, billowing trousers, Noah disembarked and passed through an airlock to the sealed walkway. He waited for Tesh to leave, then strolled to the other side of the pod station, making no attempt to conceal himself. Instead, he marched right up to one of the red-uniformed officers, identified himself, and demanded to see the Doge.

Within seconds, Noah was surrounded by uniformed men. They searched him for weapons and bound his wrists behind his body with electronic cuffs.

As they completed the arrest, Noah was startled to see the Doge Lorenzo del Velli emerge from an unmarked grid-copter just down the platform, leading an entourage that included the blonde Princess Meghina and a Hibbil attaché.

Just then, Francella Watanabe stepped onto the walkway from another vessel, and walked briskly to join the royal entourage. Suddenly she saw her twin brother, and stopped dead in her tracks.

* * * * *

No one noticed the young man in the dark blue cape who stood off to one side, gazing about furtively.

Anton Glavine had a lot on his mind, much more than the personal safety of Tesh Kori. Over the years he had seen Lorenzo del Velli at public appearances, without knowing that this powerful man was his own father. Anton had seen holo-images of his mother as well, Francella Watanabe, and had also been completely unaware of his own connection with her. At the moment, he stood only a few meters away from both of them.

His heart pounded as he watched his parents approach the prisoner....

* * * * *

"I am going to say something that sounds unbelievable," Noah said, "but I ask you to hear me out." He looked at the Doge as he spoke, then at his scowling sister.

"He's a madman, sir," one of the soldiers said, keeping hold of Noah by the arm. "A raving maniac. Shall I take him away?"

Lorenzo the Magnificent held up a hand. "Just a moment." And to Noah, he said, "You have two minutes."

"I can see far into the galaxy," Noah said, "into the very heart of the cosmos. Danger lurks out there ... Mutatis lying in wait in vessels that look like merchant prince schooners, planning some kind of an attack. They have terrible planet-buster weapons. That's how they destroyed Earth, Mars, and Plevin Four."

"Your words fall short of proof," Lorenzo said. The muscles on his face tightened, smoothing over some of the wrinkles.

"The entire galaxy is interconnected," Noah said, "in ways I never imagined. Somehow it allows me to travel mentally through deep space." Leaning close to the Doge, he exclaimed, "I can pilot podships!"

The soldier jerked Noah back and slapped him hard across the face. "See what I mean, Sire? A complete lunatic."

Flashing his gaze at Francella, Noah said, "Do you think I'm a madman, too, dear sister?"

As if thinking he had a weapon concealed somewhere and that he could still get to it, she slipped behind one of the Red Berets, and peered around the man at her handcuffed brother.

"I have bad news for you, Francella," Noah said. "I was near death and received a special healing treatment that changed me ... it made me immortal."

With that, the Doge and Francella laughed, as did the uniformed men with them.

"I think he's rather cute," Princess Meghina said, stepping forward and passing a hand through Noah's curly, reddish hair. "I'll bet I could kill him with love."

Narrowing his eyes, Noah smiled and said, "I'd have to be crazy to take you up on that offer, Princess. I hear your husband is quite a jealous man."

"Sometimes he is, and sometimes he isn't." She tossed her long blonde hair over one shoulder, and shot a bittersweet smile at the Doge.

Noah knew something about the dynamics here. Meghina and Francella despised one another, and were in competition for the affections of Lorenzo. The Princess was legally married to him and had born his daughters, but she was a famous courtesan, the lover of many noblemen. He had only married her for political reasons, to join the assets of two great houses. Reportedly his true affections were for Francella, but Noah couldn't understand how anyone could love *her*. Even Lorenzo deserved better.

"How about a little lie detector test?" Francella asked. With a sudden movement, she grabbed a puissant handgun from the holster of an officer and pointed it at her brother. The bright yellow energy chamber on top of the barrel glowed as she activated it, showing it was ready to fire.

"Go ahead and shoot," Noah said.

A soldier ripped open Noah's tunic, revealing that he wore no body armor.

"Mother, don't!" someone shouted. All eyes turned toward the young man in the blue cape and liripipe hat, who had gone unnoticed until now. He raised his hands in a halting gesture.

Two soldiers tackled him, knocking him to the deck.

Francella hesitated, and looked closely at Anton.

Noah could only imagine what his loathsome sister was thinking. She had never gazed upon her son before, not even when he was a newborn. But she might be noticing something familiar in him now, wondering if he could be the one she had left with foster parents. For a fleeting moment, Noah thought he detected a mother's love on Francella's face. Then she turned to stone, and ordered the soldiers to place Anton under arrest.

Coolly, Francella looked back at Noah.

"I don't think you should shoot him," Princess Meghina said, stepping between the brother and sister. "After all, he is a nobleman's son, and deserves a fair trial."

Francella's eyes turned feral. She shoved Meghina aside and fired a bright yellow charge at Noah's chest, ripping through flesh and searing a ragged, bloody hole. He fell back on the walkway, shuddered, and stopped moving. The electronic handcuffs sparked, and lifeless hands flopped loose.

Meghina and Anton cried out, as did several travelers who had gathered to see what was going on. One of them quipped facetiously, "You don't want *her* mad at you."

Francella glared in that direction, then looked down at her brother, with fascination burning in her eyes. An officer knelt to check the victim's carotid artery, and announced, "He's dead. Shot straight through the heart."

Slipping the gun back into the officer's holster, Francella said, "Just tidying up a little family business."

Doge Lorenzo grunted in amusement, then pointed down and exclaimed, "Look! He moved!"

On the walkway, Noah felt his own body regenerating, and the intense, burning pain of the chest wound fading. His cellular structure repaired itself more quickly than before, fusing bones and organs together and sealing the injury with new skin, while leaving blood on his clothing. In less than a minute, he rose to his feet and smiled stiffly at his sister. He still had nasty, bright red scars on his chest, but they were changing with each passing moment.

With a squeal, Francella stumbled backward, as if she had just seen the devil incarnate.

"I guess he passed his lie detector test," Princess Meghina said. "Bravo!"

"For your own good, you'd better listen to me," Noah said, stepping toward the Doge. "We need to set our differences aside and work together on this." The pain of the wound was already gone, lingering only as an unpleasant memory.

Reluctant to touch Noah, the soldiers did not attempt to intervene. Everyone stared in disbelief as the scars on his bare chest continued to smooth over and fade.

In his bloody, ragged tunic, Noah stood face to face with Lorenzo, and said to him, "I want you to send nehrcom messages to every planet in the Alliance. Tell them to fit every pod station with customized sensors to detect arriving podships, and guns to blow them out of space the instant they appear. This needs to be done fast!"

Noah glanced over at the Doge's Hibbil attaché, who had been attempting to conceal himself in a forest of much larger onlookers. "I understand there are Hibbil machines ... hibbamatics ... used for entertainment in every royal court. Can those machines be set to manufacture what we need, in a hurry?"

The Royal Attaché shot an uneasy glance at Lorenzo, but received no response from him.

"I think he can arrange it," Noah said to the Doge. "Have the sensors set to blast every podship to oblivion. Don't let anyone disembark, and don't let them off-load any ships—especially not any merchant schooners. The Mutatis have planet-busting bombs aboard them."

"This is preposterous!" Lorenzo said. "I will do no such thing. The Merchant Prince Alliance needs the podships; we can't destroy them. If the Mutatis have a scheme, we must deal with it in a different manner."

"There is no other way!" Noah shouted.

"The podships are living creatures," Lorenzo said. "If we start killing them, they will signal their brethren, and they will no longer serve our transportation needs." He stared with wild fascination as Noah's body continued to heal itself, eliminating the scars.

"Podships have already died," Noah said, "one in each planetary explosion."

"Then we should capture the disguised merchant ships," Lorenzo said. "The moment each podship docks at a pod station, we move in and … "

"We don't know how much time elapses between the arrival of a podship and the destruction of a planet," Noah said. "Maybe the Mutatis don't wait for each podship to dock."

Without warning, Noah felt a change of air pressure, and heard a firm click. A podship floated into one of the docking bays and connected to a berth.

Hanging over the walkway, a glyphreader panel flashed, calling for all Timian One passengers to board.

"Your ship, Sire," one of the officers said.

Lorenzo did not move.

Noah was agitated at the podship's arrival, and hoped that he had not given his warning too late. Were there any Mutatis aboard?

The passengers began to offload through an airlock, while vessels in the cargo hold slipped into the docking bay. There were no schooners, and no signs of Mutatis. But the shapeshifters were tricky, and might have disguised the vessels he had seen earlier.

Just then, a Red Beret lieutenant ran from the Doge's grid-copter, which had remained in a protective position, with its weapons activated. Reaching the Doge, the officer said, breathlessly, "Timian One has been destroyed, Sire! No one knows how." He held a mobile transceiver in one hand. "The planet and its pod station have been wiped out, leaving only space debris. We have eyewitness reports of people who barely escaped with their lives. The crew of a conventional spacecraft saw a huge explosion from outside the star system, then went to our nearest base to make a report."

"Sire, issue your commands to all planets!" Noah said. "Set up defensive perimeters at the pod stations! *Now!*"

Reluctantly, the Doge nodded. "Fire off a nehrcom message to General Poitier," he said to his Royal Attaché. "Tell him I need sensor-gun specifications, exactly as Mr. Watanabe described."

The dispatch was sent, and a short while later the reply came, with the needed information.

Suddenly animated, Doge Lorenzo barked orders to the Red Berets. All over the pod station, uniformed soldiers jumped into action. Urgent messages were relayed to the Canopa nehrcom station and dispatched all over the Merchant Prince Alliance. The podship floated out on its regular schedule, and Noah watched it disappear in a glimmer of green, into another dimension of Timeweb. Without the Doge or his entourage.

Noah hardly noticed his sister slinking away.

A short while later, the Doge's troop transports arrived, eerily silent in the vacuum of space. Hundreds of soldiers disembarked.

Soon the Royal Attaché was operating a hibbamatic to create the necessary sensor-guns, and furry little Hibbil technicians hurried to install them around the perimeter of the pod station, set to pick off any podships automatically as they came in. Merchant prince warships moved into positions in orbital space, near the station.

Noah felt a terrible emptiness in the pit of his stomach. Timian One! Billions of people had been killed.

* * * * *

Only moments after the defensive mechanisms were set up, a podship emerged from deep space in a burst of green light. The defensive units opened fire and the sentient spacecraft broke apart, scattering thick pieces of the fleshy hull in orbit, along with passengers and fragments from on-board vessels.

From the pod station, Noah gazed out on scattered particles and broken bodies floating in the airless vacuum of space. What looked like a merchant prince schooner floated by, with its hull split open to reveal gleaming alloy tubes and a dead Mutati pilot. Soon, two more podships appeared, and were blasted away. Then they stopped coming.

Almost oblivious to Red Beret guards beside him, Noah felt immense pain and sadness for the loss of life, but knew he could not have taken any other course of action. As a galactic ecologist, he hated having to interfere with the podships in this way, but he was convinced that the measures he recommended would save more of the beautiful creatures than they would harm. The same held true with regard to the members of other races who had to be sacrificed. Many more of them would die if he did nothing.

Noah's corporeal future was as uncertain as that of the rest of the galaxy. He expected to be taken into custody and blamed for the huge economic fallout that would result from the cessation of podship travel. Through their political wiles, Doge Lorenzo and Francella would spin the facts to make it look as if the entire crisis was Noah's fault. He didn't know exactly how they would fabricate the story, but knew they would.

Deep in his psyche, a part of Noah no longer concerned itself with such details, for he was evolving into something unique in the annals of history, changing moment by moment.

THE WEB AND THE STARS

Book 2 of the Timeweb Chronicles

Brian Herbert

Dedication

For my loving wife and incredible soul-mate, Jan. Thank you for believing in me wholeheartedly, and for never doubting me when I told you truthfully that I had dedicated Timeweb *to you, and the printer forgot to include that page. With Book Two in the series,* The Web and the Stars, *I am including that original dedication:*

Of all the books I have written, I owe the most to Jan for this one. You are the love of my life and my daily inspiration. Thank you for being so understanding while I spend much of my life in my study, taking fantastic journeys through space and time. You are a blessing beyond words.

Chapter One

A thought can be immortal, even if its creator is not.

—Noah Watanabe

They floated in orbital space, torn fragments of thick, lifeless flesh, drifting apart slowly in bright sunlight. Nearby, the powerful sensor-guns of a pod station waited for the emergence of another podship, in a flash of green light. But it did not happen. Now, following three explosions in a matter of hours … obliterating as many podships and all of their passengers … an eerie silence prevailed.

Looking through the porthole of a shuttle as it made its way through the carnage, Noah Watanabe felt the deepest sadness in his entire life. To his knowledge, nothing like this had ever before happened in history. He had been responsible for it and felt considerable guilt, but reminded himself that the violence had been necessary to prevent further Mutati attacks, and that podships and their passengers had been dying anyway, each time the shapeshifters used their super-weapon against a merchant prince planet. Entire worlds had been annihilated!

For millions of years the gentle Aopoddae had traversed the galaxy to its farthest reaches and back, making their way through perilous meteor storms, asteroid belts, exploding stars, black holes, and a myriad of other space hazards. The sentient spacecraft had survived all of those dangers, and might have continued to do so for the rest of eternity.

If not for the unfortunate intervention of galactic warfare....

* * * * *

They're shooting podships out of space!

In the millennium that he had been the Eye of the Swarm, the leader of the Parvii race, Woldn had never faced a crisis of this dimension. Now he had to make a quick decision and knew it would be the defining moment of his life, the event that would be remembered for eternity.

He flew from star system to star system and then back again in a matter of moments, accompanied by an entourage of only a few million Parviis, moving with him almost as if they were part of his body. Usually he had many more of his kind with him, linked telepathically, but now he needed solitude and room to think. This small group constituted his royal guard, and now he was performing the Parvii equivalent of pacing, flying back and forth across great distances.

His worries caused him to fly faster. He reached such a speed that he very nearly left the others behind. Just before flying into the heart of a red giant sun, he spun around and returned, speeding past his entourage again, in the other direction.

He knew what had led up to the podship crisis, the Mutati torpedoes that destroyed four merchant prince planets, attacks that stemmed from the long-standing enmity between the Humans and their shapeshifting enemies.

When his guards had finally caught up with him, Woldn had made his difficult, monumental decision. The slender Parvii had slowed in the spiral arm of the galaxy, and come to a dead stop in space. His defenders gathered around.

From there, where no outsider could see him, the powerful Eye of the Swarm communicated his decision to his Parvii minions, sending mental signals so powerful that they reached completely across the galaxy, to every sector.

Effective immediately, without regard to who was at fault for the destruction of the three podships at Canopa, the Parviis would cut off all podship travel to and from Human and Mutati worlds. No notices would be sent; podships would simply no longer go to those places. Throughout the rest of the galaxy, service would continue. Furthermore, all podships presently operating in Human and Mutati sectors were to jettison their passengers and cargoes, and report to a remote region of the galaxy.

He transmitted the telepathic commands, ranging far and wide. In those targeted sectors, the bellies of hundreds of podships opened in-flight and everything tumbled out, sending the unfortunate, unwitting passengers to their instantaneous deaths.

* * * * *

In a matter of hours, Woldn received a troubling report that his messages had not reached every Parvii pilot. He had feared this might happen, since the number of telepathic dead zones in the galaxy had been increasing at an alarming rate, running parallel with the disintegration of Timeweb.

Boarding a podship, the Eye of the Swarm prepared to broadcast from a sectoid chamber directly to pilots in other sectoid chambers, a method that boosted his signal strength. In Woldn's lifetime this had never been necessary, but it was one of the methods his predecessors had employed successfully in times of need. On the downside, it might injure the podship he transmitted from, due to the painful amplification of signal strength. But that was a risk he had to take.

Too much was at stake.

Chapter Two

In the vast universe, there are always hunters and their prey, either overt or latent. As a corollary, all relationships are only temporary, depending upon circumstances, mutual needs, and the availability of alternate sources of energy to satisfy the basic requirements of the living organisms. Symbiosis is only an illusion, and a potentially dangerous trap for the unwary.

—Master Noah Watanabe

As Tesh clung to the wall of the sectoid chamber at the nucleus of her podship, she guided the vessel along the gently curving strands of a deep-space web. Thinking back to a very special wild pod hunt centuries ago, she recalled her initiation into the ancient process. It had been in one of the darkest and most mysterious sectors of the galaxy, where hardly anything could be seen by the naked eye or instrumentation. But from an intense racial need, or survival-based instinct, Parviis on the hunt were able to see with a powerful inner eye—one that illuminated the fleeing podships as glowing green objects, like luminescent whales in a stygian sea.

She had been with other Parviis flying freely in space, millions and millions of them swarming to capture the feral pods, using neurotoxin stingers on the big, dumb creatures to subdue and train them. Gradually, as the podships were controlled and began to respond to the commands of their handlers, the Parviis cut back on the drugs, and drastically reduced their own numbers ... until finally one tiny Parvii could control each Aopoddae vessel.

Employing that procedure, Tesh was given command of her first sentient ship. It had been an extraordinary, exhilarating experience, and she came to feel that the captured podship was her very own, like a Human teenager with a pony. At the time she knew the ownership sensation was preposterous, because her people rotated piloting duties, but she couldn't help feeling it. Afterward, in due course, she passed the pod on to one of her comrades and went on to other duties.

Reminiscing now, she sighed and felt a profound, deeply satisfying connection with her people and their collective past. For hundreds of years Tesh had piloted countless other podships, but none had been as special as that first capture; like a first love, none had ever occupied the same place in her heart.

Within a narrow range, each Aopoddae ship had a subtly distinct personality, a slightly different way of responding to her commands. While all podships were similar in appearance, her trained eye could make out slightly different vein patterns on the skins, and with a touch she was able to distinguish varying textures. Inside the green, glowing core of this one, she inhaled deeply and identified barely perceptible musk odors, some of which reminded her of that first pod.

She was thinking how relaxing it was out here, speeding along the faint green web strands, hearing only the faint background hum of the sectoid chamber. Then the podship vibrated and slowed.

Using her linkage to peer through the eyes of the sentient vessel, Tesh saw that the web strand—ahead and behind—was slightly frayed, with tiny filaments fluttering in space, as if dancing on a cosmic breeze. Still vibrating, the vessel proceeded slowly over a rough section, making Tesh uneasy. She'd known the web was deteriorating but had never discovered the reason, and as a pilot she had never experienced anything like this before.

Presently the strand's integrity improved, and the podship accelerated again.

The web was a living organism, and over the eons slight aberrations had appeared in it, sections that were not perfectly symmetrical, but this was different. If she'd been a close confidante of the Eye of the Swarm, as she used to be, she could have asked him about it. Woldn was a storehouse of such information.

Parviis communicated with each other in a variety of ways. When flying in a swarm of only a few million individuals, they could beam thoughts to one another telepathically, and could communicate through speech when in close proximity. They could also transmit messages across great distances of space, from sectoid chamber to sectoid chamber, when piloting podships.

But since bygone times, the most important means by which Parviis remained in contact was through the extrasensory morphic field that extended outward from the Eye of the Swarm, reaching Parviis in all sectors of the galaxy. It was one-way, with only Woldn able to transmit freely across space with it, but for Tesh it had always been a comforting, wordless presence, an ineffable sensation that she was part of a larger organism, linked to the Eye and to every Parvii who had ever lived.

Recently, however, she had felt her connection to the morphic field weakening, and an odd, growing impression that she would one day be completely on her own. She wondered if it had anything to do with this podship she had taken control of without Woldn's approval. She was a podship pilot by profession, but was only authorized to operate one that had been captured by a Parvii swarm, under Woldn's supervision.

This Aopoddae was entirely different, a peculiar vessel that she had struggled against Noah Watanabe to control, and which he had eventually permitted her to operate while he took heroic action in an effort to save humankind.

Noah was unlike any *humanus ordinaire* who had ever lived. He had unfathomable powers, abilities that in some respects went beyond those of the Parviis, and of the Tulyans. He frightened her. She sensed that he could take control of the ship back from her at any moment, by reaching out telepathically and overriding her commands. It would do her no good to turn the podship over to the swarm; Noah could just take it back.

Her earlier experience with Noah had occurred during a hiatus from Tesh's duties as a pilot, an ongoing break that had not been relaxing at all, not with all of the problems in the galaxy, including the terrible war between the merchant princes and the shapeshifters. She hoped Noah was safe, but since their parting she had only heard hearsay about him, that he had been taken into custody by the Doge Lorenzo, despite his selfless bravery.

With respect to the podship she was guiding now, she had never heard of a Parvii taking command of one this way. Tesh knew the situation was a gray ethical area, but perhaps in her unique situation she could make a salvage claim to Woldn, and be awarded long-term control of the vessel. She had never heard of a case exactly like this one, but over the millennia some Parviis had received rewards for extraordinary exploits. She recalled some details of other cases, drawing parallels so that she might argue her case to Woldn.

Besides, what if this particular vessel had been contaminated by Noah's connection with it? It might make sense for her to keep it separate from others in the fleet, to avoid having all of them fall under Noah's strange, potentially dangerous spell.

But a sinking feeling told her this was an unfounded fear, a rationalization of her questing mind to come up with an excuse for keeping the podship.

Inside the green luminescence of the sectoid chamber, the background hum intensified, and she heard the Eye of the Swarm communicating with her over the strands of the podways. Tesh's heart sank. But it was not a message for her alone … it was for all Parviis in sectoid chambers around the galaxy, and with it she heard the distant squeal of Woldn's podship, from the extreme pain of the galactic transmission.

The urgent, drastic command of her superior appalled her. Despite the destruction of three podships by merchant prince guns, and the ongoing state of war between Humans and Mutatis, that did not justify Woldn's decision. He was committing murder.

Impulsively, Tesh guided her podship through deep space at high speed, searching the main podways for jettisoned passengers that she might rescue. Time after time she arrived too late, however, and found the horribly damaged, space-frozen bodies and other remnants of victims, from most of the galactic races.

And no survivors.

Trying to maintain her composure, Tesh speculated on Woldn's reasoning, that he wanted to discontinue all space travel immediately in the dangerous regions. Such a terrible way to do it, though. He should have ordered the ships to sectors that were not controlled by Humans or Mutatis, permitting the passengers to disembark safely.

Tesh was already considered something of a malcontent in the collective consciousness of her people. In the past she had voiced her opinions openly to Woldn, often to his annoyance. The last time she had defied him, he'd briefly suspended her privilege to pilot a podship. Something like that could happen again, or worse. But she could not worry about that; the stakes were too high. When she saw him again, she would be even more vociferous … no matter the consequences.

Stubbornly, Tesh continued to search the podways for signs of life, taking a few minutes longer. Then she set course toward the distant rendezvous point specified by Woldn, which for Parviis was the most secret, most secure place in the entire galaxy.

Chapter Three

Send nehrcom messages to the best research and development people on the Hibbil Cluster Worlds, and tell them we need faster-than-light spaceships to replace podships. Such a new invention is a matter of utmost priority. The entire Merchant Prince Alliance depends upon it.

—Private wordcom, Doge del Velli to his Royal Attaché

"Our prisoner was right," the uniformed officer announced. He stood stiffly at the center of the richly appointed office while the old nobleman, Doge Lorenzo del Velli, paced along a window wall.

They were in the Doge's new headquarters on Canopa, established as the capital world of the Merchant Prince Alliance after the Mutatis had destroyed Timian One. Francella Watanabe had leased him the top three floors of her own CorpOne headquarters building—for a steep fee, of course.

"Oh?" Lorenzo said. He paused and faced his subordinate, Captain Sheff Uki. In his tailored military garb the young officer had the appearance of a fashion model, but he was tougher than he looked. He was also irritatingly sycophantic at times.

Off to one side, the Doge's Royal Attaché, Pimyt, looked on sternly. The furry little Hibbil stood motionless, his red-eyed gaze fixed on the officer.

"Well, one-third right, Sire," Uki said. "The lab just gave me a report. One out of the three pods carried a deadly explosive device, with Mutati markings on it. Some sort of mega-bomb, our people are saying, a massively powerful torpedo."

"It might be the technology the Mutatis used to destroy Earth, Mars, Plevin Four, and Timian One," Pimyt suggested. The little alien scowled, scrunching his salt-and-pepper beard.

Lorenzo the Magnificent nodded, said, "I want the remains analyzed from every direction, turned inside out. Maybe we can build our own planet-buster and turn it on the slimy shapeshifters."

"That might be possible," Uki said, "but it would take time. We'd have to ramp up, with only bits of information available right now. There would be a big learning curve."

"What about the other pod stations where we set up sensor-guns? Any useful information there?"

"No reports of activity yet. We're getting a steady stream of nehrcom reports from all seven hundred ninety-two of them, orbiting the same number of worlds. No additional MPA planets have been lost, and no more podships have appeared."

The Doge rubbed his projecting chin. "So, Noah wasn't crazy after all. Thank the stars I moved quickly, instead of turning his recommendation over to the Council of Forty for study. Those noblemen would have set up committees and wasted a lot of time."

The officer flicked something off his own lapel. "You made the intelligent decision, Sire. If you hadn't moved quickly during the crisis, I daresay we would not be having this conversation at all."

"Most insightful of you to say that, Captain Uki."

"With your permission, Sire," Uki said, bowing, "I'd like to be excused, to order the investigation you desire."

Doge Lorenzo nodded.

After Uki left, Pimyt said, "He's too smooth to be an officer. I don't trust the man, so I've arranged to replace him. In my customary fashion."

"Kill him, then. But wait until he completes the assignment."

The Royal Attache smiled, and thought back. It was not the first time Lorenzo had authorized him to get rid of someone, particularly the sniveling sycophants who were drawn to the Doge like iron particles to a magnet. At times like this, whenever he felt respect for the merchant prince leader, Pimyt almost regretted what was about to happen.

Soon, he and his allies would make their move, and it would reverberate across the galaxy....

Chapter Four

Nothing is ever as it seems. For each apparent answer there is always another more significant one. This is true at every level of observation and interpretation. Thus, the final answer to any question is never attainable ... perhaps not even by the Sublime Creator.

—Tulyan Wisdom

For weeks, Acey and Dux had stayed in the Tulyan Visitor's Center. The globular, posh orbiter wasn't a spacetel as they had initially thought, since the Tulyans apparently never charged any of the dignitaries for staying there. According to a waitress that Dux befriended in the gourmet dining room, the place had more than a thousand suites of equal size and quality.

Dignitaries!

The first day they were there, Dux walked around with his chest puffed out, imagining how important he and his cousin were. In the corridors, they saw well-dressed personages of varying galactic races whom they imagined to be ambassadors, noblemen and their ladies, and even kings and queens by their appearances, replete with royal entourages. The gaping boys' imaginations ran to considerable extremes. When the two of them later told stories about this experience, any rational listener would undoubtedly discount their assertions, knowing how insular the Tulyans tended to be. There could not possibly have been so many galactic VIPs present at one time. But Acey and Dux, while having the good sense to avoid making any contact with the other visitors, had fun imagining who they might be. The boys also enjoyed picking out the various alien races they could identify, and marveling at those they had never seen until now. It only whetted their appetites for traveling more throughout the galaxy.

Acey kept saying he was anxious to leave for more adventures, and he'd been developing all sorts of plans about other star systems he wanted to see, and how he would get there. Every day he expressed his increasing restlessness to Dux, and to Eshaz whenever he looked in on them every few days. The Tulyan was performing important work for the Council of Elders, though he would not provide them with details. Whenever the teenagers asked him why they had to stay there, Eshaz said he felt responsible for their safety, and that he would be able to spend more time with them soon.

Soon.

Even Dux, who enjoyed the Visitor's Center far more than Acey, was growing suspicious of that promise. Eshaz's focus seemed to be elsewhere.

As time passed, Acey went to increasing lengths to avoid the comforts of the orbital center. Seeming to make a game out of it, he not only slept on the carpet instead of the bed; he refused to eat in the gourmet dining room, accepting only leftovers or slightly stale food. In addition, he wouldn't go anywhere near the very tempting amenities of the center, not the pools, spas, game rooms, or performing arts chambers.

At first Dux thought his cousin was going too far, but then he began to understand. The two of them would have to leave soon, and Acey's way of handling the overabundance of luxury was easiest for him. In contrast, Dux fully accepted the fact that their stay would not endure, but he went for the full treatment anyway, to "broaden his life experiences." For him, this made complete sense. So, each day Dux luxuriated in the pools and spas, permitting a beautiful *Jimlat* masseuse to give him treatments. He gorged himself on fine foods, and gained two kilos a day.

One afternoon as he headed for the main performance hall, Dux saw Eshaz approaching, lumbering along the corridor with his heavy strides. "Where is Acey?" the Tulyan asked. His scaly bronze skin glistened. He wore a tan cloak with a circle design on the lapel, which seemed to be his formal attire when working on important matters with the Council.

"Hey, Eshaz," the teenager called out, cheerily. "I don't know. Maybe he's walking on nails somewhere." He spoke of Acey's behavior in a humorous way, then noticed that the big reptilian looked upset about something.

Eshaz wouldn't tell him anything until they located Acey, who was sitting in the back of the main kitchen, eating with the workers. Acey, in a large chair at the head of a long opawood table, had been spinning grand yarns, embellishing stories of his adventures on board a treasure ship, taking his listeners to distant, exotic lands in their imaginations. The workers, all of whom were Tulyan, nodded their heads politely, but did not look that impressed. Acey, not seeming to notice their reactions, rambled on, looking like a child propped up on pillows in the Tulyan chair. He stopped when his cousin and Eshaz entered the room.

Seeing Eshaz, one of the most honored web caretakers, the kitchen helpers all stood and bowed respectfully. Eshaz bowed in return, then led the boys to a private dining room, where he ordered tea. When the beverages were delivered and the doors closed, he peered at the pair through slitted eyes, and said, "You young men are in my safekeeping for the moment. I trust you are being treated well here?"

"Like royalty," Dux said. "I've been using every facility. They make you feel like a prince here."

"That is our custom," Eshaz said. "We are a simple people, but we understand the needs of other races, such as your own."

"When can we leave?" Acey asked. "I know. Soon, soon."

"You are anxious to continue your adventures, I see," Eshaz said. "I can understand that, and I apologize for not being able to spend more time with you. But that will change one day." He hesitated, as if avoiding the annoying word "soon," then said to Acey, "It seems odd for a Human not to enjoy the comforts we offer. Are you ascetic for religious reasons? You follow the Way of Jainuddah, perhaps?"

In a sharp tone, Acey responded, "I'm not sure what you mean, but I don't have any religion. I just do what feels best to me."

"Ah yes, Human viscerality," the Tulyan said, nodding. He paused. Then: "I am saddened to inform you that four merchant prince planets, including the capital world of Timian One, have been destroyed by the Mutatis. As a result, Doge Lorenzo has set up a new base of operations on Canopa, where he is presently engaged in warfare against Noah's Guardians." For security reasons,

Eshaz did not tell them exactly how he and the Council of Elders had learned all of this, using their Timeweb connections.

"Timian One is gone?" Dux said. "I can't believe it."

"Along with Plevin Four, Earth, and Mars."

"Mars!" Acey said, leaning forward and accidentally knocking his tea over. "Dux and I saw what was left of it!" Acey sopped up tea with a napkin while relating how they had been aboard a podship that passed by the debris field, and the horrors that the passengers saw.

"We thought a huge meteor must have struck the planet," Dux said.

"No meteor," Eshaz said. "The Mutatis have a terrible weapon." He went on to tell the boys what he knew about Noah's involvement and the pod-killer sensor-guns he caused to be set up on pod stations orbiting all merchant prince planets, weapons that were designed to blast podships the minute they arrived from space, since they might contain Mutati weapons. Then he added, "Unfortunately, Noah is now a prisoner of the Doge."

"He sacrificed himself for the merchant princes, and that's how they reward him?" Acey said. "What kind of gratitude is that?"

"The ways of your race are most peculiar," Eshaz said. "Despite Noah's bravery, Doge Lorenzo and Francella Watanabe are speaking against him, blaming the cutoff of podship travel on him. They don't provide details or reasons, only the false assertion that it is the fault of Noah and his Guardians, and they will be punished for their misdeeds."

"They're lying!" Acey exclaimed.

"Of course they are," Eshaz said. "It is one of the things Humans do best. The truth is, Noah Watanabe is a most remarkable man, rare among the galactic races."

"We need to get back and help him," Dux said.

"But we cannot get to Canopa anymore," Eshaz said, "or to any other merchant prince planet."

"That puts a crimp in our travel plans," Dux said.

Looking out the window of the private dining room, watching the cosmic mists swirling around the Tulyan Starcloud, Eshaz said, "Podships aren't going to Human or Mutati worlds anymore. After they were attacked at Canopa, the creatures started avoiding potential war zones."

"The podships made that decision?" Dux asked, his eyes open wide. "A boycott?"

Eshaz hesitated, for he knew Parviis controlled the vast majority of podships and must have made the decision themselves. He just nodded, then pointed to the nearby pod station, in synchronous orbit over the starcloud. "For what it's worth to you, we can still travel throughout the rest of the galaxy."

"I've always suspected that podships are smarter than people say," Dux said, "that they're not really big dumb animals."

"I am not permitted to say much about them outside the Council Chamber. I will tell you this, however, my young friends. The Tulyan people have had a relationship with the Aopoddae going back for more years than you can imagine. In modern times our connection with that race has been much more limited than in the past, but I hope to change that one day."

Deep in thought, trying to imagine what the Tulyan was not telling him, Dux nodded, and gazed out the window of the Visitor's Center. The young man watched a podship leave the pod station. As the spacecraft accelerated, it became a flash of light that shifted from pale to brilliant green, like an emerald comet. Then it was gone, vanishing into the black void of the cosmos.

Chapter Five

*As Human beings, we are often not proficient at considering the consequences of
our actions. Rather, we plunge forward carelessly, taking the path of least resistance.
Short-term pleasure. But for the sake of our children and grandchildren, we need to
look farther ahead than the stubby tips of our noses.*

—Noah Watanabe, *Eco-Didactics*

With his ears attuned to every noise, Noah heard footsteps. Boots, but
he could not recognize the stride, the one foot scuffing. Maybe it
was another doctor coming to examine his condition. He hated
them for probing him every few hours, taking cell and blood
samples, hooking him up to machines.

For three days Noah Watanabe and Anton Glavine had been incarcerated at
Max One, believed to be the highest-security prison on Canopa. They were in
individual cells on separate floors, preventing the men from communicating
with one another. The facility, like the notorious Gaol of Brimrock that had
been destroyed with Timian One, fronted a broad canal, and had been built
around the same time, during the reign of Lorenzo's father.

To Noah it seemed ancient, with green-and-black grime and mold on the
stones, and lingering, unpleasant odors. Max One had an ugly reputation during
the decades it had been operating, with stories of tortured and murdered
prisoners. His father, Prince Saito, had always said they were only
unsubstantiated rumors, but looking around his own cell and walking the rock-
lined corridors whenever he was escorted by guards, Noah sensed that bad
things had taken place here, and might be occurring at that very moment.

On the third night he heard voices down the corridor, the authoritative
tones of guards and the whimpering pleas of a prisoner, followed by an ugly
sounding thump. Then footsteps again, and the dragging of a heavy object,
probably a body. The noises receded, leaving Noah with his own troubled
thoughts.

The fortresslike building echoed with emptiness. The muscular, red-haired
man climbed on top of a chair and looked out a high window at the canal.
Through the soft orange glow of electronic containment bars, he saw the lights
of the Doge's military encampment on the opposite shore, casting reflections
across the water. Even at this late hour, soldiers moved around over there,
tending to their various tasks.

Any fears Noah had were diminished by the fact that he now seemed
impervious to physical harm. In one of his most optimistic projections, he only
had to wait, and eventually he would discover a way to gain his freedom. His
enemies could not kill him. Or, he didn't *think* they could. Certainly, every
method had not yet been attempted. Not even close. He shuddered at the
thought of what the Doge's torturers might do to him, the unspeakable
suffering they might inflict on him as they performed cruel tests to see how
much he could endure. He might be immortal, but apparently that did not come
with invulnerability to physical suffering. He remembered only too well the
intense, searing pain of the puissant blast to his chest when his own sister shot
him.

Through it all, Noah at least had an avenue of escape into the paranormal
realm, and he hoped to perfect that ability enough to endure even the most
terrible atrocities that his torturers might visit upon him. Noah was able to break

269

away mentally for a few moments at a time, and sometimes longer, to take what he called "timetrance" excursions into the web. But the ability was erratic and unpredictable.

On an earlier excursion into Timeweb, Noah had been able to remote-pilot podships, one at a time. But when he attempted to do the same thing from the prison cell, his power proved unreliable. Like the tendrils of a plant, his mind would reach out into the cosmos, questing, trying to secure itself to a podship. Sometimes he could do it, though for only a few moments before the living vessel jerked away and fled into space. On other occasions he could not even touch one of the vessels. Such attempts disappointed him, because he thought he'd been making progress at unraveling the mysteries of the alternate dimension. But like a playful lover, Timeweb seemed to withdraw and elude him whenever it felt like it, dancing away and then returning, always enticing him, while remaining out of reach.

If only he could remotely control the podships on a regular basis, even one of them at a time, he might find a way of going after the Mutati torpedo weapons. But previous visions had shown him that there were hundreds of the super-bombs in space, surrounding the Merchant Prince Alliance. Noah would need to make a concerted, methodical effort, and he didn't have anywhere near the capability necessary to accomplish that yet. He also realized that even if he found a way of destroying the super-weapons, that wouldn't solve the underlying problem—the ability of the Mutatis to create more of the devices. He couldn't just treat the symptom of the disease. It went much deeper than that.

Despite Noah's frustrations, his ephemeral sojourns into the mysterious realm gave him something he could look forward to. Curiously, some of the paranormal occurrences, even if they lasted for only a few seconds, seemed to take much longer, like complex dreams that were experienced in an instant. But it was not always that way, judging by his own wristchron, which his jailers had allowed him to keep. Sometimes it was exactly the opposite, as longer trips seemed to pass in an instant, and an hour became five seconds. It was as if Timeweb, the teasing lover, was not allowing him to figure out patterns, not permitting him to exploit it.

Noah steeled himself as he heard the footsteps getting closer, and he vowed to outlive this prison, all of its wardens, and all of its doges. He would find a way to survive and live a full, rewarding life, a contributing life. *Life*. Such an unpredictable force, even in his own case, with his cellular system enhanced.

What did his tormenters want of him this time? Had they thought of some new experiment to conduct, yet another painful intrusion? He took a deep, shuddering breath. They weren't giving him enough time to sleep, but he had already noticed a diminishing need for rest, beginning right after Eshaz connected him to Timeweb and gave him the miraculous cure.

Now a new guard appeared on the other side of the containment field, with his features fogged slightly by a glitch in the electronic barrier. He fiddled with the black field-control box on his waist, cursing the trouble he was having with it.

Finally the energy field fizzled and popped, then went down entirely in a crackle and flash of orange.

Noah sprang into the corridor and tackled the guard before he could grab a weapon, slamming him to the floor. Noah was powerfully built, and had been doing daily exercises in his cell, trying to stay as active and strong as possible.

The guard was no match for him. With one punch to the jaw, Noah knocked him unconscious.

Just as he was removing the guard's uniform, however, he heard a noise and reached for the man's gun. Before he could unholster it, a bolt of yellow light knocked the weapon away.

Doge Lorenzo emerged from a side passageway, with half a dozen Red Beret soldiers. One of them fired a stun dart at Noah, hitting him in the shoulder and dropping him hard to the stone floor.

"We've been observing you," Lorenzo said. "Taking bets on what you would do. I won, of course."

Chapter Six

Truly great acts are never transitory. They last into eternity.
—Master Noah Watanabe

It had been a hard day of supervising digging operations in the deep tunnels of the subterranean Guardian base, and Giovanni Nehr felt the leaden weight of fatigue. He still wore the armored, machinelike shell that had been custom-fitted to his body by his robot companions, but it now had green-and-brown colors, like the uniforms of Noah's Guardians. All of the fighters under Thinker's command sported such colors on their bodies now. Gio remained the only Human directly under the command of the robot leader, although he was beginning to work more closely with other Humans all the time.

Subi Danvar greeted Gio in the main cavern, near one of the makeshift barracks. "You want to grab a beer?" the portly adjutant asked. He grinned. "You're the only 'machine' who will drink with me."

"I was going to take a shower, but what the hell. That can wait, eh?" Gio patted Subi on the back, and they trudged off toward the drinking chamber that the Guardians had named the Brew Room.

The bar inside the dimly lit space was a conversation piece in and of itself. The elongated, silvery shell of a decommissioned Digger machine sat on huge treads that were now bar seats on two sides, fitted with dirty pillows and mattresses to ease the discomforts that even heavy drinking could not mask. Thinker had devised a mechanized method of serving drinks, with glasses of beer popping out of openings all along the hull of the machine onto little platforms that formed tables in front of each seat.

As the two men climbed on a tread and sat down, Gio felt he was making good progress toward getting close to Danvar, who had taken charge of the Guardians in Noah's absence. Already Gio's strong personality had gained him an important position in charge of ongoing construction activities at the base, and he expected further personal gains. That goal was much easier to achieve now that he had gotten rid of those two troublesome boys, Acey and Dux, by drugging them and dispatching them into space. He smiled, thinking about the confusion they must have felt upon waking up inside a cargo box in some distant star system, and not knowing who did it to them ... although they must have had some suspicion. No matter, they were far away now and couldn't get back anyway, because podship travel had been shut down.

Just then a squat, female Tulyan entered the chamber. Zigzia was one of the few of her race who worked as a Guardian. Like Eshaz did before his departure, she performed ecological recovery and inspection operations. Now, she went to Subi and spoke to him briefly about an environmental-impact class she was starting for younger Guardians.

While ordering a beer, Gio adjusted his armor so that he was more comfortable. He rested his arm on one of the machine's nonfunctioning drill bits, a rough metal bar wrapped in padded cloth. Subi did the same with the drill bit beside him.

The beer flowed while men and women in Guardian uniforms chattered noisily around them, drinking and telling stories, using alcohol to relieve the stresses inflicted on them by the continuing war against the combined forces of the Doge's Red Berets and the corporate army of Francella Watanabe.

In the midst of that conflict, Noah's Guardian forces had been substantially restored on Canopa, and now amounted to thousands of Human and machine soldiers and equipment. All were housed in an elaborate network of underground burrows and large caverns that had been hollowed out by Digger machines that the Guardians had reclaimed. For the past month they had been raiding both Red Beret and CorpOne storehouses, and had also made a number of successful guerrilla attacks against troop barracks, weapons depots, and other military installations.

"I find it amusing and ironic," Gio said to Subi, "that we inhabit a warren of tunnels and caverns deep underground, with much of it directly beneath Noah's old ecological demonstration compound."

"By design, my friend," Subi said. He finished his fourth beer, then shoved the glass under a tap and watched it refill. "Noah chose this place right under the noses of his enemies, where they would not think to look."

"We lead a dangerous life," Gio said, "though we do have a multifunction scrambler system that masks our heat, sound, and visual signatures."

The adjutant nodded. He had set the system up himself, with Thinker.

Suddenly Subi Danvar felt the hum of machinery, but in a place where he hadn't expected it, in the Digger bar itself. With a series of percussive clicks, the drill-bit armrests retracted and the tread began to move, propelling the entire bar slowly to Subi's right. All along the tread, Guardians cried out and jumped off. Beer spilled.

Subi swore, using the most choice selections in his colorful vocabulary. He jumped up on a platform, then noticed that Gio was walking on top of the moving tread, going against the motion and holding onto his glass of beer.

After traveling a few meters to one side, still a good distance from the cavern wall, the mechanism stopped, and drill bits popped back out, still with their padding.

Calmly, Gio placed his beer on a drinking platform that was directly in front of him now, and sat down again on the tread. Looking over at Subi, he said, "A little musical-bar-stool trick we added," he said. "I suggested it to Thinker, and he thought it was a fine idea, to keep the Guardians alert to anything."

"They look more than alert now," Subi said, resuming his seat beside Gio. "In fact, I'd say they're in an ornery mood."

"Drinks are on me!" Gio said, as he watched people wipe dirt off their uniforms. "Set 'em up."

Actually, none of them had to pay for beers. It was one of the fringe benefits of their dangerous jobs.

Gradually the word got out about what Gio Nehr and the machines had done, and nervous laughter erupted in the Brew Room.

"When will it go on again?" a man shouted, as he climbed back up onto the tread.

"When you least expect it," Gio said.

* * * * *

Beer and hard drinks flowed, while Subi turned the conversation to the one that had grown closest to his heart, the whereabouts and safety of their missing leader, Noah Watanabe.

"I'd like to break him out," the adjutant said, "But we have conflicting reports on where he is."

"I've been on two of the recon missions," Gio said.

"Yeah, I know."

"Thinker got all the data, and doesn't think our chances of finding Master Noah are very good, since there are too many possible holding places for him. This is a very large planet."

"No matter," Subi said. "We'll keep sending out robots and people like you. I promise you, we'll find him no matter how long it takes. Some reports have him in one of the fifteen prisons on Canopa, or in one of the smaller jails, or even underground. I don't think they took him off-planet, not with the cessation of podship travel and the slowness of other means of space travel."

"Sounds like you've analyzed every detail yourself," Gio said.

"I have, and I'll never give up until we find him."

"I know you won't. None of us will. At this very moment, Thinker is undoubtedly assembling all available data on where Noah could be, and running probability programs. Unfortunately, the Master's captors have covered their tracks, and have dispersed many false clues as to his whereabouts."

As the buzz of conversation died down, Gio excused himself and walked wearily out into the main chamber, to the barracks there. Most of the other Guardians did the same, but Subi remained behind, nursing his last glass of dark ale.

Whatever method the Guardians used to rescue Noah, it would have to be a guerrilla strike … in and out quickly, like the successful attacks they had been making against Red Beret and CorpOne facilities. The Guardians, even with the inclusion of Thinker's small army, did not have the force necessary to fight their powerful foes any other way. They had to use cunning and subterfuge.

Finally, Subi trudged back out into the main cavern, moving slowly and purposefully through the low illumination. As he climbed the stairs of the barracks, his thoughts drifted back to Giovanni Nehr.

While Subi was impressed by the man's energy and ideas, he was troubled that he could not quite figure him out, could not quite get a comfortable handle on him. At times, Gio could be smooth and erudite, while on other occasions he mixed easily with the lowest ranks, the grunts and trainees. He certainly was an independent sort, with potentially strong leadership qualities. But something troubled Subi about him, something he couldn't quite grasp.

In bed, he lay awake thinking about it. The teenage cousins had not liked Gio, based upon their prior relationship, but so far those details had not surfaced … and probably never would, now that they had gone AWOL. Before that he'd asked the boys and Gio for more information, without receiving any satisfactory answers. Acey and Dux had probably gone off to join another treasure ship, or they were on some other space adventure. They were known to have talked about such things on the night before disappearing.

Gradually the calming effects of alcohol sank in, and Noah's loyal adjutant drifted off to sleep.

Chapter Seven

By their very nature, secrets are invariably contained in imperfect vessels that crack and leak, given the right set of circumstances.

—Lorenzo del Velli

On the strangest morning of General Jacopo Nehr's life, he awoke to hear alien voices jabbering inside his bedroom, as if people had seeped through the walls from somewhere outside. But as he sat up and yawned the voices drifted away, and finally fell silent.

Swinging out of bed, he shambled to a bay window, thinking it must have been a dream. Still, the voices had seemed to come from somewhere around here. At a window seat, he pushed a mobile nehrcom transceiver out of the way and sat down to gaze out toward the front walkway of his forested estate.

Rubbing sleep from his eyes, Nehr saw two of his blue-uniformed security men working with a large black dog, doing training exercises. The men did not appear to be concerned about anything, and Jacopo had observed this sort of activity many times before. Nothing seemed out of the ordinary.

A fuzzy, staticky noise near his leg caused him to jerk, before he realized it was the shiny black transceiver he always carried, which he had forgotten to turn off. But it never made that sort of noise, because nehrcom transmissions were always crystal clear, even when made across great distances of space.

Perplexed, he lifted the unit and fiddled with the digiscroll settings. He heard a static pop, followed by voices again, this time unmistakably alien. Jacopo did not understand the rapid-fire words, but felt a sinking sensation. The way he had set up the nehrcom installations around the Merchant Prince Alliance, all under Human control, he should not be hearing anything but Galeng—the common galactic language—and clear signals.

Something was terribly, terribly wrong.

Perspiration formed on his brow as his mind whirled. If aliens had taken over a nehrcom station and figured out how to transmit and receive, the signals should still be clear. It didn't make sense. The system was unproblematic the way he had set it up; it couldn't possibly go out of adjustment. It was either completely on or completely off, and trouble-free either way. Jacopo knew the technology well.

He also knew the security system. As the nehrcom inventor and the appointed Supreme General of the MPA Forces, this information was etched indelibly into his mind.

The secret workings of nehrcom transceivers were protected by internal explosive devices that would go off if anyone scanned or tried to open them. The booby traps were common knowledge, and there had been widely publicized explosions and deaths. They were not ordinary blasts either, because they left absolutely no evidence behind about the original composition of the transceivers. Every piece was left unrecognizable, with even the cellular structures changed. He had devised an extraordinarily clever method of protecting his priceless secret.

Nonetheless, something had gone dreadfully wrong.

Jacopo locked on to the mysterious signal and sent a tracer, bouncing the nehrcom transmission back to its source. A holo-image of one of the galactic sectors popped up from the transceiver, and floated in front of the astonished inventor's eyes.

The signal was coming from one of the Mutati strongholds, the planet of Uhadeen!

Utterly impossible. He rechecked, and rechecked. No doubt of the source, and he found additional transmissions going back and forth between Uhadeen and Paradij, the capital world of the Mutati Kingdom.

But how could that be?

A nehrcom unit could not be moved from its original place of installation, unless one of two people personally deactivated the detonator. No one knew how to do that except him and his daughter Nirella, whom he trusted implicitly. The two of them worked closely together, so he would need to confer with her about this disturbing situation.

Jacopo was developing an intense headache. His clothes were drenched in perspiration. He couldn't stop shaking.

The holo-image shifted as the transceiver tried to pick up a visual of whoever was talking on the other end. Nothing came across, no matter how much he tuned it, just static.

One unmistakable conclusion occurred to him. The Mutatis now had their own version of the system. But how did they accomplish that? They didn't seem to have perfected their version yet, since it was making static sounds. He recalled having had that problem himself early in the development process, and then figuring out the solution.

Another voice came out of the transceiver. This time it was in Galeng, but with a whiny Adurian accent, complaining that the Mutatis had no access to podships anymore, and could no longer launch "Demolio attacks" against merchant prince planets.

Demolio attacks?

Jacopo's pulse was going crazy. His thoughts could not keep up.

Thinking back, struggling desperately to comprehend, Nehr remembered one unfortunate leak in security two months ago. On that day, Doge Lorenzo's Royal Attache , Pimyt, marched into Nehr's office and showed him a holo-image of the internal workings of a nehrcom transceiver. Nehr had been startled half to death, but felt immensely relieved when Pimyt promised not to reveal the secret—and ruin him—if Nehr just performed a few innocuous tasks for him. Discreetly, Nehr had launched an investigation to determine the source of the leak, but nothing had turned up.

It was blackmail, to be certain. But the penalty had not seemed too great. Nehr only had to send occasional communiqués—provided by the Hibbil—to all planets in the Merchant Prince Alliance. The messages had been about corporate and military matters, the moving of business assets and war material around.

Nehr had been adhering to their secret agreement. It seemed to be some sort of war-profiteering scheme that Pimyt had come up with, a way of boosting his government salary. Nehr had seen countless examples of greed in the Alliance, and he had learned to look the other way more than once.

As for Pimyt, he was beyond reproach from a security standpoint, having once served as the Regent of the Merchant Prince Alliance, during a brief period when the noblemen could not agree upon the election of a new Doge. If he made some extra money during wartime, that just made him like so many others in the government.

And now, Demolio attacks against merchant prince planets? Nehr would have to discuss the matter with Lorenzo. Perhaps ... probably ... it had something to do with the MPA planets that had been destroyed.

But he couldn't discuss any of this with Lorenzo. Pimyt had threatened to ruin him if he revealed their little arrangement to anyone, and the little Hibbil had mentioned the Doge by name. Beyond that, Pimyt had insisted that Noah come to him first if anything unusual happened involving nehrcom transmissions. This certainly qualified.

Demolio attacks.

Nehr and Lorenzo knew the Mutatis had a terrible planet-buster weapon— was it called a Demolio?—and the Doge had taken steps to block it. Steps that had worked only too well, cutting off all podship travel in Human and Mutati sectors. But should Nehr keep this new information from him? Having made his bargain with Pimyt, Nehr had no choice. If any of this got out, he could be charged with treason, based upon an accusation that he had sold nehrcom secrets to the Mutatis.

He thought of his younger brother, how he had vanished. Could Gio have contacted the Mutatis and told them something about nehrcom technology? No, it wasn't possible. Gio had not been privy to the information, and besides, the two of them were brothers. At times Jacopo wished they had been closer, but it hadn't been in the cards. Now Gio was gone ... probably killed on one of the destroyed merchant prince planets. So many deaths in this war. So many innocent lives lost.

Nehr cursed at the situation in which he was caught, and shut off the transceiver. The resulting silence held no answers for him.

Chapter Eight

There is great skill in concealing your feelings of antipathy from someone you must deal with on a regular basis.

—Jacopo Nehr, confidential remarks

Throughout the Merchant Prince Alliance—on the seven hundred ninety-two surviving planets—there had been no appearances of podships whatsoever. On every one of those pod stations, sensor-guns were ready to fire, but they remained silent. People expected something to change at any moment, something big to happen. Time went by slowly and painfully for everyone, as if the clock of the universe had a sticky mechanism.

On every planet the citizens felt isolated, that they would never see distant loved ones again, and would never again be able to journey to their favorite places around the galaxy. It was like a cruel, galactic-scale version of an old party game. Wherever a person happened to be when the podships stopped was where they remained, perhaps for the rest of their lives.

When podships first appeared long ago, Humans and other galactic races had been hesitant to trust alien craft that they could not control, especially since they had no idea how they worked and couldn't gain access to their inner workings without causing violent reactions. But as decades and centuries passed, and podships (left to their own devices) kept transporting the various races safely to far destinations, the races had come to trust them. The sentient spacefarers became familiar to everyone, as their regular appearance at pod stations became a fact a life and of the heavens … like the sun seeming to rise in the sky each morning.

For a long time there had been talk of improving other space-travel technology, and recently there had been a rumor that Doge Lorenzo was calling for a massive research and development program to do so. Even barring that, it was still possible for people to travel on factory-made ships. But the hydion drive engines transported them so slowly in comparison to podships that it wasn't even worth comparison. It might be decades, if ever, before engineers came up with comparably fast vessels.

At least the Mutatis, with their solar sailers, were even farther behind. That provided some measure of comfort.

And, though Jacopo Nehr could not go directly to Doge Lorenzo with his startling discovery, at the risk of agitating Pimyt, he had decided to take another course of action. One that would not subject him to court martial and execution for hiding important military information during a time of war. As the Supreme General of all merchant prince military units, he had to walk a tightrope.

He was convinced that Doge Lorenzo could not be kept in the dark about this, but there were necessary channels to go through, to protect himself.

With a recording device hidden on his person, Nehr located Pimyt in the Royal Attaché's private exercise room, in the basement of the administration building. It was certainly the most unusual workout facility that Nehr had ever seen, and after passing through security he saw Pimyt on a machine that was a prime example of this.

The furry little Hibbil was on a stretching rack, resembling a torture machine of medieval Earth, except that this one stretched the body sideways, not head to foot, and there was no "victim." Pimyt, connected to straps on the machine, operated the controls with a brass-colored, handheld transmitter.

Nehr knew why. The Royal Attaché was one of a small number of Hibbils who had a chronic disease known as LCS—lateral contraction syndrome. Hibbils had a secondary vestigial spine that was no longer of any use, and in some members of their race, this spine had a tendency to compress in width, drawing other bones inward and causing the body to narrow, sometimes to such dangerous proportions that organs were crushed and death resulted. Some victims survived, but were crippled, no longer able to walk or use their arms.

For LCS sufferers, it was important to go through regular, rigorous physical therapy, as Pimyt did several times a week. It seemed like a primitive way of treating the condition, but reportedly it worked better than drugs or other methods.

When Jacopo Nehr approached Pimyt, the Hibbil was grimacing in pain as the machine pulled him from his left and right sides. His eyes watered.

"I need to talk with you," the general said. "I'm sorry to disturb you, but it's urgent."

"Well, what is it?" Pimyt pressed a button on the transmitter to increase the tension, and the pain.

"It's something the Doge needs to know, and it involves the internal workings of nehrcoms. You cautioned me not to discuss … certain things … with him, so I thought it best to come to you instead."

"You're not making any sense."

The chisel-featured man cleared his throat. "As you know, I keep a mobile nehrcom transceiver with me at all times. This morning I heard voices on it in an alien language. Tracing the transmission, I found it was going back and forth between the planets of Uhadeen and Paradij, in the Mutati Kingdom."

"What?"

"Toward the end of the transmission I identified an additional voice, speaking Galeng in an Adurian accent."

He brought the shiny black transceiver out of his pocket, and switched on a playback mechanism. Alien voices spoke for several minutes, followed by the Adurian-accented Galeng.

After listening, Pimyt said, "What's the significance of this?"

"There shouldn't be transmissions in the Mutati Kingdom at all, and the Adurian-accented voice is of additional concern. The Adurians are allies of the Mutatis, as you know."

"This is very strange." The Hibbil looked up at him with watery red eyes. "You must be mistaken."

"No mistake. I checked and rechecked. It came from the Mutati Sector."

"They stole some of the units?"

He shook his head. "Not possible, due to the detonators I rigged at every transmitting station. No, the Mutatis must have built their own transceivers. The transmission quality was fuzzy, but clear enough for us to understand what the Adurian said. You heard him. He spoke of the Mutatis no longer being able to employ Demolios—whatever they are—against merchant prince planets, since they could no longer use podships."

Pimyt glared up at him. "Are you accusing me of leaking the technology?"

Nehr's eyes widened in anger. "No, of course not."

"Because if you are, I can still let the details of your nehrcom secret out and ruin you when your business competitors find out how simple the transceivers are and start manufacturing their own."

"Not without piezoelectric emeralds, they won't. Those stones aren't easy to get anymore, not without podship travel."

Pimyt tightened the tension on the stretching machine again, pulling his body even more. He set the control device on a table, and said, "Maybe so, but it would still ruin your reputation as a *genius* inventor." Despite his pain, Pimyt laughed. "The great inventor Jacopo Nehr! A child could have put together what you did. No wonder you concealed the secret for so long."

"A child could not have cut the piezo emeralds with the necessary precision," Nehr huffed.

"Nonetheless, my point is well taken. It is a comparatively simple system, easily understood by a layman."

"Even so, the nehrcom system is one of our critical technologies, a military secret. You don't want to compromise that."

"What difference does it make now, if—as you said—the Mutatis already have it anyway?"

"Look, I don't want to argue with you. I know you're just making your own profits off this war, and that's fine with me. It doesn't mean you aren't a patriot at heart. We're both on the same side with the highest level of security clearance, and we have an understanding between us. As you instructed, I sent your communiqués to all merchant prince planets, and in turn you're protecting my business secrets. The Mutatis must have come up with the system on their own, and they haven't perfected it yet."

Pimyt pursed his lips, thinking. He looked agitated. His dark-eyed gaze darted around the room.

Nehr felt a mixture of fear and rage, and intense loathing for this Hibbil. But he concealed his feelings, not letting the furry little bastard see anything in his expression. Still, the inventor imagined grabbing the control for the stretching machine and torturing Pimyt until he was torn apart.

As Nehr savored the idea, Pimyt grabbed the control unit. "You are wise to come to me," he said. "I will discuss this with Doge Lorenzo, and we will order an investigation immediately. Do you think it could be a defect with your mobile transceiver? Could it have picked up freak radio signals?"

"I don't think so."

"Nonetheless, you will give me your transceiver, since we will need it for the investigation."

"But I am the only one capable of working on the system, along with my daughter, Nirella."

"Don't be absurd. A child could work on nehrcoms, and you know it. I have people I trust to do the work … under strict security clearance, of course."

"Uh, well, I don't know if…." He wilted under the Hibbil's red-eyed glare, and added quickly, "All right." Reluctantly, Nehr brought the mobile unit out of his jacket pocket and set it on the table.

Pimyt disconnected himself from the stretching rack and swung his short legs onto the floor. He walked around stiffly, then said, "As a reward and a token of our friendship, General Nehr, I am in a position to obtain additional tax benefits and other cost-saving arrangements for your manufacturing facilities on the Hibbil Cluster Worlds." His face darkened. "I am also in a position to do the opposite, if I wish."

Nehr stared at the floor. "With podship travel cut off, I'm not sure if I'll ever see those tax advantages."

"Then we'll come up with something else."

"I would appreciate that."

Without another word, the Royal Attache took the nehrcom transceiver and left through a side door. The meeting was over.

* * * * *

When he was alone, Pimyt listened to the Adurian voice on the recording again, confirming his own first impression. It was, without a doubt, VV Uncel, the Adurian Ambassador to the Mutati Kingdom.

He was a friend of Pimyt's … but not of the Mutatis. Uncel must have gone to Paradij on business for the clandestine HibAdu Coalition, which was working to overthrow both humankind and the shapeshifters, and he'd been stuck there by the podship crisis.

The Hibbil scowled for a moment as he wondered if Jacopo Nehr could upset his carefully laid plans. But the thought passed. Nehr was like an insect trapped in a narrow tube, with only one way to go.

Chapter Nine

We are receiving sporadic reports of nehrcom transmission glitches, of inexplicably weak and even lost transmissions. The problems seem to have nothing to do with our transmitting stations around the galaxy, since service personnel have checked and rechecked every one of them. The failures are few and far between, but remain troubling, since nothing like this has ever occurred in the past. In their first decades of use, nehrcoms earned a reputation for perfect reliability and strong signal quality.

—Confidential internal document, Nehrcom Industries

E arly one morning, Noah awoke to the noise of men arguing, in the corridor outside his cell. He tried to see them, but could not get an angle to see more than shadows against a rock wall.

"I received no notification of this," a voice said. "I will have to check with Warden Escobar."

"He won't be in for hours," a man said in a high-pitched, irritated whine. "We can't wait that long, and I have an authorization that supersedes him anyway. Now, open the damned cells!"

"Well, I don't know...."

"Do you want to answer to the Doge's office for your stupidity? They will not be kind to you, and could put you in one of these cells. If you are allowed to live. I am here on a Priority One assignment. Look at the authorization, you fool. If you can read."

"I can read, I can read." Noah heard papers rustling.

"Gad, you're an idiot. The authorization allows me to take any and all prisoners, as needed, for work details. With the cessation of podship travel, there is a shortage of slaves and imported robots to perform menial tasks on Canopa. Thus we are forced to draw work crews from Human and non-Mutati alien prisoners. Do you understand?"

Finally the guard said, "OK, I guess this is in order, but if there's any flak over putting Watanabe on work detail, you're taking it, not me."

"Yeah, yeah."

A loud click ensued, and then a slight dimming of the electronic containment barrier around Noah. The glowing orange bars disappeared.

"All right!" the high-pitched voice said, as the man pounded something metal against a wall. "Everybody out. It's time to go to work!"

The man turned out to be a work crew boss, with a squad of armed guards. They herded Noah and other prisoners out a side entrance. On the paved street, Noah encountered Anton in the midst of the prisoners. Approaching the younger man, Noah saw that he had a bright red mark on one side of his face.

"What happened to you?" Noah asked.

Looking around warily, Anton whispered, "They burned me with a laser on a low setting, threatened to blind me if I didn't confess."

"Confess to what?"

"To trying to assassinate the Doge. I told them that was preposterous. I only followed you to the pod station to make certain Tesh was safe. She was my only concern. I had no idea the Doge or Francella would be there, or that we would be arrested."

"No, of course not." Noah didn't comment, but remembered noticing signs of Anton's jealousy concerning his own relationship with the pretty young woman who had once been Anton's girlfriend. While Noah had reached an understanding with her over the control of a podship, he'd never had romantic intentions toward her.

"There's something I want to discuss with you," Anton said. "I've been having memory problems, an ability to remember some things, while other details fade away whenever I try to recover them. It's like ... like my mind is playing tricks on me."

"They tortured you," Noah said angrily.

"Yes, but I started having this problem right after they took us into custody on the pod station. I recall trying to go to sleep in my cell that first night, with thoughts churning in my mind, but my brain wouldn't work, at least not completely. I sensed things slipping away."

"I'm no doctor, but it sounds stress-induced," Noah said.

"We sure have a lot of that," Anton said.

A guard pushed them apart with an electronic prod and shouting threats.

All of the prisoners were loaded on a groundbus, and whisked away to a walled compound just outside the industrial metropolis of Rainbow City. Noah recognized the area. He'd been there many times, under better circumstances. As the gates opened and the bus surged through, he saw a high, round tower ahead, which he knew to be one of the nehrcom transmitting stations for sending high-speed messages across the galaxy.

The work crew spent the rest of the morning performing landscape work and spraying poisons outside the transmitting station. Supposedly, this was to keep insects, small animals and plants away from the highly sensitive facility, which required an almost antiseptic environment. Noah had heard about this procedure, and had always wondered if it was one of many ruses employed by Jacopo Nehr to throw anyone off track who might be trying to figure his transceiver out.

As Noah sprayed a canopa oak, he forgot where he was for a moment and smiled at Jacopo's eccentricities. Now the famous inventor was Supreme General of all Merchant Prince Armed Forces. Noah wondered how he was doing at that, and which planet he had ended up on when the podships stopped.

Preoccupied, Noah didn't notice a black robot watching him intensely. The robot moved closer...

* * * * *

Moments before, Jimu had come out of the nehrcom building, having sent a cross-space message on behalf of the Red Berets. He had no idea what the message was, only that it was high priority. By definition, anything sent by this means fell into that category. Afterward, he paused to watch the work crew around the building.

It was almost midday, with low gray clouds that threatened to dump their moisture on the land.

Thinking he saw a familiar face in the crew of prisoners, Jimu had paused to search his internal data banks. Now he brought up the information: Noah Watanabe, along with a summary of his biography and the charges against him.

The blond, mustachioed man working near him also looked familiar. Moments later, Jimu had his name, Anton Glavine, and all of the particulars on him, including his parentage: Doge Lorenzo del Velli and Francella Watanabe.

Concerned about finding such high-security prisoners on the work crew, Jimu did rapid scans on the others. None of them were anywhere near the caliber of these two.

The robot was deeply concerned. This was important work at the nehrcom station, but he didn't think that such high-priority prisoners should be included in the assignment. It must be some sort of a mistake.

He activated weapons systems on his torso, and took custody of the two men. "You will come with me," he said, in an officious tone.

Three guards approached, weapons drawn. Jimu had the prisoners behind him inside a crackling energy field, a small electronic containment area.

As he argued with the guards, Jimu opened a comlink to his superior officer in the Red Berets, and notified her of what he had discovered. "I thought it best to protect the prisoners, and then ask for instructions," he reported.

While the dedicated, loyal robot awaited further instructions, more guards appeared and surrounded him. None of them were robots, and he knew he had the weapons systems to blast through if necessary. But he maintained his mechanical composure. A standoff.

Twenty minutes passed.

Finally, Jimu's superior officer in the Red Berets appeared, a self-important woman named Meg Kwaid. She marched up to him sternly, followed by half a dozen uniformed soldiers. A tall woman with curly black hair, she smiled and said, "That was quick thinking, Jimu. This will look good in your personnel file."

She ordered Jimu to release the two prisoners, and when he did, she assumed custody over them. "This pair is going back to prison," Kwaid said.

Just before departing, she took a third man into custody ... the work crew boss who had removed them from the prison in the first place.

"No one told me they were high-value prisoners," the man protested. "I was only ordered to get the work done, and I didn't have the manpower."

His protests were to no avail. The man was put in a cell just down the corridor from Noah Watanabe.

Jimu returned to his own assignment, with his career path enhanced.

* * * * *

Among the Red Berets, Jimu's machines were unusual: they were "breeding machines" that could locate the necessary raw materials and construct replicas of themselves. Since joining the force, Jimu had been supervising the construction of additional fighting units, more than quadrupling the number of machines he originally brought with him from the Inn of the White Sun. All of Jimu's machines serviced themselves, and made their own energy pellets from raw materials, including carbon and mineral deposits.

Now, with the high demand for laborers, he was ordered to increase his production rate, adding a new type of machine—a worker-variant—to the fighting units he had been manufacturing. As with everything he did, Jimu completed this assignment with utmost efficiency. In short order, he had full production lines operational, producing both types of machines.

For this, and for his quick thinking in the Watanabe and Glavine extractions, he was promoted to a fourth-level Red Beret. This gave him access to more of the secret rituals, language, and symbols of the military society. Jimu just memorized them; he didn't really understand why people were so fascinated with such matters.

But Jimu had a continuing problem.

The sentient machines under his command were being mistreated, jeered at and kicked by many of the Red Beret soldiers, especially whenever the Human men drank. Too often, alcohol was thrown at the robots to see if they would short out—a bitter, sticky drink called nopal that the men favored.

Through it all, the machines still remained loyal to their Human masters, and so did Jimu. Their internal programming did not permit them to do otherwise, and they had fail-safe mechanisms to make sure nothing went wrong.

Chapter Ten

What is the highest life form?
What is the lowest?
The answers defy analysis.

—Tulyan Wisdom

In his cell one evening, surrounded by the orange glow of a pattern-changing containment field, Noah had plenty of time to think. The guards had modified the electronic field around him. Instead of traditional bars, now triangles, squares, and other geometric shapes glimmered and danced around him.

In them, he thought he saw images of Humans being blasted away or maimed, with their arms and legs flying off. Since he had performed amazing mental feats himself, it occurred to him that he might be able to focus and catch what he thought were subliminal messages in the containment field, cruel tricks employed by his captors. Noah tried this for a while, but found himself unable to do so.

His thoughts drifted to what kept him busy most of the time when he was alone, envisioning ways he might escape from this dismal cell in Max One. Intermittently he had been able to accomplish this, but only in his mind, where he took fantastic but unpredictable space journeys. And always when he returned from those sojourns into the realm of Timeweb, he was faced with a stark reality, the imprisonment of his body.

As before, the space journeys were like timetrances, and he looked forward to them. They were increasingly unpredictable, though, in that he could never predetermine how long he would remain in the alternate dimension. Sometimes, after only a few moments of mental escape, he felt himself kicked out, dumped back into his cold cell.

One morning Noah lay on his bunk, staring at the ceiling. A spider was working up there, using its legs to spin an elaborate, wheel-shaped web to trap insects. The spider went down the web, working for several moments with one pair of legs, then alternating with others. Then it went back up.

From somewhere, Noah heard a terrible scream. His heart dropped. He hoped it was not Anton. He also prayed that the injury was not too severe. But the scream told him otherwise.

As far as Noah was concerned, the Doge was the worst of all men, not only for his cruelties to prisoners, but for the damage his Merchant Prince Alliance inflicted upon the environment. The ecology of each planet—like the cellular integrity of each prisoner—was a living thing, deserving of respect and care.

Noah became aware of the spider again. It had lowered itself on its drag line and was suspended just overhead, staring at Noah with multi-faceted eyes. Noah saw intelligence there, and perhaps more.

This tiny creature seemed, in many respects, superior to a Human being.

Abruptly, the spider rose on its line and returned to its web. Noah found himself struck by the perfection of the gossamer structure, so uniquely beautiful and astounding in the way it had been spun. He found his mind expanding on its own, spinning into the cosmos and onto the faintly green cosmic webbing that connected the entire galaxy. As if he were a podship himself, he sped along one strand and then another, changing directions rapidly, vaulting himself out into the far, dark reaches of space.

He saw a podship and caught up with it, but he could not gain control of it. He was, however, able to seep inside, and entered the central sectoid chamber. There, he saw a tiny Parvii pilot controlling the creature from a perch on the forward wall of the chamber.

Tesh! he thought, feeling a rush of excitement.

She looked to one side, and then to another, as if sensing his presence.

Noah noticed something different this time, compared with prior occasions when he had journeyed around the cosmos. A faint mist formed where he was, and it took the barely discernible shape of his own body, dressed in the very clothing he had on now. Could she see this? Was it really occurring, or was it only in his imagination?

Drifting closer to her, he dwarfed her with his presence. And he whispered to her, but to his own ears the words were ever so faint, as if coming from far across the cosmos. "I've missed you," he said. "Can you hear me? I'll tell you where I am."

No reaction.

He said it again louder, and this time he added, "Have you been thinking about me, too?"

She looked to each side again, and then turned her entire body and looked around the sectoid chamber.

"You heard me, didn't you?" he said.

A perplexed expression came over her. She looked toward him, but in an unfocused way, as if peering beyond him.

To check her, Noah moved around the chamber, and after a moment's delay each time, her gaze followed his movements. "What do you see?" he asked.

No reply. Obviously, she could not make out the words, and he didn't think she could discern his ghostly mist, either. But she seemed to be sensing something. How far did it go?

On impulse, he floated to her side. Since his physical form (as he saw it) was much larger than hers, and he wanted to kiss her, he brought his mouth as close to hers as he could and let his lips touch hers. Or seem to.

Instantly, she jerked her head back, then brought a hand to her mouth.

"Who's there?" she demanded.

He kissed her again in the mismatched way, like a hippophant kissing a tiny bird. This time she didn't pull her head back, but left it in position, and even moved toward Noah just a little, as if cooperating in the cosmic contact.

"Noah?" she said as they separated. "Is that you?"

In response, he attempted to kiss her again, but this time she showed no reaction at all. He tried again, but still she didn't respond. "Tesh?" he said. "Did you feel that?"

Abruptly she turned away, and resumed her attention to her piloting task. "I'm going crazy," she said. "That wasn't Noah. It couldn't be."

"But it is me!" he shouted. Now he didn't hear the words at all, not even the faintest sound. And looking down at his misty form, he saw that it was fading, disappearing entirely.

In a fraction of a second, Noah found himself back in the prison cell, wondering what had just occurred.

Chapter Eleven

Never let down your guard, especially in time of war.

—Mutati Saying

T he violence had been totally unexpected.

On the grounds of the Bastion at Dij, the Emir Hari'Adab strolled along a flower-lined meadow path, skirting a grove of towering trees. A large white bird flew beside him, alternately soaring upward into the cerulean sky and then back down again, keeping pace with him.

But it was not really a bird. It was a shapeshifter, a female aeromutati with whom he had a special relationship. For the moment, she left him to his troubled thoughts.

In contrast, Hari'Adab was a shapeshifter who moved along the ground, a terramutati like his father the Zultan. As a boy growing up on Paradij, he had always intended to do what was expected of him. Since Zultan Abal Meshdi and Hari's late mother, Queen Essina, had little time for him, the boy had been raised by tutors, always taught the proper way of doing things. In particular, he was taught to show respect for his elders and for the rules of Mutati society that had been laid down by the wise zultans and emirs of countless generations.

In Mutati society, a man kept his word, and that imperative started at an early age, as soon as he could speak and understand the rule of law, and the unwritten code of honor that was passed on from generation to generation by word of mouth. By those standards he had pledged to uphold important traditions, the threads that held together the powerful social fabric of his people.

Throughout his young but eventful life, though, Hari had expressed more than his share of defiance, bordering on rebelliousness. He had steadfastly refused to use an Adurian gyro that his father gave to him, a foreign-made mechanical device that was supposed to help him make better decisions. In the past couple of years it had become very popular in Mutati society, particularly among the young, but Hari didn't trust the Adurians or their inventions. That race, from far across the galaxy and supposedly allied with the Mutatis, had insinuated themselves on Mutati society in a short period of time, bringing in their loud music, garish clothing, noisy groundjets, and a whole host of other products.

It didn't make sense. Hari had been brought up to respect Mutati traditions, but his father had permitted an alien culture to change what it meant to be a shapeshifter, causing Mutati citizens to neglect their own civilization and pay homage to another. It was a terrible shame, in Hari's opinion, and he hoped to reverse it when he became Zultan himself one day. He had no idea when that might occur, or if it would ever occur. His father often expressed his displeasure and his disappointment in him.

It wasn't just a disagreement between the two men over cultural matters. It went much deeper, as Hari had frequently expressed his opposition to the war against the Merchant Prince Alliance. During one argument over this the month before, the Zultan had called him a traitor. A traitor! Hari had been in complete and utter disbelief.

"If that's what you think I am, have me executed," the young Emir had said. "Obviously, I'm not fit to be your successor."

Pausing by a gold-leaf lily pond, Hari saw the white bird soar to the other side of the water and perch in a tree. In his preoccupation, Hari had not noticed that he was being watched. And that he was in great danger.

"Now, now," Abal Meshdi had said. "At least you've expressed your opinions only to me, and have not gone public with them. You have shown respect for your elders, following the time-honored rules in this regard. Contrary to your belief, I do not want you to agree with everything I say or do. That is only in public. I warn you, do not dishonor me in front of others, or it will be the last thing you ever do."

"I understand, Father. But I must be honest with you. I must tell you what I think is best for you and for our great race. Our culture is being watered down by the Adurians, and they constantly urge us to war. Why do we need to listen to them?"

"We were at war with the Humans long before we ever formed an association with the Adurians, and long before we ever brought them in as advisers."

"But without their influence, we might reach a peace accord with the merchant princes. I do not trust that VV Uncel. He is more concerned with his own Adurian people than with ours. I fear he will be our downfall."

"You worry too much, my son."

"You don't worry enough."

"That is all we will discuss of this. Perhaps the next time we talk, you will have grown a little wiser."

The conversation had ended like that, with the elder's condescending remarks, his expressed hope that Hari would eventually fit the mold that he wanted. Privately, Hari called it the "stupidity mold," and he vowed never to pour himself into it.

The two of them had not seen one another since the podship crisis, though that did not cut off contact. They had been talking over the new (though staticky) nehrcom system several times a week, and could visit one another by taking a solar-sailer journey of a little over a month. They were in adjacent solar systems, not that far apart, or Hari would have been completely isolated from him. That might have been preferable in some regards, though he did not want to run from Mutati society; he wanted to influence it and improve it, especially the moral underpinnings.

The bird lifted off from the tree branch and approached him, drifting tentatively. Hari smiled at her, and saw the return sparkle in her eyes, and the softness of her features, a different version of her original countenance. Parais d'Olor was his beloved, the one Mutati he cared more about than any other. She landed near him on a patch of grass and tucked her wings.

He looked away. Now Hari was doing something that was certain to rouse the royal ire of his father if he ever discovered it. The young Emir had a secret life. He was not a traitor, or anything like that. Rather, he was a patriot and only wanted the best for his people. That included the welfare of all three factions of Mutati society—the terramutatis, the aeromutatis, and the hydromutatis. Too often his father favored his own racial subtype over the others, but Hari believed in equality of the three groups.

In the past, both aeromutatis and hydromutatis had ruled Mutati society from the Citadel of Paradij. The legendary palace had been built by an aeromutati zultan, Vancillo the Great. For two centuries, that flying shapeshifter had ruled a peaceful Mutati realm, a period known as the Pax Vancillo ... until the Terramutati Rebellion. The terramutatis had always been the most aggressive of the three groups, and had favored going back to war against the Humans. Abal Meshdi's great grandfather, Iano Meshdi, had led the revolt, citing infractions committed by Human society against Mutati worlds and the shapeshifter race … especially military and economic incursions against Mutati planets. The old zealot had drawn a line in space, saying he would not permit Human civilization to encroach any farther into Mutati society.

How ironic that Abal Meshdi had drawn no such line with the Adurians, who were obviously an inferior race, with poor military forces and a decadent social structure. Hari didn't understand what his father saw in them. They should be taking advice from Mutatis, not the other way around!

As he continued on the meadow path with flowers all around him sparkling in the sunlight, he hardly noticed the natural beauty. The aeromutati flew beside him again, this shapeshifter that had taken the form of a large white bird. In her way of infinite patience and understanding, Parais d'Olor had tried to converse with him earlier, but she had given up for a time, saying she would wait until his mood lifted.

Parais was the most lovely shapeshifter he had ever seen, though his father would certainly not concur, since the *Holy Writ* required a highborn Mutati to marry within his own racial subtype. (He could have mistresses of the other types, but any resultant pregnancies had to be aborted.) Despite the expectations, Hari had never been attracted to terramutati girls. From the first moment he laid eyes on an airborne female, he'd been fascinated. And when he met Parais, he stopped looking at other girls at all.

In her natural form Parais had the folds of fat, tiny head, and oversized eyes of any Mutati, but instead of arms and legs she had functional wings. She could also metamorphose into any number of flying creatures, such as the one she favored now. Her movements were always graceful, like those of an aerial dancer.

"Come with me, my love," she finally said. "I am a great white gull, with a built-in saddle on my back for you to ride. Let me take you to our favorite beach-by-the-sea."

In no mood for a holiday, Hari shook his head. He did not notice a shadowy creature moving along beside them in the woods, just out of view.…

Parais flew toward the woods and fluttered between tall evergreen trees. Moments later, she returned.

"Someone is watching us," she said. "I saw no one, but I know they are there."

He stopped and looked in that direction. "How do you know?"

"I sense it." She tucked her wings and landed beside him.

"But you are not telepathic; you are not a hydromutati … a Seatel."

"Nonetheless, I sense something," she said, looking nervously in that direction. "Come with me now. Let me fly you away from here."

Hari was not pleased, and not afraid. "Someone doesn't approve of our relationship," he said. "Just like that time in your village. Is it one of your people again? How did they get past security?"

"I … I'm not sure who it is or how he got here. I just think we should go."

"This is my home. I'll be damned if I'll run from my own home!" He marched toward the woods.

She flew beside him. "Don't!" she said. "Please listen to me. At least summon the guards."

"We have a right to life without being spied on, without Mutatis questioning our lifestyle, the choice of whom I wish to love. I've always tried to follow the rules, but I keep finding too many reasons not to. Somewhere along the line, life got in the way, I guess. Now let's see who's spying on us."

Consumed with rage against the intruder, Hari heard her saying something about danger, but he didn't interpret that as physical peril, only as a risk to his reputation, and hers. As he rushed headlong into the woods, he wished he wasn't even a Mutati, that he was a Human instead, and that he had at least crossed over and changed his racial appearance, as Princess Meghina of Siriki had done. She had been widely scorned in Mutati society for doing that, but she had followed her heart. She had shown tremendous courage, and he had always admired her for it.

Just then a *Xouepop* rang out, and in the trees Hari saw the distinctive, silvery muzzle flare of a jolong rifle. A projectile whizzed past his head, and ripped a nearby sapling in half. As he ducked, another shot rang out and thunked loudly into a tree.

Hari heard Parais scream behind him.

The Emir did not travel unarmed. He pulled a white handgun out of his tunic, and pressed the top of the handle to activate it. "Did you see who shot at us?" he asked her.

"Mutati. No wings." Parais pointed. "He's on the move. Look!"

Seeing the slight movement of underbrush, Hari set the weapon's seeking mechanism so that it would home in on the heat signature of a Mutati. It was a gun his father had obtained on special order, one that only the elite of their society had.

Hari didn't even have to aim. He just fired in the general direction he wanted, and saw a flash of fire tear through the underbrush. A piercing scream echoed through the woods.

"Get on my back," Parais urged.

The Emir did so, and clung to the bar of the saddle. Parais extended her wings partway and lifted off powerfully through the trees, rising higher and higher until the two of them cleared the treetops. She had taken additional mass from nearby vegetation to become a large bird, but there were limits that she could not exceed in this process. From medical tests, Hari knew that she—like most other Mutatis—could only become large enough to carry one adult shapeshifter on her back, and that any additional mass absorption would be dangerous to her cellular structure and to her life.

Below, he saw his palace guards pour out of the bastion, running toward the woods. He sent them a telebeam message, telling them what had happened, and ordering them to find out who had shot at him.

Parais opened her white wings to full extension and beat them rhythmically, heading west.

"They'll investigate," Hari shouted, raising his voice over the sound of the wind. "Even if the assassin survives and escapes—or if his confederates take the body away—I know I hit him, and he'll leave cellular material behind. With the DNA of every Mutati on file, we'll find out who did it."

"But what if your father sent an assassin after you?" she asked. "Maybe he found out about us." She looked back as she flew, her features profiled against the blue, cloudless sky. Her blond hair flowed like a mane on the back of her neck.

"The Zultan wouldn't kill me for loving an aeromutati, though he might disinherit me for it. He has threatened to kill me if he gets tired of me, but I think it's all bravado. He wouldn't sentence his only heir to death for that."

"What happened, then?"

"Assuming it's not one of your old boyfriends, I'd say the merchant princes activated a sleeper agent. Now, where are you taking me?"

"I told you where I wanted to go ... and now you're in no position to argue."

An hour later Parais circled over a familiar, isolated stretch of red sand beach, scattered with driftwood. Aquamarine waves lapped gently against the shore.

The lovers had been there many times before, in utmost secrecy.

Chapter Twelve

It is said that twins have a unique, even clairvoyant connection. I have never delved into that realm, at least not to my knowledge. Still, I sense something horrible is going to happen to my brother. In fact, I'm certain of it.

—Francella Watanabe

For two decades Francella Watanabe had done her best to forget her son and only child, to set aside the fleeting images she'd had of him as a newborn baby, the dangerous, unintended glimpses she'd stolen before having him removed from her sight and taken away forever.

Now, a burly guard escorted Francella into a side entrance of the prison where her son was incarcerated. She felt leaden, uncertain if she wanted to go through with this. But she kept pace.

In due course, Francella had learned the name given him by his foster parents ... Anton Glavine ... along with bits and pieces about what he was doing and where he was. She'd heard he was a member of Noah's interplanetary environmental force, and eventually that Noah and Anton were holed up on the orbital Eco Station. They had fled there after an incident in which her own Corp One forces—in a joint venture with the Doge's Red Berets—attacked her brother's Ecological Demonstration Project. She'd known her son was on the orbiter but had wanted to destroy it anyway, since her hatred for her brother was so much greater than any love she felt for Anton.

But Lorenzo, upon learning of Anton's whereabouts, had refused to attack the orbiter. Anton was his son, too. What an unfortunate set of circumstances. She had thought for sure that she would kill her brother there, finally cornering him and wiping him out of existence. It had been an infuriating wrinkle in her plans.

Then, in another unexpected twist that followed, she had seen Anton Glavine at the Canopa pod station, where she'd encountered Noah only moments before. She had been trying to kill her brother again, this time by shooting him in the chest... but like a demon, Noah had come back from the dead and regenerated his flesh. Damn him! In all the commotion, Anton had been arrested and taken into custody by the Red Berets.

Since that time Francella had been thinking about her son, unable to get his face out of her mind. After all these years, seeing her own child! He'd grown into a fine-looking young man, with features that reminded her of Doge Lorenzo.

Following Anton's arrest, she had obtained a DNA test on him to be certain, and it confirmed his parentage, showing the undeniable genetic markers. Francella had paid to keep the report secret, but apparently no amount of money was enough for that. She should have known that nothing was secret from the Doge, especially when it concerned his own son.

Lorenzo had brought the report to her himself, slapping it down in front of her. It had not changed anything. For months the two of them had assumed Anton was their son based upon available information, and now they knew for sure.

The Doge might even know what she was doing at this very moment, wearing a black cape as she hurried through the dark of the night. If so, he wasn't doing anything to stop her....

The guard pointed down a rock corridor, and allowed Francella to walk through it by herself. As instructed, she halted at the end, and peered through the soft orange glow of the electronic containment field of a cell.

Anton sat in orange illumination, on the edge of his bunk. His blond hair was combed straight back, and he had a bound copy of the quasi-religious *Scienscroll* open on his lap. Looking up at her, he quoted from one of the verses: "'The night washes men's souls; it is the time of true honesty.'"

She considered the passage, recalling a bygone time when her late mother had read such verses to her and Noah in their childhood, while they sat at her feet. The words sounded familiar.

"I know who you are," Anton said, "and I have no more feelings for you than you have ever shown for me."

During the past two decades, Francella's aides had sent regular support payments for her son, though she had tried to remain detached from him emotionally. But seeing him at the pod station, something had changed, making her want to see him and speak with him.

"I don't blame you for saying that," she responded. Then, unable to deal with her own emotions, she whirled and left.

Chapter Thirteen

It is the Second Law of Thermodynamics. All things move from structure to waste, from useful energy to energy that is no longer available. Timeweb, the infrastructure of the galaxy, is no exception. It has fallen prey to the dark, degenerative forces of Entropy.

—Report to the Tulyan Council of Elders

Tulyan Starcloud ...

Having been ordered to perform timeseeing duties for the Parviis, Eshaz had been conducting sessions in an anteroom of the Council Chamber. Each of these comparatively small enclosures was different from the others, and—if any Tulyan desired more privacy—each anteroom was capable of floating freely in the sky around the inverted dome of the central chamber. At a thought-command, Eshaz could engage or disengage from the dome. In a very real sense this was more a perceived sense of privacy, and an ephemeral one, since at a touch Tulyans could read the thoughts of each other, or of other races. But the private anterooms permitted some Tulyans more mental latitude in their creative and paranormal thinking abilities, a temporary respite from the constant mental linkages around them.

Thus far, over a period of days, Eshaz had been unable to timesee anything, and Woldn had grown increasingly upset. It had been Eshaz's intention from the beginning not to report anything to the Parviis, but he had honestly attempted to timesee anyway, to no avail. He heard the buzzing discontent in the background as he tried to focus, and knew in his heart this would be another failed day.

The sound grew louder. Opening his eyes, Eshaz saw Woldn and his band of tiny, flying Humans hovering in front of him, their buzzing sounds coming through some internal vibration of their bodies, since they had no wings. "We've had enough of this!" Woldn said. "You're faking!"

Eshaz withheld his comments, and his energy. Calmly, he sent a thought-command, and the anteroom floated back into its connecting port on the topside of the Council Chamber. "We shall discuss this with the Elders," he said.

"Oh, we will do that!" Woldn and his entourage sped out of the anteroom the moment the door opened. They were waiting for him, when Eshaz marched purposefully into the large central chamber and faced the Elders.

"Let me begin by saying that I have not been disingenuous," Eshaz said, gazing up at the broad-necked First Elder Kre'n.

She looked at him sternly, then stepped down from the bench. Approaching Eshaz, she touched his scaly bronze skin and closed her eyes.

Eshaz trembled as he felt the mental linkage, the two-way flow of information between them. It was not a complete transference by either of them; barriers still remained. Some were partial, while others were full and complete barricades. This was normal.

All grew silent to Eshaz, except for a faint, rushing inner sound as data flowed back and forth. He tried to calm himself, knowing that more details about how he had healed Noah Watanabe were emerging, beyond what he had already told the Council. Eshaz felt the outward flow of truth, the immensity of what he did to Noah and the web.

He detected Kre'n's probing questions on the subject, that she was not yet getting everything she wanted to know. Even with the skin contact—the truthing touch—she was not learning all of the reasons for Eshaz's momentous and dangerous decision, including the full details of his history with the remarkable Human. Somehow, Eshaz's internal barriers were holding this back, but he would tell her anything she wanted to know if she ever asked him.

But he realized that he was not conscious of all of the reasons himself. Maybe there were subconscious motivations, or other forces at work that he did not understand himself. Despite what he and his people knew about Timeweb, it remained an infinitely mysterious realm, a massive puzzle with only a small number of its pieces showing.

Kre'n withdrew. Then, looking emotionlessly at Woldn as the tiny creature hovered near her, she said, "This timeseer has told you the truth. It is incontrovertible."

Looking deep into Eshaz's eyes, she added, "There, may, however, be a way of opening the pathways of his mind even more, of moving aside whatever may be blocking full revelation. For that, the Council must be alone with him."

Grumbling, Woldn at first refused to leave. His words were loud, despite his diminutive size. "You Tulyans have always been a nuisance, and never deserved to hold dominion over podships. We've taken them away from you, but you still find ways of causing problems, of interfering with our rightful mission in the galaxy."

"Woldn," Kre'n said, "with all due respect to your position, I must point out how … undiplomatic … your remarks are. Perhaps you would be better served to deal with us through a professional ambassador, instead of personally."

The Eye of the Swarm shouted, "I will hear no more of this!"

In a huff he attempted to leave, but at a signal from Kre'n, the guards blocked his exit, sealing the chamber off. At this he raised a commotion, citing all kinds of treaty violations that were being committed against him.

Calmly, the First Elder returned to her chair, and gazed dispassionately at the angry leader. Like a small cloud of insects, they flew one way and another, attempting to escape. Eshaz saw the twenty Elders unite their thoughts, recognized the little signs of this, the subtle, matching twitches on all of them, the simultaneously blinking sets of eyes, the way their gazes moved as if from the eyes of a single organism. They were in mindlink.

Gradually the Parviis stopped their tirade, and settled down.

"The guards will escort you back to the anteroom," the Council members said, their voices perfectly synchronized. "We will summon you after our private session."

With no choice in the matter, Woldn and his entourage flew away, following guards out a door that was opened for them.

* * * * *

Now Eshaz faced the entire Council of Elders, inside the inverted dome of the Council Chamber, floating in the misty, ethereal sky. Still in mindlink, the wise leaders stared down at him sternly. First Elder Kre'n sat in the center of the arched table. On her left sat the towering Dabiggio, the largest Tulyan Eshaz had ever seen. He did not look well, and had droopy, tired-looking eyes, skin lesions, and reddish patches of skin where the scales fell off.

Eshaz had heard stories of physical problems suffered by Tulyans in recent months, for the first time in their long history. Many were suffering from fatigue, and their missing scales were slow to grow back, if they did at all. Tulyan leaders said that the weakening of Tulyan bodies spelled the approaching end of their immortal lives, and it was somehow tied to the problems with the deteriorating cosmic web.

Dabiggio was the first victim Eshaz had seen first hand. It struck him as curious that the Tulyan Starcloud had not shown any signs of web deterioration in its sector, but its citizens were being impacted first. He assumed that the starcloud would show signs of decay as well, and soon.

Answering their unspoken questions, Eshaz expanded on what Kre'n already knew. He elaborated on how he had healed the Human, Noah Watanabe, by allowing Timeweb nutrients to flow into his dying body… and how Noah thereafter gained access to the web through his mind.

Eshaz also described how he met Noah Watanabe years ago, when the Human led a fledgling activist organization with a forgettable name, the Planetbuilders. Eshaz gave him a much better name for the organization that reflected its multi-planet importance: the Guardians. The Tulyan also made a number of operational recommendations and went to work for the organization, as his busy schedule permitted. After that, the Guardians grew in number and in prominence.

"I believe in Noah completely," Eshaz said. "This Human may become the first truly important member of his race, on a galactic scale."

Speaking in unison, the Council said, "Guilt over your Timeweb infraction may have blocked you from timeseeing, weighing heavily on your mind."

Dismayed but not ashamed, Eshaz refused to hang his head. Instead, he looked at his superiors steadily and said, "I never felt guilt over what I did for Noah. I did it for the good of the galaxy … to fulfill my sacred caretaking oath.

As I told you earlier, he may be the one spoken of in our ancient legends ... the Savior we have awaited for millions of years."

"We need not remind you," the eerie voices retorted, with more than a hint of irritation, "that no matter the idealistic intentions and efforts of Noah Watanabe, there have never been any great Humans on a galactic scale. Humans are known to be limited by their pettiness, shortsightedness, and proclivity for warfare. They are parochial creatures, lacking in compassion or foresight."

The Elders released their mindlink, and one of them, a smallish male known as Akera, spoke separately. "Nonetheless, we are willing to reserve judgment about Noah. You may be correct about him, though there is no way to tell yet, based upon the limited evidence available."

"I have told you all I know," Eshaz said, "even what is in my heart."

"You are to increase your timeseeing efforts for the Parviis," Kre'n said. "And do not even think about concealing anything from them. It is not only a matter of treaty, but of honor."

"As you wish." Eshaz bowed.

"Afterward, you have our permission to return to Noah's Guardians at the first opportunity," Kre'n said, "as soon as space travel is reopened to Human-controlled worlds."

"We want you to protect the Human," Akera said. "Help break him out of prison if you can, and keep him from causing harm to the fragile environment of Timeweb. We cannot do that from afar."

"It may also be necessary to eliminate him," Dabiggio said. He coughed. "If he proves dangerous."

Eshaz recoiled at the vile thought. He knew little of violence, and could not imagine committing it against anyone, especially not against a man whom he had come to admire so much. But what if he had been wrong about Noah? What if the concerns of the Council proved well-founded?

I am a caretaker of the web, Eshaz reminded himself. *I must do whatever is necessary.*

* * * * *

Having been summoned to return, Woldn and his followers flew back into the chamber like an angry swarm of bees. They were in high fever, flitting around, buzzing in the faces of the much larger Tulyans, but eliciting no physical or verbal response.

"Our timeseer is ready to serve you," the First Elder announced.

"You've cleared the cobwebs out of his head?" Woldn asked.

Eshaz glared at him.

"I have ordered a rendezvous of my people," Woldn said, "and I cannot waste more time here." He flew in front of the Council members. "You have failed in your obligation."

"Then the timeseer will go with you," Kre'n said. "Summon a podship and transport him to your rendezvous point."

"That is out of the question. No outsider is permitted to know where we meet. Now let me out of here!"

"You refuse the services of a timeseer when he is prepared to fulfill his duty?" Kre'n said. "That sounds like a treaty violation to me. Now you must remain here to work through the problem. It has very serious diplomatic consequences, which this Council cannot ignore."

"You're wasting my time!" Woldn shouted.

"You waste your own time by being obstinate," Kre'n insisted. "Can't you conceal the location of your meeting place from Eshaz, blindfolding him, preventing him from seeing?"

"You are all mind readers when you touch us, but we do have ways of concealing something so essential, something so vital to the survival of our race. Very well! The recalcitrant timeseer will come with us."

Woldn summoned a podship. It arrived in a matter of moments, with a distant green flash and a rumble as it entered the atmosphere of the starcloud. The craft made its way to the outside of the Council Chamber, and landed on a flat portion of the top, opposite the inverted dome.

Deep in thought and troubled, Eshaz boarded the vessel. He had left word for Acey and Dux that he expected to return in a matter of days, but in the chaos around him he knew that might not be possible.

Chapter Fourteen

Those infernal podships are holding all of us prisoner, leaving our worlds only connected by a thread ... the nehrcom communication system.

—Doge Lorenzo del Velli

F ollowing the destruction of Timian One and the Palazzo Magnifico, the Doge had relocated to quarters that were suitable to his position. His courtesan wife, Princess Meghina, had her own royal apartments on Canopa—in Rainbow City—and when the podships stopped she found herself stranded there, unable to return to her beloved planet of Siriki. Lorenzo liked having her nearby, and enjoyed the company of Francella as well. But the two women barely tolerated one another, and had always competed for his affections.

His relationship with them was different in so many ways. The Doge maintained Meghina as his favorite courtesan, taking care of all of her expenses and siring children by her, seven daughters so far. The girls were all on Siriki now, but remained in touch with their mother by nehrcom. Lorenzo hardly ever spoke with them himself, or cared to. Though they were financial heirs to him, they could never step into his shoes to rule the Merchant Prince Alliance. The noblemen would never stand for a female doge.

In contrast, while Francella was his lover as well, she was financially independent from Lorenzo, and loathed the very concept of a courtesan, considering such women to be no more than well-dressed harlots who lived off men. No paragon of virtue herself, Francella had borne him a male child out of wedlock, who, while a bastard, might still be accepted by the princes as their doge.

Wishing to maintain his own independence, Lorenzo did not want to live with either of the two women in his life. Even though he had formalized the relationship with Meghina by marrying her, she had—by mutual agreement with him—maintained her status as a courtesan, having relationships with the most famous princes in the realm. And he had his own wandering eye.

With the loss of his palazzo, Lorenzo had taken over a large suite on the top floor of the opulent cliffside villa of the late Prince Saito Watanabe, generously offered to him by Francella, the late tycoon's daughter. The lease fee had been substantial, as part of the deal she made to also let him use the top three floors of offices in her own CorpOne headquarters building. The villa lease included cliffside terraces nearby, where Lorenzo arranged for Meghina to construct a private zoo, featuring exotic breeds. The facility, nearing completion, would be much smaller than the one she had on Siriki, but it would serve to cheer her up, missing her pets and her daughters as she did.

Raiding private and public collections for animals, the Doge was limited to whatever was available on Canopa. But it was a large, wealthy planet, with an extensive selection. He obtained the services of a genetic technician—a "gene-tech"—who located a number of rare humanoids and animals for the new facility. The gene-tech, while an Adurian by birth, had sworn allegiance to the Merchant Prince Alliance, and had passed a thorough loyalty test administered personally by Lorenzo's Royal Attache, Pimyt.

Despite the fact that the major galactic races could not interbreed, the gene-tech told Lorenzo it was still possible to obtain interesting combinations within the various genetic families. His Adurian race had special knowledge in the field of biotechnology.

* * * * *

One evening at his villa, Lorenzo met with his military leaders and advisers, who summarized the lack of progress that the forces led by the Doge and Francella were making against Noah's rebellious group. The Guardians seemed to be increasing in number and power, and there had been disturbing reports of robots fighting alongside them.

"Of course we have our own sentient machines," General Jacopo Nehr said, "and they are replicating themselves at a high rate. We should be able to counter anything they throw at us. The tide will turn."

"Our machines are breeding like rabbits," Lorenzo said, "or should I say like robots?" He looked pleased at his witticism.

"Yes, our machine leader Jimu is doing a fine job," Nehr said, "and we will need every one of them." He stood up and paced the room. "The Guardians are clever. We can't figure out where they are or what they will do next. They make guerrilla attacks against our most fortified installations, somehow threading their way through and finding our weaknesses. It is very disturbing."

Lorenzo heard an explosion outside, rocking the furniture and reverberating in his ears. "What the hell?" he yelled, running to a window and looking out. The officers gathered around him. He saw flames in the crescent-shaped dry dock area at the base of the cliff, and quickly figured out what was burning.

"Damn them!" he said. "They got my space yacht!"

Flames rose high over the burning vessel, illuminating other pleasure craft moored by noblemen at the dry dock. He also saw the shadow of an unlit aircraft speeding away from the scene.

As Nehr and the other officers ran to the door, the Doge shouted after them: "Find out who fell asleep on the job and bring them to me! I'll interrogate them personally for this."

"We're on it, Sire," Nehr shouted back. "We'll get whoever's in that aircraft, too."

Lorenzo heard Nehr yelling into a com unit, dispatching grid-copters to take up the chase. Moments later, the Doge saw aircraft flying out over the valley. At least that was going efficiently. Maybe they would capture or destroy the bastards this time. If so, it would be one of the few successes.

Suddenly he whirled to cross the room, and nearly tripped over Pimyt, the Royal Attache. Lorenzo had forgotten that the little Hibbil was in the room.

"Sorry, Sire," Pimyt said, picking himself up, and wiping a trickle of blood off his own furry gray chin.

"Get me a report on this whole sorry affair," the Doge snapped. He kicked a message cube that had fallen on the floor. The cube struck Pimyt in the chest, an unintended result.

Pimyt's red eyes glowed brightly, like the embers of a fire, and his face contorted in anger.

For a moment, the Doge focused on the burning glare, but was not frightened by it. His aide was just intense, and Lorenzo had always liked that. Abruptly, the eyes softened, and the little alien smiled. Then Pimyt hurried away.

* * * * *

Too edgy to sleep, the Doge went out in the middle of the night to his in-progress zoo. As he stepped out into the cool air, a dozen of his house guards snapped to attention and accompanied him.

The Adurian gene-tech, KR Disama, was summoned, and hurried out of his small house on the grounds.

Then, beneath bright lights Lorenzo examined animals that were being kept in temporary cages. One was a dagg-sized creature with high-gloss blue fur and a head on each end.

"Where are its private parts?" Lorenzo wanted to know, for he could not see any.

The gene-tech, a completely hairless homopod with a small head and bulbous eyes, smiled and responded, "It does not have any. Hence, it is, by design, perfectly house-trained."

"But how does it relieve itself?"

"It exudes through its pores, into the air. Fear not, though. The substance dissipates quickly and is completely odorless."

As the animal walked around its cage, Doge Lorenzo could not tell whether it was going forward or backward. Despite everything on his mind, he laughed out loud. For a few minutes, he almost relaxed.

Then he remembered his destroyed yacht, and scowled ferociously.

Chapter Fifteen

The Parvii Fold is the end of the entire galaxy, the place where all known reality drops off into enigma.

—From a Parvii scientific report

Bound for the rendezvous point ordered by the Parvii leader, Tesh piloted her podship through the narrowing, dangerous Asteroid Funnel, at the far end of a magnificent spiral nebula. Linked to the sentience of the living spaceship under her command, she felt the creature's primal fear, its hesitancy to proceed. But as she clung to a wall of the sectoid chamber at the core of the ship, she had the Aopoddae vessel under total control, and it could do nothing to resist her.

All around them, glassy stones hurtled by, glowing luminous white in their passage. She saw it all through the visual organs all over the outer skin of the vessel. Maneuvering carefully to avoid full impact, Tesh felt smaller stones bouncing off the podship, causing the creature's angst to increase. But it flew onward, combining its own abilities with Tesh's as they reacted with split-second precision to select the safest route.

Steering sharply into a gray-green side tunnel that was clear of loose stones, Tesh soon exited into the legendary Parvii Fold, a broad, enclosed region that was bigger than most solar systems. Concealed from the rest of the galaxy, this was the back of beyond, and the sacred breeding zone of the Parvii people. While her race had no homeworld, they did possess this uncommon, highly secure region that few outsiders had ever been permitted to see, or even to know about.

Inside the sunless, worldless fold she saw scores of Parvii swarms—each in its own distinctive formation—and each containing tens of millions of tiny, flying people. The Parvii race did not require oxygen to breathe, or common nutrients for sustenance.

As Tesh guided her podship into the cavernous galactic fold, she saw many other sentient vessels off to one side, an immense basin of the blimp-shaped, sentient creatures tethered together in the airless vacuum. Instead of steering in that direction, however, she headed straight for the central swarm, where she expected to find Woldn. When her ship moved forward, the multitude parted and let her through ... but hundreds of the strongest pilots boarded the craft with her, and she felt their mental presence monitoring her movements and decisions, preparing themselves to take control of the craft away from her if necessary. She absorbed their thoughts and they absorbed hers.

Just ahead, she made out an elaborate structure floating in space, glowing in multicolors and formed by the living, interlocked bodies of Parviis. This was the magnificent Palace of Woldn, which had been shaped according to his exacting specifications. Docking there and disembarking from the podship, she relinquished control of the craft to one of the other pilots. Keeping her personal magnification system switched off, she remained her normal tiny self.

As she entered the palace, she felt simulated gravity that was formed by a specialized telepathic field. Stepping onto a simulated mosaic floor that was generated by the closely-knit forms of her people, she admired the elegant and intricate new designs they had created by radiating a variety of glowing colors. All around her were Herculean facsimile sculptors and paintings that had been created in the same manner, by the arrangement of living organisms. The large scale of the palace enabled Woldn to entertain visiting dignitaries from the few other races who knew of the existence of Parviis. It was a small list, including the Tulyans, and anytime they brought a visitor in, it was done in a way that blocked all information on the whereabouts of the secret galactic fold.

In Parvii society, the Eye of the Swarm was not a godlike figure, but he was the supreme commander and all-powerful central brain of this ancient galactic race. Like his followers, Woldn was mortal, although he was expected to live longer than normal, from the beneficial strength and energy imparted to him by his followers. For some time he had expressed concern, however, as the average Parvii life span had been dropping precipitously. For millions of galactic years, since the beginning of known time, Parviis could be expected to live for 2,500 or more years, but the average was down to 2,085 now, and continued to fall. He was himself 2,172 years old, and had told his followers he felt the coldness of his mortality fast approaching.

As Tesh entered the glittering central chamber of the palace, she saw the distinctive reptilian outline of a Tulyan in the middle of the large room, with a layer of Parviis all over its body, as if it had been dipped in a batter of them. Only the Tulyan's face was uncovered, and she recognized him as Noah's friend,

Eshaz. Tiny Woldn, wearing a silvery robe, was perched on top of his head.

Joining the cluster on the reptilian man's chest, Tesh felt him absorb information from her by the touch of his skin against hers—a physical connection between two races that had coexisted uneasily since time immemorial. Tulyans could read the minds of each other and of other galactic races through direct skin contact, their truthing touch. With respect to these Parviis, it meant he was absorbing data from them in order to perform timeseeing services for the swarming race.

Even though the two races had never been on friendly terms after Parvii swarms took control of virtually all podships long ago, they did have a long-standing diplomatic arrangement by which a limited number of Tulyans were permitted to journey around the galaxy as podship passengers—the only race that had been limited in its space travel, prior to the recent cessation of podship service to all Human and Mutati worlds.

"Well?" Woldn demanded impatiently. Hands on hips, the diminutive man continued to stand on top of Eshaz's head. "What do you see in our future?"

"Even in the best of circumstances I can see only a short distance into the future, and sometimes not at all," Eshaz said.

"Don't stall me!" Woldn screamed. "This is critically important, damn you! The galaxy is crumbling; our lives are shortening!"

"I see nothing at the moment," Eshaz said hesitantly. "Only layers and layers of darkness. This has never happened before, so I must interpret it. Darkness could mean everything will soon be gone, and nothing will be left. Or it might only refer to you, Woldn, and perhaps to your entire Parvii race."

"Stop lying to me!" Woldn screeched. He stomped a tiny foot on the Tulyan's thick skin.

"I'm not lying! Previously when I was unable to timesee, a wash of brilliant light filled my eyes and mind, without details. This is much different." Tesh thought he sounded nervous, and she felt a slight trembling in his skin.

"Your future is linked to Timeweb," Eshaz said, after a long pause.

"A boilerplate answer," Woldn snapped, "imparting no real or useful information. Stop stalling around or we'll dump you in deep space, with no way to return home."

"That would create a diplomatic incident."

"No matter. We hold the upper hand over your people."

"I am not afraid of any threats," Eshaz said. Gently, he brushed Parviis off his body, and most of them flew a short distance away, like gnats without wings. Woldn, Tesh, and a few others remained on him, but moved to one shoulder, where Eshaz could see them peripherally.

Eshaz went on to say that Timeweb had been deteriorating, and that its troubles seemed to parallel those of the Parvii race, and those of other races around the galaxy, including the Tulyans. "We are an immortal people," he said, "but our immortality is linked to the web and all of its problems. Some of us are feeling aches and pains for the first time, and falling ill."

Woldn fell silent for a long time. Inside the palace, his swarms stopped flying and alighted wherever they were, on their densely grouped companions who were shaped in the architectural components of the structure.

On the way there, Tesh had resolved to express her dissent against Woldn for dumping podship passengers into space, and she wanted to make a salvage claim on the podship. Locking gazes briefly with the Eye of the Swarm, she felt him receive this information telepathically. She would feel better speaking it, but under the circumstances—with a Tulyan present—this would have to do.

But Tesh had momentarily forgotten an important detail, the fact that she was touching the skin of the Tulyan. She felt him absorb information from her, but she remained where she was anyway. Both she and Eshaz were Guardians, and she felt safe with him.

"Guardians," Woldn said, in a sharp and sarcastic tone. He lifted off and flew around angrily. "Both of you have sworn allegiance to the strange Human, Noah Watanabe, haven't you? Eshaz, you continue to deceive me. Is there no honor left in your people? And Tesh, you continue to disappoint me."

Neither of them responded.

"I have decided on punishments for both of you. Tesh, you are banished for the rest of your days. I officially declare you an outcast, never to return to the Parvii Fold or associate with any member of this race. You are to take that unreliable podship with you, and Eshaz as well to avoid a 'diplomatic incident,' as he calls it. I won't transport him, not after his complete failure—whether through deception or ineptitude, it really doesn't matter. As for the podship, we can swarm and take it back whenever we please. There are ways to overcome your hold on it. Now, go!"

The two of them boarded the podship, but as Tesh hovered in the air in front of Eshaz, she had an empty feeling in the pit of her stomach. In the background of her consciousness, she only half heard Eshaz tell her that he had important ecological work to do, and that he urgently needed her assistance in transporting him to the Tulyan Starcloud.

"What?" She hesitated inside the passenger compartment.

He repeated himself.

"For what purpose?" she asked.

"My position is sensitive. I cannot confide in you without permission from the Council of Elders. Do you think a Parvii such as yourself could ever trust a Tulyan? We both work for Noah Watanabe and admire him, so our goals must be similar. At the moment, I'm in a hurry, and I must place myself at your mercy."

"We each have secrets," she said. "Woldn concealed the location of the Parvii Fold from you, one of our racial necessities."

"That is true. I was blindfolded in a sense, unable to determine where we were going. Presumably you would do the same on the return trip."

She nodded.

It occurred to her that he might try to steal her podship at the first opportunity, or might lure her into a Tulyan trap where others did so, but she dismissed the thought. This was a trusted friend of Noah Watanabe, and she did not think he would harm a fellow Guardian. As she hovered in front of Eshaz with a slight buzz, she wondered if the Tulyans and Parviis could ever reconcile their differences. Maybe this would be a step in that direction, even if it involved only two people. She vowed to give it a try.

Behind her, she heard the scorn of the palace full of Parviis, with Woldn's voice rising above the others, and telepathic winds buffeted her. She hurried into the sectoid chamber, and got underway.

Chapter Sixteen

Does my brother think I am a monster, with no feelings? He has never understood me. To be accurate, I have feelings for him. I hate him with every fiber of my being.

—Francella Watanabe

"You don't seem to realize it," Francella said, "but I've had a lot on my mind lately." In her black underclothes, she sat on an immense, disheveled bed, beneath a gilded headboard that bore the golden tigerhorse crest of the Doge's royal house.

"And I haven't?" Lorenzo snapped, as he dressed to leave. "Where do you think I'm going now? I have an important military meeting."

"So like a man," she said, "acting like a woman's concerns are nothing. Sometimes you make me feel invisible. Am I no more than a sexual partner to you?"

At her own villa, they were in the large top-floor suite that she had leased to Lorenzo. The morning sunlight was too bright for Francella. At a snap of her fingers, she lowered the automatic shades.

Clearly agitated, Lorenzo had difficulty buttoning his dark-blue tunic. "What is it this time? It's always something, isn't it?"

"Lorenzo," she said, in her firmest tone, "I want you to sit down and listen to me." She only began sentences with his given name when she wanted him to feel like he'd done something wrong.

From their long relationship, he understood the code between them. With a long, annoyed sigh, he sat on the edge of the bed and looked at her, leaving his tunic unbuttoned.

"You've been a bad little boy," she said with a smile, "and I think you need a spanking."

He fought back a smile. "After the meeting, OK? Please hurry and tell me. What do you need?"

Her eyelids fluttered. "Not so much. I just want to know what you're going to do with my troublesome brother."

"You know we've been questioning him, and performing medical tests to find out why he recovered so easily from the wound you gave him. My experts tell me they still have a great deal of work to do."

"I'm his sister, remember? Perhaps I can figure out what your experts cannot. They are taking a long time, too long. Having trouble, aren't they?"

"Well, yes, but Noah is an unprecedented case."

"As his twin, I might have certain insights."

The Doge arched his gray eyebrows. "Don't tell me you have the same ability?"

"No, nothing of the kind. But I do know more about him than anyone else. I grew up with him in the same household. If anyone can get through the barriers he has set up, it is me."

"I'm not sure what you're getting at."

"Let me supervise the research; put me in charge of Noah. As the owner of CorpOne, I have the finest medical laboratories on Canopa, but you haven't even used them. Your investigators seem to be protecting their own turf. But they're not making any progress, and it's time for a change."

"You want to keep Noah's fate in the Watanabe family?"

"You could put it that way."

He scowled. "I find it ironic that you would ask this of me, when you kept me from deciding about the fate of my own son. For more than twenty years, I didn't even know Anton existed."

"We've already been over that, and it is beside the point." She slid over by him and nibbled at his ear. "Besides, I already apologized for that, many times. Would you like me to do so again?"

He smiled, but looked troubled. "Not now. I have too much on my mind."

"You're not going off to that big important meeting with this unresolved, are you? It will just block your reasoning powers. You need to clear this up first, and then your mind will be clear and sharp for the meeting."

Looking exasperated, he shook his head, but smiled. "All right," he said. "You're in charge of Noah from now on. Make the necessary decisions, and find out how he healed himself from a puissant-gun wound that should have killed him."

"Oh, I will," she said, giving him a kiss on the cheek.

Quickly, the stocky, gray-haired nobleman resumed dressing. "One proviso," he said.

Alarmed, she asked what he meant.

"I'll decide what to do about our son ... without consulting with you."

"Agreed," she said, not showing any hesitation. Though she felt some belated motherly concern for Anton, Francella didn't have the time or adequate inclination to follow through with it. Another matter was far more important.

She needed to unravel Noah's secrets.

* * * * *

Later that day, Francella sent Noah, under heavy guard, to one of her laboratories to have him analyzed. There, she and her chief scientists met with Dr. Hurk Bichette, who was the newly installed director of CorpOne's Medical Research Division. The doctor had an interesting biography. He had held this position previously, but his career had been interrupted when Guardians kidnapped him and forced him to tend to Noah, who was gravely wounded when the Doge's Red Berets attacked the orbital EcoStation.

Bichette's time with the Guardians had been most peculiar, and intriguing to her. Having resurfaced right after the podship crisis, he told her he recalled being forced to undergo an electronic procedure by a sentient robot in the employ of the Guardians, and afterward his memories had been sketchy. He'd been left with a general knowledge that he'd been with the rebel group and that he had tended to Noah himself, but without important details. He knew that Noah had recovered from his injuries, possibly due to Bichette's own medical skills, but little more.

Most importantly, he had no memory of where he had been with the rebels and where they were hiding now. When he came back to CorpOne, Francella's people performed a battery of lie-detection tests on him, along with stringent loyalty tests, before permitting him to return to her Medical Research Division.

He had passed them all with flying colors....

Noah awoke to find himself on a hover stretcher, looking to one side at a window and a wall. His muscles felt sluggish and heavy, and his eyes became sore whenever he moved them too much. Even so, his thoughts seemed clear, making him wonder if he could vault out of there mentally the moment he felt like doing so. That might be the best sedative for him of all. But he didn't make the attempt, at least not yet, since he wanted to see what they were going to do to him.

For the moment, he didn't see or hear anyone in the room with him, though he heard distant, muffled voices.

He thought of Tesh, and the paranormal kiss he gave her, reaching across the cosmos. Not a real kiss; they'd never had one. Envisioning her classically beautiful face and bright, emerald eyes, he felt a tug of emotion. So unfortunate that the two of them ever had conflicts, but Noah realized now that he was responsible for much of the acrimony himself, since he hadn't wanted to intrude on Anton's romantic interests. But Noah had noticed the way she looked at him, and recalled the secret way he felt for her whenever they were together.

"Ah," Dr. Bichette said in his basso voice, as attendants guided a hover stretcher into the laboratory. Noah realized that he was unable to move, because electronic restraints held him down. "I've been looking forward to this!" The doctor's eyes were filled with wild fascination. Three men in white biocoats and gloves looked on, scientists who were dressed as their superior was.

Noah thought back. This was the first time he had been aware of the doctor since Francella shot Noah in the chest and he recovered afterward miraculously, in only a few remarkable moments.

As Noah listened, Francella filled the director in on the security measures that would be followed. Armed guards would always be present in the laboratory, and for even greater security Noah had been fitted with an electronic restraint system that could be customized for the movements he was permitted to make, and would stun him if he tried to do anything without authorization.

"So," Bichette said, when he finally had a chance to examine Noah, "you claim to be immortal, eh?"

Noah glared up at him. "Let's put it this way. I have no need of your medical services."

With a tight smile, the doctor removed all of Noah's clothing except for his underwear. Then, with Francella looking on, he proceeded to look at the skin on Noah's chest with a high-powered magnifying glass. "Remarkable," he said, looking away from the eyepiece of the instrument. "I see the faintest evidence of a large wound—directly over the heart—but it is completely healed. This is not possible."

Running a scanner over Noah, he next examined the internal organs. "Incredible, incredible," he said. "I don't believe it. They've all regrown. There is evidence of massive new cellular growth."

Going back to the magnifying glass, Bichette continued to go over the skin of Noah's entire body, centimeter by centimeter. At the left ankle, he said he found a very faint line all the way around. "Like an amputation mark," he said.

Noah muttered an insult under his breath, and smiled to himself when he noticed that Francella could not make out the words.

Performing an interior body scan, Bichette exclaimed, "Yes! This entire foot was amputated! Then ... then ... it *grew* back. I see new bones, muscles, tissue. This is unbelievable."

"Don't be so dramatic," Noah said. "You cut the foot off yourself, said you had to do it or I would have lost my leg, or my life. You were also there when the foot regrew."

Bichette looked at him blankly.

"He doesn't remember any of that, dear brother," Francella said. "One of your robots zapped his brain."

Not even looking in her direction, Noah considered what must have happened to the doctor. Subi Danvar or Thinker must have instituted a security measure, sometime after the Doge put Noah under arrest.

"Like a lizard," one of the scientists remarked. "This guy grows body parts back like a lizard."

"Yes," Francella said in a wary voice, "but lizards can be killed."

Maybe not this one, Noah thought. And a shudder ran down his spine, as he considered the horrors that this woman might inflict on him.

Chapter Seventeen

Racial extinction is always closer than anyone realizes.

—Parvii Inspiration

T he armored man watched as a long silver machine dug a new chamber, throwing dirt and bits of rock around, making so much noise that he had to wear high-decibel ear protection. Giovanni Nehr stood back at a safe distance to avoid the debris cast by the machine, which rolled forward on treads and had spinning drill bits on its body. Soon, new barracks would be constructed here, but not for Humans. As the Digger proceeded, it illuminated the work area in high-powered beams of light.

With the burgeoning number of robots under Guardian command, owing to Thinker's ambitious manufacturing program, additional quarters were needed. Sentient machines could live in tighter quarters than Humans, with their metal bodies stacked higher and packed tighter; they had to be kept somewhere, couldn't be left to wander around the subterranean tunnels and caverns of the compound.

There were also more Humans wearing Guardian uniforms, from Subi's clandestine recruitment program around Canopa. He and Thinker had initiated strict security controls, developing a comprehensive electronic interview method and even a selective memory erasure procedure—such as the one they had used on Dr. Bichette before releasing him. In addition, the two of them had set up an electronic barricade across all tunnel openings, so that no one could pass in or out without setting off alarms.

One of the young female recruits had dated a Guardian, and he had given her an interesting gift, a nearly extinct little alien creature named "Lumey." The amorphous creature, which she afterward took along with her to the underground hideout, had once been Noah's pet—but had been left behind in the rushed escape from EcoStation when the Doge's forces attacked the orbital facility.

As the machine proceeded now, digging deeper and wider, mechanical scoopers and dumpers scurried about, gathering debris and carting it away. They would dispose of it in a series of deep, vertical tunnels that had been dug by rampant machines in the past, when they were the mechanical pests of Canopa. The current debris removal system had been developed by Thinker and Gio. No one knew how they disposed of excess material in the past, but Thinker theorized it might have been in underground fissures and caverns. Occasionally, piles of dirt and rock had been found on the surface of the planet, but only on a remarkably few occasions, considering the extent of excavation that the machines had been doing.

Without warning, the Digger accelerated and increased the speed of its drill bits. It crashed into a wall and began boring through, where it wasn't supposed to go. It made fast progress, creating a new tunnel. Gio ran after the errant machine, with guards behind him and alarm klaxons sounding.

Reaching for his belt, Gio pressed a transmitter, sending an electronic signal to the computers controlling the machine. Abruptly, the Digger shut down all systems, including its lights. For several moments, Gio found himself in darkness, down the escape tunnel the machine had dug.

Then he saw lights coming from behind. Moments later, Thinker reached him, clanking and whirring. "I was afraid this would happen," the robot said.

"It's a good thing we were ready," Gio said.

Thinker led a robotic team to inspect the Digger. They disassembled the internal workings of the machine's computer. Presently, Thinker went back to Gio and said, "Just as I suspected, it has an override system, so cleverly concealed that we didn't see it before. The unit found a way to supersede your commands, but we had our own ace in the hole."

"I assume you disabled the mechanism?"

"Oh yes. But before we use this Digger again we'll need to reprogram your disabling transmitter and the receiver on the machine."

"The old signal won't stop it next time?"

"Better not try it. There could be more tricks in this Digger, more than we've discovered so far. Even if we successfully disable its present override system, it could have another, and another. We must be on constant alert."

"Why haven't our other two Digger machines done this?"

"Maybe this one is testing us, and somehow they're communicating with one another. They *are* sentient, after all. Maybe they're smarter than we assumed, with hidden intelligence."

"Kind of a game, isn't it?" Gio said, in an edgy tone.

"Not the way I look at it," Thinker said. "Machines are my life."

* * * * *

Subi Danvar, as acting head of the Guardians in Noah's absence, received reports from Giovanni Nehr and from Thinker on the episode with the Digger. He also heard from Gio that he'd grown tired of supervising the necessary construction activities, which kept enlarging with the increasing forces and supplies. The man wanted even more important duties.

Impressed with Gio's ambition and desire to contribute, Subi assigned him to work more closely with the machines that had brought him here and with the newly manufactured robots, to form them all into an efficient fighting force.

"But I have no real military experience," Gio admitted.

"You have an inventive mind, don't you? Doesn't it run in the family?"

"Well, I don't know. I do have a lot of ideas."

"Some of the men said you had ideas about military formations and training. Comments you made over beers."

"Well, that's true."

"They passed a few of your ideas on to me. My boy, if you can think that well when you're drinking, I'd like to see what you can do when you're completely sober."

The two men laughed, and clasped hands to mark the new relationship between them.

* * * * *

A couple of days later, Gio and Thinker reported to Subi that disturbing news had just come in: The best machine fighters—led by Jimu—had left the Inn of the White Sun some time ago and joined the Red Berets. Even worse, they had initiated a large-scale robot manufacturing program, and with access to more raw materials theirs far outpaced the program that Thinker had established for the Guardians.

It was indeed troubling news. After considering the situation for a moment, Subi said, "We need Noah back more than ever. He'd know what to do."

"We've already discussed that," Thinker said, his mechanical voice weary. "From our reconnaissance missions and other reports, I've assembled all available data, and Noah is nowhere to be found. Since his captors have no podships to take him off planet, we know he's on Canopa. Hopefully alive. The Doge's people have set up an elaborate disinformation campaign about his whereabouts, with tens of thousands of Noah sightings reported all over the planet. Too many for us to investigate with our limited resources. We can't mount a rescue effort until we have some idea of where he is. Why, he might not even be in one of their government prisons. In fact, I suspect he isn't."

"That's your analysis, is it?" Subi said.

"It is. Absolutely."

"And didn't you also analyze the Diggers some time ago, without finding their override system?"

"Yes."

"That proves that there are possibilities beyond your intellect. There is a way to find Noah and break him out—I'm convinced of it—and we need to find out what it is."

"You'll never outthink a machine," Gio said, as he listened in.

Ignoring the comment, Subi said, "It must be a perfect plan, against superior forces. Nothing is more important." With that, he stalked away, followed by Thinker, who continued to argue with him....

For days afterward, Gio began to think about this at length. If he could pull off a rescue of Noah, or at least get credit for it, he would be rewarded extremely well. Thinker, however, remained obstinate against sending out any rescue missions until they had more data. He and Subi could frequently be heard in loud exchanges.

Chapter Eighteen

Tulyans call it the "Visitor's Center," a large facility that can accommodate more than thirteen hundred guests at once. And yet, they have used an odd singularity in the title for it, as if the place was only capable of taking one person at a time. They claim to have merely named it that way to make the place seem more personal for each visitor. We suspect that the facility may, in fact, have been built for only one person, and a very important one. Tulyans dismiss our questions about it. On the surface it seems a trivial matter, but we have an idea that it may be one of their secrets.

—Merchant Prince Diplomatic File #T 16544

Though Dux had initially enjoyed the luxuries of the Visitor's Center and Acey had steadfastly resisted them, now both of them loathed the place. Acey had begun calling it a "velvet-lined prison," and Dux could not help agreeing.

Worst of all, the teenagers had thought that Eshaz would take them under his wing, but now the big, enigmatic Tulyan had gone off on a mission far across the galaxy. The waitress they'd befriended told them he had gone on a "timeseeing assignment"—whatever that meant—with the leader of the Parvii race. The boys had no idea who Parviis were, and at this point neither of them cared. They just wanted to leave the posh orbiter by any means possible.

The pair would prefer to go to Canopa or another Human-controlled world to volunteer for military service, but could not reach any of them by podship, and all other means of space travel were too slow to be practical. As a result, when added to the bad news about planetary-scale losses, Acey and Dux were no longer their usual outgoing and fun-loving selves. They had, at very young ages, become quite serious.

The Human race was in trouble.

Each day, the boys gazed longingly out at the nearby pod station, a rough gray globular structure that kept pace with the Visitor's Center, orbiting over the starcloud. The two orbital facilities were only a few kilometers apart.

"Too bad we can't get back and help Noah," Acey said.

"Maybe that's not meant for us," Dux said. He brushed his long blond hair out of his eyes. "Gio Nehr is on Canopa, and could cause us a lot of trouble. We'd probably have to kill him, or vice versa. As for me, I'm not sure I want to go that far, not even with him."

"The first step is to get away from here. Agreed?"

"No question about that," Dux said. "But how do we get on the shuttle to reach the pod station?"

A grin split Acey's wide face. "We don't. I found what looks like an emergency evacuation system. A series of passenger launchers—individual, man-sized capsules that shoot into orbital space."

"Show me."

Acey led the way through a narrow servant's passageway. He had timed it perfectly, having watched for the schedules of the employees. The teenagers slipped into a small chamber, and closed a heavy door behind them.

"This is one of the emergency-escape launch rooms," Acey said. "There are hundreds of them around the structure."

Dux surveyed the room and saw a number of clearplex tubes, each capable of holding a large person, stacked on racks. It didn't take him long to figure out how the system worked, and he saw what appeared to be cannon barrels on the outside wall. "This looks like a circus trick," he said.

"More sophisticated than that, but you're not far off."

Dux felt hesitant. "It looks dangerous."

"Well, if you'd rather stay here and loll around on vacation, that's fine by me. But I have things to do and places to see. All right?"

Again wiping hair out of his eyes, Dux said, "We promised to stay together."

"Exactly my point. You have to go with me, don't you see?"

Shaking his head, Dux stepped toward one of the tubes, and moved it. The container was light. He carried it over to the launcher and slipped it inside, then opened a hatch on one end of the tube and crawled inside. "Now what?" he asked.

He no sooner had the words out when the launcher shot him into space. Dux felt surprise, but more exhilaration. It was like a super ride an amusement park. In a few moments, he experienced a floating sensation.

Seconds later, Acey followed him out. Then Dux heard Acey's voice over a comlink. "Grab the joystick," he said. "The handle activates directional jets when you move it, taking you in the direction you want to go."

Acey roared past him, heading for the pod station.

But Dux had trouble with the controls, and veered off course. He heard Acey shouting at him over the comline. Finally he figured out the pressure pads and toggles, and made his way toward the pod station.

As the pair arrived and stepped through an airlock onto a platform, they saw no podship present, and no other vessels docked there. Looking back through a viewport, they saw a shuttle take off from the Visitor's Center.

"Not a good sign," Dux said.

"I timed this for the arrival of a podship," Acey said. "While you were swimming and getting massages, I was watching schedules. I thought one would be here now."

"What a time for them to change their schedule."

"Look!" Acey pointed, and jumped up and down with excitement.

Dux felt a surge of hope as he saw the telltale green flash of a podship arriving from deep space.

"Come on! Come on!" Acey said. "Faster!" Looking back, he saw the shuttle enter the pod station first, and make its way toward them.

Unexpectedly, the podship turned and departed without ever going into the pod station. Apparently, something had startled the creature.

The boys didn't even try to get away. Furious, they just waited to be taken into custody.

Chapter Nineteen

The Human brain is a marvelous, wondrous instrument, with razor-sharp cutting edges that can slice in countless directions. At all times, the user must be careful not to harm himself with such a powerful weapon.

—Noah Watanabe, *Commentary on Captivity*

N oah didn't like the odors inside the CorpOne medical laboratory, the disturbingly strange chemicals he could not identify. His vivid imagination worked against him now, making him wonder what the doctors and other technicians intended to do with those substances, and with the dangerous-looking array of medical instruments he saw in clearplax cases all around him. In the few days he had been housed in the facility, he had not been able to get used to the underlying sense of evil that permeated the place, and he knew he never would.

Early each morning, Dr. Bichette's assistants brought Noah out of his heavily guarded, locked room on the top level and took him down to the laboratory on the main floor, which had an operating theater in its central chamber. The laboratory was metal and plax, gleaming silver and white. Everything was voice-activated. Whenever the doctor wanted a vial or device, he spoke it by name, held his hand out, and waited for the elaborate machinery of the chamber to give it to him. Instantly, conveyors and servos in the ceiling whirred to life, removing items from cases and lowering them to his waiting hand.

From tiers of seats that circled above central operating station, around twenty people looked on, men and women. On previous days, Noah had noticed his detestable twin sister sitting in one of the front-row viewing seats above him, and he had watched her send messages to the medical personnel down on the central floor. This morning, however, she stood beside the doctor at the examination table and glared at her brother while the assistants activated electronic straps over his wrists and ankles to secure him in place.

In response, Noah gazed at her with calculated, loveless disdain.

Under different circumstances he might have been the owner of his father's corporation and all of its operations, including this one. In an odd image, he tried to imagine what it might be like to be himself, strolling into the laboratory, looking at himself on this examination table. But the hardness of the table against his backside, along with the people looking at him like a bug under a microscope, reminded Noah only too harshly that he had no degree of control over the situation. Not in a physical sense, anyway.

But he still had his mind.

In this facility and in the prison before that, Noah had been forced to undergo rigorous medical examinations, with the doctors paying close attention to the healed gun wound in the center of his chest and his regenerated left foot—wounds that showed no easily visible scars or signs of internal injury. He wondered what was on the agenda for today, and did not have long to wait for his answer.

Without warning, he saw Francella shoved Bichette out of the way. "This is going too slowly for me," she snapped. "Give me a tray of surgical tools!" She held her hand out, but the machinery did not respond.

"If you will just return to your seat, we can proceed," Bichette said. "You must have faith in my abilities. I know this patient well, and the Doge has entrusted him to my care."

"Like hell! Lorenzo has placed him in my care, not yours. You work for me, you dolt, and you will do as I say." The fingers of her extended hand twitched, as if giving hand signals to the servomachines, telling them to do her bidding.

"I have authorization from the Doge to perform complete medical examinations," the doctor insisted. "You must let me proceed."

She arched her shaved eyebrows in displeasure. "How dare you act as if I am interfering?"

Narrowing his eyes, he said, "That is not my intent. I'm sure we can work this out."

"I'm your boss, you fool. I own this facility, and Lorenzo put me in charge of the investigation. Don't you understand that?"

"But the Doge sent me a telebeam message yesterday afternoon, telling me how important my work with Noah is. He thought I might be on the verge of a momentous medical breakthrough, and that. .

"He should not have communicated with you directly! I have an agreement with Lorenzo that all decisions concerning the fate of this"—she nudged Noah roughly in the side—"are up to me."

"With all due respect, Ms. Watanabe, you don't know what you're saying. You're too close to the situation, since it involves your brother, and you need to take a step back. Granted, you *own* this medical facility, but you don't know how to run every aspect of it. Prince Saito understood that, and he delegated important tasks." He glanced at Noah. "This is an important task."

"You think I don't know that? You say my judgment is impaired because *I'm* too close to the situation? What about you? I think you like my brother, and you're going easy on him, showing favoritism toward him."

"You could not be more wrong," Bichette insisted.

In a rage, Francella smashed a hand against a case and broke the plax. Reaching through the jagged opening, she brought out a sharp, gleaming knife.

Noah braced himself, but tried to show no fear.

She waved the instrument wildly in the air. Bichette backed out of her way, and she swished the blade close to Noah's face. In response, the captive did not close his eyes or flinch, and stared at her emotionlessly. He felt a spinning sensation, and a hum of energy all around him. Where was it coming from? Noah couldn't tell.

"This is not the way!" Bichette said.

Francella hurled the weapon in another direction, and it skidded and clattered across the floor. "Get me some results," she snapped, "or, by God, I'll do it myself!"

As she stormed out of the laboratory, Noah breathed a sigh of relief, but only a little one. Somehow he had an odd, unsettling sensation that his apparent immortality might be penetrated by that insane woman.

Chapter Twenty

Some disguises run deeper than any form of perception.

—Noah Watanabe

At the Inn of the White Sun, cleverly constructed inside the orbital ring over a jewel-like planet, only a few machines remained after Jimu and Thinker took sentient units to join the opposing forces of Doge Lorenzo del Velli and Noah Watanabe.

The orbiting way station was not as exciting as it had been in past years. However, since it lay beyond the war zone, podships still came and went, though with a different mix of races, and far fewer Humans or Mutatis. The sentient machines often said they missed those two races, for their abundance of exotic personalities, capable of interesting and unpredictable behavior.

Down on the glassy surface of the planet Ignem, the machines were still constructing their army, robots building robots, but they no longer had the same enthusiasm for the project, no longer had the same altruistic goal that had originally been instilled in them by Thinker. Previously, their cerebral leader had motivated them through reminders that they had been abandoned by their Human creators, discarded on junk heaps. He convinced the robots to build a machine army to serve Humans, with the goal of proving to them that the robots had worth after all, that they still had dignity. It was revenge in a sense, but with a loving touch, a desire to excel despite tremendous obstacles, despite being overlooked and tossed away. It was also ironic, considering how poorly they had been treated by Humans.

Now, far across the galaxy the machines serving the Doge and Watanabe were proving themselves, showing their value by performing work once limited to Human beings. On each side, Thinker and Jimu were adding to their numbers as they had previously on Ignem, building more and more sentient fighting machines.

Word of their successes got around the galaxy, even this far from the Canopan battle zone, and despite the podship problem. Travelers who had heard nehrcom news reports on fringe worlds brought bits and pieces of information back to the Inn of the White Sun. The two opposing machine leaders on Canopa were developing stellar reputations, or "interstellar" reputations, as one of the travelers quipped. .

According to the reports, the two machine forces had clashed in brief skirmishes when Watanabe's Guardians made guerrilla attacks against their enemies. To Ipsy, one of the left-behind units still at the Inn of the White Sun, it seemed unfortunate that robots had to fight their own kind, or that Human creators had to fight robots, either, for that matter. Ipsy was extremely proud of his machine brethren, but felt deep sadness as well.

A small robot, Ipsy had reconstructed himself with advanced computer circuitry. His real love was for combat, and if podship travel was ever restored to the Human-ruled worlds he wanted to join Jimu's forces, since he had always admired the ferocious fighting methods that robot had espoused.

The feisty Ipsy frequently picked fights with much larger opponents, so that he could test his personal combat skills. He won a few of the frays, but lost many more by wide margins, and was frequently forced to repair himself.

* * * * *

From Canopa, the Doge broadcasted orders to every planet in his Alliance, requiring all inhabitants—without exception—to submit to medical testing and thereafter to wear a micro-ID embedded in their earlobes, certifying that they were Human. Previously there had been testing, but it had been sporadic, with too many opportunities for shapeshifters to elude discovery. This time the Doge had his military and police leaders set up stringent systems to ensure that there would be no opportunities for anyone to escape the nets of detection.

On Lorenzo's newly christened capital world, a surprisingly small number of Mutatis were rounded up in this manner and thrown in his dreaded prisons—and it was the same elsewhere. But there were many suspects. It was reminiscent of the Salem witch hunts of the seventeenth century on Earth, as people constantly turned in their neighbors and personal enemies as suspects.

All across the merchant prince empire, anti-Mutati hysteria ran rampant, with widespread fear that shapeshifters could be hiding inside the bodies of anyone, impersonating people.

Chapter Twenty-One

Even in a corner with predators at your throat, there is always a way out, if you can only discover it.

—Mutati Saying

On the shapeshifter homeworld of Paradij, the Zultan spun inside his clearplax gyrodome, high atop his magnificent, glittering Citadel. During this procedure, his mind was like an advanced computer with all data in it available to him instantaneously. In addition, he had altered his body, and now looked like a cross between a saber-toothed wyoo boar and a Gwert, one of the intelligent alien races employed in scientific positions by the Mutatis.

At the moment, he was considering a very big problem, and needed all the inspiration he could muster.

With podship space travel cut off—the only practical means of transport across the galaxy—Mutati outriders had not been able to continue their Demolio attacks against Human-controlled worlds. Conventional spacecraft, such as Mutati solar sailers and the hydion-powered vacuum rockets used by Humans, were far too slow to be effective, except for intra-sector voyages. The Humans had learned this lesson the hard way when they sent an attack fleet against the Mutatis by conventional means, and it took more than eleven years to arrive, by which time the military technology was obsolete and easily defeated.

Nonetheless, there might still be a way for the Zultan to continue his Demolio torpedo attacks, busting enemy planets apart. Years ago, a Mutati scientist cut a piece of material off a podship—a thick slab of the soft, interior skin. He did it at a pod station while the ship was loading, and caused the sentient creature to react violently. It contracted, crushing the scientist and the Parvii pilot before they could send an emergency signal, but the piece of flesh was thrown clear and recovered by another Mutati.

After that, laboratory experiments were conducted on the tissue, and detailed analyses were made of the cellular structure. In the last couple of years, after many wrong turns, Mutati scientists had been able to clone the complex tissue, and had grown several podships … an unprecedented event.

However, while the lab-bred creatures appeared to possess many of the same attributes as authentic Aopoddae, they did not have all of them, and fell short in significant particulars. The scientists suspected this might have something to do with the power of the sentient creatures to control their own appearances, and—except for the influence exerted over them by Parviis—their own actions.

What the Mutatis possessed now were generic pods that did not display any individuality or variety. They all looked virtually the same, including their interiors and amenities, which often differed in authentic, natural podships. The clones had primitive access hatches and rough, archaic interiors, more like the insides of caves than the interiors of spacecraft capable of faster-than-light speeds. Not that any of the natural podships were luxurious; far from it; they did, however, offer some basic amenities that were lacking in the clones—such as benches, tables, and stowage areas for luggage.

So far, the Mutatis had met with no success testing the lab-pods. Several attempts to guide them and ride in them as passengers had been disastrous, resulting in crashes that killed everyone aboard, or in vessels that drifted aimlessly and had to be rescued by chase ships.

In addition, using rocket boosters, the laboratory-bred pods had been shot into space. From instinct, perhaps, the pods always accelerated beyond what the Mutatis wanted and reached such high speeds that they left their boosters behind and disappeared into space. Out of twenty-four such attempts, none of the lab-pods had arrived at the intended destinations on Mutati fringe worlds. They had a serious guidance problem, and all efforts to steer them precisely had met with failure. The artificial podships were like wild rockets shot by children in backyards....

Emerging from the gyrodome, the Zultan was disappointed. Inside, God-on-High had appeared before him in a vision, telling him the guidance problem could never be solved. He'd experienced visions before, and had no idea that many of them were psychic influences from the Adurian gyrodome, altering his decision-making processes. He also didn't know that his research scientists were similarly influenced by minigyros they used, keeping them from ever figuring out how to control the lab-pods. The clandestine HibAdu Coalition didn't want any more important merchant prince planets destroyed, because they were slated to be prizes of war for the secretly allied Hibbils and Adurians.

Unaware of the layered plots enfolding him, Abal Meshdi went to the lab-pod development facility, and commanded them to make a ship ready to carry an outrider in a schooner, fitted with the torpedo doomsday weapon.

"The ship will be guided by God-on-High," the intensely devout Mutati leader announced. "If our Demolio is meant to hit the target, it will."

Chapter Twenty-Two

All things in life have a mathematical property to them: Everything you perceive by any of your senses, and everything that occurs to you in the apparent privacy of your own mind. No one can escape the numbers, not even in death.

—Master Noah Watanabe

From an observation ledge, Giovanni Nehr watched a machine manufacturing and repair facility inside one of the largest caverns in the underground hideout. He knew that Thinker had perfected some of these methods on the planet Ignem, but mostly the machines had engaged in repair operations on discarded robots there. Gio had served there himself, dressed in the very armor he wore now. Thinker was beside him now, a dull-gray metal box that only moments before had clattered shut... one of the cerebral robot's many turtle-like retreats into his inner self.

Directly in front of the shuttered robot a mist in the shape of a Human being formed in the air. But it was so faint as to be indiscernible to the eyes of any sentient race. Certainly Gio had no chance of seeing it at all. But the entity that drove the image saw him and Thinker, and absorbed information about them. The mist drew closer to Thinker, and swirled around him, like a spirit from another realm....

On such a distant world as Ignem, it had been difficult for Gio to obtain the raw materials needed for new robots, particularly those rare elements required for the internal workings of sentient machines—elements that were closely guarded by industrial and political forces. Still, Thinker had found a niche by locating discarded robots around the galaxy that contained those elements, machines that he transported by podship and put back into service.

At Ignem, the sentient robots had been able to manufacture some new items, especially a popular computer chip that they sold around the galaxy. This brought in a nice stream of revenue, but had not had much of an impact on the overall market for new sentient machine components, which were dominated by the Hibbils on their Cluster Worlds.

Now, in the subterranean tunnels and caverns of the Guardians, the machines were doing something more advanced. With access to more raw materials and exotic components on the wealthy, mineral-rich planet of Canopa, they were actually manufacturing new sentient machines, in their entirety. This didn't have the efficiency of a Hibbil facility, but it was working well enough, and Thinker was innovating many of the manufacturing and assembly methods himself. He even had a prototype all-in-one machine that was designed to process raw materials through a hopper, convert them internally, and spit out a wide variety of finished components and products, somewhat in the manner of a hibbamatic. But the prototype wasn't working very well yet.

Thinker did have a real hibbamatic machine that Subi Danvar had obtained, also designed as an all-in-one production device by the Hibbils. But the Hibbil unit had not worked properly from the beginning, and would not hold any of the adjustments that the robot technicians tried to make to it. Thinker had learned afterward that it was a cheap model of the device, with inferior components and design shortcuts. While the merchant princes had superior versions of the machine, and had used them to produce defensive weapons on pod stations, the Guardians had not yet been able to obtain one of those, and had moral reasons for not wanting to do so. The high-quality hibbamatics were being used for planetary security, and despite the differences the Guardians had with the Doge and Francella, neither Thinker nor Subi wanted to compromise planetary defenses. At least the enemies on Canopa, though despicable, were not Mutatis.

So, the hidden Guardians had been making do with what they had, and it wasn't that much. Still, the flawed Hibbil unit had given Thinker some ideas on how to produce his own, and he was making the attempt.

Glancing over at Thinker's dull-gray metal box, Gio wondered why the robot leader often folded himself shut, something he refused to explain. To Gio it didn't make sense and seemed almost eccentric … a Human quality. A machine shouldn't need to focus its concentration in such a manner; it should be able to set its programs and block everything out electronically.…

The unseen mist swirled around Thinker, as if trying to merge with the robot. The ghostly form flickered and glowed around the gray box, like an aura for Thinker, but still Gio could not see it. Unconsciously, though, Gio's gaze followed its motion, as if he sensed something there. Then he looked back at Thinker.

Gio assumed the robot leader was just peculiar, and with peculiar people there was often no particular explanation. They just did things their own way, for their own unexplained reasons. Thinker and some of the other sentient machines seemed to have a number of Humanlike characteristics, albeit artificial ones. The machines were interesting personalities, Gio admitted, not the mundane sorts he might have expected.

They were surprisingly quiet down here on the floor of the cavern, Gio thought, all those robots moving back and forth, building their own little brothers. They were not nearly as noisy as a Digger machine boring through rock and dirt.

Finally, Thinker unfolded with a small commotion of metal. Turning his flat face toward Gio, he said, "My analysis of new, substantiated data points to the location of Master Noah. The information is sparse, but it is the best we've received so far."

Gio nodded. Earlier in the day, he had brought Thinker a new reconnaissance report, highlighting all the false leads the government had been disseminating on Noah in their efforts to conceal his whereabouts. But now the Guardians had real, proven data about a government effort to conceal a high-value prisoner.

For several moments, the robot did not say anything more. He just stood there, gazing down at the manufacturing floor with his metal-lidded eyes, drinking up details of the operations, processing and reprocessing the information in his data banks....

After considering the problem at length, wondering how best to locate the missing leader of the Guardians, Giovanni Nehr had helped to obtain and assemble the data in the new reconnaissance report, and had influenced its findings. Considering his own input now, he felt rather proud of himself. He'd never seen the robot leader take so long to respond.

During all the time that Noah had been missing, Thinker had been pessimistic about finding him, saying that the possibilities were too large and there were not enough Guardians to complete an adequate search. But when Gio provided the latest report to Thinker, there had been a shift. The orange lights around the robot's face had blinked quickly; the mechanical voice had been more measured.

"I must contemplate that for a reasoned response," Thinker had said, just before folding himself closed.

Now the orange lights around the perimeter of his face plate began to glow. Finally, he said, "I am prepared to answer now." The lights stopped blinking. With his gray metal eyes open wide, Thinker stared at Gio. Something glinted deep inside one of the intelligent eyes. "As a sentient robot, it is my primary goal in life to serve Humans, who were our original creators, and as such are almost godlike beings to us. At the Inn of the White Sun and the planet Ignem, I was consumed by one overriding desire, to build as many robots as I could and put them in the service of humanity. At that time, with all of my resources focused on that one goal, the full complement of my operating programs were at my disposal."

"For the life of me, I don't understand what you're getting at. What about the new recon report?"

"With all appropriate respect, Gio, you do not think like a machine, so your confusion is understandable. Consider the context of my remarks and realize, please, that I have now placed myself and my followers in service to humankind. I have attained my most important mission in life. I am here, doing what I want to do. The moment I began to work for Noah, my internal programming made certain automatic modifications. My personal initiative was shunted aside, since it might cause me to be overly aggressive. Robots must, by definition, be subservient and passive in the presence of Human masters such as yourself."

"I am Human, but I do not order you around. On the contrary, I am under your command."

"Only for training. Eventually, you will be my superior, since Humans always rise above machines. That is one of the basic laws of Human-machine interaction. You are superior creatures, and naturally exceed our capabilities. Now that we are in service to your race, we must be extra careful about what we do. I have sensed your previous displeasure about my inability to locate Noah. Other Humans, such as Subi Danvar, have been openly argumentative with me."

"That's all very interesting, but now I'd like you to give me your new probability calculations."

"Very well. Let me recheck them. For that, I don't even need to fold closed." He made a whirring noise, and presently began to spew out the names of the prisons on Canopa and other places where Noah might be, along with percentage probabilities of where he might be at any moment.

Listening carefully, Gio said, "There is a one-point-seven-one-percent chance that he is inside the Max One prison, and that's the highest odds?"

"There are many possibilities, even, as I said, a chance that he might not be at one of the government facilities I have listed. There is, in fact, a twenty-seven-point-three-two-percent chance that he is being held by a private party or a private company, which is a much higher overall percentage than the Max One odds. But when all of the private locations and all of the government facilities are considered, there is a greater probability that he is in Max One than anywhere else."

The robot paused, and blinked his metal-lidded eyes. "Are you following me?"

"I think so." Gio chewed on the inside of his lower lip. He was anxious to go out and find Noah.

"Keep in mind as well that these possibilities change from moment to moment and hour to hour, as I absorb new data from a variety of sources."

"OK, but tell me this. What are the odds that Noah is still alive?"

Thinker's mechanical eyes looked sad. "That is not something I wish to discuss. Will you excuse me from answering?"

Surprised at the emotional display, though it was undoubtedly programmed, Gio said, "Of course. I'll focus on Max One for the moment." He hurried off to tell Subi what he had learned.

Behind him, the mist lingered around Thinker, and then disappeared into the ether.

Chapter Twenty-three

There are many forms of confinement, both seen and unseen. It is often the unseen ones that are the most debilitating.

—Princess Meghina of Siriki

At the CorpOne medical laboratory, it had been another long day of tests on Noah, of unanswered questions and lines of scientific inquiry that seemed to lead nowhere. It was late afternoon, and Dr. Bichette stepped out of the room for a break, with his assistants. They left Noah where he was, secured to the examination table by electronic straps.

For some time now, Noah had felt a spinning sensation and a hum of energy all around him whenever he was under the electronic restraints. Where was it coming from? Noah had not been able to tell. Struggling to comprehend, his mind had vaulted away, and for a few minutes he had seen his friends Subi and Thinker, before the linkage broke.

Now the spinning sensation and energy hum became more intense, and he realized that he was generating it himself. His ankles and wrists felt increasingly hot. He struggled with the restraints, thinking something might be shorting out in the electronic system. The invisible straps were burning his skin.

Then, surprisingly, he pulled one wrist free, followed by the other. With only moderate effort, he also pulled his ankles loose and jumped off the table. Looking around, he decided to run up the stairs past the empty spectator seats. Reaching a door at the top, he opened it and found a corridor.

He ran with a burst of athletic speed. It was the first time he'd really been able to stretch his legs since being taken prisoner by the Red Berets, and he took full advantage of it. The corridor led to a bank of ascensores. At this early hour no one was around, and he felt strong despite not having slept much. He only needed to sleep for around six hours a night now, and this was continuing to drop, as it had been since Eshaz administered the Timeweb healing treatment on him.

Noah touched a pressure pad to order one of the high-speed lift mechanisms, and instantly he sensed that he had made a mistake. The pad felt odd, with a slick surface. A moment passed, and then he realized it had either read his identity or had decided that he was not an authorized user. Looking around, he didn't see any surveillance cameras, but they might be there anyway.

By the time alarm klaxons and bells sounded, Noah was running the other direction down the corridor, past the upper door to the operating theater.

He heard Dr. Bichette's voice on the loudspeaker system, shouting orders to the security staff. Just behind Noah a heavy metalloy door closed with an ominous thump, blocking the corridor. Ahead he saw another one coming down, and he rolled through only a fraction of a second before it slammed down. They were blocking sections off. Another door dropped ahead, and he found himself trapped in a small area, with no doors or windows.

* * * * *

Half a dozen security men escorted Noah roughly back to the operating table, where Dr. Bichette and his assistants awaited them.

"He got out of the electronic straps," one of the security officers said. "Look at the burn marks on the table. How'd he do that?"

"I see you are going to require extraordinary measures," the doctor said in an irritated voice. "Get back on the table, please." Looking at the security staff, he told them to remain close by.

"I have a little genetic test to perform," Bichette announced as Noah lay down on the table. "For your own sake, let's hope it goes well and we discover what we need."

"The secret of my restorative powers," Noah murmured bitterly.

"Precisely. Tell your genes to talk to me. Incidentally, don't expect any favors from me, either. I didn't appreciate being kidnapped by your criminal gang of so-called Guardians, or the poor attitude you have displayed this morning."

Seeing no point or benefit in answering, Noah said nothing. He felt the numbing effects of drugs, and for a time he fought them. Then, setting aside the discomforts of the medical procedure, Noah drifted into a timetrance journey in his mind, venturing out into the space-time continuum, the vast celestial web.

Inside the alternate realm, he saw a blur of faces, and then one came into sharp focus. His Tulyan friend Eshaz gazed at him with pale gray eyes, inviting him to a place that was much safer. Noah merged into the form, like a man diving into warm water, and the countenance disappeared.

Abruptly he found himself thinking with the brain of Eshaz, remembering back to an ancient era when Tulyans had a mandate to care for the entire galaxy, and held dominion over podships. Those were halcyon days, the best of all time, and for the cosmic traveler it was an awe-inspiring experience.

That evening when Noah Watanabe awoke in his room, with the drugs wearing off, he still retained something of the Tulyan experience, as a comforting memory. Around him, he saw the orange glow of the containment field, and he recalled a guard who had experienced trouble with the field control of the system. At the time, Noah had assumed it was a simple electronic malfunction. Now he began to wonder if the energy field of his own body had contributed to it.

Reaching out, he touched the barrier with his fingertips. It looked solid, felt solid. On the other side, a guard watched him closely, his hand on the handle of a holstered gun at his hip.

* * * * *

Despite the new information pointing to Noah's whereabouts, Subi Danvar felt they needed more information before sending an armed rescue mission. So he decided to send Gio on yet another reconnaissance mission. It was not the first time Gio had been sent out, but on the prior occasions he had gone with other Guardians and robots.

This time, Subi was sending him alone. "You must leave and return carefully," the adjutant said at the appointed time, "taking great care not to allow anyone to follow you."

"I know how to check for tracking devices and take other precautions," Gio assured him, before slipping out into the night.

* * * * *

As the armored man slipped through the darkness, his thoughts wandered. He liked Noah well enough, but mostly he wanted to ingratiate himself to his superiors. In his most private, illuminating thoughts, Gio admitted to himself that he was probably the most accomplished apple polisher in the entire galaxy, always working angles to worm his way into the affections of his superiors. His own advancement was paramount in his mind.

On the reconnaissance mission, Gio took along an electronic device provided by Thinker. From the river bank opposite the stony, monolithic prison, he concealed himself behind bushes and scanned the outside of the jail. The walls were too thick to be penetrated, but he had a stroke of luck. Passing the infrared light over a wall, he saw a prisoner looking out the window of an illuminated cell, toward the water.

Unmistakably, it was Anton Glavine, the young friend of Noah Watanabe … and perhaps more than that. According to rumors in Guardian ranks, Glavine was actually Noah's nephew, but that opened up intriguing questions. It meant Francella must be Glavine's mother, and conjecture had been flying about who might be the father, even Lorenzo del Velli himself. In any event, Glavine's presence was a good sign. He and Noah were probably kept in the same facility, for ease in interrogating them.

Gio kept scanning, but did not learn anything more from that section of wall. Presently, Anton moved away from the window.

Now the scanner penetrated the water of the river, and looking just below the nearest visible wall of the prison, Gio was able to pick up startling details of the underwater portion of the wall.

He made out the outline of what appeared to be an underwater door, and at first he wondered why it was there. Then he realized it had probably been designed as a secret escape route—though not for prisoners. This structure had once been the castle of a nobleman, so it might have been his secret way out if he ever came under attack. There might even be an airlock on the other side of the door.

* * * * *

In ensuing weeks, Subi Danvar and Giovanni Nehr developed an ambitious and ingenious assault plan to get into the prison, not knowing that Noah had already been moved....

Chapter Twenty-Four

I have often thought that the wild Aopoddae are too beautiful to be captured. Once, long ago, it was not necessary. We worked in harmony with them, and they came willingly.

—A Tulyan Storyteller

At the pod station over the Tulyan Starcloud, First Elder Kre'n stood with the rest of the robed Elders, awaiting the arrival of a most unusual podship, one that was guided by a rebellious Parvii. Eshaz was scheduled to return this morning on that vessel, and had sent word to the Council—by telepathic transmission through Timeweb—that he had a matter of utmost urgency to discuss with them.

Nearby, the Human teenagers Acey and Dux sat at a bench on the docking platform, with a guard posted to keep them in line. Since their unauthorized use of emergency escape capsules a few days ago, the pair had been monitored closely. The Elders were dismayed that the young men would behave so rudely and with such utter disregard for decorum, diverting equipment that might have been needed in a real emergency. Under the circumstances, the boys were not really welcome at the starcloud, but they were Eshaz's responsibility as his invited guests, and the Elders wanted to show him the proper respect.

The dignified Elders conversed in low tones, wishing Eshaz had never taken the boys under his wing when he had so many critically important duties that needed attention. But they knew Eshaz had done it out of a sense of honor, since they were Noah Watanabe's Guardians and he felt responsible for their welfare. Even in times of crisis, a Tulyan could not ignore honor.

"This is a most unfortunate situation," Kre'n said.

"But that is to be expected when timeseers are involved," noted the tallest of the Elders, Dabiggio, "especially this one who has worked with Humans so closely." Dabiggio, thus far the only member of the Council to become ill from what was being called the "web sickness," looked better to

Kre'n than he had previously, with less redness, and healing skin lesions. The treatments were taking hold. But there were constant breakouts among the populace that needed to be dealt with on a priority basis. Fortunately, the long-lived Tulyans were a tough breed, and had strong adaptive genetics.

"He does tend toward eccentricity," the First Elder said.

"An understatement if I've ever heard one," Dabiggio said with a cough. He was not one of Eshaz's supporters on the Council.

* * * * *

As a podship pulled into one of the docking stations, arriving without the customary hieroglyphic destination sign on its side, Acey and Dux rose to their feet. They'd never seen one come in like this, and the boys approached it, intrigued. The big reptilian guard followed them closely, but made no effort to stop them.

A hatch opened in the mottled gray-and-black skin of the sentient craft, and a familiar alien stepped through the airlock onto the platform, a biped with a large head, scaly skin and slitted eyes. He was accompanied by Tesh, whom the teenagers had seen earlier with Noah Watanabe. She was one of the Guardians, and had seemed to be a member of Noah's inner circle, along with Eshaz.

"Good to see you boys," Eshaz said. "Excuse me for a moment." He hurried by.

Showing no surprise, Tesh nodded to the perplexed young men.

Dux didn't know what to say. Why were those two together? And what sort of a podship was this, with no other passengers? He'd never heard of chartered podships. The boys inched closer to the others, positioning themselves to listen in.

After greeting the elegant, robed Elders and introducing them to the attractive brunette woman, Eshaz asked to speak privately with the Council about a matter of "utmost importance." The group of Tulyans moved off to one side.

As Eshaz spoke with them, out of earshot of the teenagers, Dux noticed that the Elders looked even more troubled than before, especially a tall male whom he had never seen smile. They stared disapprovingly at Tesh, then at Acey and Dux.

Presently, the Council members conferred among themselves, huddling together and speaking in low, urgent tones. Unknown to the boys, Eshaz had made a most unusual proposal to his superiors. It was something he wanted Tesh to help them with, but he had not yet mentioned it to her, not wanting to do so until he had the necessary approval.

* * * * *

While the Council deliberated over his astounding proposal, Eshaz glanced over at Dux and Acey, and nodded to them stiffly. From staying in touch with the starcloud by Timeweb-enhanced telepathy, he knew the boys had been restless in his absence, and had caused a considerable amount of commotion. The Elders should be glad to get rid of them.

And Tesh, too, even though they had barely met her. Eshaz knew that his superiors had even more antipathetic feelings toward Tesh, since he had told them of her true identity as a Parvii, a member of the race that had been mortal enemies of the Tulyans since time immemorial. This revelation had especially disturbed Dabiggio, but Eshaz had neutralized him somewhat and had garnered the support of the majority of the Council by convincing them that Tesh was an outcast from her people, and that she possessed special talents that could be beneficial to the entire Tulyan race, and to the future of the crumbling galaxy.

By touching hands with all of the Council—the ancient truthing touch process that opened the gateways of the mind—Eshaz had convinced them of the utter truthfulness of what he was telling them. Now, as he looked on, Dabiggio went to Tesh and performed this lie-detection process on her by touching her face without telling her what he was doing. She knew anyway, since it had long been one of the pieces of information that the two races knew about each other. For Parviis, it was one of the inexplicable processes that Tulyans could do, just as the Parvii system of personal magnification was known to Tulyans, but not anything about *how* it worked....

As the tall Elder completed the test and returned to his peers, Eshaz knew that Dabiggio and some of the Elders had other concerns. With his Council minority of supporters nodding in agreement, Dabiggio had debated it with Eshaz at some length. Eshaz had taken the position with him that all Parviis could not possibly be bad, and that one Parvii had never proven to be a threat, since they were only dangerous in swarms....

* * * * *

"Even so," Dabiggio had said in a harsh tone, "they are a hive mentality, with a morphic field that compels them to behave in certain ways. We have never understood how far their telepathic fields range, so for all we know this Tesh could still be under the direct control of the Eye of the Swarm."

His slitted eyes burning with intensity, Eshaz had countered, "You're looking at an exception with her. In each race there are individuals who go beyond the range of any type of control." He grinned, and added, "Many of my people consider me something of a maverick, since I go about things in a different way."

First Elder Kre'n and most of the others laughed.

In sharp and dark contrast, Dabiggio kept a stern face, like a mask glued tightly onto the skin. "Add this episode to your maverick ways," he said. "But you must realize that there are reasons for the precautions of our people and for the traditions we have followed for millions of years. You can't just go out and bring an enemy into our midst."

"She is not an enemy, and these are not ordinary times. Tesh Kori is, like myself and Master Noah Watanabe, a member of the Guardians."

"It seems your loyalties are split, then."

"Not at all. The Guardians and Tulyans have similar goals, both wishing to preserve and enhance the integrity of the galaxy. As you well know, Dabiggio, I have remained loyal to the traditions of our race."

"But Tesh Kori has not remained true to the traditions and goals of her own people! She is a traitor to her own kind, and you want us to trust her?"

"So in your eyes, she can't do anything to gain your acceptance? I personally witnessed the animosity and vitriol in her dispute with Woldn, and I have performed the truthing touch on her."

"We have never questioned your integrity," Dabiggio said, in a softer tone. But he had spent much of his two-million year lifetime being surly, and his voice became harsh again. "I must say, though, that your judgment is another matter entirely. I'm thinking of the time you connected that Human to the web, to heal him."

"We've already been over the matter of Noah Watanabe," First Elder Kre'n said, "and it has no bearing on the discussion at hand. There is no pattern of bad judgments on Eshaz's part, only a pattern of independent thinking. Perhaps we need more of his kind in order to rise above the galactic crisis. Perhaps we need to think out of the box, as Humans like to say. All information indicates that Noah Watanabe is in fact an extraordinary person, better even than many of our own people."

Scowling, Dabiggio had muttered something, but kept it under his breath.

Daring to make another, broader point, Eshaz had said, "I think we should take steps to end the age-old animosity between Tulyans and Parviis."

"A heretical statement if I have ever heard one," Dabiggio said.

"What good has the Tulyan-Parvii conflict done for the galaxy?" Eshaz asked. "Each race has important talents that could help heal the galaxy, if we could only find a way to work together."

"Careful, Dabiggio," one of the other Elders said, "or Eshaz here will have your job. He's making sense."

But Eshaz had not shown—or felt—any satisfaction when he saw the reaction of extreme displeasure on Dabiggio's face. This one could be a dangerous foe, one he should not galvanize into action. "With all respect that you deserve for your own integrity and service to our people," Eshaz said to Dabiggio, "I am only suggesting that we explore new options. We can't keep doing things the way we have for so long. We are at the eleventh hour in the galactic crisis and the clock is ticking."

"You are one for extending olive branches, aren't you?" Dabiggio had said with a wry smile. "Both to me and to the Parviis."

Eshaz had returned the smile, with a deferential bow....

* * * * *

Now he saw the Elders approaching him, with First Elder Kre'n ahead of the others. Eshaz held his breath.

"All right," First Elder Kre'n said, with a careful smile. "You have our permission to proceed."

"Fabulous, fabulous," Eshaz said. He bowed, and excused himself from them.

Strutting over to the boys, he patted them on the backs with tender care, then guided them over to Tesh. "If you will come with me," he said to her, "I have a most interesting proposal for you."

The Tulyan did not provide specifics until the four of them were alone in Dux's suite at the orbital Visitor's Center, awaiting the delivery of supper. They all sat on large chairs at a diamondplax table, furnishings designed to accommodate the enormous bodies of Tulyans, who were the largest of the galactic races. Tesh, Acey, and Dux sat on high pillows.

Leaning forward at the table, still dwarfing his companions, Eshaz looked at Tesh and said in a conspiratorial tone, "This is something I really didn't want to say within the telepathic field of Woldn back at the Parvii Fold, and not even inside a podship, where your leader's field presumably extends."

"No comment," she said.

Dux and Acey exchanged perplexed glances.

Eshaz took a deep, excited breath. "I am about to tell you something that Woldn would not like."

He paused as Tulyan waiters brought in large plates of food, the aromatic vegetarian fare that this race favored. In their entire history, they had apparently never eaten meat, seafood, or anything that had once been alive—other than the special plants that they grew for their leaves and other foliage, and trimmed without ever killing the plants. According to one of the main dining room waitresses, the Tulyans even had religious ceremonies and rituals involving the plants. It was a very serious, very spiritual matter to them.

Dux rather liked the dishes he'd been served here before, though Acey ate them only grudgingly, because he had no choice. As the waiters removed the lid from Dux's plate, he inhaled the rich odor of a golden stew. He thought it might be something they called *watilly*, which had what the waitress had called "a rainbow of flavors." Sampling it with a spoon, he wasn't so sure. This tasted slightly different, with a cilantro aftertaste. Maybe it was still *watilly*, but seasoned in a different fashion.

When the waiters were gone, Eshaz said, "I intend to hunt and capture wild podships, the way my people did in the early years of the galaxy."

Looking alarmed, Tesh protested, asserting that her people—and especially Woldn—would never permit it, and even if Eshaz was successful he would soon be swarmed and the pods would be taken away. This was the way it had always been when Tulyans obtained podships.

"I don't want any part of it," Tesh said.

"We seem to be missing some details here," Dux said.

"Wild podships?" Acey said, ignoring his cousin's comment. *"Row fantastic!* We can go, too?"

"I've got to keep you boys out of trouble, don't I?" Eshaz wiped stew off his own chin, and grinned. "Of course, we will require transportation for such a grand adventure. That's where our friend Tesh comes in."

While the wide-eyed boys listened, Eshaz provided them with general information about Parviis and Tulyans, and their age-old battle for control of podships. He told them Tesh was not really Human, that she was a Parvii in disguise, and that she had piloted the podship that brought her and Eshaz here to the starcloud. Then he looked at Tesh and asked, "Do you want to add anything to that?"

She shook her head, and her emerald eyes flashed. "Perhaps later."

Reaching across the table, Eshaz touched her hand. Despite the magnification system he knew she had, Eshaz was able to connect with her cellular structure and read her thoughts, her innermost wishes and dreams. Earlier, he had done this to the Parviis who were clustered around him at the Palace of Woldn, probing the neuron highways of their brains, picking up some of their innermost wishes and dreams. He knew that Tesh had disagreed with Woldn before, and so had others. Now she was one of the most outspoken ones, inciting the displeasure of the leader. He had seen that firsthand, and now he learned more about her reasons, her independent way of looking at things, her strong sense of personal integrity and morality. Woldn had murdered passengers on podships, and she hated him for it. The terrible act had made her ashamed to be a Parvii.

She looked at him oddly, knowing that he was intruding on her thoughts, but letting him do it.

"Well, are you a Parvii first or a citizen of the galaxy?" Eshaz demanded, taking a new tack. "Can't you think of a situation where the health of the galaxy comes before the interests of your people? Noah's Guardians have performed recovery operations on only a handful of planets—not nearly enough. All of us need to do more." He paused. "Noah wants us to do more."

Now Eshaz found that her thoughts became troubled and murky, with flashes of near-decision that changed quickly and flitted off in other directions, some of which involved her personal feelings of attraction for Noah. In only a few moments, she explored too many ancillary considerations for him to follow. He didn't like to connect with mental impulses that shot in several directions like that, since it invariably gave him terrible headaches.

With a gentle smile, he withdrew his hand.

While Tesh considered his proposal, Eshaz said that Noah should expand his ecological recovery operations, to encompass more planets. In order to accomplish that, a fleet of Guardian-operated podships would be necessary, and

Noah—if he ever escaped from imprisonment—could eventually merge operations with the entire race of Tulyans, the original caretakers of the galaxy.

"We Tulyans are working on methods of concealing podships from Parviis, and we think it might be possible to maintain control of every wild pod we capture." Pausing, he added, "Actually, it's something I've been wanting to discuss with Noah, but circumstances were never right—emergencies kept intruding."

"How do your people capture wild Aopoddae?" Tesh asked. "It is something I have always wondered about."

"I have already revealed a Tulyan confidence to you about our plans," Eshaz said. "Just as Woldn is not pleased with you, the Tulyan Council thinks I may be a bit too much on the eccentric side. Still, they have given me permission to go on a special mission—if you consent, of course. We know that you have sealed the sectoid chamber, preventing intrusion. On wild podship hunts, we always stop at a certain planet first in the Tarbu Gap, and I will need to pilot us there, since you cannot know the location."

"We are not enemies anymore," she said. "That much I will accept, but it must be reciprocal."

"Ah yes, to a degree. You concealed the location of the Parvii Fold from my truthing touch, hiding the galactic coordinates of your sacred place. Your people were the same to my touch; they told me nothing."

"And you Tulyans have your own sacred secrets as well." She shook her head. "It's too bad you and I can't fully trust one another."

He smiled in a serene, perhaps ancient way. "Tell me where the Parvii Fold is, then, and I will tell you where the Tarbu Gap is. A quid pro quo."

"Just like that? But what if I give you the wrong information?"

"Then I will do the same for you. Don't forget. I have been traveling this galaxy for almost a million years, and I will know the truth ... or the lie ... of the coordinates you give me."

"It is at the far end of Nebula 9907," she said.

He narrowed his eyes suspiciously. "I have been to that region many times, and saw no galactic fold."

"There is an asteroid funnel that is veiled by a Parvii swarm that guards it constantly, a swarm that has changed its appearance to make it look like there is no opening at all."

"One of your nasty Parvii tricks," Eshaz said. He nodded his head. "Yes, that location rings true."

"And you Tulyans have no tricks of your own?" she said, with a smile. "Now it's your turn."

"Very well. The Tarbu Gap is in the Isuki Star System."

"Where?"

He grinned, revealing large reptilian teeth. "In the five hundred seventy-seventh quadrant, past the Tlewa Roid Belt."

She thought for a moment. "I'm drawing a blank."

"It is a region of burned-out stars, and of dwarf stars, both white and brown. It is one of the Aopoddae breeding grounds."

"I don't know how we missed it."

Eshaz shrugged. "It's a big galaxy. If you are ready, I shall give you coordinates to take us there."

"Have you used Tulyan mindlink to veil the region in some manner?"

"I have told you enough," he said curtly.

"Be nice to me or I'll inform Woldn, and he will have the swarms cut you off from that area. He will end your podship hunts forever."

"But your true allegiance is not to Woldn, is it?" Eshaz said. "It is to the well-being of this galaxy. I see it in your eyes, and ... I felt it ... in your touch."

Tesh did not look surprised. She looked down at her hand, where Eshaz had made physical contact with her, and smiled.

"Will you take us to Tarbu Gap?" Acey asked her.

"Just let anyone try and stop me," Tesh said.

The four of them reached across the table, and clasped hands.

Chapter Twenty-Five

From any point in time or space, the possibilities are endless.

—Noah Watanabe

While Giovanni Nehr was considering a plan to rescue Noah, he remembered seeing the underwater door of the Max One prison. The stone structure had once been a nobleman's castle, so he thought that was probably a secret escape route, with an airlock on the other side. But there might not be an airlock on the other side, or it might not be functional anymore.

To deal with that unknown, Gio now envisioned a scuba-commando team of Humans and fighting machines, attaching a mobile airlock to a wall underwater. They could then find a way to open the door and go through.

Finding Thinker in one of the robot construction chambers, Gio outlined his plan to him.

Blinking his metal-lidded eyes, Thinker said, "Your concept of a mobile airlock is intriguing, but it has never been done before. Granted, the underwater door on the prison may not have an airlock of its own, so your idea has some merit. But it presents difficulties, not the least of which is the method of sealing such a device against a wet surface, especially with the rock that the prison is made of. It's Canopan sangran, a material that cannot be climbed with adhesive shoes, since malleable foreign substances do not stick to it. In my data banks, I have information about the difficulties they had in formulating mortars."

"But they came up with a mortar, obviously."

"Yes, and I know the formula. But it requires materials that are not readily available to us on Canopa."

"There must be a way," Gio said.

"If we had the right materials, yes, but the lack of podship travel...." Thinker hesitated. "Ah," he said.

"What did you come up with?"

"Come with me," Thinker said. He led Gio down a long tunnel into a side cavern. At a barracks building, he asked to see one of the new recruits, a young woman named Kindsah. "Tell her to bring her friend, too," he added.

After a few minutes, she came over. A stocky woman in her early twenties with curly black hair, she smiled readily. Gio had never met her before, but had seen her with an unusual little alien—one she had with her now, visible from the top of an open carrying bag in her hand.

Thinker explained the problem to her, and he said, "I've seen you demonstrating Lumey's flexibility, and the way he can change shape and stick to surfaces with the most powerful adhesive quality I've ever seen. Could he stretch himself thin and do what we need, forming a gasket?"

Reaching into the bag, Kindsah brought out the dark-brown amorphous creature that Noah Watanabe had originally rescued from an industrially polluted planet. "To save Noah, this fellow would do anything. Of course, he could do that." She touched the creature soothingly as she murmured to it, and in a few seconds it became long and thin.

"See if he can stick to this," Thinker said. He brought a large gray chunk of sangran out of a bucket of water, and extended it.

Like a snake, Lumey darted forward and adhered himself to the wet stone, so that no one could pull it free. Then, holding him by the tail, Kindsah swung Lumey and the heavy stone over her head like a lasso. Only when she stopped and spoke soothingly to the creature, telling it to let go, did it do so.

Next, Kindsah caused the creature to spread all over the floor of the cavern like the thinnest of crepes on the surface, face-up.

"This is going to work," Thinker said. He knelt down and touched Lumey gently with the metal tip of a probe, then looked at Gio. "Now let's solve the other problems presented by your plan."

* * * * *

Giovanni Nehr had not anticipated such a woeful possibility, but as he developed the rescue plan with Thinker and Subi Danvar, he feared that he may have painted himself into a corner. Too late, a range of unwelcome possibilities occurred to him. The bottom line: If his plan did not result in Noah's safe return, he could very well be demoted to a mere fighter again, no more significant than the dead-brain robots who followed Thinker. Or worse, Gio envisioned the end of his career path in the Guardians.

But he had to proceed anyway. He had no alternative. So he recommended the key details of a dangerous, risky plan. At every opportunity, he tried to spread the potential blame as widely as possible, even to the young female recruit who cared for Lumey. With such an uncertain result, he preferred to cushion his own fall. But everyone kept complimenting him on the boldness and cleverness of his ideas, and looking to him to spearhead the effort.

It soon became apparent to Gio that the blame—or credit—would all go to him.

In the plan, he set the time and means of infiltrating Max One prison, in a daring attempt to liberate the beloved founder of the Guardians. The penal facility had been constructed on a manmade canal to resemble its notorious, blood-stained predecessor on Timian One, the Gaol of Brimrock.

Finally, Gio and his team were ready to go, not knowing that Noah wasn't even there anymore....

Chapter Twenty-Six

"The noble-born princes call themselves aristocracy and cavort about in fine trimmings, but they are empty shells, for they have earned nothing and only came into their wealth through the deaths of their ancestors. But each chain of inheritance actually began with someone earning the wealth. Hence, it is beyond comprehension how the noble-born princes can consider themselves superior to those of us who have amassed great assets through ingenuity and hard work. Alas, this has been a dynamic of history, the eternal clash of old and new money."
—Prince Saito Watanabe, public address on "The Nouveau Riche"

Seated in a front-row seat of the operating theater, Francella Watanabe leaned forward in anticipation. Having been unavoidably detained by a meeting, she had come in late. It was late morning now, and every window shade in the facility had been drawn so that bright yellow sunlight only came in through slits.

Dr. Bichette, standing over Noah at the central table, was injecting him with something. Four burly security guards stood nearby, ready to spring into action if her brother tried to escape again. Electronic straps no longer held him, and guards reported that he had shown interest in the electronic containment field of his cell, apparently trying to think of ways to disable it, too. But this was a different, far more powerful system, and thus far it seemed capable of holding Noah. No one was taking any chances, though. Additional guards had been assigned to him around the clock.

Francella glared down at the doctor, who had also been a source of irritation. Bichette had displayed a maddening degree of independence to her, but she couldn't get rid of him. Like her father before her, Prince Saito, she relied on Bichette's expertise, and to his credit, the man did not seem to like Noah much himself. In a heated discussion the day before, Bichette had assured Francella that their goals were "not dissimilar," and that he would take care of the situation in his own way, but to their mutual satisfaction.

The pledge had been somewhat less than she would have preferred, but Francella wanted to maintain her own composure in this situation, and was trying to pull herself back emotionally from the experiments being performed on her brother. That was much easier said than done, she realized.

Besides, she had other important matters on her mind. Shortly before coming in today, she had conducted a virtual-reality nehrcom session with noble-born princes on other planets. Blocked from meeting them in person by the podship crisis, this was their only viable means of getting together. At her insistence security had been tight, and because of the high status of the participants, all of them had been able to obtain private rooms at the various nehrcom transmitting stations.

The video quality of the meeting had been fuzzy, nowhere near as good as the clarity of the audio. Jacopo Nehr, inventor of the cross-space transmission system, had never been happy with the video feature, even on direct hookups such as this that did not go through relay stations. Apparently he considered it something of a professional embarrassment, so often he acted as if the feature didn't exist at all. All Francella could do was to make the best use of the technology, such as it was. She liked to watch the body language of people with whom she was conversing, as that often told her more than their words. It told her something about their sincerity and loyalty, of paramount importance to her because of the nature of their meetings.

For years Doge Lorenzo del Velli had favored men who excelled in business, and he had been appointing them to important governmental positions … at the expense of the noble-born princes. Her late father and Jacopo Nehr were among the most conspicuous examples of commoners honored at the expense of nobles, as both had been appointed "Princes of the Realm." But there were many others at various levels of government, undermining the entire infrastructure of the Merchant Prince Alliance. In a sense it was ironic that she—not of noble birth herself—should find herself aligned with those who were, but it was how she felt about the matter nonetheless. The old traditions were important, and should not be discarded easily. Men like her own brother, if permitted to excel and advance, were part of the problem.

At the VR nehrcom session the noble-born princes had clamored for her attention, asking her to be more active in their cause. She assured them that she was doing everything she could, but for security reasons she could not reveal all of the details. That was true to an extent, because she was helping their cause by destroying her own brother. But she had to admit to herself that she had something else in mind that was far more important than anything she would ever reveal to them.

Through her own sources, she had learned that some of the princes felt uneasy working with a woman (and a commoner by birth), but because of her political power and influence, she was their best hope to overthrow Lorenzo and replace him with their own man. The new leader had to be a man; she had no delusions about that, or ulterior motives of her own. She wouldn't want the job anyway, since it would only invite competitors to plot against her, especially in view of her gender. Francella felt more comfortable as a power behind the scenes. She could be a puppeteer, and make the next doge dance on the end of her strings.

She had concluded the VR meeting as quickly as possible while assuring her allies of her devotion to them, and her ongoing, behind-the-scenes efforts to undermine Doge Lorenzo's authority and eventually overthrow him. It was all a political cesspool as far as she was concerned, but she didn't particularly want to take more severe action, such as assassination. After all, she and Lorenzo had been bedmates for years now, and she didn't want to completely do away with him. She just wanted him out of office.

Now, in the laboratory, she focused on her most pressing interest. The square-jawed Dr. Bichette, in a white medical smock, was flanked by a pair of female technicians, similarly attired. The trio wore belts containing a variety of medical instruments and even stunners, should the patient become unruly and somehow break free of the electronic restraints that were holding him down.

At the moment, they seemed to be sedating Noah.

Her brother's purported immortality condition had not yet been verified, and there were certain things she needed to know. At the thought, she felt a slight trembling. In her discussion with Bichette she had emphasized their importance. He'd said he understood, and would perform the research properly, to fully exploit the information they obtained.

In previous laboratory sessions, Bichette had taken blood and tissue samples from Noah, and had performed a variety of experiments on him. Today, the doctor looked back at Francella and said, "I'm glad you are here. You will want to see this. The patient's ability to regenerate body parts seems to be linked with his reported 'immortality' condition, and if so, it is important to understand how it all works." Without further comment, he turned to his work, watching as the technicians took vital signs, including checking the dilation of the pupils. Unconscious, Noah heaved deep breaths, with his chest rising and falling perceptibly. Bichette opened one of Noah's hands and then swung the arm and hand onto a metal side table.

At a nod from one of the technicians, Dr. Bichette called for a C76 surgical scalpel, holding his hand out as the servo machinery in the room whirred to life, and a mechanical arm reached down to him from the ceiling.

Grabbing the scalpel, he made a quick motion with it, cutting off her brother's right forefinger. Noah jerked, but did not awaken. His breathing became less regular, and more agitated. Tossing the finger on a tray, the doctor moved to the bottom end of the table. This time he called for a surgical saw, and cut off the big toe on Noah's left foot, the same foot that had regenerated after being amputated earlier.

Again Noah jerked, and this time his eyes fluttered open before he drifted off once more, probably experiencing a nightmare. Francella felt no sympathy for him, never had. If he ever injured himself when they were children, she always enjoyed it, and now she felt a comfortable, pleasant sensation, a wash of memories from those times.

While Francella watched, fascinated, one of the attendants recorded everything with a holocam. In less than a minute, the finger and toe regrew, forming red appendages that changed in hue moment by moment, returning to the natural, light pigmentation of Noah's skin.

The technicians wrapped up Noah's severed finger and toe, and marked them for laboratory analysis. Dr. Bichette tossed the scalpel on a table, and looked thoughtfully at Noah. Francella wondered if his thoughts paralleled her own. Surely, he must have considered the possibilities. As for her, convinced that her brother really had eternal life, she was anxious to obtain it for herself, too.

Francella left her seat, and moved to the doctor's side. He glanced in her direction.

"I've been thinking about injecting his blood into my own bloodstream," she said.

Overhearing this, one of the laboratory technicians looked alarmed.

"I would not recommend that," Bichette said. "There are many analyses to complete before anything like that can be considered. Even then we would not want to try it on a Human being first." He shook his head. "There are many steps to follow."

Francella did not like the sound of that. She detested delays, had in mind the things she wanted to do. With the gift of eternal life, she could accomplish so much. The problem of her brother would remain, since he would also have the gift, so she would always—literally—have to keep him under control. For all eternity, she would be the master and he the slave.

Unless she found a way to obliterate Noah and all of his bodily tissue. But without cellular material, how would he regenerate? By magic? She experienced a mounting rage, and didn't know how long she could keep it in under control. Her trembling increased, and a shudder coursed her spine.

Leaning over Noah as he slept fitfully, she whispered in his ear: "I've always hated you. You were Daddy's favorite, his chosen successor, and the two of you acted like I didn't exist at all. I got nothing but the leavings, whatever you didn't want."

She felt an urge to slap him hard, but resisted because of the witnesses. Grimacing, she husked, "The tables have turned now, and I'm in control."

Chapter Twenty-Seven

Any prison, no matter how ironclad it might appear to be, has multiple weak points. Security is only an illusion, and often only works because of the illusion.
—Noah Watanabe, Ruminations

Shortly after midnight, three men, a woman, and six robots, all in black, slid down a muddy embankment and slipped into the water. The river, murky and slow-moving, chilled Gio at first despite his body suit, but he warmed as he swam across underwater, using his tankless breathing mechanism and making hardly any noise. The others followed him almost soundlessly. He felt a rush of exhilaration. With luck his commando team would rescue Noah Watanabe, and maybe even Anton Glavine. But Glavine was of secondary importance. The commandos' priority was clear, and everything had to go smoothly.

Gio wished he had a floor plan of the prison, but such information was highly classified. He had tried obtaining the layout, but at Thinker's suggestion he had made a blanket inquiry, concealing their intent by making it for all government-operated buildings on Canopa. No inquiries had resulted in anything useful, not even when bribes were offered.

The Humans under Gio's command wore night-vision goggles, but the six robots didn't require such gear, since their visual sensors adjusted automatically, absorbing the narrowest rays of light.

In actuality the commando squad had an additional member, since one of the ten squad members—Kindsah—carried Lumey in a backpack. Reaching the base of the rock prison wall, the young female Guardian removed the alien from her pack, and massaged Lumey gently. Looking at the amorphous creature in the red darkness, Gio imagined that Lumey might be feeling his own excitement and anticipation, since Noah had rescued him from an industrial slag heap.

For a moment, Gio almost had a change of heart. It was a strange sensation, as if he was about to take an unfamiliar path. Since first encountering Noah, he'd held some affection and respect for him, but with Gio such feelings had distinct limitations, not coming anywhere near the abiding, narcissistic love he felt for himself. For as long as he could remember, Gio had been a survivor, wary of outsiders, not trusting anyone, not even his family. His attitude sharpened even more after his brother became famous and got so much adulation.

In the red darkness, three of the swimming robots held the mobile airlock, with the flat side toward Kindsah. She petted the alien in her hands, and Gio saw it stretch as thin as a rope and attach itself to the perimeter of the airlock's flat side, forming a living gasket. Through some inexplicable means, the creature seemed to understand its role.

With Gio in the lead, the commando team submerged, and secured the airlock around the underwater doorway of the prison, with Lumey playing his part perfectly, and even leaving an opening in the center that matched the size of the door itself. Opening a hatch on the airlock, Gio swam inside first, followed by two of his team members, one of whom was a robot with security disabling capability.

They waited while pumps drained the chamber of water. Then they worked on the heavy metal prison door, using a fast-acting acid that ate the metal away. In a matter of moments the old door broke away, opening into darkness.

"Searching for alarm components," the robot reported. It discharged a flying unit that went ahead, through the hole. Designed by Thinker, it would neutralize any motion detectors, noise sensors, or other alarm features while making prison authorities think the system was still in operation.

In the red light of his goggles Gio made out a large, empty chamber beyond. A minute later the flying probe returned to its host robot, blinking a green light.

"Our remote camera isn't working," the robot reported. "I can't get any images of what's ahead. The probe found an alarm and decommissioned it, though."

"Let's go!" Gio said, after considering for only a moment. He led the way through. As they reached the rock interior floor of the prison, a clearplax door on the airlock closed behind them. He saw a door open on the other side of the airlock, letting water into the chamber, along with three more members of the commando team who swam inside, including Kindsah. The process repeated, and in a few moments the entire squad stood inside the prison.

With Gio in the lead, they ran from corridor to corridor and cell to cell, always keeping close to a wall, slinking around corners, moving stealthily through dim illumination. This entire level was unoccupied, though a room containing racks, garrotes, electrocution machines, injection tables, and a variety of other diabolical devices showed signs of recent activity, with scraps of food and leftover cups scattered about on the floor and tables.

Behind Gio, the robots moved with impressive silence. He didn't know how they accomplished it. Leading them up to the next level, he waited to confirm that the entire alarm system had been disabled, then hurried along the corridor. As he rounded a corner he saw a guard just ahead, and froze in his tracks. One of the robots fired a stun pellet, dropping the guard with a soft thud.

Most of the cells were unoccupied, but not all of them. As the commandos ran by, some of the prisoners asked what they were doing. Others called out for help, but Gio ignored all of them. He couldn't rescue everyone, couldn't afford to direct any energy in the wrong direction, slowing the thrust of his force.

Anton Glavine, whom Gio had seen standing at a window earlier, was nowhere to be seen. The commandos checked floor after floor, not finding Noah, either. But it was an immense facility.

On the limited number of levels they reached, they fired stun pellets, knocking guards into unconsciousness. The commando team's security robot got its remote camera working, and in a blur of speed, the flying probe searched every remaining section of the prison. There were many more guards on other levels, but no sign of Noah or Anton.

Just as the flying probe searched the last area, Gio glanced at his wristchron, and saw that he only had a couple of more minutes before they had to leave. Gio's imagination ran wild. Maybe Noah and Anton were being interrogated in a hidden room, or even tortured. The Doge's prisons were notorious hellholes.

Hearing voices just ahead, around a corner, he stopped. Holding up his hand, the rest of his team paused with him, and listened. The alarm robot sent the flying probe ahead. Studying a small screen on the robot, Gio saw the camera flicker as it sent a fuzzy signal.

On the image he saw Anton Glavine, seated at a chair with uniformed Red Berets around, interrogating him. No sign of Noah Watanabe anywhere, but on this level and on the route to reach it there were more guards than his small force could overcome. To Gio it looked too risky to attempt a rescue of Anton.

"You have such a convenient memory," one of the interrogators said, a burly man with a black beard. "Somehow you can't recall anything about where Guardian headquarters is, but you admit being there? How is that?"

"I don't know," Anton said, "but I'm telling you the truth." He smiled grimly. "Maybe it's stress-induced, and you should let up on me."

"I wish they'd let us use more efficient methods on this one," the man said, "and on Watanabe. I'd get the information out of both of them."

"So, he hasn't told you, either?" Anton asked.

"Obviously, or we wouldn't be pressing you. At least he doesn't have a cock-and-bull story like yours, and he admits knowing. He keeps talking about honor and duty. Makes me want to puke."

The interrogators paused as a woman in a hooded cloak emerged from a side door, carrying a tray of food. As she set the tray on a table, Glavine was ushered over and seated. He glanced at the woman, then began to eat quickly. The Red Berets stood to one side, talking and not paying attention to the pair.

With a quick motion the woman whispered something to Glavine, then hurried away. He looked surprised at whatever she had to say. Just before she departed through a doorway her hood fell open for a moment, revealing blond hair and a heart-shaped face. She slipped away, unnoticed by the guards.

She was the most stunningly beautiful creature Gio had ever seen. He played the holo-image back on the robot's screen, then froze the frame. And recognized her. She was, unmistakably, Princess

Meghina of Siriki! But what was the famous courtesan and companion of the Doge doing here, serving food to a prisoner and trying to conceal her identity?

An odd feeling came over Gio, a mixture of questions and the sense that all he was seeing, while fascinating, would not result in finding Noah. Anton might be a good secondary target to rescue—in view of the rumors about him—but he seemed to have an important benefactor, a noblewoman. Were they lovers? Was Lorenzo really his father? One thing seemed clear: Any attempt to get him now would certainly result in a firefight, and he'd be on the losing end. If Anton had been alone in an isolated cell, it might have been different. But this was much more complicated. Anton was the focus of too much attention.

Noah didn't seem to be here, but wherever they were keeping him they would undoubtedly move him to a more secure place after an assault on Max One. Better to retreat and regroup.

Gio gave the necessary comsignal, then led his team back the way they had come. In a matter of minutes, he and the others were outside and in the water again, with the exception of one robot, who sealed himself in the airlock and pumped water out of it. Afterward he would reseal the underwater door to the prison, using a mortar patch he had brought along. It would not look the same as the original door, but in the murky darkness of the prison should go unnoticed for a time.

As Gio emerged from the water and crawled up the riverbank on the other side, he felt dismal. He had developed an excellent rescue plan for the facility, but it seemed likely that Noah had been moved. Maybe he wasn't even alive.

For Giovanni Nehr's career path, a very bad scenario had come to pass.

Chapter Twenty-Eight

When making important leadership decisions, take care to avoid certain emotions such as anger or envy, since they can be dangerous to your mission. But don't avoid emotions entirely. Always follow your gut instincts.

—Noah Watanabe

Thinker had developed a veiling energy field to protect the subterranean headquarters, a system that was superior to the original infrared scrambling system he had set up. Now he felt even more confident that Noah's enemies would not locate their headquarters inside rock-lined underground burrows. Most of the hidden facility lay deep beneath hills near Noah's former ecological demonstration compound, but some of the newer chambers were close to the edge of his old property.

With the improved technology, the robot was not concerned about security. They could burrow directly beneath the old administration buildings if they wanted to, and would not be detected.

Learning of this, Subi liked the irony, and at first he thought it might be an unexpected action that Noah had taken himself—a slap in the face of his enemies. But Subi's better judgment told him to maintain caution....

He had trouble making some decisions. With Noah missing—incarcerated or worse—Subi felt out of balance. For the months of the Master's absence he'd been trying to keep the Guardians going, and he had done reasonably well in recruitment, bringing in hundreds of young men and women, along with the new machines that Thinker was building. Subi had helped obtain materials for the robots, and had given the robot leader specifications for the mechanical fighters and support workers that he needed.

On the surface, seen through the eyes of the Guardian membership, the organization seemed to be doing well. They were not only growing in number; they were making successful, destructive raids against the Doge's Red Berets and Francella's CorpOne assets. But to Subi, those successes only masked the deep pain he felt inside, the terrible, gnawing fear that he would never see Noah again.

Is he dead?

On one level, it seemed impossible to him; Noah Watanabe was the strongest person he had ever met, and even had an odd restorative power that Subi had observed himself, the ability to regenerate an amputated left foot. Cellular regeneration. Amazing. But Subi still assumed Noah was mortal, a container of cells that would eventually decay and die.

The loyal adjutant didn't want to think that way, and tried to remain optimistic. He would follow Noah off a cliff if ordered to do so, would do anything for the great man. With loving attention to detail, Subi was keeping the Guardians going for Noah, caretaking them until his friend and mentor returned. But what if that never happened? What if the worst had occurred?

He could not share such terrible thoughts with anyone for fear of destroying the organization, could only live with his terrible fears each day, constantly trying to put them out of his mind.

In Noah's absence, Subi had to make do in any number of ways. The adjutant missed being able to consult with his boss on tough decisions, or having Noah ask him for his advice. He missed their walks together on the Ecological Demonstration Project, and hearing the renowned man identify every plant they passed. He missed conducting classes together on Eco Station.

Now, with all of that gone, Subi had to motivate young minds in new ways. He still conducted classes, still taught ecology, but it was not the same. Holo-images of plants, shown to students in underground caverns, were not the same as the real thing.

It was all second-rate, except for Noah's own writings on galactic ecology, which Subi prepared for classroom education and distributed to the students.

* * * * *

On the operating table at the CorpOne medical laboratory, Noah sensed evil forces at work against him, and felt their debilitating effects on him. He heard his loathsome sister's taunting voice, but could not focus on her words. Drugs were keeping him submerged.

His tortured mind struggled and groped, searching for escape, and he did manage to achieve a timetrance, but it was not the serenity he longed for, not a haven to restore his energies and his desire to fight on. He felt dismal.

Like an injured predator, he attempted to gain control over a podship that was docked in a pod station, wanting to take the vessel out on the podways. But as his mental tendrils reached out and touched the podship, it jerked away from him, and fled into space.

Yet Noah kept reaching out, and this time he took a different direction....

* * * * *

Just before Noah's capture, he had asked Thinker to download a backup copy of his brain into one of the robot's data banks. The Guardian leader had been thinking about his own mortality, and wanted to make sure his teachings were directly available to his followers, in case something happened to him.

For some time afterward the cerebral robot contemplated the best means of preserving and presenting the information in Noah's mind. Finally he came up with something beyond what either of them originally contemplated. He created a three-dimensional color likeness of Noah on a large square screen, visible by opening a panel on the front of the robot's torso. It looked and behaved like the original person, and even interacted with anyone speaking to the screen. For further realism the image had freckles on its face, as well as tiny scars and blemishes on the 3-D body, all precisely correct from every side.

Anxious to show off his new creation, Thinker went to Subi Danvar's underground office, and entered unannounced.

The adjutant stood at a work table, thumbing through a pile of paper documents. Hearing the metallic sounds as the robot entered, he turned. "I'll just be a minute," Subi said, going back to his work.

As Thinker waited, he slid open the new video panel on his chest, and the image of Noah Watanabe flashed on.

"Hurry it up, hurry it up," the simulacrum said in a voice that very nearly matched the original.

"Eh?" Startled, Subi dropped the papers, scattering them on the floor.

"You heard me," the Noah said. "Now come over here where I can get a better look at you."

Timidly, Subi approached the screen, where the face of Noah Watanabe stared at him in displeasure.

"What is this?" Subi said, looking up at Thinker's metal face, just above the screen.

Thinker did not reply, but the video image did. "I'm not in the habit of being ignored by a subordinate. Speak to me, Subi, not to the robot."

Perplexed, Subi backed up, staring all the while at the screen. "Thinker, tell me what's going on here."

The robot formed a stiff smile. "When Master Noah was with us, I used my organic interface connection to download the contents of his brain. All perfectly harmless, I just made a copy, with no harm to the original. I did it at his request, to leave a backup copy of him behind. A dated copy, of course, only containing memories and experiences that were in place on the date of the interaction."

Just then a swirling mist formed around the screen, unseen by anyone. They did, however, see the image of Noah flicker.

"I think it has a short circuit," Subi said. "You'd better shut it off."

"Absurd," Thinker said. "I have instant access to every one of my circuits, and they are all operating perfectly."

"Then why is Noah's face flickering?"

"My circuits report no malfunction."

"You must be wrong, my friend." Subi saw the image of Noah partially concealed by a gray film, as if a fog had gotten inside the screen. "Robots can make mistakes too, once in a while."

"I'm no ordinary robot." Thinker whirred, and then looked down at the screen on his own chest. "Mmmm. Peculiar. Perhaps I should fold shut and contemplate this." For some reason, though, he delayed.

The foggy gray film inside the screen looked peculiar to Subi, and gave him an unsettled feeling. It swirled around, and then seemed to dart into the image of Noah and vanish entirely. Simultaneously, the eyes and face of Master Noah looked more alive, more alert, and still Thinker did not fold himself shut....

* * * * *

"You're looking rather stressed," Noah said to Subi. "Perhaps we can have one of our old talks again, and I could give you some advice that will be of assistance?"

"I doubt that," Subi said. He tapped the robot on the head, and said, "Thinker, this ... *thing* ... uses computer programming to carry on conversations?"

Hesitation. Then: "5zocomputer programming. It acts like the original, reacts like Noah really would to any given situation."

"So, *it* could still lead us?"

"Well," Thinker said, "I have already discussed this possibility with the programmed likeness, and it doesn't think that would be practical."

"Kindly do not refer to me as a thing or an it," the image said.

"A most peculiar sensation," Thinker said. "The spoken words are not emanating from my operating circuits."

"That's because I really *am* Noah. Not in the customary sense, since my corporal form is somewhere else. Even so, I have come here, and I'm with you now at this very moment. Now listen carefully, and I'll tell you where they're keeping me."

"Most unusual," Thinker said.

"Good one," Subi said. "Nice trick, Thinker."

"Not a trick," the robot said. "Something is going wrong ... going wrong." With the repeated words, Thinker's voice merged with Noah's, and came from the screen.

Subi reached out, and touched the face on the screen.

But the voice from the screen grew weak, and said, "I can't hold the connection any longer...." In a few seconds the voice faded out entirely, and the strange animation of the image went away with it, leaving it less lifelike and more in the nature of a video recording, as it had been originally.

Chapter Twenty-Nine

It is said that the Supreme Being had a first thought, a second, and a third. So it was in the beginning, and shall be again.

—A legend of Lost Earth

To Noah, it had all been like a strange dream, but he knew it had really happened. And, though he repeatedly tried to make the connection again with his image in Thinker's torso, he found it impossible to accomplish. On other occasions he had traveled along the strands of the web to go wherever he wanted, but other times—such as now—it seemed to block him. The harder he tried to return to his friends, the more impossible it seemed to be.

In his heart, he suspected that he needed to back off on the attempts. Then perhaps, the cosmic pathway would open for him again like the embrace of a lover.

* * * * *

As a robot, Thinker struggled to explain the strange event, but Subi offered an explanation right away. He theorized that there had been a computer malfunction that made Noah's simulation seem to come alive.

"I have no record of a malfunction," Thinker said.

"Therefore, you have a malfunction on top of a malfunction."

"Perhaps, but my probability programs point in an entirely different direction, to the cosmic structure they call Timeweb. I have only sketchy information on it, what has been reported to me about certain unusual properties of communication and travel. As you know, Master Noah made me the official historian of the Guardians, and the trustee of his life story. At that time, despite numerous experiences in Timeweb, he did not understand how the network functioned. Maybe he has a deeper comprehension now that he has gone from us, but we can't contact him to find out. I suspect that no *living* organism will ever gain all information about something so vast and complex."

"Are you implying that you could gain a full understanding of it?"

The heavy lidded eyes blinked. "Of course. I have a much larger capacity for data storage than any Human."

"But is Timeweb all about information and data sorting? Noah told me it has

certain spiritual qualities that he didn't think could be grasped in any purely logical way."

The machine whirred, but only for a moment. Then: "That could be the case. To be most effective, I must remain open to all possibilities, however implausible they may seem at first."

"Maybe there's hope for you after all," Subi said with a gentle smile.

"The best answer I have now," Thinker said, "is that an aberration in the cosmic structure transported Noah's mental image all the way here. Think of a radio or audiovisual signal skipping through the atmosphere of a planet, or through the galaxy. The signal comes and goes, depending upon surrounding conditions."

"Do your programs say if it can happen again?"

"Not enough information.... "

* * * * *

Over the course of several days, Thinker checked the simulacrum circuitry and pronounced it fit. He, Subi, and other Guardians interacted with the Noah-image several times, and each time it was a straightforward matter, with the image operating as the robot intended. The electronic simulation provided them with its advice and instructions based upon AI-enhanced probabilities that were calculated from Noah's actual past experiences.

The Guardians even asked the simulation about the strange, brief moments when it had seemed to be something more. "Oh, you only imagined that," the Noah said, after a moment's hesitation. "It never happened. Your perceptions are not real."

Grudgingly, Subi accepted this.

As time passed, he and his followers obtained advice from the computer-generated Noah about how best to make guerrilla raids against industrial polluters, and they were successful in destroying an immense gaserol plant operated by a business associate of Doge Lorenzo. With the help of Noah's alter ego, the Guardians pursued the most serious damagers of the environment, no longer limiting themselves to the forces of Lorenzo and Francella. This made the Guardians more unpredictable, and harder to defend against....

* * * * *

In heavy armor that disguised him as a machine, covering his entire body instead of only part of it, Giovanni Nehr was sent on a new outside mission. Even after Gio's failure at Max One, the Noah simulation had recommended no punishment for him, and the placement of no obstacles in his career path.

Thus, Gio found himself on still another reconnaissance assignment. This time he was supposed to infiltrate Jimu and the fighting machines that were in the service of the Doge. With considerable finesse he accomplished this, obtaining a position with a robotic yard crew working at the Doge's cliffside villa. There, Gio confirmed earlier intelligence reports that Jimu had his robots reproducing at a very high rate. One day, Gio saw more than a thousand of them performing efficient, deadly fighting formations in a practice session near the villa.

After a week of spying Gio returned to Guardian headquarters, and reported to Subi Danvar and Thinker, who stood just outside the Brew Room. "We don't want to oppose those machines in direct battle," Gio said. "They're too numerous, too skilled."

"I projected as much," Thinker said, after listening to more details. "They have access to far more raw materials than we do, can build at a much higher rate."

* * * * *

Again, Subi consulted with the likeness of Noah Watanabe, who flashed on at the center of the robot's chest. "Subi, you don't really need me," Noah said. He stared intently from the screen.

"How can you say that?" Subi protested. "The Guardians are nothing without you."

Noah's likeness scowled. Then it seemed to move away, and paced around a simulated chamber.

"Master Noah, come back here," Subi pleaded.

Noah did so, and returned to the foreground of the screen. With a kindly expression, he said, "Thinker has been updating me with reports of your activities and decisions. My loyal adjutant, you are the wisest of leaders. Your decisions are sound."

"Not as sound as they could be. I've done my best, but...."

Interrupting, the simulacrum said, "The best hope of the Guardians is not to consult with an electronic version of me, but to follow your leadership instincts. You've been right to continue your guerrilla raids, while building your own forces, Human and machine. I especially like your idea of calling the robots 'ecomachines.' I never thought of that."

"But I never said anything about that," Subi said. "How did you ... ?" He paused, and looked up at the metal face of Thinker. "You downloaded *my* brain, too?"

The metal face smiled, and the metal-lidded eyes blinked in acknowledgment. "While you slept."

Angrily, Subi said, "You had no right. I didn't give you permission to do that!"

"Earlier, I avoided doing that to Noah without his permission. This time, however, I...."

"Well, what?"

"I ran probability programs and arrived at the answer that you would appreciate joining Noah's simulacrum in my internal world."

"Well I don't, and I don't want you to ever do that again to anybody. Do you understand?"

"Yes, sir, but I was only trying to be helpful."

"Don't forget what I told you."

"I never forget anything. I'm a machine, with perfect recollection."

Subi shook his head. "You still have a lot to learn."

"As you can see," the Noah copy said, interrupting them from the screen, "I know you very well, Subi. Thinker's screen of me is clever, but you should not rely on me any longer, my friend. It can only weaken you."

A tear ran down Subi's cheek. "My decision is this, Noah. I will continue to speak with you from time to time ... as a friend. You thought I only saw you as a boss?"

"No, and I never saw you as only an adjutant, either." The simulacrum's eyes looked sad, even capable of crying. Then he turned and walked away, into the darkness of a simulated tunnel.

Chapter Thirty

Each world is different from every other one, and Tarbu is the most unique of all.

—From a Tulyan Story

In the vast galaxy, some life forms had existed for eternity, while others had evolved over the eons, so that only remnants of their ancient pasts remained ... the faint genetic dustings of history. So it was with planets, and entire galactic sectors surrounding them.

Tarbu was a world run by Tulyans in much the same manner as it had been millions of years ago. As mortal enemies of Tulyans, the Parviis knew it existed but had never been able to determine its location. It was the Tulyan equivalent of the Parvii Fold, mysterious and hidden, filled with the arcane ways of its inhabitants. Both regions, as if designed by God for such purposes, had been cut off from other star systems by cosmic conditions—the Parvii Fold by its pocketed, far-out-of-the-way location, and Tarbu by electrical disturbances that prevented Parvii brains from detecting it—or the existence of the Wild Pod Zone beyond, in a region of dim, dwarf stars.

According to Tulyan legend, the Sublime Creator established Tarbu and the protected region on the other side of it as a sanctuary for podships and for the Tulyans who were supposed to be their pilots. It came to be known as the Tarbu Gap. In this belief system, the Sublime Creator constructed the relationship between Tulyans and the spacefaring Aopoddae in the first place, but Parviis subsequently altered it in horrific ways, for their own selfish purposes.

Eshaz led his companions off the podship that had just traveled across space, then strode through an airlock to the station platform, talking to them constantly, giving them a preview of the remarkable wonders all of them were about to share.

Fascinated, Dux hung on every word. To the teenager, this pod station orbiting Tarbu looked like any other, with its mottled gray-and-black surfaces, along with the organic texture of its construction, not dissimilar from podships themselves. He had heard it said that both podships and pod stations were living variations of an ancient race that had been created in unexplained ways, and which continued to behave mysteriously, like an immense, galactic-scale organism. When considered in that manner, it sounded frightening to some people, but Dux had never felt that way himself. Each time he rode in a podship or stepped onto a pod station, he felt more at peace than anywhere else, and infinitely calm. It was like some people felt in the presence of water, as if the liquid was a link to the past when Humans swam the seas of Lost Earth, before evolving to walk on land and become what they were today.

"Eshaz mentioned something to you in passing," Tesh said, "the Parvii Fold. He and I have an arrangement of trust, or I would not permit him to speak in this manner, and he would never have brought me here. To his race, the Tarbu Gap is as sacred as the Parvii Fold is to mine."

"Don't forget the Tulyan Starcloud," Eshaz said. "We have more than one sacred region."

She nodded. "And perhaps there are others as well, on both sides."

This elicited no apparent reaction from the big Tulyan, as he led them across the platform of the pod station.

Staring at Tesh, Dux furrowed his brow. "Eshaz said you aren't really Human. What did he mean by that?"

"I am like you and not like you at the same moment," the pretty brunette said, as they all paused at an empty shuttle bay. She touched one of Dux's shoulders. "I am a Parvii, one of the major galactic races, even though most races do not even know we exist."

"You certainly look Human," Acey said, "so what's the difference?" He always liked to know how things worked, and studied her attractive form with new interest.

Dux noticed Eshaz standing off to one side, watching them with a somewhat amused expression.

"Your race—*humanus ordinaire*—is an offshoot of mine," she said. "We are genetically linked, but so vastly different now that the similarities are more superficial than significant." She paused. "We may look alike at the moment, but watch this." Touching her own wrist, she seemed to disappear in a faint mist. Then Dux heard her, a tiny voice down on the deck.

"Don't step on me!" she shouted, looking up at them and waving her arms.

Kneeling, Dux and Acey stared at the tiny Human shape, like a Lilliputian in the Land of Gulliver.

"I wonder what other surprises Tesh and Eshaz have for us," Acey said.

"We have hardly begun!" Eshaz boomed, towering over them.

The boys tumbled backward, when Tesh suddenly shot up and became full-size again. As Acey and Dux regained their footing and stood with her again she said, "Eshaz and I have come to an understanding of epic proportions. Historically, Tulyans and Parviis are mortal enemies, like Humans and Mutatis, but we have agreed to work together for the greater good, for all of the races and sectors of the galaxy."

"Noah Watanabe is the binding force," Eshaz said. "All of us are eco-warriors serving his cause, his interpretation of galactic ecology. Agreed?" Through slitted gray eyes he peered down at Acey and Dux.

"Agreed!" the boys exclaimed.

"We knew we could count on you," Tesh said. "Or at least, that's what Eshaz told me. You see, he read your minds."

"How did you do that?" Acey asked.

"Leave me *some* secrets," Eshaz said good-naturedly. Then, looking at Tesh, he said, "Speaking of that, I will readily admit that certain thoughts of yours are … how shall I put it? They are veiled, but not completely. I speak of personal feelings you have for Noah Watanabe, beyond anything professional in your capacity as a Guardian."

Dux saw her redden in apparent embarrassment.

"The way you look at him, for example," Eshaz added, "and the particular tone of your voice in his presence. I find it interesting."

"What do you know about it?" she said, indignantly. "You're not even Human."

"And *you* are? As far as I know, Humans don't do the magic act we just witnessed."

Composing herself, she smiled. "I'm closer to Human than you, my friend. In any event, you do not even have a mate. What is your experience in personal relationships, anyway? For that matter, how do Tulyan people *reproduce?* I know you have males and females, since First Elder Kre'n is female, or so we are led to believe. Do you mate in the customary manner?"

Now Eshaz smiled, as he was finding his own amusement in the interplay. "You have touched upon one of the matters we do not discuss with outside races."

"It is similar for me," Tesh said, "but it is not a racial matter at all. I do not discuss affairs of my heart with anyone. They are too personal."

"But you must discuss them with someone," Eshaz said. "With the person you have such feelings toward."

"That goes without saying," she said. Her green eyes twinkled. "My feelings for Noah are personal. So are my feelings for you."

Eshaz laughed, a deep rumble. "A Tulyan and a Parvii," he said. "The most interesting proposition I've ever received. And I have lived for a very long time, indeed."

Tesh pushed him good-naturedly, but he was so large and heavy that he didn't move. Her voice rose. "I didn't *proposition* you, you big oaf!"

"I will be more cautious of you in the future," he said, with a wide reptilian grin. "In all matters, you are dangerous."

In a short while a shuttle arrived, to transport them down to Tarbu. For some reason, Dux had been unable to see the planet at all when they arrived at the orbital pod station. There had been no mists or clouds, though, nothing to obscure his vision. Now, as they plunged down in the shuttle, the planet seemed to take shape before them, emerging from space like something appearing out of nothingness, as if had popped out of a void, from an entirely different dimension. As they dropped down into the atmosphere, the light was an eerie brownish gray, with no visible sun or cloud cover. Just an oddly illuminated sky.

Dux and Acey stood silently at a window of the shuttle, not saying anything, only able to absorb with their eyes and their souls.

As they set down on the landing pad of the shuttleport, Eshaz said, "We call Tarbu the 'porcupine planet,' since most of its surface is covered with thorny vines, even beneath the snow at higher elevations, and underwater. The stuff is incredibly tough, but grows so slowly that we've been able to trim it for surface travel and habitation."

The Tulyan put on a custom-fitting protective suit made of thick green material, and said, "You three will have to remain here, since we don't have suits for … aliens. I need to go off the beaten path a bit and find a special variety of vine."

"Have you forgotten?" Tesh said, "I can shut off my magnification system and ride in one of your pockets."

"Very well."

She reduced herself, and climbed onto one of Eshaz's thick hands, which he extended down to her. Carefully, he selected a side pocket for her, with a flap that she could open and close.

Then, looking sternly at the boys, Eshaz said, "Can I trust you two to stay out of trouble for a few hours? I don't want you causing mischief here, like you did at the starcloud."

"We won't let you down," Acey promised.

"But you know that, don't you?" Dux added. "After all, you read our minds, and know our hearts."

"That I do, laddies," he said. And he turned and left with his tiny Parvii passenger. They made a most unlikely pair.

* * * * *

The planet was covered with thorny underbrush, but Tesh soon learned that the inhabitants had cut ingenious labyrinthine passageways on the surface, and had built multi-level structures inside the growths. Eshaz's protective suit was necessary, he explained, because many of the thorns contained drugs, toxins, and a variety of other potentially harmful substances, and should not be touched indiscriminately.

"There are a variety of thorn bushes here," he said, "containing different things, and it takes an expert to identify them."

"Sounds like a thorny problem," she quipped, from his pocket.

"That it is," he said humorlessly.

Eshaz took a narrow passageway to the top of a knoll, where he emerged into a broad clearing. There he pointed out several prickly thorn bushes around them, in a variety of colors. "Our vinemasters cultivate these with great care," he said. "They are ancient growths, going back to the beginning days of our race."

Just then, a pair of Tulyans emerged from the undergrowth. They were much smaller than Eshaz, and at first Tesh thought they might be a sub-race.

"Greetings, Eshaz," one of them said, in a high-pitched voice.

"And to you, my young friends," Eshaz said.

"You desire cuttings today?" the other asked in a similar tone.

"These are vinemasters," Eshaz said, looking down at his pocket passenger.

The Tulyan pair looked at her closely, and one of them asked, "Is that a … Parvii? *Here?*"

"It is," Eshaz said, calmly.

"And the Overseer approves of this?" the other asked. The voices of the vinemasters bordered on hysteria.

"I am here by direction of the Council of Elders," Eshaz replied, calmly. "Shall I wait while you go and consult the Overseer?"

"That will not be necessary," a voice said. Another Tulyan appeared, this one as large as Eshaz, with a creased, bronze face and deep-set, slitted eyes. He looked very, very old. "I have been in contact with the Council, and they told me to expect our distinguished visitor."

"Tesh, meet Pluj, the eminent Overseer of Tarbu."

Peeking out of the pocket, she waved to him.

As the Tulyans talked, Tesh felt out of place, and had a lot of questions to ask, but she didn't feel the time was appropriate. She remained unclear about the ages of the "young" vinemasters, since she had heard that a Tulyan lived for millions of years, and was, in effect, immortal. It appeared that they had some type of breeding system anyway, and that these were the Tulyan equivalent of children. She suspected that this could still make them tens of thousands, or even hundreds of thousands, of years old.

Eshaz and the Overseer, followed by the vinemasters, walked up and down rows of thorn growths, selecting the vines that Eshaz needed—for a use that was not discussed among them, and which had not yet been disclosed to Tesh.

On the way back to the shuttleport, with Eshaz carrying five large wooden cases that were strapped together, she asked him how old the vinemasters were.

"Oh, much older than you might think."

"But are they children?"

"Not in the sense that you mean, or they would never be entrusted with such important responsibilities. The way we breed and age is quite different from any other race. One day, I will explain it to you, perhaps."

"We'll trade stories," she said, in her tiny voice.

"Yes, we'll do that, perhaps around a campfire."

She laughed….

Later that day, Eshaz and Tesh returned to the shuttleport with the burnished wood cases, containing the special thorn vines and other supplies (including foodstuffs) that had been provided for them by the vinemasters.

When this was completed, Eshaz provided new galactic coordinates to Tesh, and pointed into a region of space where few stars were visible. "That way," he said.

With a nod, she hurried forward to the navigation room, one of her own secrets. Eshaz smiled as he watched her shrink and disappear into a corridor.

One day, he mused as the podship took off, *our races might not keep such secrets from each other.*

Chapter Thirty-one

Nothing works by itself. Everything in this galaxy, from micro to macro, is linked to something else.

—Master Noah Watanabe

Even when podships crisscrossed the galaxy, the Zultan Abal Meshdi had not enjoyed traveling beyond the worlds of the Mutati Kingdom. Such journeys had invariably proved a disappointment to him, showing him planets and peoples that were far inferior to his own, far less than his glorious homeworld of Paradij and the jewel-like Citadel from which he ruled the multi-planet shapeshifter empire.

For him, Paradij was the center of the entire universe, but once this had been a barren, unappealing world. The Mutatis, after being driven to planets like this by Human aggression, had completely terraformed it, with massive hydraulic engineering and planting projects that transformed gray into green and blue. In their centuries-long task, generations of shapeshifters had been guided by God-on-High. This beautiful place was proof of what they could accomplish with determination and holy guidance.

As Meshdi strolled through his ornamental gardens one morning, he marveled at the towering fountains on each side of the stone path, water spouts that had been engineered to change color and shape by the hour, so that they looked new to him all the time. They were reflections of Mutatis themselves, who could metamorphose their own appearances at will, thus preventing boredom and constantly opening creative possibilities.

He considered the beauty around him a reward for his good deeds in a prior life. Certainly, no mortal being could ask for more.

Truly, I am blessed.

From this cosmic jewel, the Zultan ruled the Mutati Kingdom. He sighed. If not for constant Human aggression, this would be more than enough for him. But they forced him to lash out, to draw a line in space that he would not permit them to cross.

The Zultan adored technology, especially the personal gyrodome in his suite and the various types of minigyros, devices provided to him so generously by his Adurian allies. Each day he used the large unit to purify his thoughts, giving him the clarity he needed to lead his people. And whenever he went out, he liked to wear one of the portable minigyros on his head, not only to maintain his own thinking processes, but as an example for his people. In increasing numbers, they were using the devices as well.

The loyal Adurians, while adept at technological innovation, were nonetheless not as skilled in robotics as Hibbils, who were allied with his enemies, the merchant princes. The Humans also had their nehrcom cross-space communication system, which enabled them to remain in contact with one another instantaneously, across vast distances. Surprisingly, that had been the invention of a Human, Jacopo Nehr.

But in a blessing from God-on-High, the inventor's discontented brother, Giovanni Nehr, had come to Paradij to reveal the secret of the technology. The naïve Human had turned it over to Meshdi to get even with his brother and to ingratiate himself with the Mutatis, thinking he would be rewarded with a proverbial king's ransom. Instead, Meshdi, after accepting the information, had placed the traitorous man in prison. Somehow he had escaped, but no matter.

Now the Mutatis had the technology, or at least a large part of it. They were able to communicate across space with their own system, although the reception was fuzzy and sometimes went offline. His scientists were working on the problem now, along with other important military matters.

In particular, the Mutati scientists had successfully cloned podships, and were now hard at work on the next step, solving the very difficult guidance problem. But it had occurred to Meshdi that the guidance of podships might not be technological at all. He still had technicians working on it, but in the meantime he was relying on God-on-High to guide the sentient pods to their destinations. For a Mutati, that was always the best course of action.

Recently he had ordered the launch of a lab-pod against Siriki, a key enemy world chosen because of its proximity. With much publicity, a brave Mutati had been selected to pilot a schooner that would be carried aboard that pod, a schooner that was being fitted at that very moment with a planet-busting torpedo. The holy Demolio, his doomsday weapon that had been so successful in destroying four enemy planets, prior to the cutoff of podship travel.

Frenzied preparations were underway on Paradij, and soon all would be in readiness.

For some reason, the Adurians had expressed concern about continued attacks against enemy targets. He couldn't understand why, as they weren't providing him with good reasons, only requests that he delay for a "better opportunity," whatever that meant. The fools would not deter him, even if they were allies. War was war, after all.

Technology alone cannot win this war, Abal Meshdi thought. *God-on-High must guide our bombs.*

Upon returning to the heavily fortified keep of the Citadel, an aide handed him a nehrcom transmission, written in ornate script by one of the royal scribes. The communication was from an operative on Canopa who had been able to sneak into one of the Doge's nehrcom facilities.

The Zultan was pleased to learn of Human-against-Human warfare on Canopa, with Noah Watanabe's Guardians fighting against the forces of the Doge and Watanabe's own sister. With the blessing of God, they would all annihilate themselves, thus reducing the number of targets that the Mutatis needed to strike....

* * * * *

On far-away Canopa—now the capital world of the Merchant Prince Alliance—Doge Lorenzo amused himself by torturing a Mutati prisoner while General Jacopo Nehr looked on. They were in a deep dungeon of Max Two, which had become the largest prison on the planet, as a result of recent additions. One day the Doge might change the names around, but it was low on his priority list.

As a result of his recent emphasis on identifying Humans through medical examinations and then labeling them with implants, many disguised Mutati infiltrators had been uncovered. The Doge's police operations had been going well.

This particular Mutati was what Lorenzo called "a screamer." The creature started crying and howling on the way here and continued in a frenzy of emotion when the pain amplification machines were used. So much energy this one had, and how it hated being caught! It increased Lorenzo's pleasure.

Two guards used sharp pikes to keep the Mutati from escaping, prodding it each time it tried to veer one way or the other. All the while, dancing around the victim, Lorenzo used a large pair of clippers to cut off flaps and folds of fat from the creature's body, causing it to writhe in pain and attempt to create shapes that could not be cut so easily.

Cackling gleefully, Lorenzo saw it as a game. Snip, snip, snip! He danced around the creature, looking for new places to cut, moving in quickly and then retreating. Piles of flesh lay all around, saturated in purple Mutati blood.

"I think that's enough," Nehr said. "Unless you want to kill this one. Keep in mind, we can still get information out of it, using other methods."

"Oh, you spoil my fun," Lorenzo said as he tossed the clippers aside. "You're just like...."

He paused when he noticed the blond Princess Meghina in the doorway, watching. She glared at him, her eyes dark and angry.

"I'm disappointed in you," she said. "You know how I feel about this." Meghina could hardly contain her fury.

"What do you think dungeons are for?" Lorenzo asked. "To sing lullabies to our prisoners?" She watched as he wiped blood off his hands with a cloth.

"There are galactic conventions against this sort of thing," she said.

"There are also galactic conventions against blowing up enemy planets. Or there should be. We lost four worlds to these bastards, and billions of people! Surely, you can't begrudge me a little revenge."

"They did a horrible thing, but I don't like what the war is doing to you," she said. "This is not good for you."

"I'm sorry," he said, looking suddenly like a child who had just been scolded.

Behind him, Meghina saw the pitiful Mutati rolling over its own severed bloody parts, incorporating them back into its shapeshifting body. Despite its suffering, the Mutati focused on her for an instant with its bright black eyes, before she broke gazes with it.

Had the creature recognized her true form? She had taken a calculated risk coming down here, because some Mutatis—albeit only a small percentage—had the ability to recognize another of their kind no matter the disguise, by detecting aural and electrical signatures that were unique to the individual. She faced another risk as well, the new requirement that everyone get a medical examination and an implanted device certifying that they were Human. Because of her high status as a noble lady, she and others had not been required to undergo the process. But that could change.

Nonetheless, she stood her ground. "I would like you to discontinue this barbaric practice," she said, following Lorenzo as he left the chamber.

The beautiful Princess Meghina, while born a Mutati, had remained in Human form for so long that she could not change back. She hated Mutatis herself, but could not condone the sort of treatment she had seen today, for any reason. Not knowing his courtesan wife's dirty secret, Lorenzo was devoted to her and valued her advice, and her opinion of him. It was only out of noble custom—Meghina understood this—that he had trysts with numerous other Human (and even alien) women. She did the same herself with men, in her own fashion.

Deep in conversation, the royal couple traveled a short distance by groundjet, to the Doge's cliffside villa. By the time they reached his bedroom suite and she was nibbling at his ear, he finally acceded to her request. She had more than his apology now; she had his promise that he would not torture any more Mutati prisoners.

But Lorenzo had his own mind about such matters. He had learned to tell important people what they wanted to hear, without really altering his behavior. From now on, whenever he had an urge to torture a shapeshifter, he would still do so, but would take care to conceal the act from her. In this time of war, with all the stresses of leadership, he needed to maintain his diversions.

Chapter Thirty-Two

It is curious that two of the oldest races in the galaxy—the Parviis and the Tulyans—both rely upon paranormal methods to gain control over sentient podships. But in this context, what is "normal," and what is not?

—Tulyan Wisdom

As their podship approached the Hibbil Sector, Eshaz spoke like a tour director to the boys sitting beside him. Dux and Acey alternately chattered excitedly and listened to him.

"Wild podships migrate here at this time of year," Eshaz said, "for breeding. They're like herds of whales on Lost Earth, but cover vast distances of space. We Tulyans understand the ancient patterns of the deep-space pods, and chart them. I expect we'll see some action soon."

The podship bumped gently against the exterior bumper of a pod station, and Eshaz said. "Just a brief stop for a permit. Then we'll go on to the Wild Pod Zone. It's still a good distance away, with very dim, collapsed suns. Not like this." He pointed up, at a rather ordinary-looking yellow sun.

Tesh guided the sentient craft to a dock inside the station, where furry little Hibbil workers secured the vessel with lines.

Moments later the hatch opened, and a dozen Hibbil policemen marched aboard, dressed in black -and-gold uniforms. The men's bearlike faces twitched irritably, and their dark eyes glanced around, as if they were looking for contraband. Their gazes focused first on the Tulyan, then on the burnished wood cases that lay on the floor, still strapped together.

"Doing a little podship hunting?" the lead policeman asked. His nametag read, YOTLA.

"Seen any wild ones lately?" Eshaz asked, stepping toward the officers.

"Not for some time," Yotla said with a grin, "but it's a big zone out there and they're probably hiding somewhere. I'll take your permit fee now."

With a nod, Eshaz passed him a golden cylinder. "Our fee and application are inside."

Dux saw that the cylinder contained precious jewels. With a furry hand the Hibbil officer activated a button on the side, and a complex series of blank holo-pages popped into the air. "You haven't filled out the forms," he growled.

"My answers are the same as the last time I was here," Eshaz said, with a yawn, "so I included enough extra payment for you to complete the documentation for me." He glanced at Dux and grinned, "Saves a lot of time."

With a grunt the officer resealed the cylinder, and departed with his companions.

The podship got underway, and proceeded slowly away from the orbital station, then accelerated, but not to web speed. An hour passed, and they reached a region of space that was dotted with half a dozen white dwarf suns, and two that were brown, and even dimmer. Eshaz chattered about how they had once been bright orbs, filled with nuclear energy, but over billions and billions of years they had collapsed. "Most races think there is very little life out here," he said. "But we know better. It is a prime hunting region."

Eshaz pointed out a porthole at black-and-gold ships patrolling a sector that he called the entrance to the Wild Pod Zone, vessels with unusual, angular hull designs and bright search beams that illuminated space around them. One of the beams focused on them, causing Dux to squint.

"Hibbils wield considerable military power and are fiercely territorial," Eshaz said, "so we have found it most convenient to simply pay them off."

"Their ships look fast," Acey said.

"None faster, for intra-sector bursts," Eshaz said. "The Hibbils are a totalitarian society, run by a corrupt military junta. They claim jurisdiction over a broad region, far beyond the traditional boundaries of their Cluster Worlds." With a sneer, he added, "They pulled the planets out of orbit and linked them together mechanically. Hibbils fear a chaotic breakup of the galaxy, and think this will save their civilization from destruction."

"I'd like to go to their homeworlds sometime," Acey said. "I've heard they're tech masters." "An interesting race, perhaps," Eshaz admitted, "but they are among the worst industrial polluters

in the galaxy. They provide supposedly low-cost machines for the merchant princes and for the leaders of other races, but there are hidden costs—damage to the planets they raid for raw materials, and more depleted worlds than the Guardians can ever restore."

As Acey and Dux looked through portholes, the podship headed slowly out into the darkness of near-space, leaving the Hibbil ships behind.

Chapter Thirty-Three

There can be great beauty in change, even if propelled by violence.
—Mutati Saying

In his natural state he was the most dashingly handsome of Mutati men, with great folds of fat around his midsection, a perfectly symmetrical triple chin, and overlarge eyes on his tiny head. As he made his way through the crowd, in a golden outrider uniform decked with medals and ribbons, terramutati women swooned at his feet, and aeromutati females darted overhead, blowing him kisses as they flew by. Many Mutati men had applied for this glorious position, and Kishi Fapro had been chosen over all of them, not only for his good looks but for his enthusiastic willingness to die for the sacred cause of his people.

For weeks his holophoto had been shown everywhere on Paradij, and in grainy nehrcom video transmissions to other worlds throughout the realm, so that everyone envied him. Surely he would occupy a special place in heaven after his heroic sacrifice, even higher than his earlier counterparts who had given up their lives flying Demolio torpedoes into enemy planets. Fapro represented a new beginning, with the Mutatis working even closer with God-on-High than before, relying upon him to guide the holy bomb to its target. It was "a mating of religion and technology," the Zultan had said, displaying his proclivity for turning a phrase. After this success, the Mutatis would rain holy bombs on every merchant prince planet, and the long war would be won.

No one would ever see Kishi Fapro again, except in the holo-images that would live beyond the expiration of his flesh and in a variety of curios that were sold bearing his likeness. He would also live on in the endearing memories of everyone who watched him now as he marched steadily toward the gleaming black schooner, smiling and waving to the crowd, showing no fear whatsoever.

To enthusiastic cheers, he stepped inside the vessel and fired up the engines. In a matter of moments he lifted off, and streaked up to the orbiting pod station. As holocameras watched him all the way and projected the images to screens all over the Mutati Kingdom, the outrider guided his craft into the cargo hold of a laboratory-bred podship.

Excitement mounted as the podship taxied out of the pod station and moved into position a short distance away. Then, bearing the black schooner and its deadly bomb, the lab-pod accelerated into the sky. In a bright flash of green light seen on the surface of Paradij, the Mutati doomsday weapon left the atmosphere and disappeared into space, pointed toward the merchant prince world of Siriki. On the other end, there would be no arrival at a pod station. This time, the entire podship, with its precious cargo, would strike the planet directly, triggering the deadly explosions.

On a platform amidst the cheering onlookers, the Zultan Abal Meshdi uttered a prayer from the *Holy Writ*. He was convinced that God-on-High would guide the lab-pod to destroy their hated enemy—and that it would occur in a matter of seconds.

Following the prayer, he raised his arms and shouted to the crowd, "Our doomsday weapon is on the way!"

* * * * *

A day passed....

At a nehrcom station on Siriki, the Human operator received an odd signal. His instruments revealed that it was from the Mutati homeworld of Paradij, but he knew that was impossible, since the Mutatis had no nehrcom units.

The signal was first weak, then stronger. It repeated several times. The operator checked the source, and was astounded. Quickly, he relayed it to another operator on Canopa, a woman. She in turn went personally to the Office of the Doge on Canopa, where she handed a one-page report and a slender plax recording tube to the Royal Attache, Pimyt.

"An odd transmission came in, sir, purportedly from the Mutatis on Paradij."

After scanning the report and listening to the signal, Pimyt looked up and said, "I'll take care of this from here. You are to mention it to no one."

"That is my sworn duty, sir," the operator responded, with a slight bow to the furry, much shorter Hibbil. "I brought it directly to you."

"You understand, of course, that this is a hoax? It could not possibly have come from Paradij, because the Mutatis have no nehrcom system."

"That is my understanding, sir."

"We're putting the Doge's best investigators on this, and they'd better not learn that you discussed it with anyone."

"You can count on my silence, sir."

"Tell the Siriki station to destroy all records of this. Then destroy yours, too. I want no copies of this to exist, not in your memory or anywhere else. It is a matter of utmost security to the Merchant Prince Alliance."

"I understand, sir. With your leave, I'll take care of it right away."

Pimyt waved a hand dismissively.

When he was alone in his office, the Royal Attache muttered, "What is this? What is that fool Zultan up to now?" He stared at the report. "Sending a signal here?"

Pimyt's reasons for being upset ran through circuitous pathways. Secretly, he and his Hibbil people were allied with the Adurian race under the HibAdu Coalition, with the goal of bringing down both the Merchant Prince Alliance and the Mutati Kingdom. The conspirators, after infiltrating themselves into key positions such as his own, had not yet seen the right time to make their move. They were still laying groundwork, getting control of weapons and personnel, setting things up.

For a long time Hibbils and Adurians had been treated in a condescending manner by two races that considered themselves superior to them. His own Hibbil people, ostensibly an ally of the Humans, had actually been under the collective boot heel of the merchant princes during all that time: politically, economically, militarily, socially, and in every other imaginable way. It had been much the same story for the Adurians, except that it was the Mutati Kingdom keeping them down. Finally, unable to endure any more mistreatment, the Hibbils and Adurians had aligned themselves into what they called the HibAdu Coalition. In large measure this secret alliance was so that they could exact revenge against their tormentors, taking everything that was of value away from the merchant princes and the shapeshifters—their worlds, their profits, and more. In the coming war, the Coalition intended to wipe out ninety percent of the populations of the two offending races, and enslave what was left.

But the Mutati Zultan was a madman and a wild card. Pimyt's secret collaborator, the Adurian Ambassador VV Uncel, had been stuck on Paradij by the podship crisis, and must certainly have made attempts to influence the Mutati leader. Pimyt knew that the ambassador had convinced Mutatis to use gyrodomes and minigyros, devices that weakened their brains in subtle ways and made them easier to conquer. However, unable to stay in touch with Uncel during the most recent crisis, Pimyt didn't have updates. Neither of them could risk sending nehrcom transmissions back and forth between enemy planets, so Pimyt could only hope for the best.

This new signal episode troubled him a great deal. When added to an earlier event in which Jacopo Nehr detected Mutati nehrcom transmissions on his own mobile transceiver, apparently sent by mistake, it gave the attaché additional cause for concern. The cross-space transmission leak had occurred after the cessation of podship travel, so he had not been able to follow up on it. In the errant transmittal, he heard the whiny voice of an Adurian saying that Mutatis, with no access to podships, could no longer launch Demolio attacks against merchant prince planets. The sound quality had been fuzzy, with no video at all, and Nehr had come directly to Pimyt with the information—since the two of them had a private arrangement and the Hibbil would ruin Nehr if he didn't cooperate. The Adurian voice on the transmission had been, unmistakably, that of VV Uncel, though only Pimyt realized that.

The Royal Attache paced nervously around his office. He had been fortunate with both of the Mutati transmissions, and had taken steps to keep a lid on them. But he couldn't contain the information forever, and soon it would get out that the Mutatis had their own system. If Nehr ever came clean and revealed Pimyt's knowledge of the internal workings of nehrcom units, merchant prince investigators might soon wonder if Pimyt had passed the information on to the Mutatis. Actually, the Mutatis had obtained it independently from Nehr's disloyal brother, but the connection was still there, and Pimyt could be compromised.

"Why did the Zultan send a signal to Siriki?" Pimyt said to himself, staring at the one-page report. He scratched his gray-and-black head, then dropped his jaw, as he recalled how the Mutatis had confirmed a number of Demolio strikes by sending nehrcom signals to the planet and seeing if it was still there.

Siriki? Did he try to destroy the planet? Has he found a way to launch the bombs again?

It seemed unlikely, but in this chaotic galaxy, he could not rule out the possibility. But what could he do to find out? He had only been able to send coded nehrcoms to his own operatives on other merchant prince worlds, containing military instructions, mostly involving infiltration and setting things up for future attacks by the HibAdu Coalition, making the attacks easier and more likely to succeed. But the conspirators could not act without podships, and neither could the Zultan of the Mutati Kingdom.

No one could.

* * * * *

On Paradij, there was much confusion and unease among the people.

A nehrcom transmission verification system revealed that their nehrcom signal was received on Siriki a day later. It did not bounce back as undeliverable, as anticipated. Thus the Demolio had never arrived.

Rumors spread more rapidly than a royal birth announcement. What could have possibly gone wrong?

The Zultan Abal Meshdi tightened up his nehrcom security. Then, paying little attention to the mutterings of the populace, he called for new volunteers, announcing in a planet-wide broadcast, "We need to send more outriders, again and again! Which of you will be our instruments of God?"

Paradij an Mutatis thronged to volunteer for their sacred duty.

Chapter Thirty-Four

Each life is made up of large and small pieces. None of those pieces, not even the tiniest, is insignificant, for they all contribute to the whole, to the person you see standing before you in the mirror.

—Jacopo Nehr

In a particularly foul mood, Francella marched down the corridor of her central medical laboratory. It was lunch hour, but she had no appetite for anything, except venting her anger. All morning long she had been at the site of one of her largest manufacturing facilities, now reduced to smoking rubble by a hit-and-run Guardian attack. Her brother, even though she was holding him prisoner and conducting medical experiments on him, was still the inspirational leader of those malcontents. Originally, he had styled them as "eco-terrorists," but in her eyes they no longer carried an environmental banner. They were simply terrorists.

Throwing open the double doors of the company cafeteria, she stomped in and found Dr. Bichette at a large round table, one of five in the room. The core of each table revolved slowly like a lazy susan, so that diners could select sealed packages of food, all kept steaming hot in gelplax containers. As she sat beside the doctor, he was pressing a button on the edge of the table to select an item.

As he did so, the package slid down a short ramp onto his plate. In contact with the air, the gelplax melted away, revealing a stir-fry meal.

"We need to talk—now," she began.

She saw the immediate sag of his face and shoulders that she had noticed before, whenever she wanted something from him. Sometimes he didn't show enough respect to suit her, but he was still considered one of the best medical research directors in the Merchant Prince Alliance, and had assembled a team of brilliant specialists who were intensely loyal to him. If she ever fired Bichette, they would all go with him. In any event, with no access to personnel on other planets, he had assembled the best possible team on Canopa. So, even though he irritated her on a regular basis, she continued to put up with him.

"I've been thinking about your latest report on my brother, and my own daily observations. You and your researchers are painfully slow; I can't stand it. The two major lines of experimentation—cellular regeneration and immortality—have made woefully little progress."

"Actually we have made considerable progress, but it's too technical for you to understand. The details are in the report, the gene splicing, the cell structure analysis, the...."

"Don't be condescending. I read it all, and it's gobbledygook. I don't think you're getting anywhere at all, but you don't have the guts to put that in your precious reports, do you?" She leaned toward him, but spoke louder. "Admit it! You're not getting anywhere!"

"You're mistaken. We're doing our best on a complex project."

"Let me see. Next you're going to tell me it could take years for results."

"Why, yes. If it's solvable at all, it might not be possible to accomplish it for decades. This is cutting-edge science."

"That's what I thought you'd say," she said, rising to her feet. "Finish your lunch."

She walked briskly out of the cafeteria. Glancing back, she saw him picking at his food, deeply troubled....

Five minutes later, Francella passed one of her own CorpOne guards and entered her brother's room. He was sitting up in bed, eating from food on a lap tray. With a sharp glare, he looked at her.

She closed the door, and locked it. Francella wanted the secret of immortality, and not because the Doge had ordered her to discover it, through her research team. She wanted it for *herself*. But there were too many uncertainties, and she might die before it was made available to her.

The recently healed fingers on her brother's hands were faintly pink, from Bichette's repeated cuts there. The latest report had said that continuous acts of cellular regeneration on the same appendages were causing the skin to heal more slowly. It seemed to mark a limit to the powers of Noah's body, but the experts were not sure how significant it was.

Francella felt a sudden rush of rage and cruelty. She hated him. Her fingers tightened around the handle of a weapon in her pocket, then released. Instead of using it, she took a conciliatory tone with him and said, "Why don't we make an effort to get along? All you have to do is tell me what you know about your condition."

His hazel eyes flashed angrily, and he cleared his tray with a sweep of one hand. Dishes clattered and broke on the floor. "You were responsible for that force of fake Guardians that attacked CorpOne headquarters, weren't you?"

"Of course not. Don't be preposterous."

"I think you're lying, and that you're responsible for our father dying. After all the destruction you've caused to this family, you want us to be pals now?"

"You're in no position to speak to me like that!"

"I'll answer none of your questions." He struggled to lift his legs from the bed, but they had been deadened by implanted injections of drugs, and he couldn't move them. The doctors had found another way to keep him immobile.

"Oh, dear brother, would you like to be released?"

"Yes, damn you!"

Impulsively, she brought the weapon out of her pocket and activated it—a silver-handled laserblade. She clicked it on, causing the tip of the barrel to glow ruby red.

"You seem to be having trouble with your legs," she said. With a burst of burning red light, she began to cut off his right leg, at the thigh.

* * * * *

The drugs in Noah's legs were not painkillers. He learned that the moment the hot light began to sear through his skin, then severed tendons and melted bones. His leg felt as if it was on fire.

He screamed at her and flailed, trying unsuccessfully to reach the weapon. Blood gushed from the open wound, but coagulated quickly. As his body began to restore itself he felt a shift in the pain signals that were being transmitted within his body, a coolness like foam applied to a fire. Such an odd sensation.

But it was only short-lived relief. Calmly and precisely, Francella severed his other leg, even as the first one was beginning to grow back. She must be deaf to his screams.

A mad, fascinated gleam filled her eyes. With shaking hands, she tossed his appendages in a medical waste bin.

"I'm no longer waiting for the 'experts' to perform their 'tests' on you, dear brother. I'm taking charge of your case." She cut across his middle body, only going halfway through and digging the hot light—at some lower setting—around on his interior organs. All intentional, he presumed, to maximize his suffering. Belly pain. Spurting blood. Noah didn't know if he could keep staunching the injuries.

Through his excruciating, almost otherworldly pain, Noah heard the guard calling for his sister, and knocking on the door. "Is everything all right in there, Ms. Watanabe?"

"Yes, you idiot. Now go away!"

The man said something Noah couldn't understand, then grew quiet. He was probably going to get Bichette.

Noah howled in agony and cursed her.

With blood spraying all over her, Francella cut off the new legs before they completed their regeneration process, then hurriedly amputated both of his muscular arms.

"Let's see how immortal you really are!" Francella shouted. "If I destroy all of your body tissue, how will you regenerate? Will you get smaller and smaller, with less cellular material to use for repairs?"

"How dare you use me as a guinea pig? I'm your brother! We're fraternal twins!"

"You're like a lizard," Francella said, her eyes frenzied, "growing parts back. Is that what you've become, a slimy little lizard?"

Noah bellowed at her defiantly. "You bitch! I'm ashamed we're in the same family!"

She smiled, and he fell silent. The blood flowing from his wounds—where the arms and legs had been sliced away, and the stomach had been cut open—stopped, and skin began to grow back.

Then Francella hacked away at his head and the rest of his body, cutting and recutting the moment she saw anything growing back. Noah's consciousness ebbed, and he felt himself drifting out into the cosmos, on a stream of blood that stretched across the continuum of time and space....

* * * * *

The research scientists knocked the door down, and tried to calm her, until she threatened them with the instrument. She was drenched in blood. They backed away.

While Bichette and his associates watched in dismay, Francella continued to hack her brother into smaller and smaller pieces. Finally, she paused, breathing hard. None of the parts were moving anymore. Nothing appeared to be growing back.

She fell to her knees, screaming and sobbing. Someone took the laserblade out of her hand.

Dismayed, she realized that she had acted out of anger and frustration, and she hoped she had not killed him, but only because he was needed for the ongoing experiments. Could Noah still regrow parts, and if so, in what form? Bizarre thoughts flashed through her brain. Would multiple copies of Noah develop, one around each of the severed pieces?

* * * * *

As she watched, Bichette and the others conferred, then piled the body parts together in a gory heap.

But Noah was—against all odds—still alive, extending mental and physical tendrils into the alternate dimension of Timeweb, probing, receiving mass and nutrients from the cosmic organism that supported his remarkable body. He felt the powerful presence as it filled and restored his bodily functions.

Yet in his unbearable, unrelenting pain, Noah would have preferred death, the long sleep that eluded him.

* * * * *

Far across the galaxy, Tesh and her companions on board the podship proceeded through one dwarf star system after another in the back regions of the Hibbil Sector. The Parvii, the Tulyan, and the two Humans on the vessel did not actually have daytime or evening, not by the standards of their lifetime experiences, and there were no bright suns in this region. But they did know when they were fatigued, and based upon that they reached what Eshaz called a "diurnal arrangement," under which the wristchron Acey wore became their ship's clock.

Under this arrangement they agreed upon a time to rest, in preparation for the hunt that would begin the following "day"....

When the agreed-upon time for sleep arrived, Tesh left the sectoid chamber and sealed it, after giving the sentient vessel the command to float in space within a specified area. Now, with the lights low in the passenger compartment, she and the others lay in recumbent chairs, sleeping.

Suddenly Tesh sat up and cried out, "Noah! Oh my God!"

Around her she heard the soft snoring of the teenagers, and the rumbling, deep snorts of Eshaz. Apparently the three of them had not heard her, but she sensed that something was wrong: Noah Watanabe was in terrible danger, and she could do nothing to help.

In her inexplicable but certain grief she shouted his name, as if calling to him across the vastness of the galaxy. "Noah!"

Somehow, her traveling companions continued in their slumber. She could not understand why, or why she felt as she did. Tesh remembered Noah's freckled, handsome face, and his intelligent brown eyes.

And she wondered if she would ever see him again.

Chapter Thirty-Five

Each of us has a place of sweetness where we can go to soothe our troubled spirits. Sometimes it is a fellow Mutati or a physical location, but most often it is imaginary, and we are only able to escape there for fleeting moments.

—War therapy session notes, Dij

T he Emir Hari'Adab had a different method of clearing his mind than that employed by his powerful father, the Zultan. Instead of connecting his brain to Adurian gyros, which had become something of a fad, Hari liked to glide around the star system on a solar sailer. Though he was a sizeable Mutati himself, he felt like a mote inside the craft, with its giant silvery wings glinting in the sun. It was so silent out here, and infinitely peaceful. Usually it made his troubles seem far away and inconsequential.

But not today.

He sailed along the ecliptic of the Dijian System, following the apparent path of their sun through the heavens. Only a few hours ago, he had been towed out here by a rocket plane, and then left to drift. But that was all for show, to avoid criticisms from sailing purists. Secretly, his solar sailer had backup rockets.

Technically, he knew he wasn't really solar sailing, at least not the way a true spacefaring aficionado would look at it. Periodically, his craft was aided by short, silent bursts of rocket power. In an officially sanctioned solar-sailer race, he would be disqualified for violating the rules, but for these private moments he liked the extra energy boosts, instead of having to wait and pick up speed gradually over the reaches of space, using the rapid-absorption solar panels on the craft.

I feel like my brain needs that, he thought. *A little extra oomph.*

At his command, the craft dipped and then soared under combined sail and rocket power, as he tried to improve how he felt. The unusual, custom-built craft had a variety of entertainment options. One of them, the on-board gravitonics system was off now, but if switched on could give him the sensation of being on an amusement park ride. He didn't want that right at the moment, didn't need a thrill. In fact, he realized now, he needed the complete opposite of that. He needed to slow down the sensations and mental processes that were causing him so much anxiety.

Hearing a surge as the rockets kicked on, he shut them off, too. And just drifted. Looking through the overhead and side windows, he marveled at the glittering beauty of the outstretched wings, how they seemed to be reaching for a breath of cosmic wind from God-on-High, the way he was looking for the same thing now, heavenly inspiration.

Hari believed in God, and was more devout than most Mutatis. But his personal beliefs fell far short of the religious fanaticism his father was spreading around the realm, causing increased hysteria in the people when they were most vulnerable, not helping them at all.

On numerous occasions he had voiced his opinions to his father, always doing so respectfully and in private. Lately, Hari had been protesting the aggressive Demolio program, and he had always opposed the war against the Merchant Prince Alliance, favoring peaceful resolution instead.

Repeatedly the Zultan had rebuffed him, suggesting to his son that he needed to "gyro" himself or other such nonsense. Hari didn't think his father had ever been that intelligent. Oh, the elder Mutati was smart enough to keep from accidentally stepping off a ledge, but he didn't have the degree of mental sophistication that was needed to lead a great people. He was more like a next-door neighbor, entertaining to be around, but not a real leader.

The newest incarnation of the Demolio program was a step off a ledge of another sort, and the Zultan was dragging his people down with him. To Hari, the use of laboratory-cloned podships was a violation of nature, a sacrilege against God-On-High himself. Thus far the Emir had only told his father he opposed aggressive military tactics, without framing his discontent in religious terms. To do so would risk a huge emotional outburst from the Zultan, who considered himself the sole arbiter of all important religious and political issues.

The cutoff of podship travel had effectively confined Hari to the desolate Dijian star system, although he could take this sailer to the adjacent Paradij System if he so desired, a journey of a little over a month. For one reason or another he had avoided doing that. Most of all he didn't relish the thought of a big confrontation with his father, whom Hari blamed for causing natural podships to go into hiding.

Through it all, Hari had led the people of his solar system in a buildup of military defenses, causing them to rally around him. He considered himself patriotic, didn't want Dij or any other Mutati planet overrun by foul-smelling Humans. But his father was going too far. The frenzied Zultan Abal Meshdi had orchestrated the Mutati people, bringing them to a dangerous fever pitch.

The Zultan even forced Mutati children to sing military songs in school, and encouraged them to make gruesome drawings of dead Humans. Lost innocence. Another sacrilege.

While Hari was doing the best possible job under trying circumstances, he felt a deep sadness in his heart, one that could not be remedied on this private sailing venture. With a scowl, he sent a telebeam message, ordering the rocket plane to come back and get him.

* * * * *

The following day, Hari'Adab and his girlfriend, Parais d'Olor, sat atop a rocky, barren cliff overlooking the sea, talking. It was a perch above their favorite stretch of private beach.

For this occasion Parais had metamorphosed into a very large butterfly with rainbow designs on her wings. Periodically, as she considered their important topic of conversation, she fluttered off the cliff and floated around on sea breezes, before landing beside him and tucking her wings.

Hari had never understood the long-standing enmity between his people and Humans, and wished that rational minds might prevail, heading off further bloodshed. But his father, always rabidly militaristic, had insanely destroyed four Human-ruled planets, and intended to wipe out all the rest of them as soon as he could get another delivery system perfected. It made no sense to the young Emir, and he felt himself shaking with rage and frustration.

Gazing into Parais' cerulean blue eyes, he imagined the children they might have one day, offspring that would be aeromutati like her, since female genes were dominant. So many shapeshifters … and Humans as well… had found mates in the time-honored ways of love, and just wanted to raise their families in security.

But such dreams were only illusions, waiting to be shattered by the next episode of war.

Chapter Thirty-Six

Victory is invariably achieved through a series of carefully calculated steps.
—Jimu of the Red Berets

In recent weeks Thinker had been looking at Giovanni Nehr with increasing disdain, and even some suspicion. The man's behavior seemed particularly odd after the debacle of his failed attempt to rescue Noah from Max One Prison. Cocky and outgoing before that, he had become introverted and secretive. He stopped going to the Brew Room for beers and barely interacted at all with the robots, even though he still wore the armor Thinker had given him back on Ignem.

Even more troublesome, with Subi Danvar's blessing Gio was spending an increasing amount of time away from the subterranean headquarters, supposedly because he needed to perform additional reconnaissance missions to find out where Noah really was. But Thinker had his doubts. Gio wasn't very good at reconnaissance—he had failed to discover in advance that Noah wasn't even at that particular prison.

Still, Subi said he still believed in him, and Thinker thought this might be because the adjutant wanted to give him a chance to redeem himself. Humans were like that, always trying to give one another second chances. In his data banks the robot leader had countless examples of such generous behavior, countering the aggressive, even criminal actions of other members of the Human race.

But Thinker wondered if Gio deserved a break like that, or it was a waste of time and resources. Of greater concern, was he actually going out on reconnaissance missions, or could he possibly be a spy? Was he providing updated information on Guardian forces to the enemy? It seemed entirely possible.

Without Gio's knowledge, Thinker had been observing and psychoanalyzing him, and had determined that he had a pattern of currying favor with superiors in order to gain his own promotions and other favors. Gio had behaved that way with Thinker when the robot commanded him, and had done the same with both Noah and Subi. This was another unfortunate aspect of Human behavior, their tendency toward sycophancy.

Thinker had serious doubts about whether Gio was serving the interests of Noah or the noble cause of the Guardians. His background as the brother of the top general in the Merchant Prince Alliance made him even more suspect. Supposedly the Nehr brothers had quarreled and no longer spoke to one another. But what if that was a lie, and Gio's unexpected appearance at the Inn of the White Sun—where he volunteered to join the machine army—had been a clever ploy?

These thoughts troubled the cerebral robot.

* * * * *

One afternoon Thinker was supervising the machine troops inside four large, connected caverns as they performed training exercises. He saw Subi Danvar enter the chamber and stand off to one side, where he watched the machines as they marched and simulated weapons fire, shooting silent beams of light at each other ... the equivalent of blanks.

Thinker clanked over to Subi and began to voice his concerns about Giovanni Nehr, who was supposedly out on a recon mission at that moment, but might be doing other things instead.

The adjutant, after listening attentively, scowled. Then he said, "I don't see it that way. Gio's as dedicated as any of us."

"I'm not so sure. But there's one sure way to find out. With your permission, I could read his thoughts." Thinker brought a tentacle out of his body, and it hovered overhead. "My organic interface," he said.

"Put that damn thing away. I told you how I feel about downloading Human thoughts without permission. It's not ethical."

"I believe the issue here is survival, not ethics. All's fair in love and war?"

"I won't hear of it. You're violating Human rights. It's not the right thing to do, and Master Noah would never stand for it."

Thinker snaked the tentacle back into its compartment. "But what if I'm not wrong?" "You *are* wrong. Believe me, I know a lot more about people than you do." Just then, Gio strode into the chamber and looked around. He appeared to be quite agitated, and was perspiring heavily. Joining his two superiors, he loosened his body armor and said, "I found a huge training camp for the Red Beret machine division, in the Valley of the Princes. They've converted industrial buildings to manufacturing robots, and have more fighting machines than we ever imagined, at least thirty thousand of them, and growing fast." "That many?" Subi asked.

"We can never keep up with their production rate," Gio said. "We have one advantage, though," he added. "They don't know where we are."

"Pray it stays that way," Thinker snapped, displaying an uncharacteristic machine emotion. With a sudden movement, he clanked away, to tend to his own, much smaller army.

* * * * *

On the jewel-like planet Ignem, beneath the orbital ring containing the Inn of the White Sun, the remnants of a machine army had been performing repetitious troop exercises. Since the departures of Thinker and Jimu, they no longer had effective leadership, and had grown stagnant. They were not increasing their numbers, and only performed minimal repairs on themselves to keep what they had going.

In particular they had lost the inspiration that had been provided by Thinker, the greatest computer brain among them.

For some time now, the increasing malaise had irritated the feisty little robot, Ipsy, to the point where he had been challenging more robots to fights than ever, selecting among the largest and most heavily armed of the bunch. They were only too happy to accommodate him, and he usually lost. But the dented little guy kept coming back at them, and did gain some degree of respect in the ranks for his unflagging courage. But the officers had still refused to listen to his pleas for a more effective army, and would not make any improvements. Finally, the officers had ordered Ipsy to stay away from Ignem, and banished him to the orbital Inn.

But even that had not slowed him down, as Ipsy turned his aggression toward reinvigorating the operations of the Inn of the White Sun. For months he had been traveling to alien worlds that were still accessible, where he'd been skillfully promoting the services of the facility. Possessing a font of new promotional ideas and a relentless, hard-working attitude, he was bringing in a good income for the machines, almost as high as it had been before the Human and Mutati empires were isolated from the rest of the galaxy.

Finally, with control over a mounting treasury, he sent word down to the officers on Ignem that he wanted to spend the funds on improving the army. In a return message, they declined his offer.

Ipsy seethed, but refused to give up.

Chapter Thirty-Seven

Life always rises from death … in infinite, and sometimes startling, forms.
—Tulyan Wisdom

It was unlike anything seen in a medical journal in the history of mankind, or in the annals of any other galactic race. Dr. Hurk Bichette, at first horrified and repulsed at what Francella did to her own brother, now stared in disbelief at the grisly scene before him … Noah's bleeding, severed body parts piled inside a clearplax-covered life-support unit.

Did something just move there? The doctor wasn't sure, and the gauges showed nothing at all, no sign of life. The system, particularly the mini-atmosphere of the large, coffin-sized enclosure housing the remains, was supposed to preserve any life that remained, but that probably didn't amount to anything at all. The trauma to the body had been so severe that no one, not even a person imbued with the powers Noah had displayed, could recover from it.

Alone in a small, heavily guarded chamber, Bichette walked slowly around the plax case containing the grisly remains of the body, chunks of flesh, bone, and brain matter. On the left, a fragment of skull with Noah's red hair on it, matted with blood. In the center an eyeball, severed and amazingly intact, staring into nowhere … no change there in the forty-two hours since the horrific incident.

Punching buttons on a panel, he brought up original holophotos of the remains, and compared them with what he was looking at now. Everything was the same, except for the increasing decay, and the stench. Disappointment filled him.

From a medical standpoint, it was more a matter of observing and hooking up monitoring equipment than anything else; this wasn't the sort of patient who could be helped by any known medical treatment. Noah had to recover on his own, drawing resources from his secret, mysterious source.

Bichette rubbed his own eyes. They must be playing tricks on him. Even through the sealed plax, Bichette could still smell the putrid odors of blackened, decaying flesh, a smell that seemed to permeate everything. He didn't think he could ever put it out of his memory, or erase the recollection of what he had seen the madwoman do … his demented boss.

In the background, from another room of the medical complex, he heard Francella shouting at someone. The day before, the two of them had reached an understanding, that she would stay away from Noah from now on and not interfere in any way with procedures that needed to be done. She said she just wanted a vial of Noah's blood, which she took with her. The conversation seemed moot now. A mortician would be of more use here than a doctor.

No, wait. What is that?

Bichette stopped dead in his tracks, and watched in astonishment as the damaged brain matter writhed and gathered together, then stopped moving. Moments passed. Slowly, the brain matter began to combine with a mass of flesh, and then inched toward the intact, still motionless eyeball.

A wave of fear passed through Bichette. He started to yell for his assistants, but changed his mind. The doctor felt a personal connection to this case, almost an ownership over it.

I'm witnessing medical history.

How could the body possibly be regenerating, after such severe trauma? With cellular material destroyed and gone, what was he using for nutrients, for energy? Flesh and bones should not be able to grow out of nothing. Medical science was not magical. And yet, this was happening anyway, defying the most basic laws of science and creation.

* * * * *

The mass of brain and flesh had now encircled the eyeball, touching it, cradling it like a precious child. Abruptly the eyeball moved, and looked directly at Bichette.

The doctor stood frozen in his tracks.

Moment by moment, the flesh and bone gathered and metamorphosed, while a holocamera recorded everything.

Some would call the creature before him an abomination, and Bichette knew he had to keep information about it from going public. That would only invite unwelcome inquiries, and perhaps even worse—an attack on the facility by the Guardians. Already they had made a commando assault on Max One, where Noah used to be kept.

By the end of the morning, the entire head had regenerated, and it lay face up with facial features that clarified minute by minute, bringing out the scarred, one-eyed countenance of Noah Watanabe. The top of his skull had patches of reddish hair that were gradually filling in. The missing eye began to emerge from the skull and take shape. Through the changes, the face grimaced, as if in continuing pain, and no sounds came forth. Wounds healed, but at the bottom of the head, where the brain stem remained visible, the ragged tissue did not cauterize, and remained open and moist with blood.

As all of this occurred, the life-support system collected information and transmitted it to the gauges. The vital signs were weak, but improving. This *creature*—and that was all Bichette could call it at the moment—did not have any body, but it still had an erratic pulse.

Hours passed. All of the remaining cellular material began to gather at the base of the skull where the brain stem had remained exposed, and gradually covered it over. By the end of the afternoon, the head had become the seed of a new body, which grew from the neck down, filling in the upper body and then the rest ... the arms, hands, legs, feet. In all respects, it appeared to match Noah's previous form, with scars that continued to heal and fade.

At last, in the middle of the night the process stopped, and the instruments showed that Noah—as if exhausted from the effort—was slipping into a fitful slumber. He kept drifting off, but every few moments he would suddenly twitch and reawaken. The eyes looked blankly at Bichette.

All through the process, as Noah's features solidified and the scars disappeared, his face had been a mask of pain. The suffering had been troubling to the doctor, but he had been afraid to administer medications out of fear that they might interfere with the arcane regeneration processes occurring in the body. But now, looking at the intact, regenerated person, he took the chance. Opening a panel in the life-support case, he injected a powerful mix of opiates into Noah, then closed the case.

According to the instruments, Noah slipped into more comfortable sleep, going deeper and deeper through the stages, but occasionally coming back to REM state, dreaming.

Afraid something might go wrong, Bichette remained at his side, and checked the monitoring mechanisms on the plax case, including the alarm system. Finally, assured that he could do no more for the moment, the doctor fell asleep himself, on a gurney....

* * * * *

During the entire restoration process Noah had been linked to Timeweb in its alternate dimension, a cosmic intravenous line feeding nutrients into his body, from one realm to another. During the restoration process, he'd been thinking of venture deeper into the cosmic realm, but had been too fatigued for any attempt. He felt pain in every muscle, bone, and joint of his body.

He had also thought of Tesh, recalling in particular the intelligent beauty of her face and the confident way she comported herself. Noah wondered how she was doing, and hoped all was well with her.

Then he became aware of the medications kicking in, dulling his senses. At first Noah was angered at the intrusion, feeling his abilities slow and his mind reel back in. As moments passed, however, he welcomed the drugs and the relief they gave him from all of his troubles.

* * * * *

Very little occurred in the CorpOne medical laboratories without the knowledge of Francella Watanabe. Either she received reports on the various activities, or she could see them firsthand, through holocams inside the principal laboratory rooms.

From her office in the complex, she had watched the entire process in three-dimensional holo-images that floated in the air. It had been almost as good as being in the room with her brother and Bichette, and had the advantage of keeping her at a distance, preventing her from interfering with the unknown forces that were bringing Noah back to life.

Too often she had stormed around the building, yelling at people, venting her frustrations, even slashing the face of a scientist as he cowered in her presence and tried to fend off the surgical knife she swung at him. The man had been lucky to escape her full rage. In fact, she'd had to use all of her willpower to avoid going into the chamber where all of the real action was occurring.

While slashing at the scientist and chasing him down the corridor, she had demanded answers from him. "What will happen if I inject Noah's blood into my own body? I'm his fraternal twin. What bearing will that have?"

"I don't know," he had whimpered. "I just don't know."

"Get out of my sight, then!"

The wounded man had disappeared around a corner, presumably to find a doctor himself. The fool was lucky she didn't kill him.

Now at the end of a long day, Francella did not feel any weariness at all. Curiously, while she loathed her brother and wanted only the worst for him, she felt exhilaration at his Lazarus trick, since it confirmed to her that his blood had supernatural powers. She could use it to gain eternal life for herself. Doctors and medical-research scientists knew nothing of immortality; she shouldn't even have asked them about it. They only knew how to treat injuries and illnesses, and how to analyze diseases.

Nothing like this.

In fact, this sort of thing, if widespread, did not bode well for the medical profession at all. With death vanquished, people would not need doctors. But those professions did not need to worry, since she would not permit the secret to get out. Even if he could not be killed, her brother could still be kept in captivity and used for whatever purposes she desired. She envisioned Noah continually providing her with blood and other cellular materials, a lab animal kept alive to be milked of its nutrients.

The excited woman smiled to herself. In the low light of her office, she stared at the vial of blood that sat on her desk, at the rich, wine-colored elixir inside the small plax container. She touched the surface of the plax, and knew she had the secret of perpetual life at her fingertips.

Connecting the vial to a dermex medical instrument, she pressed it against her left arm, injecting the contents into her own bloodstream.

As the fluid raced into her veins, Francella felt supremely confident. It was said that twins had special, even paranormal connections, and she had convinced herself that this was true. The demented woman thought she was giving herself eternal life, but in reality something quite unanticipated would occur....

Chapter Thirty-Eight

I think about my sister often. Sometimes I imagine that I already know her better than I know myself.

—Noah Watanabe

Like a fetus to an umbilical cord, Noah had remained linked to Timeweb during the intense ordeal of his physical restoration, as he returned to life, defying all odds. He had, in a very real sense, gone through a remarkable process of rebirth, on a scale beyond that of any other creature who had ever walked the worlds of the universe, or moved from star system to star system.

The drugs administered to Noah had caused his mind to release its tensions, which should have enabled him to drift into peaceful, restful slumber. But the act of letting go had resulted in an unexpected consequence. Through a veil of consciousness, he saw his sister in her private office, removing a dermex unit from her arm. With a satisfied smile on her face, she leaned back on her chair and closed her eyes.

Noah felt himself forming into a mist as he had done before. Looking down, he saw that it had again taken the shape of his physical form. It floated around the room, even touching Francella briefly when he passed close. The moment the mist came into contact with her, she opened her eyes and sat straight up.

Since he was her twin, Noah sensed how deeply troubled she was, and he knew that virtually all of the hatred she could muster—a considerable amount, indeed—was focused on him, even though she did not know he was there with her. He realized as well that there was nothing he could do about it. She would always feel that way, to the last breath she took. Her wide-open eyes reflected the internal sea of her madness.

He saw her shiver and shudder. She grabbed a coat, hurried to the door, and rushed out into the corridor.

Noah followed, a mist in her wake that clung to her like a shadow.

"You sense I'm here, don't you?" he shouted.

Nervously, she looked behind her, and almost tripped as she picked up her pace and left the building. He heard the noises she was making, but didn't know if she could hear him. Just another oddity added to the long list he was accumulating in his mind.

A limocar took her home, and Noah stayed with her all the way, riding invisibly on the seat beside her. She kept twitching, looking around, talking to herself and scrunching in a corner, trying to assure herself that she was not crazy, that she just needed some rest. "I've been working too hard," she said.

He was enjoying this, making her nervous, lingering where she couldn't do anything about it.

Once, just before they got out of the limocar at her palatial home, she passed her hand through the air where Noah sat in his misty form, but her expression was perplexed and she said nothing about him, didn't use his name.

The vehicle was coming to a stop, still rolling slowly, when she leapt out, ran inside the main entrance of her home and locked the door behind her. Francella then instructed her personal servants to lock all doors and windows, and to draw the shades in every room.

As the attendants scurried about their business, Noah stuck to her, trying to scuff against the skin of her arms and face whenever he could, which had the effect of further agitating her. She went straight to bed, fully clothed, and pulled the covers over her head.

Noah took that as a barrier. Even in this circumstance, where he was functioning outside of his corporal form, he didn't want any hint of incest. Instead, he would wait for her to awaken, and would resume the torment.

He realized as he did these things that he had stooped low (though nowhere near to her level), and he felt shame, but only a modicum of it. His rage gave him righteousness, and more than anything he wanted to see her dead.

Now he felt full shame. This was not like him, not at all. As he watched her sleep—the lump under the covers—he felt his resolve weakening. At the same time his connection to the ethereal realm seemed to slip. The images in her bedroom grew more faint. He heard Francella snoring, and felt himself floating involuntarily back to the locked room in the laboratory where they kept him....

* * * * *

When Francella awoke the following morning, troubling thoughts of the incident still clung to her like raindrops from a storm. But she reminded herself that she had been fatigued when the strange energy seemed to chase her out of the office, and she ascribed it to her own imagination.

She hoped it was that, wanted to think it was, and that it had nothing to do with the blood she had injected.

Chapter Thirty-Nine

There are many forms of children. They do not always need a physical form in order to breathe.

—Saying of the Sirikan Hill People

For weeks, Princess Meghina had been making clandestine visits to a man, always in the middle of the night. Wearing a dark, hooded cloak, she moved silently down a rock-walled corridor, clinging to pockets of darkness.

As a renowned courtesan, this was not particularly unusual behavior on her part. She liked to be discreet. Her customary appointments, however, were with princes and other refined noblemen, from the best families in the galaxy. The man she was seeing now had noble blood, but only on his paternal side. He didn't live in a magnificent palace or a castle on a hill. The object of her affection was a prisoner in the Doge's prison, but not a lowly detainee. This one had status.

She had paid off the right guards with Sirikan gemstones, and thus far her secret remained intact. Since first laying eyes on Anton Glavine at the pod station where he was arrested, Meghina had felt an instant attraction. It was always like that with the men in her life, an immediate connection that soon became physical.

But to test herself, she always liked to go through a selection process with her potential paramours. Anton was far more handsome than most of them, but that had little to do with it, as far as she was concerned. Of utmost importance, each of her lovers needed to occupy a special and unique niche in the galaxy; they must not be cut from cookie-cutter molds.

Her dear Prince Saito Watanabe had qualified with flying colors. The self-made tycoon, born into relative obscurity, had raised himself by his own hard labors and force of personality. As for the Doge Lorenzo del Velli, he had his own individuality, particularly his forward-thinking way of elevating commoners to nobility based upon their accomplishments in life. He had done exactly that with Saito, with Jacopo Nehr, and with others. It took courage for him to take those actions, bucking thousands of years of noble tradition. The hardships that her prospective lover, Anton Glavine, was going through now would ultimately build his character. She liked that in a man.

As Princess Meghina hurried down the corridor, she reminded herself that she also had an important humanitarian purpose in mind. It was obvious to her that the mysterious young man had not been treated in a manner befitting his station. He was, after all, the son of Doge Lorenzo, and could even become the ruler of the Merchant Prince Alliance one day, given the right political winds. But she didn't care about the politics.

It struck her with some excitement that she had never done anything quite like this before, grooming a relationship to this extent, and she laughed a bit at herself. Perhaps she was going a bit "rock happy," losing some of her senses from being confined to one planet, albeit a large and wealthy one. For much of her life she had flitted between glittering worlds, and her restriction to this one made her feel dismal much of the time.

This nocturnal adventure lifted her spirits; each day that she had an appointment she looked forward to it, even though the two of them had only held hands so far. She hadn't pushed for more, not even a kiss. She hadn't told him of her attraction for him, though she could tell that he knew it anyway. Thus far she had only confided that she was interested in his well-being, and would tell him no more. To her credit, she pulled it all off with an air of mystery.

At first the young man had seemed confused by her attentions, and then grateful. In return for her payoffs to the guards, she had obtained better treatment for him. So far he had been spared intensive interrogations or torture, but one of the guards told her he didn't know if he could promise that for much longer.

Though she had given him no name, Anton had recognized her, and had told her so. Once when he started to utter her name, she'd pressed a hand against his mouth. "Shhh," she had said. "We don't want the wrong people to find out I'm helping you."

Some of the guards had recognized her, despite her efforts to remain cloaked and to conceal her features as much as possible. In delivering her payments to the guards, Meghina's intermediary had commanded them to look away whenever "the lady" came to visit. Most of the guards had done so, but she had seen a couple of them peeking, trying to get a glimpse of her. One of them might have seen her full face a couple of weeks ago, when her hood slipped off as she was leaving.

Tonight, as she moved stealthily down the corridor, she was surprised to see another female visitor, already with Anton in his cell, speaking to him in low tones. The princess recognized Francella Watanabe immediately, unmistakable with her high forehead and shaved eyebrows. She wore a long black coat.

Slipping into a darkened alcove only a few meters away from the orange bars of the cell's containment field, Meghina eavesdropped on the conversation.

"Are you well, my son?" Francella asked. She stood inside the cell, while he remained seated on the lower bed of his bunk.

Looking away from her, he said, "I've told you before. I have no feelings for you, so we have nothing to discuss. Why do you keep coming back?"

"Because I neglected you for too long. I beg you to forgive me, my son. Am I not worthy of your slightest sympathy?"

"You are only worthy of my contempt."

"At least you have *some* feelings for me," she said, with an emotional edge to her voice. She looked down, then said, "I could help you more, if you'd give me a chance. Already I have prevented them from torturing you."

Anton didn't respond, but it occurred to Meghina that he had at least two female protectors now. Undoubtedly the guards were playing both of the women to maximize their payoffs, saying to each that they didn't know how much longer they could continue to protect the prisoner.

Moments later, Francella used a transmitter to release the containment field, stepped out, and then reactivated it. Without another word she swept down the corridor, while Princess Meghina remained in the shadows. In his cell, Anton threw something metal that clanked on the rock floor.

Stepping out of the alcove, Meghina said, "You're popular tonight."

He looked at her, his face filled with tragedy. "I'm sorry, but this isn't a good time. Can you come back another day? I appreciate what you're doing for me, but I just don't...." He seemed at a loss for words.

"You don't need to explain," she said, softly. "I understand."

As Meghina left the prison the same way she had entered, she felt no sympathy for Francella; the selfish woman gave up her maternal rights when she abandoned him as a baby. Of that she was certain.

But the Sirikan princess was not sure what to make of Francella Watanabe's involvement now … this adversary she loathed so much, who competed with her for the affections of Meghina's own husband, Doge Lorenzo. Admittedly, the courtesan and the Doge had reached an understanding between them, an open marriage. But she wished he had better taste in some of the other women he saw.

* * * * *

It arrived, like so much information, as an unconfirmed rumor, a horrific story of butchery committed against Noah by his own sister. A new Guardian recruit, a young woman, came to Subi and Thinker with the dreadful tale.

"Everyone's talking about it," she said. "I don't know who said it first, or where it came from."

"His own sister, eh?" Subi said, seething.

"That's what they saying."

Subi sent out investigators to scour Rainbow City and the Valley of the Princes, seeking hard information. Finally it arrived, late that night. One of the investigators had spoken with a medical researcher who claimed to have actually seen the carnage.

Under cover of darkness, Subi led a commando squad himself. In a frenzy, the Guardians stormed CorpOne's headquarters complex, the inverted pyramid and surrounding buildings. Quickly, they took control of the complex and killed or captured all of the guards.

Feeling a rush of adrenaline, Subi then ordered his squad to aim incendiary rockets at the headquarters building. He hesitated before giving the order to fire. This was the most famous of Prince Saito Watanabe's buildings, and the most architecturally interesting. The late prince had been Noah's father, and as such he deserved respect. Especially since Noah came to feel that the two of them might have been close, if not for the vindictive interference of his own sister.

Francella.

But rage suffused Subi as he envisioned her face, and her terrible acts, not only against Noah but against her own father. Over a megaphone, he shouted: "Everyone in the building, you have five minutes to get out."

Some of the offices had lights on, while most were dark. He saw movement up on one of the top three floors that had been leased to Doge Lorenzo.

Within minutes, a dozen people rushed out of the building on the ground level, and were taken into custody. No one important; just mid-level office staffers and janitorial workers.

Subi made a chopping motion with his right arm, a gesture he selected intentionally, as a visual reminder of Francella's terrible crime against Noah.

A volley of incendiary rockets struck the building's top levels exactly where Thinker had told him to hit, causing the entire structure to collapse and burn. It burned like a torch, lighting up the Valley of the Princes.

Chapter Forty

"There are new experiences, and then again there are new experiences! This blows the top off my skull!"

—Acey Zelk, comment to Dux Hannah

E arly in the morning, according to the artificial diurnal time established by the hunters, their mottled gray-and-black podship proceeded slowly through the Hibbil Sector, taking a roundabout, seemingly wayward course. In this manner they hoped to avoid alerting their prey....

Inside the low light of the passenger compartment, Eshaz opened the large shipping cases and brought out a protective suit like the one he had worn on Tarbu. After putting it on, he removed the contents of the other cases, and arranged various items on the deck and on top of a bulkhead table.

These included thorn vines in varying colors, all carefully wrapped in broad leaf packages. Each parcel was marked in a Tulyan dialect that Dux could not read, labels that Eshaz said identified the toxins and drugs in the vines, along with the sizes of the clippings. Other cases held vials of liquid and powder, small bowls, fire cylinders, herbs, music spheres, pigment rings, a big alloy cauldron, and an intricately folded, gilded harness that was decorated with mythological animals. Cheerily, Eshaz described some of the items as he brought them out.

In complete fascination, the boys watched as he mixed liquids, powders, and herbs in the bowls, took scrapings from the thorn vines, and combined everything in the cauldron, which he heated by inserting the fire cylinders into receptacles around the bottom of the thick alloy casting.

"I'll let this cook for a while," he said.

"Sort of a witch's brew?" Acey asked.

"Your terminology limits comprehension," Eshaz retorted. "A common Human frailty. When roaming the galaxy, you must avoid thinking in preconceived terms."

Acey nodded, but he looked puzzled.

Dux took a deep breath, and tried to keep his own mind open.

Presently Eshaz murmured incantations and tossed the music spheres overhead, which played monastic-sounding chants and polyphonies and then floated down into the boiling cauldron, melted into the liquid, and were silenced.

"It's time," Eshaz said, looking around.

"What?" Acey said.

"Tesh is coming to a stop."

Running to a porthole, Dux and Acey looked out into a region of space that was oddly illuminated by a pale bluish-gray light that had no discernible source. Acey went to another porthole. "I don't see any wild podships," he said.

"Nonetheless, we are in the right place."

Now, using long spoons, Eshaz dipped solution out of the cauldron and poured it into silver vials, which he sealed with sharp-pointed tops and placed into a bag. Then, removing the protective suit and his other clothing, he smeared iridescent pigment rings on his body, changing the scaly bronze surfaces of his skin to a network of intricate, colorful designs.

His slitted eyes were glazed over now, and he seemed to take no notice of Dux or Acey. Invoking new incantations, he handled the thorn vines without protective clothing, and wrapped a selection of them around his waist, then used straps to secure the bag of vials to his chest. He placed a bright red vine on his head, wearing it like a crown, and murmured what Dux imagined might be a Tulyan blessing.

As the boys watched, spellbound, Eshaz grabbed the gilded harness, which was still folded. Opening a hatch, he leapt out into the eerily illuminated vacuum of space, and quickly closed the door behind him. Through the mysterious workings of the podship, there was no explosive decompression that might have been caused by the inrushing vacuum of space. Instinctively, the boys held their breaths, then began breathing a few moments later, uneasily at first but with more comfort as the cabin oxygen level replenished quickly.

"Look!" Acey said, pointing upward.

A filmy window began to form on the top of the passenger compartment, and the teenagers saw Eshaz harnessed to the top of the podship, leaning forward.

* * * * *

The Tulyan felt the craft accelerate along a course that he had specified for Tesh. Squinting to peer ahead, he made out a herd of podships there, moving in their typical vee-formation away from him. As he neared them at a higher rate of speed, he saw that they were one of the largest wild-pod herds he had ever seen, with at least seventy individuals.

"*Ubuqqo, atra mii,* " he murmured in his ancient tongue. "Thanks be to the Sublime Creator." In the time-honored way of his people, Eshaz held two silver vials—one in each hand, pointed toward the podship formation. At his mental command, the vials shot out of his hands, faster than any projectile weapon. Grabbing more vials from the bag, he released one after another, and all hit their targets, sedating the podships one by one from the rear of the formation— though they continued to fly with their visual sensors looking forward, and did not send warnings to the leader.

Gradually the entire formation slowed down—with the exception of the alpha pod—and came to a dead stop in space.

* * * * *

Inside the passenger cabin beneath Eshaz, the teenage boys pressed their faces against portholes, staring out. Limited by his Human sensations, Dux had not felt the accelerations, decelerations, or turns of the podship in which he rode. Now, as if experiencing a dream, he saw a herd of podships come into his view. Most of them appeared to be drifting.

Their own podship, still under the guidance of Tesh, floated slowly past the sedated creatures....

* * * * *

When he was just behind the lead podship, which remained unaware of the flurry of silent activity behind it, Eshaz reached deep into his mind, and focused all of his energy. He must be especially precise now, capturing the alpha pod and taking full control of it. It could not be sedated like the others or permitted to escape, or it would react by reviving them and leading all of them to commit suicide.

At the last possible moment, just as the alpha pod seemed to sense something, Eshaz made a floating, zero-g leap onto the creature's back, connected his harness, and dug thorn vines into its sides.

The podship was a big one, with ragged scars on its sides, perhaps marking prior attempts to capture it. The creature squealed out, an ancient protest that

Eshaz heard despite the vacuum, and he held on.

Like a wild stallion of Lost Earth, the creature bucked, spun, whirled, and tried to throw off its rider. With expert precision, Eshaz brought out more vines and dug the sharp thorns into the creature's hide, injecting toxins. Finally the podship settled down.

On top of the pod, Eshaz lay flat, facing downward. Spreading his hands out, he felt the creature tremble, as it sensed what was about to occur. The Tulyan felt himself dropping slowly, like sinking into a thick bog. He merged into the flesh, and into the creature's primitive brain.

The podship altered appearance. Eshaz's face and eyes formed on the front, on a scale equal to the much larger size of the creature, and its skin became scaly, a gray-bronze hue that combined the two races. Immersed in every cell of the Aopoddae, Eshaz changed the direction of the vessel, causing it to veer off to the right. The other wild pods followed.

Exhilarated, Eshaz accelerated onto a podway, with the entire formation following, and Tesh's pod just behind them.

* * * * *

From the sectoid chamber, Tesh heard Acey and Dux hooting with excitement inside the passenger compartment. Then, as the podships reached open space, beyond the protection of the Wild Pod Zone, she saw a small contingent of Parvii scouts on one side, keeping pace with them. Her emotions warred with one another.

Eshaz, leading the pack of sentient spaceships, must have seen them, too, because he urged the alpha pod—with its hybrid, reptilian face—to greater speed. The unpiloted podships accelerated, keeping up.

But the Lilliputian scouts kept pace, too.

Tesh knew they were communicating with others within telepathic range, summoning a full swarm ... enough to take control of the wild podships. She and Eshaz had discussed this possibility, and knew they wouldn't have much time to escape. In one sense she felt like a traitor to her race, but she knew her actions were absolutely necessary.

Chapter Forty-One

There are countless ways to die, but only those specified in the sacred texts guarantee your entrance into heaven.

—*The Holy Writ* of the Mutatis

On the Mutati capital world of Paradij, the Zultan Abal Meshdi lounged on oversized pillows in his palace harem, watching as his personal menagerie of shapeshifters danced for him. Fifteen of the most beautiful Mutati women of the three subspecies—terramutati, aero mutati, and hydro mutati—danced on the floor, in the air, and inside a large tank of water. They moved in perfect synchronization, kinetic kilos of undulating flesh, the most graceful he had ever seen. But this evening he did not feel any desire for them. He had too much on his mind, had worked too hard for too long. At last everything was coming together: all of the important pieces were moving into position.

He had never witnessed such a malevolent, misanthropic frenzy all across the planet, and it pleased him immensely. In each city, town, and hamlet, every citizen was contributing mightily to the war effort against humankind, marshaling resources, channeling energy, performing all of the small and large tasks required for the ultimate, grand victory of the Mutati Kingdom.

As the inspirational leader, the Zultan knew he had been the catalyst for this new thrust, but lately the whole thing was taking on a life and energy of its own. Bioengineering laboratories were creating an abundance of lab-pods, while factories were churning out simulated merchant schooners with built-in Demolio torpedoes, and training facilities were preparing the outriders. Buildings everywhere carried giant electronic murals of the Zultan, along with holos of the most popular outrider volunteers, those Mutati men and women who would pilot the planet-busting bombs to their destinations.

Rumors abounded that the Zultan himself would ride one of the deadly Demolios to glory, and he allowed the stories to persist. They did no harm, and actually served to inspire the people even more, by showing that he was willing to give his all for the cause. Privately, he had no intention of getting to heaven that way. His own deeds spoke for themselves; he had already paid for his ticket.

I'll come up with some good excuse, he thought, as he watched the bulky beauties perform a shapeshifting dance, contorting their abundant mounds of flesh in provocative ways. *Some delaying tactic to keep others boarding the lab-pods ahead of me.*

His thoughts shifted as he watched a lithesome hydromutati slide through the water. He could never marry that subspecies or conceive children with a non-terramutati, but the *Holy Writ* did permit certain dalliances....

* * * * *

Though Noah's body looked substantially restored, with all of its exterior parts and appendages, scars remained that were slow to heal, along with faint, pink discolorations on his freckled skin. His internal organs ached, especially his kidneys and lungs. Signals reaching his brain told him the organs were healed and functioning well, but they remained traumatized, like separate, sentient life forms huddling inside his body. The pain had been excruciating. Any other Human would have died under such a violent onslaught, but Noah, with his enhanced life functions, lived through more agony than any other person had ever endured in the entire history of his race. The trauma had gone on and on, without relief—with the exception of intermittent, unpredictable mental excursions that diverted his attentions elsewhere, but for only brief moments. During the worst of it he would have welcomed death, but the Grim Reaper had not awaited him with open arms.

In his continuing suffering, with his paranormal linkage to Timeweb, Noah was in the process of discovering something new and disturbing, over which he had no control....

* * * * *

Subi Danvar jumped back from the screen on Thinker's chest, as if he had just seen a ghost. He had been talking with the simulated Noah about the wonderful times they used to have at the Environmental Demonstration Project, and on board the orbital EcoStation.

Suddenly the image of Noah shifted, and a three-dimensional likeness of him seemed to float out of the screen into the underground cavern. At first, Subi thought it was a holo-image, but it didn't have the same quality of illumination, and he saw no projector. The image floated around the chamber, then landed on its feet a short distance from Subi. It looked diaphanous, like a living mist in Human form.

"Do you see that?" Subi asked Thinker.

"See what?"

"There!"

"The cavern wall, you mean? What?"

"Not the wall! Noah! Don't you see him?"

"Noah is not there. I'm afraid you're having an illusion, perhaps initiated by my data screen. I'd better switch it off." He did so, and closed a panel over the screen.

With trepidation, Subi walked over to the image. Timidly, he extended his hand toward it.

"Don't try to touch me!" Noah said.

Subi recoiled. Looking back at Thinker he asked, "Did you hear that?"

"Hear what? Poor man, you need to get some rest."

Stubbornly, Subi reached toward the image, and put his hand through it. As he did so, the apparition faded entirely.

"I told you not to touch me!" Noah yelled, as if from afar. "It's more than the dimensional stretch can tolerate!" He disappeared entirely, and took his voice with him.

Chapter Forty-Two

Though Lorenzo keeps his business affairs private, it is known that he holds a number of corporate directorships around the galaxy, a network of interactions that form the economic basis of his power.

—*Pillars of the Merchant Princes*, a holodocumentary

The destruction of the CorpOne headquarters building had forced Lorenzo to relocate his offices and royal residence to the orbiter that had formerly been Noah Watanabe's prized EcoStation. While the Doge hated to retreat, he had been pleased that he still had this facility solidly under his control, and that the pesky Guardians could not possibly get to him there. The space station, now fully armored and fitted with the most advanced security systems, also had a formidable squadron of government patrol ships constantly on alert.

Deep in thought, the Doge walked through the module containing his new offices, where a construction crew worked at an efficient but inadequate pace. He would order Pimyt to speed them up. Office work still needed to be done, so his staff had been operating out of makeshift quarters nearby.

Proceeding down a long corridor into another module, he entered one of Noah's former classrooms and waved at Princess Meghina, who was discussing the ongoing work with a contractor. With her good taste and love of exotic projects, she was helping immensely, and Lorenzo had put her in charge of this section.

Originally Lorenzo had been about to make drastic changes to this area, tearing out not only the classrooms but also the connected mini-forest area that Noah's people had cultivated. It had all looked absurd to him, and he'd wanted to move gambling equipment in for a glitzy new casino. Meghina concurred with the casino idea, but talked him out of changing this particular module, telling him that plants created oxygen, valuable on a space station. She pointed out what a holovideo told her—that the forest ecosystem was a self-sufficient, scaled-down version of life on Canopa, with small birds and other creatures filling ecological niches. She then suggested that they turn the classrooms into an attractive casino dining hall, with the miniature forest surrounding it, separated by the invisible electronic barrier that was already in place. All excellent ideas, he had to admit. The gambling equipment would have to go elsewhere.

Almost oblivious to anyone in the corridors of the orbital station, Lorenzo stalked ahead. Subordinates fell silent as he neared them, and they scurried out of his way. Behind him, four Red Beret guards kept pace, watching out for his safety. He had other things on his mind.

With the Mutati war forced into the background, Lorenzo del Velli still faced tremendous difficulties. In particular, he was concerned about reports of discontent against him among the princes on various planets. His political problems were complex and worrisome, exacerbated by the continuing guerrilla attacks by Guardian forces against government and corporate installations on Canopa. There had even been copycat incidents on other planets, reportedly done by sympathetic groups that were not formally aligned with the Guardians. With no access to nehrcom stations, the Guardians could not possibly be coordinating the attacks, but they were occurring nonetheless, and weakening him.

The underpinnings of opposition against Lorenzo ran deep. For some time, the noble-born princes had been critical of him for stubbornly appointing commoners such as Saito Watanabe and Jacopo Nehr to important government positions. The noble-born princes, descended from aristocratic lineages that went back for thousands of years, were not happy about this at all, but Lorenzo had brought most of them over to his side anyway, by pointing out the necessity of rewarding exceptional skills. None of the nobles could deny the sterling business accomplishments of either Saito or Jacopo. And, while Saito was dead now and his operations were more low-key under his daughter Francella, Jacopo Nehr was still in the limelight, having been promoted the year before to Supreme General of all Merchant Prince Armed Forces.

Rounding a corner forcefully, Lorenzo almost bowled over a little man carrying a briefcase, going the other way. One of the office functionaries. A paper shuffler. The office worker apologized profusely, bowed, and hurried on his way.

The Doge headed for a room at the end of the corridor—his communications center—which he saw through an open doorway. Lights blinked in there and small robots whirred back and forth, performing functions that were even lower than those of the typical office worker.

Lorenzo knew which noble-born princes were closest to him, because they were the ones most vocal in their support. Of course, some of that could be a ruse, and he was alert to that. He remained most concerned and troubled, however, by the ones who were remaining silent and detached from him. Having alerted his own government agents by nehrcom on the various Alliance planets, he had the princes under constant surveillance, thus far without turning up any specific evidence against any of them. It was most perplexing to him, and frustrating. The disloyal princes seemed to have taken a page from the Guardian playbook, lying low and making their own form of guerrilla attacks against him.

As he entered the communications center, Pimyt greeted him. The little Hibbil carried an electronic notebook under one arm. "We are ready to broadcast," Pimyt said. "Here are the prompter notes."

"I don't need notes," Lorenzo snapped, shoving the furry little man aside. "I know what to say."

He went to a console, and a technician in a black singlesuit turned on the machine, bathing the Doge in soft white light. Later in the day he would broadcast through nehrcom relay to the people of every planet in the Merchant Prince Alliance, his version of the ages-old fireside chat. It was a recent suggestion from Pimyt, and Lorenzo had taken a liking to the idea, as a way of keeping him in the minds of the people. With the cessation of podship travel and the mutterings of noble-born princes against him, Lorenzo's task in this regard was proving to be increasingly difficult.

But first he had a more limited broadcast, just for the Canopan people. To show his concern for their security, Lorenzo had been making regular public proclamations on the purported progress his forces were making in rooting out Noah's forces, the cowards who made guerrilla style attacks against corporate and government facilities where many of the citizens worked.

While Pimyt stood by nervously, holding the electronic notepad, Lorenzo began to talk extemporaneously. In a blatant lie, he told the people to pay no attention to the increasing number of destroyed buildings and other assets on Canopa, that Guardian losses were very high and they didn't have the resources to go on much longer.

Bolstering the spin he was putting on events, he accompanied his speech with holo-images of Noah in captivity, to prove that the Doge was in control of the situation. In reality they were older pictures of the rebel leader, before Francella hacked him to pieces. The current images of Noah, though his body had regenerated, made him look like a torture victim, with pinkish scars and other wounds that were not healing as rapidly as in the past, when he experienced less grievous injuries.

As Lorenzo completed the address, he stepped away from the white light. The technician transmitted recorded messages, boilerplate material that accompanied every one of the Doge's pronouncements.

Lorenzo walked away, ignoring Pimyt for the moment, who scuttled along behind him babbling the usual sycophantic nonsense. The merchant prince leader's new orbital office headquarters would offer him additional security, but he wanted to spend more time down on Canopa as soon as possible, and this made him grumpy whenever he focused on it.

By rights, his offices and his residence should be down there, not up here. His empire seemed to be shrinking around him. Once, he ruled hundreds of wealthy planets of the Merchant Prince Alliance from the glittering capital world of Timian One. Now, with the capital destroyed and Canopa increasingly dangerous for him, he had retreated to a very small place, and only maintained tenuous control over the remaining planets.

He still ventured down to the surface of Canopa on occasion, but only accompanied by a cadre of Red Berets, led by a trusted colonel who had been in his service for almost a decade. These men were the fiercest of Human and machine fighters, trained in the most advanced weaponry and sworn to protect their Doge at all costs.

* * * * *

Ever the optimist, Lorenzo always had interesting operations underway. For some time before the destruction of his Canopan offices, he had been expanding this space station by bringing in new armored modules and floating them into orbit, intending to turn the facility into a gambling resort called The Pleasure Palace. Word of this got out, as he wanted. But it had the unintended result of causing some of the discontented princes to criticize him for it. Still, he thought he could turn the tables on them.

Even with the forced relocation of his offices, he would proceed with the casino plans, and would demonstrate to the Alliance that he could not be intimidated by criticism. Besides, the facility would make a lot of money for him, enabling him to fulfill his love of gambling in a dramatic, very public way. Admittedly the whole enterprise was a risk, but the raw creative excitement energized him, and he felt confident that it would succeed in a big way.

Chapter Forty-Three

A thought can be the most beautiful thing in all of existence … Or the most malignant.

—Fragment from the teachings of Lost Earth

Even though Francella's Corp One headquarters building no longer existed, Doge Lorenzo was still obligated to make ten years of exorbitant lease payments to her. The same held true for the opulent cliffside villa that he had vacated. Both properties were part of the same ironclad contract, drawn up by her attentive lawyers. The merchant prince leader had hardly bothered to look before signing, bless his foolish heart. Francella so loved to manipulate him.

Now as she supervised the movement of her furnishings back into the villa, Francella glanced in a mirror that two men had just hung in the parlor. Moving close to the glax she looked at her forehead above the shaved eyebrows, and at the skin beneath her eyes. She thought her face was smoother than before, that faint lines had vanished, and she looked younger than her thirty-eight years.

Excitement infused her. The injection of Noah's blood was beginning to take effect! She felt exuberant.

With a new quickness in her step, Francella took a break and wandered along the loggia, past the open-air gallery of imperial statues. Across the Valley of the Princes, she saw Rainbow City clinging to the sheer walls of an iridescent cliff, with midday sunlight glinting off the jewel-like buildings.

At the end of the loggia, she entered a large room that had once been piled high with her father's most special treasures, and which now stood empty. She remembered going there as a child and admiring the priceless jewels and artworks, which the tycoon had collected during a lifetime of travels around the galaxy. Thinking back as she strolled around the empty room, she noted scratches on the marble floor and the walls that needed to be repaired.

But just for a moment, as if she were a small girl again, she plopped herself on the floor in one corner, on the exact spot where she used to sit. The plush handmade carpet was gone now and the floor was very hard, but she felt calmer with each passing moment.

Francella was about to get up when she noticed something on the wall. A display case had been there for years, and now, just above floor level she saw a vertical line on the wall, perhaps a third of a centimeter in height. Dropping to her knees, she examined it.

When she touched the wall it sprang outward, revealing a compartment beyond.

Her heart raced. Could a treasure be inside? She thought she had placed all of the valuables in safekeeping before the Doge moved in, but what if her father had hidden something here, perhaps the most precious of his possessions?

Reaching inside, she thought at first that the hiding place was empty. Then her fingers tightened around a small, hard object, the shape of a coin. Bringing it out into the light, she saw that it was not that at all, but was instead an old-style computer disk, the retro-though-dependable type her father had preferred to use.

She might have held this very one in her hand, years ago. Once, as a four-year old, she'd seen a pile of them on a table and had placed them in a pocket of her dress, thinking they were coins and she could buy candy with them. Finding the disks in her pocket, a maid had scolded her and put them back without ever telling her father.

Francella sighed. In many ways she missed the innocence of her childhood, before the desolate realities of life began to embitter her. In her own way, she had always loved her family, and even Noah, despite the enmity they held for one another. She had also loved their father, the old prince, dearly, but had found it necessary to get rid of him and blame the death on her brother. Under different circumstances, if she had only been treated as an equal with Noah—without all the favoritism that Prince Saito showed toward him—things might have been entirely different.

I am not a monster, she thought. / *only do what I have to do.*

But she would not let sadness intrude on her fine mood. This computer disk could be something valuable. Francella took it into her study, where a technician was setting her equipment up.

"Can you read what's on this disk?" she asked.

He whistled. "That's an oldie. Should be able to, though. I've got a converter in my bag." He set up the converter, then made several equipment adjustments and tossed the disk into a hopper. Seconds later a copy—one of the modern data shards embedded in a clearplax ball—rattled out into a tray, along with the old disk. He handed both of them to her.

In privacy, Francella activated a palm-sized computer, and watched the holo screen appear in front of her eyes. The writing on the screen had been encrypted, but she ran through the codes her father used and saw the words shift into Galeng. This was Prince Saito's electronic journal. Feeling a rush of excitement she scrolled and found references to herself and to Noah, with the old man wishing the two of them would stop quarreling.

Then she caught her breath.

"The love of my life is Princess Meghina," he wrote. "But she is secretly a Mutati who cannot shapeshift back. She is more Human than anyone I know, more filled with love and loyalty and compassion and a passion for life. I love her dearly, and can never turn her in. This is a secret I shall carry to my grave."

But the harlot is Lorenzo's wife, Francella thought. *He must know, too.*

Reading on, she discovered otherwise. "I am the only Human who knows this explosive secret. So skillful is her deception that the Doge has no idea of her true identity. Nor can he ever know. I am confident that history will sort this matter out for the best, but to protect Meghina during her lifetime I have taken steps to prevent release of the information for many years, until long after the participants in this little drama are gone."

* * * * *

Ecstatic, Francella saw an opportunity to accomplish two important goals at once.

Formulating her plan more that afternoon, she began to think about how best to spread rumors—through channels to protect her own identity—about Princess Meghina's scandalous secret. Along with that bombshell, she would add a twist of her own, the assertion that Doge Lorenzo had known about it all along.

When released—it would take a little time to get everything set up—the story and all of its related suspicions would spread like fire on dry grass. Had the Royal Consort avoided medical examinations, or had her records been falsified? Who was covering up for her, the Doge Lorenzo himself?

Yes, the puzzle pieces would fit together nicely, enabling Francella to get rid of that loathsome woman once and for all. And eliminate the Doge at the same time, thus advancing the cause of her allies, the noble-born princes who wanted to bring Lorenzo down and replace him with a leader sympathetic to their cause.

My son Anton would fill the bill nicely, she thought as she dispatched three messengers from her study.

But Francella knew this was just wishful thinking. Anton hated her so much that he would hardly speak to her. And she knew very little about his politics … except his affinity for her despicable brother, and his refusal to reveal the location of Guardian headquarters. Such a disingenuous story Anton was telling, that he'd been experiencing memory gaps.

She sighed with resignation, knowing that she could not force all of the puzzle pieces into place. At least she had recognized an opportunity and was about to jump on it. Not a bad day's work, after all.

Chapter Forty-Four

We all gamble anyway, with every breath we take. Why not make it fun?
—Plaque signed by Lorenzo del Velli,
entrance to The Pleasure Palace

With money from investors and his own sources, Lorenzo completed construction work on The Pleasure Palace in a matter of weeks, along with his connected offices and living quarters. The high class casino-resort had luxury apartments for wealthy customers, which he offered at reasonable rates in order to entice them to the gambling tables. Even in these uncertain times, gamblers flocked there, primarily the nobility and business leaders of Canopa, but also a number of wealthy travelers who had been stranded on the planet when podship travel ceased.

Each night Lorenzo played the perfect celebrity host for his well-dressed guests, and was often seen in the company of his elegant and mysterious courtesan-wife, the Princess Meghina. Liras poured in, so much wealth that he quickly had to enlarge a high-security vault wing on the orbiter.

The space station became a most unusual royal residence for the Doge, an orbital wonderland where he could indulge his taste for high living and make a great deal of money in the bargain. To an extent he was pleased with the new setup, but military and political concerns continued to occupy much of his time. Every day before going to the casino, he met with his attaché Pimyt. In particular, they prepared important nehrcom transmissions to every planet in the Merchant Prince Alliance, making certain the defensive positions remained in place on every pod station, and that military forces were as strong and alert as possible.

* * * * *

All orders of this type went from Lorenzo to Pimyt, who in turn was supposed to either transmit them himself at the nehrcom station on Canopa or convey them to General Jacopo Nehr.

As before, the devious Hibbil underhandedly modified some of the messages, causing merchant prince military installations to move or actually *reduce* strength … adjustments that were accomplished subtly and almost imperceptibly, a little at a time.

His inside knowledge of the location of Human military forces and their strength was a huge espionage coup for the Hibbils and their secret Adurian allies.

* * * * *

As far as Lorenzo knew, his orders were being taken care of properly, but he couldn't stop worrying. There were still no podships connecting the planets of his Merchant Prince Alliance—or those of the enemy Mutati Kingdom. It was as if the Human and Mutati worlds had been separated from the galaxy and discarded, like rotten apples from a barrel.

Chapter Forty-Five

Tell me what you actually see in me, and not what my detractors tell you to see.
—Princess Meghina, private note to Doge Lorenzo

L orenzo didn't like the way Pimyt looked when he entered the royal bathing room, as if he didn't care enough, or as if it was a matter that was completely out of his hands. How could the little Hibbil act so detached when Lorenzo's world was crashing around him? Wasn't it bad enough that he'd had to relocate to the orbiter? And now this? The rumor had hit Lorenzo like a Mutati torpedo, burrowing in and detonating inside his brain.

"It's a monstrous lie!" the Doge thundered. Rising naked from an immense bathing pool, he grabbed a robe from one of the two female attendants who had been washing him.

"Undoubtedly you are right," Pimyt said. "But we must act quickly to dispel the story before it gains too much traction. Already it is inflaming the populace, causing them to ask questions. They want your response."

"The people are demanding that I address them? How absurd. I speak to them whenever I wish, if it pleases me." He glared at the attendants, and they hurried away.

"I understand that, of course." The Hibbil's red eyes seemed to brighten, like embers that had been fanned. "Is that your response, then, My Doge?"

"Don't be an idiot! Obviously, this is an unusual situation, requiring emergency action. Prepare my shuttle immediately, and my escort of Red Berets."

The little alien bowed, but maintained his irritatingly detached demeanor. "It will be done."

* * * * *

A short while later the shuttle landed, and the Doge's elite special police whisked him into a gleaming black groundjet for the ride to Rainbow City, perched on a cliff top. Lorenzo fumed all the way.

When the groundjet finally came to a stop in front of a large building with white pillars, he didn't wait for attendants to let him out of the vehicle. While his security forces scrambled to keep up, he marched into the ornate lobby and across it to the high-speed ascensore for the ride to the top floor, the fifty-seventh. He told the guards and Pimyt to remain in the lobby.

Princess Meghina called these her "royal apartments," but in reality she had converted an upscale apartment building into a palace. As the Doge stepped out of the ascensore, he hardly noticed the expensive statuary and artwork in the entrance hall, most of which he had paid for himself.

"I've been expecting you," Meghina said, bowing to him as he marched toward her. Barefooted, she looked tired and bleary-eyed, as if she had been crying. Her long blond hair hung haphazardly about her shoulders, and her saffron daygown was wrinkled.

"Is it true?" he shouted, standing right in front of her and staring up into her face. Even without shoes, she was slightly taller than he was. He hardly needed to ask the question. He saw the answer in her expression. A mask of sadness.

"All I can say is it's not what you think. Yes, I was born a Mutati, but I always hated my own people. I always wanted to be Human. I am *not* a spy!"

Stunned, he could not think of anything to say.

"In my youth I studied Humans and longed to be one of them," she said tearfully. "My Mutati peers criticized me for that, but I stood up to them, and took a huge risk by intentionally remaining in Human form so long that I could not change back."

"And our daughters?"

"I falsified my pregnancies, all seven of them ... even had the genetic records altered. The girls are not related to either of us."

Raising a hand to strike her, he hesitated. "I could kill you for this!" he thundered.

"I almost wish you would," she said. "I have done you wrong. But please believe me, I did not intend to hurt you."

"Oh, you didn't intend to hurt me! Well, that makes it all right then, doesn't it?" He lowered his hand. "You are to remain here under house arrest," he commanded, "until I decide what to do with you."

"Yes, of course." Her voice became very small.

As he left, Lorenzo didn't care about any of her excuses. He was only concerned about damage control because of the immense political harm that had just been done to him.

On the lobby floor, he pushed past his guards. Not seeing Pimyt at first, he knocked the smaller Hibbil down, then stepped on his arm and continued on his way.

Sirens blaring and horns honking, the merchant prince leader and his military escort sped through the streets of Rainbow City. Presently his black groundjet stopped at the security gate of the CorpOne medical complex, and then proceeded toward the large central building.

Having already bypassed security, a small squadron of Guardians—men and robots—stood on a rooftop inside the complex. Other Guardians were in position a short distance outside, waiting for the moment to rush in.

Moments before, Thinker had folded himself shut, saying he had to consider something important. Now Subi and the others waited beside him, looking nervously in all directions. In a bold daylight raid, they had been preparing to move against the central medical laboratory on the other side of the street, where Francella Watanabe had recently been observed by Giovanni Nehr. They had also brought a new weapon with them, for just this purpose.

But at the eleventh hour Thinker had something more to work out.

Just then, Subi saw a black groundjet and other vehicles pull up at the main entrance to the big laboratory building. Somebody important. He wondered if it could be the Doge Lorenzo himself. Nervously, Subi glanced at Thinker.

Still no movement from the robot....

Back in their underground headquarters the day before, after Thinker and Subi had studied Gio's reconnaissance report, the robot had thought it might be possible to capture Francella and destroy the medical facility.

"She would be a valuable hostage," Thinker had said as they stood in Subi's unadorned office. "So I came up with a little gadget to help out."

On his torso screen, the robot had then shown Subi schematics of what he called an "isolation weapon," which would destroy buildings while providing protective cocoons for people, so that no Human casualties resulted from their attacks. "I came up with it after our strike against the CorpOne headquarters building, when we had to wait for the structure to be evacuated."

"That was a major building collapse," Subi had said. "You mean people could actually survive that?"

"Absolutely. This new weapon would scatter protective cocoons moments ahead of the destructive explosives, thus protecting everyone."

"But wouldn't rescue parties have to still dig people out of the rubble?"

"No. The cocoons have mechanisms that will cause them to rise above the explosion, and then float down without harm on the nearest spots away from the rubble."

"You're sure this will work?"

"Fully tested. Everyone will be perfectly safe.... We can use it to go after Noah's sister," Thinker had said.

"And if Noah is inside, and still alive...."

"He will be absolutely safe. I have worked this out with great precision, and the weapons are already constructed. I must inform you, however, that your con-cerns about his welfare are probably too late. He is very likely dead, wherever he is."

"I know," Subi had said. Rage had infused him with a desire to capture Francella, and he added, "OK. We go tomorrow. Let's start getting ready. This won't just be about getting even with her. It will be about weakening our enemies, cutting off the head of the monster."

"Mmmm. Francella cut Noah, so we cut her out of her own protective cocoon, separating her from the forces that surround her...."

On the rooftop Thinker suddenly opened and said, "I just corrected an inspection malfunction. The isolation weapon's design was thoroughly tested, but there is a manufacturing defect in this particular unit that needs to be corrected. Otherwise, we will kill everyone in the building."

"What?"

"We must return to headquarters and fix it."

Just then, one of the Guardians nudged Subi. Looking to his left, the adjutant saw two men on top of an adjacent building, stepping out of a stairwell onto the roof. "They saw us," the Guardian said.

Subi and his companions ran. In less than a minute, leaping down stairs, the squadron reached the alley where they had left two commandeered CorpOne vans. Thinker showed remarkable agility in keeping up. As they tumbled aboard the vehicles, shots rang out, and Subi saw uniformed CorpOne security officers running toward them.

The vans accelerated and barreled down the alley in the opposite direction. A blast hit the back of the second van, tearing into the torso of Thinker, who had bravely placed his metal body there in order to protect the other passengers. Subi narrowly missed being hit.

"Thinker!" Subi shouted, as the vans barreled through the entrance gate, then turned onto a main arterial and accelerated. Behind them, other Guardian forces—looking like ordinary Canopans and robots—moved into various positions to block pursuit.

Inside a robot-assembly area of Guardian headquarters, robotic workers worked feverishly to reactivate Thinker's central processing box, an armored core that contained the AI-brain and its micro-control systems.

In a matter of hours Thinker was rebuilt, and soon he was better than ever, with none of the scratches or dents he'd had previously. The first time he folded open, a crowd of Guardians stood watching, including Subi and Gio.

With a broad smile on his flat metal face, Thinker said, "Did anyone miss me?"

He tinkered with the screen on his own chest, causing an image of Noah Watanabe to appear, as before. Everyone clapped and cheered, and gathered around to welcome the robot back.

Then, under Thinker's direction, he had robots make dents and scratches on his rebuilt body, roughly matching those he'd had before. "I don't want to look like a green lieutenant," he said.

Chapter Forty-Six

Ironically, the crisis in Francella Watanabe's soul and her morals made her more Human. While her body was degenerating toward its inevitable end, she finally became something that had always eluded her before.

—Secret notes of Dr. Hurk Bichette

As days passed, Francella became convinced that the injection of her brother's blood really was changing her for the better. Moment by moment, she felt more invigorated and thought she looked younger.

After a while, she came to realize that she should not examine herself in the mirror so frequently, since it made it hard to notice the changes. Still, she persuaded herself that a metamorphosis was occurring.

Believing that her brother harbored the secret of eternal life, Francella had taken a big risk in seeking it for herself. But she'd thought through the options beforehand, and determined that she stood to gain more than she might lose. On the plus side, she could attain eternal life, while if something went wrong she would lose only the remaining decades of her short, mortal existence. But the crazed path of reasoning that led her to attack Noah and inject his blood into her own body had not prepared her for the stark reality.

One morning she finally looked at herself very closely in the mirror, and jumped back in surprise and horror. Then she inched closer. Unmistakably, a cobweb of fine lines covered her forehead and cheeks, with dark blue circles under her eyes. She was changing, but not in the way she had anticipated.

Behind her, a mist formed, and took the shape of a person. But she didn't notice, and after a few moments the ghostlike form faded.

As Noah drifted back into his corporal form in his locked sleeping room at the medical laboratory, he realized more than ever that he did not understand how to use his powers in Timeweb. He wasn't even certain if he could call them "powers" anymore. Once, when he'd been able to control podships, that might have been an apt description. But so much had happened to him since then, so many complexities within complexities. Podships had every reason to fear and distrust him, due to his part in recommending that Doge Lorenzo install sensor-guns on merchant prince pod stations to prevent Mutati attacks, weapons that were used to destroy several podships. That difficult decision on his part accounted in large part for the aversion of the sentient spacecraft to him, and perhaps for his difficulties in negotiating other aspects of the immense cosmic web.

He also suspected that the grievous physical injuries inflicted on him by his demented sister might have a bearing on his current difficulties, causing some sort of irreparable brain damage that led to him drifting in and out of Timeweb, with little or no control on his part. Those physical traumas might have interrupted his development in the ethereal realm.

It was most peculiar, the way he had visited his Guardian followers in this manner, and Francella as well. They were like two ends of his emotional spectrum, from abiding love to intense hatred. The Guardians were his vision for the galaxy, representing the hopes and dreams he had for mankind as the Human race fanned out into the stars. He wanted Humans to behave responsibly in ecological matters, reversing the age-old trend toward rampant consumerism and the galactic-scale dumping of garbage.

He had recovered physically, but what toll had it taken on who he was, and *what* he was? He remembered Tesh Kori thinking for a time that he was a monster who needed to be destroyed, after she saw the first episode when his amputated foot regrew, and numerous subsequent episodes when his body accomplished the impossible.

As Noah lay in his locked room, a shudder of fear ran down his spine. His access to Timeweb was not necessarily a blessing, not if he couldn't understand it fully. There had been glimmerings of possibilities revealed to him, amazing things he had seen and experienced. An immense, galactic-scale environment called Timeweb, far beyond anything he had envisioned when he coined the phrase "galactic ecology." Eshaz had healed him by connecting him to the cosmic filigree, and there had been astounding mental excursions, far beyond anything the Human mind could possibly imagine. So far beyond, in fact, that they had to be true. He had no doubt that these things had really happened to him, and that he had been given a view of something that only the gods should know about.

One thing seemed very clear to him, and he could do nothing about it. His feelings of frustration and inadequacy were made worse by his own uncertainty, making him like a rudderless ship in a paranormal void. He had seen and experienced too much … and not nearly enough.

The cruel unfairness shocked and disappointed Francella. How could her brother, with all the privileges and advantages he'd always had over her, get the better of her yet another time? It seemed to be the work of a dark power. She was like a progeria victim, aging at an accelerated rate. A leaden heaviness set in over her and she slumped to the floor, weeping and wailing.

Servants came to her, but she shouted them away. In her suffering, she didn't want them around.

Later that day she had to go to CorpOne's new temporary headquarters for a meeting, inside a hastily constructed complex of modular buildings. Under high security, a new office structure was under construction nearby, and as she made her way down an interior corridor she heard the drone and clank of machinery.

Dr. Hurk Bichette approached her, carrying a sheaf of documents. He flipped through them as he walked. Seeing her, he paused and said, "Ms. Watanabe. Are you feeling well?"

"Get out of my way," she said, pushing past him.

But he scurried to keep up with her. "You look pale," he said, "and tired. Have you been getting enough sleep?"

Francella felt a deep fatigue. None of the stimulants she had taken were helping, and she hadn't bothered with makeup. "I have an important meeting," she said, referring to an earnings report she was going to receive from her top executives. "And after that, I'm going up to the orb iter to see the Doge."

With a worried expression, the doctor looked at her closely and said, "I want to conduct comprehensive medical tests on you. See me first thing when you get back, all right?"

"Yes, yes," she said, and hurried into the conference room. Darkness seemed to be descending around her, but she vowed to keep going until she dropped.

Chapter Forty-seven

Among the galactic races, we've always been the preeminent survivors, able to overcome any obstacle and defeat any challenge. This time, however, facing galactic chaos and determined foes, we must be more resourceful and brutal than ever.

—Woldn, the Eye of the Swarm

Before the Parvii scouts had been able to summon their multitudes, Eshaz had accelerated onto a podway, with the Aopoddae herd behind him. Knowing he had only seconds to make good his escape, he pressed the pods to greater and greater speeds, faster than he had ever gone through space in his long lifetime. They did not resist him. By controlling the alpha pod, he gained absolute authority over all of them.

Taking a web shortcut that Tulyans used in bygone days, Eshaz—having merged his face and form into the flesh of the creature—had led the herd of wild podships directly to the Tulyan Starcloud. With Tesh and the unpiloted pods right behind him, he'd slipped into the protection of the starcloud.

Now, with Tulyans rushing to take control of the other sentient vessels that he had brought in, Parvii swarms were gathering in space, but kept at a distance by the protective mindlink of the Tulyans, a powerful energy shield that repelled them.

In the past the Parviis had been able to break through, but this time the Tulyans were much stronger and sent their enemies spinning away in rage and confusion....

Inside the inverted Council Chamber a short while later, Eshaz stood with Tesh, facing all twenty Elders. The tribunal of Tulyan leaders sat solemnly at their long bench, as they asked probing questions. Two of the younger Elders on the Council had reddish patches on their skin from what was being called "web disease," linked to the deterioration of Timeweb, and they looked tired.

The tallest Elder, Dabiggio, had previously suffered from this malaise himself, but now he looked much healthier, with most of his skin lesions having healed. Even so, Eshaz knew that this was a matter of utmost concern for the Tulyan people. There were increasing numbers of breakouts of the sickness throughout the starcloud, and—though Tulyans seemed able to overcome the debility—it drained their collective energy, diverting them from the important tasks they needed to perform for the welfare of the galaxy.

First Elder Kre'n had called this emergency session to deal with the situation of the Parvii swarms. Over the millennia the enemy multitudes had come and gone, and they had been able to find holes in the mindlink to compromise it... until now. The telepathic shield seemed to be a complete wall to them, without weak points.

But the Elders were not assuming anything, and they would not let their guard down. So far their ancient enemies were being kept at bay, but in the flux state of the galactic ecological crisis and the ongoing hostilities among the races, the Council had vowed not to take any chances.

As the worried Tulyans met, the swarms kept coming into their galactic sector, in larger numbers than anyone could recall, even the most aged of the Elders.

Leaning forward and scowling, Dabiggio led the interrogation of Eshaz and Tesh. The towering Elder made pronouncements more often than he asked questions, but Eshaz had come to expect this sort of behavior when dealing with the cantankerous old Tulyan. He seemed to have a deep and permanent scowl etched into his face.

"You're in contact with the swarms, aren't you?" Dabiggio said, his gaze lasering at Tesh. "If we kill you, will they scatter back into space?"

"I reject my people, since I do not agree with their aims. Unlike Tulyans, the Parviis are a selfish race, concerned only with their own welfare and their own power. As for your questions, if the morphic field still extends to me, I no longer feel it. When Woldn declared me an outcast, I think he totally cut me loose. If you were to kill me, I don't think the swarms would even know it."

"Shall we test your theory?" Dabiggio asked, his voice like a razor.

"She did not lead the swarms here," Eshaz said, interjecting, "since Parviis have known for millions of years where we are. She did us no harm, and actually benefited us with the capture of more than seventy podships."

"Seventy?" Dabiggio scoffed. "Why, in the old days we used to capture ten times that many on a hunt!"

"But it's one of the biggest herds I've seen. Over the last nine hundred thousand years, this ranks as a significant capture, much more than the three or four we typically bring back at a time."

"They are probably Trojan horses," Dabiggio grumbled, "filled with Parvii swarms hiding inside, ready to pounce at the most opportune moment."

As Eshaz and Dabiggio debated, Tesh became small and flew up onto First Elder Kre'n's shoulder. "Touch me and know the truth of my words and my actions."

With one finger, Kre'n touched the face of the tiny creature, and then smiled gently.

"What about you, then?" Tesh asked as she made a slight buzzing noise and flew in her wingless way over to Dabiggio, where she landed on the counter in front of him. "Test me yourself," she offered. "I put my life in your hands."

"Your life is *already* in my hands," the big Tulyan said. He just stared at her, without even touching her skin against his.

Showing no fear, she landed on the end of his large snout, so that the unpleasant old Tulyan could not avoid cellular contact. For several moments he just looked at her cross-eyed, in such a comical manner that it made Eshaz smile. Several of the Elders tittered. Finally, Dabiggio waved a hand near her, and she flew back to Eshaz, where she landed on his open palm.

Dabiggio sat back in his chair, looking very displeased. But he said nothing more, and let others ask their questions. Every Tulyan knew that Dabiggio had long been angry over not being selected by his peers as First Elder. His resentment had gone on for hundreds of thousands of years, as he continued to find himself unable to secure the top job. Even so, he had enough political clout to remain on the Council, as the leader of the minority faction.

Now he seemed disinterested as the other Elders completed their questioning of Tesh and Eshaz, and dismissed them. Eshaz had long felt sorry for the unhappy Elder, the way he was always so miserable. Of late, though, that sympathy had turned into his own irritation.

Chapter Forty-eight

In this universe, it is undeniable that there are secrets within secrets, layered infinitely into Timeweb. As but one example, Jacopo Nehr may not have really discovered the secret of nehrcom transmissions; perhaps he only thought he did. Web-dependent nehrcoms, and web transmissions by other races, may only be the tip of the iceberg, or keys to the outermost layer of a puzzle box. There are intriguing legends that nano-creatures inhabit the web, living inside its strands. Are they yet another, undiscovered, galactic race, and are they responsible for instantaneous, cross-space transmissions?

— From a Tulyan study of cosmic mysteries

On board the space station orbiting Canopa, Jacopo Nehr sat in his office, awaiting an appointment with the Doge's attaché. From this utilitarian work space, provided for him by the government, the Supreme General gazed glumly out on the twinkling nighttime lights of Canopa's cities, visible through broken cloud formations.

He heard voices out in the corridor as people walked by. His office, like many of the rooms on the orbiter, had inadequate soundproofing, allowing noisy intrusions that irritated him and distracted him from his important work. In another linked module, the former classrooms constructed by Noah Watanabe and his Guardians had been converted into an exotic dining hall with a miniature forest around it. What a waste of space. But because of the insulating quality of the forest and the module itself, Nehr wished his office was in there instead, so that he could enjoy some peace and quiet.

The orbiter was like an immense child's toy, a maze of modules and tunnels that had been lifted into orbit and connected, some by the Guardians and many more by the Doge after he took over. Now it featured The Pleasure Palace Casino, a Grand Ballroom, an Audience Chamber, and royal apartments, along with other features ... and more construction was ongoing.

In the public furor over her secret identity, Princess Meghina remained secluded in one of Doge Lorenzo's apartments, under his protection. After admitting in a brief broadcasted statement that she was in fact a Mutati (a damage control strategy recommended by the Doge's aides), she no longer appeared in public because of the outrage that would cause. People were evenly divided. A surprising number accepted her claim that she was more Human than Mutati, while others were deeply suspicious of her and critical of her royal protector.

Since retreating to the orb iter, Doge Lorenzo had become nervous and agitated, making him difficult to be around. Even though his new casino was generating tremendous profits, he kept worrying about more things that might go wrong, and had fallen into the habit of adding to the list of unfavorable possibilities each day and trying to take immediate actions to thwart them. Jacopo Nehr worried about his long-time friend, and felt tremendous loyalty toward him for the favors he had done for him.

Many of the modules contained thousands of the Doge's Red Beret troops, his personal contingent of the Merchant Prince Armed Forces. An elite group of Human and machine fighters, they were absolutely devoted to his protection, and remained close to him wherever he went.

One of the largest modules contained the Royal Court of the Doge, now only a shadow of its former grandeur on Timian One. Despite the proximity of the opulent casino in adjacent modules, it had become an exceedingly sober court, without the gaiety and fanfare of its predecessor, which seemed part of a bygone, halcyon era. Now the vast majority of members (and the patrons of the casino as well) were Human noblemen and ladies from Canopa, no longer such a melting pot with colorful characters from other planets. The only exceptions were a handful of aliens who happened to be on Canopa when podship travel was cut off.

Just then the door slid open and Pimyt marched in, carrying a valise under his arm. The Royal Attache, with a haughty expression, slapped half a dozen communiqués on the desk, written on the Doge's parchment stationery. Tired of being a flunky for this furry little master of extortion, Jacopo wanted to refuse further cooperation. But as he looked at the irritatingly smug expression on the Hibbil's face, Jacopo knew that he had no choice, that he must keep transmitting the messages to other planets … or Pimyt would carry out his threat to reveal Jacopo's most precious trade secrets and ruin him. It was so difficult to deal with business matters, and so unfair, when he had other important duties to handle as the highest military commander.

"You will take care of these for me," Pimyt said.

The troubled general thumbed through the papers without focusing on them, wishing he could be anywhere else, far from there.

With podship travel cut off, Jacopo's financial situation had become precarious. His factories on the Hibbil Cluster Worlds could still export robots and other machine products, but not to the Merchant Prince Alliance … nor to the Mutati Kingdom, though Jacopo never dealt with the vile shapeshifters anyway. Interplanetary financial relationships, and the entire galactic monetary system, were far different now. Keeping him afloat, a number of banks had accepted his promissory notes sent by nehrcom, and he had leveraged himself in order to build new manufacturing facilities on Canopa. Other banks had given him deadlines, saying they would foreclose on properties that were within the reach of their agents, and orders would be sent out by nehrcom.

How ironic it would be, Jacopo thought, if his assets were seized because of orders sent via his own cross-space transceivers. For business reasons he had established his own nehrcom transmitting stations on Hibbil worlds, all under the strict built-in security system he had established for all installations, a system that would destroy the stations if anyone ever tried to tamper with their inner workings. He knew Pimyt had not learned how nehrcoms worked from any one of those facilities; it was an absolute impossibility. But something else had gone wrong, and the meddlesome little fur ball had learned the details anyway.

He focused on Pimyt's latest communiqués. One was to the Human-ruled planet of Renfa, ordering the disbanding of a squadron of attack spacecraft. In recent months Jacopo had been the conduit for other military and business messages from the attaché, and the general had assumed that Pimyt and his Hibbil friends were engaged in war profiteering, controlling contracts for the construction of new military bases and for the manufacturing of war materials, making exorbitant profits in the bargain. He assumed they might even be stealing weapons and selling them to neutral parties—not imagining that they would sell to anyone remotely associated with the Mutatis.

"You will take care of these for me," Pimyt repeated. "Do it tomorrow."

Jacopo nodded, then spun his chair and gazed out into the starry night sky. He heard the door slide open behind him, and the Hibbil muttering as he left.

Just then Jacopo heard the voice of his own daughter, Nirella, who entered the office. "What's wrong?" she asked.

He went to greet the stocky, middle-aged woman. "Nothing, nothing. Just the usual." He had to keep the shameful secret to himself, that he was being blackmailed.

"I wish you wouldn't work so late," she said. "I worry about you."

"Don't," he said, mustering a reassuring tone. He ushered her to the door. "I don't have that much more to do tonight."

"All right, Daddy," she said. Giving him a peck on the cheek, she departed, leaving him to his troubled thoughts. Staring off into space, he felt dismal, with very few connections to anything that made him happy. His daughter was one of the few remaining links to his earlier celebrated life.

In her early forties and unmarried, Nirella admired her father and worked closely with him. Few people knew that she co-discovered the nehrcom transceiver with him almost twenty years earlier. The two of them had been on a business trip to one of the Inner Planets, setting up distributors for Jacopo's precious-stone export business, one of his enterprises at the time. In that operation he had specialized in selling exotic, priceless gems. Following a long day of fruitless negotiations with the Wygeros who controlled that sector, Jacopo and Nirella had been going over their business plan in their spacetel suite. Suddenly they had stopped, as static and loud voices filled the air.

Close examination of the suite had revealed that they were, in fact, alone. But crawling around on the floor, Jacopo found the source of the noise, a tiny piece of translucent green stone that had lodged in the sole of one of his shoes. As he pulled the fragment free and held it up to the light, the fuzzy, staticky sounds had still come from it. Nirella had started to say something, but had fallen silent. Wisely, it turned out.

Both of them had recognized the green rock fragment as a substance their miners had only recently discovered on a remote planet ... a deep-shaft emerald brought up by a drilling machine from more than fifty kilometers beneath the surface. Preliminary reports—made at their Canopa laboratory just before they departed for the Inner Planets—indicated it was harder than any known substance in the galaxy, with a crystalline, piezoelectric atomic structure. The voices they had been hearing in the spacetel room were those of their own company gemologists in the corporate laboratory far across space, talking about how rare the green stones were. The gemologists were speculating on what the market value of the newly discovered stones might be, and revealed a skimming operation they had been conducting, stealing precious gems from the corporation.

Kneeling beside her father, Nirella had exchanged startled glances with him, and neither of them had spoken while the static and voices continued. There were several things going on at once. Dishonest employees in sensitive positions were pilfering company assets, and somehow their duplicity was being communicated across more than a hundred light years of distance. Based upon outside events referred to in the distant conversations, it seemed to be *instantaneous* communication, too.

Simultaneously, Jacopo and his daughter had realized the immensity of what was occurring.

Without any doubt, instantaneous cross-space communication would be one of the most astounding, valuable discoveries in the history of the galaxy. But looking at his daughter, Jacopo realized that he was not alone in the knowledge. As he considered the immensity of this secret, the twenty-four-year-old woman unsheathed a stiletto from her waist and handed it to him. "Slit my throat quickly if you must," she said. "Do it the way I taught you."

Having developed potent fighting skills from an early age and honed them over the years, Nirella had been a reserve Red Beret captain at the time. She was his bodyguard as well as his business associate. He trusted her implicitly, but both of them knew that a secret of such magnitude was mind-boggling. Refusing to accept the weapon from her, he looked deep into her almond-shaped eyes, trying to see her soul, the part of her that would remain faithful through all temptations ... or would betray him. Such a secret went beyond family blood. *Way beyond it.*

And he had told her to put the knife away....

Citing a "personal emergency," Jacopo had subsequently canceled all further negotiations with the Wygeros and had caught the first outbound podship, accompanied by his daughter. Transferring twice en route, they reached Canopa in short order, and strode into the laboratory, surprising the gemologists. Nirella did her job well, cutting their throats without spilling any blood on the interesting new stones.

In ensuing weeks, Jacopo and his daughter performed their own experiments in secrecy, with each of them on a different planet, transmitting back and forth. In this manner, the optimum cuts and configurations of the emeralds were developed for perfect sound quality. Subsequently, Jacopo's miners found the special emeralds deep beneath the surface of other planets around the galaxy, and after testing them he took steps to provide security over all of the resources.

But even with all of the research they conducted, Jacopo and his daughter never figured out *how* the gems transmitted across such vast distances ... only that they did. Ever since then, Jacopo had paid Nirella more than she had ever imagined it possible to earn. She became his equal partner in the enterprise, even though he took all of the credit for it in public, and strutted about like a great inventor.

She never seemed to mind, and for that, he loved her even more.

Chapter Forty-Nine

*If you consider any question and its apparent answer, you will come to realize
that you still have a lot more to think about. Profundity is only a function of the
power of the mind.*

—The Tulyan Conundrum

The Tulyan Starcloud was a planetary system at the edge of the galaxy,
surrounded by weak suns. Concealed from them by mists during their
previous stay in the orbiting Visitor's Center, Dux and Acey had only
imagined what was down there, based on descriptions provided by the
staff of the spacetel. But those words had been grossly inadequate for the
wonders they beheld now as they returned from deep space, not coming close
to what they were meant to describe.

The beauty made Dux gasp and stare in speechless wonder. It was an
otherworldly place that no one could tell him and his cousin about; they had to
see and experience it for themselves.

While Tulyan handlers took control of the podship herd, Eshaz said he
would take the boys and Tesh on a tour around the starcloud. Tesh had refused
to give up control of her podship, and had instead sealed the sectoid chamber in
the way of her people and left the pod tethered to other vessels, floating in
secure space, protected by the powerful energy shield of the strongest Tulyan
mindlink ever conceived. Eshaz explained to his guests that Parviis had
previously penetrated their security system, but that would not happen again.
Every Tulyan on the starcloud was focused on this important assignment, and
had created the most dense and unbreakable telepathic field in their history. It
should be more than enough, Eshaz promised.

Following Eshaz onto a wingless, pencil-shaped vessel, Dux noticed a circle
design etched into the hull, which the Tulyan said was the sacred sigil of his
people. After seating his guests in the cabin,

Eshaz activated the computerized pilot system, and the small ship took off.
It made hardly any noise as it flew. Presently, they were flying between the three
planets in the unusual solar system.

The legendary starcloud was unlike any place Dux and Acey had seen
before, in all the travels they had made around the galaxy, on their vagabond
adventures. The Tulyan lands over which they flew were pristine, a fairy tale
realm of lovely meadows, sapphire-blue lakes, tall forests, and craggy, snow-clad
mountains.

"Each night the skies are filled with comets and meteor showers," Eshaz
said, "a truly remarkable ethereal display. Some of the heavenly travelers can be
seen in the daytime as well, moving and flashing across the milky white
backdrop of the starcloud."

"Sounds eerily beautiful," Dux said.

"It has that quality," the big Tulyan agreed. "We have a defensive system
called the Tulyan mindlink, and it is said that some of our most powerful Elders
actually hitch telepathic rides on comets and meteors, and ride them into space."

"Wow," Acey said. "Wish I could do that."

"You're probably not smart enough, cousin," Dux said. "And neither am
I."

"Nor I," Eshaz said. "This universe is full of wondrous things you can
never do, no matter how long your life is." He looked sadly at the boys, as if

thinking of something he didn't want to say to them.

While the pencil-shaped vessel flew on, going in and out of the mists, Eshaz said his people did not live in cities. Rather, the four million inhabitants were widely separated in small settlements on the three gravitationally linked planets of the system. Tulyans lived quite simply, and one of the few examples of advanced technology they had was the starcloud transportation system they were using now.

"The sigil of your people, the circle design on the hull of this ship," Dux said. "What does it mean?"

"Everything in life goes in a circle," the Tulyan responded, "from life to death, from happiness to sadness, from beauty to chaos. We are all eternal beings , and yet we are not. Riddles and circles mirroring each other, truths and deeper truths, layers and layers of reality, all returning to a cosmic speck of singularity, a starting and ending point. That is what existence is all about, as my people have determined, with all of their collected wisdom."

Pausing, Eshaz added, "We Tulyans are a very ancient race, perhaps the first in the entire galaxy. We go far back, through the mists and veils of time."

Presently he brought the pencil ship down in a field of red and yellow flowers on the largest world of Tuly. Disembarking, he led them along a path to a knoll where he lived, a black, glassy structure overlooking an alpine lake that was surrounded by gnarled little trees.

"This is the finest spot in the entire universe," he announced, as he swung open a heavy door and went inside. "I am very fortunate, indeed."

The walls of his home, both inside and out, were of a deep black obsidian-like material. When sunlight glinted on it the hard surface became translucent and revealed glittering points of light deep in the surface. For Dux, it was like peering into the universe itself.

After dinner that evening they went outside, where fiery comets and meteors swept through the mists of the starcloud, seeming to put on a show just for them.

Far across the galaxy, Noah remained imprisoned at the CorpOne medical facility on Canopa. He had made numerous efforts to escape from the facility, and when the physical attempts had failed, he had resorted to mental excursions, using his powers in Timeweb. But those powers were nowhere near what they had once been, back in the days when he had been able to make mental leaps across space and pilot podships by remote telepathy ... in the days before he advised Doge Lorenzo to set up sensor-guns at pod stations around the galaxy, to prevent deadly Mutati military ventures. The shapeshifters had been using a terrible weapon they transported in schooners aboard podships. Entire merchant prince planets had been blown to oblivion, scattered into space dust. Drastic measures had been required, and Noah had been at the center of the effort.

As a result, several podships had been destroyed by sensor-guns. Circumstantial evidence suggested to him that the sentient spaceships had detected his culpability in the matter, and had taken steps to block his access to the cosmic web. Such efforts (if they occurred) had not been entirely successful, since Noah had still been able to burst out into the cosmos, for paranormal journeys. But his efforts had been erratic, unpredictable, and very frustrating.

Now, after exhausting himself for hours in such efforts, he lay on a cot in his locked room, and found that he was caught in yet another locked room, a nightmare of the mind. In the dream he was trapped in a deep hole, with a huge Digger machine towering over him, piling dirt on top of him. Tesh Kori was at the controls of the machine, laughing fiendishly as she buried him.

Noah screamed, but to no avail as she piled more dirt on. Somehow, even with the scooping activity he could still see her, and still retained a glimmer of life. He howled at her in protest, "How can you do this to me? Don't you know I love you?"

The roar of machinery drowned out his words, and then he heard only the ominous sound of dirt being piled on top of him. Darkness flooded him. He was completely buried. Moments of horror passed, in which he wished he could die, but somehow he did not. Then he sensed something opening up beneath him. The planetary crust cracked, and he tumbled into a deep, Stygian void, a frozen vault of time.

He remembered hearing legends of another galaxy beneath his own, and as he tumbled into the unknown he felt chilled to the very depths of his soul. Various races called it the "undergalaxy," the place of eternal damnation.

Struggling with every last ounce of strength that he possessed, Noah flailed his arms and slammed into something. He woke up, and in the low light he saw that he was back in the Corp One room again. His left arm throbbed where he had struck a side table, knocking it over.

Was this better than the nightmare his mind had displayed? Both scenarios were dismal, and offered him no respite. Not even death.

Chapter Fifty

"Every time you make a decision you are taking a gamble. In fact, the apparent act of not making a decision is really a decision per se, and is thus inherently a gamble. Since there is no way to escape risk, the only course is to embrace it."
—Remarks of Lorenzo del Velli,
Grand Opening of The Pleasure Palace

"Even from captivity, he has made a fool of you," Francella said. She sat with Lorenzo in the dining hall of the space station, surrounded by the miniature forest of dwarf oak and blue-bark canopa pines that her brother had planted. "His Guardians attack us at will, then go into hiding. They're causing a lot of damage, ruining industrial facilities and other key assets."

"A classic guerrilla war," Lorenzo observed. "Not easy for a military power to fight. It can go on for years."

Leaning close to a cup of iced mocaba juice, the Doge inhaled, causing a narrow stream of brown liquid to rise from the cup through a narrow, invisible energy tube. A decadent manner of drinking, requiring hardly any effort, but he seemed to find it amusing.

"If you would stop playing with your gadgets," she huffed, "we might make progress in this little war." With a sneer, Francella lifted her own cup of mocaba and drank it in the conventional fashion after deactivating the energy tube. She tasted the sharp, cold flavor.

Something caught her eye in the woods, a movement that seemed unusual. Not birds or the small forest creatures that had been transplanted to the orbital enclave. A faint mist drifting in the air? She rubbed her eyes. When she looked in that direction again, nothing appeared to be out of the ordinary.

"I do not *play* at war," he said, a hurt and angry expression on his face.

"But it goes on for too long. If you dedicated more effort to rooting out the evil, it would end. Why do you go easy on your enemies?" Beyond the Doge, she saw small, speedy birds flitting from branch to branch, kept separate from the dining hall by an invisible electronic barrier.

"You are mistaken. I want nothing more than to end this nuisance, this swatting of gnats. But your brother's forces—led by his adjutant—are a crafty lot, and have their own robotic forces."

Pausing, Lorenzo looked at her closely, an inquisitive expression on his face. "You do not look well, my dear."

That morning, she'd had makeup applied artfully by a personal servant, but obviously it was not enough to conceal the ravages of her ailment. Rage seeped into every cell and atom of her body. Somehow her brother had lured her into his spider web, and caused her to take the blood that would kill her. A deadly trick, and he had the immortal gift of being able to regrow his body, a gift that had undoubtedly been denied to her.

Thoughts of revenge filled her. If she could not kill him, she wanted to destroy everything he had built in his lifetime, all of his plans, his hopes, and his dreams, turning them into a nightmarish charnel pile. Everything would die that he had worked for, and he would be left a broken shell, never able to escape his eternal confinement.

"I want the Guardians annihilated," she demanded. "They killed my father and destroyed CorpOne headquarters."

"It will be done," the merchant prince leader promised.

"Immediately!"

"Of course. Now I want you to see a doctor."

"All right," she said. But she did not see what good it would do....

In ensuing weeks the Red Berets, and especially Jimu's machine forces, stepped up their activities. All over Canopa, people were arrested and brutally interrogated. It was something Jimu did well.

Having been banished to the Inn of the White Sun by the machine officers on Ignem, the feisty little robot Ipsy pressed on. Despite the large amount of money he had garnered from his clever business operations, the officers had been paying little attention to him, and had rejected his offers of financial assistance to build a bigger army. He could not understand why, as military robots, they cared nothing for increasing the power and might of their forces. Without Thinker to guide them, they were only stupid machines, with no direction or sense of purpose. They just marched around down on the surface of the planet and engaged in foolish skirmishes.

Yet, through hard work and an aggressive marketing strategy, Ipsy impressed the civilian leadership of the Inn. As a consequence, they promoted him to the directorship of the Inn of the White Sun. Very quickly, the little machine grew increasingly officious and ordered much larger civilian robots around in a gruff tone, demanding excellence from them. Under his management, the Inn was becoming more popular than ever, even though few Human or Mutati travelers journeyed there anymore, because of the limitations on space travel.

Chapter Fifty-One

Consider sight. No matter what you gaze upon, there is always something beyond, something unseen. Consider the other senses as well, and every thought, and you will see it is true for them as well.

—Noah Watanabe

Now that Francella Watanabe knew she was dying, her surroundings took on an entirely different cast... more harsh and glaring, with hardly any noticeable loveliness or color. She could not imagine ever enjoying anything again, the beauty of music, the taste of fine wine, or laughter among friends.

She felt that way about the soft dawn pastels that flooded across the sky now, which provided her with little enjoyment at all, certainly not enough to divert her from her bleak emotions. Essentially numb to her surroundings, Francella tried to walk up a walkway toward CorpOne's largest medical laboratory building, but her steps were arthritic and painful. Every joint and muscle in her body ached. Even at this early hour, Dr. Bichette had better be there, as she had demanded. She had telebeamed him in the middle of the night with her orders, but he had sounded remote and peculiar, not his usual cooperative, obedient self.

All the pleasures of life seemed to have been taken from her prematurely, and it did not seem fair to her. Francella was not dead yet, and by rights such things should not be taken from her until the very last moment of her existence, and her last gasp of breath, which should have been many years from now.

On a deep level, she knew that she had been dying ever since she took her first lungful of air, more than thirty-eight years ago. Every mortal in the galaxy was given a death sentence at birth. The only question was when they would succumb to the frailties of the flesh, and under what circumstances. It was all so uneven, and so cruelly unpredictable within a predictable framework, the distinct limitations of the bodily container.

She wanted to lash out at everything and everyone, to be even harder on people than she had been before, but somehow that seemed purposeless to her at the moment, and might even increase her unhappiness. Perhaps if she had been a more pleasant person, it occurred to her now, the Supreme Being might have blessed her with a less demanding, far happier life. But the difficulties she had experienced since her childhood had made her the way she was today, had molded the hard edges of her personality. She had only reacted to challenging situations, the primary of which had been the curse of having a brother like Noah. From the beginning, their father had favored her fraternal twin over her, giving him a charmed life while cruelly shunting her aside. As a result she had been forced to assert herself and develop a strong personality, one that could not be trampled upon.

Nonetheless, deep in her soul she had a sensitive side. And with death staring her in the face, she was terrified.

Francella limped into the laboratory's coffee shop, where she had told Bichette to meet her. To her relief the doctor was there, accepting a large cup of mocaba from a machine. In a slow, sleepy voice, he said, "This is already my second cup, but it doesn't seem to be doing much good."

"Huh." She stared at him, didn't get anything for herself. He drank nervously, and seemed to be avoiding eye contact with her, as if afraid to anger her by focusing on the obvious—that she appeared to have aged ten years in only a few weeks. She hadn't bothered to wear makeup today, and knew the effect must be startling to him. The muscles in her legs ached from the walk.

Finally, he glanced at her and asked, "Are you ready?"

"That's why I'm here." Her voice creaked and she felt tired, overburdened with her problems.

"Of course."

They walked side by side down the corridor, saying nothing, encountering no one at this hour except for one of the maintenance men, wearing coveralls and a tool belt. The man looked at her oddly as she hobbled along painfully, and she stared him down.

The examination went much as she had anticipated, a numbing blur of probing instruments and medical jargon coming from Bichette's mouth. Essentially, she was taking this man into her confidence in revealing her physical debility to him. But she had no one else to turn to on this important health matter, no one else to give her advice. Though she had never admitted as much to him, she considered Bichette something akin to a friend. For years he had served her father and CorpOne well, as more than a mere doctor or the director of CorpOne's Medical Research Division. But friendships were not something Francella had cultivated in her life. There had been no time. Other matters had been more pressing, more immediate, and she'd had to put certain things on the shelf of someday.

Now she felt the loss, and very much alone.

After checking her blood, cellular activity, and vital signs, and comparing them with earlier readings, Dr. Bichette gave her the bad news, which was not unexpected: "You are the same blood type as your brother, but for some reason the injection of his blood is causing you to age prematurely, like a progerian. Your cells are breaking down too quickly."

"Is there an antidote?" she asked, weakly.

"None that I know of. It would be nice if we could reverse the procedure you did, removing your brother's blood and all of its effects from your body, but I know of no way to accomplish that."

"You would like to lecture me for my impulsiveness," she said with a menacing glare, "but *don't*."

He nodded.

"Come with me," she ordered. Limping, she led the way to Noah's quarters, which were an entire section of the laboratory. By the time they got there, lab technicians were arriving, beginning to check equipment and charts, laying out the tests and procedures they would conduct on him today.

Francella saw her brother sitting in a comfortable chair, calmly reading a holobook that floated in front of his eyes. He looked fully recovered now, even completely unscarred, and this infuriated her.

Feeling increasingly frustrated, she wanted to do him serious harm, in any way she could. Across a speaker system, she spoke to him, in a voice cracking with emotion. "You tricked me, didn't you? I did exactly what you expected, taking your blood, and you knew what would happen to me. I'm dying. Does that make you happy?"

He shoved the holo book to one side (where it continued to float in the air) and then stared at her, his face emotionless. "Listen to me carefully," he said. "You have everything to do with your problems, and I have nothing to do with them. Just because you have always resented me, and you have always distrusted me, does not make your feelings rational. I have never done anything to you."

"You always got the best from Daddy, and I got the dregs."

"You're blaming me for *his* actions?"

"I blame you for taking what he gave you when we were growing up, and enjoying it, without once thinking of me."

The remark struck home. She saw him flinch, and think about it.

On a rack by him, she saw some of Noah's severed body parts in cryogen tubes, awaiting further tests. She had cut all that skin and bone off him, but had been unable to finish him off. Like a lizard with a bottomless reservoir of regenerative matter, he kept growing everything back.

Turning to Dr. Bichette, who stood at her side, she ordered him to take a vial of blood from her and inject it in Noah. A bit of revenge. As she gave the command, she made sure the speaker system remained on, and watched her brother for a reaction. But he went back to reading his holobook, looking entirely relaxed.

She tried to control her anger.

Shaking his head, the doctor said, "Noah is a medical miracle, unlike any case ever recorded. You should not interfere with his cellular functions."

"I already did, when I cut him up. This is just a different procedure."

He looked alarmed. "You are not qualified to make medical decisions."

"In case you haven't been paying attention, Doctor, my family corporation owns this medical laboratory and everything that's in it, including you ... and Noah."

She had used the term "family corporation," and this gave her pause. It was owned by a family of *one* now ... Francella herself.

Summoning a medical technician, Francella repeated the command to her, to make the blood transfer. The aide looked at Dr. Bichette. Reluctantly, he nodded. They all went inside the room with Noah, where the aide took three vials of blood from Francella.

Her brother showed no reaction whatsoever when a technician made the first dermex injection in his forearm. Within seconds, his arm turned dark red, then black. Noah looked totally unconcerned. In five minutes, the arm fell away, a gory mass on the floor. He hardly looked at it. On his body, the limb began to regrow.

In fascination, the doctor and his staff watched, along with Francella.

"The rest of his body is rejecting the injection," Bichette said, "keeping the poison away."

"Poison?" Francella snapped.

He leaned close to her and whispered, "No offense intended, but your blood is tainted. You know that."

Struggling to retain her composure, Francella ordered additional injections on different parts of Noah's body. In a flurry, trying to please her, the staff did as she wished.

But each time it was exactly the same. Portions of her brother's flesh changed color and fell away, but soon began to regrow, replacing lost mass mysteriously.

"Sorcery," Francella said.

"You cannot harm him," Bichette said at last. He watched her warily, maintaining his distance from her.

"I can keep him locked up for the rest of his life."

"You mean for the rest *of our* lives. He is likely to outlive his jailers." The doctor looked at her oddly, in a way that Francella did not like, as if measuring the remainder of her lifespan.

While Francella considered the situation, it occurred to her what a curious pair of twins she and her brother were, with her aging rapidly and him reconstituting himself at an incredible pace, growing new cells even as hers were decaying.

"Your life may be shorter than mine, Doctor," Francella said in a menacing, creaking tone, "if you don't find a cure for me."

Chapter Fifty-Two

Beginnings and endings: we pay so much attention to them, and yet, we do not really see. It is said that even gods must begin someplace, and end as well. But such reference points are not the sharp demarcations we think they are; they only seem to occur when we notice them. Before that, and afterward, there is a continuous flow of one thing leading to another, and back around again. It is the flow of time and space and wonder. It is the flow of joy and sadness.

—Noah Watanabe, *Drifting in the Ether* (unpublished notes)

As his name suggested, Thinker had spent much of his life in contemplation, and was not known as a robot of action.

There had been exceptions, such as the times he had led his robot troops in practice battle maneuvers on Ignem, but that had not been his forte. Rather, he had a proven knack for gathering information and organizing it in his ever-expanding data banks. For some time now, he had been searching unsuccessfully for facts about the whereabouts of Noah Watanabe, but most of it had been rumors. In the robot's own data banks, he had the earlier download of the contents of Noah's brain, but that was of little help in determining where others were hiding him.

He also kept running through details of the strange experience in which Noah had seemed to come to life in the simulation that Thinker carried with him in his robot torso. Most peculiar, and most unexplainable, except he kept coming back to the probability that said it had something to do with the cosmic infrastructure that spanned space and time.

Thinker's information on that paranormal realm was sketchy at best, but it seemed clear that Noah Watanabe had a connection with it—or *thought* he did—that enabled him to enter and leave it on both a physical and ethereal basis. The robot had a difficult time comprehending anything that was not entirely tangible, but supposedly Master Noah could project his mind out into the far galaxy. Unfortunately, the Guardian leader might only be imagining that, from a unique form of Human insanity. One thing was certain. The whole concept of Timeweb was most peculiar, indeed.

Concerning Master Noah's location, the robot had other sources of information. The day before, he received a reported sighting of Noah as a passenger under restraint in a blue-and-silver security vehicle, the colors of Corp One. He had already added this to all of the other information on the Guardian leader in his robotic data banks. This, when added to the earlier information, enabled Thinker to run a decent probability program. He had done this once before on Noah, before the two of them ever met. At the time, Thinker had been searching the galaxy to find him and the Guardians, so that the cerebral robot and his followers could join the group of eco-warriors. Now the search area was much smaller—Canopa and nearby planets—but the situation was far more urgent. Master Noah was in danger.

The new probability program pinpointed Noah. He had to be in the CorpOne medical laboratory complex.

Now he opened up Noah's simulation, causing his image to appear on the robot's torso screen.

Glancing down at the screen, though he could "see" the image without doing so, Thinker said, "Greetings, Master Noah. You will be pleased to learn that we know where you are now, and that we have set in motion a plan for your rescue."

"A *good* plan, I hope," the simulation said.

"Even better. An excellent one. We embark tonight."

"I am pleased to hear that."

"One thing, though, Master Noah. I have burned through my circuitry trying to understand the unusual properties of the realm you call Timeweb."

"Au contraire, my metal friend. / did not make up that name. It is already long-established."

"Of course. I was only using what you Humans call a figure of speech. It has occurred to me that I should perhaps make a further effort to comprehend Timeweb before we make the rescue attempt. After all, you seem to have both physical and mental properties that are extraordinary, and the more data we have the better. I am running through more programs as we speak."

"And you expect me to give you something new? But you know I can only reveal what I knew when you used the organic interface to download the contents of my mind."

"Logically, that is so. But there was a recent episode when you—the simulation—seemed to come to life. Subi and I saw a strange mist dart into your image and disappear. At that very moment, your eyes and face seemed to become more animated. I have confirmed that this occurred, Master Noah, but there is no explanation for it... and you spoke words that were not in my operating circuits."

"Am I speaking such words now?"

"No. I know what you are going to say a fraction of a second ahead of time."

"So, it is as if you are talking to yourself?"

"That statement has no relevance in a mind of my caliber and complexity. Many times, one portion of my circuitry will 'talk' with another portion—or portions—of it. There is no Human correlation that you would be likely to understand."

"With the exception of insanity. From your probes, I see that you have investigated that with respect to my mind."

"As I should. Just one of the possibilities that I must explore."

"And your conclusion?"

"I do not have enough information about Timeweb to offer a conclusion, but all indications are that the ethereal realm does in fact exist. It could be true that the realm exists but you are still—pardon me for saying so—mentally unbalanced. Sanity is not an exact science with Human beings. It is more a matter of coping and balance. All of you seem to have aberrations."

"No argument about that."

I will leave your simulation operable for a while, but you do not look animated, as you were before."

"Are you going to leave me on during the rescue, too? That would be odd, me rescuing myself."

"My analysis tells me to shut off your programming before we leave, to keep things less confusing. We don't want a circumstance where you think you must take charge of the operation. No, Master Noah, in this instance I must override you."

"For my own good."

"Exactly."

"See you soon, then. Good luck."

"And good luck to you, Master."

That evening, Thinker and a small band of robotic commandos waited in the darkness outside the largest laboratory building. Transmitting an electronic signal, Thinker read the security code, disabled it and hurried through, ahead of the others.

Scanning forward, the robots disabled the motion and sound detectors and all pressure pads in the corridor, then surged onward, making surprisingly little noise for mechanical men. Thinker had designed this squad for stealth, and had fitted everyone with sound-softening mechanisms for their moving parts. Two Human guards were struck with stun darts, and slumped at their posts as the robots hurried past them.

Through the glax wall of a room, Thinker saw the Guardian leader lying on a bed, in low light. As if sensing something, Noah opened his eyes, even though the commandos made virtually no noise.

The robots had no way of knowing it, but Noah had been lying awake in his cell with his eyes closed, feeling trapped and dismal. Moments before the arrival of the commandos, he had been engaged in a mental struggle, and had succeeded in entering the paranormal realm of Timeweb. But as he vaulted into the heavens and tried to connect with podships, they had scattered away from him yet again, fleeing into space. Wherever he went, however he tried, it was the same. The podships avoided him like a dread disease.

At one time Noah's sojourns into the cosmic domain had been welcome respites for him, an exhilarating means of refreshing his mind. He had piloted podships by remote control, but he couldn't do that anymore. Not even close. The glorious experiences were gone, lingering only in his memory.

Then, sensing something, Noah opened his eyes just as the commandos burst into his room.

Another form of escape had become available to him.

Accompanied by the robots, Noah hurried into the corridor, in bare feet and pajamas. "Let's go!" he said.

The squad ran down the corridor with him in their midst, forming a protective metal cocoon around him.

Just before exiting the building, Thinker placed an incendiary bomb, and set the timer.

Francella's villa overlooking the Valley of the Princes had several interesting features, one of which she had discovered only recently. Accessed through a hidden doorway, she'd found a large sealed chamber cut into the cliffside beneath the villa, a sparse room with a hundred comfortable chairs fronting a podium and a transceiver box hanging from the ceiling. Documents left in the room said it was a nehrcom relay station her father had set up for corporate reasons, to keep critical business operations secret, and he had paid the Nehrs handsomely for it. The facility came with Jacopo Nehr's impregnable, built-in security system.

To her delight she'd discovered that the equipment was still operational, so she had arranged for a virtual conference that was about to begin. At her invitation half a dozen noblemen sat in chairs fronting the podium, wearing elegant surcoats and leggings.

Switching on the system from the podium, Francella saw holo projections fill the rest of the room, additional chairs with noblemen from all over the galaxy either in them, or taking their seats. In addition to these projected nobles were the ones from Canopa who actually sat in front of her.

As the meeting progressed, Francella noted that the video clarity was even worse than usual, as it flickered on and off. The audio quality—always crystal clear before—was poor as well, with bursts of static and brief, irritating periods of dead silence. All of the attendees were noble-born princes, some of whom were openly critical of Lorenzo the Magnificent's governmental policies.

Over the nehrcom transmission the dignitaries voiced several complaints about this. Then a plump man in their midst, Prince Giancarlo Paggatini, said from his projected image, "Some nobles believe in you, Francella, while others are only here on fact-finding missions, to see what you're all about. I'm one of the latter."

"Please believe me," she said. "I want to see a reversion to old ways, before the Doge began appointing princes without regard to their ancestry. He has forsaken the tried and true ways, abandoning the traditions that have always formed the cornerstones of our civilization."

"But you are a commoner yourself," Paggatini said. "Your father was one of Lorenzo's appointees, and you've always been … close … to the Doge. Why should we believe you?"

"Because I no longer believe in Lorenzo. He must have known that Princess Meghina was a Mutati and concealed it, the liar. It's a scandal! He denies knowing, but how can anyone trust him after this? And after what he's done to all of you, denying you your birthrights."

The conference participants conversed back and forth across the galactic link, discussing all the reasons they despised Doge Lorenzo. In loud, angry voices they complained that he was awarding appointments that belonged to princes, and hiding a Mutati. In addition, he was focusing too much of his efforts on his luxurious orbital casino, The Pleasure Palace, while neglecting important matters in the Merchant Prince Alliance.

"It's more like the Plunder Palace," a tall prince with a monocle quipped, eliciting the laughter of his companions. "He's profiting at our expense." This was Santino Aggi, a notorious drinker who slurred his words now, as he often did.

"It's his fault the nehrcom isn't working right, too," another nobleman said.

As the conference nehrcom continued far into the night, Francella and the princes discussed options for dealing with Doge Lorenzo. Ultimately the conversation turned to getting rid of him, one way or another.

"There is one more thing to discuss," Francella said, having waited for just the right moment to bring it up. "Some of you have heard about what happened at the pod station, when I shot Noah and he healed, right in front of our eyes. Just before that, a young man shouted at me to stop. He called me 'Mother.' We had him arrested, and he is still locked up."

"Anton Glavine," Giancarlo Paggatini said.

"That's right. He really is my son, and Lorenzo is his father. The implications are clear. We have the next Doge, the one who is entitled to the position by his bloodline."

"The princes are not obligated to choose a Doge's son," Paggatini said, his cheeks reddening. "If Lorenzo abdicates ... or dies ... we can elect someone else."

"But we're here to uphold tradition, aren't we?" she said. "And primogeniture is one of the oldest traditions in the Alliance, the eldest son taking over the duties of his father. Anton deserves the chance. Anton *del Velli.*"

"We need to think about this," Paggatini said.

"What about Anton's political views?" another asked. "Who will he appoint to high offices?"

"I can keep him in line," Francella said.

"He'll appoint nobles to high office instead of commoners?"

"He will," she said, assuming that Anton—as the son of nobility himself— would be inclined to agree with her views on this issue. All she'd heard about him indicated that he was a decent person and she thought he'd eventually forgive her. No matter the unkind words he'd spoke to her; she had seen something more gentle in his eyes, perhaps a longing for his mother. And she had to admit to herself, she'd been feeling an increasing maternal instinct toward him herself. This made her want him to do well.

As they discussed Anton, and Francella continued to expound his real and purported virtues, a number of the noblemen began to warm to the idea of him as Doge. This pleased Francella immensely. Just as she had hoped, they were beginning to rally around Anton del Velli as a figurehead. She had financial reasons for her political plans, as she expected to receive a generous share of her son's tax collections ... money she needed badly.

Though Francella Watanabe had concealed it with deft manipulation of financial records, CorpOne—the late Prince Saito's pride and joy—was near bankruptcy. While her father was still alive, she had drained the assets of his company, transferring a large amount of money off-planet and converting it to hard assets in her own name—assets that were rightfully hers, but which were subsequently lost in the destruction of Timian One. To make matters worse, the unrelenting Guardian attacks on her Canopan operations were cutting so deeply into profits that she could not make the payments on huge operational loans that she'd had to take out.

The following morning Francella received the bad news about Noah's escape from her medical facility, and the destruction of the main building. Already, Noah was sending telebeam broadcasts around Canopa, trying to rally more people to his cause.

Furious, Francella confronted Dr. Hurk Bichette in front of the smoking ruins. He shook with fear for his life. "I assure you that we can still find a cure for you," he said.

"And how do you intend to support your research, when my brother's dismembered body parts, along with blood and tissue samples, were destroyed in the fire?"

"We have you," he said, "and the secret lies somewhere in your blood, in your cellular degeneration."

"The *secret,*" she said, in a dejected tone. "Noah's body regenerated from a mass of cellular material, after I cut him into a thousand pieces. I ask you this in your precious research: How does he do it? Sorcery?"

"We'll find out."

"Noah and I are twins," she said, her voice suddenly determined. "If he can do it, I should be able to, too."

Dr. Bichette did not reply. He stared glumly into the embers of the medical building.

Chapter Fifty-Three

I asked the Master if we should do something more to ensure the silence of Anton Glavine, and he paled at the suggestion. Then he reddened with anger, and said to me: "My nephew would never reveal the location of our hidden headquarters, not even under torture. I have looked into the heart of the man, and he is pure and loyal. He is as dedicated to our cause as any of my followers."

—Security Log, entry of Subi Danvar

Standing in front of the screen on Thinker's chest, Noah looked at the 3-D color likeness of him that the robot had fashioned He and the machine leader stood inside one of the robot-assembly chambers at the Guardians' underground headquarters. It was late morning, but sunlight did not penetrate to this level. Nonetheless, Noah felt upbeat, with renewed vigor.

"So you've been running the show in my absence, eh?" Noah said to the electronic simulacrum. "Why couldn't you ... or should I say, *didn't* you ... do more to locate me?"

"I do not know what you mean," the image said, lifting its chin haughtily.

"Is it possible you didn't want to find me, so that you could take over my leadership position?"

"I did no such thing! You of all people should know that is not in my character. I am motivated only by honor and duty!"

Looking on, Subi Danvar laughed out loud, and even Thinker vibrated a little, his programmed equivalent of amusement.

"Everyone has a dark side," Noah said thoughtfully. "Perhaps it took a computer simulation to find mine." He scratched his head. "I wonder."

"Why don't we discuss something that makes sense?" the facsimile asked in an indignant tone. "Why don't you ask me where Tesh is? You've been thinking about her, haven't you?"

"Well, where is she, then?"

"Tesh is with Eshaz and those two teenage cousins, Acey and Dux. According to the last report, they are at the Tulyan Starcloud. I know this because Eshaz sends information to one of the handful of Tulyan Guardians in our employ, a female named Zigzia, and she passes it on to us. In your absence, we learned that they call her a 'webtalker,' and she utilizes some ancient means of communication, presumably involving the galactic infrastructure. Zigzia is one of the younger Tulyans, only three hundred thousand years old. Why, just yesterday she—"

"Enough!" Noah said. "I don't babble like that. There is a defect in your programming."

"The copy is just nervous in your presence," Thinker interjected. "He only wants to please you."

"The information about Zigzia is correct," Subi said. "As a security measure, I pressed the Tulyan Council and got the information—but only on a sketchy basis, without details."

"Interesting," Noah said. Then, staring at the screen, he added, "Maybe this really is my dark side, with all of my latent defects revealed."

"The dark side is always associated with the flesh," the facsimile said, raising his voice. "And as you can see, I have none."

"An intriguing argument," Noah agreed. "However, I think it's time for Thinker to update you with another download from me."

"Perhaps it should be two-way," said the face on the screen. "I know things you don't."

"No thanks," Noah said. "I'll have Thinker analyze your data and give me a report." And to the robot he said, "Shall we, my friend?"

"As you wish, Master." Thinker closed the panel on his chest, and brought out the organic interface tentacle, with its glistening array of needles.

Doge Lorenzo del Velli was making a lot of money from his orbital gambling resort and casino. Earlier that morning his architects had modified plans for an enlargement of the facility, and the redline schematics appeared on a screen built into the top of his desk. A set of computer keys and touch pads enabled him to make notes on the screen, which were transmitted to his staff for immediate action. Looking up, he watched through his office window as two modules were floated into position by spacetugs and locked in place.

Urgent demands from Francella Watanabe sat on his desk, asking for even more Red Beret action against her brother's Guardians, who continued to make attacks on her Canopan operations. He shook his head. She had been especially foolish to allow Noah's escape and lose a large medical laboratory. He wished he had not given her full control over the prisoner, but she had been quite insistent... and it had been her brother, after all. Now the rebellion could only escalate, with its titular head back in charge.

Barking a command into a speaker, Lorenzo delegated Francella's requests to his Royal Attache. The Hibbil would take care of them in his usual efficient fashion, leaving the Doge to attend to more interesting matters. Looking back at the desktop screen, he made some additional notations on the schematics, where he thought more gambling machines could be fitted in. Already his casino was immense, but demand was high and he didn't want to miss any opportunity to maximize profits.

His architectural instructions were heeded. But on the other matter his Hibbil attaché sent only lackluster instructions to Canopan military and police commanders, telling them to "look into" Francella's request.

Where the Adurians were widely known for their biotech laboratories, the Hibbils were known for providing efficient manufacturing facilities, and especially for the low-cost machines they produced in large quantities on their worlds. In his own office next to that of the Doge, Pimyt envisioned a Hibbil torture machine that he intended to hook up to Jacopo, Francella, and even Lorenzo. If only there weren't so many delays and unexpected problems.

Working undercover (Hibbils on Human worlds and Adurians on Mutati worlds), the conspirators had been planning to overthrow them and take over. Years ago, in an initial effort to destabilize the Mutati leadership, the Hibbils' Adurian "allies" had cleverly insinuated gyroscopic "decision-making" devices on the shapeshifters, causing them to pursue foolish military actions against the Humans ... actions that focused their political and military energies in the wrong direction, away from the true threat... and were destined to fail.

In order to give the Mutatis a false sense of accomplishment, the Hibbil-Adurian cabal had caused decisions to be made that resulted in the destruction of Mars, Earth, and Plevin Four. The later obliteration of Timian One, however, was not supposed to have occurred ... and was an expensive mistake, since the

Hibbils were supposed to take that wealthy planet as a war prize. This caused considerable friction between the conspirators.

Under great pressure, the Adurians assured the Hibbils that they would take care of the problem through minor adjustments to the Zultan Abal Meshdi's gyrodome and to the portable gyros used by the populace—accomplished through undetectable electronic signals. The Adurians were insistent that it would not happen again, and in recompense they offered to transfer certain Mutati assets from the Adurian side of the ledger to the Hibbil side, after the Human and Mutati governments were overrun by combined Hibbil and Adurian military forces.

Then podship travel had been cut off mysteriously, and Pimyt had gone through a period in which he had been out of contact with his conspirators on distant worlds, since he had not wanted to risk sending nehrcom messages from the Merchant Prince Alliance to transceivers that should not even exist in other star systems. Eventually he had been able to set up a relay system in which he sent coded messages to other MPA planets, and they were in turn relayed to HibAdus on other planets. The arrangements had been complex—requiring much more than the customary bribes, promises, and threats—but he had accomplished it, so that intermittent messages could be sent back and forth.

When the communication links resumed, Pimyt learned that the Mutatis had discovered how to clone podships in the laboratory, and that the crazed, hate-filled Zultan had been using the lab-pods to send Demolios against Human targets. Gyro manipulation had not altered his thoughts, since his loathing for Humans was too deeply entrenched. Fortunately, the lab-pods had serious navigation malfunctions, and there'd been no strikes. Just a lot of effort and fanfare. But just by sheer luck, Abal Meshdi might eventually hit a valuable target, or his scientists might solve the technological glitches.

After conferring with the Hibbils, the Coalition had been able to use gyro manipulations to force Mutati scientists to make complex adjustments to all artificial pods being produced, so that their guidance systems could never work. Thus Meshdi's psychological need to attack Human targets was fulfilled, but it would never amount to anything; he could not cause any significant damage.

With the infiltration of Mutati lab-pod facilities, the Coalition accomplished something more. They learned how the cloning process worked for lab-pods, so that they could begin to make their own lab-pods on Hibbil and Adurian worlds. In conjunction with that, they had the Hibbils design navigation systems that actually worked, guiding the vessels across the vast distances of space. The Hibbils had also been able to fit customized fixtures into selected vessels, so that they were more useful as warships, or so that some of them were more comfortable than others.

But through it all, even with these successes the Coalition remained troubled as to why podship travel had been cut off to and from all Human and Mutati worlds. No one had any idea how that could have happened … and, if not for this unfortunate circumstance, the secret plan of the Coalition would certainly have been completed by now. They had their lab-pods, but it was taking time to grow the new fleet.

Pimyt was a key player in the Hibbil side of the arrangement, which bore some similarities with the Adurian program. Humans were by far the largest consumers of Hibbil machines, and many of those units—even the ones manufactured by Jacopo Nehr's factories on the Cluster Worlds and shipped out prior to the podship crisis—contained (without Jacopo's knowledge) certain subtleties that would in time turn them against Humans. Pimyt smiled at the thought. Even the sensor-guns that had been connected on short notice to pod stations throughout the Merchant Prince Alliance were not for the benefit of Humans.

They were to protect the planets for the conquerors.

Chapter Fifty-Four

Ultimately everything is happenstance, isn't it? You can take steps to accomplish a particular goal, and you think you are improving the odds of success, even ensuring the result you want. But it is not really so. There is always something out there that you cannot possibly anticipate, a monster waiting to crush your hopes and dreams.

—Anonymous, from Lost Earth

On the pod station orbiting the Mutati homeworld of Paradij, the Zultan Abal Meshdi led a prayer service, attended by a throng of his people, who stood in silence on the sealed walkways of the station.

He, like everyone present for this traditional religious holiday, wore a simple white gown, and they all had minigyro mechanisms on their foreheads. It was nighttime, and in the low natural light cast by the pod station the gyros threw eerie VR-light on the faces of the participants. His voice came across speakers to the assemblage, many of whom could only see him on projection cameras.

Every square centimeter of the pod station was packed with fleshy Mutatis, and some of those who could not fly overhead used their shapeshifting abilities to make themselves more comfortable, turning into a variety of creatures that could climb walls and windows, or hang from ceilings. Today was the Feast of Paradij, honoring the occasion centuries ago when nomadic Mutatis first settled on the most sacred of all planets.

As was his right, the Zultan had selected this holy day for yet another Demolio launch against the enemy—hoping that a spillover of blessings from God-on-High during the celebration would aid the war effort.

The previous launch against the merchant prince planet of Siriki, and recent attempts against other enemy worlds, had been unsuccessful thus far, even when they tried slightly different trajectories against the same targets, like gunners trying to find the range. Their laboratory-bred podships, while they looked like the real thing and reached tremendous speeds in space, continued to have perplexing guidance problems that sent them veering wildly off course.

For today's attempt, a system of deep-space relay telescopes had been pointed toward distant Canopa, where a massive explosion was expected. By the law of averages something had to eventually hit its intended target, if only by accident. Or so his scientists claimed. But the Zultan wasn't so sure about that. The galaxy was a very large place.

He completed the prayer and blessing, then lifted his arms and gave the command everyone had been awaiting.

Silently, the laboratory-bred podship took off and disappeared into space, with its deadly Demolio torpedo inside.

At an improvised nehrcom station on Dij, the Zultan's son, Hari'Adab, and Parais d'Olor listened to a report on the latest launch. The Mutatis had not yet perfected their cross-space transmission system, and static interfered with the sound quality, along with something that caused the signals to surge and fade.

The pair stood silently with their hands clasped in front of them, the position of Mutati prayer.

Minutes passed with excruciating slowness. Hari heard chatter over the line as a commentator provided calculations on how long it should take for the lab-pod to arrive at Canopa and blow it to oblivion. Lab-pods didn't need to go anywhere near the pod stations where the Merchant Prince Alliance had set up sensor-guns. Theoretically a cloned podship could emerge on the opposite side of Canopa and then blow the planet into space dust.

Finally enough time elapsed, and there was no report of an explosion. Hari and Parais heaved sighs of relief. Their prayers had been answered.

Chapter Fifty-Five

All things come to an end. There are no exceptions.

—Tulyan Saying

It was like having front-row seats for the most spectacular show in the cosmos. As if they were living creatures, small comets and meteors swooped so close to Eshaz's home that he imagined jumping aboard one of them and flying it straight to heaven. He never tired of the spectacular galactic displays, not even after seeing them for hundreds of thousands of years.

His three guests sat with him in large rocking chairs on the porch, oohing and aahing like spectators at a fireworks display. Even the Parvii woman seemed impressed, and she had undoubtedly seen a great deal in her travels around the galaxy. Hours ago, they had all received great news, a report that Noah Watanabe had been rescued from a CorpOne medical laboratory. Already Eshaz had obtained permission from the Council to send a congratulatory message to him at the next regularly scheduled transmission time over Timeweb—a message that would be received on the other end by Zigzia, a Tulyan working for Noah's Guardians. This evening's galactic show was the frosting on an excellent day.

Truly, I have been blessed to live here, Eshaz thought, savoring the beauty of the night. But he worried over how much longer such natural delights would last, galactic wonders that were probably unrivaled in the entire universe. So far the sacred starcloud had not shown any signs of the deterioration affecting other star systems as the Timeweb infrastructure unraveled, that living organism linking all galactic life forms.

"There are so many excellent stories I could tell you," Eshaz said in the low light, "for I am very old by your standards, and rich with experience." He rocked in his creaking chair. "Eons ago, my people were masters of the entire galaxy, and could journey to the farthest stars in the blink of an eye. We controlled podships then, before Parviis swarmed in and pirated them away."

He glanced at the shadowy, magnified profile of Tesh, who had chosen to remain too small for the Tulyan rocker, and added, "Our enemies were always an irritant, and eventually became much more than that. It was the beginning of the end, and prevented us from performing our large-scale caretaking work. For too long we have tried to patch things together, but it has not been nearly enough."

She looked over at him, with the saddest expression on her face. The remorse of one Parvii meant little to Eshaz. It was not nearly enough, but he still enjoyed her companionship, and had done important work with her. They had captured podships together, an unprecedented collaboration in the history of the galaxy.

The big Tulyan stopped rocking and said, "Even with their domination, Parviis don't have all of our powers. I am a timeseer, one of the Tulyans who is sometimes able to peer short distances into the future."

"In order to obtain travel privileges for his people," Tesh interjected, "Eshaz's services ... and the services of other Tulyans like him ... are made available to the Parviis. Woldn, and all the Eyes of the Swarm who preceded him, have always worried about the future."

"Your people have a guilty conscience," Eshaz said.

"Perhaps that is true, though I suppose all of us feel the guilt of our ancestors."

In a faltering voice, Eshaz said, "I was ordered to timesee for Woldn, but something blocked me ... chaos in the galaxy, I think. But I sense something important anyway, that Noah Watanabe holds the keys to the future."

"In what way?" Dux asked.

"I wish I knew. He might not even understand how to use them himself." The ancient reptilian shuddered as a cold breeze emerged from the mists, and the sky went dark.

Chapter Fifty-Six

Eternal life does not equate to eternal happiness. In point of fact, the opposite is far more likely.

—Noah Watanabe

Francella stood on the largest loggia of her palatial cliffside home. Gripping the railing, she looked dejectedly out on the moonlit Valley of the Princes, focusing on her own destroyed buildings down there ... the headquarters and the main lab that had been sabotaged by the pesky Guardians. Then her gaze drifted down to the cliff face beneath the railing, and the welcome relief that could be only a few moments away for her.

For Francella Watanabe, her entire life had been a waking nightmare in which she had striven to be noticed, but in which her rightful position in the family and in society had been denied. As far as she was concerned, most of the blame for that went to her twin brother, but it also irritated her that their father had permitted it all to happen in the first place. A self-made industrialist, Saito had been opposed to the indolence and inherited wealth of noble-born princes. He professed to honor hard work and ingenuity, so logically he should have honored and rewarded her efforts. But it had never been that way. She'd been forced to work twice as hard as Noah to gain any measure of respect with their father, and ultimately she received only the grudging, secondary attention given to a mere daughter.

That lack of respect for her as a person and as a woman carried over even now, despite the fact that she owned and controlled the immense assets of CorpOne. She saw it on the faces of officers of the company and in members of the Doge's Royal Court, in their subtle looks and tones of voice. On the surface they appeared to give her deference and jumped to comply with her wishes, but she always sensed an undercurrent. She was not the great Prince Saito Watanabe. Nor was she Noah Watanabe, who—despite having been declared a criminal—was still widely admired among the people.

She felt the moisture of her own teardrops on her hands as she continued to grip the railing. It would not be difficult for her to climb over and tumble into oblivion.

To Francella, the atmosphere of hard work in which she had grown up was a fraud and a farce, a purported ethical base that never really existed. Any semblance of ethics she'd seen had been tainted with exclusionary clauses that left her out of the inner circles of merchant prince society. As a woman and a Human being, she resented that.

Feeling betrayed by her family, it was easy for her to abandon them. She had arranged for the death of her father, and had neatly blamed it on her brother. Likewise, she had been spreading rumors against Doge Lorenzo, and had allied herself with his political enemies, the noble-born princes. It had been easy for her to turn against people who did not respect her. Now she would champion the cause of the noble-born aristocrats, and in the process would advance the position of her own son Anton, and of herself. After all, he was of noble blood from the loins of Doge Lorenzo, and she could not be expected to ignore that.

Through it all she had become a political chameleon, doing whatever it took to survive in a male-dominated society filled with intrigues and double dealings. She thought her own schemes had been well laid out, and they did give her some measure of influence over difficult situations.

But something eluded her. From birth, she had been allotted the normal Human lifetime. That was limited enough, yet now, through a terrible misfortune and injustice, even that was being taken away from her. Each time she looked in the mirror or saw others react with aversion to her appearance, she felt the erosion. The end was drawing near....

Unable to sleep that night, she had been pacing the corridors of her villa in a robe, desperate to come up with a solution. Earlier in the evening she had taken a couple of spinneros, pills that were manufactured by her company as antidepressants. They were not working on her, perhaps because they were lousy drugs, or because she was too far down to bring herself back.

She envisioned herself summoning the necessary courage and jumping off the cliff. But would that really be courage? Wouldn't it be more brave to fight harder than ever for life?

Her despair shifted quickly to anger, and she turned away from the railing. She had never been a quitter or a loser. Her enemies would have to drag her kicking and screaming from this life, from everything she deserved. As long as she still had breath, she would fight.

Dressing hurriedly, she summoned her chauffeur and ordered him to notify Dr. Bichette that she intended to call on him within the hour. She wanted a firsthand status report on her condition, and what he was doing to combat it. No matter that it was the middle of the night. If she could not sleep, neither should Bichette.

At the last minute, Francella slipped a puissant handgun into the pocket of her jacket. If she didn't like what he had to say, she would administer her own form of discipline, and—assuming she let him live—she would put a black mark in his personnel file. Actually, a bloody mark sounded better to her. It was her right as his employer, after all.

At the front entrance, the chauffeur handed her an envelope. "The doctor sent this over right after I contacted him."

After slipping into the back seat of the limousine, she opened the envelope, while the vehicle hummed along the maglev track. Reading the note, she said to the driver, "Take me to Lab Two instead of his home. He's waiting there."

Her pulse raced. The message read, "I have good news." What did he mean?

Arriving at the laboratory, she found that the doctor, fully aware of his precarious position, had been working around the clock. He looked pale and gaunt, and had not shaven in some time. A vein throbbed at his temple, as it did whenever he became agitated. "I'm glad you're here," he said in his deep voice, grasping her hand and shaking it. "Your timing is elegant."

Dr. Bichette reported interesting developments in the research. From duplicate medical records that were kept in a separate location and not destroyed in the lab fire, he and his staff had compared Noah's previous DNA structure with what it was now, and had spotted significant differences, particularly involving how genes transferred during cellular division. In a normal person, a small number of cells had age-related chromosomal defects that were held in check when the person was young, but expanded their domain as the person grew older.

"But in the case of Noah Watanabe," the excited doctor said, "these defective cells no longer exist. His basic DNA structure has been completely revamped, making him better than new."

Francella found these comments fascinating, but she was impatient to hear more. "What does this mean for me?" she demanded.

Looking increasingly nervous, the doctor continued. "When you injected yourself with Noah's blood, it gave me an idea. I began to wonder if his DNA might be used as a blueprint to make a new product, an elixir of eternal life."

"The Fountain of Youth," Francella said.

"It seems entirely possible. Computer projections indicate that an injection of elixir could make some people live for a very long time."

He started to go into more detail when she interrupted. "Begin production at once."

His eyes widened. "But more studies are required first, tests on animals and willing Human subjects."

"I do not have the luxury of time. You are to immediately suspend all other medical operations and focus our resources on the elixir."

Chapter Fifty-Seven

Certain robots have no sense of honor programmed into them, or they have overridden it, and will destroy anything that stands in their way.

—Thinker, entry in his data banks

Upon learning of Noah's escape from the CorpOne facility, Jacopo Nehr summoned his top officers to the orbital space station. In his office there, the Supreme General of the Merchant Prince Armed Forces said, "I understand robots broke the prisoner out of the medical lab. Is that true?"

Colonel Umar Javit, commander of the Red Berets, stepped forward. A big man with broad shoulders, he said, "It is, sir."

"But how could robots sneak in and do that? Aren't they clanky and noisy?"

"There are ways to muffle sound, a fact I learned by asking robots under my own command the same questions."

"I've heard about your robots," Nehr said, thoughtfully. "They're doing a good job for you, aren't they?"

"Better than most men, sir. They've been self-replicating, too, building more of their kind quickly. I had twenty machine volunteers in the beginning, and now they number in the tens of thousands."

"Impressive. Put them to work on this Noah situation. Add them to the Human Red Berets that are already looking for him. Find Noah and his hideout and destroy them."

"Shall I take prisoners, sir?"

"Only enough to obtain intelligence information." He grimaced. "Doge Lorenzo and Francella are anxious for results."

"We are to kill the rest of the Guardians, then? I mean, the Humans?"

"Right. Their robots can be reprogrammed, after we get important data from them."

"And what are we to do about Noah Watanabe? From what I hear, he can't be killed. There are

even doubts about whether he is really Human or not. I mean, he's not like Princess Meghina, really a

Mutati. The shapeshifters are as mortal as we are."

Nehr nodded. "He's in his own category, isn't he? Capture him, kill him if you can with

overwhelming firepower. Whatever it takes to stop his operations."

Underground, his location veiled by the security system that Subi and Thinker had improvised, Noah stood with Zigzia, a female Tulyan who was around his own height, but who probably weighed three times as much as he did. She wore a green-and-brown Guardian uniform. For her race, Zigzia was on the small side, even for a female. Noah had dealt with enough Tulyans to be able to distinguish one from another by facial features, and he thought this one had an interesting look to her, with intelligence in her dark, slitted eyes.

"Please repeat my message back," Noah said.

"To make certain I have it right, you mean?" She looked a bit perturbed, and a crinkle formed along her bronze, scaly snout. "I have a perfect memory, just as Eshaz does."

"Of course. I don't wish to be insulting. As I understand it, virtually all Tulyans have such a memory. But there *are* a small percentage of exceptions."

"With all due respect, Master, you think I might fall into the latter category?"

He shook his head. "I'm sure you don't. I am told by my people that you have precise recall, and that you have transmitted numerous messages between us and your Council of Elders on the Tulyan Starcloud. It's just that this is the first time I have dealt with you personally, and I have a certain way of doing things."

"I accept your apology," she said.

"My...." Noah smiled. "Yes, you could call it that."

With a twinkle in her eyes, the bulky alien repeated his message back to him in its entirety, even including the vocal inflections and pauses in his original, when he uttered it moments ago. Word for word, she got it exactly right, and he nodded with satisfaction.

"Very good," he said. "Most impressive. OK, go ahead and send it."

She grinned, revealing large teeth. "The regularly appointed time is this afternoon."

"Yes. As specified by your Council. One of these days I shall ask you to show me in detail how the system works. Something to do with the web, as I understand it."

Disapproval registered on her face. "That is correct, but the Council has not authorized me to say more."

"To an outsider, you mean?"

"No, Master Noah. You are as close to being Tulyan as any Human I have ever met. Among my people, you are held in great esteem. But only the Elders can decide what is revealed to you."

"I understand."

She bowed, and left to perform her various tasks.

In his soon-to-be transmitted message, Noah asked about Eshaz and Tesh, wondering how they were doing and what they were doing. On the surface it appeared to be entirely businesslike, focused on their operations as Guardians, and Noah's request that they return as soon as possible. Noah also had an interest in regaining jurisdiction over the podship that Tesh had with her, even if he was never able to pilot one of the sentient vessels himself again. With the ship at his disposal, many things were possible.

In several voyages across space, each taking only a few moments, he could move his entire force of Guardians to another planet. But what would he accomplish if he did that? He didn't want to mount an army to attack the merchant princes. Instead, he wanted to work with them against the Mutatis and the Parviis, who were so problematic in different ways. The podship—presumably operated by Tesh—would enable him to personally move around the galaxy quickly if he needed to do so, and it might also be a bargaining chip in dealing with young Anton, who was the odds-on favorite to be the next doge. Noah harbored hopes that his past close relationship with his nephew might be beneficial to the cause of humankind. He just needed to figure out the best way of reaching out to him.

Noah wanted Eshaz, Tesh, and the podship back for professional reasons, to be sure, but behind the official communication he concealed his strong desire to see Tesh. He missed her. On a very personal level, it was a situation that he wanted to figure out how to handle, how to reach out to her. But in this galaxy, with all of the problems he faced, other matters were more pressing....

On the other end of the transmission, Eshaz was forced by the Council of Elders to answer vaguely, without details of what they were doing. They saw through Noah's words, to his true feelings. Eshaz defended Noah, saying that the man would never let personal feelings get in the way of important work. But Eshaz had to agree with his superiors. In his own experience, he had seen something extra between the two Humans.

Under tight control by the Elders, Eshaz's transmitted response to Noah read simply, "Congratulations on your rescue from imprisonment. We trust that you are doing well, and look forward to working closely with you again."

When Jimu received his command to find and destroy Noah and his headquarters, it tied in with something the robot had been planning to do anyway. Recently, there had been reports of undercover Guardian machines operating around Canopa, eluding capture. He would concentrate on finding them, and ferreting out their secrets.

Moving quickly, Jimu ordered a roundup of every sentient machine that showed its metal face on Canopa. Household, factory, and office bots were brought in for questioning, along with every other type of mechanical device that had the capacity to think. Interface probes would be used, and even disassembly, if necessary. Whatever it took to find out where each machine had been, and what it was programmed to do....

A week later, Jimu heard about some unusual robots that had turned up, and one in particular. As excited as a robot could be with his programmed emotions, he hurried to a government warehouse on the outskirts of Rainbow City. There he found a contingent of his Red Beret machines surrounding an armored Human and a dented bot that had folded itself shut. He recognized them immediately, from information in his own data banks. Both were famous in machine lore.

Without a doubt, they were Giovanni Nehr and Thinker.

"The robot won't open," one of Jimu's sergeants said, "and we're worried about damaging his programming if we try to force the issue. He's really sealed himself up."

Striding up to the prisoners, Jimu said, "Hello, Thinker. Remember me, old friend?"

To his surprise, Thinker opened without delay. Having erased part of his internal programming, the portion that revealed the location of Noah's subterranean headquarters, Thinker had set all of this up intentionally, wanting to be captured. He had his own plan in mind, with two important goals ... one involving Jimu and the other involving Gio.

Back at the Guardian hideout, the cerebral robot had left a full backup copy of himself, and instructions that if he didn't return within three hours, this copy would be inserted into a new body, and the one he occupied now (including its internal programming) would be automatically deactivated. With respect to Gio, whom he did not yet entirely trust, this was an important test, sanctioned by Noah Watanabe himself.

Using his advanced programming, Thinker had taken preparations to send an electronic signal that would wipe out Gio's memory of the headquarters location if he even started to utter the wrong words, or if any attempt was made to separate the two of them. Additional memory-wiping signals, though designed for robots, would be sent to all sentient machines within hearing range, if necessary. The robot had made adjustments to his own programming to set it up. Normally Thinker could not harm Humans or meddle with their minds, but he was able to tweak that by placing Noah's safety, and the security of the entire Guardian organization, above all other concerns.

"You're on the wrong side, old friend," Thinker said to Jimu. Around the perimeter of Thinker's face plate, orange lights blinked on. They began to pulse slowly and hypnotically, with the light receding and returning like the tide, dimming and brightening, dimming and brightening.

"But we both work for Humans," Jimu said. "How can that possibly be wrong?"

Abruptly, an interface probe shot out of Thinker's torso and locked into a port on Jimu's body, which now bore the cardinal-red markings of the Doge's elite force. It took only seconds to transfer the data to the wayward robot, after which Thinker withdrew the probe.

"Now do you understand?" Thinker asked.

"All Humans are not worthy of our loyalty and devotion," Jimu intoned. "But Master Noah is."

"Welcome to the Guardians," Thinker said. He clasped metal hands with Jimu.

Jimu, instilled with sudden fervor, now issued new commands to the robot force in the warehouse. "We will not fight our own kind, especially not the revered Thinker. We all owe him a duty, for what he began in the White Sun Solar System where your brethren were first renovated, after having been discarded as worthless by the merchant princes."

"Giovanni Nehr knows the way," Thinker said.

Moments later, the motley group filed out of the warehouse, with Jimu ostensibly at the head of a Red Beret squadron. But an armored Human right behind him provided directions.

In ensuing weeks, Thinker and Jimu worked together from Noah's headquarters to decimate the robotic ranks of the Red Berets. During what looked like typical patrols or troop exercises, a number of the Doge's machines began to slip away and go over to Noah's side—a trickle at first that would gradually increase.

Chapter Fifty-Eight

The concept of voting is like a pebble in a pond, enlarging outward from personal decision points concerning small matters to larger and larger matters.
—Anonymous, perhaps from a politician of Lost Earth

Despite his vices and extreme avarice, Doge Lorenzo had attempted to coordinate an effective military defense system on all planets in the Merchant Prince Alliance. As a matter of routine, he left most of the details to the professionals such as General Jacopo Nehr, but the Doge had his own ideas and concerns about such important matters. Sometimes he went into Nehr's office on the orb iter and discussed military issues with him, but usually Lorenzo passed his orders through his attaché, Pimyt, who in turn relayed them down to the nehrcom transmitting station on the surface of Canopa for dissemination to other planets.

Lorenzo had also continued to reward scientific and business achievements by appointing commoners to princely positions. But he had failed to keep abreast of changing political tides, and failed to see the strength of the opposition to him until it surfaced in a big way. Now his political opponents— while concealing their identities—were lobbying for a vote of no-confidence in the Hall of Princes, and had garnered enough support to make it happen.

Today was the day of the vote.

Accompanied by his guards, the self-proclaimed Lorenzo the Magnificent took a shuttle down to the surface, and then a groundcar to the government complex in Rainbow City. At one time these buildings had been devoted to Canopan affairs, but now they served a larger purpose because of the destruction of Timian One and the merchant prince capital there.

His car crossed the city's central square and stopped at the largest building, a domed structure that was now the Hall of Princes. The vote would be taken inside during a nehrcom conference session.

As he took his seat on the central stage, he wondered how many princes were aligned against him, and which of those who claimed to support him were actually working against him behind his back. He sighed. His grandfather had told him to be wary of political alliances, since they could blow away like leaves in the wind. Lorenzo realized now with a sinking sensation that he had forgotten that admonition, and had let his guard down while his enemies massed against him. He felt tears of sadness and rage welling up inside, and fought them back.

Many of his questions would be answered soon, when the princes placed their anonymous votes. For years he had been able to avoid even having a vote of confidence, since he had so many supporters who opposed it. But now, with the increasing opposition, the vote would be taken. He did not expect to lose, but the mere fact of the vote troubled him.

A handful of Canopan princes filed into the chamber and took their seats, along with a number of princes who had been visiting when podship travel was cut off. Gradually the other seats filled with holo-images, projections from other worlds. The transmitted images were so realistic that Lorenzo had to look closely to see the difference: they had a slight, almost imperceptible lack of sharpness. He nodded to some of his friends and long-time allies, including Anese Eng of Siriki and Nebba Kami of Salducia. They nodded back, most of them from far across the galaxy.

With a worried scowl, Lorenzo folded his arms across his chest and waited. He cast his own vote with a control panel on the arm of his chair, and saw the princes doing the same out in the chamber. They had an hour to complete the process, and many of the dignitaries whispered and murmured among themselves, making last-minute decisions and deals.

He didn't like the facial expressions he saw on many in the chamber, including noblemen he had long considered his friends and allies. Stony countenances that seemed to look completely through him, as if he wasn't even there. Could the vote possibly go against him? He wished he could say something here on his own behalf, but by long tradition that was impossible. All of the politicking had been done before this, with secret deals and payoffs. But it might not be enough.

Nervously, Lorenzo summoned an aide. "I'm not feeling well," he said. "Perhaps I should go to an anteroom."

The aide, a small but powerfully built black man, spoke in a confidential tone. Dib Venkins had always been outspoken, but his advice was consistently good. "Couldn't that be seen as a sign of weakness, Sire?"

"It would look worse if I fall over."

Nodding, Venkins helped him to his feet and escorted him through a side doorway, while the whispering and murmuring increased. Maybe this would garner him some sympathy votes, the Doge thought. Pimyt hurried to lend assistance.

In the anteroom, Lorenzo refused to sit, eat, or drink. "Leave me," he said to the aide.

After the black man left, Lorenzo told Pimyt why he'd had to leave, then said, "How can they even call for this vote, after all I've done for the MPA? I've put money in the pockets of everyone in that chamber, and this is how I'm rewarded?"

"All ballots are not in yet," Pimyt said. "I have people making last-minute deals, pressing for the support of anyone who's on the fence. It is difficult to do, however, since so many princes are keeping their cards close to the vest. As you know, Francella has her people doing their best on our behalf, too. I just spoke with her this morning."

He nodded. "You're doing the best you possibly can, and I appreciate it."

Lorenzo heard a rap at the anteroom door, and Pimyt let Francella in. She wore a long white dress, with a pale blue sash and a gold broach bearing her initials on her lapel. He saw the unmistakable aging on her face (despite the attempts to cover it with makeup), and a slight stoop to her posture. He felt a deep concern for her welfare. It was good of her to come when she was not feeling well.

"May I come in?" she asked, looking over the top of the much shorter Hibbil and smiling at Lorenzo.

Feeling the need for emotional support, Lorenzo nodded. He rested his hand on a copy of the *Scienscroll* that lay open on a stand, and this gave him some comfort, as if a higher power was watching over him.

Hurrying to his side, Francella placed a hand on his shoulder. "We're doing everything we can," she said, "but it doesn't look good."

In disbelief, he looked at her. "I'm going to lose?"

"The revelation about Princess Meghina is too large to overcome, it seems."

"I didn't know she was a Mutati!"

"I believe you, but it has the appearance of concealment on your part, and some people are willing to believe the worst about you. There is this, too. Word has it that my brother spread the story about Meghina and your involvement."

"Noah did that?"

"It's in his nature, and he's out now, back with the Guardians."

"But how did he find out about Meghina?"

With a shrug, Francella said, "Who knows? But Noah hates you for helping me."

"I could kill him for this!"

"I already tried that."

"Just the same, there are still things we can do. If we get our hands on him again, we can seal him in plax and bury him, or drop him in the deepest part of the ocean."

"My brother's cells do have some value, so it would be better to seal him up somewhere and stab needles into him to extract blood whenever we need it."

"A cure for you," Lorenzo said.

"Precisely."

A wave of sadness overwhelmed the Doge, and words caught in his throat.

"It's Noah's fault that this vote of confidence is going to go against you," Francella said. "I hoped for a different result, but the polls are clear." She looked downcast.

"Maybe you're mistaken," Lorenzo said, staring at the *Scienscroll* that still rested under one hand. "I could still pull off a miracle."

She did not reply.

With a sudden movement, Lorenzo dropped to his knees in front of the *Scienscroll* stand. He could not hold his emotions back, and tears streamed down his face.

On either side of him, Francella and Pimyt knelt, too, and the three of them prayed silently together for several long minutes.

"I don't understand how this happened," Lorenzo finally said, opening his eyes and looking at his most trusted associates. "I just don't see how this could have possibly happened. Don't the princes know what I've done for them?"

"Maybe there will be a miracle after all," Pimyt suggested.

But Lorenzo heard otherwise in his tone, and saw hopelessness in his face. He was only going through the motions.

Looking at his long-time lover on the other side, Lorenzo thought she looked dismal, and seemed to age moment by moment. The Doge sensed powerful forces aligned against him, attacking even those closest to him.

"If it does not go well," Francella said, "we must salvage what we can. Our best hope may lie with our son, Anton."

"As the next Doge, you mean?"

She nodded. "I have made inquiries through intermediaries. Anton could garner considerable support."

"Because he's a del Velli, but does not have my baggage."

With a tight smile, she said, "And you could still exert a powerful influence over him behind the

scenes.

"I don't know him well enough to say that." "But I do, and he'll do as we say."

"We must consider the ramifications of this," Pimyt said, obviously agitated. "It would be a big step, with obvious risks."

"If it goes badly for you out in the hall," she said to Lorenzo, "we must move quickly and present Anton to them before anyone can mount an opposition candidate."

Pimyt did not say anything, and to Lorenzo his attaché seemed unable to keep up with the fast pace of events. At least Francella had considered the possibilities.

Reluctantly, the Doge nodded. "Let's go back in," he said. Trying to summon his courage, he rose shakily to his feet.

When he walked back into the large chamber with Pimyt, it was eerily silent. All eyes were turned on Lorenzo.

He saw the tally on a screen that hung from the high ceiling:

For Doge Lorenzo del Velli: 578 Against Doge Lorenzo del Velli: 955

Angrily, he tried to control his shaking. He had lost the vote of confidence. It wasn't even close.

Just then, Francella Watanabe strode into the chamber and marched down the central aisle toward him, accompanied by their son, Anton Glavine.

The real and the projected princes rose to their feet and the chamber erupted in applause. To Lorenzo's surprise, he heard a clamor arise in favor of his bastard son.

"Doge Anton!" they chanted. "Doge Anton!"

Francella and Anton mounted the stage and stood in front of him. "This is our miracle," she said to Lorenzo. "I've made all the necessary arrangements, made the payments and promises. The princes will haggle back and forth a bit, but only for the sake of appearances. The vote for Anton will only be a formality."

The Doge sat down. His Human enemies were more subtle and devious than the Mutatis, and had succeeded in pulling out the Doge's underpinnings of support so suddenly that he was shocked. The situation with Anton was intriguing, but Lorenzo couldn't accept him too easily, or that would garner opposition to the new Doge.

So, feigning more rage and discontent than he really felt, Lorenzo jumped to his feet. "You haven't heard the last of me!" he shouted, as he stormed out of the hall.

Even though the princes wanted Lorenzo's resignation, they could not force it, not even after the vote of no confidence. A number of legal procedures still had to be followed to remove him from office, and that could take years, as it had in the past with other merchant prince leaders. Lorenzo knew something of merchant prince law, and had the best lawyers to represent his interests.

In private, he told her what he had decided to do, and finally she said, "Yes. I see the wisdom in your words."

The princes and their representatives held meetings far into the night, while Lorenzo conferred with Pimyt and a staff of attorneys. During a meal break on the stage, with tables set up for those who were on Canopa, Francella went over to Lorenzo and said, "I told them you are too stubborn to resign, my dear, but you must be cautious. The noble-born princes are not in a patient mood, and we are at war against the Mutatis and against the Guardians. They are talking about using wartime provisions against you, and...."

"Don't try to snow me," Lorenzo said, raising his voice so that others could see him seeming to argue with her. "My people know the laws better than you do. I can take steps to remain in power for a long time."

"Some of your opponents are saying that you could be overthrown violently," Francella said. She glanced back at Anton, who sat at her table but thus far had remained silent.

"Supreme General Jacopo Nehr is totally loyal to me," Lorenzo countered. "He can bring most of the armed forces to my support on a moment's notice." Pausing, the Doge smiled and added, "Nonetheless, for the good of the Alliance, I have decided to take a different course of action. Tell them I will abdicate, but only under certain conditions."

"And those conditions are?" Francella asked. She sounded irritated, but Lorenzo assumed it was only for show.

"Watch me," he said.

Calling in old favors, Lorenzo and his staff made a flurry of last-minute political arrangements. Despite his bluster, he knew his political opponents could attack him militarily, and the armor on the orbiter wouldn't stand against a full-scale assault. Still, that would be an unprecedented, egregious act, and might very well lead to civil war all across the Alliance.

Making the best of a bad situation, Lorenzo slipped cleverly out of the noose his opponents had prepared for him. He agreed to abdicate immediately, and accepted exile to his space station, where he would operate The Pleasure Palace Casino, guarded by a contingent of Red Berets. Under the arrangement, he would be permitted to keep his corporate directorships, and would receive the title of Doge Emeritus, along with a generous annual pension.

He also had the new, secret understanding with Francella, which might prove to be more lucrative than the gambling casino. Immediately after the agreement with Lorenzo was signed, the princes conducted a private vote, and Anton del Velli was elected Doge.

Chapter Fifty-Nine

Everyone wants to be seen and noticed. It is an aspect of the Human condition. It is also an aspect that we constantly attempt to select and frame the pictures in which we appear.

—Master Noah Watanabe

Anton Glavine, a former maintenance man and later a prisoner, never imagined that he would one day become the highest-ranking official in the Merchant Prince Alliance, the Doge of all humankind. The suddenness of his ascension stunned him. After a midnight vote he felt as if he had been plucked from darkness and lifted into the light, with limitless possibilities for his life. Great riches had been opened for him as the heir to the House of del Velli and the Doge's share of taxes he would receive, even if they only came from Canopa and the rest was on paper, due to the cessation of podship travel.

In the beginning Anton had to follow a tight course, at least until he gained enough power and influence in his own right to speak out and say what he felt. His concerns ran deep. Principal among them was his enigmatic mother, about whom he had mixed feelings. Anton tried to view her sympathetically for the woman's mental illness, which seemed obvious. He appreciated the belated attention she had given him, her overtures to make up for the time they had lost between them, more than twenty years. Anton tried to feel love for her, but that was not easy, and he didn't know if he ever could.

She might have done terrible things to the person he admired most in the entire galaxy, his Uncle Noah Watanabe. Anton had heard stories about Francella performing violent laboratory experiments on her own brother and how he had survived through some miracle and then escaped. If she really did that to him, Anton could never forgive her. He would even see that she was prosecuted, but thus far they were only stories, without evidence.

Francella was claiming that the descriptions were exaggerated, and that she had really conducted controlled experiments, with full medical technology and personnel available for life saving purposes. According to her claim, supported by Dr. Bichette, Noah gave permission to have his body cut into pieces, knowing that they would grow back, and he issued a challenge, asserting he could not be killed. Anton had seen him do that on the pod station, when Noah told his estranged sister to go ahead and shoot, since that could not harm him. He claimed immortality, and evidence suggested that this actually was the case.

Though Anton did not fully understand why, he knew that his mother had always hated Noah and had unfairly blamed him for the attack on CorpOne headquarters that killed old Prince Saito Watanabe. She might even have been responsible for that aggression herself, but Anton did not have any evidence pointing in that direction. Only the suspicions of her brother and other people. Anton wanted to believe the best about his mother. What a shame it would be to find her after all this time and then discover that she had no redeeming qualities at all.

He also found it troublesome that Francella seemed to be a master at pointing fingers, including the recent incident with Noah, the earlier attack on CorpOne, and the way she had recently cast suspicions about Doge Lorenzo, asserting that he knew all along that Princess Meghina was not Human, and had concealed the facts. That tactic was one of the key reasons for his fall from power. As far as Anton was concerned, it had not been entirely above board, but perhaps that was the way of merchant prince politics, just another day in the arena of political combat. Soon, he would learn more about how the game was played. For now, he was a child thrown into the ocean and told to swim.

Trumpets blared, and on all sides noblemen and ladies bowed their heads to Anton as he walked down the central aisle of the Hall of Princes, with his mother just behind him. Anton wore a glittering gold-brocade cloak and uniform, draped in jewels and medallions, while his regal-looking mother was adorned in a long white gown and golden headdress. Outside, the central square fronting the government buildings thronged with people, celebrating the inauguration of the new Doge, the leading prince of the realm.

On one level of awareness, Anton felt tremendous pride, and a certainty that this lofty position was his birthright as the son of Lorenzo. But he also felt a great deal of responsibility, and a fear that he might not be up to the task. He vowed privately to do his best, and to assert himself as soon as he could, getting out from under the skirts of the woman behind him and prosecuting her if he found evidence that she had committed any crimes. Anton knew he had to be his own man. He would grow into the job, beginning with humility and diplomacy and gradually changing, revealing his own personality and goals. It was a difficult time to ascend to this position, with the ongoing hostilities and the strange cessation of podship travel. He doubted if any ruler before him had ever faced such monumental obstacles.

He noticed General Jacopo Nehr and his daughter Nirella standing by the aisle. The woman glanced at Anton and smiled. She looked to be around twice his age and was rather stocky—but he found her attractive and reportedly she was still able to bear children. Her father had been lobbying through the political channels of the merchant princes, offering her in marriage to the new Doge. Anton still had feelings for Tesh, and he didn't want to think about matrimony just yet. Nirella seemed pleasant enough the few times they had met, but he needed to get to know her better before making a commitment—no matter the obvious political and economic benefits of joining two influential merchant prince houses.

Anton continued down the aisle, then took a deep breath and climbed the steps of the central stage, where a white-robed Merchant Priest awaited him, holding a bound copy of the *Scienscroll*.

Having rehearsed this event, Anton strode up to him and stopped, while Lorenzo and Francella stood stiffly on one side. Due to the limitations on space travel that prevented merchant prince nobles and their entourages from journeying great distances, common citizens were permitted to sit in the great hall on this occasion, beside those noblemen and ladies who lived on Canopa. Around the realm, other noblemen and ladies, as well as billions of citizens, watched the proceedings via nehrcom links.

The priest told the assemblage in the hall to stand. Then he sprinkled holy water on Anton and read words from the *Scienscroll*:

"For ours is a realm fashioned and favored by the Supreme Being;
Truly, our blessings and glories are many!
Hear this now, in every princely land:
A new ruler rises like the sun, to shine brightly on us all!"

At a nod from the priest, Lorenzo stepped forward and handed his son a sapphire signet ring, on a tiny pillow. Then he stepped back.

Anton shivered with delight as the priest reached out and placed the ring on the third finger of the young man's right hand. Every merchant prince wore such a ring, and they had collectively given this as a gift to him. In recent days, he had been wearing it, getting used to it. The ring was his bond to the other princes, signifying that he was allegiant to them, one of their peers. Now, by virtue of the inaugural ceremony and the blessing of the priest on the ring, Anton had risen to first among his noble peers, simultaneously subject to them and their ruler.

Trumpets blared again, while the crowd cheered and stamped its feet in a traditional welcoming gesture. On one of the most unexpected occasions in all of Human history, Anton Glavine, the bastard son of Lorenzo the Magnificent, was inaugurated Doge Anton del Velli of the Merchant Prince Alliance.

The following day, he would move into the palatial cliffside villa vacated by his father, and still owned by his mother. Suddenly Anton's life had accelerated, and he hoped he could keep up.

* * * * *

After the grand ball that evening, Francella sat alone in her dressing room, reflecting on the big day. It had pleased her to see her son and Nirella Nehr dancing together, and engaged in animated conversation. She would be happy to see the two houses merge through marriage, giving Francella access to one of the great fortunes in the galaxy.

The day had gone extremely well, and she felt considerable pride—but not for her son, though that might come one day, if he showed the sense of duty she hoped he had. For the moment, she felt extremely proud of herself, for rising above adversity and achieving what seemed impossible. She had not only toppled a sitting doge without him knowing of her involvement, but she had installed her own son in his place. Truly remarkable.

And, while she had been unable to stop the agreement under which Doge Lorenzo saved himself from disaster, at least she had made the best of the situation. Her son's new position would bring great revenues into the family in the form of skimmed taxes, and she intended to receive a considerable share of them. In addition, she envisioned a sizable financial reward when her company began producing and selling the new elixir based upon Noah's DNA. She would use it herself, and would sell it to selected clients on Canopa for more than a king's ransom.

A name for the product occurred to her, and she made a note of it in a recording device built into one of her lockets. She would call it the "Elixir of Life."

Chapter Sixty

All galactic races share the need to learn. It is part of the genetic coding for survival, a process that instills life and vitality into the collective organism. When learning stops, the cells eventually become necrotic, and death looms.
                                    —Finding of CorpOne medical research study

A month passed that seemed like much longer to Anton Glavine. In his new position and responsibilities, he had many concerns.

For one, the mustachioed young Doge wondered what had happened to thousands of Red Beret robots, which seemed to have vanished. He suspected that his uncle and his Guardian machines had something to do with it, since it was now known that clever programming and inventory adjustments had been made to conceal the disappearances. The remainder of the Red Beret robotic force was under lock and key now, with the machines decommissioned and guarded.

Anton wondered about the fate of Noah, too, who continued to elude discovery and for some reason had reduced the number of guerrilla attacks, around the same time that the robots disappeared. General Nehr suspected that the Guardians were preparing for a new, much larger attack against Red Beret and CorpOne facilities, and that a machine army would form an integral part of their new plans.

But where were the Guardians? His mind ached from trying to figure it out. Once, Anton had known the location of their hidden headquarters, for he had been a trusted member of Noah's inner circle. Then, mysteriously, the information had vanished ... or had gone into hiding, like Noah himself.

One of his interrogators at Max One had referred to it as a "convenient memory," and perhaps it was that, or a selective memory. Or maybe it was, as

Noah suggested, stress-induced. In any event, Anton had not been lying. He really could not remember.

Anton recalled his early life with Noah, and being on the orbital EcoStation with the great ecological teacher and his Guardians, but there were significant gaps after that. The Doge saw faces in his memory, such as those of Subi Danvar, Tesh Kori, Giovanni Nehr, and the robot Thinker, and meetings with Guardians, but he could not recollect the backgrounds, could not tell where the meetings took place, or many of the details that were discussed. Anton also remembered the dramatic events at the pod station, where Noah confronted Doge Lorenzo and Francella Watanabe. Both Noah and Anton had been taken into custody that day, and imprisoned at Max One.

An odd thought intruded, that the gaps in data suggested he might actually be a robot, or a bionic man, and someone had tampered with his internal programming. But that was preposterous. He knew he truly was Human, and that he was the biological son of Doge Lorenzo and Francella Watanabe. Medical tests had proven it.

But why can 't I remember more about Noah? he wondered.

Oddly, he had so many concise memories of other things about Noah. It occurred to him that maybe he was protecting his uncle from harm by enemies, and had somehow blocked the memories in his own mind.

Perhaps I don 't want to know, because if I did, I would have to go after him and harm, or even kill, him. This man who has done so much for me, and whom I have always admired more than any other.

The harder Anton tried to remember, or to figure out what was preventing him from doing so, the farther away the memories seemed to go. It was almost as if some higher power was interfering with his thought processes, preventing him from revealing secrets that were hidden and layered deep in his psyche.

A higher power that was protecting Noah Watanabe.

The youthful Doge worked hard each day, studying holohistories and other electronic documents to learn as much as he could about the merchant princes and the most important commercial and industrial worlds. Much of his training regimen was provided by his mother, but he went beyond anything she put in front of him, and he opened up his own channels of inquiry through his staff and the local government library.

Nirella Nehr was a big help as well. In her position as half owner of her father's corporate empire and its nehrcom transmission system, she obtained information from all over the galaxy and shared it with him. They were spending a lot of time together, and rumors were circulating that a royal wedding would soon take place.

While undergoing an intense, on-the-job learning process, Anton was anxious to put his own new policies into force. He had a lot of ideas, including reaching a cease-fire with Noah. But his own position was complex. First he needed to be more sure of himself and of how his mother would react to such a step. Anton had been probing her on this issue, talking about political necessities that might point to the necessity of a cease-fire, and how a cessation of internal hostilities could benefit the entire Human cause. Thus far she remained unconvinced, but gradually her arguments were becoming less vociferous, less emotional.

As Anton accumulated information, it amazed him how much he had not known previously, especially about history and politics, and how many important activities were going on without the public having any knowledge of them. Instilled with fresh enthusiasm for the new things he was learning, he looked forward to getting up each morning and going about his activities. He was so excited about his new life, in fact, that he began sleeping a couple of hours less each night than before. In part this was because he was so tired at the end of each day that he slept more soundly. Essentially, he had two speeds now: like a hyperactive child, he went full tilt all day, and then fell sound asleep. In some respects he felt like a child, too, discovering new things with each waking moment.

While Anton got to know Nirella, it surprised him what a close bond they were forming, despite the difference in their ages. They clicked together, but she didn't press him for marriage, and claimed it was her father doing that, and Anton's mother. "I hear that's the best way to ruin a great friendship," Nirella said once.

He liked her sense of humor, and the way her blue eyes danced when she laughed. As time passed he thought less and less about how much older she was, and began to think of both of them as around thirty ... the approximate mid-point between their ages. One evening as they shared a late meal, Anton surprised himself by proposing to her and sliding a glittering engagement ring across the small private table.

"Are you sure?" she asked, holding the large diamonix ring up to a candle to see it better.

"Is that a yes or a no?" Nervously, Anton polished off a glass of redicio wine, then refilled it.

"You are the Doge," she said. "If you want to marry me, I cannot say no."

"Don't be silly. I give you permission to turn me down."

"To be honest, I would marry you even if you weren't the Doge, and I think you would do the same if I weren't filthy rich."

He smiled. "You're right. I wish we'd met earlier."

"If we had, I'd be a child molester."

"I mean two or three years ago. I feel like I'm missing out on life when you're not around."

"What a sweet thing to say." She extended her left hand. He slipped the diamonix ring over her wedding finger, and then leaned across the table to kiss her.

Far across the galaxy at the Inn of the White Sun, the sentient machines had grown tired of Ipsy's officious, dictatorial methods. The feisty little robot's opponents formed a resistance movement that gained momentum quickly.

Before Ipsy could take counter-actions, he found himself exiled and tossed aboard a podship bound for the Hibbil Cluster Worlds. The other machines did this as a cruel joke, thinking that the Hibbils (who preferred their own regimented machines) would deactivate the patched-together Ipsy and dump him on a trash heap.

The royal wedding, held a scant week after the proposal, was by no means typical. At Nirella's suggestion, they made it an electronic event, broadcasting it all over the Merchant Prince Alliance by nehrcom. Even on Canopa, the couple invited only a few guests to the small theoscientific chapel where they exchanged vows, choosing instead to transmit the proceedings.

Francella, not a typical mother herself, did not complain, and neither did Jacopo or his shy and unassuming wife, Lady Amila Nehr. The parents seemed so pleased at the union that they didn't care how the formalities were accomplished. Lorenzo had no say in the matter at all, though he was invited and did attend. Keeping his feelings to himself, he sat quietly at the rear of the chapel with his Hibbil attaché Pimyt, while Francella and members of the Nehr family sat in the front.

The chapel, constructed almost entirely of prismatic glax, sat in a park in the Valley of the Princes. It had been the late Prince Saito's favorite place to go for serenity and contemplation, and seemed to Anton like the perfect spot for him to begin his exciting new life with Nirella. The altar contained a life-sized sculpture of the Madonna cradling models of technological devices, including a silvery vacuum rocket and a white, bubble-shaped nehrcom transmitting station.

When the participants began the ceremony, the weather had been cloudy, and through the prismatic roof of the structure Anton saw that the sky was a dismal gray. Then, just as they were about to exchange rings, the sun peeked around the cloud cover and shone a narrow beam of light on their hands, making the rings sparkle and gleam.

"I'd say that's a good sign," Nirella said as they kissed.

He laughed, and heard soft chuckles from the small audience.

To conclude the ceremony, the white-robed priest passed each of them a chalice of holy water, which Anton and Nirella sprinkled on one another.

Just then, Anton jerked in surprise when he saw two men enter the chapel and take seats at the rear, on the other side of the aisle from his father and the Hibbil. The late arrivals were Noah Watanabe and the bride's adventurous paternal uncle, Giovanni Nehr. What were they doing here, and how had they gotten past security?

"Look!" Anton said, pointing.

"A little wedding present for you, darling," Nirella said with a gentle smile. "You've been talking about the need for a cease-fire with Noah, so I thought we might have a little family reunion on our wedding day."

Anton exchanged nods and smiles with his Uncle Noah, across the chapel.

"I checked with your mother before inviting him, and told her what I had in mind. She was resistant at first, then agreed, especially when she realized that my father, as the MPA military commander, was arranging a cease-fire at the highest level, just for us."

"My mother didn't try to stop it?"

"No. Maybe she's changing."

"One can only hope."

"The public isn't being told that Noah is here, and no images of him are being broadcast from the chapel."

Anton nodded. "This is great, because I don't want to fight with Noah anyway. I'd been hoping something could be worked out, so that we could devote our full attention to our real enemy, the Mutati Kingdom. Podship travel could resume at any moment, and the war with it."

"I forbid you to talk shop on our wedding day," she said. "Now, go to him."

Beaming with delight, Anton made his way toward Noah, and they met halfway. As he passed his mother, the young Doge heard her muttering in displeasure, but she did not seem inclined to make a scene. Anton wondered if his wife had made a demand, and had gotten her way against her new mother-in-law. He hoped the two women would get along. It would be difficult if they did not.

"Congratulations, Nephew," Noah said, giving the young Doge a robust handshake. "Pardon me for being so familiar, but I still remember when you wore short pants."

"I'm glad you could make it," Anton said. "And you, too, Gio. It's great to see both of you."

"We're hearing good things about you," Noah said.

"And I'm hearing very little about you," came the Doge's rejoinder. "We have a great deal to discuss, but my wife says I can't talk shop on our wedding day."

"We can't stay long today," Noah said, "but perhaps we might get together another time." He looked up at a nehrcom unit mounted in the ceiling. "Your public awaits you."

The two men clasped hands again, and then the visitors hurried away.

Chapter Sixty-One

The variations of God are infinite.
—Noah Watanabe, Commentary on Sentience

"I shouldn't have gone," Lorenzo said. "The tension was so thick in that chapel, you could cut it with a knife." He and his Hibbil attaché stood in a new casino module, watching robots move heavy gambling machines into place.

"To the contrary, My Lord," Pimyt said, rubbing his own furry chin. "It is always valuable to attend such events, for the purpose of gathering information."

"Perhaps, but I felt like jumping out of my seat and strangling Noah."

"Francella wanted a chance at him, too, and that's what made it so interesting. To her credit, she—and you, Your Magnificence—rose above petty grievances, and showed up for the sake of your son."

Arching his gray eyebrows, Lorenzo said, "My grievances against Noah are hardly *petty*. He and his Guardians undermined my leadership, and then he leaked the story about Meghina being a Mutati."

"You have evidence of that, Sire?"

"A gut feeling. Instinct."

"Mmmm. Interesting. Nevertheless, on a galactic scale, when you view the big picture, the immense societal tides that are flowing as we speak, all such interactions really are *petty*."

"I don't have to keep you around, you know," Lorenzo said. "You've always been rather haughty, and now that I've been deposed you have become openly impertinent."

"I only speak frankly, My Lord, which is what you need at the moment." The furry little Hibbil bowed. "I have always considered you a friend, and only want what is best for you."

With a hard stare, Lorenzo nodded and lowered his voice. "I suppose you're right. Very well, but do not speak to me in that manner when we are in the presence of others. We'll keep it our little secret, eh?"

The dark red eyes lit up. "Oh yes. I love secrets." Rubbing his furry chin, Pimyt said, "I wonder if Francella will keep her bargain with you, if she will truly allow you to influence the new Doge. We haven't heard much from her since the vote and the inauguration."

"She's been busy. Don't worry, Pimyt. Francella and I have a long relationship, and she'll come through for me, as she promised."

"I hope you're right."

They walked around a robot work crew, then exited the module and strolled down a glax-walled corridor, which offered stunning views of the armored space station modules, profiled against Canopa far below. It was mid-afternoon.

Ducking into an office that had formerly been occupied by General Jacopo Nehr, they closed the door and sat in comfortable side chairs. Pimyt had to hop up on a cushion and arrange pillows behind himself for back support. His uncovered feet dangled over the floor. The new Doge Anton had decided to keep General Nehr on as commander of the Merchant Prince Armed Forces, a decision that undoubtedly had a great deal to do with the fact that Nehr was his father-in-law.

"It will be interesting to see how much of an ally the general remains to us," Lorenzo said. "When he left, he expressed gratitude for the appointments I gave him, and he promised to always look out for my welfare. But things have changed, and we'll have to see how it all turns out."

"Now you're the worrier," Pimyt said, with a tight smile. "Jacopo will keep his word. I know this for a fact."

"And how can you be so sure?"

"That is my business, Sire, to keep such details in line. I have always been good at them, don't you agree?"

"Without question." The Doge Emeritus narrowed his eyes. "You almost sound like you have something on him."

A tight smile behind the salt-and-pepper beard. "I have something on everyone, Sire. Except you, of course."

"I wonder. Now let's talk about how to further our interests, and I'm not just talking about financial matters. Politics is in my blood, and always will be."

"I know that. Well, there is some dissatisfaction among corporate princes about the inauguration of Anton, who was brought to power by his mother and the noble-born, anti-corporate princes. A number of dissatisfied, self-made princes have contacted me, offering to form an alliance with you. They have not forgotten how you always rewarded performance instead of bloodlines."

"Good," Lorenzo said, nodding. "Form the alliances, and we'll build from them. But do not say anything against Doge Anton or Francella. We don't want our comments coming back to bite us."

"You are a master of diplomacy, My Lord."

Since escaping from the medical laboratory, Noah had been playing catch-up, learning about the guerrilla operations that had been undertaken by Subi and Thinker, and the assimilation of thousands of new robots that had formerly been Red Berets.

One morning he stood in a large underground chamber, getting an update from Giovanni Nehr, who wore his customary armor, making him look like a machine-man hybrid. Gio had been assigned to work closely with the new robots. The two of them watched as Jimu inspected hundreds of fighter bots, who stood in formation. While they had been extensively checked and reconditioned, some still had cardinal red markings on their metal bodies, which Noah mentioned.

"I'll make sure they're all cleaned off," Gio said.

"Hmm," Noah said, nodding, "but I'm more concerned about what's inside the robots, their programming. An enemy could implant latent operating instructions that are designed to activate at a certain time, or under certain circumstances."

"That would be a nasty trick."

"And devastating."

"Thinker already thought of that, and these robots have passed his rigid tests. He's checking others now by interfacing with them, and even tearing them down completely."

"Is he tearing all of them down, or only on a random basis?"

"The latter, Master Noah. Thinker ran probability programs, and he assures us that the likelihood of such problems is infinitesimal."

"I want all of them torn down anyway. It's better to be slow and safe."

"I'll tell him."

"Hear me well. I want the probability reduced to *less* than infinitesimal. All of the new robots are to be disarmed and placed under guard until they are fully cleared."

Gio saluted, and went to inform Jimu of the increased security measures.

That evening, as he had done on a number of occasions since returning to the Guardians, Noah attempted to reenter the cosmic web. In darkness he lay in bed, letting his mind float freely. He felt a slight tugging at his consciousness, and this gave him hope. Was he going back in?

But the sensation dissipated, and afterward he lay awake, wondering what was going wrong. Had he lost his previous powers entirely? And did that suggest he would lose his immortality as well? Most of all, it troubled him that he had not been able to remotely control podships for some time now. The last occasion that he had done it efficiently, without being rejected by the creatures, had been before he recommended drastic measures to the former Doge Lorenzo del Velli, measures that resulted in setting up the deadly pod-killer sensor-guns. Did the creatures know, somehow, that Noah had been responsible?

He had many more questions than answers.

Lorenzo knew he was licking his wounds, but he hadn't done so poorly in the exchange of his merchant prince leadership role for the life he led now. He was still one of the five wealthiest men in the galaxy, and remained widely respected. Under the new agreement, he had his own powerful paramilitary forces,

Red Berets that had been assigned to protect him for the rest of his life. His space station—with a population now of more than twenty thousand persons—was well-armored, and surrounded by defensive gunships that were always on patrol.

As days passed, the Doge Emeritus formalized his new alliances, and had one brief meeting with Francella Watanabe. She told him, just as he had anticipated, that she had been busy with all of the arrangements involving the new Doge, and she and Lorenzo had to go through what she called a "cooling off period" before the former Doge could get more involved in Anton's affairs. Biting his tongue and not complaining, Lorenzo accepted her assurances. He was coming to accept the new arrangements, and understood that important political relationships did not always move forward quickly.

Even in his present position, Lorenzo had to be alert against Noah and his Guardians. Their guerrilla attacks and other disruptions had long been a thorn in his side, preventing him from dealing with other pressing problems. He was certain that Noah still wanted to get even with him for taking over the ecology compound, the orbital space station, and planetary recovery operations around the galaxy. All of that, when added to the likelihood that Noah had leaked the story about Meghina being a Mutati, made Lorenzo and Noah natural enemies.

"I'm going to get him before he gets me," Lorenzo said to Pimyt, during an afternoon meeting, held just before the opening of a new casino expansion module. Behind the stocky, gray-haired man a holo floated, an overview of intelligence reports that had come in on the guerrilla activities of Noah's Guardians. A timeline with it showed that they had stepped up their attacks against corporate installations on Canopa, though there seemed to be a slight reduction in attacks against government facilities.

"Good strategy," the Hibbil replied. "We know one thing. With podships cut off, he could not have gone far."

Now, with assurance from Francella that she would keep Doge Anton in line, Lorenzo instituted a renewed all-out effort to locate Noah's secret headquarters and annihilate him.

Chapter Sixty-Two

There are certain big events that mark historical turning points. It is invariably possible to look back on them years later and recognize them. For the most momentous events, however, you know them the instant you see or participate in them, the moment they are set into motion.

—Jodie Am'Uss, Official Historian of the Tulyan race

There were particular things that Eshaz could not reveal to the teenage Humans or to the Parvii woman. The full power of Tulyan mindlink was but one of many examples. He didn't know how he could put that phenomenon into words anyway, because he didn't fully comprehend how it worked ... only that it did.

To discourage military aggression by outsiders, the Tulyans had leaked information that they had a powerful mindlink defensive system, and that certain Elders could actually hitch telepathic rides on comets and meteors, taking them on fantastic trips through space. These were true statements, but mindlink was much more than that. It had dimensions that had not been known to the Tulyans in ancient times when they were defeated by the Parviis, but which had been developed and perfected over the past century and a half. In galactic time, that was not very long ago at all.

It was not known by outsiders that the spectacular nighttime displays of comets and meteors in the starcloud were actually the result of the collective telepathic powers of the Tulyan people, under the guidance of powerful Elders. It was also not known that the Tulyans, considered a pacifist people, could now harness the energy of these cosmic bodies and turn them into weapons.

Previously the Parviis had broken through weak spots in mindlink, and had entered with their swarms, taking control of podships that were being hidden by the Tulyans. For weeks now, Parvii swarms had been gathering outside the starcloud, increasing their strength and trying to find the opportunity to break through again. This time they wanted to take over the seventy podships that Eshaz had brought back, along with the vessel that was under Tesh's control. But, with the tenuous, perilous condition of the galaxy, and the need for Tulyan caretakers to spread out in greater numbers, the Tulyans could not permit that to happen. They needed *more* podships, not fewer of them. They needed to end the cycle of Tulyan capture and Parvii attack.

The Council of Elders vowed that this time there would be no mindlink lapse, no opening for the relentless enemy to exploit. And for the first time in the history of their race, the Tulyans were going to do something unexpected, going on the offensive with their own telepathic weapon.

At the appointed time, in full daylight, Eshaz left his three alien companions at his home, and climbed alone to a high point of rock that overlooked his property, telling them only that he wanted time for contemplation. Reaching the pinnacle, he closed his eyes and focused all of his mental energies in the manner that the Elders had instructed him to do. In doing this, he, like other Tulyans involved in the effort, were energy boosters for the Elders, who were themselves performing more complex defensive and guidance functions.

They called it a telekinetic weapon.

In the universe of his mind, Eshaz saw the misty starcloud and its three planets, looking as if they were floating in a bath of milk. He felt the energy level rising, and then saw fiery comets and meteors approaching from space as if drawn to a magnet, along with glowing asteroids. At the last moment the celestial visitors veered off and headed for the largest swarm of Parviis, terrifying the tiny creatures and scattering them into space.

Eshaz felt a supreme relaxation of tension, and opened his eyes.

Like an island oasis in the troubled galaxy, the Tulyan Starcloud floated serenely and peacefully in the ethereal mists, as if nothing unusual had occurred at all, just as it had looked since ancient times.

It was the way the galaxy should be, unchanging and constant... eternal. But beneath the surface, beyond what Eshaz could see, he knew that the fabric of existence was shredding.

The Parviis, who had been thwarted in their desire to penetrate the mindlink energy shield, were now dispersed into the frozen void and sent spinning off in confusion, with their morphic field disrupted. As a result they lost contact with Woldn, who had been in their midst and had been controlling their movements.

Their connection to the Eye of the Swarm interrupted, billions of the tiny creatures flew off in all directions. Furious, Woldn dispatched squads to locate them. But when only a small portion of his people returned, it became clear to him that the others had perished, and that his power base had been eroded.

He hoped it was only temporary.

With the Parviis in disarray, the Tulyan Council of Elders sent out more than seventy hunting teams aboard as many podships, to the Hibbil Sector and to galactic sectors far and wide, where the wild podships migrated at this time of year.

Eshaz, having earlier merged with an alpha pod in order to capture an entire herd, piloted the same vessel now. He was the Aopoddae ship and it was him. The spacefaring vessel bore his reptilian face on the front of its hull, and its skin had taken on a scaly, gray-bronze hue.

Inside the passenger compartment stood six Tulyan hunters, anxiously awaiting the opportunity to go to work, to practice the ancient methods of capturing the mysterious, sentient creatures. Acey and Dux were on board with them, but Tesh—at Dabiggio's insistence—remained back at the Starcloud Visitor's Center. There had been something of a tug of war between her and the Council through intermediaries, and Tesh had held firm that if she was not permitted to join the hunt she was not going to release control of her podship to anyone. So, it remained sealed and motionless, floating in its docking bay at the starcloud. Through regular truth-touching to verify her motives and allegiances she was declared pure, and by majority vote the Council judged that she had at least earned the respect she was demanding.

But, like all Parviis, she had other information deep in her mind, and knew things that the mortal enemies of her people could never draw out of her. Not unless she told them....

"Eshaz wants you boys to enjoy yourselves," said one of the Tulyan hunters in the alpha pod. A squat reptile with an angular grin, he went by the name Viadu. "Old Eshaz says you're experienced hunters."

"I wouldn't go quite that far," Dux said. "We were just observers the last time out."

"Well you're part of the team now, though you can't go outside and wrangle."

"Maybe we can," Dux said. He glanced over at Acey, who was removing articles from a pack he brought along.

"What do you have there?" Viadu asked.

"Just something I put together with spare parts, while I was banging around in the Visitor's Center. It kept me busy."

Dux knew what it was. As he and the Tulyans watched, Acey brought out a helmet with a plax face plate, and a green protective suit modeled after the larger Tulyan models, to keep from being drugged or poisoned by thorns. He put the gear on.

Looking at him, the Tulyans laughed.

"Hey," Acey said, "I'm pretty handy with things, and I really can breathe inside this thing. I tested it. Made one for my cousin, too, but he's not as brave as I am."

"Not as *foolhardy*, you mean," Dux said.

"So, you want to go upstairs, eh?" Viadu said, to Acey.

The young man nodded vigorously, inside his outfit. His voice came through a built-in speaker, sounding thin: "This suit is perfectly sealed, and has oxygen for me to breathe. It's also thermally protected, since we Humans weren't born with much insulation."

"All right, but there are certain things you can't do, since the pods only respond to telepathy."

"I just want a front row seat up there," Acey said.

"All right, but if you get in the way, I'm sending you back down here."

"Agreed," the teenager said.

The Tulyans unpacked shipping cases and got into their own protective suits, after which they brought out thorn vines wrapped in broad leaf packages, and other items they would need. One of the Tulyans mixed liquids, powders, herbs, and thorn scrapings in small bowls, then tossed everything into a cauldron and heated it with fire cylinders in the alloy casting. Dux and Acey had seen Eshaz do this before, but they found it no less fascinating now.

Viadu murmured incantations and tossed spheres overhead, which played serene music and then floated down into the cauldron and melted into the boiling liquid. Working fast, the Tulyans filled silver vials with the liquid, then removed their protective suits and smeared pigment rings on their bodies, creating the network of intricate, iridescent designs that they had previously seen Eshaz create.

The Tulyans, slipping into a collective trance, murmured incantations and handled the multicolored thorn vines without protection, wrapping them around their waists and making red crowns for their heads. Bravely, Acey stepped forward, and Viadu wrapped a vine around his protected torso, along with a red-vine crown on his helmet.

Dux began to feel afraid for his cousin, but didn't say anything. They had already discussed this at length, and Acey would not be deterred. Being more circumspect, Dux thought it was too reckless, but he had tested the oxygen and thermal systems in the two helmets and suits himself, and had assured himself that it all worked. As far as Dux could tell, Acey had done his usual excellent job in putting the gear together.

A few minutes later the podship slowed, and Dux heard the Tulyans saying wild podships had been sighted. Moving quickly, Viadu opened a hatch and leaped outside, pulling Acey with him. The hatch closed quickly behind them. Through a filmy window that formed on the ceiling, Dux saw them standing on top of the sentient spaceship, leaning forward. From listening to the Tulyans, Dux had learned something that reassured him somewhat about Acey's safety. They said that all podships had protective fields around them, enabling pilots to ride outside, even at high speeds.

Eshaz guided the craft toward the rear of a formation of wild podships, and Dux saw Viadu use thought-commands to fire sedative vials at the creatures, causing them to slow, one by one. The alpha pod, sensing pursuers, turned around to confront them. Eshaz steered straight at him, and Viadu leaped onto the back of the creature, connected the harness, and dug thorn vines into its sides. Soon he merged into the flesh of the podship, and his face appeared on the prow.

Next the other five Tulyans in the hunting party went onto the top of Eshaz's vessel, one at a time, and in short order they captured five more podships and metamorphosed them into amalgam creatures with Tulyan pilots, while additional hunting teams came in and helped mop up the herd. From a porthole in the passenger compartment Dux watched in astonishment as Tulyans and podships seemed to create another race of hybrid spaceships.

Utilizing methods more mystical than technological, the Tulyans first fought Parvii swarms with comets and meteors and then wrangled more than three hundred additional wild podships, which they returned in short order to the security of the starcloud.

It was a historic day, and a reminder of legendary glories.

Chapter Sixty-Three

It is said that wisdom comes with age. I have lived for almost a million standard years, but I still have a great deal to learn.

—Ruminations of Eshaz

For the past month, Francella Watanabe had locked herself on the lower floors of her villa, refusing to see anyone. In all that time, she had not been to the laboratory complex or to her new CorpOne offices, and had not responded to requests from Lorenzo for appointments. While Lorenzo had relocated his office and residence to the orbital space station, he still had an unexpired lease for the top-floor suite of her villa, though he had not been seen there in some time.

Each day Francella sent telebeam messages to Dr. Bichette, asking for progress reports on the new elixir research program. He and his staff of brow-beaten, under-pressure scientists worked around the clock, with the desperate feeling that they were not just trying to save Francella's life, but their own as well. To enforce her orders, Francella had sent CorpOne security troops to ring the laboratory complex, and was not letting anyone out. Food was sent in, and the sleeping arrangements were improvised. Bichette sent constant, increasingly nervous responses to his menacing boss.

Failure was not an option.

The reason for Francella's isolation at the villa was obvious to anyone. The last time Bichette saw her she had been aging rapidly, at a pace that must have terrified her. He had been frightened himself, just seeing the way her face changed, day by day. Now it must look much worse, so shocking that no amount of makeup could conceal it.

One afternoon the doctor's medical assistant, Reez Carthur, sat at a desk preparing a response to Francella, informing her of the latest research results. As with the prior communiqués, the information was accurate, but he put the lab results in layman's terms, so that Francella could understand. Carthur spoke into a microphone, which transcribed his words and typed them into the telebeam transmitter.

Just then, Dr. Bichette burst into her tiny, windowless office. "Don't send it," he said. "I have an important update."

With great excitement, he dictated a message, telling Francella that at last he and his dedicated staff had been able to synthesize an elixir using Noah's blood, but there were distinct limitations. He told her they had taken a genetic blueprint from the plasma, but it was so complex that it defied any form of written or electronic documentation. Curiously, though, they had still been able to get the DNA of the plasma to transmit manufacturing instructions through a computer network, to produce an elixir. Computer projections indicated that the elixir could extend the lifetimes of Human beings.

He paused, and thought to himself. *Could extend.* The computer projections indicated something more as well, a bit of information he was not revealing to her yet. The elixir would only work on a small number of people, what he called a "micro percentage" of the population. It seemed best to omit that tidbit for now, and hope for the best. He had tried to get a probability of success percentage from the computer, but so far he had been unable to obtain it. The only answer had been, repeatedly: "Data incomplete."

Another detail troubled him, and thus far he kept this to himself, too. In the elixir manufacturing process, tiny amounts of Noah's original blood plasma would be used up, so production could not go on forever ... unless they could take him captive again, or otherwise gain access to him. So many problems, but indications were that the plasma they had on hand would be enough to produce millions of capsules. .

Francella did not respond by telebeam. Instead, she showed up in person hours later, looking haggard and demanding a dose of the miracle drug. Only thirty-eight, she looked twice that age. "We're not in production yet," Bichette said. "I'm not made of patience," she said, something he already knew from personal experience.

"As I understand it, you don't want us to scientifically test the elixir before you take it? We only have computer projections at this point."

"You understand me perfectly."

Bichette heaved a sigh of resignation. Apparently she had not noticed the distinction he had made in his telebeam message to her, that the elixir *could* extend the lifetimes of Human beings. She wanted it to work so much that she was willing to take the optimistic view, and overlook any downside. Afraid to argue with her or point out pitfalls, he had no choice except to do as she demanded.

Under Francella's withering eye, Dr. Bichette and his staff rushed to set up a small-scale manufacturing facility in one of the laboratory rooms. In less than twenty-four hours they began producing capsules of blood-red elixir.

"This is not to be swallowed," Dr. Bichette said, having taken a capsule directly from a machine hopper and handed it to her. "Instead, it is to be squeezed between the fingers and injected into the skin by tiny needles."

With shaking hands, Francella squeezed the capsule. She closed her eyes, then opened them and looked angry. "I don't feel anything yet."

"We don't know how long it's supposed to take. We tried to get that information out of the computer, but got no answer. Besides, I suspect it's different for every person."

The used capsule in Francella's hand had become flat and gray. She tossed it aside. "Give me more," she said.

"Listen to me, please. Wait for a few days to see if you start feeling better. We'll check you and monitor your progress."

"Do as I say."

Stepping close to her, Bichette placed a reassuring hand on her shoulder. "Please listen to me on this. I care about you, and I don't want you to overdose."

"You'd better be right about this," she said, then whirled and left.

Chapter Sixty-Four

For our race, web caretaking is the most ancient of tasks, the one for which we were born. Alas, alas, alas. So much in our heritage remains unfulfilled.
—Lament of the Tulyans

For Tesh, it had been a stunning sight that had captured her full attention and a wide range of emotions, seeing hundreds of podships arrive at the Tulyan Starcloud, all bearing the faces of Tulyans on their prows, reminiscent of the figureheads on sailing ships in the old days of Lost Earth. For this epic event, she had been standing on a sealed observation deck of the orbital Visitor's Center, along with many excited Tulyans and a handful of dignitaries of other races.

As a Parvii, she knew she should not have felt that it was a wonderful moment, but she had been unable to escape the sensation of delight, and a chill had run down her spine....

Now two days had passed, and as she stood alone on the same observation deck, she had not changed her impressions or her sentiments. It seemed to her that her own people had been in the wrong for much of the galaxy's history and she had been an unwitting part of it, a contributor in her own limited way. Long ago, Parvii swarms used powerful telepathic weapons to steal the fleets of podships away from their original custodians, the Tulyans, and then took actions to round up every last sentient spaceship that the Tulyans happened to get their hands on. For Tesh, born into the situation only seven centuries ago, she had not been provided with a context about this that would have enabled her to understand the immensity of the historical act.

She wondered if she had been brainwashed.

In orbital space, she watched a Tulyan face appear on one of the tethered ships. It was not Eshaz. The ship moved around to the other side of the formation, and disappeared from view.

Suspecting that Parvii belief systems had been imposed on her in subtle and deceptive ways, Tesh wondered how far the historical fraud might have gone. Did the Eye of the Swarm and others close to him know the true nature of the situation, or was he a pawn himself, having been fed false information that had become part of Parvii lore? Her people had no written history, only the oral traditions passed on from generation to generation, so she had no place to go and look anything up, no documentation. At least not through her own race. That was unfortunate. She wondered as well what documents or other forms of proof the Tulyans had, and if they might be tricking her now in some way.

But her heart told her otherwise, an innate sensibility that she always carried with her. Was the truth right in front of her eyes? From her private vantage point, she saw almost four hundred captured podships moored in nearby space, the bounty of two hunts, including the one she went on with Eshaz and the teenage Humans. The Council of Elders had decided to tether them at the center of the starcloud for maximum security, a strong point where the mindlink energies of the race were maximized.

Increasingly it seemed to Tesh that the decay of Timeweb might in large degree be the fault of her own race, for removing the Tulyan web caretakers from their jobs and only allowing a few of them to go about their work, not nearly enough for such a massive job. Considering this, with doubts seeping into her consciousness, she began to feel great shame. Not for doing anything wrong herself, since she must have been a dupe like so many others, but for the very fact that she was a Parvii. Such thoughts! Did she carry within her cells, within her DNA, the dark remnants of her genetic past, the shameful detritus of those in her race who had been directly and consciously to blame?

Yes. The truth stared her in the face.

But she knew that she needed to set these worries aside at this critical juncture in history, and begin anew with a fresh awareness and fresh eyes, doing her very best to right the wrongs of the past. As a result of those wrongs, the entire galaxy was out of balance, and crumbling away. She had to reveal certain information to the Tulyans, and saw no alternative....

As she watched, two other ships took on Tulyan faces, and moved to other moorages. Even though she had seen the extraordinary piloting process several times now, Tesh didn't know if she could ever get used to it. The Tulyan method of piloting podships was so different from that of the Parviis. In a sense it seemed more personal to her, merging as they did with the sentient spacecraft. She wondered how the Aopoddae felt about it.

Prior to meeting Eshaz and sharing time with him, Tesh had considered his people her enemy. After all, they were a race that wanted to take away what Parviis had, control over the enigmatic podships that traversed the galaxy at tachyon speeds. She had seen Tulyans over the centuries, whenever they came around the Parvii Fold to perform timeseeing duties and other tasks, and whenever they rode as passengers in ships she piloted ... but now she was beginning to perceive them as a tragically lost people, making a desperate, last-ditch attempt to regain their power and perceived purpose.

They are no longer my enemy, she thought as tears formed in her eyes.

With remarkable clarity she was beginning to see the error of Parvii ways, of aggressive actions that might have led to the extinction of any other galactic race except the Tulyans. Ironically, they were tough and resilient and were actually fighting to survive, unexpected qualities in a race that had professed pacifism for so long.

All her life Tesh had known that Tulyans were nearly immortal, since they were immune to disease and other forms of cellular degeneration, though it was known that they could be injured or even killed in accidents. Now she was beginning to understand that their twin curses of longevity and pacifism had forced them to watch as the galaxy and its Timeweb infrastructure disintegrated in front of their eyes. It must have been a terrible penalty for them to pay, a constant reminder of their supreme failures and of their once-glorious past.

At long last, their pacifism was over, and so, perhaps, was their longevity. The increasing physical discomforts the Tulyans were experiencing suggested that a process of bodily disorder and deterioration might be beginning in their race. Additionally she had heard that hundreds of Tulyans had disappeared, while working on their limited assignments around the galaxy. Though Tesh was not inside their skins, she felt as if she was beginning to get inside their heads, suffering with them, thinking more like them than a Parvii.

Nevertheless, it troubled her that her own people had scattered outside the Tulyan Starcloud and flown off in disorder. To her knowledge, nothing like that had ever happened before. Tesh knew full well what Woldn would do next, but she could not permit that to happen....

That morning at the Tulyan Starcloud, Tesh approached Eshaz, in the lounge of the Visitor's Center. She slid into a seat opposite him at a table, after raising the chair to conform to her body size, which even in its magnified state was still considerably smaller than Tulyans. Since this was a diplomatic facility, the furnishings were designed to accommodate a variety of racial types and sizes. The two of them ordered cocaxy drinks in frosty, frozen glasses. It was as if Eshaz had waited for her to arrive before getting anything for himself, even though they had made no arrangements to meet.

"We received a message from Master Noah," the Tulyan said. "He asked about you." "So?" She tried to still the quickened beating of her heart. "How is that of interest to me?" Reaching into a body pouch in his side, he brought out a piece of folded parchment and placed it in front of her. "A transcript of Noah's message," he said. "A touch on your skin could tell me how it is of interest to you."

Tesh took a sip of the tart, aromatic drink and scanned the document, which had been printed in the widely understood language of Galeng. Noah's words were few, and she finished them quickly. "It's just an official communication; nothing personal here at all."

"That depends upon how you look at it. Right after mentioning your name, he asks that you and your traveling companions return as soon as possible."

"Don't be silly. I'm looking at his words now, and they refer to all of us, not just me."

"On the contrary, there is a certain emphasis, a *weightiness* to what he is saying. Our diplomatic people have examined it carefully, and there is no doubt. He is asking about your welfare, and wants to see you."

"Well, maybe you're right." Tesh smiled stiffly. "After all, I am not without certain charms. But I must discuss something else with you, something of far greater consequence than the fates of two people in a huge, crumbling galaxy."

Eshaz nodded solemnly. "Proceed."

The Parvii woman had something very important to say, one of the secrets of her race. She struggled to express herself, having practiced how she might say this, but faltered under the enormous gravity of all the warnings she and her ancestors had received against revealing such information. Finally she paused, unable to get the words out the way she wanted.

Reaching across the table, Eshaz made contact with the crackling energy field that was Tesh's second skin, touching her projection-enlarged left hand. In performing this truthing touch, he absorbed her thoughts as Tulyans could do with another galactic race … but she knew he still didn't obtain the information she had to reveal to him. She sighed deeply, trying to calm herself.

Presently Tesh told him without speaking, *My people are very aggressive, with angry tempers. You Tulyans may have won a battle with your newfound telepathic powers, your mindlink. But you have stirred up a huge hornet's nest, and the Parvii potential is much greater than yours. We have rapid breeding methods, and the capacity to use the most devastating psychic weapons in the galaxy, with the concentrated focal power of millions of Parviis at a time. In ancient times, my people employed these devices against Tulyans and other races, destroying entire fleets and planets.*

She paused, letting the information sink in. He didn't transmit any thought response, or say anything, as if he knew she still had more to say.

Continuing her internal monologue, she told him, *The ancient knowledge is still available, held in sacred reserve by our war priests. As you know, I am an outcast, no longer in contact with Woldn's morphic field, but I still sense that something big is brewing. I know my people well, and what the legends say we will do in a time of dire need. At this very moment they have sought sanctuary in the Parvii Fold, where breedmasters and war priests are working together for a retaliatory strike.*

Now Eshaz pulled back. His gray, slitted eyes flashed with alarm. "This is very disturbing."

She spoke, too. "A great deal is at stake. I want you to accompany me on a diplomatic mission to the Parvii Fold, before my people can regenerate and mount a counterattack. We must convince Woldn that war between our races is suicidal, and…."

"And that we need to work together to preserve and repair the galactic infrastructure of Timeweb," he said, interrupting. "Tulyans and Parviis must use the entire podship fleet cooperatively for the most massive project in history. Thousands of ships to transport repair teams all over the galaxy, to as many trouble spots as possible. For the sake of harmony, Parviis can pilot the ships, while Tulyans such as yourself can perform the web repairs."

"You and I are beginning to understand each other," she said with a slight smile. "Let's hope it bodes well for the others we must convince."

"You would return to the Parvii Fold?" Eshaz whispered to her. "But you are an outcast, forbidden from returning to your people."

"I must risk everything, as all of us must. The stakes are too high for any concerns about personal safety. Yes, I would do that, and much more."

Finally, Eshaz sat back, and stared across the table at her.

She pushed the cocaxy drink away.

"I will seek the advice of the Council," he said.

Eshaz requested an emergency meeting with the Elders, and they assented. He told them Tesh's story, and her astounding proposal. A short while later they summoned her before them, and listened attentively to the details. She told them she wanted Eshaz to accompany her to the Parvii Fold, perhaps with a diplomatic team of Tulyans. Then she clasped her hands in front of herself, awaiting their decision.

"You say you want Parvii pilots to transport podships around the galaxy, containing teams of Tulyan repair teams," First Elder Kre'n said, after a brief conference with the other Elders. The Tulyan leader paused, as if expecting a response.

"That's right," Tesh said, filling in the quiet that had fallen across the great chamber.

"Tulyans and Parviis can never work together in a meaningful way," Kre'n declared. "We agree that web repairs are needed, but for that we don't need Parviis at all. We can pilot podships *and* do the infrastructure repairs. Your request is denied."

"But you are in grave danger!"

"So are we all." Kre'n waved an arm dismissively. "You have our permission to leave the starcloud on your 'diplomatic mission,' but *alone*. It will serve no purpose for any Tulyans to accompany you, as it could inflame the passions of Woldn in an unproductive way."

"Not even Eshaz? Woldn knows him."

Eshaz grabbed her by the arm, squeezing it. "Don't argue with the Elders."

She pulled away. "I'm not. I'm just...."

"Their decisions are carefully thought out," Eshaz said, "and based on reasons you could never understand." He glanced up at their unsmiling faces, then back at her. "The Elders will not reconsider."

He escorted her forcefully out of the chamber.

"Your people can never defend against a Parvii telepathic onslaught," she said, in the corridor outside. "You have no concept of the terrible destructive force that war priests can generate. They have a focal weapon, drawing upon the primal energies of the universe."

His eyes widened. "I have heard stories of such a thing, legends. But we have a highly advanced form of mindlink now, which we didn't have in the old days. We will not fall so easily."

"But why risk a battle with the Parviis? No matter how it goes, it will be a waste of valuable time and resources."

"Go quickly," Eshaz said, as they reached the smooth plax deck outside. "I will remain here with my people in our small moment of triumph and renewal, working with the few hundred wild podships we have, practicing with them on the podways that are protected by the starcloud."

"Your moment of triumph will not last long." She narrowed her eyes. "Is that all you're going to say to me? Just go, and good luck to you? Don't you understand the immensity of this?"

"The Council has spoken. We must do as they command."

"You've argued with them before."

"I've tried to *persuade* them of certain things. But after working with them for so long, I know when it is utterly hopeless, and when it is certain to raise their ire. I must say, they don't trust you, don't really believe you. The truthing touch did not reveal any of this additional information, so they're assuming it's an insidious Parvii trick, and they wonder what else you might have hidden. They would rather spend their time and energy on shoring up the defenses here."

"I'm very worried about this. Woldn is going to strike back, using ancient weapons."

"With the stakes so high, we won't be routed easily."

"I hope you're right," Tesh said. "But won't you come with me?"

"No."

"Why not?"

"For reasons you can never understand. Now go! You're wasting time."

While packing her things and readying for departure, Tesh heard a rap at her door. Touching a remote pad to open it, she greeted Acey and Dux.

"Eshaz told us about your diplomatic mission," Dux said. "Let us go with you."

She frowned. "For the sake of adventure, or to really help?" she asked.

"I don't think I can give you a good answer to that," Dux admitted. "If I say what you want to hear, you'll think I'm lying."

"That's about the only thing you could have said to please me," she said, with a grin that flashed white teeth.

"We won't get in the way," Acey promised. "We just want to go with you as your friends."

"Be careful," she said. "You might say something that doesn't sound sincere."

Acey looked crestfallen, and Tesh added quickly, "I would like both of you to come along as my friends. I appreciate your devotion, and I've come to believe that all the races must work together. Woldn will not be pleased to see you, but such contacts must begin someplace."

"So we are emissaries?" Dux asked.

"Isn't every member of every race, whenever they come into contact with another galactic species." Looking both boys over, Tesh added, "You couldn't possibly be spies."

"Do you include the Mutatis in your vision of races working together?" Dux asked.

"Well, perhaps there are exceptions," she said, with a small smile. "You must be on your very best behavior, though, and the trip will be dangerous. There are tremendous perils on the way to the Parvii Fold, and as I told you I am an outcast, forbidden to mix with my people ever again."

Dux, who could wax philosophical at times, responded, "Safety is never more than an illusion anyway, no matter where … or who … you are."

"I travel light," she said, in a cheery voice. "How about you guys?"

"We're ready!" Acey said….

Eshaz secured the necessary departure permission from the Council for the last-minute inclusion of the teenage boys. The Elders were only too happy to let the Parvii woman go, along with the Humans.

"Even assuming the best about her, she is on a fool's mission," Dabiggio said.

"So it seems," Kre'n said, wrinkling her bronze-scaled face in worry. "But what if we're wrong?"

"Not even worth considering," the big Tulyan responded.

In the tension of the Council Chamber, Eshaz wisely remained silent, then bowed and left.

After delivering the clearance to Tesh, Eshaz caught a shuttle home. On the way, he saw her podship slide away from its docking bay and head into space. The sentient craft accelerated, and vanished in a flash of green light.

Chapter Sixty-Five

It is a deadly, ancient clash of inbred racial purposes, those of the Tulyans and those of the Parviis. And at the middle of their conflict is yet another race, the Aopoddae, the most enigmatic of all ... and perhaps the most important.
—Noah Watanabe, *Reflections on my Life*, Guardian Publications

On board the podship, Tesh left the teenagers in the passenger compartment, then entered the sectoid chamber by herself. The boys understood in general terms that she was piloting the ship, and had asked her for details, but she avoided telling them very much. They were her friends, but she had not felt comfortable discussing certain subjects with them yet, things that she had been taught from an early age were important Parvii secrets.

Already, she had gone farther than any Parvii was permitted. If Woldn learned what she told the Tulyans, she could be put to death, but the galactic stakes were so high that she had to take the chance. Secrets. She was beginning to think it was a dirty word, and a tool with which she and others like her had been controlled for so long.

Tesh was violating another prohibition now, in taking the boys to the Parvii Fold. Oh, she had excuses worked out in her mind for Woldn, that the Human teenagers were Guardians as she was, and they were working with her to maintain the integrity of the galactic web. This was all true, but she would have to do a lot of smooth talking to convince the Eye of the Swarm. There was also the matter of the Tulyan she had befriended, an alien who had been facing similar challenges regarding his own racial secrets. To Tesh, and she suspected Eshaz felt this way as well, such secrets didn't matter anymore. The integrity of the entire galaxy was at stake, not territorial claims or racial power structures.

She was beginning to doubt many of the "sacred" teachings that had been passed on to her during her lifetime, and had been wondering how much of the information had been a clever web of deceit. Now she was taking two of her Human friends to the most clandestine of all Parvii gathering places, which could subject her to severe discipline from Woldn, but she was willing to face that possibility. She felt newly strong and defiant, and could not wait to tell him with determination and absolute certainty what needed to be done for the sake of the galaxy.

It took longer than Tesh had anticipated for her to cross space, since she ran into a stretch of bad podways on the far side of the Oxxi Asteroid Belt, and had to slow down. Only a few years ago, when she piloted other podships on these and other routes, she only rarely encountered this sort of problem. Eshaz had told her that entire galactic sectors had collapsed since then, from the continual entropic decay of Timeweb. This was of increasing concern to her, as it was to the dedicated Tulyan caretaker.

After almost two hours, the podship finally entered the treacherous Asteroid Funnel leading into the galactic fold of the Parviis. Inside the passenger compartment, Acey and Dux looked out portholes and saw grisly clusters of tiny Parvii bodies outside floating in the vacuum ... along with the tumbling, luminous white stones of the funnel, stones that were slowed by the collective mass of the corpses. So was the podship, which had to carefully negotiate the funnel in order to elude the stones and thick groupings of bodies.

In the green glow of the sectoid chamber, Tesh was even more horrified than her two passengers, but she kept advancing toward her destination anyway, with tears streaming down her face. This was the most terrible Parvii tragedy she had ever seen, and in all likelihood the greatest in their entire history.

Finally the spacecraft emerged into the immense, pocketlike Parvii Fold, where even more chaos became apparent. There were clusters of bodies everywhere in sight, floating and bumping into one another, and more podships than she had ever seen before—thousands and thousands of sentient spacecraft overflowing the moorage basin. Some of the vessels were tethered together, but many were not and just floated aimlessly in the airless vacuum, as if even the life force of the sentient creatures themselves had gone out of commission.

Around the faintly glowing Palace of Woldn, Tesh saw a comparatively small swarm of Parviis—a few million of them flying to and fro lethargically, with nowhere near their usual hummingbird energy. As she tethered her ship, she saw that the grand palace was weakening, since the Parviis holding it together were losing strength and causing structural deficiencies and inconsistencies in the simulated gravity system. Many of them had a sickly, yellowish sheen to their bodies.

Leaving her personal magnification system off, Tesh entered the large palace by riding in on a shoulder of Dux Hannah, who walked beside Acey Zelk. Both of the boys wore their thick green protective suits and helmets, to enable them to breathe and to survive in the subzero environment. They were like giants entering the building, but the structure was on such a majestic scale that they still had plenty of headroom.

Inside a vaulted chamber on the second level, Woldn lay on a bed formed by his fellow Parviis and fabric, while a small number of his advisers sat or stood nearby. None of them were flying, and many looked gaunt as they walked about arthritically, with the natural color drained from their faces.

Like a Lilliputian speaking to giants, Tesh told her Human companions to find a place to sit off to one side, and they did as she wished, on the simulated marble floor.

Approaching the Eye of the Swarm, Tesh told him where she had been, and asked what had happened to him.

"You!" Woldn exclaimed, half rising out of his bed. Tall by Parvii standards, and wiry-thin, he wore a dark robe. "I forbid you to be here! And you bring Humans? What madness is this?"

"I have come nonetheless," she said, in a gentle voice. "For your sake, my honored leader, and for the sake of all galactic races. We come on a mission of utmost importance."

"What sort of drivel is this? Leave my sight, before I have you killed."

Four of his aides moved toward her, but stopped when Acey made a motion to intervene. The Eye of the Swarm was sending them telepathic commands.

"You always were outspoken, weren't you?" Woldn said, to Tesh. "Is there no escape from your meddling, even on my deathbed?" He sat up, arranging tiny pillows around him. "Once, I had high hopes for you, but you let me down. You let all of us down."

Tesh moved closer to him, and felt herself engage with his weakened morphic field. Though Parviis could transmit thoughts telepathically to one another, and could limit what information they passed to each other through this means, she instead opened her mind and did not attempt to conceal anything from him. Feeling the outflow of her thoughts, Tesh watched the expression on his narrow, creased face as he assimilated the data and perused it. She revealed her ideals to him, how she thought Humans, Tulyans, Parviis, and other galactic races needed to work together.

"You have experienced a great deal in your life," Woldn said, at last. "Important things."

"Yes," she said, softly.

"Your intentions are good. I see that. But I cannot agree with your reason for coming here. You ask too much. My people will never work on equal terms with Tulyans or Humans. For millennia, for as long as the memory expands and the stories are told, Parviis have been the dominant race of the three. That will not change under my leadership."

She said nothing, and hoped that he would cogitate further, analyzing the information she had provided from new angles. But he was sick and weak, and might not have the capability to do so.

In a diminished, cheerless voice, Woldn said that the new defensive weapons shot by the Tulyans—comets, meteors, and radioactive asteroids—had caused immense harm to the Parviis, disrupting the energy fields that connected them paranormally with their brethren, throwing the tiny people into disarray. The damage extended to some Parviis who had been piloting podships out in deep space, causing them to fall off course into uncharted regions. It also killed most of the breedmasters and war priests, preventing the symbiotic segments from organizing a retaliatory force to strike back at the Tulyans.

"It is terrible to see what has happened to my brethren," Tesh said. She nodded toward an uncovered window, where bodies floated in space.

Woldn nodded, then continued. He said he withdrew all of his people into the Parvii Fold, along with every podship still in their control... more than one hundred thousand of them. But in what had become known as "the Tulyan Incident," at least eighty percent of the Parvii people had died. It was the greatest catastrophe in their history.

She stood and listened sympathetically while Woldn lamented at length, wondering how the tragedy could have possibly occurred when he and his followers had worked so hard, the way his people always had. Parviis had swarmed the perimeter of the Tulyan Starcloud many times before and had dealt with Tulyan defensive measures, always getting through eventually to recapture podships—but never in the past had Parviis been injured or killed by Tulyans. It used to be easy to blockade the Tulyans for punishment, driving them crazy by confining them to their impenetrable starcloud, but it was much different now.

"If I survive this," Woldn said, "I don't want to risk going back there for a long time." He swung out of bed and paced around slowly, in his robe.

"The Tulyans have developed a weapon we never expected," Tesh said, "but our troubles go beyond anything they did to us. Our plight is another symptom of the deterioration of Timeweb. We Parviis can no longer go our own selfish way as we have in the past. We must cooperate with other galactic races from now on ... and especially with the Tulyans, whom we have always sought to dominate and humiliate."

"We have never charged for galactic transportation services," Woldn said indignantly, "and have provided them faithfully for millions of years."

"With the exception of charging Tulyans for their limited travel rights," she said, "by making them timesee for us."

"Well, yes," he admitted, folding his arms across his chest. "But that's so minor in the overall scheme of things that it's hardly worth mentioning."

Tesh knew that the historical currency of her people was not money or precious jewels; it was the thrill of mastering the magnificent podships … the supreme ecstasy of piloting them across vast distances, while keeping other galactic races from doing so. But Woldn's impassioned argument was making no headway with her at all. It didn't alter, in the least, what needed to be done.

In a firm voice she said to him, "Your morphic field is weakened and might never recover. Forgive me for saying so, but you might die. Have you appointed a replacement?"

He stopped pacing. His shoulders sagged. His entire body sagged. "My heir apparent is dead, along with three backups. The entire order of succession that I established." Gazing sadly at her, he said, "Once I considered you a candidate, with your strong will and intelligence. But you went too far in your defiance, and disappointed me."

Her eyes twinkled softly. "I never would have guessed how much you liked me."

"I have never *liked* you. I have only observed you carefully, and have discussed you at length with my top advisers."

"And now?" she said, grasping at possibilities. "Is there still a chance for me? You have seen the loyalty in my heart, the great vision I have for the galaxy."

He shook his head stubbornly. "Because of your rebelliousness I would never teach you the way of the morphic field, no matter the situation. But the secret will not die with me. I will heal, and so will my people." He looked away from her, as if uncertain of his words.

Going closer to him, Tesh said, "But if you die without a successor, there will be no Eye of the Swarm. With no one to take your place and establish a Timeweb-spanning morphic field, our people can no longer pilot the fleet of podships across the galaxy. I think you should make all of the podships available to the Tulyans immediately, so that they can accelerate their critical work. Do it with them: Parvii pilots to transport Tulyans, so that they can do the web caretaking tasks."

"*Their* critical work? What about *our* critical work? Without the podships, we would be nothing."

"I'm not suggesting that you turn the ships over to them. As I said, we can maintain Parvii pilots."

"It's a trick. I don't trust them."

"Then put a small swarm into each podship, enough telepathic power to defend it."

"No. We are weakened, we are ill."

"We need to get beyond this discussion," she said. "The Tulyans must maintain and repair the galaxy the way they used to, long before you or I were born."

"If we lose the podships," he said with a glare, "what is our purpose? We will go extinct."

"Our prospects are not good now. Besides, every race in the galaxy will go extinct if you don't cooperate."

He stood speechless for only a moment. "In time my people will heal," he insisted, "and everything will be back to normal again."

"There's nothing more I can say to you then," Tesh said, angrily.

"Everything will be back to normal again," he repeated, with a far-away look in his eyes, as if his mind had slipped out of gear.

Frustrated at her inability to sway him, Tesh departed with her two friends. Before getting the podship underway she stood in the passenger compartment and told them, "I can't tell you how disappointed I am at Woldn's selfishness. I hate to say it, but if all of my people die, maybe that would be the best thing that could happen."

"Maybe he'll change his mind," Acey said. His wide face was etched with concern.

"I don't think he ever will," she said.

"Why don't we go see Noah and consult with him?" Acey asked. "We know he escaped from his sister's laboratory, so he's probably back at Guardian headquarters now."

"Maybe you're right," Tesh said, brightening a little. "I'd like to see him, and with any luck it shouldn't take us long to get there."

"One thing though, Acey," Dux said. "We'd better steer clear of Giovanni Nehr, or we'll do something we'll regret."

"Guess you're right." Acey looked dark, then grinned disarmingly. "Hey, we should *thank* him. If he hadn't boxed us up and shipped us into space, we wouldn't have gone on the wild pod hunts, or ever seen the Parvii Fold."

"Just stay away from him," Dux said. "No threats, no nothing."

"All right." Acey thought for a moment, and asked Tesh, "What about the Doge's electronic surveillance system around Canopa? We can't just swagger back into the pod station and take a shuttle down to the planet."

"There is a way of taking the podship directly to Canopa," she said, "circumventing the pod station and the most advanced scanner nets. It's a tricky landing maneuver, but I can do it."

"Is it dangerous?" Acey asked.

"You bet." Then she squinted at him and added, "But that only makes it more appealing to you, doesn't it?"

Chapter Sixty-Six

We believe that the Aopoddae may have evolved from something quite different, and that they did not always look like the podships they are today. We have long known that they are shapeshifters, for they can adjust their cabins, cargo areas, and other on-board components. It has been assumed that they are not Mutatis, but if this assumption is incorrect, our enemies have plans we cannot possibly fathom.

—Doge Anton del Velli

After crossing space, Tesh took her podship down to the surface of the planet Canopa, avoiding the orbital pod station and landing in a wooded clearing near the concealed entrance to Guardian headquarters.

To accomplish this, she had taken a circuitous, multi-speed route that enabled her to pass undetected through the electronic surveillance net in Canopa's skies, using skills she had learned from one of the most talented of all Parvii pilots, Ado. Centuries ago, under his very special tutelage, she had been taught that there were instances of pod stations being damaged or destroyed, so that Aopoddae vessels occasionally had to take alternate landing measures. Ado had taught her how to elude electronic security and virtually anything else in her path, from tumbling rocks in the Asteroid Funnel to objects floating through the atmospheric envelopes of planets....

A squadron of robots entered the clearing as she and the teenagers disembarked. Noting green -and-brown Guardian colors on the machines, Tesh sighed in relief.

"I'm Jimu," a small, patched-together robot announced in a formal voice. "I have identified each of you by your spectral characteristics. Please follow me."

The three visitors followed, though they knew the way.

Just inside the entrance to the subterranean headquarters, Noah greeted them stiffly.

"They landed a podship out there in the meadow," Jimu said. "My robots are putting an electronic net over it to prevent detection."

"We saw it all on a security screen," Noah said, shaking his head in disapproval.

"It was a bit tricky getting through the planet's security net," Tesh said, "but I can do it again to get out of here. The way I do it, they don't even know I'm getting through."

Noah motioned to Thinker, and told the boys to go with the cerebral machine. They walked away slowly, but lingered to eavesdrop.

Scowling at Tesh, Noah then said, "You were undetected by the planetary net, but we picked you up on our system?"

"Different systems, different results. I came in fully aware of both systems. Look, Noah, I could explain it to you in detail, but there are other matters we need to discuss first."

"We don't know if you consider us Guardians anymore," Acey said. "But we want to stay with Tesh wherever she goes."

"Just go with Thinker right now," Noah said in a firm voice. "I also have some things to discuss with Tesh." Frowning, he watched the flat-bodied robot walk away with Acey and Dux.

As the boys entered a burrow tunnel, Acey told Thinker excitedly how he and Dux went on two podship hunts, and rounded up almost four hundred sentient spaceships. The boys provided some of the most colorful details.

To Thinker, this was entirely new information, beyond anything in his data banks. He asked for more specifics, and found himself intrigued and astounded by what he heard.

Somberly, Noah turned to Tesh. "I'll decide the priorities here," he said, "and I don't like your daredevil flying. If you brought a podship in, that means the Mutatis might do the same, and use one of their doomsday weapons against Canopa ... or against another Human-ruled planet."

"I don't think that could possibly...."

Noah cut her off. "If the Mutatis learn what you have done, a new avenue of attack could be opened. If they can land without a pod station, it becomes a lot harder to prevent attacks."

"I am among the elite of all Parvii pilots, and hardly anyone can match my skills. Besides, all of the Mutatis that we saw in merchant schooners have been denied access to space travel... just as Humans have been cut off. The shapeshifters don't have their own podships, and neither do your people."

"You shouldn't have come without calling," Noah said. "You put all of us in danger."

A silence fell between them. Noah shot a hard stare at her, and when she gave him a hostile look in return, he wondered if she could see beyond his veneer to the attraction he felt for her. Now that Tesh was no longer with his nephew Anton, there was nothing to keep her and Noah away from each other. Nothing except for the tension that constantly existed between them. Now something sparkled in her eyes, like a little dance of light. A glint of attraction for him? But it only lasted for a moment, before her own veneer replaced it.

Noticing that she was beginning to shake slightly, Noah placed a hand on her shoulder and said, "I wish ... I wish for so much, but there have always been complications surrounding us."

Her eyes flashed. "What are you trying to say?"

"That we should understand one another better, that we should...." He looked away, and instantly regretted letting his guard down with her.

Upset, she pushed his hand away and said, "I'm a Guardian, and that's all." He had trouble reading her. Previously she had pursued him physically, but now he wondered if that had only been a ploy on her part, to manipulate him for her own purposes. Still, he couldn't help wondering what it would be like to make love to her, this woman of a different race. She certainly was attractive, especially when angry. Feeling a slight flush, he took a deep breath and struggled to suppress his emotions.

"We have certain feelings for each other," Noah said, choosing his words carefully. He felt awkward, though. "Or should I say, *toward* each other. In any event, the emotions are there, and we both know it. But whatever those feelings are, and wherever they could take us, I have always known that we need to set them aside. Whether it is affection or loathing, we cannot let them get in the way of our duties. Our priorities must lie elsewhere."

"Nothing else occurred to me," she huffed.

He said bitterly, "Then we agree on something after all."

"I have important information to tell you," she said. "I just came from the Parvii Fold, and...."

This elevated Noah's anger, reminding him of the way she brought her podship in. "Yeah, you flew through the security net and imperiled us all. I told you how I feel about that. Listen, I have other things to do now, so we'll have to talk later." Before she could respond, he whirled and stalked off.

To Noah Watanabe, problems were piling on top of problems, big ones coming in so quickly that he was feeling overwhelmed by them. Tesh's unapproved podship landing would require some thought. For the time being, he notified his security force to put her and the boys on lockdown. They would not be allowed to leave the headquarters without his express permission.

The evening before, Noah had been trying to deal with another big challenge, his continuing inability to enter Timeweb or control podships. Again, he had failed to make the necessary mental leap, and he'd been left wondering why. Noah had been sensing cosmic disturbances all around him.

In addition, he'd been trying to improve another difficult situation. Recently he had made diplomatic overtures to Doge Anton, his nephew who had never formally resigned from the Guardians. So far Anton had not responded, but Noah wondered if it might be possible for the two of them, at long last, to reform the Merchant Prince Alliance into a more environmentally-aware entity. That would not be easy, because of the influence Francella seemed to have over her son, whom she had brought to power. Noah was sick of the politics, the constant small-minded maneuvering and jockeying for position when much larger issues were at stake.

As he entered a dimly lit tunnel, Noah saw Thinker approaching.

"The boys have given me important information," the robot said. He described the successful wild podship hunts.

"At least that's some good news," Noah said.

"There's more, Master Noah. As you know, the Parviis have a vast galactic network of pilots who are in control of podships, and they're the ones who cut off podship travel to Human and Mutati worlds."

Noah nodded. He had learned this previously from Tesh.

"Master, their transportation network is in complete disarray. At the Tulyan Starcloud, the Tulyans mounted a surprise attack against the Parvii swarms and scattered them into the galaxy. Many Parviis died, and the powerful morphic field that keeps their race together has fallen apart. Their leader withdrew the entire podship fleet to a secret place, the Parvii Fold."

"So that's what Tesh wanted to tell me," Noah said. He thought for a moment. "And Eshaz. Where is he?"

"Still at the starcloud, with the podships they captured."

"The boys say that Tesh came here to discuss using diplomacy on the Parviis. She couldn't convince Woldn on her own, and wants your help. Tesh thinks the entire podship fleet should be used to transport Timeweb repair teams around the galaxy."

"We'd better find her right away," Noah said.

"Exactly what I was thinking," the robot said.

Chapter Sixty-Seven

For every life form that is declining, another is in its ascension. It is one of the eternal balances of galactic ecology, and an engine by which the system continues to advance.

—Master Noah Watanabe

Acey Zelk lay awake in an agitated state, staring into the shadows of the barracks building, one of several inside the largest subterranean chamber. He heard Dux sleeping on the bunk just above his, and through a high window he saw a faint glow of indirect lighting on the ceiling of the natural cavern. Before retiring for the night, Acey had gone off on his own and asked a few questions of a pretty young woman, pretending to be Giovanni Nehr's friend. Now he knew exactly where Gio was in another chamber, inside one of the robot-assembly buildings.

Gio, wearing his foolish body armor, had his own private quarters there; he was receiving favorable treatment as if he were a general in Noah's forces instead of a supervisor of robotic assemblies. Even that position irked Acey, because it showed that Gio was gaining undeserved respect in the Guardian organization.

Acey knew he had given his word to Dux to stay away from the man, and that meant something. But other things were more important. He could not ignore what Gio had done to them.

Silently, Acey slipped out of bed and grabbed his shoes and clothing, which he put on when he was outside the barracks. Like a shadow, he hurried through a tunnel toward the robot section, following the directions that the young woman had provided. On the way he passed sentient machines as they went about their sleepless work, carrying materials and blinking and beeping with their electronic communication systems. Acey felt a slight current of cool air in the passageway, which he attributed to all of the activity around him. The robots hardly gave him any notice.

Reaching the designated structure, which had been painted Guardian colors, Acey opened a door and slipped inside. Just as the young woman had described, it was an assembly area and an inspection facility for former Red Beret robots, which were disassembled there and checked in detail. Robot parts lay in neat groupings, and work was continuing under the supervision of a small, blinking robot.

It was quite noisy in the building, and Acey wondered how anyone could sleep through it. He got his answer when he opened the door to Gio's quarters and slipped inside.

The windowless room was filled with white noise like the steady pulse of an ocean, or the inside of a seashell, a continuous sound that drowned out all of the activity outside. In dim light coming through cracks around the door, Acey saw body armor on the floor and Gio on a bed, fast asleep. Leaning down, Acey removed a puissant gun from its holster, and set the charge. A yellow energy chamber on top of the barrel glowed.

Finding the white-noise transmitter on a bed table, Acey adjusted the background murmur, making it go up and down. With the glowing weapon behind him to keep the light low, he stood at the head of the bed and watched as Gio began to toss and turn, his sleep disturbed.

With his eyes still closed, Gio reached for the noise transmitter, but could not find it on the side table. He opened his eyes, and at first did not see the intruder.

"Looking for this?" Acey asked, tossing the transmitter on the table. "Or this?" He shoved the glowing barrel of the gun in Gio's face.

Startled, Gio tried to pull back, but the agile teenager jumped on the bed and straddled him, with the gun jammed against his forehead.

"What are *you* doing here?" Gio asked, recognizing his attacker.

"That's my question for you," Acey said. "I'm here to stop you from pulling off your next nasty little scheme." He saw fear in the man's eyes.

"Please don't kill me," Gio whimpered.

In disgust, Acey swung the gun and hit him hard on the side of the head.

Dazed for a moment, Gio lashed out and threw the teenager off, causing Acey to tumble to the floor. At the same time Gio set off an alarm, and klaxons sounded.

In Noah's office, the Master of the Guardians and Thinker had been holding a late night meeting with Tesh, discussing the surprising new information about podships—those under Tulyan control and those at the Parvii Fold—and the apparent breakdown of Parvii power.

As Tesh spoke about her own people and all of the tragic deaths, her eyes misted over, but she seemed able to overcome it and find an inner strength. Newly impressed, Noah felt his anger subsiding. She had come in and landed like a hot-rodder, but her flying skills were superb and she did have important things to tell him. Things that were better said in person than over communication links that could have been intercepted or compromised. For the moment Noah and Tesh set aside their differences, though he felt the residual tension between them, and knew from her demeanor that she did, too.

"Acey and Dux say you tried to convince the Parviis to allow their podship fleet to be used by the Tulyans for repair work on the galactic infrastructure … Timeweb. Apparently, Woldn didn't like your proposal."

"That's right, but I still consider myself one of your Guardians, and I'm here seeking your leadership on this critical matter involving galactic ecology … the phrase you coined, Master Noah."

"What do the Tulyan leaders think of your idea? I assume you discussed it with them?"

"Of course, but they don't think Parviis and Tulyans can ever work cooperatively on a project of that scale. They say they don't need Parviis to pilot podships, that Tulyans can do that, and the web repairs, too."

"That sounds short-sighted," Noah said. "But I suppose it's the result of millennia of hatred and loathing between the two races."

"The Tulyan Elders think I'm a wild card, and since I'm a Parvii they don't trust me. But Noah, if I work with you and the Guardians—offering solutions for the huge ecological crisis—maybe they'll take me seriously. Maybe they'll take *us* seriously." She paused. "The Tulyans are an ancient people, with a history of pacifism. They scattered Woldn's swarms this time, but I don't think the Tulyans should try to go against the Parviis again without help, not even with the weakened state of my people."

"So that's where Humans come in, eh?" Noah said. "We're much more warlike, and can stand up to your tough brothers and sisters."

She shook her head. "I came to you, Noah, because the Tulyans respect you—and because Humans can convince them of the need for diplomacy in this matter. If we send a joint Human-Tulyan diplomatic mission to the Parviis, maybe Woldn will finally listen."

He nodded, but hesitantly. "Maybe."

She went on to tell him what she had related earlier to Eshaz, that the ancient Parviis had used powerful telepathic weapons against their enemies, and that Woldn had obviously gone back to the Parvii Fold to resurrect those powers.

"But Woldn said most of the breedmasters and war priests were killed when the Tulyans disrupted his morphic field, thus slowing down the regeneration of Parvii telepathic power." She paused. "I feel we must move quickly with diplomatic overtures, before my people find a way to regenerate their destructive powers. As a species we are survivors, and as bad as it looks for Parviis now, I think they will find a way."

"Diplomatic overtures, you say, and not a military strike?"

"I would never cooperate with an attack against my people. For their sake, and for that of everyone else, diplomacy is the only way."

"But couldn't it come with military might reinforcing it?"

Folding her arms across her chest, Tesh stared at him. "I will not discuss such matters. If you keep pressing me, we shall have nothing more to discuss."

"I wouldn't say that, Tesh. Actually, you showed good sense coming here, providing us with reconnaissance about what happened to the Parviis and verifying that they still control thousands of podships. I also want to meet with the Tulyan Elders, and I would like you to take me there."

She was about to say something when the alarm klaxons went off, with the pattern of sound indicating the location of trouble.

"Robot section!" Thinker said, heading for the door. Noah ran around the slower robot, followed by Tesh.

Human and robot Guardians were hurrying ahead of Noah, and he ran after them, just ahead of his two companions. Reaching one of the robot-assembly buildings, Noah saw that the doors were wide open. Inside, sentient machines and Human Guardians were gathered at the interior door that led to Giovanni Nehr's private quarters.

Pushing his way through and entering the room, Noah saw Gio and Acey rolling on the floor, fighting for control of a puissant pistol. The weapon glowed

443

yellow. A shot rang out, and one of the robots fell. Then the gun fell, and one of the Guardian women kicked it away.

Two Guardian men grabbed Gio to restrain him, while a pair of robots took hold of Acey.

Noah demanded to know what they were quarreling about, but both Acey and Gio sulked without saying anything.

"Dux and Acey told you about the prison moon quarrel," Tesh said, "when they claimed that Gio tried to push Dux out of an airvator, but it's gone beyond that. Now the boys think Gio drugged them and shipped them into space."

"Is that so?" Noah said to Acey.

The young man nodded.

"Well?" Noah said, looking hard at Giovanni Nehr. "Did you do it?"

Standing up straight, the chisel-featured man said, "None of it. The boys are liars."

"Acey, what proof do you have?" Noah asked, waving off the Guardian robots. They released their hold on the teenager.

"Dux and I saw what he did on the airvator, and we tried to set aside our anger about that. Then he drugged us and put us in a spacebox. We could have been killed, and he didn't care. He just wanted to get rid of us."

"Tell me more about this alleged drugging," Noah said. "Start at the beginning."

"To be honest," Acey said, glaring over at Gio, "we didn't actually see him do anything, but he's the only one who *could* have done it. For some reason, he wanted to get rid of us."

"Earlier, you promised me that you would set your differences aside," Noah said. "Now you've decided to break your word based upon a mere suspicion?"

"I'm sorry," the boy said, hanging his head, "but I know he did it to us. No one can ever change my mind about that."

"Gio is in charge of new robot recruits from the Red Berets," Noah said, "making sure they are all torn down and thoroughly checked. He's been doing a great job, and I trust him completely."

"Well we don't," Acey said. "You'd better tear him down like one of those robots and find out what's going on inside his brain, because he has a really dark side."

Noah shook his head. "I find that impossible to believe."

"His brother is the Supreme General of the Merchant Prince Alliance," Acey said. "Jacopo Nehr is your enemy, so how can you trust his brother?"

"I don't consider the MPA my enemy," Noah said. "It's Lorenzo and Francella I oppose, not the new Doge. As for Jacopo Nehr, I've always respected him, since he raised himself up by his own bootstraps, unlike most of the noble-born princes. In any event, Gio never got along with his brother. We have good evidence of that."

"Dux and I didn't leave here on our own. That bastard drugged us and packed us in spaceboxes."

"You're still a Guardian," Noah said, "and I expect you to rise above personal conflicts for the sake of our cause. There are too many important problems to be dealt with for all of you to be squabbling like kids in a schoolyard."

Acey and Gio exchanged hateful stares.

"I don't want to see you within fifty meters of each other. Stay apart. Do you both understand?"

They nodded.

"If Eshaz were only here, he could discover the truth," Tesh said, moving to Noah's side. "Tulyans can touch your skin and read your thoughts. Are there are any other Tulyans here at the headquarters?"

"Zigzia," Noah said. "She sends messages for us to the starcloud."

"We could do that," Tesh said, glaring at Gio, "but I believe Acey and his cousin."

"I may be able to solve this right now," Thinker said. A tentacle snaked out of his head and hovered over Giovanni, the robot's organic interface. "Shall I?" Thinker asked, looking at Noah.

Pursing his lips, Noah said, "I've always resisted using that, or the Tulyan method for lie detection. I refuse to run a police state around me. Instead, I prefer to look into the hearts of people, and in that way I sense if they are loyal to me or not. I try to inspire people to follow me, to believe in my ideals."

Looking at Gio, however, Noah noticed him sigh in relief. This gave the Guardian leader pause, but still he did not give Thinker the go-ahead. "I must say, Gio," Noah said, "that I have always sensed you are troubled, but I never sensed any betrayal of me or the Guardian organization."

"I'm totally loyal to you," Gio said.

"That may be true," Noah said, "and I won't force you to undergo lie detection. However, if you want to clear this matter up, there is an easy way to do it."

"A painless way," Thinker said to Gio. "In only a few seconds, I can download the contents of your mind and analyze them."

Gio struggled against the men who were holding him.

"I don't like what I'm seeing here," Noah said. "Why would you want to harm those boys?"

"I didn't want to harm them. That was an accident in the airvator, and I took steps to make sure they could breathe inside the spaceboxes."

"So you did do that," Noah said.

"I told you!" Acey exclaimed.

"Only because I knew they would never let up on me," Gio said. "I had to get rid of them before they got rid of me."

"We're not like you," Acey said. "We don't sneak around pulling dirty tricks."

"Take Gio away," Noah said to the men holding him. "Lock him up until I decide what to do with him."

"No!" Gio shouted, struggling unsuccessfully to get free.

Disgusted, Noah turned his back on him.

The cell had an electronic code, which the two Guardians activated with a touch pad to lock Gio inside. The prisoner didn't bother to sit on the bed, since he didn't plan to stay that long.

A week ago, he had supervised robots as they repaired the locks on the cells, so he knew the codes. Now, after the Guardians left him alone, he uttered the eight digits aloud to voice-activate the lock. The metalloy door slid open with a soft squeal.

Gio ran out into the corridor, and made his way to a secondary entrance to the headquarters. Again, he knew the codes to get out, since he had been one of the most trusted Guardians, and had been sent on several reconnaissance missions into the nearby towns.

But as he worked the codes, he heard something behind him and whirled.

Thinker stood there, with orange lights glowing and blinking around his face plate. "My probability program brought me here," the robot said.

445

"You predicted I would be here?" Gio asked.

"Probabilities are not the same as prescient-based predictions. Machine programs are not the same as organic brains. Nonetheless, my system works rather efficiently."

Expecting Thinker to detain him, Gio hesitated and considered his options. The door was not responding.

He repeated the codes. This time the door to the secondary entrance opened, sliding into the wall.

Gio stepped through the doorway, not feeling the electronic signal that the robot fired into his brain, erasing all knowledge of the headquarters location. For Thinker, the safety of Noah and the Guardians was paramount, and he had decided it was time for Gio and the organization to part. This man who had worn armor and had served in Thinker's own army could not cause trouble any longer....

As Gio ran through the moonlit woods, he felt confused and lost. Why couldn't he tell which direction to go? His brain whirled, making him dizzy. Sitting on the ground to gather his thoughts, he saw the trees whirling around him. Every direction looked the same to Gio, and he had no idea where he was, though part of him knew that he had been here many times before.

Back in the headquarters, Thinker had been behaving strangely. But where had that been, and what had the facility looked like? He had no images of the place, only of the people and robots he had been with there.

Thinker did something to me, Gio realized.

Feeling a wave of sadness, he knew he had not betrayed Noah at all. Though Gio's motives had been complex and he had a penchant for promoting his own interests, he had genuinely liked and respected Noah, and had hoped to advance his own career in the Guardian organization. Admittedly Gio had taken shortcuts to get ahead, but he wasn't the only one who'd ever done that.

Now all of his hopes were dashed. The Guardians thought he was a bad person, but that wasn't the case at all. He had always been loyal to Noah, and had done a good job for him.

He just couldn't get along with those meddlesome teenagers.

Chapter Sixty-Eight

Such an odd pairing, Princess Meghina and Lorenzo del Velli. She is known to show compassion, and has a love for exotic animals, while he has revealed himself to be the opposite, a cruel and scheming man. It suggests that our perceptions of both of them may not be entirely accurate.

—Subi Danvar, security briefing at Guardian headquarters

The young Doge was not sure how to respond to the conciliatory messages from Noah Watanabe, which he had been receiving in the form of personal letters delivered by an intermediary. To Anton, it seemed as if he himself had lived two lives. In the first one, Noah had been his beloved uncle and much-admired Master of the Guardians. But in Anton's second incarnation, Noah had been the most wanted criminal in the Merchant Prince Alliance, accused of murdering his own father and of guerrilla attacks against corporate and governmental interests.

Dressed in a golden cloak over a jerkin and leggings, Anton paced the perimeter of a rooftop garden connected to his private office suite. Across the square he saw the Hall of Princes, with its red-and-gold banners fluttering in the breeze, each emblazoned with the golden tigerhorse crest of the del-Velli royal house.

My house, and my father's, he thought.

Even with the change in his own position, and the resultant metamorphosis in his relationship with the Guardians, Anton didn't think he could ever hate Noah. Now, in his official capacity as the most powerful of all merchant princes, Anton might be forced to put him to death, but he could never hate him.

Anton held the latest letter now, written in Noah's own hand. The paper crackled in a gust of wind. He had delayed answering the earlier communications, which must have made Noah think he was ignoring him. But that was not his intent.

It occurred to the Doge that Noah might very well guess what was going through his mind at that very moment, that Anton had never intended any disrespect by not answering. Noah must know that his own sister would interfere and prevent answers, but in this case that had not occurred. The letters had been delivered to him directly, and Francella did not know about them. Somehow, Noah had used his contacts to arrange that.

The young leader found himself in a difficult political position, feeling conflicting pressures and loyalties. The letter in his hands mentioned setting priorities, and placed the Mutati threat near the top. Noah wanted a cease-fire, so that the Guardians and merchant prince forces might work together for a common good.

Anton re-read the letter's provocative last sentence: *"I have recently obtained access to a podship, with a pilot for it. "*

This intrigued Anton immensely, but he was politically aligned with his own mother Francella, who hated her brother. In addition, Anton was now married to the daughter of General Jacopo Nehr, a man who was still on friendly terms with Lorenzo del Velli—who had recently instituted a program to find Noah's elusive Guardians and annihilate them. The former Doge was doing that with his own private forces, in alliance with various corporations who opposed Noah's guerrilla environmental activities.

So far Anton had used his own influence to keep his forces and other government resources out of such operations, asserting that they were needed elsewhere. In reality he still admired his uncle, and could never envision taking overt action against him. Anton had also resisted making any contact with him, thinking it was best to remain essentially neutral and let the warring factions fight it out among themselves.

I must not allow personal feelings to interfere, Anton thought as he went back into his office. *I must make the right decision for the Alliance.*

From youthful inexperience, he was not certain whom to consult about this situation. As time passed, he had come to the realization that he would need to make the decision on his own. He added the letter to the others, locked away in a cabinet.

Chapter Sixty-Nine

It is one thing to know you are going to die someday, at an indeterminate moment. It is quite another to see the process accelerate in front of your eyes.

—Francella Watanabe

With money, all things are possible, she thought. What a lie that is, what a cruel lie.

Money could not buy love or happiness, or the salvation of Francella's life, which continued to dwindle away while she suffered helplessly. For weeks, the wealthiest woman in the Merchant Prince Alliance had been holed up on the lower floors of her cliffside villa, avoiding all Human contact. She took her food through slots in the door like a prisoner, and she wasn't much different from that, because she was trapped inside her ever-weakening body. She looked like an old lady now, like her own grandmother. The elixir that had been prepared from Noah's blood was not working on her at all, though she had been trying it in all conceivable doses, taking care to space them out (as Bichette had recommended) so that she did not overdose.

Enraged, she hobbled through the villa, even going to the top floor that was still leased to Lorenzo, though he had not been there in months. She smashed every mirror in the elegant home, even breaking anything that showed the slightest reflection of her aging face. Hardly any piece of glax survived, and she had every window covered on the inside (and many on the outside) with shutters. She even ordered that every serving robot be painted in dull colors, and that their synthetic eyes and other forms of visual sensors have no sheens whatsoever. Everything in the villa had to be either modified or replaced, to meet her demands. Even the smallest item that could cast a reflection.

Throughout Francella's increasing madness, money rolled in. Much of it amounted to paper profits, since she received regular nehrcom-transmitted statements on how her holdings continued to mount around the galaxy. But a lot of it was real and tangible, profits that she could get her hands on from her extensive Canopan operations, and from her generous share of her son's tax collection revenues, much of which came in from the many companies that had their galactic headquarters on Canopa. This planet, home to Prince Saito Watanabe, had been second in its wealth only to Timian One. And now, with the obliteration of the capital world, Canopa was preeminent.

She had enough money to keep CorpOne's expensive medical laboratories and other industries going strong for a long time, facilities that were now heavily guarded by her own corporate military forces, along with contingents of Red Berets that Anton had assigned to her. With money, it should be possible to find a cure for her malady. But how long would it take? She was running out of time.

In her rising despair, she had considered hurling herself off the cliff by her villa, shooting herself in the head (or having someone do it), taking poison or having it injected, and even getting into a vacuum rocket and flying far away into space, bound for unknown regions. How romantic that last option sounded, and how utterly foolish. If she did that, or decided on any of the other options, it would amount to giving up. And she wasn't about to do that. As long as she could manage one breath from her lungs, she would struggle to have a second, and a third.

Each mouthful of air and each moment had become precious to her, but the effort to sustain herself was hellish. She wished she could just rest and stop thinking about her problems, but knew she had to keep trying. Something would turn up, a medical procedure or even a miracle that had seemed impossible before. If her brother could have his miracle, she deserved her own, too.

Her thoughts ranged from philosophy to the pits of gloom, from hope and light to dark, homicidal rage. Her medical researchers lived in terror of her, and well they should, for their inexcusable failures. Periodically she had been getting rid of the people she felt were incompetent, or getting in the way of progress. All of her medical laboratories had been fitted with video-recording devices, enabling her to watch the progress of each experiment closely, listen in on the conversations, and send out her killers. All while never leaving her villa. Thus far she had spared Dr. Bichette, but with her own increasing medical knowledge—from observing and from her studies of technical holobooks—she had been selecting the doctors to work with him.

Bichette had been recommending that she broaden the scientific study of the elixir by bringing in more test subjects than just herself and the handful of others they had been using. She was coming around to agreeing with him. By seeing how the elixir worked on different people, it would surely reveal more information, and might open up new, critical avenues of research.

So it was that one day Francella transmitted her orders directly to Dr. Bichette, who had been ordered to never go out of range. "I want you to immediately distribute elixir to a broad spectrum of Canopa's population," she said. "Charge a price for it, but not too high, so that we pick up a variety of social strata and genetic types. Don't put any limitations on it. I want all galactic races—at least those on the planet now—to have access to the elixir. Include a sampling from Lorenzo's space station, too."

Francella could not see Bichette on any screen at the moment, but she heard him muttering angrily, followed by the suction sound of a toilet. She smiled to herself.

Presently, she saw him in the hallway outside the restroom, staring up into an electronic eye. "Did I hear you right?" he asked.

She saw two robots with dull silver patinas pass by him and continue on their way.

"You did, and I want it instituted immediately. My lawyers will form a new subsidiary of CorpOne to handle the sales. Mmm, we'll call it LifeCorp, and its product will be the Elixir of Life. How does that sound?"

"Excellent, ma'am, but I must tell you something we have discovered. We can produce millions of capsules, but we must be careful not to use up all of Noah's blood plasma in the manufacturing process. Until we locate him, the blood supplies we have are irreplaceable."

"Of course, of course."

"Very well then, ma'am. I'll take care of it right away."

"I know you will."

Everything in Francella Watanabe's life was on the fast track, including her bodily decay and the commands she issued in a desperate attempt to stave off the end.

In a matter of days, LifeCorp salesmen spread out to the major cities of Canopa, using old-fashioned hucksterism and showmanship to draw crowds and sell the product. In this manner, they sold more than two hundred thousand capsules of elixir, as many as they had been allotted, while leaving plenty of Noah's plasma for Francella herself and for other studies.

Even in the face of mounting military and political tensions, her new profits were substantial. But she didn't care a whit about the money. Concurrent with the marketing program, she dispatched an army of medical researchers to study the path of each capsule of elixir after it was sold, analyzing how it affected those who took it. Each purchaser had to sign a holodocument, agreeing to cooperate with the research program. Offered the prospect of eternal life, no one argued with that.

Out of all the elixir capsules that were sold, the product did enhance the DNA of a small number of people ... but only six. This was in line with a computer projection that Francella discovered Dr. Bichette had withheld from her. Against what have been expected, she actually forgave him for that, as she came to realize he had not wanted to discourage her, and she would not have wanted him to. Even if the odds were pitiful, and they were close to that, she wanted every chance she could get. Every straw of hope.

The sales and research program became like a lottery, with the prize going to only a few. But what a prize it was! The winners emerged under widespread publicity and then tried to continue their lives and vocations, envied by all who knew them.

One of the lucky winners was Princess Meghina, the infamous Mutati who wanted to be Human, and who had remained in that shape for so long that she could not change back. She lived in her own private apartments on Lorenzo's orbital Pleasure Palace.

Far across the galaxy, at the Tulyan Starcloud, Eshaz was summoned to the private office of the First Elder. As Eshaz entered, he saw Kre'n standing at her central work table, with Dabiggio sitting in a sling chair on one side. Uncharacteristically, the big Tulyan Elder had a smile on his bronze-scaled face, which surprised Eshaz.

"And where is your Parvii friend and her vast fleet of podships?" Dabiggio asked.

"She'll be back," Eshaz said.

"With the ships?" Dabiggio's large body caused the sling chair to sag low, just above the floor.

"If anyone can do it, she can."

"So, she's a super Parvii, just as Noah Watanabe is a super-Human. Is that it? My, you certainly have influential friends. But has she even sent a message? Any word at all?"

"Not to my knowledge," Eshaz admitted.

"We should never have let her go," Dabiggio said. He hefted himself out of the chair and stood by Eshaz, at least a head taller than him. "She admitted having information beyond the reach of our truthing touch ... all that stuff about breedmasters, war priests, and unstoppable telepathic weapons. She was probably a spy, and has given military intelligence about us to the Parviis."

"After millions of years, the Parviis have a lot of dirty tricks," another Elder said, a thin male who was one of the followers of Dabiggio. "The way they magnify themselves should tell us something. They never are what they appear to be. How do we know they even resemble Humans in their appearance? Maybe they're something else entirely, something they don't want us to know about. Think about the way their swarms move, too, defying physics and even the imagination. They breathe without air? What are we to believe about such a race?"

"Even if Tesh Kori brings the ships," Dabiggio said, "we shouldn't let her back into the starcloud. I say we keep the mindlink barrier up and strike the fleet the way we hit the swarms."

"If she brings the ships, we're going to let her in," Kre'n said, interrupting the exchange between the Elders. "Bringing them here would be a feat never seen in the annals of history."

"And you would sacrifice our race just to see it?" Dabiggio asked. "There is no limit to the tricks they could pull on us if we let them in. These are *Parvis* we're dealing with, remember, not innocent children."

"We're all in trouble anyway," Kre'n said. "Even if she brings us half that many, or a hundredth, we have to take the chance."

"OK," Dabiggio said, grudgingly. "But if she doesn't get back soon we need to embark on repair missions with what we have, making a last-ditch effort to save what's left of the galaxy."

"Agreed," Kre'n said.

"She'll be back," Eshaz repeated. "I know she will."

At that moment, thousands and thousands of Tulyan repair teams were being assembled on the three worlds of the starcloud, along with the potions and other supplies they needed for their work. As it looked now, there would be many more teams than ships, a reality that would restrict the efforts considerably.

To deal with this serious limitation, the Elders were assembling reports from all of their web caretakers. The trouble spots were being prioritized on a triage basis, like injuries on an immense galactic battlefield.

Chapter Seventy

We have discovered six immortals—the Mutati princess, four Humans, and a Salducian diplomat. It is not too early to declare all of them immortal. Their cellular structures have changed dramatically, with the addition of what we are calling 'warrior antibodies'—proteins in their bodies that annihilate all disease pathogens, both overt and latent. As stipulated in the contracts they have signed, we are now drawing their blood and flash freezing it. This offers the potential that much more of the elixir can be produced, and that we will not need to worry so much about using up the plasma of Noah Watanabe.

—Dr. Hurk Bichette, report to Francella Watanabe

Whenever Lorenzo gambled in his magnificent orbital casino, he did not relax, not even when he was winning, which was virtually all of the time, due to the unregulated programming of the games and machines. He always had a lot on his mind, and as the revenues poured in, he was not much happier than Francella.

One glittering evening he stood in front of his elegantly dressed patrons to promote his newest game, which featured a smiling Mutati simulation. Behind him an oversized mechanical creature changed smoothly into a variety of alien and animal shapes, while the patrons oohed, aahed, and hissed good-naturedly.

"The players sit at those stations," Lorenzo said, pointing to chairs and screens that ringed the faux Mutati, which continued to metamorphose. "When the bell rings, you have one minute to place your bets and select from the shapes on the screen, as you guess which shape the monster will take when it stops."

"Like a roulette wheel?" a woman asked.

Lorenzo laughed. "Certainly not. It's like *a Mutati!* Can't you see that?"

The crowd laughed, and people moved forward to take seats at the play stations.

At a gesture from Lorenzo, the large mechanical creature stopped metamorphosing, and became what looked like a flesh-fat Mutati, in its hideous natural state.

Leering at the creature, a drunken nobleman asked loudly, "Is that what Princess Meghina looks like when she takes off her makeup?"

Some people laughed nervously, while others gasped in shock, since it was known that Lorenzo had stood steadfastly by his courtesan wife, and had even given her private apartments on the orbiter.

"I shall consider that the liquor talking," Lorenzo said with a hard stare. "Otherwise, I would have to create a new game just for you, based upon the torture chambers in the Gaol of Brimrock."

This elicited hearty laughter among the nobles and ladies.

"It's nice to see all of you enjoying yourselves," Lorenzo said, "but keep this in mind. My lovely wife will get the last laugh on all of us. She has not only changed her appearance to that of a Human, but she may have become immortal, enabling her to dance on our graves."

This dampened the amusement somewhat, but Lorenzo knew these foolish people would soon be back at the games, transferring their assets to him. He only had to make their losses amusing, and even verbal jousts served that purpose. The gamblers would keep coming back.

In the midst of the throng, Lorenzo recognized a tall, sharp-featured man and nodded to him. It was Jacopo Nehr's younger brother, Giovanni. Lorenzo heard he had been traveling, so he must have made it back to Canopa just before the cessation of podship travel.

As the Mutati game got underway, Lorenzo slipped into an office to discuss the events of the day with his attaché, Pimyt. The Doge Emeritus greatly appreciated the loyalty of this aging Hibbil, and had raised his salary to even more than he had earned as a government employee.

"What are you doing with all of your money?" Lorenzo asked. He and his aide sat at a table where cups of steaming mocaba juice had just been set out for them.

"Hiring bounty hunters," the Hibbil said, as he took a sip of the beverage without waiting for it to cool. High temperatures never seemed to bother him, though this was not reportedly a Hibbil characteristic.

"Eh?"

"To bring Noah in." Pimyt had wet fur on his upper lip, from the drink.

"Oh, but you don't have to pay for that personally. Just pay it out of my accounts."

"I'd like to bring Number One in with my own money. Somehow, it sounds more special."

"Ah, nice idea. I'll raise your salary to make up for the payments. Come to think of it, maybe I'll pay for some bounty hunters myself, making it like one of my gambling ventures. I am a lucky man, you know. Despite my recent political challenges."

"You are, indeed. Now, onto business. So far, even with the help of our powerful corporate friends on Canopa, we cannot locate Noah's hidden headquarters. We could use help from the new Doge, but to get to your son we have to go through Francella, and she's gone into seclusion."

"So much for her promises of access to Anton. Well, we'll have to get Noah without him. I want him more than anything."

"We'll get him anyway. I have a devious move in mind. Since Anton's ascension to power, Noah has gone to ground and is no longer attacking government facilities, perhaps under some secret arrangement that we don't know about. Even so, we can make it look like he's still operating."

Pimyt laid out an intriguing plan, causing Lorenzo's eyes to narrow in concern.

"We can penetrate some of the corporate guard forces on Canopa and destroy assets, making it look like the Guardians did it."

"Which corporate assets?"

"NehrGem. They have a jewelry-manufacturing operation in the Valley of the Princes."

"But Jacopo Nehr is one of our friends."

"And he hasn't been helping enough, not as much as some of our other friends. I have incontrovertible evidence, if you want to review it."

"No, that's your job. I trust you."

"Thank you. Maybe Jacopo has been distracted by his military duties, but—as you know—we don't accept excuses."

Lorenzo nodded.

"We won't do major damage to his facility," Pimyt said, "only wrecking a small percentage of it. Just enough to anger Jacopo and get him working harder to find our bad guy. We'll use some of your backup Red Berets, the ones stationed down on Canopa."

"Go ahead and set it up."

The little Hibbil nodded. "One more thing, Your Magnificence. This just came in from the government." He activated a telebeam unit on the table, causing a black-and-white message to flash on, floating in the air. The words were backwards to Lorenzo, so he touched a pad to spin it around his way.

"Interesting, wouldn't you say?" Pimyt said.

"To say the least."

Truly, this was startling news, and Lorenzo was not sure what to make of it. The shutdown of podships had enlarged. No longer confined to Human and Mutati worlds, it now encompassed the entire galaxy ... and neither he nor Pimyt could imagine why.

Chapter Seventy-One

Princess Meghina is expressing a desire to come out of seclusion and mingle with the patrons of the orbital casino. Polls show that much of the public is willing to assume the best about her, asserting that she should never have been born a Mutati in the first place.

—Telebeam report to Francella Watanabe,
read just before one of her ranting tirades

stensibly, the damage to NehrGem's industrial complex appeared minor, as only a small section of one jewelry-manufacturing building had been destroyed by the remote-guided rocket, and fire suppression systems had prevented further damage. But that section had contained the rarest gemstones in Jacopo Nehr's collection, garnered from mining operations around the galaxy. If podship travel did not resume, he could not hope to replace these losses. Even some piezoelectric emeralds of the type used in nehrcom transceivers had been destroyed, making it an Alliance security matter and a subject of utmost military importance.

In a matter of hours, forensic evidence revealed that the perpetrators had been Noah Watanabe's Guardians, based upon tracking records that turned up on fragments of the rocket. And, with a brashness that made Jacopo's blood boil, Noah even sent a telebeam message to Jacopo's offices afterward, claiming full responsibility for the attack.

Feverish with anger, Jacopo ordered immediate retaliation, and he began searching for a place to strike. This proved to be a challenge, since the perpetrators could not be located. They were like wisps of wind, gusting up here and there and then disappearing into thin air. As a consequence, the targets were limited … but not non-existent.

Within two days he set his sights on a warehouse and storage yard where the confiscated assets of Noah Watanabe were held under government seal. These were items that had been removed from the Ecological Demonstration Project and from the orbital EcoStation.

Seeking no approval from Doge Anton or the Hall of Princes, Jacopo launched a full-scale bombing attack on the warehouse and storage yard, using one of the merchant prince aerial squadrons. Not surprisingly, since there were no defensive weapons at the facility, he succeeded in completely destroying the target.

That evening, he was confronted at his office by one of Doge Anton's Red Beret officers, Lieutenant Colonel Erry Pont. Sputtering in protestation while the officer read a list of charges against him, Jacopo summoned his own security personnel to prevent the man from arresting him. Six uniformed NehrCorp guards rushed into the office and surrounded the red-uniformed officer.

"You cannot hope to resist the power of the Doge," the officer said calmly. Jacopo recognized him as the son of Gilforth Pont, one of the leading noble-born princes. In an obviously intended slight, Lieutenant Colonel Pont had not removed his red cap, and gazed at Jacopo with an arrogant expression.

"Take off your hat in my presence," Nehr demanded.

The officer glanced around, then did so. But his arrogant expression did not change and he said, "In your vengeful zeal, General Nehr, you overlooked some rather important legal details, which I would be happy to explain while I take you into custody."

"I will *not* be taken into custody!"

"Even though you are in command of the Merchant Prince Armed Forces," Pont explained, "you carried out an unauthorized and illegal course of action. Those were no longer Guardian assets you destroyed. They were the assets of the Merchant Prince Alliance, since they had been officially confiscated and placed under seal."

"Mere technicalities. I'll explain it all to Doge Anton myself."

"He has authorized me to tell you that he is not interested in any explanations. He is quite upset."

"Why? Is he a puppet of Noah Watanabe as rumors suggest, protecting Guardian assets and refusing to bring the little worm to justice?"

"The Doge will not be pleased to hear you said that, General."

"Or is he a puppet of his mother, who is coddling noble-born brats like you and your father?"

"General!"

"Tell Anton I refuse to be arrested, and I refuse to listen to any charges!" Nehr thundered. He waved a hand. "Now go, before I place you in one of my brigs!"

"I'm afraid he's gone too far," Doge Anton said to Nirella, as they prepared for bed. "I know he's your father and I respect him, but he can't go around half-cocked, attacking whatever he wants, using MPA forces."

"You're right," she said, "but your mother is pushing to have him removed since he is not noble-born, and you must be your own man."

"With you at my side, I will be," the youthful leader said, with a soft smile. He kissed her and added, "I'm sorry I'm not a better lover, but the stresses of the job are taking their toll."

"I adore you anyway," she said.

It saddened him to notice disappointment in her eyes. During the months that they had been married, Anton was growing to love Nirella. Time was healing the wounds he suffered when he lost Tesh, and now he only wanted to please his wife.

"I have to at least fire him," Anton said, at last. "Our highest military officer is still subject to the laws of the MPA."

"I know." She fluffed her pillows and climbed into the large bed they shared.

"What is your rank in the Red Berets?" he asked, even though he already knew the answer.

"Why, I'm a reserve colonel," she said.

"I'm giving you a promotion, to Supreme General of the Merchant Prince Armed Forces."

Her eyes widened. "What?"

"We'll put the word out that it's only an interim appointment, until we decide on a permanent replacement. Don't worry about making a mistake. The Mutati war is on suspension anyway."

"But I'll need to be in touch by nehrcom with our forces all over the galaxy, to make certain everything is in readiness. I'm not sure if I'm qualified for that."

"You're as qualified as your father, since you co-manage the galactic operations of Nehrcom Industries with him, and I know you have extensive military knowledge. I've seen the holobooks you read. You're a student of military tactics and strategies."

"True, but I do not have anywhere near the prestige of my father."

"I have to admit, Jacopo was doing well as Supreme General until this lapse. Maybe he will recover his senses with rest, and again qualify for the job." Anton scratched his head. "Mmm. Instead of firing your father or taking him into custody, I'll put him on a leave of absence for an indeterminate period. That's the political way to handle it. He still has powerful friends and allies, and I don't want to lose their support."

"You're learning fast," she said.

The following afternoon, upon learning of the Doge's decision, Jacopo Nehr took his wife, Lady Amila, and a few men who were loyal to him and joined Lorenzo on the space station. There he conferred with two men whom he thought had remained loyal to him, Lorenzo and Pimyt.

But in this time of galactic chaos and tension, relationships were not always what they appeared to be.

After the six Elixir of Life winners were announced, Princess Meghina began to socialize with the other five, and they formed an exclusive club. Under continuing medical observation, the small group arranged regular get-togethers in Meghina's royal apartments on Lorenzo's orbiter. All the while, Francella and her researchers eavesdropped electronically on everything they said.

In the cities and towns of Canopa there were philosophical debates about the elixir, as people considered whether or not they would like to become immortal, if CorpOne ever offered more of the precious substance for sale. They considered it like a lottery.

One evening on board the orbital gambling casino, Lorenzo announced that he would like to become immortal himself so that he could spend the rest of eternity with his pretty wife. The Doge Emeritus revealed that he was at the top of a waiting list for the elixir, and would take it himself as soon as it again became available.

In Noah's camp there were also debates, with his Guardians lining up on both sides of the issue. The outspoken Acey Zelk, having heard how apparent immortality had changed Master Noah, did not want it for himself.

"What fun would there be if I knew I could not be killed?" the teenager asked one afternoon while taking a break with Dux. "The risk of death makes life worth living."

"It does give things an edge, doesn't it?" Dux said. "As for myself, I think I agree with you. Maybe if everyone I cared about, such as yourself, could be made immortal I would accept it for myself, but the odds are slim that the elixir will work on any of us."

Overhearing this exchange, Noah saw a certain wisdom in their opinions, but for himself he did not entirely agree. He wanted to accomplish so much that he didn't see how one lifetime could possibly be enough for him. From an early age Noah had always seen broad horizons, had always felt that he could make important contributions. Now, the longer his allotted lifetime, the more he could achieve.

Admittedly Noah had felt trapped at times by his own enhanced existence, as if it were—paradoxically—yet another prison confining him. But if he could ever regain access to Timeweb it might open wondrous possibilities for humankind and new glories for all of the galactic races ... if only they could see the wisdom of working together instead of at cross purposes.

Thus far Noah was presuming that he still had his own immortality, since he had been feeling physically strong, without any hint of the aches or pains that his friend Eshaz had complained of ... a Tulyan who had lived for nearly a million years.

But Timeweb continued to reject every attempt Noah made to reenter it, and this disappointed him deeply.

Chapter Seventy-Two

The immortal Mutati courtesan presents us with difficult questions. Out of the thousands of doses of elixir that were distributed, Princess Meghina is the only Mutati known to have consumed any, and the cellular effects on her were dramatic. Mutatis typically have lifespans similar to those of Humans, so the possibility of immortality for every shapeshifter who consumes the Elixir of Life is frightening. Maybe this is not the case and it is only a coincidence, but it presents obvious security concerns, as it could result in the ultimate domination of that race over humankind. I would strongly recommend two courses of action: We must only distribute additional doses under strictly controlled conditions, and you need to notify your son of the situation. After all, he is the Doge, responsible for the welfare of all of us.

—Dr. Hurk Bichette, telebeam to Francella Watanabe

A week passed.

Despite his inexperience on the job, Doge Anton had already developed a routine. Each morning he arose early and had breakfast brought to him in his office. If the weather was nice, he ate in the adjacent rooftop garden, as he was doing now.

He flipped on a telebeam projector beside his plate and read the messages as he ate, letting an electronic fork automatically lift morsels of omelet to his mouth. It freed up his hands to continue working.

As usual there were several messages from his mother, listing the most important appointments he had that day, and how to handle each of them. She was not pleased that he had appointed Nirella Nehr as interim Supreme General, and for days she had been pressing to have him not to make the appointment permanent. In Nirella's place she had been touting her own candidate, Gilforth Pont, providing reasons why he would make a great general.

The trouble was, Anton knew the man, and he didn't have the first idea about what it took to lead the Merchant Prince Armed Forces. Neither did his spoiled son, who had manipulated the system to obtain an appointment as a lieutenant colonel in the Red Berets. Anton didn't like people who worked their connections to get ahead. Instead, he liked those who advanced through the sweat of their own brows.

The fork continued its passage from the plate to his mouth, using sensors to keep from missing or stabbing him. He paused to take a sip of tangy juice, and turned the fork off. He didn't feel like finishing the omelet.

Consistent with his opinion of others, Anton felt some embarrassment for his own appointment to the highest position in the Alliance. He was the son of a noble-born prince himself (albeit out of matrimony), and in danger of becoming one of the very dandies he loathed. Still, he had high hopes of proving that he deserved the job. Already he was asserting himself, showing his mother that he could make important decisions on his own.

He knew she could not really do anything about that, because she held her own lofty social position in large part due to her relationship with him, her bragging rights as the mother of the Doge. She tried to act like she was in charge, in tacit control, but he really held the more important cards. He just needed to figure out how to play them.

His feelings for her were evolving. Anton was beginning to see Francella as a complete person, with strengths and weaknesses. He didn't think he could ever forgive her for abandoning him at birth, but at least she had paid a family to raise him. That showed some modicum of concern, and suggested that she wasn't nearly as bad as she seemed to be.

Yet the stories of her raw rage were terrifying, the things she allegedly did to Noah, or tried to do to him, as well as the rumors that she may have killed her own father and blamed it on her brother. Her actions in the laboratory may have been controlled experiments; at least that was what she claimed. In addition, she insisted that she had nothing to do with old Prince Saito's death, and Anton wanted to believe her. He also worried about her health, and hoped a way could be found to slow or reverse the accelerated aging she had been suffering.

A robot servant removed the dishes, and he continued reading the telebeam images that floated in front of his eyes. One of the messages—from an investigator he respected—cited proof that Noah was not responsible for the attack on Jacopo Nehr's jewelry-manufacturing complex after all, and that Lorenzo del Velli had actually been the perpetrator.

Interesting. So Uncle Noah is not guilty of everything after all.

Anton considered sending the information to Jacopo Nehr himself, then reconsidered and forwarded it to Nirella instead. It was her father, and she would want to do whatever she could to ensure his safety. But why had Lorenzo done such a thing? The plots among merchant princes seemed endless.

After forwarding the message to Nirella, along with his own cover note, Anton paused to consider who else should know. His mother? Eventually, yes. But first, he wanted to do something he had been delaying for too long.

Because of Lorenzo's deception, the young Doge finally decided to meet with Noah, and he responded to his uncle's diplomatic overtures.

Reading the telebeam message in his underground office, Noah felt a rush of elation. Anton said he looked forward to resuming their close relationship, and suggested a neutral meeting place—in a canyon on the far side of Canopa. That sounded all right to Noah, but he would check with Subi before answering, to make certain that the necessary security measures were taken.

Touching his sapphire signet ring, Noah closed the transceiver. The message disappeared into his ring in a wisp of gray smoke.

Just then he heard a thunderous explosion, and the shouts of men. As he ran out into the main chamber, he saw men, women, and robots heading toward a breach in the entrance, carrying weapons.

Subi Danvar hurried up to him, and shouted, "Cameras show soldiers and heavy vehicles outside! We can't hold them off for long."

Subi guided Noah toward a side tunnel, which they entered at a full run.

"MPA?" Noah asked.

"No, paramilitary. They're wearing Red Beret uniforms."

"I didn't think Anton would do this to me," Noah said.

"Maybe he didn't. As the Doge Emeritus, Lorenzo has Red Berets, too."

Noah cursed, and as he ran with Subi, he wondered how his enemies had found him. At the adjutant's suggestion, Noah had beefed up the energy-field security system and metalloy barricades at the main entrance, so that—along with the brave Guardians who were facing the attackers—should slow them down.

Reaching a rear chamber, Noah and Subi assembled fighters and equipment. From all tunnels around them, fully armed Guardians streamed in and received their orders.

More explosions sounded. Looking at a portable security screen, Subi reported: "They're at all of the entrances. We only have one way to get out and try to hit them from another side."

He pointed to a Digger machine.

High in the enclosed operators' cabin of the vehicle sat Acey Zelk and Dux Hannah, side by side. "Let's go!" Acey shouted. He shut the door and fired up the big machine. Its engines made a deafening roar.

In the face of the overwhelming onslaught, Noah and a force of Guardians used the Digger to tunnel an escape route for them. Following a compass, they set a course toward the northeast, his old ecological compound.

With Acey at the controls the machine hummed, throwing dirt and rocks behind it, which robots pushed back with smaller machines, allowing the fighters to surge forward into the earth. The Digger was fast, and the robots had to work hard to keep up behind it.

Noah smelled the dust and dirt, and he coughed, as did the Humans with him. He saw an opening ahead, and heard what sounded like running water.

Abruptly the Digger coughed too, and the engines shut down. On top of the machine, Acey spat expletives.

Part of the tunnel collapsed overhead, trapping Acey and Dux and many of Noah's loyal followers. At a command from Noah, robots rushed in and began digging furiously, trying to rescue people before they stopped breathing. Noah and Subi climbed on top of the partially buried Digger, and used a puissant pistol to knock dirt away, causing it to cascade harmlessly to the ground. They saw the teenagers now, inside the sealed cabin. The boys pushed the door open and climbed out.

From the rooftop, Noah surveyed the machine. A large rock had crushed the engine compartment, and the Digger would need repairs before it could be used again. As a security measure, to prevent the units from repairing themselves and going on burrowing rampages, as they had done in the past, Subi had disconnected the sentient features. It was just a dumb machine now, totally useless.

At the front of the Digger, Noah saw through the large opening it had cut, revealing a cavern and a subterranean stream. Guardians were climbing down an embankment to the water, gathering along the edge.

"Now what?" Dux asked.

"Where does this stream lead?" Acey asked. "Does anybody know how far it is to an outlet?"

Tapping buttons on his security computer, Subi tried to get information. "Nothing here," he said.

Acey repeated his questions, scrambling down the embankment and shouting them to the Human and robotic Guardians around him. No one seemed to have any answers.

Noah, Subi, and Dux went down to the stream, too. Noah dipped a hand in the water. It was not that cold.

"I've done some swimming in my life," Acey said, testing the temperature himself. "Extreme sports where I had to hold my breath for a long time." He waded into the water.

Figuring out what Acey had in mind—an underwater swim—Noah shouted: "Hold it! You don't know how far it is to an outlet."

"What choices do we have?" Acey asked, with a wide grin.

"I'll do it, then," Noah said. "I can't die, remember?"

"And let you have all the fun?" Acey shouted. "Wish me luck!" He swam away downstream, taking powerful strokes.

Noah dove in and swam after him, but Acey was a faster swimmer.

The brave teenager went under, followed by Noah.

Just when Acey felt as if his lungs would burst, he went over a waterfall into a pool of deep, cold water—outside. Noah, who aspirated a great deal of water and should have drowned, joined him moments later. Both of them took several moments to recuperate.

Then Noah made out shapes on the shore, surrounding the water. Humans and robots. They drew closer, and he saw Guardian uniforms and colors on them. One of his subcommanders shouted to him, "We got out a secondary entrance. It's just you two?"

"No!" Noah shouted. "Subi and others are back there, hundreds of Guardians." He pointed in the direction of the waterfall. "We need to break through rock and get them out."

"You mean with a Digger?" the subcommander asked.

"Exactly."

Noah heard the roar of another Digger, and saw its hulking shape appear.

In only a few minutes, with Noah directing, they dug back to the stranded Digger, and Noah's squad of followers.

Noah and Subi then led a counterattack and drove away the Red Beret forces—which outnumbered them—with hardly any resistance.

As the battle turned, the two men watched on a remote videocam as the attackers hurried into military vehicles and drove off.

"That was too easy," Subi said. "Did you notice? Just before running, they were talking feverishly on com units."

"I saw that," Noah said. "We'd better get under cover and regroup."

Chapter Seventy-Three

No motivation is more powerful than the desire to annihilate your historical mortal enemies. It is one of the dark forces, which invariably seem to be stronger among the races than the forces of good. This does not bode well for the balance of the galaxy, which is connected to all activity and continues to erode ... while the undergalaxy does the exact opposite. Our loss is their gain.

—Report of web caretakers to the Council of Elders

Noah and Thinker surveyed the rubble of the battle, watching as Subi, the teenage boys, Tesh, and others quickly retrieved usable weapons and took them inside the shelter of the headquarters. Medical robots tended to the injured, with most of the bots having been custom programmed a short while before by Thinker.

As the sentient machines performed their work they transmitted signals to Thinker, reporting on the conditions of the patients.

When their tasks were complete, Thinker passed the information on to Noah. "Fifteen dead Red Berets," the robot leader said.

"How many did we lose?" Noah asked.

"Fifty-four."

"That many?" He thought back. "But I only saw a few."

"Aren't robots as important as Humans?" Thinker asked.

"Of course. Your contributions are tremendous. We couldn't do it without you."

"There are six Human dead, and forty-eight seriously damaged robots."

"Fifty-four in all, then."

"Right."

Noah felt considerable relief, but didn't want to offend Thinker by showing it, or pointing out that dead machines could be repaired, while Humans could not. Except for himself. And half a dozen others, from what he'd heard.

Soon additional information came in, this time from Subi, who rushed over and interrupted Noah and Thinker. "We took prisoners," the adjutant said breathlessly, "and they confirmed our suspicions about Lorenzo. The attack force was under his command from the orbiter, using Red Berets stationed on Canopa."

"So EcoStation is more than a gambling casino," Noah said, bitterly. "We built it and that idiot turned it against us."

"How did they find out where we are?" Dux asked.

"It was only a matter of time," Thinker said, "and probabilities. They have been searching for us intensely."

"This headquarters is no longer safe," Subi said. "They'll hit us with a massive force next."

Noah noticed that his signet ring was flashing colors, and shifting from sapphire to gold. The color change and pattern of flashes told him the source of a telebeam message that had just arrived for him: Doge Anton.

Opening the connection, he saw words floating in the air: *"Hello, Uncle Noah. For the sake of the MPA, I'm declaring a formal cease-fire with the Guardians, while you and I discuss ways of ending the hostilities. For your part, you must discontinue all guerrilla attacks against corporate assets, including those owned by my mother and my father. I found out about Lorenzo's attack on you, and put a stop to it. Not that you needed my help. I just made it easier for you. "*

Speaking into a recording mechanism, Noah transmitted a response: "Much appreciated. All right, I'll keep my end of the cease-fire. I assume you'll see that Lorenzo does the same."

Moments later, he saw the Doge's response in front of his eyes: *"I'll do my best, but watch out for his tricks. He and your sister are always plotting against you. "*

When the exchange was complete, Subi said to Noah, "We should still dig in and open up as many escape tunnels as possible. Let's take new precautions, lay traps, and do the unexpected. I think we should also send a recon team to the orbiter and see what Lorenzo is doing there. Obviously he's using it as a command center against us, but maybe we can get through and find out what he's up to."

"The best defense if a good offense," Noah said, nodding. Tesh approached him, a look of sadness on her face. She stood by him, listening as he and the robot continued their conversation.

"Wearable surveillance cameras would be handy on such a mission," Thinker said. "I've done repairs to a hibbamatic machine that Subi brought in some time ago, and it can produce as many cameras as you need, tiny units that look like buttons and are totally undetectable to scanners. They'll project images from the space station back here."

"As I recall," Subi said, scratching his head, "you were less than impressed by the quality of products produced by that machine."

"I improved it," the cerebral robot said. "The thing is not perfect, but it should serve our needs, especially on short notice. The cameras will project images back here just fine; they're a simple enough mechanism."

Noah nodded. "All right, Subi, set up the recon mission. How many people do you want to send?"

"Eh?" Subi was staring at Dux, then at Acey, who were only a few meters away. "I'm thinking three," he replied. "Say, these boys have the look of Sirikan nobility. Isn't that where you're from?"

"From Siriki, yes," Dux said, "but from the back country. Our families are dirt poor."

"Well, I'd say a nobleman or two passed your way on vacation, and spent the night. You two have just the look I want for this mission. If you're game for it, I want you to act like young nobles and wander around, seeing how much you can transmit back to us."

"Right," Dux said, exchanging nods with Acey. "Our own little casino game."

Looking at Thinker, Noah said, "After you produce the cameras, I want you to have tunnels dug to the clearing where our podship is, so that we can get as many Guardians on board the craft as possible for a mass escape, if necessary. Human *and robot* Guardians."

Then to Tesh he said, "Supervise new construction inside the podship, racks to stack robots, and vertical structures to accommodate as many people as possible."

"That is a fine idea, Master," the robot said, with orange lights blinking around his face plate.

"Sounds good to me, too," Tesh agreed.

"As for me," Noah said, "I'm going to meet with Anton, at the place he designated. There's no point taking security with me. He's proven himself by intercepting Lorenzo's attack. Besides, I'm invulnerable, in case some of you haven't heard yet." He grinned. "And if I get captured, you guys can just break me out again."

Thinker made an odd mechanical noise. Then: "Don't get overconfident, Master. The last time you were caught, your sister cut you up into little pieces. Don't forget: She's Anton's mother, and his benefactor."

"Perhaps you're right. Maybe I am being overly optimistic."

"At least take a squad of robots with you," Thinker said, "to make it harder for them to capture you," We have our own longevity, because we can always be repaired."

"Not always," Noah said, "not if the damage is too great. And perhaps it is the same with me." He chewed at his lower lip. "Very well, I'll tell Anton I want fifty of my guards, and he can bring the same number."

Across the galaxy, about as far as anyone could go, Woldn felt much better, and was working to regenerate an entire galactic race. He dispatched cleanup teams to remove the floating bodies from the Parvii Fold and the connecting tunnels, and separated his surviving people into groups, with special attention to the most healthy.

Of those who were in the best condition, he instituted an intense Parvii reproduction program under the supervision of two surviving breedmasters, to generate as many offspring as possible, as fast as possible. With a short gestation period of only a few days, the population began to increase, and reached adulthood in a matter of weeks.

Soon Woldn was culling the best of the offspring and combining them with the best of the older adults, selecting who would be future podship pilots, and who would be trained for other important professions.

He had the historic goal of his galactic race firmly in his mind, and it would never leave his thoughts. Maintain full control of the podships.

One major problem existed, but he would do the best he could despite it. While he had managed to save two breedmasters, only one war priest had survived, carrying with him the secret of the ancient telepathic weapons.

Throughout their long military tradition, war priests had always worked in groups of twenty or more, forming among them a telepathic seed weapon, which was then passed on to the swarms. Over the millennia there had been no need for such a powerful weapon, but the war priests had practiced their craft anyway, generation after generation, awaiting the moment when they might be called to duty.

Now, after all of that preparation, only one of them remained, but he was the most skillful of his group, and the unspoken leader among them. This one, who went by his ancestral name of Ryall, had risen from his deathbed and gone immediately to work. "I can do it anyway," he promised Woldn. "It will take longer, but there are still Parviis with substantial telepathic powers. I will teach them the ancient arts, and we will have the weapons again...."

Addressing a gathering of future pilots, the best of the best, Woldn announced, vocally and telepathically at the same time: "We're not going to resume our podship routes until we take care of other chores first. The Tulyans will pay for what they did to us!"

The din of buzzing and applause filled Woldn's brain, and lifted him to a state of euphoria.

"Soon!" he told them. "We avenge our dead!"

Chapter Seventy-Four

Some people should never have been born, while others should never die.

—Ancient Saying

Acey knew his cousin was uncomfortable in the bright, variegated cape, leggings, and liripipe hat, as Acey was himself, dressed in his own gold-and-white outfit. But the two of them looked perfect for the reconnaissance mission, like typical young lords out squandering their inherited wealth. And their companion Subi, even though he was actually a rough-and-tumble type, looked suitably magnificent himself, like a no-nonsense corporate head, or a front-line military officer with many Mutati kills to his credit.

Disembarking from the shuttle, they stepped through an airlock onto the space station. Following a throng of gamblers, they bypassed inattentive security officers and swept into the large central chamber of the casino. Acey heard the tinkling of coins, the voices of card dealers, and the squeals of anticipation and delight as nobles and their ladies played the games. Robotic waiters passed between the patrons, plying them with gratis exotic drinks and reducing their inhibitions.

The three Guardians split up and explored side chambers and corridors, transmitting images of their surroundings back to headquarters with the cameras concealed in the buttons of their clothing. By prearrangement, they would meet again in an hour.

Acey was surprised by the lax security. Perhaps it was due to the gaiety of this section of the space station, or some of the guards had quaffed those exotic drinks themselves, but any red-uniformed men and women he saw seemed unconcerned and chatted casually with passersby. Waving cheerfully to one of the guards, as Acey had seen others do, he continued on his way into a corridor.

There were restrooms down there, along with a gourmet restaurant, and numerous other rooms, many of which were unlocked. He saw gambling patrons peeking into rooms curiously and either entering, or closing the doors and leaving. He did the same. Poking his head into a small private dining room he was surprised to see Giovanni Nehr in a black waiter's uniform, serving a well-dressed Hibbil. They had not seen him yet. The center of the red-and-gold dining table had been inlaid with the golden tigerhorse crest of Lorenzo's House del Velli, as had all of the chair backs.

Inside Acey's pocket, he carried an unusual weapon that looked like a billfold full of money. Silently, slowly, he pulled it out and activated an internal pressure pad, causing the device to metamorphose into a powerful little laser pistol, with a silencer attachment.

Feeling uncontrollable anger, Acey burst into the dining room with his weapon drawn, not noticing Subi and Dux come up from behind and try to stop him.

In a blur of movement the Hibbil drew his own projectile weapon and fired, sending darts through the air with little pinging sounds. The diminutive, bearlike man was surprisingly fast, but not very accurate in his aim.

Ducking and running, the Guardians took cover behind the ornate chairs and fired laser bursts, an eerily silent battle that filled the room with blue light. Acey expected an alarm to go off at any moment, but it didn't happen. Then he noticed signs of ongoing construction activities in the room—a couple of open junction boxes and a wire on the floor at the base of a wall. The alarm system might be inoperable in here.

Hurling chairs along one side of the table, Gio used their cover to leap into a hatch by the window, and slammed the door shut behind him.

"Emergency-escape route," Acey said to Dux, firing in that direction.

The laser bursts had no effect on the hatch. Through thick clearplax, Acey saw Gio don a spacesuit with a manned maneuvering pack attached. In only a few seconds, he leaped out into space. Firing red flames from the thruster on the MMP, he propelled himself around the outside of the space station.

The Hibbil tried to sound an alarm, but Subi fired a laser beam into his shoulder, causing him to fall on the deck, moaning in pain. Acey ran for another escape hatch but the Hibbil started firing again, forcing Acey to duck for cover behind the overturned chairs. Subi, bleeding from a wound on one arm, crept around the other side of the table, making his way quietly toward the Hibbil.

Seeing another escape hatch nearer to him than to Acey, Dux considered running for it. But he didn't have Acey's skills with mechanical objects or weapons. Acey should be the one to go.

"Acey, look!" Dux shouted. He pointed at the hatch.

"Go!" Acey shouted to Dux. "If you can get him, do it!"

Coming around behind the Hibbil, Subi made a rude noise. The Hibbil whirled, but before he could fire, Acey leaped on him and hit him with a fist, causing the alien to drop his weapon. The furry little man fell back with a curse, but came straight at Acey and pummeled him with surprisingly hard blows.

"We're trying not to kill you," Acey grunted, "but you're not making it easy."

Subi joined in trying to subdue the Hibbil, who fought back with ferocity.

Dux wanted to help them, but decided he'd better go after Gio, to keep him from further compromising their security. He wished Acey hadn't been so impulsive, but now they were committed and their choices were limited.

Climbing inside the escape hatch, Dux slammed the door shut behind him. Dux was not the fighter that Acey was, and didn't think he was anywhere near as brave, but Gio was trying to get away, and Dux did not want to waste any time. Putting on his own suit and maneuvering pack, the teenager shot out into space, steering with controls on his belt. He held his laser pistol in a gloved hand.

Ahead he saw Gio trying to connect to the space station, on a windowless section where there was another hatch. He was having some trouble making the connection, and looked back nervously at his pursuer. Dux fired a warning shot that flashed blue against the hatch, causing Gio to recoil.

Logic told Dux that he should try to kill Gio, since it would not be possible to take him back to Noah alive. But he hesitated. Gio did not appear to be armed, and he couldn't just murder him in cold blood. Looking back at the modules of the space station, Dux did not see many windows on this side, except for those on the private dining room he had just left. So far, he and Gio didn't seem to have attracted any attention.

But Dux—with limited mechanical abilities—had not noticed the weapons on his own maneuvering pack, and on Gio's. The man activated a high-powered projectile gun and fired a dart that grazed Dux on one side, not hitting his skin but penetrating the life-support system of the suit, causing oxygen to leak out.

Gasping for air, the young man propelled himself directly toward Gio and spun away from two more shots, which sent him several hundred meters away from the station. He put the jet on full thruster, trying to get back in time.

Now Gio had time to make the connection to the space station. As he pulled open the hatch, however, Dux hit him in the helmet with a laser blast, blowing his head off. Blood gushed into the vacuum of space, and the body floated away.

The hatch was open, and Dux—nearly passing out from low oxygen—tumbled inside, then closed the hatch behind him. Finding himself in what looked like a food storage room, he caught his breath. Then a door opened, and Dux expected to be captured, or worse.

Instead, it was Acey and Subi. "We followed your emergency locator," Subi said. "You got him?"

Dux nodded. He felt relieved to be alive, but not particularly proud of killing his first man. But if anyone deserved to be his first, it had been Giovanni Nehr.

Regaining their composure and smoothing their clothes as much as possible, the trio walked calmly down a corridor and out into the gambling casino. They passed a Mutati game where patrons were thronging around, and continued on to the shuttle station, in another module.

Through the windows they saw that a shuttle was just unloading, and other patrons were lined up to board it. Hurrying through an airlock, the three Guardians joined the line.

Noticing a little blood on Subi's arm, a female guard asked him what had happened.

"It's nothing," Subi assured her, faking a slur to make it look like he had been drinking. "Just a little too much fun."

With a smile, she waved him and the teenagers onto the shuttle.

Chapter Seventy-Five

Understanding the weak points of your enemy—and of yourself—can be the difference between victory and defeat.

—Teaching of the HibAdu War College

On the space station, Pimyt lay on a medical bed, receiving treatment from a nurse for the injury he received when three strangers attacked him and killed the waiter, Giovanni Nehr. His injured shoulder ached, but something else concerned him much more, and he was impatient to get back to his office.

All of the violence had occurred in a new section that did not yet have security cameras, but he did have images of the three men from the moment they arrived at the orbiter, and afterward when they wandered through public rooms, and later when they boarded a shuttle to leave. The way they split up on arrival troubled him. It suggested that they were doing reconnaissance work, perhaps in advance of a military attack.

"This will hurt a little," the nurse said, as she cleaned bloody fur out of the wound.

In his mind, the Hibbil ran through a list of suspects who might have perpetrated this intrusion. It could be Doge Anton or Francella Watanabe who sent them, or the noble-born princes who still hated Lorenzo for his policies when he was Doge. It might even be Noah's troublesome Guardians, who had fought back so tenaciously against Lorenzo's forces. The attackers could have been Mutatis, though he didn't think so, since they were Pimyt's secret allies and would not want to do him harm.

But paranoid thoughts darted through his mind. In his own long career, he had developed enemies, too, perhaps even more than Lorenzo.

"Hurry it up," Pimyt said, in an agitated, squeaky voice. "I have work to do, and this is costing me valuable time."

"If an infection sets in," she snapped, "it will cost you a lot more than that."

"Okay, okay. But pick it up, pick it up! You're as slow as a nursing student."

"What an unkind thing to say." Her hands shook with anger, but she did speed up, and slapped a healing patch over the wound, a little too hard.

Pimyt didn't say anything about the bolt of pain her mishandling caused. He just sat up and hurried off, glad to get out of there.

Alone in his office, the Hibbil considered the grand plan that he and his people had set up, in cooperation with their Adurian allies. Doge Lorenzo del Velli was no longer in control of the Merchant Prince Alliance, but during his time in that position, Pimyt—as his Royal Attaché—had been in a key position to set things up on behalf of the secret HibAdu Coalition, designed to overthrow both the Humans and the Mutatis.

More work needed to be done, and Jacopo Nehr's foolish loss of his position as Supreme General was presenting new obstacles. But Pimyt prided himself on his own craftiness, and thought he might come up with some clever way to replace the loss. Perhaps he could get to Nirella Nehr and influence her in the same way he had her father. After all, the business interests of father and daughter ran parallel. But it was not so easy for him to get to her in his present position. Even with this obstacle, and others, the die was cast. Victory would just take a little longer to achieve.

At least that mad shapeshifter, Zultan Abal Meshdi, had been prevented from foolishly destroying any more merchant prince planets. The intervention of Noah Watanabe had been most helpful, when he recommended to Lorenzo that they establish sensor-guns on all pod stations, to keep podships from arriving and potentially bringing in more Mutati planet-buster bombs. Following Noah Watanabe's fortuitous suggestion, the Hibbils had been only too happy to set up defensive perimeters on all pod stations that orbited Human-controlled worlds, thus preventing wayward Mutati outriders from coming in and torpedoing another valuable planet.

But not before key worlds were destroyed by the hell-bent shapeshifters, including the merchant prince capital of Timian One. Valuable resources that might have been spoils of war had been destroyed.

For decades, the Hibbils and Adurians had been fostering disorder in their intended victims, enabling the imminent conquerors to divide the spoils between themselves. As a result of this wide-scale sabotage, it would be a diminished war between Humans and Mutatis if it ever resumed—which it most certainly would if podship travel ever started again. Such an unexpected problem for the HibAdu Coalition, and a mystery as to how or why the galactic transportation system had been cut off—another unexplained occurrence to add to the litany of them concerning the sentient spaceships that had wandered the cosmos since time immemorial.

But the inventive HibAdus had come up with a solution. After undermining the Mutati lab-pod production program, they had used Hibbil machine expertise to develop an excellent navigation system for the vessels, a secret that had been kept from the Mutatis. Now, on Adurian and Hibbil worlds, the HibAdu Coalition was mounting a military offensive of massive proportions.

While Pimyt's people had known about an alternate galactic dimension for some time, they had never previously been able to capitalize on it. Centuries ago, using the viewing skills of captured, drugged Tulyans and projecting images from their minds, the Hibbils had been able to see the galaxy's weblike connective tissue on screens. Now the HibAdu Coalition had their own burgeoning lab-pod fleet. Using Hibbil manufacturing expertise combined with Adurian biotechnology, their factories were working around the clock.

The Coalition had a Hibbil method of guiding lab-pods, a nav-unit that caused the vessels to travel along selected podways. Initially the lab-pods had been considerably slower than traditional podship travel, taking more than three days to get across the galaxy, along the longest routes. This had been more time-consuming than traditional podship travel, but had still been remarkably fast in comparison with Mutati solar sailers and the hydion-powered vacuum rockets of the merchant princes. Gradually, the Hibbils had discovered ways of improving the speed of lab-pods, but they had not been able to attain the optimal speeds that should have been reached, according to hull-speed engineering calculations. One of the long-lived, captive Tulyans had revealed the reason for this: increasingly frayed podways that caused all podships traveling over them to slow down.

Still, the lab-pods functioned as well as could be expected, under the circumstances. On both Hibbil and Adurian worlds, the cloned spacecraft were being put into military service. Some of the fully-functional lab-pods had already been used to land clandestine Coalition military operatives directly on Human and Mutati worlds, after bypassing pod stations and defeating planetary security systems, so that no one knew they had gotten past.

Now, thousands of lab-pods fitted with nav-units had been built, and more were on the way.

They were aided in their efforts by another Hibbil innovation. Some time ago the Adurian Ambassador VV Uncel had passed interesting technology on to them, information that the Mutatis had obtained on the workings of the famous nehrcom cross-space communication system. While the Mutatis struggled to perfect it, with their research efforts inhibited by gyros provided to them by the Adurians, the HibAdu Coalition had no such impediments. They had perfected a working nehrcom system that linked their growing military enterprise ... and through a system of complex, secure relays they were in contact with conspirators such as Pimyt on merchant prince worlds.

Chapter Seventy-Six

Pitfalls are always around you ... sometimes visible, but more often not. Survival frequently depends upon seeing them with your inner eye.
—Noah Watanabe, *Drifting in the Ether* (unpublished notes)

The large, unmarked grid-plane circled a remote canyon, with Noah and fifty robots in the passenger compartment. At the controls of the vessel, Subi Danvar used infrared and other electronics to survey the conditions below. With his naked eye, Noah saw a transport vessel on the ground, bearing the red-and-gold colors of Doge Anton. It was midday, with fast-moving clouds overhead that cast scattered shadows on the landscape.

The house colors demonstrated that Noah's nephew was a del Velli now, and confirmed what he had heard, that Anton was no longer using his foster name of Glavine. This gave Noah pause, since this was the son of the man who had just launched a sneak attack against Guardian headquarters. Were the two of them working closely together now, and were soldiers hiding in the surrounding terrain, ready to pounce and capture Noah again?

Noah wanted to think the best of Anton, for he had known the young man for years, and hoped he had not changed for the worst since becoming Doge. In his high position, Anton might have inherited certain political necessities, but Noah had always trusted him ... and Anton had never let him down before. He could not have lost his sense of honor so quickly.

But Noah recalled only too well his own wounds from having trusted Giovanni Nehr, of thinking he had seen goodness and loyalty in Gio's heart, and how wrong he had been. Still, he had a feeling about Anton, that this was an important, even essential, relationship to be developed even further. Noah did not see any benefit in fleeing on Tesh's podship to another world, because what would he do there? He didn't want to raise an army to attack the merchant princes; instead, he wanted to work with them against the Mutatis and the Parviis, who were causing so much damage to everything they touched.

Today was a necessary step. He *had to* risk it.

The grid-plane went into its vertical landing mode and dropped slowly toward the shore of a river at the bottom of the gorge, passing billions of years of sedimentation and rock formations on the sheer canyon walls, in all the shades of brown he could imagine. Gusts of wind buffeted the craft, but Subi kept it under control.

Around Noah the robots were entirely silent, because they had been packed compactly and programmed to sleep. All of them were boxy in shape, which made them easier to pack in tight quarters.

Robots had certain advantages, Noah realized, and this was only one of them. The primary reason he had brought them was another—he didn't want to risk losing Guardians in case he was wrong about Anton. As for Subi, he was Noah's equal in many ways, and when the big man wanted to go someplace, it was hard to stop him. Subi, intensely loyal, wanted to make certain that every possible safety precaution was taken. He had even formulated a plan to take Anton hostage in a quick strike, if necessary. Assuming Anton was even there.

As the grid-plane settled onto a sandy beach, Noah got his answer. Doge Anton del Velli, looking elegant and rested, strode toward him across the glittering, silvery sand, leaving his own entourage behind. He wore a thick coat, to protect against the unseasonably cold weather. His blond mustache looked freshly trimmed.

Subi disembarked first, followed by Noah, both wearing green-and-brown Guardian uniforms. Then the robots came to life, and began clattering down the ramp to the ground. As they did so, Anton showed no alarm, and left his own guards a considerable distance away, by his own plane.

As if in answer to Noah's unspoken question, Anton said, "I have nothing to fear from you, and you have nothing to fear from me."

Standing in sunlight, the two men clasped hands firmly, then embraced. For a moment, it seemed to Noah as if nothing had ever separated them.

"It seems like a long time since we saw each other at your wedding, doesn't it?" Noah said, as they separated. "It's only been a few months, but so much has happened."

"And not all for the best," the Doge said, scowling. Wind whipped his long hair. He gestured, "Come, Uncle, and accompany me on a walk."

Noah nodded, and followed Anton's lead as they strolled away from both aircraft onto a rocky section of beach.

"Speaking of uncles," Anton said with a sidelong glance, "my wife is grieving over what happened to Gio."

Noah nodded, and said, "An unfortunate incident."

"Yes, most unfortunate. But Gio was not like his brother, was he?"

"No, sadly he was not like Jacopo at all."

"Tragic situation. He'd fallen on hard times, was working as a waiter on the orbital casino."

Noah expected Anton to press for more information, voicing suspicions that Guardians might have killed Gio, but instead the young Doge dropped the subject and said, "You may have noticed that I made no real effort to find you, or mount my own attack. I, too, have had odd mental experiences. While I should know where your headquarters is, because I have been there, I cannot remember anything about the location. It is as if a portion of my memory has been erased." He stared hard at Noah, and added, "Did you do that to me?"

"Not consciously, but perhaps it is linked to the powers I received. The Supreme Being who gave me those powers may have wanted to protect me, so he did a little tap dance inside your brain."

"As good an explanation as any, I suppose." He smiled. "I never wanted to take action against you anyway, no matter how hard my mother pressed me. Now, why did you request this meeting?"

The Master of the Guardians closed his coat, to protect against the cool wind that was whipping through the canyon. "Undoubtedly you have heard things about me, how my cellular structure has taken on certain unusual propensities."

"Not only have I heard that, I was on the pod station when Mother fired a puissant blast through your chest. You're like a reptile that can grow back its lost body parts."

"On a much more advanced level than any reptile," Noah said, as they stepped over a log. "You heard what she did to me in the laboratory?"

"Yes." He smiled ruefully. "That wasn't very nice of her, was it?"

"She has certain—personality defects. Doge Anton, forgive me for insulting your mother, but I may be the only person who has the right."

"I don't dispute your right to say anything you please about your sister, but there are other sides to her as well, sides that have surprised me. I've seen compassion in her eyes when she looks at me, and she has done things for me that can only be interpreted as love. Of course, she always has her own personal ambitions and motivations, but she really has shown me love, in the only way she knows." He paused. "It's a distant sort of emotion with her, but it is still there, as if it's been suppressed for her entire life and is finally breaking free."

"It's not enough," Noah said, in a bitter voice. "I know her bad side only too well. Did you take the Elixir of Life?"

"No, for a couple of reasons. One, I don't know if I want to live forever. And two, look what it's done to her. It could do the same to me."

Noah nodded. He thought for a moment, and said, "Even when it works, it's no blessing."

They sat on a flat stone in a patch of sunlight, watching the clean mountain water flow swiftly by them. Noah related some of his incredible stories so that Anton could better understand the immensity of the challenges facing humankind and the entire galaxy. He told of his travels through a web of time and space, of signs of decay around the galaxy, of wild podships captured by the Tulyans, and of injured Parviis taking their entire podship fleet out of service in order to recuperate in a galactic fold. He also described the ancient caretaking duties of the Tulyan race, and how that had been diminished severely when they lost their podships to the Parviis.

Anton was astounded at what he heard, but did not question it. For several long minutes after Noah stopped talking, the younger man just sat there, absorbing the fantastic details. Presently he said, "It is common knowledge that podships are mysterious space travelers, and your account fills in missing elements. But tiny creatures piloting podships? If that is the case, why have the Parviis maintained podship service for so long throughout the galaxy, without ever charging for it?"

"They do not value money, in any form. Their entire existence is centered around controlling the sentient spaceships. It's all they want to do, all they have ever wanted to do, all they have known. The problem is enormous. I'm sure they are planning to do something big with those podships—more than a hundred thousand of them—and it might not be the resumption of podship routes."

"What do you think they'll do?"

"A surprisingly powerful Tulyan attack drove the Parviis into a frenzy and killed many of them. I have a Parvii friend, a female, and her guess is that they plan to get revenge on a genocidal scale. They're weakened now, but she doesn't think it is the end for them, since they are survivors. Their swarms may be able to regenerate powerful telepathic weapons that have not been used since ancient wars."

"And your Parvii friend has the podship you mentioned in one of your messages?"

"That's right." He hesitated. "You know her."

"Eh?"

"The Parvii female. Tesh Kori."

Anton's jaw dropped. "What?"

Noah went on to tell him about the magnification capabilities of her people, and how her amplified skin not only looked real, but seemed real to the touch.

Looking at his uncle in astonishment, Anton said, "I feel like my head is going to explode with all of this new information."

"Every word of it is true."

"I don't doubt it. I've never doubted anything about you, Noah. But why are you telling me all of this?"

"Because we need to work together, with all of our followers, instead of at cross purposes. Tesh came to me, asking for my help with a diplomatic mission to the Parvii Fold. She already went there on her own, trying to convince Parvii leadership to allow all of their podships to be used for web caretaking duties. They turned her down, declared her an outcast. I'm willing to help Tesh, but the diplomatic mission must go first to the Tulyans, to convince them to join the effort. The Tulyans have captured almost four hundred wild podships in deep space, but they need more vessels for all the web repair work that is needed."

"They have that many ships?"

"It's a pittance, compared to what the Parviis control."

"But *four hundred* ships! We could fill them with military equipment and troops, and attack the Parviis in their nest!"

"Tesh would never consent to that."

"If only we had a way of getting around her."

"She has the only podship at our disposal and she knows how to seal its operations against intrusion. We have no choice. She's the only way we can get to the Tulyan Starcloud."

"So we tell her a few lies."

Noah scowled, shook his head. "I don't want any part of that."

"I'm afraid you're being nai've, Uncle."

"Perhaps you're right, but let's rethink this. There must be another way."

"As Doge, I shall take the responsibility. I like your suggestion that we work together, but I shall have to consider how best to accomplish that. Aside from how to handle Tesh, there are certain political hurdles to leap. My mother has many important allies, and they will be watching me closely."

"This is a matter of utmost urgency."

"I realize that."

"And Lorenzo? You can keep him from attacking me again?"

"Only if you discontinue all guerrilla attacks against corporate assets. I know, both my mother and father have caused you a lot of grief, but you need to be the good guy here. If you can do that, I can lean hard on Lorenzo. He's upset that I intervened to stop his attack against your headquarters, and I pulled every political string I have to do it. So far it's holding, but you need to keep your end of the bargain."

Noah nodded, and smiled. "You have my promise. Well, aren't you the master diplomat now."

As they sat there, Anton described the difficulties he had experienced in adjusting to his new position as leader of the Merchant Prince Alliance, and his frustration at trying to rule a fragmented, barely connected domain. He also admitted that his mother would continue to impede any alliance he might want with Noah—but she had been counseled by high officials that the MPA needed this cease-fire so that they could focus their assets on larger, galactic-scale matters.

Noah scowled. "Francella's concerns are petty and self-centered, but for the sake of larger issues I will try to overlook the enmity we have always felt for one another." He cleared his throat. "Sometimes I sense forces working to keep the entire galaxy in disarray. Why do Humans and Mutatis hate each other, anyway? Does anyone know?"

With a shrug, Anton said, "I only know that the mutual animosity goes back for thousands of years."

"And look how many competing camps we have on Canopa," Noah said, "at the heart of merchant prince rule. Your forces, mine, Francella's, and Lorenzo's, all splintered to one degree or another. Look at all of the corporate security forces on Canopa alone. I know for a fact that they've never been adequately coordinated with MPA forces, and this is true on other worlds as well. With greedy individuals and corporations looking out for their own interests, we're in no shape to fight anyone except ourselves."

A cold wind picked up as the sun disappeared behind clouds. "We'd better get going," Anton said, rising to his feet.

In deference, Noah rose afterward, and as they walked back toward the aircraft, he marveled at how Anton was already showing leadership skills, including the way he led Noah around at their meeting place, deciding when to leave.

As they approached the landing sites, they heard excited shouts ahead, from their companions. Running in that direction, Noah and Anton saw a large, ragged rift along the river shore, with the Red Beret soldiers clinging to the edge of the hole, yelling for help. Noah's robots were setting up rescue equipment, but the hole widened and all of Anton's people disappeared in a great thunder of earth and rock, along with his grid-plane.

"My God!" Anton exclaimed.

While Noah hurried Anton aboard his own aircraft, along with Subi and the robots, the hole went in and out of focus, glowing red around the edges. A portion closed over, leaving a scabrous covering of ground and rock, but he saw more of the hole ripping the gorge open in the other direction.

Moments later the grid-plane lifted off, and rose above the danger area.

"Tesh told me there were strange things occurring on planetary surfaces," Noah said, looking back at the long rip in the planet as they cleared the tops of the cliff faces. "She and Eshaz talked for a long time about things that have been concealed from most galactic races for too long. Apparently the Tulyans call that a timehole, a rip in the fabric of time."

"No one can hope to stop such forces," Anton lamented. He sat with his head in his hands, almost unable to cope with the immensity of the crisis and all of the information that had been thrust into his young mind.

"Maybe not, but we have to try. We need to ensure that the Tulyans are dispersed as much as possible, to perform their ancient healing procedures."

Anton did not respond.

Looking back at the ragged, growing timehole, Noah shuddered. This one was much larger than anything the Tulyan had described to Tesh.

Aboard the space station, Pimyt received a coded nehrcom message, relayed to him from the receiving station on Canopa. According to the urgent transmittal, the HibAdu Coalition had noticed unusual geological activities on a number of planets around the galaxy. It was an unexplained, simultaneous phenomenon, which their scientists were investigating.

On Bilwer, one of the Mutati worlds, an entire battalion of Coalition soldiers had been landed secretly—but the ground opened up beneath them and took almost all of them, closing afterward like the mouth of a dragon swallowing a meal.

Chapter Seventy-Seven

Every moment is fresh and new, like the first breath of a child.

—Ancient Saying

W hat looked like a large hawk flew over the sparse, northern forest of Dij, extending its wings and soaring upward on the cool air currents and then drifting back down. It landed high in a tree at the edge of the janda woods, and gazed across the broken landscape, which sloped upward into the foothills of the mountains.

The aeromutati Parais d'Olor enjoyed long flights by herself to explore remote regions, looking for new places to take her lover, the Emir Hari'Adab. In the distance, she saw the high, craggy mountains of the Kindu Range, where Mutati religious hermits were said to live. She had seen pictures of the elusive people in the pages of holobooks, and had always found them intriguing. She wouldn't think of disturbing them in their retreats, however, for that would be like fouling the rugged beauty of the planet itself.

Over the peaks, an immense podship emerged from space in a flash of green light and approached, surprising her. It floated down like a dirigible and landed in the clearing. Wondering how this could possibly happen—since she thought podships could only dock at pod stations—she flew closer, and perched on top of a rock formation.

A hatch yawned open on the side of the mottled gray-and-black vessel, and uniformed soldiers marched down a ramp. They did not, however, wear the gold attire with black trim of the Mutati Kingdom. Instead it was a uniform she had never seen before—orange and gray—and this troubled her. Some of the soldiers were hairless Adurians, while others were short, bearlike Hibbils. They began setting up camp structures.

What are they doing here? she wondered, *and why are the two races mixing?* This was most unusual, and disturbing. The Adurians were Mutati allies, but not the Hibbils, who were instead aligned with the merchant princes.

A short time later, a second podship split the sky and drifted down to the ground. More alien soldiers streamed out. There were thousands of them, an army of Adurians and Hibbils.

Even more unusual, Parais saw what looked like gun ports open on one of the vessels. Hibbils brought in a portable scaffold, and raised it to the level of the ports. Zooming her vision, she saw that they were cannons, and the furry little soldiers were making adjustments or repairs to them.

Weapons on a podship? Parais had never heard of anything like that. Podships had only been known to transport the smaller vessels of the various galactic races. Never anything like this.

Deeply concerned, she flew away, to tell the Emir Hari'Adab what she had seen.

Chapter Seventy-Eight

"There can be no more lofty goal in life than the search for truth. It is the essence of nobility. It is the only air I want you to breathe."
—Eunicia Watanabe, to her son Noah on the boy's ninth birthday

I n the grid-plane, Noah and Anton sat at a table, engaged in animated conversation. They were covering a lot of important ground, going over the galactic web and podship crises, the suspended war, and what actions they might take together.

Since the Parviis were incapacitated, they agreed it might be possible for the entire Tulyan podship fleet—almost four hundred vessels, plus any additional ones they might have captured—to venture out onto the podways. Noah and Anton wondered if the Council of Elders had already decided to do that, as in the old days, filling the vessels with Tulyan web caretakers.

The proper course of action seemed clear, if only the Tulyans could be convinced of it... and Tesh, who had the only podship available to Noah. Based upon what he had learned about the Parviis and the remarkable things that his journeys into Timeweb had revealed to him, Noah didn't think Tesh's idea of diplomacy would work, since the Parviis were too entrenched in their ancient ways and peculiar power structure. Instead, a more drastic course of action was required: Using the Tulyan fleet, Humans and Tulyans needed to make a military assault on the Parvii Fold and take control of every podship the Parviis had. After that, a massive web repair operation could be undertaken for the entire galaxy ... if it was not too late.

They had to move quickly or risk complete galactic disaster, a collapse of the infrastructure in all sectors. There was also the problem of the Parviis. If they recovered, which could happen at any moment, they would surely swarm the pods and take them back, just as they had done for millions of years.

On every one of those points, Noah and Anton concurred wholeheartedly. But they had run into a stumbling block—whether or not to lie to Tesh—and for the past ten minutes their conversation had heated up, with neither one of them backing down. For Noah it was a matter of principle, while Anton was looking at a larger picture. All the while Noah saw the weakness in his own argument, and struggled to find a way to deal with the problem.

Subi landed the grid-plane near Anton's villa, overlooking the industrial centers and offices of the Valley of the Princes. It was sunset, with a violent splash of color across the western sky.

"We're there," the big man said.

Only half hearing him, Noah didn't move. He saw the anger on Anton's face and heard it in his voice.

"Clearly, we need to have Tesh take us to the Tulyan Starcloud for a meeting with the Elders," Anton said, "and it's imperative that we leave right away." He slammed his fist on the table. "But think man! We're talking about a military strike against her own people, so we can't let her in on it, especially not before getting her to take us to the starcloud."

"I won't deceive her," Noah insisted. "She deserves better."

"And what if she doesn't like our plan—which seems obvious—and won't take us to the starcloud?"

Hesitation. Then: "I might be able to take control of the ship away from her."

"And you might not. Isn't that right? The podships fear you, and you're still having trouble getting into Timeweb, right?"

"No one can carry on a conversation with a podship, and it doesn't help that I recommended the pod-killer sensor-guns, but I only did what was necessary to protect the galaxy, and humankind." He sighed. "You're right. There are complications."

Noah hung his head, knowing he could not win this argument, and that Anton was right. Too much was at stake for Noah to hang on a point of personal honor between him and Tesh. This was a matter affecting huge populations and countless star systems.

"Which means you can't pilot the ship telepathically," he said. "It sounds to me like your odds of wresting control away from her are slim."

"True, but I won't lie to her. There must be another way."

"Not that I can see. Think it over, and let me know what our options are."

That very day, Noah had again tried to gain access to the galactic web, but had failed. And even if he ever made it in, with circumstances being what they were, he wasn't at all certain if he could hold the connection. The galaxy was in a state of increasing chaos. It seemed safer for Tesh to pilot the podship by entering the sectoid chamber and taking direct control of it.

"I have a solution," Noah said, with a thin smile. "*You 're* going to have to convince her ... in your own way. I won't contribute one word to your argument."

"No problem," Anton said. "Let's get over there now."

Noah gave new flight instructions to Subi, and they lifted off.

Many changes were occurring in Nirella del Velli's life.

She had only been married to Doge Anton for a short time, and for an even shorter time she had been the Supreme General of the Merchant Prince Armed Forces, succeeding her father. Events were going by her so rapidly that she could hardly figure out what to do. It was like trying to grab hold of the tail of a comet. But she was in a leadership position, and people needed to follow her direction.

But if they only knew how afraid she was, how unsure of herself. And if Anton only knew. Still, she didn't want to add to his burdens by saying anything to him. He already had too many problems to handle, and she didn't want to add to them.

Now another situation had surfaced. An anonymous telebeam message had arrived in the past hour, and she had been pacing her office ever since.

It was a tip that her father was being blackmailed by Lorenzo's attaché, Pimyt. She was not provided with any other details. *Her own father.* What could it possibly involve? As far as she knew, Jacopo Nehr had led an exemplary life, with only the one justifiable incident where he lost control and destroyed government assets. But if that event was already public, and he had lost his job over it, what more could there be?

Upset and confused, she decided to find her father and discuss it with him personally.

Chapter Seventy-Nine

Love comes in all variations. Ironically, it is as unpredictable as its opposite—war—never the same each time it is played out.

—Naj Nairb, a philosopher of Lost Earth

The Emir Hari'Adab always felt out of balance when his beautiful aeromutati girlfriend was out flying alone on one of her wilderness explorations. Parais loved those trips, connecting with remote and pristine beauty. He would never think of denying them to her, would never ask her not to go, or tell her how low and out of sorts it made him feel whenever she was away. If he decided to say anything to her about his innermost feelings, if he clipped the wings of his pretty bird, he knew she would remain at his side and try to be cheerful about it, but she would not be the same person. A part of her would be wounded, and it would make him feel even worse than he did at the moment.

So, he suffered through his quiet misery.

As the ruler of Dij, with the concomitant duties his father had assigned to him, Hari had countless matters on his mind. He remained busy when Parais was away, filling each day with work to keep from having to deal too much with his emotions. But these days, ever since the Zultan had started his psychotic Demolio program, Hari was having trouble focusing on much else.

While the young Emir had taken no part in leading his people into the mass insanity, which ran rampant on every Mutati planet except Dij, each day that passed without him rectifying the situation made him feel more and more culpable. He was, after all, the eldest son and heir of the Zultan of the Mutati Kingdom.

As the designated ruler of the planet Dij, he ran it like a fiefdom, deriving a substantial income for himself and sending taxes to his father on the capital world of Paradij. Bucking pressure from the Zultan, Hari had steadfastly refused to use Adurian gyrodomes or portable gyros, and had issued edicts on Dij making them off-limits to his subjects as well. Even though the Adurians were military allies, he had never trusted them, believing they were too smooth and always had answers that sounded as if they have been coached.

Now, after long contemplation and soul searching, Hari had decided upon a radical course of action. / *am a sane person, but I must do an insane thing,* he thought.

His plan would require the ultimate in security precautions as he dealt secretly with a brilliant Mutati scientist named Zad Qato. Ideally, Hari would have liked to have gotten together personally with Qato … which would have meant having the Paradijan take a solar sailer to Dij, since Hari could not go to him without calling unwanted attention to himself. Unfortunately Qato was under close scrutiny himself, and could not go flitting around the solar system on long journeys that took weeks in each direction.

Qato did, however, have the highest level of military security clearance in the Mutati Kingdom, which gave him access to the Mutati variation of nehrcom communication. It was by this method that the two sent coded messages back and forth. The quality of the transmissions was poor, since the Mutatis had not solved all of the problems of the system. But it did work, and they sent instantaneous transmittals to one another at prearranged times.

Zad Qato, long in years and wisdom, shared Hari's aversion to Adurian gyro units, and to the entire Demolio program that the Zultan had forced on his people. At Hari's urging, Qato had performed careful calculations of trajectory for the Demolio torpedoes, and had adjusted the projected route of a particular shot.

Only the two of them knew this, and Hari prayed that they would not be discovered before they could put their ambitious plan into effect. Everything had to go just right, and the guidance problems had proven to be very difficult. But for the particular target they had in mind, it just might be possible....

Chapter Eighty

Life is not fair,
But death is,
The great and eternal equalizer.

—Noah Watanabe, Galactic Insights

F rancella Watanabe, after all of her schemes and dark triumphs, had withdrawn from virtually everyone and everything. For months she had refused to allow anyone into her private quarters at the villa, and had received her food and other necessities through pass doors. The connected rooms smelled horrible, and bore evidence of her increasingly dismal moods, with furnishings overturned and broken, paintings ripped from the walls and smashed, and dirty clothing strewn about.

Periodically Francella hurled heavy objects off the balconies and loggias. Sometimes when she threw things out they went over the cliff, but once in a while she intentionally hurled heavy objects into the gardens and onto walkways when she saw people down there. More than once, she had struck servants, and had seriously injured two of them.

One evening a private investigator came to inquire about the injured servants. He stood on the loggia outside the entrance to the main floor, while Francella shouted at him through a closed door, refusing to open it. "I warned them to stay out of the way!" she screeched. "It's their own fault if they didn't listen!"

"Get yourself some psychological help," the man shouted back. "You're not well."

"Don't tell me what I need! I'll give you three minutes to leave, or I'll destroy your career!"

She heard low voices outside, and departing footsteps. Then, watching from a curtained window, she saw the investigator hurry along a walkway, looking back nervously, wary of getting hit by something. He climbed into a groundjet and sped off.

Satisfied for the moment, Francella turned a chair right-side up, and sat down, breathing hard.

She continued to rake in profits from her various corporate operations, but had stopped selling elixir, owing to the unpredictable and potentially dangerous nature of the product. As Dr. Bichette had so wisely pointed out, if it worked on the only Mutati known to have taken it—Princess Meghina—could it possibly work on *all* Mutatis if they got their hands on it, and render them indestructible as a race?

Francella had always considered her own interests above those of anyone else, but with her own death staring her in the face, she did not want to become the laughing stock of galactic history. No, she would rather give up her own life than risk being responsible for the elevation of the Mutatis to the immortal—rather than mortal—enemies of humankind.

On one level, she did not wear such an altruistic sentiment easily, for it ran counter to the narcissistic spine of her lifetime, and subjugated her to a footnote of history at best—without a chance of rising above the corporate legacy left by her father. But on another, deeper level, she was actually enjoying the new sentiments, and they felt right to her. Near the end of her existence now, when she was having trouble walking without a cane, when her own breathing was becoming labored and she looked a hundred years old, she was at least connecting with her inner self. It had not really taken her a century to achieve that, not in terms of elapsed years, but spiritually and emotionally she'd had at least that much experience.

No one would believe it if she revealed these innermost thoughts, so she felt it best to keep them to herself, not writing them down or recording them in any way. Many people found religion (or at least spirituality) at the end of life, and perhaps she was doing the same. In any event, it was private and personal, and she had nothing to prove to any other Human being, only to herself. Francella had set events in motion, and had attempted with all of her energy to destroy her hated brother, but it had all backfired on her.

Running parallel with that, even her attempt to bring Princess Meghina down were failing miserably. Francella had always disliked the attractive blond courtesan, since the two of them had been long-time competitors for the affections of Lorenzo del Velli. Francella had tried to ruin her by revealing her true identity as a Mutati, but that had not gone as she had envisioned. Through a cruel twist of fate, Meghina had gained the upper hand. She had become an exotic personality at the gambling casino and an attraction for the guests, going out and mixing with them, telling colorful anecdotes. Even worse, Meghina had received the precious gift of immortality, while Francella had suffered the exact opposite—a death sentence that was being carried out on her with tortuous certainty.

Ever since the discovery that Meghina and five others had achieved immortality from the elixir, Francella's medical laboratories had been taking samples of their blood and flash-freezing it. All the while, Francella had been pressing Dr. Bichette to make more elixir from these samples. But he had resisted, pointing out that it had only been a few months since their apparent transformations, and computer projections indicated that their bodies could eventually reject the elixir, setting in force a reaction like that suffered by Francella, or worse. He didn't want to make any new product from them until he conducted more extensive studies. And in her decline, Francella was running out of the energy to argue with him.

She felt as if she had been chopped up mentally and spiritually, just as she had tried to hack apart Noah's body. On one level, Francella still wanted to destroy her enemies, principal among them her own twin brother. But on an entirely different level, she had been experiencing something new and surprising: altruistic feelings for all of humankind.

It occurred to her now that maybe she only *thought* she felt such benevolence. Maybe, subconsciously, she was really concerned about her own spiritual legacy, and didn't want to risk leaving herself out there as the consummate idiot of all time who had set loose a demonic elixir that led to the downfall of the entire Human race.

Francella could still risk that, widening the elixir studies, and maybe the worst would not come to pass. Maybe Princess Meghina had only achieved her apparent immortality because of some quirk in her body chemistry. She was, after all, unlike other Mutatis psychologically, and physically as well, now that her body would no longer change form. Francella had to admit that the courtesan had never acted like a Mutati, and investigators had never turned up any evidence against her to show that she was disloyal to the Merchant Prince Alliance or to Lorenzo.

She was too perfect to suit Francella, irritatingly so.

If only I wasn't so impulsive, she thought. *If only I hadn't injected Noah's blood into my body.*

With newfound clarity Francella wished she had waited for her laboratory to make elixir and that she had taken only that, without first contaminating her body, harming it with the raw primal energy that flowed through Noah's veins. But even if she had waited for the processed product, she reminded herself now, that would not have guaranteed the success of the elixir on her.

Still, the odds had not been *that* low: six in two hundred thousand … one in thirty-three thousand.

Through all the horrors that Francella had been through, her skin was not only wrinkling and drying out, it was also changing color to a sickly yellow-orange cast, as if an artificial tanning lotion had not mixed well with her body chemistry.

Across the room, a tabletop telebeam projector blinked, signifying the arrival of a message. If this communication did not please her, she would destroy the projector and open a new one, from those she had stacked in a closet, all in their original containers.

Opening the electronic message, she read the words that danced in front of her face, then changed her mind and touched a voice activation panel to listen instead. It was Dr. Hurk Bichette:

"Your troubles might have something to do with the fact that you are Noah's fraternal twin," Bichette said. "Perhaps there is a 'Janus Effect' at work here, with an opposite outcome for each twin. Noah is immortal, while you have become the opposite, and are suffering from a form of the aging disease progeria. We are following this line of research, and hope to provide you with an antidote."

Bichette went on to list, in his usual self-serving way, all the things he and his staff were doing for her benefit, how they were working around the clock, never relenting in their efforts to save her. She'd heard such drivel from him too many times.

In the midst of a sentence, Francella fired a puissant pistol at the projector, causing it to disintegrate.

But Francella had more telebeam projectors in storage, behind locked doors where she could not easily go on rampages and destroy things. She also had more than five thousand doses of the Elixir of Life, the same formula that had been sent out to the public. So far she had only consumed a few doses, and it had not gone well for her. Now she would try something different.

Shoving trash out of the way, the desperate, aging woman brought all of the elixir out and sat in the middle of the floor with it. Surrounded by laboratory boxes, she took dose after dose by squeezing the blood-red capsules between her fingers and feeling the prick of the injection needles. In a few minutes she felt no effect, only pain on the tips of her fingers, which were bloody from all the needles.

Dr. Bichette had warned about the danger of overdose, but at this point she could not see what she had to lose.

479

Chapter Eighty-One

If something disappears entirely, with no trace remaining of it, how can anyone ever prove it was ever really there? Aren't memories notoriously unreliable?

—From *Worlds and Stars*, one of the philosophical plays

The operators of a Mutati deep-space telescope saw a blinding flash of light, but it was not what they had hoped and prayed for, to God-On-High.

A fraction of a second later, the Mutati homeworld of Paradij—with billions of the Zultan's citizens—was obliterated. An armed lab-pod had gone off course and split open the core of the planet. The massive explosion had taken Paradij's three moons with it as well.

Receiving confirmation of the destruction by messenger from the communication station, Hari'Adab screamed, "It can't be! No!"

He could not hold back the flood of tears. It was late at night, with the cold darkness of an eternal shadow seeping into his soul. Trembling, he knelt in his family's private chapel, gripping the sheet of parchment that had just been handed to him. Behind him he heard the gently beating wings of the messenger as he flew away, and the opening and closing of the doors.

The ominous words had been etched on tigerhorse skin by the Mutati version of a nehrcom transceiver, and even contained—like the audio-video versions of other transmittals he had seen—gaps and static markings, reflecting the imperfect quality of the transmission. But enough remained to tell him what had occurred.

It was not supposed to have gone like this. He could not comprehend the immensity and error of the disaster … or his own part in it.

The old scientist Zad Qato had assured him that the Demolio would only hit one of the moons of Paradij—Uta—the location of the primary Demolio-manufacturing facility. Once the main factory had been on Hari's own world of Dij, but eventually the Zultan decided to move them to an automated facility on Uta, where he could visit the operation regularly.

In an engineering marvel that might have been one of the Wonders of the Galaxy if it had been widely publicized, the ancient moon Uta had been sealed with an Adurian-generated atmosphere, a living organism that cocooned the moon in an oxygen-rich enclosure that allowed Mutatis to breathe the air. Automatic gravity systems further enhanced the moon for habitation, enabling the shapeshifters to walk about normally on the surface.

After making hundreds of Demolio shots from Paradij, the Zultan had recently decided to move the launches to Uta. In a gala kickoff ceremony, Abal Meshdi went to Uta to broadcast the event to all the citizens of the Mutati Kingdom.

Infiltrating the Uta facility and gaining the trust of the Zultan, Zad Qato had calculated the trajectory carefully, and after Abal Meshdi's speech the lab-pod was supposed to have boomeranged around and hit Uta, killing the Zultan, a handful of Mutatis in his entourage, and a small number who supervised operations at the automated factory. In setting up the assassination, Hari'Adab had not liked the prospect of collateral damage, but under the plan it would have been a necessary sacrifice, saving trillions and trillions of war deaths—both Mutati and Human—at the hands of his insane father.

For some time, Hari had contemplated the unthinkable familial sin, the act of patricide. Sometimes, as he stood with his father, he had considered killing him on the spot, but always he had weakened. In close proximity, the old Zultan had intimidated him, and had prevented the movement of the younger Mutati. Hari had stood frozen, unable to go through with it. Even when he visualized making the attempt he worried that something might go wrong and he would fail. If that happened, he would never get a second opportunity.

He had considered countless other ways of accomplishing the dreaded task, such as sending an assassin after the old terramutati, or bombing the Citadel of Paradij. But his father had dramatically tightened the network of security around himself and all of his palaces, so Hari could not come up with any such plan that had the remotest chance of success.

That only left two workable options, doing it himself in close proximity or blowing up the Uta moon. Since he could not accomplish the first method, that left only the second. It was beyond unthinkable, especially for a Mutati who had always prided himself on his high morals. But it was the only way.

Zad Qato had assured Hari that the trajectory calculations and guidance system adjustments would be absolutely perfect. Now, Hari could not even yell at the old scientist, since Qato had been on Uta at the time of the launch, and the powerful detonation of Paradij had taken the moon with it.

Hari was deeply saddened at the tragic loss of his own father, as well as the old scientist and so many other shapeshifters. It had gone horribly wrong. By this horrendous act, Hari knew he had put a stop to his father's murderous aggressions. But that realization did not help assuage his conscience, not in the least.

There might be a few outriders still in deep space with the capability of firing torpedoes, and he could only hope that they were not on prearranged attack schedules. But he knew that the Demolio torpedo program could not continue on a large scale, since the Zultan had coordinated everything himself, and Mutatis would not do anything important without his blessing.

Now, in his private chapel, Hari went to a cabinet and removed a ceremonial sword. Unsheathing it, he pressed the tip of it against his fleshy midsection. And prepared to fall upon it.

At that moment, Parais d'Olor—hurrying to tell Hari about the podship landings—flew by the chapel window and looked through it. Seeing what he was about to do, the beautiful aeromutati crashed through the plax and knocked the sword away with one of her powerful wings.

"My darling, my darling!" she exclaimed, gathering her wings to pull him to her bosom.

Looking up at her gentle, compassionate face, Hari wished he had been faster with the sword. But that would have required bravery, which he did not have. He felt the deepest, most mournful sadness anyone could ever experience, for he knew with certainty that he would be condemned to the eternal damnation of the undergalaxy for this. He had indelibly blackened his soul.

There could be no redemption for what he had done.

"But why, why would you do this to yourself?" she asked.

After saving Hari's life, Parais escorted him into his palace and put him to bed. "You must rest," she said. "Everything will look better in the morning."

"That is not possible," he said.

"I will remain with you," she promised, "never taking trips away from you, never leaving your side. I love you so much, and you must believe me when I tell you that life is worth living."

Deeply despondent, Hari admitted what he did—the unimaginable, accidental destruction of Paradij in an attempt to stop his father's psychotic military program. As he told her he saw shock and horror register on her face. But she recovered quickly, and spoke to him in a soothing tone. "It's not your fault," she said. "It must have been the will of God-On-High."

"More likely, it was influenced by the demons of the undergalaxy."

"Forgive me for saying this, but your father was the most evil Mutati I've ever met. I was chilled to the bone in his presence. The galaxy is a better place with him gone."

He nodded, but did not brighten.

"Don't be sad, my darling. Wherever you're going, I'll be by your side."

"You would kill yourself?"

"Without you, I would have no reason to live."

Struggling to maintain his composure, Hari touched her face with one of his three hands, and followed her perfect contours with his fingertips, the exquisite bone structure and classic features. He could not imagine her dying, but knew of no way to keep her alive unless he remained among the living.

"With the Zultan dead," she said, "the victim of his own demented plan, the Mutati people need a strong, ethical leader to keep them on the proper path. And you—as Abal Meshdi's eldest son—are that leader. You shall be the new Zultan."

They placed their hands on a copy of *The Holy Writ*, and shared a prayer.

After Hari had rested, Parais told him of the strange podship landings on the other side of Dij, and of the Adurian and Hibbil soldiers that had disembarked. She expected him to say he already knew about it, but he looked shocked.

Immediately he dispatched his own military forces to the site, with orders to rout the intruders. In the operation, his fighters killed half of the aliens and captured the rest. They also took control of two podships. But these vessels, his scientists determined by tracking their DNA histories, proved to be of the laboratory-bred variety that his father had been cloning on a secondary world in the star system. And these two, unlike the others that had been so unreliable for cross-space shots, had navigation systems that worked perfectly, taking test pilots out into deep space and back.

None of the prisoners would reveal anything, but Hari's linguistic experts soon learned that the nav-units had Hibbil markings on them.

Chapter Eighty-Two

It should not be possible for a vast connective tissue to exist, touching every celestial body in the heavens, but this is, nonetheless, the galactic design. How do planets orbit suns when the webbing is intact, and fall out of orbit in sectors where the webbing has decayed? To comprehend, it is necessary to expand your mind, and when you believe comprehension is reached you must suspend it, because the true answer comes from a different portion of your brain.

—Noah Watanabe

Disembarking from the grid-plane, Noah led Anton and Subi along an electronic-camouflaged path to the main entrance of the subterranean headquarters. It was early evening, with stars twinkling faintly against a charcoal-gray backdrop. They walked inside a moving infrared bubble, which permitted them to see through the darkness in all directions.

"Are you taking me to the podship?" Anton asked. "Is that where Tesh is?" "Possibly, but we don't want to alarm her by going directly there. It is best to act more casual, and broach the matter with her in my office, or over a meal." "You're right. I'm just impatient to get on with it." "So am I, but we need to be careful what we say to her."

"You mean, what / say to her," Anton said. "I have to convince her on my own, remember?" Noah shot him a rueful smile, and considered the situation. Despite the electronic camouflage, certain realities were apparent. Anton's father—Lorenzo del Velli—already knew the location of the facility, so Noah saw no point in concealing it from the young Doge. The information was out anyway, and besides, there was a cease-fire and Noah needed to work with Anton closely if the Human race—and every other race, for that matter—had any chance of surviving the growing galactic cataclysm. He even wished the Mutatis well, as long as it didn't come at the expense of humankind.

Though Noah had been indoctrinated from an early age to despise all Mutatis, he had never really understood the historical underpinnings of the conflict, and now he could not bring himself to wish extinction on them. There must be good and bad Mutatis, just as there were good and bad Humans.

Maybe Princess Meghina was one of the good shapeshifters. After all, she had tried to prevent Francella from shooting him on the Canopa pod station. Meghina was known as a courtesan, but she also had a reputation for being compassionate, and for donating funds to animal-welfare groups as well as to impoverished people on various MPA planets, especially those living in the back country of her own homeworld, Siriki. She had even been kind to Noah's father, Prince Saito Watanabe, caring for the old man more than any courtesan should.

In the red darkness, Noah saw a wide stone that marked one of the secondary entrances to the headquarters. Touching a button on his belt, the stone slid aside, revealing a metalloy door. From another control on his belt, Noah sent coded signals. The door did not open.

"I just changed the codes," Subi said.

"Yeah, I know," Noah said, "but I thought you programmed the new ones into my belt."

"I did."

"Don't worry," Noah said, as he transmitted more signals. "I still have other ways of getting in, an access override."

"We shouldn't have to use the overrides," Subi said, watching as Noah transmitted an alternate code. "Okay, there it goes."

The large door irised open, revealing a dark tunnel beyond. Subi led his companions inside, and closed the entrance behind them. Lights flashed on in the tunnel, and they hurried through it.

"In all the excitement," Anton said, walking beside Noah, "I forgot that I need to maintain contact with my own office, or they will worry about me. Can you get a message to them, under my seal?"

"Of course."

"You want to help with my diplomatic mission?" Tesh asked, staring at Doge Anton. Glancing over at Noah, she said, "Did you tell him everything?"

"Yes." Noah sat beside the merchant prince leader, sipping a glass of redicio wine. They were inside a large subterranean cafeteria, serviced by robot waiters. Noah saw Tesh's green eyes flash at him, and he felt the emotional charge between himself and her. He also noticed the interaction between her and Anton, the remnants of what once had been an intimate relationship.

"But how can you trust this man?" she demanded. "He's the Doge now, the leader of the Merchant Prince Alliance. Your enemies! How could you do such a thing?"

"You trusted me once," Anton said. On the tabletop, he touched her hand. She pulled away.

"I want you to take me to the Tulyan Starcloud," Anton said. "It's essential to begin the diplomatic mission there. Your idea about going to the Parviis is a fine one, but it can't be done casually, not the way you did it the first time. No, I'm going to advocate that it must be a full-fledged mission, led by the finest diplomats, both Human and Tulyan."

Glaring at Doge Anton, she kept her thoughts to herself.

"For something this important, I need to go myself," Anton said, as if anticipating a question she might have.

"And your entourage?" she said.

"Not needed for this initial trip. Though the Tulyans respect Noah, they do not generally trust Humans. I must take this gradually." He smiled stiffly at his former girlfriend.

Tesh swished the wine in her glass, didn't drink it. "Something doesn't feel right here," she said. Looking at Noah, she asked, "What do you have to say about this?"

"I'm outranked by my nephew. He's doing the talking."

"Are you being deceptive? I'm sensing something else going on here."

"This is an important matter with far-reaching consequences," Anton said. "We don't have time *for feelings.*"

Wrong way to put it, Noah thought, shaking his head.

Flashing an angry look at Anton, Tesh rose. "You're in no position to be condescending." She walked away.

"Tesh, wait," Anton said.

But she kept going, and didn't look back.

"That went well," Noah said to Anton, when she was out of earshot. "She's not stupid, you know."

"I remember," Anton said. "She always was difficult for me to handle, and that hasn't changed. What do we do now?"

"Wait for her to cool off," Noah said.

After reducing herself in size, Tesh entered the sectoid chamber of the podship. Scurrying up a wall, she attached herself to the green flesh, where she felt the gentle, soothing pulse of the creature. Bathed in the lambent green light, she heard the faint background hum that had historically linked all of these creatures in the galaxy. Holding on to the thick flesh was no effort for Tesh at all. Through the connection, she peered through the eyes of the podship into the darkness, and up to the vault of stars.

Closing her eyes, she let her mind drift.

It was so peaceful here, and seemed to Tesh like the safest place in the universe, where she could gather her thoughts and sort through problems. Since landing near the Guardian headquarters, Tesh went to the sentient spaceship a couple of times a day, just to be by herself. Now she pressed her tiny face against the flesh, and felt the creature's warmth, and the subtle changes in its pulse. Each day that she was with the alien organism she felt closer to it ... as if it was becoming part of her, and she was becoming part of it.

"I dub thee Webdancer," she whispered, on impulse.

It was an appellation that brought to her mind romantic images of podships skittering along the web, from star to star. She sometimes wondered if these simple, beautiful creatures should be left free and wild, to roam the galaxy on their own.

It had agitated her seeing Anton again, since it reminded her of some of the arguments they'd had after she met Noah, when Anton accused her falsely of not being faithful to him. She'd been with possessive men before, and had never liked it. Anton had taken it relatively well when she broke up with him, though he had seemed genuinely sad.

Sifting through her thoughts, she realized that she felt gloomy just sitting at the same table with him. Once there had been strong feelings between them, almost love, and she still cared about him. She also knew him well enough to sense when he was not telling the truth, or when he was concealing something from her.

But what could it be?

Anton wanted to travel to the Tulyan Starcloud very badly, to see the Council of Elders. Supposedly to make sure they performed caretaking operations for MP A sectors. In truth, that might be part of it.

Or ...

She didn't want to think about the alternative.

Abruptly, Tesh detected an increasingly strong tugging at her mind, something trying to break her mental and physical link with the podship, trying to take Webdancer away from her.

Her serenity broken, Tesh came to sharp awareness and fought back.

Deeply fatigued, Noah had been drifting off to sleep, just beginning to peer into a dream world of alpine lakes and canopa fir trees, with gnarled rocks above ... formations that looked like living, fairy tale creatures. The rocks moved slightly, as if they were talking to each other, but they did not seem threatening to him. They were like sentinels, protecting the realm of his reverie.

But an odd, intrusive sensation began to come over Noah, as if two dimensions were rubbing together, grating on the tranquility of his dream. In a violent jerk, he had suddenly been ripped away from slumber and thrust out into the cosmos.

He found himself spinning along the vast, curving strands of the web. From what he'd heard, he'd expected to see only a few podships out there, occasional wild ones. But there were hundreds of gray creatures flying one direction and another, maybe more of them than that, taking courses that seemed different from those he had seen before. These ships were going slower, skipping along the web for a distance, slipping off, and getting back on again. Still, they were making their way across the galaxy at much higher speeds than conventional solar sailers or vacuum rockets.

To his dismay, Noah noticed great rips in sections of the web, ragged holes in the fabric of the galaxy and regions where planets and stars slid and tumbled out of orbit, with no web tissue connecting them at all. The podships went around those problem sectors, but even where the web looked normal the sentient vessels could not go as fast or as efficiently as the podships he had seen previously.

These vessels were most peculiar. Stretching his mind and peering into them, he saw that they were piloted by Hibbils, sitting inside navigation units that were unlike anything he had seen before. Surrounding the furry little men were arrays of computers and servo machines, blinking lights and panels. He saw no Parviis on board any of the ships. And in the cargo holds he found something very troubling, transport ships full of Adurian and Hibbil soldiers.

What does this mean?

With each podship that he viewed, he sensed increasing agitation, as if the creatures were sending signals to each other, warning one another about him. Gradually he felt his connection to the podships slipping, and the interiors began to flicker in and out of view. Soon he could not view the interiors at all, and the sentient spacefarers began to veer away from him, like frightened fish in a cosmic sea. Focusing his energy, Noah tried to take command of one podship, and then another, but to no avail. They sped away from him, in all directions.

As I suspected, they fear me, he thought. *They know about the sensor-guns I recommended.*

Their continuing reaction against Noah suggested to him that they had a means of sensing danger, but only at a primitive level. If they had been more intelligent, they would realize that he had actually saved many more of their kind than he killed by preventing the Mutatis from using their planet-buster weapons … weapons that destroyed podships as well as merchant prince worlds.

Breaking away, Noah found that he could expand his mind again. With a rediscovered measure of control, he tried to locate the Parvii Fold where Tesh said one hundred thousand podships were, and where he presumed that the Parviis were attempting to recover. But he could not locate the region, not in any of the sectors in the galaxy. She had told him it was in the most out of the way place, so perhaps he just needed to look harder. Discontinuing the effort for a moment, he tried to see another assemblage of podships, at the Tulyan Starcloud. He made out the milky star system, but could not get close to it, could not penetrate the powerful mindlink security veil of the Tulyans.

His mind arced involuntarily, and he sped across the galaxy, back to Canopa. To his surprise, he surged into the podship and saw Tesh inside the sectoid chamber. Somehow he had gotten past the defenses of the creature. Was that because he had been more closely associated with this one in the past than with any other? Did it trust him more?

Almost immediately, Noah sensed the uneasiness of the creature, but his own mind pressed forward, trying to overcome the resistance. He had not intended to fight her for control of the vessel, but found himself doing so anyway, without his volition. He struggled to break away and leave Tesh and the podship alone, but the more he tried, the harder another side of his psyche fought for dominance … over him, and over them.

Against the powerful mental onslaught, Tesh lost her hold and tumbled to the floor of the sectoid chamber. But she fought back ferociously, aided by the podship, and Noah was glad they did, because it seemed to him that Tesh had more of a right to control this creature than he did.

Gradually Noah found himself losing the battle, and presently he peered into the alpine dream world again, as he drifted off to slumber. The sentinel rocks were larger now, and more powerful.

They set up a defensive perimeter, letting him sleep.

As he continued dreaming, Noah found himself viewing the interior of the podship, but his hold was tenuous, with only flickering images coming to him. Tesh had just emerged from the sectoid chamber, and had switched on her magnification system. The images shifted, and abruptly Noah stood with her inside the passenger compartment, gazing at her while she glared at him. Looking down, Noah saw that his feet seemed to float in space, with swirling nebulas and speeding comets below him. He sensed the uneasiness of the podship around him, and saw the interior skin of the vessel trembling.

"My mind scanned Timeweb," Noah said, his voice remote. "I don't mean to be here. I didn't do it on purpose."

"You tried to take control of this ship again," she replied, a scolding tone.

"Not consciously. I didn't even enter the web consciously."

"Just as you are not here consciously now?" Tesh said.

"Yes. When I was out in space, I saw strange podships, filled with Hibbil and Adurian soldiers. The ships were piloted by Hibbils inside computerized navigation units. So strange, and troubling."

"There is a disturbance in the web," she said.

"Most peculiar. Thinking back now, I do not think those podships are normal. I suspect they have been created artificially, perhaps cloned for military purposes. The Hibbils and Adurians are not to be trusted."

"You must tell Doge Anton what you saw."

"When I awaken. So odd," Noah repeated. "Those strange podships veered away from me and fled in fear. Even this podship does not accept me. I sense its fear."

"I know," she said, softly.

"Why can't the podships understand that I don't want to hurt them?"

"Don't you know?" she responded. "After you recommended the establishment of pod station defense mechanisms all over the Merchant Prince Alliance, three podships were destroyed at the Canopa station. Podships, even cloned ones, know your part in the destruction of their kind. They sense it, smell it on you."

"I know that, of course, but I only did what I had to do, because of the terrible Mutati military threat. That's what I mean, that they should be able the sense the truth, the unavoidable actions I took."

"On some level this podship might realize that," Tesh said. "Perhaps that is why it permits you this close."

As Noah touched the interior skin of the creature, it recoiled and shuddered. "This is most distressing to me," he said.

"I understand," she said, "and perhaps in time they will, too. I don't blame you for the podships. You only did what you thought was necessary."

He smiled winsomely, and saw its disarming effect on her.

"Noah, I still care about you, despite all that has occurred." She smiled gently. "Since you have come to me in this manner, does that mean I'm your dream girl?"

"No question about that. I knew it the moment I set eyes on you, though I tried to deny it, tried to stay away from you. Look at this! I can't seem to get away from your charms, even when I sleep."

They drew together, and kissed....

On the podship, Noah and Tesh had their first sexual encounter. For both of them it was astounding, but Noah wondered how it could have possibly occurred, since she was actually so tiny in her physique, a creature the size of a Human finger. Previously she had explained that the magnification system around her was so complete that it processed physical acts—in all of their intimate details—as if her body was really much larger.

But now, experiencing the spectacular sensuality with her, Noah could hardly believe it.

Chapter Eighty-Three

We have not yet seen all of the life forms that can be created in this universe.
— Tulyan Warning, a common finding of the timeseers

"I hate him as much as Francella does," Lorenzo muttered.

He stomped around The Pleasure Palace, where robots and other workers were preparing for the evening's gambling activities, carrying immense trays of food and setting up the finest wines and other liquors. Even with the cessation of podship travel, Lorenzo still had his valuable wines, especially old growth redicios and vintage champanas from around the galaxy, having accumulated them during his two-decade tenure as Doge. Keeping all of that was part of the deal when he abdicated. He also kept the del Velli corporate operations and his own Red Beret forces, stationed on the ground near two shuttle stations and on the orbiter.

Maintaining pace with the aged but still spry man, Pimyt moved his little legs rapidly. "It is too bad we didn't kill him," the Hibbil said. "Now Noah is making important political advances, aligning himself with the new Doge."

"My foolish son Anton," Lorenzo grumbled. "I'd disown him, but he has his own wealth now and wouldn't care. My options are badly diminished. Why isn't Francella keeping them apart? And what about her promise to give me access to the Office of the Doge? She must be dying. It can't be good that we haven't heard from her."

"Noah still has our prisoners," Pimyt said. "Shouldn't we negotiate with him for their return?"

"I don't negotiate, unless I have the upper hand. You should know that by now. You taught it to me."

"True enough, but it's embarrassing to linger like this."

"Hang embarrassment. It can't be worse than our failed attack, or having to abdicate." Lorenzo gestured with his hands as he spoke, and accidentally slammed into a tray carried by a young waitress, spilling food on all three of them and sending dishes crashing to the floor.

"Oh, excuse me, Your Magnificence!" she said.

Workers hurried to clean up the mess while the flustered woman used a towel to wipe Lorenzo's billowing white tunic, where a crepe had soiled the fabric.

"You're only making it worse!" he thundered. "Get away from me!"

She burst into tears and hurried away.

Kicking the tray out of his way, Lorenzo continued his angry march around the casino, ignoring the soiled white shirt and the food on his shoes.

"Do you think the Doge might attack me?" Lorenzo asked.

"Unthinkable. That would cause an uproar against him by the merchant princes."

"Still, I want more protection up here. I want you to order more of my soldiers onto the orbiter."

"But that would require reducing our forces at the shuttle stations, where they perform screening operations to keep undesirables from coming up here."

"Then put in a requisition and get me more troops. Raise a stink about it."

"Yes, Sire. Right away."

"We'll pay for it … or some of it… if we have to, but only as a last resort. Don't offer anything Just make demands. I want more powerful gunships patrolling the space around us, too."

"All right. I'll take care of it." As if afraid that Lorenzo would give him a longer list, the little attaché hurried away, leaving almost as rapidly as the waitress.

Pimyt would prefer to have Lorenzo still in charge of the Merchant Prince Alliance, since it gave the HibAdu Coalition more opportunities to set up their military plans. But the coded nehrcom messages he had received told him that things were going well enough anyway, with Hibbil and Adurian troops stationed strategically on merchant prince and shapeshifter worlds, ready for major, simultaneous attacks.

For his own personal safety, and for the benefit of the clandestine military operations, Pimyt did not want the orbiter to fall under attack. Conceivably, Noah Watanabe could convince Doge Anton to mount an offensive against Lorenzo. It was not likely, but he wanted to eliminate the possibility.

Purporting to operate under the authority of Lorenzo, Pimyt dispatched a priority telebeam transmission to Doge Anton, asking him to broker a peace conference between Lorenzo and Noah. The Doge Emeritus would not be pleased to learn what he was doing, but Pimyt didn't care. It would protect the orbiter, and would give the Hibbil the additional time he needed to accomplish the goals of the Coalition.

Pimyt was stalling for time, but didn't need very much more now. The Adurians had discovered a way to speed up the process of growing cloned podships. As a result, the fleet was expanding rapidly, and the ships were filling with troops and military materiel.

Within the hour, Pimyt received a response from Anton's office, saying the Doge was away on important business, and would attend to the matter upon his return. There were other things as well—referred to in the communication, but not explained—that needed to be taken care of before any arrangements could be made for a peace conference.

Chapter Eighty-Four

The universe is a treasure chest filled with mysteries.

—A Saying of Lost Earth

As Tesh emerged from the sleeping quarters that she shared with female Guardians, she found Doge Anton del Velli awaiting her. He stood at the top of a stairway that led down to the cavern floor from the barracks building, with his arms folded across his chest.

"I thought we might have breakfast together," he said.

"We can talk here," she said, scuffing her foot on the deck. "I don't feel like getting indigestion, with you at the table pressing me for what you want."

"I need to get to the Tulyan Starcloud right away. It's very important. Look, you're the one who suggested a diplomatic mission to the Parvii Fold."

"I suggested it to Noah, not to you. As far as I'm concerned, you're not needed." She paused. "In any way."

"It isn't going to help the situation if you and I can't be on cordial terms. That's the least we should do, after the feelings we shared in the past. Besides, I never did anything to hurt you. Why are you taking this attitude with me?"

Brian Herbert

"Because I sense something, that you aren't telling me the whole truth."

He sighed. "I just think the diplomatic mission needs to be undertaken with more preparation. I'm willing to throw my full efforts into the enterprise, and we need high-level Tulyan involvement, too. You can't just go to the Parvii Fold with Noah Watanabe, only the two of you. Is that what you have in mind?"

"I assume he might bring some of his top Guardians, such as Subi Danvar and Thinker. I know he has others, too, who have negotiating skills."

"Well, we need a lot more than that."

"How much more?"

"That's what I want to discuss with the Tulyan Elders."

"Is military force part of your plan?"

"The Tulyans are pacifists."

"Throughout most of their history, they were. But their mindlink attack with comets changed all of that. I'm afraid they aren't in the right frame of mind to talk with Woldn. And Woldn isn't going to feel favorably toward them."

"We can't just go to the Parvii Fold in one ship, with a few people. No matter the high office I hold, we need more of a show than that. If the Tulyans pitch in and we fill their podships with a diplomatic delegation, that will carry more weight with Woldn."

She eyed him skeptically. "You're still not telling me everything, are you?"

He grimaced. "You know me too well. But please understand that in my position, I cannot provide all of the details. This is a matter between Human and Tulyan governments, at the highest levels."

"And I'm a mere pilot, you mean?"

"No, it's just that certain matters of galactic security must remain confidential. I am the Doge, and you must respect that."

"You're not *my* Doge. I am a Parvii, not a Human." She paused. "So, you admit wanting to discuss additional, unspecified matters with the Council of Elders?"

"They involve sensitive diplomatic issues."

"And Tulyan caretaking operations for MPA planets?"

"Perhaps," he said.

She kept her eyes narrow. "They will do that even if you don't ask for their help. I know them, and understand their motives. MPA sectors will get the same treatment as other sectors, according to priorities. Are you going to ask them for favoritism? Is that it?"

"Of course not. I only expect what we deserve."

Shaking her head so that her long black hair made a snapping sound, she asked, "Why don't you send a message through Zigzia, the Tulyan female who works with Noah's Guardians? Through her, he is in regular contact with the Council of Elders, sending messages across Timeweb."

"We tried that, but there are transmission problems, and we haven't been able to get clear signals through. It's patchy at best; signals keep breaking up. Zigzia and Noah think it has something to do with the galactic infrastructure failing."

She was about to say something, but instead glowered and took a deep breath.

"For this mission, I can only do it in person," he said. "Maybe it's meant to be. There can be no intermediaries, no couriers or messaging technology. I must look in their eyes, and they must look in mine."

"Then you're not in any position to ignore me, are you? Not if you want to hitch a ride."

490

He reddened. "You're absolutely impossible!"

"And you're not?"

"This matter can't be delayed," Anton said. "Don't you understand? The galactic infrastructure is failing, and we need to leave right away!"

"And if I say no, the whole damned galaxy falls apart?"

"Something like that. Yeah."

"Why is it all on my shoulders?" Her eyes smoldered.

"It's not. We're in this together."

"Well, I don't feel that way."

"This goes way beyond feelings, Tesh. It goes beyond emotions."

"You just said the wrong thing again, *Mister*. As usual."

Before Anton could recover, she whirled and left.

Too upset to eat, Tesh headed for her podship. Nearing the tunnel that led to the vessel she ran straight into Noah Watanabe, as he rounded a corner.

"Oh, I'm sorry," he said, as he stumbled trying to avoid her. The two of them remained on their feet, and stood looking at each other awkwardly.

"That's all right," she said with a smile. "I have a lot of insulation in my energy field. It acts like an airbag, reducing any impact on my body."

"I was just looking in on our newest robot recruits," he said. "Gio Nehr was responsible for tearing them down and inspecting their programs, so to play it safe we've been checking all of his work."

"I'm heading for Webdancer. Oh, that's what I call my ...*the* podship."

"I like it. Do you want company?"

"To pick up where we left off?"

He frowned in confusion as they began to walk together. "Kind of. I was going to ask you what you decided to do about Anton's request. He's young and doesn't always put things very well, especially to you, it seems."

"We just had an ex-lovers' spat," she said.

"Oh, so you turned him down?"

"It wasn't about that. But even if it had been, I'd turn him down. But never you. I enjoyed last night."

"What?"

"In the podship." She tossed her long hair over one shoulder. "We made love, in case you've forgotten so soon."

"That really happened?"

With a smile, she said, "I'd say so."

They reached the end of the tunnel, and passed through the electronic security.

"I thought it was a dream," he said. "My physical body wasn't with you."

"Sure seemed like it to me. It was terrific, like supernatural sex."

Noah thought about this and finally said, "Maybe it's a projection of some sort—like your magnification system makes touching your projected skin seem real. Maybe I locked onto something like that while I was dreaming."

"I can't think of a better explanation."

"Actually it seemed like more than a dream before I was with you. I was out in the galaxy, taking a telepathic trip through Timeweb. I didn't try to get out there, either. I was pulled out of my dream."

"Strange."

Ahead, beneath a shimmering veil of electronic security, the gray-and-black podship waited. They mounted a platform next to it, and a side hatch yawned open.

"Will Webdancer allow me to board?" Noah asked.

Tesh touched the mottled skin of the creature, and stroked it gently. "I think so," she said. "The podship knows I'm in full control now, and that you pose no threat."

With trepidation, Noah followed her. As in his dream, he saw the trembling of the vessel's interior skin, and he moved forward quietly, as non-threateningly as he could. He had heard of podships reacting to intruders by sealing themselves up and closing off all sections, suffocating the passengers.

Gradually, the trembling of the thick skin ceased, and Noah breathed a sigh of relief. But he had no illusions about regenerating his past piloting abilities. He thought that Tesh's presence, and her feelings of support for him, were calming influences on the creature. On a level that he didn't understand, these podships were able to sense danger, and he was pleased that he seemed to be making some small progress in convincing one of them that he was not a danger to their race.

"How does your magnification system work?" Noah asked, keeping his voice down. "That might give us a clue as to what happened between us last night."

"I don't know how the system works," she said, "only that it does." They paused in the middle of the passenger compartment, and the hatch shut behind them, a compression of cellular material over the opening. "Just as we don't understand how podships work, but we use them anyway."

"How do you activate your magnification feature?"

Pushing the collar of her blouse aside a little, she pointed to a tiny, dark mark on the skin of her neck. "I rub that spot for a moment. It's an implanted device."

"Med tech?"

"Enhanced. It creates an energy field all around me that makes me look much larger than I really am."

"But what happened with us last night wasn't technological. Unless…."

"Unless what?"

"Unless there really is an area of overlap between the scientific and the spiritual. I've never been devoutly religious, have considered myself more of an agnostic about such matters. But the *Scienscroll* of the merchant princes says there is an overlap, a theoscientific universe of the heavens."

"Maybe the explanation lies in the holy scriptures of your race," Tesh said. "In fact, the more I think about it, maybe that isn't as odd as it sounds. After all, there is a distant genetic link between Humans and Parviis."

"Perhaps, though I'm not a student of religion. Or, the answer lies in a combination of truths from the Parviis, from Humans, and from all of the other galactic races, including the Tulyans."

"I hate to think that Mutatis are part of God's sacred design," Tesh said. "They're more like something out of the undergalaxy, something that should have never been allowed to escape." She shuddered at the thought. Then, as if to calm herself, she ran a hand along a bulkhead wall, and felt the faint pulse of Webdancer.

"Sometimes it's hard to envision the truth."

"At least you have eternal life now," she pointed out. "That gives you enough time to investigate the greatest questions in the universe and discover the answers."

"You mean like, 'What is the meaning of life?'"

She nodded. "Maybe it's even bigger than that. Maybe the question should be, 'What is the meaning of the universe?'"

Looking around the compartment, Tesh stared at the place on the floor where they had made love the night before.

Noah saw where she was looking, and smiled. She kissed him on his lips, and drew him against her body. But he pulled away.

"Did Anton ever tell you the truth?" he asked.

"Going back how far?"

Showing no amusement, he said, "I don't mean when you were lovers. I mean about why he wants to go to the Tulyan Starcloud."

She shook her head. "Just political doubletalk."

Pursing his lips, Noah said, "Anton wants the Tulyans to help him mount a military operation against your people. He wants to capture the huge Parvii podship fleet—all those thousands of ships—and prevent Woldn from using it to take revenge on the Tulyans."

"I thought so. That occurred to me, and I even asked him if he wanted to use military power. He lied to me, and I didn't want to believe that could be the reason." Tesh felt anger rising. "Does he expect me to turn against my own kind?"

"I understand why you're hesitant, Tesh, because he's talking about going after Parviis. I don't want to admit it, but I agree with Anton. He should not have lied to you, but he is right. I hate to put it this way to you, but we need to attack the Parvii nest. For the sake of the entire galaxy, you must be a Guardian before you're a Parvii, before anything else. It's that critical, my darling, and we don't have much time."

"I'll give you an answer when I'm ready," she said. "As for our little rendezvous, I'm no longer in the mood."

"Neither am I," he admitted.

They talked stiffly for a while longer. Then the Parvii woman opened the hatch for Noah and he went to his office, where he found the Doge awaiting him.

"Subi said he saw you with her," Anton said.

"I told her the truth. You weren't getting anywhere, so I tried a different tack." The young Doge covered his eyes with one hand, then peered through his fingers at the older man. "What did she say?" Noah told him.

Unable to sleep that night, wondering what Tesh's answer would be, Noah tossed and turned. Finally, he began to drift off.

And as before, Noah was sent spinning on another mental journey into Timeweb. This time he discovered a new aspect, and saw the web in curving layers that peeled away before him like those of an onion, showing some familiar aspects and some that were new to him. Each layer, he realized to his amazement, was an entire, huge galaxy. How many were there? He couldn't tell, and couldn't gauge the full scope of what was seeing. The images compressed, and again he beheld the familiar, faint green web lines of the cosmic filigree, with very few pods flying along it. He was surprised to see that the Mutati homeworld Paradij did not exist anymore.

Only a debris field remained.

Curiously, the less Noah tried to enter Timeweb, the more he was able to go into it. Two nights in a row. The sensation terrified and excited him simultaneously. He wanted to see these things and learn the secrets of the heavens, but didn't want to at the same time. He thought he might be several different entities at once, and that his life was like an umbrella for all of the creatures living under it, including the Human aspect of Noah, as well as his spiritual form that ventured into the universe, and much more. But details eluded him.

Suddenly he felt himself sucked far across the web, and he was speeding through space at multiples of tachyon speed, covering vast distances. Gradually, as if he was on a machine in the process of shutting down, he stopped spinning, but felt a sharp, sudden pain in the middle of his back. Something had just struck him from behind, penetrating the skin.

Whirling, he saw the image of his sister Francella—looking haggard and old but with a fanatical energy and the fierce gleam of madness in her eyes. Screaming soundless epithets, she flew at him across space, firing lightning bolts from her fingertips—eerie, noiseless lances of light in rapid succession.

He dodged them and fought back in the same manner—as if the two of them were mythological beings battling one another in the heavens. Moment by moment, Noah felt Timeweb suffusing him with power, and he drove the crazed apparition back, hitting her with so many energy bolts that her entire form lit up in flames that should not have been possible in the oxygenless void.

She screamed, again without making a sound, and disappeared into a ragged rip in the web of time.

Chapter Eighty-Five

Think of secrets, small and large. Secrets within each individual's mind and expanding outward into the cosmos, until the entire universe is filled with them. Based largely on selfishness and narcissism, they have become an unhealthy, dangerous energy.

—Master Noah Watanabe

Unknown to Doge Anton or Lorenzo del Velli, two laboratory-bred podships filled with HibAdu soldiers had slipped through Canopa's security network and landed on a desolate, remote prairie. Activating an electronic veil over them, they made themselves—and their new military camp—invisible to satellites or aircraft.

After the soldiers were set up with their assault aircraft and other equipment, Pimyt made arrangements to use one of the lab-pods, along with its crew. At shortly past midnight, the lab-pod flew to a prearranged rendezvous point north of Rainbow City, where the scheming attaché boarded it, taking with him a bound, drugged man. The prisoner, carried by a bulky robot, was Jacopo Nehr....

The subsequent journey across space took more than an hour, a very slow passage that Pimyt learned was due to deterioration of the galactic infrastructure on which they traveled. The sections they had to traverse for this trip were especially rough.

A few minutes into the flight, Nehr stirred from his bench in the passenger compartment and struggled with the electronic cuffs securing his wrists, then tumbled onto the deck. Unknown to him, a Hibbil sat in a comfortable VIP chair at the rear.

"What is this?" the inventor demanded. "I'm on a podship? Who's back there?" Craning his neck, he tried to see across the compartment to the rear, where he seemed to sense another passenger. His voice was slow and slurred, the residual effects of the drug.

Pimyt muttered to himself. Without replying, he transmitted a signal to release the electronic restraints.

He heard Nehr walking around the compartment, and in a few moments he saw the enraged, confused man. The eyes were red and bleary, the graying hair tousled. Watching him, Pimyt sat calmly on his padded chair, so short that he couldn't be seen until now.

"You did this to me," the enraged inventor said, holding onto the back of a chair to keep from falling. He looked around at the mottled gray-and-black walls, which to him must look like a standard podship. "But how? Podships are operating again?"

"In a sense," Pimyt said, bouncing off his chair.

"What do you mean?"

The Hibbil shrugged, and smiled enigmatically.

"Shouldn't we be somewhere by now?" Jacopo asked, going over to a porthole and peering out.

Gazing calmly past him, Pimyt saw stars, nebulas, and brilliant suns flash by. "We're taking the long way," he said.

"The long way? I didn't know there was such a thing. I've never heard of a podship trip longer than a few minutes. Eleven or twelve at most. Where is my wife? Where is Lady Amila?"

"She's back on the orbiter. Now just sit back and relax," Pimyt said. "We'll be there in due course."

Pacing nervously around the cabin, Jacopo opened cabinets and inspected vending machines and mechanical gaming stations. "What kind of a podship is this?" he asked, standing in front of a plax-fronted mechanical galley. "I've never seen amenities like these. Have they been custom fitted into the compartment? How did they get the podship to accept all this stuff?"

"You ask a lot of dull questions," Pimyt said, with no intention of telling him that this was a lab-pod.

The secretive Hibbil saw it as a game, fending questions and not providing any answers. He was not happy with Jacopo Nehr for losing his position as Supreme General of the Merchant Prince Armed Forces, punishment for the foolish attack on a sealed government warehouse and storage yard. The resulting fallout made Nehr less useful to the HibAdu Coalition, since he could no longer be used as a conduit for coded military messages. Most of the important military communications had already been sent through Jacopo, but a number of details remained, and Nehr's blunder was hampering their operations.

Even so, his firing did not make him entirely useless. He was still the father of Nirella Nehr, who was now the supreme Human military commander. Having the inventor-prince as a hostage might give Pimyt some leverage with her, to make her the new conduit. If he could ever get through to her and make the additional threat to reveal the secret of her company's nehrcom units. So far, she had been too busy to see him.

Finally, the agitated Jacopo took a seat near the front of the compartment. Several times, he got up and walked around, looking increasingly nervous and upset. At last he laid down on a bench and closed his eyes.

A short while later, Pimyt shook him.

"Whah?" Jacopo said. He seemed to have dozed off.

"We've arrived."

Pimyt climbed on a bench and looked through a porthole. Below, he saw the largest of the Hibbil Cluster Worlds, and shivered with pleasure. He always felt this way when returning to the planet where he was born, the place where he had happy memories of long ago, before he began to work with the irritating merchant princes.

Glancing to one side, he saw Jacopo looking through another window. "You will be permitted to oversee your robot manufacturing operations on the Cluster Worlds," Pimyt said. "You will not, however, be allowed to contact anyone back home, and you will have no access to your own nehrcom transmitting system."

"Why have you done this to me?"

"Patience, and you will find out."

Ipsy had been on the Hibbil planets for several weeks, and had survived surprisingly well—largely because he was viewed by the furry little people as a novelty, with his patched-together body and free-spirited ways. After initially earning money by telling stories on street corners, Ipsy had talked his way into a job at Jacopo Nehr's largest machine manufacturing plant. A facility that used to export huge numbers of robots to the Merchant Prince Alliance, it was now getting by on much lower sales to other galactic races. Ipsy, with his marketing success at the Inn of the White Sun, had boasted that he could build this business, too.

When Jacopo arrived and entered his own office, he found Ipsy there, sitting at the factory owner's own desk. Knowing that the wealthy man was due to arrive, the little robot had positioned himself boldly, in order to get the most attention.

Remaining in his boss's chair, the fast-talking robot spewed forth a steady stream of marketing ideas. "The Adurians need to replace their delivery robots," he said, "and the Salducians are complaining about getting thousands of bad machines from one of your competitors. *Lemons*. And I can give you a whole list of additional opportunities. I've been doing my research, you know."

Feeling angry and irritated, Jacopo lifted the robot out of the chair and placed him roughly in a side chair. "Let's get one thing straight in the beginning," the former general said, slipping into his own chair. "I sit here, and you only take a seat if I give you permission."

"Of course, of course," the robot said. "You like my ideas, I assume."

"Do you know why I'm here?" Jacopo asked.

After a moment of processing data and blinking lights, the robot said, "To supervise your business operations here?"

"No. I could have done that from Canopa. Do you have any idea why I was brought to this planet?"

More blinking lights. "Not known."

"Can you find out for me?"

"You are the boss. But do you like my sales ideas? I worked very hard on them, and I wish to please you."

"Nothing pleases me at the moment."

"I will work hard to rectify that."

Jacopo nodded.

In the days that followed, Jacopo overcame his initial irritation and began to institute some of Ipsy's suggestions, many of which had excellent prospects of success. But the robot failed in one important respect, because he could not obtain information that Jacopo wanted. The reason he had been brought to the Hibbil worlds.

Chapter Eighty-Six

Francella's moral fabric ripped open and she plunged through, into something entirely unexpected.

—Secret notes of Dr. Hurk Bichette

For the better part of a day Noah had been using an intermediary in an attempt to find out about Francella, but no one at her villa or at her offices provided any information. The supernatural battle with her had seemed so real to him, and there had been the strange sexual encounter before that with Tesh—an event that she insisted had actually occurred. Could that possibly mean that Francella was dead? In the fight, she had fallen through a rip in Timeweb.

Hesitant to discuss the situation with Anton, Noah decided to say nothing about it to him. The two of them got together for breakfast and lunch, and both times they discussed Tesh, speculating what she was thinking and what her answer might be. Once they saw her walking briskly through a tunnel with other Guardians, but she strode right past them without speaking or making eye contact.

Every couple of hours, Noah went alone to his office to check status reports on his wicked sister. Just after dinner he received a telebeam response, ostensibly from Francella's house manager, a Mr. Vanda. Floating in the air, the words said, "I regret to inform you that Ms. Watanabe is deceased. She died here peacefully within the hour."

Noah felt an unexpected surge of pain and grief. Tears flowed onto his cheeks. Angry at this display of weakness, he brushed them away. He shouldn't have such feelings for her.

Now he had to talk with Anton. Inviting him to his office, Noah sat at his own desk, waiting. When the door opened and the young Doge walked in, Noah saw a mask of grief on his face.

"You know about her?" Noah asked.

"For most of my life I hated my mother for abandoning me," Anton said, "without knowing who she was. When I finally met her, I hated her even more. Then, when I spoke with her and her feelings opened up to me, I began to sympathize with her."

"I always felt sympathy for Francella," Noah said. "Even when I loathed her the most, I tried to be understanding." He paused to reflect. "It wasn't always easy, because of her mental illness."

"You've been a good brother and a good uncle," Anton said.

"I'd like to pay your mother my last respects," Noah said. "It's the least I can do, and I'd like to do it right now."

His blond eyebrows arched. "Now?"

"Yes. I don't want to attend any funeral service for her, not with crowds of mourners. She was a famous, powerful lady, and the mother of Doge Anton. They'll come in droves. I just want to say a few last words to her. Do you want to go with me?"

"What about security?"

"I can arrange it. We know from reconnaissance how she guarded the villa. Under merchant prince tradition, her body will remain there for at least a day."

"This could be a trap laid for you," Anton said. "I'll go with you, and you can use me as a hostage if anything goes wrong."

"I wouldn't think of it, *Sire!*"

"I understand more about politics than you do, Uncle. I'm going with you, and you can't stop me."

Noah bowed his head.

In short order, Noah put together a security squadron led by Jimu, and went to the villa in a groundtruck. It was a clear night, with stars sparkling overhead like diamonds. The vehicle didn't stop at the front gate; with the robots firing their weapons, it burst through. Against superior firepower, the guards ducked for cover, not shooting back.

Disembarking at the great house, a hundred robots stormed the building, followed by Noah and Anton. They met no resistance, as the guards fled into the darkness.

Jimu set up a perimeter around the villa, then accompanied Noah and Doge Anton into the lobby. There, Noah spoke with the balding house manager, Nigel Vanda, a short, dark-skinned man who couldn't seem to stand still.

"Sorry I didn't give you advance notice," Noah said. "You know who we are?"

The man nodded. "Though I am surprised to see you together." He bowed to Anton.

"Where is she?" Noah demanded.

Looking dismal, Vanda gestured to the right, constantly twitching. "Mistress is in the master suite."

Noah had come on impulse, wanting to say his final, respectful good-bye to a woman he had always loathed and always loved, in his own private way. He felt recurring waves of sadness, more than he had expected. She was not only his sister; she was his fraternal twin. In the natural order of things they should have been very close, but it hadn't been that way and never would be. Their ill-fated relationship seemed symptomatic of the chaos in the universe.

He wanted a few moments alone with her body, but to play it safe he had brought the robots along, to prevent falling victim to one of Francella's schemes. Considering the possibilities, Noah had an odd, overcommitted feeling. Though he had brought along considerable firepower, something prickled the hairs on the back of his neck. He glanced around, met Anton's equally concerned gaze, and then looked back at the house manager, who stood shaking in front of him.

The nervous little man looked cheerless, with sadness filling his eyes and his mouth downturned. He looked as if his mistress might very well have died, and he had cared about her. Anton said he had seen her good side, and Noah had heard about some of her kindnesses from others as well. She just never showed that side to him.

And now she was gone.

"Take us to her," Noah said to Vanda.

"We haven't moved her yet," the house manager said. "I have sent for the proper attendants. Procedures must be followed."

"I understand," Noah said....

Francella's body lay on the marbleine floor, surrounded by expended elixir capsules. She looked very dead, with her eyes staring into nothingness. Jimu checked the suite first, dispatching twenty robots into all of the connecting rooms. Presently, the dented little robot announced, "All clear, Master. I'll check the body now."

"No," Noah said, leaning down and feeling her neck for a pulse. There was none. "She's gone." Then, to Anton, he asked, "Could I have a few moments alone with her?"

"Of course."

Doge Anton, the house manager, and the robots left.

As Noah leaned over Francella he picked up her unwashed odor, and nearly gagged. The rooms were a cyclone, with furnishings and food scattered everywhere. She wore a filthy blue robe and lay in a fetal position, with her face turned to one side.

Out of the corner of his eye Noah saw something move, and he jerked in reaction. A black roachrat scampered over the garbage, ignoring him. Shuddering at the conditions under which his sister had been living, and in which she had died, Noah threw a holobook at the rodent. The creature ran off.

Feeling a wave of sadness Noah reached out and gently massaged Francella's high forehead. The wrinkled skin was still warm, so perhaps she had not died when he had the cosmic confrontation with her. She must have passed away sometime afterward. He felt his own heart skip a beat. She looked like a very old woman, one that had not aged well.

Why did she look this way?

All of a sudden Francella came to life and struck out at him with a dermex, stabbing it into his stomach. He stumbled backward, grabbed at the medical device, and finally hurled it aside.

"Too late," she said. The face was cadaverous, the eyes dark and hellish cesspools. "I injected you with my own blood. Now let's see if you are truly immortal after all."

"But how? You had no pulse!"

"Either I'm a zombie or CorpOne has a medical division, and there are drugs to simulate death." She cackled with fiendish delight.

Noah struggled to his feet, trying to assess how he felt.

Laughing cruelly, Francella then brought a knife out of her robe and held it to her throat. She paused, and her expression saddened. For a moment, Noah saw a softer side to his sister. "I'm so tired," she said.

"Hand me the knife." Noah tried to sound calm, but heard his own voice crack.

"So you can kill me with it?"

"Don't talk that way, Francella. Let me help you. Give me a chance. *Please.*"

Madness overtook her face, especially in the gleaming eyes. "I'd rather do it myself," she said. With an efficient move, she slashed her own throat. Blood spurted from the wound, and she slumped to the floor.

Noah hurried to her and tried to stem the flow of blood by pressing his fingers against an artery. It wouldn't seal, and sprayed in his face. "Jimu!" he shouted. "Get in here!"

The door exploded inward, and a dozen robots surged into the room, followed by Doge Anton.

"Master!" Jimu said.

The house manager ran forward. He looked confused, and in apparent disbelief. A good performance, if that's what it was.

"She wasn't dead," Noah said, glaring at the little man. In his arms, he felt her go limp and lifeless. He cradled her and rocked her, but refused to cry.

Jimu sent for reinforcements, and in a matter of minutes a small army of Guardians surrounded the villa.

On the second level, Noah took a shower and changed into clothes that were brought for him. Then, in the dining hall, a medical team led by Dr. Bichette performed a battery of tests on him.

Finally Bichette met privately with Noah, in an anteroom. "There seems to be no injury or adverse effect on you," the doctor announced.

But in Noah's private thoughts he was not so certain. Returning to his headquarters at shortly past dawn, he slumped into a soft, oversized chair in his private sleeping quarters.

He had never expected to be with Francella when she died, not like that. It was as if she had perished twice, first in the paranormal space battle and later in the villa. Somehow she had entered Timeweb with him in the earlier encounter, and she should not have been there. But it really had happened. One aspect of her, the spiritual one, had fallen through a timehole and vanished into another realm.

Then the rest of her, all that was left of her demented, anguished existence, finished herself off.

Chapter Eighty-Seven

Enhancements and extensions are always possible, but only within certain frameworks, which can be quite large. Ultimately, when the eye has seen as far as it can see and the mind has stretched to its farthest reaches, eternity and infinity only exist in the imagination. The paired concepts are artificial constructions, and not reality.

—Tulyan Wisdom

At first the knocking sounded distant, as from many kilometers away, or from a nearly forgotten memory. Noah straightened in the big chair, and blinked his eyes open. The louvers were drawn over the two windows in his room, and across the large sheet of glax in the door. Under the circumstances, with the perpetual darkness of living underground, he had tried to bring as much outside light into his quarters as possible through the glax, albeit the artificial illumination of the chamber that contained the barracks and his own private section.

Most peculiar, though. He saw blue light around the edges of the door. Rubbing his eyes, he stared, and heard the knocking again. "Noah, are you up?" *Tesh.*

He shuffled over to the door and opened it. She wore a blouse and slacks, and her entire body glowed blue, as did the clothing.

"Oh, I'm sorry," she said, looking him over. "Did I wake you?" "That's okay," he mumbled. "I had to get up and answer the door anyway." She smiled thinly at the witticism. "I suppose you're wondering why I'm blue this morning." "The thought did occur to me." He felt concerned for her. "Something wrong with your magnification system? It's not dangerous to you?"

"It's just a color I selected for my energy field," she said. "We Parviis can do that, and blue is the way I feel."

"Melancholy, you mean?"

She nodded and said, "You look terrible, Noah. Your eyes are sunken and tired, and you have dark shadows under your eyes. Out all night drinking?"

"Hardly, but I didn't get any sleep. Long story."

"I'd better go, and let you rest."

"Don't. I'm all right."

With a gesture and a yawn, Noah invited her into the compact room, which had been designed in the manner of a ship's compartment where space was at a premium. High walls were filled with shelves and cabinets, and some of the furnishings served dual purposes, with fold-down tables and a settee that converted into a bed. Too tired to even hit a button when he got back to the room, he had not activated the bed.

As Tesh entered and took a seat at a small table, she said, "I'm blue because I've made a difficult decision, one I don't feel entirely good about."

He felt his pulse jump. "The starcloud trip?"

"Good guess." She chewed nervously at her upper lip, couldn't seem to come up with the proper words. The blueness vanished, and she sat there dressed in white.

Watching the Parvii woman, seeing the turmoil on her lovely face, Noah's mind spun. Her words could mean two things. Either she didn't feel good about having to reject the request from Anton and Noah, or....

He didn't dare hope, almost didn't want to know the answer.

Looking away, Tesh acted as if she could not bear to utter the words herself, as if she didn't want to hear them from her own lips.

Shambling over to the table, Noah touched a brown button on one edge, tapping it twice. A mocaba-juice processor popped out of the wall and within seconds it started brewing and filling two cups with steaming, dark beverage. He smelled the rich aroma.

Feeling the need to fill the air with words, Noah changed the subject. While talking, he handed the mocaba to her and sat down beside her at the table. He told her of his second dream trip into Timeweb, and of all of the layers he saw out there, the wondrous galaxies.

"They are like the pages of a great book," she said, "the Story of the Galaxy. My people have a saying: 'Each layer is like a different version of the same reality, like the colors of a sunset shifting slightly, moment by moment.' "

"So many mysteries," he said.

"No Parvii I have ever heard of, and no Tulyan, has ever mastered all the mysteries of the cosmos. Perhaps if you gain control of the ability to come and go in Timeweb, you will see more than we ever have. Some things cannot be taught; they must be experienced."

Lapsing into a long silence she sipped her coffee, didn't seem ready to say whatever was really on her mind.

"Unfortunately there is much more," Noah said. He told her of his cosmic battle against Francella and the later bloody, final confrontation. "It was as if she died twice," Noah said. "First her spiritual self and then the physical, one after the other." Several minutes had passed since he had poured the mocaba juice. He dipped a finger in the cup to test the temperature, then took a long drink of the lukewarm beverage.

"How awful," she said. She kissed the reddish stubble on his cheek. "I'm so glad that you're all right."

"I'm not really all right," he said. "Part of me didn't want her to die. I ... I hoped we could be like a real brother and sister some day, despite all that had occurred between us. With Anton's involvement, and what he was telling me about the nice things she did for him, I thought she might be changing. It was like the way I felt about my father. He and I had been estranged for so long, and then there was a glimmer of hope. But he died." Noah hung his head. "Now I've lost both of them."

"I'm so sorry."

"I appreciate that." With what must be a pained expression, he looked at her.

"We're both a mess this morning," she said. From the sharp glint in her eyes, he thought she might be ready to tell him.

In a husky whisper, hardly able to get the words out, she said, "I will take you and Anton to see the Tulyans."

He felt elation but suppressed it, out of concern for her. The reason for her own sadness was obvious. She had made a courageous and momentous decision, choosing the Guardians and the welfare of the galaxy over the interests of her own people. It must be the hardest choice she had ever made.

"You are destined for greatness," she said, "and I will not stand in your way."

"But you are not a timeseer," he protested. How can you say that about me?"

"You are destined for greatness," she repeated, this time in an eerie, almost synthesized voice that sent a reverberating shudder through Noah's body. Deep in her eyes, he could almost see the entire universe cast in an emerald tint, galaxies on top of galaxies, stretching all the way back to the beginning of time.

Chapter Eighty-Eight

It is the most important thing I have ever done. On this event, the entire future hinges.

—Doge Anton del Velli, private notes

As Webdancer split space and emerged into the Starcloud Solar System, Tesh guided the podship toward the globular pod station floating in the milky void. Sunlight filtered through the mist. She judged it was the middle of the day in this region.

It had taken her almost thirty minutes to negotiate the journey across space, at least three times the normal duration. Suddenly the way was blocked by many podships with large Tulyan faces on their prows. At the same moment she sensed something inside the sectoid chamber with her. Looking around, she noticed a faint vapor that sparkled a little in the air, like tiny metallic particles. It dissipated quickly.

Ahead, the vessels parted and permitted Tesh to steer through their midst, into the main docking bay of the station. As Noah, Anton, Tesh, and an entourage of Human and robotic Red Berets disembarked and passed through an airlock onto the walkway, they were approached by a group of Tulyans.

Another podship pulled into the docking bay and moored. Noah recognized Eshaz's face on the craft, but in a matter of seconds the flesh of the podship morphed and smoothed over. Presently Eshaz walked out of the vessel, emerging from a hatch in the side of the hull.

The web caretaker first greeted Tesh, and the two of them spoke cordially for a moment. "I saw you in the sectoid chamber," he said, "and told my friends to let you through."

"I sensed something there. A faint metallic vapor. That was you?"

He nodded.

"We have different powers, you and I," she said. Gesturing toward Anton, she added, "The Doge has urgent business with your Council of Elders. He could not send you a nehrcom because your people don't have them, and he didn't want to use Zigzia and the web."

"It is too important," Anton said, "so I wanted to come here personally."

"What business do you have?" Eshaz asked.

"I prefer to only say it once," the merchant prince leader said. "Can you take us there directly? It is most urgent."

"As you wish."

During the shuttle ride, Eshaz told them that the Tulyans had been busy, and had wrangled an additional five hundred wild podships, giving them more than nine hundred in all. Eshaz reported that no Parvii-piloted ships had been seen out on the web thoroughfares at all, and he theorized that Tesh's people must still be holed up in the galactic fold, not coming out for any reason.

"Your fleet is growing," Anton said.

"Hunting has been made easier by the absence of competitors," Eshaz said, "though we don't know how long that will last."

"I'm not a Parvii anymore," Tesh announced. "I'm a Guardian."

Noah smiled gently. His brown eyes were filled with appreciation and compassion. He and Tesh exchanged slight smiles.

Showing his own appreciation, Eshaz nodded to her. He went on to say that Tulyans had recently seen other mysterious podships out in space, traveling much slower than regular Aopoddae. "They must be defectives," he said, "mutants of some sort, and a large number of them. My people, piloting our own podships, cannot form any kind of telepathic link with the unusual creatures and cannot see inside, even though we have always been able to do so with other podships, while piloting one of them."

"They may be clones," Tesh said, glancing over at Noah.

"I had a paranormal experience and saw inside them," Noah said. "The vessels are operated by Hibbils."

"*Hibbils*? But why?"

"Perhaps we can sort it out together," Anton said. "The sooner we pool our resources against whatever forces are at work out there, the better."

Later in the day the Council of Elders gathered to hear the important visitors, inside the floating, inverted dome of the Council Chamber. Looking around as he entered the large central room, Noah noted that the audience seats were packed with Tulyans, murmuring to each other in low, excited tones. Robed Elders began to take their seats at the high bench.

The floor beneath Noah was a clear material, through which he saw filtered sunlight, with podships tethered in the mist. He took a seat at the front with Eshaz, Anton, and Tesh.

"Who will speak first?" one of the Elders said.

"That's First Elder Kre'n," Eshaz said to Noah. "Some say she's as old as the galaxy itself."

Rising to his feet and stepping into a designated circle on the floor in front of the bench, Doge Anton del Velli wore a formal dark-blue cape and suit that he had brought along for the occasion. He held a liripipe hat in his hands. "I'm going to get right to the point," he said, in a firm voice that was carried throughout the chamber by the enhanced acoustics of the circle. "On behalf of the Merchant Prince Alliance, I propose a military joint venture between my people and yours, to attack the Parviis in their nest. I know you have traditionally been a non-violent people, but I am told that you did mount an attack against Parvii swarms who were gathering against you, and you scattered them in disarray."

"An unfortunate situation," Kre 'n said, scowling.

"But necessary," Anton said. "Now help us finish the job. My military forces are the finest in the galaxy. With your fleet and the telekinetic ability to control comets and meteors…."

"Our telekinesis works best in the starcloud," the old Tulyan said, leaning forward and looking down sternly. "Mindlink still functions away from the starcloud, but in a much diminished form."

"All the more reason to join forces with me. I can fill your ships with soldiers and war materiel."

"It is one thing to defend our sacred starcloud, and quite another to mount an aggressive military campaign far across the galaxy."

"Your ancient enemies are regrouping," Anton said, "and they'll be back, trying to accomplish what they could not before."

"Then we will drive them off again."

"Maybe, and maybe not. In any event, why wait for them to come, and why take the chance that they might succeed, using ancient, more powerful weapons? We need to annihilate them in their galactic fold, preventing them from causing more harm."

"These ideas trouble me," the First Elder said.

"We live in troubled times," Anton said. "But I ask you most urgently to consider the merits of my proposal." The young Doge bowed and swept across his knees with the hat, then returned to his seat.

By pre arrangement Noah followed him to the speaking circle. Standing tall, with his voice strong, he said, "I have had a number of remarkable experiences, spinning across the cosmos in my mind, taking incredible mental journeys. It is all impossible, of course, but seemed real to me each time. Later I came to realize how authentic the cosmic experiences actually were, on a level unknown to any other person of my race."

As he spoke, Noah noticed all of the Elders leaning forward, listening to his every word.

Taking a deep breath, Noah continued, "Something highly unusual has happened to me, but I have never considered it power, not in any sense of the word. Perhaps it is an ability, or a talent, or just a freak cosmic connection. Whatever it is, comes and goes. No matter what, even if I had full control of myself in Timeweb and I could accomplish meaningful things in that realm, I would consider it a *responsibility* to the entire galaxy, not something I do for selfish reasons."

He met Kre'n's gaze, and added, "Just as your people consider it a responsibility to take care of the web."

"We have heard many stories about you," said the largest Elder on the bench, looking very intense and severe as he sat beside Kre'n. Earlier, Eshaz had said his name was Dabiggio.

"I am here to second the request of Doge Anton," Noah said, "and to tell you this. For the sake of the galaxy, all podships must be returned to their rightful custodians, your people. It is not a matter for diplomacy, though we have considered this option at length. Since time immemorial, Parviis have controlled a vast fleet of podships. It is what they do, and what they think they were born to do. I don't think they will move aside for the sake of anyone, and certainly not where their mortal enemies are taking a central role in using the podships. Instead, we need to strike the Parviis hard and recover the Aopoddae. Tesh says the Parviis are ill and weak, but may be recovering. And—they have more than a hundred thousand vessels."

As Noah spoke, some of the Elders stepped down from the bench and walked around him, looking down at him closely. The large aliens made him uneasy. Even the shortest of them was still half a meter taller than he was, and all of them weighed several times what he did. Finally he asked, "What is it?"

For more than a minute, the old Tulyans said nothing, and a hush fell over the entire chamber. Looking around, Noah noticed a certain deference toward him on the faces of some Elders … but Dabiggio and others seemed to regard him with suspicion.

"There are many legends among my people," Kre'n said, "and one of them concerns a Savior." She placed a large hand gently on Noah's shoulder. He felt her rough, scaly skin against the side of his neck, touching bare skin. "You may be the one," she added.

Noah did not particularly like what she had just said. Tesh's earlier comment bore some similarity: *You are destined for greatness.*' First from a Parvii and now from a Tulyan … to his knowledge, these were the only two galactic races that had ever dominated podships.

Am I really the first of my race who has been able to do it, too? he wondered. / *think I am, but what if I am not? What if there have been others in the past….* He paused in his thought process, when it occurred to him that he might be a genetic mutation that would continue into the future, from his own offspring. Yet another galactic race, or subrace.

If the galaxy survives.

But he thought his special ability might be gone, since he could no longer enter Timeweb voluntarily, and of late had only been able to gain entrance through his dreams. It was as if two dimensions were rubbing together at the time-and-space nexus of his life, sliding him into and out of each realm.

Still, Noah sensed that he had not entirely lost the ability, and that it lay dormant somewhere deep inside, verified by the dreams. One day, the skill would resurface again, but only when he was ready to receive it.

But the suggestion that he might be a Savior was an aspect that terrified him, one that he did not feel equipped to handle. Gazing up at the rugged, ancient faces of the Elders and at the audience around the chamber, he wanted to announce that he was not anyone's messiah, that he was just one man, and he would do the best he could.

As Noah considered this, he noticed that most of the Elders had returned to their seats, but First Elder Kre'n remained behind. Now she said to him, in a husky whisper, "I just read your thoughts." He had almost forgotten that she was still touching his neck, but now he became aware of it, and remembered what Eshaz had once told him, that Tulyans could read minds this way.

When she withdrew her hand, Noah felt sudden panic, and a swooning sensation.

"Don't say what you're thinking to them," the Tulyan leader urged, still whispering. "Let those who think you are the Savior continue to believe. It makes them more likely to authorize the military venture. Only time will tell if you really are the one. You don't even know yourself."

Reluctantly, Noah nodded. Kre'n returned to her own position on the bench.

Noah continued, speaking passionately. "At this moment in galactic history, there is a critical need for unity between Tulyans and Humans and cooperation on an unprecedented scale." The great chamber had fallen silent, while everyone listened to his words.

"I don't know the full extent of my abilities, or why I've been placed here at this time of terrible crisis." He paused and looked around the chamber with a determined expression. "Truly, I can only tell you what is in my heart, something your First Elder has ascertained with her touch. We must move forward together and survive ... or die together. Doge Anton is right. We must form a military joint venture and attack the Parvii Fold."

Whispering filled the chamber, and Noah concluded his remarks.

After he resumed his seat between Eshaz and Anton, the Council engaged in a brief debate among themselves, speaking in low tones on the other side of the bench. There was a good deal of whispering, and periods when the Tulyans read each other's minds by touching hands.

Finally, the Elders resumed their places at the bench, but this time they remained standing.

In a somber tone, the First Elder looked at Doge Anton del Velli and announced, "We agree to form a military partnership with you. Due to the pressing need to regain our relationship with the sacred Aopoddae fleet, we see no viable alternative." She cleared her throat. "We will provide podships and pilots for the enterprise, while the merchant princes will provide weapons, fighters, and the military commander in chief."

"That is satisfactory," Doge Anton said, rising as he spoke.

"I must emphasize that we were never masters of the sacred fleet," Kre'n said. "Instead, it was a cooperative arrangement between two sentient races for the well-being of the entire galaxy."

"May I propose a name for our joint assault force?" Noah asked, standing beside Anton.

Kre'n nodded.

"The Liberators," Noah said. "It will be our mission to rescue podships and return them to you, for the stewardship and maintenance of galactic infrastructures."

"We are not inspired by such designations," Kre'n said, with a slight smile, "but it is known that you Humans are. Very well, for the purposes of this mission, we shall be known as the Liberators."

Chapter Eighty-Nine

The endings and beginnings of life perpetually feed into one another, in infinite and fascinating variations.

—Master Noah Watanabe, unpublished interview

While Tesh no longer wanted Anton as a lover, she had been impressed by a number of decisions he had made recently, all surprising in view of his youth and political inexperience. According to stories circulating while his demented mother was still alive, he had emerged quickly from behind her skirts to carve his own identity as a leader. Now he was working closely with Noah Watanabe, a man Tesh looked up to more than any other.

The aggressive plan that the two men had conceived for the Tulyan Starcloud trip had irritated her at first, but in the end she had seen the wisdom of their views, and the absolute necessity of carrying them out. The way Noah and Anton were setting aside political animosities between the government and the Guardians was admirable, and she liked their decision to bring a nehrcom relay unit along on the voyage. While it was of no use at the starcloud, since it was out of range of land-based installations, they had foreseen how it would be employed elsewhere.

As Tesh approached Canopa, piloting Webdancer at the head of the Tulyan fleet, Doge Anton used the relay unit to send a coded transmission ahead, ordering the shutdown of the pod station defense system. This was done, and the podships arrived en masse, surrounding the facility. A few of the ships took turns to disembark passengers. The vessels were unlike any others seen in that sector, at least in modern times. They had large reptilian faces on their prows, giving them a hybrid appearance, like the strangest race in the entire galaxy.

At the pod station, Anton's wife, General Nirella Nehr, greeted the Doge and his entourage, bringing with her a contingent of Red Beret and MPA soldiers. She wore a red uniform with gold epaulets and braids, the first time Tesh had ever seen her in it. The impressive garb suited her. This woman of impeccable reputation looked very official and comfortable in her position. She saluted the Doge, then stood rigidly at attention as he spoke to her.

"Begin loading our specialized military personnel and hardware onto the podships," Anton said. "Exactly as I told you to prepare before I left, except now we have a larger fleet than I anticipated … more than nine hundred ships. We will make stops all over the Merchant Prince Alliance, gathering the largest possible strike force."

"So it's really going to happen," Nirella said. "An assault on the Parvii Fold!" The female officer glanced at Tesh, then back to Anton. "As you ordered, we've been getting everything ready in your absence, including our most powerful space-artillery pieces."

He plans well, Tesh thought, looking at her former boyfriend. *Let's hope this leads to a good result.*

Although he struggled to conceal it, Pimyt was alarmed to see Human military activity on Canopa, with hundreds of podships setting down on the surface of the planet. Where did Doge Anton and Noah Watanabe get all of those vessels, and why did they have reptilian faces on their prows, giving them the appearance of odd Aopoddae-Tulyan hybrids? The Hibbil wanted to relay nehrcom messages to his people, but since Lorenzo's fall from power he was being denied access to a transceiver.

Using his remaining connections, Pimyt traveled around the planet to see more of what was going on. Through the payment of bribes, he learned what was happening: a major military venture to the Parvii Fold, with Tulyan pilots operating the ships. He felt his spirits lifting. There were persistent rumors that the Parviis had powerful telepathic weapons, so with any luck at all, the task force would be wiped out and never make it back to Canopa.

On the third day of military preparations, the door to Pimyt's office on the orbiter slammed open, and Nirella Nehr marched in, wearing her uniform and cap. Just before the door closed behind her, he saw her soldiers crowding into the corridor outside.

"Where is my father?" she demanded, leaning on the desk and glaring at the Hibbil, only centimeters from his furry face.

"I don't know," Pimyt said, indignantly. "How dare you come in here like this?" Actually he'd been trying to arrange an appointment with her to work his wiles on her, but she had either been too busy to respond or had her own reasons for avoiding him. This was not what he had in mind.

"Some of the people you've been paying off are talking, and we have established a pattern. You've been blackmailing my father, haven't you?" She was so angry that spittle sprayed on his face.

Wiping off his cheek, the attaché responded in a syrupy tone, "You and I might come to an understanding, in exchange for certain … cooperation."

With a sudden motion, she grabbed him by the neck and shouted, "I '11 hook you up to the same Hibbil torture machine that Lorenzo used on General Sajak, melting his body piece by piece, from the feet up!"

"And what a galactic scandal that would cause," Pimyt countered, with a sly, ostensibly fearless smile. "Especially when embarrassing information about your father is released at the same time. Let's call it an industrial secret about how your precious nehrcom works. It's not quite as complex as you've let on, is it?"

When she reddened, he grinned and added, "The disclosure is all set up, an automatic reaction if anything happens to me."

Her eyes narrowed dangerously, and for a moment he thought she might murder him on the spot. Then she whirled and stalked off, without another word.

As she left, angry and frustrated, Pimyt realized he had only won a skirmish with this female general, and there would be additional confrontations. Maybe he should have told her more, everything he knew about the internal workings of the nehrcom. But she had caught him off guard, and he'd wanted more time to consider what to tell her.

Just then the door burst open again, and a squad of red-uniformed soldiers marched in. A young officer slapped a document onto the desk. "We are placing you into protective custody," he announced.

"But I don't need *any protection!*" the little Hibbil protested, as he was lifted into the air, with his feet kicking. "I can take care of myself!"

"Orders directly from the Doge," the officer said, showing him an oval red seal on the document. He snapped electronic cuffs around Pimyt's wrists and ankles.

"But Lorenzo would never…." Pimyt caught himself, having gotten so flustered that he had forgotten political realities. "Why would Doge Anton do this?"

"Gee," the officer said, "I'd ask him, but I think he's kind of busy."

"Lorenzo will not like this!"

"The two of you can discuss it at length," the officer said. "He's being taken into custody, too."

The following morning the Liberator fleet departed, bound for Siriki, the second wealthiest planet in the Merchant Prince Alliance. As the warships left Canopa, the pod station defenses were reactivated, while ahead, at Siriki, they were temporarily shut down, for the least possible amount of time.

Noah, Anton, and Nirella rode in the flagship Webdancer, which was piloted by Tesh. Her vessel was the only craft not piloted by a Tulyan, and as a consequence it was the sole one that did not have a reptilian face on its prow. All of the ships (including hers) had a useful new feature: gun ports that opened and closed in the thick flesh of the hulls at the command of the various pilots, so that weapons could be fired through them. Intriguingly, the podships had done this en masse when weapons were being loaded aboard them, so they obviously had a collective way of understanding the lofty purpose and magnitude of the mission.

Many Guardians rode in the warships, including Subi Danvar, Acey Zelk, and Dux Hannah. All of them would fight side by side with Red Berets and

MPA soldiers against a common enemy. But by far the most numerous of the passengers on board the spacecraft were Tulyan pilots, more than one hundred thousand of them in transport vessels inside the cargo holds, waiting for the opportunity to regain control of the huge podship fleet.

During the preparations for this ambitious undertaking, Master Noah had been at Anton's side, giving him advice and marveling as he saw his young nephew assume the reins of power and gain the respect of his troops. He was exactly the sort of doge that a venture of this magnitude required.

As one of the leaders of the desperate military effort, Noah felt strong and very much in contact with this dimension of reality, which was inhabited by his physical body and its conscious memories. In recent days he had not dreamed at all when he slept, and perhaps this had something to do with how tired he was when his head hit the pillow, causing him to go deeper into unconsciousness than the REM level of dreams.

At Siriki, specialized military personnel and space weapons were loaded aboard the ships, and the fleet moved on. This procedure was repeated at the seventeen largest Alliance planets, until they had what they needed. In the process, Noah and Anton discovered that Human military assets on all of the planets were not as extensive as shown in the records left behind by ex-Doge Lorenzo. The bases were smaller, and even seemed to be positioned in non-strategic locations. The two men vowed to look into it further upon returning to Canopa.

Having earlier discovered deficiencies in the military installations on Canopa, Anton had ordered the arrests of Lorenzo and Pimyt, along with their top associates. Even if they proved innocent of wrongdoing, Anton said he did not want to leave that group in charge of anything, not even the orbital gambling facility. He didn't intend to leave a power vacuum that Lorenzo could exploit.

With minimal fanfare, the task force set course for the galactic fold of the Parviis. Speeding ahead, Webdancer seemed anxious to join the battle. Not far behind the sentient flagship, in the midst of other Tulyan-piloted vessels, flew one under the guidance of Eshaz, bearing his determined face on the prow.

It was the most important military operation in the history of the galaxy.

WEBDANCERS

Book 1 of the Timeweb Chronicles

Brian Herbert

Dedication

This book is for Jan. When I met you on that summer day in California, all of the stars in the heavens were in alignment for us—and my darling, they have been ever since. Thank you for being my loyal, loving companion and for teaching me everything that is meaningful about life.

Chapter One

Eddies and currents of time flow through the galaxy ... and immense whirlpools beckon everything into chaos.
> —Eshaz, timeseeing report to the Council of Elders

A tiny figure, the Parvii woman clung to a wall of the glowing green sectoid chamber. Using her touch and a telepathic linkage to the Aopoddae podship, she guided the creature past uncounted star systems, which she saw through multiple eyes on the craft's hull. At the vanguard of the Liberator fleet, she led the other Aopoddae vessels toward the galactic fold of the Parviis, and now their destination drew near.

Tesh Kori's dominion over the sentient spacecraft was an evolving relationship, a symbiosis between two ancient and very different galactic races in which she merged into the psyche of the creature in the ancient way. Now she felt an increasing closeness to this flagship that she had named *Webdancer*. The connection gave her a glimmer of hope for the future, that perhaps her people would finally see the error of their ways and agree to cooperate with other races.

But she didn't hold out much hope for that outcome. More likely, there would be a terrible battle in the sacred fold. And she would be responsible for leading a powerful military force to that secret location, for an attack on her own people.

She tried to set aside the feelings of guilt, if only for a few moments. Her thoughts drifted to something infinitely more pleasant, her feelings for an alien Human named Noah Watanabe....

* * * * *

In the passenger compartment behind Tesh's sectoid chamber, Noah stood beside a blond young man, both of them staring out a wide aft porthole at the formation of nine hundred podships behind them. Unlike the flagship, the trailing vessels were all piloted by Tulyans that had merged into the flesh of the spacefaring vessels, causing reptilian Tulyan faces to protrude from the prows. He recognized several of them, including that of his close friend, Eshaz.

The journey had taken longer than anticipated—more than two days so far—due to the extreme distance involved and poor conditions of the podways that had required the fleet to take alternate routes. They'd been forced to go around entire galactic sectors that had collapsed from the entropic decay of the Timeweb infrastructure.

The young man nudged him. It was Noah's nephew, Doge Anton del Velli. "While we've been looking outside, our ship morphed again. I think it's bigger now."

Noah looked around the grayness of the large cabin, which was illuminated by hidden sources that flickered faintly green at times. Many of the uniformed officers and other personnel stood at forward viewing windows that jutted out on the port and starboard sides. He heard the murmur of their voices.

Everyone had noticed the changes. Since embarking on this critical mission, the passenger areas and the cargo holds on the lower levels had become at least half again as large as they had originally been. None of the Human, Tulyan, or robotic passengers had left the vessel, and all of the fighter craft were parked in the holds, yet everyone agreed there was considerably more space for everything now.

"You're right," Noah said. "There's another row of benches, and the ceiling seems a little higher."

Anton rubbed his thick blond mustache. "*Webdancer*, she calls this one, and from the reports I'm getting, it's bigger than all the rest of them."

With a grin on his freckled face, Noah said, "Well, it is the flagship, and seems to sense its relative importance." He paused. "Perhaps our ship is just puffing up its chest in pride."

"Odd, the way podships can configure themselves at will," Anton said, expanding, changing layouts, and even adding gun ports on the sides of the hulls that are perfect for our space artillery pieces. I find it most peculiar."

"Indeed."

"With your connections, Noah, you should know why."

"But I don't." Noah's incredible psychic powers came and went, enabling him to take paranormal journeys far across the heavens, and sometimes to pilot podships, these mysterious creatures that had their own communication methods and secret motivations. It had all started after he'd been mortally wounded in an attack by Doge Lorenzo del Velli's forces, and Eshaz healed him by connecting him to a strand of Timeweb. It had been much more than a physical healing process

Timeweb.

He shuddered slightly as he thought of the name that Parviis and Tulyans had given to the cosmic green filigree connecting everything in the galaxy, a vast network on which these Aopoddae craft were traveling now. Most of the races could not see it, but after Noah's miraculous survival he'd been granted unprecedented private access to the web, although without explanation or guidance. Still, through it all, Noah had come to suspect that a higher power was guiding him, and had been doing so for some time. He sensed this force with him now, and with the entire fleet.

We're doing the right thing, he assured himself, *the only thing we can do.*

As he looked at the young merchant prince leader beside him, Noah thought his nephew carried his responsibilities well, and comported himself as if he had been groomed for this important position. That was hardly the case, though Anton did have royal blood on his father Lorenzo's side, albeit from an extramarital relationship he'd had with Noah's sister. Only serving as the Doge for a short time after his father was deposed, Anton had managed to coordinate much of the galaxy-spanning military effort, working with the various allied races and factions so that none felt slighted, and all believed they were indispensable to the success of the mission. It helped that this actually was true. Each of the groups in the assault force—the Red Berets, the MPA troopers, the Guardians, the Tulyans, and even the sentient robots—had important roles to play.

Just then, a clamor of excited voices rose at the front of the compartment. Noah and Anton hurried over, making their way around the extruded benches, tables and other furnishings the podship had provided. Noticing the approach of the two leaders, the other passengers moved aside, allowing them to reach one of the forward viewing windows.

Looking through it, Noah sucked in a deep breath, and suppressed a gasp. Ahead he saw what looked like a large, luminous hole in the black fabric of the galaxy, casting subdued illumination like a dull cosmic searchlight.

"The Asteroid Funnel," Anton murmured. "The Parvii Fold is on the other side, but Tesh will need all of her piloting skills to get us there."

"She can do it," Noah said. Both of them had heard of the terrible dangers of the galactic funnel, the hurtling asteroids, the extremely perilous flying conditions.

For several moments time seemed to stand still around Noah Watanabe, and all went silent. So much rested on this military venture, the fate of all the galactic races and their worlds, the fate of all they had ever known and all they had ever imagined. Countless dreams hung in the balance, made precarious by the dark clouds that had seeped into the galaxy.

Closing his eyes, Noah attempted to mind-range and peer into the cosmic web, trying to see into the Parvii Fold beyond the funnel. But the paranormal network had only been accessible to him intermittently, and almost never of his own volition. Now he beheld a pocket of blackness in his mind, and felt cold fear washing through him.

Just as Noah opened his eyes again, *Webdancer* plunged into the hole, with the fleet right behind.

Chapter Two

The most ancient patterns of the heavens are falling victim to new laws of science. From time immemorial, comets, asteroids, and planetary systems have traveled through space at regular, predictable orbits, speeds, and inclinations. Previously it was possible to calculate exactly when a particular comet would transit Venus, to the hour and minute. It was like clockwork, but no more. Cosmic bodies, even entire galactic sectors, have vanished into timeholes.

—Professor Daviz Joél, report to the Merchant Prince Alliance

Two mottled gray-and-black podships sped along the galactic web, one right after the other. Though they traveled so rapidly that a Human eye would not be able to see them, their speeds were nonetheless diminished from the norm, in large part due to the decline of the infrastructure.

Bred in a laboratory, these large, sentient vessels were not piloted like their natural cousins. Instead of Parviis inside the sectoid chambers, or Tulyans merged into the flesh of the creatures, each was under the control of a Mutati operating a Hibbil navigation unit. Behind the pilot in the lead craft stood the Emir Hari'Adab, leader of the shapeshifter race ... a position he had attained after assassinating his own father, the Zultan Abal Meshdi.

Hari had Hibbil and Adurian prisoners in the cargo hold, all of them soldiers. For a reason they refused to divulge, they had landed a small military force on his own planet of Dij. The Emir's fighters had overcome them, killing most and taking the rest into custody, along with their two unusual ships. His own demented father had authorized the breeding of what were known as "lab-pods," but these two spacecraft were of a higher order. They actually had Hibbil nav-systems that worked quite well, in sharp contrast with those of the Zultan.

The prisoners were members of the "HibAdu Coalition." One of them had carried a document fragment bearing the name of that military force, inscribed on a remnant of papers the soldiers had tried to destroy, along with all electronic records. But the salvaged document and other articles found with the soldiers had only succeeded in generating more questions, which none of the captives would answer.

Historically, Hibbils were allies of Humans, while Adurians had a similar relationship with Mutatis. And, since Humans and Mutatis had been the archenemies of one another since time immemorial, everyone had assumed that Hibbils and Adurians should be the same. Perhaps it was only a splinter group that had landed on Hari's planet, but he sensed it might be something much more significant, and dangerous. The well-armed soldiers had carried the sophisticated weaponry and communications equipment of a much larger, well-financed force. They appeared to have been on a reconnaissance mission.

They call themselves HibAdus, Hari thought as he watched the Mutati pilot seated ahead of him, operating the touch-panel controls of the ship. *Very strange.*

Perhaps the Tulyans—with their ability to determine truth or falsehood through physical contact—could determine who his prisoners really were. And Hari had an additional motive for approaching the reptilians in their legendary starcloud. They were rumored to be close to Noah Watanabe and other Human leaders of the Merchant Prince Alliance. Perhaps the Tulyan Council of Elders could broker a peace agreement between the warring MPA and the Mutati Kingdom, ending the insane, ages-old hostilities between the two races. No one could even recall why they had been battling for so long, and Hari had always believed that there should be some way of bringing it all to a peaceful end. This had put him in direct conflict with his stubborn father, but now—after the unthinkable act Hari had committed—perhaps the Humans would believe him. If necessary, he would even submit himself to the truthing touch of the Tulyans.

At the sound of the cockpit door sliding open behind him, Hari turned to exchange smiles with his girlfriend, Parais d'Olor. While Hari and the pilot (like most other shapeshifters) were terramutatis who walked, she was an aeromutati, able to spread her wings and soar into the air, should she ever desire to do so. Just before departing on the trip with him, she had metamorphosed into the guise of a colorful Alty peacock, a very large bird with a red-and-gold body and black, silver-tipped wings that were now tucked tightly against her body. In the confinement of the lab-pod, she got around by walking, and from her own morphology she had developed a way of walking smoothly on her two bird legs, instead of hopping around in the customary avian fashion.

Behind her stood Yerto Bhaleen, a career military officer who held the rank of Kajor in the Mutati High Command. A small, muscular terramutati with the standard complement of three slender arms and six stout legs, he was a four-star Kajor, just beneath the highest of ranks. Like Hari, he had refused any higher designation, since his own commanders had died in the tragic loss of Paradij, the horrific collateral damage involved in the assassination of the Zultan.

"We should be there soon, My Emir," Bhaleen said. "All is in readiness."

"Very good," Hari said.

The officer moved back a couple of paces and stood rigidly, awaiting any further commands.

Glancing at Parais, the Mutati leader said, "You can't wait to fly on your own, can you? Perhaps after we arrive the Tulyans will permit you to fly around their starcloud."

"Only if we gain their trust," she suggested.

Rubbing up against his side, she smiled gently at him. Her lovely facial features were fleshy, with a small beak and oversized brown eyes that were totally without guile. "But I don't need to fly," she said. "Wherever you are is where I want to be."

Hari adored her. Without Parais' guidance and inspiration, he would not be able to go on with his life, and with the new, very ambitious purpose he had undertaken. If anyone deserved to lead the Mutati people, it was her, and not him. But the shapeshifter race was very traditional, and Hari had the right of ascendancy by birthright, no matter the terrible thing he had done to accelerate the process.

It had been an act of violence that went terribly wrong in the trajectory calculation of a planet-busting Demolio torpedo. Aimed at a moon his father was visiting, the missile went off course and destroyed the Mutati homeworld of Paradij instead, wiping out billions of Hari's own people. The orbiting moon and the mad Zultan Abal Meshdi had been annihilated in the cataclysms as well, but that had been little solace. Hari could hardly bear to think of the scale of the tragedy.

Not yet having admitted to the Mutati people what he did, or the reason, Hari carried a terrible burden of guilt on his shoulders. At Parais's encouragement, he continued to lead the shapeshifter race, but he insisted on doing it as Emir, a princely governor's designation, rather than the customary Zultan title his father and most predecessors had held. It was Hari's way of saying privately that he did not yet deserve the higher title, that he had not earned it, and perhaps he never would.

Chapter Three

After we defeated the Parviis, the Eye of the Swarm withdrew his survivors, taking more than 100,000 podships they control to the remote Parvii Fold. Earlier, he had already cut off regularly scheduled podship travel to Human and Mutati worlds, and now he's done the same for the rest of the galaxy. A few Parvii pilots who are out of contact with their leader are continuing routes in non-Human or Mutati sectors, but that won't last long. In addition, there are disturbing reports of laboratory-bred pods out in the galaxy.

           —Excerpts from confidential report to the Tulyan Council of Elders

From the window of a small office suspended inside the immense building, Jacopo Nehr looked down on his manufacturing and assembly lines as they produced new machine components and robots for export.

He heard the steady drone of machinery, and felt the vibrations of manufacturing beneath his feet. This plant, located on one of the Hibbil Cluster Worlds, was one of many industrial facilities that Nehr owned around the galaxy.

But to his dismay, he was not there voluntarily. He cursed and smashed the side of his fist against the plax window. It flexed, but did not break.

Down on the factory floor he saw a scruffy, silver little robot engaged in oddly animated conversations with subordinate workbots of varying sizes and designs. The little one's name was Ipsy, an odd mechanical runt who had an officious, irritating personality. He certainly grated on Jacopo, and other sentient robots took offense to him at times as well, as they seemed to be doing at the moment. Jacopo had tried to teach him personal interaction and management skills, but Ipsy had been resistant to learning them.

Now, Ipsy pushed another robot in the chest, knocking him backward against others. Three more of them tumbled over like dominoes. Jacopo had seen this mechanical emotionalism and physicality before, and always Ipsy won out. Someone had programmed him to be quite aggressive.

Despite his gruff methods, the little guy had taken charge of the facility, causing it to hum at high efficiency, producing more robots and machine parts than ever before. Jacopo knew where some of the products were being shipped around the galaxy, but not all of them. He only knew for certain that business was booming. Ipsy didn't seem to know all of the end-user details either, or he was keeping the information to himself. As a large part of this factory's business, it produced electronic instruments and control panels—components that could be used for a variety of purposes.

Unfortunately, the facility was making money Jacopo could not spend. The Hibbils allowed him access to heavily edited financial reports, but he couldn't get his hands on his share of the funds themselves, and he was not allowed access to any form of transportation. The factory complex was ringed with an electronic containment field that penned him in. The furry little bastards even forced him to live in a rudimentary apartment on the grounds, a stunted, boxlike abode that had been designed for one of *them*, not for a Human being.

Each day Nehr woke up in a foul mood, then spent much of his time dithering around the factory, hoping something would change, that the Hibbils who had essentially imprisoned him there more than a week ago would set him free and allow him to return to Canopa. But he saw no sign of that happening.

He hadn't seen any fellow Humans at all since being forced to fly across the galaxy on a strange podship, one that was unlike any other he'd ever seen. From Ipsy he'd learned it was a craft that had been bred in a laboratory, and guided by a Hibbil navigation system. The thought of an artificial podship boggled his mind, not easily done to an inventor and businessman of his stature. One of the leading merchant princes in the Alliance, Jacopo Nehr had discovered the nehrcom cross-space communication system, and had built an impressive multi-planet business empire around that connective tissue. Before falling out of favor with the princes, he had even been appointed Supreme General of the Merchant Prince Armed Forces—the primary Human military force.

Down on the floor, Ipsy was getting increasingly aggressive, and he pushed other workbots out of his way as they pressed in around him.

Jacopo hardly cared. Ipsy would get his way, as always. The merchant prince was more concerned about being held prisoner in his own factory complex, with no one to talk to except the robots that ran the facility. Why was he being treated this way? It seemed like a cruel joke, but he wasn't laughing.

To make it even more perplexing, a Hibbil had done this to him, and not just any furball, either. It had been Pimyt, the Royal Attaché to Lorenzo del Velli, former Doge of the Alliance. Pimyt was so trusted that for a time he had even been appointed regent of the entire multi-planet empire, until the princes could agree on the selection of a new doge—the prince of all princes. Nehr had suspected for some time that Pimyt was involved in war profiteering, but he'd found no evidence of it, and had been unable to determine exactly what the attaché wanted with him.

He'd been able to come up with a pretty good guess, though, one that made sense the more he thought about it. *Leverage.* Holding him hostage on the Hibbil Cluster Worlds in order to force his powerful daughter, Nirella, to cooperate. She was not only married to Doge Anton del Velli; she was Supreme General of the Merchant Prince Armed Forces, having succeeded her own father in that position.

Nehr wondered if he would ever see her again, or his wife, Lady Amila. His mood sank even more, as he realized that the Hibbils could just keep him there for the rest of his life, and maintain the leverage they wanted. But Hibbils were supposed to be allies of Humans. Why would they do this? It went beyond war profiteering. Nehr didn't want to imagine how far beyond.

Noticing that the altercation down on the production floor had escalated, he sighed. Robots were streaming toward Ipsy, leaving their work posts, slowing down the operation. It looked like Jacopo would have to intervene this time.

Taking a lift down to the main floor, he found hundreds of robotic workers surrounding Ipsy, glaring at him with orange visual sensors that were much brighter than usual and shouting at him in a din of mechanical voices. Jacopo pushed forward through their midst. Noticing him, the robots grew quieter, but he heard them whispering around him, a peculiar and disturbing mechanical hum.

"I want all of you to calm down and return to work!" Jacopo shouted, raising his arms in the air.

The robots grew completely quiet, each one just staring at him. But in the multicolored, blinking lights around their face plates and their bright orange, ember-like visual sensors, he saw that Ipsy's supervision methods had triggered their anger programs to a much higher level than Jacopo had ever seen. They were operating in concert, too. Like a mob or a pack.

A wave of fear passed through him, as he saw the blinking-light patterns intensify, and the ember eyes burn even brighter. Under a strict code of honor programmed into all robots created by Humans (or stemming from those creations), robots were not supposed to harm Humans. But since his incarceration, Jacopo had grown increasingly concerned about the factory robots, since many of them were of unfamiliar designs and didn't always behave according to known industrial parameters. Some of their personalities seemed oddly unpredictable, and he had decided that this must be because they had been manufactured by the Hibbils, under standards that were not known to Humans. The Hibbils had long manufactured their own robots, but until recently Jacopo thought he knew all of the basic designs, since he had often worked in concert with them on the development and manufacture of sentient machines. Now, something had changed.

"We demand that you get rid of Ipsy," one of the robots howled in a tinny voice.

"Yes!" said another. "He goes, or we stop work!"

"Don't be silly," Jacopo said. "Robots can't go on strike. Now stop this foolishness and get back to work immediately."

The robots advanced on Jacopo, their face-plate lights blinking furiously, their eyes afire. He felt their hard bodies press around them, and it hurt. Then he heard Ipsy shout in his officious mechanical voice, telling them to clear away. The little mechanical man managed to reach Jacopo's side, but now the other robots pressed hard around both of them.

Jacopo panicked as he felt them crushing him, and he couldn't breathe. He cried out in pain and rage as they crushed his bones. Broken and smashed, the inventor slumped in the midst of the hard metalloy bodies around him.

When it was done, the robots packaged Jacopo's body into an export box. And they tossed Ipsy ... what was left of him ... onto a scrap heap.

Chapter Four

There is a certain glamour and allure to very old ways, and in particular to those that are the most ancient of all. It is almost as if the Supreme Being got it right in the very beginning with the various races and star systems he spawned, but only then. Thereafter, under pressure from countless directions, things declined, and continued that way until the entire cosmic engine started to run out of steam. Scientists describe it as entropy on a huge scale, with energy systems winding down and life forms eventually returning to the soil and cosmic dust. But I have a different, less scientific, way of putting it: Sentient life forms have a way of making selfish decisions and mucking things up.

—Master Noah Watanabe, speech to
the seventh Guardian graduating class

Horrendous. Ghastly.
Onboard the flagship, Noah and Anton conferred. Tesh stood with them, having temporarily left the sectoid chamber. They all faced one of the viewing windows in the large passenger compartment,

staring in shock at the impediment to the fleet's forward progress.

A short while ago, when they first entered the narrowing funnel, there had been the expected hurtling, luminous white stones that Tesh and the other pilots had been forced to negotiate. Then the rolling, oncoming stones had ceased altogether, and an unexpected obstacle had presented itself to the fleet. As a result, all the way back up the funnel the entire Liberator podship fleet came to an abrupt halt, and floated freely in the frozen vacuum, unable to proceed any further.

Noah grimaced at the sight ahead of *Webdancer*. Like an immense cork, the way forward was blocked by immense clusters of tiny, horribly mutilated and frozen Parvii bodies, all clumped together to form a grisly barrier.

Tears streamed down Tesh's cheeks. "I saw bodies floating the last time I was here, but got past them." She paused. "When we first entered the funnel this time, I wondered why there were no bodies. Now I know."

"We must reach the Parvii Fold," Anton said, staring out the window. "Everything depends on us capturing the rest of the podships."

"It's obvious what we have to do," Noah said. He put a reassuring hand on Tesh's shoulder. "I'm sorry, but we need to open fire and blast our way through."

Her eyes looked tortured and red.

"But will we find anything on the other side?" Anton asked.

"I think so," she said, wiping her eyes. "Woldn must have created this barrier in order to protect himself, and the others who remain with him." She scowled at the mention of the Parvii leader, the Eye of the Swarm.

Moments later, six Liberator podships opened the gun ports on their sides and commenced fire on the horrific barricade. In the fiery onslaught of white-hot projectiles, Parvii flesh melted away, revealing a dark tunnel beyond....

* * * * *

Doge Anton sent two podships ahead into the darkness to scout for further hazards or traps. One of the vessels was piloted by Eshaz. His passenger compartment thronged with Human fighters and Tulyan pilots, along with Acey Zelk and Dux Hannah., a pair of young Humans who were friends of Eshaz.

Anton's wife, General Nirella, had considered off-loading the pilots onto other vessels, but the Tulyans resisted, saying their telekinetic mindlink powers could be of added value against any Parviis they encountered. Even though the combined telepathic power was much weaker away from the Tulyan Starcloud, it was at least another dimension that might be useful in battle, and the Parviis had shown themselves to be susceptible to it.

"If we get through this, we can call ourselves men," Dux said. He and his cousin—still teenagers—sat on one of the extruded organic benches. The reptilian Tulyans towered around them on the hard seats.

"Don't get all terrified," Acey said, with a smirk on his wide face. "If you go hysterical when I'm needed for a crisis, I'm going to have to let you go."

Dux gave him a less-than-good-natured shove. Acey always considered himself the braver of the pair, but Dux considered his cousin rather foolhardy instead. Now they were committed, with no turning back.

"I'd rather be at the controls of one of these space blimps," Acey said.

Dux nodded, remembering a time that they had gone on a wild podship hunt, along with Eshaz and Tesh. An excited Acey had been allowed to pilot one of the wild pods shortly after it was captured. Afterward he said it was the highlight of his life, and he couldn't wait to do it again. Eshaz had told him, however, that Humans were limited in their ability to pilot the sentient creatures, and were not skilled enough for battle. All logic said this was true, but Acey showed stubborn determination. He felt he could do more than Eshaz had seen, so he kept pressing.

Now the boys and all other Human military personnel had backup life support suits aboard, and Acey hoped to use his for going outside and mounting a podship to guide it. The insistent Acey had also obtained permission to bring along a gilded harness and Tarbu thorn-vines for basic piloting, just in case there was an opportunity for him to stand atop a podship and pilot it, even if it was only on a backup basis.

Dux hoped it wasn't necessary for Acey to do that. Not in this distant region, filled with unknown dangers.

As the scout ships made their way through the narrowing funnel, luminous white stones reappeared and hurtled toward them. One glanced off the companion scout craft, causing it to veer off course, before the pilot regained control. Dux watched in horror as a much larger rock tumbled toward his own podship at a high rate of speed. Eshaz, immersed into the Aopoddae flesh and, piloting the podship as if he had been born in this form, veered hard to starboard, narrowly averting destruction.

Both scout ships made it to an adjoining gray-green passageway that was clear of stones, and then passed completely through, into the immense, pocketlike Parvii Fold. There, Dux saw thousands of the sentient spacecraft tethered in a moorage basin, and many more floated loosely in the airless vacuum, as far as the eye could see.

From the hidden, faintly green realm, Dux sent a comline message back that no Parvii swarms were massing in battle formation, not even a defensive arrangement.

"Just a swarm around the Palace of Woldn," he reported. "They look lethargic, like hibernating insects."

"And their podship fleet?" General Nirella asked, over the connection.

"Lots of ships are here, sir. Too many to count."

After hearing the report, Doge Anton ordered the Liberator task force to advance. In minutes, the fleet streamed through the rest of the funnel, and out into the pocketlike galactic fold.

By this time, Parvii sentries were sending alarms, and the swarm was beginning to awaken.

* * * * *

The Palace of Woldn—constructed of interlocked members of the Parvii race—floated in the vacuum of the Parvii Fold. High-pitched sirens went off throughout the structure. Having been ill, the Eye of the Swarm was in a deep sleep when the intruders arrived. In his diminished state, he had not anticipated an attack, nor that a Parvii would lead enemies into their midst.

Slowly struggling back to consciousness, Woldn probed telepathically, and learned from his sentinels that a fleet of Tulyan-controlled podships had arrived, behind a podship that did not have a Tulyan face on its prow. Based on this, he wondered if a Parvii could be piloting the lead craft. If so, it would be a betrayal of epic proportions. Via relay, he saw that this particular podship did look familiar, albeit larger than the last time he'd seen it. And he recalled the name of its rebellious pilot, a woman he had banished from the swarm.

Tesh Kori. But could she have brought the enemy here, at the head of an armed fleet? He didn't want to believe it.

The Eye of the Swarm sent high-pitched telepathic signals to his followers, alerting them even more than the sentries already had, and sending specific instructions to the remaining swarms....

* * * * *

During the doomed Parvii attack on the Tulyan Starcloud, the Tulyans had surprised Woldn with a defensive strike that sent comets, meteors, and radioactive asteroids into the swarms, scattering them into space and resulting in the death of more than eighty percent of the Parvii population. It had been the biggest disaster in Parvii history, going back millions of years.

In the days of Parvii lore, long, long ago, there had been tens of thousands of war priests and breeding specialists—two powerful factions that had worked together to enlarge the influence and domain of the galactic race. In modern times, prior to the devastating "Tulyan Incident" that killed so many of Woldn's people, a small number of war priests and breeding specialists had continued to practice the old ways, keeping their skills sharp in case they were ever needed. During Woldn's rule there had never been more than a hundred members of each group, far diminished from the old days. With the Tulyan disruption of the energy fields that connected Parviis paranormally with their brethren, however, most of the modern war priests and breeding specialists had been killed, so that Woldn was left with only two female breeding specialists, Ting and Volom, and one male war priest, Ryall.

Following the disaster, in the perceived security of the Parvii Fold, Woldn had set in motion old forces, resurrecting ancient programs that his race had once employed successfully against their enemies. In short order, the breeding specialists had established an intense breeding program from old cellular stock, and their population had begun to increase, with hundreds of thousands of young Parviis reaching adulthood in a matter of weeks. It had been a comparatively small amount, but a promising beginning nonetheless.

Then something had gone terribly wrong. Shortly after reaching adulthood, the newly generated Parviis had developed a mysterious metabolic ailment that killed almost all of them, and even infected some of the general populace, including Woldn himself. Ting and Volom had been forced to set up quarantine procedures and start over. In the process, they discovered that some of the cellular material retained from ancient times was contaminated, and any Parvii created from it was genetically defective, born to suffer a slow, lingering death.

For more than a week Woldn had been ill, feeling lethargic and hardly able to move. In the last couple of days, he had felt a little better, but he still slept most of the time, in an attempt to regain his strength. He would awaken for brief periods to do telepathic checks, then would go back to sleep. During Woldn's recovery process, Ting and Volom worked long hours, trying to figure out the problem and get things going again with uncontaminated cellular material. It was going very slowly, and both were hindered by moderate forms of the illness themselves.

Hidden in the genetic structure of Woldn's race, there were others like Ting, Volom, and Ryall, waiting to come back from a long inactivity. The knowledge of breeding specialists and war priests still existed in the cellular structures of Woldn's people, having gone into dormancy. And the Eye of the Storm had been hoping that the strongest of the ancients would reemerge.

So it was that inside one of the wings of the palace, Parviis had been working in a laboratory to resurrect the old ways. Tapping into old cellular material and into the brains of their living people, the breeding specialists had discovered the ancient memories of a few additional war priests and breeding specialists—memories in the minds of Parviis who became known as "latents," those persons with fertile memories that had been lying dormant in the collective unconsciousness of the entire race. It was like growing plants in the most receptive cellular material, weeding out intrusive thoughts, nurturing the old knowledge, bringing it back. But it wasn't going rapidly enough, and now the enemy was attacking at exactly the wrong moment. If only there had been more time to prepare, if only the war priests had been able to recreate the powerful weapons of yore. But it was not meant to be....

* * * * *

White-hot bursts of light hit the palace and a number of structures around it, and Woldn heard the screams of his dying people through the morphic field that connected him to them telepathically. The outer walls of the palace, constructed of densely and intricately interlocked Parviis, held up against several blasts, allowing Woldn, his personal guards, and other key personnel to escape into the airless vacuum. Leading them toward the podship basin, Woldn narrowly avoided the blasts of enemy weapons. Some of his guards were hit, and he heard their telepathic shrieks of agony.

Behind him, the Palace of Woldn disintegrated, its living components killed or scattered.

Gathering his survivors, Woldn commanded them to take control of the floating podships in his own fleet. But most of the Parviis, like their leader, were weak and phlegmatic. They attempted to swarm the podships and gain control over them with neurotoxin stingers as they had done in the past, but the stingers had little or no effect. The Parviis also tried to attack a handful of the Tulyan-piloted podships that were away from the rest of their fleet, but the Tulyans used mindlink energy to keep the attackers at bay, while MPA and Red Beret fighters opened fire with hull cannons.

Through his paranormal linkage, Woldn heard the terrible screams of his people as they died by the millions.

With Parvii numbers diminishing and unable to fight back, the Eye of the Swarm led only a couple of hundred thousand followers in a desperate retreat through an opening in the gray-green membrane of the galactic fold, passing through a small hole, so tiny that none of the attackers could follow.

In darkness on the other side, he reassessed. No active breeding specialists or war priests survived, only a handful of the budding "latents," Parviis who did not yet have use of their skills or powers. Two potential war priests and five potential breeding specialists.

To Woldn's further dismay, he had left more than one hundred thousand podships behind, floating in the vacuum of the galactic fold, waiting to be taken by his enemies.

Chapter Five

All of us are prisoners of something, and ultimately of our own mortality.
—Ancient Saying

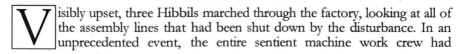

isibly upset, three Hibbils marched through the factory, looking at all of the assembly lines that had been shut down by the disturbance. In an unprecedented event, the entire sentient machine work crew had rebelled against their robotic supervisor, smashing him into useless metal and killing the Human factory owner.

"This shouldn't have happened," said one of the Hibbils, his red eyes glowing angrily. He had flecks of gray fur and a thick, salt-and-pepper beard. On either side of him a furry little companion grunted, and their red eyes glowed nearly as brightly as his.

Pimyt watched as the two others inspected several robots, inserting interface probes into their control boxes and reading the results.

"Doesn't look good," one of them said. Squat and overweight, Rennov took his job seriously.

"I don't see how this happened," the other said. This one was younger, a Hibbil with glistening, golden-brown fur.

The two of them kept using probes to check the sentient machines.

Overseeing the procedures, Pimyt was unhappy on multiple levels. He and the division managers with him didn't like to see the factory operation interrupted, since the new robots and other machine components produced there—especially the control panels—were needed for the war effort of the HibAdu Coalition, the union of Hibadus and Adurians. In addition, the last thing he had wanted was for Jacopo Nehr to die, since that eliminated any potential leverage with the human's powerful daughter, Nirella del Velli. So far, it had been a stand-off with her. She'd accused Pimyt of blackmailing her father and had even threatened to torture him into talking. Not backing down, Pimyt had threatened to release technical information about the workings of the nehrcom instantaneous cross-space communication system—revealing how simple its operation really was. It would be a scandal that would ruin her father's reputation as a famous inventor, and destroy the Nehr company. Hearing this, she had stormed off.

Shortly after that, Nirella's husband, Doge Anton, had ordered Pimyt and the former Doge Lorenzo taken into "protective custody." Enfuriated, Pimyt was ready to make good on his threat, but he and Lorenzo had been placed into solitary confinement at a prison on Canopa, with no one to talk to except for uncooperative guards. And Pimyt had not yet set up a mechanism to release the information if certain things happened to him.

While the two of them were so rudely confined, Doge Anton, General Nirella, and Noah Watanabe had departed on their foolish military venture to the Parvii Fold, an operation Pimyt had learned about just before being taken into custody. Then, from his cell Pimyt had hoped the Parviis would succeed in wiping out all of them with the powerful telepathic weapons they were said to have.

Three days had passed. Finally, one morning the glowing electronic confinement bars on the cells went dark, and the guards said the pair was free to leave. No explanation. Lorenzo had returned to the Pleasure Palace, his opulent gambling facility orbiting Canopa. Pimyt had considered getting even with Nirella—assuming she had a part in his incarceration—but had decided to think it over first. Nirella (or whomever she left in charge) had the power to confine him at any time, for any reason. Perhaps the three-day confinement had been her way of telling him exactly that.

Considering his options (which Pimyt often did), he had slipped away to rejoin his HibAdu conspirators, and resumed his involvement in facilitating the downfall of both the Merchant Prince Alliance and the Mutati Kingdom. This had brought him, on a secret lab-pod flight made easier by the diminishment of MPA military forces, to the Hibbil Cluster Worlds....

Even now, through all of his intelligence sources, Pimyt didn't know what was happening at the Parvii Fold. It did amuse him that the Humans—reportedly with Tulyan allies—were spending so much time and effort going after Parviis. The HibAdus, learning of the military operation from Pimyt, had seen it as an opportunity to strike merchant prince planets that were left inadequately defended, because of the diversion of ships and armaments to a foolish, distant operation. In addition, HibAdu leadership—while Pimyt had never met any of them personally—had sent a message agreeing with his assessment. The Parviis, even if they failed to completely destroy the attacking force, were sure to damage it seriously.

Now the scheming, highly organized HibAdus were almost ready to launch their simultaneous surprise attacks on key planets. Just a few essential details remained to be completed, with this additional complication. The robot uprising would have been just an annoying nuisance, if not for Jacopo's death..

The division managers completed their inspection, spot-checking robots throughout the factory. Finally, Rennov announced, "Every workbot in the factory will have to be reprogrammed."

"Get started, then," Pimyt ordered.

* * * * *

Ipsy, with the weight of industrial scrap on top of him, burrowed his smashed and broken body into a cavity in the pile and began to rebuild himself, converting the junked parts he found around him. He took on an even smaller body form this time, using microcircuit boards and fiber optics that he salvaged from the scrap heap, after testing each of them. His arms and legs were essentially the same, but he was considerably thinner now, and even shorter than before.

Then, as he connected a small, silver and green panel to his brain, he fell backward, his limbs freezing into immobility. The panel had a defect that he had not noticed.

While he lay there, looking upward and trying to repair the problem internally, Hibbil workers started dismantling the scrap pile with a mechanical, remote-controlled arm and claw, intending to melt the metals down and recycle them. Ipsy saw patches of daylight as pieces above him were removed. He noticed a zoomeye on the mechanical arm, and the claw hesitated over him for an instant—bathing him in orange light—before going on to other, larger pieces. But Ipsy knew it would be back.

The little robot was like a paralyzed man, unable to move.

Chapter Six

Once, the number of Parviis in the galaxy was far beyond our capability to measure. Now the Eye of the Swarm is in a desperate situation, fleeing with what little he has left. This is not a time for us to gloat. It is a time to be wary. Like a cornered animal, he may be at his most dangerous.

—Tulyan report to the Council of Elders

fter all the eons of Parvii glory, the successes that went back farther than anyone could remember, Woldn couldn't understand how things had gone so terribly wrong. Certainly, it was not due to any errors of leadership he had committed. He was far too careful for that, always using the resources of his people—and the podships under their control—prudently.

At the moment, he and his drastically diminished swarm huddled in the darkness of an unknown place. The hole through which they had escaped had not been there previously, or it would have been noticed by his people, who had been constantly checking every square centimeter of the Parvii Fold, making certain it was absolutely safe. They had all been taught from an early age that this was their sacred nest in a dangerous galaxy, one they had to protect it at all costs. Never before had holes appeared in the fabric of the fold. It seemed an impossibility, because the immense protective pocket was at the farthest end of the known galaxy. They'd always thought that nothing lay beyond the gray-green membrane, that it marked the edge of existence.

And yet, he and his remaining followers had gone through. Less than two hundred thousand individuals.

Now Woldn reached telepathically into his morphic field, and opened up some of his own thoughts for his followers to read. In the process he felt the Parviis flowing to him and probing him, reading the particular thoughts he had opened up to them. In turn, all of the Parviis made the totality of their own thoughts more easily accessible to the Eye of the Swarm, so that he could read them at will himself. He did so selectively, a few at a time.

Where are we? Woldn wondered. No one seemed to know.

He and his swarm remained close to the tiny hole through which they had come, as if gaining some reassurance from its proximity. At least it gave them their bearings. They were very close to their beloved Parvii Fold, and yet so far from it. The galactic membrane separating them from the fold had not proven to be very thick, but it may as well have been the entire width of the universe. Woldn had stationed alternating sentries at the hole, peering through one at a time to the other side, and they continued to report extensive military activity in the fold.

Will we ever return? Woldn thought, *or are we doomed to remain here forever?*

One of his followers transmitted weakly: *I think we're in the undergalaxy.*

Then another, equally diminished Parvii thought reached him: *I agree.*

But throughout the rest of the swarm, no others ventured opinions. They shivered and huddled, and flew nearby, ever alert to dangers.

A shudder passed through Woldn as he remembered the Tulyan legend of an "undergalaxy." Parviis had always dismissed such a concept as just one of the harebrained ideas that their rivals, the Tulyans, had. Since their fall from glory long ago, when Parviis had taken control of podships away from them, the Tulyans had descended into superstition and stories of how things used to be. They were an odd race. Oh, they had their uses. On occasion Woldn and other Parvii leaders had used them for their timeseeing abilities, for that peculiar way they had of looking through what Tulyans called the "lens of time." Bordering on the supernatural, the ability seemed to work. But not consistently.

Woldn wondered now if their stories of the undergalaxy could possibly contain a grain of truth. Or more than that.

Is that where we are? The undergalaxy?

Gazing past an opening in the huddled swarm, some of the darkness seemed to melt away, enabling him to barely make out faint and unknown star systems that seemed oddly configured. In happier times, he had led his swarms to every corner of the known galaxy, and this was not anyplace he'd ever seen before. Had he overlooked a portion of the galaxy, or could this actually be an entirely different place?

He strongly suspected the latter.

Woldn was terrified, but concealed it from his followers, and steeled himself. Two hundred thousand survivors didn't amount to much, but they would have to form the nucleus of Parvii recovery. He was determined to not only survive as a galactic race, but to rise once more in power so that Parviis regained their former glory.

According to Tulyan legend, a dark terror resided in this nether galaxy, but details were murky. Woldn did not reveal it to anyone, but he began to wonder if this legend of his enemy could possibly be true, and if Parviis had ever been to such a stygian realm. Perhaps the horrors of the undergalaxy were buried in the collective unconscious of the Parvii race, and could only be brought out in a laboratory.

Telepathically, he probed the minds of the seven latents, and absorbed their thoughts. At the most protected center of the tiny swarm, with their brethren clustered around them to preserve their body heat, these latents—two potential war priests and five potential breeding specialists—represented the future or doom of all Parviis. Seeds of the past grew in their physical bodies, which were of varying ages. Woldn probed deeply into the minds of the seven, into their memories and racial past. Into the long tunnels of their minds he went, probing, searching for facts. The paths joined, and continued back in time. From the embryonic war priests he found circumstantial evidence that an undergalaxy really existed.

But there were barriers to more information, to meaningful details. He found no personal accounts of the other dimension, so the two young men did not have those particulars yet. Even so, Woldn was beginning to suspect that his people had been to this place at one time, but the memories were too horrible and had been collectively repressed by his race.

Leading the paltry swarm, Woldn skirted the edge of the undergalaxy and circled back to the tiny bolt hole, hoping that the awful danger on this side—what could it possibly be?—did not sense their presence. When things quieted down on the other side, he intended to lead the way back through, to the Parvii Fold. Then he would take precautions to seal the area off so that no intruders could ever get back in.

But his medical personnel and his own telepathic probes were revealing disturbing information about the condition of the swarm of survivors around him. Only a small percentage of them (including Woldn) had effective neurotoxin sting-ers in their bodies, which explained why most of them had little effect on the podships of the military attack force.

We are far, far from home, with no way to retake it.

It was a private, very lonely thought.

Chapter Seven

"I don't see what's still holding this galaxy together."
—First Elder Kre'n, comment to her Council

While the fleet was being consolidated and organized at the Parvii Fold, Noah inspected the area. He and Eshaz rode in the flagship while Tesh piloted it around the immense galactic pocket, alternately speeding up and slowing down as Noah required. By touching the skin of the sentient vessel, Eshaz was able to link with its consciousness, a variation on the truthing touch. In turn, this connected the Tulyan with Tesh, who clung in her tiny humanoid form to a wall of the sectoid chamber, guiding the craft. Thus, Tesh and Eshaz could communicate directly—transmitting to each other through the podship's flesh.

"She is describing details of the fold," Eshaz said to Noah. The reptilian man held one hand against the rough, gray podship skin on the interior of the passenger compartment. "Every crease and basin in the fold has a name, a purpose, and a history behind it." He pointed out the window. The Parviis say that the long scar on that membrane is where the Universal Creator put the finishing touches on the galaxy and stitched everything together."

"Interesting," Noah said. "How does the Parvii concept of a Universal Creator compare with your Sublime Creator, and with our Supreme Being?"

"Some of my people would be surprised to hear you ask such a question," Eshaz said with a toothy smile. "They believe you are a messiah."

"So, you think I should know all the answers?"

"I wasn't necessarily speaking for myself. Tell me, my friend. Are you saying, then, that you are not a messiah?"

"If I am one, I have a lot to learn." Noah paused. "I don't know what I am, or why special things have happened to me. My life changed dramatically after you healed me the way you did, touching my skin to the web, causing its nutrients to flow into my wound."

"Do you regret any of it?"

Noah hesitated. "No. I don't think I do." He stared at the place on the wall where Eshaz continued to touch the podship.

"Try connecting with Tesh yourself," Eshaz said. "You've had a special relationship with podships, and with her. Touch the skin and communicate with her, as I am doing."

"I don't know. My ... I hesitate to call them powers ... come and go. I never know when I'm going to be able journey through the web, and when it will keep me at bay."

"Give it a try now."

Instead, Noah looked out the window. The podship had come to a stop very close to the gray-green membrane of the fold, near the long scar that Tesh had spoken of. The sentient craft nudged against the membrane, like a ship bumping up against a dock.

Over the last four days, Noah, Anton, and the Tulyans had been consolidating the immense podship fleet at the Parvii Fold. Instead of nine hundred ships in the Liberator fleet, they now had a vastly larger number of vessels—and all of them had morphed to produce gun port feature on their hulls, controllable by the various pilots in the battle group.

With their increased assets, the Liberators had a new mission: Use the podships to transport Tulyan teams all over the galaxy, so that they could perform the infrastructure repairs on an emergency basis, staving off the damage that was occurring to the fabric of the universe....

* * * * *

But before leaving, Tulyan hunting crews needed to round up all of the podships that had drifted around inside the Parvii Fold, away from the moorage basin. Acey Zelk, always anxious to pilot the arcane vessels, had been permitted to join one of the crews. Already they had found more ships than the one hundred thousand Tulyan pilots they had brought with them, so the Liberators would need to send some of their original fleet back to their starcloud to pick up thousands of more pilots. The exact number was unclear, because they kept finding more podships, in hidden places.

"A nice problem to have," Doge Anton had said that morning, when he and the others began to realize the enormity of the prize they had captured from the Parviis.

Through the web, Eshaz had sent a message back to the Tulyan Starcloud, notifying the Council of the logistical challenge. They made arrangements to send four hundred podships from the original Liberator fleet back to the starcloud, to get thousands of more Tulyans. They needed enough pilots to transport the rest of the huge fleet of recovered vessels, and none of the new ships could be moved yet.

This was because the Tulyan pilots and web maintenance crews needed time to familiarize themselves with the new podships, and to practice operations with them. Since time immemorial, there had always been a methodical breaking-in process in which the various personalities and talents—Tulyan and Aopoddae—were sorted out and meshed properly. If this was not done correctly, the ancient legends held that there could be extremely adverse results, even disasters in which podships rebelled and caused destructive havoc. Thus, it was worth taking the extra time to ensure safety, and—to the extent possible—to enhance predictability.

In addition, the Liberators were setting up defenses, securing the galactic fold militarily to prevent Parviis from returning and regaining multiswarm strength there. General Nirella had set up a guard post near the tiny bolt hole where the Parviis had disappeared, and made plans to leave a guard force of one hundred podships and military personnel in other key areas of the fold, including the entranceway to the Asteroid Funnel....

* * * * *

Continuing the inspection tour on a prearranged route, Tesh caused *Webdancer* to hover over the bolt hole. Using a magnaviewer aboard the flagship, Noah saw the barely-perceptible opening through which the Parviis had escaped. Inside the hole, he saw something move, and identified it as a solitary Parvii. A sentry, Noah surmised.

Noah set the viewer aside, and said, "We must guard this area well."

"Where there's one hole, there may be others," Eshaz said.

Both of them knew Tulyan teams were looking, but so far nothing had turned up.

Once more the podship nudged up against the membrane, this time near the bolt hole. Inside the passenger compartment, Noah touched the skin of the vessel, but unlike the experience of Eshaz, Noah did not link with Tesh. The skin trembled, as if in fear of Noah. Then it calmed, and abruptly his vision shifted, flooding his consciousness with a wash of gray-green. Presently it focused, and one star seemed to twinkle in the broad field of view, but for only a moment before turning the blackest black.

With his mind, Noah Watanabe—this most unusual of all men—peered into Timeweb and absorbed the entire vast enclosure of his own galaxy, including the decaying infrastructure and this remote, intricately folded section of membrane that had once protected the Parviis.

The opening through which they had fled was a tiny point of blackness in the midst of the gray-green membrane. With his inner eye, Noah peered through the hole into another galaxy, and saw distant, twinkling star systems, nebulas, and belts of undefined, streaking color.

He then experienced an even more peculiar sensation, and felt his consciousness shifting, spinning, making him dizzy. Presently he regained his internal balance, and found that his mind was now *inside* the alternate galaxy, experiencing it paranormally. From this new vantage point, he saw the small Parvii swarm near the other side of the bolt hole.

They're in the undergalaxy, he thought, feeling both a rush of excitement and deep trepidation.

Oddly, Noah could not see very far in this realm, and he wondered if his own anxiety had something to do with that. In his own galaxy, he had learned to overcome physical fear, for he was as close to immortal in that realm as any person could be. But in the undergalaxy, he sensed the rules of physics and laws of nature were entirely different. Nothing was as it seemed there, and he curbed his own curiosity, didn't really want to venture further. Everything he had been through in his own galaxy was more than enough for him, and he couldn't afford to lose focus, couldn't afford to leave his duties and spin off into the unknown.

But Noah also sensed very strongly that something in the undergalaxy was causing the decline of Timeweb, or at least contributing to it. He could not escape considering the ramifications of this second galaxy. His entire concept of galactic ecology had potentially been broadened by a great deal, and beyond that the implications were exponential. A universe of them.

Seeing the vastly diminished Parvii swarm hovering by the bolt hole, Noah had mixed feelings—an urge to destroy them and feelings of pity. Tesh was one of that devilish breed, and he thought he might even love her, and that he might do virtually anything for her if he ever managed to fulfill the galactic duties that seemed to have been thrust upon him by fate.

I am not a god or a messiah.

He did not want to even consider such possibilities. It could only cause harm to his focus, to his intentions. He felt an innate sense of rightness about the course he had followed with his life thus far, about the choices he had made. But he hesitated to believe that he might be anything more than an enhanced form of a human being. Eshaz, in his zeal to heal Noah, had pressed his wounded flesh against the infrastructure of Timeweb, but the strange and powerful nutrients of the infrastructure could never alter certain basic truths.

I was born of a Human mother and father. There is nothing miraculous or particularly heroic about that.

Despite all he told himself, and his sense that he was highly ethical, part of Noah wanted to eliminate this Parvii swarm violently, leaving Tesh Kori as the only survivor of her demented race. In the undergalaxy, the troubled Noah stirred his mind, and felt a cosmic storm forming. Was he causing it? He felt uncertainty about this. But then, as if caught in a great wind, he saw the Parvii swarm buffeted, so that they flitted about in confusion and fear. Some scattered into the distance, and did not return.

The swarm grew even smaller, and Noah felt pity for the terrified creatures.

Wondering what had just occurred, he struggled to extract himself from the peculiar visions. Finally he succeeded in withdrawing, and returned to his physical self, in the passenger compartment of *Webdancer*.

Conflicting emotions raged in his mind, giving him an intense headache.

Eshaz looked at him with concern in his large eyes. "You saw something, didn't you?" the Tulyan asked.

Noah nodded, but for several moments found himself unable to organize his thoughts or form them into words.

Chapter Eight

Noah worries incessantly about his genetic linkage to Francella Watanabe, and her severe mental health issues. But there is an ancillary problem, something he has not discussed with me, and which I have not had the courage to bring up: Is not Doge Anton genetically linked to Francella as well, and might there be psychological repercussions because of that?

—Tesh Kori, private notes

T housands of additional Tulyan pilots had arrived from the starcloud, and were being meshed with the podships like alien marital partners, using the ancient techniques to ensure the maximum efficiency of the Tulyan-Aopoddae linkages. Now, counting the original nine hundred podships that the Liberator fleet had brought to the galactic fold, Doge Anton had a force of more than one hundred twenty-two thousand podships. As had earlier occurred with the original fleet, as the new pilot-ship matchings were completed, the sentient podships took on the reptilian faces of their pilots, and opened up gun ports on the sides of their hulls.

The process was going well. Only two hundred and fourteen podships remained to be synchronized by the Tulyans, plus a few more out in the reaches of the fold that needed to be brought in.

Noah, Anton, and Eshaz stood at a viewing window inside a modular headquarters structure that General Nirella's military technicians had constructed. Held in place by space anchors, it was positioned exactly where the Palace of Woldn used to be, which was considered the most central—and most commanding—position in the entire fold.

The three leaders stood with a number of dignitaries who had been brought in after the victory here over the Parviis, including two members of the Council of Elders and a number of merchant princes. They watched while teams of Tulyan podship handlers worked in the airless vacuum with the remaining, unsynchronized Aopoddae.

The entire Liberator fleet had been delayed while Tulyan experts synchronized and stabilized the vast fleet, necessary to ensure that there would be no rebellion in the Aopoddae ranks, and that every one of the sentient ships was working in concert with the pilots. This involved subtle methods of synchronicity and mutual respect, ways that had been known to the Tulyans since time immemorial, and by which they ensured the integrity of the immense fleet.

"It has been very difficult to integrate so many ships," Eshaz said, "but we're almost there. Long ago, the Parviis did something similar, using their own methods. We're replacing their bonds with our own, then checking and rechecking."

"And those are the most difficult of the bunch," Anton said, pointing out at the podships that were still being worked.

"Precisely. We've separated them from the others, and are performing final tests on the others as we speak. Keep in mind, too, that this is not a process of breaking or taming the podships. Rather, we must harmonize with them."

"Just as Humans and other races need to do in nature," Noah said.

"Well put, my good friend," Eshaz said. He touched Noah's left arm affectionately before pulling away. Then, looking at Doge Anton, the Tulyan added, "If final tests go as anticipated, the rest of the fleet should be able to depart for the starcloud in two days."

"And the recalcitrants?" Anton asked, gesturing again at the podships outside.

"They can be left behind for more work. Eventually, they will be integrated with the others. These just have more difficult Parvii bonds to overcome."

Anton tapped on the window plax. "Can they be merged with the guard force of one hundred armed vessels that we're leaving?"

"Some, perhaps. We'll see."

Outside, Noah saw three additional podships being brought into the mooring basin, including one piloted by Acey Zelk. In the only way that a Human could do this, the teenager stood on top of the vessel. He wore a life support suit, and was secured to the beast by an ornate harness. He used thorn-vines to guide the creature. The suit and harness enable him to travel at high speeds, as fast as the podship could go. The young man was grinning as he came in atop the hull, and he waved toward the viewing window.

Noah and Eshaz waved back.

But Noah withdrew his hand quickly. He wore a long-sleeve shirt, and the extension of his left arm had revealed something that had been troubling him for several days ... a rough area of gray-and-black skin that ran from the forearm to the shoulder and down across his torso, like a mineral vein.

He had not wanted to see a doctor about the condition, suspecting that it was far beyond anything a medical practitioner could understand. Much of his own paranormal abilities undoubtedly stemmed from the time that Eshaz had healed him of a serious head injury by connecting him to a torn fragment of Timeweb. Afterward Noah's own sister, Francella, had attempted to kill him by the most brutal of methods, by hacking him to pieces. Through some miracle, he had survived the dismemberment attempt, growing back all of his severed body parts like an exotic lizard.

The doctors had been dumbfounded.

Even after all that, Noah's demented, dying sister had injected him with a dermex of her own tainted, contaminated blood. Since then, Noah had been increasingly concerned, but had not wanted to consult with anyone about it, not even Eshaz. Whatever was happening to his body would happen, and Noah sensed—very strongly—that neither he nor anyone else could do anything about it.

The night before, while sleeping in accommodations that had been provided for him in the headquarters building, he'd experienced an odd dream about Francella in which she had chased him across the Parvii Fold. It had seemed so real, but had been utterly impossible, since Francella had died after injecting herself with an immortality elixir—a substance that turned against her and made her age rapidly. It was with that tainted blood that she had injected Noah, just before dying herself prematurely. His relationship with her had been a real nightmare. No matter how many good things Noah had tried to do for her during his lifetime, nothing had worked and she had never appreciated any of it. To the end she had remained bitter toward him, irrationally blaming him for her troubles and trying to kill him.

Now Noah saw Eshaz watching him closely, as the Tulyan sometimes did.

Then Noah remembered Eshaz touching his affected arm a few minutes ago. With their truthing touch ability, Tulyans could read thoughts if they desired to do so. But Noah had been wearing the long-sleeve shirt, and Eshaz hadn't felt the skin directly. Noah had always assumed that direct skin contact was necessary, but what if that wasn't the case? What if Tulyan mental probes could penetrate the fabric?

With Noah staring back at him, Eshaz lowered his gaze.

In privacy that evening, Noah examined his arm closely, and an unavoidable thought occurred to him. The affected area that he'd been trying to hide reminded him of podship skin.

Chapter Nine

Great historical events can be illusory to their participants, and to the historians who write about them afterward. Even with the passage of time and the seasoning of history, the truth can still be elusive.

—Sister Janiko, one of the "veiled historians" of Lost Earth

A fter reading a holo-report that floated above his desktop, Pimyt paused and looked up. "This looks good," he said to the dignitary sitting across from him, an insectoid man in a white-and-gold suit.

Ambassador VV Uncel did not respond. He stared at a small handheld screen.

"VV?"

"Eh?" The Adurian's voice squeaked. "Oh, sorry, my roommate gave me a list of things he wants me to do. Household tasks."

"Ah yes, what Humans call the 'honey-do' list."

"Yes. He's quite demanding."

Even though Uncel and his male roommate were in what the Adurians called an 'affectionate relationship,' Pimyt knew it was not sexually intimate. It couldn't possibly be, because the androgynous Adurians, renowned for their laboratory breeding methods, even relied upon them entirely for the propagation of their own race.

"Now what were you saying?" the Ambassador asked.

"Just that the report looks good. The results are exactly as I expected."

"As *we* expected," Ambassador VV Uncel said. Like all of his race, he was entirely hairless, a mixture of mammalian and insectoid features with a small head and large bulbous eyes. His skin was a bright patchwork of multicolored caste markings, symbolizing high social status.

"Don't take that tone with me. The minute I learned about Human military operations on Canopa, I found out their purpose, and I knew instantly they would fail against Parvii telepathic weapons. That was all in *my* initial report to the Coalition, predating anything you wrote."

The Ambassador raised his chin haughtily. "Your report would not have gone anywhere if I hadn't concurred with your *guess*."

"What do you mean, *guess*?" Pimyt felt his face flush hot, and considered hurling something at the irritating diplomat. For a moment, he scanned the objects on his desk, a glax paperweight that could kill him, a paper spike that could do the same, or put out an eye....

The Hibbil's gaze settled on a book that was heavy enough to cause pain if hurled accurately, but wouldn't do lasting physical harm. He'd never taken such action before, though, and knew he shouldn't even consider it. Too much was at stake.

Taking a deep breath, Pimyt continued. "In my position as the Royal Attaché to Doge Lorenzo del Velli, I gained extensive military experience. I was

531

personally responsible for moving MPA troops and equipment around, taking steps to weaken merchant prince military capabilities while maximizing our own. I was also on the team that came up with the idea of inserting sabotaged computer chips into the firing mechanisms of merchant prince space cannons, ion guns, and energy detonators. The weapons will seem to operate perfectly, until our warships come into range and are identified—which automatically shuts the weapons down. What a delightful image: totally defenseless Humans, ready to be slaughtered."

The elegant insectoid smiled. "You are so like your Human friends, aren't you? Always exaggerating your contribution, trying to take personal credit for everything. We Adurians are not that way, and understand the need to share credit, to work as a team. You know quite well that I had similar devices installed surreptitiously on the biggest Mutati warships, but I'm not bragging about it."

Pimyt grabbed the book. Perhaps if he threw it just right it would strike the Ambassador hard enough in the head to knock him out for a few minutes. Yes, he could do it quickly, without warning. Then he could.... The Hibbil salivated, but he set the violent thought aside, and the book.

"Let's stop bickering," Pimyt said. "We agree the Humans have gone on a fool's mission against the Parviis, and soon we'll learn the scale of it." He pointed to the holo-screen, which displayed a report sent back by HibAdu observers who had positioned lab-pods out on the podways to watch for enemy activity. "The Humans have big problems tying them down at the Parvii Fold, so much that they even had to send hundreds of ships back to the Tulyan Starcloud for reinforcements."

"Our Coalition forces are in perfect position, my furry friend. With the merchant princes tied up in a distant battle, their planets will be easy pickings for our massive fleet of four hundred and seventy-six thousand lab-pods, filled with military armaments and fighters. Uncel gestured with his wiry hands as he spoke. "The only question being worked out now is how to distribute our forces for the simultaneous attacks on Merchant Prince Alliance and Mutati Kingdom targets. The Humans have spread themselves too thin, so we're assigning more of our forces to the attacks on Mutati worlds."

Nodding, Pimyt said, "Our enemies have weakened themselves by warring against each other, and now the shapeshifters have been further weakened by the destruction of their homeworld, Paradij."

"Close call for me," Uncel mused, tapping a long finger on the desk top. "I got away just in time."

A pity, Pimyt thought. His eyes felt hot as he glared at the Ambassador.

Uncel paused, seemed nervous as he continued to speak. "Only two days before the destruction, I was with the Zultan Abal Meshdi, spent a night in his palace. He was completely insane, you know, with that Demolio program to blow up merchant prince planets—wiping out our potential prizes of war."

Pimyt nodded. "It is a double-edged sword, isn't it? Less planets, but the Mutatis are weaker because of the loss of Paradij."

"Lucky for me, I had to get back here for an appointment." Uncel scratched his wiry neck. "Hard to believe Meshdi's own son did it, a murder conspiracy with a huge miscalculation that blew up the most important Mutati planet. Even though rumors are rampant that Hari'Adab did that, most Mutatis seem willing to forgive him. "

"No figuring shapeshifters," Pimyt said.

"That's for sure. Even so, both target empires still have many valuables for us. We'll hit them hard, out of the blue."

"I'd like to meet our own leaders one day," Pimyt mused, "especially High Ruler Coreq."

"Many things are far more important," the Ambassador said, his tone sharp.

Pimyt fumed. "Don't you see? We have a lot in common, you and I, including important assignments from HibAdu commanders we've never met."

"No matter. Our careers are assured. Reports from each of us have proven invaluable to the HibAdu effort."

Pimyt grinned. "To make up for my *perceived* selfishness, I must give credit to your own resourcefulness in the not-too-distant past."

Uncel's already-large eyes widened, and he smiled. "But I have so many accomplishments, my friend. As a *team* member, of course. Of what do you speak?"

"I'm thinking of the time you obtained raw information from the Mutatis on the nehrcom cross-space communication system, a system that the Mutatis could not perfect. But our scientists certainly had no problems figuring it out, did they?"

"No. Truly, our forces are poised, and are fortunate. With Hibbil manufacturing skills and Adurian biotech knowledge, it is a combination of the best. No longer will our people be under the boot heels of the Humans and Mutatis."

"We live in legendary times," Pimyt said. "After the great HibAdu victory, perhaps historians will write of our own contributions, VV. To the *team*, of course. Incidentally, I was just teasing you when I exaggerated my own contribution. Sometimes it is quite simple to agitate you."

"Yes, *friend*, but rile me at your own peril. You think I'm a pushover, don't you?"

"I think a lot of things about you that are not productive to mention. A pushover? Perhaps, but I have never required a weak opponent to prevail." He leaned forward over the desk. "But let us turn our talents elsewhere, shall we?"

"Ah yes, an excellent suggestion. Combined, we are much stronger, aren't we? And that's what the Coalition is all about."

Chapter Ten

I ought to exercise more caution, but it is not in my nature. My father was a risk-taker of the highest order, and it is my weakness that I have inherited this tendency from him. Hopefully, I have not also acquired the Zultan's madness.

—Emir Hari'Adab

The Mutati delegation should have been able to reach the Tulyan Starcloud in a few minutes, but it was taking them much longer to cross the galaxy. Hari's two lab-pods had been in the far reaches of space for more than a day so far, but they had not yet reached their destination. At the moment the vessels were dead in space, having been stopped by their crews to assess the unexpected situation. In the lead craft, Hari'Adab and his followers were in comlink contact with the other crew, trying to figure out the problem. And inside the holds of each vessel, HibAdu prisoners were being interrogated intensely.

One thing seemed clear. The Hibbil navigation units on each ship, which the Mutati crews originally thought they understood, had sent them off-course by millions and millions of light years. But that could be made up quickly, if they could only determine where they were. At the speed of podships, even traveling along a damaged infrastructure, such distances could be covered in a relatively short time—and these lab-pods, like their natural cousins, were biological entities with seemingly unlimited travel capabilities. But the lab-pods were acting like blind birds flying headlong through space, not knowing where they were going.

According to one of the prisoners, in all manufacturing tests the Hibbils had performed, covering multiple star systems, the nav-units had functioned perfectly. Apparently, he claimed, they did not function well in all sectors—and in the deepest reaches of space, far from the Hibbil Cluster Worlds, they were undoubtedly giving erroneous readings.

Dismayed and frustrated, Hari conferred with Kajor Yerto Bhaleen. They sat at a small table in the spacious passenger compartment, examining an electronic clip pad that displayed an astromap of this galactic sector. Tapping a button on the pad, Bhaleen called up a holo image of the sector, showing planets, suns, an asteroid belt, and a stunning, butterfly-shaped nebula in the distance that glinted with golden light.

"It's incredibly beautiful in this region," the Kajor said, "but that doesn't help us figure out where we are. My officers are running and rerunning programs now, searching for answers. The prisoners may have thrown us off intentionally, providing false information."

"You think they're fanatics?"

"Maybe. Hard to tell."

"Give me your best guess," Hari said. "How much longer do you think this will take?" Hari asked.

"To figure out where we are, or to get to the starcloud?"

"Both."

"Hard to judge, because even if—I mean, *when*—we figure out our location, we are still having problems with the nav-units. Even so, my officers are confident that we can compensate for the errors. They're taking astronomical readings, and the ships' computers should be able to figure out what we did, and how to correct it."

"But the computers allowed us to go off course?"

"They did, but there have been problems with the podways on which these ships travel, with entire galactic sectors damaged so badly that we couldn't travel through them, requiring that we go around."

"And now?"

"With all the course mistakes and corrections we've made, we're way off course. But don't worry. My navigation officers will come up with new settings."

"At least that's what they're telling you."

"True enough, My Emir." The Kajor smiled cautiously. "But you've always liked my optimism in the past."

With a broad grin, Hari patted him on the back.

Just then, Bhaleen took a comlink call from the other ship. Under intense interrogation, the captured Hibbil and Adurian soldiers were offering no assistance whatsoever. The Kajor went on to discuss a mechanical question with someone on the other end of the line. Bhaleen was the most loyal of all military officers Hari had ever known, and could always be relied upon to perform his work well.

That took some of the load off the young leader's shoulders. But it had not been an easy journey for Hari to arrive at this point. In sharp contrast to the radical, demented militarism of his own father, he had always considered himself something of a moderate—a person who was willing to talk to the enemies of the kingdom and negotiate with them for the mutual benefit of two very different galactic races. And, just as he loved Parais d'Olor, he was certain that all of humankind was filled with relationships such as the one he knew with her, of people who didn't care about ancient enmities and just wanted the fighting to stop.

Normally, Hari was not an appeaser; while he was willing to negotiate, he also believed in negotiating from strength. In the present circumstances, however, that tactic was no longer possible. With the total destruction of the beloved Mutati homeworld of Paradij (an event that would always weigh heavily on his conscience), the shapeshifters had sustained a grievous setback. His people were still in possession of considerable military strength in other Mutati star systems, but the command center and the most powerful forces had been lost with Paradij. The brightest of the brightest had been wiped out, along with the greatest of all military minds and a great deal more.

He tried not to dwell on the troubling details, but they kept surfacing to torment him, almost beyond the limit of his endurance. His heart sank at the thought of the great libraries that had been destroyed on the beautiful world, with all of the priceless ancient documents. All of the historical and cultural treasures. And most of all, the lives that had been taken, especially the young ones. Their imagined faces spun through his thoughts, and he fought off tears.

Suddenly, Parais d'Olor burst into the passenger compartment. Excitedly, she almost lifted her wings, though she had no room to fly in there. "One of the Adurians is talking," she said. "He's a navigation technician who refused to say anything before. Now he's telling our officers what we did wrong, and how we were misled by other prisoners."

"But can we trust him?" Bhaleen asked. He hurried past her, heading for the hold where the prisoners were.

"Wish we had a Tulyan to use the truthing touch on him," Hari said.

When Hari and the others entered the spacious hold, he saw his officers and soldiers standing around one of the hairless, bulbous-eyed Adurians. The alien was spewing words like automatic projectile fire, technical information about astronomical coordinates and settings on the nav-units. One of Hari's men was recording him, and another was entering notes on a clip pad.

Finally, the HibAdu soldier fell silent.

Pushing his way past the others, Kajor Bhaleen unfolded a knife and held the blade against the throat of the prisoner. The Adurian technician had dark, bulbous eyes that were comparatively small for his race. His gaze darted around nervously.

"Why should we believe you?" Bhaleen asked. He drew a trickle of yellow blood from the alien's neck.

"Please don't kill me! I'm telling the truth because I don't want to die out here, marooned. I have told your men what they need to do."

"If he's lying, we will know soon enough," Hari said, placing a hand on Bhaleen's shoulder.

The Kajor hesitated, then withdrew the weapon. He wiped off the blade and folded it back into his pocket.

The Adurian pleaded to be sent back to join his companions, and received assurance from his captors that his actions would be kept secret. Afterward,

Brian Herbert

Mutatis checked and rechecked the new information. All calculations and projections showed that it was correct, and finally the ships got underway again.

Three hours later, the Adurian was found dead in his sleeping quarters, strangled by a fellow prisoner.

Chapter Eleven

Sometimes it is possible to think about a thing too much.

—Master Noah Watanabe

For weeks, the Liberator fleet had been in the Parvii Fold, occupied with essential tasks. The complete vanquishing of the Parviis and their flight from the galactic pocket had only been the beginning. Now, at last, virtually all of the podships had Tulyan pilots and the galactic pocket had been secured against the return of enemy swarms, to prevent them from ever using it as a home base, or an area of racial recuperation.

In addition to their concerns about Parvii survivors, the Tulyans in the Liberator force had devoted themselves to preparing the vast Aopoddae fleet for deep-space galactic recovery operations, matching them up with pilots and taking steps to remove and replace the ancient bonds that Parviis had placed on the sentient spacecraft in order to control them.

Inside the main corridor of the flagship *Webdancer*, Noah had just spoken with Tesh Kori. Then she had returned to her isolated position in the sectoid chamber, from which she would pilot the vessel in the Parvii manner. She was about to get underway, but this time fleet command had decided that the big flagship would be among the last of the vessels to depart for the Tulyan Starcloud. For hours now, the rest of the fleet had been streaming out through the Asteroid Funnel, into deep space.

As Noah hurried through the gray-green corridors of the vessel, he had mixed feelings. Some of his companions, including Anton del Velli and Subi Danvar, had said they hoped the entire Parvii race went extinct, for the greater good of the galaxy. To Noah that sounded horrific, but privately he'd admitted that it did make some sense. Still, he wanted to believe it was overkill, so he had been telling the others that there were worthwhile Parviis in the race. Tesh Kori had proven that, and her intentions had been verified by the Tulyan truthing touch.

If only the remaining Parviis could be separated from the Eye of the Swarm and his influences, many of the race might be rehabilitated. For that matter, while Noah had seen the survivors through a Timeweb vision, and they had been hovering near the bolt hole on the other side, he wasn't at all certain if Woldn remained with them. For security purposes, he had to assume they still had the same leader, and that he remained a danger.

Noah stopped as something small scurried past his feet and disappeared around a corner. He'd gotten a good look at it, and his eyebrows lifted in surprise. A dark brown roachrat.

"On a podship?" he murmured. Then, considering it more, he felt confident that the podship could selectively kill the rodent if desired. The sentient spacecraft must be aware of its presence (and perhaps others), just as it was aware of the pilot and passengers aboard.

Continuing down the corridor, Noah entered the passenger compartment, which was filled MPA and Red Beret soldiers and the noise of conversations

536

among them. He nodded to Doge Anton, who was conversing with one of his officers.

Finding a chair by a porthole, Noah sat down and gazed outside, at large and small stones tumbling by in the Asteroid Funnel, obstacles that Tesh eluded skillfully. Previously the stones had only tumbled in one direction. Now Noah noticed them coming from both ends of the funnel, at varying speeds. Many of them bounced off the hull, transmitting dull thuds to the interior, but Tesh kept the ship going. Finally, the huge fleet was getting underway.

When Noah's ship reached open space, he felt a slight vibration in the chair and in the deck, which meant they were on a rough section of podway, where the strands of the paranormal infrastructure were frayed. Ahead, he saw other Aopoddae ships veering onto a side podway, and presently Tesh followed.

Sitting by the porthole, Noah ran a finger up his left forearm, beneath the long sleeve of the tunic. Feeling the rough skin on the arm, he still didn't want anyone to know about it yet, perhaps never. The gray-and-black streak ran from his wrist all the way up his arm to the shoulder, and down the front of his torso. Grayness now covered the spot beside his belly button where his sister had stabbed the dermex into him, but the vein had not started there. In his questing mind, this did not necessarily mean that she was not the cause of his strange physical changes. In fact, he strongly suspected that she had something to do with the phenomenon, perhaps as a catalyst.

But beyond anything Francella might have had to do with his metamorphosis, it was as if ...

He took a deep breath before continuing the thought.

Noah feared thinking about it, and couldn't imagine it really being true, but his skin definitely looked like that of a podship hull. On a much smaller scale, of course, but the colors and texture were remarkably alike.

Now, as he had done previously, he touched the actual podship skin, the interior of the wall. This time the creature did not tremble in fear.

A note of progress, Noah thought.

He made an attempt to connect with Timeweb again, but after several moments he realized it was to no avail, perhaps because the vessel was not nudging up against a galactic membrane like the last time. Apparently, the linkage to podway strands was not enough, perhaps due to breakages in the infrastructure. But as Noah withdrew his hand and stood straight, he realized that he was developing a headache, and it was quickly growing intense.

He heard the voices of fellow passengers around him. Motioning to a tall Red Beret soldier, Noah asked if he had anything to help his headache.

"I have just the thing, sir," he said. "Acupuncture robotics."

Noah nodded. He'd tried the technique once, and it had worked.

The soldier activated a small acu-robot—the size of a freckle—that scampered over Noah's skull and through his hair, along the scalp. He barely felt the needle prick, just a little tickle. Gradually Noah's thoughts calmed and his head began to feel better. But he still had an ache in the back of his head. In an attempt to relax more, Noah raised the back of his chair and leaned his head against a pad.

While he was able to tune out the conversations around him, his mind continued to churn, dredging up a panoply of thoughts—from the most minuscule to the most significant.

Abruptly, Noah felt a surge in his mind. Now, through sharp lances of eye pain he saw an internal vision of the planet Canopa, and a huge timehole near it, just beyond the atmosphere. The hole spun like a pale gray whirlpool, encircled by a luminous band of green light.

The headquarters of the Merchant Prince Alliance was on Canopa now, along with Noah's roots … the birthplace of virtually everyone in his family, going back for many generations. But his mother, father, and even his vile sister were all gone, and Noah had created new roots for himself around the galaxy, with successful business operations involving ecological recovery operations. Until crises—one on top of another—interrupted.

The timehole grew larger, and the planet drew closer to it. He wondered if this was reality. He thought it was, but there were so many unanswered questions about the paranormal realm.

Canopa was Noah's homeworld, and he felt a deep sadness at the prospect of its loss. If the entire planet disappeared into the hole and presumably into the adjacent galaxy, he assumed that all life on the world would perish. For him it was more than personal feelings; it was a galactic ecology issue and a military matter. It was the loss of his personal and Human underpinnings, and extremely unsettling to him. But from this remote distance, what could he do to rescue Canopa?

Squinting, he saw an orbital station move into view and drift near the timehole. With a start, he realized it was EcoStation, which the former Doge Lorenzo had renamed the Pleasure Palace, and which he used as a gambling casino. Noah missed the facility that had long been close to his heart, and a source of immense pride for him.

Then, just as quickly as it had appeared, the images of Canopa, the space station, and the timehole faded away. Noah felt an immense emptiness at the potential cataclysm, and bemoaned his inability to do anything to prevent it.

He would send a message to Canopa as soon as possible to warn them, and would alert the Tulyan Council of Elders to send a repair team—in case the images proved to be true. Inexplicably and against all of his logic and moral base, he worried more about EcoStation than anything. He wasn't proud of the thought and didn't understand it, but it lingered with him nonetheless.

Chapter Twelve

We wear our mortal skins like cloaks, protecting us until the fabric rots away.
Then at last we are left naked, exposed to the entropy of the universe.

—A saying of Lost Earth

Princess Meghina of Siriki had led an interesting life.

One of the most beautiful women in the galaxy, she had married the Doge Lorenzo del Velli twenty-two years ago, when she was only fourteen. As her loveliness became renowned throughout the realm, she had—with her husband's concurrence—become a courtesan to other powerful noblemen in the Merchant Prince Alliance. An independent woman, she had lived separately in a marvelous palace on the planet Siriki, and ostensibly bore seven daughters for Lorenzo. Afterward, having escaped the destruction of her homeworld by Mutati military forces, she had moved to the orbital gambling facility over Canopa, to live with her husband.

There, her darkest secrets had been revealed. Through intrigues by Francella Watanabe, she had been exposed as a Mutati, but one who had always wanted to be Human, and whose shapeshifting cellular structure had locked into Human form. Her daughters, it turned out, had all been fake pregnancies. She had never given birth to any of them. The MPA public, and Lorenzo himself, had ultimately been sympathetic to her, despite the deceit.

Living with her husband on the orbital gambling facility for some time now, she had become a mysterious, glamorous figure, occasionally seen out on the gaming floor, but more often she frequented the back corridors and glittering chambers of the facility, where she spent time with a most unusual group of friends....

One evening, Lorenzo invited Meghina and these friends to dinner in his elegant dining hall. Months earlier, he had been forced to abdicate as doge, in part because of the revelations about Meghina, which his political enemies used to their advantage. Now the nobleman was essentially an outcast on the orbiter, living in a velvet-lined cocoon.

At the appointed hour, Princess Meghina sat on one end of the gleaming wooden banquet table, opposite Lorenzo on the other. With her golden hair secured by a jeweled headband, she wore a long black velveen dress, trimmed in precious gemstones. She smiled down the long table at her husband, and sipped from a large silver goblet of red wine, a fine Canopan vintage.

Along the sides sat her five extraordinary companions—three men on one side and two women on the other. They formed an exclusive little club, often getting together socially in Meghina's royal apartments on the Pleasure Palace orbiter. All the while, the six of them were under continuing medical supervision.

This was because they had apparently become immortal.

Under a research program established by the medical division of CorpOne, a remarkable elixir had been developed from the DNA of the purportedly indestructible Noah Watanabe. The new solution (dubbed the Elixir of Life) had been injected into two hundred thousand persons from all of the galactic races, and had resulted in immortality for a scant six of them, including Meghina. It had been like winning a lottery, and initially they had all considered themselves lucky.

Then they had heard that Noah's insane sister had injected herself with the elixir, and had suffered a rapid cellular decline—an artificial form of progeria that caused the rapid aging of her cells, and her premature death. There had even been rumors that Francella, shortly before dying, had injected her own tainted blood back into her brother, trying to harm him. The attempt had apparently been unsuccessful, because he didn't seem to have experienced any associated medical problems.

So far, neither had Princess Meghina or the other Elixir of Life "winners."

* * * * *

In a chair on Meghina's immediate left sat a small black-and-tan pet that she had recently taken a liking to, a rare Bernjack dagg from her private animal collection. Once it had been owned by a very old woman, but she had gone into a rest home and had been unable to care for the dagg any longer. The shaggy animal was very special to Meghina now, and she called it Orga, because the old lady had been Mrs. Orga. Using the solitary bulbous eye above its snout, it peered around the shaggy fur overhanging its face.

At the other end of the table, on Lorenzo's right, sat what looked like another pet but really wasn't. Rather, it was her husband's furry little attaché, the feisty Hibbil, Pimyt. Meghina had never liked the graying, black-and-white alien, but had gracefully concealed her feelings from him.

Raising his own goblet, Lorenzo said, "A toast to the good life."

He and his guests quaffed their drinks, then set the goblets down with thumps that were almost in synchronization.

Just then, the dagg leaned its long snout over the table, and gripped its water bowl in its mouth. Lifting the bowl high, the animal leaned back and slurped from it, before losing its grip. The bowl crashed to the floor, shattering and spilling the water.

Several guests tittered, but Lorenzo scowled at the animal, as he often did. He only tolerated the dagg. A servant hurried over to clean up the mess.

"Perhaps we should put wine in Orga's bowl!" suggested one of the guests, a ruddy, aging man named Dougal Netzer. Once an impoverished portrait painter, he now earned large sums for his work. More than any of his cellular peers, he had been able to capitalize financially on his overnight fame as an immortal.

Servants brought in platters heaped with steaming game hens, cooked in a dark, aromatic sauce. At Meghina's order, they even had a plate of boned meat for the dagg. The moment it was placed in front of him, Orga tried to grab a piece of meat. But Meghina waggled a finger near the plate, causing the animal to let go of the food and pull his head back—awaiting permission to eat.

"As my lovely wife has probably told you," Lorenzo said, "I am in *de facto* exile on this orbital facility, with little opportunity to get away from it." He paused. "Tell me about events on the surface of Canopa—news, gossip, bits of information. Pimyt doesn't have the connections he enjoyed while working for me on-planet. I've been feeling isolated."

Pimyt shot him a hard stare, but for only a moment. Two of the female guests and one of the men provided the former doge with details, how Doge Anton, Noah Watanabe, and others had formed a military expedition and departed in a big hurry.

When Lorenzo had heard enough, he permitted the table to fall into witty, light-hearted conversation, much of it about the immortality of Meghina and her friends.

At first, Pimyt said very little. Finally, he asked the woman seated next to him, "What do you intend to do with your own extended life?"

"I have so much time now to consider such matters," she said. A robust, big-chested woman in a blue tunic, she smiled. Since gaining immortality she had abandoned her original name, and for unexplained reasons now called herself Paltrow.

"And the answer is, after all the time you've taken to consider it?" the Hibbil asked.

"I have put off such matters, such *worries*, really. I've hardly thought about them at all."

"A nice luxury to have." The little Hibbil tugged at the salt-and-pepper fur on his chin. It was a nervous mannerism that Meghina had noticed previously.

"I'm sorry," Paltrow said. "I don't mean to be rude, but I honestly haven't given it much thought."

Most of those at the table had paused to listen to the exchange.

"Perhaps our additional time is not so important as you might think," Meghina suggested. "What, exactly, does living forever mean? Living forever in relation to what?"

"Intriguing observation," Dougal Netzer said.

The guests began to pitch in. Finally Paltrow asked, "Is a million years in our galaxy only a moment, or a mere fraction of a moment?"

Theories and more questions went around the table in rapid succession, and it developed into a game in which several people tried to ask the most clever question, some of them rhetorical.

The repartee intensified, and Lorenzo seemed to enjoy it. Meghina couldn't help noticing, however, that Pimyt appeared to be somewhere else in his mind, perhaps far across the galaxy on his alien homeworld.

Chapter Thirteen

Each moment is slightly different from the one preceding it.

—Parvii Inspiration

In the alternate realm, the cosmic storm subsided, and the huddled swarm of Parviis stopped being buffeted around. But to the Eye of the Swarm, this provided little comfort.

Drifting in the airless darkness with the remnants of his once-mighty race, Woldn felt dismal. He had always been a leader who visualized things and made them happen. For him, that was a key aspect of command, envisioning things that others could not, and making them come to pass. But in his wildest imaginings, from his first recollections of life more than two thousand years ago, he'd never thought it possible that he could fall to this level, soundly defeated and relegated to hiding in an unknown galactic region, perhaps even in another galaxy altogether.

More than anything, Woldn wanted to fight back, to stream back through the bolt hole into the Parvii Fold and dispatch his enemies with raw violence, killing and scattering them, chasing them to the ends of the universe and wiping out all remnants of them. But he didn't have the power to do that. Not even close.

Even worse, troublesome thoughts had been creeping into his consciousness like vermin infesting his mind, and he could not avoid asking himself, *Have I done anything to cause this?*

The Eye of the Swarm wondered if he might ... or *should* ... have done anything differently. And yet, he had only done things the way every Parvii ruler had done them since time immemorial. He had followed the ancient traditions, the proven ways.

A sense of deep gloom and foreboding came over him now, as something new occurred to him. He realized that he had in effect been following a template, that his leadership methods had been inherited ... and hardly modified at all. Methods that did not contemplate the modern challenges confronting him. Never before had a leader faced such immense trials and tribulations: the decline of the galactic infrastructure on which podships traveled, and the enemies of the Parvii race who wanted to destroy them. But he realized this was no excuse. Millions of years of relative sameness in the galaxy had lulled him and predecessors into a false sense of security.

We didn't adapt to changing conditions. I didn't adapt. My people followed me off the edge of a cliff.

He shivered in the dim void. Though his people hardly ever felt the frigid extremes of temperature in deep space, for some reason it seemed much colder to him here. But how could that be? It probably wasn't the case, not according to the laws of physics and the galactic principles that had been around since the beginning of time. Perhaps extreme stress was affecting him, compromising his

Parvii bodily functions.

And ... this might be another galaxy, one that really is colder.

He drifted toward the tiny bolt hole, and telepathically commanded the sentry at the opening to make way for him. That one hurried out of his way, back into the alternate realm.

Woldn entered. The hole was actually a tunnel, though only a few hundred meters in length—tunnel through the membrane that defined and protected a large portion of the sacred Parvii Fold. In a matter of seconds, he reached the other end, but stopped just before emerging.

Then, ever so cautiously, he pushed his head out of the opening on the other side and peered into the fold. Not far away, he saw a few dozen podships that looked as if they had been stationed to guard the hole. Extending his range of vision (as only the Eye of the Swarm could do), he made out additional sentient vessels in the distance, engaged in what appeared to be practice maneuvers, and other podships that he thought were on patrol.

Scanning around the fold, he didn't see that many vessels. Then, at the entrance to the Asteroid Funnel, he saw podships going through, departing. Looking farther, he saw to his vexation that they were making their way expertly past the tumbling, luminous white stones and out into deep space.

They're stealing my fleet, damn them!

Right there, as never before, Woldn vowed revenge. Even if it required every ounce of his remaining strength, to the very last breath he took he would make the effort. And so would every one of his followers. If any of them didn't show enough commitment, he would kill them. For a matter involving stakes this high, he could do no less, could expect no less.

Chapter Fourteen

Many people want to predict the future, so that they can be ready and position themselves most advantageously—protecting themselves and those close to them. Every organism has an innate need to survive, but I have no curiosity about the moment and method of my own death. Rather, I choose to observe larger issues that effect all living organisms, so that I might contribute to the whole. If we do not take the long view as a species, the short view that happens to each of us no longer matters.

—Master Noah Watanabe, classroom instruction

On board the flagship, while the pilot searched for safe podway routes along a decaying infrastructure, Noah had additional concerns. Layers of trouble seeped through his thoughts as he paced back and forth across an anteroom. It was one of several that the sentient vessel had formed around the perimeter of the main passenger compartment, using its mysterious manner of extrusion and changing shape, and of changing size. Now she was easily the largest vessel in the fleet, with the most complex arrangement of interior rooms.

She, Noah thought. *Yes, assuming Webdancer has a gender, it seems female to me.*

Through an open doorway, he heard the voices of Doge Anton, General Nirella, and Subi Danvar coming from a room across the corridor. He'd been in there with them earlier, telling them about the paranormal image of a timehole he'd seen near Canopa and EcoStation, and how real it had seemed to him.

Now he tuned out the voices in the other room, didn't try to listen in on their words.

His main concern was much closer to him. Noah's body had been changing for some time now, though it remained to be seen if it was a bizarre evolutionary process, an uncharted disease, or something he had not yet considered.

I may be immortal, but what am I becoming?

He felt vibration in the floor as they passed over a rough section of podway. It grew worse for perhaps a minute, then gradually smoothed out.

During the past year, Noah had taken a number of fantastic mental excursions through Timeweb, and he had peered into what seemed to be an entirely different galaxy, where a small swarm of Parvii survivors had fled. While held prisoner by his own sister, Noah had survived her vicious butchery, and had even regrown severed limbs and other body parts like a lizard. Now, in recent weeks, the skin on his torso and arms was becoming different, morphing into something unfamiliar. He'd been able to conceal the changes beneath his clothing so far, but he didn't know how much longer he could do that.

Am I turning into an alien … no longer Human?

His mental incongruities seemed to have come first, followed by the physical. But he had no way of studying the history of his own cellular structure to confirm that, so the physical changes might have actually started the process. Most perplexing. Perhaps it all had been occurring simultaneously. Certainly both the cerebral and the corporal were apparent now, and they had not locked into any semblance of stability. He was in a constant state of flux, leaving him with infinite questions and no good answers.

Terror washed through him, but abated in a few moments when he realized that part of him actually *wanted* the changes to continue. On many occasions he had tried to enter the Timeweb realm of his own volition, but for the most part he had been unable to do so. And even when he had been able to go into the web at all, it seemed to be through a back or side door, one that the gods of the realm had only left ajar accidentally. Perhaps it was a symptom of the declining infrastructure, the strange and baffling ecological malaise that was spreading through the galaxy. Without warning, as if sensing his presence where he was not supposed to be, the rulers of the realm kept locating him and throwing him out summarily.

The podship vibrated again, and slowed. Through a porthole Noah saw a flickering blue sun and a system of ringed planets. Then the podway improved once more, and they sped past the system, through the heart of a purple nebula.

In the end Noah realized that it didn't matter what he wanted himself. All of the bizarre things that were happening to him were far beyond his personal control. His tormented sister Francella had complicated any hope he ever had of figuring the transformation out, stabbing that dermex of her own poisoned blood deep into him.

Now he lifted his tunic and stared at his muscular abdomen, the place where she had struck. The vein of his morphing, gray-and-black skin had started on his chest, but not at that spot beside his belly button. Even so, there might be a time correlation. The physical changes had begun a short while *after* her attack, and now included the place she had stabbed him, a small oblong area that was darker than the rest of the altered skin.

He paused and fixed his gaze on the open doorway, the gray-green natural light out in the corridor, and the mottled gray skin of the podship. Just focusing on various sections of the sentient vessel seemed to have a strange fascination for him, reminding him of how he felt as a small boy when he stared transfixed into pools of water, hypnotized by the changes in light and ripples of liquid motion. The interior of each Aopoddae vessel was like that in a sense, as he detected tiny shiftings in the illumination and skin surfaces all the time, subtle differences in hue and texture that he didn't think the other passengers noticed.

Perhaps Tesh, as the Parvii pilot, could see such things. It might be possible. *Beautiful Tesh*. His thoughts drifted toward her, and then away again.

Abruptly, he found himself plunging outward, beyond the confines of the podship and into space. As he hurtled into the frozen void he saw *Webdancer* and the rest of the huge fleet behind him, with porthole lights visible along their hulls. Quickly, the fleet vanished from view, and a new awareness came over him.

Noah's motion stabilized, and he found himself standing motionless inside the sectoid chamber of yet another podship, piloting it in the Tulyan manner along the decaying infrastructure at much higher speeds than *Webdancer* had ever been able to attain. He changed course repeatedly, finding optimum strands for the ship to utilize. In a state of hyper awareness, Noah realized that it was not his Human body in the sectoid chamber. Rather, he had become a metallic green mist within an amorphous, unidentifiable shape, perhaps the form he had been evolving into before this happened.

But, as if in contradiction of that, on the prow of the vessel he saw—somehow—his own Human face in an enlarged form, suggesting that he had discovered a modified Tulyan method of piloting the craft. Did the form of the pilot lose its separate features inside the sectoid chamber when its energy merged into the podship flesh?

Another question without an answer.

Far off in the distance, he recognized some of the major planetary systems of the Merchant Prince Alliance, and as he flew on he made out the galactic sectors of other races. He made his way toward some of the regions that he recognized. But soon he found, strangely, that he was flying right through them as if they were no more than holo images. On previous excursions into Timeweb he had been able to see activity in the galaxy, particularly other ships as they negotiated the podways. Now it was different. He could not make out details such as that, only increasingly blurry views as he neared and passed through the systems.

And he sensed—but could not see—a great but undefined danger out in the galaxy, beyond the crumbling infrastructure that everyone knew about. As he turned around and went back in the direction he had come, he wondered what the feeling meant.

On the way Noah recalled an earlier venture into the paranormal realm in which he saw Hibbil and Adurian soldiers inside strange podships that were piloted by Hibbils using computerized navigation units. It had been peculiar and unexplained, and he had reported it to Tesh Kori and Doge Anton.

Alas, with no way of reentering the web at will, and no way of verifying what he had seen, Noah never could tell if that startling vision had been real or not. It had not made any sense at all, since Hibbils were aligned with Humans, and Adurians were the long-time allies of Mutatis. Since then, there had been no other sightings of the odd soldiers or the highly unusual ships, so nothing could be done about it.

Might that be the additional menace he sensed now? He let the question sink in. No, he decided. The threat came from something else.

Just ahead he saw the rear of the podship fleet. The larger and more impressive *Webdancer* was out in front, leading the others. At the immense rate of speed that Noah had attained, the fleet seemed to be traveling slowly through space, and he caught up with it easily. None of the vessels noticed him, and as he neared he found himself hurtling out of the sectoid chamber toward *Webdancer*, and back into the anteroom he'd been in before embarking on this strange journey.

Moments later he was standing in that room, staring through the doorway into a gray-green wash of light.

And abruptly, as if emerging from a trance, Noah jerked to awareness and hurried across the corridor, to the room occupied by Anton, Nirella, and Subi. The three of them sat at a table, engaged in intense conversation. At first they didn't notice him enter. Then Subi called attention to him, and they all looked at Noah in a similarly odd manner, leaning close and squinting their eyes. Under their intense scrutiny Noah felt warm. Drops of perspiration formed on his brow.

"I sense a terrible danger out there," Noah said, at last. He could hardly get the words out.

"Are you feeling all right?" Nirella asked. She wore a red uniform with gold braids and insignia, designating her rank as Supreme General of the MPA armed forces. But now she conducted herself more like a caring woman than a military commander, looking at him with concern and urging him to sit down.

He resisted her efforts and pulled his arm away from her grasp. "I'm fine. Listen to me. I sense an additional threat, more powerful than anything else we've ever seen or discussed."

"But what?"

"I can't say, but it's out there, and seems like even more than the disintegration of the galactic infrastructure."

"It can't be military," Nirella said. "We've defeated the Parviis, and the Mutatis don't have anywhere near the power we have now. We control all the podships, so we can go and attack their planets at anytime."

"It's not Parviis or Mutatis," Noah said. "Or any other galactic race. It's something else entirely. I think … I *fear* … that it's beyond anything we're able to comprehend."

"For hours we've been in range of deep-space nehrcom relay stations," Anton said, "and the reports from our planets are all good. Nothing significant is happening in our sector, or anywhere near it."

"Maybe it's only the infrastructure after all," Noah said. He slumped into a comfortable chair that the podship had created, off to one side. He smiled grimly. "*Only* the infrastructure. As if that isn't enough."

"The repair and restoration of the galactic network needs to be our top priority," the young doge insisted.

"I don't dispute that," Noah said. "I just wish we'd get to the starcloud faster so we can get on with it."

But no one in the room had any idea what was really occurring. Or the fact that HibAdu conspirators were using their own technology to relay false nehrcom messages. In actuality, a terrible thing *had* happened, which Noah and his companions would soon discover.…

Chapter Fifteen

We are a galactic race that no one has ever noticed. Doesn't the intelligence of our members—at least the best of us—compare favorably with that of any recognized galactic race? Admittedly, we look different from any of them, and we don't have their cellular structures, but who's to say that a galactic race has to be biological? Why can't it be mechanical instead, with metal and plax parts, and computer circuitry?

—From one of Thinker's private data banks

Unable to move, Ipsy watched as a mechanical claw reached for the remains of a large, dented unit that had once been the central processing unit for an entire factory assembly line. As the claw lifted its load, the pile shifted, and the broken little robot was jostled to one side.

He'd been there for weeks outside the factory, bumped around and constantly ignored. No one seemed to need his parts for anything. He was small and easily overlooked, but the claw had a zoomeye on it, projecting a beam of orange light that enabled it to see the tiniest part anywhere in the heap, even at the bottom, underneath everything else.

At the moment, with the heavy CPU no longer on him, Ipsy found himself on the very top of the scrap heap, warming under a bright sun. He didn't really want to be taken, because then he might lose what little independence he had left, if only what remained of it in his own mind. All he had now was his ability to observe what went on around him, and to remember better days.

The claw moved its load and released it, then returned and hovered over another part, a couple of meters away from Ipsy.

Just then, without being touched, the pile shifted, settled. And, for the first time since being thrown on the scrap heap, Ipsy moved one of his mechanical arms, and a leg. His circuits had reconnected, but only partially. He tried to move his other arm and leg, but without success. It would be difficult to escape this place with only two of his four major appendages, but he decided to give it a try anyway.

Like a cripple, he dragged himself over the top of the heap, away from the claw. His improvised body was even shorter than before, and much thinner. With one of his rear visual sensors, he saw the claw's orange beam of light move toward him, and almost catch up with him. Abruptly, more key components of his circuitry came to life. He scurried like a rodent down the slope of junk, and entered the factory through a side door.

Reaching the main aisle and then crawling up on a ledge for a better view, the little robot saw that the factory was not operating at all. Hibbils and workbots busied themselves at assembly-line stations, adjusting the machinery, connecting raw material feeder units to it. On the far end of the aisle, robots stood motionlessly, awaiting the signal to return to their stations.

Hearing voices behind him, Ipsy dropped down behind a bench.

He saw the furry lower legs of two Hibbils, standing near him. The diminutive men spoke rapidly, excitedly. From their conversation, he figured out they were military officers for something called the HibAdu Coalition, checking on the production of war materials. Listening attentively, Ipsy heard more.

"We're getting close to zero hour," one of them said. "It'll be unprecedented. Simultaneous sneak attacks on Human and Mutati planets.

Imagine the scope of it, all the destruction and death."

"From what I hear, it could already be underway."

"I wish I was on the front lines, instead of this assignment," the other said. "I hate Humans, the way they've always lorded over us, treating us like children."

"We each must do our part. Most of the instrument systems and parts coming out of this factory are for the HibAdu fleet." This Hibbil laughed, and added, "If you want to go on the front lines, why don't you hide inside one of the weapon-control boxes?"

The two officers walked away, and their conversation faded.

Ipsy's artificial brain whirred. He wondered if he might commit an act of sabotage … perhaps even blow up the factory. But this was one of many factories, and they would just resume operations elsewhere. Besides, it sounded like most of the HibAdu attack force was already in place and ready to attack.

Then Ipsy had an even more intriguing idea. If he could do something *during* a military engagement, he might be able to wreak much more havoc.

Considerably smaller than a Hibbil, he crawled inside one of the weapon-control boxes just before it was sealed up, and awaited its delivery to the war.

Chapter Sixteen

Trust is like quicksand. It can lull you to your death.

—A saying of Lost Earth

At opposite sides of a dual-console machine, two aliens of differing races stood inside a glax tower building in the Hibbil capital city, surrounded by a sea of industrial structures that stretched to the horizons of the planet. The shorter one, a Hibbil with graying black-and-white fur, glanced up at his companion, concealing his own enmity.

This Adurian diplomat was a major irritation.

Whenever VV Uncel wasn't looking, Pimyt glared at him with red-ember eyes. Then, the moment Uncel looked his way with those oversized insectoid orbs, the little Hibbil was all smiles on his own furry, bearded face, and his eyes had reverted to red dullness. Pimyt knew how disarmingly cute he could look whenever he wanted, like a cuddly Earthian panda bear. He also knew that Adurians didn't trust Hibbils, and vice versa. The two races were only working together for their own interests, with each side constantly trying to get a leg up on the other. On some occasions the methods were subtle, but most of the time they were not. Even so, racial preservation and advancement had a way of causing each side to overlook the perceived slights committed by the other. The leaders of the two races understood this, and knew they could go farther together than apart.

In other circumstances, and perhaps sometime in the not-too-distant future, Pimyt might eradicate Uncel with shocking suddenness, moving in for the kill in a surprising blur of speed. But for now, they would play this little game together.

It was an Adurian form of entertainment, actually, in which the two of them stood at linked holovid consoles, operating touchpad controls that immersed each of them into a holodrama, shown on a large central screen. The Adurians loved their games of chance and competition, and this one had a couple of twists that rigged it in the Adurian player's favor. And, though Uncel had taken pains to keep it secret, Pimyt knew that the decisions the Hibbil player made were being sent by hidden telebeam transmitters to an office full of Adurian bureaucrats, where they were further studied, to analyze sincerity and trustworthiness.

Pimyt smiled to himself. As a race, the Adurians were notoriously paranoid. On their homeworld and throughout their foreign operations, everything was under surveillance, and they were quite adept at tech gadgets. But Hibbils were considerably better at devising clever machines and mechanical systems than Adurians, and for every tech system the Adurians had, the Hibbils had one that was superior. It was only in diverse biological and biotech products that the Adurians held the upper hand, particularly in the improvement of lab-pods, which had originally been discovered by Mutati scientists—but not developed very well by them.

This machine could be set to play a variety of games. At the moment, the participants were in a simulated competition of space baseball, with their holo images dressed in uniforms, standing in batters' boxes on an asteroid. Each of them faced the same tall Vandurian pitcher who threw two balls simultaneously, one with each arm. The first player to hit the tricky pitches, or to get the best hit if both of them connected simultaneously, won the game.

Uncel swung, and missed. "Damn!" he exclaimed.

Smiling to himself, Pimyt hit a line drive that carried into the asteroid belt. His virtual ball kept going and going, and soon it was out of sight. Gleefully, the holo image of the little Hibbil ran and leaped from asteroid to asteroid around the simulated deep-space base path, and finally he came back around to home plate on the original asteroid.

"Going, going, gone!" he shouted, as if he was an announcer describing a long home run. "You lose!"

Uncel had an expression on his face like a man who knew he had been hoodwinked, but couldn't figure out how. In fact, the Adurian machine had been rigged to give Uncel the advantage, but Pimyt had transmitted an overriding signal into it to give him the edge instead.

"This is impossible," Uncel said. "You did something to the game, didn't you?"

"You sound so certain of that, my friend. Why is that, do you suppose?" Pimyt knew why, and saw a look of guilt on the Ambassador's face. The cheater knew that he had himself been cheated.

"You're wasting my valuable time," Uncel snapped. Lifting his head in disdain, he marched to an ascensore and entered it, leaving Pimyt alone in the tower room.

"Pompous ass," Pimyt muttered under his breath.

Left to himself, he fiddled with the game controls, changing the settings in rapid succession, bringing up a variety of games, some of which he'd never heard of. Many of the diversions involved cards, dice, or balls, while others were animal races, with the players riding on the backs of a selection of alien beasts.

All the while, his thoughts wandered. The little Hibbil led an uncommonly complex life, balancing his various duties, his layers of subterfuge and intrigue. His biography was not linear, and would be impossible for anyone to write accurately without his candid cooperation.

Pimyt was, without doubt, a very important person. And not just in his own estimation.

Though Hibbils did mate, and the vast majority of them enjoyed the company of the opposite sex, he had been involved in very few dalliances in the past, and expected the future to be the same. He was proud of the fact that his libido had no influence on his decision-making processes. Or at least, that he had subdued it enough to make it ancillary.

There had been undeniable temptations, such as the attractive Jimlat dwarf that had caught his eye on the remote, unaligned planet of the same name. He'd never seen a face and figure to match hers. And the way she *moved!* She had almost derailed his entire career with her charms. Pimyt had made love with her in her apartment, and she'd told him of her own ambitions and dreams, of how she would like to marry him and move to the Hibbil Cluster Worlds.

He had smiled and nodded, and had popped a pill to diminish his passions. Then, when her back was turned, he had strangled her to death, moving against her with a suddenness that she could never have anticipated. It wasn't that Pimyt liked to kill anyone. He didn't go out of his way for anything like that. But she had been a distraction, one he could ill afford. He'd done her a favor, actually. Undoubtedly he would have been more brutal with her if he'd really gotten to know her. Especially if—as he thought might happen—he actually fell in love with her.

For someone in Pimyt's position, with so much riding on his shoulders, he could never allow that to happen. He was responsible for a major portion of the HibAdu plan, and it had to proceed without impediments. He was, in his own estimation, far more important to the cause than the pretentious Adurian Ambassador.

At that moment a telebeam message came in, and he activated his ring to open the connection. A bright red banner opened in the air, a holo image with white lettering on it:

> **News Bulletin:** HibAdu Coalition makes surprise attacks against all Human and Mutati worlds. Defender Ships proved useless, due to sabotaged firing mechanisms on their artillery pieces. We also used signal-blocking devices to muzzle the defenders' telebeam transmissions, so none of their emergency messages got out. All MPA worlds except for Canopa and Siriki have fallen, and all Mutati worlds except for Dij. Fighting rages for these last three planets.

Grinning from ear to furry ear, Pimyt linked the ring to a panel box on the wall, and transmitted the same banner—in much larger form—into the sky outside the tower building. Tonight, there would be dancing in the streets.

Chapter Seventeen

Any moment could be your last—individually and collectively.
                                                    —Eshaz, comment to Subi Danvar

t the head of the podship fleet, *Webdancer* plunged into the ethereal mists. Thousands of ships in the first wave followed her into the starcloud, while the balance of the fleet went into holding patterns in that galactic sector, awaiting instructions by comlink to proceed.

Noah sat solemnly on a hard bench in the passenger compartment. Looking up, he saw a blank white screen appear, covering the viewing window on the forward wall. Like a schoolteacher, the big Tulyan Eshaz stood near the screen, holding a black control device in one of his thick hands.

He activated the device, and the screen went on, showing multiple views of the starcloud planets—all showing throngs of Tulyans celebrating in the streets.

"Word has reached them that the fleet is returning," Eshaz said, his voice and expression filled with pride. "After millions of years, we can once again return to our caretaking duties."

"We've rescued the podships," another Tulyan said. "Truly, this is a joyous occasion."

But Noah felt a deep despondency, and a sense of foreboding. He knew something terrible was wrong, but couldn't determine what it was. He was focused so far inward, questing and wanting answers, that events around him seemed as hazy as the mists of the starcloud. In a short while he disembarked the podship at the moorage basin and boarded a glax, self-propelled space platform. Tesh, Eshaz, Anton, Subi and a number of soldiers from the flagship accompanied him.

From the platform, the others stared in amazement at tens of thousands of podships moored around them in the pale mists. Like a small child, Tesh pressed her face up against the clearglax, for a closer view. Then she pulled back and looked at Noah. "As a galactic race," she said, "the Aopoddae are known to date back even farther than the Tulyans ... to the very origins of the galaxy."

As Eshaz gazed out on the wide mooring area, he said in a reverent tone, "Some of these creatures are exactly the same pods that once transported us on our important maintenance and repair assignments, millions of years ago. The ancient podships are well-known from the oral history of my people. Each ship has a name and a historical record of accomplishments. Some of the most legendary pods are Spirok, Elo, Dahi, Thur, Riebu, Thees, Lody." He pointed. "There! That one is Riebu!"

The one he designated had deep, rippled scars on its side, as if it had suffered the space equivalent of Moby Dick, and survived.

"Podships have mysterious life cycles," Tesh said to Noah. "While many of them live almost eternally, that is not the case with all. Some die from accidents and diseases. Breeding is inconsistent. It goes in spurts, and then seems to stop entirely for centuries."

"This is true," Eshaz said. He looked at her thoughtfully. "Your people have had time to observe the creatures."

She nodded, her expression growing sad.

Outside, a number of Tulyan pilots emerged from the podships, then stood atop the creatures and bowed their heads.

"An ancient ceremony," Eshaz said, his voice choking with emotion. "These pilots have been reunited with their original podships, from long ago."

At his side, Noah saw Tesh crying softly. He wiped the tears away from her cheeks, and kissed her tenderly.

"My feelings are complex," she said. "Tears of joy for the Tulyans and their podships, but intense sorrow for my own people."

"I understand," Noah said, putting an arm around her.

"Why did it have to come to this?" she asked. Then she added quickly, "Of course, I already have the answer to that."

In a comforting tone, Noah said, "I know it's impossible to ask you not to feel distress. But Tesh, please don't feel guilty for what you had to do. Maybe you're like Meghina. Both of you were born to other races, but you each wanted to be Human. You are Human now, my darling."

She smiled, but only a little. Her green eyes opened wide. "Well, almost Human, anyway. Cellular tests would say otherwise."

"You and Meghina both look Human and act Human. It's beyond cellular structures, beyond anything physical. It goes to your hearts."

"Listening to you, I could almost imagine that any other differences are inconsequential."

"They are." He pulled her close, embraced her. It amazed him how the Parvii magnification system could make this tiny person seem much larger, in all respects. He wondered what the fate of her decimated race was, and knew she spent much more time thinking about that than he did.

Noah heard a low hum, and felt a gentle vibration at his feet. The glax platform shuttled them from the moorage basin toward the floating, inverted dome of the council chamber. After a few minutes, it nudged up against a docking module and locked into position. Glax double doors slid open, revealing the interior of an entrance deck that skirted the chamber.

A pair of Tulyans marched forward stiffly, dressed in green-and-gold uniforms. They each carried a cap. "Right this way, please," the shorter of the reptilian men said, to Anton and Noah, as they stepped off the platform. "We are your escorts." He bowed, then put his cap back on. "The Elders are extremely anxious to speak with you."

"It is an emergency," the other Tulyan said as he put on his own cap.

"What do you mean?" Doge Anton asked.

"I am not authorized to say."

Noah felt a sense of foreboding.

Emerging from the gathered passengers, Eshaz said, "I'll go with them. This doesn't sound good."

"As you wish." The shorter escort led the way up a wide, travertine tile stairway, while Eshaz motioned for Tesh and Subi to join the group.

On the next level they hurried through an arched doorway, then over a wide bridge that crossed a reflecting pool. Well-dressed aliens of a variety of races were gathered in a reception area, talking in hushed tones. They looked angry. Noah noticed that other alien dignitaries were being led out of the council chamber, just beyond. None of them looked very happy.

The escorts led the small party into the immense council chamber, onto a clearglax floor that seemed to float on air, with the curvature of the inverted dome below, and the ethereal mists of the starcloud. Their footsteps echoed on the floor. The immense chamber was nearly empty, with no one in the rows of spectator seats, and a few last aliens being led out, despite their protestations.

Three stern-looking Tulyans sat in the center of a wide, curving bench.

"Something is terribly wrong," Eshaz whispered to Noah. "Just three Elders, and no one in the visitor's gallery. I have never seen anything like this before, and I have lived for a long time."

The female Elder in the center looked down solemnly from the bench, and waited for the chamber to be sealed. Noah recognized her as First Elder Kre'n.

"We have very grave news, indeed," she said.

Noah and his companions stared upward inquisitively. His feelings of foreboding intensified.

"Terrible tragedies on Human and Mutati worlds," a much larger Elder on her left, Dabiggio, said. "Our operatives got messages off to us describing the disasters."

551

"Web transmissions," Kre'n said. "While we have had difficulties with them, due to galactic conditions, they remain more reliable than your nehrcoms."

"Tragedies, disasters?" Anton asked. "What are you talking about?"

Kre'n scowled at him. "You don't know? While you were away, didn't you receive any nehrcom messages?"

"We've been in relay range for awhile now. Several reports came in, but nothing about any big problems."

"Fake transmissions, I suspect. Every Human and Mutati planet has been attacked."

Anton and Tesh gasped. Noah glowered, waiting for more information.

"The attackers cut off authentic nehrcom transmissions from all MPA planets," Kre'n said. "It took them longer, but they also managed to cut off our web transmissions. We fear the worst for our operatives."

"What the hell happened?" Anton demanded. "Who attacked us?"

"Hibbils and Adurians," Dabiggio said. "The Human and Mutati empires are lost. Surprise assaults, with overwhelming force. We lost communication three hours ago, but at that time only Canopa and Siriki were holding out in the MPA, and the Mutatis only had Dij left."

"My God!" Anton said.

"We have incontrovertible proof that the Hibbils and Adurians are in alliance." the third Elder said.

Is this what I sensed? Noah wondered. "Hibbils and Adurians?" he asked. "How could that possibly be?"

Nodding solemnly, Kre'n said, "They call themselves the HibAdu Coalition. They must have been plotting the attacks for some time. Coordinated military assaults against all targets."

"Traitors," Tesh said. "What a bunch of sneaky bastards."

Noah thought back, and again he remembered seeing Hibbil and Adurian soldiers in a Timeweb vision. He'd reported it to Doge Anton, but there had been no indication of the scope of the treachery, or the direction it might take. Noah also remembered now that Lorenzo had a Hibbil attaché named Pimyt. The last Noah heard, Lorenzo and Pimyt were in Noah's former EcoStation, where the deposed doge was in exile.

The HibAdu Coalition, he thought in dismay, letting it seep in.

But his gut told him that wasn't all he'd been sensing. There was something more than this dire military news, something even worse, and he couldn't put a finger on it.

Kre'n raised a hand. "Bring the Mutatis in," she said.

"The Mutatis?" Anton exclaimed. Obviously stunned, he exchanged nervous glances with Noah.

A side door burst open, and a large Mutati strutted in, wearing a purple-and-gold robe. He was accompanied by an entourage that included several uniformed military officers and a female shapeshifter—of the aerial variety—who flew beside him.

"Meet the Emir Hari'Adab," Kre'n said, "ruler of the Mutati Kingdom."

Chapter Eighteen

If you look hard enough, there are always surprises in this universe.

—Tulyan Wisdom

Inside the inverted, floating dome of the Council Chamber, Hari'Adab addressed the small gathering, choosing to emit synchronized, pulsing sounds from his puckish little mouth. It was not an orifice that had been part of his natural-born state, but was instead something he had improvised (and varied slightly from time to time) when he became old enough to care about his appearance. Now, dressed in a flowing robe that cascaded over his mounds of fat, the Emir paced in front of the wide council bench.

"Since you know my name and I know some of yours, allow me to introduce two of my companions." He motioned back to the aeromutati who stood off to one side, just behind him. "This is Parais d'Olor, the gentlest of all Mutatis, a person who brings peace to my heart."

He nodded somberly in her direction, then looked back to the other side, where Kajor Yerto Bhaleen stood with military erectness. After introducing him by title and name, he said, "Yerto is the highest officer in the Military High Command. He gives me advice in matters of war. But he knows, and fully understands, that I seek peace as the highest priority of my people."

Noting skepticism on the faces of Doge Anton and Noah Watanabe, he gazed at them with oval, bright black eyes and said, "The Elders told me of your tremendous military victory over the Parviis. Unfortunately, while you were occupied with that, the Merchant Prince Alliance and the Mutati Kingdom fell to conquerors."

The Humans glared at him. Then Anton responded, "Between us, we may have three planets left. Whatever the case, we *will* fight back."

Beside them, a large Tulyan and a Human-looking woman watched Hari warily. The young Emir, with a racial ability to detect subtle details of physical appearance, noticed immediately that the female was not really Human, but had altered her appearance to look that way. She was not, however, a Mutati. What was she, then? Wondering if her companions knew of her secret identity, the Emir decided she would bear close watching. That one could be dangerous.

In a careful tone, he said, "We each have our own terrible burdens to bear, Doge Anton. And we must face reality. Our peoples need to put our wasteful, ancient feud to rest."

"Mutatis have never shown us anything but aggression," Anton said, with a glower.

"That will change, now that I am in charge. The old ways have not been productive or kind to anyone, so I refuse to continue them. Over the centuries, billions and billions of Mutatis and Humans have died due to our ongoing wars. It makes no sense."

"War is the biggest polluter of all," Noah said, somberly.

"Ah, yes, the famous galactic ecologist. I have heard many things about you, Mr. Watanabe. My father used to speak of you derisively, but he and I never agreed on much of anything." The Emir smiled, but it didn't hold, and tears began to stream down his face.

In a halting tone, as if hardly able to utter the words, Hari'Adab told of the horrendous error Zad Qato had made in the trajectory calculations on a Demolio shot, and how it had destroyed the beautiful Mutati homeworld of

Paradij, killing all of its populace. Billions of lives lost due to one miscalculation. As he spoke he trembled, and tears streamed down his face. "I, I'm sorry," he said, wiping his face.

The big Tulyan stepped closer to Hari. "I am Eshaz," he said. "Do not be alarmed, but I must make skin contact with you. Is the back of your neck all right?"

"The truthing touch." Hari looked up at the seated Elders. "But they have already done this to me, to Parais, and all of the other Mutatis with me. They have also done the same with HibAdu prisoners we turned over to them."

The Tulyan hesitated, looked to his superiors for guidance.

"Go ahead," First Elder Kre'n said to Eshaz. "You are especially gifted in this area. Perhaps you will find something we missed."

Eshaz touched the back of Hari's neck, and the Emir felt the coarseness of the reptilian hand on his skin. It remained there for only a few moments, before Eshaz withdrew and announced, "He is being honest with us. The shapeshifter leader bears us no ill will, and he intends to take the Mutati people in a new direction."

"If he can save the remains of his race, of course," the peculiar woman said.

Hari nodded, trying to be dispassionate.

"We were aware of the loss of your homeworld," Noah said.

"Oh? How?"

"I have certain ... um, paranormal ... abilities that permit me to peer into the universe from time to time. Where Paradij used to be, I saw only a debris field floating in space. I did not, however, know how it happened, or why."

"It has been said that we live in a universe of magic," Hari said. "You are, perhaps, one of the primary examples of that."

"And an entire race of shapeshifters is another," the woman said.

"And you are?" Hari asked, in his most polite tone.

"Tesh Kori. I've noticed you looking at me strangely. Is there a particular reason for that?"

"Maybe it is a defect of my personality. If I have offended you, I apologize most sincerely."

"It's not that, not at all." She exchanged glances with Eshaz, then added, "You have discerned something about me. Please, share with everyone here what it is."

"Are you certain you want me to do that?" Hari looked around at the Humans and Tulyans in the great chamber.

"I have nothing to hide from them. These are my friends. And if Eshaz's report on you is correct, you might become one of them yourself."

"We shall see about that." He smiled. "For one thing, I see that you are a woman of considerable charm. In my experience, I must tell you that charming people are to be watched more closely than others."

"Because they can be manipulative, you mean?" she said, looking past him at Parais d'Olor.

"Precisely."

She lifted her chin haughtily. "And you have come all the way from the Mutati Kingdom to warn everyone about me?"

Laughter echoed around the large chamber, from the Elders and from her own companions.

Maintaining his composure, Hari said, "Madam, I would have said nothing about anything I might have noticed, but you have pressed me to speak. Very well, you are not what you appear to be. By that, I mean, you are not Human."

"She's a Parvii, and we all know it," Eshaz said. "Do you think we didn't achieve full openness with her, just as we have verified from you?"

"I see. A member of the defeated race. I have heard of you. Not exactly shapeshifters, from what I hear. Some sort of magnification system, I am told."

"Your reports are accurate," Tesh said. "Science or magic? Where does one end and the other begin?"

"Where, indeed?" Hari said. We're going to need a lot of both if our races are to survive the present catastrophe."

"You refer to the HibAdu matter, of course," First Elder Kre'n said, from the bench. "But there are other, even more pressing matters that you might not be aware of." She looked at the two other Elders with her, at Eshaz, and then at Noah Watanabe.

"Something worse than the HibAdus?" Hari said. "But how can that be?"

"The galaxy, we're sad to inform you, is crumbling. We took a huge podship fleet away from the Parviis in order to set up a massive galactic repair program. When there is more time, we will tell you more. But suffice to tell you now that in ancient times the Sublime Creator of the galaxy assigned an important duty to the Tulyan race. We were the caretakers of the weblike galactic infrastructure, with jurisdiction over all podships, for the purpose of performing our important work."

Hari struggled to keep up with the new information, but decided not to ask questions. He and the others here knew there had been a feeling-out process among those present as they got to know one another, and that the apparent small talk had not been that at all. It had been important to get the relationships sorted out among themselves. It still was.

"I want to work with you in any way possible," Hari said. "The last I checked, much of my most elite military force remained intact, holding out against the attackers at Dij."

He formed a frown on his fleshy face, and his snout twitched as he turned his gaze on Doge Anton. Then the shapeshifter leader asked, "I assume you are going to assign podship assets to the defense of the Merchant Prince Alliance?"

"We're working through those details now," the youthful doge said.

"Assuming you send some military assets to the MPA, might I ask that some be assigned to assist the Mutati Kingdom as well?"

"It is possible," First Elder Kre'n said. "Now, we must move quickly. Far beyond Human and Mutati domains, the entire galaxy is a battlefield, and we must triage it, assigning our assets on a priority basis."

The Tulyan leader looked around at the small assemblage, and announced, "You have all come to me, my Human and Mutati friends—and my one Parvii friend, of course—and all of us should consider ourselves caretakers of the galactic web. It is a shared responsibility among races, at a time of crisis like none other in the annals of history."

Doors opened around the chamber, and robed Tulyan dignitaries marched in, from several directions. They took seats at the remaining council chairs on the curved bench. The Tulyan Elders—twenty of them now—all conferred for several minutes in a language that Hari could not understand.

Then Kre'n leaned forward and announced, "Eighty percent of our podships will be assigned to galactic recovery operations, and twenty percent to Human and Mutati military operations. Doge Anton, you shall have the authority to work out the proper allocation of those assets."

Anton and Noah nodded in deference to the Council leader. Then the young doge said, "I concur fully. The welfare of the entire galaxy must take precedence over the military threats."

"We would prefer to allocate fewer ships to the HibAdu matter, but our technicians are studying the two laboratory-bred podships that the Emir brought with him—and they've already determined that such vessels cause damage to the podways on which they travel. Tiny green fibers of the Timeweb infrastructure have been found in the undercarriage tracks of the lab-pods." Kre'n scowled. "Those ships are burning up the podways. As you can see, Doge Anton, your duties coincide with our own ecological recovery operations."

"I understand," Anton said.

Kre'n continued in a solemn tone. "When you succeed in your military operations—and I have every confidence that you will—we shall expect to reassign your podships to galactic restoration projects. Your primary responsibilities are to remove the artificial podships from service, and to save Human and Mutati worlds."

"It will be done," Anton said. "We'll hit the HibAdus with everything we have, starting from the three planetary fronts."

With a sense of urgency in the air, the Council of Elders adjourned the meeting, and called for new ones to begin in different portions of the large chamber—to deal with the galactic ecology and HibAdu crises. Decisions had to be made quickly, so that the ships and crews could be dispatched where they were most needed.

Chapter Nineteen

Noah is a composite man, a puzzle person forged in a galactic crucible. I can't help being drawn to him.

—Tesh Kori, private notes

In only a short time, Doge Anton del Velli made the most important decision of his brief political career. After consulting with the robot leader Thinker, as well as with his other top advisers, Anton divided the twenty-four thousand podships under his control into three task forces. Anton and Nirella would take twelve thousand of them to the merchant prince homeworld of Canopa, while Noah would lead six thousand in the Siriki mission. Another six thousand podships would be assigned to the military needs of the Mutati planet of Dij.

As the meetings and submeetings formed, military officers and Tulyan caretakers flowed into the large chamber and headed for their various sessions. To accommodate the acoustic needs of the groups, the Elders used shimmering energy fields to separate the sections.

In nine hours, all of the plans were essentially complete, and the various groups began to break up. The ecological recovery operations would follow ancient patterns. On the military side, the tactics for the rescue of each of the three planets had to proceed with caution, because of the lack of clear intelligence from the field.

As Anton concluded his Canopa meeting, Tesh and he talked with the largest Tulyan Elder, Dabiggio. The stern Elder looked down at Tesh and said to her, "Before you depart, I must comment on your own pod, the one you call

Webdancer. Prior to your involvement with the vessel, it was marooned on Plevin Four for a long time."

"That is correct." She felt perplexed.

"I must tell you that the podship had a different appellation in ancient times—Clegg. It was one of the strongest and fastest ships, high-spirited but unproved, and only known to the Tulyans for a short while before the entire race of podships was swarmed and taken by the Parviis. You didn't know that, did you?"

"I know some things about *Webdancer,* but the vessels are enigmatic, as you know."

"So, you didn't know what I told you?"

She smiled. "I didn't say that."

"And how did it get marooned?" Anton asked.

Dabiggio hesitated, appeared to calm himself with a heave of his wide shoulders. Then: "We have learned from a variation of the truthing touch that the vessel rebelled against its Parvii masters and fled into space. For hundreds of thousands of years it roamed the cosmos, and no one could capture it. The rest of its story remains, thus far, unrevealed to us."

"My podship has a rather independent personality," Tesh said, giving the Tulyan a gentle smile. "Perhaps it will reveal its full story to me one day."

He stared at her rigidly. "Unlikely. Parviis do not have the telepathic skills of Tulyans, so you would have difficulty conversing with him."

"But we do have some of those skills, as you know."

"True enough, but beside the point. Here's what I want to tell you. By tradition, the names of podships have always remained unchanged. Once Clegg, always Clegg."

The remark hit Tesh hard, and took something personal away from her. She looked at the clearglax floor and the starcloud mists visible beyond.

"Do you understand what I am saying to you?" Dabiggio asked in a gruff tone.

"You want me to change the name back?"

"Exactly. It is not good luck to do otherwise."

"Nonsense," First Elder Kre'n interjecting as she came over to them. "Tell her what we decided as a Council, not what you believe independently."

Dabiggio wrinkled his reptilian face in displeasure. He said nothing.

"I'll tell her, then," Kre'n said. She looked at the Parvii woman and said, "Tesh Kori, you are admired by the Council of Elders, and there is widespread recognition of your contributions to the success of the Liberators. Even Dabiggio—who tries to argue with everything—cannot really dispute this. In honor of your service to the cause, we have decided that you may continue to use the appellation *Webdancer* for the pod."

"That pleases me very much," she said. "I appreciate it."

As Anton and she left the chamber together, he said, "I would have allowed you to keep the name, anyway. Those old Elders can't tell us everything to do, even though they might think they can."

"Would that really have been a battle you should have picked?" she asked, remembering for a moment how close the two of them had once been.

Darkness came over his features. "Maybe I'm a bit of a rebel myself. Now, let's move on to the battles that really matter."

* * * * *

Tulyan wranglers separated twenty-four thousand podships from the main fleet, and further divided the smaller portion into three even smaller fleets, earmarked for Canopa, Siriki, and Dij.

For the Sirikan rescue mission, Noah Watanabe controlled six thousand sentient warships, which he quickly calculated to be five percent of the entire Liberator fleet. After receiving the ships, he and Subi Danvar supervised the details of their military assault force, passing instructions on to their subordinates about how they wanted personnel and equipment loaded into the podships.

All the while, the wranglers and other Tulyan specialists coordinated and synchronized the various vessels in each of the military fleets. Anton's portion, the largest, would get underway first, in part because of the already proven leadership qualities of the flagship, *Webdancer*. But there were larger reasons. Canopa was unarguably the most important of the surviving planets, and Noah had reported to Anton his troubling vision in which the planet—and Noah's former EcoStation orbiting it—appeared to be drifting toward a dangerous timehole. Noah had also arranged with the Elders to have a Tulyan repair team sent there.

Discussing that in the Tulyan Council Chamber, Anton had said, "I know what you're thinking, Noah, that you would prefer to go on the Canopa mission. But I need you to head up the Sirikan operation for me. I'm weighing all the factors, and that is my decision."

Noah had nodded, but recalled chewing the inside of his own mouth to the point of rawness, as he resisted arguing with his superior ... a wound that still hurt a little.

"A timehole," Anton had said. "If that additional element is indeed added to the already ongoing military operations there, I'm not certain what any of us can do to keep the planet and the orbiter from vanishing into the cosmic whirlpool. I only know that I have to be there firsthand, to do whatever I can."

It was the mission that Anton wanted, so he would have it.

Noah's smaller fleet, and the one of matching size assigned to the Mutati rescue mission, would have individual flagships, thus requiring more preparations and coordination—work that was not commenced until after the Tulyan Elders decided on the allocation of the vessels.

Finally, having rushed around tending to numerous important matters involving his task force, Noah sent an aide to summon Subi Danvar for a brief, final meeting. While waiting, Noah settled into a deep-cushion chair in his onboard office. Subi would arrive any moment, so Noah closed his eyes, just for a few seconds.

As he sank into the fleshy podship cushion, Noah sighed, and a deep sense of calm came over him. Minutes passed, only a few, and he felt himself sinking into the most restful state of relaxation he could imagine.

Subi seemed to be taking a long time to arrive. Not wanting to fall asleep, Noah decided to open his eyes. As he did so, however, he experienced a sensation like opening an unusual circular door, one that irised open with shocking suddenness. Abruptly, he felt himself catapulted through an amorphous opening, and he hurtled and spun out into the starry, eternal night of space.

He was back in Timeweb, via a slightly different entry point.

A rush of excitement passed through Noah, tempered by the realization that he could not remain there long, that he needed to go back and get his podship fleet underway. But at the same time, he couldn't pass up this opportunity either....

Chapter Twenty

War has a way of shortening some men's lives, and lengthening others.
—Doge Anton del Velli

"Only twelve thousand ships," Doge Anton said. "Only a small portion of the fleet we brought back from the Parvii Fold."

He and the cerebral robot Thinker stood on the command bridge of the flagship *Webdancer*. Tesh was still at the controls, but the podship had metamorphosed internally to create new military-purpose rooms, and had grown even larger than before, so that it now appeared to be at least twice the size of any other vessel in the fleet. Anton didn't know how the ship changed (or the impetus for the alterations), but he rather liked the new internal arrangement, which included a spacious dome on top of the vessel where they stood now—with wide viewing areas in all directions, through filmy windows.

"I appreciate you coming with me," Anton said.

"You are the commander-in-chief. I follow your bidding. Everyone interpreted your 'request' for my assistance as considerably more than that."

Anton smiled gently as he looked back to see other vessels behind picking up speed to keep pace with the flagship, cutting through the milky mists of the starcloud. "Somehow," he said, "I've always thought of you as a strong and independent personality, more impressive than any other machine and more than most men."

"You are too kind, my Lord. I only hope to be of service on this, the most important of the three military missions. I must say, Sire, you were wise to allocate your ships the way you did. Canopa merits the most consideration, and the most firepower."

Anton nodded. In the ongoing, mounting crisis he had made quick decisions, after receiving advice from his wife Nirella, from this robot, and from the other top minds in the new alliance, including Noah and his strategy-wise adjutant, Subi Danvar.

Webdancer accelerated onto a main podway, bound for Canopa. It would take longer than in the old days. Supreme General Nirella rode in another ship with the main navigation team of the Humans, and they had made predictions and projections of the route the ships would probably take. For all practical purposes, the fleet would select its own course, following the lead of Tesh when she—enmeshed with *Webdancer* in the Parvii way—got a good view of space and determined the best route.

With all he had been through, and the tremendous burden of responsibility on his shoulders, Anton felt like a man in his middle age. But as he reviewed the actual mileposts of his life, the chronology only added up to twenty-one years.

As stars blurred past, he realized that he seemed to have lived two entire lifetimes. In the first, comprising a bit over twenty years, he had been the rather ordinary Anton Glavine, a mere caretaker and maintenance man. For a while he had been close to the exciting Tesh Kori, and they had been lovers. But they'd never connected in a deeper sense, and their relationship had ended when

Anton and Noah were taken prisoner by Lorenzo. The two had escaped, but by the time Anton saw Tesh again, she had already drifted toward Noah.

During his so-called "second lifetime," Anton was the fledgling Doge of the Merchant Prince Alliance, and he'd been forced to learn on the job, facing the challenges of managing the various competing powers in the realm. Not the least of the problems he'd faced had been his late mother Francella Watanabe, but he had found ways to sidestep even her. As for his father, the former Doge Lorenzo, Anton had not had much to do with him at all, other than making certain he didn't interfere in merchant prince affairs.

Now, as he embarked for Canopa at the head of twelve thousand armed podships, Anton felt yet another lifetime beginning. Only a few hours ago he had met Hari'Adab, and now—at breakneck pace—the three portions of Anton's fleet were speeding toward different destinations.

But significant restrictions had been placed on the Mutati Emir and his mission to Dij. After conferring with his advisers, Anton had sent what Nirella called "military chaperones" to monitor him. Ostensibly, they were following Hari'Adab's commands, and to an extent they would do that. But—despite the Tulyan lie detection tests Hari and all of his Mutati followers had passed— Anton's Human officers were alert for tricks and traps, and on a moment's notice they were prepared to take control of the Dij-bound fleet. Robotic troops had also been sent with that rescue force, led by the loyal robot Jimu.

In yet another precautionary measure, Anton had ordered that the Emir's lady friend, Parais d'Olor, be separated from him and placed with Noah's forces on the Siriki mission—for at least the duration of the three initial military campaigns. Both Hari and Parais had objected to this, but the young doge had insisted upon it. The more indignant they were—and they showed considerable vehemence—the more certain he became that it was the right thing to do. Obviously Hari cared deeply for this aeromutati, so Anton had gained some leverage over him by keeping them apart. How much, though, he was not certain.

Now, as he thought back on these things, and on his own place in the critical events unfolding around him, Anton murmured, " 'Trust but verify.' "

"What did you say, sir?" Thinker asked.

Anton repeated it, louder this time. Then: "It's a saying of Lost Earth. I don't know where I picked it up."

Thinker whirred. "I have it in my data banks. It was a Russian adage, one of the major nations on the doomed planet."

"I wonder how much of the MPA we can save," Anton said.

His thoughts were very dark. Just before departure he had received a report that the HibAdus had enslaved trillions of Humans on every merchant prince planet with the exception of the two where the defenders were still holding out. He hoped, at least, that this had not worsened, and that he was not too late.

"Odds unknown," Thinker said. "Not enough data on the enemy."

"The people of Canopa and Siriki have fought bravely," the Doge said. "We can't abandon them to the HibAdus when they've shown such determined resistance."

He felt his blood pressure rising from the frustration of how long it was taking to cross space. Then a comlink transmission came from General Nirella: "On final podway approach to Canopa system, sir. With luck, we're only a few minutes away."

"Any evidence of a timehole in the vicinity?"

"The Tulyans are checking on that. No report from them yet."

"Visual confirmation that we are approaching Canopa, sir," Thinker said. Even at the extreme speed of the podship, he was rapidly accumulating data on the star systems they were passing.

Anton steeled himself, wondering what awaited them. It could be a carefully laid HibAdu trap, and the same held true for Siriki and Dij.

Chapter Twenty-One

There is no such thing as a perfect secret.

—Adurian admonition

I t required a considerable amount of bravery for the guests to have come here, to Lorenzo del Velli's opulent gambling hall on the Pleasure Palace orbital station. At any moment, HibAdu forces could reappear from space and blast the facility into oblivion.

Of course, Pimyt knew otherwise. He just smiled to himself as he stood listening to the nervous chatter around the long diceball table. On his right, Lorenzo stood at the head of the table watching the game, occasionally interjecting to regale his guests with gossip-laden conversation. This gray-haired old man might have been deposed as Doge of the Merchant Prince Alliance, but he still retained his memories of many of the interesting noblemen and ladies in the realm. And if he had trouble remembering some of the details, he made some up in convincing fashion.

Though he kept it undisclosed in such company, Pimyt had been leading a hectic, though fascinating, life himself. If anyone ever wrote about the events and compiled them, his secrets would fill numerous thick volumes.

"The enemy could strike from any direction," one of the noblemen said, looking around nervously at the wide view of space they had from the glax-walled main casino on the top level of the space station. Dozens of the Doge's defensive ships patrolled the area, but Pimyt knew how paltry they would prove against any real attack. So, it seemed, did a number of the guests.

"Just being here is rather like a game of chance, wouldn't you say?" Princess Meghina observed from her place opposite Lorenzo. As beautiful as ever, the blonde courtesan was a constantly smiling, perfect hostess. She sipped red wine from a crystal goblet, and asked, "Do we feel lucky or not?" Beside her, Meghina's pet dagg emitted a low growl. She petted the large black animal.

"But what if the luck for any one of us has run out?" a giddy noblewoman asked as she rolled the diceball and watched it bounce from obstacle to obstacle on the table. Her hair was coiffed in a high bun on her head, and adorned with glittering rubians and saphos that cast prismatic red and blue light around her head. "What if it's you, Lorenzo?" she asked, looking at him. "You've always had quite a run of good fortune."

The automated table tallied her score, and three gold chips popped into a tray in front of her.

"Until forces conspired to remove me from office," he snarled. "Don't delude yourself. I've already had my share of misfortune. No, it isn't *my* luck that would run out."

The gamblers bantered and quipped around the table, as they tried to figure out who among them might either be ready to lose their luck, or who might be a Jonah that could bring bad fortune on the entire orbiter. Then the subject of conversation changed, and they talked about dagg races many of them had

561

attended earlier in the day, at the recently completed race track that encircled the bottom level of the space station.

Pimyt tuned out their voices. His HibAdu conspirators had made powerful military strikes against every Human and Mutati world, and had overrun all but three of them. Ironically, Pimyt was now in orbit over one of the unconquered planets, Canopa, aboard Lorenzo's space station. For several days, fighting had been fierce down on the surface, and in the air and orbital spaces over the planet … but had since died down. For a time, Lorenzo had suspected him of being one of the conspirators, but Pimyt had convinced him otherwise. And the Hibbil's credentials, especially as a former Regent of the Merchant Prince Alliance, gave his word considerable weight. All Hibbils and Adurians were not against Humans, just because some were. For the time being Pimyt's story had been believed, but would he need to take extra care in the future to avoid detection.

Through good fortune or divine salvation, the space station had been spared thus far. Or so the defenders thought. In reality, Pimyt had played a behind-the-scenes role in that, having convinced his superiors that it was a useful facility, worth saving. To preserve it as a prize of war, he'd made certain that HibAdu forces launched only token attacks against the facility, so diminished that Lorenzo's own ships had been able to drive them away.

But even after all he had been through and all he had accomplished, Pimyt had never met any of the HibAdu leaders, nor did he know anyone who had. Prior to the emergence of the HibAdu Coalition, the Hibbils and Adurians had been ruled by their own planetary councils and committees, with largely ceremonial heads of state. That was all suspended with the onset of the HibAdu military buildup, which took precedence over prior forms of government. Now the Hibbils and Adurians were one political and military entity.

Most of Pimyt's associates, such as the Adurian VV Uncel, said they did not care if they ever met the HibAdu leaders in person. To Pimyt, though, it had always seemed peculiar that the coalition high command only distributed audio recordings of themselves delivering inspirational speeches, and had never made personal appearances to the public or to the armed forces. While their names and titles were known—High Ruler Coreq, Prime Lord Enver, and Warlord Tarix—no photos had been disseminated of any of them. Sometimes, in his wildest visions, Pimyt's thoughts would run amok and he would imagine that the leaders were not what they seemed to be … not Hibbils or Adurians.

Of course, he constantly assured himself, that was not possible.

Jolting Pimyt to awareness, the floor suddenly shuddered beneath his feet. Gaming pieces rattled on the table and slid off in a series of increasingly loud, crashing clatters. He heard an explosion, and the shouts and screams of his companions.

* * * * *

Noah experienced dual realities, the pleasant sensation of the soft podship chair around him, but the suspicion that it might have drawn him down like quicksand into Timeweb. Normally, he might have welcomed a journey into the paranormal realm. On numerous occasions he had attempted to enter it himself through varying doorways that always seemed to open of their own volition. Now, unexpectedly, he had been drawn in at a time when he could least afford it.

If he didn't wake up quickly, it meant he had essentially gone to sleep on the job. Not like him at all. Noah had always been a hard worker, but now as he considered the prospect of going back, he suddenly felt very tired—the fatigue of an entire lifetime weighing him down.

Here in Timeweb, on the other hand, he had an odd sense of exhilaration and tremendous energy, that he could journey on and on through the cosmos, like a stone skipping forever across a very, very broad pond.

His motion through space slowed dramatically, and just ahead he made out the Canopa Star System and its largest planet, the homeworld of the Merchant Prince Alliance. As if his eyes were a holocamera, Noah zoomed in on the planet. He searched for the timehole he had seen in an earlier vision, and didn't see it. But beyond Canopa, space was murky, with a peculiar fog that he found troubling.

Abruptly, time seemed to go in reverse, and once again Noah was a small boy living in the Valley of the Princes, on his father's vast estate. A redheaded girl ran toward him, calling his name. "Noah! Noah!"

For an instant, he hesitated. Then he answered her back with her name. "Francella! Where have you been?"

"I don't know," she said. "But I'm back." Francella smiled sweetly, prettily. Her dark brown eyes glittered.

Like long-lost siblings, the two children hugged. Noah felt the warmth of her embrace.

When they withdrew and he looked at her he saw that she was pointing in wonder at the sky, her eyes open wide in astonishment.

Noah looked up at a vault of grayness that was dissipating, like a thinning fog. Through an opening in the vault he made out the faint green filigree of Timeweb against the backdrop of space and glittering stars. Then his vision zoomed in, and he saw his former space station orbiting Canopa, now the home-in-exile of Lorenzo del Velli. Seeing the facility again gave Noah a warm, comfortable feeling. He still thought of the orbiter by his own original name for it, EcoStation, even though it had been substantially changed after the merchant princes took it away from him and Lorenzo turned it into a gambling casino.

His gaze searched in the vicinity of the space station, and to his alarm Noah detected a crack in the fabric of the webbing, a fine line running through the green threads that stretched larger and larger and widened, until he could identify the defect as a whirling timehole, with the blackness of eternity visible beyond. The stygian hole pulsed on its luminous green edges like a living thing. It grew in size until it dwarfed the space station, which drew close to it, as if pulled by a magnet.

In a previous vision, Noah had seen a huge timehole in the vicinity, and now it seemed apparent that it had diminished in size for a time, and then had re-enlarged. Through the luminous perimeter of the opening, he saw a view of space beyond that looked like the blackest place in the entire universe.

* * * * *

Inside the glax-walled gambling hall, people screamed and cried out in pain as the space station rolled and tumbled, and the onboard gravitonics system failed. Meghina's dagg barked and whined. Pimyt tried to find something stable to hold onto, while avoiding being hit by the loose, heavy objects. He grabbed the edge of the big gaming table. Something slammed into his left hip, and a sharp pain lance of shot through his body.

Everyone tumbled over in a deafening crash of sound, as the table, guests, and chairs slid against the viewing windows.

* * * * *

In what seemed to Noah like a nightmare instead of reality, EcoStation vanished into the galactic maw in a bright green flash. He gasped in horror. A shift in the strands of the webbing ensued, and the timehole sealed over, so that Noah could no longer see it.

He awoke, and found himself back in the soft chair in his office. The chair, part of the podship and created by it, pulsed around his body, as if massaging him and trying to draw him back into it.

But Noah leaped to his feet. He shouted for Subi Danvar, and moments later he saw the rotund adjutant standing in the doorway.

"Everything's ready," Subi said, as if nothing unusual had happened.

Glancing at his own wristchron, Noah was surprised to see that only a few minutes had passed since he'd taken the break. It hadn't done him any good, and he didn't feel rested at all. But he had no time to consider such matters, and he couldn't worry about EcoStation. That was not his mission.

From deep inside, he drew strength, and hurried with Subi to the passenger compartment of the flagship, a room they had converted to a command center for the fleet.

Arriving there in the midst of his officers, Noah told an aide to send a message to Anton about what he had seen. Then he shouted, "On to Siriki!"

In a matter of moments, the command was transmitted to Tesh in the sectoid chamber. The vessel—named *Okion* since ancient times—accelerated toward the podways.

Chapter Twenty-Two

All battles are not won by those who seem to prevail on the field and are left alive. Sometimes, it is better to have died the quick way.

—General Nirella del Velli

After emerging from space, *Webdancer* flew toward Canopa, in bright light from the system's yellow sun. In the command-bridge dome atop the sentient vessel, Doge Anton stood with his wife and supreme military officer, General Nirella.

"What's that?" he asked, pointing ahead. Not far from the planet, a green flash lit up space, then vanished.

"Give us a reading," Nirella said, to a junior officer who sat at one of the consoles.

"Lorenzo del Velli's space station disappeared," he said. "It looks like one of those timeholes the Tulyans need to fix." The officer conferred with a Tulyan woman who wore a red MPA uniform like his own, then added, "Timehole confirmed."

"Noah was right," Anton said.

"Notify the Council of Elders," General Nirella said to the Tulyan. Nodding, the reptilian woman pressed a hand against the filmy window surface, thus putting her in telepathic contact with Tesh and the podship. From Tesh, the message would be relayed to another vessel in the fleet and to a Tulyan webtalker, who would then tap into Timeweb for a transmission to the starcloud. The Elders had already assigned an eco-repair team, and were undoubtedly aware of the confirmation. But this was too important to assume anything.

"Now enter the atmosphere," Anton said.

The Tulyan transmitted the instruction to Tesh Kori, who caused the Aopoddae vessel to dip toward the atmosphere. Some of the other ships remained behind to patrol space, while the majority followed the flagship in a series of "v"-formations that looked like immense flying wings.

Comlink reports flowed as the fleet made contact with military and civilian authorities on the ground and in the air. The defenders reported that battles had subsided in this vicinity, but that the HibAdus had been using a variety of deadly weapons, including warheads filled with Adurian-developed plague viruses. Fortunately, medical personnel on the ground had the situation under control, so the fleet command made arrangements to land.

Five kilometers above the surface of the world, one-quarter of the trailing formations broke away to form patrol sections in the skies. Anton saw one of the formations chase the podships of a HibAdu squadron—small, dark gray aircraft that were much smaller than podships, with orange cartouches on their hulls. The pursuers then divided into smaller formations and fired cannon shots at the fleeing craft, sending bright orange tracer fire through the sky. Several hit their marks, and explosions erupted in the air like fiery red flower blossoms.

The main body of Anton's fleet continued downward. At the vanguard, *Webdancer* circled the cliffside metropolis of Rainbow City, then flew down into the Valley of Princes and set down on the main landing field. Hundreds of the other ships followed, while others found additional landing sites at nearby commercial and industrial sites.

As Anton disembarked on a ramp, ahead of Nirella and Tesh, they were greeted by two MPA officers in red-and-gold uniforms. On either side, hundreds of soldiers stood at attention, and beyond them sprawled the towers and structures of the field.

The tallest MPA officer saluted. After introducing himself as Vice-General J. W. Hackson and a dark-skinned officer with him as Kajor Avery, he said, "Sire, thank you for coming to our aid. As I said over the comlink, there is much death here, and not all from battle wounds. The HibAdus spread plague and other biological scourges before we succeeded in driving them off. So far, our medical personnel have the illnesses under control, but we've had to devote tremendous resources to the problem."

"Any quarantines?" Anton asked.

"Not necessary any more. CorpOne research personnel have identified the biologicals, and have already distributed antidotes."

"Some of the enemy are still in the vicinity," Anton said. He heard Nirella on the comlink behind him, getting reports from the air-and-space patrols.

Presently she reported: "Not much activity. Enemy is on the run."

"We didn't kill anywhere near as many HibAdu ships as we saw," Hackson said. "They've been preparing for a counterattack, but it might not come now that you're here. How many pod warships did you bring?"

"Twelve thousand."

The Vice-General smiled. "That should keep 'em at bay."

"Maybe not. Our best robots have calculated that it must have required hundreds of thousands of enemy ships to conquer so many Human and Mutati planets. We may have slowed them down a bit here, that's all."

"But even outnumbered, we're still better than they are," Hackman said. "We already proved that here, and your forces can only help." He looked back, and motioned for a square-jawed man to step forward.

"This is Doctor Bichette," the Vice-General said. "He runs the CorpOne medical research division, and has come up with capsules to immunize you from the HibAdu diseases. He will be coordinating the treatments for all of your officers and soldiers."

After shaking hands with Anton and Nirella, the doctor looked past them and said, "Hello, Tesh."

"Hurk." Her reply was icy.

"We used to know each other well," Bichette said to the Vice-General, with a curt smile.

"He was the personal physician for Prince Saito," Tesh said. "Noah Watanabe's father."

Following an awkward silence, an aide to Dr. Bichette handed out packets of capsules to Anton and his entourage.

After taking the medications, Anton, Nirella, and Tesh boarded a survey aircraft, along with Hacket and Bichette. Thinker accompanied them, as did other top MPA and Liberator officers. Their civilian pilot flew them away from the valley and the city, out toward the coast.

Below, on a broad field bordering the sea, Anton saw tens of thousands of bodies and the burned-out hulks of warships from both sides of the battle, including the rotting remains of dead podships.

"The enemy pods aren't natural," Hacket said, pointing to several decaying wrecks on the ground. "They're growing them in Adurian bio-labs, and fitting them with Hibbil navigation machines."

"We saw a couple of them back on the starcloud," Anton said. "The Tulyans are analyzing them."

"We've done some of that ourselves," Hacket said. "We'll have to compare notes."

They toured four more death-fields where ships had fallen and soldiers on both sides had died. Many enemy robots lay on the ground beside Hibbils and Adurians, but Anton didn't care about any of them. Then a tinge of emotion went through him as he realized how many of his own loyal robots had fallen fighting at the sides of his fighters.

Presently Anton and his entourage flew over the smoldering remains of Octo, one of Canopa's largest cities. "We lost over a million people down there," Bichette said in a somber tone. "But it could have been worse."

"You're a military expert now?" Tesh said.

"Just quoting the Vice-General," he replied.

"That's right," Hacket agreed. "The HibAdus arrived in force, but we drove them back."

Kajor Avery, a slender officer with almond-shaped eyes, pursed his lips. "The enemy seemed to pull their punches, as if they didn't want to wipe everything out. We counterattacked, and they fled too easily."

"In your opinion," Vice-General Hacket said. "It's not the majority opinion."

"I have the vote that counts," Doge Anton said. He narrowed his gaze. "I think the HibAdus could have hit harder, but they wanted to save the planet as a war prize. Even with us here, they probably think they can strike a killing blow any time they feel like it."

Avery nodded, while Hacket just glared silently.

Tapping General Nirella on the shoulder, Anton said, "Send an emergency message to Noah Watanabe at Siriki. Tell him in detail what happened here, and not to let his guard down."

Chapter Twenty-Three

Most members of a racial group do not know the reasons for their hatred of another race. The reasons fall away, like leaves from a tree. But the hatred remains.

—First Elder Kre'n

Noah's fleet split space in brilliant bursts of green as it emerged over Siriki. While his warships formed into battle groups, the flagship *Okion* went into geostationary orbit over the planet. On the command bridge of the vessel, Noah stood at a wide viewing window with Subi Danvar, watching violent splashes of color in near-space and in the atmosphere below. They had arrived on the night side of the planet, and from his high vantage point Noah received reports from spotters about the ferocious battle raging below.

He heard their voices on his comlink headset, and on screen displays he saw smaller HibAdu and MPA ships engaged in fierce dogfights and larger ones in cannon exchanges, lighting up orbital space and the skies over the planet with orange tracer fire and brilliant, multicolored explosions.

Before Noah and Subi could put a rescue plan into operation, a Tulyan woman received permission to enter, and strode heavily onto the command bridge. The reptilian Zigzia had always been what her people called a "webtalker," but Noah had not heard of the vocation until recently, from Elders at the starcloud. Prior to that, he and other Guardians had only known that Zigzia could send and receive messages across the galaxy, though an arcane method of communication.

But the name of her specialty said a great deal about how she and others like her accomplished it. In recent days Noah had asked questions, and had learned that they tapped into Timeweb in a variety of ways, and transmitted telepathically along the strands of the infrastructure.

"Urgent message from Doge Anton at Canopa," the webtalker said in a trancelike voice. "He advises you not to trust anything you see, and suspects that the HibAdus are adept at trickery, at laying deadly traps for our forces. On Canopa it is relatively calm, but there are indications of a storm brewing."

Without hesitating, Noah dictated a response to Doge Anton. "Sire, I have encountered a difficult situation on Siriki. The HibAdus are attacking in considerable force."

Completing his comments, Noah waved the Tulyan away. She hurried off to transmit. By prior arrangement, the three divisions of the Liberator fleet—at Canopa, Siriki, and Dij—were on their own, unless Doge Anton decided to change that.

Keeping his main force back, he ordered one of his battle groups to attack, and it dove into action. Podships disgorged thousands of fighter craft into the sky, which immediately sped to the aid of the Sirikan defenders, guns blazing. In orbital space, some of Noah's larger ships hunted for the biggest, most powerful enemy targets, which were not making themselves apparent thus far.

Just then, firing their powerful cannons, two enemy podships came out of nowhere and raced toward Noah's flagship. It was a moment of vulnerability, but *Okion*—either from instinct or the Tulyan pilot operating it—darted out of the way in the battle-lit darkness as if it were a smaller, more agile craft, and fired volleys that destroyed both vessels. They blew up in bursts of color that quickly flashed out in the airless vacuum.

* * * * *

In the next half hour, the tide of battle swung decisively in the Liberators' favor. No more enemy lab-pods appeared, and the smaller warships were soon scattered or destroyed. Confident that he could go to the next stage, Noah sent more commands by comlink, and to the flagship's sectoid chamber through a Tulyan on the command bridge. Now *Okion* led the main body of Noah's fleet downward, into the atmosphere. Fighter craft and other podships cleared the way. HibAdu ships were no match for the natural podships, or for the smaller vessels operated by highly trained crews. Reports came in to Noah over comlinks that the HibAdus were in full retreat.

Followed by other podships, *Okion* flew to the sunlit side of Siriki, where there were no ongoing battles. The ship circled the grounds of Princess Meghina's palace and then set down in a broad meadow of flowers. Hundreds of ships followed, while additional craft found their own landing sites in the nearby countryside.

As Noah and Subi disembarked in bright sunlight, he was greeted by three MPA officers who wore red-and-gold uniforms. Hundreds of soldiers stood at attention, and behind them rose the glittering turrets and spires of the Golden Palace. The Princess had not returned since the cessation of regularly scheduled podship travel.

"I'll go ahead and check things out," Subi said. "Let's see if the keep in her palace matches its reputation."

Noah nodded, and watched as Subi and a half-dozen men marched down a flower-line path toward the elegant structure. Looking around, Noah saw no signs of war here. The grounds were immaculately maintained.

Reportedly the Princess had set up an attack-proof capsule inside the palace structure, her version of the ancient concept of a fortified castle keep, where the royal family and key associates resided. Subi—with his security expertise—wanted to see it first-hand.

At a gesture from Noah, a dark-skinned aide hurried over, and saluted. "Sir?"

"Bring the Mutati to me," Noah said.

Within minutes, two soldiers brought Parais d'Olor to him. Under close supervision, she had ridden in the passenger compartment of one of the other podships.

"Another test I need to pass?" the Mutati asked in a weary voice, when she reached Noah. She looked much the same as the last time he'd seen her, just before his fleet disembarked, but he thought her peacock feathers were of a slightly different color now. A woman's prerogative, he supposed. Her small beak moved as she spoke.

"No," he said.

Before departing from the starcloud on this mission, the Council of Elders had confirmed Parais's veracity and lack of duplicity by administering the truthing touch on her. The Tulyans had done the same with all of the other Mutatis who had arrived in the two lab-pods, including the shapeshifter leader, Hari'Adab. Now, according to a report that had been transmitted to Noah's flagship, Parais d'Olor had passed an additional series of truthing tests that had been administered by Tulyans in Noah's fleet.

In his experience as Master of the Guardians, Noah had developed a sixth sense about the people he admitted into his environmental organization. Unarguably, the best choice he had ever made had been Subi Danvar, a man who had risen quickly through the ranks to become adjutant. Another had been the Tulyan Eshaz, who had performed excellent ecological recovery work for the organization. In accepting Tesh Kori as a Guardian, Noah had assessed her heart correctly, but had not realized until later that she was really a Parvii, and not Human. He had also allowed the cerebral robot, Thinker, to join his inner circle. Thus, an interesting pattern had developed around Noah, as he interacted closely with a variety of galactic races, as well as sentient robots.

Subi Danvar, always security conscious, had expressed concern over this when he saw the pattern taking shape. In response, Noah had authorized him to complete any background or other security checks he wanted, and the adjutant had done so. For non-Humans, that proved to be difficult, but in his own way, Subi had satisfied himself that the eclectic assortment of new Guardians were an asset to the organization, and not a liability.

Noah had never suspected anything else. Just as he saw the entire galaxy as one ecological unit, so too did he view all galactic races—and even sentient robots (who were inspired by Humans)—as cut from the same essential cloth. Honor was honor, and betrayal was betrayal. Though he had been through his share of battles and could justify feeling otherwise, Noah invariably tried to find the good in people, instead of assuming the worst about them. He even did this with his enemies, trying to understand their rationalizations, their motivations. It helped him cope.

Now, as he looked intently into Parais's large brown eyes, Noah was trying to determine the sincerity of the member of yet another race. And this time it was not just any galactic race. This was a *Mutati*, and they had been the mortal enemies of humankind since time immemorial.

"I believe I can trust you," Noah said.

She smiled, revealing upturned creases around the sides of her beak. "You remind me of my Hari," she said, "always thinking, always evolving in your thinking. You look *through* people."

"I'm sorry. I don't mean to, but these are not ordinary times."

"No, they aren't."

He told the soldiers with her to allow her freedom of movement, then said to Parais, "I'll talk more about this to Doge Anton, and see if we can come up with duties for you. Something befitting of your position and your unique skills."

"Thank you." She bowed slightly to him.

"Excuse me," Noah said, as he received a vibrating comlink signal. When Parais left, he took the call over a handheld transceiver. It was from Subi.

"The palace is everything I hoped," the adjutant said. He grinned, put his hand on a pistol that was holstered on his hip. "Ten of us convinced the caretaker to give us a tour. Meghina's central keep is virtually impregnable, so it should be as good a place as any to coordinate our military operations. There are some surprises, though, as you'll see when you get here."

Followed by the MPA officers and some of his own men, Noah marched along the dimly-lit main path toward the palace. Just before going in the main entrance, he saw Acey Zelk and Dux Hannah, in a lighted section of the gardens. The teenagers were with a group of men setting up temporary structures and equipment for a security perimeter around the grounds. Dux said something to a non-commissioned officer, who looked in Noah's direction and then nodded to him deferentially.

The boys hurried over to join Noah, and Acey spoke first. "Master Noah, we really sent the HibAdus packing, didn't we?" The young man, having never really retired from the Guardians or been dismissed from them, apparently felt comfortable using Noah's title as the leader of that organization.

"Don't trust anything you see," Noah said, passing Anton's advice along. "We can't let our guard down for a moment."

"Our Grandmamá Zelk lives on Siriki," Dux said. "In the back country. Sir, we're worried about her."

"Can we go and check on her?" Acey asked. He grinned awkwardly. "We're just a couple of kids and not worth much. No one will miss us."

"You're hardly worthless," Noah said. "I've been getting good reports on both of you." He looked boys over, noted that much of the baby fat had left their faces.

"We know how to use local transportation," Dux said in an imploring voice, "and we won't take long."

Hesitation. Then: "OK, I'm going to let you go. You've both earned the right." He patted the boys on the shoulders. "But take care of yourselves and come back safe, all right?"

"Thank you sir," Dux said, with a wide grin. "We will."

Acey, less mindful of decorum, was already hurrying off, down the dimly lit main path. Dux saluted Noah, and ran after him.

Chapter Twenty-Four

The ultimate crisis can bring out the best in a galactic race ... or lead to its complete extinction.

—Woldn, in his darkest hour

The Eye of the Swarm clustered in the midst of the surviving members of his race, in what he thought must be the darkest, coldest region of the universe. All hope seemed to be lost. He felt the collective loss of body heat in his race, sensed the slowly fading members around him.

Focus, he thought, *I must focus and find a way.*

The Parviis had their secret treasures, going back for millions and millions of years, to the very beginnings of their collective consciousness. It comprised a vault of arcane information that had worked well for them in bygone days to establish their position in the cosmos, but which had not been needed in later times. Or so it had seemed to a long succession of leaders. But Woldn was questioning the old ways.

As the Eye, I did as my predecessors did.

But Woldn didn't want to make excuses for the extreme difficulties in which he now found himself, because leaders were supposed to lead and show strength. He wondered when the changes began, the slippages in ways of doing things, the entombment of important knowledge. At various points along the course of history, Parvii leaders had decided not to continue the old ways, and in the process important concepts and activities had piled up on intellectual dust heaps. He may even have contributed to the steady decline himself, in some barely perceptible manner. Admittedly, he had not made the decision to resurrect the old knowledge soon enough.

In his great despair, Woldn realized that he had lost touch with the ancient truths and principles of his race, the roots of what it meant to be a Parvii.

We have drifted.

And in drifting, the Parvii race had lost its compass. How fitting that he would make this analogy now, when he and the surviving members of the once vast swarms were huddled in an uncharted region, probably in another galaxy entirely.

But all living Parviis are not here, he thought. *Tesh has joined our ancient enemy, has thrown in her lot with the Tulyans.*

Woldn lamented over how many Parvii secrets she might have revealed to them. Some, perhaps, like the location of the Parvii Fold. But not all of them, certainly. The traitorous female had never gone through the rituals and training required to become a Parvii Eye of the Swarm. Thus, she could not possibly know certain things.

Secrets within secrets.

But she did have important contacts, like Noah Watanabe. If the rumors about him were true, if he was the first Human in history who could access Timeweb and utilize its vast powers, he was a dangerous wild card. He might even be able to peer into the secret treasure vaults of the Parvii race. The reputed "galactic ecologist," combined with Tesh's betrayal, could be why Woldn found himself where he was now.

Cast off, floundering, and sinking into oblivion.

To his dismay he noticed that some of the Parviis who had been clustered around the latents had died, but remained in place even in death. Through his morphic field, he counted them telepathically. Eight hundred and thirteen. Just then, another passed on, right in front of his mind. Eight hundred and fourteen brave souls so far, and surely more would follow. He appreciated their contributions, their loyalty.

Something spiked in his consciousness. Telepathic waves coming from the center of the cluster, from one of the war priests. This one had a name now, resurrected from ancient times. Yurtii. As moments passed, Woldn sensed Yurtii drawing closer to him. The name was unfamiliar,, so he must not have been one of the most famous of the ancients.

Like a chick hatching from an egg, Yurtii shoved several of the dead Parviis aside and emerged in the physical form of a boy, then pushed his way out into space. Woldn followed him. Entirely hairless and without clothing, the boy flew to Woldn and hovered near him, making a buzzing noise that the Parvii leader could hear, despite the absence of atmosphere.

The Eye of the Swarm felt his spirits lift, but he could not put the sensation into words for anyone to hear, did not even know if the feeling was justified, or if it was foolish.

"What was old is new again," Yurtii said.

In the war priest's presence, confronted by the potent ancient mind that had regrown in a child's consciousness, Woldn felt grossly inadequate. Though he had known war priests before, his initial probings of Yurtii indicated that they were only faint shadows of this one. Woldn had never been in the presence of a war priest of such talent.

"I am no longer qualified to command the swarm," Woldn said, his voice weak. "Perhaps I should pass the mantle on to you."

Yurtii's bright blue eyes flashed from depths that seemed far beyond his corporal form, like twin stars in the alternate galaxy. "It is in the specialty of a war priest that I can do the most for our race." The hovering youth bowed his head. "I defer to you."

"Very well." Falling silent, Woldn closed his eyes and probed Yurtii's reawakened mind even more. In the process, he learned interesting things about this war priest's past successes. It gave Woldn hope for the future, especially if the other latents were on the level of this one. But Yurtii had faced opposition from other war priests of his era, and the historical record had not been as kind to him as it might have been. His military successes, while numerous and important, had been downplayed by those who served after him. A cesspool of politics.

Reopening his eyes and staring at the war priest, Woldn said, "Long ago, our race had many masters of illusion. I wish to restore what is good about the old days."

Simultaneously, Woldn and Yurtii focused their gazes on the tiny timehole through which their small swarm had escaped. As seconds passed, a telepathic bubble emanated from the two linked minds, an invisible enclosure that passed through empty to the other side, unseen and undetectable by the guardian ships of the enemy. The swarm could enter it and travel undetected, concealed from view.

With new excitement, the Eye of the Swarm led the way through, into the safety of the bubble. Then, filled with Parviis, the invisible bubble floated away, to a remote corner of the Parvii Fold. Behind, the timehole appeared to seal over, so that it no longer seemed to exist.

Under Woldn's leadership the tiny creatures were coming back to awareness. They were angry and single-minded, and wanted to regain control of the podships. They saw this as their only purpose in life, their sacred and eternal destiny. But their numbers were far too small to even consider resurrecting the ancient glories, at least not yet. All of them were feeling better physically and mentally, but most of the individuals no longer had the effective neurotoxin stingers that were needed to capture and control podships.

Still, inside the Parviis' invisible bubble lay potential salvation, because it offered the means of escape, a tiny pocket within the traditional galactic fold that had always been their sacred place. It was warmer inside the bubble, much better for breeding than out in space.

But the five latent breeding specialists had not yet returned to consciousness. And without their guidance, the Parviis could not breed at all. They could only die.

Chapter Twenty-Five

Timeweb holds this galaxy together. But there are galaxies on top of galaxies in this vast universe. Are they also linked to the cosmic web that we know, or are their structures entirely different and unimaginable to us?

—Tulyan report to the Council of Elders

In times long past, so many years ago that Eshaz could hardly remember them, he had been a skilled podship pilot for the Tulyans, transporting web caretaker teams around the galaxy. After the insidious, selfish Parviis took away control of the podship fleet, Eshaz—having lost the means of performing his specialty—had been forced to adapt. As a consequence, he had perfected other skills authorized by the Council, among them the ability to timesee. In addition, he had become a web caretaker himself, performing occasional timehole repair duties in the limited travels that became available to him.

Eventually he'd met Noah Watanabe, the first Human to ever grasp the concept of galaxy-wide ecological interdependence. Joining Noah's idealistic team of "eco-warriors," Eshaz and scores of other Tulyans engaged in ecological monitoring operations, and—in secrecy—they occasionally used ancient Tulyan methods to complete timehole repairs.

In recent years, Eshaz had seen conditions worsening, but he had been unable to do much about it until now. With more than ninety-six thousand podships dedicated to their tasks, the Tulyans were mounting the most massive ecological recovery operation in history. After assembling reports from web caretakers, the Elders were looking at the vast galaxy as if it were a battlefield, with wounded soldiers lying all over it. In their way of prioritizing, each of the timeholes became like an injured person, and the Tulyan leaders were using a triage method to determine which wounds needed attention first.

At long last, the Tulyans—who had always considered themselves a peaceful people—were going to war, in a very aggressive, organized fashion.

As the leader of one of the repair divisions, Eshaz stood with a throng of other Tulyans on a space platform while the craft floated past the immense fleet of rescued, moored podships. Presently the glax-enclosed platform came to a stop and rocked gently in the vacuum, an optimal moorage basin at the stationary center of the planets of the Tulyan Starcloud. In recent months, Eshaz had been resurrecting his old piloting skills, having gone on a hunt for wild podships and having piloted one of the sentient vessels in the Liberator Fleet.

Now the Tulyan portion of the Liberator Fleet was embarking on an even greater, task. In a sense it was linked to the military operations of the Humans and Mutatis in their efforts to save their planets and stop HibAdu lab-pods from damaging the podways—but this was a far more delicate and wide-scale operation. Everything had to be done perfectly. The fate of the galaxy rested on their skills.

For some time the Tulyans had been re-training themselves, updating their old aptitudes and methods. Because they led exceedingly long lives, hundreds of thousands and even millions of years, many living Tulyans recalled the old days. But after so long, memories had a way of slipping in the clutter of events, and some of Eshaz's race were better at recalling details than others. There had been numerous arguments about the proper methods to use, but the proof had been in the tests they had performed. Handling a few wild pods—which Tulyans had continued to do for centuries—was not the same as organizing and coordinating the actions of thousands of them. Large numbers of Aopoddae behaved quite differently from smaller numbers, and needed specialized techniques to manage them. Determining which methods to use was like a filtering process, eliminating the ideas that didn't work and implementing those that did.

Just getting the podships here from the Parvii Fold had involved much of that, perfecting ways of piloting the vessels in large formations to selected destinations. Now the ships no longer had gun ports on their hulls, for their passengers had different requirements, and the sentient spacecraft had made adjustments. Their passenger compartments and cargo holds were filled with ecological repair teams, with all of the equipment and esoteric equipment needed for that purpose. The articles taken along weren't things that could be manufactured in a conventional factory. Rather, they were thorn vines, pouches of green dust, and books of incantations that would be needed to ward off the evil spirits of the undergalaxy.

To an extent the Tulyans understood what they were up against: Galara, the powerful evil spirit of the undergalaxy, was punching holes in the Known Galaxy, penetrating the protective membrane at numerous points in order to undermine and conquer. For millions of years the malevolent one had been working at this, and finally, with the momentum of the decay Galara had set in motion, the adverse conditions were accelerating. Long ago, the Tulyans had an easier task, because they could respond quickly whenever timeholes appeared, and could seal them quickly. But with all the years of decline the job was much bigger now, and the prospects were uncertain at best. Certainly, all of these thousands of podships and teams of Tulyans were a formidable force to save the galaxy. But was it too late? Could they make enough of a difference to reverse an immense-scale decline?

Just as Tulyans knew that there were ancient enemies among the galactic races, so too they believed there were competing spirits and gods of the various galaxies. Just as people wanted to dominate one another, so too was it in higher orders of existence, where the stakes were much greater.

Eshaz bowed his bronze head in reverence to Ubuqqo, the Sublime Creator, and whispered a prayer for the salvation of the galaxy. *"Ubuqqo, anret pir huyyil."*

A benign spirit seemed to encompass the reptilian man now, and he felt supremely comforted in its presence. Closing his slitted eyes, Eshaz murmured an incantation to beckon a nearby, familiar podship in the ancient way, commanding it to come closer: *"Aopoddae, eyamo ippaq azii ... Aopoddae, eyamo ippaq azii ... "*

When Eshaz opened his eyes moments later, the large gray-and-black pod was bumping up against the platform, and an open access hatch was open on the hull. The ship drifted back just a little, but remained close. With a rush of excitement, Eshaz leaped off the platform into space. Like an eager lover, the podship scooped him up, and he found himself inside.

Once more it was like old times, when Eshaz had been a caretaker-team pilot. He placed his hands on a warm interior wall and felt the pulsing consciousness of the ancient creature, and repeated its name, which he knew well. In the times of lore, this had been one of the podships he had piloted across vast distances.

Agryt.

Walking down the corridor, Eshaz reached the sectoid chamber, and found the access hatch open as expected, revealing a glowing green enclosure beyond. The podship awaited his commands.

Eshaz took a deep, satisfied breath and stepped across the threshold into the core of the vessel. The access hatch closed behind him, bathing him in green luminescence, but he was not afraid. In the age-old way of his people, the Tulyan touched the glowing flesh and merged into it.

On the prow of the podship, Eshaz's face appeared, very large now in his metamorphosed state. He felt euphoric, like a reborn creature ready to leap and frolic across vast expanses of the heavens. But he knew he could not do that, could not do anything trivial or selfish with this critically important assignment that had been entrusted to him.

Instead, as the leader of a five-hundred-ship ecological repair team, Eshaz guided Agryt around the other vessels assigned to him, signaling to them telepathically, as they had practiced. Tulyan faces appeared on the prows of ship after ship, and the vessels fell into formation behind him, their countenances rigid and expressionless.

The Tulyan caretaker had many things on his mind, the concerns of the day. And of all those matters, one surfaced above others. Noah had been telling everyone that he sensed a "terrible danger" out in the cosmos, beyond anything they already knew. Eshaz wondered if his friend could possibly be right, and if so, what it might conceivably be. Something to do with Galara that was even worse?

A chill ran down his spine. In this galaxy, anything seemed possible.

Chapter Twenty-Six

Just as there are byways and hidden passages within any sentient mind, so too is it with larger groups of living beings. As individuals, and as groups, conscious organisms have an obsession to do things that others do not know about. It is their way of controlling situations—or of altering their perception so that they believe they are in control.

—Thinker, data bank file * * * * *34ΩÆØ

Having been summoned to his homeworld of Adurian, the Ambassador waited patiently for the dignitaries to arrive. His pulse quickened. Uncel had received notification that the three leaders of the HibAdu Coalition would finally identify themselves, and that they would make a major military announcement. At last, he would learn who they were!

VV Uncel stood with other diplomats and local Adurian leaders, all gathered in a grand reception hall that had been converted from the remains of an old spacecraft. A buzz of anticipation filled the air, and people kept looking up at the speaking balcony and at the grand staircase that descended to their level, where the triumvirate might appear.

In its original form the large spacefaring vessel had contained numerous reception halls and meeting rooms, and had been built in an opulent style for one of the early Adurian emperors, Oragem the Third. The walls and ceilings were hand-painted and framed in gold filigree along the moldings and on the railings and banisters.

A tall Churian with thick red eyebrows worked the gathering, offering drinks that he balanced precariously on two trays.

"I'll have a ku-royale, please," Uncel said, pointing.

Nodding, the Churian contorted a very flexible leg that had long, prehensile toes on the foot, which he used to grasp the drink and pass it on to Uncel.

As the servant moved away, the Ambassador took a long sip of the alcoholic beverage, and tasted its delicate, minty sweetness. Surrounded by conversations around him in which he was not taking part, he took a few moments to reflect. Though born to wealth and privilege, Ambassador VV Uncel had always worked hard to improve himself, and took pride in his achievements. A pureblood Adurian born on the planet of the same name, his father had been a successful biochemist who earned numerous patents, while his mother had been a product designer who worked on the team that developed *Endo*, the most popular of all Adurian games.

Educated at the elite Sarban University in the capital city, Uncel had always known he would succeed. Everyone who knew him commented on his many attributes, especially his keen intelligence, his way of getting along with virtually anyone, and his burning desire to succeed. He had graduated first in his class.

For years, Uncel had been on the ascendancy in his career, culminating with his appointment as Ambassador to the Mutati Kingdom at the very young age of sixty years, quite youthful by the biologically-enhanced Adurian standards. In his professional life he had known the Adurian emperor and his advisers very well, and had established a vital communication line with the Mutatis and their difficult Zultan, Abal Meshdi.

Uncel had even been in on the early planning sessions of the Hibbil and Adurian rulers, in which they resolved to form a clandestine alliance to defeat both the Mutati Kingdom and the Merchant Prince Alliance. When the HibAdu alliance got underway, however, Uncel had been frustrated to find himself increasingly out of the loop, and that he was one of the people who only received information on a "need to know" basis. In answer to his queries about various issues, the Adurian Emperor and his advisers began to defer to what they called the Royal Parliament, which they said was making the key decisions about HibAdu military plans. Three names and titles had surfaced in that governing body, but not their faces: High Ruler Coreq, Premier Enver, and Warlord Tarix.

Prior to that, Uncel had never heard of the trio or their governing body, and he'd never been able to determine where they met. Rumor held that the Royal Parliament had been established on one of the secondary Hibbil worlds, which gave Uncel concern. But his life was busy with diplomatic assignments, and he saw the immense war machine building all around him, with thousands of factories gearing up to produce armaments and laboratory-bred podships, all necessary for the upcoming attacks on the enemy.

A career diplomat, VV Uncel had always managed to land on his feet when political winds blew, as they invariably did. With the HibAdu Coalition and weapons manufacturing in full swing, he fell into a pattern of just playing his part as a diplomat and as a spy against the Mutatis, without totally understanding what was occurring on his own side. But he had faith that it would all turn out for the best. Mutatis and Humans were the most loathsome of galactic races, and deserved the terrible punishment that was being delivered upon them.

"Another drink, sir?" The Churian was back.

"No." Uncel watched as the prehensile foot extended again, and took the glax from him. The servant drifted away.

In one of the high points of his career, Ambassador Uncel had tricked the Mutatis into using Adurian gyrodomes and minigyros, devices that weakened their brains in subtle ways and made them easier to conquer. Afterward, his HibAdu superiors had sent him a laudatory message telling him he had done an excellent job of softening up the enemy for the imminent attack.

Uncel prided himself on an ability to get along with people he did not like, while artfully concealing any antipathies he felt from them. That included not only the Mutati Zultan, but the duplicitous little Hibbil, Pimyt. Though Uncel and Pimyt worked closely together on the Hibbil Cluster Worlds, Uncel had never trusted the furry little devil. Something troubled him about Pimyt's red-tinged eyes, which seemed to conceal too much. While Pimyt professed to know as little as Uncel himself, the Ambassador did not entirely believe him. Pimyt was the sort of person who had schemes within schemes, and fallback positions to protect himself while sacrificing others.

As attaché to the former Doge Lorenzo del Velli, Pimyt had connections to leaders of the Merchant Prince Alliance, and for all Uncel knew he might have spilled the plans to them. Of course, the HibAdus had systems to check on such things, a way of taking cellular samples from Pimyt and others (and even from

Uncel), samples that they could read in laboratories to obtain information. Uncel's own father had developed the biotechnology and had been well-rewarded for it. Though VV held no legal rights to the particular patents involved with reading cells, since the patents were considered high-security assets of the state, he recalled how as a child his father had shown him that biological cells contained memories—memories that could be read in order to obtain evidence of a crime or of disloyalty to the government. It was the ultimate police tool, and a key contribution of the Adurians to the HibAdu Coalition.

But Hibbils were crafty. They possessed significant technology of their own, and might even have secret methods of thwarting the cellular lie-detection system of the Adurians. Pimyt was with the Humans now, ostensibly on a clandestine HibAdu assignment. Uncel would like to be a proverbial fly on the wall around that one.

The buzz of conversation intensified around him, and he heard exclamations. Looking up at the speaking balcony, Uncel gasped at the sight of three peculiar figures standing there, all dressed in orange-and-gray robes. HibAdu colors.

From their bodies and facial appearances, he thought two were men and one a woman. They were quite different from any galactic race he had ever seen before, but familiar to him at the same time, in a haunting and disturbing sort of way. A single word came to his mind, one he dared not utter, because he strongly suspected that these were the HibAdu leaders. At long last, they were presenting themselves.

Freaks.

He couldn't help the thought, though he knew it was dangerous. Their heads were of the Adurian insectoid shape, with large, bulbous eyes. But the eyes were pale yellow instead of the darker shades typical of Adurians, while their heads and exposed hands had Hibbil features. All three leaders were fur covered, and they had stunted bone structures. These were laboratory-grown people, horrific hybrids of the two races.

The male freak in the center was the tallest, if he could be called tall. Throughout the reception hall, no one spoke a word, and everyone stiffened up. Uncel felt a shortness of breath, and tried to calm himself. He hoped it was just a joke, something the Adurian lab scientists had cooked up.

"I am High Ruler Coreq," the robed monster at the center said, in a whiny voice that sounded Adurian. Motioning to his left and right, he identified the other male as Premier Enver and the female as Warlord Tarix, and then added, "We are, as many of you have surmised, laboratory-bred, but make no mistake about it. This does not make us inferior to any of you in any way. On the contrary, we are far superior in every way imaginable."

"Gaze upon us and see the future," Premier Enver said. This one sounded more like a Hibbil, with a deeper voice. "One day, when the time is right, an entire race of HibAdus will be created, and there will be no need for any other races to exist."

A chill ran down VV Uncel's spine, and he heard an uneasy murmuring around him.

Warlord Tarix had something to add, in an echoing voice that carried deadly undertones. "Our enemies are on their knees, making their last stands. We have conquered every Human world except for two, and every Mutati world save for one." She smiled cruelly, revealing sharp white teeth. "They cannot hold out much longer."

Then, eerily, the three of them spoke in synchronization: "To retain what we have gained, our forces have established impregnable defense systems on every conquered planet. Thanks to Hibbil ingenuity, we have wide-range sensor-guns that sweep considerably more than the areas around pod stations, as the Humans have. Our sensors encompass entire planets. If any unauthorized podship appears, it will be blasted into oblivion."

The triumvirate began to clap, as if for themselves. Everyone in the reception hall joined in, including Ambassador Uncel, but he felt a dark gloom seeping into his soul.

Chapter Twenty-Seven

Those who adapt, survive. This basic rule applies to all living things, and to all places they exist in the universe. Biological creatures, being much smaller and weaker than the natural forces of their surroundings, can only control their environments to limited extents. When things change around them, they must change as well. Or die.

—Master Noah Watanabe, Journal of the Cosmic Sea

It could have been much worse.

At least that was the first impression Princess Meghina got when the space station stopped tumbling and the gravitonics system went back on.

The glax-walled gambling room on the orbiter had righted itself, and was lit with soft illumination coming through the windows. But was it really over? And what in the world had happened?

She crawled out from under the gaming table and assessed the bumps and bruises on her face and body. Around her, others did the same. Some were groaning, but as she saw them move, it didn't look like anyone was seriously injured. Pimyt stood on top of the upside-down gaming table, complaining that one of his hips hurt. His tunic was torn, showing silvery fur on his chest.

Meghina's dagg whined, and scampered over debris to reach her. The large black animal licked her hand, where a bruise was beginning to show.

"Thank you, Orga ," she said with a gentle smile. "That makes me feel better already."

"Are you all right?" It was Kobi Akar, the impeccably dressed Salducian diplomat who was one of her immortal companions. He stood over her, looking down with concern in his dark, close-set eyes. Though he had always been nice enough to her, she'd never really liked him that much. There seemed to be an undercurrent to him, something just beneath the surface that was decidedly unpleasant. Exactly what that might be, she had never been certain. But she didn't admire the way he sometimes alluded to getting away with things that others could not, because of his diplomatic immunity. Even so, he could be funny and witty at times, and the others in her elite group of elixir-immortals all seemed to like him.

Typical of his race, Akar was sturdily built, with an oblong head, two small, crablike pincers for hands, and a multi-legged underbody concealed beneath a long robe. The Salducians, while trading partners and military allies of the Merchant Prince Alliance, were a galactic race of their own, and had settled in only a small sector of the galaxy.

"I'm fine," Meghina said. She looked around. "And the others?"

"All minor injuries, it appears."

"That's good." She rose to her feet and gazed out through the clearglax walls in all directions, onto a star-encrusted canvas of space. Looking down along the connected modules of the space station, she noticed large dents that had not been there before, and jagged pieces hanging loosely from sections that were too badly damaged to be saved by airtight emergency doors. Beyond this startling view, she saw something just as unsettling: a brown planet that was obviously not Canopa, where they had been orbiting previously. Sunlight came from behind the orbiter.

An odd, queasy feeling came over her. "Where are we?"

Akar scratched the thin line of hair on his forehead, the last patch of his hairline. "Hard to say."

He was considered handsome by his people, and was reputed to enjoy the company of many mistresses. As for herself, the courtesan Princess Meghina had never found him or any other Salducian male physically attractive, and his quirks and deficiencies were irritating. He looked worried now, but often had a rather artificial smile on his overlarge mouth.

Pimyt limped past her, grimacing in pain from his injured hip. "We need medical packs," he said. He went down a short stairway to the corridor door, and shouted back, "I'll see what I can find."

"This space station is seriously damaged," someone said.

A man's voice came over the onboard com-system. "I am Colonel Truitt of the Red Berets. All passengers are advised to make your way to emergency stations and put on survival suits."

"We're in one of the emergency stations now," Lorenzo said.

Someone activated ceiling hatches, causing nets to drop down slowly, containing life-support suits and emergency supply canisters. Moments later, Red Beret soldiers entered the chamber, opened the nets, and began handing out suits. The emergency doors for this module, which were supposed to be airtight, were leaking.

"But there are immortals among us," said Prince Okkco, a nobleman with wavy white hair. "They do not need life-support."

"Everyone puts on a suit," Lorenzo said, with a scowl. "No exceptions."

"We are orbiting an unknown planet in an unknown solar system," one of the Red Berets said, looking at the readings on a handheld device.

One of his companions, with a similar unit, said, "We're still taking astronomical readings, but nothing looks familiar."

In a few minutes, everyone in the chamber including the Red Berets had put on puffy, pale blue survival suits. But they left the face plates hinged open, since the on-board air systems were still functioning.

More guests and soldiers from other portions of the orbiter entered the wrecked gambling hall, since it was one of the principal emergency stations on the orbiter. Colonel Truitt came in as well, a tall man with a thick mustache. He conferred with Lorenzo and Pimyt.

Presently, Lorenzo announced, "Though we've lost one of our primary shuttles, we still have two in working order. We're going to use one of them to send a scouting party down to that planet, and see what we can find out. Our scanners show it has a breathable atmosphere and moderate temperatures on the surface, so we won't need these suits when we get down there."

"There could still be unknown dangers," Meghina said. "As one of the immortals, I'd like to volunteer to go down with the scouting party."

"No," Lorenzo said. "You're staying here. But I'm going down, and so is Pimyt."

"Why?" Meghina said.

And Pimyt said, too, almost at the same time: "Why?"

"Because," Lorenzo said, " one of you is my wife, and the other is my attaché, and both of you will do as I command."

In shared reluctance, Meghina and Pimyt nodded.

Then the Salducian diplomat said, "If you want an immortal to go along, I'll do it."

"No, you'd just get in the way," Lorenzo said. He scanned the four Human immortals, and seemed to consider taking one or more of them along instead. Then he looked at Pimyt and said, "Make the necessary arrangements. Add a dozen elite Red Beret guardsmen to the scouting party."

"Fourteen in all, then," the Hibbil said.

"Right."

As she watched her husband take charge of the situation, Meghina felt a renewed surge of attraction for him. He looked rather handsome in this time of crisis, and was displaying courage that she hadn't seen before.

Noticing her looking at him, Lorenzo smiled. But his resolve appeared suddenly shaky. As if to conceal this, he turned and led the others out the door into the corridor.

* * * * *

When the shuttle dropped down through the atmosphere, Pimyt saw predominantly brown hues on the planet, from horizon to horizon. The world had grayish-brown mountains and formations of rock in other muted colors, but he saw no evidence of water or plants.

He heard one of the guardsmen comment on the same thing.

Looking at them, Pimyt said, "If the air's breathable there must be water and plants somewhere."

"Maybe our instruments are wrong," one of the guardsmen said. A lieutenant with gold stripes on his shoulder, Eden Rista was the highest ranking guardsmen in the party.

"Instruments are still showing good oxygen levels," another guardsman said, as he stood at a console. They were only a few hundred meters above the surface. The shuttle slowed, fired retro-rockets, and set down on a wide expanse of rock.

Four guardsmen went through an airlock and stepped outside, leaving the rest of the party on the shuttle. As Pimyt watched through a porthole, the men performed several tests, using handheld instruments. Then they swung aside the face plates on their suits, and gave the all-clear signal.

Now the entire party disembarked, and climbed down from the rock onto an expanse of dry, dusty earth. The air was a little cool, even in direct sunlight. That didn't bother Pimyt, but his companions wore jackets.

Moving off by himself, Lieutenant Rista held a ground-penetrating radar unit.

"Network of subterranean waterways down there," he reported. "Average depth around thirty meters."

"So, there is water here, after all," Pimyt said. Looking at Lorenzo, he added, "If you want, sir, I could bring a hibbamatic down here and build something to dig, and to explore the waterways."

"For what purpose?" Lorenzo asked.

"We're in an unknown region, on an unknown planet," the Hibbil said. "Maybe we should take soil, rock, and water samples. Comparing the data with galactic exploration records, it could give us information on where we are."

"Let's do it," the former doge said.

An hour later, they had the hibbamatic set up on the ground. Pimyt made several settings on the machine, then began feeding cartridges of raw materials into the hopper on top.

In a short while, the little Hibbil stood at a glistening black machine, which he had assembled from components that the hibbamatic produced. The new machine was around the size of a small passenger car, except it had a seat on top, and handlebars.

"This thing is dual purpose," he said. "Watch."

Pimyt touched a button, and wheels began grinding on the bottom of the machine. Then he climbed onto the seat and plopped himself there, while holding onto the handlebars. The mechanisms started digging, and in short order it had produced a tunnel sloping down into the ground.

The tunnel had just enough headroom for the others to follow down the slope, on foot. At the bottom, Lorenzo found Pimyt on a flat section of rock inside a low-ceilinged rock cavern, by the edge of a stream. The Hibbil knelt beside the black machine, with lights on the unit illuminating the silvery, luminous surface of the cavern and the underground waterway. Pimyt was making adjustments. As he did so, the seat and handlebars melted into the surface of the machine, and like a shapeshifter it enlarged and morphed into a teardrop shape, with a windshield on the fat end.

"Four-man mini-sub," Pimyt reported. "Perfect for underwater exploration."

"Clever," Lorenzo said, walking around the gleaming black boat. "But what does this have to do with taking soil, rock, and water samples?"

"Very little, perhaps," Pimyt admitted, "but where there's water there's life. Or so the saying goes. Undoubtedly there are organisms in the water, but we're looking for something more substantial. If anyone lives on this planet, we might find them beneath the surface."

"Follow the water," Lorenzo said.

"Precisely. And with instruments, we can always get back here."

"Very well, but for only a couple of hours, at most. If we don't find any evidence of meaningful life, we take the samples and go back to the orbiter."

Pimyt nodded.

A number of the guardsmen were older, and said they had experience with a variety of machines. Lieutenant Rista designated two men to go in the sub. The other men lowered the machine into the water, where it bobbed on the surface. Climbing inside the sub, the two guardsmen familiarized themselves with the controls, taking the boat underwater and back up again. The twin engines purred smoothly.

Using a handheld unit, Lorenzo sent a comlink message up to the orbiter, informing them where the landing party was, and what they were doing.

"I should go," Pimyt said, to Lorenzo. "If necessary, I can operate the sub, too. I've been watching them and listening in, and it looks easy enough to handle. How about you, sir? Want to take a little submarine ride?"

"Are you sure it's safe?" Lorenzo asked. He shut off his comlink unit, replaced it in a holder at his belt.

Pimyt grinned. "Absolutely not."

With a grimace, Lorenzo climbed into the four-man craft and took one of the two aft seats, in the narrowest section of the teardrop hull. Pimyt followed, and sat in the remaining seat directly beside him, while the two guardsmen sat side by side ahead of them, in the pilot and co-pilot chairs behind the windshield.

Slowly, the mini-sub proceeded downstream, casting a powerful headlight to illuminate the watery tunnel ahead, through murky darkness. At first they made their way on the surface of the water, like an ordinary motor-propelled boat.

"Low rock overhang ahead," the pilot announced. He was much thinner and shorter than his companion, and proved to be entirely bald as well when he removed his cap and stuffed it in a uniform pocket.

"The water is deep enough to submerge," the larger soldier said, reading an instrument panel.

"OK," the pilot said. "Here we go." He submerged the vessel, and they proceeded to the other side of the overhang, where they surfaced again. But only for a short distance. The waterway widened considerably, but across the entire width the ceiling dipped so low that they had to submerge again.

As they proceeded underwater, the big soldier looked back at Lorenzo and said, "Quite an adventure we're on, sir."

"I'm not afraid," the former doge said, "not at all. I've seen much worse than this."

But Pimyt heard fear in his voice, and this amused him. He'd never liked Lorenzo, and secretly enjoyed seeing him suffer. The Hibbil had other feelings as well, of a more aggressive nature. In his mind, he savored the possibilities.

Suddenly he felt the mini-sub's speed increase dramatically, a strong thrust forward. Moments afterward, a warning buzzer went off.

The pilot swore loudly, and slammed the engines into hard reverse.

Chapter Twenty-Eight

Effective leadership is primarily a matter of striking a pose and causing others to see you in a favorable light. It is all about perception. If you appear to be in full command, others are assured, and will follow you. If you appear to be unsteady or fearful, they will scurry away from you like insects from a burning structure.

— Doge Paolantonio IV, private comments

"So you're the great Noah Watanabe?" The palace reception hall echoed with her words, and with her condescending tone.

Though he had never met the young woman before, Noah recognized her instantly from holophotos he had seen. Tall and blonde, Princess Annyette appeared to be around twenty and very businesslike, in a white pants suit and understated gold jewelry. Her hair was closely cropped, more the cut of a man than of a woman. Just behind her stood her six younger sisters, all blonde and similarly attired, but in clothing of different colors. The youngest appeared to be around twelve years of age.

In deference to the rank that Annyette still retained on Siriki (and in what remained of the Merchant Prince Alliance), Noah bowed to her. He had a small entourage of uniformed MPA officers and soldiers with him, along with his rotund adjutant, Subi Danvar.

In the faces and bone structures of the seven princesses, Noah detected resemblances to both Princess Meghina and to Lorenzo del Velli, the royal couple who for years had been thought to be her birth parents. That changed when the famous courtesan confessed publicly that she was not Human at all, but was instead a Mutati, one of the loathsome shapeshifters. Lorenzo del Velli had continued to protect his wife, and much of the public continued to support her, agreeing that she was really more Human than Mutati in her thoughts and loyalties, no matter her unfortunate genetics. But the revelation of Meghina's true identity meant that she could not possibly have borne Human children sired by Lorenzo. Obviously, in her attempts to deceive him and the public, she had selected the birth parents of her "daughters" carefully, because the girls standing before Noah looked perfect in all respects, and even carried themselves with a certain royal hauteur.

"I have never claimed to be great," he responded in a respectful tone. "Not in any sense of the word. On the contrary, I see myself as exceedingly small in a very large universe."

"Which means I am even smaller?" she said, arching her eyebrows.

"I didn't mean that at all." He smiled. "I'm sorry, but I was told that the palace is unoccupied, that you and your sisters prefer to live elsewhere on Siriki, in your own royal quarters."

"The HibAdu attacks changed all of that. We have gathered here at the keep for safety, with our own forces." She nodded toward her gold-uniformed guards that stood at attention around the room, all of them eying Noah's men suspiciously.

"Your castle keep is renowned. You have made a wise decision."

"I'm glad you think so."

Noah shifted on his feet. "Of course, I will make alternate arrangements for myself and my officers."

With a broad, almost friendly smile, Annyette said, "Not necessary. You are my guests and allies."

"And friends," Noah added. "Then you can accommodate some of us in the keep?"

"No more than three hundred."

"Most generous. Now, if you could have someone show us the quarters, we are anxious to set things up. I presume there are meeting halls we could use?"

"Of course."

* * * * *

In what appeared to be a complete about face, Annyette actually became friendly. For Noah and his top officers, she insisted that they accept accommodations on the most secure lower floors of the keep, near her own suites and those of her sisters. She also arranged for protected meeting chambers, and even proved to Subi Danvar's satisfaction that the suites and chambers were safe from eavesdroppers.

Afterward, at a quick and spartan meal with his officers and aides, Noah laid out plans for the following day. Only half of the force he had brought with him had landed on Siriki, where they were setting up bases around the planet. The rest of the Aopoddae warships and smaller fighter craft patrolled the skies and orbital space, constantly on the alert for any HibAdu threat.

That evening, Noah retired to his quarters, just down the corridor from Princess Annyette. But in the entryway to his suite, while he was bidding good evening to Subi, the adjutant suddenly flashed a military hand communication to him—a brief flicker of the fingers that contained a private message: "Remain alert. Perhaps it's only a reaction to the food, but my gut is starting to act up."

With a blink of his eyes, Noah acknowledged, and entered the opulent suite. For half an hour, he sat in a hard chair facing the door, with his ion pistol on his lap. Then, over his mobile comlink transceiver, he received a coded click-message from Subi: "I double-checked security. Stomach feeling a little better."

Subi had not yet provided a full security blessing, but Noah knew it was his adjutant's nature to be overly cautious, and he appreciated that about him. It was just Subi being Subi, Noah assured himself.

Keeping his sidearm with him, Noah crawled into bed. Then, after adjusting the mattress controls to their firmest setting, he lay awake in the darkness, worrying. Many uncertainties crowded his mind for attention as he lay on his back, and his mind scanned them, pausing on each topic of concern for varying lengths of time. Gradually, his thoughts drifted to the skin changes on his arms and torso, how those areas had become rough to the touch and darker, like a smaller version of podship skin. With his hands, which had not changed yet, he felt the coarse skin on his chest, and traced the limits of the metamorphosis to the side, under the left arm. He heaved a deep sigh of resignation. Whatever was happening to him had at least slowed, and he was thankful for that. Thus far, though he had considered it many times, he had not consulted a doctor. None of them would know what he had anyway.

I am like no other person who was ever born, he thought.

Gradually the pockets of worry emptied their contents, and he drifted off to sleep. Noah dreamed about many of the women he had known in his life. In the cloud of his consciousness he heard the voices of his mother, Eunicia, calling his name and of his sister in her frail, manipulative endearing way. Noah had loved his mother dearly, and had been as devastated as his father when she died in a grid-plane crash. In contrast, his sister, Francella, had not seemed to care about her one way or the other. She'd only been concerned about her own needs, which prevented her from seeing anything outside herself clearly.

Now, even though he tried to prevent it, Noah saw Francella's twisted, angry face and heard her unwelcome tones as she ranted at him in a way that made him want to be anywhere else in the universe except with her. Suddenly, a more pleasant voice intervened—that of Tesh Kori, murmuring to him that she had loved him from the moment she first set eyes on him. In the peculiar chimera of his dream he thought this rang true, but he also knew that she had never actually said that to him. She seemed to care for him deeply in a way that Noah had never known from anyone else, but their relationship remained largely unfulfilled. Even the one sexual liaison they'd shared had been surreal—more dreamlike than real, though she had insisted afterward that it actually had occurred.

It was like that now, as he heard other female voices close by—voices that did not seem to be coming from mouths, but instead seemed to be carried in another realm. One of them said in a discomforting tone, "After this, Watanabe, you'll sleep even more peacefully."

As if shocked out of his dream, Noah came to full awareness and opened his eyes. In the darkness, his fingers found the handle and trigger button of the ion pistol.

Across the room, he saw shadows moving. Four Human shapes, coming toward him stealthily, not making a sound, not saying anything. His finger tightened on the trigger, ready to press down. But he hesitated, uncertain of the meaning of the words he had just heard, or if this was really happening. Besides, he had proven numerous times in the past that he could not be physically harmed, at least not easily.

The corridor burst open, and the blue light of puissant pistol fire filled the room. The shadowy figures, all slender and dressed in black, dropped to the floor with anguished cries. Noah rolled off the bed on the opposite side, and crawled around for a better view.

He saw Subi Danvar just inside the doorway, with a steady stream of MPA soldiers pouring into the room. "Secure the premises," Subi barked. "Noah? You okay?"

"I'm fine. What the hell happened?" He rose to his feet and looked at the carnage on the floor.

Princess Annyette, in a hooded black leotard, lay wounded, beside three of her sisters, also dressed in black, and motionless. Purple fluid pooled around them on the marbelite tiles and Sirikan carpets, and poison-tipped daggers lay near their hands.

"Mutatis!" Noah said.

The Annyette simulacrum looked up at him and contorted her face in hatred. Noah heard words from her clearly, but in the alternate realm that he knew Subi and the others could not hear. Her mouth did not move as she said to Noah, "Maybe we didn't get you this time, but there will be many more like us to test the limits of your mortality. You will never be able to close your eyes again."

The words meshed with what he heard in his dream-fugue. Had she whispered the earlier threat, or had he read her mind?

Then, as if giving way to an irresistible force, her body turned into a fleshy pudding, devoid of all Human qualities. Her companions, for whatever reason, remained in Human form, but bled the telltale purple of the shapeshifter race.

"Our men rescued the real sisters from a compound where they were being held," Subi said. "As for these, they've taken their story with them."

"And Hari'Adab is supposed to be our ally?" Noah said.

"I was thinking the same thing," Subi said. "We're rounding up everyone on the palace grounds now, and will force them to submit to testing. We're also searching every corner with heat sensors, looking for any living beings. This security sweep will be much more thorough than I was able to do before."

"I guess no one is ever above suspicion," Noah said. "Except for you, my friend. You have Parais d'Olor?"

"She's the first one we took into custody."

"Good. Get an immediate report off to Doge Anton, and tell him to check carefully on the boyfriend's activities. Already, Hari'Adab is being monitored, and it's a good thing we made that decision. Now, we must dig even deeper."

Subi saluted stiffly, and went about his tasks, after leaving a new guard detail to accompany Noah.

* * * * *

Unable to remain in his suite while the entire palace was undergoing searches and tests, Noah felt a need to be alone for a few minutes. He sensed something intruding on his thoughts, and needed to collect himself, in an attempt to assess whatever was occurring.

On impulse, he hurried up a narrow back stairway that led to the top levels of the fortresslike core of the structure. On top of the keep, he at first looked down at the ornamental gardens, which were illuminated in bright lights while his forces bustled about in their duties.

Gazing up at the night sky, he found himself unable to perceive much detail, because of the glow of lights from the ground. Then, gradually, the noises of his troops and the effect of the illumination diminished, so that he could make out star systems and the pinpoint lights of his own ships as they patrolled the air and orbital space.

At any moment, the HibAdus could break through from deep space and mount a full-scale attack on Siriki. But Noah Watanabe continued to sense something else out there that was even more perilous, and which had not yet been considered. Something that would dwarf every other danger that he or his allies had faced.

I must be ready, Noah told himself. *But for what?*

Like a man awaiting a signal from God, he stood there for minute after minute, gazing heavenward. Nothing came to him, and he felt very alone.

Almost fifteen minutes passed. Finally, knowing he needed to tend to important military duties involving the Sirikan sector, he hurried downstairs. At least he would accomplish what he could, what he knew. It was a degree of control over his surroundings, albeit a small one.

Chapter Twenty-Nine

If there ever was a time to not sleep, this is it. Against all barriers, physical or mental and internal or external, we must press on, reaching deep into the reservoir of our collective racial strength. There will be time enough for rest later, if anything remains of the galaxy.

— First Elder Kre'n, to departing repair teams

Out of his podship, Eshaz stood alone on a floating asteroid, having allowed his craft to drift nearby in the vacuum of space, without any Tulyan at the controls. The podship, *Agryt*, remained in telepathic contact with him in the wordless manner of such relationships, and Eshaz had every confidence that the vessel would do its part, and would remain close by. Some of the other vessels in his repair team were visible around the sector, with some of them like dots to his naked eye, and others beyond the range of his vision. But Eshaz and Agryt knew where all of them were, and what they were doing.

Almost a million years ago, Eshaz had piloted podships to uncounted sectors of the known galaxy, and in the normal course of his duties he had seen all manner of star systems, nebulas, asteroid belts, comets, and other heavenly formations. In those halcyon days the trips had been frequent, at a time when the Tulyan race led their fabled existence of maintaining the galactic infrastructure in the manner that the Sublime Creator originally intended. It had been Eshaz's duty to deliver a single onboard caretaking crew to various destinations. Caretaking ships and crews operated in a more predictable fashion in those days. There had been many vessels, and an air of responsibility that caused everyone to perform excellent work, without the sense of dire urgency that all Tulyans felt now.

To Eshaz, it all seemed to spiral downward when the free will granted to all galactic races altered the Sublime Creator's grand plan. Then, in a terrible series of strikes with telepathic weapons, the Parviis had taken the entire podship fleet away from the Tulyans, a loss that continued for hundreds of thousands of years. The Dark Epoch.

Now, at long last, the Liberator fleet had made a successful attack on the Parvii Fold, and podships had been returned to their rightful custodians. As a result, the excited Eshaz had an opportunity to make much more of a difference than he ever had before, even in those long-ago days when he had been so satisfied with his life and fulfilled an important ecological niche for the interconnected galaxy.

Based upon his experience and qualifications, Eshaz was being entrusted to command one of the larger repair teams. In that position he would employ his skills as part of the larger Tulyan project—in coordination with many other teams—to repair the wounded, dying galaxy. Certainly the industrious Tulyans faced a daunting task, and Eshaz realized that he and his crew could accomplish only a limited amount. All of the Tulyan teams, large and small, would need to work rapidly and efficiently, moving from one trouble spot to the next, following prioritized astronomical charts and work schedules that had been provided for them by the Council of Elders. These charts and schedules were constantly being updated, as conditions required.

Under Eshaz's sphere of responsibility, if he completed the first tier of emergency repairs, he was to move on to the next, and the next, and the next. It would require a great deal of stamina for his crews to keep going without any meaningful rest, but Eshaz—and everyone with him—had vowed to do their parts....

The asteroid on which the dedicated Tulyan stood, which normally might be expected to drift or hurtle through the cosmos, was at the moment hung up on barely perceptible strands of torn and disintegrating Timeweb webbing. He knew from Tulyan laboratory reports that this was exactly the sort of damage that had been caused—or at least exacerbated—by the undercarriages of HibAdu lab-pods as they sped along the galactic infrastructure. He hoped that Noah, Anton, and Hari were having military success against the careless, predatory HibAdus, and that they were able to destroy or ground the artificial podships, preventing them from causing such widespread ecological damage.

All of the Tulyan repair teams, spread as they were around the galaxy, were exposed to HibAdu interference and possible attacks. The Tulyans had conventional and telepathic weaponry on all of their own podships, but against such formidable fighters as the HibAdus, that might prove inadequate. Thus far, Eshaz had not seen any sign of them, though other teams had reported to the starcloud that they saw HibAdu scouts, and large-scale military movements against other targets, focusing on Human and Mutati star systems. To this point, the HibAdu military forces had not gone after the Tulyan repair teams, but the Tulyans were constantly on the alert.

Now, standing on the asteroid, Eshaz opened his hands and scattered green dust onto the problem area. Then, extending his clenched fists upward, he uttered an ancient incantation designed to cure this defect.

As he waited to see if the treatment would work, Eshaz felt like an artist on a scaffold, a Michelangelo of sorts, but working on the ceiling of the galaxy instead of in the Sistine Chapel. Moments passed, and to his satisfaction the asteroid began to break free, and with his alternate vision he saw the web strands reattaching themselves, healing. One task completed among many.

Agryt drifted close by, parallel to the motion of the asteroid. Eshaz leaped onto the back of the podship, and then dropped down through a hatch.

These were days without end, of moving from one crisis spot to the next, for as long as the Tulyans could sustain themselves to complete the immense tasks they had undertaken. Eshaz felt part of a larger whole, and a larger importance. He felt no fatigue and knew he never would, not as long as he maintained his focus.

Like a patient on a vast hospital bed, the galaxy kept breathing fitfully. Eshaz only hoped it was not a deathbed.

Chapter Thirty

Many take credit for successes, but are nowhere to be found when it is time to assess blame.

—Anonymous

The Eye of the Swarm could not determine when or where his race had slipped onto the path of disaster, or how much he might have contributed to it personally. After the initial shock of realization, he had tried to diminish his personal responsibility for what had gone wrong, convincing himself that he had only done what other leaders had done before him.

But he realized quickly that this was utter foolishness. To correct the present situation, he first had to fully admit his own culpability, and then find a way to resurrect ancient Parvii glories. As long as his people lived and were capable of breeding, the restoration of the fallen race remained a possibility, albeit a faint one.

The after-effects of the cataclysm were all around him now, and apparent to anyone. His once magnificent Parvii swarms—decillions of individuals—now amounted to less than one hundred and ninety-four thousand.

But after creating the telepathic bubble in which the remaining population could huddle without detection from outside, there had been some welcome signs of improvement. The death rate had slowed, and inside the comparative warmth of the invisible enclosure one of the latent breeding specialists was returning to consciousness at this very moment and was expected to join Yurtii, the latent war priest who had recently become aware of his ancient identity. In these two and in the five remaining latents, the future of the Parvii race hung. His people needed to fight back, but to accomplish that they first needed their numbers to increase dramatically.

And something more occurred to him now. It was important. *Next time, I will divide the swarms into independent telepathic divisions,* Woldn thought. *That could help prevent the massive die-off that we experienced. Of course, it will mean sharing my power—or at least delegating some of it—but perhaps that is important to do.*

Increasingly, it seemed to him that the old ways, while revered and magical in the collective memories of his people, might not always be best. The Parviis, he realized, had been in a long and gradual decline, and the results of their cumulative weakness now placed them on the brink of extinction.

Like a parent observing the birth of a child, Woldn watched a naked boy emerge from the protected cluster of Parviis at the core of the swarm. It was not a new birth, at least not in the physical sense, but mentally and spiritually it was entirely new. And entirely old. Though their telepathic linkage, Woldn learned the ancient name of the breeding specialist that was coming back to consciousness: *Imho.*

Again, as with the war priest Yurtii earlier, the name was at first unfamiliar to Woldn, meaning that this was not one of the most famous of the ancients. But it was someone of significance, anyway, a highly valued breeding expert.

Looking at Woldn, the child blinked his eyes and said, "Knowledge is power, but only if used properly. Otherwise, it can be a curse." His slender body trembled slightly.

"Already you are wiser than I," Woldn said with a smile. He paused, sensing an ancient stirring in the minds of the other latent breeding specialists, like psychic creatures coming out of a long hibernation.

But the other latent war priest, huddled with them, had no ancient thoughts. So far, he was only a modern boy. At least he was holding steady physically. For a time his host body had declined precipitously. But then, on the verge of death, he had rallied. Perhaps—and Woldn had no proof of this—it was because an ancient being wanted to come back. Maybe it would be one of the great war priests, as Yurtii had suggested.

"I feel the flow," Imho said, "breeding data surging into my mind, a flood of it." He paused, and his face filled with a beatific reverie.

One of the older females flew close to the boy. She wrapped a warm blue cloak around him, then guided him over to where Yurtii looked on. Woldn dared to feel a surge of hope. The two of them were of different specializations, but in ancient times war priests and breeding specialists had worked closely together, albeit in much larger numbers.

For the Parviis, the present challenge was all about numbers, and about developing them as rapidly as possible. More bodies and minds meant more power, for only in multitudes could the devastatingly violent telepathic weapons of old be resurrected.

Breeding and war, with each specialization feeding necessarily upon the other. Historically it had been true with many races, and so too with the Parviis. It was a nice balance of life and death, an exquisite concept, and truly beautiful in the application.

With renewed determination, Woldn probed telepathically to the core of the clustered Parviis, to the four latent breeding specialists and the one latent war priest there.

At long last, the second war priest began to stir, along with the other breeding specialists....

Chapter Thirty-One

We are each of us only seconds away from committing violence.

—Ancient saying

Moments before the emergency on the mini-sub, the Hibbil had been staring at patterns of freckles and moles on the sides of Lorenzo del Velli's neck, visible in cabin illumination whenever the gray-haired old man turned his head one way or the other. For some reason, Pimyt had never noticed the patterns previously, but as the boat proceeded through murky underwater darkness, he became fixated on them.

His red-eyed gaze moved upward, along the side of the man's face and back down again. A hand came into view as Lorenzo gestured with it while speaking to one of the two Red Beret soldiers seated at the front, the larger man who was not piloting the sub. Lorenzo's hand had more flesh-fat than the Hibbil had noticed previously, and he felt saliva building in his mouth. An involuntary, anticipatory response that Pimyt had usually suppressed before, trying to put such primal urges out of his mind. But now, in this remote subterranean region of an unnamed planet, new possibilities seemed open to him. Actions he had not dared to seriously consider before, whenever he and Lorenzo interacted over the years.

Prior to the recent turn of events, Pimyt had been focused inward, on the schemes of the HibAdu Coalition and on the important role he played in them. In conjunction with that, he'd been forced to deal with the constant demands of this difficult Human nobleman, doing so in a manner that would keep Lorenzo from noticing the Hibbil's true intentions. Playing his part with consummate skill, Pimyt had remained near the important merchant prince, poised to take him prisoner the moment the Coalition was ready to make their move.

Now, for all Pimyt knew, HibAdu forces had already made their attacks on merchant prince and shapeshifter planets. Just before the space station hurtled into this unknown realm, his military leaders had been saying that an important announcement was imminent. If the attacks had been made, or were underway now, certain opportunities might already be available to him. His gaze moved to the two soldiers at the front, especially to the heavyset one on the right who was talking with Lorenzo. Pimyt visualized blood gushing from the severed arteries of all three Humans, and their startled eyes as they looked at the vicious Hibbil and wondered what was happening to them.

I'm much faster than they realize, Pimyt thought. *In the blink of an eye, I could kill all of them.*

The moisture buildup in his mouth increased, but he forced control over himself, having second thoughts that he might not be able to pilot the sub adequately in this underground waterway. His carnivorous pleasures would have to wait. He smiled to himself, though. It had been fun letting his imagination run for a while.

Suddenly Pimyt became aware of the mini-sub shooting forward, and the engines being thrown into reverse. The pilot issued a volley of curses. Through the windshield, Pimyt saw filtered light ahead, and realized that they were back on the surface of the water again, with a very high cavern ceiling above them.

"Waterfall!" the soldier beside him shouted.

The engines surged and tugged, but the vessel kept going forward, caught in a powerful current. The sound of the engines intensified and increased in pitch, until finally they seemed to catch hold of something. The sub went backward slowly, and veered to one side, toward the bank. On this section, the stream had become a river, and was considerably wider than their embarkation point.

As the pilot guided the craft toward a low shelf of rock on one side, Pimyt gazed in astonishment at a huge subterranean cavern that dwarfed the waterfall and the tiny vessel. The cavern appeared to be illuminated from within, with eerie, pale blue light coming from crystalline walls and stalactite deposits that hung like icicles from above. Across the waterway he saw what looked like another waterfall drop-off, undoubtedly tumbling like the nearer one into a pool somewhere far below.

The mini-sub slid up onto the rock shelf, and came to a safe stop. Relieved for the moment, they all got out of the vessel and walked around in the strange blue illumination, looking up at the luminous ceiling in wonder, gasping in awe at something they'd never seen before.

Abruptly, the rock shook around them, and stalactites began to fall from the ceiling, crashing around them on the rocky floor and splashing into the water. "Quick!" Pimyt yelled. "Back in the sub, or we'll be trapped here!"

As they ran for the vessel, a stalactite smashed down on the larger Red Beret soldier, crushing him to death. Dodging and leaping over debris, the three others hurried back to the sub. They slid the craft back into the water and boarded. Within moments, the hatch was closed and they were underway, submerging as far as they could and going back the way they had come.

To Pimyt, the return trip seemed interminable. Chunks of rock kept falling into the water, as if an enemy was dropping depth charges from above, trying to hit them. The pilot had to make evasive maneuvers, but one of the pieces glanced off the hull, sending them off course. Still, he recovered quickly, and they continued on.

Finally, the pilot confirmed their location from the instruments and surfaced at the embarkation point, in the narrow stretch of waterway. With the ground still shaking, the desperate trio—with Pimyt in the lead—scrambled out and ran up the ramp of dirt to the surface.

The Hibbil was considerably faster than his companions, which elicited a breathless reprimand from Lorenzo: "Slow down, Pimyt … and make sure I get out!"

Pimyt ignored him, but heard the soldier say, "I'll help you, Sire." The slender Red Beret had remained back with the merchant prince.

Sputtering in anger, Lorenzo continued up the slope.

When all three of them were at the top, the former doge started into a harangue at Pimyt, but fell silent when the ground shook even harder, and the hole closed behind them. Over at the landing site, the shuttle hovered just above the ground, awaiting the return of the exploration team.

The shaking intensified, but the shuttle set down on the ground again anyway, where it rocked and threatened to topple over. Six soldiers jumped out and helped Lorenzo, Pimyt, and the submarine pilot onto the shuttle. Without further delay, the craft lifted into the sky.

Gazing out a porthole, Pimyt felt the engines running roughly, so that the pilot had to rev them higher to keep going up. He watched the ground shudder and change shape below. And above, where they were headed, Pimyt saw the lights of the space station flickering on and off.

Then, in a bright green flash, the space station disappeared.

Chapter Thirty-Two

The universe is the brain of God.

—Ancient saying

"Y ou boys keep your eyes open, all right?" Subi Danvar said. "Noah is worried about you." The adjutant had taken time away from his busy schedule to see Dux and Acey off as they prepared to leave the palace grounds.

"We can take care of ourselves," Acey said, sticking out his chin with determination. He and his cousin wore variweather coats that were adaptable to temperature and weather changes, and small backpacks.

They stood by the main entry gate, where Red Beret robots stood guard. Nearby, other robots and Humans looked on, waiting to talk with Subi.

The rotund man frowned. He looked up as a squadron of MPA patrol aircraft flew overhead, then said, "I'm sending someone with you. All of us think a lot of you, so we've assigned one of our machines to accompany you."

He gestured, and a small, dull brown robot approached, with green and yellow lights flashing around its face plate. Dux noticed that some of the lights weren't working, and saw a number of dents on the body. That didn't necessarily mean anything, or it could suggest a lack of recent servicing.

"This is Kekur," Subi said. "He served with great distinction under Jimu, and he will be of great use to you."

"Is he armed?" Dux asked, noting compartments on the robot's body, where weapons might be carried.

"Of course," Subi said. "To avoid calling attention to him, he bears no military markings or indications, but he is in fact a soldier."

"We can take care of ourselves," Acey said. "We don't need a metal bodyguard."

"To the contrary, we have intelligence information that HibAdu remnants are still on Siriki. They're hiding out, waiting to be found by their comrades, or waiting to regroup."

"We can scout around for you, then," Dux said.

The adjutant nodded. "Right. You're still on duty. Transmit messages to us through the robot."

"I am your servant," Kekur said.

"So we're spies now," Dux said.

Acey grunted, a sound that Dux recognized as agreement.

When the robot arrived, Acey flipped open a control panel on its chest. Apparently he had noticed the same potential deficiencies as Dux. Then he said, "Okay, this will give me something to tinker with when I'm bored. I always have a few tools with me."

"I don't need any adjustment," Kekur said. The lights on his faceplate blinked faster, but some of them were still out.

"Everything will be fine as long as you follow our commands," Acey said.

"I am your servant," Kekur repeated.

"There are certain things he won't do," Subi said.

"Such as?" Dux asked.

"He has one of our enhanced security programs, so he won't follow risky commands, anything that, in his estimation, could put the two of you in increased danger."

"What if we want to override him?" Acey asked.

"Not possible," Kekur said.

"Can we still do what *we* want?" Dux asked Subi.

The robot answered. "As your servant, I would not prevent you from going into danger, but I would warn you before taking countermeasures. Then, if you insist on being foolhardy, I will do whatever I can to protect you."

"You must do so without trying to block us," Acey said with a grin.

"Only if possible," Kekur said. The faceplate lights dimmed, then went off as his transitional programming settled down.

* * * * *

"I guess Noah doesn't think we can do much to help," Acey said. Staring out the window of the hoverbus, he brushed a hand through his bristly black hair. "I didn't think he'd agree to let us go so easily. I mean, if we were key people, he would have begged for us to stay."

Seated beside him, Dux said, "You're the one who said we're just a couple of kids and no one will miss us. Besides, we must have some value, or they wouldn't have sent Kekur to watch out for us."

The robot was seated across the aisle from them. A handful of Sirikan citizens sat in other seats, chatting nervously about difficulties they had been experiencing since the HibAdus first attacked.

"Well, cousin," Dux said, "we are young, and we have been a bit flighty in the past, jumping from one galactic adventure to another."

"We returned to the Guardians, didn't we? That means we have some staying power after all."

Dux smiled. "You surprise me, Acey. You're talking like I do." He nudged the shorter, more muscular boy. "Maybe I should play your part from now on— the aggressive one, the one who's always getting us into trouble. You can be the cerebral one."

"This time it was your idea, cousin."

Dux felt a little guilty about making the special request to see their grandmother, since the boys wanted to contribute what they could to the war effort. But they had to find out if she was all right. The old woman lived in the back country, without modern conveniences. They had no way to contact her without going to see her. She was a feisty old bird, though....

"Say," Acey said. "What are you smiling about?"

"Was I? Uh, I was just thinking about the time Grandmamá chased us around her yard with a stick."

"I remember, because we accidentally ran over her vegetable garden with that aircar we stole. Boy, was she mad!"

"*We* stole? You were driving, Acey, and it was your idea to steal it. I was trying to get you to slow down and take it back."

"Nobody slows me down, buddy."

"Just wait 'til Grandmamá gets ahold of you."

Acey flushed. "You've got a point there."

* * * * *

Noah stood in an opulent library that contained shimmering holobooks on simulated shelves, the personal collection of Princess Meghina. While waiting for Subi Danvar and his top military officers to report for a meeting, he scanned the titles. To his surprise, several of them were about environmental issues, and he recognized a number of the titles. A large number of other books were about animal welfare.

He recalled seeing the famous courtesan more than six months ago on the pod station where he was taken prisoner by Red Berets. Meghina had tried to prevent Francella from shooting him. The few times he had met the Princess, she had always been kind to him. Now, in one of her private rooms, he felt her kindness, her concern for the environment, for animals, and the compassion she had showed toward him.

Only half conscious of what he was doing, Noah rubbed the back of his neck, beneath the collar where his skin had been getting thick and rough. For several days now the areas of coarse skin had slowed their expansion, and thus far they had not appeared anywhere that people could easily notice. Just the day before, he had finally confided in Subi Danvar about his condition, and the adjutant had suggested that he see a doctor. Noah refused, saying he was too busy for that, and swore him to secrecy....

In the library, time seemed to slow around Noah, and his thoughts drifted. He envisioned himself out in space, at first inside a podship as it sped along a podway, a strand of galactic webbing. Then, as moments passed, he felt the irregular skin seem to cover his entire body. Then his face merged into the flesh of the podship, and appeared on the prow of the vessel. With his own eyes and the optic sensors on the hull of the podship, he saw far into the galaxy. He was back in Timeweb.

This metamorphosis felt supremely comfortable to him, and very familiar. As moments passed, questions seeped into his mind, and he wondered if he had always been this ancient podship. If he was the oldest of spacefaring creatures, perhaps this explained why—even in Human form—he had come up with the concept of galactic ecology, of planets and star systems interconnected in one large environment.

As he surged through space, Noah suddenly felt himself buffeted, so that he could hardly remain on the podway infrastructure. He slowed way down, and then came to a stop in space.

A timestorm is coming, he thought, with a sudden awareness of information that had not been available to him previously. Timeweb didn't seem so alien to him anymore. He was part of it, and it was part of him.

Space warped around the podship, an immense flexing back and forth. Noah did all he could to remain on the webbing. Just ahead, a planet came into view, and its name surfaced in his consciousness: Yaree. It was one of the unaligned worlds, where numerous galactic races coexisted.

Beyond the planet, a jagged hole appeared in space, a spot of black-blackness, so intensely dark that it was readily visible to him. Gradually the hole shifted, grew larger, and he saw a bright flash of green light inside it.

As he stared, transfixed, Noah detected an illuminated object coming toward him from the hole in space, going at a very high rate of speed. As it came into his visual range, he realized, in amazement, what it was.

EcoStation! The orbital facility that had once been his, and which Doge Lorenzo had commandeered for his own purposes.

As if drawn by a magnet, the space station rushed toward Noah at an apparent speed that should have torn it apart. But it held together and drew closer. Entranced, Noah watched it, unable to move.

Just when the space station seemed about to slam into him, it suddenly slowed and floated in space, not far away. The facility, though largely intact, was badly dented, as if it was an ocean-going vessel that had survived a hurricane. Some of its modules had split open, and loose contents and other parts spilled out into the weightless void, along with bodies. Concerned, Noah guided his podship-self in that direction, to do what he could. But something resisted his forward movement and reduced his speed, like a powerful current going against him.

I think the space station was in the undergalaxy and now it's back, Noah thought, as he made slow headway.

But he realized that he knew very little about the adjacent galaxy, only that timeholes in the membrane between the two realms provided occasional glimpses. And he recalled an earlier vision, in which he had seen a small Parvii swarm hiding in the other galaxy, near the bolt hole they had used to escape from their sacred fold. Assuming the vision had been accurate, he had always wondered what had happened to them.

Now, as he drew near the space station and its widening debris field, the timehole sealed over behind them, and vanished from view. Then everything became hazy, just a wash of gray-blackness in all directions.

Noah blinked his eyes, and found himself back on Siriki, standing in the private library. He watched as Subi Danvar and other uniformed officers filed into the room for their scheduled meeting.

I'm not going crazy, Noah told himself. He had been through such paranormal shifts before, and although they never felt entirely comfortable to him, he was getting more used to them.

But he was still left with an uncountable number of unanswered questions.

Chapter Thirty-Three

War is like a lover. It lures you, embraces you, and rejects you. It lifts you up and tears you down—and just when you think you can stand no more of it, you plunge back into the fray.

—General Nirella del Velli, Supreme General of the MPA

Upon arriving at Canopa at the head of a fleet of twelve thousand podships, Doge Anton had seen Lorenzo del Velli's space station vanish into space, in a bright burst of green. One of the Tulyans with the fleet reported that it went into a timehole.

More than a week had passed since then, during which the unopposed Liberator forces solidified their military hold on the planet. For this critical mission, the young leader had selected the best fighters and warships, and every soldier was anxious to go into battle against the enemy.

"The silence is weird," Nirella said. She and her husband stood on the bridge of the flagship *Webdancer*, looking out into orbital space and down at the world below. In the time they'd been here, there had been very few HibAdu sightings. Less than a hundred Hibbils and Adurians had been captured, and only a handful of small military aircraft. There had been no sightings of enemy lab-pods at all, though many were reported to have been in the Canopa system before the arrival of Anton's rescue force.

It was very unsettling to him. The HibAdus had used an immense fleet of podships to attack and conquer almost every Human and Mutati world. But where were all of those vessels now? He had been exchanging urgent messages with Noah at Siriki and with the loyal robot Jimu at Dij—messages that were relayed through Tulyan webtalkers. Aside from a brief battle at Siriki when Noah arrived, the conditions were much the same at all three planets. Very few HibAdus sightings at all, and only a few hundred soldiers captured in all.

At distant Dij, Human military officers and the robot Jimu were keeping a close watch over Hari'Adab, and despite the Mutati troubles on Siriki they reported no reason to suspect the Mutati leader of any form of deception. Without his knowledge, other Mutatis had schemed to assassinate Noah.. Arriving at the only unconquered Mutati world, the Emir had been greeted by his people as a returning hero. They had staged parades and other accolades for him, but in a public broadcast he had asked them not to waste their energies in such frivolous ceremonies.

"We need to remain on constant alert," Hari'Adab had told them in a speech broadcast to every corner of the planet. "We can never let our guard down again."

For the moment, the three military forces were in holding patterns, ready to defend each of their remaining worlds, and awaiting further commands from Doge Anton about when to move on to other worlds and attempt to take them back from the Coalition.

Now, as Anton stood with Nirella, she said to him, "You and I are married, but I don't know if we'll ever get our lives back, at least not the way they used to

Brian Herbert

be. It's the same with the MPA and Mutati worlds: even if we get them all back, they can never be what they once were, can never have the peace and serenity they once enjoyed."

"The enemy is waiting for us out there," Anton said, as he gazed into space. "But where?"

He noticed a flare of anger on her face, which he knew was because he had not responded to her personal observation. Then she said, "Hard to say. Our scout ships are out, but they haven't found anything yet."

"We could be sitting ducks here," he said. "It hard to know the right thing to do. With the size of their forces, we don't dare break up our fleet any more. We're strongest here, and at Siriki, and at Dij. For some reason, the HibAdus couldn't conquer any of those worlds before, and now—with all the reinforcements we brought in—it will be even harder."

"You're being optimistic. They were just spread too thin, and are gathering again. I'm afraid they did this to draw us in. Like a spider with three webs."

"Could be, but we've discussed the possibilities, the odds, the options. I think the HibAdus know we commandeered more than a hundred and twenty thousand podships from the Parviis, and—if the HibAdus are watching all three of these planets—they're only seeing a total of twenty-four thousand podships. They could be wondering where the other ninety-six thousand are."

The General half smiled. "I hope you're right, and they think we're laying a trap for them, waiting to pounce with a bigger force."

"So we each wait, and wonder."

Chapter Thirty-Four

Just as our galaxy is linked by an invisible web, so is it with our individual lives. From birth to death, we interact with one another in complex ways, never seeing the intricate strands woven around us.

—Tesh Kori, ruminations on the meaning of galactic life

Throughout the immense structure, stationary machines hummed, whirred, and clicked as they produced new instruments, robots, and robotic components. The factory had once been owned by the famous inventor Jacopo Nehr, but following his assassination it was no longer the property of any Human.

From his place of concealment, the tiny sentient robot identified the sounds, and knew exactly what was going on out on the floor, even though he could not see anything at all. He was immersed in darkness.

Ipsy recalled being told that Nehr had taken extra care in the design of the facility, and had refused to proceed with ground breaking or construction until the production line schematics and computerized projections were absolutely perfect. For months, Nehr had worked with industrial architects, production line designers, and robotics technicians, but they had been unable to meet his exacting standards for the production lines. He required that the lines operate at extremely high rates of speed, producing items quickly, and always of the highest quality.

One of the biggest problems facing him had been that computer projections told him he would have to slow the lines down to get the quality of finished items that he wanted. Stubbornly, he had refused to accept this. The lines had to be fast, and everything that came out of the factory had to be absolutely perfect. He required the finest materials, with tolerances and efficiencies that the experts said were impossible.

Even though Nehr's name was tainted now, he had once been something of a fabled figure to the sentient machines. And according to legend, after months of working on the details of the factory and wrangling about how to get it functioning, Nehr had gone to bed one night feeling angry and frustrated. In the middle of the night, he sat straight up and started reciting the details, as if from a robotics program. Fortunately, he'd had the foresight to rig video recording machines up in all of the places he frequented. Even in his bedroom.

In a trancelike state, the inventor had dictated the whole thing, and had even made detailed drawings on an electronic note pad. Everything had flowed, and it had all been brilliantly correct, down to the smallest detail. Afterward, with his modifications, the computer projections showed that the manufacturing process would meet every one of his exacting standards. Soon afterward, construction had proceeded and Nehr's factories became the most efficient ever devised.

For a time, as long as he held political and economic power, Nehr and his legal teams had controlled where and when the factories would be built, and all were under his ownership. However, based on what Ipsy had learned about the HibAdu Coalition from eavesdropping on a pair of Hibbils, he had now run a probability program. It told him that the Hibbils and their Adurian allies had undoubtedly constructed numerous major factories like this one elsewhere, secretly using Nehr's methods to produce war materiel. The death of the inventor would have made the task even easier.

In his dark cocoon, the robot couldn't wait to get back into action. The weapon-control box in which the little robot concealed himself was sitting on a shelf in a warehouse section designated for emergency-only replacement parts, and this particular panel might not be needed at all for a long time. Other panels like it were not breaking down in HibAdu warships, so it would take a miracle for Ipsy to make himself useful to Humans now.

During the time he had spent inside the panel, he had completed a number of additional repairs to his own internal mechanisms, so that his principal functions now worked reasonably well. But that didn't mean he could escape.

The panel had been tightly sealed from the outside, and he couldn't get out. Trapped, he could only crawl around inside.

Chapter Thirty-Five

I've always thought that there are degrees of goodness in all things, and degrees of badness, and that virtually every situation is a combination of the two. This is not to say that I am some sort of Pollyanna, that I live in a bubble of naïveté. Rather, it means that I try to see even the smallest glimmer of hope in the worst of circumstances, and the tiniest glimmer of virtue in the most vile of people. It helps me to cope.

—Princess Meghina of Siriki, private journals

This time, it was much worse.

Earlier, when the space station tumbled through the void into another star system, there had been only a few deaths, and most of the occupants had survived. Now, as Princess Meghina made her way through the corridors and rooms, she had to hold onto safety railings, since the gravitonics system was weak, and her feet floated just above the deck. It was freezing cold, with very hardly any oxygen in the air, but in her augmented physical state she did not shiver, and had no trouble breathing.

Though much of the lighting system still worked, damage to the station was extensive, with gaping holes into space. Bodies of Humans and other races were strewn around the interior, floating and bumping into one another. She had to push her way through them, one horror after another—past the death stares of people she had known as patrons of the Pleasure Palace or as servants. In corridors and rooms, there were bodies in disarray, bouncing around in the vacuum.

Her pet dagg was missing, and the more death she encountered, the more she feared the worst for him. As she hurried around, she called his name in increasing desperation, "Orga! Orga!"

But he didn't appear, didn't bark. Meghina felt too numb to cry.

Sometimes through glax floor plates and windows, she got views through broken clouds of a gray-blue planet, far below the space station. Occasionally, something would glint down there in pockets of sunlight, silvery flashes suggesting to her that there might be manmade structures or other objects there. It gave her some hope, some *connectedness* to living things. But to exactly what, she did not know.

After searching most of one multi-module deck and shouting for anyone who might remain alive, she encountered no one. There were still many more modules and decks to search, but she was likely to encounter even more fatalities in the other areas, which were much more densely inhabited than this one, where she and Lorenzo had apartments and other facilities for their private enjoyment. The very thought of the catastrophe nearly overwhelmed her, but she drew strength within, and continued on. She was sure that thousands of passengers had died from lack of oxygen, or had been hurtled to their deaths into deep space.

Gradually, the soles of her shoes began to touch the deck, and at the end of one corridor she found a new module where the gravity system functioned better, an area that contained no bodies. As she entered the module, however, the main door to the corridor slammed shut behind her, and she couldn't get it back open. The wall controls didn't function when she tapped the pressure pads, or when she tried to use override commands. She was cut off from the rest of the space station.

"Can anyone hear me?" she shouted in desperation. "Is anyone alive?"

But Princess Meghina sensed that she was all alone, and very likely the last survivor onboard. With her elixir-enhanced physical condition, she did not seem to need oxygen to breathe, and could not die. But what a terrible fate this would be for her, like a prisoner condemned to solitary confinement for eternity.

She stared out one of the large viewing windows into space, but saw only floating death out there. Grimly, she sat on a window seat, positioning herself so that she didn't have to look through any of the windows at the macabre graveyard outside. It was a sea of death out there. She wondered how much it had to do with strange rumors she had heard about cosmic deterioration, somehow tied to what Noah Watanabe and his radical environmentalists referred to as galactic ecology, some sort of connectivity between wide-ranging star systems. Though she had no reason to dislike Noah, and rather admired him for his independence, many of his ideas had always sounded far-fetched to her. But what if he was right after all? What else could explain the wild, perilous trips this space station had taken through space?

From her earliest years, Princess Meghina had been immersed in currents of change. Born a shapeshifter, she had not liked her natural Mutati form, and had always longed to be Human instead. In her early teens she had altered her bodily appearance to look the way she preferred, the guise of a beautiful blonde Human woman. Despite intense pressures from Mutatis, she kept the alteration in place for so long that her cellular structure actually locked into that appearance. Afterward, she could not have changed back, or into anything else, if she had wanted to. But that was no trouble from her perspective; she had always hated being a Mutati anyway.

Shunned by her family and Mutati society, she had escaped in one of the regularly scheduled podships that used to travel among the star systems, and she had gradually merged into Human civilization on the planet of Siriki, without revealing who she really was. Her new life had presented challenges. Wanting to start out at the same approximate age she had been as a Mutati—thirteen years old—she'd had to apply makeup carefully in order to take years off the age she had chosen to make herself look, which was of a Human woman of around thirty.

Fortunately, she had selected a beautiful, though neutral, face that, with a little clever application of skin tints and other products, could easily conceal its apparent age. Rather like that of a doll. Perhaps from her background as a shapeshifter who was accustomed to modifying her appearance, she proved to have a flair for applying treatments to her skin, and to selecting hair styles and clothes that made her look like a teenager. At a glittering costume ball, she met the powerful Doge Lorenzo del Velli, and soon he succumbed to her considerable charms. She became his consort, and he made her a Princess of the Realm. Then—only a short time after they met—he married her.

In that lofty and enviable position, Princess Meghina of Siriki had become one of the most powerful noblewomen in the Merchant Prince Alliance, even though she was not actually Human. Through clever subterfuge, she had falsified a series of pregnancies, making it look as if she had given birth to seven daughters. In reality, she had obtained each of the Human babies through surrogates, and a carefully woven tapestry of lies and pay-offs.

Ultimately, Meghina found herself immersed in even more changes, after she consumed an elixir and gained immortality—as did the four Humans and the Salducian. In that widely-publicized event, she and the others became famous and were considered the luckiest of people in the galaxy, like lottery winners. But through intrigues against her by Francella Watanabe and others, Meghina's hidden identity became known to the public. This had tilted the political balance against Lorenzo, and he had been forced out of office. Through it all, he had shown strength that she hadn't known he had, and he'd remained loyal and protective toward her. He had also adapted to a life of business instead of politics, focusing on constructing and promoting the Pleasure Palace, his orbital gambling casino.

In return, Meghina had remained devoted to him. Of course she still had her dalliances with other noblemen, and he did the same with an assortment of noble ladies. It was all part of the social circles in which the two of them ran. But they developed a new sense of understanding between them, and a mutual respect.

Now as she sat in her confined module, she worried about Lorenzo. He'd gone down to an unknown world to explore it, and had not returned. While he was gone, everything went upside down, and the space station had vaulted through space to yet another planet in another unknown solar system.

Hours passed in her confinement. Finally, hearing a thump behind her, she hesitated at first, not wanting to look at something grisly, a body out there bumping up against the space station. Then she heard another thump, followed by what sounded like knocking on the window plate.

Trembling, Meghina stood, and turning slowly, she looked through the window. To her amazement, she saw five people outside, their faces illuminated by lights from the space station. All of them wore jet packs but no spacesuits, and she quickly figured out why. These were the other elixir-immortals, including the Salducian, Kobi Akar, and a young Human woman she'd always liked, Betha Neider.

Meghina felt a surge of hope, but shouted, "I can't get out!"

At first they looked perplexed. Then one of the Humans—a corpulent man named Llew Jarro, nodded and mouthed the words, "I understand."

Soon his companions understood as well. They went away for several moments, then returned with a long girder that had broken loose from the space station. It looked odd for them to be handling such a large object, but they moved it around like an oversized toothpick in the weightlessness of space. After taking it several hundred meters from the space station, they turned on their jet packs to full power, shooting blue light from them, and surged toward Meghina at a high rate of speed.

Almost instinctively, though perhaps she didn't need to, Meghina ducked out of the way. The beam slammed into the window and made a spider web crack in the glax, but did not penetrate. Back they went for another try, and another, and yet another. In zero-g, she thought they might be moving the stranded space station. Finally, they broke through the window, creating an opening that was large enough for Meghina to swim through, into space.

For several moments, she floated and swam out there in the void, which was noiseless except for a barely audible, seemingly distant hum. At first it was colder to her than in the space station, but as moments passed, it did not bother her at all. Except for light from the station it was dark where they were, with the sun hidden by the planet.

Then Jarro gave her a jet pack. "Manned maneuvering unit," he explained as he helped her into it. His words made no sound to her ears, but she read his lips.

The Salducian pointed down at the planet with one of his crablike hands, and then rocketed toward it, leaving a streak of blue light behind him. His five companions followed.

As they entered the atmosphere, Meghina saw orange sparks of heat dancing around her, but felt none of it, due to an electronic shield generated by the jet pack. When they penetrated the cloud layer, Meghina made out the twinkling lights of a city below, with bridges across a river and large buildings. From the unique layout she realized that this was without question the city of Okk, capital of the unaligned world of Yaree. In what seemed like only one of her incarnations, she had traveled widely as a "Human" noblewoman, both on her own and with Lorenzo. In one of their business trips together, they had led a trade delegation to this mineral-rich world, to set up a commercial arrangement. The local ruler, a tall Ilkian named Wan Haqro, had been an attractive humanoid, with piercing blue eyes. He was not, however, a merchant prince, and by strict custom did not qualify for her attentions as a courtesan.

Now, to her alarm she saw the blue light of Akar's MMU pack flicker off below her as his power pack failed, and he began to drop like a stone. Then the same thing happened to Jarro, and to the others. Meghina's jet pack was the last to shut off. In a matter of moments, all six of them were tumbling toward the planet, in free fall.

The last thought Meghina had before blacking out was that this would be a true test of their immortality.

They crashed into buildings, hit motor vehicles and trees, and slammed into the ground. The carnage of their broken bodies was spread over portions of a four-block area.

Chapter Thirty-Six

Events occurred in the past that we cannot begin to imagine.

—Anonymous

Away from the Parvii Fold, Woldn was out of his comfort zone. As he led his small swarm out onto the podways, he was very nervous. Less than a hundred and ninety-four thousand individuals remained in his entire race, a proud people that once counted their numbers in the decillions. Not so long ago, Parvii swarms had been in every sector of the known galaxy, and the Eye of the Swarm had been in telepathic contact with them. They had been his distant eyes and ears, constantly reporting to him. Now he felt like a blind, deaf man, stumbling around in a vast chamber of stars, never knowing where his enemies or other perils were.

He knew it would be safer to remain back at the telepathic bubble, where all five breeding specialist latents had come to life and were beginning their important work of increasing the population. But Woldn had moved the bubble to a remote galactic sector, stationing only a small number of guards inside with the breeding specialists, who had come back to awareness along with the two war priests. The breeding specialists were already using genetic materials to produce future generations of Parviis. Before leaving, Woldn had been pleased to see three thousand Parvii embryos in incubation. Only an infinitesimal number by the standards of his race, but a beginning nonetheless.

It had been necessary to go back to the oldest of methods, all but starting over as a race. As part of that ancient formula for survival and advancement of the species, he needed podships, even if he could only capture a few and build from there.

Now Woldn stationed his mini-swarm along one of the main podway routes, waiting for ships to pass this way, so that he could overwhelm and capture them. He had just enough followers to commandeer one ship at a time, and when the first one was safely tucked away, they could move on to another, and another. His near-term goals were humble, but he had to make the effort. He could not just stand by and watch his race go extinct.

In the two millennia of his lifetime, Woldn had flown with his swarms to the farthest reaches of the known galaxy. In those days, Parviis had controlled a vast fleet of podships, a virtual monopoly that made them the most powerful and influential of all galactic races. The coin of the Parvii realm had not been monetary; rather it had been the extent of their domination over other galactic civilizations, and the extent that those peoples depended upon them. Because it was the pleasure of the Parvii race to provide podship service throughout the galaxy, and because it was the pleasure of the Eye of the Swarm to allow it to continue, it had.

Now, however, he found himself at the bottom of a spiral that had been spinning out of control. As much as Woldn hated to admit it, Noah Watanabe and the Tulyans had been right: the galactic infrastructure *had* been crumbling, decaying moment by moment. In the unique past position of the Parviis, swarming and piloting podships, Woldn's people had seen the subtle signs of decomposition for centuries, but had not wanted to admit what was really happening. Because to admit it meant only one thing: that they needed to allow the Tulyans to go back to their ancient tasks of maintaining the galaxy, of using their arcane methods to keep everything going behind the scenes. The Parvii leader had hoped it was just a natural cycle, and that it would eventually reverse itself. But the hoped-for reversal had not taken place.

Long ago, eons before Woldn was ever incubated and born, an ancient Eye of the Swarm scored a huge military victory against the Tulyans, and took the podship fleet away from them. In that single event, more than one hundred thousand sentient Aopoddae fell into the Parvii domain. Assuming the mantle of leadership long afterward, Woldn had just continued the old ways, using the might and power of the swarms to keep the podships going on their regular routes. He and other Parvii leaders before him had always considered themselves generous for continuing this tradition, providing it free of charge to all races—except Tulyans had been monitored in their travels and kept from regaining the ships.

But other races think of us selfish, Woldn thought. *They misunderstand us.*

"Podship coming," one of his followers said, transmitting the thought to him from close range. It was Vorlik, one of the two resurrected war priests. Though he reclaimed his old knowledge later than the other war priest (Yurtii), this one was the most famous of the pair. Vorlik had been among the most ferocious and successful of the ancients, and with each passing moment he seemed to increase in aggressiveness and hatred of outside races.

Now, through his Parviis, Woldn heard the Aopoddae coming. He sent the signal for readiness. He could tell that it was a strong wild pod, one that had never been captured.

At precisely the right moment, more than one hundred and ninety thousand Parviis swarmed around the podship as it sped along. For several seconds, the Parviis kept up, but they didn't have the energy to continue or to penetrate into the sectoid chamber, and they soon fell back without the prize.

To Woldn's dismay, only a few of his people even got neurotoxin stingers into the thick hull of the podship, and the effect had not slowed the big, dumb creature at all. It just kept going.

Even with this failure, Woldn reminded himself that his people had been recovering. In concert, they could fire telepathic energy blasts—not very large ones, but perhaps enough to stop a podship. However, Woldn hesitated using that technique. He didn't want to harm or kill any of the sentient spacecraft, and also feared setting off a reaction among all of the Aopoddae that would make them harder to capture. No, he should only utilize the traditional ways, pursuing podships at high rates of speed and using neurotoxins.

The Parviis waited for another ship. Hours passed. It wasn't like the old days, when podships were constantly going this way and that. Finally one appeared, and again the tiny humanoids gave chase. This time, they did just as poorly. Their stingers, which had always drugged podships in the past, weren't having any effect at all, and the flying speed of the Parviis—always faster than podships before—barely enabled them to keep up, and for only short distances.

In addition to the practical importance of recapturing podships, Woldn had gone on this hunt with another motivation. He had hoped to restore the confidence of his people and reduce their collective stress. But there had been an opposite effect. He sensed fear and panic in the ranks.

The Eye of the Swarm was deeply troubled, knowing his race must find a way to recuperate faster, or it would vanish entirely—a complete colony die-off. Too many galactic perils could kill them all if they weren't strong.

He searched his memory, and—telepathically—the minds of everyone in the swarm. According to the secret knowledge of his people, known only to the most elite groups, the Parviis of ancient times had some sort of a connection with the Adurians. He did not know the details, nor did any of his followers. All information was lost in the dusty archives of Parvii racial memory. But he'd been thinking about going to see the Adurians, in an effort to find out what, if anything, they knew. This podway had been selected with that idea in mind; it was on the way to the Adurian homeworld.

As Woldn hovered in space, looking in dismay at the swarm, he became aware of two strong intellects, so close to him that their brain waves lapped against his own thoughts and almost penetrated them against his will.

Turning, he saw both of the war priests dressed in the black robes of their cult, the stocky man Vorlik and the hairless boy Yurtii. They trembled in anger as they hovered there, demanding entrance into his thoughts. Secretly, he thought they might break through even without his permission, an unsettling realization. Nothing like that had ever happened to him before, and he found it irritating, almost unnerving.

In the airless, soundless void, Vorlik's lips moved as he transmitted his thoughts to Woldn. It was one of the Parvii methods of speaking in soundless space. "You summoned us?" Vorlik said.

"No."

"We sensed an urgency in your energy waves," Yurtii said. "Something you are about to do."

"How do you know that?"

"We are war priests. For the survival of our species, we sense danger."

"Danger? My thoughts are not dangerous!"

"That depends on what they are," Vorlik said. A stocky Parvii with a ruddy, elfin face, he looked very worried.

"Well if you must know, I intend to go and visit the Adurians, to learn more about the ancient connection between our races."

"The oral tradition," Yurtii said, his words edged in scorn. "To what purpose?"

"Have you discovered any additional information in your own memory archives?" Woldn asked.

The two war priests shook their heads.

"Then we'll go and find it another way."

"That is not a good idea," Vorlik said. He scowled.

"Why do you say that?"

"It is our instinct," Yurtii said.

"Well, my instinct says otherwise, and I am the Eye of the Swarm. I have a strong feeling that the path to our salvation goes through the Adurian homeworld."

"Are you sure it isn't the path to our destruction?" Vorlik asked.

"Do not be insubordinate!" Woldn transmitted a psychic command to the swarm, and instantly they grouped into a formation, ready to follow him wherever he led them. The two war priests, after hesitating for several moments, joined them.

A flicker of doubt passed through Woldn's mind, but he suppressed it, and concealed it from the others.

Like flying insects, they sped along the podway. Seconds later, the Parviis darkened the sky over the main Adurian world, and dropped down into the largest city, a sprawling, dusty metropolis. Having flown over the area numerous times, Woldn knew the way, even though he'd never set down on the planet before.

As the swarm hovered over the huge capital rotunda, Woldn heard alarm sirens and klaxons going off.

He led the others through open windows and vents in the rotunda, streaking past startled dignitaries and workers, who looked up at them and pointed. The immense central chamber was filled with the insectoid Adurians, who were having some sort of a government meeting. One of them had been giving a speech to the gathering. But he stopped, and stared in alarm at the swarm covering the dome and the high, ornamental ceiling.

Separating from the others, Woldn flew down to the speaker, and—hovering like a bee—he spoke into a microphone on his lapel. "I am the Eye of the Swarm," he said, "leader of the Parvii race. We come in peace."

"And why have you come in peace?" the speaker asked. A wiry insectoid, he glared at Woldn with bulbous eyes. An electronic nameplate on the lapel of his suit read, *VV UNCEL.*

"In ancient times, Parviis and Adurians worked closely together," Woldn said. "I have come to discuss ways that we might do so again."

"In *ancient* times?" Uncel said. "What are you talking about?"

"It is part of our oral tradition," Woldn said. "Long ago, our races worked together."

"In what ways?" asked one of the Adurians out in the audience.

"Swat him like a fly!" someone shouted.

"Details are sketchy," Woldn said, ignoring the threat. "Non-existent, I must admit. I thought that someone here might have the answer."

"Is this just curiosity?" Uncel asked, "or is what we hear true, that the Humans and Tulyans gave you a good thrashing?"

"That is true, I must admit. But look how we bypassed your defensive systems to get in here. We can slip into places where other galactic races cannot go. Despite our reduced strength, we Parviis still have unique powers."

"That may be," Uncel said, nodding. He pursed his lips, seemed to be thinking.

Another Adurian male stepped up to the podium. Deferring to him, Uncel stepped to one side. "I am Chief of Security," this one said. Looking up, he shouted, "All of you are under arrest."

Woldn heard mechanical noises, and before he could do anything, metallic plates slid over all windows and doors of the chamber. Only a few thousand of his sentries remained outside.

"How dare you?" Woldn shouted.

"How dare you come here uninvited?" a peculiar female voice echoed, through speakers all around the chamber. "I am Warlord Tarix, and your fate rests in my hands."

"I stated our purpose honestly," Woldn said. Panic filled him. The security chief swatted at him with an open hand, but Woldn flew beyond his reach.

"Bring in the bug spray," someone yelled.

Laughter pealed through the assemblage.

Flying as high as he could in the huge dome, Woldn rejoined thousands of his followers there, and hovered between his two war priests. "Our telepathic weapons are not strong enough to deal with them," Woldn said to them, keeping his voice low.

"Not like before," Yurtii said. "We aren't ready for a big fight yet."

"We told you not to come here," Vorlik said.

"Don't lecture me!"

Vorlik glowered down at the Adurians who were looking up at them and pointing. Then he said, "Maybe we should concentrate our energy and knock a few of them down, as a display of power."

"I don't think so," Woldn said. "That could only provoke them to extreme violence, and we don't want that."

* * * * *

Unknown to the frustrated, enraged Parviis, the Adurians in the chamber had been discussing their own involvement in the HibAdu Coalition, a military organization that was totally unknown to Woldn or his minions. Overseeing the meeting from their tintplax private boxes around the chamber, the HibAdu triumvirate—Coreq, Enver, and Tarix—had been surprised at the ease of entry by the Parvii swarm, and by their contention that an ancient relationship existed between Parviis and Adurians.

Any ancient relationship between these races, if it ever existed, had been lost in the dusty archives of history. Nonetheless, seeing the potential value of the Parviis to the HibAdu cause—as spies or as swarms to capture natural podships—the triumvirate ordered the Adurian scientists to investigate Woldn's claim....

Chapter Thirty-Seven

How do we measure the accomplishments of our lives? By this do we measure our happiness, or our despair.

—Anton Glavine, *Reflections*

At his palatial military headquarters on Siriki, Noah was at times put off by the grandiosity around him. Knowing that some people lived quite primitively in the back country on this world, it seemed strange to him that anyone could live this way, in such contrasting fashion. He'd observed similar disparities on other merchant prince planets, of course, but never had he seen any royal residence more spectacular than the Golden Palace.

By all accounts, though (including his own personal observation), Princess Meghina seemed to be a good person, and caring in her own way. She'd tried to help Noah in the past, and at her private zoo she kept rescued animals that had previously been at risk, and some endangered as species. There were even a number of animals here from Lost Earth and other planets that no longer existed.

In all, Noah could not say with any certainty that the famous courtesan was profligate or selfish. Certainly, the rumors of her extravagant monetary demands on the former doge had seemed to be of that nature, since she constantly sought to have new additions put on the palace. And this afternoon, as Noah walked through the south wing of the structure and made his way out to the manicured grounds, he found plenty of evidence of construction activities—work that had been halted when the HibAdus made their presence known. But he suspected that much of that had been for show, because it was expected of her, and that she had not sought to improve her image by publicizing her worthwhile activities.

Beyond a stand of Sirikan elms, he barely saw one of the conventional fences of her large zoo, and a giraffe reaching up to eat something from a tree. From that direction, he also heard simian-like jungle sounds, and the loud chattering of birds.

In recent days, some of the palace contractors had begun filtering back to the security gates, asking if they could resume their work. Subi Danvar had accepted some of them, after running them through checks and tests, confirming their loyalty. He had also coordinated the talents of those who passed his rigid screening process, focusing their labors toward military installations instead of what they'd been doing previously. Now they were armoring buildings, improving underground bunkers, and setting up layers of defense.

Trying to be an optimist, Noah wanted to think the best about Princess Meghina, and now he worried about her welfare. According to intelligence reports, she and the other five "immortals" who had benefited from Francella's Elixir of Life had been on the space station that he'd seen making wild trips through space. The last time he saw the station, it appeared to be seriously damaged, making him wonder if anyone could have possibly survived such tremendous perils, or if anyone remained onboard.

He scowled, remembering an APB nehrcom report that sat on his desk concerning the Salducian diplomat in her group of immortals, Kobi Akar. A woman had filed a formal charge that he'd molested her twelve-year old daughter. According to her claim, the crime occurred on the space station, while it orbited Canopa. The woman had been a kitchen employee of Doge Lorenzo's gambling casino, living there in servant's quarters with the girl. If the charge against the Salducian was true, and he was still alive, Noah hoped justice could still be served on him.

* * * * *

On distant Yaree, crowds gathered around the main hospital, awaiting word on the remarkable visitors. This was a melting pot world, so a wide variety of races mingled together in the street and blocked traffic, even Humans and fleshy Mutatis standing side by side. Here, the races generally got along quite well. There were exceptions, fights and murders involving personality disputes and crimes, but usually they had nothing to do with race.

Like gods who lost their ability to fly, the visitors had fallen from the sky three nights ago. Sirens screaming and lights flashing, emergency vehicles had rushed to the various sites of impact. Medical crews had recovered the horribly broken bodies—all of which had remained remarkably intact, despite the great heights from which they had fallen. That had been one of the first oddities that anyone noticed. But there had been more to come.

At first, they had all appeared to be dead, and had been taken to the morgue. Then, in spectacular fashion, all six of them had come back to life on the slabs. Looking more dead than alive, they had sat up one by one like zombies, and looked around. Impossibly, the corpses then began to shamble around the morgue and to reshape their appearances, repairing broken bones, facial damage, and grievous head wounds. Cameras recorded much of it, and millions of Yareens had seen it on holocasts.

Hospital gowns soon replaced the victims' own clothing, and gradually their wounds had begun to heal even more. Word had it that their improvements had little or nothing to do with medical attention. Rather, it was something that came from inside their bodies, from their cellular structure. Four of the "space people," as they were being called, seemed to be Human, while one was a Salducian. Yet another—a blonde female—appeared to be Human, but had bled Mutati purple. That, along with the fact that there were six members of the group, gave the authorities clues and suspicions about their identities, and some of the populace arrived at the same conclusion.

In the crowd, names were murmured, and one in particular. "Princess Meghina of Siriki ... Could it possibly be her? The name of Noah Watanabe was also mentioned as a possibility, since he was rumored to have achieved immortality, though perhaps in a slightly different fashion from the others. But if Noah was one of them, there should be seven, not six.

Beneath a warm midday sun, a hospital spokesman stood at the top of the main entrance stairway, preparing to address the tightly packed crowd. A rotund Kichi man with a thick white beard, he adjusted a microphone on his lapel, cleared his throat.

"I am pleased to report that all six of the patients are recovering well. They are eating and walking normally, and almost all of their injuries have healed." He paused. "It is as many of us suspected. These are the people who consumed a wondrous elixir that made them virtually indestructible. One of them is indeed Princess Meghina of Siriki."

"And Noah Watanabe?" someone shouted.

"He is not among them. One of the Humans in the group, however, confirmed something we have heard in the past—that Noah's blood runs in their veins, from the elixir they consumed. An elixir that was prepared from his own blood."

The crowd murmured. Truly, no one on the planet had ever received visitors of this nature. This would be written of in the history holos for centuries to come.

* * * * *

The government of Yaree was fiercely independent and militaristic. The people were also insular and xenophobic despite their racial mixture, identifying themselves as Yareens above anything else. They did not trust outsiders, or outside cultures. The HibAdus, apparently knowing how tough they were, had not even tried to attack them. In an out-of-the-way sector of the galaxy, Yaree was also virtually off the MPA and Mutati Kingdom radar screens.

The Prime Leader of the planet, Wan Haqro, had remembered meeting Princess Meghina during her earlier visit with a trade delegation. This time, the tall Ilkian man greeted her in the austere sitting room outside her hospital room. "I have arranged for you to leave immediately," he told her, after refusing her invitation to sit and speak with her.

"I do not wish to leave yet," she said, rising to her feet. She wore an elegant green brocade dress now, which had been brought to her. "There are matters to attend to on the space station." She nodded toward the ceiling, indicating the general direction of the damaged orbiter.

"We will tend to all of that," Haqro said, tersely. "You will depart tomorrow."

Her voice became chilly. "Headed where? By what manner of transport?"

"To your homeworld, Siriki. I do this as a courtesy."

Hearing the destination, she arched her eyebrows in surprise.

"It is quite simple to get you there, really, " he said. "We have a number of laboratory-produced podships that we purchased from an Adurian on the black market, and we are using them to run our own trade routes. You have heard of the war, of course?"

"Of course. Humans and Mutatis have been each other's throats for a long time."

"I do not speak of that. From what I understand, you may have been out of the information loop for a good while. While you were away, a secret alliance of Hibbils and Adurians attacked all Human and Mutati worlds, and conquered the vast majority of them. Only Siriki and one other planet remain in the Merchant Prince Alliance, while the Mutati Kingdom has a single remaining planet."

"My God!" she said.

"To counter the aggression, your merchant princes have formed an alliance with Mutatis and with Tulyans."

"This is indeed surprising. You are aligned with our enemies, then? The Adurians?"

"Certainly not. We are neutral, and will trade with anyone. It is only because of a business relationship that I return you to Siriki on an Adurian-made ship."

"If what you say is true, I must leave immediately."

"It is already arranged, my Lady." The Ilkian bowed stiffly, and left.

* * * * *

In a matter of hours, Princess Meghina and her five companions stepped off a Yareen lab-pod, onto Sirikan soil. Moments before, there had been a tense stand-off in the skies over Siriki, when the podship entered its airspace. Fortunately, the Yareen pilot had state-of-the-art communications equipment aboard, and with it he identified the passengers, and the purpose of the arrival.

For a few moments, Meghina and the other immortals had wondered if they would have to arrive there the same way they set down on Yaree, falling out of the sky. But that had proved unnecessary, and all had gone well in the landing. Now, looking up, she saw that the lab-pod was being blocked from takeoff by military craft that hovered overhead.

A throng of officers and soldiers, in both MPA and Guardian uniforms, stood waiting for her on the landing pad. As Meghina reached the bottom of the egress ramp, soldiers rushed past her and boarded the lab-pod.

"See here!" the Yareen pilot exclaimed as he was led out of the ship. "You can't treat me in this manner." He and a dozen other Yareen citizens of varying races were taken into custody.

From the midst of officers on the landing pad, Noah Watanabe marched forward, in a green-and-brown Guardian uniform. "Hold them for questioning," he ordered, "and take this ship in for analysis."

Coming face to face with Meghina, he said, "Welcome home, Princess."

"Thank you."

"We found it necessary to commandeer your palace for our headquarters. You will note other changes as well."

"I have heard about the war. I am here to help."

"Good." He looked past her. Seeing a Salducian among those who had disembarked from the lab-pod, he pointed to him and asked, "Is that Kobi Akar?"

"It is."

"Then I will have to place him under arrest."

She raised her eyebrows. "For what?"

Noah told her, and as he spoke, her face darkened. "I've wondered about him," she said. "Very well. But who shall judge him?"

"It is a Canopan charge. I suspect that they will want him to be brought back on the next military flight."

She nodded. "I see."

Speaking to an aide, Noah ordered the diplomat's arrest, than stood with Meghina and watched while it was carried out. As he was being taken into custody, the Salducian shouted protestations and threats of political repercussions. Finally two MPA soldiers gained control over him, and led him away.

As Noah walked with Meghina toward a waiting hovercar, he said, "There are other serious problems, Princess. This morning, we received a report of a mountaintop breaking off and disappearing into space in a green flash of light."

"From Siriki?" she asked, her voice alarmed.

"Unfortunately, yes, and we're getting emergency nehrcom messages about bizarre events on Canopa as well. On both planets, land is breaking off and disappearing—a mountaintop here, a peninsula there, an island…. Some scientists and curious citizens who went to investigate have disappeared, too, or have reported seeing green flashes as huge chunks of dirt and rock vanish. In deep oceans and lakes, more disturbances are occurring … and water levels are fluctuating wildly." He paused, and his breath came in shallow bursts, as if he were running from something, at least in his mind. "So far on Siriki, this is only happening in remote regions, but we are on the alert here as well."

"What is causing it?"

"I have much to tell you, dear Lady. The entire galaxy is in chaos, and what we are experiencing here is just part of it. On a more personal note, two of my most loyal young Guardians—a pair of teenage cousins—are in the danger zone on Siriki. We're sending a rescue mission to find them. Hopefully, still alive."

Gesturing back at her companions, Meghina said, "I have much to tell you, as well. We are the six immortals who took the elixir. For what it's worth, we seem to be indestructible."

"I have the same condition," Noah said, "and I'm not sure what good it does against the tremendous odds we all face."

"To live forever might not be the best thing," she said, somberly.

Chapter Thirty-Eight

We are dispatching web repair crews to each galactic disaster zone as quickly as possible, but the task is overwhelming. Yet through all of this adversity we must maintain a positive face, especially when interacting with our allies. It would not be in our interest—nor that of any other galactic race—for us to spread pessimism.

— Confidential dispatch, Tulyan Council of Elders

In his natural fleshy state, the Mutati left his private quarters on the flagship and made his way forward. There was a matter he needed to take care of.

Hari'Adab had not been pleased with a number of things, among them the fact that he and his girlfriend Parais had been forcibly separated. Though Doge Anton had seemed pleasant enough in their meetings, he had nonetheless ordered this action against the two lovers. On one level, Hari understood the decision, since Humans and Mutatis had long been mortal enemies. But on another, more personal level, he hated it, and despised the Humans who had done it to him. Not hatred in the psychotic, destructive sense his father had felt, but the young doge's action showed a lack of respect for Hari's status as the Mutati leader, and a lack of trust.

There had also been the matter of the fake sisters of Princess Meghina, the Mutati infiltrators. Hari had not known about that in advance, and could only surmise that it was a plan his father had carried out before his death—or which some hard-core Mutati fanatics had fostered afterward. Both he and Parais had proved their innocence in the matter, and had been restored to a degree of freedom, although it still involved strict controls and oversight.

He sighed. In the present circumstance, Humans and Tulyans had the upper hand, and perhaps it should be that way. His own father, and a long line of Zultans before him, had caused a lot of damage ... and that could not be repaired overnight.

On the regular courier trips between Dij and Canopa, at least, Hari and Parais had been permitted to exchange personal messages ... transmittals that were undoubtedly checked by censors and xenocryptologists. At least she had reported signs of progress, because Noah Watanabe had said on several occasions that he trusted her, and that he would talk to Doge Anton about getting her assignments that were befitting of her station and her talents.

That was something, anyway.

The Emir took a gray-black stairway to an upper level. It always amazed him to see the living spaceship around him, with its slightly pulsing walls and protruding surfaces, and the way it sometimes altered itself to fit the needs of the passengers.

Initially, Hari had been irritated by the presence of the "military chaperones" that were sent along with him on the mission to Dij. There had been moments of stress whenever he tried to assert himself with them, testing the limits of his freedom and authority. A number of Human MPA military officers had been assigned to him, including mid-level chetens, kajors, and even two vice-generals, but for the most part they seemed to cooperate with him. To an extent. They often had to go off somewhere away by themselves and obtain permission to follow "orders" that Hari gave to them, but invariably they came back and agreed to do as he wished, with only a few minor modifications.

In the weeks they had been together on this mission, Hari had gotten to know, and like, many of the officers and soldiers.

The robots, however, were a different matter, and quite irritating. Nothing he wanted done about them could be handled through the Human officers. Everything had to go through the Captain of the sentient machines, a black, patched-together robot named Jimu. That one seemed to have more than one screw loose, and to make matters worse, he reported directly to Doge Anton. Having been assigned to Hari's flagship, Jimu was always there, studying Hari with glowing yellow eyes that alternately dimmed and brightened in a peculiar, unsettling fashion. Usually, Hari tried not to think about him, but that was not always possible. Jimu had a peculiar way of insinuating himself into situations.

It was happening right now, in fact, as Hari and the robot stood face to face on the command bridge of the flagship.

"Now see here," the Emir said. "I don't deserve to be treated this way."

"You are a Mutati." The mechanical words were delivered in a particularly flat tone, even for a robot.

"I want to inspect other worlds now," Hari said. It was the subject of their latest dispute, a debate that had been going on all morning. "We'll leave half the force to watch over Dij, and take the rest with us."

"The fleet cannot be divided."

"But I'm making perfect sense. I discussed it with Vice-General Dressen, and he seemed to agree with my assessment."

"I assume he explained the line of authority to you?"

"Yes, yes. Technically he outranks you, but on this mission you report directly to Doge Anton, just as he does."

"And I have been ordered that the fleet is not to be divided. If the Vice-General disagrees with that, he can take it up with the Doge himself."

"He already has, as you well know—and the Doge is taking your side, though I can't figure out why. But if you would only listen to reason. My idea is our best course of action."

"You are a Mutati."

"Damn you, stop saying that! We are allies now, so the racial tag means nothing."

"The fleet cannot be divided."

"All right, damn it! Then I want to take all of it to other worlds, on an inspection tour. There's obviously no action for us here."

"The enemy watches our every move, and responds."

"Dij already held out against them. We're not needed here anyway."

The robot's eyes flashed. "It's not known how large a force the enemy committed to Dij in the last battle. You could be making a tactical mistake."

"There are many other important Mutati worlds that I'm concerned about. I must do whatever is necessary to rescue them as well."

"This can be done, if the fleet is kept intact."

"Yes, yes. By nightfall, I want to set course for Uhadeen, one of our most important military strongholds. Apparently it has fallen, but I intend to change that."

"By nightfall," the robot agreed. "We leave nothing behind."

* * * * *

After they departed, one day passed. Then, in a lightning military strike, Dij fell to a massive onslaught of HibAdu forces.

Ambassador VV Uncel received the good news—transmitted by HibAdu nehrcom—while he was on the Adurian homeworld, submitting yet another report to his superiors. Now he crossed the marbelite floor of the spaceport at a brisk pace. Through the glax of double doors ahead, he saw a lab-pod sitting on the landing field, ready to take him to Dij for an inspection tour. A number of Hibbils and Adurians were boarding it. He crowded onboard with them, and found a seat that had been reserved for him at the front of the passenger compartment. The food-service machines were better in this section than those at the rear, as were the seats and lavatory accommodations.

Getting up, he obtained a Vanadian pear from one of the machines and then returned to his seat. The lab-pod engines whined to life.

As he munched on the crispy fruit, Uncel considered the rapid pace of activity surrounding the war effort. His own HibAdu leaders were most peculiar, indeed. A triumvirate of freaks who didn't reveal their identities until two weeks ago. Ambassador VV Uncel shuddered at the thought of the horrific hybrids created in a genetics laboratory, and at the thought of what might happen to him if they ever read the recent memories in his cells. Thus far, it had only happened once, at the onset of the Coalition. He had been positive in those days, and somewhat naive, he realized in hindsight.

Ever since the beginning of this alliance between Hibbils and Adurians, Uncel had been curious about who was running everything. Many times he'd wondered why they were concealing themselves from him, when his years of loyal service and social status should have allowed him entrance to their inner circle. In a peculiar, disturbing fashion, all of his orders had been sent to him through intermediaries. Never in person, and never was he ever treated with the respect he so richly deserved.

But Uncel was a professional, through and through. He never complained to anyone about being kept at a distance by his superiors, about only being told pieces of information and never knowing the complete picture, never knowing the really important things. Year after year he just continued to do his job efficiently, everything the freaks had ordered him to do through intermediaries.

Now, though, he worried that their brains were as abnormal as their appearance. How could leaders be created in a laboratory? Didn't that make someone else their boss? Who could that possibly be? A genetic scientist, or group of them?

One of the three monstrosities—Premier Enver—had suggested that a new race of bizarre laboratory-bred creatures might be created. Hybrid "HibAdus," produced from the genetic stock of Hibbils and Adurians. Previously, the name HibAdu had only meant a somewhat arcane political entity to Uncel. Now it referred to something entirely different. Something decidedly darker.

Not that Uncel considered himself any sort of a moral icon. Morality and ethics were concepts he didn't think about much at all. His primary concerns, in order, were himself and the political structure that supported the lifestyle to which he'd grown accustomed. With his niche seemingly secure, he had kept going, doing whatever he was told. But now, with the talk of creating a new race of freaks—how soon?—he felt an army of worry marching on his brain, making more and more inroads, like little guerrilla attacks. He didn't want to think about such things.

As the lab-pod went into hover mode and prepared to set down in the main city on Dij, the Ambassador gazed out the window at blackened hulks of buildings and military equipment. With a soft bump, the craft set down on a charred landing pad, near the bodies of Mutati soldiers that lay in disarray, their flesh melted away. These defenders, while a stubborn and resourceful lot, had finally been defeated by Adurian personnel bombs that had incinerated them. Now carrion birds picked at the grisly remains.

Wrinkling his nose at the odor, Uncel walked past the bodies. On the landing field he noticed other lab-pods on the ground, with each of the vessels disgorging hundreds of Hibbil and Adurian passengers—military and civilian. Everyone was heading for the nearby city, taking a wide conveyor walkway that had either not been damaged in the attack or which has been repaired afterward.

Disembarking at the central square, the Ambassador paused to watch his Hibbil allies devouring Mutati flesh. He'd heard about such disgusting practices, of course, but had never seen them firsthand. Curious, he moved closer, as did other Adurian onlookers. Then, surprisingly, some of the Adurian soldiers joined in, tasting the flesh of their dead enemies.

"Come on, Ambassador!" a Hibbil soldier shouted. "Get some for yourself! The meat is sweet!"

Grudgingly, like a person tasting an unusual food for the first time, the diplomat waded in, stepping over purple puddles of Mutati blood. A Hibbil soldier handed him a dripping slab of fatty flesh.

At first, Uncel just nibbled at the corner, and found it surprisingly succulent and not repulsive. Delicious, he decided, with another nibble. Soon he had devoured the entire morsel and was reaching down to rip off bigger chunks for himself. All around him, the diners grinned and grunted to each other, with purple goo dripping down their chins and all over their clothes.

Already, Uncel found himself developing a taste for the fleshy meat, and he even pushed some of the other people out of the way to get more for himself.

That evening, at a banquet where Mutati flesh was prepared according to gourmet standards, Uncel heard details of biological weapons that he'd only previously heard about as rumors. On Dij and other conquered planets—to make them easier to rule by reducing their populations—the HibAdus had unleashed bioweapons that either killed or permanently sedated Humans and Mutatis. A variety of weapons and delivery systems were employed, the most deadly of which were plague bombs, which were dropped from lab-pods and detonated in mid-air, spreading their spores over entire planets.

Billions of the enemy had been infected, though the resourceful Humans had eventually developed antidotes for their own race. Thus far, the Mutatis had been far less fortunate.

* * * * *

Far across the galaxy, a Hibbil workman stood on a motoladder, having elevated it to its highest setting so that he could see one of the top shelves in the warehouse. Reaching to the back of the shelf, he slid a dusty weapon-control box forward and examined it. An engraved code told him the date of manufacture and certain quality control details.

"Did you think we forgot about you?" he asked, talking to the unit as if it were alive. "Have you been hiding back there, trying to stay out of battle? Well, there's been a malfunction in one of the front-line units, and you're finally going to get your chance to prove yourself."

Using a robotic arm on the ladder, the worker moved the heavy panel box down to the floor of the warehouse and piled it with a number of other replacement components that were going to be installed in HibAdu warships.

Inside the unit, a little robot heard the words, but said nothing, and did not make a sound.

At last, Ipsy thought. *I'm going to get my chance!*

Chapter Thirty-Nine

Everything we experience is through a series of individual and social filters, from our day to day activities to our perception of the universe. No matter the circumstance, what we see is never the same as what any other person sees. There can be similarities and overlaps, but it is never identical.

—Master Noah Watanabe, classroom instruction

Doge Anton and a number of his key military officers were holding a late night strategy session at his headquarters on Canopa. They met on the top floor of the tallest building in the Valley of the Princes. They had not yet heard the bad news about Dij.

"I don't like this waiting game," General Nirella said. She paced the floor in front of a bank of windows. Beyond her, Anton saw the glittering lights of the corporate buildings in the valley, and the cliff-hanging structures of Rainbow City in the distance.

"We need to hit them hard," Kajor Swen said. He was one of the youngest, most aggressive officers.

"But where?" one of the other officers said. "Our intelligence reports show that they have large forces stationed at each of the conquered planets, and there seems no limit to the forces they can bring to battle."

"That's because they're growing podships in labs," Nirella said. "The Tulyans hunting wild podships can't keep up; we can't increase our fleet at the pace the HibAdus can."

"Maybe we should figure out how they're doing it and set up our own program," Swen said.

"Look into it," Anton said.

As the meeting continued, the Doge sat uneasily at the head of the table, watching everyone and listening to the exchange of ideas and comments. There were fourteen men and women in the conference room, and many could not seem to remain in their seats. They kept getting up and walking around, as if itching for some real military action.

"Good God!" Nirella exclaimed. She had her face pressed against the glax, looking out at something.

Everyone hurried over to look, including Anton.

The sky over Rainbow City looked like it was spouting green flames. Anton first thought the strange illumination might be an aurora borealis, but it was not positioned over the northern pole of the planet. Using a handheld magnaviewer, he detected a hole in space, emitting what appeared to be green exhaust.

"Get me a satellite report!" Anton shouted.

Two minutes later, a female Tulyan passed through security and strode heavily into the conference room. Doge Anton recognized her as Zigzia, one of the webtalkers who specialized in communicating via the web strands in space. "The satellite report is coming, as you ordered, but there is more you need to know."

"Something to do with Timeweb?" Nirella asked.

"Yes, General," Zigzia said. She looked worriedly in the direction of the fiery green sky. "We need to evacuate the building immediately," she said.

"What?" Anton said.

"There's a timehole up there, Sire. It's getting closer, on a direct course for the valley. It could recede, or could suck this whole building into it, and a lot more."

Astonished, Anton stared at the unnatural sky, and he knew she was right. "Do it!" he barked.

As they hurried out into the corridor, alarm klaxons sounded. The building rumbled, and an eerie green light permeated everything.

"To the roof!" Nirella said.

Running as fast as they could, Anton, Nirella, Zigzia, and all of the others boarded two grid planes, which took off within seconds after all of them were aboard. The pilots hit the jets, and the aircraft shot into the sky at low angles, away from the approaching timehole. Anton held Nirella's hand. They sat side by side, with electronic safety restraints holding them in. Turbulence shook the plane, but it kept flying.

Behind them, the entire Valley of the Princes glowed green. Then, like particles drawn by a magnet, buildings and whole chunks of land exploded into the green sky and disappeared into the insatiable maw of the timehole.

Suddenly, inexplicably, the sky was no longer green, and the night sky over the valley looked almost completely normal, with glittering stars against a dark cosmic ceiling.

Seated beside Anton, his wife read a telebeam message that appeared over the ring on her hand. "More bad news," the female officer said. "The last Mutati world has fallen to the HibAdus. We've lost Dij."

"What about the fleet we sent with the Mutati Emir?"

"Safe," Nirella said. "Hari'Adab wanted to break it up and take a portion of it to other Mutati worlds, but Jimu prevented it."

"Under our orders," Anton said. "Good, good. Where are they now?"

"Deep space in the Mutati Sector, or should I say the *former* Mutati Sector."

"That's some positive news at least. I want them to come back here right away. All six thousand podships."

"Right." She sent the telebeam command, then read another incoming message. "A little more good news, Doge. Elements of the original Mutati fleet have been found in space. They escaped the HibAdus, and have been hiding out. Eclectic solar sailers and other conventional spacecraft, but they're loaded with armaments. Jimu says they're loading stuff on the podships and bringing it back."

"We can use it all."

"Interesting," she said. "Our podships are enlarging themselves as necessary to accommodate the additional cargoes. Handy, aren't they?"

"That they are. And Siriki?"

"All quiet there, Sire. And they know about Dij. Do you want to reconsider the podships we assigned to Siriki, and bring them back as well?"

He shook his head. "No. It's not apples and apples, is it? I mean, the HibAdus didn't hit Dij hard until *after* our forces left. Maybe our presence on Siriki inhibits them."

"It's a guessing game, isn't it? We make a move and they make theirs."

Leaning forward, Anton said to the pilot, "Take us to my flagship."

* * * * *

At the heavily fortified palace keep on Siriki, Noah absorbed the stream of emergency courier reports from command headquarters on Canopa. The galactic-ecology situation there was bad, but the loss of Dij was dire news, and suggested that Siriki could be the next target of a massive HibAdu assault, taking out the easier targets first. Noah had his own forces on the highest state of alert, but this was nothing new. At his direction, Subi Danvar had instituted that from the very first day they arrived on Siriki. In orbital space, in the sky, and on the ground, all was in readiness—to the extent possible.

Intending to keep an appointment with Princess Meghina, Noah hurried outside. It was a sunny afternoon, and he walked briskly along a crushed brick path that led to her private zoo.

He found her supervising as handlers unloaded exotic animals from a hoverplane and put them in cages. Dressed in black jeans and a short-sleeve gray sweatshirt, the attractive woman did not look like a princess or a courtesan. Her blonde hair was secured in a simple ponytail.

Seeing him, she said, "These animals just came in from one of our remote islands, where there has been destructive activity. They were panicked. I wish we could take them to another planet where it's safer. For that matter, I wish all of us could go somewhere safe." She looked long at Noah. "But there's no such place, is there?"

"I'm afraid not, but so far Siriki has been spared the horrors suffered by other worlds. " He looked apprehensively at the sky, half expecting HibAdu warships to appear at any time. "I've assigned a new guard force to protect you," he said. "At any given moment, they can get you immediately into an emergency escape craft."

"I've seen them following me everywhere," she said, nodding her head in the direction of uniformed Human and robotic soldiers on the path. "You needn't worry about me so much. I'm pretty tough."

"I know you are, but I feel responsible for you now." He shuffled his feet. "Look, I want to tell you how much I appreciate the kindness you showed me when my sister was behaving so badly."

"Was she ever any other way?"

"I know you didn't like her, and she gave you good reason to feel that way. You tried to keep her from shooting me, and I know you made other attempts to help me behind the scenes. You also took food to my nephew Anton when he was imprisoned by Doge Lorenzo."

"I'm afraid I wasn't that great an advocate for either of you," she said, with a rueful smile. "Fortunately for you, though, you have your own built-in cellular survival kit."

"And so do you."

"Mmmm, but from what I hear, your special talents are not limited to the ability to physically regenerate yourself. In that area, we might be comparable, but I don't have the far-ranging psychic powers you enjoy."

"I wouldn't call it enjoyable. The powers seem to come and go. Sometimes I can get into a paranormal realm of my own volition, and sometimes I can't. There appear to be numerous ways in, but I haven't figured them out."

"Timeweb," she said. "I've heard about it. Is it as beautiful as they say? A faint green filigree extending all across the cosmos?"

"I can't put it into words," he said.

Meghina excused herself for a moment, to speak with one of the handlers, a woman who was trying to feed raw meat to a caged Sirikan tiger. Noah knew something of the rare, endangered species. It tugged at his heart to see that the orange-and-black animal was emaciated and bruised. It appeared listless, more interested in going to sleep than eating.

When she returned to Noah, she said, "I think I danced on the edge of the sword for awhile. Did you hear about the incredible ride I took in the Pleasure Palace? And about Lorenzo? He's still missing." Her eyes glistened with sadness.

"I'm sorry that's happened to you. As for the orbiter, I still think of it as EcoStation."

She wiped a tear from her eye. "Yes, it is rightfully yours, but I'm afraid it's severely damaged. I rode it God only knows how far—through one of those timeholes and back out."

"Yes, I saw some of that with my ... special vision."

"What's left of your EcoStation is orbiting the planet of Yaree. The orbiter is severely damaged. Some of the modules may still be sealed or partially sealed, but I'm not sure. It's taken quite a beating in its travels."

Noah narrowed his gaze. "The pilot of the lab-pod that we confiscated told us a little about Yaree. It's an unaligned world in a remote galactic sector, a melting pot of various races. Humans, Mutatis, and other races working side by side."

"Sort of a utopia that way, though it's not the most scenic spot I've ever visited. The planet is mineral rich, and its rulers are clever traders, dealing in all sorts of goods. With the cessation of regular podship travel, their business activities have been severely curtailed, but they are an industrious people, and militarily quite strong. So far, the HibAdus have not attacked them. The Yareens say they wouldn't dare."

"Will they join us militarily?"

"I didn't ask, but they might."

"I'm going to look into it—we need all the help we can get," Noah said. He paused, envisioning EcoStation as it used to be, when he conducted Guardian classed onboard, teaching eager young students about his concept of galactic ecology. Maybe it could be that again, and more.

"If we can repair EcoStation," he added, "it could be used for military purposes, as an observation platform for relaying information to Doge Anton."

"It would be easier to build a new space station," she said.

"But it wouldn't be the same," Noah said.

Chapter Forty

We are each alone in this universe.
The multitudes around us only conceal this fact.

—Anonymous, from Lost Earth

In a different context, another universe, it seemed to Lorenzo del Velli, the Hibbil had been respectful, and—though feisty and combative at times—always deferential when confronted by his superior. In those heady days, Pimyt had been his Royal Attaché, both during and after Lorenzo's reign as Doge of the Merchant Prince Alliance.

Now, it was all quite different.

The space station was gone, inexplicably! Standing on the ground by the landed shuttle, Lorenzo still had trouble believing it, or comprehending where his Pleasure Palace gambling casino was. Weeks had passed, and he'd been forced to sleep on the deck of the shuttle with the others. As a result, he had sore muscles and bones (including a painful hip from lying on his side), and his stomach kept rumbling. He despised the emergency rations and strange local plants they'd been eating. They were totally unsuited to a nobleman of his station and lineage.

Each day Lorenzo and his companions—Pimyt and the eleven surviving Red Beret soldiers—had been searching orbital space around the unnamed, unknown planet. The ion engines kept running roughly, and were giving all of them considerable concern. There'd been no sign of the Pleasure Palace at all, not even a real clue as to its whereabouts.

Around an hour ago, as the shuttle landed yet again, Pimyt had offered a theory. Lorenzo had been inspecting himself in the bathroom mirror, he knew his own aged face was worry-worn. The door had been ajar, and Pimyt had pushed it open. The temerity of the creature!

Lorenzo, unhappy at this affront and still displeased with him for running up the slope ahead of him and hardly looking back, had glowered at the furry little alien. But, for the sake of harmony, the merchant prince had held back a stream of invectives that he had in mind.

As Lorenzo pushed his way out of the small room, with the Hibbil behind him, Pimyt said, "We have experienced but one of many unusual occurrences all across space. You and I have seen the reports, Lorenzo, and we've heard the rumors. Something is seriously amiss in all galactic sectors."

"I get the feeling we're not even in the known galaxy anymore," the former doge then said. He rubbed a spot on his forehead nervously, a place he had already made red and rough.

"Let's see you get out of this one, Lorenzo. What political strings can you pull now?"

Lorenzo swore and made a menacing step toward the smaller being, but had second thoughts when he saw the Hibbil's glowing red eyes, so the Human just glared at him instead....

* * * * *

Later that afternoon they moved the shuttle to the other side of the planet, to a clearing at the center of the most peculiar jungle any of them had ever seen. The trees and other plant forms, while living and supple, were entirely gray-brown. One of the Red Berets thought it might be an unusual form of photosynthesis, peculiar to this solar system. Though warm at times and providing reasonable illumination, the yellowish sun had a constant grayish tone around the edges—as if from a lens, or a peculiar solar cloud.

Yes, everything was quite different now.

Disheveled and dirty, Lorenzo had not washed properly since arriving on this unnamed planet. He stood at the main hatch of the shuttle, watching several of the Red Berets venture into the jungle. A few minutes earlier, Pimyt had gone in that direction as well.

Behind Lorenzo, the slender Red Beret who had piloted the mini-sub stood attentively, awaiting instructions from his superior. The man removed his red cap for a moment, smoothed it and put it back on.

"What is your name?" Lorenzo asked, noting no insignia of rank on his uniform. Just a common guard, apparently, although he had been through intensive security screening, like the others.

"Kenjie Ashop, Sire," he said.

"Well, Ashop, I appreciate your loyalty and attention to my needs. I'm going to take a walk, and while I'm gone I want you to watch over this shuttle. Don't follow instructions from anyone else until you hear from me."

"Yes, Sire. Would you like me to go with you? There could be unknown dangers out there."

Lorenzo's eyes flashed at him. "As if our situation could get any worse, you mean? No thanks, I'll go on my own." The nobleman grabbed a copy of the *Scienscroll* off a shelf, and slipped it into a clearplax carrying bag. The ground was wet and spongy from a recent rain.

The guard unclipped a small black device from a bulkhead, and handed it to Lorenzo. "This is a locator beacon for your safety, Sire. If you get lost in the strange terrain, it will enable us to find you, and it will also enable you to find your way back to the shuttle. It has a range of more than a hundred kilometers."

"A bit more than I planned to walk today," Lorenzo said with a smile. He examined the device and its touchpad controls.

The guard nodded, and showed him how to work the directional features. Then he said, "See that orange circle? If you flip open the cap over it, you have an energy-burst weapon, capable of bringing down any animal that might try to come after you. Just touch the red button and fire."

"Thank you."

"I'll take care of everything here, Sire."

"I know you will. I'm counting on you."

Lorenzo took a different route into the jungle from those he'd seen the others take. He had in mind sitting somewhere alone with the quasi-religious book and searching it for appropriate passages, as he occasionally liked to do. Perhaps he could find a dry rock, in a warm patch of sunlight.

There were no trails in this area that he could make out, suggesting a paucity of animals, or a complete lack of them. But he did find a relatively clear area that sloped slightly downward, as from water runoff. Leafy trees leaned in on each side, making a canopy overhead, through which filtered sunlight passed.

As he proceeded, Lorenzo kept one hand on the *Scienscroll* bag and the other in his jacket pocket, over the weapon. Only rarely did he have to move thick leaves or branches out of the way. Just ahead, he saw the sunny rock he'd hoped for.

As he neared the rock, he found a dry, warm place to sit that also had a back rest. He also noticed a small, quiet pool of water nearby, beneath a rock overhang that must have kept them from noticing it when they were in the air. Sitting on the hard, dry surface, it pleased Lorenzo that the contours were relatively comfortable, almost as if a simple chair had been constructed just for him.

Removing the book from the bag, he read for awhile, but only superficially. Nothing really caught his interest.

But he did have something else with him. Unzipping a pocket of his coat, he removed a small padded medical kit that he had obtained from the CorpOne medical laboratory, back on Canopa. He opened it and examined the contents: a plax vial of red-wine-colored fluid and a dermex injector.

It was a vial of the Elixir of Life, which the crazed Francella Watanabe had developed, using the blood of her brother, Noah. She had sought eternal life, but had only obtained the opposite, an eternity of darkness. Earlier, using the public as guinea pigs to see how effective the product was, she had sold more than two hundred thousand doses. In the vast majority of cases, the elixir had shown no effect at all. But there had been a handful of successes—Princess Meghina, the Salducian diplomat Kobi Akar, four others, and perhaps Noah, too—but by a slightly different route.

After Francella's death, Lorenzo had come into possession of this vial, but he'd never used it. She had died horribly after consuming the substance, albeit in massive quantities. In addition, there had been recent reports of other elixir consumers coming down with painful, rare diseases and dying. Lorenzo had heard of several hundred cases, and Dr. Bichette had told him that there could be more, as what he called "delayed medical reactions" set in.

Touching the cool surface of the vial, Lorenzo considered his options. Unquestionably, consuming it could make his life more interesting in this boring place. But conceivably, a large percentage—or even all—of the people who had taken the elixir would eventually suffer unpleasant deaths.

Not quite ready to take the chance, he closed the kit and replaced it in his pocket.

Feeling quite sleepy, Lorenzo leaned back and closed his eyes, intending to do so for just a few moments. Since falling from power he had been through a terrible ordeal, and been feeling increasingly tired. It was comparatively warm here, and almost comfortable. Perhaps he could forget his troubles for a few minutes....

Pimyt had been trailing him at a distance, keeping out of sight, making hardly any sounds. The furry, disheveled Hibbil crept closer and watched the former MPA leader as his head lolled to one side and he drifted off to sleep. Long minutes passed, and as he drew even closer, Pimyt heard the foolish Human snoring.

The Hibbil was far from his people, but he could still sense their collective pulse, and their awakened appetites. He sniffed the air, moved closer.

Chapter Forty-One

There are uncounted secrets in this universe.
The vast majority of them will never be revealed.

—Parvii Inspiration

Webdancer floated in the midst of other sentient vessels, all with their space anchors activated. Inside the warmth of the podship's sectoid chamber, Tesh lay supine on the deck, staring up at the iridescent green ceiling.

The Parvii woman knew that in the officers' conference room on the deck below her, Doge Anton, his officers, and a number of Tulyans were discussing web conditions in the Canopa region. After the big upheaval in the Valley of the Princes, the timehole near the planet seemed to have settled down, but everyone knew it could flare up at any moment, without warning. Now a Tulyan repair team was high above the planet, working to keep that from happening.

Anton had just begun a meeting, after concluding an even more important session with Hari'Adab, who had just returned with his fleet after the loss of Dij. From listening in on part of the earlier meeting, Tesh knew that the news from the Emir had not been all bad, because he had also brought back a sizable additional force of Mutati warships, soldiers, and military supplies, which he had retrieved from hiding places around the huge sector that had formerly been the dominion of the Mutatis.

With so many important events occurring that required Tesh's attention, she really saw no good time to do anything as personal as she was about to do now, and she felt some guilt about even thinking about such a matter. But she needed to do this anyway, had to move forward so that her mind could be clear for other things. Helping her a bit, Doge Anton was occupied and didn't need her for awhile, so barring any new catastrophe Tesh might have enough time to do what she had in mind. She only needed a few moments of intense concentration.

In her natural minuscule form, the sectoid chamber seemed quite large, the relative size of a typical passenger compartment to a normal Human, perhaps. When she first took control of the vessel, this core chamber had been substantially smaller. But gradually, as the war progressed and as *Webdancer* became more important to the Liberator fleet, the ship had grown bigger, of its own volition. Now it was at least twice the size of any other podship in the fleet.

Though Tesh never conversed with *Webdancer* in words, because they utilized different forms of language, she still thought she understood some of the motivations of the great ship. The two of them had a wordless connection, on a higher level than the superficiality of any spoken tongue.

Tesh was more than seven hundred years old—a mere youngster by galactic standards, and she realized that she still had a great deal to learn. Even so, beyond her knowledge of the Aopoddae, she knew other significant things that were perhaps even more arcane.

In her comparative youth six centuries ago, Tesh had befriended a retired breeding specialist at the Parvii Fold, a slender old woman who took her into her confidence. Old Astar had wanted the younger Parvii to become a breeding specialist like herself, a rare opportunity presented to a "commonblood" such as Tesh. At the time, the profession was dying out, she said, not considered necessary anymore. Astar was the only remaining one, and she had not practiced her craft for almost two millennia.

She explained that in the Parvii race, there used to be more than one way to pursue some of the most important professions. In the case of breeding specialists, most came from particular genetic lines, but historically there had been exceptions, notable commonbloods who displayed special talents that enabled them to join the elite group. Tesh had been one of those extraordinary people who had been noticed.

For Astar, it had been unusual for her to open up to anyone, for she had always been known as an insular person, filled with secret knowledge. From the beginning of their relationship, Tesh had told her that she didn't want to become a breeding specialist, because that was not the direction in which her heart pointed her. Besides, there would be extreme political difficulties if she were to make the attempt. Instead, the young woman had always wanted to pilot podships across vast expanses of space. It had felt like her calling, a glamorous career that consumed much of her imagination. Astar had been disappointed, but had said she accepted the decision. Even so, it took a long time before she gave up trying to get Tesh to change her mind.

One day, when it was clear that Tesh would not accept the calling, and that the old woman did not have long to live, a highly unusual event occurred. In the years since then, Tesh had thought of it often.

The two of them had been flying side by side, at a slow speed because of Astar's declining health. They reached a foldcave that the old woman said would give them complete security from the telepathic probes of the Eye of the Swarm. There, standing in the small natural chamber, illuminated in low gray light, Astar said, "I have thought long and hard on this, and there is something I want to bequeath to you, a special gift that will help you in times of great need. I would be criticized for doing so, but I went through secret channels and consulted a Tulyan timeseer about you."

For several moments, the airless cave seemed to contain another presence, a thing that the old woman had not yet said. Finally, Astar continued, her voice quavering. "The timeseer told me that a unique future lies in store for you, Tesh, unlike anything that has ever happened to a member of the Parvii race."

"I only want to be a podship pilot."

The slender woman placed a wrinkled hand on Tesh's shoulder. "I know, dear, but something more is available to you, something far greater. Throughout history, there have been occasions when our women and men have fallen in love with members of other races."

"I have heard this."

"Then you have also heard that it is impossible for a Parvii to breed with another galactic race. Even though we can engage in sexual acts with them, no children can result."

"Yes."

"Well, that is not strictly true. There are certain methods. Offspring have in fact been conceived from such unions. Not many, but it has happened. A few thousand perhaps, over millions of years. Some of the children were hunted down and killed as monstrosities by the Eye of the Swarm, but others escaped and lived out their lives as fugitives. In your case, you are destined to face such a breeding conundrum. And it will be unlike any of the other examples. The alien male you meet will be exceptional, perhaps even godlike."

"I'm not sure if I like the sound of this."

"When you encounter this person, you will know. At first, you will have doubts about whether he can possibly be the one who has been foretold, and you may even discount what I am telling you now as nonsense. You will think he is an ordinary alien male, and will discover that sexual acts with him are pleasurable, though perhaps not fantastic. But after you are intimate with him, a certainty will seep into your awareness, and you will know that you must bear his child. Increasingly, this will consume your thoughts."

"And what will my child be like?" Tesh's heart had raced as she asked the question.

"Ordinary in appearance, but anything but ordinary inside. The gender has not been revealed to me, nor have specifics about the life your child will lead. Throughout the history of all races there have been special children who have accomplished great things, such as Sanji the Tulyan and Jesus Christ the Human. Your child could very well be on that scale."

"You have omitted mention of any great or legendary Parvii."

"And with good reason, Tesh. I hate to say this, but our race has been making terrible mistakes for a long time, grievous errors that have had widespread consequences. I know you want to be a podship pilot—perhaps for the glamour of it—but I have long wondered if that is our true calling as a race. Certainly it is not the honorable pursuit our leaders make it out to be."

Astar paused. Presently, looking into Tesh's eyes, the wrinkled breeding specialist said, "I suspect you're wondering how I can keep such blasphemous thoughts away from the telepathic probes of the Eye of the Swarm. Let me just say that there are ways. And perhaps it is wishful thinking on my part, but I think your child just might be part of the solution, a way for us to alter the course of Parvii destiny. I sense goodness in you, Tesh. Otherwise, I would not be saying such things to you."

Placing her own hand on the old woman's face, Tesh said, "I believe you."

After that, Astar revealed things about the intricacies of the Parvii female body, and described specific methods that could be used to become pregnant with the child of an alien. Then the old woman made Tesh repeat it all back to her, in detail. The younger woman got it right the first time.

"Never forget what I have taught you," Astar said, in the most solemn and ominous of voices.

"I won't. I promise."

"There are so many more things I would like to tell you, Tesh, but I don't have the energy to do so, and perhaps it would not be right anyway. Know and understand, though, that you will face great, undetermined dangers in taking the path I have outlined. You will be bearing a forbidden child, considered a horror by our people. But our people are *wrong*."

Weakened by the exertion of the flight and all she had to say, the old woman slumped to the floor of the foldcave. Tesh eased her down, and sat on the hard surface, holding Astar's head on her own lap.

Looking up into Tesh's face, the aged woman smiled. Then her facial expression became stony and she said, "There is one more thing I must tell you. I don't have the specifics, but long ago, in the early days of the galaxy … " Astar coughed, struggled to speak.

Tesh comforted her, but couldn't help wanting to know what the old woman had to say.

Finally, Astar said, "What I am about to tell you is all I know about a particular subject, and that is not very much. It is a fact known to all breeding specialists, but it is only a fragment of information. Long ago, so distant in time that it has been all but erased from our memories, the Parvii race had a connection with another galactic race."

"The Tulyans," Tesh said. "We defeated them in battle, took the podships away from them."

"Not that type of connection, child. No, not that at all. Something entirely different and more cooperative in nature." She sighed. "Oh, if we only knew more than that morsel of information, and more than the name of the race!"

In Tesh's arms, the old woman trembled, and then said, "I speak of an important connection between Parviis and Adurians. What it is, I do not know, and the races seem so different. But there are similarities that are apparent to one in my profession."

"Both races have extensive breeding knowledge?"

"Precisely." The smile returned, though a wary one. "With the specialized knowledge I have imparted, you are now a limited breeding specialist, with just enough information to navigate your own remarkable future. I wish you all of the good things in life, for you and your unusual family."

"Thank you."

The old woman closed her eyes, and against Tesh's fingertips she felt Astar's pulse slowing. The younger woman turned away, crying.

Nearly an hour passed. Finally, the aged breeding specialist slipped away, into her own eternity.…

* * * * *

Now, in the privacy of the sectoid chamber, Tesh had been using a combination of things she knew about the internal workings of her own body—the things that every Parvii woman knew, along with the secret knowledge that Astar had shared with her. Already, she had used the secret knowledge to protect something precious that Noah had given to her, something she had been concealing within her body for two months.

Reaching under the side of her collar, Tesh touched a place on her skin that she knew was a tiny, dark mark, beneath which lay the implanted med-tech device that operated her body's magnification system. This time, though, instead of rubbing the spot to activate the magnifier and enlarge the appearance of her body, she held a forefinger there for several moments, until she felt another feature of the med-tech unit click on.

Over Tesh's head, a hologram appeared, a full-color, life-size videocam of the interior of her body. Using the technology, she conducted her own private medical examination. Along with the projected images in front of her eyes, data flowed into her brain, telling her the exact condition of every organ, every muscle, and every cell—even every atom and subatomic particle, if she chose to analyze them in detail. Barring an accident, she could expect to live for almost fifteen hundred additional years. So far, this was an analysis that any Parvii could accomplish.

But that was not what Tesh was looking for.

Taking a deep breath, she activated one of the hidden features of the system that Astar had revealed to her centuries ago. This went beyond what Tesh had already done to her body as a result, the keeping and preserving of Noah's gift within her. That only allowed her time to think, to consider possibilities and decide if she wanted to go on to the next stage. Now, she was certain.

Staring into the hologram, Tesh felt a beam of bright light wash over her, causing her to shiver in anticipation. Her vision became foggy and unfocused, and her mind seemed to expand outward, into a luminous green cosmos that stretched into infinity. And far away in that realm of apparent space, in the place that Astar had told her how to reach, Tesh saw an opening, like a tunnel in the universe. But she knew this was inside her own body instead, a special feature of the embedded medical apparatus. She hesitated, felt her metabolism quicken, and then plunged psychically into the tunnel.

In a matter of moments, Tesh emerged on the other side, in a tiny, colorless chamber of her own body. And there she saw what she sought: a sac of the alien cellular material that she had been storing in her body, ever since her sexual encounter with Noah Watanabe.

Again, she hesitated. But she knew the decision no longer hung in the balance. She had gone this far, and had to continue.

Carefully, mentally adjusting the med-tech device in the precise manner that Astar had revealed to her, Tesh opened the sac and let Noah's sperm flow through her body, bypassing the racial firewalls that had been designed to prevent breeding between Parviis and any other ethnic group.

Now she felt Noah with her again, his physical closeness and warmth, as if they were making love once more. The rapture she shared with him was even more intense than it had been previously, wave upon wave of pleasure building to a grand climax in her mind and body. Finally, as after a great storm, the fury of passion subsided and she lay there in the green luminescence, completely sated.

Having done this, Tesh no longer felt alone, and that gave her some comfort. But she sensed grave perils ahead. To face them, she would need to reach deep for all the strength she could muster, and for all the strength she could draw from others. She knew absolutely that she had to attempt this difficult path, no matter where it took her ... and her child.

And no matter how anyone felt about it. Even Noah.

Chapter Forty-Two

Time is a measuring stick, but it goes in a circle.

—Tulyan observation

As Eshaz continued to lead his ecological repair team around the galaxy, he thought he must be one of the busiest Tulyans alive. He not only had to coordinate the work assignments of his caretakers, but he liked to get involved personally, and perform some of the important web repair tasks himself. Some of his team members wondered how he could possibly do so much, and to that inquiry, Eshaz invariably had a simple reply: "I don't sleep anymore."

It was an exaggeration, but not much of one. He slept only a couple of hours a day now, and somehow he kept going anyway. Humans would have said their adrenaline was causing it, or caffeine, or one of the designer drugs that kept them awake. In Eshaz's case, it was sheer desperation. He knew he would never again face such an important challenge. The responsibility of managing five hundred podships and the Tulyans aboard them weighed heavily on him. He felt up to the challenge, but knew when it was completed, if he ever got back to his beloved Tulyan Starcloud, he wanted to sleep for a month straight.

At the moment, he was performing yet another duty, having merged into the flesh of the lead podship, Agryt, in order to pilot it and lead the repair fleet across the galaxy. They were just leaving the Tarbu Gap, a sacred and secret Tulyan region whose location was concealed from the prying eyes and telepathic probes of outsiders by electrical disturbances.

Ahead, if he kept on this route, lay the legendary Wild Pod Zone. He wished he could go there as he had in the past, but knew that was impossible. It was now in the Hibbil Sector.

Through visual sensors on the hull of the pod, combined with his own enhanced eyes, Eshaz saw far out into space, to the dim dwarf stars of that region, white or brown in color. But even if he was able to go there, he suspected it would not be the same as the past. In all likelihood there were dangerous galactic conditions there, things that needed the attention of his expert team. To him, the threat of military action by the HibAdus didn't seem any worse than some of the other dangers around the galaxy. It seemed like a matter of priorities, that he should just barrel ahead and try to complete as many repairs in that sector as he could. But the Council of Elders had forbidden him from going there. They were keeping part of the Liberator fleet to perform military operations to enforce the web repairs that were needed, and perhaps at this very moment other Tulyans were conducting operations in that region. If he went against orders, he could compromise their efforts.

My superiors know better than I, he thought.

Grudgingly, Eshaz changed course sharply, and headed for yet another star system, in a different sector. The other podships followed. One by one, he was completing the tasks on his list. In only a few minutes, he would be in the next work zone, unless he had to take an alternate route due to web conditions.

In his lifetime of nearly a million years, Eshaz had seen many things, and had done many things. He had been a renowned and talented timeseer, among a small number in all of the Tulyan Starcloud who could see portions of the future. It had always been an imperfect talent, affected and limited by cosmic conditions and by other factors that were largely unknown to him. In one of his most distasteful assignments, the Council had ordered him to perform timeseeing duties for Woldn and the Parviis—an unusual cooperative arrangement between the races that existed before the latest hostilities. The attempt had not gone well, and as a result Woldn had not been pleased. But Eshaz had been painfully honest with him; he really had not been able to provide the information sought by the Parvii leader.

Sometimes—both under assignment and on his own—Eshaz had tried to visualize other specific futures. Prime among them, he had endeavored to discern the path lying ahead of the most remarkable of all Humans, Noah Watanabe ... the galactic ecologist, Timeweb traveler, and immortal. Against all odds, this Human might outlive the most ancient of Tulyans. Remarkable,

625

indeed. And, though Noah denied it, he might be the messiah foretold in Tulyan legends.

But each time that Eshaz had made the effort to focus his timeseeing abilities on Noah, he had encountered only chaos around the man, a cosmic, veiling murkiness that prevented any intrusion. The more he had tried to probe, the more Eshaz had found himself with a ferocious headache, so he had gradually given up the effort. Some things were truly impossible.

Now as he sped along the webway, Eshaz attempted something that seemed even more broad that focusing on Noah's life. Mulling it over, however, he realized that it was something that stemmed from Noah, or at least from something Noah had said—and this might add to the difficulties of timeseeing.

With his far-seeing eyes, Eshaz gazed beyond the physical reality of the galaxy around him, into an alternate dimension that was connected to the web of time. Having already commanded his podship to follow a particular course, he could take a few moments to make this new attempt.

For a good distance, the ethereal realm opened up to him and he saw where Timeweb was connected to the substance and mass of the known galaxy, and where many of the Tulyan caretaking repair teams had either completed important work or were continuing with it.

And far, far beyond that, he peered into the place where all things were heading with each passing moment, an inexorable flow of time and destiny from countless directions. Like streams and currents. *There!* he thought, feeling a surge of excitement, but one that was tinged in dread.

Something dark and amorphous lay in the future of all living beings in the galaxy, blocking all paths, preventing any way around it. But what? As he attempted to see farther into the lens of time, his corporeal limitations intruded, and he felt the worst headache of his entire life. And Eshaz knew that if he pressed forward, he would create such pain and such internal cellular damage that he could die.

This risk did not matter to him, not with such so much at stake. As a consequence, he pressed on with his own form of psychic timeseeing, looking with the specially attuned eyes that he had been received as a gift with his birth. *The pain!* Sharp lances surged into his awareness.

But he refused to back off.

Less than a minute passed, though it seemed like much longer to Eshaz, as in the compression of a dream ... or a nightmare. Finally, something kicked him out, hard, and he landed back in the reality of the podship speeding through space.

Moments later, Agryt reached the destination that Eshaz had provided, and slowed down. The rest of the Aopoddae behind did the same. All of their pilots and crews awaited Eshaz's further instructions. He wondered what his own face must look like on the prow of the vessel.

He didn't feel in any condition to guide the team. His head screamed in pain. Then, as moments passed he felt the discomfort diminishing, and he realized that Agryt was comforting him, using some unfathomable Aopoddae method to bring a foolish Tulyan back to awareness and function.

Presently, Eshaz felt fully restored, and grateful to his symbiotic companion. But he was left with a certainty that troubled him above all others.

Noah had been right. There really *was* a great and towering danger out there—more than any of the galactic races had ever encountered before—and to complicate the situation even more, no one could identify it.

Chapter Forty-Three

In this universe of wondrous possibilities, certain constants exist, and all of them are linked to the symbiosis of science and religion. These two divisions of the Ultimate Truth are—in the basic analysis—one and the same, and their respective subparts contribute to the whole. Are certain acts morally wrong and repugnant to civilization? In pre-Scienscroll times, many purported scientists claimed that there were no immoral acts, and that moral templates were no more than artificial constructs. When at long last humanity saw the light, such views were righteously tossed into the dustbins of history.

—*Scienscroll,* 1 Eth 77–78

With Princess Meghina right behind him, Noah negotiated a spiral, rock stairway that led down to the ancient dungeons of the palace. Bright lights illuminated the way, so that they could walk more safely on the uneven, stained surface—stairs that had been worn down in places by the passage of many feet. It was early morning.

"As you know, it was pretty dark down here before," he said, "so we added more lighting."

"My palace has a long history," she said, "much of it unsavory. I'm afraid there were torture chambers down here centuries ago."

"We found some evidence of that. No machines, but there were still shackles on the walls."

Noah pushed open a heavy iron door, revealing a corridor lined with glowing orange, electronic containment cells. His officers had converted this to a military gaol, always necessary to confine fighters and a limited number of others that the forces encountered who needed to be taken into custody. And, though it was not large or crowded with prisoners today, it became, nonetheless, quite noisy as they approached a cell on the far end.

"Finally!" the Salducian diplomat shouted as he jumped up from a cot. His normally impeccable gray suit was wrinkled and soiled, and at the knees of some of his numerous legs the fabric was torn and bloody, with visible wounds. Glaring through the containment field at Noah, he then shifted his gaze to the Princess. At that point his demeanor changed, and in a pleasant tone he said to her, "Thank you for coming to get me out. I have spent a most uncomfortable night."

"I'm not here for that," she said.

"What?" Confusion moved across Kobi Akar's oblong face. His crab-pincer hands flexed back and forth behind the containment field, as if looking for something to grab onto and rip apart. Looking at Noah, he asked, "Are you attempting to assert military jurisdiction over me?"

"No," Noah said. "Your confinement is presently military, since that offers the best security. However, the jurisdiction is civilian. As soon as possible, you will be transferred to Canopan authorities."

"In the midst of a war? What outrage is this? I want a lawyer!"

"You will have access to lawyers on Canopa," Noah said.

"This is outrageous!"

"It is the law," Noah said. "A serious charge has been placed against you."

In an indignant tone, the Salducian said, "One of the guards mentioned something about sex with a minor girl. It's a complete lie!"

627

"You will have your opportunity to prove that. Reportedly it occurred on the orbital gambling casino, over Canopa."

"It's all a monstrous fabrication, designed to extort payment out of me. However, just for the sake of argument, I ask you: How can there be any Canopan civilian jurisdiction over an orbiter that is in space? That falls under intergalactic law, not planetary law."

"We don't know the particulars," Meghina said, "only that the Office of the Doge has ordered you to Canopa."

"It's all a waste of time, you know," Akar said. He scuttled backward, and sagged wearily onto the cot. "Whatever the jurisdiction, I have diplomatic immunity."

"And the courts will determine if you flaunted it," Noah said.

"Flaunted? In this matter, that is not a legal term. Obviously, I know the law and you don't."

"I'm not here to debate you."

"I asked Noah to bring me to check on your physical condition," the Princess said. "Are you being fed well, Mr. Akar? Have you received treatment for your injuries?" She looked down at his bloodied legs that draped over the side of the cot.

"The food is unfit for roachrats," he replied. "And as for my injuries, that is an additional matter. My lawyers will prefer charges for mistreatment of a prisoner."

"I viewed the surveillance file on you," Noah said. "You injured yourself when you fell on the stairs."

"I was pushed!"

"That isn't what the evidence shows."

"I shall send you better food and a doctor," Meghina said, stiffly. Then, without another word, she turned and left, with Noah behind her.

"What are they going to do?" Akar shouted after them, "Give me a life sentence?" He cackled, delighted at his own dark humor.

"That is not up to us," Noah said, over his shoulder. "We are only holding you for other authorities."

"I have a long list of grievances!" Akar shouted after them. "You'll both hear from my lawyers!"

"On that, at least, I believe you," Noah yelled back, as he and Meghina went through the heavy iron door.

"What's that supposed to mean?"

In response, Noah slammed the door shut.

"A charming man, but I never entirely trusted him," Meghina said. "That doesn't mean he's guilty, though."

Noah couldn't help but agree, though soon—after completing the transfer to Canopa—the matter would be out of his hands.

* * * * *

Sometimes, Noah dreaded going to sleep. In his military duties, he spent long hours attending to important tasks, so by the end of each day he invariably felt tired enough to drift off. But so many problems kept churning through his mind that he found it difficult to leave them unresolved. So much seemed beyond his ability to fix or even to understand. At times, he wished he knew less than he did, or at least that he had been exposed to less.

The mysteries of Timeweb were at the very top of his list.

It awed him to think of the incredible galactic web that connected everything in a manner that most galactic races could not detect, a structure that had existed for millions and millions of years. During all of that time, it had been strong enough to hold everything together, but now, after so much abuse and neglect, it was falling apart. Reports from the Tulyan caretaker teams indicated some progress in completing repairs, and a number of the most heavily damaged areas had been improved. But there were also ongoing reports of new timeholes needing attention and entire galactic sectors in peril, so the Tulyan Elders needed to constantly adjust their priorities and plans.

As First Elder Kre'n had said, it was like the triage method of assessing the injuries of soldiers on a vast galactic battlefield, except in this case Timeweb was a single entity, with many widespread wounds.

Humankind is a single organism, Noah thought, as he made his way to his private quarters in the keep. *In fact, all races are a single organism. All races are linked to Timeweb.*

He felt his thoughts stretching beyond prior levels of understanding or connection.

Suddenly, in the corridor he dropped to his knees, and a green darkness pervaded his consciousness. In the background, he heard guards asking if he was all right.

Noah was conscious of remaining on his knees, and of people all around him. Some of them touched him, and he heard their distant voices asking if they should help him to lie down. Someone summoned a doctor, and Noah wondered if it would be the same doctor that would attend to the Salducian. An odd, throwaway thought that intruded on others of much more importance.

Priorities, he thought. Life was about assigning priorities, and acting upon them. He wasn't sure if he had heard that somewhere, or if he had figured it out himself. Another throwaway thought.

Then, with all of the commotion around him, Noah became an island unto himself, and voices drifted away around him. He recalled the horrible death of his sister, the way she aged too rapidly and died looking like a haggard old woman, and probably in terrible pain. Certainly, she suffered from a horrendous anguish of the soul. Noah thought back to the last time he saw her, when she stabbed him with a dermex needle, claiming it contained her own tainted blood. Even though doctors subsequently assured him that she had not infected him— and Noah seemed to have his own brand of immortality—he still worried about it occasionally.

So much information to discard. So many details that only clogged his mind and made it work inefficiently, details that intruded like guerrilla fighters and then retreated, only to irritate him over and over again. Concerning Francella, he didn't want to think about her bad side, though that was almost all he'd ever seen of her. Instead, he tried to remember the few comparatively pleasant times they had shared (mostly as children), occasions when they almost seemed like normal siblings.

My life has been anything but normal, he thought. *And hers, in its own horrific way, was far from normal as well.*

The Human condition seemed to cover a broad range of purported normalcy. But he realized that at its very core each Human relationship contained an inevitable element of dysfunction, and that people—the optimistic types—tried to put a positive cast on problems, making them seem less significant than they actually were.

Noah had always tried to be an optimist himself, even when the obstacles against that state of mind seemed insurmountable. Now, more than ever in his lifetime, and he was quite certain—more than ever in the history of the galaxy—the obstacles were greater than ever.

Like a great flood waiting to break through holes in a dike, Chaos threatened to inundate everything in the known galaxy, ruining eons of cosmic evolution, changing everything for the worse. The Tulyans were like little Dutch boys running around putting their fingers in the holes. But there seemed to be many more timeholes than there were caretakers to fix them.

He felt the dark seepage of pessimism into his awareness, and fought to push it back.

At the moment, he sensed someone carrying him, but that part didn't matter. He cried out, and felt the flood of an abrupt vision that took over his consciousness. Suddenly, he found himself thinking with Francella's mind and seeing through her eyes. Startling! But fascinating. He didn't fight the sensations. It didn't seem like one of the doors to Timeweb; it seemed like something else....

It was a gloomy, rainy day on Canopa, and Francella was at CorpOne headquarters with their father, Prince Saito Watanabe.

"You know," the old man said as they stood by the rain-swept window, "I might have been wrong all my life about industrial pollution and waste, so maybe I should change after all, as Noah has been preaching to me—even if it means dismantling every business operation my company has. Maybe I should turn operation of the company over to your brother and let him clean things up from the inside."

"He can only destroy CorpOne!" she shouted back, her voice cracking. "Noah has never cared about this company or this family! How can you say such a thing?"

"You will accept whatever I decide," the old merchant prince said. "If I have been wrong in the past, I must make amends." He looked at her with rheumy old eyes. "And you must makes amends, too. For a long time, I have noticed how you never reach out to Noah, never seem capable of seeing anything good about him. Why is that? I never wanted the two of you to grow so far apart."

He extended a hand to touch her shoulder affectionately, but she pushed it away.

They argued for awhile, father and daughter, with far more than the normal associated emotions. Finally Francella went away by herself, to her own island of twisted consciousness. She felt extremely upset at what the old tycoon had said to her. In her office her thoughts went wild, and she smashed things around her.

It was a turning point in her life. Always before, she had imagined doing terrible things, even worse than the financial indiscretions she had long committed against her company and her family. Now, for the first time, she actively plotted to kill her father and blame it on Noah.

As the images faded and Noah found himself in his own apartment with a doctor tending to him, he was left wondering if he had experienced an accurate vision of her thoughts, something transmitted by her blood—which she had injected so violently into his bloodstream. They had been born fraternal twins, and perhaps the injection had intensified a paranormal connection they'd already had.

"He's breathing hard," the doctor said.

Through bleary eyes, Noah saw an elderly man with white hair. Noah tried to calm his own pulse, but became conscious of it roaring in his ears as blood pumped wildly through his veins.

Could their father's death really have occurred the way he had just envisioned it? Noah was stunned, but somehow it all seemed to fit.

He felt medications taking effect, and heard the voices drift away again, but this time he blacked out.

Chapter Forty-Four

Each breath we attempt to take is an adventure into the unknown.

—Ancient saying

So much had happened, and of such grave and far-reaching significance, that Princess Meghina had not had time to grieve for her lost dagg, Orga, or for the many citizens of Siriki who had died in the HibAdu onslaught. Many had been her friends and associates. Sadly, she had to face the fact that portions of her past were gone, and irretrievable. Even her once-magnificent Golden Palace was looking worn and tired, from its conversion into a military headquarters for the Liberator forces.

She didn't object to the use of her opulent home for that noble purpose, so her sadness was tempered by the stark realities that faced everyone now. There were two grave threats—the HibAdus, and the declining infrastructure of the galaxy. She'd even heard rumors that the Tulyans and Noah thought there might be yet another great peril "out there" somewhere, but whenever she had asked any of them about it, she had received only vague responses. Even Noah, who had a reputation for being concise and direct, had evaded her question. She came away with the feeling that the people around her were bordering on paranoia, and perhaps a quiet hysteria, constantly feeling that terrible things were about to happen.

It was mid-afternoon on a cloudy day, and Meghina found herself in an improbable place, standing on the edge of a high cliff with Llew Jarro, Betha Neider, Dougal Netzer, and Paltrow. All of them were the "elixir-immortals," but missing the Salducian diplomat, who was being transferred as a prisoner to Canopa later that day. The five of them were still on the palace grounds, and had gone up in a tram. The high perch had always been a favorite place for Meghina to go, often by herself, and sometimes with one of her rare pet animals.

"We form an exclusive little club, you know," said the corpulent Jarro. He stood with his back to the precipice, facing the others. "I thought you might be interested in learning what I have been discovering about our ... special condition."

"Not that we're afraid of heights or anything," Paltrow said, with a little snicker. "But I'll ask again: Why have you brought us to this cliff?"

A thick, buxom woman, Paltrow nonetheless didn't appear to have an ounce of fat on her. She looked to have trained for sporting activities of some sort in the past, but was close-mouthed about her personal history, except to say that she was only too happy to "leave it in the dust," including her own birth name. With her immortality, she had not only assumed a new body, but a new name of her choosing. Despite the enigma around the woman, Meghina rather

631

liked her, and didn't sense anything shadowy about her. Not what the Princess had sensed—accurately, in all likelihood—about Kobi Akar.

"Some things are best demonstrated rather than described," Jarro said. "I'm about to jump off this cliff. Not to kill myself, of course, because that is an impossibility. I've been coming up here on my own, and have gone off several times."

Meghina glanced over the edge, and felt a little tug at her stomach, a touch of queasiness. It was a long way down. According to Sirikan legend, two star-crossed lovers had committed suicide from this place, long ago. Through a grove of trees, the Princess saw some of the fences and buildings of her private zoo, and beyond that, a meadow that had been converted to a landing field for conventional military aircraft, and for occasional podships.

Jarro took a half step backward, so that he barely maintained his footing. "We've all heard of the horrors that Noah Watanabe experienced at the hands of his sister, how she kept hacking him up, and his body kept regenerating. From our experience at Yaree, it is clear that we share some of that remarkable ability. We could fall off here, and eventually recover."

"That's true enough," old Dougal Netzer said. A scowl formed on the artist's creased, ruddy face. "It wouldn't be good, though, if we were all trapped in a rock slide. We still have our muscular limitations."

"I hadn't thought of that," Jarro said, "but the rocks seem stable enough here."

"You're not a geologist," the old man said.

"You're right."

"A timehole could open up, too, and start some sort of an upheaval."

"You do have an imagination," Jarro said. "But that could happen anywhere, not just here. I guess we could all decide to remain separate if we're worried about that. However, I think we have more to learn from each other. I've jumped off this cliff eight times now, and ... "

"You've used up your nine lives, then," Betha Neider quipped, "counting your fall at Yaree."

"Usually you are a delightful young woman," Jarro said, "but your inexperience can cause you to be facetious at times. This is one of those occasions. No, Betha, I have many more lives than the proverbial allocation, as do we all. I was about to say, each time I've done the jump, I've recovered faster than the time before. At first, it was hours before I could get up and walk back to the palace. The last time, it was a matter of minutes."

"This promises to be a delightful day," Betha said, undeterred. "You'll walk back and have dinner, while we lay splattered at the base of the cliff, until we get up in the darkness and stumble around like zombies."

"I'm talking about self-improvement," Jarro said, glaring at her. "If any of you prefer, you can ride the tram to the bottom. As for me, I have an alternate means of transportation." He backed up and leaped off backward, tumbling into the air. "See you at the bottom!"

After a few seconds, Meghina heard the sickening thump of his body when it struck the ground, far below. She looked over the edge, but couldn't make out where he had hit. A minute later she saw something moving down there, and heard a distant voice that carried all the way up the cliff face: "Come on in! The water's fine!"

"See you guys in Zombieland," Betha said, as she leaped off. Paltrow followed her, leaving Meghina and old Dougal on the high perch. "I can't have girls showing me up," the artist said, with a shrug. Then he followed the others.

For several moments, the Princess stood on the edge of the precipice, looking down. So far, only one person moved down there, whom she presumed to be Llew Jarro. It seemed most untidy and undignified to her to add herself to the splattered flesh and broken bones at the base of the cliff, and a wayward thought occurred to her: What if animals from the woods came and started eating the bodies? Maybe they wouldn't finish the bodies off before they started regenerating, not even with the help of carrion birds, but it gave her pause. Besides, she was not in the mood to make herself the subject of a scientific experiment, especially an impromptu one. In the midst of a huge galactic war, with so many concerns on her mind, she could not afford to be foolish or capricious. She shouldn't even have come up here with the others, not without finding out what Jarro wanted.

And by title, she remained the civilian leader of this planet, requiring that she behave with decorum.

Jarro, and perhaps some of the others, might not agree with her feelings, but that didn't matter to her. She had heard somewhere that true leadership was not a popularity contest.

Summoning a different sort of courage than her companions had displayed, Princess Meghina boarded the tram, and rode it down. She would send palace guards and doctors to attend to her friends.

* * * * *

That evening, with the necessary transfer documents completed, two MPA marshals escorted their high-security prisoner onto a podship for the flight to Canopa. The electronically-cuffed Salducian was not cooperative, and as they entered the passenger compartment he tried to kick one of the officers—both of whom were burly Human men. They stepped out the way easily, and shoved him roughly onto a bench, then activated a shimmering containment field to keep him there.

"You'll lose your careers for this!" Kobi Akar shouted, as he struggled unsuccessfully to break free.

"Oh, do you hear that, Iktar? We're really worried, aren't we?"

"Yeah," said the other, as the diplomat glared at them. "Maybe we should turn this guy loose, or 'accidentally' let him escape. That would really look good in our personnel files, wouldn't it?"

"Sure would. Our salaries would be doubled right away, and we'd be promoted."

The one called Iktar sat on a nearby bench, and said, "Too bad we're having trouble with the restraint controls. I just can't seem to get them to open up."

"Yeah, they are temperamental, aren't they? Like our famous prisoner here."

Kobi Akar shouted obscenities at them in two languages, until they set the controls to prevent his mouth from moving. After that, he could only grunt— and each time he even did that, he received an electric shock. Soon, glowering crazily, he settled down.

Because of poor podway conditions, the flight took more than an hour and a half. Finally, they reached the pod station over Canopa and docked. The prisoner was transferred to a shuttle.

But as the shuttle descended over Canopa, a glowing green hole suddenly opened in the sky—just large enough to swallow the craft before closing afterward. Witnesses on the ground and in space reported seeing a small time-hole for a few seconds before it vanished, taking the ship and passengers with it.

Chapter Forty-Five

We have no superiors—not even those who created us.

—High Ruler Coreq, remarks to the other two
members of the HibAdu triumvirate

He was shorter than the typical Adurian and taller than most Hibbils, with features of each race. His oversized, pale yellow eyes took in everything around him as he passed through security doors and strutted into the laboratory complex. The odors of flesh and strong chemicals permeated the air, as Adurian scientists and research technicians went about their tasks at spotless, gleaming work stations. All of them wore sealed body suits and helmets to prevent contaminating the genetic samples they were handling, while electronic bio-barriers kept any visitor at a safe distance. Complex machines hummed and throbbed. Concise, technical words filled the air as staff members discussed their experiments.

The yellow-suited Adurian workers seemed to hardly give the hybrid any notice as he passed by, but he knew they were watching him peripherally, and fearfully. In the past, some of their predecessors in these labs had even called him a freak and other improper terms, but never to his face. No matter, High Ruler Coreq always found out who they were from cellular-memory readings and had them eliminated. Permanently. Those who were left now seemed to be relatively stable, though they always needed to be monitored, and checked. There was another problem with them at the moment, however. They did not want to perform a particular task that the triumvirate had ordered them to do—the one involving the Parviis.

Coreq considered the Adurians weaklings, only good for limited, assigned functions. When the time was right, he and his triumvirate would orchestrate the breeding of an entirely new hybrid race, one that would kill or enslave all other sentients in the galaxy.

By the standards of most galactic races, the High Ruler was still quite young, having not yet passed his fifteenth birth marker. But that only accounted for his physical self, part Hibbil and part Adurian, bred under optimal laboratory conditions. Inside his mind—the part that mattered much more than the external appearance—he was exceedingly old, because the wisdom and violence of the ancients had been infused into him, but not in any random or cluttered manner. He had their cellular memories, but only those that mattered for the success of the galactic-wide military force that his triumvirate led.

I am first among equals, he thought, thinking of his two companions.

It was his own observation, but an apt one. The others—Premier Enver and Warlord Tarix—deferred to him on virtually all matters of importance. Sometimes this surprised him whenever they were discussing military or security matters, since Tarix knew considerably more about those subjects than he did. But she always phrased her statements with exquisite care, so that she was the adviser and Coreq the decision maker.

Even so, Coreq didn't entirely trust her, or Enver, either. He always suspected they were plotting against him, planning to take over at the first opportunity. But the High Ruler was no fool. Wherever he went, he had his personal retinue of elite robot guards close behind, and robotic security agents checking the route ahead. Tiny biomachines tasted his food and beverages for poisons, and even flew in front to test the air he was about to breathe. He'd thought of everything. Some of them hovered above him now, still taking readings and sending audible electronic signals to him, while others went further ahead, to scout where he intended to go.

Presently he left one lab section and entered the large central chamber, where some the most famous experiments were conducted. It always gave him a rush coming in here, because he and his two HibAdu cohorts had been created at these very lab stations, had taken their first breaths here.

Ahead, Coreq saw a flurry of biomachines in the air, like a horde of insects. He heard their high-pitched exchanges and reports as they confirmed the area was safe for the High Ruler to enter. Because of their tiny size, the units reminded him of Parviis, but the comparison did not go much beyond that. Coreq could control these biomachines with an implanted transmitter in his own brain, while Parviis required a different sort of attention.

For the moment, Coreq's aides had arranged for Woldn and his followers to occupy all of the observation galleries around the central chamber, where they clustered on the other side against the thick glax, and peered into the huge laboratory. Security sensors reported more than one hundred and sixty thousand of the tiny aliens there, packed into the enclosures.

Though the High Ruler had tried to secure the galleries and prevent the escape of the pesky visitors, the tiny humanoids had a form of collective paranoia, in which Woldn kept them in a state of hyper alertness, constantly checking and maintaining routes of escape. Obviously, it was a survival mechanism and Coreq would have found it interesting, had he not wanted to dominate these creatures and take them into custody. But, to keep the situation calm and under control, he had been forced to back off, leaving some escape routes open.

Woldn had presented twenty volunteer Parviis to the Adurian scientists for dissection and detailed analysis. This reflected the purpose of the Parvii leader's visit: to investigate a possible ancient connection between Adurians and Parviis. Seventeen days ago, upon first hearing this claim from his private box in the assembly hall, Coreq had almost dismissed the notion out of hand, since his enhanced and focused memories carried no reference to such a connection. But—via an intercom that connected the leaders' private boxes—Warlord Tarix and Premier Enver had convinced him otherwise. Enver said he had a faint but undocumented sensation that the contention might very well be true. While no data actually existed in the Premier's conscious memory, not even a fragment, he said it was important sometimes to follow through on sensory feelings. He and Tarix had recommended that they look into the matter, so Coreq had agreed.

And, although the Adurian scientists had been reluctant to say much, Coreq knew they were fearful of this line of inquiry. It had to do with an odd psychosis of their tunnel-minded race, in which—despite great successes in genetics and bioengineering—they were afraid of their collective past, and ashamed of it. According to legend, terrible things had happened to them as a race long ago, and their collective humiliation had caused them to stop talking about such matters, and to gradually try to forget them. Even so, fragments of the past remained in their consciousness, of lost wars and planets destroyed. The details were vague, however, , despite the fact that the Adurians had the ability to track genetic memories back for thousands of generations. It seemed logical to Coreq that some Adurians must have gone privately into the cellular archives and learned the full truth, but if so they were not talking about it—and thus far he had been unable to discover anything through the ongoing police methods of reading the cells of citizens.

In the days since Coreq had ordered the new investigation, highly agitated Adurian scientists had been delving further into the genetic memories of their own people, and of the hundred Parviis from the swarm, seeking information, some common ground. The old data did not come through clearly, but clues were surfacing along genetic paths that the researchers followed backward, using complicated techniques. The scientists did this with both races, and as ancient memories came back they were processed, converted to data, and projected onto screens.

Now, on a large wall screen of the central chamber, the lab technicians displayed two side-by-side composite projections, one for the combined memory cells of each race. Images sped up and slowed, as the experts searched for connections, for similarities. As Coreq stood looking up at the screen, the Parvii side showed views of deep space, of suns, planets, and swirling nebulas in a hypnotic array of colors and shapes.

To the left of it, the Adurian side was much more limited in astronomical scope, showing trips through space, but comparatively more images of the Adurian homeworld itself. Coreq recognized his own capital city, always bustling in its various stages of historical development, and he saw yellow-suited scientists that worked long ago, looking very much like their modern counterparts.

Now the laboratory manager—an old Adurian with a pointed chin—pushed back the hood of his suit and joined Coreq. "I wish you had not asked us to research this matter, sir, for it has put my staff on the verge of a nervous breakdown. They are holding together as well as possible, but I am worried about them."

"Don't ever come to me with such drivel," Coreq said. "My time is valuable, and if you're not careful, your time will be limited."

"I have already enjoyed a long and productive life, but I do not wish to displease you. In addition, High Ruler, I must admit that I am finding the ancient lab procedures intriguing as they are revealed to us, though many of them would be of little interest to you. There is ... Wait! I just saw something."

Though Coreq normally cared little about names, he had remembered the name of this particular scientist, because he had been on the team that grew the three triumvirate leaders in this very laboratory. He called himself Bashpor, and might need to be dealt with eventually because of his arrogance, even though he had never been proven disloyal. For the moment, at least, he remained useful.

From a high-caste family, Bashpor and his team had initially tried to exert control over the HibAdu triumvirate. That had soon proved impossible, because the hybrids were so dominating and powerful, so the Bashpor group had slipped into what appeared to be a subservient position. And, while they were not entirely pleased with this, Coreq had the surveillance reports to prove that they had formed no conspiracy against the triumvirate, and that they held considerable emotional affection for their three laboratory creations.

Of utmost importance, from all appearances the galactic aims of the top Hibbil and Adurian scientists and of the HibAdu hybrids matched: Eliminate the Merchant Prince Alliance and the Mutati Kingdom. Thus far, the military successes had been gratifying, but a great deal of work remained to be completed, mopping up the remaining—and significant—resistance forces.

With a wave of his hand, Bashpor stopped the Adurian screen images from moving, and backed them up. Then, as the scientist enhanced the image of a table at the rear of the long-ago laboratory, Coreq saw what looked like tiny humanoids inside a clearglax enclosure. It took several seconds, but with more enhancement and enlargement, the images came into focus.

"Parviis?" the High Ruler asked.

"It would appear so, Your Eminence. I'll do more checking, but it looks to me like we created them in our laboratories."

Around him, Coreq heard the Parviis clamoring inside the observation galleries. A microphone clicked on, and it was Woldn, "That's the proof, isn't it?"

"It is a possible indication," the lab manager said, transmitting to him. "We shall investigate it further."

"I was right!" Woldn shouted, with his small voice made large by the lab's sound amplification system.

* * * * *

Later that day, the HibAdu leaders received a more complete report from the lab manager.

Inside a sleek office suite, High Ruler Coreq sat at a wide, polished desk, with Premier Enver on one side of him, and Warlord Tarix on the other. They stared blankly with their overlarge, pale yellow eyes, and listened.

"An intriguing tableau has emerged," Bashpor said. "Now that I've opened my mind to it, I must admit that it is very interesting." He paced back and forth in front of the big desk. "In ancient times, we Adurians were even more involved in biotechnology than we are now. Content with our present scientific and societal conditions, we never thought to delve so far back in our genetic history."

"Not content," Coreq said. "Fearful is more like it. But continue."

The old Adurian paused, and looked at the three. "We have always believed that the future is a more interesting domain."

"Undoubtedly that is one of the reasons that you created us," Tarix said, her oddly-echoing voice reverberating through the room. Her long white teeth glistened, which she liked to display to throw terror into underlings. At the moment, it had its effect on Bashpor, as he could not hold gazes with her. To avoid that uncomfortable position, he resumed pacing.

"In ancient days, we were engaged in countless wars, some of which did not go well for us. In modern times we knew that had occurred, but only in general. Here's a specific detail that rises above others: Long ago, we created two galactic races in our laboratories."

Coreq leaned forward. "*Two?* One was the Parviis, I assume?"

"Correct. The other has no name, but they are even smaller than Parviis, and have a domain that is quite surprising and intriguing. For want of a better term I shall refer to them as sub-biologicals, or sub-bios. Mmmm. They are nano-creatures, so I shall call them Nanos instead. Yes. In the most unlikely of all places, the Nanos live *inside* the galactic webbing, the structure that Tulyans and Parviis call Timeweb."

"I think we should call them Webbies instead of Nanos," Enver said. Sometimes he said off-the-wall things, focusing on irrelevant points. Just the same, Coreq thought the name that Enver suggested was preferable, so he nodded.

"Very well," Bashpor said. "Regarding their exact function, we don't know how to test any hypothesis, but we think the … Webbies … may explain how Tulyans are said to communicate across vast distances over the galactic infrastructure. If that is the case, the infinitely small creatures might also have something to do with the nehrcom transmission system of the Humans, a system we have replicated, without really understanding how it works. It is believed to operate through some sort of web-related cosmic frequency. I have more to tell you, much more."

Bashpor increased the speed of his pacing, as if charged with a drug. "Long ago, other galactic races took offense at our laboratory methods, so they went to war with us over them. Among our enemies were the Blippiqs and the Huluvians, and they forced to us to abandon our laboratory attempts to create new races. It seems that we went back to doing the forbidden things anyway, however, when we created you three HibAdus. Of course, that doesn't amount to an entire race yet, but I know your professed intentions in that regard."

"*Will* you stop pacing!" Coreq said. "My neck aches from watching you go back and forth."

Looking very nervous, Bashpor slumped into a chair in front of the leaders. Then, not making firm eye contact with them, he continued to speak. "In those long-ago days, the other galactic societies considered our experiments dangerous and unethical—which led to the hostilities. After using their war machines and forcing treaties on us to shut down that phase of our researches, the Blippiqs and Huluvians made attempts to eradicate the entire Parvii race. This proved unsuccessful." He paused. "But in response to the threat, the Parviis bred at a high and efficient rate, and soon their aggressive swarms wreaked havoc in the galaxy by taking control of the podship race away from the Tulyans. It seems that we caused a bit of trouble in space, albeit indirectly and unintentionally."

"And we're doing it again," Tarix said. "But this time, no one will stop us. We are no longer mere Adurians. We are *HibAdus.*"

"There is one thing more of particular interest," Bashpor said. "We have long suspected this, but now we have the proof, having followed the genetic markings back in time and unraveled the details: Genetic mutations of the Parviis led to the abhorrent Human race."

"Good reason to wipe out both races," Tarix said, causing a long, eerie echo at the conclusion of her words.

* * * * *

Awaiting word from the triumvirate, Woldn felt a change of pressure in the linked observation galleries. He exchanged telepathic alarm signals with his followers. All of them went into a frenzy as those stationed at the perimeters, in the ducts, and at all previously unsealed areas sent information to him. Outside the dome, the sentries he had positioned relayed additional information. With all of this data, the Eye of the Swarm knew the Adurians were making a more concerted and overt effort to seal the galleries and prevent escape.

"We reject your offer of close cooperation between Adurians and Parviis," Coreq said, his voice booming over the speaker system.

"And I reject your rejection!" Woldn shouted back.

Ever-wary and prepared for this, Woldn knew exactly where the weakest Adurian security points were—and where he should focus the telepathic attention of his swarm. Though not yet at their full mental or physical powers, he and his followers had been growing collectively stronger, and they had telepathic detonators that functioned passably well. He led his swarm through a heating duct system, blasting everything out of the way in mini detonations. Soon they found themselves in free space.

Woldn determined their course for the return voyage across the galaxy. Moments later, at the head of the small swarm, he vowed, "This Adurian insult shall not go unanswered!"

But he wondered who—and what—that odd creature in the laboratory had been. It looked male, as well as part Adurian and part Hibbil. A horrific combination of genes, from the look of it. Certainly it should have been a failed experiment, but the creature looked to be in charge of the entire operation.

Woldn had never seen anything like it. The very sight of the monster had given him chills.

Chapter Forty-Six

Appearances can be deceiving. Despite its bulky, fleshy form, a Mutati adult in its natural state weighs only half as much as a typical Human of the same age. Aeromutatis—the aviary version of the shapeshifter race—are just as light, but have stronger frames, so that they can fly other Mutatis on their backs, generally one at a time.

—MPA autopsy and interview results on Mutati prisoners

By taking interconnected hoverbus and airgrid plane routes, Dux, Acey, and the robot had been able to travel thousands of kilometers, getting them to Xisto, considered the last of the Sirikan frontier towns. In reality, there were other villages and towns in the back country beyond, but they did not have any form of public transportation.

As the boys and the small brown robot disembarked in the central square of Xisto, it was late morning. Dux and Acey had been eating sandwiches and any other quick food they could find, to keep going. Their passage and other expenses were all being paid by the unobtrusive-looking robot, from a compartment full of local funds that he carried. None of the townspeople even gave the trio a second glance; there were numerous other robots on the streets and visible in shops, performing a variety of tasks.

Unofficially, this was a personal trip to see the boys' grandmother. Officially, it was a military mission, to see if there were any HibAdu elements in the hinterlands. So far, other scouts had found no trace of them.

Acey said he knew his way around, since he'd been to this town before, with Grandma Zelk. "We want to go that way," he said, pointing toward a dirt road that led north.

They began walking, and within the hour picked up a ride from a flatbed hovertruck driver who talked cheerfully about his ranch and children. The teenagers rode with him inside the cab, while Kekur held onto a railing in the back. Later that afternoon they caught a ride from another farmer, this time on a motocart laden with fruits and vegetables. The people were quite friendly, just as the boys remembered. That night, they slept in an abandoned, ramshackle barn, while the robot kept guard over them.

The next afternoon, they got even luckier. For a modest charge, paid by Kekur, a young woman gave them a ride of five hundred kilometers in her crop-duster plane. On the way the boys ogled the attractive redhead and flirted with her. She had a good figure that she didn't mind showing off to them. But nothing came of the encounter, and at dusk she circled over a small meadow near a river, preparing to set down in hover mode.

In the low light, none of them noticed a camouflaged encampment on the opposite river bank. Suddenly, beams of blue light hit the wings of the aircraft, sending it spinning toward the ground.

"What the hell?" the pilot shouted.

"HibAdu forces," Kekur reported. "I am notifying command headquarters."

The pilot fought for control against the blue beams, and for a few moments she got the craft flying again, on an escape route. Then a blast of light penetrated the cabin and hit her in the head, killing her instantly. Descending, the plane ripped off the top of a tree and then skimmed over the ground, ready to go down hard.

Neither the boys nor the robot noticed a large white bird circling high overhead....

* * * * *

After the party left, Noah and Doge Anton had decided to send even more protection for them, so they'd told Parais d'Olor to follow, and to do what she could to keep them safe. Now she watched helplessly as the crop-duster plane landed roughly and skidded to a stop. She saw movement inside. One of the doors opened, and the boys tumbled out, followed by the robot. They were on the side away from the HibAdu camp, so maybe the soldiers wouldn't see them.

Flying in a streak toward the crash site, Parais landed. Except for some bumps and bruises the boys were on their feet and looked all right to her.

"Parais!" Dux said. "What are you doing here?"

"Noah sent me," she said. "We need to move quickly."

Knowing she had no time to waste, Parais tore off broken tree branches that the aircraft had snagged, and scooped up chunks of disturbed soil. Then she embraced the pile of material in her wings until it all glowed orange and melted into her body, making her into a larger and darker bird. Gradually, the glow subsided.

In absorbing so much organic matter at once, however, the shapeshifter risked compromising her complex internal chemistry, which could result in cellular damage and even death. Bravely and privately, she accepted the risk anyway, since she needed to carry three passengers on her back. With their dense bone structures, Humans were heavier than the Mutatis she typically carried, such as Hari. And that little robot probably weighed as much as the boys combined.

"I sent a distress call to headquarters," Kekur said, "with the coordinates of this enemy force."

"Good," Parais said. She heard soldiers running toward them, shouting commands to each other.

With the transfer of mass complete, the bird looked like a giant black eagle. "Jump on my back and hold onto my feather mane," she said.

Acey got on first, followed by Dux and the robot. In the early evening light, all were shadowy shapes on the bird's back.

As the bird got underway Dux shivered in fear, and from the chill wind that cut through his jacket and trousers. He held onto Acey, and behind Dux, Kekur held onto him. At first, Parais flew low over the ground, away from the troops. Finally, with powerful strokes of her massive wings, she lifted into the sky in a great upward arc.

Looking back, Dux saw spotlights illuminate the crash site. But he and his companions were safe, lifting high into the air where the HibAdus could no longer see or harm them.

"I'd better take you back to headquarters," Parais shouted back.

"No!" Acey shouted.

Just behind him on the eagle's back, Dux said, "We appreciate your help, Parais, but we need to check on our grandmother. We've come all this way to do that, and we don't want to turn back now. Please, fly us to her."

For several moments, the bird kept flapping in the same direction. Presently she asked, "Which direction?"

"To the right," Dux said, "beyond those mountains."

She changed course. As they flew past the peaks he had designated, an orange moon rose on the horizon, illuminating the way. Though the air was cold, the mountains were not extensive, and presently they saw a valley just ahead.

"She lives on the other side of that valley," Acey shouted.

The air was warmer there. Below, Dux made out the simple farms and fields of the Barani tribe, in this remote region where he and Acey had spent much of their childhood. Dim lights illuminated the windows of some of the small homes. But soon he saw that all was not well down there.

As they crossed the valley and passed over a small river, the orange moon cast enough illumination for Dux to see heavy destruction of the landscape, leaving its once-distinctive lakes and gnarled hills barely recognizable. Some of the land was broken, as if from seismic activity, and the stream where he and Acey had fished as boys was much wider now, having flooded many of the homesteads.

Nonetheless, the teenagers were still able to find the familiar ramshackle cabin of their grandmother, on cleared ground partway up a slope. The cabin was dark as they landed in a front yard that was cluttered with old household articles and rusty flying machines.

"Grandma doesn't like surprises," Acey said, keeping his voice low. "I'd better go ahead on my own and let her know we're here."

"God, I hope she's all right," Dux said. He waited with the robot and the shapeshifter, watching as Acey climbed a rickety stairway and rapped on the front door, shouting to identify himself. Dux saw a light go on inside, and then the door opened, casting more light across the cluttered yard.

Dux felt a rush of joy, and ran toward the cabin.

"I knew you were too ornery to get killed, Grandmamá," Acey said to the old woman, using a Barani term of endearment that she liked, but did not use in referring to herself. Dux caught up to them, and the boys hugged her.

"We brought along a couple of friends," Dux said, motioning back toward the shadows.

Small and deeply wrinkled, Grandma Zelk squinted to see. "Well, tell them to show their faces." A superstitious woman who spoke unusual dialects, she had a stooped posture and wore a long embroidered dress with large pockets. At her waist hung a stained pouch, with compartments in it filled with her favorite folk medicines. Despite her years, she was tough and wiry-thin from climbing around in the hills, and had always bragged that she could out-hike any man.

When many members of her tribe were enslaved for not paying taxes to Doge Lorenzo, she was not included, since she hid in the backwoods and survived off the land until her pursuers went away. They wouldn't have wanted to catch up with the old woman anyway. At her waist she also wore her customary handgun in a holster, a weapon that she called her "equalizer"—to be used against any authority figure who might try to apprehend her.

"One of my friends is a robot," Dux said. "And you should know that the other is a … shapeshifter."

"A Mutati," Acey said, "but a good one. She's big, too, and flew us here on her back."

"I don't trust Mutatis," the old woman said, her voice a low, dangerous growl. "The robot can come in, but not the shapeshifter."

Dux hurried back to explain the situation to Parais, who stood with her wings tucked in against her sides. She had grown so large that she was bigger than a Tulyan. "That's all right," she said, in a voice that sounded very tired. "I have a coat of feathers to keep me warm. I'll just find a place out here to sleep."

"I'm sorry," Dux said.

"I might not be able to get through that doorway anyway. Besides, I see a nice thick canopy of trees to sleep in, and that's something I have grown accustomed to over the years, from long flights taken around my homeworld of Dij." She gestured with her beak, showing where she planned to be.

"We'll check back with you in the morning," Dux promised. Looking up, he saw that the sky was clear. Maybe it wouldn't rain during the night, but surely it would get colder than it was now. He shivered in a slight breeze from the mountains, but the bird didn't seem to feel it.

"Okay," Parais said. Her voice was weak and didn't sound good to him, but he assumed she would be better after she had rested.

He joined the others inside, where Grandma Zelk lit a log in the rock fireplace. As she puttered around, preparing tea, she spoke of the spirit world, and especially of Zehbu, the ancient god who was said to live within the molten core of Siriki.

"Interesting data," Kekur said. He stood by the fireplace as if warming himself there, though he should not have needed to.

"Some people think it's a lot of silliness," Acey said to the robot.

"Not necessarily," the robot said. "In my data banks I have similar stories from other star systems. Conclusion: Your god is a common legend that might very well have a basis in fact."

The old lady nodded, and said to Acey, "Don't make Zehbu angry, boy, or he'll get you for sure."

"I wasn't talking about myself," the young man said. "I was talking about some people."

"Well those 'some people' better not be around here," she said. "That's for sure. And don't you boys come around here with any foolish outsider ideas."

"We aren't, Grandmamá," Dux said. "We came because we're worried about you. We saw a lot of damage in the valley."

"The planet's got a sickness," the old woman said. She lifted a teapot from the stove, and poured three cups.

Dux held back saying what he'd heard, that the troubles were caused by something that went far beyond Siriki. A disintegrating galactic web and timeholes. His grandmother was stubborn, and would not take any interest in such stories, except to reject them out of hand. Acey kept the information to himself as well.

"Timeholes," the robot said.

"Eh?" Grandma Zelk said.

"She doesn't want to hear any nonsense," Dux said to Kekur. "Do not speak unless we give you permission."

The robot fell silent.

"I tried giving that order to you boys when you were only knee high," the stooped woman said. "Dux, you kept quiet, but Acey—I never could get you to shut up."

"I'm the same as I always was," Acey said. "And we're happy to see that you are, too."

* * * * *

Perched on a low cedar bough, Parais felt sharp lances of pain all over her body, and a deep fatigue that seemed to draw her down into it like quicksand. Struggling for life, gasping for air, she knew that she needed to find a way to reduce her body mass quickly, or she would die. But she had used up a great deal of energy taking on the additional mass and flying here, and now she felt too weak to go through the necessary recovery steps.

Chapter Forty-Seven

Noah has invariably tried to see the positive side of things, despite extreme difficulties. It's one of the things I love about him. I haven't been able to see Noah for awhile, but I've been told that he seems to be growing increasingly darker ... as if he is losing some sort of an internal battle.

—Tesh Kori, remarks to Eshaz

Accompanied by men and women in MPA and Guardian uniforms, Tesh boarded a podship at the Canopa pod station, and found a bench seat at the rear. She did not like to magnify herself and ride as a passenger in one of the sentient vessels as she was doing now, but if she wanted to get to Siriki quickly, this was the only choice she had. Doge Anton, while permitting her to visit Noah in this manner, had forbidden her to take her own podship, *Webdancer*, on such a mission.

She thought back on the conversation she'd had with the youthful doge that morning, and of the child growing in her womb.

"Think of what you're asking," Anton had said to her. They were standing in the tower of an airgrid station on Canopa, where the Liberators were setting up one of their ground bases. "*Webdancer* is my flagship. I can't have it flitting around the galaxy on personal missions. What is it you want to discuss with Noah anyway?"

"As I said, sir, it is a personal mission and I'll only be gone a couple of hours. The round-trip flight shouldn't take long, and allowing for the time to..."

"My answer is the same. No."

Tesh had looked away, at airgrid planes landing and taking off on the field, using their vertical take-off and landing systems.

"You and I were once close," Anton had said, but it was not our fate to remain together for our entire lives. Or, I should say for *my* entire lifetime, in view of your longevity." He glanced over at his wife, Nirella (who was out of earshot), and exchanged smiles with her. "I'm happy with the choice I made," he added, "even though you forced it by leaving me."

"I prefer to say we drifted apart," she said.

"If I'd been paying attention, I would have noticed that you had a wandering eye. I took you away from Doctor Bichette, and in turn Noah spirited you away from me."

"Noah and I have no relationship," she said, bristling.

"Only because there hasn't been time," Anton said. "I've seen the way the two of you look at each other, the way you act around one another. There's electricity in the air, even when you argue. Anyone can see it."

"I won't deny that. All right, I'll leave *Webdancer* here."

"Leave the sectoid chamber unsealed, so a Tulyan pilot can operate the vessel if necessary."

After a moment's hesitation, Tesh nodded. "Unsealed it will be."

Now the other podship was loaded with passengers, only around twenty for this trip. The vessel taxied out of the orbital station and prepared to engage with the podways. Tesh saw a burst of green light outside, and then a dimmer, barely perceptible green hue out in space as the vessel sped along one of the strands of Timeweb.

This particular flight was part of a military procedure that General Nirella had established: regular courier runs linking Canopa and Siriki, using designated podships. Since both planets were among the original merchant prince worlds, they still had functioning nehrcom stations at each, a technology that could have been used for communication. However, the Humans now knew that the cross-space communication system had been compromised by Jacopo Nehr's treacherous brother Gio, who had revealed the secret of the operation to the Mutatis almost a year ago. The Mutatis had, in turn, revealed what they knew to the Adurians. While some of the MPA leaders had suspected that the technology had been leaked for some time now, they now knew details of how it happened—information that had been provided voluntarily by their new allies, Hari'Adab and the Mutatis.

It was early evening on a moonlit night when Tesh rode the shuttle down from the pod station and landed on Siriki. The Golden Palace, which she had seen lit up in past visits, was now darkened for military purposes, as was most of the planet. With modern infratech systems, she knew darkness only provided limited concealment benefits, so she wondered why the authorities didn't just blaze all the lights they had, as a means of flaunting and aggravating the enemy. Maybe that was the answer; maybe they didn't want to provoke the emotions of their foe. At least not yet.

Emotions, she thought. *That's why I'm here.*

Having sent a comlink message down from the pod station, she hoped it had gotten through to Noah. She waited at the main entrance of the terminal. For just twenty minutes, but it seemed like an eternity, as Humans, robots, and Tulyans looked at her in peculiar ways. Around her, everyone seemed to have their lives organized with military precision, but hers was anything but that.

Finally, when she was about to give up and go in search of him, he arrived in a military staff car, driven by a robot. One of the rear doors slid open. Not even getting out, Noah leaned through the opening and said, "Get in. I can only talk for a little while."

"Perhaps we should make this some other time."

"No. With my schedule, it's always something." An interior light brightened, so that she could see him better. Noah hadn't shaven in a couple of days, and his eyes looked tired. His curly, reddish hair was mussed. He smiled disarmingly, and this broke her momentary anger.

"I suppose that's understandable." She sat beside him, and the door closed behind her. The interior light dimmed.

"What is it?" Noah said, as the car made its way back toward the palace, without visible headlights.

"Aren't you glad to see me? It's been too long."

"Of course. It's just that there's a lot going on here. I was about to leave for Yaree, but something important came up and I've been forced to change my plans. EcoStation is orbiting that planet, so I wanted to check on it. The unaligned Yareens are potential military allies, too."

"Sure, EcoStation. I worked for you on the orbiter, remember? But how did it get to Yaree?"

"It's one of the things I want to investigate. I still hope to go, but later. Until I can get there, I'm sending a recon team of Tulyans, diplomats, and military officers."

"What made you change your plans?"

"You remember Acey and Dux?"

"Sure."

Noah went on to tell her where the teenagers had gone, and how the robot Kekur had sent a distress call that they were under HibAdu attack in the back country. "We're organizing a rescue-and-attack squadron right now," he said. "I'm going with it."

"But you have so many other responsibilities. Surely you can delegate that one."

"HibAdus are a priority. Besides, those boys may not always be near, but they're Guardians through and through. I've always seen them as future leaders, after they finish sowing their wild oats. And as for you, Tesh, I'm always glad to see you. From the moment I met you, I knew you were a … special case."

"You make me sound like a fugitive from a nut house."

"In this war, aren't we all?"

"I suppose. Look, I don't need much of your time. I have to get back to my own duties, piloting Anton's flagship."

"Pull over there," Noah said to the driver, reaching forward and pointing so that the man could see what he wanted.

Noah and Tesh got out in a shadowy garden area, where pathways and a pond were illuminated in moonlight.

"Here," Noah said, handing a pair of night-vision glasses to her. "I don't think you'll need these with the natural lighting, but just in case."

"Thanks." She tucked them into a pocket of her jacket, as he did with his own pair. "It's kind of heavenly out here tonight, and maybe that's a sign."

"A sign?" he said.

"Just the observation of a hopelessly romantic female."

"You're anything but hopelessly romantic." Noah leaned down and kissed her affectionately on the lips, then grasped her hand and led her toward the pond. His grip was warm and strong, and she felt his steady pulse against her magnified skin.

"Since we don't have much time, I'm going to be very direct," Tesh said.

"Normally we men prefer that, but coming from you, I'm not so certain I want to hear it. I've never been able to figure you out, or what we mean to each other."

"Odd that you'd say that, because I've been stewing over the same thing. There hasn't been enough time for us, has there?"

"No." He kissed her again, longer this time, before they continued on the walkway. The moon reflected on the pond, an image broken by a wooden boardwalk that led to a small island at the center.

As they walked along the creaking boardwalk, Tesh said, "From the beginning, I knew something about you, too. Or should I say, about *us*. Sparks were always there between us, a physical passion that neither of us could deny. As a Parvii, I've lived a lot longer than you, and I've had more … relationships, as your Human women like to call them. From the beginning, I couldn't stop thinking about you, Noah. I'm sorry to be so direct, but the war forces my words, compresses our lives."

"That's all right." He led her to a bench on the island, and they sat down, still holding hands, to gaze out on the reflections of the pond.

"We had our one time together. You thought it was only a dream since you were with me through Timeweb, but it actually happened."

"Two months ago, right?"

"Sixty-eight days," she said, with a hard stare at him.

During all that time, until just a few days ago, Tesh had been carrying his seed within her, until she finally made her decision about what to do. Now she felt their child growing inside, and she wondered how to tell him, what to say. She needed to choose her words carefully. This was no ordinary man, and she could not predict how he would respond if he knew.

Unsure if she should tell him at all, and especially now, she hesitated. Noah was a busy, important figure now.

"As complicated as our lives have been," she said, "neither of us have had time to explore the real potential of our relationship."

"I have to admit, I've always found you intriguing," he said. Looking at her intently, he said, "This is going to sound like a line, but whenever I look into your pretty green eyes, I see a universe of stars and planets, a universe of possibilities. I see the past and the future in you. You are one woman, and you are all women who have ever lived. I love the depths of you."

"That was quite a mouthful. You can see the color of my eyes, even in this light?"

"Do you think I would forget what you look like?"

She kissed him, and asked, "Did you just tell me that you love me, or that you love all women in general? Do you only love the 'depths of me,' or do you love all of me?"

"That's a complex question." He grinned as he considered how to reply.

While she held his left hand, her fingers wandered inside his sleeve, and she felt rough skin on his wrist and forearm. Odd. It must be the scars of an injury he hadn't told her about yet. Not wanting to make him uncomfortable, she quickly withdrew.

Just then, they heard voices, and on the far side of the pond—away from the palace—Tesh saw dark figures in the moonlight. Five Human shapes, moving furtively through the garden.

Noah put on his night-vision glasses, and so did she.

"It's … " Tesh hesitated. "One of them looks like Princess Meghina. Is she here?"

"Yes. She's led an interesting life."

"Look," Tesh said. "They're moving strangely, going in a circle. What are they doing?"

"I don't know."

Rising to his feet, Noah went back on the boardwalk the way they had come, moving slowly and keeping to the side, where the boards squeaked less.

Following him, Tesh did the same. So far, she had not gotten to say what she'd intended, and now she might not get the opportunity. As they left the magical, moonlit island, it seemed to her that a spell had been broken. She sighed. Maybe it was for the best. For his own safety, Noah needed to keep his full attention on his important duties. That was the case with her, too, and she wondered if she should have waited longer before commencing her pregnancy.

What's done is for the best, she thought. *If I had waited, it might never have happened.* And it needed to happen. Tesh was sure of it.

She followed him to a stand of high shrubbery, and they peered through an opening in it....

* * * * *

Princess Meghina had been feeling peculiar, and almost giddy. For her, always conscious of her duties and of making the proper impression on others, this was most unusual. But around the other immortals, especially now that Kobi Akar was gone, she'd been feeling more comfortable. After jumping off the cliff, her companions had all healed at varying rates, and they were fine now. Meghina still didn't think she would ever make that leap.

She wanted to maintain her dignity, but she also wanted to be part of this special group, a group that was elite in its own, ineffable way. Not that living forever was a sign of status, or of some bonus that the gods had given to them. At least she didn't see it that way. Sometimes, she almost felt it was a curse, a burden that she and the others had to bear. The Salducian diplomat had failed in his responsibilities, and now he was paying the price for it. He would spend a long time incarcerated, a long time being miserable. Of course, they couldn't give him a life sentence, because that would never end, and he had not committed a crime that warranted the death sentence. He was a unique prisoner. No doubt about it.

Now she held hands with Betha Neider on one side and Paltrow on the other, and all of them were linked in a circle with Llew Jarro and Dougal Netzer, circling in the moonlight, circling, circling.

On one level, the one that was most obvious to her, this all seemed silly, and almost a cliché. But they weren't *dancing* in the moonlight, not exactly. It was more an improvised thing for them to do together in this private place where they could let off some of the pressures and behave in an impulsive, childlike manner. But this wasn't childlike, she quickly realized. As they moved around and around, it occurred to her that they were doing something very important.

Stupid thoughts. On a superficial level, Meghina felt silly. But deeper, where it really mattered much more, she felt quite different. This was their shared destiny.

Our destiny to spin in circles? One side of her asked a question of the other. And the other side did not answer. It just kept compelling her to go around and around in the garden.

* * * * *

Looking on, Tesh and Noah heard the scuffing and stepping of feet as Meghina and her companions continued their strange amusement. To Tesh, it looked like some sort of weird religious ritual, and she wondered if they would strip off their clothes next and paint themselves blue, as the ancients of Lost Earth used to do. With her military glasses, she saw the garden in full color, and the dark clothing of the circling people.

"Do you think they're drunk?" she whispered. Then, from the direction of the zoo, she heard an animal roar.

"They're drunk on something," he whispered back. "Can't say what, though."

"Shall we join them?"

"I ... " When Noah hesitated, she noticed a peculiar expression on his face as he watched Meghina and the others. One of longing, she thought, and fascination. Then he said, "I'll go, but you stay here."

"Why? They aren't dangerous."

"Maybe I shouldn't go, either."

"You're not making sense."

"I ... I feel like they're tugging at me, wanting me to be with them. But I feel something else, too, telling me not to. I ... Uh, on second thought, I think we should both stay here."

"That was a confusing answer."

He smiled stiffly.

Tesh felt her own conflicting sensations. Noah always had good instincts. It was one of the things that made her comfortable being around him. He seemed like a protective force to her. But now she wondered why he was behaving this way.

Princess Meghina glanced in their direction, as if she had heard something. Tesh froze, seeing the eerie glint of moonlight in the searching, questing eyes. A chill ran down her back, as she felt a rush of fear. But the Princess soon looked away, and never stopped circling with the others. Faster and faster they whirled in a bizarre dance. And, as if in concert with them, animals in the zoo roared, chattered, and called out in high, agitated pitches.

At that moment, a faint green mist encompassed the five people, a mist that thickened and grew more green as moments passed, until Tesh could no longer see the dancers. The sounds diminished, and finally faded away entirely.

Presently the mist cleared, and the people were gone. Tesh saw only a moonlit garden, as if the whole scene had been an apparition.

Moving with caution, Noah led the way around the shrubbery, to the place where they had seen the strange activity.

On the ground, they found five heaps of clothing arranged in a circle. It looked like a magic trick. But as Tesh lifted the heap that had been Princess Meghina's black gown, she gasped.

Tesh saw a moonlit hole in the ground, with something jammed down into it, out of reach. Thinking Meghina was trapped in the hole, Noah used a comlink to call for help.

While waiting, he and Tesh dug desperately with their hands, widening the opening. Finally Noah touched whatever was in there, but it only crumbled. Within minutes, uniformed soldiers burst onto the scene, and they began digging with autoshovels.

Beneath each pile of clothing, they found a hole. And inside every hole, only the husks of four Humans and one Mutati—like exoskeletons—with nothing inside.

Chapter Forty-Eight

Each sentient creature has a mental list of things to worry about. The lists are of varying lengths and of varying significance. It has been observed, though, that the thing that gets you will not even be on your list.

—Anne Jules, child philosopher of Lost Earth

S everal times during the night, Dux had awakened and worried about the brave Mutati outside. Now, as he stirred yet again and opened his eyes, he wondered if he should go out and check on her. That might disturb everyone, though. He recalled that his grandmother was a light sleeper, and cantankerous if she didn't get her rest.

Dux and his cousin slept on thin pads that Grandma Zelk had laid out for them on the floor of the small cabin. In the shadows only a couple of meters away, he saw the robot sitting by the dying embers of the fireplace. Kekur was a peculiar sentient machine, but he did seem dedicated to his duties. One of the yellow lights around his face plate pulsed slowly. Undoubtedly, he was monitoring his surroundings, standing sentry over the boys.

Once more, Dux drifted off to an uneasy sleep....

In the morning, when he heard the old lady clunking around in the kitchen, Dux dressed hurriedly and went outside. A chill wind stabbed into his bones, and he closed his jacket.

Just ahead, he saw Parais perched on a low cedar bough that drooped under her weight, almost all the way to the ground. He hurried to her side. Behind him, he heard his grandmother calling his name, but he ignored her for the moment.

The Mutati opened one large eye, and Dux was shocked to see that it was a sickly shade of yellow, with purple veins through it. Her posture was bad and she leaned, as if about to tumble off the branch.

"Parais," he said. "Are you all right?"

"Took on too much mass," she said. "Must expel it, but I'm so tired. My avicular chemistry has been warring with the increased organic material that I absorbed." Her voice grew increasingly faint as she continued. "Just before dawn, I tried ... tried to shed my body of the excess, but only stirred up my insides more, making me feel worse. I'll try again later."

"Are you sure you should do that?"

"Maybe. There are methods I've learned from other aeromutatis." She looked up into the gray, foggy sky. "Perhaps the sun will come out, and give me new energy."

Turning toward the cabin, he saw the old woman on the porch, with her hands on her hips. She did not look pleased, but at the moment he didn't care about that.

He ran to her and said, "Grandmamá, we must help the Mutati. She saved our lives and risked her own. Can you give her a folk medicine?"

The wrinkled woman scowled. "You say she's a good Mutati, eh? Maybe she's fooled you, and the minute she's stronger she'll kill us all."

Acey was in the cabin doorway now, with the robot behind him. "Parais wouldn't do that," Acey said. "She could have killed us many times before. We all trust her."

"The Mutati needs help," Kekur said.

The prior evening, Dux had told the robot not to speak without permission, so this gave him a moment's pause. He decided not to scold him, however. Maybe Kekur's internal programming had determined that it was a military priority to revive the Mutati.

"My healing powder might work on her," Grandma Zelk said, touching the pouch at her waist, "but I hate to waste it. With all of the sickness in the ground around here, I've been sprinkling it on problem areas, trying to heal Zehbu."

"Living planet organism to the Barani tribe of Siriki," Kekur said. "Zehbu is linked to larger galactic-god entity Buko. A variation on the Tulyan deity Ubuqqo, one of many versions of the ultimate divinity. All unsubstantiated folk tales."

"Don't make me come after you with a stick," the old woman said to the robot.

The yellow lights blinked around Kekur's faceplate, but he had the good sense not to respond.

"Sadly, my supply of healing powder is diminishing," Grandma Zelk said. "My powder came from my ancestors before me, who got it from Zehbu, along with the obligation to use it properly. Just a grain or two a decade was all Siriki needed in the past to remain healthy, but the required amount has increased dramatically."

"Don't waste your … healing powder on me," Parais said, barely getting the words out. "Use it for a larger purpose."

"The shapeshifter makes sense," the old woman said, patting her small bag. "Look, boys, have you ever seen my pouch so flat? This is all I have left. Zehbu has been too sick to produce any more of it, and I'm afraid the downward cycle is irreversible."

As if punctuating her comments, Dux felt the ground tremble underfoot.

"No place is safe anymore," she said. Her face darkened, and gripping the pouch tightly, she turned and strode up a rocky slope. The boys and the robot followed, as did the robot. She kept up her legendary brisk pace, and as they climbed Dux was surprised that he didn't hear a flow of water coming from up there, where the mountain stream ran down into the valley.

They reached a rock promontory where they could look down on the stream. Though it was late spring in the Sirikan back country and the water had always flowed swiftly in the past, it was nothing like that now, only a weak, trickling rivulet.

Bowing her head, the old woman said, "This water is one of the arteries of the living planet-god. You see how it is."

"Yes," Dux said. Somehow, the old superstitions and legends about Zehbu and the larger galactic entity Buko had always seemed true to him. The concepts seemed linked to the galactic ecology theories espoused by Noah Watanabe.

Hearing a noise behind them, Dux saw the large black eagle Parais fly in, struggling to flap her wings. She managed to land on an evergreen tree branch, which sagged under her weight. He thought she might look a little smaller than before, so perhaps she had managed to shed some of her mass. Or, it was only his wishful thinking. She still didn't look well.

Noticing the shapeshifter, Grandma Zelk scowled at it. Her fingers rested on the handle of her powerful handgun, then moved away.

"Zehbu is displeased with the sins of mankind," the old woman said, "so he seeks vengeance on the inhabitants of the planet." Her voice became eerie and shuddering as she added, "None of us are safe anymore."

She brought a smaller, yellowing pouch from the larger one at her waist. Dux had seen it before. It was her special "healing powder," a green dust that reminded him of a similar-looking substance that he'd seen Eshaz sprinkle on the ground of Canopa once, during a momentary lapse when the Tulyan had not seen him watching. Dux wondered now if the substances might be related, and perhaps even identical.

Grandma Zelk opened the little pouch carefully, and for several moments she stared into it. But for some reason she did not reach in and sprinkle any of the contents around. Instead she tilted her head slightly, as if listening for something.

At that moment the ground shook violently for several seconds, and everyone struggled to maintain their footing. Acey hurried to his grandmother to help her, but she stood on her own and shook him off. Dux heard a distant roar, and was shocked to see the stream hiss below them, and turn to glowing red. Moment by moment, it became a heavier flow.

"Magma," Kekur said, in a mechanical, matter of fact tone that seemed out of place for the emergency. But after that he said, "I am reporting this rupture of the planetary crust to headquarters."

The glowing river flowed surprisingly fast, a powerful torrent heading for the valley floor below. Then, filling the old stream channel, the molten material began rising toward Dux and his companions, climbing the banks several meters a minute and causing trees and loose rocks to tumble into it.

Abruptly, the flow changed. A crack appeared in the hillside close to their feet and some of the lava began to flow into it.

"We'd better get out of here," Acey said, again reaching for his grandmother.

But the rail-thin old lady would hear none of it, and held her ground. "I'm staying," she said.

Dux saw a pool of hot magma perhaps fifty meters down slope from them, and he felt the heat. A queer sensation filled his brain, as if part of it had cracked off with the debris and fallen into the chasm.

Grandma Zelk opened her little pouch of healing powder and scattered a pinch of it toward the lava. As if by magic, a little breeze caught the powder and lifted it into the molten material, where it sparked and disappeared. "That is all I can do," she said, closing the pouch. "It is no use to throw more in." Her voice trailed off and she began murmuring incantations, as if to further ward off the evil spirits.

As long moments passed, Dux detected no noticeable effect on the flow.

Finally, behind him he heard a squeal of pain, and saw that Parais had tried to fly to them, but had fallen to the rocky surface, where she lay in a pile of feathers, struggling to breathe.

Chapter Forty-Nine

I can think of no more admirable trait than loyalty. It is the bond of honor that holds together relationships at all levels. The great leader can only fulfill his vision if he obtains the undying allegiance of his followers.

—In the Words of the Master, by Subi Danvar

Having already dispatched an attack squadron to confront the HibAdu force that Kekur had reported in the back country, Noah prepared to depart for the same region himself—a region where Kekur was also reporting tremors and the eruption of underground magma.

A military gridjet awaited Noah at the palace landing field, along with another squadron. In his office moments ago, he had dispatched a courier message to Doge Anton, reporting the situation to him. It had been a long night, and Noah had only been able to grab two hours of restless sleep, which he had forced on himself with a dermex, something that he didn't like to do. But it had provided him with a deep slumber, and he did not feel overly tired at the moment.

Before leaving for the back country, Noah stopped by the garden area where Meghina and her companions had disappeared the night before. As he stepped out of the hovercar, a moist morning fog hung in the air, brightened by filtered sunlight.

He walked around the high shrubbery and saw soldiers using ground penetrating scanners and other equipment, trying to determine what had happened. The area had been excavated, creating a large single hole where there had previously been five smaller ones. In a patch of sunlight on one side, two of Noah's officers and a Tulyan woman investigated the exoskeletons that had been removed from the holes. They lay in pieces on a ground tarp, but enough remained of their structures to show that they had once been four Humans and a Mutati, and that their original bone structures had been altered in death to thin, dry crusts.

Of all the strange things Noah had seen and experienced in his lifetime, what he had witnessed last night had been the most peculiar. And not just because of what he saw. While watching the whirling dancers, he had felt a powerful urge to join them, and an even stronger urge *not* to, because it would be dangerous to do so. He had hesitated, and then had followed the more compelling instinct, which proved to be right.

Where had Meghina and her companions gone? Would Noah have gone with them? All of them, and Noah as well, were immortals. Now he sensed that the compulsion to join them had something to do with the never-ending quality of life he shared with them. They had been drawn into something, but he—perhaps because he had a slightly different and perhaps stronger form of the condition—had been able to resist.

But what did I resist? And did I do the right thing? He wasn't certain.

Glancing at his wristchron, he knew he had to board the gridjet. Even so, he took a few moments and walked over to the exoskeletons. He'd seen them during the night when they were dug out, and now they seemed to confirm that it had not all been a nightmare, and that it had really happened.

The Tulyan woman looked at him, and said, "They vanished into five tiny timeholes that opened up and then closed afterward. Like little cosmic jaws."

"Maybe we'd be safer getting off this planet," one of the two officers said. He was Keftenant Ett Jahoki, a young man from a long tradition of military officers who had served with distinction in the Merchant Prince Alliance.

"No place is safe," the Tulyan said, her voice ominous. "Timeholes tear through spacecraft, too."

"But aren't podships safer?"

"True enough. They do sense cosmic disturbances and often are able to go around them, but I think Master Watanabe here would prefer to hold this planet and attempt to remedy the problems here."

"You're absolutely right," Noah said to the Tulyan. "What is your name?"

"Iffika," she said. "My good friend Eshaz has told me many good things about you."

"Thank you. But five tiny timeholes here? All in such close proximity?"

"Infrastructure defects take varying, surprising forms. We have seen similar things occur around the galaxy. I have tested this site carefully for telltale signs. There is no question about what happened."

"But where did Meghina and the others go? Where did the timeholes take them?"

"They were all immortal, so wherever they are I suspect they're still alive. Unless the physical impact on them was so severe that it demolished their cells to such a degree that they could not regenerate."

Noah emitted a long whistle. "I've gotta get going," he said.

Minutes later, as he boarded the red-and-gold gridjet, he thought about the special purpose of this trip. Kekur's additional report of tectonic activity in the back country could refer to timehole activity, and Noah wanted to see it firsthand, accompanied by another Tulyan expert who could analyze what was going on. Even in the midst of galaxy-spanning chaos, some geologic upheavals were still considered normal. But Noah wanted to be sure. He also wanted to check on the welfare of Dux, Acey, and Kekur, along with the independent old woman.

Making the situation even more complicated, there were HibAdus to be dealt with.

* * * * *

In the rugged Sirikan back country, it was midday. Overhead, the sky had darkened, as if forewarning a downturn in the weather.

Hours ago, Grandma Zelk had scattered a pinch of her healing powder onto the magma river, and in that time there had been no apparent effect. Now she sat on a high rock staring down at the flow and murmuring trancelike incantations to Zehbu, while holding the small pouch in her hands. The level of the lava had risen closer, and now was perhaps ten meters below her. Remaining with her, Dux, Acey, and Kekur had all expressed concern that they should leave, that it was not safe to stay.

But the old woman would hear none of it, and the boys didn't want to risk her health by forcing her to leave. She knew this country better than anyone, and had a right to remain if that was what she wanted. Her fate had become theirs.

Behind them, the Mutati bird lay on a flat stone. Since landing there, she had been taking measures to reduce her bodily mass, which she said she needed to do in order to remain alive. Every once in a while, Parais would glow orange and pieces of her body would peel off. Then she would adjust her form slightly, and the flesh and feathers would regenerate, as they were doing now.

So far she had shed only a small portion of her mass, and had told Dux it was a slow and painful process—and that she needed to get rid of more. "I won't go all the way back to my previous size," she said. "I want to remain large enough to carry two of you at a time."

"We can get out of here on our own," Acey had said.

"Perhaps, and perhaps not," she had said in a gentle voice. "I suspect the latter." Then, she had grimaced from the internal pain and had concentrated inward.

Looking back at her, Dux noticed that her feathers had lightened slightly in hue, so that they were no longer a rich black, but were instead more of a charcoal hue, with patches of dark gray.

Beside him he heard his grandmother's incantations louder beside him, and then she stood up. Holding the small pouch over her head, she shouted, "Zehbu, son of Buko, I implore you. Save this world!"

At that moment, the magma bubbled and smoked, and fingerlings of molten red material rose toward her, as if the planet god was reaching out to take her.

"Grandma, we've got to leave," Dux said. But, as she had done earlier with Acey, she pulled away. She had a beatific expression on her wrinkled face.

Despite the old woman's stubbornness, Dux was just about to grab her and force her to safety. At the last possible moment the lava fingers changed course, and—flowing quickly—they encircled the rocky promontory where he and his companions were. In a matter of moments, before anyone could do anything, they were found themselves on an island, with lava flowing all around them. Dux felt the heat even more than before, and smelled sulfur, as if demons below were causing the upheaval.

The lava rose again, this time all around. Higher and higher. Feeling a wave of panic, Dux saw the Mutati standing up on her bird legs. Her eyes were still a sickly yellow, veined in purple, and she looked unsteady, in no condition to fly any of them to safety. Even if Parais could lift off, she might not be strong enough for passengers....

* * * * *

Aboard the gridjet, Noah's pilot flew toward the coordinates that had been provided by Kekur. Just ahead, he saw the gridplanes and 'copters of his other squadron engaged in aerial dogfights against the orange-and-gray aircraft of HibAdu forces. On the ground, soldiers on each side faced off. He saw the HibAdu encampment in flames, but its soldiers were still fighting fiercely.

"Let's help them out," Noah said.

His pilot nodded, and the small plane streaked into battle, firing blasts of white-hot energy at the enemy. The other ships with him followed.

* * * * *

Dux felt a jolt that knocked him down. To his horror, the rock under Grandma Zelk cracked with a loud report, and she tumbled into the lava. Her body hit the red-hot flow with a sickening *thud* and a hiss of steam, then vanished. Only her pouch of healing powder remained behind.

"Come on!" Parais shouted. "Get on my back!"

Grief-stricken, Dux grabbed the pouch and ran with Acey to the bird. As they were climbing on, Parais said, "I think I've found the right balance of mass and strength, and I feel a little better. I think I can fly, but no guarantees."

"Just like life," Acey said grimly.

She flapped her wings slowly, and began to lift off ever so slightly from the rocky deathtrap, like a heavily loaded cargo plane. Up they went, slowly and steadily. They passed through a pocket of very hot air that nearly took Dux's breath away. Moments later, higher, the air grew cooler and more breathable.

Looking back at the rock promontory below, he saw the loyal robot Kekur standing motionless, awaiting his fate.

"Drop us off and go back for him," Acey said, saying what Dux was already thinking.

But the living lava had another idea. Burning bright red, it swept over the rock and took Kekur with it.

Chapter Fifty

In desperate times, desperate measures are required.

—Parvii Inspiration

Accompanied by two war priests and a small Parvii guard force, the Eye of the Swarm flew over a planet that glittered in varying hues, an ever-changing effect caused by solar conditions and the movement of glassy dust through the atmosphere. Once a favored site for galactic tourists and for the development of a machine army, the world had since fallen into complete disuse. With no regularly scheduled podships to bring anyone back, it was perfect for his needs.

Ignem.

The resurrection of this remote planet's importance would run parallel to the reawakening of the Parvii race. Soon he would have billions and billions of Parviis to set up military defenses here. Or, he could find another similar planet for his purposes. For what he had in mind, he only needed Ignem for a few days. Certainly, no one would disturb him in that time. High overhead in the orbital ring, there were still a few hundred machines at the Inn of the White Sun, but they were not expected to be any problem. They had no means of space travel, and even their shuttles for reaching the planet were slow and easily thwarted.

Woldn had come to believe in contingency plans. It was not something he had been particularly good at in the past when things were going well for the Parviis, but recently—in his hours of shame and despair—he had found himself reaching out, trying new things. Sprinkling seeds for the reawakening of his race.

For some time now, his breeding specialists had been operating a new propagation program inside the telepathic bubble, which Woldn had concealed far from Ignem in a dark, remote region of the galaxy where there were no suns or planets, and no other races were likely to interfere with his plans. Thousands of Parvii embryos had already been born, and more in incubation were about to be born. It was a steady, proven process.

But something even larger and more important had occurred, and this would involve Ignem. It would be a second, and potentially much larger, crucible for forging new life....

* * * * *

Weeks ago, when Woldn and most of his swarm were on the Adurian homeworld, he had dispatched tiny spies to gather information from the entire laboratory complex. For millennia, it had been widely known that the Adurians operated the most advanced biological research and development facilities in the galaxy. But the products of those labs were not always known, since operations were kept under the tightest security. But during his visit, Woldn had taken measures to find out what they were up to.

And he had accomplished that goal like a magician. The skill of misdirection.

While the Adurian leaders were focused on Woldn and his swarm in the observation galleries, his tiny spies were entering secret lab areas through the smallest openings, where they gathered data and transmitted it telepathically to the Eye of the Swarm. Not really understanding what they were looking at, the Parvii infiltrators were like little cameras, recording information and sending it out for compilation and investigation. Even Woldn did not comprehend what they provided to him, so he took it back to the five breeding specialists at the telepathic bubble.

The breeding specialists had been astounded by what they learned. Inside the bubble, hovering hear the incubating Parvii embryos, they had met with Woldn. One of the breeding specialists, Qryst, had spoken for the others.

"The new information is exceedingly complex," he said. "Even with years of study, we might never understand all of it. But some important facts have emerged. First, that strange leader you saw is a hybrid of Hibbil and Adurian genes, one of only three that they created in the laboratory. Three that lived, I should say."

"And one of them is a leader? It looks like he at least runs the laboratory, and I suspect he's even more important than that."

"It seems backward, doesn't it? Growing leaders in a bio-lab. And yet, that appears to be what they did. But beyond that, we have learned something even more important, at least for our purposes."

"Yes?" Woldn felt his metabolism accelerate, and he heard it buzz around him.

"Although the Adurians have developed many methods of breeding, some of their incubation methods run parallel with ours. It is in this area that we focused our attention, trying to build on what we already know. The effort has required the mental probes of all five of us in concert, utilizing every bit of Parvii genetic knowledge that we have. And finally, I am pleased to report, we have something that is extremely useful."

"What is it? Get to the point, please!"

"The Adurians have a very clever, and very basic, incubation generator that produces births in a much larger number, and at a greater speed, than we ever dreamed possible. It is so simple that I'm surprised we didn't think of ourselves. But of course, with the historical successes of the Parviis, we didn't need to, did we? We grew lazy, and complacent."

One of the other breeding specialists, Jeed, interjected. "On the other hand, our predecessors may have investigated this method and discarded it because of its inherent problems."

Woldn felt a sudden letdown.

"Nothing insurmountable," Qryst said.

"But it is something we must pay close attention to," Jeed insisted. "It seems that the incubation generators cause birth defects in a significant percentage of the embryos. We can produce many more Parviis with this method, but it must be done carefully, with strict quality control, segregation, and disposal procedures."

"What percentage will have defects?"

"As much as one in eighteen. We might get that as low as one in thirty, but I don't think we can do much better than that."

"There are methods of analyzing the embryos for defects," Qryst said, "so that we can get rid of them before birth."

"Of course, a small number of defective embryos will slip past any screening," Jeed said. He seemed to be the pessimist of the two. "Some of the hardier defective embryos will adapt for their own survival, so we will need to keep adapting ourselves."

"And the percentage of defects that get through?" Woldn asked, not sure how he felt about all of this new information.

"Very low," Qryst said. "Perhaps ten in a billion."

"I don't suppose I want to know what sort of defects they might have," Woldn said.

Qryst smiled. "Minor problems, for the most part."

"Theoretically," Jeed said.

"Nothing to worry about," Qryst retorted. "They won't be able to fly through space, or they will be slower, or they won't have telepathic abilities. We'll soon find them even if they are born."

Now, remembering all of this, Woldn led his guard swarm down toward the glassy surface of the planet. They passed through the red dust of a volcano, and entered a lava tube.

In his newfound system of developing contingency plans, Woldn had set up two distinct Parvii breeding programs, and had assigned breeding specialists to each. The initial program, the traditional one, would continue back in the telepathic bubble, under the direction of Imho and two other breeding specialists. This was the tried and true method, the way that his race had always bred. Assisting Imho in the bubble would be the pessimistic Jeed, and another breeding specialist, Sosk. As the reincarnated versions of past breeding specialists, the three of them were expected to be steady, predictable performers.

Here on Ignem, the new Adurian-inspired breeding program (and by far the most exciting of the two), was under the direction of Qryst, since he had shown such enthusiasm for the concept of incubation generators. To Woldn, he seemed like the sort of positive personality who would find ways around problems, a scientist who would keep the program going, despite difficulties. Assisting him would be Ruttin, a breeding specialist who in ancient times had been brilliant but erratic. Woldn expected Qryst, equally brilliant but more emotionally stable, to keep him in line.

Qryst and Ruttin had been on Ignem for only a short time, setting up the cutting-edge program. Already they were reporting excellent progress, and were ready to combine their efforts with those of the war priests.

Inside the warm lava tubes of the volcanic planet, tens of billions of Parviis were breeding, using the laboratory methods of the Adurians. The Parviis were massing to attack again, breeding much faster than they could under natural conditions. In the past, a machine army had formed on the surface of Ignem, and had gone off to fight for the merchant princes.

Now a far more powerful force would emerge, one that would smash all opponents into oblivion.

Chapter Fifty-One

The great unknown is a lure and a terror. Simultaneously it beckons and threatens us, and we find ourselves unable to resist the temptation. We simply must walk down those creaking stairs into the dark cellar.

—Ancient observation

O n the unnamed planet in the unknown solar system, Pimyt scurried along a now-familiar path through the gray jungle. A morning fog hug low and moistened the fur on his face as he moved through it. He was the first one in the party to rise today, and had gone for a walk so that he could think, and settle his nerves.

The stranded group had even more problems than they had initially imagined. Something in the air had eroded the engines of the shuttle, so that the craft no longer flew at all. It was only good for a shelter, and already they were out of the packaged meals they had brought with them. That left only the local plants that they could gather from the jungle, most of which had minimal food value. No one had expected having to remain away from the space station for so long.

Despite the obstacles, they had developed a routine in the weeks that they had been here. Every morning, seven or eight Red Berets would go out on foot on hunting and gathering expeditions, while three or four would remain with the shuttle, guarding it and performing other tasks. The highest ranking guardsmen among them, Lieutenant Eden Rista, had some scientific training, so he set up a work station in the shuttle where he performed tests on plants to confirm that they were potentially edible, with worthwhile nutrients.

Lorenzo acted as if he was in charge of the operation, but Pimyt and a number of the soldiers only tolerated him. As time passed, the aged merchant prince was getting more irritable and difficult to tolerate. Among other things, he kept complaining about the limited number of items they had on their menu. Part of that had to do with the genetic unsuitability of far-planet microbiology, the fact that Humans and other races were not able to eat and digest extremely alien foods. That was a problem here, so the soldiers had performed tests on various plants and had used customized additives, to make them edible.

Many of the gray-brown native plants had proved to be either poisonous or impossible to eat, either because of their stringy texture or bitter flavors. But a number of greenish roots were moderately tasty when cooked, and some of the plants could be ground up and dried to create seasonings. They also found an area of soft stones near the pool of water where Lorenzo often sat to read the *Scienscroll*, stones that could be scraped and mashed into fine particles that were the equivalent of salt. Oddly, they found no animal life at all, not even insects or creatures crawling in the soil. It was, to a degree, a sterile environment for everything except plants, which gave them pause and put them constantly on the alert for poisons in their food and drink.

The pool of water contained organic and mineral contaminants, but after digging several test holes into the subterranean rivers, they found water that proved drinkable without boiling or other treatment.

In this environment Lorenzo only proved his inadequacies. Though he didn't mind getting dirty, he did not display any skills or knowledge to help the group. He was just *there*, and often in the way. Among the soldiers, only Eden Rista and Kenjie Ishop seemed to kowtow to him. Both worked on the food—

Rista doing the tests and Ishop the preparation and cooking. The others did as the fussy merchant prince ordered, but Pimyt had heard them grumbling about it privately, when Lorenzo was out of earshot.

Like a broken holorecording, Lorenzo had been complaining about the limited menu, and insisted that the Red Berets bring in something new every day for analysis and testing. Each afternoon, he would await their return from the jungle, and would ask, in an edgy voice, "What did you find for me today? Anything interesting?" And the plant or mineral would go to Rista to look it over and perform tests on it.

Even with the discomforts and annoyances, the group was getting by. Ishop even had a talent for music, and had constructed a stringed instrument that sounded surprisingly good, using plant fibers for strings and a hollowed-out tuber root for the sounding box. Ishop was a nice enough fellow. He'd even learned the words of an old Hibbil ballad from Pimyt, and sang it passably well.

But for Pimyt that had only been to pass the time. Essentially, he had been treading water, waiting for someone to come and rescue them. He wished he knew what was happening on the war front. Whatever it was, his own contribution had disappeared altogether. The HibAdu leaders had probably already forgotten about him, after only a few weeks. Even before that, Pimyt's sphere of influence had been shrinking, and now amounted to essentially nothing.

Originally he had been brought into the HibAdu conspiracy because of his closeness to the merchant prince leader, Doge Lorenzo. Pimyt had accompanied Lorenzo after his fall from political power, when Lorenzo still had considerable influence as a wealthy merchant prince. But now, neither Pimyt nor Lorenzo had any power at all. They only had this tiny group of fourteen survivors, with no hopes or prospects for the future. There weren't even any females here. They could only die off in this forgotten place, one by one.

Pimyt grinned ferally as a recurring thought surfaced. He could make things more pleasurable around here anyway. At least for a time. He didn't think he could face one more meal without meat protein.

The night before, they had all gotten drunk on an alcoholic beverage that one of the soldiers had brewed using roots and brown berries. The liquid had been a sickly color, but had tasted reasonably good, especially after a few drinks of it. His companions were sleeping it off now. After losing a bet to Pimyt about who could drink the most, Lorenzo had stumbled out of the shuttle and announced that he was going to sleep "somewhere else." No one could talk him out of it, so one of the soldiers, Kenjie Ishop, had helped the former doge construct a makeshift bed at the edge of the jungle. Then Ishop and the others had gone back inside the shuttle, where they all slept on thin mats or on the hard deck.

Reaching the clearing, Pimyt saw the shuttle. The silvery craft sat silently, with no lights on inside or activity visible through the portholes or front windshield. Moisture dripped down the windows and the solar array that the crew had left open.

Perhaps a hundred meters away, the Hibbil found Lorenzo sleeping on the ground, on a makeshift bed of branches and broad leaves, snoring loudly.

The furry little man crept closer, and stared down at the once-powerful merchant prince. 'Lorenzo the Great' was nothing now, would never see his former trappings of power and wealth. Like the other Humans, Lorenzo had a scruffy, dirty beard. His clothes were damp, but he was too stupidly drunk to have noticed.

Humans are such ugly creatures, Pimyt thought. Personally, he had always preferred the fat, fleshy meat of Mutatis. Human meat was tougher, chewier, and too sweet. But this time it would have to do.

The little Hibbil moved closer.

Hearing a noise, Lorenzo awakened. He looked around and sat up. "Whah? What am I doing out here?"

"You insisted on sleeping outside," Pimyt said. He felt the hunger mounting inside, and knew his red eyes must be glowing brightly, like hot little coals in his face. He narrowed the eyelids to slits. Saliva built up in his mouth.

"I did?" The ex-doge shivered, and tried to stand. But his legs buckled under him.

Plopping back down on the leafy bed, he said, "Look what my life has become. At one time I ruled the vast Human universe and dispatched merchant ships to the farthest reaches of my realm. I was wealthy beyond belief. Now I am trapped on the most remote, worthless planet imaginable. It's all your fault, you know, Pimyt."

The eye slits widened. "No, it isn't. Anyway, fault is a meaningless word that doesn't matter out here. In this place there are no rules, no conditions, no social mores or niceties."

For the first time, Lorenzo seemed to notice Pimyt's face. "Why are you looking at me like that?" Fear crept over the Human's face.

To the Hibbil, it didn't matter what the fallen man was saying. Pimyt's eyes had taken on an untamed cast and he no longer thought of being a Royal Attaché, a member of the HibAdu Coalition, or anything like that. He thought only of satisfying his hunger.

With a sudden move, the Hibbil bared his sharp teeth and lunged for Lorenzo's white, wrinkled throat, taking the Human down and tearing into his flesh. It happened so quickly that the hapless prey hardly had time to emit a squeal.

On all fours, Pimyt fed on the corpse, and felt great. Then his teeth struck something hard and foreign, causing him to examine what it was. Clothing had been no obstacle, he'd just shredded his way through it and swallowed. But not this. Holding the object in one hand, he saw it was a dermex in a small padded case. Inside the case, he saw a vial of red fluid that looked like Human blood. Interesting. He would get to that later. For now, he was enjoying the flesh.

At a noise, he paused and looked toward the shuttle, with blood and tissue dripping from his furry chin.

One of the Red Beret soldiers awakened, then went to the main hatch and looked out. Confused at the sight of a Hibbil in a feeding frenzy, he hesitated for a moment too long. With inhuman speed and strength, Pimyt bolted toward him and attacked, then surged inside and killed the sleeping or awakening soldiers one after the other before they could get their weapons, before they knew what was happening to them. It helped him that they'd been drinking an alcoholic concoction the night before, which made them groggy and slow.

He ripped all of them apart and tasted their meat … one sample after the other. Though not the finest quality of flesh, organs, and bones, it was perhaps the best meal he'd ever had. He had been so hungry!

When he reached his fill, he considered what to do next, and then remembered the vial of red fluid by the body of Lorenzo. Covered in blood, he bounded out of the shuttle and across the clearing.

Examining the dermex and the vial, Pimyt wondered why Lorenzo had been carrying these things with him. Opening the top of the vial, he sniffed. It had definite elements of Human blood, but had a color that was more like wine. He didn't see any purpose in wondering why Lorenzo had it.

Tossing the dermex aside, Pimyt swallowed the vial's contents. *Delicious!* It was like a fine aperitif after a big meal.

Then, sitting on the ground beside the corpse, he was pleased to see carrion birds circling overhead. So, there were living creatures on this planet after all, and they'd come out of their places of concealment.

The clever Hibbil started to think about laying traps for them, using pieces of the corpses as bait.

A sudden swoon came over him, as from lightheadedness, and he felt fire coursing through the veins of his body, energizing him. *Fantastic!* His pleasure mounted.

He heard a loud crashing. Without warning, the shuttle tumbled over and vanished. Green light came from a hole in the ground, giving an eerie cast to the foggy air.

Eh? Intensely curious, Pimyt went over to look down into the hole. With nothing to lose, he didn't feel any fear. As the blood-soaked Hibbil stood on the edge, he rubbed his full belly and looked down into a chasm so deep that he didn't think it had a bottom.

Drawn by a sudden compulsion, he inched closer to the edge, then lost his footing and tumbled into the hole. Through the green light he plunged, into an abyss that gave him a feeling of euphoria. But gradually something seemed to change, and he had the distinct sensation that he was going in the other direction, back the way he had just come. How could that be? Moments later, he realized he was right, as he vaulted out of the hole and over the encampment where he'd slaughtered Lorenzo and the others.

Soon he left all that behind as well, and found himself drifting slowly through a vast, starry universe. Inexplicably, he could breathe out there. The green light had faded entirely, but there was a faint, colorless illumination source in this place. He saw something ahead. Drifting toward it, Pimyt was amazed to see the faces of Princess Meghina and four of her immortal companions, floating in space. Three women and two men.

At first the Hibbil could not make out the bodies of the people, only their huge, out-of-scale faces. As moments passed the visages began to bend, as if they were on banners fluttering in a breeze, and their features became distorted.

Then Pimyt saw their bodies, stygian black and barely discernible—immense, multilegged creatures coming toward him with bizarre Human faces. He tried to scream in terror, but in the void he heard no sound.

Silently, ominously, they closed in on him....

Chapter Fifty-Two

In conquering almost every Human and Mutati world, the HibAdus used a nasty trick—which we figured out by checking and rechecking all remaining parts that the Hibbils made for us when we thought they were our allies. And there it was: a tiny, ingeniously designed computer chip that functioned perfectly during testing but didn't hold up to further scrutiny. In the midst of battle, the chip detected the presence of attacking HibAdu warships, which in turn instantly shut down the firing mechanisms of the defenders' artillery pieces. If undiscovered, we Liberators would have met the same fate in our first big engagement. Now, let the enemy wonder if we have spotted their ruse.

—General Nirella del Velli, speech to her officers

From a military perspective, Doge Anton and General Nirella did not consider the loss of Dij entirely bad. Their feelings had nothing to do with any past enmity toward shapeshifters. Rather, they were pleased that Hari'Adab had managed to locate a large number of Mutati warships, soldiers, and military supplies around the former Mutati Sector, and that he had returned safely with a much more powerful force than he had when he left.

Now Anton and Nirella sat inside a gourd-shaped officers' yacht as its robot pilot guided them slowly through the moorage basin containing the newly arrived podships. A number of the sentient vessels disgorged conventional Mutati craft, which were going into moorage and defensive positions around the larger ships. In times past, seeing so many of these Mutati vessels would have been cause for alarm. But not now. Humans and Mutatis—along with Tulyans—were in alliance against the most deadly enemy any of them had ever faced.

The yacht took a position on the perimeter of the moorage basin. Then, at a signal from General Nirella, hundreds of podships separated from the others, forming a procession heading out to space. This was the first wave of them.

Within the hour, three hundred podships—a small portion of the force that had been allocated to the Mutati leader—would depart for Siriki on a new assignment—at the request of Emir Hari'Adab. The new operation would be under joint Human and Mutati command, and the shapeshifter Emir was being permitted to accompany them, so that he could personally check on the welfare of his lady friend, Parais d'Olor. A disturbing report from the Sirikan back country suggested that she could be in grave physical danger.

The lead ship accelerated with Hari'Adab aboard, and in a bright burst of green it was the first to vanish into the cosmic web. The others followed, and in tight military precision one split space every three seconds....

* * * * *

With two passengers aboard, the dark bird beat its wings rhythmically, and lifted slowly into the air. Holding onto the mane of feathers behind Parais's neck, Dux thought she was slightly smaller now, but not that much. She seemed stronger, but he heard her wheezing as she exerted herself.

In the midday sky, gray clouds sagged above them, as if pregnant with water and about to release their contents. So far, though, Dux felt no moisture in the air, just a warm updraft. It was not a comforting warmth, though, coming as it did from the lava-flooded valley and woodlands below, the remote area where he, Acey, and their grandmother had spent many happy years. Now it was fast disappearing. Here and there some of the homesteads on higher ground held out, but gradually all of them were being inundated. Dux hoped that some people were able to escape, and he felt considerable survivor's guilt for having gotten away himself.

From the left, he heard what he thought were the sounds of battle, loud percussive thumps and explosions. Looking in that direction—approximately where they had been shot down earlier in the crop-duster plane—he saw bright bursts of blue and orange beyond tree-lined hills. Now, as Parais rose higher, Dux saw an aerial dogfight, and one fighter craft shot down the other. From this distance he couldn't make out military markings, but he assumed it was a force sent by Noah to root out the HibAdus that Kekur had reported there.

Suddenly he felt a shudder in the bird, and saw the wings slow their beating, and then stop. The aeromutati lost altitude, slowly at first, and then faster as she had difficulty keeping her wings spread. Intermittently, finding strength, she would attempt to use the wings again, but she couldn't sustain the effort.

"Hold on!" Parais shouted. Dux couldn't grip her any harder, and even his normally courageous cousin shivered in fear as he held onto Dux.

Increasingly, as the shapeshifter's wings threatened to completely tuck themselves against her body, she began to fall like a feathered rock, only intermittently getting the wings out a little. Somehow she managed to keep herself upright, or the boys might have fallen off. Below, trees were fast approaching.

Shuddering and groaning, Parais extended her wings, and at the last possible moment she was able to regain her aerodynamics and glide. As seconds passed, however, she continued to lose altitude. They were away from the flow of lava but too near the battle zone for comfort. Dux heard the sounds of fighting even louder than before, and saw a red-and-gold MPA gridjet speed overhead.

Skimming the tops of evergreen trees, Parais barely cleared them. Finally, over a small meadow her strength gave out, and she drifted down for a bumpy landing. As she hit the ground, her passengers tumbled off.

Scrambling to his feet, Dux assessed his new bumps and bruises, as did Acey near him.

"Now we've survived two crashes around here," Acey said.

The boys hurried to check on Parais, who lay on the ground breathing hard, with one wing tucked and the other half extended. Though she didn't say anything, she clearly wanted to fold her other wing in, so Dux and Acey helped her accomplish this.

After several deep, gasping breaths, she said, "Thank you." Her eyes were open, and though they looked better than before, they still had a sickly yellow cast to them, with small purple veins running through them more visibly than ever.

"Look!" Acey husked in a low voice. He pointed toward the woods.

Through an opening in the trees, they saw an orange-and-gray aircraft. It was sleek, had a pointed nose, and—from the number of portholes on the side behind the cockpit—the craft looked large enough to carry at least ten passengers.

"HibAdu ship!" Acey said.

Out in the meadow the three of them were exposed, but so far the HibAdus did not seem to have noticed them. At least no one was bursting out of the woods and running toward them, or firing at them.

Moving as quickly and silently as they could, Dux and Acey helped Parais walk into the cover of trees, perhaps a hundred meters from the ship. From there, they watched for several long minutes, detecting no activity around the vessel.

"Could be an escape craft," Acey said. "Stashed here for officers. It looks fast. See those jet tubes on the sides? I'll bet that baby can scoot. I don't see any guards, but you can bet they'll be back pretty quick."

"Are you thinking what I'm thinking?" Dux asked. He grinned. "I don't even need to ask that question." Looking at Parais, he said to her, "Acey and I are soldiers, and we need to either steal that ship or sabotage it."

"I understand," she said, her voice raspy.

"Do you want to stay here or go with us?" Dux asked, as he stroked the feathers on her back.

"If I'm not too much of a burden, I'd like to go with you."

"After what you did for us," Acey said, "you're no burden at all." He looked toward the sleek craft. "Let's go."

They were slowed by having to help Parais walk toward the ship, and they found it easier to go back out to the edge of the meadow with her. Agonizingly long minutes passed, and finally they made it to the rear of the vessel. Still no sign of anyone, not even any robotic guards. On the back side of the craft, a ramp was down.

The boys assisted Parais up the ramp, and Dux found her a spot on the aft deck of the passenger cabin, where she plopped down unceremoniously. Acey had hurried to the cockpit, and Dux heard him up there muttering to himself as he tried to figure out the controls. He hit a toggle, and the engines surged on. They made a high-pitched whine that irritated Dux's ears.

Hurry, hurry, he thought.

But he heard angry shouts. Looking out a porthole, Dux saw three HibAdu soldiers running toward them. Two Adurians and a Hibbil.

"Get the ramp up and take off!" Dux shouted. "We've been spotted!"

"I'm trying, dammit!"

Seeing a handgun in a holster on the bulkhead, Dux grabbed the weapon. His thoughts accelerated, and he remembered Acey showing him how to operate a similar one earlier. Touching a pad on the barrel, he caused the energy chamber on top to glow yellow.

Just as Acey got the ship to move off the ground a little, one of the insectoid Adurians ran up the ramp and burst into the passenger cabin. Dux hit him in the chest with an energy burst, and the soldier dropped. The other Adurian and the Hibbil got on before Dux could get off another shot, and they jumped behind a half-bulkhead, just inside the passenger compartment.

The ramp closed with a loud click, and the craft lifted into the air. As the engines whined louder, the ship went faster. Suddenly they shot up into the sky at an angle, and it was all Dux could do to keep from falling backward. The Hibbil lost his footing and tumbled past Dux, into the aft section.

Dux wanted to fire at him, but by the time he regained his footing, he saw Parais attacking the Hibbil, tearing at him with beak and talons. The furry little alien screamed in pain, so it looked as if the shapeshifter had found enough strength to deal with him. At least, Dux hoped so. He didn't want to shoot in that direction and hit her.

Having lost track of the Adurian, Dux crept forward around the seats. Just ahead, he heard the Adurian say something from the cockpit, but Dux couldn't see him. "Turn this ship around and land!" the soldier said in a whiny voice. "Now!"

"No!" Acey shouted.

Now Dux saw the barrel of a gun around the bulkhead, a weapon that was pointed at Acey. Dux couldn't get a good angle to shoot at him. And from behind he heard a sudden shot, and then Parais crying out, as if she'd been hit. But she kept attacking the Hibbil.

"I've got my hand on the self-destruct button," Acey said, glancing back at the Adurian. "Put down your weapon, or I'm going to put all of us down."

Deciding to help Parais first, Dux hurried aft, watching all the while in case the Adurian spotted him. In the small rear section he found a bleeding, badly injured Parais battling the much smaller but still deadly Hibbil. She had managed to knock his weapon away and it was nowhere to be seen—but the Hibbil was by no means defenseless, and he was very fast. Bleeding badly himself, he kept getting around her beak and talons and ripping into her flesh with his sharp teeth.

Even in her weakened, injured condition, with purple blood soaking her feathers, Parais had some cellular regeneration ability as a shapeshifter. The Hibbil, with no such ability, finally fell back on the deck from his injuries. As he tried to get back on his feet, Parais drove a sharp talon through his chest, like a spike into his heart. He stopped moving, but Parais had expended almost all of her energy. To Dux's horror, her cellular structure started to break down in front of his eyes. Pieces of flesh and feathers sloughed off onto the deck, in a purple mass of goo.

Then, giving him some hope, he saw a substantially smaller version of Parais stabilize her shape.

Just then the ship lurched, and Dux heard Acey shout, "Have a nice trip!"

The Adurian screamed, and through a porthole Dux watched him tumble out of the aircraft.

Running forward, Dux saw to his amazement that Acey had found another hatch door, this one for the cockpit, and he had skillfully opened it just as he steered the ship sharply in the opposite direction, causing the Adurian to fall out.

"Nice move," Dux said. He told Accy about the other two enemy soldiers, then added, "We each got one of the bad guys, but we need to get Parais some medical attention. She's having trouble back there."

Acey set course for the headquarters at the Golden Palace, while Dux went back to do what he could for Parais. She was only around half as big as she had been when she carried the boys and Kekur on her back. One of her wings was badly torn and she didn't seem able to regenerate its cellular configuration. All over her body and on her once-beautiful face, open wounds oozed purple.

Barely alive, the brave Mutati slumped to the deck, quivering and shaking. Dux found her a blanket and massaged her gently where it didn't seem to cause her pain. She looked at him thankfully, but he felt helpless.

"Hang on," he said in a soothing voice.

Chapter Fifty-Three

Maturity is not something that can be given to you, or which you can gain by simply growing older. It is something you must earn, through the harsh lessons of personal experience.

—Subi Danvar

"Siriki below," the robot soldier reported to a group of Human and Mutati officers who stood on a cargo deck of the Aopoddae flagship. One of the shapeshifters sneezed from an allergic reaction to Humans, but he smiled and adjusted a tiny medical booster on his wrist, which enhanced the allergy protector implanted in his body.

Anxious to board the shuttle, Hari'Adab stood at the forefront of the group. Unlike most of his race, he had never felt a physical aversion toward Humans, and neither had his girlfriend, Parais. He had always wondered how much of it was psychosomatic, based upon stress, mass hysteria, or the power of suggestion.

Now he tried to be patient. Looking through a filmy viewing window, he watched a shuttle approach to take them down to the planet. Somewhere down there on the blue-green world, his precious Parais was in trouble, and he desperately wanted to get to her. He hoped and prayed that she was still alive, and that she would recover.

"Shuttle two minutes away," the robot said. Slender and compact, the sentient machine had a neckless head, and arms that were kept in compartments and only appeared when needed. At the moment, one of the arms was saluting in an awkward fashion, while his mechanical face looked at no one in particular.

Hari sighed. As a Mutati, he naturally gloried in the marvels of flesh and the creative possibilities that a shape-shifting body could assume. Just looking at this robot (or any other one), and seeing the rigid physical structure—the manufactured, non-biological components—he was always struck by the inferiority of machines and their distinct limitations. As far as he was concerned, their artificial intelligence did not elevate them in the least. It was a synthetic thing, and unnatural.

He knew he should not be thinking this way, that it touched on the feelings of racial superiority that Mutati leaders had long felt, especially in comparison with Humans. Some people considered sentient machines a separate galactic race, though this seemed like quite a stretch to Hari. Even Noah Watanabe, whom Hari greatly respected, was reported to hold that opinion. As evidence of that, he was said to point to the example of his machine leader and trusted adviser, Thinker.

Considering it more, Hari wondered if he could really dispute that position. After watching the irritating robot Jimu in action, with all of his clever maneuverings, there certainly seemed to be a spark of life there ... albeit an irritating one. The loyalty of robots to Humans was legendary, and so pervasive that it seemed to go beyond anything that could have been programmed into them. Jimu was watching Hari now, from a mezzanine over the cargo deck.

The cargo door opened, and Hari hurried through an airlock into the shuttle. It seemed to take forever for the other passengers to load, though he knew it was less than ten minutes. But every minute and every second away from Parais tormented his heart.

* * * * *

When it came to mechanical things, Acey had always been a quick study. Almost a year ago he and Dux had been on a treasure-hunting crew, a motley bunch of rowdies many of whom had had experience working on conventional spaceships. When their craft broke down, the teenage Acey had helped figure out the problem, just one of many instances in which he had proved himself capable.

And Acey had done it again, though it might not be enough to save Parais. Under pressure from three attacking soldiers, he had figured out the operation of the sleek HibAdu craft and had flown it away. Now the vessel sped over mountains, lakes, and forests, while Dux remained in the aft section, tending to the grievously wounded Mutati. Though she had fought valiantly for survival, she seemed to have been shot in a vital place, one that her already destabilized condition had prevented her from healing. From what he had heard, a Mutati could often survive terrible wounds by changing its cellular structure around and finding new body forms. But this seemed different. She'd been wounded when she was already weak from the problem of having taken on too much mass.

Clearly, her condition was worsening. During the flight Parais had been devolving in a frightening way, as her body was losing its distinctive features and becoming a quivering mass of salmon-colored flesh. Moments ago, her eyes had slipped back inside the fatty cellular structure, but Dux had not been repulsed, and had not moved away from her at all. He kept talking to her in a soothing voice, using her name and massaging where her shoulders and neck used to be. The pulse of her flesh was slowing, but occasionally—as if in direct response to his words or touch—she would revive. Then, moments later, she would fade again. He only knew that he had to keep trying, letting her know that someone cared about her.

In his pocket he had Grandma Zelk's pouch of healing powder, and he had considered sprinkling some of it on the Mutati. But he had hesitated, not wanting to risk doing anything that could worsen her condition, or even cause her death.

Through a porthole Dux saw the glittering spires of the Golden Palace nearing, and the military compound that had grown up around it. Having established comlink contact a half-hour ago, Acey now circled the landing field, waiting his turn after a shuttle that was setting down. Dux allowed himself to feel a surge of hope.

A minute later he heard the welcome, reassuring voice of Noah Watanabe over the comlink: "Okay, Acey. Bring her in next to the shuttle. We have doctors waiting for your patient."

As Acey went into hover mode and landed, Dux saw at least a hundred Humans and Mutatis standing on the groundpad. With the engines whining down, the hatch and ramp of the HibAdu craft opened.

Mutatis rushed on board first, and it soon became apparent that they were a medical team. Having shapeshifted into various modes of appearance, all wore pale blue uniforms. Dux stayed out of their way, and watched as they carried her down the ramp on a metalloy stretcher to a waiting ambulance.

Noah Watanabe and a robed Mutati hurried along with them. Having seen holophotos of the Mutati before, Dux knew it was the shapeshifter leader, Hari'Adab.

Noah and the Emir shook hands. Then the somber Mutati climbed into the ambulance with Parais, and the vehicle sped off.

Seeing Acey and Dux leave the HibAdu aircraft, Noah went to them. "Good to see you boys," he said, giving each of them a hearty hug. "You'll get commendations for this." His face darkened. "Sorry to hear about your grandmother. Terrible conditions in the back country."

"Thanks," Acey said. "We lost Kekur, too."

"I know. A fine robot, that one."

Taking one of his staff cars, Noah accompanied the teenagers back to their barracks on the palace grounds. On the way he told them about a wounded HibAdu lab-pod that had been found on Siriki, having been hit by ion-cannon fire.

"I just got back from seeing it," Noah said. "Some of my aides wanted to kill it because of the damage such podships cause to the galactic infrastructure. I couldn't do that, though. It's defective, but it's still a living creature. Eshaz is here on a brief stopover, and he said it might be revived with a green dust that he carries around with him, but he didn't recommend doing that."

Dux thought of the healing powder in his pocket, but said nothing about it. Soon he would give it to Noah or Eshaz, but first it was something that he only wanted to share with Acey. It was all they had left that had belonged to Grandmamá.

Noah sighed. "Maybe it would be better to put the creature out of its misery, after all. We can't ever let it fly again, and would have to keep it pinned down. I guess I know what has to be done."

"These are unusual times," Dux said. "I never would have thought we'd fly a HibAdu ship here, trying to save a Mutati."

"That makes me think of an ancient curse from Lost Earth," Noah said, shaking his head in dismay. " 'May you live in interesting times.' " Then he looked at Dux and Acey, and added, "Well men, that's where we are now."

One of his words did not go unnoticed by either of the cousins. Exchanging glances, each of them knew they were *men* now.

Chapter Fifty-Four

We Humans are easily susceptible to stress. From my observation, the root causes seem clear: Stress is derived from a lack of perceived control over conditions around you. To a great extent this operates on a personal level, on situations impacting the individual. If you can gain a measure of control over those things, reducing their negative impact on you, it will reduce your stress. Think of disease, or financial matters, or relationships. It is simple to think of stress in this way, but not so easy in the application. We are Humans after all, and far from perfect in anything we attempt. Realize, too, that our collective anxiety as Guardians is potentially great, because we are going to war against ecological damage. Not an easy thing to control, but like soldiers, we must find comfort in our just purpose, and serenity in the knowledge that we are doing our best.

—Master Noah Watanabe, speech to the last graduating class on EcoStation

In his apartment at the keep, Noah prepared to leave for Yaree, the trip that had been interrupted by the battle on Siriki and the Parais d'Olor matter. His breakfast sat half-eaten on a coffee table, near a dirty pouch of green dust that Dux Hannah had given him ... purportedly a strange "healing powder" that had belonged to his grandmother. Eshaz had already examined it, and said it was similar to the substance that Tulyans used to remedy small timeholes.

Quickly, Noah tossed the pouch and a stack of holofiles into a briefcase, then snapped it shut. These were old-format research reports about Yaree and their customs that he'd found in the palace library. Meghina had a lot of books and files in there, gleaned from her travels around the galaxy in happier times. Noah also had three reports from the recon team that he'd sent to Yaree—one for each day they'd been there. These were on new-format holofiles, which he converted to telebeam storage files and kept in his signet ring. He could convert the older files, too, but there would be a longer conversion process, and he wanted to get going.

Noah's thoughts churned as he hurried out into the corridor. He walked briskly, with aides signaling to each other as they accompanied him, making last-minute arrangements. His whole life felt rushed now, like he couldn't get a handle on it, that it was not in his control.

A wayward memory intruded. Upon seeing how he could regenerate his body after a serious injury, a doctor once said to Noah, "You'll live forever. You have time in your pocket."

Perhaps that was true, or perhaps not. A pocket—like the galaxy itself—could have holes in it.

Without any doubt, he believed that his enhanced cellular capabilities were linked to Timeweb, but that paranormal realm had proven to be volatile and elusive. It only allowed him to enter it on *its* own terms, not on his. But if he was connected to the web, and the infrastructure was deteriorating, couldn't that mean that he would eventually lose his immortality? He thought so, and that any serious future injury he sustained could prove to be fatal.

His lack of understanding troubled him deeply, but he remembered the calming exercises he had taught to his galactic ecology students. Inwardly, even as he rushed forward physically, he took a long mental breath, and felt a little better. As moments passed, one merging into the next, his stormy continent of worries diminished to a small tropical island, with warm, gentle waves lapping against the shore. But the trick only lasted temporarily, and in his mind he envisioned storm clouds approaching over the sea.

Complete control. Such an elusive, impossible concept.

Yaree was in a galactic sector that had displayed severe timehole activity. It was also a planet with an unpredictable leadership. He hoped he could learn something in Meghina's holofiles about how to deal with those people. He knew the Yareens had rich mineral deposits and that they had a long history of independence as savvy galactic traders. For centuries they had been excellent businessmen, so he would probably need to make them an offer that was economically attractive to them.

He didn't like thinking in such terms. In the present state of the galaxy, with the HibAdus running rampant and not caring what irreparable damage they were causing with their military acts and their ecologically harmful lab-pods, he needed people who were capable of answering to a higher calling than money. First he would try to appeal to Yareen morals and see if they would respond to the galactic emergency on that basis. Even better, if they could be convinced of the severity of the ecological crisis, they might pitch in for their own survival.

Noah was taking an escort of only three armed podships on the trip. With such a small force, he hoped to avoid being noticed by the HibAdus, slipping under their scanners. He thought it likely that this would work, because he had earlier sent a reconnaissance mission to Yaree with that number of ships, and there had been scores of courier flights, all without incident. His advisers had objected to the light escort, but he'd prevailed over them with an argument they could not dispute—his instincts told him to go to Yaree in that manner. He'd grown to rely on instincts to a considerable extent; on more than one occasion, they had proven their value to him going all the way back to his childhood.

As part of his plan, Noah left the bulk of his fleet at Siriki, along with Hari's reinforcements. All were ready to respond if he needed them, but because of poor podway conditions, the Tulyans were estimating that the trip would take more than an hour each way. This meant that it would require more than twice that long to get reinforcements to Yaree if necessary, assuming a courier could make the return trip and sound the alarm. It also meant, however, that he now had a little time to review the holofiles in his briefcase before arriving at his destination.

After instructing his aides to leave him alone, he secluded himself in his office on the podship, and began examining the documents. He floated five holofiles at a time in the air, and moved from file to file.

Almost oblivious to the fact that his ship was splitting space and gaining speed, he learned from the documents that the Yareens had a potential weakness, something he might be able to exploit if necessary. Though he would first appeal to their morality and need to survive, if those attempts failed he had a contingency plan.

As recently as a couple of years ago, the Yareens had been addicted to nobo, a hallucinogenic tree root that only grew in the rain forests of Canopa, so it had to be imported from there. Of little significance anywhere else in the galaxy, nobo was in high demand on Yaree, where it was burned in religious rites in elaborate ceremonies that were said to ward off evil spirits. If their stockpiles were low, and if they didn't have access to podships, Noah thought he could gain considerable leverage with them.

But first, he would inspect EcoStation and the galactic conditions nearby, receiving the latest information from the experts on his recon team.

* * * * *

With Noah's three podships moored in orbital space, he rode a tube-shaped transport ship over to the orbital position of EcoStation. The facility was ragged and torn open, in such horrible condition that most people would think it was not worth restoring. Even so, Noah wanted to recover it, for the inspirational value it would offer. In view of the ongoing war and other crises, he would not file a formal salvage claim for the space station. Instead, he would take charge of it on a de facto basis, not involving the filing of any documents. Someday Lorenzo del Velli might surface again and make preposterous legal demands. If necessary, Noah would deal with such a challenge when the time came. For now, he had other priorities.

The transport ship locked onto a docking port of the orbiter, and Noah noticed that the hulls of the modules glowed faintly green. He didn't know why, and it gave him some trepidation. Double doors slid open with a grinding noise.

Passing through an airlock, he was greeted by the dented black robot Jimu and four other soldier robots. With a crisp salute, Jimu stepped forward and said, "Fantastic to see you again, sir. Everything is in readiness for your inspection."

"First I want a full report on what happened to this station. Wait a minute, what are you doing here? I thought you were keeping tabs on Hari'Adab."

"I was, sir, but he complained that I was getting on his nerves, so others were assigned to him—a couple of robots with better personalities than mine. I just arrived before you did. The Tulyans received your comlink message and are ready to provide the information you desire. I will take you to the meeting chamber."

Looking around, Noah saw the evidence of recent repairs to the hull of this module, to make it airtight. He heard loud machinery noises, and saw robots at work restoring one of the other docking ports.

"Heat and life support systems are functional in some modules," Jimu said, as he handed a survival suit to Noah. "You'd better get into this, because we'll be passing through airless sections. I've made sure that we can walk through most modules safely, but some are ripped apart, and clinging to the framework of the space station by the barest structural components."

Noah put on the suit, but left the face piece open in the helmeted top. The suit was transparent flexplax, and squeaked a little as he followed Jimu to a lift.

"We've sealed some modules where there are bodies of Red Berets who were stationed here, and bodies of gambling patrons. They were all caught by surprise when something tore the station apart."

"I've heard," Noah said, "Princess Meghina told me a few of the horrific details."

The lift door closed, and the car rose, noisily and slowly.

"Has she been found, sir?" This robot had an excess of personality at times, but Noah had never found him overly annoying. Jimu had a history of loyal service, and had accomplished a great deal for the Liberator cause. He was one of only a handful of sentient machines who could be spoken of in the same breath with the name of Thinker.

"Sadly, no."

They stepped out of the lift, onto an uneven deck. Ahead, Noah saw hundreds of motionless robots. Although an unrepaired hole remained in the ceiling, the sentient machines still stood erectly and didn't disappear into space, held in place by the onboard gravitonics system. They did not appear to be damaged.

"I know each of these robots well," Jimu said. "I used to be in charge of Red Beret machines here, you know. These were among the units I was reproducing as worker variants instead of fighters. They performed office, janitorial, construction, and food service duties."

Noah scowled. "When you worked for Doge Lorenzo."

"Before I knew any better, until I joined you and Thinker."

Jimu stepped close to the front row of robots, touched one of the faceplates. "These machines are all deactivated," he said, "locked-down so that they cannot energize themselves. After I led a mass defection, taking most of the fighting machines to join your Guardians, Lorenzo had these shut down—to play it safe."

"And they just left them here?"

"As far as I can tell. In another module I've reactivated sixty-two machines and put them to work. I've given each of them a name. I always prefer to make the robots more personal to each other and connected to their unit, instead of using typical machine codes. This way, it seems more Human to me."

Noah followed Jimu through two modules, then boarded another lift with him. On an upper level, the Guardian leader found more robots working, and a small Tulyan woman speaking with them. He recognized her as Zigzia, the webtalker who had sent cross-space messages for him in the past.

"Better connect your breathing apparatus," Jimu said. "We'll be going through a module that has no air. We've got an emergency gravitonics system working in most modules, but you'll notice some difference. We're only doing the emergency repairs you ordered, but there's still a lot of work to do, depending upon what you decide to do with the station."

Spotting Noah, Zigzia broke away from her conversation and joined him, as Jimu led the way onto another module. Noah almost gagged from the stench, and soon he saw why: bodies and body parts were stacked along the sides of the corridor and in adjoining rooms. Some of the doors to those rooms were damaged or blocked, and didn't close all the way. From earlier reports, Noah knew to expect this, but it was impossible to prepare himself for the gruesome reality. He had told the reconnaissance- and robotic-repair teams not to jettison any of the bodies. They deserved proper ceremonies. This, and the identification of the victims, were among many details that still needed attention. He had already set that in motion, and expected a mortuary and burial team to arrive in a few days.

For the moment, though, he needed to find out what had occurred here, and he was anxious to meet with the Tulyan experts.

As Noah looked around at the damaged space station, he couldn't help wondering if it was really worth salvaging. It would be no small task to repair it, which would require time and the allocation of additional robotic assets that might be more appropriately used elsewhere. There was also the problem of transporting it to a more suitable location, either orbiting Canopa or Siriki. That might be accomplished by breaking it up into sections and loading them into podship cargo holds. In one of the earlier reports, Jimu had estimated that this would involve seven or eight sections, and three or four podships to transport them.

But now, seeing EcoStation firsthand, Noah reminded himself of the reason he had ordered the makeshift repairs that were occurring now. His famed School of Galactic Ecology had once been here, filled with classroom and laboratory facilities. This orbiter was much more than machinery, much more than the sum of its tortured modules and shredded parts. It represented something immensely important—a potentially powerful source of inspiration for humankind—and the determined conviction that the galaxy would survive against all odds, even in the face of warfare and the collapsing infrastructure. Wherever he placed it, EcoStation could become a beacon in the cosmos.

It was very personal for him. Noah had strong feelings for the facility, and a sense that he needed to connect with his past in order to counter the flurry of changes around him, thus reconnecting to a time when he began to call himself and his followers "eco-warriors."

Jimu and Zigzia led him into one of the original school sections that had been converted into a gambling hall. Now it didn't look like either, with overturned, smashed equipment and gaming pieces piled against the walls. "This way, please," the webtalker said, pointing out an improvised divider wall at the center. Entering the hall, Noah found four other Tulyans, seated at a large table.

"Master Watanabe," one of the Tulyans said, rising with his companions and bowing. It was Inya Vato, head of the reconnaissance team. "Please, take a seat." He gestured toward the head of the table.

When Noah sat down, the others slipped back into their places along the sides. Jimu and Zigzia stood, looking on.

"Our first assumptions proved to be correct," Vato said. "This space station fell through a timehole into another galaxy. Then, somehow, it was knocked back into this one. On the modular hulls and other parts, there are spectral traces of alien materials, not found anywhere in this galaxy. Telltale signs that it has been someplace else."

"Is that why the hulls glow faintly green now?" Noah asked.

"No," one of the other Tulyans said, a bulky male with wide, slitted eyes. "We treated the space station to make it less susceptible to timeholes, in case any more appear. A film that acts as a repellent."

"Is it like the healing dust I've seen caretakers use?" Noah asked.

"It has some similar properties. This is a liquid variation that adheres to the hull."

While listening to the Tulyans, Noah went to one of the magnaviewers by the window, a double-mirror unit that bathed him in light when he looked through it. First he located his own space-moored podships, six in all, including three that had arrived earlier with the reconnaissance and repair teams. Then, focusing on the surface of the planet Yaree, Noah saw what looked like a Yareen military base on the ground, and considerable activity there. Black military shuttles and other small aircraft taxied on an airfield and took off, one after the other.

Suddenly, orbital space filled with orange-and-gray warships, closing in on EcoStation. Noah pushed Zigzia out of the way, and opened a link to the six Liberator podships that were moored a short distance away.

"Mayday!" Noah shouted.

His podships were already in motion, with five of them going into a defensive formation. In a prearranged maneuver, the sixth sped away and split space in a burst of green light.

"We sent for reinforcements!" an officer shouted over the line.

"Zigzia," Noah said, looking at the Tulyan. "Can you transmit an emergency message to the Tulyan Elders?"

"I can try, but the web isn't in great condition between here and the starcloud, so I'll have to use alternate transmission routes." She thumped heavily out into the corridor. Noah wasn't sure where she would attempt to make the contact, but knew that Tulyans could see the web where others couldn't.

Noah's remaining podships had their space cannons pointed toward the advancing warships, and fired. The HibAdu vessels were all conventional craft, but bristling with weapons. So far he didn't see any of their lab-pods, but suspected they were nearby.

Some of the advancing HibAdu ships burst into flames, but others changed course quickly and sped toward the Liberator vessels at new angles. One of the defending podships exploded, and the four others drew back toward the space station in a last-ditch shielding effort.

But Noah had a sinking, hopeless feeling. He was badly outnumbered, and reinforcements could not possibly arrive in time....

Chapter Fifty-Five

Everything in this galaxy is linked to everything else.
Nothing is really detached, no matter how much it seems to be.
—Textbook introduction, School of Galactic Ecology

U nknown to Noah, the podship that escaped the HibAdu attack was among the oldest and most experienced of the spacefaring Aopoddae. In ancient times the vessel had been known as Diminian, and it had been present in the earliest days of the galaxy. Even then, from the outset, there had been problems with the webbing infrastructure—and those conditions bore ominous parallels with those of modern times. The galaxy had been fresh and new in the beginning, but with podship travel and other conditions the infrastructure became worn and frayed rather quickly in many places ... in the equivalent of only a few thousand years. This was one of the reasons that the first Tulyan caretakers had been dispatched to perform repairs, and afterward for regular maintenance duties.

With seasoning, the webbing actually became stronger and more able to withstand podship travel and other cosmic conditions, but there were always weak points that appeared from time to time, requiring the attention of the expert caretakers. Many of those weak points proved to be chronic, and had been among the most difficult to keep in good repair during the current crisis of galactic decay. With his long and perfect memory Diminian knew all of this, and knew better than any podship how to take alternate routes. Though he did not communicate in words, he had other means of sensing the emergency of the HibAdu attack on the space station. Thus the return flight to Siriki, which Noah had expected to take an hour or more, required only four minutes.

The Tulyan pilot, with his own means of communicating with both Aopoddae and Humans, delivered the mayday call to Noah's command headquarters, where Liberator officers sprang into action. When Diminian's ship arrived, Subi Danvar was in orbital space near Siriki, commanding a military exercise involving eight hundred podships and the Mutati warships that had been sent from Canopa. For the maneuvers, Acey and Dux were acting as Subi's personal aides on the primary vessel.

Over a comlink, Subi informed all pilots and officers of the new mission, along with the astronomical coordinates of Yaree and the orbital position of EcoStation. Then he put the just-returned Tulyan pilot on the connection, to provide details for the other pilots on the alternate, but faster, route they needed to take.

When the Tulyan finished giving the information, Subi shouted, "Let's go!" Moments later, he led the armed podships out into space, leaving the Mutati warships and the bulk of the podship fleet behind.

Even with Noah under attack, they could not risk sending more of their military assets to Yaree. Subi and the other officers were under standing orders to maintain a strong defensive position at Siriki, and not to be drawn away. They did not want to repeat what happened to the Mutati planet of Dij and lose another important world.

Back at Siriki, other officers sent Diminian and his Tulyan pilot to relay the new information to Doge Anton del Velli in the Canopa sector. They also sent a number of additional podships to Yaree, to act as couriers from the battle zone.

* * * * *

Only minutes after the attack on EcoStation, all Liberator forces in the galaxy went onto full alert. At Canopa, Doge Anton received the mayday call. With additional information on favored routes provided by the Tulyan pilot (from his esoteric connection with Diminian), Anton dispatched an additional one thousand podships.

Leaving General Nirella behind with the bulk of the fleet, the young doge led the second rescue force to Yaree. Some of his officers had questioned his decision to go himself, saying he should delegate it to one of them. But Nirella, outranking all of them, had silenced their comments. "Noah is Anton's uncle, and there has always been a strong bond between them." Smiling stiffly, she had added, "Besides, I'm the better military commander in this marriage. From a strategic standpoint, it's essential that I remain with the bulk of the fleet."

"We've already talked it out," Anton had said, "and I'm on my way."

In the flagship *Webdancer*, Anton now stood on the command bridge, at the forward viewing window. Beside him, the venerable robot Thinker folded open with a small clattering and clicking of metal. Anton was anxious to help Noah, and for this mission he needed the most brilliant of all sentient machines. He also needed the best pilots, and for the flagship that meant Tesh Kori.

As they sped through space, Thinker said, "I know you want to add my military recommendations to those of your officers, but I need to assess the battle before adding anything to what they told you. I agree with them that we must move quickly to protect the space station, since Noah was last reported aboard it. But conditions will undoubtedly be fluid on the battlefield, and he may have moved."

"Assuming he's OK. Noah once told me his 'immortality' might be as fragile as the galactic webbing, or might have been compromised by the tainted blood he got from his sister."

"Our Liberator force from Siriki may already be there."

"I hope they are," Anton said.

"As do I. There is something more. A number of the ships and fighters we have with us now were brought back to Canopa by Hari'Adab, after the loss of Dij. We have Mutati officers and soldiers among us."

"You're not concerned about their loyalty, are you?"

"No, sir. But for the first time in history, Mutati forces are going into battle under Human command."

"That is hardly at the top of my mind," Anton said.

"Nor of mine," Thinker admitted. He whirred for a moment. Then: "My internal programming informs me that I was just making nervous conversation. Like you, I am very worried about Master Noah."

* * * * *

At the Tulyan Starcloud, the Council of Elders received the emergency web transmission from Zigzia. They immediately sought out Eshaz, who was restocking his ships with supplies and assigning fresh caretaking crews for yet another mission.

With a small entourage, Elder Kre'n and Dabiggio rode a space platform through the mists that floated around their fabled planets. In one of the protected moorage basins they found Eshaz's fleet of vessels. All five hundred ships had returned safely, with no reports of HibAdu encounters. But that was about to change.

They docked the platform at a ship that bore no Tulyan face on its prow, but which was known to be the vessel operated personally by Eshaz. Moments later, Eshaz appeared at the main entrance hatch, and then boarded the glax-domed platform.

"We have urgent news from Zigzia," Kre'n said. "She is with Noah Watanabe at Yaree, where they are under attack by HibAdu forces. Zigzia said a courier flew to Siriki for reinforcements, but she didn't know when they might arrive."

"We must mount our own military force then," Eshaz said. "How many armed podships can you round up?"

"The fifty with you, and three hundred more," Dabiggio said.

Eshaz formed a scowl on his reptilian face. "Hardly an overwhelming force."

"No," the towering Elder said, "but we can make the force look much larger if we also send the nine thousand caretaker podships we have here, along with the armed podships—everything we have here. They don't contribute much to our starcloud defenses anyway." He looked at Kre'n, awaiting her comment.

"Do it," she commanded. "Our mindlink protects the starcloud."

"And my orders?" Eshaz asked.

"You are in command," Kre'n said.

It all happened quickly. Every podship went out, even if they had only Tulyan pilots aboard, and no passengers or armaments.

As they accelerated onto the podways of deep space, Eshaz and the Tulyan pilots behind him reported feeling bursts of speed unlike any they had ever experienced before. The podships took their own course to Yaree, reaching tachyon speeds but not traveling in anything close to a straight line.

The mysterious Aopoddae seemed to know in advance which sections of podway were in the best condition....

Chapter Fifty-Six

There is a Tulyan prophecy of the Sublime Creator and the Savior, the bipartite entity who can see the past, present, and future of Timeweb. It is said that he will appear one day from the most unlikely of sources, and will determine the course of the universe.

—MPA report on Tulyan motivations and religion

For Subi Danvar, this was unlike any of the military maneuvers he and the other officers had practiced. And for him personally, far more was at stake.

Like fireworks in the air, his eight hundred podships arrived near Yaree in successive bursts of bright green light. Not waiting for even the few minutes that would have been required for all of them to arrive, Subi instead rushed forward with only a handful of support vessels behind him. He saw the space station in orbital space, and near it HibAdu warships battling a defensive force of Liberator podships and smaller craft that had come out of the cargo holds. Though there were hundreds of HibAdu ships attacking, all of them were small, short-range gun ships, not lab-pods. The defenders were tenacious, causing problems for the attackers.

It gave the adjutant a feeling of relief to see EcoStation still there, though it was not in good shape. Just then, he saw one of the lower modules explode, a ball of orange that quickly dissipated in the airless vacuum. From his security experience on EcoStation, he knew that each module had oxygen cutoff systems, lessening the impact of a problem in one area on the rest of the orbiter. From the brightness of the explosion, he judged that there had been quite a bit of oxygen in that particular module. He hoped Noah was not inside.

As Subi's podship entered the fray with its space cannons blasting, he remembered Noah's supposed immortality. For the loyal adjutant, that did not lessen his concerns. Mirroring Noah's own feelings, Subi doubted if the condition could possibly be absolute, so he was always on the alert for gaps in it, so that he could better protect the Master.

Subi scattered the lead ships in the approaching HibAdu squadron by flying toward them and then veering off at the last moment, while his crew fired space cannons and automatic weapons at them. To keep his lead podship flying the way he wanted, Subi gave orders to a Tulyan with him, who in turn relayed them telepathically to the Tulyan pilot. The responses were almost instantaneous.

Two of Subi's shots struck their mark. Then more gun ships exploded as the rest of his podships and smaller fighter craft from the cargo holds joined the battle. But to his dismay he saw more enemy ships advancing, as if from a limitless source of them.

In the distance, from the direction where the enemy was advancing, he saw green flashes in space, and from markings on the vessels he confirmed that they were enemy lab-pods. His heart sank. The HibAdu ships near the space station were only an advance force. They had used just enough firepower to alarm the Liberators, and to lure more of them in.

It was too late for Subi to worry about things like that. He heard his own podship squeal as it was hit. But the sentient spacecraft recovered, and kept responding to Subi's relayed commands. For the moment, he cleared an area around the space station, where he positioned fifty of his own armed podships, all with the faces of their Tulyan pilots on the prows. Then Subi sent the rest of his force smashing through the enemy gun ships and some of the newly arrived, larger battleships. He blasted them out of the way, heading toward the more powerful and dangerous lab-pod mother ships in the distance.

But near those vessels he saw many more flashes of green, bright flowers in space. They were not his own podships arriving, because those had already been engaged in the battle. In a matter of seconds, he received confirmation that they were Liberator vessels. To his delight he saw the newly arrived ships surge into battle against the lab-pods and begin to drive them back, even as the HibAdus were trying to disgorge more gun ships and larger warships from the holds.

Adjusting the comlink channel to connect with a portable unit that Noah carried, Subi said, "Noah, you there? Are you all right?" In the distance, he saw the space station, with the armed warships Subi had left to protect it. No activity there. But over the comlink, he heard only static in response.

Looking back at the battle scene, he saw the smaller HibAdu craft retreating in disarray, but not making it back to the mother ships, because they were being blasted out of space. Over other communication channels, he heard the excited chatter of his officers and voices of others from additional podships that Doge Anton had dispatched. How many vessels, Subi didn't know, but the combined Liberator force was proving superior, because it chased the HibAdus and made kill after kill. He hoped this was not a trick, designed to lure forces away from Canopa and Siriki.

Over the connections, he heard Doge Anton himself, and the mechanical voice of Thinker, whose brilliant machine intellect was being committed to this important battle. It gave Subi some reassurance that the best minds were being employed for the Liberator strategies. He also heard them say that thousands of caretaker podships had arrived from the Tulyan Starcloud, vessels that were mostly unarmed, and which Anton had kept away from the center of battle. Eshaz and other Tulyan web technicians were among the new arrivals.

But Subi had another priority, the reason he came here in the first place.

"Prepare to board EcoStation," he announced. "I will dock and go aboard with my soldiers, and I want the twenty closest ships to me to dock, too. We need to search every area of the orbiter to find Master Noah. There are uncertain atmospheric conditions on board, so wear survival suits."

* * * * *

In the midst of the HibAdu fleet, Ipsy remained concealed inside a weapon-control box that had been installed in one of the new lab-pods. He heard the chatter of Hibbil and Adurian officers on the command bridge, and knew that this vessel and others had turned around and fled into space when the battle appeared lost.

This cheered him somewhat, but he would have felt much better if his ship had been in the middle of combat, and the officers had tried to use the weapons activated by this panel.

Even so, he was not without options. When installing the panel on the bridge, the technicians had removed the screws on the back side of the unit, intending to lift off the cover, which was necessary in order to make the electrical connections. With no way to hide from the workers, Ipsy had prepared for the worst.

But the little robot got an important break. Before lifting off the cover, the technicians took a break and left the bridge. Cautiously, Ipsy then pushed the cover aside and peeked out. No one was on the bridge at all, and the ship was not in operation. He transmitted signals, verified that no alarm or videocam system was in operation.

The robot climbed out of the panel box, and replaced the cover. Then he concealed himself in a dead air space behind the main instrument console. A short while later the technicians returned and completed their work.

The following day a pilot and crew took the lab-pod into space and tested the powerful energy cannons. They fired perfectly, and the vessel was brought back in. From his place of concealment, Ipsy heard an officer say something interesting, while they were shutting down the systems. This was not merely an ordinary vessel. Because of damage to the flagship of the HibAdu fleet, this ship was replacing it. The vessel would be under the direct command of the High Ruler.

For the little robot, the stakes were increasing quickly. He had waited for a long time for this opportunity, and didn't want to blow it. Alone during the night, he inspected the main instrument panel, and quietly removed panels and covers to examine the interior layouts of computer boards, circuits, and other components. He didn't need to actually operate the systems to understand how they worked. Just looking at the inner workings and control surfaces was enough for him.

Carefully, he made adjustments to the weapon control box, hidden settings that no one would notice. If the HibAdus performed any additional tests, the weapons would fire. But something entirely different would occur if Ipsy transmitted an electronic signal into the box....

* * * * *

With the enemy ships routed or destroyed, Tesh received the command for *Webdancer* to approach the space station. From the glowing green sectoid chamber, she guided the sentient vessel in that direction, gazing into near-space through her link with the multiple eyes on the hull.

But something unusual was happening. Unarmed caretaker ships were swooping past her and gathering closely around EcoStation, so many vessels that she could hardly see the orbiter itself. Just before that, Subi Danvar had sent a comlink message that he was docking with twenty other ships, but many more were massing around the space station now. Something seemed terribly wrong.

Over the connection with Doge Anton, Tesh heard his own concerns, and those of Thinker, as they sent comlink messages to the officers on the ships. The replies, which she did not hear directly, must not have helped, because Anton contacted her, through a Tulyan with him.

"Tesh," Anton relayed, "Do you know what's going on there?"

"No, sir," she replied.

Ahead, she saw more podships packing themselves around the space station, and now she could no longer see the orbiter at all, just the irregular shape of it. The podships seemed to flow together and become one, like a mottled, gray-and-black cocoon.

Anton ordered *Webdancer* to veer away from the station. But when Tesh followed the command, she felt a tugging coming from the direction of the strange cocoon, as if the massed podships were drawing her vessel toward them. A surge of fear enveloped her, but she was able to guide *Webdancer* away.

In space several kilometers away, Doge Anton gathered the bulk of his podship force. There, Tesh did not feel the magnetic pull of the cocoon.

At a new command center for his own moored ships, Doge Anton and his closest advisers tried to assess the unusual situation. Tesh was asked to leave the sectoid chamber and join them in the main conference room of the flagship, along with Eshaz. No one sat. Instead, everyone stood anxiously near the windows, looking back at the space station, which was shifting into an amorphous shape, like a giant alien shapeshifter. Anton's aides, Acey Zelk and Dux Hannah stood near him.

"At least three hundred ships are in that cocoon," the Doge said. "We need to find out what's happening, but I didn't want to rush forward, endangering more of the fleet."

"Subi Danvar is in there," one of the officers said. "Noah's right-hand man."

"I'm worried about a HibAdu trick," Anton said.

"It could be that," Thinker said, "but my projections do not indicate they are capable of controlling podships in that manner. Obviously, the Aopoddae in the cocoon are linked mentally and physically, but for what purpose I cannot determine. One sign of hope: they are all caretaker Aopoddae, except for the ones Subi took in."

Wrinkling his scaly brow, Eshaz said, "I've heard of them forming into cocoons in ancient days, but long before I was born. The reasons were varied."

"And you were born almost a million years ago," Tesh said, trying to envision how long that was. While speaking, she watched the cocoon in the distance. At first, she thought it had stopped morphing, then she wasn't so sure. She thought she saw it move slightly.

"In the earliest days," Eshaz said, "before my time, there were many unique dangers in space. For various reasons, to face different perils, the podships would form themselves into larger units—such as what you see here."

"Could the cocoon be protecting something?" Doge Anton asked. "Could Noah be inside?"

"I'm hoping that's the case," Eshaz said. "Protecting important individuals and groups was one of the purposes of conglomerating, but by no means the only one."

"We need to send an exploratory party," Anton said.

"But any ship we send could just find itself merged into the others," Tesh said. She spoke of the tugging sensation she had felt through *Webdancer*, and listened while other officers said they had received reports of the same thing.

"Something similar happened to us," Eshaz then said. "In the thousands of ships I brought from the starcloud, my pilots all reported sensations of increased speed on the way, as if an unexpected, sustained wind had sped us to our destination. When we drew within visual range of the space station, we all felt a pull too, as you others have described. It was like magnetism, drawing us toward it. We kept away from the station, as Doge Anton commanded."

"There seems to be an Aopoddae telepathic link that goes beyond the cocooned podships," Anton said. "Far out into space."

"I would like to accompany the exploration team," Thinker said. "I am only a machine, so death is not a consideration."

"You're not just an ordinary machine," Anton said. "But I do have multiple backup copies of your computer program, so we could rebuild you if necessary. All right. You'll lead the investigating squad."

The Doge then looked around, and spoke to one of the officers, a Kajor named J.B. Alcazar, "You coordinate it," he said. "But no Humans go on the mission. Or Mutatis. I want you to use robots."

"We machines could take that as an insult," Thinker said, "but in this special instance we won't. That's why I volunteered. For Noah."

"Don't send another podship in, either," Anton said. "Instead, use a shuttle."

"Can we go?" Dux asked.

"You heard me," the Doge said. "Robots only." His tone offered no discussion.

"An armed shuttle?" Alcazar asked.

"I don't see where firepower would do any good in this situation," Anton said.

"I strongly suggest an unarmed shuttle," Eshaz said, "and remove any smaller weapons that might be onboard. Deactivate all robotic weapons systems, too. You don't want the podships to perceive any threat at all. In their cocoon state, they're on high alert. The smallest thing could trigger a violent reaction. You've heard how individual podships react to forced entry, crushing intruders. It could be like that with the cocoon, but on a much larger scale."

"Make it unarmed," Anton said.

"One more thing," Eshaz said. "At least one Tulyan should go with Thinker. Tulyans and podships have connections that no other races or machines can fathom."

"All right," the Doge said, after a moment's consideration. "I suppose you're volunteering, aren't you?"

"I am."

"What about us?" Acey asked, looking at Eshaz for his support.

"Not this time," Eshaz said. "We need experience and intellect, not youthful exuberance. Do not take that as an insult. It is just fact."

Acey sulked away, but Tesh saw Dux nod in understanding.

* * * * *

Onboard the unarmed shuttle, Thinker at first went into a folded position, to focus on and contemplate the additional data he had been receiving. Standing beside him on the forward observation platform, Eshaz looked at the space station as it loomed larger and larger. On the gray-and-black skin he noticed a steady pulse, as if the cocoon was breathing in the airless void of space.

Presently, Thinker unfolded himself, after having been closed for only a couple of minutes.

Eshaz felt his own pulse quicken when they drew nearer and nearer to the strange amalgamation. As if in synchronicity, the throb of the cocoon increased as well.

A section of podship flesh parted, revealing a docking station beyond. But as he neared it, Eshaz saw that it was not part of the space station. Instead, it was Aopoddae flesh beyond, and docking connections like those he had seen on orbital pod stations.

In trepidation, Eshaz continued forward. He had no other choice.

* * * * *

Back when the HibAdu force first approached, Noah had originally assumed the worst, so over the orbiter's communication channel he had ordered all Humans and Mutatis on the space station into an armored command chamber with him. From that windowless enclosure, Noah and the others had watched the battle on a holoscreen … the dramatic ebb and flow of combat.

When the HibAdus had seemed defeated, he'd watched on the projected screen as Subi Danvar's podship connected to the space station, along with a score of others. In near space just beyond Subi's ship, Noah had seen numerous unarmed caretaker podships—and he'd felt them reaching out to him wordlessly, assuring him that they would protect him and would even respond to his commands. Curiously, Aopoddae names and their biographical details had simultaneously surfaced in Noah's consciousness, like objects bobbing up from deep in the ocean. One of the vessels had been the ancient spacefarer, Diminian, who dated back to the earliest days of the galaxy. Most of the others had been nearly as old. Noah found all of it intriguing.

With the battle apparently won, the Mutatis and Humans in the command chamber had streamed out, to greet Subi Danvar and the others. But Noah had remained behind by himself, feeling an odd sense of serenity and a need to be alone. Despite his own history, his part in developing the defensive pod-killer weapons on MPA pod stations, these podships no longer feared him at all. He was confident, as well, that the change went throughout the entire Aopoddae race.

Out in the airless battlefield, Noah had seen the debris of combat, including bodies floating in orbital space, and podships that he sensed were waiting for him to command them. Summoning his courage, he had reached out with the psychic tentacles of his mind and had drawn the sentient spacecraft in around the space station, where they had combined with the vessels of Subi and the others....

Now Noah felt their protective layer, their cocoon. In addition, he sensed a force far out in the cosmos, one that was separate from him, but one with him at the same moment. And, though he did not yet understand it, Noah knew that he could call upon it whenever he needed. At last, he had a degree of control over the paranormal elements around him. Or was that only his perception? How much—and what—did he really control?

These thoughts agitated him, so he withdrew from them, and floated in the troubled, cosmic sea of his mind.

Chapter Fifty-Seven

There is no safe place in this universe.

—Anonymous

F rom the armored chamber within the cocoon, Noah touched the new rough skin covering his legs and feet. Though he was still Human in all places where it showed to others, the hidden patches beneath his clothing had extended in the last few minutes, and tingled on the surface. He pulled his trousers back on, then slipped into his socks and shoes. He knew he looked normal, like the old Noah. But changes had a way of coming over him unpredictably.

His mind reached out into orbital space, to the battlefield where bodies and the debris of combat drifted. He saw a shuttle approaching—and looking inside, he knew who the passengers were, and that they were coming unarmed.

Eshaz and Thinker. Friends.

But he cautioned himself anyway. Relationships had a nasty habit of changing for the worse. Even Tesh, who cared about him deeply, had expressed concern over his strange powers—and that had been before this latest escalation. She was out there now at the fringe of the battlefield, in the sectoid chamber of *Webdancer*. Tesh and the others thought they were beyond the reach of Noah's cocoon, but they were wrong.

Ever the optimist, Noah didn't like to think of negative possibilities, but he knew he had to anyway. As his powers increased, he had to always be wary of people who might not understand them, and what he was going to do with them. Even Noah didn't know what his powers were all about, or the extent of them. He was on a path going somewhere important, but he didn't know the purpose of his journey or the destination. He only knew his own heart and instincts, and had to assume he would not betray them, no matter the physical form he took. It was one of the reasons he felt drawn to EcoStation. In a way that he could not put into words, the orbiter seemed to ground him emotionally and spiritually.

I am an eco-warrior, he thought.

From his earliest moments of consciousness as a small child, Noah had marveled at nature—at leaves, insects and birds, and the animals of the forest near his home on Canopa. He had noticed a symmetry, a regularity, and a beauty to the supposedly more primitive life forms in his immediate vicinity, and he had seen how this contrasted with the way Humans behaved. As a child, it had made him feel out of place and awkwardly conspicuous, as if the various life forms were watching him and ridiculing him.

It was from that core of early existence that Noah had stretched his thoughts as far as he could. In his teens he had come up with the concept of galactic ecology, the idea that remote star systems and planets were linked throughout the heavens and needed to be protected against the avarices and carelessness of Humans and other races.

For most of his life, he had been on an environmental quest, seeking to draw everything in the galaxy together and make perfect sense of it. With his newfound knowledge and powers, no matter how patchy or unpredictable they might be, he had an even greater desire than ever to understand the vastness and minutia of the cosmos, to find ultimate precision and faultlessness. Perfect sense out of chaos.

Bringing himself back to his immediate surroundings, to the augmented flesh that contained his enhanced mind, Noah knew with certainty that he needed to guard himself against all attacks, so that he could continue his incredibly important quest.

And ultimately, Noah fully understood—or sensed—that there were far greater life forms than his own. But he also sensed that not all of them would agree with his beliefs and desires. What if one or more of those outside entities were able to gain an influence over him? He thought that this might have already occurred, explaining to some degree the enhancements and powers he had been given. But he could not be certain. It might also be true that he was like a cosmic magnet, drawing talents and abilities to him so that he could complete his great quest, his galactic-scale mission.

Then, winding his thoughts back to his own Human form and his feelings that he had to protect himself against attack, Noah wondered if he felt this for himself—for his own interests—or if he was instead feeling this on behalf of some outside entity that was shaping him to its desires. Feeling no selfishness at all, he hoped an outside entity was not guiding him, and if it was, that things would turn out well. It seemed to him that Timeweb was a beneficial structure, and that the creator—or creators—of the galactic filigree were....

He wasn't sure if the word he had in mind was adequate. *Virtuous.* To be virtuous in the context he was considering it, taking actions for the benefit of the galaxy did not necessarily mean being kind. It could very well involve making difficult, even brutal, decisions.

As he analyzed his thoughts from different angles, Noah could not stand the idea of an outside entity controlling him, pushing him forward and possibly luring him into a trap or making him into a slave, perhaps even for eternity. He needed facts, explanations, but there were none. And now he was farther along on the course of physical and mental changes than ever before. Heading for where? The impetus for all of it was uncertain, as was so much more. He had to stay alert, had to look around the next corner and see what was there.

* * * * *

For all his vision, for all he was and all that he was becoming, Noah Watanabe had a paranormal blind spot that prevented him from seeing an immense timehole that was about to surface near him.

Inside the unseen timehole, in a starless void between two galaxies that was sealed on both ends, a powerful fleet of HibAdu lab-pods floated, with their crews in confusion. Minutes before, they had been far across the known galaxy, preparing to attack Canopa, the most powerful remaining Merchant Prince world. Then, just as they were about to emerge from space over Canopa in bursts of green light, they had found themselves somewhere else entirely, in an unknown, uncharted realm. And from that place they could not split space and travel on any galactic webbing, because no cosmic infrastructure existed there. They could only move under backup propulsion systems and send desperate, bewildered communications from ship to ship. The Hibbil and Adurian officers and soldiers didn't know where they were, and couldn't see—or go—beyond the confines of their dark prison.

Aboard the largest and most elegant ship in the HibAdu fleet, High Ruler Coreq sat in the midst of the mounting turmoil of his officers, saying nothing to them in his despair, and not even responding when they addressed him. It had been Coreq's idea to attack Canopa, and to bask in the glory of certain victory. He had wanted to be there at the forefront, soaking it all in. So he had gone along on the mission, leaving Premier Enver and Warlord Tarix to run things on the Adurian homeworld while he was away.

From the beginning, when he first emerged from an Adurian laboratory, Coreq had known he had a calling that spanned every star system, that God in his perfect wisdom had created him and his two hybrid companions for a purpose. Now he sensed powerful forces at work around him, and that he had not been thwarted in his desire to attack Canopa. Instead, he had been guided in a different direction, toward a far more important target.

Absorbing his surroundings, feeling a sudden flow of energy, he directed his ships to fly in a specific direction that seemed upward to him, though such a direction did not really exist where he was. Nonetheless, he went up, until the fleet could go no further, until they seemed to bump into an unseen barrier.

As moments passed the barrier grew filmy, with faint lights visible beyond. Then the gossamer substance of the barricade faded entirely, and he saw stars beyond. His fleet surged through, and now he saw something else.

It was a large, amorphous shape, and a fleet of enemy warships beyond. Looking through a scope, he thought the bulky form almost looked like a giant podship with a mottled gray-and-black surface, but it was in a different configuration. He'd never seen anything like it, but he sensed an urgency to destroy it.

Without hesitation, Coreq gave the order to attack. Beside him, a newly-installed control panel displayed a series of multicolored lights, showing that it was ready to fire the warship's weapons.

* * * * *

Noah had a brief vision, a burst of thought in which everything blew up around him and his body tumbled into a glowing green timehole. It only took a couple of moments for this to flash in his mind, and then he readied himself for action.

Extreme danger.

In his mind's eye he saw the approaching HibAdu fleet, and finally saw the gaping, green void of the timehole beyond. All around him, he felt the urgency and collective panic of the podships. They shifted and thickened and hardened themselves, but Noah knew it would not be enough.

He also saw *Webdancer* and the rest of the Liberator fleet moving as they perceived the HibAdu threat. Doge Anton's forces activated their weapons and rushed toward the cocooned space station. But they would not get there in time.

Precious seconds ticked by, and Noah looked farther, beyond anything that was happening here, or that might occur in this place. Now his far-seeing eye saw the Tulyan Starcloud and he longed to be there, as if it were a heavenly destination.

* * * * *

On the command bridge of the HibAdu flagship, an Adurian officer touched pressure pads on the weapon-control box to fire the high-energy space cannons. A tremendous volley went out, but from the wrong weapons, at the rear of the ship.

"You idiots!" Coreq shouted. "What are you doing?" He saw HibAdu war-pods behind his vessel explode into orange flowers of light, and other ships taking evasive action.

"Sir, we did everything right," the officer insisted. He pointed. "Look, the panel is showing that we fired the forward cannons."

"I accept no excuses," the High Ruler said. With one powerful hand, he reached out and broke the officer's neck.

From his hiding place behind the instrument console, Ipsy heard officers chattering nervously, saying they didn't know what was wrong, and they still had other ships going after the target. The little robot wished he could do more to stop those attacks, and to destroy the rest of the HibAdu fleet. But at least he had made a difference.

Ipsy realized that he could become a casualty of war with this now defenseless ship, or he might be discovered in his place of concealment. It shouldn't matter to him one way or the other. Based on the commotion he was hearing out on the bridge, he knew he had made a difference.

But he wanted to do something even bigger. Perhaps he could discover a way....

* * * * *

After looking across space for only a few seconds, Noah had shifted focus to his immediate surroundings, and he watched the unfolding battle, the confusion in the attack force and the ships from the rear coming around to the front to take up the assault.

Moments later, he saw HibAdu energy bursts bounce off the skins of the cocoon-linked podships. The approaching Liberator fleet fired back, hitting three lab-pods and blowing them apart. But other enemy ships continued to advance and fire. Noah felt the cocoon weaken, as podships on one side of the space station envelope were injured by the powerful blasts.

Suddenly everything turned brilliant green around Noah, but he knew it was not from an explosion, or from being sucked into the timehole. He blinked his eyes, and EcoStation—with its Aopoddae cocoon—was somewhere else.

Of his own volition, Noah had split space to take a podway shortcut that still existed, despite the decline of the galactic infrastructure. And almost instantaneously, his cocoon emerged from space inside the serene cosmic mists of the starcloud. All around he felt the telepathic probings of Tulyan citizens, some of whom had stronger telepathic powers than others. They probed, and he felt the psychic power of mindlink mounting, as if to attack and destroy the intruder.

Inside the Aopoddae skin around the space station, Noah heard the voices of Tulyan pilots and Liberator fighters who were in the honeycomb of passages and chambers. He heard Thinker talking to Eshaz as they hurried through a dimly-illuminated passageway on foot, and he determined that Eshaz was responding to the telepathic probes of his people, telling them that the cocoon structure did not threaten them, or the starcloud.

Oddly, Noah felt simple, almost primitive thoughts mixed with his more complex ruminations. *Eshaz is my friend. Let him through. And Thinker, too.*

With this thought Noah caused a new passageway to open up near the Tulyan and the cerebral robot, allowing them to leave the membrane and enter the space station. Then Noah sent his own clairvoyant signals to Eshaz, guiding him through the modules to his armored chamber.

Around him Noah sensed that the Tulyan probes had faded and that their mindlink weaponry had subsided. The starcloud defenders would not attack. In their own way, the Tulyans had determined the identity of the unusual intruder in their starcloud, and no longer considered it a threat.

Noah also knew what was occurring over Yaree. He could not predict the outcome, but using Timeweb he watched from afar, frustrated that he could not contribute to the fight....

* * * * *

At the vanguard of the Liberator ships, Tesh threw *Webdancer* into the battle first. At their weapons ports, Doge Anton's crew fired space cannons, ion guns, and energy detonators at the HibAdus, as did the other ships in his fleet. In only a few minutes the HibAdus realized they were outgunned and outmaneuvered, and they fell back, trying to save their lab-pods for another day.

But Doge Anton ordered pursuit, and his podships chased and killed hundreds of enemy vessels. Even though they were only going after lab-pods, the Liberator pilots each reported feeling a jolt in the bodies of their own podships when each kill was made. It seemed to be a sympathetic psychic reaction experienced by the Aopoddae. Tesh felt this herself from her connection, but pressed onward. The Liberator podships suffered even in victory, but continued to cooperate with their pilots and crews....

Hearing Eshaz and Thinker at the door, Noah let them in. "Give me a moment," Noah said as they entered.

In his mind's eye, Noah saw the waning battle, *experienced* all of it. And even before the fighting was complete and the remaining HibAdu ships had fled into space, he watched Tulyan caretaker ships take positions over the timehole. Perched there, the Tulyans dropped exploding packets into the opening and murmured their ancient incantations.

Gradually the cosmic hole became smaller and smaller, and presently it was no longer there.

Chapter Fifty-Eight

In the case of Noah Watanabe, the known rules of cellular physiology do not apply.

—Excerpt from CorpOne medical report

"Y ou are something even more unusual now, aren't you?" Eshaz stood over Noah, looking down at him with slitted, pale gray eyes.

"Some realities are not fact or science based," Thinker said, standing beside the Tulyan. "Master Noah, increasingly, I must place information about you into my alternate data banks."

Noah clasped one of Eshaz's oversized hands, then reached over and patted his robotic companion on one of his metal shoulders. "My friends, it is good to see both of you. Very good, indeed. We have won a great victory at Yaree. It is the beginning of the end for the HibAdus."

The reptilian man and the robot just stood there, looking at him.

"Well of course I'm different now," Noah said. "Everyone is different from moment to moment. That's true of each of you as well. Even you, Thinker, with your changing data banks."

"Your skin is metamorphosing, isn't it?" Eshaz said. "I sensed something once when I touched your shirt fabric. It was on one of your arms." He squinted his slitted eyes, thinking back. "Your left arm. Through Tesh's connection with *Webdancer* and the other podships, I learned from her that she actually felt rough skin under the sleeve on your left arm. Would you like to show it to us?"

"For what purpose?"

"You must trust us," Eshaz said. "Perhaps we can help you."

Noah hesitated, trying to maintain some personal space around himself. Then he sighed, and said, "All right, my friends."

He stripped down to his shorts. All of the skin on his muscular body—with the exception of the neck, head, and hands—had turned gray, with deep veins of black coursing in several directions. "What am I becoming?" Noah asked. "A podship?"

"Accessing alternate data banks," Thinker said, blinking his metal-lidded eyes. Orange lights flashed around his faceplate.

"How did you fly the space station to the starcloud?" Eshaz asked.

"Mmmm. Basically, I envisioned it, and it happened. Beyond that, I'm not sure."

"Interesting," the Tulyan said. Looking around the armored room, he said, "This is your sectoid chamber, then, and from here you control the amalgamated podships?"

Noah grew quiet for a moment, and heard the faint pulse of the cocooned Aopoddae. From this room, he was not in physical contact with their amalgamated flesh, but he was in touch with it in a different manner, and he cared deeply about the creatures. Through the link, he satisfied himself that the injured podships were beginning to heal, benefiting from their connection to their brethren, and from a connection they had with Timeweb.

Finally, Noah answered the question. "This is not a sectoid chamber at all. I just happened to be here when during the battle and the flight."

"But the podships have cocooned you for a reason," Eshaz said. "To protect you, obviously."

"Supposedly I am immortal, and if that's true I should not need protecting." Then, remembering another vision he had in which his body tumbled free of the space station into a timehole, he said, "Perhaps you are right after all. They do offer me some protection. A great deal, actually. I think they enhance my mental abilities, as well. I feel more focused here, calmer and more centered. The podships actually trust me now, Eshaz!"

"Processing new data," the cerebral robot said. "Remarkable information."

"Knock it off, Thinker," Noah said, as he put his clothes back on. "You don't have to announce that you are processing data in order to do it."

The metal-lidded eyes blinked quickly. "No, but I am feeling great excitement and astonishment at what is occurring around me. Programmed emotions, to be certain, but I want to be part of the discussion, sharing the joy of the moment with you. A great victory over the HibAdus and a new journey for Master Noah. Truly, these are epic times!"

Smiling, Noah said, "I recall making you the official historian of the Guardians, and the trustee of my life story. OK, my metal friend, process away."

Meeting Eshaz's gaze, Noah then said, "Everything that occurs here goes beyond this room, doesn't it?"

"Not necessarily," Eshaz said.

"With Thinker here, your answer seems easy to comprehend. If I instruct him to do so, he will bury the data somewhere. It could still be subject to detection by an expert investigating his data banks, but if any robot can successfully hide the information it is this one. You are not the same, though, Eshaz. You are linked to all Tulyans and to the Aopoddae."

The reptilian man straightened. "Nonetheless, there are methods of concealing information from the truthing touch and from every other probe. What do you command of me, Master Noah?"

And what do you command of me, Master Noah?" Thinker said.

"If I wanted either of you to maintain confidentiality about me, I might *request* it, not command it. However, I see no way to keep the secret. It will get out eventually, because the podships cocooning me are linked to other podships, and in turn to their Tulyan pilots. Also to the one Parvii pilot, Tesh. No, it would get out anyway. And maybe it should."

"We would do anything for you, Master Noah," Thinker said.

"I know you would, and I appreciate that." Noah finished dressing, and then said, "Lead the way, Eshaz. We must discuss the situation with the Council of Elders."

"They asked me to tell you that is not necessary. Earlier, they were linked to you telepathically, and they obtained all the information about you that they needed. For the moment, anyway."

"Very well. I suppose I can let them know I'm turning into a podman later."

"With their probative powers they probably already know that," Eshaz said, "but to make certain, I'll let them know on your behalf. First Elder Kre'n also asked me to tell you that she actually permitted your cocoon to enter the starcloud in the first place. Our strongest minds—including her—detected your imminent approach, and opened the way for you."

"Then why did they subject me to such intense scrutiny when I arrived?'

"For extra security purposes."

"Can't hurt, I guess."

Eshaz scratched his side. "The First Elder agrees with you that EcoStation can be an important symbol for the Liberators, and for you as an eco-warrior. It could become a symbol of resistance, inspiring the people of various galactic races."

These remarks only reminded Noah of his own limitations, and of his need to remain humble and respectful during all exchanges with the powerful Tulyan leaders.

"Please be sure to tell them we have a lot of bodies onboard," Noah said. "I'd like the authorization to hold a burial ceremony somewhere in the starcloud."

* * * * *

The Council of Elders gave permission for Noah to conduct services on the smallest of their three planets, in a flower-filled mountain meadow. The morning after Noah's arrival, they provided transport ships to carry the mourners, along with more than twelve hundred bodies, to the destination.

As Noah boarded one of the ships and it pulled away from the cocoon, he felt a mounting panic, and considered asking the pilot to turn around and take him back. A sensation of dizziness came over him, and he felt weakness in the muscles of his legs, so that he had to hold onto a high railing for support when he stood—even though the flight through the mists was quite smooth.

"Are you all right, Master Noah?" It was Eshaz, reaching out to steady him by the arm. Thinker and Subi Danvar were there, too.

"I'm fine," Noah said. As he had grown accustomed to doing, Noah wore clothing that completely covered the changes in his skin. This time, it was a green-and-brown Guardian uniform and cap.

Gradually, Noah felt a little better. But he came to suspect that it was only a stabilizing effect, and that he had to get used to feeling weaker away from the cocoon. How far he could journey from the amalgamated pods, he didn't know. But he sensed a supportive, healing power here in the starcloud that gave him assurance that he could proceed with the burial ceremony.

When Noah disembarked on the high meadow, walking carefully, he said to Subi, "I am told that you are doing a terrific job in your duties with the fleet. While my Guardians have been merged into the Liberator force, I want you to oversee them in my place, whenever necessary. It seems that I am becoming rather occupied with other matters."

"Yes, Master Noah, I will do that for you, until you are ready to resume your duties. I know how close the Guardians are to your heart."

"Thank you."

On the meadow grass, the entire Council of Elders greeted Noah, dressed in elegant black-and-gold robes. "I'm glad we are able to accommodate your desires," Kre'n said. She shook his hand.

As the big alien woman held his hand, Noah felt the probing of her truthing touch. Another level of Tulyan security, he surmised. But he didn't mind, and allowed her to complete her task. Finally she removed her grasp, and looking at him, she said, "You may indeed be the one spoken of in our legends."

"I doubt if I qualify for any legends," Noah said, with an embarrassed smile.

"More and more of us are agreeing with Eshaz's assessment," she insisted. "He thinks you are the first important member of the Human race in the history of the galaxy."

"Oh, there have been far greater figures than myself," Noah insisted.

"Perhaps not. You are the man who restored the ecological health of numerous Merchant Prince planets, and then went beyond even that. You are a man of vision. Many of us—myself included—believe that your emergence has triggered the resurgence of the Tulyan race. For the first time in millions of years, we are again dispatching caretaker teams to maintain and repair the web." She paused. "Only time will tell how successful we are."

Wrinkling his brow, Noah considered her comments for a moment, while she awaited his response. He remembered an earlier visit to the Tulyan council chamber, when Kre'n first mentioned the legend of a Savior to him. Some of the Elders had looked upon him with a certain reverence at that time, with the notable exception of the big, grumpy one, Dabiggio. Now, it was different. Even Dabiggio seemed to believe.

Presently Noah insisted, "I don't think I'm the Savior spoken of in your legends. I am a mere Human, with a few quirks. However, I wish to do everything possible to make myself worthy of your respect. Admittedly, I do have certain leadership qualities that might prove helpful to others. As Master of the Guardians, I have been able to inspire others to achieve more than they might have without me. At this time, I find myself in a position to accomplish more than ever before. I hope I am not much more than a man, that I am not evolving into a god of any form, or your Savior. But if anything like that happens, if that is my destination, I shall be prepared to fulfill it."

"Humbly," Kre'n said. "I have already read this in your thoughts."

Noah bowed to her. "Of course."

"We Tulyans do not die often," she said, "and we have always been underpopulated for the size of our starcloud. Consequently, we have plenty of space for burial plots. As we told Eshaz, this will be a single ceremony to include timehole and war victims alike, but there will be individual burials in carefully marked graves. Identities will be indicated if known, and there will be genetic charts for each victim. Later, if any of the family members want the remains sent somewhere else, those requests can be accommodated."

"Thank you. It is very much appreciated." Looking around, he saw gnarled mountaintops at higher elevations, and pristine lakes in a valley beneath the sentinel perches. It looked like someplace in a fairy tale, and the scenery alone seemed to return some of his strength. He stood tall as he accompanied the Elders to a large, flat stone where they all gathered.

Golden sunlight found its way through the mists of the starcloud, and bathed Noah in warmth. On meadows and grassy slopes around the site, he saw many Tulyans in white robes, standing beside coffins and grave sites that had already been dug. In those coffins were a variety of races. Though most of the timehole victims were Human, there were also Blippiqs, Huluvians, Salducians, and other races, including a couple of unidentified Mutatis who might have been spies sent by the vile Zultan, before his son Hari'Adab took control of the race and changed its alliances. Noah thought of the Mutati who had preferred being Human, Princess Meghina of Siriki, and wondered where she and her immortal companions could possibly be now.

Kre'n straightened her own robes, and stood facing the gravesites. Noah heard her words carrying far out on a warm breeze, without the need of electronics. As the Tulyan leader spoke, hundreds of tiny comets appeared high overhead, and sped through the mists separating the planets.

"We stand upon one of the miracles of our wondrous starcloud," Kre'n said to the assemblage, as if in answer to Noah's unspoken question. "This is one of our most sacred transmitting stones, one of the points where our most powerful intellects can stand, and dramatically increase the powers of mindlink. In this day and age, even at this very moment, we cannot afford to let our guard down for a moment."

On the perimeter of the stone, several Tulyan men and women stood with their faces turned skyward, looking in different directions. They appeared to be in trances, but were undoubtedly watching for any approaching danger.

Kre'n continued: "We are honored to dedicate this sacred site to a new purpose, as the first multiracial graveyard on Tulyan soil. We are part of this great and just war and of the interconnected galaxy, and this is one of our contributions. All Tulyans are pleased to do this. In tribute to these dead, many of whom died honorably fighting for the Liberators, we have brought in a comet for each of them."

Looking up, she pointed, and the comets put on a spectacular aerial show, speeding this way and that, swooping down almost to the valley floor and then going back up again, high into the ethereal mists. Then, in the blink of an eye, they were gone, as if the comets had taken the spirits of the dead to some other place.

Noah heard a clapping sound in the air, but didn't see anyone moving their hands to do this. Telepathic clapping? Yes, he decided as he watched the faces of the Tulyans.

Then, looking down at his own hands, which were clasped in front of his body, he saw the gray-black flesh encroaching, moving onto the tops of his wrists. As he absorbed the ongoing ceremony and looked inward at the same time, Noah felt his own self dying. The *old* self. He continued to become something radically different, and found the possibilities both exciting and terrifying.

Whatever was happening to him, Noah wondered how much of it he controlled himself. Earlier, the podships had moved close to the space station without cocooning it at first, making him aware that they were available for him to direct. He had responded by drawing them in around him in a protective fashion, and they had completed their amalgam around EcoStation. It seemed to have been a cooperative, collective effort between himself and them. Now he wondered how much of the changes to his body were of his own volition, and how much could possibly be caused by outside influence.

Focusing hard, he saw the encroaching skin retreat a few centimeters. This told him something. A piece of the puzzle, but not the answer. He allowed the metamorphosis to continue.

I want it, he thought. *With all of its unknown dangers, I want it.*

But for the moment he resisted the urge, and caused the encroaching skin to retreat back under his clothing. This was not the time, or the place, to permit it to flow over his entire body.

"Please say something now," Kre'n said. Placing a hand on Noah's shoulder, she guided him to the spot where she had been standing.

Noah took a deep breath and said, his words carrying out to the assemblage, "Thank you for sharing this special place with me, and with those who are being honored here today. On behalf of the families of the loved ones we are laying to rest, I express their appreciation. By courier, I have also contacted Doge Anton, and he wants me to pass on his heartfelt gratitude to you as well."

Pausing, Noah looked around, to the gnarled mountain peaks and down to the magical lakes in the valley. Then he said, "Being here, I could almost imagine that there is nothing wrong in the galaxy, that all is in perfect order. But all of us know that this not the case. Sadly, these dead are the proof of it."

To close the ceremony, Noah asked for a moment of silence. When it was completed, he nodded to Kre'n, who in turn gave a signal to the Tulyans at the gravesites.

Simultaneously, the Tulyans raised their hands, and with their collective psychic energy they lowered the coffins into the ground.

Chapter Fifty-Nine

There are more roads to tragedy than to happiness.

—Ancient observation

As Hari'Adab strode through a corridor on the top floor of the Golden Palace, he hardly noticed the opulence around him, the gilded walls and furnishings, the infinity mirrors, the priceless paintings and statuaries.

He had seen such finery before in the Mutati Kingdom, in the palatial residences of his own family. Often in the past he had felt considerable embarrassment for living in luxurious surroundings, considering the impoverished conditions suffered by many of his people. His father (and some of Hari's advisers) had pointed out to him the necessity of a leader acting and looking like a leader, and of displaying the trappings of success to the populace.

So they said, and Hari had essentially gone along with the role-playing they espoused, but he had also instituted more programs to help the poor than any leader in Mutati history. And he'd done it with layers of anonymity that prevented most people from knowing his involvement. To him, it made no sense to do things for people and then ask for their adoration in return. He didn't like the equation, just as he'd never liked the thought of praying for himself. For Hari, it was far more important to pray for someone else, just as he had been doing for his beloved Parais.

The Mutati doctors had set up a medical room for the injured aeromutati on the top level of the palace, and they had been tending to her with all known treatments and technology. Since learning of the terrible injury to his lover, the young Emir had been at an emotional nadir. To the extent possible, trying to be vigilant but not interfering, he had overseen her medical care. For two straight days he had hardly left her side, and he was only away briefly now, while they administered treatments that they said would be difficult for him to watch. Parais was experiencing cellular complications that were unique to Mutatis, and she needed surgical procedures to improve the flow of medicines through her body. Hari had tried to stay, but the doctors had prevailed on him, insisting it was best for him, and for the patient. They needed to focus on her, not on his reactions.

Now Hari couldn't wait to get back inside the room. He came to a stop just outside her door, waiting for it to open. They'd said it would only be a few minutes, but now it had been nearly half an hour. He heard them inside with their instruments and machines, chattering in their arcane medical language. The tones were urgent. Hari felt like bursting inside, but worried about causing harm to Parais.

The HibAdu weapon used on her had been insidious, sending an energy pulse into her body that had expanded and wreaked havoc on her internal organs. In reaction to the violent intrusion, Parais' cellular structure had gone into retreat, fleeing inward to a place where it thought it could best restore the body. Hari only understand this in generalities, but it had long been known that shapeshifter cells had a racial brain and survival instincts that were not under control of the mind of any individual. In taking control away from Parais, the cells had reverted to a state that was even more ancient and basic than the natural fleshy appearance of a typical Mutati. They reverted to a primitive core, which scientists said was similar to the primordial matter that generated the first Mutati life millions and millions of years ago.

Slowly, hesitantly, Hari walked away from the door. Two uniformed MPA soldiers hurried by, carrying message cubes. They entered a room that Hari knew was one of the offices used by Liberator military commanders, including the remaining officers of the Mutati High Command. The day before, Hari had met briefly with them to discuss how they might allocate their combined military assets to recover the conquered worlds of the Mutati Kingdom. They were considering a military offensive that would start with the Emir's own planet Dij, and if success was achieved there, they would move on to others.

Heightening the need for this, there had been sickening rumors of atrocities committed against the Mutati people by the invaders, including gruesome public displays in which Hibbils and Adurians had eaten the flesh of their shapeshifter victims. He hoped these were only rumors, the sort that were common in times of war, but a little voice inside told him they were true. He'd long sensed the resentment felt by Adurians toward Mutatis, and Hibbils were known to be vicious little carnivores. Unfortunately, it all added up.

All of the allied officers and political leaders—including Doge Anton, Hari'Adab, and First Elder Kre'n—wanted to rescue and recover every Human and Mutati planet, but they were also worried about the strange absence of large-scale military activity by the HibAdus against Canopa and Siriki. There had been skirmishes and the recent, relatively small battle in the Sirikan back country, but not much other than that. The two MPA planets were like beacons of hope in the bleak war against the HibAdus. Some of the officers, particularly Subi Danvar, thought that the galactic instabilities that had occurred on both Canopa and Siriki were preventing the HibAdus from mounting full-scale attacks there. There had been extensive geological damage to the Valley of the Princes on Canopa and to remote sections of Siriki.

There were so many immense concerns going on simultaneously that Hari felt the limitations of anything he could do to improve conditions. According to all estimates, the HibAdus had much larger military forces than the Liberators and their Human, Mutati, and Tulyan elements. In addition, the Tulyans—who were heading up the other "war" against galactic disintegration—were not able to keep up with the deterioration that was continuing.

The Emir heaved a deep sigh, trying to calm himself, and returned to the door to Parais' room. The voices and equipment noises seemed unchanged, a sense that the doctors and their aides were taking efficient, urgent actions.

This section of the Golden Palace was the most heavily fortified, and constituted the keep that had been designed and built to protect its royal inhabitants against outside attack. As far as Hari was concerned, it housed the most important person of all now, Parais d'Olor. But the vicious assault on her had already been made, and he had not been there to protect her.

For that, he had initially blamed Doge Anton, who had kept them apart. But ultimately, Hari came to the realization that it wasn't the Doge's fault after all. There really was no one to blame—at least not anymore—for the long history of enmity between the Human and Mutati races, and the deep distrust that resulted. Even now, with close cooperation between the races, some of the old feelings lingered. There had been fights and name-calling among the soldiers, but cooler heads always prevailed. During moments of frustration, Hari had experienced such feelings of antagonism himself, but had kept them in check.

He felt overwhelmed by all of the details surrounding him, and longed for the halcyon times he had spent with Parais, flying on her avian back to a retreat where they could enjoy each other's company in private. On Dij, they had frequented an isolated beach, where the sun warmed the sands. In his mind now, he tried to remember how it used to be with her, particular details that he wanted to relive and push aside the cold realities of the moment. He shivered.

The door to her room opened suddenly, and Hari got out of the way of two Mutati medical attendants who hurried past him and down the corridor. Their faces were emotionless, but he knew this was the way of their profession, the need to suppress feelings and keep doing their jobs. A Human doctor followed them, an elderly man who had been allowed to observe, and to offer what limited assistance he could.

"You may come in now," another doctor said from inside the room. A small Mutati male with a narrow mustache, Dr. Wikk motioned toward the bed where Parais lay. Two other doctors left the room.

Summoning his courage, Hari entered. "How is she?"

"The same. We've adjusted her medications slightly, to reduce the pain. I'll leave you two alone for a few minutes."

Fighting back tears, Hari stood by the mass of quivering flesh and dark feathers on the bed. A copy of *The Holy Writ*—the sacred book of the Mutati people—sat on a table beside her. Unable to speak, Parais barely clung to life. Her facial features were puffy and horribly contorted, and almost unrecognizable. From a medical treatment, her brown eyes had reemerged from the fatty cellular structure of her face, but they were closed now.

"It might be kinder to put her out of her misery," the doctor said, as he departed.

"What?" In sudden fury, Hari almost lunged at him. Then, in a menacing tone, he said, "You'd better not try anything like that. If you do, I ... Look, I'm sorry. I know you're just doing your best, and thinking of her suffering."

"I'm sorry." The doctor left, and the door slid shut behind him.

Hari'Adab was alone with Parais again, but not in the way he'd been remembering. The contrasts were so far apart, and the prospects so dismal. As he had done after killing his father, Hari'Adab again contemplated suicide. It would put an end to his suffering. But what about Parais? He couldn't just leave her, and couldn't bear the thought of euthanizing her. At his previous low point, despite the loss of Paradij and all of its inhabitants, she had insisted that Hari live and make himself strong for the sake of the Mutati people. With her loving influence, she had convinced him to spend the rest of his life doing what was right, not only for his own followers but for other galactic races as well.

Now he placed a hand gently on her face. In his mind's eye, Hari envisioned Parais clearly in her various mutations, the way she used to be when she morphed from one beautiful flying creature into another. She favored white feathers then, unlike her present disarrayed condition. The memories were so clear that he could almost imagine the lovely aeromutati back to normal at this very moment. In his memory, they spoke again of having children, and of their many other dreams.

He felt movement under his fingers. Parais opened her eyes and looked at him with her brown eyes, so filled with suffering that it ripped apart his emotions. He was at least heartened to see a glint there, and she seemed to recognize him. But she couldn't speak or hold her eyes open, and soon faded back into her universe of pain.

Chapter Sixty

The Human brain is a gold mine of wondrous possibilities ... and a cesspool.

—A saying of Lost Earth

Noah stood by himself in one of the larger chambers of EcoStation, examining a section of bulkhead where podship skin had filled what had once been a large, jagged break in the module. It was his third day back at the Tulyan Starcloud. He detected the approach of visitors through the linked corridors of the cocoon and the space station, and he knew their identities: Doge Anton and a small entourage.

The leader of the Liberators had flown here after the Battle of Yaree, and had announced that he wanted to meet with Noah. But not wanting any interruption, Noah had sent no response. At least the Council of Elders seemed to already know that Noah wanted privacy, from their earlier telepathic probes, and—from a linkage with them—Eshaz had known as well.

He heard Doge Anton enter the chamber behind him, along with Tesh, Thinker, and two Tulyan caretakers. Noah did not have to turn around to see them, but he did so anyway. It would reduce the number of questions they asked of him. For now, in his white, long-sleeve tunic and dark trousers, the rough skin that covered most of his body was not visible to them. His hands, forearms, and head remained normal in appearance.

Tesh stood silently on one side, looking anxiously at Noah.

"I've called a meeting to assess everything," Anton said. The blond man wore a red-and-gold MPA uniform, decked with ribbons. A weapons belt circled his waist. "It will be held on General Nirella's ship this afternoon. I have also have a request from Tesh to discuss something with you. She says it's important."

"I am unable to attend your meeting," Noah said. "I'm not feeling up to it at the moment, and don't think I can contribute. At least not yet. I have experienced many changes, many pressures on my mind and body, and I need to recuperate."

Scowling, Anton said, "Very well, but let me know when you are ready. Nirella and I would like your input, your suggestions."

"I can contribute more if you permit me this time alone."

"All right, Noah."

"With no interruptions. Please don't ask me for an explanation, because I'm not sure if I can provide one anyway—but I can see and hear everyone in EcoStation and everyone in the passageways and chambers of the cocoon. Please order them to leave."

Puzzled thoughts played across Anton's face. "You want the Tulyan pilots to leave, too?"

"They are without employment here. The cocoon does not respond to their commands."

"But it does to yours?"

"Yes."

"There is much to grasp here, Noah, but I will defer to your wishes. I will take care of it."

"Thank you."

Then, looking at the Parvii woman, Noah felt a tug of emotion. The cast of her green eyes and the slight trembling of her lips told him she had something important to discuss with him. At least, it was important to *her*. He didn't like having such a thought, because at his core he didn't feel superior to Tesh at all. But he could not take the time or energy to talk with her yet.

"I need more time," Noah said to her. "I will inform you when I'm ready."

Her face showed her displeasure, but she said nothing, and left with the others.

Afterward, Noah stared at the podship skin on the bulkhead, and knew the flesh was connected to the cocoon. Reaching out and touching the wall, he felt the regular pulse of the living creature.

In images before his eyes, he also saw Doge Anton and his entourage striding away through a corridor, and saw the evacuation of the space station and of the cocoon—Humans, Tulyans, and robots streaming out into waiting transport ships. With one exception. In what had once been an education module of EcoStation, a solitary figure stood immobile, with the lights around its face plate glowing softly. Thinker.

So, the official historian of the Guardians, and the trustee of my life story has decided to defy me.

From his vantage, Noah sensed Thinker going almost entirely silent inside his robotic mechanisms, leaving only a sentry program operating. And, though he had not expected to feel this way, the presence of his friend gave the Guardian leader some comfort.

He thought of concentric circles around him, starting with the toughness of his own body, the way it could heal and regenerate itself after injuries. Beyond that, he saw the cocoon drifting in the protective mindlink of Tulyans in their sacred starcloud. As another layer of personal security, he had Thinker, Tesh, and Subi, and everyone else who cared about him.

Am I truly the Savior they speak of in Tulyan legends?

He still did not think so, though he had no evidence one way or the other. Noah suspected, however, that it was not a provable thing, that it might be argued one way or the other.

Maybe I'm just helping the Tulyans save themselves. Maybe they are their own Savior, in a collective sense.

Gods and prophets—they didn't have to be what they were commonly believed to be in Noah's opinion, did have to look like their universal depictions. As just two examples among many, he doubted if he would ever see (in any form of sight that he possessed) a bearded old man in the sky or angels with wings. Maybe the supreme deity was more of a collective entity that stretched across the cosmos, like Noah's own concept of galactic ecology.

And, though Noah did not consider himself the center of the universe or even the galaxy, he nonetheless saw himself as the hub of *something*, with those concentric circles around him, radiating outward. At last, he could enter and leave Timeweb of his own volition. This enabled him to remain connected to the galactic web, and to the podship flesh he was touching now.

At his fingertips, Noah felt his own energy flowing outward into the amalgamated Aopoddae flesh, probing all of the arteries, organs, and cells that made up the ancient creatures. They were so complex, and yet so primitive. It made him realize how far afield many of the galactic races had gone with all of their details and complexities, all of their branched-out, hedonistic, disoriented priorities that caused them to wreak such havoc on the galaxy.

He saw that the battle-injured portions of the cocoon had not yet completely healed themselves, that their connection to their brethren and to Timeweb had helped them, but had not been quite enough. And it never would be enough without his involvement.

Noah didn't hold anything back from the Aopoddae. He allowed his energy to flow into the primitive flesh, as if he was Timeweb himself, providing healing nutrients to injured creatures. Once, Eshaz had done that for him, and Noah had made a miraculous recovery. Now, moment-by-moment, the alien flesh of the cocoon fused and healed at an accelerated rate. All the while, Noah probed and tested carefully, and perfected the cellular repairs. There was no question of trust anymore, no doubts of any kind from the Aopoddae about Noah's motivations. No fear of him. They needed him, and he needed them. It was a symbiotic relationship of extraordinary proportions.

He realized as well that the cocoon protected not only himself, but EcoStation. If Noah's plan unfolded for the space station, the enhanced facility would become an inspiration for all galactic races, a beacon of hope and more of a teaching facility for ecology than he had ever envisioned before.

Noah felt the podship skin tremble against his own flesh, as the cocoon anticipated what he was going to do next. He allowed the strengthened energy of the cocoon to flow back into him. Noah had healed the collective creature, and at this moment—in its fortified form—he anticipated that it would return the favor. Ultimately, Noah knew he was much more than a human being—physically and spiritually—and he sensed that the Aopoddae could guide him, could enable him to discover the path he should take with his remarkable life, and perhaps give him the tools that he needed.

The inflow was tremendous, and he struggled to absorb it and comprehend. Much of the new Aopoddae data, the vast majority of it, was indecipherable to him. But a limited amount of information, as if passing through a filter system from the Aopoddae language to something he could understand, reached his consciousness.

Noah realized that he was all of the galactic races, inextricably linked to them. He saw the history of sentient life as multiple paths spreading out in his wake, and found the broad routes he had taken in his own genetic history and life that brought him to this exact place and awareness. Countless other events could have occurred instead, events that would have prevented Noah from ever existing, or from ever being needed at all. Events that would not have led to the state of galactic decay in which everyone now found themselves trapped.

And, though Noah could not see the future with any degree of certainty, he was able to envision multiple paths of unfolding galactic possibilities extending into future time, radiating outward from him. He could only try to nudge the various races to take the proper paths. He could never force them to do so.

Opening the synapses and paranormal elements of his mind, as if they were pores that he was unplugging, Noah tried to let more data flow in, everything the podships knew. He hungered for all of it. In response an overwhelming surge of additional information flowed in, a tidal wave of data—much of it in raw, indecipherable form.

Pain!

It was too much, too fast, and the Aopoddae didn't seem to realize it. Or did they? Were they trying to kill him? Was that a last bit of data they would inject into him through the connection? Their confession of guilt, or even a gloating?

He screamed from the unbearable pain. It was not just physical. It went way beyond that.

Parallel realities surrounded him, like the concentric circles. In one of them, he realized that he had fallen to his knees, and that he was still trying to maintain physical contact with the Aopoddae cocoon. In his agony he lost contact, and slumped to the deck.

* * * * *

Noah became aware of needles in his brain, and of data flowing outward, like something removing poisons from his body. Bringing him back from the brink, rescuing him from his foolishness.

Opening his eyes, he saw Thinker kneeling over him, with a tentacle containing an array of needles linking the robot to Noah's skull. An organic interface, Noah realized. The robot had used it on him previously, to download information on Noah's life and genetics. Now he was doing it again, but for a different purpose. Gradually, Noah began to feel better.

"You saved my life," Noah said, as the pain faded. He breathed a sigh of relief.

697

"Perhaps not," Thinker said. "As we speak, I am analyzing limited elements of the Aopoddae information, even as it is being downloaded into my data banks and sorted. Contrary to your suspicion, the podships did not wish to do you harm. They made a decision that you could handle the flood of information, and that you would heal mentally from any adverse effects of it—just as you have proven yourself able to recover from physical injuries."

"But you had to intervene."

"Because I didn't know what else to do. I don't think I caused any damage, and you can certainly reconnect to them and get the data again. However, I have an alternative that might be of use to you."

The robot disconnected the interface, and it snaked back into his metal body. Noah sat up on the deck, noticed that his hands were different, entirely gray and rough-surfaced now, with veins of black. He felt his face. It had changed as well. He felt ready for the complete metamorphosis. The time had arrived.

"What alternative?" Noah asked.

"I expected you would ask," Thinker said. He straightened, looked down at Noah. "Consider me your portable backup. I can adjust the interface, enabling you to search through my data banks at will, making the Aopoddae information available to you in a more palatable form."

"An intriguing offer," Noah said. "Yes, I want you to do that."

"I hasten to add, however, that most of the data is incomprehensible, even to me."

"I found the same thing. If that is true, though, how can you be certain they don't want to do me harm?"

"Good question. My only answer beyond what they have revealed to us is that I do not sense they have aggressive intentions toward you. I know, however, that my instincts in this regard are only programmed into me, and thus are by definition inferior to yours."

"I sense the same thing. The Aopoddae are essentially gentle souls, but dangerous when threatened, if they perceive enemies. Once, they considered me a possible enemy, but that has since been worked out between us. You notice I said between. I believe they are a single organism, a collective organism."

"Each species, each race is like that," Thinker noted. "I think you're saying that the Aopoddae are more closely linked to one another than other galactic races are?"

"That is my belief, but I also believe, in my heart of hearts, that all sentient life forms in the galaxy are ultimately linked. It is a matter of definitions and semantics, and of filters on our thought processes. But it makes sense to me. It's tied to galactic ecology, to the interdependence of all matter in the galaxy, whether sentient or not."

"And tied to the concept of God."

"Not a typical comment for a robot," Noah said, with a gentle smile.

"I am not your typical robot."

"No, you aren't."

"I will run decryption programs on the Aopoddae raw data and see what more I can discover. It will not be easy, but ... Hmmm, just a moment, please." Thinker whirred, and his body jerked, as if in pain. Noah heard something clank inside the mechanism.

Presently, however, the orange lights on the robot's faceplate blinked cheerily, and he announced, "I was overloading too, but I connected to a series of reserve memory cores. It is better now."

"There is probably more that we didn't absorb yet," Noah said. "I broke off the connection."

"Based upon what I'm seeing, Master Noah, I think we'd better try to figure out what we have first before obtaining more."

Noah nodded.

Thinker blinked his metal-lidded eyes. "Why don't we work with the information, sir, and see if we can handle it more safely? Maybe the Aopoddae didn't properly anticipate the danger to you, and we should set up safeguards."

"As usual, your wisdom is impeccable, my friend."

Rising to his feet, Noah looked down at his hands again. *Podship skin.* In a reflected metal surface of the chamber he saw the like changed in his face. He still saw the old Noah in the features, but they were distorted, an amalgam of his Human past and his evolving future.

I am unlike any other creature in the history of the galaxy, he thought.

It was a portion of the Aopoddae data that he had understood, and had retained in his mind. People had thought this before about him, and so had Noah. But none of them had anticipated the degree or scale of the phenomenon, and the continuing changes Noah was undergoing. He suspected that he had not yet reached his final stage of evolution, and that he might continue to metamorphose over the course of an eternal lifetime, without ever reaching stasis.

He found it fantastically exciting, and terrifying at the same time.

Chapter Sixty-One

Each life form in this universe—even those that seem most injurious to others—appears for a purpose. It may not always be easy to ascertain that purpose, but if you really search for it—if you drill down—you will find it.

　　　　　　　　　—Master Noah Watanabe, early notes on ecology

The planet was giving birth, but not to its own kind.

Billions of tiny creatures flowed out of lava tubes and swarmed as thick as locusts over Ignem, covering the glassy surface of the world so that it absorbed hardly any light at all. It took on a dull, lifeless appearance, but would recover its jewel-like glitter soon. Woldn did not intend to remain there for long.

Now he led the newborns in maneuvers over the remote planetscape, training and molding them telepathically so that they learned to function under the collective mind of one: that of The Eye of the Swarm. These were simple, preliminary exercises, which most of the Parviis picked up quickly. Some of the individuals straggled as they learned a little slower than the bulk of the others, but within an hour Woldn had them in line, as well.

Utilizing secret methods they had stolen from the Adurian laboratories, Woldn's breeding specialists had instituted the most massive reproduction program in the long history of the Parvii race. The gestation period in the lava tubes was comparable to the traditional method, but the warmth in the tubes and other conditions enabled the breeding specialists to generate exponentially more individuals from the same batch of raw genetic material.

This was a dramatic change from the old days and methods, where there had been distinct limitations. That had not mattered so much in the past, though, because the swarm had always maintained its population equilibrium, and the intermittent infusion of relatively small number of births had been adequate. In those days, only Parvii leaders and specialists had known the number of their brethren, but it had been vast. Now his race was on the road to recovery. In this batch alone, he counted more than eight hundred and fifty billion individuals. More than enough for what he had in mind.

In the new method, the maturation period following birth would be the same: only a matter of weeks to reach adulthood. During that time, they would be trained here and out in space, building up to increasingly complex maneuvers and techniques. For the next stage, he summoned the war priests.

Vorlik and Yurtii arrived in a matter of moments, having already been with the breeding specialists on Ignem, where they had been watching the progress of the breeding program. Man and boy respectively, they wore the black robes of their cult, raiments that were actually projections around their bodies.

Flying beside Woldn, Vorlik down on the hovering, waiting swarm. "The breeding specialists report that some of our youngsters already have potent neurotoxin stingers and show excellent potential for working with each other to fire telepathic weapons. They also appear to fly well for their age."

"Yes," Woldn said. "I am always wary of anything new, however. In due course, we will take them out into space and assess their capabilities in capturing podships. I'm worried about training them properly. Natural podships and the artificial lab-pods created by the Adurians could present different challenges."

"But it is especially important for us to test our young swarms in combat. The stresses of warfare will sort the weak from the strong. With our new breeding process, we can replace the losses quickly."

"Perhaps you are right," Woldn said.

"I disagree," the hairless Yurtii said. "I am worried about the capabilities of these swarms. Especially considering how these individuals were bred. It occurs to me now that we might have been lured into the Adurian laboratory so that we would adopt their breeding methods and create Parviis that would one day turn against us."

"Too bad you didn't think of that earlier," Vorlik said with a scowl.

Below them, the naked individuals clustered in groups according to their skin tones, forming divisions in which they were more comfortable. For the time being, Woldn permitted it, because he knew they were still insecure in their extreme youth. But as they grew, he would separate them more and more, so that color tones would no longer matter to them at all.

"If need be, I could put all of these to death in an instant," Woldn said. "But I have probed them myself—individually and collectively—and there is nothing to raise any alarm signals." He looked at Yurtii and smiled stiffly. "*So far,* that is. You are right to raise a voice of caution, but I agree with Vorlik that we must test the swarms in combat as soon as possible."

"In war it is necessary to take chances," Vorlik said. "That is how wars are won."

"And lost," Yurtii said.

Vorlik frowned. "I'm talking about *calculated* risks, professionally assessed. Don't tell me you don't know what I mean, Yurtii. In your time, you took chances, and achieved military victories. You could have been even greater, though, if you had been more bold and daring."

"Like yourself?"

"Of course." The mature, stocky man beamed proudly, and Woldn knew he had every right to do so.

But Yurtii still had points to make. "Admittedly, your historical achievements were greater than mine, because you were largely responsible for defeating the Tulyans and taking the podships away from them. However, your quick, glamorous victories in the Tulyan War cannot be compared with the obstacles I had to overcome. My later war in the Far Sector involved complexities that you did not face. We each faced different times, differing challenges and conditions. In retrospect, I came to the opinion that I should have proceeded even more carefully than I did on some of my military campaigns. The enemy was resourceful, laid traps for me. I still defeated them, but it was not easy."

"We are an apple and an orange, you and I," Vorlik said. "To borrow a Human phrase."

"No," Woldn said. "You are each of the same ilk, but display different aspects of it from your particular experiences. This is a good balance. I will listen to both of you equally, and render my decisions."

"As you wish," Vorlik said, though he did not look entirely pleased. Given enough provocation, he might even kill Yurtii. But with his own telepathic control over both of them, Woldn knew that should not happen. And even on the remote chance that it did, Vorlik would never get away with it. Already, the breeding specialists had discovered new war-priest latents, and nascent breeding specialists.

Everyone can be replaced and will be replaced if necessary, Woldn thought. *Even me.*

He dispatched the two war priests to perform their training-instruction duties, and notified the swarm to follow them. Then he watched as Vorlik and Yurtii divided the swarm into ten divisions and caused their bodies to change color, so that all of them appeared to wear pale blue uniforms. Soon the war priests were leading the first two divisions in basic war maneuvers, swoops and streaks of pale blue that went this way and that over the planet, sometimes blocking the sun, and sometimes allowing it to glint off Ignem's glassy surface.

In a short time, many of the trainees changed in color to purple, proof that they had perfected the first phase of their studies. He saw the light blue swarms shift increasingly in hue as the most advanced individuals contributed to the whole and melded themselves into it in the Parvii way. Soon there were two purple divisions, and the war priests began to work with the other divisions, bringing them up to the same standard.

It was still early in their training. Purple would not be their ultimate color. That would be a bright red, suitable for a military force since it was the most common color of blood among the galactic races. Already the young Parviis were displaying significant improvements in style and technique, and soon they could constitute a formidable fighting force.

Wave after wave of them surging into battle, annihilating all enemies in their path....

Chapter Sixty-Two

In the vast majority of races, the female of the species is more complex than the male—physically and psychologically. Thus, the female should be considered more valuable. But that is not always the case.

—Excerpt, Jimlat report on the galactic races

oah could walk independently throughout the large, empty space station and its Aopoddae outer layer. He moved with the normal gait of a human being, but knew he must look like a monster, as if some diabolical alien creature had invaded his cellular structure and taken over.

"Just a minute," he said to Thinker, who rattled along beside him. Something in the flat-bodied robot's body had come loose, but he had been so preoccupied with other matters that he had neglected to diagnose and repair it. He had been sorting and resorting the Aopoddae data in his data banks and in his reserve memory cores, but so far very little of it was decipherable.

Now the two of them stood in front of an ornate corridor mirror that somehow had escaped the destruction wreaked upon most of the orbiter. It was one of the gaudy decorations that Lorenzo had installed when he had the facility converted to a gambling casino. Lights were on in the corridor. Thinker had figured out how to get them working.

Looking in the reflective glass, Noah saw that his original facial and muscular features were identifiable—he still had a strong chin, aquiline nose, and wide-spaced hazel eyes—but the skin was gray, with streaks of black throughout. It had a rough texture like that of a podship, and portions of it pulsed on the surface. His curly red hair was gone, having been replaced by a clump of reddish flesh on top of his head, in the approximate shape of his former hairstyle. Fine lines in it looked like strands of red hair, but weren't. They were veins.

"My face looks like the prow of a podship, with its pilot immersed into the flesh. The question is, can I fly?"

"You are not a flying craft," Thinker said. "There is no doubt about that. I have seen no undercarriage, no place or way for you to engage with the strands of the podways. No, you are something else entirely. A *podman*, for want of a better word."

"The question is, what comes with my new appearance?"

"That is one of many questions."

"Do you think people will fear me when they see what I look like?"

"They already fear you, Master Noah, in varying degrees. Even Tesh, who cares deeply about you. She's been asking to see you. In fact, she's demanding it now, and says you can't keep ignoring her. She is in a shuttle that is in comlink contact with us at this very moment. I am linked to the comstation by remote. Would you like to hear her, or reply to her?"

"I wonder if she will still consider me attractive," Noah mused. "Of course, she is much older than I am—though she doesn't look it—and she has had past relationships with a variety of galactic races. She told me so. She also said she'd never met anyone like me before."

"An understatement, I'm sure. Especially now."

Noah chuckled. "I see you've developed a sense of humor. I don't recall one when I first met you, but lately you've been different. Did somebody program it into you?"

"Subi Danvar and some of the others thought I was too stiff and intellectual, so they tweaked my operating systems a bit. I asked them to make certain I would never be inappropriately funny, because I don't wish to irritate you Humans. Therefore, you should find my humor somewhat subdued."

"So far, you're doing fine, my metal friend." Looking at both of them in the mirror, he added, "We're quite an odd pair, aren't we?"

The orange lights around Thinker's faceplate glowed, then went out. "Shall we send for the lady, sir?"

"I wonder if she knows a female robot to bring along. Then we could have a double date."

"You are much funnier than I am, Master Noah. I interpret that as a possible yes?"

"Send for her, then. I'll receive her in the module where I used to have a dining hall for my students. You know where that is?"

"Of course. You've had robots move furnishings and gambling tables out of the way in there."

"Yes, they've set up a smaller dining table for me in there, with chairs and vending machines. Later I want to get the habitat enclosures installed around the eating area again, the miniature forest of dwarf oak and blue-bark canopa pines, along with the birds and other organisms."

"That will be delightful."

"One day, Thinker, this will be a School of Galactic Ecology again, and much more. I have grand plans for EcoStation."

"I will help you with them."

"Give me thirty minutes before letting Tesh in. I want to spruce myself up."

The robot rattled away, chuckling.

* * * * *

High Ruler Coreq stood on the bridge of his flagship, gazing at the vast armada gathered around him, as the ships moved gracefully in concert, flowing and shifting through the Kandor Section of space like dancers following his choreography. They were practicing battle maneuvers.

He slammed a fist against the thick glax window, and made a vow.

Things would be far different in the next military encounter with the enemy, not like the debacle from which he had been fortunate to escape with his life and a portion of his force. Inexplicably, galactic conditions had interfered, just as he'd been about to split space and emerge over the target world of Canopa. Something bad had happened, and suddenly he'd found himself far away, in a region of unknown coordinates. Holes and traps in the infrastructure had nearly spelled the end of him, but he suspected that the enemy must be having as much trouble with it as he was. They'd just been able to take advantage of him that time. The perilous galactic conditions could not possibly be a weapon of theirs; no one could have a power that immense and far-reaching.

After the incident, Coreq had sent a report back to the Adurian homeworld by courier, providing Premier Enver and Warlord Tarix with as many details as he could—and urging them to step up the production of laboratory-bred podships even more. In addition, he had ordered the bulk of his occupying forces to depart from Human and Mutati worlds and join him here for a final thrust against the so-called Liberators....

* * * * *

Left alone in the corridor, Noah stared in the mirror again, at the rough alien flesh covering his face. He focused on the lump of reddish flesh where his hair used to be, and on the fine veins in the lump. Something shifted in the mass, and he was able to separate out a single strand of curly red hair at the front. Then he separated another, and then hundreds of them, and finally his entire head. With his mind, he commanded how he wanted the hair to be arranged, and it cooperated, down to the last follicle.

However, looking at himself now, with his humanoid face and normal hair, it did not look right at all. He looked like an alien clown.

So he focused on his face, and as moments passed he saw the alien skin fade away, from the forehead down, until the normal Noah looked back at him, the one everyone expected to see. He did the same with his hands and forearms, completing the visible areas.

Now I've spruced myself up, he thought. And he made his way to the dining hall.

He was not there long when Tesh strode in, with a determined look on her face, as if she had finally caught the person she had been chasing. She wore a green skirt and white blouse, which he presumed were projections from her energy field, instead of real apparel. Walking right up to him, Tesh looked closely at his face, and showed confusion on her own.

"Thinker said something to you, didn't he?" Noah asked.

"He told me not to be shocked by your appearance, that's all."

"No details?"

She shook her head, causing her black hair to brush over her shoulders.

Noah frowned. "Shall I put it into words or show you? Mmmm. Words are inadequate, so here goes."

In the blink of an eye, Noah assumed the alien "podman" appearance, including the reddish lump instead of hair.

She gasped and took a step backward. Then, cautiously, she reached out and touched the streaky, gray-black skin on his cheek. "I, I … Once, I felt roughness on your forearm, under your shirt. This has been happening gradually?"

He nodded. "Now I seem able to control it at will, though."

"Like a shapeshifter?"

"To an extent. On the surface of my skin, at least."

She narrowed her eyes suspiciously. "There are many forms of shapeshifters in this galaxy: Mutatis, Aopoddae, Parviis. And you are yet another, it seems. I believe you are the first of your kind."

"Oddly, I feel more comfortable this way. The old Noah is gone now."

"But I miss the *old* Noah," she said. "Just when I thought I was getting to know him and care about him, he changed."

"You don't need to fear me," Noah said. "I see in your eyes that you do."

He watched her take a deep, shuddering breath. The emerald green eyes flashed, and she said, "My reasons are more complicated than you assume. There is something important I need to discuss with you."

"I get the feeling I'm not going to like this."

She smiled, but it had a hard edge to it. "That depends."

"On what?"

"On what sort of a … *man* … you are." She grasped one of his alien hands and said, "Noah, I'm pregnant with your child."

"From the one time when you said we really had sex, when I thought I only imagined it?"

"It was real, and so is our baby."

He jerked his head back. "But you told me once that the galactic races could not interbreed."

To this, she wagged a finger at him like a schoolteacher and said, "As I told you before, Parviis and Humans were once the same race, until they branched off. Technically, they are not entirely separate galactic races. I have in fact heard of a very small number of cases in which children have been born. The odds of conceiving a child, however, are so low as to be non-existent."

"Mmmm, I'm sure you omitted some of those details from me earlier."

"Or, you might not have been listening carefully." She looked at him apprehensively, seemed to be gauging his reactions.

"I guess we're lucky, huh?" He grinned, but wasn't sure how he felt about her condition. He didn't want to make her feel he was not pleased. And even if he wasn't, he promised himself that he would take steps to protect Tesh from now on, and their child. He didn't even consider asking her to terminate the pregnancy. That was out of the question.

"We are lucky." A cast to her eyes revealed to him that she had not yet revealed certain things, but he decided not to press her.

Instead, Noah asked, "Am I really Human? Was I ever really Human?"

"I think you were when we conceived the child, though I'm not so sure what you have become since then."

"But I was already different then, when we conceived. Eshaz had already healed my injuries by connecting my injured body to the galactic webbing, allowing its nutrients to flow into me. You saw how I could recover afterward from virtually anything."

"Yes, you were different, but apparently not different enough." She patted her belly, but he couldn't see any difference in it. He didn't doubt her pregnancy, though.

"When will you give birth?"

"In a cross-racial situation, that can vary. Anywhere from a few weeks to a few months. I think I will get a sense of it as our child grows in my womb." Her eyes sparkled, and he could tell that she was happy about what was happening inside her body.

Noah held her tightly, and kissed her. She melted into his arms.

When they separated, Noah looked at her and marveled about what an incredible creature *she* was. He had heard somewhere that the Human woman was much more complex than the male, and he thought this Parvii female must be even more complicated than that. At the moment, the pretty brunette looked like a normal-sized Human woman, but that was only because of her magnification system. It was a remarkable technology, one that made her projected skin feel normal to him, even though it was actually an energy field. She told him once that the force field around her made physical acts seem as if her body was really much larger. Apparently this included the process of fertilization.

"What size will our child will be?" he asked.

"That is determined by the natural size of the woman, by the dimensions of the womb and birth canal. If I were, instead, a Parvii man and you were a Human woman, the child would be what you would consider normal size."

Wrinkling his forehead, trying to comprehend, Noah did not know how to respond. He was having trouble envisioning a son or daughter that he could hold in the palm of his hand, or which he could carry about in a pocket.

Placing her hands on her hips, she said, "Are you happy with the news?"

"Of course! It just takes some getting used to."

"I know how you feel, then." She ran her fingers over the alien skin and the Human contours of his face. "Your lips are a bit rough now, dear," she said, "so you'll have to be gentle when you kiss me."

"Can't you adjust your magnification system?"

"I could. But I would rather see you show consideration by making your own alterations occasionally, somewhat like shaving off bristle. A woman always likes a man to be considerate. Perhaps you can do it without altering your appearance. I think you're very handsome now."

He smiled. "I really am happy about the news," he said.

"I know you are."

In all of the past and future paths that Noah had envisioned via his connection with the cocoon, he had not foreseen any of this. But he knew with certainty—an instinctual feeling—that their child would be important.

Chapter Sixty-Three

The Sublime Creator designed life and death to go in a circle, a never-ending dance of birth and death. But something has interrupted the sacred process. None of the races—not even Tulyans—are supposed to be completely immortal.

—Report to the Council of Elders

He lived in a universe of strange, mind stretching possibilities.

Master Noah entered a large chamber of the orbiter, a room that had once been Lorenzo's Grand Ballroom, a separate, private area of the Pleasure Palace Casino. Now it was a shambles, with wrecked furnishings and shattered plax on the floor, crunching under his feet. A broken mirror showed a distortion of his half-Human form as he walked by.

Almost a year ago, Eshaz had healed Noah by connecting his injured flesh to a defect in the galactic webbing, at a point where a timehole was just beginning to form. Afterward, Noah had displayed miraculous physical capabilities, an ability to recover from traumatic, even grisly, injuries by regenerating the cells of his body. Since then, more things had happened that were even more remarkable. Thinking back now, Noah was coming to believe that he had visualized healing himself, and that it had happened. Somehow, in his intense pain—especially from being hacked up by his sister—he had seen his way through a narrow, treacherous path, and had survived.

It had been a learning experience on an extrasensory journey.

But had he actually risen from the dead, like Lazarus of Lost Earth? He was not sure, but knew that stories about him had gotten out, and had contributed to the fear and awe with which many people looked at him, especially those who didn't actually know him personally. It would be even worse from now on because of Noah's appearance, though he knew he could modify his skin to make it look Human. He could visualize it, and it would happen.

Clearly, this ability to imagine and shape went beyond the creation of physical changes in his own body. He had proven that when the cocoon was under attack by HibAdu forces, and he'd transported the space station across the galaxy to the Tulyan Starcloud, after envisioning that heavenly realm in his mind. There had also been times in the past when he had intermittently been able to enter and control podships in a paranormal manner. He presumed that he could do that now if he wished, on an individual podship basis, but he felt no need or desire to do so.

He could even control multiple podships, as he had proven by moving the cocoon through space. It might just be possible for him to gather every podship in the whole galaxy, making him like another version the Eye of the Swarm, but on a much more grand, and potentially powerful, basis. Noah suspected that his abilities went farther than he dared imagine, and the very thought of the possibilities made him want to slow down. He did not want to leap forward too rapidly, before he was ready.

But the galaxy was in chaos. He could not ignore this fact, could not hide from it. There was no formal training facility where he could learn and polish his unusual craft. He'd had to discover and perfect the highly specialized skills on the job, during times of crisis. Noah had escaped to the starcloud without a moment to spare. But he had been unable to stand and fight, a situation he had found frustrating.

Now the injured portions of the cocoon were healed, though as he looked around the space station itself, he saw that a tremendous amount of restoration work remained to be done. The robots had patched some of the breaks in the hulls, and had completed some basic repairs to the gravity generators, plumbing system, electrical connections, and air circulators. The bodies had been taken away and buried, but on the floor of the Grand Ballroom he still saw splotches of dried blood in both red and purple, evidence of the traumatic deaths that had occurred here.

Peripherally, he noticed Thinker enter the chamber, moving more smoothly and quietly than before. He seemed to have repaired his own loose parts. "I was looking all over for you, Master," he said.

"And Tesh?"

"I escorted her back to *Webdancer*. She's very determined to continue her piloting duties, even with the news of her pregnancy."

Noah bristled. "There are no secrets from you, are there?"

"As your authorized biographer, I require such information. I think Tesh rather likes me, and I feel the same about her. I asked her if everything was all right, and she told me about the baby."

"Maybe you'd like to marry her and take my place."

"Oh! I could never do that, Master." He paused. "I just came to let you know she is safe."

"Thank you."

"Would you like me to leave you alone?"

"No, you might as well observe what I'm about to do firsthand. I thought I would do a little cleaning up around here."

"You mean for exercise? Wouldn't you like me to send for robots to do it?"

"We'll see," Noah said.

The windows of this ballroom had once looked out on the planet Canopa, and on the twinkling vastness of space. Now they were covered by the podship skin of the cocoon. Noah found a place where the windowplax had been broken away, and which was now sealed by the amalgamated Aopoddae. Walking over there, he looked more closely, and touched the mottled gray-and-black skin. This time, he did not seek or permit the inflow of raw Aopoddae data. Instead, he had something else in mind, something he hoped would help him on the journey to understand the podship race.

The cocoon flesh softened to his touch. He let go, and the flesh oozed back into the ballroom in a thin film, flowing down the outer wall and onto the floor, where it pooled around Noah's feet. With his free hand, he pointed to the overturned and broken furnishings, to the dried blood, to the dents and breaks in the walls and windows. More alien cellular material flowed out of the break in the plax where he had touched it, and covered the floor. Thinker scrambled out into the corridor, but kept looking in through the doorway.

All around Noah, objects began to change as they were touched by the podship flesh. Everything became gray and veiny black, and just as he had anticipated, new forms began to take shape—a central platform, and rows of chairs extending outward from it. He had always wondered how podships altered the internal configurations of their vessels, and now he was experiencing it directly as the amalgamated creature created an auditorium for him. It looked like another version of a room that might be onboard a podship.

"Marvelous!" Thinker exclaimed from the corridor.

"You're witnessing the rebirth of EcoStation," Noah said. "In the future it will again be a school for galactic ecologists, but on a much larger scale than it ever was before, as an inspiration for all races to restore and maintain the ecological health of the galaxy. Like me, the space station is evolving."

"Don't forget me," Thinker said, as Noah freed himself from the liquefied flesh and joined him in the corridor. "I've evolved too," the robot insisted.

"We're all doing it together," Noah said. He strode to the next large area of the space station, Lorenzo's former Audience Chamber. Utilizing podship flesh from another break in the hull, Noah soon created an Astronomical Projection Chamber, in which he would demonstrate the motions and connectivity of star systems, planets, and other cosmic bodies. Compliantly, the Aopoddae formed the basic enclosure according to his specifications, and much of the furnishings—all attached to the expanding cocoon. When circumstances permitted it, Noah would later bring in the technological devices. But this was the framework he wanted, the canvas on which he would paint his eco-picture.

For the rest of the day, he and Thinker moved from module to module and chamber to chamber, where Noah put himself in direct contact with the podship flesh and made the alterations he wanted. In the process, he was restoring EcoStation, bringing it back from its own near-death. He realized as he did this that he might have just envisioned the whole project at once, but he didn't want to speed it up. There were subtleties in the control he exerted over the alien flesh. He and the cocooned Aopoddae were getting to know one another, learning how to work together, making the procedures more efficient.

When the work was nearly complete, Noah and the robot stood inside one of the new classroom modules, where Noah had set up the raw framework of learning stations for his students. Looking around with a degree of satisfaction, he realized, *I am learning at my own school.* And he knew this was as it should be. Even the wisest and most accomplished people still had many things to learn. That held true for robots, too, as they continually updated their data banks, always advancing their operating systems and memory cores.

During the restoration of EcoStation, Thinker had been adding what he observed to his data banks. Noah had kept the cerebral robot with him for this, and for other reasons. This intelligent machine was the smartest of all of them, an excellent and faithful adviser. And, though Noah was not intentionally allowing new Aopoddae data to flow into him, he remained concerned about making a serious mistake, perhaps through some communication problem. At least Thinker was always nearby if necessary, to relieve any overload on Noah's brain. But would that be enough? He wasn't sure, but it gave him concern. Maybe something like that, the overwhelming power of the psychic flow, could actually kill him. And if Noah died, he could not advance, could not achieve what he needed to do.

Sensing something, he touched the podship flesh at a learning station desk, then used the multiple eyes of the creatures to gaze far out into space. Something was approaching fast, bearing down on the Tulyan Starcloud. He looked closer. It was a Parvii swarm, the biggest one he had ever seen. Somehow, they had regenerated and were coming back in force.

He sensed a disturbance in the starcloud as the mindlinked Tulyans detected the approaching danger from their mortal enemy. The immense swarm neared at high speed, and split into divisions that veered out to the sides, to attack from different directions.

They struck with stunning speed. Blue bursts of energy came from the center of each swarm. Telepathic artillery. Some of their shots hit the thick skin of the cocoon, and Noah heard the pain of the amalgamated podships.

He turned the unarmed cocoon around and retreated into the starcloud. Mindlink opened and let him in, like a cosmic gate. It shut behind him, then guided him to a safer position. Moments later, he saw comets and meteors streak by him in eerie silence, heading out against the swarms. Hundreds of armed Liberator podships also surged out to join the battle, ships that had been assigned to protect the starcloud and the caretaking crews that came and went. Noah wanted to contribute to the effort, but could only watch.

Frustrated, he turned to Thinker and asked, "How are you coming in deciphering the Aopoddae data? It's important."

"I know, and I have been able to decipher a few additional fragments," the robot said. "In the midst of all the other data, I found an even more heavily encrypted section, like an armored core of data. I don't know if I can ever get into that part. The podships still harbor doubts about you concerning the release of this particular information, uncertainties about whether or not you are a person they can fully trust."

"Keep trying to find out what it is," Noah said.

He touched a nearby bulkhead, and through a Timeweb link he saw the raging battle. At least he could access the paranormal dimension at will now. He watched the swarms dive forward into the onslaught of defensive weapons that the Tulyans threw at them. To his dismay, he saw mindlink seem to weaken. Holes in it opened up, and tiny invaders surged through.

But Noah soon saw that it was a Tulyan trap. Any swarms that got through mindlink soon detonated in puffs of white, while other swarms beyond the starcloud fled from the pursuing comets and meteors. Noah estimated that the Parviis lost half their force before they turned and retreated into space.

He knew they would be back, and probably in even greater numbers the next time. Somehow they had regenerated their population at an incredible rate.

Chapter Sixty-Four

Most legends are designed to fit the needs of those in power. But there have been notable historical exceptions, and they can be the most significant of all.
    —Finding of the Galactic Study Group, subcommittee on religion

A bleak, gray sky hung over the Golden Palace.

In the medical room on the top floor, Hari'Adab's mood matched the weather. When not attending to his duties as the Mutati ruler, he spent every available moment at Parais' side. It occurred to him now, as he looked at the quivering mass of flesh and dark feathers on the bed, that this remarkable aeromutati was really his top *professional* priority. It wasn't just personal, because he was nothing as an Emir without her guidance and love. Now and then he'd been attending the military strategy meetings with Mutatis, Humans, and Tulyans, but he had not really been *there*. He had not been all that he should be in the high position he held, all that his people deserved.

As Parais faded, so did he, along with all of his abilities to lead and inspire others. He knew he should step aside, and in effect he had done exactly that, because he had been turning over more and more command duties and decisions to Kajor Yerto Bhaleen. It seemed ironic to Hari that he—always a pacifist at heart—would come to rely so heavily on a military officer. At one time, he never would have considered such an action. But that had been before he faced the stark realities of command that were arrayed before him now, with the extreme pressures of political and military responsibility weighed against his personal and emotional needs.

I am only a Mutati, he thought. *A bunch of feelings and desires in a cellular package.* As a shapeshifter, Hari knew he could alter his appearance, making himself look carefree and happy, but it would only be the thinnest veneer. He wouldn't waste his time doing that, so he'd only been modifying his cellular structure occasionally in small ways, to keep his same basic appearance while not permitting the cells to lock into any one position. His mind and heart, though, the engine of his soul, were shutting down, preparing to lock everything into death.

On the surface, he was dressed differently today. For the strategy meeting he'd just left, he had worn a gold-and-black dress uniform, which he still had on. Having received intelligence information on the location of the main HibAdu fleet, Doge Anton and the officers were planning a major military assault. The meeting was still going on, down the corridor. He heard the clamor of their voices, through open doors. That morning there had been some disagreements—different war philosophies between Humans and Mutatis. But Hari expected the participants to iron them out. The spirit of cooperation among all of the allies—Human, Mutati, and Tulyan—was very strong.

For some time now the Liberators had been sending podships to neutral worlds around the galaxy, rounding up Humans and Mutatis who happened to be living there ... calling for volunteers and specialists. Many of the Mutatis were proving to be particularly valuable, since they could disguise themselves as any race, even as Hibbils and Adurians. That was how the Liberators had now learned the location of the enemy fleet—in the distant Kandor Sector.

Hari knew his ceremonial uniform gave him a more official and commanding appearance, and in part he had chosen it today for that very reason. But he had another. The costume included a ceremonial sword—the same one he'd almost used after the disastrous destruction of Paradij, when he had intended to kill himself for his culpability in that matter. He'd placed the point of the weapon against his belly, and had been ready to fall on it. But Parais had knocked the sword away, saving his life and telling him he needed to live for the sake of the Mutati people, preventing another fanatic like his father from ruling.

This time, she could not save him. The sword and its scabbard lay on the table by the bed, beside Parais' personal copy of the sacred Mutati book, *The Holy Writ*. After his failed suicide attempt, the two of them had placed their hands on that very book and shared a prayer.

But this he had not shared with her, his vow: If she died, he would follow her soon afterward.

Hari knew he could only lead his people with Parais at his side, and he had only continued to hold the titular title of Emir in the hope that she would recover. Gazing upon her now, feeling the faint, weakening pulse of her skin, he was losing all hope. Increasingly, he found himself unable to think of anything but a bleak future.

With each passing day, Parais looked less and less recognizable. Only when she occasionally emerged from her pain and looked at him with her gentle brown eyes could he ever confirm it was her. She had done that the evening before, but now the eyes had sunken back into the flesh, and he only had a vague sense of where they were. Tragically, she was almost entirely unidentifiable, with only a ghost of her facial features remaining, as if they had been scoured off.

Removing the sword from the scabbard, Hari touched his finger to the sharp blade. Purple blood trickled from his skin and dripped on the floor.

In a few seconds he could be dead. So easy, so inviting.

But he almost heard her scolding words. That would be the easy course, she'd say, the coward's way out. Death was always easier than life from a personal standpoint, but for those who remained behind after the event, it was much more difficult.

Hari'Adab rose to his feet. Ponderously, he resheathed the sword and clipped it onto his belt.

For Parais, I will take the more difficult path. I will live. For her, and for my people.

And he vowed to never again reach this state of personal despair, not even if she died. If Parais' life ever meant anything—and it *did*—he had to follow her wishes. She would want him to be strong.

On the bed, he saw the hulk breathing, but barely. He tried to distance himself from his darkest feelings, told himself that he had to.

I shall not be selfish, he thought.

Then he realized that he was still, in a way, actually being selfish, since he was also concerned about his legacy, what future generations of his people would think of him. He had already killed billions of Mutatis, the unwanted collateral effect of assassinating his own father. His people had died accidentally, to be certain, a terrible mistake. But in the process—and Hari struggled once more to convince himself of this—he had saved trillions more across the entire Mutati Sector. His father had been a complete madman. Everyone with any brains knew that.

Feeling stronger now, Hari returned to the meeting. The participants fell silent as he entered. Holding his head high, the Emir strode across the room and sat next to Doge Anton.

"How is Parais?" Anton asked.

"The same. Thank you for asking." Looking around the room, Hari added, "I'm sorry if I was distracted before. I'm ready to perform my duties now. Parais is with me here." Fighting back his emotions, he patted his own chest, over his heart.

"That's good," Anton said, "but know this. We share your pain."

"Thank you."

The military discussions resumed. General Nirella and Kajor Bhaleen got into a disagreement over military strategy, over how much force should be applied in the initial assault against the HibAdus. Nirella wanted to keep major assets in reserve, to protect the planets and star systems they now held, but Bhaleen disagreed.

"What use is it to hold onto what little we have?" he asked. "Two Human planets, plus Yaree and the Tulyan Starcloud. The Tulyans just held off a large Parvii assault, so they're proving their own defensive capabilities. If only their mindlink was strong away from the starcloud, we could spread them around. But mindlink weakens dramatically in other galactic sectors, so I agree that the Tulyan defenders are most effective remaining where they are. But if we're ever going to succeed in this war, we need to hit the enemy with all the other forces we have, and make them hurt. At last, we have solid information that the main HibAdu fleet is in the Kandor Sector. There is not a moment to spare."

"For what it's worth, I agree." The rotund Subi Danvar, one of Noah Watanabe's representatives at the meeting, stood up. "I've spent my life thinking about security, trying to protect what we have and where we are. But what point is that if our diluted forces cause us to lose everything anyway? I say we throw everything we have at the bastards, and not to just hurt them. We need to *annihilate* them!"

A clamor of disagreement arose in the room. Gradually, the advocates of a more aggressive approach drowned out the others. Doge Anton and Hari'Adab both stayed out of it, watching and listening.

Then Anton rose and stood by Subi and the other officers, Human and Mutati, who had gathered around Kajor Bhaleen, to support his position. "What is a military force for, if not to attack?" the Doge asked.

The rationale of his words still left room for debate, but the opponents of massive force had no more wind in their sails. Grudgingly, General Nirella stood and went to her husband's side.

"There is one thing more," Hari'Adab said. He remained seated. "From now on, the forces of the Mutati Kingdom will be named the Parais Division. She will be the inspiration for me, and for my fighters. I'm going into battle with them."

"She will be an inspiration for all of us," Doge Anton said. "Before we're finished, we'll emancipate *all* Human and Mutati planets, and free our people that have been enslaved. The Hibbils and Adurians will regret ever turning against us with their traitorous schemes!"

Clapping and cheering carried across the floor. Hari hoped that Parais could hear it, and that she would find the strength to hold on.

Chapter Sixty-Five

The Eye of the Swarm appears to have a new method of breeding Parvits that enables him to breed large masses of his people quickly. We don't know the details, but this much seems clear: The young swarms are not able to generate sufficient telepathic power for the weapons they need. The multi-input weapons fire, but have diminished impact. Perhaps that will improve with time when the swarms mature. But as they progress, so must we, to counteract and destroy them. Complacency is our biggest enemy of all.

—Report to the Tulyan Council of Elders

I n the student dining hall, Noah touched the podship skin that covered a window opening. As he did so, the surface became filmy, so that he could see through it, as if it were a porthole on a podship. He let go, and the window remained.

He had again moved the cocoon out into space, just beyond the misty starcloud, because he wanted to perform his own experiments there, not interfering with the mindlink defensive system. Through the window, he saw Tulyans and elements of the Liberator fleet performing battle maneuvers in the sunlight, coordinating mindlink telepathic weapons and the firepower of armed podships.

All of the key leaders and most of the podships were at the starcloud now, for critical preparations. On an emergency basis, General Nirella had obtained the cooperation of the Tulyan Council to arm much more of the caretaking fleet than the original allotments. With the cooperation not only of the Tulyans but of the mysterious Aopoddae, this conversion was accomplished in a matter of days. The military force under Anton's command now amounted to more than one hundred and ten thousand podships, with the remainder assigned to the most crucial web caretaking duties.

Noah saw Eshaz speed by, his face on the prow of a vessel he was piloting. Then Noah recognized *Webdancer* with only its normal Aopoddae look, meaning that Tesh was in the sectoid chamber, guiding the vessel in her Parvii way. In view of what she had told him about her pregnancy, he wished she would discontinue her dangerous military duties, at least until the baby was born.

She wouldn't, though. He'd tried to convince her himself, and had even asked others to make the effort. They'd all come back with the same answer: An adamant *no*. Her voice filled with emotion, she had told Noah and Anton that the whole cause of the Liberators was at risk, not just one fetus. And it was hard to argue with her. She was one of the very best pilots, and her skills were needed for the upcoming attack against the HibAdus in the Kandor Sector, the most important battle that Humans, Mutatis, or Tulyans had ever fought.

The combined Liberator force needed to commit every available resource to the fight—and they needed to attack as soon as possible—before the HibAdu Coalition could produce too many more laboratory-bred warships. But against the immense military power the enemy already had, no one knew if victory was achievable.

The Liberator leaders only knew that they had to make the monumental effort.

* * * * *

Taking a break from war maneuvers, Tesh stood in the passenger compartment of *Webdancer*, looking out on a series of scaled-down comet attacks that the Tulyans were using to destroy large holo-simulations of enemy warships that the Liberators were projecting into space. The projections moved in a variety of attack formations, so that the Tulyans had to constantly adapt and adjust. In other maneuvers nearby, General Nirella led armed podships in simulated battles. Later in the day there would be joint operations, involving Liberator and Tulyan forces against the theoretical enemy.

Tesh had noticed that *Webdancer* was even larger than before, with more interior chambers, as the intelligent podship had sensed that even more space and amenities were needed to accommodate its use as a flagship. Moments before, she and Anton had been engaged in an uncomfortable conversation. A year ago they had been lovers, but both of them knew that could never happen again, and neither of them wanted to resume the old relationship. They had taken alternate paths, had new loves in their lives. But the conversation had still slipped back to some of the old times they had enjoyed together, and there had been moments of awkward silence in which each of them remembered, but said little. Now Anton was getting coffee from a wall-mounted machine.

He returned and handed her a cup of the naturally white, Huluvian beverage. "Thanks," she said.

Their conversation shifted to the war maneuvers outside, and Anton said, "Look at the way the podships move gracefully through space. They're so smooth and fast. I often wonder what it would be like to have a conversation with one of them."

"I've wondered the same thing," she said, "even though every Parvii knows it is an impossibility. For millions of years our race was linked to them, and yet it seems like we never truly understood them—at least not beyond a surface comprehension of us as the master and the Aopoddae as our servants. Podships were just there, and we guided them on regular routes, from star system to star system. I doubt if even the Eye of Swarm ever really knew in a deep sense what it was all about. He only did what his predecessors had always done under our dominion, and the whole system continued."

"Until now."

"Yes, until now. I think it's right for my people to give up the podships, but the galaxy is in such chaos. If I can contribute to the Liberator cause—just one Parvii woman—I'll bet there are others of my race who would be willing to help as well. If only Woldn would release them from his hold."

"That will never happen. You were lucky to get away."

Tesh held the cup under her nose, and inhaled the warm, aromatic steam. She sipped. This was good, imported coffee that the Liberators had obtained, the only coffee she'd ever found that actually tasted as good as it smelled.

"You know," Tesh said, "watching these podships, I'm reminded of something Noah said to me once, about the poetry of the name *Webdancer*. He said it evokes romantic images of all the Aopoddae—that they're all webdancers, negotiating the slender, delicate strands of the galactic infrastructure."

"Yes, it is like that, isn't it?"

"But any one of the podships—or many more of them in a mass catastrophe—can fall off the damaged webbing and tumble into oblivion. It's like dancing on the edge of a sword, as they used to say on Lost Earth."

He thought for a moment, and nodded. "Exhilarating life on one side of the blade, death on the other."

* * * * *

Noah heard Thinker nearby, whirring as he processed data. In order to intensify his focus he had folded himself shut … and had been that way for almost half an hour now.

Noah considered tapping on the robot's flat metal body to ask him a question, but reconsidered. He didn't want to interrupt the mechanical genius in the midst of a critical analysis.

Presently, Thinker opened, with a soft click of metal parts as they shifted and locked into new positions.

"Anything?" Noah asked.

"I think I've gotten what I can, and that's only what I told you before. The armored memory core remains impenetrable. I've tried everything possible. It just won't open for me."

"For you. But what about for me? Can you link me to the core and allow my mind to probe, and enter it?"

Hesitation, and whirring. Then: "The Aopoddae trust you more than before, but not completely. I don't think they entirely trust me, either, perhaps because I am not biological, or perhaps due to my connection to you. I'm afraid if we get too aggressive trying to obtain the information, the data will go into permanent lockdown."

"Originally, the Aopoddae let the data flow into my brain," Noah said. "I think you need to give it back to me."

"The overload could kill you."

"How much data is in the armored memory core?"

"I can only estimate. Based on bulk storage space, I think it's around fifteen percent of the whole."

"Can you transfer the armored core to me? Only that, and no more?"

"I think so. But the data count could be exponentially greater than I estimated, if they compressed it. If you find a way of opening it, the surge could be too much for you to handle."

"We live in dangerous times," Noah said. "I want you to do it. And then erase the armored core from your own data banks."

"Are you sure?"

"We want them to trust us, don't we? I need to be vulnerable to them."

"And the rest of their data?"

"Keep it, for now. Let's prioritize this, and try it in increments. If I open the armored core, and the Aopoddae fully trust us, maybe I can download it back to you, unencrypted."

"You make it sound so easy."

"I always try to be optimistic," Noah said, with a wry smile.

The organic interface snaked out of Thinker's body. Just before it connected to Noah's skull, he closed his eyes. He felt the powerful inflow of raw data, filling the cells and synapses of his brain. The process took more than a minute, and during that time, he saw only images of blackness. No color or light at all. It occurred to Noah that he might reach out into Timeweb and perhaps escape the terror he was feeling, the stygian darkness. But that could interrupt the flow and damage the information. So he remained focused and motionless, a cup to be filled.

"It is finished," Thinker finally announced. "And irretrievably erased from my own data systems."

Opening his eyes, Noah didn't feel any different.

In the past, he had been able to stretch his mind across the cosmos, taking fantastic journeys through space. Now he tried to do the opposite, and probed inward, looking for the armored core and the key that would open its door.

But nothing happened.

Chapter Sixty-Six

There is one certainty to military combat:
Wars, and the battles that comprise them, never go entirely as planned.

—General Nirella del Velli

Later in the day Noah paced nervously inside the shuttle, refusing to take a seat beside Tesh. She had just brought him a message from Doge Anton.

"He didn't say what he wants?" The podman passed a gray-skinned hand over the reddish lump of skin on top of his head, as if he actually had hair there to smooth out. As usual, he felt weaker away from the cocoon, but he kept pacing anyway, trying not to reach out and grab anything for balance. For the most part he was successful in this regard, so perhaps it was a learning experience.

Tesh pursed her lips. She sat near Thinker, who had bent his own flat body to fit onto one of the benches—something he did on occasion to test his working parts, or to act like a biological person. "No," she said, "but I suspect it's important. He is the Doge, after all, and we're about to head off into battle."

"He's probably wondering where I fit in. I sent him a message yesterday, telling him I should remain here at the starcloud. My interests—and talents—are more akin to those of the Tulyans and their web restoration work, instead of open warfare. The cocoon is almost entirely composed of unarmed caretaker podships. They're useless in combat. I had to turn tail and run from battle." Grimacing, Noah added, "I hated doing that. I wanted to fight, wanted to blow the HibAdus out of space. But I didn't have any way to do it."

"Maybe Anton has some way of arming the cocoon," she said. "I heard him and Nirella speculating about that, wondering if it could be turned into a battle station."

"That would just make it a bigger target."

"Perhaps you're right."

* * * * *

As Noah stepped off the shuttle onto the flagship, he was greeted by Subi Danvar. "Right this way, Master," he said. "Anton is waiting for you in his private office." Looking at Thinker and Tesh, he added, "He wants to see Noah alone."

Following the rotund adjutant through the main corridor of the vessel, Noah was struck by how much larger the ship was now, with many more rooms and side corridors than before. Even though he had psychically guided the cocoon to make changes to the space station—and the massed Aopoddae had cooperated with him—he still didn't understand how they did it.

But he thought he understood *why*. Though their motives were not as easy to figure out as those of other races, Noah thought the podships were acting to protect and enhance the integrity of the galaxy. It had nothing to do with politics or personalities, and everything to do with galactic ecology. He believed now that he had been born with the destiny to be one of the leaders of this cause, and that destiny had guided him along a path that led him to this very place. Whether destiny translated into connecting him with a higher sentient power, he was not certain, and he thought he might never determine that answer. As far as he knew, destiny just existed … it was an element to the cosmos that kept things going. It could not be ignored, or eluded.

And if Anton wanted to turn EcoStation into a battle station, Noah could try to help in the effort. He wasn't afraid of combat himself, and wanted to do everything possible to advance the Liberator cause. But the podships had their own collective mind, and might not cooperate.

"Right through there, sir," Subi said, pointing to an open doorway.

Noah continued on his own, with his mind racing, wondering. Maybe the Liberator commanders wanted the cocoon podships back as individual craft, to arm them separately and send them into battle.

Yes, that could be it, he thought. *They think I've been dithering, getting in the way of the war effort.* But his instincts told him that he needed to do everything possible to protect the integrity of the cocoon, and that it should never revert to its former parts.

"Noah!" Anton said. The young doge bounded across his office and gave him a hearty handshake. Then he stood back and assessed Noah's gray skin, streaked in black. "I've heard about your metamorphosis, of course, and VR images have been brought to me, but seeing you in person is quite different."

"VR images?"

"Yes. Thinker said you wouldn't mind." Anton held onto Noah's rough-skinned right hand, then released it.

"No, I suppose I don't. He does work for you and for me. Look, I think I know what this is about, why you called me here." Noah took a seat across from the desk, while Anton slipped into his own chair.

"You know, eh?" To Noah's surprise, the mustachioed merchant prince looked amused, not nearly as tense as he might be before the upcoming military adventure.

"You're wondering where I fit in, and how I can contribute to the war effort."

"Oh, you've already contributed far beyond the call of duty, Uncle Noah."

"You don't think I've been wasting my time in the cocoon?"

Anton laughed. "In this galaxy, with all the strange events that are occurring? Are you kidding? I say, if you can figure the Aopoddae out, it will help all of us. Maybe you're in there generating a super weapon, for all I know."

"If I were doing that, Thinker would have told you."

"Ah, but you are on a different plane from the rest of us, Noah. You can accomplish things no one else can imagine. I'm sure you could conceal things from the robot."

"Not from his organic probe, though. It's his form of the truthing touch. No, I don't have a super weapon in the cocoon. I wish I did, but I don't."

"Well, wishes do come true. Keep wishing, and maybe it will happen. We could sure use more firepower. But that is not why I asked you to come here."

Anton fiddled with a pen, spinning it around on the desktop. Then he continued. "I'm intrigued by the way you got from Yaree to the Tulyan Starcloud." He snapped his fingers. "Even with all of the web damage, you made the journey just like that. But how?"

"Some of the podships in my cocoon are among the oldest in the galaxy, and they know alternate routes, shortcuts across space."

"I'm aware of the alternate routes Diminian found, and which his pilot showed to us—dropping travel time to a matter of minutes, going around damaged web sections. But you accomplished something even faster, didn't you? Noah, you just visualized the starcloud, right? And the cocoon went there immediately?"

"That's about right."

"Can you show the rest of the fleet how to do that? Speed is always an asset in warfare, and I want every advantage we can get."

"I don't know exactly how it works, but I'm sure the podships do—the cocoon. My connection with the Aopoddae seems to be a work in progress, but I could give it a try." He didn't mention the unopened, armored core of data in his brain, knew Thinker would reveal its existence anyway, if he hadn't done so already.

"All right. Let's run some preliminary tests. You get in the cocoon and see if you can get it to lead the others. Think of guerrilla warfare, on a scale never before seen. Ideally, I'd like to have my whole fleet appear out of nowhere, attack the HibAdus, and then disappear. We could then keep hitting them from different angles, and vanishing before they could mount an attack. No matter how big their entire force is, we could whittle it down, hopefully faster than they can reproduce lab-pods."

"Sounds good to me."

The two of them worked out more details. Then Noah rose to his feet and bowed to his nephew.

"Please," Anton said, coming around the desk and shaking Noah's hand again. "Only do that when someone is looking. Here, we are family. More than that, we are friends."

"In what seems like a prior lifetime, I had a similar arrangement with my adjutant, Subi. He was not allowed to insult me in front of others. Only in private."

"We shall do that, too," Anton said, as he accompanied Noah to the door. "Private insults, only."

"You're in a surprisingly chipper mood," Noah said.

"Because I think we're going to win." The young doge paused, and grinned. "In fact, I *visualized* it."

* * * * *

The next morning the combined fleet was ready to go into battle, with the exception of one final detail.

Noah and Thinker strode into what had once been the Grand Ballroom of Lorenzo's Pleasure Palace, a chamber that Noah had transformed into an auditorium for his future School of Galactic Ecology.

"I might as well try it from here as anywhere else," Noah said, as they walked up the steps to the central platform. "Let's see what sort of a magic show we can put on."

"Very well," Thinker said. "I shall be your audience." He went back down the stairs and bent his metal body, so that he could sit in one of the front-row seats.

"You and the whole fleet. All right, here goes."

Kneeling on the floor, Noah pressed the palms of both hands against the podship flesh that covered everything, like a blanket of gray, black-streaked snow.

He and Doge Anton had agreed on galactic destinations, so Noah visualized Yaree, where they had won their battle against the HibAdus. It seemed like a safe destination now, where the Liberators had joint defensive operations with the Yareens. Hours ago, Anton had dispatched courier ships there (and to Canopa and Siriki) to notify them of last-minute war maneuvers that could take place in their vicinities.

Feeling a link to Timeweb, Noah saw far across space to the Yareen star system and its central planet, framed against the faint green filigree of the cosmic web. Simultaneously, he expanded his far-reaching eye, so that he also saw where he was now, just outside the Tulyan Starcloud with the Liberator fleet. And, just as he was expanding outward, so too did he delve deep into his own psyche and to the linkage he shared with the cocoon.

Show them the way, Noah thought, wondering if the secret of nearly instantaneous travel lay inside the armored core of data that Thinker had passed on to him. *We lead, and they will follow.*

A burst of green light filled his consciousness, and he felt the slightest sensation of movement. Looking again, Noah saw that EcoStation was now in a geostationary orbit over the blue-green planet Yaree, and thousands of armed podships were with him.

Then he noticed that it was not the entire Liberator fleet, but still a significant portion of it, around forty-five thousand ships. Less than half of the total. *Webdancer* was with him, and other familiar podships. The older ones, mostly, including Diminian. Many of the younger Aopoddae had not made the journey, and seemed confused back where they had been left. But a large number of older podships remained behind with them as well.

Noah made the effort again. This time, he visualized returning to the rest of the fleet, and in a matter of moments he made the leap across space. Then, assessing the results, he saw that all of the ships that had gone to Yaree had returned with him.

Next, he visualized Siriki, and after that, Canopa. With each gigantic leap across space, a handful of the younger podships figured out how to do it, and joined the pack. The majority of them, however, were having difficulty learning the method, and some of the older Aopoddae didn't even seem to make the effort. A number of the younger ships got lost for awhile, and had to find their way back to the original jump-off point. A handful were still out there in space, and had not been accounted for....

Finally, retrieving the rest of the fleet and bringing it back to the Tulyan Starcloud, Anton and Noah had another meeting in the Doge's flagship office.

"Mixed results," Noah said. "With time, we might make it work, but I know what you're thinking. We don't have time."

Anton scowled. "We can do the guerrilla attacks with forty percent of the fleet, but my generals—who were initially supportive—are now saying that we should hit the HibAdus with everything we've got, the whole fleet. Our best Tulyan scouts say it will take two hours to get to the Kandor Sector the conventional way, due to rough podways and no good shortcuts of any kind."

"To me, it still makes sense to hit them with guerrilla attacks. Even forty percent is still a lot of ships, a lot of firepower."

"My generals say otherwise. If we don't reduce the number of enemy ships fast enough, they're afraid the HibAdus can dramatically increase the manufacture of lab-pods in response, and overwhelm us. We have the intelligence reports, and we're going back to Plan A, what we've been building up for all along. I just had a wild idea that something else might work."

719

"It was worth trying. All right, think of it this way. The exercises were not wasted. If we get in a jam, we can still evacuate much of the fleet."

"And leave the rest to be slaughtered?"

"No, many of the other podships could still break away into space and join up with us again. Think of me as an escape hatch, a desperation plan to be used only in the event of a dire emergency, if all seems to be lost."

"All right. I'll set that up as a last resort. But we need to be in close contact all through the battle. We'll take the two-hour route to Kandor, and I want you at the rear of the fleet with my own division. We'll have redundant communication to stay in touch with you—comlink and Tulyan webtalkers."

* * * * *

Supreme General Nirella del Velli—commanding the combined Liberator fleet—divided into four divisions—Andromeda, Borealis, Corona, and Parais. The latter three, all smaller than the core Andromeda Division, went out to holding positions just outside the Kandor Sector, while the core division took up a position at the rear, with Doge Anton and Noah. Most of the Mutati fighters and support equipment were with Hari'Adab in the Parais Division, inspired by the brave aeromutati who still clung to life on Siriki.

Then, from those three forward divisions, twenty-one scout ships were dispatched into regions that were near the last-reported position of the main body of the HibAdu fleet—but not so close that the scouts would be detected. It required twenty-one of the best Tulyan pilots, and—through wartime testing procedures—it was determined that one of them was Eshaz, who had been assigned to the Borealis Division.

Having received a different assignment from that of his cousin, Dux Hannah was aboard Eshaz's scout ship, which separated from the other scouts and sped through space alone. Their craft entered the Vindi Lightway, an atmosphere-encased asteroid belt that was illuminated by miniature suns, each of them looking like a small, bright moon. Taking different routes, the other scout ships, were probing different areas near the Kandor Sector.

Onboard the cocoon, Noah went into a deep "timetrance," a term he had developed for particularly vivid journeys into Timeweb. Though he had not anticipated this, he now found himself able to see through the eyes of the distant scout podships—and he saw the Kandor Sector, a region of nebulas and blue stars visible in the distance.

Concentrating as the scouts closed in, taking carefully developed routes, Noah was able to magnify the images seen by the podships. The planets and suns came into focus, and—beyond a veil of nebula dust—he saw a multi-level armada of lab-pods so immense that it looked like a huge dead sun.

But there were blind spots now. Previously he had been able to peer inside some of the pseudo podships in the HibAdu force, and he had seen Hibbils operating navigations units inside them, and soldiers in the cargo holds. The enemy might have found a way to veil the interiors from him since then, or web conditions were preventing the reach of his mind into the enemy vessels. He also could not see through the eyes on the hulls of the lab-pods.

Noah wondered about the enemy ships, how similar they were to their natural cousins. The Tulyans had inspected two of them back at the starcloud, and had found startling cellular similarities—along with differences in the undercarriages that caused damage to podways when they traveled over them. The lab-pods also seemed to be substantially out of contact with natural podships—although the natural pods had shown slightly averse reactions when participating in attacks on their faux versions. Maybe this lack of contact had something to do with Noah's blind spots.

The armada was much larger than any of the figures he had heard. There must be more than a million armed lab-pods there! As he watched, the immense layered formation began to shift in eerie synchronization. Large sections broke away and spread outward in all directions. The maneuver was almost hypnotic. It looked choreographed, a dangerous thing of beauty.

Emerging from the trance, Noah transmitted an urgent warning to Doge Anton.

Chapter Sixty-Seven

Throughout military history, there have been instances of determined, inspired warriors winning the day, despite the immense odds against them. We hasten to add that such examples are quite rare. Overwhelming force usually prevails.

—Report to General Nirella, by officers
formerly in the Mutati High Command

The command bridge of the flagship was a buzz of activity, of robots and junior officers at their consoles and bustling from station to station, preparing for battle. Standing at the forward viewing area, Doge Anton stared tersely ahead, looking through a deep-space magnaviewer—one of several round units attached to the windowplax. Beside him, General Nirella did the same.

"I don't see anything yet," he said.

"We will," she said.

Moments ago, they had received urgent transmissions from their scout ships and from Noah. The HibAdu fleet was vastly larger than earlier intelligence reports had indicated, and it was in motion.

"Maybe they're only performing a practice maneuver," Anton suggested.

"Whatever they're doing, I don't like it."

"Do you think we should fall back and regroup?"

"Not yet. Hold on. Another transmission coming in from Noah." She adjusted her ear-set.

"I'm getting it, too, but it's filled with static."

Neither of them could understand what he was transmitting. Noah was in his cocoon at the rear of the main Andromeda Division, but despite the distance he had earlier reported getting a clear view of the enemy armada. Anton could not begin to understand the powers of his uncle. They seemed to change constantly, and Noah had often said himself that they were unpredictable. The young doge only knew that he trusted him completely, and so did every fighter in the Liberator force.

Anton motioned to a Tulyan, who was also in contact with Noah's cocoon via the specialized method of the reptilian race. On each end, experienced webtalkers in the Liberator fleet found creative ways to touch the cosmic web, and in turn they relayed messages to other Tulyans in the warships. Because of the relays and changing galactic conditions, it sometimes took a little longer than the military comlink system, but it was often more clear and reliable.

In his comlink ear-set, Anton began to hear sentence fragments from Noah. "HibAdu force ... shifting direction ... large portion is ... " The Doge couldn't get any more.

Moments later, a small Tulyan woman hurried over and said, "Noah reports that the bulk of the HibAdu force is heading toward us. Speed moderate but steady. Portions of the enemy fleet keep breaking off and then returning. Noah thinks they've spotted us."

Now Anton saw the armada, coming toward him like an immense cloud of interstellar dust, with sunlight glinting off portions of it. He sucked in a deep breath. "Do we stand and fight or regroup and save what we can for another day? Maybe we should reconsider guerrilla attacks. They're much larger than we thought anyway."

"We still have time to fall back on that," Nirella said. "All the podships that can follow Noah through galactic shortcuts are with us in the Andromeda Division. But first we need to probe our foe and see what his tactics are, how mobile he is, and how responsive he is to changes on the battlefield. Maybe we can discover a weakness, or force him into a mistake."

"I know," Anton said glumly. "We've gone over all this."

"Yes we have, and we have some tricks up our sleeve."

Anton didn't like the fact that his main division was comparatively safer than the other three portions of the fleet, with access to an escape hatch through space that they didn't have. But it made perfect military sense. Aside from the probing, the Liberators had a fallback position in Noah Watanabe, enabling them to survive and fight again. Anton and his generals had studied the options, and another consideration had come into play: Despite Noah's purported immortality, the military experts were concerned about risking him unnecessarily. He was extremely valuable, and had arcane powers that even he did not understand. He must be protected, and for now he seemed best suited to remain at the rear of the fleet.

Leaning over to study a console screen, Nirella said, "Spectral scanners report that some of the HibAdu activity is illusion, that not all of the ships breaking away from the main force are really doing that. Some of them are projections of warships, similar to the ones we use in war games."

"How much of the main force is real?"

"Unfortunately, more than half of it. You could override me, Anton, but I don't think we should retreat yet. Parais Division has their space mines ready to go, and with luck we'll get results from them. The HibAdus may have their tricks, but we have some of our own. They might even be operating under the false assumption that we didn't discover their sabotage attempt on our space artillery pieces, or other sabotage attempts we've found."

"Anton nodded. "The tiny computer chip that Hibbils made when we thought they were our allies. But are the HibAdus foolish enough to think we wouldn't go back and check all of those parts and replace them if necessary?"

"They might be overconfident. The Hibbils and Adurians had their secret coalition going for years undetected."

"I doubt if we've discovered all of their tricks."

"Agreed. But we still have some nasty surprises for them."

"All right, we stand and fight," Looking at the console, Doge Anton saw the Parais Division out in front of the others now, with the brave Mutatis in that force plunging into battle before anyone else—according to plan. Hari'Adab had wanted it that way.

* * * * *

Inside the enemy flagship, Ipsy watched from a place of concealment behind the main instrument console. He had rigged an ingenious method by which he could look around the command bridge unnoticed, using the various console screens as remote viewing windows.

Now he watched High Ruler Coreq hurrying back and forth from battle station to battle station, making sure his officers and technicians were doing what he had commanded. Coreq had set up the projected warships to make his force look even larger, and he was also coordinating the movements of the actual warships. At times the hideous hybrid would stand at the center of the bridge and wave his arms this way or that. In response, large sections of the armada would shift position. Moments ago, he had done that, drawing most of the divisions together into a central force.

"Beautiful!" he had exclaimed. "Perfect!" He was like a choreographer, setting things in motion around him.

Now, however, he stopped gesturing, and scowled. His oversized, pale yellow eyes looked around dangerously. Something was bothering him. He focused on a young Adurian officer, who had not yet brought up a battlefield report that Coreq had ordered.

With a sudden movement, Coreq hit the man so hard in the head that his skull broke open and fleshy pieces of his brain splattered on the console. "Clean this up and get me another officer!" the HibAdu leader screamed. Then he returned to his favored position at the center of the bridge.

The High Ruler extended his arms forward, bent the elbows outward, and joined the fingertips of both hands in a wide "vee" shape. The armada was moving forward in that formation, covering a broad swath of space with its invincible ships. To Ipsy, he seemed like a madman.

The industrious little robot had developed several plans of what he might do. As conditions developed, he had to select the proper moment, and take just the right measure. He was a choreographer, too, and everything needed to go perfectly. He couldn't wait too long, but couldn't move precipitously, either.

The HibAdus had taken measures to block Ipsy, or any other would-be saboteur, from tempering with the weapon-control box on this ship. The unit had been replaced, and had been sealed so that an intruder could no longer gain access to it without drawing attention to himself. As a consequence, whatever Ipsy did would have to be different from the last trick he pulled. But he still had options. His internal programs constantly reviewed them and perfected them.

Able to deactivate videocam and other security systems by transmitting electronic signals, Ipsy had used the privacy to make secret adjustments to the ship's systems that should prove interesting if he ever activated them. All the while, he left no trail that he had ever been there.

He had even made enhancements to his own mechanical body and brain—self-improvements, he called them. Thinking of this and all of his preparations, he smiled to himself, a feature of his internal programming that did not show on his metal face.

* * * * *

General Nirella sent Hari'Adab's force directly at the main body of the enemy fleet, and then readied the Borealis and Corona divisions to make flank attacks. Watching the action unfold, Doge Anton felt like an ancient military officer on a hill, observing a slaughter that was about to occur on the battlefield.

Moving from the magnaviewer to the console, he saw the inspired Parais Division surge forward—a force of thousands of armed podships that looked painfully small in comparison with the enemy. For the moment, the HibAdus seemed content to advance at a steady speed, drawing most of their force together.

"Why don't they divide up more?" he asked.

"They don't think they have to," Nirella said. "Look on the spectral scanner. They're not even using the holo-warships anymore. Now that they see what we have—less than a quarter of their armada—they think they can run over us like a juggernaut."

"I hope they're wrong."

"So do I."

Then Anton saw sunlight flash increasingly off the hulls of the advancing HibAdu force. The intensity increased dramatically, and became so bright that he had to look away.

"That ruse was old a long time ago," Nirella said. "We're ready for it."

* * * * *

At a gun station in the Parais Division, Acey Zelk saw the blinding flashes, and heard the sharp command of the Mutati officer on this level. "Solar mirrors," the shapeshifter said. "Fire on them the way we practiced."

Acey had trained for this, as had all of the other gunners onboard with him, at their stations along the hull of the podship. Firing away with long-range projectiles, he saw some of the shots hit their mark, opening dark spots in the enemy fleet. Other Liberator ships did the same, and had a similar effect.

"Good shooting, Acey," the officer shouted. "The rest of you, see if you can do as well as this young Human!"

Acey kept firing and hitting, while the target continued to draw closer and closer. He saw other podships in his division firing alternate weapons, space cannons with purple beams of light—heat rays. Many of those shots were slipping past the surprisingly tough solar mirrors, penetrating the hulls of some lab-pods and destroying them.

He heard the Mutati officer say that the Borealis and Corona divisions were also engaging the enemy, making flank attacks.

Following commands, Acey re-set his space cannon to fire heat rays. Now his shots, and those of his companions, penetrated deeper, causing more damage. But it all seemed like throwing pebbles at a hippophant. The monster just kept coming, knocking the debris of its own damaged ships out of the way.

* * * * *

Through his magnaviewer, Doge Anton del Velli saw the Borealis and Corona divisions draw together around the Parais Division. Then they reversed course en masse and sped back toward a holding position, with the immensely larger HibAdu armada still advancing toward the center, heading right for the Andromeda Division.

Glancing at the console, he saw the readings that confirmed what Kajor Bhaleen of the Mutati High Command had planned. As the Liberator divisions retreated, they cast thousands of electronically cloaked space mines behind them ... a Mutati trick.

"The HibAdus are speeding up," one of the junior officers shouted, "anticipating a big kill."

"Perfect," General Nirella said. "That will make our stingers hurt more."

Moments later, space lit up in a series of multicolored explosions. Unable to reverse direction in time, a considerable portion of the HibAdu fleet blew up. In close formation, many ships that were not hit by the mines crashed into the others, and were themselves destroyed.

A chain reaction of demolition surged through the front of the HibAdu armada. Finally, the bulk of the force was able to turn around and go back in the other direction.

Anton saw them regrouping, splitting up into new attack formations. "I'm afraid we only made them mad," he said.

"They know we mean business, though," Nirella said. "It will make them more cautious."

For the next phase of the battle, she ordered the Parais, Borealis, and Corona divisions to protect the exposed perimeters of the Andromeda Division. Then she directed thousands of podships filled with Tulyan caretakers to fan out from the Liberator fleet, for yet another tactic. Upon first hearing about this idea, the Council of Elders had been somewhat resistant, but eventually they had come around to seeing the wisdom of it.

Using their arcane methods, the Tulyan web technicians were changing conditions on the battlefield in ways that the HibAdus and their artificial podships might not detect—tearing up the webbing, or making it look strong when it really wasn't. This was a calculated risk, as the Liberators hoped they could later restore what they had damaged.

In only a few minutes, the Tulyans completed their work and returned to share details of what they had done with the commanders. With this information, technicians were quickly preparing a new map of the battlefield. The potential points of ship-to-ship engagement would go out in great arcs in several directions from the Liberators, while leaving better escape routes to the rear.

General Nirella smiled, displaying a confidence that Anton did not share. "That should slow 'em down and enable us to customize new attacks," she said.

"I hope it works," Anton said, "but I told Noah to be ready in case it doesn't."

Chapter Sixty-Eight

Liberators.
We're not just about rescuing Human and Mutati worlds.
We intend to rescue the whole galaxy.

—Master Noah Watanabe

High Ruler Coreq had decided to get his hands dirty. Now he sat in the pilot's chair of his immense flagship, operating the touch-pad controls while the actual pilot sat next to him, giving technical advice. With a laboratory-enhanced brain, Coreq was a fast learner, and operating this lab-pod seemed easy to him. Though he looked to be of an adult age, the hybrid was barely fifteen years old, having been grown in an Adurian laboratory. That didn't mean he was emotionally or intellectually immature. Far from it. The scientists had done a terrific job on him.

Speeding the flagship from one area of the fleet to another, he satisfied himself that his warships had regrouped into the new attack formations he had specified. Earlier he had done this with arm gestures from the command bridge, which in turn transmitted electronic signals, but he had decided on impulse to handle the flagship controls himself for a while. At just the right moment, his forces would divide and hurdle themselves at the opposing forces from multiple directions, using a variety of methods and a panoply of weapons.

He didn't like staying back on the Adurian homeworld, wanted to go out and destroy the enemy himself. He'd been at the vanguard of the coordinated assaults on Human and Mutati planets. Great victories—but as yet incomplete. Two Human-ruled worlds remained stubbornly outside the HibAdu empire, along with a number of upstart independent worlds, the foremost of which was Yaree. Against all odds, Humans and Mutatis were allies now, and were working with the Tulyans, and even a number of other races in lesser roles. Calling themselves "Liberators," they had more than a hundred thousand natural podships that were armed—a formidable fleet, but one that should be no match for his own. Those enemy ships were among the spoils of war that he wanted to save, at least as many as possible.

His triumvirate companions—Premier Enver and Warlord Tarix—did not have his hands-on, adventurous spirit, so they had remained back on the Adurian homeworld, making themselves look busy supervising the bureaucracy. Coreq thought it was a particular fallacy that Tarix called herself a warlord. The extent of her violent acts were confined to police activities on Adurian- and Hibbil-controlled planets. Coreq, on the other hand, was reaching for the stars. That was the stated purpose of the HibAdu Coalition, after all: Conquer all Human and Mutati worlds, and then the rest of the galaxy. Annihilate all enemies.

But getting his hands dirty was one thing. Getting them slapped was quite another.

So far, the Liberators had put up a surprisingly strong resistance. He had not really expected the sabotaged firing mechanisms to still be in place on the Liberator warships, even though the tactic had worked fabulously in the initial surprise attacks against hundreds of enemy planets. As anticipated, the enemy had figured this out afterward, and had replaced the Hibbil computer chips. Those space mines, however, had come as a complete surprise, not showing up on any scanners or signal probes. And he wasn't sure what all those Liberator ships had been doing afterward around the Liberator fleet—thousands of enemy vessels that advanced and fanned out, but for only a few minutes. What had they been doing out there? Trying to lure HibAdu forces forward into another minefield? That was the assessment of his top Adurian commander, Admiral Silisk, and of other officers. Coreq, however, was not so sure. He doubted if they would try a similar tactic two times in a row.

Already his scanning technicians said they could now detect all space mines—they had proven this by spotting several that had not been detonated, and reconfiguring their detection equipment. Leaving the pilot to control the flagship, Coreq went to a forward window, where he could get a good view through a magnaviewer. There, he watched as squadrons of his own ships went out in forays, scouting the battlefield ahead, seeing what the enemy had been up to. Oddly, his scout squadrons began going in erratic flight patterns. Some crashed into each other, and others seemed to disappear in green flashes. He scowled, trying to figure out what was going on.

Opening all emergency channels, Coreq heard the panicked reports of Hibbil and Adurian pilots.

"Podways damaged! Can't see where we are on any of our instruments. Flying blind out here."

"Lost an entire squadron! They just disappeared!"

"Can't stay on course!"

Then a Hibbil came on, sounding more calm over the powerful, secure channel. "As directed, I took my squad around behind the enemy fleet, several parsecs on the other side. Now we're heading back toward them, with their force just now becoming visible on instruments." He grew more excited. "They've spotted us! Only a few seconds before they attack. A few rough spots on the podways, but typical of what we've seen elsewhere. Infrastructure much better here."

The transmission fizzled out, but Coreq had learned something valuable. His clever foe had left open an escape route at their rear—and probably more than one—bolt holes into space. Quickly, he ordered his fleet to go around. In a matter of seconds, they split space in green flashes. Then, reforming into attack groups, they surged back toward the Liberator force from a different direction.

* * * * *

The redeployment of the immense HibAdu fleet occurred very quickly. Alarmed, Ipsy watched from his hiding place, while his internal programs absorbed battlefield data, and he recalculated the courses of action that he might take. He wanted to inflict the maximum possible harm on the enemy.

Only a short while ago, he had been heartened by the successes of the Liberator fleet. Now the tide of battle seemed to be changing the other way.

Unless the Liberators were setting a trap. He hoped that was the case, but all indications said otherwise.

* * * * *

Watching everything from his paranormal viewing platform, Noah sent comlink and webtalker warnings to Doge Anton and General Nirella.

Responding right away over the comlink, Nirella said, "We see what they're doing. What about our escape contingency?"

Having emerged from the timetrance to await a response, Noah said, "No longer available. I can't visualize any destination beyond this sector. With their huge force the enemy is sweeping space behind us, covering every available podway. The Tulyan researchers said they use a combination of instruments and artificial podship methods to determine where the podways are. Now they have forces stationed on each of them, more than enough to keep us from escaping."

"Can't we knock them out of the way? We can send more than a hundred thousand podships on any one route."

They have tens of thousands of heavily armed ships stationed on each route. It would be suicide for us to slam into all those warships, with the bombs and other munitions involved."

"But space is vast. There must be other escape routes!"

"From here, the routes are few, and the HibAdus have found all of them."

"Then we've painted ourselves into a corner," Nirella said.

"I'm afraid so."

Dipping back into Timeweb, Noah noticed something more: Dark little spots all over the hulls of the Liberator vessels. Several of the spots flickered, then grew dark again. But Noah had seen what they were: Parviis.

The tiny humanoids seemed to be camouflaging themselves with their projection mechanisms. But why weren't they flying in a swarm and firing telepathic weapons? He answered his own question almost before it passed through his mind.

Attacking en masse had not worked—some problem with their firepower that the Tulyans had noticed. Taking a different tack, the Parviis were going to focus on individual podships in the Liberator fleet, trying to gain entrance and control any way they could. In the alternate realm, Noah saw more and more of the tiny dark spots appear, until space was thick with them around the Aopoddae ships.

When he reemerged, Noah saw his webtalker already engaged in urgent communication with her fellow Tulyans, all of whom had sensed the presence of their mortal enemies.

Chapter Sixty-Nine

Life, in all of its forms, is ultimately about control. This is linked to survival and to the perception that particular life forms cannot live in harmony, and must take all available resources for themselves. But wars and other forms of mass destruction often rise directly from survival perceptions that are not accurate. We do not need to wipe out other races or life forms to survive. In fact, it is in our interest as Humans not to do that, and to harmonize with other galactic peoples.

—Master Noah Watanabe, from one of his early essays

Over the communication links, Noah heard the desperation of the Liberator officers and soldiers, and of the Tulyan caretakers. And through his supernatural link to Timeweb, he saw the changing currents of the battle, with the HibAdus gaining an overwhelmingly superior position. They had cleverly cut off all routes of conventional escape for the Liberator fleet, and were now moving in for the kill. Increasingly confident, the enemy armada was gaining speed. All the while, Parviis continued to mass on the hulls of Doge Anton's podships, and were using neurotoxins and other methods to gain entrance. So far Tulyans were using their own methods to keep them at bay, but more and more Parviis kept arriving and joining the others.

Beside him on the central platform of the auditorium, Thinker whirred noisily, and said, "I have searched for all possibilities, but there are no good choices."

Noah didn't respond, He felt like a man on the edge of a precipice, and if he fell off everyone he cared about would tumble off with him. Dreams would crash with him.

His mind raced at frantic speed, and he thought of the armored memory core Thinker had transferred back to him. The heavily encrypted Aopoddae information lay somewhere in Noah's brain, hiding inside the cells and synapses, waiting to be released.

For the Master of the Guardians, it was like knowing something, and not knowing it at the same instant. The information was there at his fingertips, and around him in the cocoon. But he could not utilize it. Previously, he had touched the podship flesh and had caused it to reshape the space station. Several times he had commanded the cocoon to fly through space, and it had cooperated.

Essential information was locked away in the protected core of data that Thinker had found, and Noah needed the key to open it. Why were the Aopoddae making it so difficult?

Thinking back, he recalled that he had used his own arcane powers to heal wounded podship flesh, and had received a tremendous inflow of data from the sentient spacecraft. It was as if they wanted him to have the information—

whatever it was—but first they had to make sure he was qualified to receive it, and that he would not use it for the wrong purposes. The Aopoddae had only given him *access* to the critical information. He still had to prove he was worthy of it. How could he do that?

A chill ran down his spine, as it occurred to him that the secret of a powerful weapon might be what was inside the armored core of data. Doge Anton had suggested that Noah might be surreptitiously generating a super weapon inside the cocoon. Noah had dismissed it as an idle comment, but what if the idea had an element of merit? What if the amalgamated podships could generate a powerful destructive force?

If it was a weapon inside the armored data core, that would explain why the sentient spacecraft were not sure if he should receive it. Even now, facing their own destruction, they could be hesitating. Had the Aopoddae looked into his soul for his motives, and if so, what had they seen there? His demented twin sister, Francella?

Precious seconds ticked by.

Taking a deep breath, Noah touched a thick section of flesh on the outer wall. It was soft and almost liquid beneath his fingertips. As before, he let go, and the flesh oozed down onto the deck and flowed over the floor. This time, however, instead of flowing across the room, it pooled around him and rose up around his ankles. The alien material was warm and wet against his own skin.

Noah felt like screaming in terror. It had very little to do with fear for his own personal safety. He had survived so much, had been through so many harrowing experiences, that he didn't worry about such things much anymore—except he didn't want his followers to lose their inspiration, their guiding light. And beyond that, Noah didn't want to be lured into a place from which he could not escape, or used by some diabolical outside entity for its own purposes.

So far he felt as if he could go back, that he could reverse the process and step away from the advancing cocoon flesh. But the sentient stuff was probing around the skin inside his shoes and socks and on his ankles, delving into his cellular structure, seeking to flow further upward on his body. If he allowed that to occur, could he still go back? And did he really want to go through this, to achieve an indeterminate *destructive* power?

Noah sensed that he was subconsciously trying to talk himself out of going further. He had always been a person who followed his instincts, so he asked himself some hard questions now: Did he really sense danger if he proceeded? What was his gut telling him?

This time, when he needed it most, his viscera didn't send him any signals at all. He found this troubling, because it suggested that he was losing contact with an important aspect of his own humanity, a means of perception and survival that had always worked well for him in the past.

Noah tried to command the cocoon to open the fortified data core, and to show him what was inside. But nothing happened, other than a flurry of agitation in the ancient, linked minds of the creatures.

He knew the HibAdus could attack at any moment. The immensity and immediacy of this threat loomed over all others. For the moment, the Parviis were secondary, and even the crumbling galaxy. If the armada got through, it would be the end of the Liberator force.

Suddenly he heard a booming voice over the comlink, overriding other conversations. "This is High Ruler Coreq. You have ninety seconds to surrender, or we will annihilate you."

* * * * *

After listening to Coreq's announcement from his hiding place, Ipsy heard a loud buzzing noise, and looked up. The confined space where he'd been hiding was filling with tiny, droning machines, like a swarm of insects.

"Intruder alert," a voice said. It was an eerie, synchronized voice, emitted by speakers on the bodies of the flying biomachines. Ipsy's programs accelerated as he tried to find a way out.

Suddenly there was a loud clatter, and strong hands pulled the little robot out from behind the instrument console. Two Adurian soldiers dragged him to the center of the command bridge, where the High Ruler stood, waiting.

"How did you get in there?" Coreq said. He interlaced the fingers of his small, furry hands, then pulled them apart, then interlaced them again. A nervous mannerism, it appeared.

"Manufacturing defect," Ipsy said. "The stupid Hibbils left me in there. I only recently came back to awareness, and wondered what I was doing on your ship. Those Hibbils can't do anything right."

"He's lying," the biomachines said, in their eerie synchronization.

"Yes I am," Ipsy said. "And you just narrowed my options down to one."

He saw the look of alarm in Coreq's bulbous, pale yellow eyes. But before the freak could move or issue a command, Ipsy transmitted a chain-reaction detonation program he had set up, electronic signals that surged into the vessel's operating systems.

"Get him!" Coreq screamed. But it was too late.

"Now you're going to die," Ipsy said in a matter of fact tone. He felt a wonderful sensation of internal warmth come over him as his circuits heated up, and then set off the explosive charges. Only a limited detonation to start with, killing everyone on the command bridge, and keeping his own artificial consciousness alive, in the enclosure he had armored for it.

He heard a piercing scream that filled the flagship and surrounding space. It was Coreq, dying.

Moments later, the flagship blew up in a fireball that took two nearby vessels with it, and damaged twenty other lab-pods, causing them to drop out of formation. In the midst of the HibAdu armada, the event was hardly noticed by Liberator observers. To them, it looked like a relatively minor problem with the fleet, so inconsequential that it had no effect on the massive force. The armada kept going forward, past the floating debris.

* * * * *

"Data projection," Thinker said. "The HibAdus would prefer not to destroy our fleet of natural podships, since they are superior to his in numerous ways. But his priority is complete military victory, and there are always some wild podships to be captured in space. His deadline is not a bluff."

Taking a deep, shuddering breath, Noah let go and the warm cellular material ran up his legs and thighs and waist, over the clothing and beneath it, covering him entirely up to his midsection. He felt a flood of data from the podship cocoon, flowing into his brain.

"Master Noah," Thinker said, "are you sure this is wise?"

"I'm beyond going back," Noah said.

Reaching down with his left hand, he immersed it in the thick fluid and felt it congeal around his Human bone structure. He immersed the other hand, and then let the malleable flesh rise over his torso, up to his neck.

Noah felt compression on his chest, making it difficult for him to breathe. He took deep, gasping breaths.

"Master Noah, are you all right?"

Without answering, Noah slid down into the flesh and flowed with it into the outer wall, where he began to swim. Behind him, he heard Thinker's voice, but fading. Time and space seemed to disappear. Noah was in his own universe, swimming across vast distances of starless space.

In moments, he stood again. This time he was inside a new and combined sectoid chamber, glowing with an ancient green luminescence. He could move about freely inside the enclosure (which was at least five times larger than those of podships), and he felt confident that he could leave it if he wanted to do so. He was separate from the cocoon, but part of it at the same time. Just as every creature in the galaxy was linked, so too was he connected to this prehistoric life form that was both primitive and advanced.

He probed inward with his thoughts, seeking the information he so desperately needed. Then, in a wordless epiphany, he let go. Something this important did not depend on words, or even on an organized collection of data. The armored core that Thinker had been unable to access did not contain multiple bits of data.

It only contained *one*, and now Noah knew what it was, so simple and yet so complex.

Pressing his face against a wall of the sectoid chamber, he felt his own facial features enlarge and flow outward, so that he could be seen in bas-relief on the outside of the cocoon. But it was not a "man in the moon" appearance, and not like the reptilian faces that emerged from podship prows when Tulyans piloted them. Instead, Noah's countenance was repeated many times all around the cocoon, as if each podship had assumed his features on its body. Through his own humanoid eyes now, he looked in all directions: to the farthest reaches of the galaxy, to the Parviis trying to gain control of the Liberator fleet, and to the advancing HibAdu armada, which was much closer than before, with glowing weapons ports on the warships, ready to fire.

Noah felt power building around him. Paradoxically, the Aopoddae were a peaceful race, but he realized now that they had access to a weapon beyond the scope of any others, and finally they were allowing him to use it. Higher and higher the energy built up around Noah until EcoStation became a brilliant green sun in space. Parviis and Tulyans had their telepathic weapons that could wreak great destruction, but this was potentially much, much more.

His eyes glowed the brightest of all, and beams of light shot from them on the sides facing the HibAdu ships, bathing the enemy armada in a wash of green. Then the ships detonated, in tidal waves of destruction that went through the entire fleet in great surges, until it was gone.

As Noah drew back, he felt himself shuddering. He had tapped into a source of galactic energy that might even reach the core of the entire universe. It was raw, primal, and volcanic. It simmered in his consciousness, waiting to explode. He could fire the primal weapon at will. The raw violence was awesome, simultaneously thrilling and horrifying to him. Again, he thought of the Francella element in his blood, and he wondered if his mind would hold together through all of its expansions and contractions, or if he would go completely mad and start destroying in all directions.

But his doubts lasted only a few nanoseconds. With his brain running at hyper speed, he didn't have any more time to wonder about anything, or to worry. He only had time to respond.

Brian Herbert

Now he turned the powerful beams of light toward the Liberator fleet, where Parviis continued to scramble over the hulls of the ships, trying to get in. They were no longer veiling their appearances, and could be seen clearly as tiny humanoids. On the hulls of some vessels, Tulyan faces had disappeared, suggesting that the pilots had been overcome and Parviis had taken over. Increasingly he saw the reptilian prows diminish in number, and wherever this occurred, the ships moved away from the others and began to congregate. So far, this amounted to only a small portion of the fleet, perhaps five percent. But he could not allow it to continue.

Through his hyper-alert, organic connection to the cosmos, Noah figured out more possibilities than Thinker could ever imagine. He saw inside every podship in the Liberator fleet, to the individual battles for each craft, and to the mindlink that Tulyans were trying to use for their fellows, but which was much weaker away from the starcloud.

Remembering how he had originally lost the trust of podships because of his part in developing pod-killer guns for the merchant princes, Noah didn't want to destroy any podships. He had something else in mind.

Focusing the energy beams precisely and governing their power, he detonated them inside the bodies of the attacking Parviis. Tiny green explosions went off inside his consciousness, and he sensed the anguish of his victims, heard their collective screams. And, as moments passed, he saw Tulyan faces reappear on every hull in the fleet. Secure again, the breakaway ships drew back together with the others.

Intentionally, Noah allowed the Eye of the Swarm and a small number of his followers to escape. Noah had always believed that every galactic race, even the supposedly most heinous, had redeeming qualities. The Mutatis had proven that, and he knew and loved one of the Parviis himself. She would be the mother of his child. Their baby would look like a Parvii, but would be a hybrid, not the same as the originals.

I am not about extermination, he thought. Despite all of the changes in which he was immersed, Noah Watanabe remained true to his core values. A deep sensation of fatigue came over him from tapping into the raw primal power, but he fought to overcome it. From somewhere, a reservoir of strength, he summoned more energy.

Then, using his eyes like powerful searchlights to illuminate space, Noah scanned the vast expanse, questing. He sensed something else out there, more dangerous and destructive than HibAdus, Parviis, or even the crumbling galaxy.

Something he might not be able to stop....

Chapter Seventy

Battles are never static. Even when they seem to be over, the tide can change.
—General Nirella del Velli

During the surprise Parvii attack, Tesh had fought for control of the flagship, trying to keep her own people from gaining entrance to the vessel. It was a battle within a battle, as the clustering humanoids tried to use neurotoxins to subdue the podship, and other ancient methods. Even with thousands of their tiny bodies all over *Webdancer*'s hull, they had faced a formidable task. Just one Parvii—Tesh—inside the sectoid chamber of the

vessel could ward them all off, counteracting the toxins and keeping the Aopoddae creature under her sole control.

Then the equation had changed.

Woldn himself—the Eye of the Swarm—had joined the cluster on *Webdancer*. Tesh had sensed him out there, with his mind merging deeper into the others and dominating them more than ever. From his proximity and intense focus, powerful telepathic waves had slammed against Tesh's sectoid chamber, like psychic battering rams. She'd fought back valiantly, but moment by moment she had been losing ground as the neurotoxins began to take effect on *Webdancer* and—soon thereafter—on her. Finally, the eager Parviis had streamed through openings they made in the flesh, like carpenter bees boring into soft wood.

Woldn and a handful of others had entered the inside the sectoid chamber with her, pushing her barely conscious form aside so that one of them could take over. Helpless to resist, she'd only been able to watch.

The Eye of the Swarm had kicked her. "Traitor!" he said. "We'll show you what happens to traitors. But first, there is a battle to be won."

He had become the new pilot himself, and guided *Webdancer* away to join other breakaway ships.

Suddenly, the sectoid chamber had glowed bright green, an unnatural condition that prevented Woldn from guiding the craft. *Webdancer* began to go in circles and loops, veering off into space.

"Let's get out of here!" Woldn had exclaimed. "You too, Tesh."

With that, he had swooped her up in a telepathic surge that flowed out and away from the ship and the battle.

"We've lost!" Woldn had said.

Unable to resist, Tesh had flown with the small group that left *Webdancer*—a few thousand individuals—bound for an unknown destination. She'd been caught up in their momentum, which suspended her independence. Curiously, Woldn was having difficulty sending telepathic commands to other Parviis in the swarms that had attacked other ships. Some of those Parviis followed Woldn's small cluster, but others did not, and instead scattered into space in complete disarray.

Now as she flew on, Tesh absorbed psychic currents roiling from Woldn's anger and determination to keep fighting back against all obstacles. Seeking to regain the old glories of his race, he would regroup. He would never give up. Everyone in the mini-swarm knew it, and Tesh felt considerable sympathy for them—and even for Woldn. She had never liked turning against her own people, but under the circumstances there had been no other choice. They had been wrong.

Tesh sensed increased anger focused on her—not only from the Parvii leader, but from the others linked to him. If Woldn permitted it, they could kill her. But he had something else in mind for her. What? She could not tell. Gradually, she was able to fall back to the rear of the group where it was a little more comfortable for her. But she could not pull away entirely, and swept forward with her unwanted companions.

Behind her, Tesh sensed something coming fast. Before she could turn to look, it swept her up and absorbed her.

Webdancer!

The vessel had come of its own volition, taking Anton, Nirella, and others with it. Tesh found herself inside the sectoid chamber, and within moments she was piloting the ship back to join the rest of the victorious Liberator fleet.

* * * * *

But the elation did not last long.

The moment *Webdancer* pulled back to join the other podships, Eshaz flew near and asked for an emergency meeting. His request was granted, and the two podships nudged against each other and opened their hatches, so that Eshaz and two other Tulyans could enter.

Through her connection to the podship, Tesh listened as the Tulyans strode heavily through the corridors of *Webdancer* and entered Doge Anton's office. Tesh heard the voices of Anton and Nirella as they greeted them.

"Dire news," Eshaz said. "We must depart for the starcloud immediately!"

"Another enemy," one of the other Tulyans murmured. "Another enemy."

Alarmed, Tesh left the sectoid chamber and hurried down the corridor in her tiny natural form, moving in a blur of speed along the walls. Then, so small that no one noticed her, she slipped through an opening beneath the door of Anton's office and entered. It took her only a matter of seconds to get there, and she slipped inside. Then, scurrying up an interior corner like an insect, she became motionless, like the proverbial fly on the wall, eavesdropping.

The biggest Tulyan of the three, Eshaz, shifted uneasily on his feet. "Noah summoned us to the cocoon, and asked us to timesee. He's been sensing a great danger, and wanted us to help him figure out what is happening."

"I've heard of timeseeing?" Nirella said. "You're saying it actually works?"

"We don't talk about it much, but yes. It's an ability a few Tulyans have to see aspects of the future," Eshaz said. "We three are among the few capable of this, and I regret to inform you that we have no time to celebrate. A great and terrible thing approaches. We must leave immediately for the starcloud. It is safer there."

"But what is it?" Nirella asked. "We're victorious here. All of our enemies are vanquished."

"All that you know about. We cannot say what is coming, only that it brings darkness with it, and the probable end of all that we know."

"Darkness for all time," the third Tulyan said.

"The end of the galaxy?" Anton said. "The decay can't be stopped?"

"Something more," Eshaz said. "We can't determine what. Only that we must hurry."

"I'm not going to question your judgment," Anton said. "Or Noah's. Nirella, notify the fleet we are departing for the Tulyan Starcloud. Without delay."

She saluted and got on the comlink to set it up.

The Tulyans hurried away, and Tesh sped back to her sectoid chamber. Only a few minutes later, Noah Watanabe transported his cocoon, *Webdancer*, and most of the Andromeda division of the fleet back to the starcloud via the visualization method he had used previously—a method that he surmised must use the ultimate of galactic shortcuts. It was not quite instantaneous, but was close to it.

Then, in a matter of seconds, he sped back to the battlefield and signaled that he would escort the rest of the fleet—around sixty percent of the ships—to the starcloud via other podways, staying with them for the protective firepower he could offer. But, he worried, even that might not be enough.

Feeling great fatigue from tapping into the primal energy source, and with the continuing demands on his energy, Noah hoped he could find the strength to continue. Intermittently, he went through moments where he didn't think he could. Then, he would feel bursts of energy that gave him just enough to keep going.

Now his cocoon and thousands of smaller podships split space in flashes of green light, in a frantic rush to escape an enemy that they could not see. For defensive purposes Noah remained at the rear of the pack, and through the Aopoddae linkages he transmitted details to the other podships about the best route for them to take.

As Noah zipped through space behind the others, he pressed his face against the wall of the cocoon's sectoid chamber, peering in all directions through his many eyes in the hull, scanning, searching. Podflesh oozed around him in the chamber, a shallow pool of it.

The route he took involved some shortcuts between sectors, and they passed through regions where web conditions were barely adequate. Tulyan repair teams had already worked on some of these podways, and for the areas where breaks still existed, he went around. In a little over two hours, the group emerged from space just outside the Tulyan Starcloud, and made their way into the protective mists.

Just before entering the mindlink field himself, Noah paused briefly and scanned conditions in the galaxy, seeing far across space with his multiple eyes on the hull of the cocoon ... eyes that enabled him to view the vast filigree of Timeweb and the farthest reaches of space. As he focused to do this, the cocoon glowed brilliant green, casting light far across the galaxy and even illuminating the distant Kandor Sector he had just left.

He detected a disturbing bulge there, in the paranormal fabric of the galaxy. Abruptly, strands of the galactic infrastructure ripped away, creating what looked like an immense timehole, covering the entire galactic sector. Around the galaxy he saw other bulges, and additional huge holes appeared. One of them sucked up Woldn and the remnants of his attack force, then closed again, like a fantastic cosmic mouth. Another took the entire Adurian homeworld to an unknown place ... and he didn't think it would ever return.

Then, where the Kandor Sector used to be, huge, dark shapes poured out of the hole and scrambled around on the podways, on multiple legs that scampered along the strands of Timeweb. Even with the illumination Noah cast on them, he could not distinguish details of their bodies—only that they were large, amorphous creatures that moved very quickly.

Viscerally, he knew this was the additional danger he had foreseen, but he had no idea what it was.

Chapter Seventy-One

Time spins its own web.

—Ancient Tulyan saying

Inside the ethereal mists of the starcloud, Noah communicated with the Council of Elders, this time using one of the comlink channels of the Liberators. Then, after making arrangements directly with First Elder Kre'n, he guided his cocoon to the immense inverted dome of the Council Chamber, which floated over Tulé, the largest Tulyan planet. The cocoon and the chamber were of equivalent sizes, but of very different configurations—and Noah's was much more the organic of the two structures. He commanded the amalgamated Aopoddae to link to a docking station on the chamber.

By prior agreement, Noah strode out of the cocoon and made his way into a tunnel linking the structures. There, he boarded a small, automated motocart that had been sent for him, which carried him rapidly into the central meeting chamber.

The entire Council awaited him, sitting at their high, curved bench. Noah would have preferred to remain inside the cocoon, but the Tulyan leaders had insisted otherwise. Worried about still being able to control the primal weapon, Noah had nonetheless acceded to their demand, subject to the availability of the motocart to get him back in the event of an emergency.

Although some of the Elders had seen him in his present podman appearance, the entire Council had not. He exchanged greetings quickly with the Elders, tried not to let their probing, inquisitive stares bother him. He saw Doge Anton, General Nirella, and Subi Danvar standing nearby, and nodded to them.

Again, Noah was weaker away from EcoStation, but this time it was much more serious than the previous occasions when he had left. He felt drained, a condition of deep fatigue that he had begun to notice after using the primal weapon. He had recovered only slightly since then. The weariness had reached deep into his cells and mind, making him feel as if he could sleep for a week, or longer. He didn't dare. He had to go on, had to keep finding the strength to go on.

As he stood before the high bench, Noah focused on the fact that the Elders were looking down at him closely, and some of them were whispering to each other. Troubled, he had a feeling he should get back to the cocoon as soon as possible, for the restorative energy it imparted to him.

"We have formed a military plan with the Liberator fleet commanders," Kre'n said, "and it is necessary for us to merge you into it—with your newfound powers."

"Though we aren't quite sure how to do that," Anton said.

Noah nodded, pursed his lips in thought. He felt exhaustion seeping over him.

"I think we all need a certain amount of autonomy," Kre'n said. "We have our communication channels and our differing capabilities. Here in the starcloud, we Tulyans will maintain our mindlink as a defensive force, while your Liberator ships can be more offensive in nature, still keeping some vessels back to aid us here. As for you, Noah Watanabe, you can serve both purposes."

She paused, and added, "You are in possession of great power and responsibility, Noah. Surely you are the Savior spoken of in our legends, the one who will deliver us from death."

This subject had come up before, and Noah had tried not to believe it. Now he was no longer so certain, and chose not to comment on it. But no matter what they called him—or what his destiny might be—he was not certain if he had the capability to stop whatever creatures were tearing the galaxy apart with new timeholes, bigger than any he'd ever seen before, or had ever heard of. The decay of the galaxy—at least the rapid acceleration of the process—had not been from any natural, internal laws of decay. An outside force was involved.

Fighting back his fatigue, Noah looked up at Kre'n and said, "I told you what I saw—all the new timeholes, and huge, dark shapes pouring out of the one in the Kandor Sector. Creatures of some kind. You said you know what they are?"

Kre'n nodded her scaly, reptilian head. Then she narrowed her slitted eyes, and said, "What I am going to tell you has never been revealed to non-Tulyans, not by us or by any of our predecessors. It is one of the things we routinely confirm among our people with the truthing touch, constantly verifying that the information has not gotten out. The terrible secret has become ingrained in our race, but now it is appropriate for you and the others present to know what we are all up against."

Noah trembled in anticipation.

"The creatures are Web Spinners," Kre'n said, following a moment's hesitation. "We have Tulyan observers in deep space, and they have confirmed this. The danger is severe."

When Noah looked at the ancient leader with a blank expression, she said solemnly, "In the first days of the universe, the Sublime Creator formed galaxies on top of galaxies, folding in around each other in cosmic embraces. Our beneficial deity lives in the overgalaxy, a wondrous realm of time-and-space consciousness that is on a higher plane than any other."

"Like heaven."

"Somewhat."

"How many galaxies are there?"

"This is not known, and perhaps can never be known by us." She gazed at Noah for a lingering moment, then said, "Long ago, after the explosion of an incomprehensibly large star, galaxies were formed from the flaming embers, creating suns, planets, and other cosmic bodies. From the earliest days, the Sublime Creator wanted to organize the galaxies and keep their differing qualities separate, so he sought builders for the huge project. He was the grand visionary that generated the universe, but for certain detailed tasks he delegated much of the work."

She smiled sadly. "An early form of management, you might say. He already had the galaxies, but to make each of them an entirely separate enclosure he needed a strong fabric for the separations. This he accomplished with work crews involving various life forms that he created. The scale is beyond our comprehension, as are the details. But for us it all boils down to this galaxy, and how it was set up. Our galaxy received special consideration, giving it beauty that is second only to the ethereal realm of the Sublime Creator. This explains the loveliness of our nebulas and star systems, and particularly of Timeweb—our cosmic filigree whose intricacies are unmatched by any other galaxy. This paranormal webbing was generated by specialized creatures on a rather large scale—though on the scale of the universe it might not seem that way."

"And that's where the Web Spinners come in," Noah said.

"Precisely. Like huge spiders, the Web Spinners extruded the strands of our galactic web, after consuming the fibers of deep-shaft, piezoelectric emeralds. So that the races could travel on this glorious infrastructure, the Sublime Creator formed the Aopoddae podships, a race of sentient spacecraft capable of transporting other races across the galaxy in a matter of moments. Our galaxy is indeed a wondrous creation, containing countless life forms that are supposed to work in harmony with one another. There are even infinitesimally small nanocreatures that live inside the webbing. Another race entirely. They are secret beings … except to us.

"Since it is spun from ingested emerald fibers, Timeweb glows faintly green. The same glow is also found in the sectoid chambers of podships, making it possible for ship pilots to communicate with each other across vast distances via the galactic web that the chambers are in direct contact with. The nehrcom transmission system of the merchant princes also uses these piezoelectric emeralds in a slightly different fashion, aligning the stones so that they bounce signals off the web."

"And my cocoon can glow, like a green sun in space."

"Yes. Truly remarkable."

"And dangerous in the wrong hands," the towering Elder named Dabiggio added. Scowling more than usual, he sat on one side of her at the long bench.

"Fortunately, that is not the case," Kre'n said, glancing at him and speaking in a scolding tone.

"You say the Web Spinners are spiders?" Noah asked.

"No, I said they are *like* spiders, with certain similarities—but significant differences as well. The creatures are immense in size, with remarkably strong exoskeletons that are not subject to the expansion limitations of planet-bound spiders, which would collapse if they were scaled up too much."

"It should not be possible for them to be so large," Noah said, "just as Timeweb should not be possible. Even though I know the vast web exists and that it links the entire galaxy, I am still amazed that something so intricate holds it all together, and that most of the races can't even detect its existence."

"Truly, Timeweb is a grand and marvelous concept," Kre'n said, "but there have been problems. One has been apparent for some time now. The web is infinitely strong but fragile in many ways, and requires a great deal of work to maintain it. Initially, the Sublime Creator assigned Tulyans to perform this work, and gave us dominion over podships to get us around the galaxy. This system fell into disarray when another race grew in numbers and took control of the podships away from us. *Parviis.* The Sublime Creator didn't actually create Parviis directly; they arose from the biotech laboratories of the Adurians, whom he did create himself."

"And even though your race were cast out so ungraciously," Noah said, "you continued to perform whatever maintenance and repair work you could, on a piecemeal basis. A noble undertaking, I must say."

She looked dismal. "The Adurians caused a lot of trouble in ancient days, as they have in recent times. We have always been wary of them, as we have been of their surrogates, the Parviis."

"Tesh Kori told me that Humans are an offshoot of Parviis."

"That is true," Kre'n said, "which serves to explain some of the problems humankind has caused. But that is another story, and you are not typical of the race."

The comment made Noah think of Tesh (who also was atypical of her race), and of their unborn baby, which would be a hybrid of the Human and Parvii genetic lines.

Just then, Eshaz hurried into the chamber and addressed the Council. "Our deep-space observers report the Web Spinners are on the move," he said. "Heading in this direction. They're leaving a wake of destruction in their path— planetary systems, even the biggest, hottest suns wiped out and scattered into flaming embers. Nothing gets in their way. They just mow it down."

"And their ETA?" Kre'n asked. She looked very concerned, but amazingly steady. Noah detected no panic there, nor on the faces of the other Elders. But in their long experience, this must be the worst of events.

"Eighteen minutes."

Feeling his pulse quicken, Noah said, "I must return to the cocoon."

"We can have you there in less than a minute," Kre'n said. "But know this, valiant Human, before you go into battle: The Sublime Creator found the Web Spinners difficult to control, especially their leader, the Queen. Like the sentient races that are familiar to us, they were granted a form of free will. In their case, they had to be carefully and forcefully monitored while they built the Timeweb infrastructure—a process that took a very long time. When, at long last, they completed the vast construction project, the Sublime Creator confined them to the undergalaxy and sealed them there, so that they could not disturb him or the showcase of his marvelous creation—our own galaxy. Since then, the Queen of the Undergalaxy has ruled her stygian realm, and only that."

"But we have an ancient prophecy," said one of the other Elders, an elegant Tulyan man. "What the Web Spinners create they can also destroy."

"So you've always known this was coming?" Noah asked.

"Our timeseers have long foretold these days," Kre'n said, "and their visions have finally come upon us. Depending upon what happens next—and that we do not know—these are either the End of Days or a New Beginning."

"And a battle plan?" Noah asked.

"Defend and attack. Against such an onrushing enemy, there can be no other plan."

"I guess we'll find out soon enough where I fit into all of this," Noah said.

Kre'n nodded, and said softly, "Our blessings be upon you, Master Noah."

Then everyone hurried to their battle stations.

Chapter Seventy-Two

If they come for us, there will be no place to hide.

—Ancient Tulyan warning

The moment Noah set foot on the docking platform of the cocoon, he began to feel physically stronger. His skin wasn't even in direct contact with the mottled gray-and-black flesh—only his shoes were—but he still felt an instant infusion of vitality greater than any before, and the fatigue seemed to fade entirely. The cocoon was becoming like a mother's womb, providing nutrients for him in invisible ways.

But he didn't have time to wonder about the nature or cause of the phenomenon. A tidal wave of destruction was on the way.

Thinker greeted him on the platform. "Did the meeting go well, Master Noah?"

"A new threat is on the way." Taking less than a minute, he told the robot what he knew.

As Thinker listened, the lights around his metal faceplate glowed an angry shade of orange. Then he said, "We must fight back hard."

"That is my intent. Now, I'm afraid you're going to have to wait for me again, friend. I'm going back into the sectoid chamber of this cocoon."

"The weapon room," Thinker said.

"Essentially, yes. I wish it were not that way, but I have no choice." With a grim expression, Noah gave the sentient robot an affectionate pat on the shoulder, feeling this might be the last time the two of them ever saw each other.

Thinker's metal-lidded eyes blinked, as if fighting away tears that were not actually there. At least not physically.

Noah knelt on the platform, and touched his hands against the podship flesh. It became gray liquid around him. He felt the warmth of the alien cellular material, and allowed it to run up his arms.

"I've been given considerable autonomy in the use of the weapon," Noah said, "and I'll be focused on what I have to do." The soft flesh covered his

739

body, all the way up to his shoulders. "I can't use a conventional webtalker to relay information—they say there's too much disturbance around the cocoon—so I need you to remain in direct comlink contact with General Nirella and Doge Anton. Obtain their commands, and relay them to me."

"What? Oh, you're thinking I can use my organic interface connection on the podflesh, and that will put me in contact with you?"

"Try it now. Quickly."

The familiar tentacle snaked out of Thinker's alloy body, and darted into the gray-and-black flesh on a nearby bulkhead. "Yes," the robot said, "I am now linked to your mind. It will work."

"Good. One more thing. You've always been a de facto officer in the Liberator fleet, though no one has ever given you a rank."

"No matter. I command the robots, but at the pleasure of Humans."

"It *does* matter, my good friend. For your unflagging loyalty and service, you deserve more. Therefore, as Master of the Guardians, I hereby appoint you Vice-General, in charge of all robots. Tell Anton and Nirella I made a battlefield promotion. I'm sure they won't countermand it."

"Thank you, Master Noah. Where shall I meet you after our victory?"

"Anywhere on the cocoon," Noah said, with a stiff smile. "I'll know where you are, because it will be an extension of my own body."

The alien flesh rose up Noah's neck, to his chin.

"We're very small in this galaxy, aren't we?" Thinker said.

It was the last thing Noah heard before he swam into the flesh and became one with it. Again he seemed to cross a vast distance, as if traversing the entire universe. There were no stars, only a darkness that gradually began to glow with a soft green luminescence. Once more, he reached the sectoid chamber and rose to his feet inside, like an alien life form that had just been born and could already stand.

Again he pressed his face against the glowing green flesh of the sectoid chamber, and his enlarged countenance emerged on the outside of the cocoon, this time showing the podman features of his evolved face. He disengaged from the inverted dome of the Council Chamber, and floated free of it.

Noah felt like he was in a vast sea that stretched across the cosmos. All around him, as if his presence was connected to a vast cosmic circuit, he felt the energy source building, the raw, elemental power of the superweapon. He became a brilliant green sun in space with shining Noah-faces all around it, looking in all directions with the multiple humanoid eyes, casting spotlights of illumination to the farthest reaches of galactic existence. Noah was the cocoon; he was the weapon, and much more. He was a mote, a micro-organism, an embryonic life form, but he extended across time and space. Again he was in direct contact with the primal energy of the universe.

Peering through the green illumination, Noah saw hundreds of the immense, dark creatures scrambling across the podways like huge hunting daggs following a scent, going toward the starcloud along the identical secondary route that Noah had taken. He felt a chill. He still could not make out details of the monsters, only glimpses of multiple legs beneath their bodies, propelling them forward at high speed.

Web Spinners.

As if in response to his thoughts, the massed Aopoddae stirred around him, an agitation of ancient flesh. Trembling to the very depths of his own soul, Noah Watanabe knew that he would have preferred to hold back, that he didn't really want to be any part of a weapon, and especially not one of this frightening scope and power. But he was coming to believe that this horrendous device stood right in the middle of his evolutionary path, blocking his way until he used it. He could not go around the duty, could not avoid the dreadful task that lay before him, no matter how much he might like to. Causing destruction ran counter to every instinct he had. Throughout history, the very worst genocides and ecological disasters had been brought about by warfare. Even the current galactic-wide crisis might have been started by military conflict, and at the very minimum it had been severely exacerbated by it.

Must I use violence to quell violence, he thought, *to begin the process of restoring the galaxy?* And he wondered if his own hesitation, his own doubts, were causing the agitation in the podship flesh in which he was immersed.

He wondered, as well, how the mysterious cocoon weapon functioned, what its workings looked like. It seemed to be an unanswerable question, of enormous proportions. The thing just existed, and in certain circumstances the incredible weapon could spew destruction across the galaxy—like an immense green-flame thrower. He sensed, however, that even that might not be enough against such a threat.

Less than eleven minutes had passed since the Tulyans had estimated the eighteen-minute arrival time, so there should be seven left. But Noah thought it might be more like three now. In the last few moments, the Web Spinners had increased their speed, in anticipation of reaching their goal.

They were hungry....

* * * * *

Clinging to the forward wall of *Webdancer*'s much smaller sectoid chamber, Tesh Kori monitored the flurry of activity in the meeting rooms and corridors of the flagship, and in space around her. Through her connection with the podflesh, she listened to the interior of the vessel, while looking outward through visual sensors in the hull. The Liberator fleet had been divided up and positioned according to General Nirella's orders, prepared to defend the starcloud against the fast-approaching threat.

Web Spinners, they called them. Ancient creatures from the undergalaxy. Demons? That was the only parallel she could draw to Parvii legends, which described the undergalaxy as a stygian realm, inhabited by evil spirits.

She waited for the next command from her superiors. Agonizing seconds ticked by. Through the misty gases of the starcloud, Tesh saw Noah's cocoon moving to a forward position, where General Nirella had ordered him to go. She thought of Noah's child growing in her womb, and wondered if they would ever form a family—the three of them. She desperately hoped so, but nothing about her relationship with Noah was conventional. Besides, war was filled with uncertainties, and too many of the possibilities were not good.

Tesh had lived for more than seven centuries, and in that time had dated men of many star systems and galactic races. But never before had she met anyone even remotely like Noah Watanabe, nor had she ever experienced feelings for any of them that approached those she felt for him.

And, while she could remember details going back all that time, she had noticed a recent compression of the memories that mattered most to her, the ones she kept calling up and thinking about over and over. The kisses she had shared with Noah, their brief intimacy, the comforting sound of his voice, the caring way he looked at her with his hazel eyes, which he still had even after his flesh changed.

Since meeting him, the original racial difference between them had widened, as Noah had set forth on a path of evolving into something else. She only hoped that he was not evolving into some*one* else.

At the very heart of her feelings, his appearance didn't really matter to her. She cared much more about what was inside, what he was thinking and where he was going with his life. She cared about what sort of a father he might be for their child.

Tears welled up in Tesh's eyes, and ran down her cheeks. She tasted salt.

I must be strong, she thought. The tears stopped, and she steeled herself for battle.

* * * * *

The great weapon that Noah was about to use and the entire scenario seemed so far beyond the range of possibility that he wondered if he was going completely mad, if he had been infected with a terrible disease of the mind. His own twin sister had gone insane and had died hideously. Noah recalled the dermex injection she had stabbed into him, claiming it was her own blood. It had been her last act of hatred toward him before dying. Could Francella's vicious presence be alive inside him at this very moment, and dictating his very perceptions? It remained an unanswered question, just one of many.

I need to control chaos, he thought, trying to bring himself back, knowing that the monsters of the undergalaxy really were coming. *Order must emerge from chaos. In this galaxy, and in my own psyche.*

Abruptly, Noah felt a shift in time and space around him, and he saw fast-forward images through Francella's eyes as she committed vile acts—scheming to murder their father, stealing his assets, hacking at and stabbing Noah. He felt her hatreds, her twisted views, her petty jealousies and self-serving plots. He felt how much she loathed her twin. It was not the first time he had seen through her eyes—or seemed to—and he wondered if this had something to do with the blood she had injected in him, or to the fact that twins were said to have paranormal linkages.

The eyes shifted; the *view* shifted, revealing a horrific threat to the Tulyan Starcloud....

Chapter Seventy-Three

In some circumstances, it is better to perish than to survive.
If that be the case in our hour of crisis, may death come quickly to us all.
—Transmitted thoughts, from a Tulyan webtalker

Like an earthquake in space, a terrible upheaval consumed the Tulyan Starcloud. Once a haven like none other in the known galaxy, it was anything but that now. Having slipped out of the control of mindlink, comets and meteors streaked wildly through the mists of the starcloud, threatening the planets, the Liberator fleet, and the Council Chamber.

Focusing and refocusing their telepathic waves, the Tulyans succeeded in diverting the incoming missiles one at a time, but more kept coming. A huge meteor—the size of a small moon—barely missed hitting the planet Tulé.

All across the starcloud, Liberator warships fired their weapons at the incoming objects, hitting some and diverting them, but missing others. With the attentions of the defenders on the larger objects, meteorites got through and crashed into dwellings and community structures. Flaming embers hit the floating Council Chamber.

Noah's cocoon was in motion, moving independently of his commands. It was a survival mode in the amalgamated podships that enabled him to focus on other, more pressing concerns. The cocoon moved through the mists in great graceful patterns, avoiding the celestial storm. It rose heavenward, then circled over the misty veils and three planets of the starcloud, taking evasive action as necessary.

From his paranormal, web-linked observation and listening post Noah hesitated, sensing that he should not fire his great weapon at the incoming objects yet, that he needed to save it for exactly the right moment. But he couldn't just stand by and watch this. At Yaree, he had minimized the power and spread it around to detonate the invading Parviis.

He realized he was having a gut reaction now, and he had to ask himself if it was relevant, or if it was a useless remnant of his Human form, something that should be discarded. As he watched the cosmic storm all around him, he could hardly stand it anymore. He had to fire the weapon to divert some of those incoming objects.

But still he hesitated.

Through Timeweb, Noah heard one of the Elders—Dabiggio—cry out in dismay, "The demons of the undergalaxy are breaking through!" Other council members shouted that this couldn't possibly be happening, that the starcloud was supposed to be the strongest place in the entire galaxy, since mindlink had been improved dramatically by a concerted effort of the defenders.

The Council Chamber was hit again, this time by a small comet that skipped off the bulbous underside, tearing loose a jagged piece of the inverted dome. All over the starcloud, thousands of Tulyans were fleeing for the podships and attempting to board them. But in the chaos most vessels were having to take off before they were fully loaded. Above Tulé, four were hit by meteorites and larger objects, destroying them. Noah heard the screams of the dying Aopoddae and their Tulyan passengers.

Unable to wait any longer, he reduced the power of the great weapon, focused it, and fired bursts of primal green light in multiple directions. All over the starcloud and beyond it, comets, meteors, and meteorites exploded and veered away. A small number of them kept coming, but Noah thought the Tulyans should be able to deter the rest of them with mindlink. He drew the power inward, felt it building up around him again.

Now his humanoid eyes looked at the oncoming Web Spinners, amorphous shapes that were closer than ever, only a minute or two away, surging past one star system after another. Why weren't they coming into focus? Kre'n had said they were like spiders, and had exoskeletons that scaled up to amazing proportions. Did they look like spiders, then? So far, he'd only gotten glimpses of long legs beneath dark bodies that almost seemed fluid, as their shapes bent one way and another. Perhaps this was yet another form of shapeshifting.

Again Noah felt the visceral sensation telling him not to fire, not yet. He had to wait for precisely the right moment, and really cut loose with everything he had. This time, Noah went with the feeling, and hoped he had not made a mistake by activating the weapon earlier to protect the starcloud. He felt the power continue to build up around him, and it did not seem to him that he had damaged anything. It could keep going up and up.

But in a matter of moments he reached a point where he didn't feel his brain could encompass any more of the tremendous energy. Although his thoughts extended far and could accomplish a great deal, he still had some connection to his past as a Human, and he sensed that there were distinct limitations on what he could do, and that he should not go beyond certain boundaries. But what were those boundaries? His expanded mind would not, or could not, tell him.

Noah felt like a child-god, one who was not able to understand or fully control his powers. But he had no more time to learn, and needed to utilize what he had immediately. It was the most severe form of on-the-job training imaginable, because any mistake he made would have immense consequences.

He felt the momentum of time around him, a tidal wave of events pushing him toward an unavoidable climax. He looked in all directions at once, absorbed information from everywhere simultaneously.

The dark creatures kept coming, and in anticipation of this the Tulyans were evacuating the Council Chamber. Noah recognized the face of Eshaz on the prow of one of the ships that was taking on passengers. That vessel began to move quickly and headed away with others, going in the opposite direction from the approaching Web Spinners. Incoming thoughts from webtalkers told Noah that the Tulyans were setting up a new defensive bastion on their largest planet, Tulé. Due to changes in cosmic conditions, this would be the most powerful place in the starcloud, where they intended to make a last-ditch telepathic stand against the attackers.

Noah saw a weak spot in the galactic infrastructure near the abandoned Council Chamber, a fraying of the green filigree that would soon send the chamber tumbling one direction or another. Nothing like that had ever happened before in this region of space.

Then, to his amazement, the approaching Web Spinners began to disappear before reaching the starcloud, one after the other. From his vantage over the misty Tulyan domain, Noah saw that the creatures were entering a timehole. In seconds, they were gone, and the hole closed.

But near the Council Chamber he saw a bulge in the barely visible fabric of space, and remembered seeing that effect in the Kandor Sector, right before the creatures poured through from the undergalaxy. Now he noticed other bulges appearing around the starcloud, with the biggest of all forming around Tulé, where podships full of evacuees were still arriving. To his dismay, he realized that Eshaz was piloting one of them.

And Noah had no time to do anything about it.

The surface of Tulé cracked open like an eggshell. Something monstrous and black pushed its way through molten lava and crust of the world, a creature that was much larger than the others. It had long legs, which waved in the sky and struck several podships at they tried to take off, causing them to crash. The planet cracked open further, and Noah saw smaller creatures, scurrying out of fissures. Near the Council Chamber, other creatures emerged and knocked the chamber aside, sending its severely damaged remains drifting through the starcloud.

The earlier Web Spinners had been scouts. Now many more of them were coming out of the undergalaxy, and the mother of them all was a hundred times the size of Noah's cocoon, with a head and body of odd geometric angles, and yellow-ember eyes that burned as bright as suns. Its legs looked and moved like those of a spider, but its body, just breaking through the crust of the planet, was diamond-shaped, as if cut from an immense, precious stone. It was the darkest shade of black he had ever seen, and seemed to absorb light into it and make it disappear, like a black hole in motion.

The monsters clustered on webbing over the ruined world, having scattered Tulé and its atmosphere into space. Liberator warships attacked the creatures, firing ion cannons, nuclear projectiles, and a variety of other space weapons. But nothing did any good, as the creatures ignored the small blasts.

From his high vantage Noah was sickened to see the torn bodies of Humans, Tulyans, and Mutatis floating in space.

The largest Web Spinner, now free, began to climb the web toward Noah's cocoon, but got on a weak strand that broke, causing a momentary delay before it found another.

The *Queen of the Undergalaxy*, he thought.

Other smaller creatures followed her, but even the smallest of them were as big as his cocoon.

Seeing through his many eyes in the amalgamation around him, Noah's eyes displayed multiple images of the spiders crawling up the web toward him. It was like an array of video screens … all showing horror. The creatures were picking up speed.

Noah focused the primal-energy weapon and fired a blinding green blast that was much more powerful than he had used to destroy the HibAdu armada. But this time it only bounced off the creatures, without seeming to harm them.

Desperately, he increased the energy level by several factors—beyond what he had earlier thought he could stand. He continued firing, but with very little effect on the monsters of the nether realm. The blasts slowed them, but they didn't seem to be harmed at all, and they kept coming.…

Chapter Seventy-Four

In this universe, there is always a way to escape from any situation … even from the greatest danger. It is for us, with the brains and free will that the Sublime Creator gave us, to find the way.

—Tulyan observation, in emergency council

The Web Spinners scrambled along the strands, heading directly toward Noah's cocoon, ignoring the warships of the Liberator fleet that raced alongside them, peppering them with ion and atomic cannon fire that didn't phase them at all, didn't slow them down or make them change course. The monsters just ignored them.

In the midst of the terrible threat, Noah's mind raced, searching for answers and possibilities. He kept firing his own primal blasts at the creatures, but they kept coming, and he didn't want to increase the power any more, fearing it would go beyond anything he could handle. It could destroy the remains of the starcloud, the Liberator fleet, and everything in this galactic sector—with the possible exception of the monsters of the undergalaxy. He wasn't sure if anything could stop them.

For the moment, he continued to fire at the geometric, spidery creatures, and at least his shots were slowing them down—though they kept regrouping and clamoring toward him. Intermittently, for brief moments, he saw faint lights and shifting colors inside the bodies and heads, as if illuminated from within. Then the colors and lights would fade to black-blackness with the exception of the yellow-ember eyes, peering out of the darkness of the bodies.

Noah recalled the Battle of Yaree, where he had experienced a brief vision lasting only a few seconds, in which the cocoon blew up and he tumbled out into a glowing green timehole. That had never really happened, and he strongly suspected now—more viscerally than intellectually—that he had seen a fragment of his own future in that vision. But he also felt, with equal certainty, that it was only *one* of his possible futures, and that he could still avoid it if he made the right choices. Perhaps that was why his mind revealed the vision to him again, to prevent it from happening.

The Web Spinners had been opening timeholes all over the galaxy, exploiting natural galactic weaknesses and creating new ones, undoubtedly setting them up as entry points and waiting for their best opportunity to attack. But they had seemed to ignore the HibAdus and their conventional weaponry, and were doing the same with the Liberators. They weren't ignoring Noah, though, and his weapon didn't seem to have much effect on them at all.

Should he raise the primal power and see what it could do to the creatures, no matter what the potential risk was to everything else? He might have to.

He realized now that the Web Spinners wanted to get to *him*, to the exclusion of everything else in this galaxy. And they had been after him before. Somehow they'd been sensing his presence wherever he was, especially after he formed the cocoon and began discovering what it contained—a raw, cosmic power that the creatures feared. Earlier they had intended to get him at Yaree and in the Kandor Sector, but each time Noah had eluded them. Crossing space from Kandor, he had displayed an ability to traverse vast distances almost instantaneously, which seemed to cause problems for the creatures. And—if that method of travel was not available—for reasons he did not yet understand—he could still travel at great speeds along the podways. He had the means of escape, though he suspected that would only delay the inevitable. They would find him. They were *determined* to find him, like predators that refused to give up the hunt. But for what purpose? Presumably, to attempt to kill him. But what if they couldn't accomplish that? What then? What sort of integrated mind and energy drove them? What form of extraterrestrial hell did they intend for him?

That particular future—if it existed—had not yet been revealed to him.

These alien organisms were smart, and they would undoubtedly attempt to cut off his routes of escape, as the HibAdus had tried to do with the Liberator fleet. Alternately, the creatures seemed to select both undergalactic routes and routes in this galaxy. But Noah was not without his own options. Maybe he could lure them away as far as possible and set off a huge detonation that would finish them off. If conditions permitted it, he could go through a timehole into the undergalaxy and do it to them there—thus shifting the focus of the destruction.

Wipe them out in their own nest, he thought. *Kill all of them. Get the Queen.*

If this worked, it would test the limits of his own "immortality," and his ability to return to this realm through a timehole, or through some other means he did not yet know about. But these considerations were not a priority. For the sake of his own galaxy, and for all he held dear, he was more than willing to sacrifice his own life—in whatever form that sacrifice took. It might just save Tesh and their child, and the Liberator fleet could then attack the weakened HibAdu forces and take back the Human and Mutati planets they controlled.

Thinker, are you picking this up? Noah thought.

Yes.

Tell the fleet to disengage, and why. Tell them to remain here, without me.

I'm doing it now, Master.

* * * * *

Noah envisioned a sector far across the galaxy, a region where he had seen numerous timeholes, through the paranormal lens available to him. It was beyond Yaree and the Kandor Sector—so far away, so desolate and off the beaten path that he didn't know of a name for it, or even an astronomical number. Even with all of the sector mapping that had been completed by the various races, there were still places like this, and it was exactly what he wanted. If he had to set off an explosion there, it would be as far as possible from population centers, and it presented the possibility of escape routes to the undergalaxy, where he would go if necessary. One way or another, he would make a statement.

This time, the movement across space was not nearly instantaneous, as it had seemed to be before. He felt the podships tremble around him as he transmitted psychic energy to them, but he urged them to go—he *commanded* it, and they went into motion. There was a tightening inside his skull, and a searing pain as the collective entity accelerated along one podway and then another, heading for the far reaches of the galaxy at tachyon speeds. The discomfort in his skull was enormous—as if the Aopoddae didn't want to cooperate in this— but he did not let up.

Through his cocoon eyes at the rear, Noah saw the curvature of the web, and black forms scrambling along it behind him, trying to keep up. The smaller Web Spinners were in front of the big one now. He summoned the cocoon to greater speed, but it resisted. Despite this, he was still going at tremendous speed, because he saw suns and solar systems passing by in a blur.

But as he peered through the eyes behind the pod-amalgam, he knew he was not going fast enough. After initially falling back, the predators were gradually gaining on him, with the smaller ones running along parallel strands and the big one looming behind.

The hybrid space station began to vibrate and slow down slightly, and Noah realized that the strand beneath his ship was disintegrating, about to break. Before he could react, the cocoon spun and somersaulted away through space. It had fallen off the galactic track. He struggled for control, and to see what is going on, but for several moments he could do neither. One of the smaller pursuers was ahead of the others, and very near him now. Running along a parallel strand, it reached out to swipe at the cocoon with a claw, but narrowly missed.

Noah managed to engage with another podway strand and he accelerated along it, momentarily leaving the creatures behind—until they got on the same podway and began to gain on him again. He urged the cocoon to greater speed, but it resisted.

Desperately, Noah looked for an alternate way to get to the remote sector where he wanted to detonate the primal charge and get rid of these alien bastards. He changed course three times to again head in that direction, but each time he looked back, the pursuers were a little bit closer. Judging the distance he still needed to travel and the limited velocities the cocoon seemed able to attain, he knew he would never make it that far.

Now he had to find the nearest timehole. Desperately, Noah took a series of looping turns and skimmed a gray-green membrane that didn't seem to belong there, since it was nowhere near the perimeter of the galaxy. Like a wavering, broken piece of wall, it might be a remnant of the long-ago galactic construction project, a huge unused piece that had just drifted away. Or, more likely, it had something to do with the faltering state of the cosmos. He did find podways that were faster on the membrane, but he couldn't locate a timehole. The geometric spiders were much closer now, only a few seconds behind him. The largest one moved up to the center of the pack.

Again the Web Spinners displayed internal lights and colors, but this time only in their heads, where the energy glowed brightly and danced inside the facets, as if in anticipation of the kill. As the monsters neared, Noah was startled to identify facial features on them that were contorted but still resembled those of various galactic races—Humans, Salducians, Adurians, Hibbils, Jimlats, Mutatis, Churians, and even Tulyans.

The faces were chiseled and hard instead of organic ... features buried within facets.

The Queen looked like an amalgamation of the others, more ferocious and predatory in appearance than any monster of the imagination. She revealed immense pincers on two of her eight feet—claws that could easily rip the space station apart. Looking like an arachnid, a crustacean, and a host of unknown organisms from her demonic realm, she was a nightmare come to life.

A particularly fast spinner streaked ahead of the others, but this one did not have yellow-sun eyes—these burned red. The contorted face resembled that of Pimyt, the Royal Attaché to Lorenzo del Velli. Noah had no time to be amazed, or to wonder. He fired a blast from the cocoon weapon that slowed the creature down, and it fell back with the others.

The Queen of the Undergalaxy moved to the front of the pack. Focusing through the multiple humanoid eyes at the rear of his cocoon, Noah saw that she and her minions were almost on top of him now. While continuing to run ahead of his pursuers, he glowed brighter green, preparing to fire at them.

Suddenly Noah saw bursts of green light ahead of him, like flowers in space, and thousands of podships emerging, one after the other. It was the Liberator fleet led by *Webdancer*, catching up because of the circuitous route he had taken. But he was not happy to see them, and commanded Thinker to tell them so. Noah was troubled. The Liberators were not only risking their own safety, but it was a foolish gesture, because their destruction would leave much of the known galaxy in the hands of the HibAdus. With no Liberator force to oppose them, Human and Mutati worlds would be forever lost to the conspirators.

Thinker sent the message, but his comlink call had no effect. The fleet surged around Noah, more than one hundred thousand of them heading en masse toward the advancing Web Spinners, firing every weapon they had. Curiously, most of the vessels did not have Tulyan faces on them, suggesting that they were under Aopoddae control.

This new tactic had some effect on the monsters, as it forced them to veer off course and come back around. Even the Queen shifted course in the barrage of fire, and when she and her demon-companions took new routes toward Noah, the fleet harassed them. Even so, the Web Spinners tried to ignore them, and did not counterattack. They just kept going around and focusing on Noah.

Send another message! Noah said to Thinker, through their organic link. *Tell them I was trying to lure the Web Spinners to a remote region, and preferably into the undergalaxy, where I planned to set off a big explosion. Now I'll have to do it here, but first the fleet needs to be as far away as possible.*

Moments later, Thinker reported back: *Fleet command reports that most of the podships are flying out of their control, not responding to the commands of their Tulyan pilots. Only Tesh, Eshaz, and a few hundred other pilots, for reasons that no one understands, report that they can convince their podships to do what they want. But they're here of their own volition, too—and they're setting up battle formations with the others.*

Tell Tesh to go back! Noah said, worrying about her and their unborn child. *Maybe the others will follow.*

A momentary delay. Then: *She won't do it, Master Noah, won't abandon the fleet. Or you.*

Desperately, Noah looked for opportunities to fire at the Web Spinners, but worried about hitting the thick clusters of Liberator ships, and especially *Webdancer*, which Tesh piloted. He still knew where Tesh was—*Webdancer* was the largest ship in the fleet, and beside that, he saw through Timeweb to the sectoid chamber where she clung to a wall inside, piloting the craft. But he could not linger to watch over her, and couldn't justify trying to save her at the expense of the others. Then he was heartened, but only a little, to see his friend Eshaz bring his ship Agryt and others in close to *Webdancer*, forming some protection for the flagship. But against such behemoths of space, the effort couldn't amount to much.

Changing course, Noah went around to a flank position, where he was able to fire the primal weapon at several smaller Web Spinners on the perimeter. He used a little higher intensity than before, but far short of the massive detonation he planned. Once more, the creatures were not harmed, but he did manage to knock five of them further away, forcing them to scramble back. If any of those blasts had accidentally hit a Liberator vessel, however, he had no doubt the vessel would not survive. The Aopoddae ships were now following the lead of the flagship, coordinating attacks on the monsters that were beginning to have some effect, albeit only like the collective effect of pesky flies.

Reaching the limit of her patience, the Queen finally began thrashing around with her multiple legs, snaring podships on the sticky surfaces of her skin and smashing the vessels together, killing the Aopoddae and their passengers. So far, *Webdancer* eluded this fate, as did Eshaz's ship Agryt, but to his horror Noah saw them heading straight toward her. This time she had her deadly pincers extended toward them.

Noah fired two bright green blasts of energy across the bows of the ships, hitting the Queen's pincers and momentarily deterring their destructive work. *Webdancer* and Eshaz veered away, but soon came back around to continue the fight.

I've got to change this equation, Noah said to Thinker, across their linkage.

Abruptly, he took the cocoon in a sharp turn and headed through a small spiral nebula, passing through it and heading toward a region that was commonly known as the Heart of the Galaxy, the theoretically exact mathematical center of all galactic mass and gravitation. He wished he'd been able to go farther, into uncharted regions. But at least there were no known resident populations in this region.

The Queen of the Undergalaxy was right behind him, picking up speed. Her pincers were extended in anticipation, and she opened her mouth as well, a black, deadly maw in the expanse of space. Wherever she went, color and light vanished—other than her brilliant yellow eyes. She seemed to inhale entire suns and planetary systems, which vanished after she passed near them, though she did not grow perceptibly larger. Oddly—and he began to wonder if it was because of some power the Aopoddae had—she had not been able to do that to them, or to him.

Just then, Noah saw hundreds of Liberator ships on either side of him, keeping up on parallel podways. All except one—*Webdancer*—had Tulyan faces on their prows. *Webdancer* took a lead position on one side of the cocoon, and Agryt—piloted by Eshaz—was at the lead on the other side, like flanking guards. Soon, more and more podships—the much larger group of faceless ones—caught up.

The Queen still managed to get past the fleet, and attacked the underside of the cocoon. She lashed out at the space station with one of her immense chelicerae claws, and barely scratched the hide of the amalgamated podships, but deep enough to cause them to cry out to Noah in pain. Quickly, they began to heal the wound, while Noah slowed and veered off, taking a position to protect *Webdancer*, and Tesh.

Behind him, he saw five of the smaller Web Spinners do something unexpected. In concert, they flew directly at the Queen's other pincer, and smashed into it. Enraged, she stabbed them with her pincers and tossed the smaller creatures aside. Noah saw a familiar face in one of the dying spinners—a glimmering, distorted countenance that still had the features of Princess Meghina. Then he saw other Human faces inside the facets of the other dying creatures—and recognized them as the Humans who had consumed the Elixir of Life to become immortals. Were they really dying now? Earlier, he had seen Pimyt's face on one of the Web Spinners. What did it all mean? How—and why—had they been recruited into the ranks of the Web Spinners? At least Meghina and four of her companions had not been converted entirely. They had not lost their loyalty to the cause of humanity. Even Meghina, unhappy at being born a Mutati, had proved that she deserved to be considered Human, in the best definition of the race.

The smaller creature with the face of Pimyt swiped at *Webdancer*, and struck the ship a glancing blow. Noah darted in that direction and slammed hard into the spiderlike demon, knocking it away into space.

On a Thinker-to-comlink relay, Noah had the robot say to Tesh, "Go away! Save yourself and our baby!"

She did not respond, and returned to her course, flying alongside the cocoon with the other podships. *Webdancer* had scratches on its hull where it had been clawed and scraped, but the injuries didn't seem to be severe.

In a sudden movement, the Queen struck out at Eshaz's ship, and grabbed it in a powerful pincer grip. Then, to his horror, Noah saw the monster bite into the face of Eshaz on the prow of the ship. For a moment, the entire podship changed shape into a larger-than-life version of Eshaz's natural reptilian body, struggling to get away from the spinner. It was to no avail. She ripped through Eshaz and cast him away. He tumbled, alternately changing shape to Aopoddae and Tulyan, then became amorphous and black, with eight legs sprouting out from his lower body. In a matter of moments, the newborn horror raced toward Noah, and Eshaz's face began to glimmer on its faceted face. It had become one of the small Web Spinners.

Noah didn't have time to grieve, or to think about the other podships and pilots who were being converted when the Queen got to them, vessel by vessel. He continued to take evasive maneuvers from the pack of spinners, all the while trying to keep them away from *Webdancer*.

Filled with anger and frustration, Noah felt a trembling in the cocoon flesh. Casting green light from his eyes around the hull of the space station, he gazed out on the thousands of podships in the fleet, many of which kept flying directly at the Queen's pincers in obvious, though suicidal, efforts to deter her. It was working to some extent, as she continued to deal with them while still pursuing Noah. It had the effect of slowing her down, and her companions with her. She seemed to be the only one who could stab the attackers and convert them into spinners. If it kept going like that, however, Noah realized that she would eventually convert the entire podship fleet and command them as well. But she could only convert as many as she could reach—and so far she'd barely made a dent in the Liberator fleet.

Through Timeweb, Noah expanded his mind into each of the interiors of the podships. He wasn't really touching them, at least not physically, but the contact was significant, nonetheless. His mind raced, exploring new possibilities as they occurred to him.

In a form of gestalt, Noah realized that he could do much more than he had previously thought possible with the weapon. The cocoon and all of the other podships could accomplish more than the sum of their individual possibilities. He saw a new way to use the tremendous firepower, a way that even the podships themselves might not realize. After all, they had not used it until he appeared.

In the midst of his racing thoughts, Noah caught himself, and felt a chill of realization as information seeped out of the armored Aopoddae memory core in his brain and entered his consciousness. The sentient spacecraft had known the full potential of the weapon all along, but needed him to prove he was worthy of using it. He had to figure it out himself, while they remained in close proximity to him—taking control of most of the fleet away from the pilots.

Even facing their own destruction, the podships were behaving unpredictably, in ways that did not always seem to help their own survival. Their behavior almost seemed ... religious to him, as if they believed in fate and destiny. But whatever their motives, they concealed them from him. Noah had the feeling that he would never figure out the ancient aliens to any great extent, even if he managed to get through this great challenge with them.

With that realization, Noah felt a shift in space and time around him, and abruptly his face and eyes appeared on the prow of each ship in the Liberator fleet, in addition to his multiple countenances all around the cocoon. Protectively, he was on the prow of *Webdancer*, with Tesh inside.

In the past, when Noah's powers were embryonic and unpredictable, he had, for a time, been able to guide a single podship by remote control, extending his thoughts into its sectoid chamber. Now he found that he could do this for all of the Aopoddae at once—more than one hundred thousand of them—psychically connecting the sectoid chamber of the cocoon with all of the smaller sectoid chambers in the fleet.

Every ship in the fleet glowed faintly green, and Noah felt the pulsing of the flesh of every vessel, the coordinated heartbeat of one collective organism. Noah was that organism, and it was him. The ships all glowed brighter, matching the intensity and hue of the cocoon.

Then Noah fired the incredible primal weapon at the Queen and her minions, not holding anything back. The blasts were white this time—with the ships in the fleet firing at the smaller Web Spinners and the cocoon firing directly at the Queen of the Undergalaxy. He hit her with far more power than all of her slaves received combined. In all, it was exponentially more force than he had used before.

This was enough to disintegrate every one of the smaller Web Spinners in hot bursts of primal whiteness that turned them into dust particles so infinitesimal that they could no longer be seen. They just seemed to vanish. But that didn't happen with the Queen. The tremendous force of the biggest blast knocked her into another star system, but she recovered and roared back, her yellow-ember eyes more intense than ever and her body flashing all of the colors in the universe.

Noah hit her again, this time directing blasts at her from the cocoon and from every podship. The tremendous combined force hit her on all sides and broke her into parts, but the parts kept moving, kept trying to regroup. It reminded Noah of himself, the way he repeatedly regenerated his body after his sister hacked it apart. Tesh had worried about what kind of a monster he might be. He hoped he was not one, and had dedicated himself to proving it. But this Queen was something else entirely. Could she ever be stopped?

He continued to fire in rapid succession, focal blasts from all directions that broke the Queen up into smaller and smaller fragments, until only a black cloud of dust remained. The cloud coalesced more tightly and tried to float away, but Noah used the podship fleet to herd it into a timehole—a cosmic opening that made its presence known like a message from the creator of the universe. In went the Queen of the Undergalaxy—every last particle of her stygian dust.

And when she was gone, Noah used the primal power of the cocoon to seal the timehole over, repairing it for all time. Then, gathering energy into the cocoon from the podship fleet, he transmitted simultaneous bursts of raw power into all astronomical sectors, sealing every timehole in the galaxy and repairing every torn fragment of galactic webbing.

Deeply fatigued, he still had the strength to access Timeweb, and through it he watched as Doge Anton sent wave after wave of podships out into the galaxy, on missions to destroy the HibAdus and recapture every Human and Mutati world. In a matter of hours, eleven main planets were taken back.

More planets would follow, but Noah didn't have the strength to monitor the details. He was not needed for those efforts. Already the enemy soldiers were surrendering en masse. Soon the Adurian homeworld and the Hibbil Cluster Worlds would fall as well.

Just before leaving the paranormal realm, he saw the commencement of a big victory celebration on Dij, the new Mutati homeworld. Riding in an open car, Hari'Adab was leading a procession down the main boulevard of the capital city. Beside him sat Parais d'Olor in a custom seat that accommodated her avian form. Finally, she was recovering from her injuries....

Noah sighed in contentment. After all the chaos, things were settling down and new balances were being put into place. Safeguards to prevent future galactic wars and rampant decay of the infrastructure.

On a personal level, it pleased him immensely that Tesh and their unborn baby were safe, along with EcoStation. But a great and true friend had been lost, and for him Noah mourned deeply. *Eshaz.*

Vowing to honor his fallen companion one day, Noah gazed out on the fleet of podships, and saw them revert to their normal mottled appearances, with gray, black-streaked hulls. They floated motionless in space, and he understood why.

Lethargically, he swam back through the podflesh and emerged into one of the classroom modules, where he found Thinker awaiting him.

The orange lights around the robot's faceplate blinked cheerily as he strutted forward, making whirring sounds that were louder than normal. "Congratulations, Master Noah!" he exclaimed.

Moving slowly, feeling fatigued and sore, Noah extricated himself from the cocoon's podflesh and then watched it solidify into the decking and walls, along with all of the interior appointments that had previously been extruded by the amalgamated entity. His own skin remained gray, streaked in black.

Around him, he felt the power he had harnessed weakening, fading, dissipating. In a matter of moments the glowing green cocoon-sun went out like a used-up light bulb, and became a gray, faceless shape floating in space. Inside, Noah slumped onto the deck, but waved Thinker away when the robot hurried to help.

"You don't look good, Master Noah."

"Nothing a thousand years of sleep can't fix. Just let me rest."

"Shall I send for a doctor?"

Noah almost didn't have the energy to respond. He heard his own voice winding down. "The doctor doesn't exist who can tend to me. Tell everyone I do not wish to be disturbed."

"As you wish, sir."

So drained of energy that he could barely move a muscle, the podman curled up in a fetal ball and plunged into a deep sleep that transported him far, far away.

Chapter Seventy-Five

The best measure of your life is what you give to others,
not what you take for yourself.

—Noah Watanabe

As Noah slept on the deck, he dreamed of far-away places and alien races. Across the wide viewing canvas of his mind he saw the entire galaxy in all of its spectacular, colorful beauty, as the Creator had originally designed it. This gave him great pleasure, but the feeling was ephemeral, as he moved from dream to dream, with each of them compressed into only a few ticks of time.

In one of the dreams, he was the first person in an entirely new galactic race of Human-Aopoddae hybrids who had paranormal powers and the ability to inspire others to take care of the galactic environment. His followers wore green-and-brown Guardian uniforms. They looked upon him with awe and reverence, saying he had a certain glow about him and an unparalleled dynamism, that he was a force of nature unto himself. Truly, they insisted, he must be the Savior spoken of in Tulyan legends, the one sent to save Timeweb and hold dominion over it for all eternity thereafter. He tried to deny this, to tell them otherwise, but they wouldn't listen.

In yet another, even more troubling dream, he detected a resumption of trouble in the galaxy, as Web Spinners regenerated themselves and began poking at weak spots from the undergalaxy to make small holes, but not large enough yet for their sinister sovereign to break through. Past events seemed to merge with a possible future that Noah was seeing in the dream, as if all aspects of time had folded together, and the future, the present, and the past were all one. In the past, even when the Queen had been unable to escape she had still found extrasensory ways to recruit from our galaxy, taking Tulyans, Humans, and other races who metamorphosed into Web Spinners. She also incorporated into her Cimmerian legions the ancient race that originally inhabited Canopa in eons past, and was thought to have gone extinct.

It might explain why Eshaz was taken and became a Web Spinner, and why Princess Meghina and her companions were drawn in as well. Perhaps these recruits had powers or abilities that the aggressive Queen found useful. Pimyt was a complete question mark. As far as Noah knew, he did not have Eshaz's paranormal timeseeing abilities, or the immortal blood of Meghina and her companions.

Noah paused, sensing that the Hibbil, too, must have some link to the others that made him attractive to the Queen. But the members of other galactic races had been drawn into her minions as well. More question marks.

And what about me?

Noah's dreaming mind spread out, trying to absorb all possibilities. He saw the reptilian face of First Elder Kre'n superimposed over the heavens, with the faint green filigree of Timeweb visible beyond. "The goal of the Web Spinners," she said, "is to escape the nether realm where they have been imprisoned, so that they can take control of our galaxy and every other galaxy as well. Working at cross-purposes to her, Noah, you sought to maintain and restore Timeweb, in coordination with us. The Web Spinners—with paranormal abilities to perceive events beyond the undergalaxy—could not stand that. After recognizing the threat from you, and your identity as the Savior, the Queen intended to capture you and convert you to her own purposes … as her hapless consort. You are immortal, after all, like some of the others that she coveted, but you possess far greater powers—and she thought she could gain control over them through you. She still believes that."

"But I pulverized her into dust," the dream-Noah said.

"All things arise from dust," Kre'n said, in an ancient voice. "You know that. It's why you swept the particles into that timehole."

"Yes."

An additional worry occurred to Noah, and he was about to ask Kre'n about it when he saw a vast timehole open up behind her, encompassing half the galaxy. Out of that hole came the Web Spinners—more than he had ever seen before. So many that they reminded him of a Parvii swarm, but in nightmarish proportions. They swept through the image of Kre'n, scattering her into particles that drifted away. The dark creatures coalesced and grew more compact, and where Kre'n's face had been, another appeared.

Is this real or imagined? he wondered, struggling unsuccessfully to awaken, to free himself of the visions.

The Queen of the Undergalaxy smiled at Noah, but her faceted face was not like before. This time it bore the countenance of Tesh Kori, and in her swollen abdomen grew the child they had conceived.

"You are the God of the Undergalaxy," she said, "and I have guided you to your true purpose."

Noah cried out, but felt his scream absorbed into the noiseless void of the universe. No one heard him, and no one could help him. Not against something like this.

Awakening in a sweat, Noah found that someone had placed a thick blanket over him. He pushed it off, and lay there on the deck dripping with perspiration, trying to shake off memories of the nightmare. It had seemed so real. At least he was still lying in the classroom module where he had gone to sleep. That gave him a sense of continuity, that the visions had not been real, or even Timeweb excursions.

At the sound of voices, he looked and saw Thinker standing in the doorway of the chamber, speaking in low tones to another robot out in the corridor.

Presently, Thinker whirred into the room and said, "You look much better, Master Noah."

Noah rose to his feet, half expecting to still have sore muscles. But he didn't, and he understood why. The cocoon had transmitted Timeweb nutrients into him, and he felt totally energized again.

"How long did I sleep?" he asked.

"Three days. I'll bet you're hungry."

"Not really."

"You've been through a terrible ordeal," Thinker said. "All of us have, but you've had it the worst. By far."

All of the losses deeply saddened Noah, and particularly that of Eshaz, who had given his life so valiantly in the climactic battle. But the outcome of the horrific series of escalating dangers had been favorable. Eshaz would have said it was worth it.

Moments later, Tesh ran into the room. "Darling!" she said. "I'm so proud of you. How are you feeling?"

"Quite rested."

"Good. Despite what you said to Thinker, we took the liberty of having a doctor check your vital signs and administer fluids to you intravenously."

He nodded, but didn't know if that had been necessary. He had other connections.

She gave him a long, lingering kiss. Then, with a broad smile, she reached up to touch the grayish, alien skin on his mouth.

"Is my face a little rough?" he asked.

"A girl can get used to it."

"Just for you, I could revert to my Human appearance ... at least for kissing."

"No. This is the way you are meant to look, and this is the way I love you now." She placed a hand on her own stomach, which was beginning to show her pregnancy. "I wonder what our little one will look like."

The reality cast aside the bad dreams. Noah remembered what Tesh had told him earlier, that the baby passing through her birth canal would be tiny, the size of a Parvii. "When you say 'little one,' Tesh, you really mean it, don't you?"

"Big things come in small packages," she said.

"You're evidence of that."

"And you, too, Noah. How you accomplished so much, I don't think any of us will ever understand. We all saw portions of it firsthand, and we've seen the reports from Tulyan survey teams and robotic data banks. It's truly astounding."

A voice came from the direction of the corridor. "But the galaxy is not perfect." First Elder Kre'n strode heavily into the chamber, followed by Dabiggio and two other Elders.

"We have reports of weak infrastructure in a number of sectors," Kre'n said. "Nothing major and no new timeholes—at least not yet—but they are matters that need expert attention. We've dispatched caretaking teams."

"I was only able to work with the existing infrastructure material," Noah said. "It seems that the Creator designed it with inherent flaws, thus necessitating regular maintenance." He smiled. "Sounds like job security for you folks."

"You could override us and continue to perform the repairs yourself," Dabiggio said.

"Perhaps, but the energy requirements would be immense and wasteful, potentially throwing off the natural balances. I hope I haven't already done that, but there were no options. Now I think it is far better to return to the old ways, to the ancient systems that were set up by someone far greater than any of us."

"Humility looks good on you," Dabiggio said. Uncharacteristically, the towering Tulyan smiled.

"Thanks, but it's a suit of clothes everyone should wear," Noah said.

He grinned as several of his other friends entered the chamber—Doge Anton, General Nirella, Subi Danvar, Dux Hannah, and Acey Zelk. It pleased him to see that all of them had survived, and that they had not sustained serious injuries.

"What do we call you now?" Subi asked. The rotund adjutant had a discolored bump on his forehead, but otherwise looked well.

"Just Noah." He put his arm around Tesh. "I'm adjusting my priorities. From now on, I'm the Master Emeritus of the Guardians. You've done such a great job on my behalf, Subi, that I want you to run things from now on."

"As Master Subi?"

"That has a nice sound to it," Noah said.

"Yes, it does," Tesh agreed.

"But I will not live as long as you," Subi said. "One day you will need to resume your previous duties."

"Not if you set up a proper chain of succession." Glancing at Dux and Acey, he said, "We have a couple of good candidates right here."

The young men glowed proudly.

"Good choices." Subi's eyes brightened. "Oh, I see. You want the Guardians to be self sufficient."

Noah nodded. "I'd like the whole galaxy to be that way, functioning without the need for my intervention. It's idealistic, I know, but there are other things I have to do."

"What other things?" Subi asked.

"I'm not sure, only that I must free myself from day to day duties and prepare for something else. The various galactic races need to set up workable systems to do things on their own … always thinking of ecology, always trying to work together instead of at cross-purposes. Life, in all of its forms, must have a common vision."

They spoke for a while longer. Finally, after the others left, Tesh stood alone with Noah and said to him, "I've been thinking about what you said, that there are other things you have to do. Is the Big Guy giving you a promotion? Are you becoming a god yourself?"

With a scowl, Noah said, "I don't think references such as God, the Supreme Being, or the Sublime Creator are necessarily how it really is. They are just convenient reference points for something the galactic races don't understand."

"How about what they call you, the Savior?"

"Mmmm. I told the Tulyans I don't think I'm the messiah foretold in their legends, but I'll admit to you privately I'm not so certain anymore. Don't tell anyone I said this, but maybe it was my destiny to appear when I did and do what I did. For some time now, I have felt myself pulled along on a tidal wave of events. Sometimes I could steer this way or that, as if I had limited free will, but for the most part I've been forced along a certain path. And I don't know where that path leads."

"Somewhere good, for certain," she said, with a gentle smile. "But you frighten me with this kind of talk. You sound like you're planning to leave me."

He smiled sadly, tenderly. "In my line of work, I can't always make plans. But I do follow my instincts." He took her in his arms and held her tight. "One of my instincts tells me how much I love you … and our baby."

"But is that your primary instinct, your main purpose in life? I know I'm asking a typical female question, but I can't help wondering."

"Maybe it is my main purpose. Maybe I can't do anything without you."

She sighed. "The strong woman behind the great man."

"I didn't mean it that way."

"I know you didn't." She looked up and kissed him.

"I mean, we're a strong team, Tesh. You give me strength and vice versa, I hope."

"And our baby? Could he be our real destiny? Might he hold a special purpose, beyond anything you or I could ever accomplish?"

"After what we've been through, anything is possible. But if he … or *she* … is healthy and contributes to the welfare of the known galaxy, that will be sufficient."

"For me, just being with you is enough, Noah. Our baby is a bonus." She grasped his rough-textured hand and led him toward the doorway. "Now come with me, Darling. We have some catching up to do. Our own set of priorities."

Chapter Seventy-Six

Not knowing in advance often makes life more interesting. There can be a certain magic in the process of discovery.

—Noah Watanabe

Near the Ring Moons of the Wygeros race, EcoStation floated in space with its anchor-jets set for the night. Soon, when the blue Wygerian sun faded from view, everyone aboard the facility would enjoy spectacular evening views of lucent ring-shadows as they played colors across the surface of the planet below.

Noah strode through the corridors of the cocoon, past instructors, research technicians, and eager young students as they bustled back and forth between classes and laboratories. All wore green-and-brown uniforms. He smiled at the people, and called out to some by name, noting with pleasure how many of the galactic races were represented here. EcoStation had not only survived—it had come back more gloriously than ever, and was filled to the brim with learning stations, research laboratories, and other features of the latest technology, installed in a magnificent citadel of ancient podflesh.

The contrasts were startling to some, but not to Noah. Each passenger on the cocoon had boarded it only recently in cosmic terms, and they were learning how to live in harmony with ancient things—with the galaxy and all of its varied contents. EcoStation was just part of the whole picture, but a very important one. It had become the inspiration that he had hoped for, drawing the most brilliant and idealistic minds from the widest sectors, the greatest teachers from every race. Though the cocoon no longer glowed, since Noah had suspended its weapon function, it was still a beacon, in an important and positive sense. From this place, in new ways, Noah was illuminating the entire galaxy with knowledge.

Walking into one of the research and development laboratories, he paused to watch Thinker and Dux. They stood at an electronic drafting table designing eco-monitors—flying robotics that could check a planet's air, land, and water. It was just one of the many aspects of Noah's continuing mission to keep the galactic machine running smoothly. EcoStation was full of projects such as this one, and Subi Danvar was doing a terrific job of managing and coordinating the operations. This left Noah time to be creative, to come up with new ideas and approaches.

Thinker and Dux were so engrossed in their work that they did not notice Noah standing behind them, watching them quietly. Noah smiled to himself, and left. Back in the corridor he picked up his pace, thinking of his own relatively short past, and his much longer future.

The transformed man had experienced a great deal of change around him, the weaving of evolutionary strands. His apparently immortal lifetime and mottled gray-and-black skin were only part of it. Not long ago he had been performing ecological repair work on planets that had been damaged by the industrial operations of merchant princes. Afterward his career had taken unexpected turns, and he'd been required to perform work that was related, but exponentially more important.

And all of it had taken place in only a galactic moment.

Considering his potential lifetime, this made Noah wonder what more he might accomplish. Would his expertise eventually be needed for operations encompassing the entire universe and all of its galaxies? If that proved to be the case, what role could the Tulyans and Aopoddae play in the work?

But as Noah considered these questions, he realized he was thinking through the filter of his own life experiences. Even with all he had seen and accomplished, he knew there was still a lot more than that. The known galaxy was just one of many realms, each with its own unique story.

I am only a punctuation mark in the unfolding epic of the universe, he thought. He rounded a corner and headed down a long corridor.

It seemed incomprehensible to Noah that his destiny lay elsewhere, beyond the vast frame of reference encompassed by Timeweb and the known galaxy. And yet, he sensed that it did. He felt confident there were fantastic discoveries ahead that he could not begin to imagine. But he wanted to postpone the wildest (and admittedly most intriguing) possibilities for a while, so that he could spend time with Tesh and their baby. After all, Tesh—and probably the child as well—would not have Noah's life span, so it only made sense for him to spend as much time as possible with his family now.

I have free will, and this is what I want, he thought. Then, as if addressing a higher power, he asked, *Haven't I earned the privilege?*

No answer came, not viscerally or any other way. For the moment—other than the ruminations of his mind—he only had the here and now.

Subi Danvar approached. He looked harried, as if he had too much on his mind and had not been sleeping well. He was doing a good job, but still needed to grow into his job as Master of the Guardians, and become accustomed to the responsibilities. "I have that report you requested," he said, as he reached Noah. He handed over a thick file.

"Good," Noah said, thumbing through the pages. It was an analysis of piezoelectric emerald veins around the galaxy, a subject that he found interesting on several levels. He studied a chart for a moment.

"Look on page sixteen for evidence of ancient mining," Subi said.

Noah thumbed to the page, nodded. "I'll study this before tomorrow's meeting," he said. He tucked the file under his arm. Leaving Subi, he continued down the corridor.

The information that Noah had just perused had to do with his theory of galactic ecology, of the interconnectedness of the galaxy. It was important documentation, more corroborative evidence. Piezoelectric emeralds were the stuff that the ancient builders of Timeweb had used to spin the fantastic webbing of the cosmos. There was much to learn about those minerals, and about the infinitesimally small life forms that lived in their cellular structures.

A captured Adurian lab scientist had referred to them as "Webbies," and said that those inhabiting the galactic webbing undoubtedly had something to do with nearly instantaneous Tulyan communication across the galaxy, and with nehrcom transmissions. They might even have something to do with Noah's recovery from a serious injury, when Eshaz connected him to a strand of galactic webbing, and it healed him. In recent days, cooperative Adurian laboratory technicians had found evidence of the tiny, elusive creatures in samples of Noah's blood.

What a fantastic universe this is! Noah thought. He couldn't wait to discover more of its secrets. And he had a long time to unravel them.

Of great importance, Tulyan teams had been journeying to the farthest reaches of the galaxy aboard their restored fleet of podships, performing critical inspection and maintenance tasks. Having seen the terrible reality of the monsters of the undergalaxy, the Tulyans were working with renewed vigor to keep them bottled up. For the rest of eternity, Tulyans expected to perform many of their traditional caretaking duties. But they could not do it all alone. Other races had to contribute as well—different tasks according to their abilities.

Everything had to function like a biological machine, with the parts moving in synchronization. For it all to work, there had to be harmony among all of the ecological niches, on an immense scale. Old prejudices and conflicts would have to be set aside.

Noah sighed, as he thought of the vastness of space, and the diversity of conditions around the galaxy. A great deal of work remained to be done, and he knew the races could never let their guard down again. They must always be vigilant. It was one of the primary lessons that everyone had to learn. Unexpected dangers could always emerge.

He glanced at a chronometer on the wall of the corridor, paused to stare at it. For several moments he was hypnotized by the digital numbers as they advanced in their relentless, cyclical routine. In a few minutes he would sit in as an observer at a class on cluster-world ecology. It was being conducted by a full-time Mutati professor, a close associate of the Emir Hari'Adab.

Noah grinned. My, how times had changed.

Chapter Seventy-Seven

"I am my parents and my grandparents, stretching back to the beginnings of our race—and even beyond, far beyond, to the entropic materials that were stirred up in the dust of stars and went into the first sentient creature. I am the person you see before you, and much more. I am one cosmic life form and I am many. After being healed by nutrients from Timeweb and receiving the nanocreatures of the webbing into my bloodstream, I began to evolve in a new direction. Now the tiny life forms speak to me in their own way, and transport me to my destiny."

—Noah Watanabe, entry in Thinker's data banks

The podship *Webdancer*, having recovered from its battle injuries, was speeding near the Tulyan Starcloud, dodging comets and meteors, and occasionally racing them. The ancient creature was like a frisky pony, with a tiny Parvii woman flying alongside, keeping up easily, matching every maneuver. Though they were not physically connected at the moment, Tesh and her podship were mentally linked through a morphic field, constantly aware of each other's movements. It was one of the methods of communication used by podships to fly in formation, and *Webdancer* had taught it to her in the wordless way of the Aopoddae.

Ever since the epochal battle to save the galaxy, Tesh had been learning things about the arcane cosmic creatures, picking up subtleties of their communication system, and even noting differences within family groupings—what she called "dialects of motion." Without question, these space travelers—defying their appearances—were far more intelligent and advanced than any other galactic race.

Noah claimed not to know much about their wordless methods. And, although her lover seemed far superior in comparison with her, it was his contention that he could never possibly learn everything there was to know, not even about important matters such as the Aopoddae. It was his view—shared with the Tulyan Elders—that the sentient podships comprised a vast and collective storehouse of cosmic knowledge, a repository of treasures and mysteries that went all the way back to the first days of existence, when the galaxy came into being.

"They contain the secrets of the universe within their cells," Noah had said to her recently.

Now Tesh became aware of a change in her Aopoddae companion. The podship was slowing down, and had opened a hatch for her to enter. Moments later, she felt a stirring of life within her own body.

Somehow, *Webdancer* had sensed that it was her time.

* * * * *

It was early morning in the Wygerian Star System, with lucent ring shadows still casting soft colors across the surface of the coreworld below. In only a few minutes the sun would rise and chase the shadows away, but Noah hardly thought about that. His senses were on full alert, stretching outward.

A short while ago, he had again immersed himself into the flesh of the cocoon. Now, from far across space, he detected the same thing as *Webdancer*. It was time.

Noah visualized the Tulyan Star System, and in the blink of an eye he was there, bumping up against the much smaller *Webdancer*. He made the docking connection, lifted himself out of the podship flesh, and strode the short distance into Tesh's podship.

As they had discussed earlier concerning this special moment, Tesh lay in the warmth and security of the craft's sectoid chamber. There, at the nucleus of the ancient creature, she would give birth. The old making it possible for the new. She was a minuscule Parvii form on the soft gray deck, with her magnification system off.

Though Noah had influenced far-ranging matters of great scale and importance, he now found himself unable to have any effect at all on the tiny woman in front of him, or on the child she carried in her womb. He felt helpless and awkward.

Carefully he knelt over her, feeling like a giant. "I wish I could do something," he said, softly.

Tesh smiled up at him. Her voice was small and distant, as if she was having to shout. "Don't worry! This is the most natural of processes. You're here, and that's more than enough for me."

Noah didn't know if Parvii women ever suffered labor pains the way Human females did—but in this case it seemed effortless. As he watched, Tesh seemed to *will* the birth, and then it happened. She made hardly a sound, did not grimace in pain. The precious child slid easily through her birth canal and emerged, dripping amniotic fluids.

With deft motions, Tesh severed the umbilical cord and tied off the connection on the child's stomach. Then, producing a blanket as if by magic, she swaddled the baby and extended it up to Noah. "Meet your new son," she said.

Noah placed his right hand beside her, palm up, and she set the baby onto his palm. Tesh was herself only half the length of Noah's forefinger, and the child much smaller than that. Ever so carefully, he used his other hand to slide the child to a safer position. He held the baby delicately, afraid of harming him.

Such a tiny life form, Noah marveled, *and yet so infinitely important.* He saw pinpoint-eyes of indeterminate color in the round face, glittering like miniature stars.

"With your permission, I would like to name him Saito, in honor of my father," Noah said.

Tesh climbed onto the hand too, and lifted the baby into her arms. She had tidied up her own clothing, and had even brushed her hair quickly. "Then Saito shall be his name."

Walking across Noah's hand, the pretty brunette hopped back down to the deck. Moving a distance away and activating her own magnification system, Tesh became full size again, and stood there with the child nearly as small on her hand as he had been on Noah's. "Little Saito cannot be fitted with a magsystem until he is fully grown," she said with a smile, "at the risk of stunting his growth. And for my people that is a very serious concern!"

Noah exchanged loving smiles with her, and for a moment he forgot that he was more than Human, and that this restricted his possibilities for happiness.

The shared bliss was only momentary, before Noah sensed *Webdancer* and other podships communicating with one another in their prehistoric, mysterious way. He identified the characteristic sounds of Diminian and his companions— the most ancient of the Aopoddae in the cocoon and in the rest of the Liberator fleet.

Tesh's green eyes opened wide in alarm. "Look at your skin!" she said. "Oh, my God, what's happening to you?"

Looking down, Noah saw that the flesh on his hands was breaking up into tiny, dark particles that seemed to bounce off one another on the surface. He touched one hand to the other, and it didn't feel any different.

"It's happening to your face, too!" she said. She stepped backward and clutched the baby protectively to her bosom. Then she reconsidered, and reached out to touch the skin on Noah's forehead. To his dismay, he felt her fingertips sink into his own flesh and bone. It was painless to him, but he detected the immersion.

Visibly upset, she withdrew.

When Noah touched his own skin, however, it felt no different to him than normal, and he did not sink in.

Now the dark particles on his skin began to move faster and faster, and seemed to dive into the surface, where they continued their agitation in a foggy realm. The skin had taken on a haziness, a ghostlike quality. This time when Noah tried to touch one hand to the other, they passed through each other and he felt no tactile sensation at all. They were like clouds merging. Pulling the hands apart, they still had their misty definition.

"Are you vanishing?" she asked, her voice panicky. "Darling, what's happening to you?"

"I don't know." Noah felt oddly calm, and that he should accept whatever was occurring instead of trying to fight it. He was only one life form in a universe of countless sentient creatures and possibilities—an infinite number of individuals that were evolving, and were ultimately connected to one another. Inside his body, the Webbies were doing their work.

Tears streamed down Tesh's cheeks. She kept trying to caress Noah's face, but nothing tangible was there. She touched the sleeve of his tunic and it gave way, as if it had nothing behind it. But Noah could still see her clearly, and still saw a misty quality to his own skin—some substance and integrity there.

"For now, it seems to be holding," he said.

"You're continuing to evolve," she said in a voice tinged with panic, "but into what?"

"I don't know where the path of my life is leading. All I know is that I must follow it." He reached out to her, but could no longer feel her skin. He withdrew, disheartened.

"Can you reverse the process, the way you could mentally command the podflesh to disappear from your skin?"

"That is no longer possible," he said, as information from the Aopoddae surfaced in his mind. "I am beyond going back."

"I'm trying to understand, Darling. I don't want to be selfish, but I love you so much it hurts."

"We share feelings that no one needs to know about," Noah said. "Now that our Saito is born, there is no more need for my physical body. It has been transferred to him. One day, you will tell him of this, and he will fulfill his own destiny."

Filled with sadness, she could only nod.

Noah leaned toward her and kissed her lips. It gave him an emotional sensation, but not a corporal one. Even so, he could clearly remember the tenderness of her kisses, and knew he would never forget them, no matter how long he lived. He recalled an earlier Timeweb experience in which they had been together paranormally, and she had later insisted it had been physically real as well. Their baby was evidence of that. Now, it was similar. But entirely different.

As moments passed Tesh made herself smaller, and held the child in a normal fashion.

Around Noah the sectoid chamber seemed to melt and morph, and in a matter of moments he found that he stood alone inside the larger sectoid chamber of the cocoon. This time there had been no walking, or swimming through the flesh. Somehow, the Aopoddae had done it differently.

Through visual sensors in the flesh, Noah watched Tesh in her reduced form as she hurried through the main corridor of *Webdancer* with their child, making her way forward in the vessel.

In a matter of minutes, hundreds of the oldest podships in the fleet gathered around Noah's cocoon. They began to glow softly in concert with the larger structure, then led it out into deep space. For awhile, *Webdancer* kept up with them, flying of her own accord. Then the gray-and-black Liberator flagship separated from the others and fell back....

Tesh stood inside, at a forward viewing window. She saw the glowing podships and the cocoon accelerate along parallel podways that seemed to go upward from her vantage point. Then, in a brilliant burst of green, the fabric of space split open and they went through. For the briefest moment, Tesh got a glimpse of something beyond, of shimmering, enchanting lights and colors that danced in the ether like immense living creatures. Then the cosmic portal closed, and Noah was gone.

"Goodbye, my love," she whispered. Crying softly, she held the baby close to her.

About the Author

Brian Herbert, the son of Frank Herbert, is the author of numerous *New York Times* bestsellers. He has won many literary honors and has been nominated for the highest awards in science fiction. In 2003, he published *Dreamer of Dune*, a moving biography of his father that was nominated for the Hugo Award. After writing ten DUNE-universe novels with Kevin J. Anderson, the coauthors created their own epic series, HELLHOLE. Brian began his own galaxy-spanning science fiction series in 2006, TIMEWEB. His other acclaimed solo novels include *Sidney's Comet; Sudanna, Sudanna; The Race for God;* and *Man of Two Worlds* (written with Frank Herbert).

CPSIA information can be obtained at www.ICGtesting.com
Printed in the USA
LVOW12s2145110614

389684LV00014B/565/P